# American Short Stories Since 1945

John G. Parks
*Miami University of Ohio*

New York Oxford
OXFORD UNIVERSITY PRESS
2002

*For Joel M. Jones, Ferenc Szasz, and F. Thomas Trotter*
*The best of teachers, the finest of men*

Oxford University Press

Oxford New York
Athens Auckland Bangkok Bogotá Buenos Aires Calcutta
Cape Town Chennai Dar es Salaam Delhi Florence Hong Kong Istanbul
Karachi Kuala Lumpur Madrid Melbourne Mexico City Mumbai
Nairobi Paris São Paulo Shanghai Singapore Taipei Tokyo Toronto Warsaw

and associated companies in
Berlin Ibadan



Published by Oxford University Press, Inc.
198 Madison Avenue, New York, New York 10016
http://www.oup-usa.org



**Library of Congress Cataloging-in-Publication Data**

American short stories since 1945 / [selected] by John G. Parks.
p. cm.
Includes bibliographical references.
ISBN 0-19-513132-0 (pbk. : acid-free paper)
1. Short stories, American. 2. American fiction—20th century. 3. United States—Social life and customs—20th century—Fiction. I. Parks, John G. II. Title.

PS648.S5 A475 2001
813′.01054—dc21

2001021237

Printing number: 9 8 7 6 5 4 3 2

Printed in the United States of America
on acid-free paper

# CONTENTS

# PREFACE

A preface is a brief speaking before a more lengthy speaking. It is often the place where an author gives the reader clues, hints, previews of coming attractions, as it were, and acknowledgments of gratitude to various and sundry individuals for different sorts of help. A preface, in short, is often a generous, optimistic, and hopeful presentation. "Come on in," it says, as agreeably as possible, "I have much in store for you!" And indeed I do.

However, in an age of many and often massive anthologies, a preface may need to take on the role of an *apologia. Another* anthology?! Yes, *another* anthology. Why an anthology on the American short story since World War II? It serves a number of needs. Now that the twentieth century is over, it makes a certain sense to break the period in half in the teaching of American literature. Just as was the case with World War I, the Second World War marked the entry of a new generation of American writers with new sensibilities and agendas. This anthology includes the best writers of fiction since 1945, most with well-established reputations, some with reputations in the making. It is an excellent and varied collection for courses in the short story and for creative writing classes on recent fiction. More generally this anthology comprises American fiction that will appeal to readers outside of schools. For, taken together, these stories document the ever-changing reality of American life since the Second World War—who we are, where we have been, and where we might be going. Thus, this anthology serves as a kind of necessary archive of our lives, a multifaceted narrative of our pilgrims' progress. However, when readers reflect on the range of human experience chronicled here, and the pain, suffering, and uncertainty recounted, they may wonder about our progress. At the same time, there are some wonderfully comic moments in many of these stories, richly ironic, sometimes even with redemptive effect. Ultimately, the authors included in this collection write as honestly as they can about the truth of our lives and do so with great skill and passion. Reading these stories is to be in excellent company.

While many of the stories and authors included here are also found in other anthologies, no other anthology concentrates on the period of 1945 to the present. In addition, I have tried to choose stories that, for the most part, are not overly anthologized. (Although, in some instances, I had to keep some familiar titles, such as Shirley Jackson's "The Lottery.") Moreover, unlike most recent anthologies, I have included authors who have fallen into neglect but whose work deserves a place in the archive. I refer to writers such as J. F. Powers, James Purdy, Wright Morris, John Gardner, and

Leonard Michaels. I am pleased also to include one of James Alan McPherson's fine stories, for he has slipped from inclusion in recent anthologies. Three authors are represented by two stories each—Flannery O'Connor, John Cheever, and Raymond Carver, arguably among the best practitioners of the short story in the last half century.

America is increasingly becoming a culture of minorities. Woven rightly throughout this collection are key African-American and new immigrant writers such as Ralph Ellison, Ernest J. Gaines, Alice Walker, James Baldwin, Jamaica Kincaid, and Bharati Mukherjee, as well as important Asian-American and Latino writers such as Hisaye Yamamoto, Maxine Hong Kingston, Amy Tan, Helena María Viramontes, Sandra Cisneros, and Frank Chin. Altogether there are seventy-six authors represented by seventy-nine stories, over half of which were published in the last twenty years.

And now some sincere thanks. I am especially grateful to Anthony English, senior editor at Oxford University Press, for his help and guidance in this project. I also deeply appreciate the assistance of Christine D'Antonio and Yarisa Paulino during the production of the text. Two of my colleagues, James Reiss and Stephen Bauer, were generous in giving good advice in the development of my list of authors. And I am grateful to the outside reviewers of the text for their thoughtful suggestions.

So, come on in and enjoy some of the finest stories of our time.

# INTRODUCTION

In the beginning is the story. Narrative is the rhetoric of duration. It has to do with the finite, the transient, and the contingent, which is to say it has to do with infinite possibility, a few possibilities at a time. Along with the story is voice; indeed, voice or voices constitute the story. The voices call worlds into being, worlds with listeners and readers to participate in the event of storytelling or story-making. While stories doubtless exist in the mind of God, as most certainly they do within human minds, they do not fully exist without the utterance—spoken or written—for listeners and readers. Only then is a story real, made real through acts of intersubjective exchange, more commonly known as listening and reading. Narrative is the way the human mind both creates and makes sense out of reality, the way it negotiates life. Because of this, stories have authority, they make claims upon our attention, they give us pleasure, they give us news, they give us the language we need to comprehend our lives. Some stories do these things so well that we save them and listen to them or read them again and again, for in a real sense they have become essential or necessary to who and what we are. In literate cultures, stories are saved in books, in collections called anthologies.

The canon wars of the last decades of the twentieth century challenged and undermined the authority of traditional literary anthologies. Those collections were criticized for being narrow and exclusive, for their lack of or underrepresentation of women and minority writers. Whatever claims for historical significance or for aesthetic excellences that older texts might make for their contents, they were strongly repudiated by new theories that were antiaesthetic and antifoundational. These academic and textual debates, of course, reflected the radical social and political movements of the 1960s: civil rights, antiwar, Black Power, women's liberation, the counterculture, and, later, the rise of gay rights and of identity politics. While some critics argued for abolishing the idea of a canon altogether (after all, isn't everything a text?), most seemed to prefer an expanded and open canon, one that is inclusive and truly representative of the polyphonic American culture that has emerged since the Second World War. Heretofore marginalized groups have moved to the center of literary and cultural significance. Or, perhaps better, literary culture has been decentered so that there are multiple centers vying for our attention. In any event, the authority of anthologies has come to be based largely on representation and inclusiveness, essentially sociological and political criteria, rather than on traditional aesthetic principles or values.

These challenges and changes in literary and academic culture carry with them both gains and losses. Both American culture in general and academic culture in particular have gained from the infusion of the energies and talents of women and minorities in all areas of cultural activity. America at the beginning of the twenty-first century is more inclusive and more pluralistic than it was at the end of the Second World War. Our literature, in all genres, has grown from the presence and active participation of formerly mostly silent or invisible groups: women, African Americans, American Indians, Asians, Latinos. As a result, we have new answers to the old question, posed by Michel-Guillaume-Jean de Crevecoeur back in 1782, "What is an American?" Moreover, new waves of immigrants to the United States add further relevance to this question. All the old boundaries have been broken down or are vanishing.

The losses concern the issue of authority. If the often courageous and self-zsacrificing movements for social reform were largely motivated by claims of moral universality, the last few decades of the twentieth century saw the emergence of a radical skepticism and of the "hermeneutics of doubt." The German philosopher Jürgen Habermas describes our era as undergoing a "legitimation crisis," a situation where newer generations no longer feel connected to or bound by cultural or religious traditions. Programs and projects of demythologizing and demystification make liberatory claims to free us of the last vestiges of superstition, religious metaphor, transcendent beliefs. As a result, what remains is just language, rhetoric, and history. Formerly universal claims were now regarded as merely generalizing upon local practices. The antifoundationalist and antiaesthetic critique repudiates all grand narratives, all claims of ultimacy, and regards all authority and truth as partial, relative, and contingent. Such a critique makes moral and aesthetic judgments difficult if not impossible, for all standards are called into question. Irony has been the dominant mood or style of our skeptical era. An analogous situation existed in the years between the world wars. Writing in his book *A Preface to Morals* (1929), Walter Lippmann spoke of the "acids of modernity" that were eating away at the foundations of our beliefs. In our own times we might speak of the "oils of postmodernity" that permit us to slip, slide, and avoid all standards that may make claims upon our attention and responsibility. Reflecting on this situation and the apparent triumph of science and secularity in his book *The Death of Satan* (1995), Andrew Delbanco fears the split of our culture into two sensibilities—belief and irony—a split with a potential for great animosity. Increasingly, however, there are signs of a renewed interest by serious scholars in moral and ethical criticism, as well as in aesthetics, though we cannot predict that such interest will bring about a reorientation of academic and intellectual culture. In an age without a name, many may share the sensibilities of the writer Dencombe, Henry James' character in his novel *The Middle Years,* who says at the end: "We work in the dark—we do what we can—we give what we have. Our doubt is our passion, and our passion is our task."

Because of this social, intellectual, and political context, compiling this anthology of American stories written since the Second World War has been both enjoyable and risky. In the first instance, an editor faces the limitations imposed by the publisher on length and budget for permissions, and some of those prove too dear for a work to be included. Then there is the occasional writer who prefers not to be included. I had hoped to include a story by J. D. Salinger, but Salinger will not permit his stories to be anthologized. Even so, there is an abundance of fine stories and authors to choose from. I wanted an anthology that would be representative in the fullest sense—representative of all literary voices and representative of the best writing the period has produced. I wanted the anthology to do what all good anthologies should do: tell a story of how we have lived. In short, I wanted the anthology to represent a kind of social, intellectual, and spiritual history of American life since 1945. As such, the collection will serve the general reader, as well as college classes in the short story, creative writing, and American literature. While I cannot expect all readers to agree with all of my choices, I do believe that the stories in this collection are strong and worthy and bear witness to our lives. Indeed, in an era where it appears that many academic critics have largely abandoned literature for theory, it has been writers themselves who have sustained a faith in the intrinsic value of the literary imagination and in literature as a way of knowing essential to living.

In a real sense, the short story developed as America developed. As a creature of the magazine, the short story flourished in conditions of expanding literacy and, with the growth of the railroads, better systems of distribution. Washington Irving's *The Sketch Book* (1819) marks the beginnings of American short-story history. The collection, containing his well-known tales "Rip Van Winkle" and "The Legend of Sleepy Hollow," interestingly was an Americanizing of some old German folktales. William Austin's 1824 story "Peter Rugg, the Missing Man" developed on Irving's model in its use of the legendary and the picturesque. In addition to the growing magazine market, there was the popularity of annual gift books that contained a lot of new fiction, much of it by women writers like the best-selling Catharine Maria Sedgwick, and emphasizing romantic themes. While numerous women authors wrote tales of domestic distress, others addressed issues of larger social import and the need for reforms, such as poverty and slavery. Harriet Beecher Stowe's influential and best-selling *Uncle Tom's Cabin* (1852) was serialized in the magazine *National Era.* In the 1830s and 1840s, Edgar Allen Poe published his tales of gothic terror and of rational analysis, and in his criticism he argued that a short story should always strive to achieve the unity of a "single effect," a view that has influenced many writers. In the same years, Nathaniel Hawthorne produced his tales exploring the darkness of sin and guilt and the inescapability of history.

The Civil War marked the turn away from the romantic preoccupations with the picturesque, the legendary, and the fanciful that dominated the antebellum period. Realism became the dominant mode of writing, and author and magazine editor William Dean Howells became the literary arbiter of the late nineteenth century. The forces of industrialization, immigration, urbanization, and new technologies created a new America and a new agenda for writers. The magazine market expanded and became more national in scope. Regional writers flourished—Bret Harte and Mark Twain in the West, Mary Wilkins Freeman and Sara Orne Jewett in the Northeast, George Washington Cable and Kate Chopin in the South, and Hamlin Garland in the Midwest, among many others. Henry James published dozens of stories, and many of his novels were serialized in magazines. Reflecting the influence of Darwin's thought, naturalism, a darker, more deterministic form of realism, emerged in the 1890s in such writers as Stephen Crane and Jack London.

After what Theodore Roosevelt called our "splendid little war" with Spain in 1898, America began the new century as a world power flush with optimism. It was the Progressive Era in politics and all sorts of reforms were in the air. It was an exciting era for journalism, as "muckrakers" attacked the social ills stemming from corporate monopolies, the corruption in urban politics, the exploitation of labor and our natural resources. The election of Woodrow Wilson to the presidency in 1912 seemed to mark the triumph of the progressive program and idealism. But it was short lived. For just as the Civil War marked the division between two Americas, the Great War brought an end to American innocence, idealism, and optimism, especially among writers and intellectuals. As Ezra Pound and T. S. Eliot would have it, our civilization has been "botched," it was a "heap of broken statues," it was a "wasteland." We were all now inescapably modern.

Technical improvements in printing lowered production costs and helped raise circulation of new magazines, many of which paid well for new short stories. The early years of the century saw the publication of stories by Henry James, Edith Wharton, Theodore Dreiser, Jack London, Willa Cather, Mary Antin, Susan Glaspell, and the ever-popular O. Henry (William Sydney Porter). Sherwood Anderson's *Winesburg, Ohio* (1919) marks a shift to modernist techniques and concerns. F. Scott Fitzgerald's stories, many appearing in the *Saturday Evening Post,* chronicle the lives of a new generation of Americans coming of age after the Great War. The spare and stoical stories of Ernest Hemingway appeared in the 1920s and implied more with less, a style that has had strong influence on writers throughout the twentieth century. In 1915, the annual publication of what has become *The Best American Short Stories* was inaugerated, as well as the O. Henry Award volumes, both of which continue today. In 1925, *The New Yorker* magazine began, and it has been one of the major publishers of literary fiction in the country and an important arbiter of taste. The 1920s also saw the emergence of a new generation of black writers, including Jean Toomer, Zora Neale Hurston, Arna Bontemps, and Langston Hughes—all part of the Harlem Renaissance that flourished from 1917 to 1930. William Faulkner and Katherine Anne Porter began publishing stories in the late 1920s as well.

In contrast to the fads and rebellions of the 1920s, the 1930s was an angry decade. The economic collapse of the Great Depression spawned new concerns in the writers of the decade. If the 1920s were preoccupied with the self, the 1930s were concerned with the community, with what happened to us. The fiction of John Steinbeck and Richard Wright addressed powerfully the social crises of the time.

The first half of the 1940s was preoccupied with the Second World War, another watershed event in national and world history. With the dropping of the atomic bombs in 1945, we entered what W. H. Auden called an "age of anxiety." Now, no one was safe. The terrible slaughter of the Great War was unimaginably surpassed in this Second Great War by massive bombing raids and the revelations of the horrors of the Holocaust. All the world were witness to the heart of darkness. With the Iron Curtain dividing Europe between East and West, the world endured a Cold War for over four decades. In a real sense, the Korean War (1950–1953) and the war in Vietnam (1964–1975) were Cold War wars, conflicts acting out Cold War ideologies and tensions. The conformity of the 1950s was fueled by Senator Joseph McCarthy's anti-Communist probes and the pursuit of affluence. The central cities were abandoned for the expanding suburbs, leaving black ghettos of poverty and unemployment. After the historic *Brown v. Board of Education* decision in 1954, the civil rights movement took off in earnest—sit-ins, marches, boycotts, voter registration drives, massive rallies in Washington, D.C., as well as urban riots and assassinations. Landmark civil rights legislation and antipoverty programs were passed in President Lyndon B. Johnson's administration (1965–1968). The baby-boomer generation came of age in the mid to late 1960s and began to challenge the values and lives of the previous generations. The

New Left developed a political agenda. Many youths were involved in communitarian experiments. The Vietnam War and the draft polarized the nation as no other event since the Civil War. There were many demonstrations on and off college campuses against the war. A new women's movement took shape in the second half of the 1960s and has had far-reaching impact on all areas of American life in the years since.

And present throughout all of these movements was television, the dominant medium of the postwar period. It not only recorded events, it virtually created a new sense of reality. Old forms of verbal literacy were challenged and increasingly dominated by the new visual media. New freedoms in the culture allowed all the arts to deal openly and explicitly with all subjects. Films, protected by a new rating system, treated sex and violence in ever more graphic terms. And the exponential growth of computer systems has brought us closer to Marshall McLuhan's "global village."

After the Watergate scandal and the resignation of President Richard Nixon in 1974 and the conclusion of the Vietnam War in 1975, the culture appeared adrift with a kind of fatigue or exhaustion from all the tumult of the past decade. Internationally, various terrorist organizations began to pose threats to national and personal security, while the collapse of the Soviet Union opened up new prospects of international cooperation. President Ronald Reagan's elevation of greed to a virtue in the 1980s led Americans to the pursuit of "more." Despite the brief scare of the 1987 stock market fall, the last years of the twentieth century have been properous ones. And yet for some observers of our time, a kind of melancholy and joylessness attend our pursuits. We appear to lack purpose and meaning in our drive for wealth. Andrew Delbanco writes movingly of this situation in his book *The Real American Dream: A Meditation on Hope* (1999). Earlier generations placed their hope in God and then later generations put their hope in the nation. Our own time appears to have nothing left but the self and the urge to consume. And one wonders if that is enough.

In order to explore the development of the American short story since 1945, I have divided the period roughly into three segments. The stories published in the postwar years 1945 to 1960 I describe as reflecting "the strains of accommodation and consensus." The stories reveal the hidden tensions of an era of change and adjustment, an era requiring conformity to corporate and organizational systems, an era of anxiety about Communist conspiracies and nuclear war. Social critics wrote about the "organizational man," the "lonely crowd," and the "status seekers." Existentialism portrayed life as absurd, with meaning coming only from the self. Rejecting the hopelessness of existentialism, American writers probed deeply into our moral failures and our capacity for evil, but could still point to the possibility of redemption and affirmation, even if hard won.

The second segment, the 1960s and 1970s, I describe as a period of "breakdowns and breakthroughs." The new energies unloosed in the 1960s broke down, or at least weakened, all prevailing authority systems: political, economic, class, racial, gender. The terrible violence of assassinations and civil unrest created suspicion about official authority and official versions of events. Many writers called into question conventional and traditional fictional devices. A highly self-conscious self-referential fiction, called metafiction, emerged, practiced by such writers as John Barth, Robert Coover, William Gass, and Donald Barthelme. It was a literature turned against itself in an attempt to write itself free from predetermined plots and linguistic structures—for some there was no escape from the prison house of language. It called attention to all literary artifice, indeed, to the narrativity of all modes of thought. In these fictional innovations lay the beginnings of later postmodernist thought and practice. Nevertheless, while realism has been roundly attacked and proclaimed dead by most of the metafictionists and postmodernists, it continues to thrive, though often freely employing innovative devices. The fiction in this period both subverts the ways the world makes sense of itself and engages the wounds and sufferings of that world.

The fiction of the 1980s and 1990s reflects a culture whose center and margins interpenetrate or one in which, as Yeats said long ago, the center no longer holds—an era of many new voices engaging the ever-changing American landscape. For many writers who began publishing in these years, the fiction of Raymond Carver was the major influence. His own career shows a move from the margins to the center, and his pared-down, minimalist style opened up new possibilities for the short story. But there is great richness and variety in the fiction of the final years of the twentieth century. Indeed, despite the changing circumstances of the production of short stories today—the decline of the number of magazines that pay well for stories; the growth of smaller, academically based journals; the role of creative writing programs in the development of new writers and their support of established writers, to mention a few—the short story in America is as strong as it has ever been.

Reading Robert Coles' book, *The Call of Stories: Teaching and the Moral Imagination* (1989), a few years ago, I remember being impressed by Coles' story of his psychiatric internship and how he learned to see patients as "storytellers" and not as subjects with "problems"to anaylze and diagnose with proper psychoanalytic terminology. For Coles, doctor and patient best meet one another in the give-and-take of storytelling, an enterprise that honors and respects the particularity of individual lives. Analogously, Coles argues, as readers we best meet stories when we let them engage us deeply and penetrate our moral imaginations—not so much in providing solutions or resolutions, but in "a broadening and even heightening of our struggles" as human beings. The best stories stimulate in readers an essentially spiritual quest, they call to us at the deepest levels of our lives. It is my hope that the stories in this collection will provoke this level of engagement in its readers. In this regard, I recall how Russell Banks concludes his novel *Continental Drift* (1985). He claims that stories "deprive the world as it is of some of the greed it needs to continue to be itself." He then sends his book outward as an agent of "sabotage and subversion." He sends it forth to "help destroy the world as it is," which is also and profoundly an act of creation. So do I send this one.

# 1

# 1945–1960

## *The Strains of Accommodation and Consensus*

# ⁑ SHIRLEY JACKSON
## (1919–1965)

Born in San Francisco, Shirley Jackson lived most of her childhood years in Burlingame, California, with her mother, a housewife, and father, a lithographer. She showed an interest in writing early, winning a poetry prize at age 12. At age 14 she moved with her family to Rochester, New York. She began college at the University of Rochester but withdrew due to a bout with depression, a condition with which she struggled periodically in later years. In 1937 she resumed her education at Syracuse University, where she majored in English and founded and edited the literary magazine. There she met Stanley Edgar Hyman, whom she married just after graduation in 1940. After a year in New York City, the couple moved to Vermont, where Hyman taught at Bennington College, they raised their four children, and both led intense literary lives.

In addition to writing many short stories, published in numerous magazines, Jackson wrote six novels: *The Road Through the Wall* (1948), *Hangsaman* (1951), *The Bird's Nest* (1954), *The Sundial* (1958), *The Haunting of Hill House* (1959), and *We Have Always Lived in the Castle* (1962). Her first collection of short stories was published in 1949 under the title *The Lottery, or, The Adventures of James Harris.* A novel fragment and sixteen stories appeared posthumously in 1968 under the title *Come Along with Me,* edited by Stanley Edgar Hyman. Another collection of unpublished stories appeared in 1997 entitled *Just an Ordinary Day: The Uncollected Stories of Shirley Jackson.*

In our overly stimulated age, it is hard to imagine a short story creating the sensation "The Lottery" did in 1948 when it was published in *The New Yorker.* No other story in *New Yorker* history evoked so many letters, mostly of shock, anger, confusion. Jackson herself noted that the letters exhibit "a kind of wide-eyed, shocked innocence." So much of her fiction, like Hawthorne's tales, reveals the possibilities of evil and madness beneath the ordinary surfaces and patterns of daily life, never something most people find comfortable contemplating.

## The Lottery

THE MORNING of June 27th was clear and sunny, with the fresh warmth of a full-summer day; the flowers were blossoming profusely and the grass was richly green. The people of the village began to gather in the square, between the post office and the bank, around ten o'clock; in some towns there were so many people that the lottery took two days and had to be started on June 26th, but in this village, where there were only about three hundred people, the whole lottery took less than two hours, so it could begin at ten o'clock in the morning and still be through in time to allow the villagers to get home for noon dinner.

The children assembled first, of course. School was recently over for the summer, and the feeling of liberty sat uneasily on most of them; they tended to gather together quietly for a while before they broke into boisterous play, and their talk was still of the classroom and the teacher, of books and reprimands. Bobby Martin had already stuffed his pockets full of stones, and the other boys soon followed his example, selecting the smoothest and roundest stones; Bobby and Harry Jones and Dickie Delacroix—the villagers pronounced this name "Dellacroy"—eventually made a great pile of stones in one corner of the square and guarded it against the raids of the other boys. The girls stood aside, talking among themselves, looking over their shoulders at the boys, and the very small children rolled in the dust or clung to the hands of their older brothers or sisters.

Soon the men began to gather, surveying their own children, speaking of planting and rain, tractors and taxes. They stood together, away from the pile of stones in the corner, and their jokes were quiet and they smiled rather than laughed. The women, wearing faded house dresses and sweaters, came shortly after their menfolk. They greeted one another and exchanged bits of gossip as they went to join their husbands. Soon the women, standing by their husbands, began to call to their children, and the children came reluctantly, having to be called four or five times. Bobby Martin ducked under his mother's grasping hand and ran, laughing, back to the pile of stones. His father spoke up sharply, and Bobby came quickly and took his place between his father and his oldest brother.

The lottery was conducted—as were the square dances, the teen-age club, the Halloween program—by Mr. Summers, who had time and energy to devote to civic activities. He was a round-faced, jovial man and he ran the coal business, and people were sorry for him, because he had no children and his wife was a scold. When he arrived in the square, carrying the black wooden box, there was a murmur of conversation among the villagers, and he waved and called, "Little late today, folks." The postmaster, Mr. Graves, followed him, carrying a three-legged stool, and the stool was put in the center of the square and Mr. Summers set the black box down on it. The villagers kept their distance, leaving a space between themselves and the stool, and when Mr. Summers said, "Some of you fellows want to give me a hand?" there was a hesitation before two men, Mr. Martin and his oldest son, Baxter, came forward to hold the box steady on the stool while Mr. Summers stirred up the papers inside it.

The original paraphernalia for the lottery had been lost long ago, and the black box now resting on the stool had been put into use even before Old Man Warner, the oldest man in town, was born. Mr. Summers spoke frequently to the villagers about making a new box, but no one liked to upset even as much tradition as was represented by the black box. There was a story that the present box had been made with some pieces of the box that had preceded it, the one that had been constructed when the first people settled down to make a village here. Every year, after the lottery, Mr. Summers began talking again about a new box, but every year the subject was allowed to fade off without anything's being done. The black box grew shabbier each year; by now it was no longer completely black but splintered badly along one side to show the original wood color, and in some places faded or stained.

Mr. Martin and his oldest son, Baxter, held the black box securely on the stool until Mr. Summers had stirred the papers thoroughly with his hand. Because so much of the ritual had been forgotten or discarded, Mr. Summers had been successful in having slips of paper substituted for the chips of wood that had been used for generations. Chips of wood, Mr. Summers had argued, had been all very well when the village was tiny, but now that the population was more than three hundred and likely to keep on growing, it was necessary to use something that would fit more easily into the black box. The night before the lottery, Mr. Summers and Mr. Graves made up the slips of paper and put them in the box, and it was then taken to the safe of Mr. Summers' coal company and locked up until Mr. Summers was ready to take it to the square next morning. The rest of the year, the box was put away, sometimes one place, sometimes another; it had spent one year in Mr. Graves's barn and another year underfoot in the post office, and sometimes it was set on a shelf in the Martin grocery and left there.

There was a great deal of fussing to be done before Mr. Summers declared the lottery open. There were the lists to make up—of heads of families, heads of households in each family, members of each household in each family. There was the proper swearing-in of Mr. Summers by the postmaster, as the official of the lottery; at one time, some people remembered, there had been a recital of some sort, performed by the official of the lottery, a perfunctory, tuneless chant that had been rattled off duly each year; some people believed that the official of the lottery used to stand just so when he said or sang it, others believed that he was supposed to walk among the people, but years and years ago this part of the ritual had been allowed to lapse. There had been, also, a ritual salute, which the official of the lottery had had to use in addressing each person who came up to draw from the box, but this also had changed with time, until now it was felt necessary only for the official to speak to each person approaching. Mr. Summers was very good at all this; in his clean white shirt and blue jeans, with one hand resting carelessly on the black box, he seemed very proper and important as he talked interminably to Mr. Graves and the Martins.

Just as Mr. Summers finally left off talking and turned to the assembled villagers, Mrs. Hutchinson came hurriedly along the path to the square, her sweater thrown over her shoulders, and slid into place in the back of the crowd. "Clean forgot what day it was," she said to Mrs. Delacroix, who stood next to her, and they both laughed softly. "Thought my old man was out back stacking wood," Mrs. Hutchinson went on, "and then I looked out the window and the kids was gone, and then I remembered it was the twenty-seventh and came a-running." She dried her hands on her apron, and Mrs. Delacroix said, "You're in time, though. They're still talking away up there."

Mrs. Hutchinson craned her neck to see through the crowd and found her husband and children standing near the front. She tapped Mrs. Delacroix on the arm as a farewell and began to make her way through the crowd. The people separated good-humoredly to let her through; two or three people said, in voices just loud enough to be heard across the crowd, "Here comes your Missus, Hutchinson," and "Bill, she made it after all." Mrs. Hutchinson reached her husband, and Mr. Summers, who had been waiting, said cheerfully, "Thought we were going to have to get on without you, Tessie." Mrs.

Hutchinson said, grinning, "Wouldn't have me leave m'dishes in the sink, now, would you, Joe?," and soft laughter ran through the crowd as the people stirred back into position after Mrs. Hutchinson's arrival.

"Well, now," Mr. Summers said soberly, "guess we better get started, get this over with, so's we can go back to work. Anybody ain't here?"

"Dunbar," several people said. "Dunbar, Dunbar."

Mr. Summers consulted his list. "Clyde Dunbar," he said. "That's right. He's broke his leg, hasn't he? Who's drawing for him?"

"Me, I guess," a woman said, and Mr. Summers turned to look at her. "Wife draws for her husband," Mr. Summers said. "Don't you have a grown boy to do it for you, Janey?" Although Mr. Summers and everyone else in the village knew the answer perfectly well, it was the business of the official of the lottery to ask such questions formally. Mr. Summers waited with an expression of polite interest while Mrs. Dunbar answered.

"Horace's not but sixteen yet," Mrs. Dunbar said regretfully. "Guess I gotta fill in for the old man this year."

"Right," Mr. Summers said. He made a note on the list he was holding. Then he asked, "Watson boy drawing this year?"

A tall boy in the crowd raised his hand. "Here," he said. "I'm drawing for m'mother and me." He blinked his eyes nervously and ducked his head as several voices in the crowd said things like "Good fellow, Jack," and "Glad to see your mother's got a man to do it."

"Well," Mr. Summers said, "guess that's everyone. Old Man Warner make it?"

"Here," a voice said, and Mr. Summers nodded.

* * *

A sudden hush fell on the crowd as Mr. Summers cleared his throat and looked at the list. "All ready?" he called. "Now, I'll read the names—heads of families first—and the men come up and take a paper out of the box. Keep the paper folded in your hand without looking at it until everyone has had a turn. Everything clear?"

The people had done it so many times that they only half listened to the directions; most of them were quiet, wetting their lips, not looking around. Then Mr. Summers raised one hand high and said, "Adams." A man disengaged himself from the crowd and came forward. "Hi, Steve," Mr. Summers said, and Mr. Adams said, "Hi, Joe." They grinned at one another humorlessly and nervously. Then Mr. Adams reached into the black box and took out a folded paper. He held it firmly by one corner as he turned and went hastily back to his place in the crowd, where he stood a little apart from his family, not looking down at his hand.

"Allen," Mr. Summers said. "Anderson. . . . Bentham."

"Seems like there's no time at all between lotteries any more," Mrs. Delacroix said to Mrs. Graves in the back row. "Seems like we got through with the last one only last week."

"Time sure goes fast," Mrs. Graves said.

"Clark. . . . Delacroix."

"There goes my old man," Mrs. Delacroix said. She held her breath while her husband went forward.

"Dunbar," Mr. Summers said, and Mrs. Dunbar went steadily to the box while one of the women said, "Go on, Janey," and another said, "There she goes."

"We're next," Mrs. Graves said. She watched while Mr. Graves came around from the side of the box, greeted Mr. Summers gravely, and selected a slip of paper from the box. By now, all through the crowd there were men holding the small folded papers in their large hands, turning them over and over nervously. Mrs. Dunbar and her two sons stood together, Mrs. Dunbar holding the slip of paper.

"Harburt. . . . Hutchinson."

"Get up there, Bill," Mrs. Hutchinson said, and the people near her laughed.

"Jones."

"They do say," Mr. Adams said to Old Man Warner, who stood next to him, "that over in the north village they're talking of giving up the lottery."

Old Man Warner snorted. "Pack of crazy fools," he said. "Listening to the young folks, nothing's good enough for *them.* Next thing you know, they'll be wanting to go back to living in caves, nobody work any more, live *that* way for a while. Used to be a saying about 'Lottery in June, corn be heavy soon.' First thing you know, we'd all be eating stewed chickweed and acorns. There's *always* been a lottery," he added petulantly. "Bad enough to see young Joe Summers up there joking with everybody."

"Some places have already quit lotteries," Mrs. Adams said.

"Nothing but trouble in *that,*" Old Man Warner said stoutly. "Pack of young fools."

"Martin." And Bobby Martin watched his father go forward. "Overdyke. . . . Percy."

"I wish they'd hurry," Mrs. Dunbar said to her older son. "I wish they'd hurry."

"They're almost through," her son said.

"You get ready to run tell Dad," Mrs. Dunbar said.

Mr. Summers called his own name and then stepped forward precisely and selected a slip from the box. Then he called, "Warner."

"Seventy-seventh year I been in the lottery," Old Man Warner said as he went through the crowd. "Seventy-seventh time."

"Watson." The tall boy came awkwardly through the crowd. Someone said, "Don't be nervous, Jack," and Mr. Summers said, "Take your time, son."

"Zanini."

* * *

After that, there was a long pause, a breathless pause, until Mr. Summers, holding his slip of paper in the air, said, "All right, fellows." For a minute, no one moved, and then all the slips of paper were opened. Suddenly, all the women began to speak at once, saying, "Who is it?," "Who's got it?," "Is it the Dunbars?," "Is it the Watsons?" Then the voices began to say, "It's Hutchinson. It's Bill," "Bill Hutchinson's got it."

"Go tell your father," Mrs. Dunbar said to her older son.

People began to look around to see the Hutchinsons. Bill Hutchinson was standing quiet, staring down at the paper in his hand. Suddenly, Tessie Hutchinson shouted to Mr. Summers, "You didn't give him time enough to take any paper he wanted. I saw you. It wasn't fair!"

"Be a good sport, Tessie," Mrs. Delacroix called, and Mrs. Graves said, "All of us took the same chance."

Warner = past + not willing to change

against lottery

"Shut up, Tessie," Bill Hutchinson said.

"Well, everyone," Mr. Summers said, "that was done pretty fast, and now we've got to be hurrying a little more to get done in time." He consulted his next list. "Bill," he said, "you draw for the Hutchinson family. You got any other households in the Hutchinsons?"

"There's Don and Eva," Mrs. Hutchinson yelled. "Make *them* take their chance!"

"Daughters draw with their husbands' families, Tessie," Mr. Summers said gently. "You know that as well as anyone else."

"It wasn't *fair,*" Tessie said.

"I guess not, Joe," Bill Hutchinson said regretfully. "My daughter draws with her husband's family, that's only fair. And I've got no other family except the kids."

"Then, as far as drawing for families is concerned, it's you," Mr. Summers said in explanation, "and as far as drawing for households is concerned, that's you, too. Right?"

"Right," Bill Hutchinson said.

"How many kids, Bill?" Mr. Summers asked formally.

"Three," Bill Hutchinson said. "There's Bill, Jr., and Nancy, and little Dave. And Tessie and me."

"All right, then," Mr. Summers said. "Harry, you got their tickets back?"

Mr. Graves nodded and held up the slips of paper. "Put them in the box, then," Mr. Summers directed. "Take Bill's and put it in."

"I think we ought to start over," Mrs. Hutchinson said, as quietly as she could. "I tell you it wasn't *fair.* You didn't give him time enough to choose. *Every*body saw that."

Mr. Graves had selected the five slips and put them in the box, and he dropped all the papers but those onto the ground, where the breeze caught them and lifted them off.

"Listen, everybody," Mrs. Hutchinson was saying to the people around her.

"Ready, Bill?" Mr. Summers asked, and Bill Hutchinson, with one quick glance around at his wife and children, nodded.

"Remember," Mr. Summers said, "take the slips and keep them folded until each person has taken one. Harry, you help little Dave." Mr. Graves took the hand of the little boy, who came willingly with him up to the box. "Take a paper out of the box, Davy," Mr. Summers said. Davy put his hand into the box and laughed. "Take just *one* paper," Mr. Summers said. "Harry, you hold it for him." Mr. Graves took the child's hand and removed the folded paper from the tight fist and held it while little Dave stood next to him and looked up at him wonderingly.

"Nancy next," Mr. Summers said. Nancy was twelve, and her school friends breathed heavily as she went forward, switching her skirt, and took a slip daintily from the box. "Bill, Jr.," Mr. Summers said, and Billy, his face red and his feet overlarge, nearly knocked the box over as he got a paper out. "Tessie," Mr. Summers said. She hesitated for a minute, looking around defiantly, and then set her lips and went up to the box. She snatched a paper out and held it behind her.

"Bill," Mr. Summers said, and Bill Hutchinson reached into the box and felt around, bringing his hand out at last with the slip of paper in it.

The crowd was quiet. A girl whispered, "I hope it's not Nancy," and the sound of the whisper reached the edges of the crowd.

"It's not the way it used to be," Old Man Warner said clearly. "People ain't the way they used to be."

"All right," Mr. Summers said. "Open the papers. Harry, you open little Dave's."

Mr. Graves opened the slip of paper and there was a general sigh through the crowd as he held it up and everyone could see that it was blank. Nancy and Bill, Jr., opened theirs at the same time, and both beamed and laughed, turning around to the crowd and holding their slips of paper above their heads.

"Tessie," Mr. Summers said. There was a pause, and then Mr. Summers looked at Bill Hutchinson, and Bill unfolded his paper and showed it. It was blank.

"It's Tessie," Mr. Summers said, and his voice was hushed. "Show us her paper, Bill."

Bill Hutchinson went over to his wife and forced the slip of paper out of her hand. It had a black spot on it, the black spot Mr. Summers had made the night before with the heavy pencil in the coal-company office. Bill Hutchinson held it up, and there was a stir in the crowd.

"All right, folks," Mr. Summers said. "Let's finish quickly."

Although the villagers had forgotten the ritual and lost the original black box, they still remembered to use stones. The pile of stones the boys had made earlier was ready; there were stones on the ground with the blowing scraps of paper that had come out of the box. Mrs. Delacroix selected a stone so large she had to pick it up with both hands and turned to Mrs. Dunbar. "Come on," she said. "Hurry up."

Mrs. Dunbar had small stones in both hands, and she said, gasping for breath, "I can't run at all. You'll have to go ahead and I'll catch up with you."

The children had stones already, and someone gave little Davy Hutchinson a few pebbles.

Tessie Hutchinson was in the center of a cleared space by now, and she held her hands out desperately as the villagers moved in on her. "It isn't fair," she said. A stone hit her on the side of the head.

Old Man Warner was saying, "Come on, come on, everyone." Steve Adams was in the front of the crowd of villagers, with Mrs. Graves beside him.

"It isn't fair, it isn't right," Mrs. Hutchinson screamed, and then they were upon her.

# ⁂ EUDORA WELTY

## (1909– )

Place is of signal importance to many writers, and this is especially true for Mississippi-born Eudora Welty, whose stories and novels keenly observe the tone and texture of life in the Deep South since the late 1930s. Welty was born in Jackson, the capital of Mississippi. She attended Jackson State College for Women between 1925 and 1927, and then transferred to the University of Wisconsin, from which she graduated in 1929. After a year studying advertising at the Columbia University School of Business, Welty returned to Jackson in 1931 and wrote for various newspapers and a local radio station. A job with the Works Progress Administration during the Depression allowed her to travel about Mississippi meeting and observing people who would later become characters in her fiction. Encouraged by such prominent southern writers as Cleanth Brooks, Robert Penn Warren, and Katherine Anne Porter, Welty began publishing stories in such journals as the *Southern Review* and the *Atlantic Monthly.* Her first collection of stories appeared in 1941 under the title *A Curtain of Green.*

Other collections of stories include *The Wide Net* (1943), *The Golden Apples* (1949), *Selected Stories* (1954), *The Bride of Innisfallen* (1955), *Thirteen Stories* (1965), and *The Collected Stories of Eudora Welty* (1980). Her stories have won four O. Henry Memorial prizes, fellowships, and awards. Welty's talent as a photographer is exhibited in her books *One Time, One Place* (1946) and *Eudora Welty: Photographs* (1989). Her novels include *The Robber Bridesgroom* (1942), *Delta Wedding* (1946), *The Ponder Heart* (1954), *Losing Battles* (1970), and the Pulitzer Prize–winning *The Optimist's Daughter* (1972).

Avoiding a tendentious aesthetics, Welty's fiction brings readers into an empathic engagement with keenly imagined and localized characters whose interior lives emerge through their distinctive voices and social interconnections. At times comic, at others nostalgic, sad, and portraying people longing to be understood or at least heard, her stories capture closely observed lives whose fates echo human life everywhere. In "Why I Live at the P.O." readers may see a parallel with a parable about a certain prodigal child.

# Why I Live at the P.O.

I WAS getting along fine with Mama, Papa-Daddy and Uncle Rondo until my sister Stella-Rondo just separated from her husband and came back home again. Mr. Whitaker! Of course I went with Mr. Whitaker first, when he first appeared here in China Grove, taking "Pose Yourself" photos, and Stella-Rondo broke us up. Told him I was one-sided. Bigger on one side than the other, which is a deliberate, calculated falsehood: I'm the same. Stella-Rondo is exactly twelve months to the day younger than I am and for that reason she's spoiled.

She's always had anything in the world she wanted and then she'd throw it away. Papa-Daddy gave her this gorgeous Add-a-Pearl necklace when she was eight years old and she threw it away playing baseball when she was nine, with only two pearls.

So as soon as she got married and moved away from home the first thing she did was separate! From Mr. Whitaker! This photographer with the popeyes she said she trusted. Came home from one of those towns up in Illinois and to our complete surprise brought this child of two.

Mama said she like to made her drop dead for a second. "Here you had this marvelous blonde child and never so much as wrote your mother a word about it," says Mama. "I'm thoroughly ashamed of you." But of course she wasn't.

Stella-Rondo just calmly takes off this *hat,* I wish you could see it. She says, "Why, Mama, Shirley-T.'s adopted, I can prove it."

"How?" says Mama, but all I says was, "H'm!" There I was over the hot stove, trying to stretch two chickens over five people and a completely unexpected child into the bargain, without one moment's notice.

"What do you mean—'H'm!'?" says Stella-Rondo, and Mama says, "I heard that, Sister."

I said that oh, I didn't mean a thing, only that whoever Shirley-T. was, she was the spit-image of Papa-Daddy if he'd cut off his beard, which of course he'd never do in the world. Papa-Daddy's Mama's papa and sulks.

Stella-Rondo got furious! She said, "Sister, I don't need to tell you you got a lot of nerve and always did have and I'll thank you to make no future reference to my adopted child whatsoever."

"Very well," I said. "Very well, very well. Of course I noticed at once she looks like Mr. Whitaker's side too. That frown. She looks like a cross between Mr. Whitaker and Papa-Daddy."

"Well, all I can say is she isn't."

"She looks exactly like Shirley Temple to me," says Mama, but Shirley-T. just ran away from her.

So the first thing Stella-Rondo did at the table was turn Papa-Daddy against me.

"Papa-Daddy," she says. He was trying to cut up his meat. "Papa-Daddy!" I was taken completely by surprise. Papa-Daddy is about a million years old and's got this long-long beard. "Papa-Daddy, Sister says she fails to understand why you don't cut off your beard."

So Papa-Daddy l-a-y-s down his knife and fork! He's real rich. Mama says he is, he says he isn't. So he says, "Have I heard correctly? You don't understand why I don't cut off my beard?"

"Why," I says, "Papa-Daddy, of course I understand, I did not say any such of a thing, the idea!"

He says, "Hussy!"

I says, "Papa-Daddy, you know I wouldn't any more want you to cut off your beard than the man in the moon. It was the farthest thing from my mind! Stella-Rondo sat there and made that up while she was eating breast of chicken."

But he says, "So the postmistress fails to understand why I don't cut off my beard. Which job I got you through my influence with the government. 'Bird's nest'—is that what you call it?"

Not that it isn't the next to smallest P.O. in the entire state of Mississippi.

I says, "Oh, Papa-Daddy," I says, "I didn't say any such of a thing, I never dreamed it was a bird's nest, I have always been grateful though this is the next to smallest P.O. in the state of Mississippi, and I do not enjoy being referred to as a hussy by my own grandfather."

But Stella-Rondo says, "Yes, you did say it too. Anybody in the world could of heard you, that had ears."

"Stop right there," says Mama, looking at *me.*

So I pulled my napkin straight back through the napkin ring and left the table.

As soon as I was out of the room Mama says, "Call her back, or she'll starve to death," but Papa-Daddy says, "This is the beard I started growing on the Coast when I was fifteen years old." He would of gone on till nightfall if Shirley-T. hadn't lost the Milky Way she ate in Cairo.

So Papa-Daddy says, "I am going out and lie in the hammock, and you can all sit here and remember my words: I'll never cut off my beard as long as I live, even one inch, and I don't appreciate it in you at all." Passed right by me in the hall and went straight out and got in the hammock.

It would be a holiday. It wasn't five minutes before Uncle Rondo suddenly appeared in the hall in one of Stella-Rondo's flesh-colored kimonos, all cut on the bias, like something Mr. Whitaker probably thought was gorgeous.

"Uncle Rondo!" I says. "I didn't know who that was! Where are you going?"

"Sister," he says, "get out of my way, I'm poisoned."

"If you're poisoned stay away from Papa-Daddy," I says. "Keep out of the hammock. Papa-Daddy will certainly beat you on the head if you come within forty miles of him. He thinks I deliberately said he ought to cut off his beard after he got me the P.O., and I've told him and told him and told him, and he acts like he just don't hear me. Papa-Daddy must of gone stone deaf."

"He picked a fine day to do it then," says Uncle Rondo, and before you could say "Jack Robinson" flew out in the yard.

What he'd really done, he'd drunk another bottle of that prescription. He does it every single Fourth of July as sure as shooting, and it's horribly expensive. Then he falls over in the hammock and snores. So he insisted on zigzagging right on out to the hammock, looking like a half-wit.

Papa-Daddy woke up with this horrible yell and right there without moving an inch he tried to turn Uncle Rondo against me. I heard every word he said. Oh, he told Uncle Rondo I didn't learn to read till I was eight years old and he didn't see how in the world I ever got the mail put up at the P.O., much less read it all, and he said if Uncle Rondo could only fathom the lengths he had gone to get me that job! And he said on the other hand he thought Stella-Rondo had a brilliant mind and deserved credit for getting out of town. All the time he was just lying there swinging as pretty as you please and looping out his beard, and poor Uncle Rondo was *pleading* with him to slow down the hammock, it was making him as dizzy as a witch to watch it. But that's what Papa-Daddy likes about a hammock. So Uncle Rondo was too dizzy to get turned against me for the time being. He's Mama's only brother and is a good case of a one-track mind. Ask anybody. A certified pharmacist.

Just then I heard Stella-Rondo raising the upstairs window. While she was married she got this peculiar idea that it's cooler with the windows shut and locked. So she has to raise the window before she can make a soul hear her outdoors.

So she raises the window and says, *"Oh!"* You would have thought she was mortally wounded.

Uncle Rondo and Papa-Daddy didn't even look up, but kept right on with what they were doing. I had to laugh.

I flew up the stairs and threw the door open! I says, "What in the wide world's the matter, Stella-Rondo? You mortally wounded?"

"No," she says, "I am not mortally wounded but I wish you would do me the favor of looking out that window there and telling me what you see."

So I shade my eyes and look out the window.

"I see the front yard," I says.

"Don't you see any human beings?" she says.

"I see Uncle Rondo trying to run Papa-Daddy out of the hammock," I says. "Nothing more. Naturally, it's so suffocating-hot in the house, with all the windows shut and locked, everybody who cares to stay in their right mind will have to go out and get in the hammock before the Fourth of July is over."

"Don't you notice anything different about Uncle Rondo?" asks Stella-Rondo.

"Why, no, except he's got on some terrible-looking flesh-colored contraption I wouldn't be found dead in, is all I can see," I says.

"Never mind, you won't be found dead in it, because it happens to be part of my trousseau, and Mr. Whitaker took several dozen photographs of me in it," says Stella-Rondo. "What on earth could Uncle Rondo *mean* by wearing part of my trousseau out in the broad open daylight without saying so much as 'Kiss my foot,' *knowing* I only got home this morning after my separation and hung my negligee up on the bathroom door, just as nervous as I could be?"

"I'm sure I don't know, and what do you expect me to do about it?" I says. "Jump out the window?"

"No, I expect nothing of the kind. I simply declare that Uncle Rondo looks like a fool in it, that's all," she says. "It makes me sick to my stomach."

"Well, he looks as good as he can," I says. "As good as anybody in reason could." I stood up for Uncle Rondo, please remember. And I said to Stella-Rondo, "I think I would do well not to criticize so freely if I were you and came home with a two-year-old child I had never said a word about, and no explanation whatever about my separation."

"I asked you the instant I entered this house not to refer one more time to my adopted child, and you gave me your word of honor you would not," was all Stella-Rondo would say, and started pulling out every one of her eyebrows with some cheap Kress tweezers.

So I merely slammed the door behind me and went down and made some green-tomato pickle. Somebody had to do it. Of course Mama had turned both the niggers loose; she always said no earthly power could hold one anyway on the Fourth of July, so she wouldn't even try. It turned out that Jaypan fell in the lake and came within a very narrow limit of drowning.

So Mama trots in. Lifts up the lid and says, "H'm! Not very good for your Uncle Rondo in his precarious condition, I must say. Or poor little adopted Shirley-T. Shame on you!"

That made me tired. I says, "Well, Stella-Rondo had better thank her lucky stars it was her instead of me came trotting in with that very peculiar-looking child. Now if it had been me that trotted in from Illinois and brought a peculiar-looking child of two, I shudder to think of the reception I'd of got, much less controlled the diet of an entire family."

"But you must remember, Sister, that you were never married to Mr. Whitaker in the first place and didn't go up to Illinois to live," says Mama, shaking a spoon in my face. "If you had I would of been just as overjoyed to see you and your little adopted girl as I was to see Stella-Rondo, when you wound up with your separation and came on back home."

"You would not," I says.

"Don't contradict me, I would," says Mama.

But I said she couldn't convince me though she talked till she was blue in the face. Then I said, "Besides, you know as well as I do that that child is not adopted."

"She most certainly is adopted," says Mama, stiff as a poker.

I says, "Why, Mama, Stella-Rondo had her just as sure as anything in this world, and just too stuck up to admit it."

"Why, Sister," said Mama. "Here I thought we were going to have a pleasant Fourth of July, and you start right out not believing a word your own baby sister tells you!"

"Just like Cousin Annie Flo. Went to her grave denying the facts of life," I remind Mama.

"I told you if you ever mentioned Annie Flo's name I'd slap your face," says Mama, and slaps my face.

"All right, you wait and see," I says.

"I," says Mama, "I prefer to take my children's word for anything when it's humanly possible." You ought to see Mama, she weighs two hundred pounds and has real tiny feet.

Just then something perfectly horrible occurred to me.

"Mama," I says, "can that child talk?" I simply had to whisper! "Mama, I wonder if that child can be—you know—in any way? Do you realize," I says, "that she hasn't spoken one single, solitary word to a human being up to this minute? This is the way she looks," I says, and I looked like this.

Well, Mama and I just stood there and stared at each other. It was horrible!

"I remember well that Joe Whitaker frequently drank like a fish," says Mama. "I believed to my soul he drank *chemicals.*" And without another word she marches to the foot of the stairs and calls Stella-Rondo.

"Stella-Rondo? O-o-o-o-o! Stella-Rondo!"

"What?" says Stella-Rondo from upstairs. Not even the grace to get up off the bed.

"Can that child of yours talk?" asks Mama.

Stella-Rondo says, "Can she what?"

"Talk! Talk!" says Mama. "Burdyburdyburdyburdy!"

So Stella-Rondo yells back, "Who says she can't talk?"

"Sister says so," says Mama.

"You didn't have to tell me, I know whose word of honor don't mean a thing in this house," says Stella-Rondo.

And in a minute the loudest Yankee voice I ever heard in my life yells out, "OE'm Pop-OE the Sailor-r-r-r Ma-a-an!" and then somebody jumps up and down in the upstairs hall. In another second the house would of fallen down.

"Not only talks, she can tap-dance!" calls Stella-Rondo, "Which is more than some people I won't name can do."

"Why, the little precious darling thing!" Mama says, so surprised. "Just as smart as she can be!" Starts talking baby talk right there. Then she turns on me. "Sister, you ought to be thoroughly ashamed! Run upstairs this instant and apologize to Stella-Rondo and Shirley-T."

"Apologize for what?" I says. "I merely wondered if the child was normal, that's all. Now that she's proved she is, why, I have nothing further to say."

But Mama just turned on her heel and flew out, furious. She ran right upstairs and hugged the baby. She believed it was adopted. Stella-Rondo hadn't done a thing but turn her against me from upstairs while I stood there helpless over the hot stove. So that made Mama, Papa-Daddy and the baby all on Stella-Rondo's side.

Next, Uncle Rondo.

I must say that Uncle Rondo has been marvelous to me at various times in the past and I was completely unprepared to be made to jump out of my skin, the way it turned out. Once Stella-Rondo did something perfectly horrible to him—broke a chain letter from Flanders Field—and he took the radio back he had given her and gave it to me. Stella-Rondo was furious! For six months we all had to call her Stella instead of Stella-Rondo, or she wouldn't answer. I always thought Uncle Rondo had all the brains of the entire family. Another time he sent me to Mammoth Cave, with all expenses paid.

But this would be the day he was drinking that prescription, the Fourth of July.

So at supper Stella-Rondo speaks up and says she thinks Uncle Rondo ought to try to eat a little something. So finally Uncle Rondo said he would try a little cold biscuits and ketchup, but that was all. So *she* brought it to him.

"Do you think it wise to disport with ketchup in Stella-Rondo's flesh-colored kimono?" I says. Trying to be considerate! If Stella-Rondo couldn't watch out for her trousseau, somebody had to.

"Any objections?" asks Uncle Rondo, just about to pour out all the ketchup.

"Don't mind what she says, Uncle Rondo," says Stella-Rondo. "Sister has been devoting this solid afternoon to sneering out my bedroom window at the way you look."

"What's that?" says Uncle Rondo. Uncle Rondo has got the most terrible temper in the world. Anything is liable to make him tear the house down if it comes at the wrong time.

So Stella-Rondo says, "Sister says, 'Uncle Rondo certainly does look like a fool in that pink kimono!' "

Do you remember who it was really said that?

Uncle Rondo spills out all the ketchup and jumps out of his chair and tears off the kimono and throws it down on the dirty floor and puts his foot on it. It had to be sent all the way to Jackson to the cleaners and re-pleated.

"So that's your opinion of your Uncle Rondo, is it?" he says. "I look like a fool, do I? Well, that's the last straw. A whole day in this house with nothing to do, and then to hear you come out with a remark like that behind my back!"

"I didn't say any such of a thing, Uncle Rondo," I says, "and I'm not saying who did, either. Why, I think you look all right. Just try to take care of yourself and not talk and eat at the same time," I says. "I think you better go lie down."

"Lie down my foot," says Uncle Rondo. I ought to of known by that he was fixing to do something perfectly horrible.

So he didn't do anything that night in the precarious state he was in—just played Casino with Mama and Stella-Rondo and Shirley-T. and gave Shirley-T. a nickel with a head on both sides. It tickled her nearly to death, and she called him "Papa." But at 6:30 A.M. the next morning, he threw a whole five-cent package of some unsold one-inch firecrackers from the store as hard as he could into my bedroom and they every one went off. Not one bad one in the string. Anybody else, there'd be one that wouldn't go off.

Well, I'm just terribly susceptible to noise of any kind, the doctor has always told me I was the most sensitive person he had ever seen in his whole life, and I was simply prostrated. I couldn't eat! People tell me they heard it as far as the cemetery, and old Aunt Jep Patterson, that had been holding her own so good, thought it was Judgment Day and she was going to meet her whole family. It's usually so quiet here.

And I'll tell you it didn't take me any longer than a minute to make up my mind what to do. There I was with the whole entire house on Stella-Rondo's side and turned against me. If I have anything at all I have pride.

So I just decided I'd go straight down to the P.O. There's plenty of room there in the back, I says to myself.

Well! I made no bones about letting the family catch on to what I was up to. I didn't try to conceal it.

The first thing they knew, I marched in where they were all playing Old Maid and pulled the electric oscillating fan out by the plug, and everything got real hot. Next I snatched the pillow I'd done the needlepoint on right off the davenport from behind Papa-Daddy. He went "Ugh!" I beat Stella-Rondo up the stairs and finally found my charm bracelet in her bureau drawer under a picture of Nelson Eddy.

"So that's the way the land lies," says Uncle Rondo. There he was, piecing on the ham. "Well, Sister, I'll be glad to donate my army cot if you got any place to set it up, providing you'll leave right this minute and let me get some peace." Uncle Rondo was in France.

"Thank you kindly for the cot and 'peace' is hardly the word I would select if I had to resort to firecrackers at 6:30 A.M. in a young girl's bedroom," I says back to him. "And as to where I intend to go, you seem to forget my position as postmistress of China Grove, Mississippi," I says. "I've always got the P.O."

Well, that made them all sit up and take notice.

I went out front and started digging up some four-o'clocks to plant around the P.O.

"Ah-ah-ah!" says Mama, raising the window. "Those happen to be my four-o'clocks. Everything planted in that star is mine. I've never known you to make anything grow in your life."

"Very well," I says. "But I take the fern. Even you, Mama, can't stand there and deny that I'm the one watered that fern. And I happen to know where I can send in a box top and get a packet of one thousand mixed seeds, no two the same kind, free."

"Oh, where?" Mama wants to know.

But I says, "Too late. You 'tend to your house, and I'll 'tend to mine. You hear things like that all the time if you know how to listen to the radio. Perfectly marvelous offers. Get anything you want free."

So I hope to tell you I marched in and got that radio, and they could of all bit a nail in two, especially Stella-Rondo, that it used to belong to, and she well knew she couldn't get it back, I'd sue for it like a shot. And I very politely took the sewing-machine motor I helped pay the most on to give Mama for Christmas back in 1929, and a good big calendar, with the first-aid remedies on it. The thermometer and the Hawaiian ukulele certainly were rightfully mine, and I stood on the step-ladder and got all my watermelon-rind preserves and every fruit and vegetable I'd put up, every jar. Then I began to pull the tacks out of the bluebird wall vases on the archway to the dining room.

"Who told you you could have those, Miss Priss?" says Mama, fanning as hard as she could.

"I bought 'em and I'll keep track of 'em," I says. "I'll tack 'em up one on each side the post-office window, and you can see 'em when you come to ask me for your mail, if you're so dead to see 'em."

"Not I! I'll never darken the door to that post office again if I live to be a hundred," Mama says. "Ungrateful child! After all the money we spent on you at the Normal."

"Me either," says Stella-Rondo. "You can just let my mail lie there and *rot,* for all I care. I'll never come and relieve you of a single, solitary piece."

"I should worry," I says. "And who you think's going to sit down and write you all those big fat letters and postcards, by the way? Mr. Whitaker? Just because he was the only man ever dropped down in China Grove and you got him—unfairly—is he going to sit down and write you a lengthy correspondence after you come home giving no rhyme nor reason whatsoever for your separation and no explanation for the presence of that child? I may not have your brilliant mind, but I fail to see it."

So Mama says, "Sister, I've told you a thousand times that Stella-Rondo simply got homesick, and this child is far too big to be hers," and she says, "Now, why don't you all just sit down and play Casino?"

Then Shirley-T. sticks out her tongue at me in this perfectly horrible way. She has no more manners than the man in the moon. I told her she was going to cross her eyes like that some day and they'd stick.

"It's too late to stop me now," I says. "You should have tried that yesterday. I'm going to the P.O. and the only way you can possibly see me is to visit me there."

So Papa-Daddy says, "You'll never catch me setting foot in that post office even if I should take a notion into my head to write a letter some place." He says, "I won't have you reachin' out of that little old window with a pair of shears and cuttin' off any beard of mine. I'm too smart for you!"

"We all are," says Stella-Rondo.

But I said, "If you're so smart, where's Mr. Whitaker?"

So then Uncle Rondo says, "I'll thank you from now on to stop reading all the orders I get on postcards and telling everybody in China Grove what you think is the matter with them," but I says, "I draw my own conclusions and will continue in the future to draw them." I says, "if people want to write their inmost secrets on penny postcards, there's nothing in the wide world you can do about it, Uncle Rondo."

"And if you think we'll ever *write* another postcard you're sadly mistaken," says Mama.

"Cutting off your nose to spite your face then," I says. "But if you're all determined to have no more to do with the U.S. mail, think of this: What will Stella-Rondo do now, if she wants to tell Mr. Whitaker to come after her?"

"Wah!" says Stella-Rondo. I knew she'd cry. She had a conniption fit right there in the kitchen.

"It will be interesting to see how long she holds out," I says. "And now—I am leaving."

"Good-bye," says Uncle Rondo.

"Oh, I declare," says Mama, "to think that a family of mine should quarrel on the Fourth of July, or the day after, over Stella-Rondo leaving old Mr. Whitaker and having the sweetest little adopted child! It looks like we'd all be glad!"

"Wah!" says Stella-Rondo, and has a fresh conniption fit.

"*He* left *her*—you mark my words," I says. "That's Mr. Whitaker. I know Mr. Whitaker. After all, I knew him first. I said from the beginning he'd up and leave her. I foretold every single thing that's happened."

"Where did he go?" asks Mama.

"Probably to the North Pole, if he knows what's good for him," I says.

But Stella-Rondo just bawled and wouldn't say another word. She flew to her room and slammed the door.

"Now look what you've gone and done, Sister," says Mama. "You go apologize."

"I haven't got time, I'm leaving," I says

"Well, what are you waiting around for?" asks Uncle Rondo.

So I just picked up the kitchen clock and marched off, without saying "Kiss my foot" or anything, and never did tell Stella-Rondo good-bye.

There was a nigger girl going along on a little wagon right in front.

"Nigger girl," I says, "come help me haul these things down the hill, I'm going to live in the post office."

Took her nine trips in her express wagon. Uncle Rondo came out on the porch and threw her a nickel.

And that's the last I've laid eyes on any of my family or my family laid eyes on me for five solid days and nights. Stella-Rondo may be telling the most horrible tales in the world about Mr. Whitaker, but I haven't heard them. As I tell everybody, I draw my own conclusions.

But oh, I like it here. It's ideal, as I've been saying. You see, I've got everything cater-cornered, the way I like it. Hear the radio? All the war news. Radio, sewing machine, book ends, ironing board and that great big piano lamp—peace, that's what I like. Butter-bean vines planted all along the front where the strings are.

Of course, there's not much mail. My family are naturally the main people in China Grove, and if they prefer to vanish from the face of the earth, for all the mail they get or the mail they write, why, I'm not going to open my mouth. Some of the folks here in town are taking up for me and some turned against me. I know which is which. There are always people who will quit buying stamps just to get on the right side of Papa-Daddy.

But here I am, and here I'll stay. I want the world to know I'm happy.

And if Stella-Rondo should come to me this minute, on bended knees, and *attempt* to explain the incidents of her life with Mr. Whitaker, I'd simply put my fingers in both my ears and refuse to listen.

# ISAAC BASHEVIS SINGER

(1904–1991)

Writing traditional stories in Yiddish, rejecting the experiments of modernism and postmodernism, Isaac Bashevis Singer is an example of the artists who led the increasing internationalization of American literature and indeed of all the arts in the twentieth century. Singer was born in Radzymin, Poland. His father was a rabbi in the strict Orthodox tradition, with strong views against secular learning and literature. Despite his father's views, Singer early developed an interest in writing. After a year in the rabbinical seminary in Warsaw, in 1921, he turned to journalism and literature. He published his first story in 1935.

Following his brother Israel Joshua Singer, Isaac Bashevis Singer immigrated to the United States in 1935. He made a living writing for the *Jewish Daily Forward,* a Yiddish-language newspaper. A prolific writer, Singer wrote novels, stories, and memoirs. It was not until the 1950s that this work became available to wider audiences through English translations. Singer's first collection of stories was translated by Saul Bellow and published as *Gimpel the Fool and Other Stories* in 1957. His *Collected Stories* appeared in 1982. His work won two National Book awards, in 1970 and in 1974, and the Nobel Prize in Literature in 1978.

Singer's fiction recovers lost worlds, Jewish communities in the small towns of Poland or in Warsaw. Many of his stories retain the quality of the oral tale, negotiating among several levels of reality. Somewhere between Market Street and the heavens a miracle may occur, human life itself being perhaps the most unlikely of miracles.

## The Spinoza of Market Street

I

Dr. Nahum Fischelson paced back and forth in his garret room in Market Street, Warsaw. Dr. Fischelson was a short, hunched man with a grayish beard, and was quite bald except for a few wisps of hair remaining at the nape of the neck. His nose was as crooked as a beak and his eyes were large, dark, and fluttering like those of some huge bird. It was a hot summer evening, but Dr. Fischelson wore a black coat which reached to his knees, and he had on a stiff collar and a bow tie. From the door he paced slowly to the dormer window set high in the slanting room and back again. One had to mount several steps to look out. A candle in a brass holder was burning on the table and a variety of insects buzzed around the flame. Now and again one of the creatures would fly too close to the fire and sear its wings, or one would ignite and glow on the wick for an instant. At such moments Dr. Fischelson grimaced. His wrinkled face would twitch and beneath his disheveled moustache he would bite his lips. Finally he took a handkerchief from his pocket and waved it at the insects.

"Away from there, fools and imbeciles," he scolded. "You won't get warm here; you'll only burn yourself."

The insects scattered but a second later returned and once more circled the trembling flame. Dr. Fischelson wiped the sweat from his wrinkled forehead and sighed, "Like men they desire nothing but the pleasure of the moment." On the table lay an open book written in Latin, and on its broad-margined pages were notes and comments printed in small letters by Dr. Fischelson. The book was Spinoza's *Ethics* and Dr. Fischelson had been studying it for the last thirty years. He knew every proposition, every proof, every corollary, every note by heart. When he wanted to find a particular passage, he generally opened to the place immediately without having to search for it. But, nevertheless, he continued to study the *Ethics* for hours every day with a magnifying glass in his bony hand, murmuring and nodding his head in agreement. The truth was that the more Dr. Fischelson studied, the more puzzling sentences, unclear passages, and cryptic remarks he found. Each sentence contained hints unfathomed by any of the students of Spinoza. Actually the philosopher had anticipated all of the criticisms of pure reason made by Kant and his followers. Dr. Fischelson was writing a commentary on the *Ethics.* He had drawers full of notes and drafts, but it didn't seem that he would ever be able to complete his work. The stomach ailment which had plagued him for years was growing worse from day to day. Now he would get pains in his stomach after only a few mouthfuls of oatmeal. "God in Heaven, it's difficult, very difficult," he would say to himself using the same intonation as had his father, the late Rabbi of Tishevitz. "It's very, very hard."

Dr. Fischelson was not afraid of dying. To begin with, he was no longer a young man. Secondly, it is stated in the fourth part of the *Ethics* that "a free man thinks of nothing less than of death and his wisdom is a meditation not of death, but of life." Thirdly, it is also said that "the human mind cannot be absolutely destroyed with the human body but there is some part of it that remains eternal." And yet Dr. Fischelson's ulcer (or perhaps it was a cancer) continued to bother him. His tongue was always coated. He belched frequently and emitted a different foul-smelling gas each time. He suffered from heartburn and cramps. At times he felt like vomiting and at other times he was hungry for garlic, onions, and fried foods. He had long ago discarded the medicines prescribed for him by the doctors and had sought his own remedies. He found it beneficial to take grated radish after meals and lie on his bed, belly down, with his head hanging over the side. But these home remedies offered only temporary relief. Some of the doctors he consulted insisted there was nothing the matter with him. "It's just nerves," they told him. "You could live to be a hundred."

But on this particular hot summer night, Dr. Fischelson felt his strength ebbing. His knees were shaky, his pulse weak. He sat down to read and his vision blurred. The letters on the page turned from green to gold. The lines became waved and jumped over each other, leaving white gaps as if the text had disappeared in some mysterious way. The heat was unbearable, flowing down directly from the tin roof; Dr. Fischelson felt he was inside of an oven. Several times he climbed the four steps to the window and thrust his head out into the cool of the evening breeze. He would remain in that position for so long his knees would become wobbly. "Oh it's a fine breeze," he would murmur, "really delightful," and he would recall that according to Spinoza, morality and happiness were identical, and that the most moral deed a man could perform was to indulge in some pleasure which was not contrary to reason.

2

Dr. Fischelson, standing on the top step at the window and looking out, could see into two worlds. Above him were the heavens, thickly strewn with stars. Dr. Fischelson had never seriously studied astronomy but he could differentiate between the planets, those bodies which like the earth, revolve around the sun, and the fixed stars, themselves distant suns, whose light reaches us a hundred or even a thousand years later. He recognized the constellations which mark the path of the earth in space and that nebulous sash, the Milky Way. Dr. Fischelson owned a small telescope he had bought in Switzerland where he had studied and he particularly enjoyed looking at the moon through it. He could clearly make out on the moon's surface the volcanoes bathed in sunlight and the dark, shadowy craters. He never wearied of gazing at these cracks and crevasses. To him they seemed both near and distant, both substantial and insubstantial. Now and then he would see a shooting star trace a wide arc across the sky and disappear, leaving a fiery trail behind it. Dr. Fischelson would know then that a meteorite had reached our atmosphere, and perhaps some unburned fragment of it had fallen into the ocean or had landed in the desert or perhaps even in some inhabited region. Slowly the stars which had appeared from behind Dr. Fischelson's roof rose until they were shining above the house across the street. Yes, when Dr. Fischelson looked up into the heavens, he became aware of that infinite extension which is, according to Spinoza, one of God's attributes. It comforted Dr. Fischelson to think that although he was only a weak, puny man, a changing mode of the absolutely infinite Substance, he was nevertheless a part of the cosmos, made of the same matter as the celestial bodies; to the extent that he was a part of the Godhead, he knew he could not be destroyed. In such moments, Dr. Fischelson experienced the *Amor Dei Intellectualis* which is, according to the philosopher of Amsterdam, the highest perfection of the mind. Dr. Fischelson breathed deeply, lifted his head as high as his stiff collar permitted and actually felt he was whirling in company with the earth, the sun, the stars of the Milky Way, and the infinite host of galaxies known only to infinite thought. His legs became light and weightless and he grasped the window frame with both hands as if afraid he would lose his footing and fly out into eternity.

When Dr. Fischelson tired of observing the sky, his glance dropped to Market Street below. He could see a long strip extending from Yanash's market to Iron Street with the gas lamps lining it merged into a string of fiery dots. Smoke was issuing from the chimneys on the black, tin roofs; the bakers were heating their ovens, and here and there sparks mingled with the black smoke. The street never looked so noisy and crowded as on a summer evening. Thieves, prostitutes, gamblers, and fences loafed in the square which looked from above like a pretzel covered with poppy seeds. The young men laughed coarsely and the girls shrieked. A peddler with a keg of lemonade on his back pierced the general din with his intermittent cries. A watermelon vendor shouted in a savage voice, and the long knife which he used for cutting the fruit dripped with the blood-like juice. Now and again the street became even more agitated. Fire engines, their heavy wheels clanging, sped by; they were drawn by sturdy black horses which had to be tightly curbed to prevent them from running wild. Next came an ambulance, its siren screaming. Then some thugs had a fight among themselves and the police had to be called. A passerby was robbed and ran about shouting for help. Some wagons loaded with firewood sought to get through into the courtyards where the bakeries were located but the horses could not lift the wheels over the steep curbs and the drivers berated the animals and lashed them with their whips. Sparks rose from the clanging hoofs. It was now long after seven, which was the prescribed closing time for stores, but actually business had only begun. Customers were led in stealthily through back doors. The Russian policemen on the street, having been paid off, noticed nothing of this. Merchants continued to hawk their wares, each seeking to outshout the others.

"Gold, gold, gold," a woman who dealt in rotten oranges shrieked.

"Sugar, sugar, sugar," croaked a dealer of overripe plums.

"Heads, heads, heads," a boy who sold fishheads roared.

Through the window of a *Chassidic* study house across the way, Dr. Fischelson could see boys with long sidelocks swaying over holy volumes, grimacing and studying aloud in singsong voices. Butchers, porters, and fruit dealers were drinking beer in the tavern below. Vapor drifted from the tavern's open door like steam from a bathhouse, and there was the sound of loud music. Outside of the tavern, streetwalkers snatched at drunken soldiers and at workers on their way home from the factories. Some of the men carried bundles of wood on their shoulders, reminding Dr. Fischelson of the wicked who are condemned to kindle their own fires in Hell. Husky record players poured out their raspings through open windows. The liturgy of the high holidays alternated with vulgar vaudeville songs.

Dr. Fischelson peered into the half-lit bedlam and cocked his ears. He knew that the behavior of this rabble was the very antithesis of reason. These people were immersed in the vainest of passions, were drunk with emotions, and, according to Spinoza, emotion was never good. Instead of the pleasure they ran after, all they succeeded in obtaining was disease and prison, shame and the suffering that resulted from ignorance. Even the cats which loitered on the roofs here seemed more savage and passionate than those in other parts of the town. They caterwauled with the voices of women in labor, and like demons scampered up walls and leaped onto eaves and balconies. One of the toms paused at Dr. Fischelson's window and let out a howl which made Dr. Fischelson shudder. The doctor stepped from the window and, picking up a broom, brandished it in front of the black beast's glowing, green eyes. "Scat, begone, you ignorant savage!"—and he rapped the broom handle against the roof until the tom ran off.

## 3

When Dr. Fischelson had returned to Warsaw from Zurich where he had studied philosophy, a great future had been predicted for him. His friends had known that he was writing an important book on Spinoza. A Jewish Polish journal had invited him to be a contributor; he had been a frequent guest at several wealthy households and he had been made head librarian at the Warsaw synagogue. Although even then he had been considered an old bachelor, the matchmakers had proposed several rich girls for him. But Dr. Fischelson had not taken advantage of these opportunities. He had wanted to be as independent as Spinoza himself. And he had been. But because of his heretical ideas he had come into conflict with the rabbi and had had to resign his post as librarian. For years after that, he had supported himself by giving private lessons in Hebrew and German. Then, when he had become sick, the Berlin Jewish community had voted him a subsidy of five hundred marks a year. This had been made possible through the intervention of the famous Dr. Hildesheimer with whom he corresponded about philosophy. In order to get by on so small a pension, Dr. Fischelson had moved into the attic room and had begun cooking his own meals on a kerosene stove. He had a cupboard which had many drawers, and each drawer was labelled with the food it contained—buckwheat, rice, barley, onions, carrots, potatoes, mushrooms. Once a week Dr. Fischelson put on his wide-brimmed black hat, took a basket in one hand and Spinoza's *Ethics* in the other, and went off to the market for his provisions. While he was waiting to be served, he would open the *Ethics.* The merchants knew him and would motion him to their stalls.

"A fine piece of cheese, Doctor—just melts in your mouth."

"Fresh mushrooms, Doctor, straight from the woods."

"Make way for the Doctor, ladies," the butcher would shout. "Please don't block the entrance."

During the early years of his sickness, Dr. Fischelson had still gone in the evening to a café which was frequented by Hebrew teachers and other intellectuals. It had been his habit to sit there and play chess while drinking a half a glass of black coffee. Sometimes he would stop at the bookstores on Holy Cross Street where all sorts of old books and magazines could be purchased cheap. On one occasion a former pupil of his had arranged to meet him at a restaurant one evening. When Dr. Fischelson arrived, he had been surprised to find a group of friends and admirers who forced him to sit at the head of the table while they made speeches about him. But these were things that had happened long ago. Now people were no longer interested in him. He had isolated himself completely and had become a forgotten man. The events of 1905 when the boys of Market Street had begun to organize strikes, throw bombs at police stations, and shoot strike breakers so that the stores were closed even on weekdays had greatly increased his isolation. He began to despise everything associated with the modern Jew—Zionism, socialism, anarchism. The young men in question seemed to him nothing but an ignorant rabble intent on destroying society, society without which no reasonable existence was possible. He still read a Hebrew magazine occasionally, but he felt contempt for modern Hebrew which had no roots in the Bible or the Mishnah. The spelling of Polish words had changed also. Dr. Fischelson concluded that even the so-called spiritual men had abandoned reason and were doing their utmost to pander to the mob. Now and again he still visited a library and browsed through some of the modern histories of philosophy, but he found that the professors did not understand Spinoza, quoted him incorrectly, attributed their own muddled ideas to the philosopher. Although Dr. Fischelson was well aware that anger was an emotion unworthy of those who walk the path of reason, he would become furious, and would quickly close the book and push it from him. "Idiots," he would mutter, "asses, upstarts." And he would vow never again to look at modern philosophy.

4

Every three months a special mailman who only delivered money orders brought Dr. Fischelson eighty rubles. He expected his quarterly allotment at the beginning of July but as day after day passed and the tall man with the blond moustache and the shiny buttons did not appear, the Doctor grew anxious. He had scarcely a groshen left. Who knows—possibly the Berlin Community had rescinded his subsidy; perhaps Dr. Hildesheimer had died, God forbid; the post office might have made a mistake. Every event has its cause, Dr. Fischelson knew. All was determined, all necessary, and a man of reason had no right to worry. Nevertheless, worry invaded his brain, and buzzed about like the flies. If the worst came to the worst, it occurred to him, he could commit suicide, but then he remembered that Spinoza did not approve of suicide and compared those who took their own lives to the insane.

One day when Dr. Fischelson went out to a store to purchase a composition book, he heard people talking about war. In Serbia somewhere, an Austrian Prince had been shot and the Austrians had delivered an ultimatum to the Serbs. The owner of the store, a young man with a yellow beard and shifty yellow eyes, announced, "We are about to have a small war," and he advised Dr. Fischelson to store up food because in the near future there was likely to be a shortage.

Everything happened so quickly. Dr. Fischelson had not even decided whether it was worthwhile to spend four groshen on a newspaper, and already posters had been hung up announcing mobilization. Men were to be seen walking on the street with round, metal tags on their lapels, a sign that they were being drafted. They were followed by their crying wives. One Monday when Dr. Fischelson descended to the street to buy some food with his last kopecks, he found the stores closed. The owners and their wives stood outside and explained that merchandise was unobtainable. But certain special customers were pulled to one side and let in through back doors. On the street all was confusion. Policemen with swords unsheathed could be seen riding on horseback. A large crowd had gathered around the tavern where, at the command of the Tsar, the tavern's stock of whiskey was being poured into the gutter.

Dr. Fischelson went to his old café. Perhaps he would find some acquaintances there who would advise him. But he did not come across a single person he knew. He decided, then, to visit the rabbi of the synagogue where he had once been librarian, but the sexton with the six-sided skull cap informed him that the rabbi and his family had gone off to the spas. Dr. Fischelson had other old friends in town but he found no one at home. His feet ached from so much walking; black and green spots appeared before his eyes and he felt faint. He stopped and waited for the giddiness to pass. The passers-by jostled him. A dark-eyed high school girl tried to give him a coin. Although the war had just started, soldiers eight abreast were marching in full battle dress—the men were covered with dust and were sunburnt. Canteens were strapped to their sides and they wore rows of bullets across their chests. The bayonets on their rifles gleamed with a cold, green light. They sang with mournful voices. Along with the men came cannons, each pulled by eight horses; their blind muzzles breathed gloomy terror. Dr. Fischelson felt nauseous. His stomach ached; his intestines seemed about to turn themselves inside out. Cold sweat appeared on his face.

"I'm dying," he thought. "This is the end." Nevertheless, he did manage to drag himself home where he lay down on the iron cot and remained, panting and gasping. He must have dozed off because he imagined that he was in his home town, Tishvitz. He had a sore throat and his mother was busy wrapping a stocking stuffed with hot salt around his neck. He could hear talk going on in the house; something about a candle and about how a frog had bitten him. He wanted to go out into the street but they wouldn't let him because a Catholic procession was passing by. Men in long robes, holding double edged axes in their hands, were intoning in Latin as they sprinkled holy water. Crosses gleamed; sacred pictures waved in the air. There was an odor of incense and corpses. Suddenly the sky turned a burning red and the whole world started to burn. Bells were ringing; people rushed madly about. Flocks of birds flew overhead, screeching. Dr. Fischelson awoke with a start. His body was covered with sweat and his throat was now actually sore. He tried to meditate about his extraordinary dream, to find its rational connection with what was happening to him and to comprehend it *sub specie eternitatis,* but none of it made sense. "Alas, the brain is a receptacle for nonsense," Dr. Fischelson thought. "This earth belongs to the mad."

And he once more closed his eyes; once more he dozed; once more he dreamed.

## 5

The eternal laws, apparently, had not yet ordained Dr. Fischelson's end.

There was a door to the left of Dr. Fischelson's attic room which opened off a dark corridor, cluttered with boxes and baskets, in which the odor of fried onions and laundry soap was always present. Behind this door lived a spinster whom the neighbors called Black Dobbe. Dobbe was tall and lean, and as black as a baker's shovel. She had a broken nose and there was a mustache on her upper lip. She spoke with the hoarse voice of a man and she wore men's shoes. For years Black Dobbe had sold breads, rolls, and bagels which she had bought from the baker at the gate of the house. But one day she and the baker had quarreled and she had moved her business to the market place and now she dealt in what were called "wrinklers" which was a synonym for cracked eggs. Black Dobbe had no luck with men. Twice she had been engaged to baker's apprentices but in both instances they had returned the engagement contract to her. Some time afterwards she had received an engagement contract from an old man, a glazier who claimed that he was divorced, but it had later come to light that he still had a wife. Black Dobbe had a cousin in America, a shoemaker, and repeatedly she boasted that this cousin was sending her passage, but she remained in Warsaw. She was constantly being teased by the women who would say, "There's no hope for you, Dobbe. You're fated to die an old maid." Dobbe always answered, "I don't intend to be a slave for any man. Let them all rot."

That afternoon Dobbe received a letter from America. Generally she would go to Leizer the Tailor and have him read it to her. However, that day Leizer was out and so Dobbe thought of Dr. Fischelson whom the other tenants considered a convert since he never went to prayer. She knocked on the door of the doctor's room but there was no answer. "The heretic is probably out," Dobbe thought but, nevertheless, she knocked once more, and this time the door moved slightly. She pushed her way in and stood there frightened. Dr. Fischelson lay fully clothed on his bed; his face was as yellow as wax; his Adam's apple stuck out prominently; his beard pointed upward. Dobbe screamed; she was certain that he was dead, but—no—his body moved. Dobbe picked up a glass which stood on the table, ran into the corridor, filled the glass with water from the faucet, hurried back, and threw the water into the face of the unconscious man. Dr. Fischelson shook his head and opened his eyes.

"What's wrong with you?" Dobbe asked. "Are you sick?"

"Thank you very much. No."

"Have you a family? I'll call them."

"No family," Dr. Fischelson said.

Dobbe wanted to fetch the barber from across the street but Dr. Fischelson signified that he didn't wish the barber's assistance. Since Dobbe was not going to the market that day, no "wrinklers" being available, she decided to do a good deed. She assisted the sick man to get off the bed and smoothed down the blanket. Then she undressed Dr. Fischelson and prepared some soup for him on the kerosene stove. The sun never entered Dobbe's room, but here squares of sunlight shimmered on the faded walls. The floor was painted red. Over the bed hung a picture of a man who was wearing a broad frill around his neck and had long hair. "Such an old fellow and yet he keeps his place so nice and clean," Dobbe thought approvingly. Dr. Fischelson asked for the *Ethics,* and she gave it to him disapprovingly. She was certain it was a gentile prayer book. Then she began bustling about, brought in a pail of water, swept the floor. Dr. Fischelson ate; after he had finished, he was much stronger and Dobbe asked him to read her the letter.

He read it slowly, the paper trembling in his hands. It came from New York, from Dobbe's cousin. Once more he wrote that he was about to send her a "really important letter" and a ticket to America. By now, Dobbe knew the story by heart and she helped the old man decipher her cousin's scrawl. "He's lying," Dobbe said. "He forgot about me a long time ago." In the evening, Dobbe came again. A candle in a brass holder was burning on the chair next to the bed. Reddish shadows trembled on the walls and ceiling. Dr. Fischelson sat propped up in bed, reading a book. The candle threw a golden light on his forehead which seemed as if cleft in two. A bird had flown in through the window and was perched on the table. For a moment Dobbe was frightened. This man made her think of witches, of black mirrors and corpses wandering around at night and terrifying women. Nevertheless, she took a few steps toward him and inquired, "How are you? Any better?"

"A little, thank you."

"Are you really a convert?" she asked although she wasn't quite sure what the word meant.

"Me, a convert? No, I'm a Jew like any other Jew," Dr. Fischelson answered.

The doctor's assurances made Dobbe feel more at home. She found the bottle of kerosene and lit the stove, and after that she fetched a glass of milk from her room and began cooking kasha. Dr. Fischelson continued to study the *Ethics,* but that evening he could make no sense of the theorems and proofs with their many references to axioms and definitions and other theorems. With trembling hand he raised the book to his eyes and read, "The idea of each modification of the human body does not involve adequate knowledge of the human body itself. . . . The idea of the idea of each modification of the human mind does not involve adequate knowledge of the human mind."

## 6

Dr. Fischelson was certain he would die any day now. He made out his will, leaving all of his books and manuscripts to the synagogue library. His clothing and furniture would go to Dobbe since she had taken care of him. But death did not come. Rather his health improved. Dobbe returned to her business in the market, but she visited the old man several times a day, prepared soup for him, left him a glass of tea, and told him news of the war. The Germans had occupied Kalish, Bendin, and Cestechow, and they were marching on Warsaw. People said that on a quiet morning one could hear the rumblings of the cannon. Dobbe reported that the casualties were heavy. "They're falling like flies," she said. "What a terrible misfortune for the women."

She couldn't explain why, but the old man's attic room attracted her. She liked to remove the gold-rimmed books from the bookcase, dust them, and then air them on the window sill. She would climb the few steps to the window and look out through the telescope. She also enjoyed talking to Dr. Fischelson. He told her about Switzerland where he had studied, of the great cities he had passed through, of the high mountains that were covered with snow even in the summer. His father had been a rabbi, he said, and before he, Dr. Fischelson, had become a student, he had attended a yeshiva. She asked him how many languages he knew and it turned out that he could speak and write Hebrew, Russian, German, and French, in addition to Yiddish. He also knew Latin. Dobbe was astonished that such an educated man should live in an attic room on Market Street. But what amazed her most of all was that although he had the title "Doctor," he couldn't write prescriptions. "Why don't you become a real doctor?" she would ask him. "I am a doctor," he would answer. "I'm just not a physician." "What kind of a doctor?" "A doctor of philosophy." Although she had no idea of what this meant, she felt it must be very important. "Oh my blessed mother," she would say, "where did you get such a brain?"

Then one evening after Dobbe had given him his crackers and his glass of tea with milk, he began questioning her about where she came from, who her parents were, and why she had not married. Dobbe was surprised. No one had ever asked her such questions. She told him her story in a quiet voice and stayed until eleven o'clock. Her father had been a porter at the kosher butcher shops. Her mother had plucked chickens in the slaughterhouse. The family had lived in a cellar at No. 19 Market Street. When she had been ten, she had become a maid. The man she had worked for had been a fence who bought stolen goods from thieves on the square. Dobbe had had a brother who had gone into the Russian army and had never returned. Her sister had married a coachman in Praga and had died in childbirth. Dobbe told of the battles between the underworld and the revolutionaries in 1905, of blind Itche and his gang and how they collected protection money from the stores, of the thugs who attacked young boys and girls out on Saturday afternoon strolls if they were not paid money for security. She also spoke of the pimps who drove about in carriages and abducted women to be sold in Buenos Aires. Dobbe swore that some men had even sought to inveigle her into a brothel, but that she had run away. She complained of a thousand evils done to her. She had been robbed; her boy friend had been stolen; a competitor had once poured a pint of kerosene into her basket of bagels; her own cousin, the shoemaker, had cheated her out of a hundred rubles before he had left for America. Dr. Fischelson listened to her attentively. He asked her questions, shook his head, and grunted.

"Well, do you believe in God?" he finally asked her.

"I don't know," she answered. "Do you?"

"Yes, I believe."

"Then why don't you go to synagogue?" she asked.

"God is everywhere," he replied. "In the synagogue. In the marketplace. In this very room. We ourselves are parts of God."

"Don't say such things," Dobbe said. "You frighten me."

She left the room and Dr. Fischelson was certain she had gone to bed. But he wondered why she had not said "good night." "I probably drove her away with my philosophy," he thought. The very next moment he heard her footsteps. She came in carrying a pile of clothing like a peddler.

"I wanted to show you these," she said. "They're my trousseau." And she began to spread out, on the chair, dresses—woolen, silk, velvet. Taking each dress up in turn, she held it to her body. She gave him an account of every item in her trousseau—underwear, shoes, stockings.

"I'm not wasteful, she said. "I'm a saver. I have enough money to go to America."

Then she was silent and her face turned brick-red. She looked at Dr. Fischelson out of the corner of her eyes, timidly, inquisitively. Dr. Fischelson's body suddenly began to shake as if he had the chills. He said, "Very nice, beautiful things." His brow furrowed and he pulled at his beard with two fingers. A sad smile appeared on his toothless mouth and his large fluttering eyes, gazing into the distance through the attic window, also smiled sadly.

## 7

The day that Black Dobbe came to the rabbi's chambers and announced that she was to marry Dr. Fischelson, the rabbi's wife thought she had gone mad. But the news had already reached Leizer the Tailor, and had spread to the bakery, as well as to other shops. There were those who thought that the "old maid" was very lucky; the doctor, they said, had a vast hoard of money. But there were others who took the view that he was a run-down degenerate who would give her syphilis. Although Dr. Fischelson had insisted that the wedding be a small, quiet one, a host of guests assembled in the rabbi's rooms. The baker's apprentices who generally went about barefoot, and in their underwear, with paper bags on the tops of their heads, now put on light-colored suits, straw hats, yellow shoes, gaudy ties, and they brought with them huge cakes and pans filled with cookies. They had even managed to find a bottle of vodka although liquor was forbidden in wartime. When the bride and groom entered the rabbi's chamber, a murmur arose from the crowd. The women could not believe their eyes. The woman that they saw was not the one they had known. Dobbe wore a wide-brimmed hat which was amply adorned with cherries, grapes, and plumes, and the dress that she had on was of white silk and was equipped with a train; on her feet were high-heeled shoes, gold in color, and from her thin neck hung a string of imitation pearls. Nor was this all: her fingers sparkled with rings and glittering stones. Her face was veiled. She looked almost like one of those rich brides who were married in the Vienna Hall. The bakers' apprentices whistled mockingly. As for Dr. Fischelson, he was wearing his black coat and broad-toed shoes. He was scarcely able to walk; he was leaning on Dobbe. When he saw the crowd from the doorway, he became frightened and began to retreat, but Dobbe's former employer approached him saying, "Come in, come in, bridegroom. Don't be bashful. We are all brethren now."

The ceremony proceeded according to the law. The rabbi, in a worn satin gabardine, wrote the marriage contract and then had the bride and groom touch his handkerchief as a token of agreement; the rabbi wiped the point of the pen on his skullcap. Several porters who had been called from the street to make up the quorum supported the canopy. Dr. Fischelson put on a white robe as a reminder of the day of his death and Dobbe walked around him seven times as custom required. The light from the braided candles flickered on the walls. The shadows wavered. Having poured wine into a goblet, the rabbi chanted the benedictions in a sad melody. Dobbe uttered only a single cry. As for the other women, they took out their lace handkerchiefs and stood with them in their hands, grimacing. When the baker's boys began to whisper wisecracks to each other, the rabbi put a finger to his lips and murmured, *"Eh nu oh,"* as a sign that talking was forbidden. The moment came to slip the wedding ring on the bride's finger, but the bridegroom's hand started to tremble and he had trouble locating Dobbe's index finger. The next thing, according to custom, was the smashing of the glass, but though Dr. Fischelson kicked the goblet several times, it remained unbroken. The girls lowered their heads, pinched each other gleefully, and giggled. Finally one of the apprentices struck the goblet with his heel and it shattered. Even the rabbi could not restrain a smile. After the ceremony the guests drank vodka and ate cookies. Dobbe's former employer came up to Dr. Fischelson and said, "*Mazel tov,* bridegroom. Your luck should be as good as your wife." "Thank you, thank you," Dr. Fischelson murmured, "but I don't look forward to any luck." He was anxious to return as quickly as possible to his attic room. He felt a pressure in his stomach and his chest ached. His face had become greenish. Dobbe had suddenly become angry. She pulled back her veil and called out to the crowd, "What are you laughing at? This isn't a show." And without picking up the cushion-cover in which the gifts were wrapped, she returned with her husband to their rooms on the fifth floor.

Dr. Fischelson lay down on the freshly made bed in his room and began reading the *Ethics.* Dobbe had gone back to her own room. The doctor had explained to her that he was an old man, that he was sick and without strength. He had promised her nothing. Nevertheless she returned wearing a silk nightgown, slippers with pompoms, and with her hair hanging down over her shoulders. There was a smile on her face, and she was bashful and hesitant. Dr. Fischelson trembled and the *Ethics* dropped from his hands. The candle went out. Dobbe groped for Dr. Fischelson in the dark and kissed his mouth. "My dear husband," she whispered to him, *"Mazel tov."*

What happened that night could be called a miracle. If Dr. Fischelson hadn't been convinced that every occurrence is in accordance with the laws of nature, he would have thought that Black Dobbe had bewitched him. Powers long dormant awakened in him. Although he had had only a sip of the benediction wine, he was as if intoxicated. He kissed Dobbe and spoke to her of love. Long forgotten quotations from Klopfstock, Lessing, Goethe, rose to his lips. The pressures and aches stopped. He embraced Dobbe, pressed her to himself, was again a man as in his youth. Dobbe was faint with delight; crying, she murmured things to him in a Warsaw slang which he did not understand. Later, Dr. Fischelson slipped off into the deep sleep young men know. He dreamed that he was in Switzerland and that he was climbing mountains—running, falling, flying. At dawn he opened his eyes; it seemed to him that someone had blown into his ears. Dobbe was snoring. Dr. Fischelson quietly got out of bed. In his long nightshirt he approached the window, walked up the steps and looked out in wonder. Market Street was asleep, breathing with a deep stillness. The gas lamps were flickering. The black shutters on the stores were fastened with iron bars. A cool breeze was blowing. Dr. Fischelson looked up at the sky. The black arch was thickly sown with stars—there were green, red, yellow, blue stars; there were large ones and small ones, winking and steady ones. There were those that were clustered in dense groups and those that were alone. In the higher sphere, apparently, little notice was taken of the fact that a certain Dr. Fischelson had in his declining days married someone called Black Dobbe. Seen from above even the Great War was nothing but a temporary play of the modes. The myriads of fixed stars continued to travel their destined courses in unbounded space. The comets, planets, satellites, asteroids kept circling these shining centers. Worlds were born and died in cosmic upheavals. In the chaos of nebulae, primeval matter was being formed. Now and again a star tore loose, and swept across the sky, leaving behind it a fiery streak. It was the month of August when there are showers of meteors. Yes, the divine substance was extended and had neither beginning nor end; it was absolute, indivisible, eternal, without duration, infinite in its attributes. Its waves and bubbles danced in the universal cauldron, seething with change, following the unbroken chain of causes and effects, and he, Dr. Fischelson, with his unavoidable fate, was part of this. The doctor closed his eyelids and allowed the breeze to cool the sweat on his forehead and stir the hair of his beard. He breathed deeply of the midnight air, supported his shaky hands on the window sill and murmured, "Divine Spinoza, forgive me. I have become a fool."

TRANSLATED BY
MARTHA GLICKLICH
AND CECIL HEMLEY

# TILLIE OLSEN
## (1913– )

Tillie Olsen was born in Omaha, Nebraska, in 1912 or 1913, of working-class Russian Jewish immigrants who had fled Russia during the Czarist repression after the 1905 revolution. Her parents were deeply involved in the Socialist party, and Eugene Debs visited their home after the father was released from jail for protesting World War I. At age 16, Olsen had to drop out of high school to help support her family. She became a member of the Young Communist League, and was active in labor union organizing in Kansas City.

Olsen began her first novel *Yonnondio,* at age 19, writing four chapters over the next four years. She married, but her husband deserted her and their baby due to their impoverished circumstances. She met Jack Olsen through her labor and political activities, and married him in 1936. They had three children. Raising her children and supporting various causes kept Olsen from taking up writing again until 1953, when her youngest daughter started school. She then took writing classes at San Francisco State College, and in 1955 she went to Stanford University on a writing fellowship.

The four exquisite stories that make up her collection *Tell Me a Riddle* were published in a paper edition in 1961; this book established her reputation. The title story won the 1961 O. Henry Memorial Award. In 1972 Olsen wrote an introduction to a new edition of Rebecca Harding Davis' nineteenth-century novel, *Life in the Iron Mills*. With the help of grants and fellowships, Olsen was able to finish her novel *Yonnondio* in 1974. A series of reflective essays on the circumstances that promote or silence creativity were published as *Silences* in 1978. She now resides in Berkeley.

The intensity, beauty, and honesty of Olsen's stories, especially as they explore the lives of women, have led to Olsen being embraced and esteemed, indeed revered, by a whole generation of women coming of age with the reemergence of the women's movement in the 1960s. Her stories reach into the depths of all readers.

# I Stand Here Ironing

I STAND here ironing, and what you asked me moves tormented back and forth with the iron.

"I wish you would manage the time to come in and talk with me about your daughter. I'm sure you can help me understand her. She's a youngster who needs help and whom I'm deeply interested in helping."

"Who needs help." . . . Even if I came, what good would it do? You think because I am her mother I have a key, or that in some way you could use me as a key? She has lived for nineteen years. There is all that life that has happened outside of me, beyond me.

And when is there time to remember, to sift, to weigh, to estimate, to total? I will start and there will be an interruption and I will have to gather it all together again. Or I will become engulfed with all I did or did not do, with what should have been and what cannot be helped.

She was a beautiful baby. The first and only one of our five that was beautiful at birth. You do not guess how new and uneasy her tenancy in her now-loveliness. You did not know her all those years she was thought homely, or see her poring over her baby pictures, making me tell her over and over how beautiful she had been—and would be, I would tell her—and was now, to the seeing eye. But the seeing eyes were few or nonexistent. Including mine.

I nursed her. They feel that's important nowadays. I nursed all the children, but with her, with all the fierce rigidity of first motherhood, I did like the books then said. Though her cries battered me to trembling and my breasts ached with swollenness, I waited till the clock decreed.

Why do I put that first? I do not even know if it matters, or if it explains anything.

She was a beautiful baby. She blew shining bubbles of sound. She loved motion, loved light, loved color and music and textures. She would lie on the floor in her blue overalls patting the surface so hard in ecstasy her hands and feet would blur. She was a miracle to me, but when she was eight months old I had to leave her daytimes with the woman downstairs to whom she was no miracle at all, for I worked or looked for work and for Emily's father, who "could no longer endure" (he wrote in his good-bye note) "sharing want with us."

I was nineteen. It was the pre-relief, pre-WPA world of the depression. I would start running as soon as I got off the streetcar, running up the stairs, the place smelling sour, and awake or asleep to startle awake, when she saw me she would break into a clogged weeping that could not be comforted, a weeping I can hear yet.

After a while I found a job hashing at night so I could be with her days, and it was better. But it came to where I had to bring her to his family and leave her.

It took a long time to raise the money for her fare back. Then she got chicken pox and I had to wait longer. When she finally came, I hardly knew her, walking quick and nervous like her father, looking like her father, thin, and dressed in a shoddy red that yellowed her skin and glared at the pockmarks. All the baby loveliness gone.

She was two. Old enough for nursery school they said, and I did not know then what I know now—the fatigue of the long day, and the lacerations of group life in the kinds of nurseries that are only parking places for children.

Except that it would have made no difference if I had known. It was the only place there was. It was the only way we could be together, the only way I could hold a job.

And even without knowing, I knew. I knew the teacher that was evil because all these years it has curdled into my memory, the little boy hunched in the corner, her rasp, "why aren't you outside, because Alvin hits you? that's no reason, go out, scaredy." I knew Emily hated it even if she did not clutch and implore "don't go Mommy" like the other children, mornings.

She always had a reason why we should stay home. Momma, you look sick. Momma, I feel sick. Momma, the teachers aren't there today, they're sick. Momma, we can't go, there was a fire there last night. Momma, it's a holiday today, no school, they told me.

But never a direct protest, never rebellion. I think of our others in their three-, four-year-oldness—the explosions, the tempers, the denunciations, the demands—and I feel suddenly ill. I put the iron down. What in me demanded that goodness in her? And what was the cost, the cost to her of such goodness?

The old man living in the back once said in his gentle way: "You should smile at Emily more when you look at her." What *was* in my face when I looked at her? I loved her. There were all the acts of love.

It was only with the others I remembered what he said, and it was the face of joy, and not of care or tightness or worry I turned to them—too late for Emily. She does not smile easily, let alone almost always as her brothers and sisters do. Her face is closed and sombre, but when she wants, how fluid. You must have seen it in her pantomimes, you spoke of her rare gift for comedy on the stage that rouses a laughter out of the audience so dear they applaud and applaud and do not want to let her go.

Where does it come from, that comedy? There was none of it in her when she came back to me that second time, after I had had to send her away again. She had a new daddy now to learn to love, and I think perhaps it was a better time.

Except when we left her alone nights, telling ourselves she was old enough.

"Can't you go some other time, Mommy, like tomorrow?" she would ask. "Will it be just a little while you'll be gone? Do you promise?"

The time we came back, the front door open, the clock on the floor in the hall. She rigid awake. "It wasn't just a little while. I didn't cry. Three times I called you, just three times, and then I ran downstairs to open the door so you could come faster. The clock talked loud. I threw it away, it scared me what it talked."

She said the clock talked loud again that night I went to the hospital to have Susan. She was delirious with the fever that comes before red measles, but she was fully conscious all the week I was gone and the week after we were home when she could not come near the new baby or me.

She did not get well. She stayed skeleton thin, not wanting to eat, and night after night she had nightmares. She would call for me, and I would rouse from exhaustion to sleepily call back: "You're all right, darling, go to sleep, it's just a dream," and if she still called, in a sterner voice, "Now go to sleep, Emily, there's nothing to hurt you." Twice, only twice, when I had to get up for Susan anyhow, I went in to sit with her.

Now when it is too late (as if she would let me hold and comfort her like I do the others) I get up and go to her at once at her moan or restless stirring. "Are you awake, Emily? Can I get you something?" And the answer is always the same: "No, I'm all right, go back to sleep, Mother."

They persuaded me at the clinic to send her away to a convalescent home in the country where "she can have the kind of food and care you can't manage for her, and you'll be free to concentrate on the new baby." They still send children to that place. I see pictures on the society page of sleek young women planning affairs to raise money for it, or dancing at the affairs, or decorating Easter eggs or filling Christmas stockings for the children.

They never have a picture of the children so I do not know if the girls still wear those gigantic red bows and the ravaged looks on the every other Sunday when parents can come to visit "unless otherwise notified"—as we were notified the first six weeks.

Oh it is a handsome place, green lawns and tall trees and fluted flower beds. High up on the balconies of each cottage the children stand, the girls in their red bows and white dresses, the boys in white suits and giant red ties. The parents stand below shrieking up to be heard and the children shriek down to be heard, and between them the invisible wall "Not To Be Contaminated by Parental Germs or Physical Affection."

There was a tiny girl who always stood hand in hand with Emily. Her parents never came. One visit she was gone. "They moved her to Rose Cottage" Emily shouted in explanation. "They don't like you to love anybody here."

She wrote once a week, the labored writing of a seven-year-old. "I am fine. How is the baby. If I write my leter nicly I will have a star. Love." There never was a star. We wrote every other day, letters she could never hold or keep but only hear read—once. "We simply do not have room for children to keep any personal possessions," they patiently explained when we pieced one Sunday's shrieking together to plead how much it would mean to Emily, who loved so to keep things, to be allowed to keep her letters and cards.

Each visit she looked frailer. "She isn't eating," they told us.

(They had runny eggs for breakfast or mush with lumps, Emily said later, I'd hold it in my mouth and not swallow. Nothing ever tasted good, just when they had chicken.)

It took us eight months to get her released home, and only the fact that she gained back so little of her seven lost pounds convinced the social worker.

I used to try to hold and love her after she came back, but her body would stay stiff, and after a while she'd push away. She ate little. Food sickened her, and I think much of life too. Oh she had physical lightness and brightness, twinkling by on skates, bouncing like a ball up and down up and down over the jump rope, skimming over the hill; but these were momentary.

She fretted about her appearance, thin and dark and foreign-looking at a time when every little girl was supposed to look or thought she should look a chubby blond replica of Shirley Temple. The doorbell sometimes rang for her, but no one seemed to come and play in the house or be a best friend. Maybe because we moved so much.

There was a boy she loved painfully through two school semesters. Months later she told me how she had taken pennies from my purse to buy him candy. "Licorice was his favorite and I brought him some every day, but he still liked Jennifer better'n me. Why, Mommy?" The kind of question for which there is no answer.

School was a worry to her. She was not glib or quick in a world where glibness and quickness were easily confused with ability to learn. To her overworked and exasperated teachers she was an overconscientious "slow learner" who kept trying to catch up and was absent entirely too often.

I let her be absent, though sometimes the illness was imaginary. How different from my now-strictness about attendance with the others. I wasn't working. We had a new baby, I was home anyhow. Sometimes, after Susan grew old enough, I would keep her home from school, too, to have them all together.

Mostly Emily had asthma, and her breathing, harsh and labored, would fill the house with a curiously tranquil sound. I would bring the two old dresser mirrors and her boxes of collections to her bed. She would select beads and single earrings, bottle tops and shells, dried flowers and pebbles, old postcards and scraps, all sorts of oddments; then she and Susan would play Kingdom, setting up landscapes and furniture, peopling them with action.

Those were the only times of peaceful companionship between her and Susan. I have edged away from it, that poisonous feeling between them, that terrible balancing of hurts and needs I had to do between the two, and did so badly, those earlier years.

Oh there are conflicts between the others too, each one human, needing, demanding, hurting, taking—but only between Emily and Susan, no, Emily toward Susan that corroding resentment. It seems so obvious on the surface, yet it is not obvious. Susan, the second child, Susan, golden- and curly-haired and chubby, quick and articulate and assured, everything in appearance and manner Emily was not; Susan, not able to resist Emily's precious things, losing or sometimes clumsily breaking them; Susan telling jokes and riddles to company for applause while Emily sat silent (to say to me later: that was *my* riddle, Mother, I told it to Susan); Susan, who for all the five years' difference in age was just a year behind Emily in developing physically.

I am glad for that slow physical development that widened the difference between her and her contemporaries, though she suffered over it. She was too vulnerable for that terrible world of youthful competition, of preening and parading, of constant measuring of yourself against every other, of envy, "If I had that copper hair," "If I had that skin. . . ." She tormented herself enough about not looking like the others, there was enough of the unsureness, the having to be conscious of words before you speak, the constant caring—what are they thinking of me? without having it all magnified by the merciless physical drives.

Ronnie is calling. He is wet and I change him. It is rare there is such a cry now. That time of motherhood is almost behind me when the ear is not one's own but must always be racked and listening for the child cry, the child call. We sit for a while and I hold him, looking out over the city spread in charcoal with its soft aisles of light. *"Shoogily,"* he breathes and curls closer. I carry him back to bed, asleep. *Shoogily.* A funny word, a family word, inherited from Emily, invented by her to say: *comfort.*

In this and other ways she leaves her seal, I say aloud. And startle at my saying it. What do I mean? What did I start to gather together, to try and make coherent? I was at the terrible, growing years. War years. I do not remember them well. I was working, there were four smaller ones now, there was not time for her. She had to help be a mother, and housekeeper, and shopper. She had to set her seal. Mornings of crisis and near hysteria trying to get lunches packed, hair combed, coats and shoes found, everyone to school or Child Care on time, the baby ready for transportation. And always the paper scribbled on by a smaller one, the book looked at by Susan then mislaid, the homework not done. Running out to that huge school where she was one, she was lost, she was a drop; suffering over her unpreparedness, stammering and unsure in her classes.

There was so little time left at night after the kids were bedded down. She would struggle over books, always eating (it was in those years she developed her enormous appetite that is legendary in our family) and I would be ironing, or preparing food for the next day, or writing V-mail to Bill, or tending the baby. Sometimes, to make me laugh, or out of her despair, she would imitate happenings or types at school.

I think I said once: "Why don't you do something like this in the school amateur show?" One morning she phoned me at work, hardly understandable through the weeping: "Mother, I did it. I won, I won; they gave me first prize; they clapped and clapped and wouldn't let me go."

Now suddenly she was Somebody, and as imprisoned in her difference as she had been in her anonymity.

She began to be asked to perform at other high schools, even in colleges, then at city and statewide affairs. The first one we went to, I only recognized her that first moment when thin, shy, she almost drowned herself into the curtains. Then: Was this Emily? The control, the command, the convulsing and deadly clowning, the spell, then the roaring, stamping audience, unwilling to let this rare and precious laughter out of their lives.

Afterwards: You ought to do something about her with a gift like that—but without money or knowing how, what does one do? We have left it all to her, and the gift has as often eddied inside, clogged and clotted, as been used and growing.

She is coming. She runs up the stairs two at a time with her light graceful step, and I know she is happy tonight. Whatever it was that occasioned your call did not happen today.

"Aren't you ever going to finish the ironing, Mother? Whistler painted his mother in a rocker. I'd have to paint mine standing over an ironing board." This is one of her communicative nights and she tells me everything and nothing as she fixes herself a plate of food out of the icebox.

She is so lovely. Why did you want me to come in at all? Why were you concerned? She will find her way.

She starts up the stairs to bed. "Don't get *me* up with the rest in the morning." "But I thought you were having midterms." "Oh, those," she comes back in, kisses me, and says quite lightly, "in a couple of years when we'll all be atom-dead they won't matter a bit."

She has said it before. She *believes* it. But because I have been dredging the past, and all that compounds a human being is so heavy and meaningful in me, I cannot endure it tonight.

I will never total it all. I will never come in to say: She was a child seldom smiled at. Her father left me before she was a year old. I had to work her first six years when there was work, or I sent her home and to his relatives. There were years she had care she hated. She was dark and thin and foreign-looking in a world where the prestige went to blondness and curly hair and dimples; she was slow where glibness was prized. She was a child of anxious, not proud, love. We were poor and could not afford for her the soil of easy growth. I was a young mother, I was a distracted mother. There were the other children pushing up, demanding. Her younger sister seemed all that she was not. There were years she did not let me touch her. She kept too much in herself, her life was such she had to keep too much in herself. My wisdom came too late. She has much to her and probably little will come of it. She is a child of her age, of depression, of war, of fear.

Let her be. So all that is in her will not bloom—but in how many does it? There is still enough left to live by. Only help her to know—help make it so there is cause for her to know—that she is more than this dress on the ironing board, helpless before the iron.

# RALPH ELLISON

## (1914–1994)

Ralph Ellison was born in Oklahoma City, Oklahoma, and raised in a close-knit black community. His father died when he was 3 years old, and his mother went to work as a domestic servant. His mother also was an activist recruiting for the Socialist party.

Ellison's first love was music: he began playing the trumpet at age 8 and later played in his high school band. He went to the Tuskegee Institute in Alabama in 1933 to study music, but left after three years to go to New York City. There he met the writers Langston Hughes and Richard Wright; the latter influenced and encouraged his writing ambitions. He worked with the Federal Writers Project in the late 1930s and began publishing stories, essays, and reviews in various periodicals. In 1942 Ellison became managing editor of the *Negro Quarterly*.

Ellison achieved international fame for his novel *Invisible Man* (1952), which won both the National Book Award and the Pulitzer Prize for fiction in 1953. A collection of essays entitled *Shadow and Act* was published in 1964, and another, *Going to the Territory,* in 1986. His stories were collected in *Flying Home and Other Stories,* published in 1996.

Ellison taught in a number of universities abroad and in the United States. He held the Albert Schweitzer Professorship of Contemporary Literature and Culture at New York University until his retirement. A long-awaited second novel was lost in a fire at his summer home in the Berkshires, although segments of it had appeared in various periodicals from 1960 to 1977. The novel he was working on at the time of his death was compiled and edited by John F. Callahan and was published in 1999 under the title *Juneteenth.*

For Ellison, America was a frontier culture of "infinite possibilities," a conception expressed quite well throughout his fiction. While some readers criticized him for not being strongly militant on racial issues in his work, Ellison continued to believe in the universality of human experience, one person's journey reflecting everyone's journey. The struggle to define one's self and achieve dignity is both particular and universal.

## Battle Royal

IT GOES a long way back, some twenty years. All my life I had been looking for something, and everywhere I turned someone tried to tell me what it was. I accepted their answers too, though they were often in contradiction and even self-contradictory. I was naïve. I was looking for myself and asking everyone except myself questions which I, and only I, could answer. It took me a long time and much painful boomeranging of my expectations to achieve a realization everyone else appears to have been born with: That I am nobody but myself. But first I had to discover that I am an invisible man!

And yet I am no freak of nature, nor of history. I was in the cards, other things having been equal (or unequal) eighty-five years ago. I am not ashamed of my grandparents for having been slaves. I am only ashamed of myself for having at one time been ashamed. About eighty-five years ago they were told they were free, united with others of our country in everything pertaining to the common good, and, in everything social, separate like the fingers of the hand. And they believed it. They exulted in it. They stayed in their place, worked hard, and brought up my father to do the same. But my grandfather is the one. He was an odd old guy, my grandfather, and I am told I take after him. It was he who caused the trouble. On his deathbed he called my father to him and said, "Son, after I'm gone I want you to keep up the good fight. I never told you, but our life is a war and I have been a traitor all my born days, a spy in the enemy's country ever since I give up my gun back in the Reconstruction. Live with your head in the lion's mouth. I want you to overcome 'em with yeses, undermine 'em with grins, agree 'em to death and destruction, let 'em swoller you till they vomit or bust wide open." They thought the old man had gone out of his mind. He had been the meekest of men. The younger children were rushed from the room, the shades drawn and the flame of the lamp turned so low that it sputtered on the wick like the old man's breathing. "Learn it to the younguns," he whispered fiercely; then he died.

But my folks were more alarmed over his last words than over his dying. It was as though he had not died at all, his words caused so much anxiety. I was warned emphatically to forget what he had said and, indeed, this is the first time it has been mentioned outside the family circle. It had a tremendous effect upon me, however. I could never be sure of what he meant. Grandfather had been a quiet old man who never made any trouble, yet on his deathbed he had called himself a traitor and a spy, and he had spoken of his meekness as a dangerous activity. It became a constant puzzle which lay unanswered in the back of my mind. And whenever things went well for me I remembered my grandfather and felt guilty and uncomfortable. It was as though I was carrying out his advice in spite of myself. And to make it worse, everyone loved me for it. I was praised by the most lily-white men in town. I was considered an example of desirable conduct—just as my grandfather had been. And what puzzled me was that the old man had defined it as *treachery.* When I was praised for my conduct I felt a guilt that in some way I was doing something that was really against the wishes of the white folks, that if they had understood they would have desired me to act just the opposite, that I should have been sulky and mean, and that that really would have been what they wanted, even though they were fooled and thought they wanted me to act as I did. It made me afraid that some day they would look upon me as a traitor and I would be lost. Still I was more afraid to act any other way because they didn't like that at all. The old man's words were like a curse. On my graduation day I delivered an oration in which I showed that humility was the secret, indeed, the very essence of progress. (Not that I believed this—how could I, remembering my grandfather?—I only believed that it worked.) It was a great success. Everyone praised me and I was invited to give the speech at a gathering of the town's leading white citizens. It was a triumph for the whole community.

It was in the main ballroom of the leading hotel. When I got there I discovered that it was on the occasion of a smoker, and I was told that since I was to be there anyway I might as well take part in the battle royal to be fought by some of my schoolmates as part of the entertainment. The battle royal came first.

All of the town's big shots were there in their tuxedoes, wolfing down the buffet foods, drinking beer and whiskey and smoking black cigars. It was a large room with a high ceiling. Chairs were arranged in neat rows around three sides of a portable boxing ring. The fourth side was clear, revealing a gleaming space of polished floor. I had some misgivings over the battle royal, by the way. Not from a distaste for fighting but because I didn't care too much for the other fellows who were to take part. They were tough guys who seemed to have no grandfather's curse worrying their minds. No one could mistake their toughness. And besides, I suspected that fighting a battle royal might detract from the dignity of my speech. In those pre-invisible days I visualized myself as a potential Booker T. Washington. But the other fellows didn't care too much for me either, and there were nine of them. I felt superior to them in my way, and I didn't like the manner in which we were all crowded together in the servants' elevator. Nor did they like my being there. In fact, as the warmly lighted floors flashed past the elevator we had words over the fact that I, by taking part in the fight, had knocked one of their friends out of a night's work.

We were led out of the elevator through a rococo hall into an anteroom and told to get into our fighting togs. Each of us was issued a pair of boxing gloves and ushered out into the big mirrored hall, which we entered looking cautiously about us and whispering, lest we might accidentally be heard above the noise of the room. It was foggy with cigar smoke. And already the whiskey was taking effect. I was shocked to see some of the most important men of the town quite tipsy. They were all there—bankers, lawyers, judges, doctors, fire chiefs, teachers, merchants. Even one of the more fashionable pastors. Something we could not see was going on up front. A clarinet was vibrating sensuously and the men were standing up and moving eagerly forward. We were a small tight group, clustered together, our bare upper bodies touching and shining with anticipatory sweat: while up front the big shots were becoming increasingly excited over something we still could not see. Suddenly I heard the school superintendent, who had told me to come, yell, "Bring up the shines, gentlemen! Bring up the little shines!"

We were rushed up to the front of the ballroom, where it smelled even more strongly of tobacco and whiskey. Then we were pushed into place. I almost wet my pants. A sea of faces, some hostile, some amused, ringed around us, and in the center, facing us, stood a magnificent blonde—stark naked. There was dead silence. I felt a blast of cold air chill me. I tried to back away, but they were behind me and around me. Some of the boys stood with lowered heads, trembling. I felt a wave of irrational guilt and fear. My teeth chattered, my skin turned to goose flesh, my knees knocked. Yet I was strongly attracted and looked in spite of myself. Had the price of looking been blindness, I would have looked. The hair was yellow like that of a circus kewpie doll, the face heavily powdered and rouged, as though to form an abstract mask, the eyes hollow and smeared a cool blue, the color of a baboon's butt. I felt a desire to spit upon her as my eyes brushed slowly over her body. Her breasts were firm and round as the domes of East Indian temples, and I stood so close as to see the fine skin texture and beads of pearly perspiration glistening like dew around the pink and erected buds of her nipples. I wanted at one and the same time to run from the room, to sink through the floor, or go to her and cover her from my eyes and the eyes of the others with my body; to feel the soft thighs, to caress her and destroy her, to love her and to murder her, to hide from her, and yet to stroke where below the small American flag tattooed upon her belly her thighs formed a capital V. I had a notion that of all in the room she saw only me with her impersonal eyes.

And then she began to dance, a slow sensuous movement; the smoke of a hundred cigars clinging to her like the thinnest of veils. She seemed like a fair bird-girl girdled in veils calling to me from the angry surface of some gray and threatening sea. I was transported. Then I became aware of the clarinet playing and the big shots yelling at us. Some threatened us if we looked and others if we did not. On my right I saw one boy faint. And now a man grabbed a silver pitcher from a table and stepped close as he dashed ice water upon him and stood him up and forced two of us to support him as his head hung and moans issued from his thick bluish lips. Another boy began to plead to go home. He was the largest of the group, wearing dark red fighting trunks much too small to conceal the erection which projected from him as though in answer to the insinuating low-registered moaning of the clarinet. He tried to hide himself with his boxing gloves.

And all the while the blonde continued dancing, smiling faintly at the big shots who watched her with fascination, and faintly smiling at our fear. I noticed a certain merchant who followed her hungrily, his lips loose and drooling. He was a large man who wore diamond studs in a shirtfront which swelled with the ample paunch underneath, and each time the blonde swayed her undulating hips he ran his hand through the thin hair of his bald head and, with his arms upheld, his posture clumsy like that of an intoxicated panda, wound his belly in a slow and obscene grind. This creature was completely hypnotized. The music had quickened. As the dancer flung herself about with a detached expression on her face, the men began reaching out to touch her. I could see their beefy fingers sink into her soft flesh. Some of the others tried to stop them and she began to move around the floor in graceful circles, as they gave chase, slipping and sliding over the polished floor. It was mad. Chairs went crashing, drinks were spilt, as they ran laughing and howling after her. They caught her just as she reached a door, raised her from the floor, and tossed her as college boys are tossed at a hazing, and above her red, fixed-smiling lips I saw the terror and disgust in her eyes, almost like my own terror and that which I saw in some of the other boys. As I watched, they tossed her twice and her soft breasts seemed to flatten against the air and her legs flung wildly as she spun. Some of the more sober ones helped her to escape. And I started off the floor, heading for the anteroom with the rest of the boys.

Some were still crying and in hysteria. But as we tried to leave we were stopped and ordered to get into the ring. There was nothing to do but what we were told. All ten of us climbed under the ropes and allowed ourselves to be blindfolded with broad bands of white cloth. One of the men seemed to feel a bit sympathetic and tried to cheer us up as we stood with our backs against the ropes. Some of us tried to grin. "See that boy over there?" one of the men said. "I want you to run across at the bell and give it to him right in the belly. If you don't get him, I'm going to get you. I don't like his looks." Each of us was told the same. The blindfolds were put on. Yet even then I had been going over my speech. In my mind each word was as bright as a flame. I felt the cloth pressed into place, and frowned so that it would be loosened when I relaxed.

But now I felt a sudden fit of blind terror. I was unused to darkness, it was as though I had suddenly found myself in a dark room filled with poisonous cottonmouths. I could hear the bleary voices yelling insistently for the battle royal to begin.

"Get going in there!"

"Let me at that big nigger!"

I strained to pick up the school superintendent's voice, as though to squeeze some security out of that slightly more familiar sound.

"Let me at those black sonsabitches!" someone yelled.

"No, Jackson, no!" another voice yelled. "Here, somebody, help me hold Jack."

"I want to get at that ginger-colored nigger. Tear him limb from limb," the first voice yelled.

I stood against the ropes trembling. For in those days I was what they called ginger-colored, and he sounded as though he might crunch me between his teeth like a crisp ginger cookie.

Quite a struggle was going on. Chairs were being kicked about and I could hear voices grunting as with terrific effort. I wanted to see, to see more desperately than ever before. But the blindfold was as tight as a thick skin-puckering scab and when I raised my gloved hands to push the layers of white aside a voice yelled, "Oh, no you don't, black bastard! Leave that alone!"

"Ring the bell before Jackson kills him a coon!" someone boomed in the sudden silence. And I heard the bell clang and the sound of the feet scuffling forward.

A glove smacked against my head. I pivoted, striking out stiffly as someone went past, and felt the jar ripple along the length of my arm to my shoulder. Then it seemed as though all nine of the boys had turned upon me at once. Blows pounded me from all sides while I struck out as best I could. So many blows landed upon me that I wondered if I were not the only blindfolded fighter in the ring, or if the man called Jackson hadn't succeeded in getting me after all.

Blindfolded, I could no longer control my motions. I had no dignity. I stumbled about like a baby or a drunken man. The smoke had become thicker and with each new blow it seemed to sear and further restrict my lungs. My saliva became like hot bitter glue. A glove connected with my head, filling my mouth with warm blood. It was everywhere. I could not tell if the moisture I felt upon my body was sweat or blood. A blow landed hard against the nape of my neck. I felt myself going over, my head hitting the floor. Streaks of blue light filled the black world behind the blindfold. I lay prone, pretending that I was knocked out, but felt myself seized by hands and yanked to my feet. "Get going, black boy! Mix it up!" My arms were like lead, my head smarting from blows. I managed to feel my way to the ropes and held on, trying to catch my breath. A glove landed in my midsection and I went over again, feeling as though the smoke had become a knife jabbed into my guts. Pushed this way and that by the legs milling around me, I finally pulled erect and discovered that I could see the black, sweat-washed forms weaving in the smoky-blue atmosphere like drunken dancers weaving to the rapid drum-like thuds of blows.

Everyone fought hysterically. It was complete anarchy. Everybody fought everybody else. No group fought together for long. Two, three, four, fought one, then turned to fight each other, were themselves attacked. Blows landed below the belt and in the kidney, with the gloves open as well as closed, and with my eye partly opened now there was not so much terror. I moved carefully, avoiding blows, although not too many to attract attention, fighting group to group. The boys groped about like blind, cautious crabs crouching to protect their midsections, their heads pulled in short against their shoulders, their arms stretched nervously before them, with their fists testing the smoke-filled air like the knobbed feelers of hypersensitive snails. In one corner I glimpsed a boy violently punching the air and heard him scream in pain as he smashed his hand against a ring post. For a second I saw him bent over holding his hand, then going down as a blow caught his unprotected head. I played one group against the other, slipping in and throwing a punch then stepping out of range while pushing the others into the melee to take the blows blindly aimed at me. The smoke was agonizing and there were no rounds, no bells at three minute intervals to relieve our exhaustion. The room spun round me, a swirl of lights, smoke, sweating bodies surrounded by tense white faces. I bled from both nose and mouth, the blood spattering upon my chest.

The men kept yelling, "Slug him, black boy! Knock his guts out!"

"Uppercut him! Kill him! Kill that big boy!"

Taking a fake fall, I saw a boy going down heavily beside me as though we were felled by a single blow, saw a sneaker-clad foot shoot into his groin as the two who had knocked him down stumbled upon him. I rolled out of range, feeling a twinge of nausea.

The harder we fought the more threatening the men became. And yet, I had begun to worry about my speech again. How would it go? Would they recognize my ability? What would they give me?

I was fighting automatically when suddenly I noticed that one after another of the boys was leaving the ring. I was surprised, filled with panic, as though I had been left alone with an unknown danger. Then I understood. The boys had arranged it among themselves. It was the custom for the two men left in the ring to slug it out for the winner's prize. I discovered this too late. When the bell sounded two men in tuxedoes leaped into the ring and removed the blindfold. I found myself facing Tatlock, the biggest of the gang. I felt sick at my stomach. Hardly had the bell stopped ringing in my ears than it clanged again and I saw him moving swiftly toward me. Thinking of nothing else to do I hit him smash on the nose. He kept coming, bringing the rank sharp violence of stale sweat. His face was a black blank of a face, only his eyes alive—with hate of me and aglow with a feverish terror from what had happened to us all. I became anxious. I wanted to deliver my speech and he came at me as though he meant to beat it out of me. I smashed him again and again, taking his blows as they came. Then on a sudden impulse I struck him lightly and we clinched. I whispered, "Fake like I knocked you out, you can have the prize."

"I'll break your behind," he whispered hoarsely.

"For *them?*"

"For *me,* sonafabitch!"

They were yelling for us to break it up and Tatlock spun me half around with a blow, and as a joggled camera sweeps in a reeling scene, I saw the howling red faces crouching tense beneath the cloud of blue-gray smoke. For a moment the world wavered, unraveled, flowed, then my head cleared and Tatlock bounced before me. That fluttering shadow before my eyes was his jabbing left hand. Then falling forward, my head against his damp shoulder, I whispered.

"I'll make it five dollars more."

"Go to hell!"

But his muscles relaxed a trifle beneath my pressure and I breathed, "Seven?"

"Give it to your ma," he said, ripping me beneath the heart.

And while I still held him I butted him and moved away. I felt myself bombarded with punches. I fought back with hopeless desperation. I wanted to deliver my speech more than anything else in the world, because I felt that only these men could judge truly my ability, and now this stupid clown was ruining my chances. I began fighting carefully now, moving in to punch him and out again with my greater speed. A lucky blow to his chin and I had him going too—until I heard a loud voice yell, "I got my money on the big boy."

Hearing this, I almost dropped my guard. I was confused: Should I try to win against the voice out there? Would not this go against my speech, and was not this a moment for humility, for nonresistance? A blow to my head as I danced about sent my right eye popping like a jack-in-the-box and settled my dilemma. The room went red as I fell. It was a dream fall, my body languid and fastidious as to where to land, until the floor became impatient and smashed up to meet me. A moment later I came to. An hypnotic voice said FIVE emphatically. And I lay there, hazily watching a dark red spot of my own blood shaping itself into a butterfly, glistening and soaking into the soiled gray world of the canvas.

When the voice drawled TEN I was lifted up and dragged to a chair. I sat dazed. My eye pained and swelled with each throb of my pounding heart and I wondered if now I would be allowed to speak. I was wringing wet, my mouth still bleeding. We were grouped along the wall now. The other boys ignored me as they congratulated Tatlock and speculated as to how much they would be paid. One boy whimpered over his smashed hand. Looking up front, I saw attendants in white jackets rolling the portable ring away and placing a small square rug in the vacant space surrounded by chairs. Perhaps, I thought, I will stand on the rug to deliver my speech.

Then the M.C. called to us. "Come on up here boys and get your money."

We ran forward to where the men laughed and talked in their chairs, waiting. Everyone seemed friendly now.

"There it is on the rug," the man said. I saw the rug covered with coins of all dimensions and a few crumpled bills. But what excited me, scattered here and there, were the gold pieces.

"Boys, it's all yours," the man said. "You get all you grab."

"That's right, Sambo," a blond man said, winking at me confidentially.

I trembled with excitement, forgetting my pain. I would get the gold and the bills, I thought. I would use both hands. I would throw my body against the boys nearest me to block them from the gold.

"Get down around the rug now," the man commanded, "and don't anyone touch it until I give the signal."

"This ought to be good," I heard.

As told, we got around the square rug on our knees. Slowly the man raised his freckled hand as we followed it upward with our eyes.

I heard, "These niggers look like they're about to pray!"

Then, "Ready," the man said. "Go!"

I lunged for a yellow coin lying on the blue design of the carpet, touching it and sending a surprised shriek to join those around me. I tried frantically to remove my hand but could not let go. A hot, violent force tore through my body, shaking me like a wet rat. The rug was electrified. The hair bristled up on my head as I shook myself free. My muscles jumped, my nerves jangled, writhed. But I saw that this was not stopping the other boys. Laughing in fear and embarrassment, some were holding back and scooping up the coins knocked off by the painful contortions of others. The men roared above us as we struggled.

"Pick it up, goddamnit, pick it up!" someone called like a bass-voiced parrot. "Go on, get it!"

I crawled rapidly around the floor, picking up the coins, trying to avoid the coppers and to get greenbacks and the gold. Ignoring the shock by laughing, as I brushed the coins off quickly, I discovered that I could contain the electricity—a contradiction but it works. Then the men began to push us onto the rug. Laughing embarrassedly, we struggled out of their hands and kept after the coins. We were all wet and slippery and hard to hold. Suddenly I saw a boy lifted into the air, glistening with sweat like a circus seal, and dropped, his wet back landing flush upon the charged rug, heard him yell and saw him literally dance upon his back, his elbows beating a frenzied tattoo upon the floor, his muscles twitching like the flesh of a horse stung by many flies. When he finally rolled off, his face was gray and no one stopped him when he ran from the floor amid booming laughter.

"Get the money," the M.C. called. "That's good hard American cash!"

And we snatched and grabbed, snatched and grabbed. I was careful not to come too close to the rug now, and when I felt the hot whiskey breath descend upon me like a cloud of foul air I reached out and grabbed the leg of a chair. It was occupied and I held on desperately.

"Leggo, nigger! Leggo!"

The huge face wavered down to mine as he tried to push me free. But my body was slippery and he was too drunk. It was Mr. Colcord, who owned a chain of movie houses and "entertainment palaces." Each time he grabbed me I slipped out of his hands. It became a real struggle. I feared the rug more than I did the drunk, so I held on, surprising myself for a moment by trying to topple *him* upon the rug. It was such an enormous idea that I found myself actually carrying it out. I tried not to be obvious, yet when I grabbed his leg, trying to tumble him out of the chair, he raised up roaring with laughter, and, looking at me with soberness dead in the eye, kicked me viciously in the chest. The chair leg flew out of my hand and I felt myself going and rolled. It was as though I had rolled through a bed of hot coals. It seemed a whole century would pass before I would roll free, a century in which I was seared through the deepest levels of my body to the fearful breath within me and the breath seared and heated to the point of explosion. It'll all be over in a flash, I thought as I rolled clear. It'll all be over in a flash.

But not yet, the men on the other side were waiting, red faces swollen as though from apoplexy as they bent forward in their chairs. Seeing their fingers coming toward me I rolled away as a fumbled football rolls off the receiver's fingertips, back into the coals. That time I luckily sent the rug sliding out of place and heard the coins ringing against the floor and the boys scuffling to pick them up and the M.C. calling, "All right, boys, that's all. Go get dressed and get your money."

I was limp as a dish rag. My back felt as though it had been beaten with wires.

When we had dressed the M.C. came in and gave us each five dollars, except Tatlock, who got ten for being the last in the ring. Then he told us to leave. I was not to get a chance to deliver my speech, I thought. I was going out into the dim alley in despair when I was stopped and told to go back. I returned to the ball-room, where the men were pushing back their chairs and gathering in small groups to talk.

The M.C. knocked on a table for quiet. "Gentlemen," he said, "we almost forgot an important part of the program. A most serious part, gentlemen. This boy was brought here to deliver a speech which he made at his graduation yesterday . . ."

"Bravo!"

"I'm told that he is the smartest boy we've got out there in Greenwood. I'm told that he knows more big words than a pocket-sized dictionary."

Much applause and laughter.

"So now, gentlemen, I want you to give him your attention."

There was still laughter as I faced them, my mouth dry, my eyes throbbing. I began slowly, but evidently my throat was tense, because they began shouting. "Louder! Louder!"

"We of the younger generation extol the wisdom of that great leader and educator," I shouted, "who first spoke these flaming words of wisdom: 'A ship lost at sea for many days suddenly sighted a friendly vessel. From the mast of the unfortunate vessel was seen a signal: "Water, water; we die of thirst!" The answer from the friendly vessel came back: "Cast down your bucket where you are." The captain of the distressed vessel, at last heeding the injunction, cast down his bucket, and it came up full of fresh sparkling water from the mouth of the Amazon River.' And like him I say, and in his words, 'To those of my race who depend upon bettering their condition in a foreign land, or who underestimate the importance of cultivating friendly relations with the Southern white man, who is his next-door neighbor, I would say: "Cast down your bucket where you are"—cast it down in making friends in every manly way of the people of all races by whom we are surrounded. . . .' "

I spoke automatically and with such fervor that I did not realize that the men were still talking and laughing until my dry mouth, filling up with blood from the cut, almost strangled me. I coughed, wanting to stop and go to one of the tall brass, sand-filled spittoons to relieve myself, but a few of the men, especially the superintendent, were listening and I was afraid. So I gulped it down, blood, saliva and all, and continued. (What powers of endurance I had during those days! What enthusiasm! What a belief in the rightness of things!) I spoke even louder in spite of the pain. But still they talked and still they laughed, as though deaf with cotton in dirty ears. So I spoke with greater emotional emphasis. I closed my ears and swallowed blood until I was nauseated. The speech seemed a hundred times as long as before, but I could not leave out a single word. All had to be said, each memorized nuance considered, rendered. Nor was that all. Whenever I uttered a word of three or more syllables a group of voices would yell for me to repeat it. I used the phrase "social responsibility" and they yelled:

"What's the word you say, boy?"

"Social responsibility," I said.

"What?"

"Social . . ."

"Louder."

" . . . responsibility."

"More!"

"Respon—"

"Repeat!"

"—sibility."

complicates / He is still trying to please white guy.

The room filled with the uproar of laughter until, no doubt, distracted by having to gulp down my blood, I made a mistake and yelled a phrase I had often seen denounced in newspaper editorials, heard debated in private.

"Social . . ."

"What?" they yelled.

" . . . equality—"

The laughter hung smokelike in the sudden stillness. I opened my eyes, puzzled. Sounds of displeasure filled the room. The M.C. rushed forward. They shouted hostile phrases at me. But I did not understand.

A small dry mustached man in the front row blared out, "Say that slowly, son!"

"What, sir?"

"What you just said!"

"Social responsibility, sir," I said.

"You weren't being smart, were you boy?" he said, not unkindly.

"No, sir!"

"You sure that about 'equality' was a mistake?"

"Oh, yes, sir," I said. "I was swallowing blood."

"Well, you had better speak more slowly so we can understand. We mean to do right by you, but you've got to know your place at all times. All right, now, go on with your speech."

I was afraid. I wanted to leave but I wanted also to speak and I was afraid they'd snatch me down.

"Thank you, sir," I said, beginning where I had left off, and having them ignore me as before.

Yet when I finished there was a thunderous applause. I was surprised to see the superintendent come forth with a package wrapped in white tissue paper, and, gesturing for quiet, address the men.

"Gentlemen, you see that I did not overpraise the boy. He makes a good speech and some day he'll lead his people in the proper paths. And I don't have to tell you that this is important in these days and times. This is a good, smart boy, and so to encourage him in the right direction, in the name of the Board of Education I wish to present him a prize in the form of this . . ."

He paused, removing the tissue paper and revealing a gleaming calfskin briefcase.

" . . . in the form of this first-class article from Shad Whitmore's shop."

"Boy," he said, addressing me, "take this prize and keep it well. Consider it a badge of office. Prize it. Keep developing as you are and some day it will be filled with important papers that will help shape the destiny of your people."

I was so moved that I could hardly express my thanks. A rope of bloody saliva forming a shape like an undiscovered continent drooled upon the leather and I wiped it quickly away. I felt an importance that I had never dreamed.

"Open it and see what's inside," I was told.

My fingers a-tremble, I complied, smelling fresh leather and finding an official-looking document inside. It was a scholarship to the state college for Negroes. My eyes filled with tears and I ran awkwardly off the floor.

I was overjoyed; I did not even mind when I discovered the gold pieces I had scrambled for were brass pocket tokens advertising a certain make of automobile.

When I reached home everyone was excited. Next day the neighbors came to congratulate me. I even felt safe from grandfather, whose deathbed curse usually spoiled my triumphs. I stood beneath his photograph with my briefcase in hand and smiled triumphantly into his stolid black peasant's face. It was a face that fascinated me. The eyes seemed to follow everywhere I went.

That night I dreamed I was at a circus with him and that he refused to laugh at the clowns no matter what they did. Then later he told me to open my briefcase and read what was inside and I did, finding an official envelope stamped with the state seal: and inside the envelope I found another and another, endlessly, and I thought I would fall of weariness. "Them's years," he said. "Now open that one." And I did and in it I found an engraved stamp containing a short message in letters of gold. "Read it," my grandfather said. "Out loud."

"To Whom It May Concern," I intoned. "Keep This Nigger-Boy Running."

I awoke with the old man's laughter ringing in my ears.

Door opened a little for him.

Know your place

# ⁂ GRACE PALEY
## (1922– )

One of the distinguishing features of Grace Paley's fiction is the quality of its voice—clear, simple, Jewish, urban. And it is no wonder, for she grew up in a family of great talkers, people of passion and political action. She was born in the Bronx, New York, of parents who emigrated from Russia and who were Zionists and political activists. She left high school at age 16 and entered Hunter College in New York City, but left without completing a degree. She married Jess Paley in 1942, with whom she had two children. They separated three years later, but did not divorce until 1971.

Like those of her friend Tillie Olsen, Paley's life and work are imbued with a deep faith in and compassion for humanity. This faith shows itself in her lifelong activism for peace, social and political justice, and women's rights. She began to write poety at first, but the short story proved to be her natural form. In the 1950s her work began to appear in such periodicals as the *Atlantic Monthly* and *Esquire*. Paley's first collection of stories was *The Little Disturbances of Man* (1959). This collection established her reputation as a writer whose stories reveal the depth and vitality of the lives of essentially ordinary people. Her second volume of stories, *Enormous Changes at the Last Minute*, appeared in 1974, and her third collection, *Later the Same Day*, in 1985. She has published two volumes of poems, *Leaning Forward* (1985) and *New and Collected Poems* (1992). Her *Long Walks and Intimate Talks* (1991) contains both stories and poems. Her *Collected Stories* was published in 1994. She divides her time between a farm in Vermont and an apartment in New York City.

# An Interest in Life

MY HUSBAND gave me a broom one Christmas. This wasn't right. No one can tell me it was meant kindly.

"I don't want you not to have anything for Christmas while I'm away in the army," he said. "Virginia, please look at it. It comes with this fancy dustpan. It hangs off a stick. Look at it, will you? Are you blind or cross-eyed?"

"Thanks, chum," I said. I had always wanted a dustpan hooked up that way. It was a good one. My husband doesn't shop in bargain basements or January sales.

Still and all, in spite of the quality, it was a mean present to give a woman you planned on never seeing again, a person you had children with and got onto all the time, drunk or sober, even when everybody had to get up early in the morning.

I asked him if he could wait and join the army in a half hour, as I had to get the groceries. I don't like to leave kids alone in a three-room apartment full of gas and electricity. Fire may break out from a nasty remark. Or the oldest decides to get even with the youngest.

"Just this once," he said. "But you better figure out how to get along without me."

"You're a handicapped person mentally," I said. "You should've been institutionalized years ago." I slammed the door. I didn't want to see him pack his underwear and ironed shirts.

I never got farther than the front stoop, though, because there was Mrs. Raftery, wringing her hands, tears in her eyes as though she had a monopoly on all the good news.

"Mrs. Raftery!" I said, putting my arm around her. "Don't cry." She leaned on me because I am such a horsey build. "Don't cry, Mrs. Raftery, please!" I said.

"That's like you, Virginia. Always looking at the ugly side of things. 'Take in the wash. It's rainin'!' That's you. You're the first one knows it when the dumbwaiter breaks."

"Oh, come on now, that's not so. It just isn't so," I said. "I'm the exact opposite."

"Did you see Mrs. Cullen yet?" she asked, paying no attention.

"Where?"

"Virginia!" she said, shocked. "She's passed away. The whole house knows it. They've got her in white like a bride and you never saw a beautiful creature like that. She must be eighty. Her husband's proud."

"She was never more than an acquaintance; she didn't have any children," I said.

"Well, I don't care about that. Now, Virginia, you do what I say now, you go downstairs and you say like this—listen to me—say, 'I hear, Mr. Cullen, your wife's passed away. I'm sorry.' Then ask him how he is. Then you ought to go around the corner and see her. She's in Witson & Wayde. Then you ought to go over to the church when they carry her over."

"It's not my church," I said.

"That's no reason, Virginia. You go up like this," she said, parting from me to do a prancy dance. "Up the big front steps, into the church you go. It's beautiful in there. You can't help kneeling only for a minute. Then round to the right. Then up the other stairway. Then you come to a great oak door that's arched above you, then," she said, seizing a deep, deep breath, for all the good it would do her, "and then turn the knob slowly and open the door and see for yourself: Our Blessed Mother is in charge. Beautiful. Beautiful. Beautiful."

I sighed in and I groaned out, so as to melt a certain pain around my heart. A steel ring like arthritis, at my age.

"You are a groaner," Mrs. Raftery said, gawking into my mouth.

"I am not," I said. I got a whiff of her, a terrible cheap wine lush.

My husband threw a penny at the door from the inside to take my notice from Mrs. Raftery. He rattled the glass door to make sure I looked at him. He had a fat duffel bag on each shoulder. Where did he acquire so much worldly possession? What was in them? My grandma's goose feathers from across the ocean? Or all the diaper-service diapers? To this day the truth is shrouded in mystery.

"What the hell are you doing, Virginia?" he said, dumping them at my feet. "Standing out here on your hind legs telling everybody your business? The army gives you a certain time, for godsakes, they're not kidding." Then he said, "I beg your pardon," to Mrs. Raftery. He took hold of me with his two arms as though in love and pressed his body hard against mine so that I could feel him for the last time and suffer my loss. Then he kissed me in a mean way to nearly split my lip. Then he winked and said, "That's all for now," and skipped off into the future, duffel bags full of rags.

He left me in an embarrassing situation, nearly fainting, in front of that old widow, who can't even remember the half of it. "He's a crock," said Mrs. Raftery. "Is he leaving for good or just temporarily, Virginia?"

"Oh, he's probably deserting me," I said, and sat down on the stoop, pulling my big knees up to my chin.

"If that's the case, tell the Welfare right away," she said. "He's a bum, leaving you just before Christmas. Tell the cops," she said. "They'll provide the toys for the little kids gladly. And don't forget to let the grocer in on it. He won't be so hard on you expecting payment."

She saw that sadness was stretched worldwide across my face. Mrs. Raftery isn't the worst person. She said, "Look around for comfort, dear." With a nervous finger she pointed to the truckers eating lunch on their haunches across the street, leaning on the loading platforms. She waved her hand to include in all the men marching up and down in search of a decent luncheonette. She didn't leave out the six longshoremen loafing under the fish-market marquee. "If their lungs and stomachs ain't crushed by overwork, they disappear somewhere in the world. Don't be disappointed, Virginia. I don't know a man living'd last you a lifetime."

Ten days later Girard asked, "Where's Daddy?"

"Ask me no questions, I'll tell you no lies." I didn't want the children to know the facts. Present or past, a child should have a father.

"Where *is* Daddy?" Girard asked the week after that.

"He joined the army," I said.

"He made my bunk bed," said Philip.

"The truth shall make ye free," I said.

Then I sat down with pencil and pad to get in control of my resources. The facts, when I added and subtracted them, were that my husband had left me with fourteen dollars, and the rent unpaid, in an emergency state. He'd claimed he was sorry to do this, but my opinion is, out of sight, out of mind. "The city won't let you starve," he'd said. "After all, you're half the population. You're keeping up the good work. Without you the race would die out. Who'd pay the taxes? Who'd keep the streets clean? There wouldn't be no army. A man like me wouldn't have no place to go."

I sent Girard right down to Mrs. Raftery with a request about the whereabouts of Welfare. She responded R.S.V.P. with an extra comment in left-handed script: "Poor Girard . . . he's never the boy my John was!"

Who asked her?

I called on Welfare right after the new year. In no time I discovered that they're rigged up to deal with liars, and if you're truthful it's disappointing to them. They may even refuse to handle your case if you're too truthful.

They asked sensible questions at first. They asked where my husband had enlisted. I didn't know. They put some letter writers and agents after him. "He's not in the United States Army," they said. "Try the Brazilian Army," I suggested.

They have no sense of kidding around. They're not the least bit lighthearted and they tried. "Oh no," they said. "That was incorrect. He is not in the Brazilian Army."

"No?" I said. "How strange! He must be in the Mexican Navy."

By law, they had to hound his brothers. They wrote to his brother who has a first-class card in the Teamsters and owns an apartment house in California. They asked his two brothers in Jersey to help me. They have large families. Rightfully they laughed. Then they wrote to Thomas, the oldest, the smart one (the one they all worked so hard for years to keep him in college until his brains could pay off). He was the one who sent ten dollars immediately, saying, "What a bastard! I'll send something time to time, Ginny, but whatever you do, don't tell the authorities." Of course I never did. Soon they began to guess they were better people than me, that I was in trouble because I deserved it, and then they liked me better.

But they never fixed my refrigerator. Every time I called I said patiently, "The milk is sour . . ." I said, "Corn beef went bad." Sitting in that beer-stinking phone booth in Felan's for the sixth time (sixty cents) with the baby on my lap and Barbie tapping at the glass door with an American flag, I cried into the secretary's hardhearted ear, "I bought real butter for the holiday, and it's rancid. . . ." They said, "You'll have to get a better bid on the repair job."

While I waited indoors for a man to bid, Girard took to swinging back and forth on top of the bathroom door, just to soothe himself, giving me the laugh, dreamy, nibbling calcimine off the ceiling. On first sight Mrs. Raftery said, "Whack the monkey, he'd be better off on arsenic."

But Girard is my son and I'm the judge. It means a terrible thing for the future, though I don't know what to call it.

It was from constantly thinking of my foreknowledge on this and other subjects, it was from observing when I put my lipstick on daily, how my face was just curling up to die, that John Raftery came from Jersey to rescue me.

On Thursdays, anyway, John Raftery took the tubes in to visit his mother. The whole house knew it. She was cheerful even before breakfast. She sang out loud in a girlish brogue that only came to tongue for grand occasions. Hanging out the wash, she blushed to recall what a remarkable boy her John had been. "Ask the sisters around the corner," she said to the open kitchen windows. "They'll never forget John."

That particular night after supper Mrs. Raftery said to her son, "John, how come you don't say hello to your old friend Virginia? She's had hard luck and she's gloomy."

"Is that so, Mother?" he said, and immediately climbed two flights to knock at my door.

"Oh, John," I said at the sight of him, hat in hand in a white shirt and blue-striped tie, spick-and-span, a Sunday-school man. "Hello!"

"Welcome, John!" I said. "Sit down. Come right in. How are you? You look awfully good. You do. Tell me, how've you been all this time, John?"

"How've I been?" he asked thoughtfully. To answer within reason, he described his life with Margaret, marriage, work, and children up to the present day.

I had nothing good to report. Now that he had put the subject around before my very eyes, every burnt-up day of my life smoked in shame, and I couldn't even get a clear view of the good half hours.

"Of course," he said, "you do have lovely children. Noticeable-looking, Virginia. Good looks is always something to be thankful for."

"Thankful?" I said. "I don't have to thank anything but my own foolishness for four children when I'm twenty-six years old, deserted, and poverty-struck, regardless of looks. A man can't help it, but I could have behaved better."

"Don't be so cruel on yourself, Ginny," he said. "Children come from God."

"You're still great on holy subjects, aren't you? You know damn well where children come from."

He did know. His red face reddened further. John Raftery has had that color coming out on him boy and man from keeping his rages so inward.

Still he made more sense in his conversation after that, and I poured fresh tea to tell him how my husband used to like me because I was a passionate person. That was until he took a look around and saw how in the long run this life only meant more of the same thing. He tried to turn away from me once he came to this understanding, and make me hate him. His face changed. He gave up his brand of cigarettes, which we had in common. He threw out the two pairs of socks I knitted by hand. "If there's anything I hate in this world, it's navy blue," he said. Oh, I could have dyed them. I would have done anything for him, if he were only not too sorry to ask me.

"You were a nice kid in those days," said John, referring to certain Saturday nights. "A wild, nice kid."

"Aaah," I said, disgusted. Whatever I was then was on the way to where I am now. "I was fresh. If I had a kid like me, I'd slap her cross-eyed."

The very next Thursday John gave me a beautiful radio with a record player. "Enjoy yourself," he said. That really made Welfare speechless. We didn't own any records, but the investigator saw my burden was lightened and he scribbled a dozen pages about it in his notebook.

On the third Thursday he brought a walking doll (twenty-four inches) for Linda and Barbie with a card inscribed, "A baby doll for a couple of dolls." He had also had a couple of drinks at his mother's, and this made him want to dance. "La-la-la," he sang, a ramrod swaying in my kitchen chair. "La-la-la, let yourself go. . . ."

"You gotta give a little," he sang, "live a little. . . ." He said, "Virginia, may I have this dance?"

"Sssh, we finally got them asleep. Please, turn the radio down. Quiet. Deathly silence, John Raftery."

"Let me do your dishes, Virginia."

"Don't be silly, you're a guest in my house," I said. "I still regard you as a guest."

"I want to do something for you, Virginia."

"Tell me I'm the most gorgeous thing," I said, dipping my arm to the funny bone in dish soap.

He didn't answer. "I'm having a lot of trouble at work" was all he said. Then I heard him push the chair back. He came up behind me, put his arms around my waistline, and kissed my cheek. He whirled me around and took my hands. He said, "An old friend is better than rubies." He looked me in the eye. He held my attention by trying to be honest. And he kissed me a short sweet kiss on my mouth.

"Please sit down, Virginia," he said. He kneeled before me and put his head in my lap. I was stirred by so much activity. Then he looked up at me and, as though proposing marriage for life, he offered—because he was drunk—to place his immortal soul in peril to comfort me.

First I said, "Thank you." Then I said, "No."

I was sorry for him, but he's devout, a leader of the Fathers' Club at his church, active in all the lay groups for charities, orphans, etc. I knew that if he stayed late to love with me, he would not do it lightly but would in the end pay terrible penance and ruin his long life. The responsibility would be on me.

So I said no.

And Barbie is such a light sleeper. All she has to do, I thought, is wake up and wander in and see her mother and her new friend John with his pants around his knees, wrestling on the kitchen table. A vision like that could affect a kid for life.

I said no.

Everyone in this building is so goddamn nosy. That evening I had to say no.

But John came to visit, anyway, on the fourth Thursday. This time he brought the discarded dresses of Margaret's daughters, organdy party dresses and glazed cotton for every day. He gently admired Barbara and Linda, his blue eyes rolling to back up a couple of dozen oohs and ahs.

Even Philip, who thinks God gave him just a certain number of hellos and he better save them for the final judgment, Philip leaned on John and said, "Why don't you bring your boy to play with me? I don't have nobody who to play with." (Philip's a liar. There must be at least seventy-one children in this house, pale pink to medium brown, English-talking and gibbering in Spanish, rough-and-tough boys, the Lone Ranger's bloody pals, or the exact picture of Supermouse. If a boy wanted a friend, he could pick the very one out of his neighbors.)

Also, Girard is a cold fish. He was in a lonesome despair. Sometimes he looked in the mirror and said, "How come I have such an ugly face? My nose is funny. Mostly people don't like me." He was a liar too. Girard has a face like his father's. His eyes are the color of those little blue plums in August. He looks like an advertisement in a magazine. He could be a child model and make a lot of money. He is my first child, and if he thinks he is ugly, I think I am ugly.

John said, "I can't stand to see a boy mope like that. . . . What do the Sisters say in school?"

"He doesn't pay attention is all they say. You can't get much out of them."

"My middle boy was like that," said John. "Couldn't take an interest. Aaah, I wish I didn't have all that headache on the job. I'd grab Girard by the collar and make him take notice of the world. I wish I could ask him out to Jersey to play in all that space."

"Why not?" I said.

"Why, Virginia, I'm surprised you don't know why not. You know I can't take your children out to meet my children."

I felt a lot of strong arthritis in my ribs.

"My mother's the funny one, Virginia." He felt he had to continue with the subject matter. "I don't know. I guess she likes the idea of bugging Margaret. She says, 'You goin' up, John?' 'Yes, Mother,' I say. 'Behave yourself, John,' she says. 'That husband might come home and hacksaw you into hell. You're a Catholic man, John,' she says.

But I figured it out. She likes to know I'm in the building. I swear, Virginia, she wishes me the best of luck."

"I do too, John," I said. We drank a last glass of beer to make sure of a peaceful sleep. "Good night, Virginia," he said, looping his muffler neatly under his chin. "Don't worry. I'll be thinking of what to do about Girard."

I got into the big bed that I share with the girls in the little room. For once I had no trouble falling asleep. I only had to worry about Linda and Barbara and Philip. It was a great relief to me that John had taken over the thinking about Girard.

John was sincere. That's true. He paid a lot of attention to Girard, smoking out all his sneaky sorrows. He registered him into a wild pack of Cub Scouts that went up to the Bronx once a week to let off steam. He gave him a Junior Erector Set. And sometimes when his family wasn't listening he prayed at great length for him.

One Sunday, Sister Veronica said in her sweet voice from another life, "He's not worse. He might even be a little better. How are *you,* Virginia?" putting her hand on mine. Everybody around here acts like they know everything.

"Just fine," I said.

"We ought to start on Philip," John said, "if it's true Girard's improving."

"You should've been a social worker, John."

"A lot of people have noticed that about me," said John.

"Your mother was always acting so crazy about you, how come she didn't knock herself out a little to see you in college? Like we did for Thomas?"

"Now, Virginia, be fair. She's a poor old woman. My father was a weak earner. She had to have my wages, and I'll tell you, Virginia, I'm not sorry. Look at Thomas. He's still in school. Drop him in this jungle and he'd be devoured. He hasn't had a touch of real life. And here I am with a good chunk of a family, a home of my own, a name in the building trades. One thing I have to tell you, the poor old woman is sorry. I said one day (oh, in passing—years ago) that I might marry you. She stuck a knife in herself. It's a fact. Not more than an eighth of an inch. You never saw such a gory Sunday. One thing—you would have been a better daughter-in-law to her than Margaret."

"Marry me?" I said.

"Well, yes. . . . Aaah—I always liked you, then. . . . Why do you think I'd sit in the shade of this kitchen every Thursday night? For godsakes, the only warm thing around here is this teacup. Yes sir, I did want to marry you, Virginia."

"No kidding, John? Really?" It was nice to know. Better late than never, to learn you were desired in youth.

I didn't tell John, but the truth is, I would never have married him. Once I met my husband with his winking looks, he was my only interest. Wild as I had been with John and others, I turned all my wildness over to him and then there was no question in my mind.

Still, face facts, if my husband didn't budge on in life, it was my fault. On me, as they say, be it. I greeted the morn with a song. I had a hello for everyone but the landlord. Ask the people on the block, come or go—even the Spanish ones, with their sad dark faces—they have to smile when they see me.

But for his own comfort, he should have done better lifewise and moneywise. I was happy, but I am now in possession of knowledge that this is wrong. Happiness isn't so bad for a woman. She gets fatter, she gets older, she could lie down, nuzzling a regiment of men and little kids, she could just die of the pleasure. But men are different, they have to own money, or they have to be famous, or everybody on the block has to look up to them from the cellar stairs.

A woman counts her children and acts snotty, like she invented life, but men *must* do well in the world. I know that men are not fooled by being happy.

"A funny guy," said John, guessing where my thoughts had gone. "What stopped him up? He was nobody's fool. He had a funny thing about him, Virginia, if you don't mind my saying so. He wasn't much distance up, but he was all set and ready to be looking down on us all."

"He was very smart, John. You don't realize that. His hobby was crossword puzzles, and I said to him real often, as did others around here, that he ought to go out on the '$64 Question.' Why not? But he laughed. You know what he said? He said, 'That proves how dumb you are if you think I'm smart.' "

"A funny guy," said John. "Get it all off your chest," he said. "Talk it out, Virginia; it's the only way to kill the pain."

By and large, I was happy to oblige. Still I could not carry through about certain cruel remarks. It was like trying to move back into the dry mouth of a nightmare to remember that the last day I was happy was the middle of a week in March, when I told my husband I was going to have Linda. Barbara was five months old to the hour. The boys were three and four. I had to tell him. It was the last day with anything happy about it.

Later on he said, "Oh, you make me so sick, you're so goddamn big and fat, you look like a goddamn brownstone, the way you're squared off in front."

"Well, where are you going tonight?" I asked.

"How should I know?" he said. "Your big ass takes up the whole goddamn bed," he said. "There's no room for me." He bought a sleeping bag and slept on the floor.

I couldn't believe it. I would start every morning fresh. I couldn't believe that he would turn against me so, while I was still young and even his friends still liked me.

But he did, he turned absolutely against me and became no friend of mine. "All you ever think about is making babies. This place stinks like the men's room in the BMT. It's a fucking *pissoir.*" He was strong on truth all through the year. "That kid eats more than the five of us put together," he said. "Stop stuffing your face, you fat dumbbell," he said to Philip.

Then he worked on the neighbors. "Get that nosy old bag out of here," he said. "If she comes on once more with 'my son in the building trades' I'll squash her for the cat."

Then he turned on Spielvogel, the checker, his oldest friend, who only visited on holidays and never spoke to me (shy, the way some bachelors are). "That sonofabitch, don't hand me that friendship crap, all he's after is your ass. That's what I need—a little shitmaker of his using up the air in this flat."

And then there was no one else to dispose of. We were left alone fair and square, facing each other.

"Now, Virginia," he said, "I come to the end of my rope. I see a black wall ahead of me. What the hell am I supposed to do? I only got one life. Should I lie down and die? I don't know what to do anymore. I'll give it to you straight, Virginia, if I stick around, you can't help it, you'll hate me. . . ."

"I hate you right now," I said. "So do whatever you like."

"This place drives me nuts," he mumbled. "I don't know what to do around here. I want to get you a present. Something."

"I told you, do whatever you like. Buy me a rat trap for rats."

That's when he went down to the House Appliance Store, and he brought back a new broom and a classy dustpan.

"A new broom sweeps clean," he said. "I got to get out of here," he said. "I'm going nuts." Then he began to stuff the duffel bags, and I went to the grocery store but was stopped by Mrs. Raftery, who had to tell me what she considered so beautiful—death—then he kissed me and went to join some army somewhere.

I didn't tell John any of this, because I think it makes a woman look too bad to tell on how another man has treated her. He begins to see her through the other man's eyes, a sitting duck, a skinful of flaws. After all, I had come to depend on John. All my husband's friends were strangers now, though I had always said to them, "Feel welcome."

And the family men in the building looked too cunning, as though they had all personally deserted me. If they met me on the stairs, they carried the heaviest groceries up and helped bring Linda's stroller down, but they never asked me a question worth answering at all.

Besides that, Girard and Philip taught the girls the days of the week: Monday, Tuesday, Wednesday, Johnday, Friday. They waited for him once a week, under the hallway lamp, half asleep like bugs in the sun, sitting in their little chairs with their names on in gold, a birth present from my mother-in-law. At fifteen after eight he punctually came, to read a story, pass out some kisses, and tuck them into bed.

But one night, after a long Johnday of them squealing my eardrum split, after a rainy afternoon with brother constantly raising up his hand against brother, with the girls near ready to go to court over the proper ownership of Melinda Lee, the twenty-four-inch walking doll, the doorbell rang three times. Not any of those times did John's face greet me.

I was too ashamed to call down to Mrs. Raftery, and she was too mean to knock on my door and explain.

He didn't come the following Thursday either. Girard said sadly, "He must've run away, John."

I had to give him up after two weeks' absence and no word. I didn't know how to tell the children: something about right and wrong, goodness and meanness, men and women. I had it all at my fingertips, ready to hand over. But I didn't think I ought to take mistakes and truth away from them. Who knows? They might make a truer friend in this world somewhere than I have ever made. So I just put them to bed and sat in the kitchen and cried.

In the middle of my third beer, searching in my mind for the next step, I found the decision to go on *Strike It Rich.* I scrounged some paper and pencil from the toy box and I listed all my troubles, which must be done in order to qualify. The list when complete could have brought tears to the eye of God if He had a minute. At the sight of it my bitterness began to improve. All that is really necessary for survival of the fittest, it seems, is an interest in life, good, bad, or peculiar.

As always happens in these cases where you have begun to help yourself with plans, news comes from an opposite direction. The doorbell rang, two short and two long—meaning John.

My first thought was to wake the children and make them happy. "No! No!" he said. "Please don't put yourself to that trouble. Virginia, I'm dog-tired," he said. "Dog-tired. My job is a damn headache. It's too much. It's all day and it scuttles my mind at night, and in the end who does the credit go to?

"Virginia," he said, "I don't know if I can come anymore. I've been wanting to tell you. I just don't know. What's it all about? Could you answer me if I asked you? I can't figure this whole thing out at all."

I started the tea steeping because his fingers when I touched them were cold. I didn't speak. I tried looking at it from his man point of view, and I thought he had to take a bus, the tubes, and a subway to see me; and then the subway, the tubes, and a bus to go back home at 1 A.M. It wouldn't be any trouble at all for him to part with us forever. I thought about my life, and I gave strongest consideration to my children. If given the choice, I decided to choose not to live without him.

"What's that?" he asked, pointing to my careful list of troubles. "Writing a letter?"

"Oh no," I said, "it's for *Strike It Rich.* I hope to go on the program."

"Virginia, for goodness' sakes," he said, giving it a glance, "you don't have a ghost. They'd laugh you out of the studio. Those people really suffer."

"Are you sure, John?" I asked.

"No question in my mind at all," said John. "Have you ever seen that program? I mean, in addition to all of this—the little disturbances of man"—he waved a scornful hand at my list—"they *suffer.* They live in the forefront of tornadoes, their lives are washed off by floods—catastrophes of God. Oh, Virginia."

"Are you sure, John?"

"For goodness' sake. . . ."

Sadly I put my list away. Still, if things got worse, I could always make use of it.

Once that was settled, I acted on an earlier decision. I pushed his cup of scalding tea aside. I wedged myself onto his lap between his hard belt buckle and the table. I put my arms around his neck and said, "How come you're so cold, John?" He has a kind face and he knew how to look astonished. He said, "Why, Virginia, I'm getting warmer." We laughed.

John became a lover to me that night.

* * *

Mrs. Raftery is sometimes silly and sick from her private source of cheap wine. She expects John often. "Honor your mother, what's the matter with you, John?" she complains. "Honor. Honor."

"Virginia dear," she says. "You never would've taken John away to Jersey like Margaret. I wish he'd've married you."

"You didn't like me much in those days."

"That's a lie," she says. I know she's a hypocrite, but no more than the rest of the world.

What is remarkable to me is that it doesn't seem to conscience John as I thought it might. It is still hard to believe that a man who sends out the Ten Commandments every year for a Christmas card can be so easy buttoning and unbuttoning.

Of course we must be very careful not to wake the children or disturb the neighbors, who will enjoy another person's excitement just so far, and then the pleasure enrages them. We must be very careful for ourselves too, for when my husband comes back, realizing the babies are in school and everything easier, he won't forgive me if I've started it all up again—noisy signs of life that are so much trouble to a man.

We haven't seen him in two and a half years. Although people have suggested it, I do not want the police or Intelligence or a private eye or anyone to go after him to bring him back. I know that if he expected to stay away forever he would have written and said so. As it is, I just don't know what evening, any time, he may appear. Sometimes, stumbling over a blockbuster of a dream at midnight, I wake up to vision his soft arrival.

He comes in the door with his old key. He gives me a strict look and says, "Well, you look older, Virginia." "So do you," I say, although he hasn't changed a bit.

He settles in the kitchen because the children are asleep all over the rest of the house. I unknot his tie and offer him a cold sandwich. He raps my backside, paying attention to the bounce. I walk around him as though he were a Maypole, kissing as I go.

"I didn't like the army much," he says. "Next time I think I might go join the Merchant Marine."

"What army?" I say.

"It's pretty much the same everywhere," he says.

"I wouldn't be a bit surprised," I say.

"I lost my cuff link, goddamnit," he says, and drops to the floor to look for it. I go down too on my knees, but I know he never had a cuff link in his life. Still I would do a lot for him.

"Got you off your feet that time," he says, laughing. "Oh yes, I did." And before I can even make myself half comfortable on that polka-dotted linoleum, he got onto me right where we were, and the truth is, we were so happy, we forgot the precautions.

# J. F. POWERS

## (1917–1999)

James Farl Powers was born in Jacksonville, Illinois. He moved to Chicago after high school and held a number of odd jobs. Too poor to pursue a full-time degree program at Northwestern University, he took classes in English and philosophy at night. During World War II, he was a conscientious objector and spent thirteen months in a federal prison for draft refusal. After marrying in 1946, Powers taught creative writing for a year at St. John's University in Collegeville, Minnesota. He also taught briefly at Marquette University, the University of Michigan, and Smith College. Powers and his family lived in Ireland for several years before returning to a position at St. John's University and the College of St. Benedict from 1975 to 1993. Powers avoided publicity and never pursued fame or fortune.

While his total output was modest—often battling procrastination and agonizing over virtually every sentence—his work is highly esteemed. His story

"The Valiant Woman" received the O. Henry Award in 1943. In 1948 he received a National Institute of Arts and Letters grant and a Guggenheim fellowship. He was awarded three Rockefeller fellowships. Most of his stories appeared in *The New Yorker, Nation,* and *Colliers.* He published three short story collections: *Prince of Darkness and Other Stories* (1947); *The Presence of Grace* (1956); and *Look How the Fish Live* (1975). His novel *Mort d' Urban* (1962) won the 1963 National Book Award. His second novel, *Wheat That Springeth Green* (1988), was nominated for the National Book Award and the National Book Critics Circle Award. He was a member of the National Institute of Arts and Letters.

Although sadly rarely anthologized, Powers' stories are among the best of the twentieth century. Most of his fiction deals with Roman Catholic priests. But, unlike those of his European counterparts, Powers' priests are worldly—much like corporate managers—and they do not reveal much of their inner spiritual agonies. Rather, their struggles are with a very seductive, and very American, secular material world. In Powers, as in Henry James, the hidden forces of life are implied and must be imagined by the reader.

# Prince of Darkness

## I. Morning

I should've known you'd be eating breakfast, Father. But I was at your Mass and I said to myself that must be Father Burner. Then I stayed a few minutes after Mass to make my thanksgiving."

"Fine," Father Burner said. "Breakfast?"

"Had it, Father, thanking you all the same. It's the regret of my life that I can't be a daily communicant. Doctor forbids it. 'Fast every day and see how long you last,' he tells me. But I do make it to Mass."

"Fine. You say you live in Father Desmond's parish?"

"Yes, Father. And sometimes I think Father Desmond does too much. All the societies to look after. Plus the Scouts and the Legion. Of course Father Kells being so elderly and all . . ."

"We're all busy these days."

"It's the poor parish priest's day that's never done, I always say, Father, not meaning to slight the ladies, God love 'em."

Father Burner's sausage fingers, spelling his impatience over and over, worked up sweat in the folds of the napkin which he kept in view to provoke an early departure. "About this matter you say Father Desmond thought I might be interested in—"

"The Plan, Father." Mr. Tracy lifted his seersucker trousers by the creases, crossed his shining two-tone shoes, and rolled warmly forward. "Father . . ."

Father Burner met his look briefly. He was wary of the fatherers. A backslider he could handle, it was the old story, but a red-hot believer, especially a talkative one, could be a devilish nuisance. This kind might be driven away only by prayer and fasting, and he was not adept at either.

"I guess security's one thing we're all after."

Father Burner grunted. Mr. Tracy was too familiar to suit him. He liked his parishioners to be retiring, dumb, or frightened. There were too many references made to the priest's hard lot. Not so many poor souls as all that passed away in the wee hours, nor was there so much bad weather to brave. Mr. Tracy's heart bled for priests. That in itself was a suspicious thing in a layman. It all led up to the Plan.

"Here's the Plan, Father . . ." Father Burner watched his eye peel down to naked intimacy. Then, half listening, he gazed about the room. He hated it, too. A fabulous brown rummage of encyclopedias, world globes, maps, photographs, holy pictures, mirrors, crucifixes, tropical fish, and too much furniture. The room reproduced the world, all wonders and horrors, less land than water. From the faded precipices of the walls photographs viewed each other for the most part genially across time. Three popes, successively thinner, raised hands to bless their departed painters. The world globes simpered in the shadows, heavy-headed idiot boys, listening. A bird in a blacked-out cage scratched among its offal. An anomalous buddha peeked beyond his dusty umbilicus at the trampled figures in the rug. The fish swam on, the mirrors and encyclopedias turned in upon themselves, the earless boys heard everything and understood nothing. Father Burner put his big black shoe on a moth and sent dust flecks crowding up a shaft of sunlight to the distant ceiling.

"Say you pay in $22.67 every month, can be paid semiannually or as you please, policy matures in twenty years and pays you $35.50 a month for twenty years or as long as you live. That's the deal for you, Father. It beats the deal Father Desmond's got, although he's got a darned good one, and I hope he keeps it up. But we've gone ahead in the last few years, Father. Utilities are sounder, bonds are more secure, and this new legislation protects you one hundred per cent."

"You say Ed—Father Desmond—has the Plan?"

"Oh, indeed, Father." Mr. Tracy had to laugh. "I hope you don't think I'm trying to high-pressure you, Father. It's not just a piece of business with me, the Plan."

"No?"

"No. You see, it's more or less a pet project of mine. Hardly make a cent on it. Looking out after the fathers, you might say, so they'll maybe look out after me—spiritually. I call it heavenly life insurance."

Slightly repelled, Father Burner nodded.

"Not a few priests that I've sold the Plan to remember me at the altar daily. I guess prayer's one thing we can all use. Anyway, it's why I take a hand in putting boys through seminary."

With that Mr. Tracy shed his shabby anonymity for Father Burner, and grew executive markings. He became the one and only Thomas Nash Tracy—T. N. T. It was impossible to read the papers and not know a few things about T. N. T. He was in small loans and insurance. His company's advertising smothered the town and country; everybody knew the slogan "T. N. T. Spells Security." He figured in any financial drive undertaken by the diocese, was caught by photographers in orphanages, and sat at the heavy end of the table at communion breakfasts. Hundreds of nuns, thanks to his thoughtfulness, ate capon on Christmas Day, and a few priests of the right sort received baskets of scotch. He was a B. C. L., a Big Catholic Layman, and now Father Burner could see why. Father Burner's countenance softened at this intelligence, and T. N. T. proceeded with more assurance.

"And don't call it charity, Father. Insurance, as I said, is a better name for it. I have a little money, Father, which makes it possible." He tuned his voice down to a whisper. "You might say I'm moderately wealthy." He looked sharply at Father Burner, not sure of his man. "But I'm told there isn't any crime in that."

"I believe you need not fear for your soul on that account."

"Glad to hear it from you, a priest, Father. Ofttimes it's thrown up to me." He came to terms with reality, smiling. "I wasn't always so well off myself, so I can understand the temptation to knock the other fellow."

"Fine."

"But that's still not to say that water's not wet or that names don't hurt sometimes, whatever the bard said to the contrary."

"What bard?"

" 'Sticks and stones—' "

"Oh."

"If this were a matter of faith and morals, Father, I'd be the one to sit back and let you do the talking. But it's a case of common sense, Father, and I think I can safely say, if you listen to me you'll not lose by it in the long run."

"It could be."

"May I ask you a personal question, Father?"

Father Burner searched T. N. T.'s face. "Go ahead, Mr. Tracy."

"Do you bank, Father?"

"*Bank?* Oh, bank—no. Why?"

"Let's admit it, Father," T. N. T. coaxed, frankly amused. "Priests as a class are an improvident lot—our records show it—and you're no exception. But that, I think, explains the glory of the Church down through the ages."

"The Church is divine," Father Burner corrected. "And the concept of poverty isn't exactly foreign to Christianity or even to the priesthood."

"Exactly," T. N. T. agreed, pinked. "But think of the future, Father."

Nowadays when Father Burner thought of the future it required a firm act of imagination. As a seminarian twenty years ago, it had all been plain: ordination, roughly ten years as a curate somewhere (he was not the kind to be sent to Rome for further study), a church of his own to follow, the fruitful years, then retirement, pastor emeritus, with assistants doing the spade work, leaving the fine touches to him, still a hearty old man very much alive. It was not an uncommon hope and, in fact, all around him it had materialized for his friends. But for him it was only a bad memory growing worse. He was the desperate assistant now, the angry functionary aging in the outer office. One day he would wake and find himself old, as the morning finds itself covered with snow. The future had assumed the forgotten character of a dream, so that he could not be sure that he had ever truly had one.

T. N. T. talked on and Father Burner felt a mist generating on his forehead. He tore his damp hands apart and put the napkin aside. Yes, yes, it was true a priest received miserably little, but then that was the whole idea. He did not comment, dreading T. N. T.'s foaming compassion, to be spat upon with charity. Yes, as a matter of fact, it would be easier to face old age with something more to draw upon than what the ecclesiastical authorities deemed sufficient and would provide. Also, as T. N. T. pointed out, one never knew when he might come down with an expensive illness. T. N. T., despite himself, had something. . . . The Plan, in itself, was not bad. He must not reject the olive branch because it came by buzzard. But still Father Burner was a little bothered by the idea of a priest feathering his nest. Why? In other problems he was never the one to take the ascetic interpretation.

"You must be between thirty-five and forty, Father."

"I'll never see forty again."

"I'd never believe it from anyone else. You sure don't look it, Father."

"Maybe not. But I feel it."

"Worries, Father. And one big one is the future, Father. You'll get to be fifty, sixty, seventy—and what have you got?—not a penny saved. You look around and say to yourself—where did it go?"

T. N. T. had the trained voice of the good and faithful servant, supple from many such dealings. And still from time to time a faint draught of contempt seemed to pass through it which had something to do with his eyes. Here, Father Burner thought, was the latest thing in simony, unnecessary, inspired from without, participated in spiritlessly by the priest who must yet suffer the brunt of the blame and ultimately do the penance. Father Burner felt mysteriously purchasable. He was involved in an exchange of confidences which impoverished him mortally. In T. N. T. he sensed free will in its senility or the infinite capacity for equating evil with good—or with nothing—the same thing, only easier. Here was one more word in the history of the worm's progress, another wave on the dry flood that kept rising, the constant aggrandizement of decay. In the end it must touch the world and everything at the heart. Father Burner felt weak from a nameless loss.

"I think I can do us both a service, Father."

"I don't say you can't." Father Burner rose quickly. "I'll have to think about it, Mr. Tracy."

"To be sure, Father." He produced a glossy circular. "Just let me leave this literature with you."

Father Burner, leading him to the door, prevented further talk by reading the circular. It was printed in a churchy type, all purple and gold, a dummy leaf from a medieval hymnal, and entitled, "A Silver Lining in the Sky." It was evidently meant for clergymen only, though not necessarily priests, as Father Burner could instantly see from its general tone.

"Very interesting," he said.

"My business phone is right on the back, Father. But if you'd rather call me at my home some night—"

"No thanks, Mr. Tracy."

"Allow me to repeat, Father, this isn't just business with me."

"I understand." He opened the door too soon for T. N. T. "Glad to have met you."

"Glad to have met you, Father."

Father Burner went back to the table. The coffee needed warming up and the butter had vanished into the toast. "Mary," he called. Then he heard them come gabbing into the rectory, Quinlan and his friend Keefe, also newly ordained.

They were hardly inside the dining room before he was explaining how he came to be eating breakfast so late—so late, see?—not *still.*

"You protest too much, Father," Quinlan said. "The Angelic Doctor himself weighed three hundred pounds, and I'll wager he didn't get it all from prayer and fasting."

"A pituitary condition," Keefe interjected, faltering. "Don't you think?"

"Yah, yah, Father, you'll wager"—Father Burner, eyes malignant, leaned on his knife, the blade bowing out bright and buttery beneath his fist—"and I'll wager you'll be the first saint to reach heaven with a flannel mouth!" Rising from the table, he shook Keefe's hand, which was damp from his pocket, and experienced a surge of strength, the fat man's contempt and envy for the thin man. He thought he might break Keefe's hand off at the wrist without drawing a drop of blood.

Quinlan stood aside, six inches or more below them, gazing up, as at two impossibly heroic figures in a hotel mural. Reading the caption under them, he mused, "Father Burner meets Father Keefe."

"I've heard about you, Father," Keefe said, plying him with a warmth beyond his means.

"Bound to be the case in a diocese as overstocked with magpies as this one." Father Burner threw a fresh napkin at a plate. "But be seated, Father Keefe." Keefe, yes, he had seen him before, a nobody in a crowd, some affair . . . the K. C. barbecue, the Youth Center? No, probably not, not Keefe, who was obviously not the type, too crabbed and introversive for Catholic Action. "I suppose," he said, "you've heard the latest definition of Catholic Action—the interference of the laity with the inactivity of the hierarchy."

"Very good," Keefe said uneasily.

Quinlan yanked off his collar and churned his neck up and down to get circulation. "Dean in the house? No? Good." He pitched the collar at one of the candles on the buffet for a ringer. "That turkey we met coming out the front door—think I've seen his face somewhere."

"Thomas Nash Tracy," Keefe said. "I thought you knew."

"The prominent lay priest and usurer?"

Keefe coughed. "They say he's done a lot of good."

Quinlan spoke to Father Burner: "Did you take out a policy, Father?"

"One of the sixth-graders threw a rock through his windshield," Father Burner said. "He was very nice about it."

"Muldoon or Ciesniewski?"

"A new kid. Public school transfer." Father Burner patted the napkin to his chin. "Not that I see anything wrong with insurance."

Quinlan laughed. "Let Walter tell you what happened to him a few days ago. Go ahead, Walter," he said to Keefe.

"Oh, that." Keefe fidgeted and, seemingly against his better judgment, began. "I had a little accident—was it Wednesday it rained so? I had the misfortune to skid into a fellow parked on Fairmount. Dented his fender." Keefe stopped and then, as though impelled by the memory of it, went on. "The fellow came raging out of his car at me. I thought there'd be serious trouble. Then he must have seen I was a priest, the way he calmed down, I mean. I had a funny feeling it wasn't because he was a Catholic or anything like that. As a matter of fact he wore a Masonic button." Keefe sighed. "I guess he saw I was a priest and ergo . . . knew I'd have insurance."

"Take nothing for your journey, neither staff, nor scrip," Quinlan said, "words taken from today's gospel."

Father Burner spoke in a level tone: "Not that I *still* see anything wrong with insurance. It's awfully easy," he continued, hating himself for talking drivel, "to make too much of little things." With Quinlan around he played the conservative; among the real right-handers he was the *enfant terrible.* He operated on the principle of discord at any cost. He did not know why. It was a habit. Perhaps it had something to do with being overweight.

Arranging the Dean's chair, which had arms, for himself, Quinlan sank into it, giving Keefe the Irish whisper. "Grace, Father."

Keefe addressed the usual words to God concerning the gifts they were about to receive. During the prayer Father Burner stopped chewing and did not reach for anything. He noted once more that Quinlan crossed himself sloppily enough to be a monsignor.

Keefe nervously cleared the entire length of his throat. "It's a beautiful church you have here at Saint Patrick's, Father." A lukewarm light appeared in his eyes, flickered, sputtered out, leaving them blank and blue. His endless fingers felt for his receding chin in the onslaught of silence.

"*I* have?" Father Burner turned his spoon abasingly to his bosom. *"Me?"* He jabbed at the grapefruit before him, his second, demolishing its perfect rose window. "I don't know why it is the Irish without exception are always laying personal claim to church property. The Dean is forever saying *my* church, *my* school, *my* furnace . . ."

"I'm sorry, Father," Keefe said, flushing. "And I'll confess I did think he virtually built Saint Patrick's."

"Out of the slime of the earth, I know. A common error." With sudden, unabated displeasure Father Burner recalled how the Dean, one of the last of the old brick and mortar pastors, had built the church, school, sisters' house, and rectory, and had named the whole thing through the lavish pretense of a popular contest. Opposed bitterly by Polish, German, and Italian minorities, he had effected a compromise between their bad taste (Saint Stanislaus, Saint Boniface, Saint Anthony) and his own better judgment in the choice of Saint Patrick's.

Quinlan, snorting, blurted, "Well, he did build it, didn't he?"

Father Burner smiled at them from the other world. "Only, if you please, in a manner of speaking."

"True," Keefe murmured humbly.

"Nuts," Quinlan said. "It's hard for me to see God in a few buildings paid for by the funds of the faithful and put up by a mick contractor. A burning bush, yes."

Father Burner, lips parched to speak an unsummonable cruelty, settled for a smoldering aside to the kitchen. "Mary, more eggs here."

A stuffed moose of a woman with a tabby-cat face charged in on swollen feet. She stood wavering in shoes sliced fiercely for corns. With the back of her hand she wiped some cream from the fuzz ringing her baby-pink mouth. Her hair poked through a broken net like stunted antlers. Father Burner pointed to the empty platter.

"Eggs," he said.

"Eggs!" she cried, tumbling her eyes like great blue dice among them. She seized up the platter and carried it whirling with grease into the kitchen.

Father Burner put aside the grapefruit. He smiled and spoke calmly. "I'll have to let the Dean know, Father, how much you like *his* plant."

"Do, Father. A beautiful church . . . 'a poem in stone'—was it Ruskin?"

"Ruskin? *Stones of Venice,*" Father Burner grumbled. "*Sesame and Lilies,* I know . . . but I never cared for his *style.*" He passed the knife lovingly over the pancakes on his plate and watched the butter bubble at the pores. "So much sweetness, so much light, I'm afraid, made Jack a dull boy."

Quinlan slapped all his pockets. "Pencil and paper, quick!"

"And yet . . ." Keefe cocked his long head, brow fretted, and complained to his upturned hands. "Don't understand how he stayed outside the Church." He glanced up hopefully. "I wonder if Chesterton gives us a clue."

Father Burner, deaf to such precious speculation, said, "In the nineteenth century Francis Thompson was the only limey worth his salt. It's true." He quartered the pancakes. "Of course, Newman."

"Hopkins has some good things."

"Good—yes, if you like jabberwocky and jebbies! I don't care for either." He dispatched a look of indictment at Quinlan.

"What a pity," Quinlan murmured, "Oliver Wendell couldn't be at table this morning."

"No, Father, you can have your Hopkins, you and Father Quinlan here. Include me out, as Sam Goldwyn says. Poetry—I'll take my poetry the way I take my liquor, neat."

Mary brought in the platter oozing with bacon and eggs.

"Good for you, Mary," Quinlan said. "I'll pray for you."

"Thank you, Father," Mary said.

Quinlan dipped the platter with a trace of obeisance to Father Burner.

"No thanks."

Quinlan scooped up the coffeepot in a fearsome rush and held it high at Father Burner, his arm so atremble the lid rattled dangerously. "Sure and will you be about having a sup of coffee now, Father?"

"Not now. And do you mind not playing the wild Irish wit so early in the day, Father?"

"That I don't. *But a relentless fate pursuing good Father Quinlan, he was thrown in among hardened clerics where but for the grace of God that saintly priest, so little understood, so much maligned . . .*" Quinlan poured two cups and passed one to Keefe.

"For yourself, Father." Father Burner nudged the toast to Keefe. "Father Quinlan, that saintly priest, models his life after the Rover Boys, particularly Sam, the fun-loving one."

Quinlan dealt himself a mighty *mea culpa.*

Father Burner grimaced, the flesh rising in sweet, concentric tiers around his mouth, and said in a tone both entrusting and ennobling Keefe with his confidence, "The syrup, if you please, Father." Keefe passed the silver pitcher which was running at the mouth. Father Burner reimmersed the doughy remains on his plate until the butter began to float around the edges as in a moat. He felt them both watching the butter. Regretting that he had not foreseen this attraction, he cast about in his mind for something to divert them and found the morning sun coming in too strongly. He got up and pulled down the shade. He returned to his place and settled himself in such a way that a new chapter was indicated. "Don't believe I know where you're located, Father."

"Saint Jerome's," Keefe said. "Monsignor Fiedler's."

"One of those P. N. places, eh? Is the boss sorry he ever started it? I know some of them are."

Keefe's lips popped apart. "I don't quite understand."

Quinlan prompted: "P.N.—Perpetual Novena."

"Oh, I never heard him say."

"You wouldn't, of course. But I know a lot of them that are." Father Burner stuck a morsel on his fork and swirled it against the tide of syrup. "It's a real problem all right. I was all out for a P. N. here during the depression. Thought it might help. The Dean was against it."

"I can tell you this," Keefe said. "Attendance was down from what it used to be until the casualties began to come in. Now it's going up."

"I was just going to say the war ought to take the place of the depression." Father Burner fell silent. "Terrible thing, war. Hard to know what to do about it. I tried to sell the Dean the idea of a victory altar. You've seen them. Vigil lights—"

"At a dollar a throw," Quinlan said.

"Vigil lights in the form of a V, names of the men in the service and all that. But even that, I guess—Well, like I said, I tried. . . ."

"Yes, it is hard," Keefe said.

"God, the Home, and the Flag," Quinlan said. "The poets don't make the wars."

Father Burner ignored that. "Lately, though, I can't say how I feel about P. N.'s. Admit I'm not so strong for them as I was once. Ought to be some way of terminating them, you know, but then they wouldn't be perpetual, would they?"

"No, they wouldn't," Keefe said.

"Not *so* perpetual," Quinlan said.

"Of course," Father Burner continued, "the term itself, perpetual novena, is preposterous, a solecism. Possibly dispensation lies in that direction. I'm not theologian enough to say. Fortunately it's not a problem we have to decide." He laid his knife and fork across the plate. "Many are the consolations of the lowly curate. No decisions, no money worries."

"We still have to count the sugar," Quinlan said. "And put up the card tables."

"Reminds me," Father Burner said earnestly. "Father Desmond at Assumption was telling me they've got a new machine does all that."

"Puts up card tables?" Quinlan inquired.

"Counts the collection, wraps the silver," Father Burner explained, "so it's all ready for the bank. Mean to mention it to the Dean, if I can catch him right."

"I'm afraid, Father, he knows about it already."

Father Burner regarded Quinlan skeptically. "Does? I suppose he's against it."

"I heard him tell the salesman that's what he had his assistants for."

"Assistant, Father, not assistants. You count the collection, not me. I was only thinking of you."

"I was only quoting him, Father. *Sic.* Sorry."

"Not at all. I haven't forgotten the days I had to do it. It's a job has to be done and nothing to be ashamed of. Wouldn't you say, Father Keefe?"

"I dare say that's true."

Quinlan, with Father Burner still molesting him with his eyes, poured out a glass of water and drank it all. "I still think we could do with a lot less calculating. I notice the only time we get rid of the parish paper is when the new lists are published—the official standings. Of course it's a lousy sheet anyway."

Father Burner, as editor of the paper, replied: "Yes, yes, Father. We all know how easy it is to be wrathful or fastidious about these things—or whatever the hell it is you are. And we all know there *are* abuses. But contributing to the support of the Church is still one of her commandments."

"Peace, Père," Quinlan said.

"Figures don't lie."

"Somebody was telling me just last night that figures do lie. He looked a lot like you."

Father Burner found his cigarettes and shuffled a couple half out of the pack. He eyed Quinlan and the cigarettes as though it were as simple to discipline the one as to smoke the others. "For some reason, Father, you're damned fond of those particular figures."

Keefe stirred. "Which particular figures, Father?"

"It's the figures put out by the Cardinal of Toledo on how many made their Easter duty last year." Father Burner offered Keefe a cigarette. "I discussed the whole thing with Father Quinlan last night. It's his latest thesis. Have a cigarette?"

"No, thanks," Keefe said.

"So you don't smoke?" Father Burner looked from Keefe to Quinlan, blacklisting them together. He held the cigarette hesitantly at his lips. "It's all right, isn't it?" He laughed and touched off the match with his thumbnail.

"His Eminence," Quinlan said, "reports only fifteen per cent of the women and five per cent of the men made their Easter duty last year."

"So that's only three times as many women as men," Father Burner said with buried gaiety. "Certainly to be expected in any Latin country."

"But fifteen per cent, Father! And five per cent! Just think of it!" Keefe glanced up at the ceiling and at the souvenir plates on the molding, as though to see inscribed along with scenes from the Columbian Exposition the day and hour the end of the world would begin. He finally stared deep into the goldfish tank in the window.

Father Burner plowed up the silence, talking with a mouthful of smoke. "All right, all right, I'll say what I said in the first place. There's something wrong with the figures. A country as overwhelmingly Catholic as Spain!" He sniffed, pursed his lips, and said, "Pooh!"

"Yes," Keefe said, still balking. "But it *is* disturbing, Father Burner."

"Sure it's disturbing, Father Keefe. *Lots* of things *are*."

A big, faded goldfish paused to stare through the glass at them and then with a single lob of its tail slipped into a dark green corner.

Quinlan said, "Father Burner belongs to the school that's always seeing a great renascence of faith in the offing. The hour before dawn and all that. Tell it to Rotary on Tuesday, Father."

Father Burner countered with a frosty pink smile. "What would I ever do without you, Father? If you're trying to say I'm a dreadful optimist, you're right and I don't mind at all. I am—and proud of it!"

Ascending to his feet, he went to the right side of the buffet, took down the card index to parishioners, and returned with it to his place. He pushed his dishes aside and began to sort out the deadheads to be called on personally by him or Quinlan. The Dean, like all pastors, he reflected, left the dirty work to the assistants. "Why doesn't he pull them," he snapped, tearing up a card, "when they kick off! Can't very well forward them to the next world. Say, how many Gradys live at 909 South Vine? Here's Anna, Catherine, Clement, Gerald, Harvey, James A., James F.—which James is the one they call 'Bum'?"

"James F.," Quinlan said. "Can't you tell from the take? The other James works."

"John, Margaret, Matthew—that's ten, no eleven. Here's Dennis out of place. Patrick, Rita and William—fourteen of them, no birth control there, and they all give. Except Bum. Nice account otherwise. Can't we find Bum a job? What's it with him, drink?"

Now he came to Maple Street. These cards were the remains of little Father Vicci's work among the magdalens. Ann Mason, Estelle Rogers, May Miller, Billie Starr. The names had the generic ring. Great givers when they gave—Christmas, $25; Easter, $20; Propagation of the Faith, $10; Catholic University, $10—but not much since Father Vicci was exiled to the sticks. He put Maple Street aside for a thorough sifting.

The doorbell rang. Father Burner leaned around in his chair. "Mary." The doorbell rang again. Father Burner bellowed. "Mary!"

Quinlan pushed his chair away from the table. "I'll get it."

Father Burner blocked him. "Oh, I'll get it! Hell of a bell! Why does he have a bell like that!" Father Burner opened the door to a middle-aged woman whose name he had forgotten or never known. "Good morning," he said. "Will you step in?"

She stayed where she was and said, "Father, it's about the servicemen's flag in church. My son Stanley—you know him—"

Father Burner, who did not know him, half nodded. "Yes, how is Stanley?" He gazed over her shoulder at the lawn, at the dandelions turning into poppies before his eyes.

"You know he was drafted last October, Father, and I been watching that flag you got in church ever since, and it's still the same, five hundred thirty-six stars. I thought you said you put a star up for all them that's gone in the service, Father."

Now the poppies were dandelions again. He could afford to be firm with her. "We can't spend all our time putting up stars. Sometimes we fall behind. Besides, a lot of the boys are being discharged."

"You mean there's just as many going in as coming out, so you don't have to change the flag?"

"Something like that."

"I see." He was sorry for her. They had run out of stars. He had tried to get the Dean to order some more, had even offered . . . and the Dean had said they could use up the gold ones first. When Father Burner had objected, telling him what it would mean, he had suggested that Father Burner apply for the curatorship of the armory.

"The pastor will be glad to explain how it works the next time you see him."

"Well, Father, if that's the way it is . . ." She was fading down the steps. "I just thought I'd ask."

"That's right. There's no harm in asking. How's Stanley?"

"Fine, and thank you, Father, for your trouble."

"No trouble."

When he came back to the table they were talking about the junior clergyman's examinations which they would take for the first time next week. Father Burner interrupted, "The Dean conducts the history end of it, you know."

"I say!" Keefe said. "Any idea what we can expect?"

"You have nothing to fear. Nothing."

"Really?"

"Really. Last year, I remember, there were five questions and the last four depended on the first. So it was really only one question—if you knew it. I imagine you would've." He paused, making Keefe ask for it.

"Perhaps you can recall the question, Father?"

"Perfectly, Father. 'What event in the American history of the Church took place in 1541?' " Father Burner, slumping in his chair, smirked at Keefe pondering for likely martyrs and church legislation. He imagined him skipping among the tomes and statuary of his mind, winnowing dates and little known facts like mad, only at last to emerge dusty and downcast. Father Burner sat up with a jerk and assaulted the table with the flat of his hand. "Time's up. Answer: 'De Soto sailed up the Mississippi.' "

Quinlan snorted. Keefe sat very still, incredulous, silent, utterly unable to digest the answer, finally croaking, "How odd." Father Burner saw in him the boy whose marks in school had always been a consolation to his parents.

"So you don't have to worry, Father. No sense in preparing for it. Take in a couple of movies instead. And cheer up! The Dean's been examining the junior clergy for twenty-five years and nobody ever passed history yet. You wouldn't want to be the first one."

Father Burner said grace and made the sign of the cross with slow distinction. "And, Father," he said, standing, extending his hand to Keefe, who also rose, "I'm glad to have met you." He withdrew his hand before Keefe was through with it and stood against the table knocking toast crumbs onto his plate. "Ever play any golf? No? Well, come and see us for conversation then. You don't have anything against talking, do you?"

"Well, of course, Father, I . . ."

Father Burner gave Keefe's arm a rousing clutch. "Do that!"

"I will, Father. It's been a pleasure."

"Speaking of pleasure," Father Burner said, tossing Quinlan a stack of cards, "I've picked out a few lost sheep for you to see on Maple Street, Father."

## II. Noon

He hung his best black trousers on a hanger in the closet and took down another pair, also black. He tossed them out behind him and they fell patched at the cuffs and baggy across his unmade bed. His old suède jacket, following, slid dumpily to the floor. He stood gaping in his clerical vest and undershorts, knees knocking and pimply, thinking . . . what else? His aviator's helmet. He felt all the hooks blindly in the darkness. It was not there. "Oh, hell!" he groaned, sinking to his knees. He pawed among the old shoes and boxes and wrapping paper and string that he was always going to need. Under his golf bag he found it. So Mary had cleaned yesterday.

There was also a golf ball unknown to him, a Royal Bomber, with one small hickey in it. Father Desmond, he remembered, had received a box of Royal Bombers from a thoughtful parishioner. He stuck the helmet on his balding head to get it out of the way and took the putter from the bag. He dropped the ball at the door of the closet. Taking his own eccentric stance—a perversion of what the pro recommended and a dozen books on the subject—he putted the ball across the room at a dirty collar lying against the bookcase. A thready place in the carpet caused the ball to jump the collar and to loose a pamphlet from the top of the bookcase. He restored the pamphlet—Pius XI on "Atheistic Communism"—and poked the ball back to the door of the closet. Then, allowing for the carpet, he drove the ball straight, *click,* through the collar, *clop.* Still had his old putting eye. And his irons had always been steady if not exactly crashing. It was his woods, the tee shots, that ruined his game. He'd give a lot to be able to hit his woods properly, not to dub his drives, if only on the first tee—where there was always a crowd (mixed).

At one time or another he had played every hole at the country club in par or less. Put all those pars and birdies together, adding in the only two eagles he'd ever had, and you had the winning round in the state open, write-ups and action shots in the papers—photo shows Rev. Ernest "Boomer" Burner, par-shattering padre, blasting out of a trap. He needed only practice perhaps and at his earliest opportunity he would entice some of the eighth-grade boys over into the park to shag balls. He sank one more for good measure, winning a buck from Ed Desmond who would have bet against it, and put the club away.

Crossing the room for his trousers he noticed himself in the mirror with the helmet on and got a mild surprise. He scratched a little hair down from underneath the helmet to offset the egg effect. He searched his eyes in the mirror for a sign of ill health. He walked away from the mirror, as though done with it, only to wheel sharply so as to see himself as others saw him, front and profile, not wanting to catch his eye, just to see himself. . . .

Out of the top drawer of the dresser he drew a clean white silk handkerchief and wiped the shine from his nose. He chased his eyes over into the corner of the mirror and saw nothing. Then, succumbing to his original intention, he knotted the handkerchief at the crown of the helmet and completed the transformation of time and place and person by humming, vibrato, "Jeannine, I dream in lilac time," remembering the old movie. He saw himself over his shoulder in the mirror, a sad war ace. It reminded him that his name was not Burner, but Boerner, an impediment removed at the outset of the first world war by his father. In a way he resented the old man for it. They had laughed at the seminary; the war, except as theory, hardly entered there. In perverse homage to the old Boerner, to which he now affixed a proud "von," he dropped the fair-minded American look he had and faced the mirror sneering, scar-cheeked, and black of heart, the flying Junker who might have been. "*Himmelkreuzdonnerwetter!* When you hear the word 'culture,' " he snarled, hearing it come back to him in German, "reach for your revolver!"

Reluctantly he pulled on his black trousers, falling across the bed to do so, as though felled, legs heaving up like howitzers.

He lay still for a moment, panting, and then let the inner-spring mattress bounce him to his feet, a fighter coming off the ropes. He stood looking out the window, buckling his belt, and then down at the buckle, chins kneading softly with the effort, and was pleased to see that he was holding his own on the belt, still a good half inch away from last winter's high-water mark.

At the sound of high heels approaching on the front walk below, he turned firmly away from the window and considered for the first time since he posted it on the wall the prayer for priests sent him by a candle concern. "Remember, O most compassionate God, that they are but weak and frail human beings. Stir up in them the grace of their vocation which is in them by the imposition of the Bishops' hands. Keep them close to Thee, lest the enemy prevail against them, so that they may never do anything in the slightest degree unworthy of their sublime . . ." His eyes raced through the prayer and out the window. . . .

He was suddenly inspired to write another letter to the Archbishop. He sat down at his desk, slipped a piece of paper into his portable, dated it with the saint's day it was, and wrote, "Your Excellency: Thinking my letter of some months ago may have gone amiss, or perhaps due to the press of business—" He ripped the paper from the portable and typed the same thing on a fresh sheet until he came to "business," using instead "affairs of the Church." He went on to signify—it was considered all right to "signify," but to re-signify?—that he was still of the humble opinion that he needed a change of location and had decided, since he believed himself ready for a parish of his own, a rural one might be best, all things considered (by which he meant easier to get). He, unlike some priests of urban upbringing and experience, would have no objection to the country. He begged to be graced with an early reply. That line, for all its seeming docility, was full of dynamite and ought to break the episcopal silence into which the first letter had dissolved. This was a much stronger job. He thought it better for two reasons: the Archbishop was supposed to like outspoken people, or, that being only more propaganda talked up by the sycophants, then it ought to bring a reply which would reveal once and for all his prospects. Long overdue for the routine promotion, he had a just cause. He addressed the letter and placed it in his coat. He went to the bathroom. When he came back he put on the coat, picked up the suède jacket and helmet, looked around for something he might have forgot, a book of chances, a box of Sunday envelopes to be delivered, some copy for the printer, but there was nothing. He lit a cigarette at the door and not caring to throw the match on the floor or look for the ashtray, which was out of sight again, he dropped it in the empty holy-water font.

Downstairs he paused at the telephone in the hall, scribbled "Airport" on the message pad, thought of crossing it out or tearing off the page, but since it was dated he let it stand and added "Visiting the sick," signing his initials, *E. B.*

He went through the wicker basket for mail. A card from the Book-of-the-Month Club. So it was going to be another war book selection this month. Well, they knew what they could do with it. He wished the Club would wake up and select some dandies, as they had in the past. He thought of *Studs Lonigan*—there was a book, the best thing since the Bible.

* * *

An oblique curve in the road: perfect, wheels parallel with the center line. So many drivers took a curve like that way over on the other fellow's side. Father Burner touched the lighter on the dashboard to his cigarette and plunged his hams deeper into the cushions. A cloud of smoke whirled about the little Saint Christopher garroted from the ceiling. Father Burner tugged viciously at both knees, loosening the binding black cloth, easing the seat. Now that he was in open country he wanted to enjoy the scenery—God's majesty. How about a sermon that would liken the things in the landscape to the people in a church? All different, all the same, the handiwork of God. Moral: it is right and meet for rocks to be rocks, trees to be trees, pigs to be pigs, but—and here the small gesture that says so much—what did that mean that men, created in the image and likeness of God, should be? And what—He thrust the sermon out of mind, tired of it. He relaxed, as before an open fireplace, the weight of dogma off his shoulders. Then he grabbed at his knees again, cursing. Did the tailor skimp on the cloth because of the ecclesiastical discount?

A billboard inquired: "Pimples?" Yes, he had a few, but he blamed them on the climate, the humidity. Awfully hard for a priest to transfer out of a diocese. He remembered the plan he had never gone through with. Would it work after all? Would another doctor recommend a change? Why? He would only want to know why, like the last bastard. Just a slight case of obesity, Reverend. Knew he was a non-Catholic when he said Reverend. Couldn't trust a Catholic one. Some of them were thicker than thieves with the clergy. Wouldn't want to be known as a malingerer, along with everything else.

Another billboard: "Need Cash? See T. N. T."

Rain. He knew it. No flying for him today. One more day between him and a pilot's license. Thirteen hours yet and it might have been twelve. Raining so, and with no flying, the world seemed to him . . . a valley of tears. He would drive on past the airport for a hamburger. If he had known, he would have brought along one of the eighth-grade boys. They were always bragging among themselves about how many he had bought them, keeping score. One of them, the Cannon kid, had got too serious from the hamburgers. When he said he was "contemplating the priesthood" Father Burner, wanting to spare him the terrible thing a false vocation could be, had told him to take up aviation instead. He could not forget the boy's reply: *But couldn't I be a priest like you, Father?*

On the other hand, he was glad to be out driving alone. Never had got the bang out of playing with the kids a priest in this country was supposed to. The failure of the Tom Playfair tradition. He hated most sports. Ed Desmond was a sight at a ball game. Running up and down the base lines, giving the umpires hell, busting all the buttons off his cassock. Assumption rectory smelled like a locker room from all the equipment. Poor Ed.

The rain drummed on the engine hood. The windshield wiper sliced back and forth, reminding him a little of a guillotine. Yes, if he had to, he would die for the Faith.

From here to the hamburger place it was asphalt and slicker than concrete. Careful. Slick. Asphalt. Remembered . . . Quinlan coming into his room one afternoon last winter when it was snowing—the idiot—prating:

> Here were decent godless people:
> Their only monument the asphalt road
> And a thousand lost golf balls . . .

That was Quinlan for you, always spouting against the status quo without having anything better to offer. Told him that. Told him golfers, funny as it might seem to some people, have souls and who's to save them? John Bosco worked wonders in taverns, which was not to say Father Burner thought he was a saint, but rather only that he was not too proud to meet souls halfway wherever it might be, in the confessional or on the fairways. Saint Ernest Burner, Help of Golfers, Pray for Us! (Quinlan's come back.) Quinlan gave him a pain. Keefe, now that he knew what he was like, ditto. Non-smokers. Jansenists. First fervor is false fervor. They would cool. He would not judge them, however.

He slowed down and executed a sweeping turn into the parking lot reserved for patrons of the hamburger. He honked his horn his way, three shorts and a long—victory. She would see his car or know his honk and bring out two hamburgers, medium well, onions, pickle, relish, tomato, catsup—his way.

She came out now, carrying an umbrella, holding it ostensibly more over the hamburgers than herself. He took the tray from her. She waited dumbly, her eyes at a level with his collar.

"What's to drink?"

"We got pop, milk, coffee . . ." Here she faltered, as he knew she would, washing her hands of what recurrent revelation, rather than experience, told her was to follow.

"A nice cold bottle of beer." Delivered of the fatal words, Father Burner bit into the smoking hamburger. The woman turned sorrowfully away. He put her down again for native Protestant stock.

When she returned, sheltering the bottle under the umbrella, Father Burner had to smile at her not letting pious scruples interfere with business, another fruit of the so-called Reformation. Watch that smile, he warned himself, or she'll take it for carnal. He received the bottle from her hands. For all his familiarity with the type, he was uneasy. Her lowered eyes informed him of his guilt.

*Was* he immoderate? Who on earth could say? *In dubiis libertas,* not? He recalled his first church supper at Saint Patrick's, a mother bringing her child to the Dean's table. She's going to be confirmed next month, Monsignor. Indeed? Then tell me, young lady, what are the seven capital sins? Pride, Covetousness . . . Lust, Anger. Uh. The child's mother, one of those tough Irish females built like a robin, worried to death, lips silently forming the other sins for her daughter. Go ahead, dear. Envy. Proceed, child. Yes, Monsignor. Uh . . . Sloth. To be sure. That's six. One more. And . . . uh. Fear of the Lord, perhaps? Meekness? Hey, Monsignor, ain't them the Divine Counsels! The Dean, smiling, looking at Father Burner's plate, covered with chicken bones, at his stomach, fighting the vest, and for a second into the child's eyes, slipping her the seventh sin. *Gluttony,* Monsignor! The Dean gave her a coin for her trouble and she stood awkwardly in front of Father Burner, lingering, twisting her gaze from his plate to his stomach, to his eyes, finally quacking, Oh Fawther!

* * *

Now he began to brood upon his failure as a priest. There was no sense in applying the consolations of an anchorite to himself. He wanted to know one thing: when would he get a parish? When would he make the great metamorphosis from assistant to pastor, from mouse to rat, as the saying went? He was forty-three, four times transferred, seventeen years an ordained priest, a curate yet and only. He was the only one of his class still without a parish. The only one . . . and in his pocket, three days unopened, was another letter from his mother, kept waiting all these years, who was to have been his housekeeper. He could not bear to warm up her expectations again.

Be a chaplain? That would take him away from it all and there was the possibility of meeting a remote and glorious death carrying the Holy Eucharist to a dying soldier. It would take something like that to make him come out even, but then that, too, he knew in a corner of his heart, would be only exterior justification for him, a last bid for public approbation, a short cut to nothing. And the chaplain's job, it was whispered, could be an ordeal both ignominious and tragic. It would be just his luck to draw an assignment in a rehabilitation center, racking pool balls and repairing ping-pong bats for the boys—the apostolic game-room attendant and toastmaster. Sure, Sarge, I'll lay you even money the Sox make it three straight in Philly and spot you a run a game to boot. You win, I lose a carton of Chesters—I win, you go to Mass every day for a week! Hard-headed holiness. . . .

There was the painful matter of the appointment to Saint Patrick's. The Dean, an irremovable pastor, and the Archbishop had argued over funds and the cemetery association. And the Archbishop, losing though he won, took his revenge, it was rumored, by appointing Father Burner as the Dean's assistant. It was their second encounter. In the first days of his succession, the Archbishop heard that the Dean always said a green Mass on Saint Patrick's Day, thus setting the rubrics at nought. Furious, he summoned the Dean into his presence, but stymied by the total strangeness of him and his great age, he had talked of something else. The Dean took a different view of his narrow escape, which is what the chancery office gossips called it, and now every year, on repeating the error, he would say to the uneasy nuns, "Sure and nobody ever crashed the gates of hell for the wearing of the green." (Otherwise it was not often he did something to delight the hearts of the professional Irish.)

In the Dean's presence Father Burner often had the sensation of confusion, a feeling that someone besides them stood listening in the room. To free himself he would say things he neither meant nor believed. The Dean would take the other side and then . . . there they were again. The Dean's position in these bouts was roughly that of the old saints famous for their faculty of smelling sins and Father Burner played the role of the one smelled. It was no contest. If the Archbishop could find no words for the Dean there was nothing he might do. He might continue to peck away at a few stray foibles behind the Dean's back. He might point out how familiar the Dean was with the Protestant clergy about town. He did. It suited his occasional orthodoxy (reserved mostly to confound his critics and others much worse, like Quinlan, whom he suspected of having him under observation for humorous purposes) to disapprove of all such questionable ties, as though the Dean were entertaining heresy, or at least felt kindly toward this new "inter-faith" nonsense so dear to the reformed Jews and fresh-water sects. It was very small game, however. And the merest brush with the Dean might bring any one of a hundred embarrassing occasions back to life, and it was easy for him to burn all over again.

When he got his darkroom rigged up in the rectory the Dean had come snooping around and inquired without staying for an answer if the making of tintypes demanded that a man shun the light to the extent Father Burner appeared to. Now and again, hearkening back to this episode, the Dean referred to him as the Prince of Darkness. It did not end there. The title caught on all over the diocese. It was not the only one he had.

In reviewing a new historical work for a national Catholic magazine, he had attempted to get back at two Jesuits he knew in town, calling attention to certain tendencies—he meant nothing so gross as "order pride"—which, if not necessarily characteristic of any religious congregation within the Church, were still too often to be seen in any long view of history (which the book at hand did not pretend to take), and whereas the secular clergy, *per se,* had much to answer for, was it not true, though certainly not through any superior virtue, nor even as a consequence of their secularity—indeed, he would be a fool to dream that such orders as those founded, for instance, by Saint Benedict, Saint Francis, and Saint Dominic (Saint Ignatius was not instanced) were without their places in the heart of the Church, even today, when perhaps . . .

Anyway "secular" turned up once as "circular" in the review. The local Jesuits, writing in to the magazine as a group of innocent bystanders, made many subtle plays upon the unfortunate "circular" and its possible application to the person of the reviewer (their absolute unfamiliarity with the reviewer, they explained, enabled them to indulge in such conceivably dangerous whimsey). But the direction of his utterances, they thought, seemed clear, and they regretted more than they could say that the editors of an otherwise distinguished journal had found space for them, especially in wartime, or perhaps they did not rightly comprehend the course—was it something new?—set upon by the editors and if so . . .

So Father Burner was also known as "the circular priest" and he had not reviewed anything since for that magazine.

The mark of the true priest was heavy on the Dean. The mark was on Quinlan; it was on Keefe. It was on every priest he could think of, including a few on the bum, and his good friend and bad companion, Father Desmond. But it was not on him, not properly. They, the others, were stained with it beyond all disguise or disfigurement—indelibly, as indeed Holy Orders by its sacramental nature must stain, for keeps in this world and the one to come. "Thou art a priest forever." With him, however, it was something else and less, a mask or badge which he could and did remove at will, a temporal part to be played, almost only a doctor's or lawyer's. They, the others, would be lost in any persecution. The mark would doom them. But he, if that *dies irae* ever came—and it was every plump seminarian's apple-cheeked dream—could pass as the most harmless and useful of humans, a mailman, a bus rider, a husband. But would he? No. They would see. I, he would say, appearing unsought before the judging rabble, am a priest, of the order of Melchizedech. Take me. I am ready. *Deo gratias.*

Father Burner got out the money to pay and honked his horn. The woman, coming for the bottle and tray, took his money without acknowledging the tip. She stood aside, the bottle held gingerly between offended fingers, final illustration of her lambishness, and watched him drive away. Father Burner, applying a cloven foot to the pedal, gave it the gas. He sensed the woman hoping in her simple heart to see him wreck the car and meet instant death in an unpostponed act of God.

Under the steadying influence of his stomach thrust against the wheel, the car proceeded while he searched himself for a cigarette. He passed a hitchhiker, saw him fade out of view in the mirror overhead, gesticulate wetly in the distance. Was the son of a gun thumbing his nose? Anticlericalism. But pray that your flight be not in the winter . . . No, wrong text: he would not run away.

The road skirted a tourist village. He wondered who stayed in those places and seemed to remember a story in one of the religious scandal sheets . . . ILLICIT LOVE in steaming red type.

A billboard cried out, "Get in the scrap and—get in the scrap!" Some of this advertising, he thought, was pretty slick. Put out probably by big New York and Chicago agencies with crack men on their staffs, fellows who had studied at *Time.* How would it be to write advertising? He knew a few things about layout and type faces from editing the parish paper. He had read somewhere about the best men of our time being in advertising, the air corps of business. There was room for better taste in the Catholic magazines, for someone with a name in the secular field to step in and drive out the money-changers with their trusses, corn cures, non-tangle rosary beads, and crosses that glow in the dark. It was a thought.

Coming into the city limits, he glanced at his watch, but neglected to notice the time. The new gold strap got his eye. The watch itself, a priceless pyx, held the hour (time is money) sacred, like a host. He had chosen it for an ordination gift rather than the usual chalice. It took the kind of courage he had to go against the grain there.

* * *

"I'm a dirty stinker!" Father Desmond flung his arms out hard against the mattress. His fists opened on the sheet, hungry for the spikes, meek and ready. "I'm a dirty stinker, Ernest!"

Father Burner, seated deep in a red leather chair at the sick man's bedside, crossed his legs forcefully. "Now don't take on so, Father."

"Don't call me 'Father'!" Father Desmond's eyes fluttered open momentarily, but closed again on the reality of it all. "I don't deserve it. I'm a disgrace to the priesthood! I am not worthy! Lord, Lord, I am not worthy!"

A nurse entered and stuck a thermometer in Father Desmond's mouth.

Father Burner smiled at the nurse. He lit a cigarette and wondered if she understood. The chart probably bore the diagnosis "pneumonia," but if she had been a nurse very long she would know all about that. She released Father Desmond's wrist and recorded his pulse on her pad. She took the thermometer and left the room.

Father Desmond surged up in bed and flopped, turning with a wrench of the covers, on his stomach. He lay gasping like a fish out of water. Father Burner could smell it on his breath yet.

"Do you want to go to confession?"

"No! I'm not ready for it. I want to remember this time!"

"Oh, all right." It was funny, if a little tiresome, the way the Irish could exaggerate a situation. They all had access to the same two or three emotions. They all played the same battered barrel organ handed down through generations. Dying, fighting, talking, drinking, praying . . . wakes, wars, politics, pubs, church. The fates were decimated and hamstrung among them. They loved monotony.

Father Desmond, doing the poor soul uttering his last words in italics, said: "We make too good a thing out of confession, Ernest! Ever think of that, Ernest?" He wagged a nicotined finger. Some of his self-contempt seemed to overshoot its mark and include Father Burner.

Father Burner honked his lips—*plutt!* "Hire a hall, Ed."

Father Desmond clawed a rosary out from under his pillow.

Father Burner left.

* * *

He put the car in the garage. On the way to his room he passed voices in the Dean's office.

"Father Burner!" the Dean called through the door.

Father Burner stayed in the hallway, only peeping in, indicating numerous commitments elsewhere. Quinlan and Keefe were with the Dean.

"Apparently, Father, you failed to kill yourself." Then, for Keefe, the Dean said, "Father Burner fulfils the dream of the American hierarchy and the principle of historical localization. He's been up in his flying machine all morning."

"I didn't go up." Sullenness came and went in his voice. "It rained." He shuffled one foot, about to leave, when the Dean's left eyebrow wriggled up, warning, holding him.

"I don't believe you've had the pleasure." The Dean gave Keefe to Father Burner. "Father Keefe, sir, went through school with Father Quinlan—from the grades through the priesthood." The Dean described an arc with his breviary, dripping with ribbons, to show the passing years. Father Burner nodded.

"Well?" The Dean frowned at Father Burner. "Has the cat got your tongue, sir? Why don't you be about greeting Father O'Keefe—or Keefe, is it?"

"Keefe, " Keefe said.

Father Burner, caught in the old amber of his inadequacy, stepped over and shook Keefe's hand once.

Quinlan stood by and let the drama play itself out.

Keefe, smiling a curious mixture more anxiety than amusement, said, "It's a pleasure, Father."

"Same here," Father Burner said.

"Well, good day, sirs!" The Dean cracked open his breviary and began to read, lips twitching.

Father Burner waited for them in the hall. Before he could explain that he thought too much of the Dean not to humor him and that besides the old fool was out of his head, the Dean proclaimed after them, "The Chancery phoned, Father Burner. You will hear confessions there tonight. I suppose one of those Cathedral jokers lost his faculties."

Yes, Father Burner knew, it was common procedure all right for the Archbishop to confer promotions by private interview, but every time a priest got called to the Cathedral it did not mean simply that. Many received sermons and it was most likely now someone was needed to hear confessions. And still Father Burner, feeling his pocket, was glad he had not remembered to mail the letter. He would not bother to speak to Quinlan and Keefe now.

## III. Night

"And for your penance say five Our Fathers and five Hail Marys and pray for my intention. And now make a good act of contrition. *Misereatur tui omnipotens Deus dimissis peccatis tuis* . . ." Father Burner swept out into the current of the prayer, stroking strongly in Latin, while the penitent, a miserable boy coming into puberty, paddled as fast as he could along the shore in English.

Finishing first, Father Burner waited for the boy to conclude. When, breathless, he did, Father Burner anointed the air and shot a whisper, "God bless you," kicking the window shut with the heel of his hand, ejecting the boy, an ear of corn shucked clean, into the world again. There was nobody on the other side of the confessional, so Father Burner turned on the signal light. A big spider drowsy in his web, drugged with heat and sins, he sat waiting for the next one to be hurled into his presence by guilt ruddy ripe, as with the boy, or, as with the old ladies who come early and try to stay late, by the spiritual famine of their lives or simply the desire to tell secrets in the dark.

He held his wrist in such a way as to see the sweat gleaming in the hairs. He looked at his watch. He had been at it since seven and now it was after nine. If there were no more kneeling in his section of the Cathedral at 9:30 he could close up and have a cigarette. He was too weary to read his office, though he had the Little Hours, Vespers, and Compline still to go. It was the last minutes in the confessional that got him—the insensible end of the excursion that begins with so many sinewy sensations and good intentions to look sharp at the landscape. In the last minutes how many priests, would-be surgeons of the soul, ended as blacksmiths, hammering out absolution anyway?

A few of the Cathedral familiars still drifted around the floor. They were day and night in the shadows praying. Meeting one of them, Father Burner always wanted to get away. They were collectors of priests' blessings in a day when most priests felt ashamed to raise their hands to God outside the ceremonies. Their respect for a priest was fanatic, that of the unworldly, the martyrs, for an emissary of heaven. They were so desperately disposed to death that the manner of dying was their greatest concern. But Father Burner had an idea there were more dull pretenders than saints among them. They inspired no unearthly feelings in him, as true sanctity was supposed to, and he felt it was all right not to like them. They spoke of God, the Blessed Virgin, of miracles, cures, and visitations, as of people and items in the news, which was annoying. The Cathedral, because of its location, described by brokers as exclusive, was not so much frequented by these wretches as it would have been if more convenient to the slums. But nevertheless a few came there, like the diarrheic pigeons, also a scandal to the neighborhood, and would not go away. Father Burner, from his glancing contact with them, had concluded that body odor is the real odor of sanctity.

Through the grating now Father Burner saw the young Vicar General stop a little distance up the aisle and speak to a couple of people who were possible prospects for Father Burner. "Anyone desiring to go to confession should do so at once. In a few minutes the priests will be gone from the confessionals." He crossed to the other side of the Cathedral.

Father Burner did not like to compare his career with the Vicar General's. The Archbishop had taken the Vicar General, a younger man than Father Burner by at least fifteen years, direct from the seminary. After a period of trial as Chancellor, he was raised to his present eminence—for reasons much pondered by the clergy and more difficult to discern than those obviously accounted for by intelligence, appearance, and, post factum, the loyalty consequent upon his selection over many older and possibly abler men. It was a medieval act of preference, a slap in the face to the monsignori, a rebuke to the principle of advancement by years applied elsewhere. The Vicar General had the quality of inscrutability in an ideal measure. He did not seem at all given to gossip or conspiracy or even to that owlish secrecy peculiar to secretaries and so exasperating to others. He had possibly no enemies and certainly no intimates. In time he would be a bishop unless, as was breathed wherever the Cloth gathered over food and drink, he really was "troubled with sanctity," which might lead to anything else, the cloister or insanity.

The Vicar General appeared at the door of Father Burner's compartment. "The Archbishop will see you, Father, before you leave tonight." He went up the aisle, genuflected before the main altar, opened as a gate one of the host of brass angels surrounding the sanctuary, and entered the sacristies.

Before he would let hope have its way with him, Father Burner sought to recast the expression on the Vicar General's face. He could recall nothing significant. Very probably there had been nothing to see. Then, with a rush, he permitted himself to think this was his lucky day. Already he was formulating the way he would let the news out, providing he decided not to keep it a secret for a time. He might do that. It would be delicious to go about his business until the very last minute, to savor the old aggravations and feel none of the sting, to receive the old quips and smiles with good grace and know them to be toothless. The news, once out, would fly through the diocese. Hear about Burner at Saint Pat's, Tom? Finally landed himself a parish. Yeah, I just had it from McKenna. So I guess the A. B. wasn't so sore at the Round One after all. Well, he's just ornery enough to make a go of it.

Father Burner, earlier in the evening, had smoked a cigarette with one of the young priests attached to the Cathedral (a classmate of Quinlan's but not half the prig), stalling, hoping someone would come and say the Archbishop wanted to see him. When nothing happened except the usual small talk and introductions to a couple of missionaries stopping over, he had given up hope easily. He had seen the basis for his expectations as folly once more. It did not bother him after the fact was certain. He was amenable to any kind of finality. He had a light heart for a Ger—an American of German descent. And his hopes rose higher each time and with less cause. He was a ball that bounced up only. He had kept faith. And now—his just reward.

A little surprised he had not thought of her first, he admitted his mother into the new order of things. He wanted to open the letter from her, still in his coat, and late as it was send her a wire, which would do her more good than a night's sleep. He thought of himself back in her kitchen, home from the sem for the holidays, a bruiser in a tight black suit, his feet heavy on the oven door. She was fussing at the stove and he was promising her a porcelain one as big as a house after he got his parish. But he let her know, kidding on the square, that he would be running things at the rectory. It would not be the old story of the priest taking orders from his housekeeper, even if she was his mother (seminarians, from winter evenings of shooting the bull, knew only too well the pitfalls of parish life), or as with Ed Desmond a few years ago when his father was still living with him, the old man losing his marbles one by one, butting in when people came for advice and instructions, finally coming to believe he was the one to say Mass in his son's absence—no need to get a strange priest in—and sneaking into the box to hear confessions the day before they took him away.

He would be gentle with his mother, however, even if she talked too much, as he recalled she did the last time he saw her. She was well-preserved and strong for her age and ought to be able to keep the house up. Once involved in the social life of the parish she could be a valuable agent in coping with any lay opposition, which was too often the case when a new priest took over.

He resolved to show no nervousness before the Archbishop. A trifle surprised, yes—the Archbishop must have his due—but not overly affected by good fortune. If questioned, he would display a lot of easy confidence not unaccompanied by a touch of humility, a phrase or two like "God willing" or "with the help of Almighty God and your prayers, Your Excellency." He would also not forget to look the part—reliable, casual, cool, an iceberg, only the tip of his true worth showing.

At precisely 9:30 Father Burner picked up his breviary and backed out of the stall. But then there was the scuff of a foot and the tap of one of the confessional doors closing and then, to tell him the last penitent was a woman, the scent of apple blossoms. He turned off the light, saying "Damn!" to himself, and sat down again inside. He threw back the partition and led off, "Yes?" He placed his hand alongside his head and listened, looking down into the deeper darkness of his cassock sleeve.

"I . . ."

"Yes?" At the heart of the apple blossoms another scent bloomed: gin and vermouth.

"Bless me, Father, I . . . have sinned."

Father Burner knew this kind. They would always wait until the last moment. How they managed to get themselves into church at all, and then into the confessional, was a mystery. Sometimes liquor thawed them out. This one was evidently young, nubile. He had a feeling it was going to be adultery. He guessed it was up to him to get her under way.

"How long since your last confession?"

"I don't know . . ."

"Have you been away from the Church?"

"Yes."

"Are you married?"

"Yes."

"To a Catholic?"

"No."

"Protestant?"

"No."

"Jew?"

"No."

"Atheist?"

"No—nothing."

"Were you married by a priest?"

"Yes."

"How long ago was that?"

"Four years."

"Any children?"

"No."

"Practice birth control?"

"Yes, sometimes."

"Don't you know it's a crime against nature and the Church forbids it?"

"Yes."

"Don't you know that France fell because of birth control?"

"No."

"Well, it did. Was it your husband's fault?"

"You mean—the birth control?"

"Yes."

"Not wholly."

"And you've been away from the Church ever since your marriage?"

"Yes."

"Now you see why the Church is against mixed marriages. All right, go on. What else?"

"I don't know . . ."

"Is that what you came to confess?"

"No. Yes. I'm sorry, I'm afraid that's all."

"Do you have a problem?"

"I think that's all, Father."

"Remember, it is your obligation, and not mine, to examine your conscience. The task of instructing persons with regard to these delicate matters—I refer to the connubial relationship—is not an easy one. Nevertheless, since there is a grave obligation imposed by God, it cannot be shirked. If you have a problem—"

"I don't have a *problem.*"

"Remember, God never commands what is impossible and so if you make use of the sacraments regularly you have every reason to be confident that you will be able to overcome this evil successfully, with His help. I hope this is all clear to you."

"All clear."

"Then if you are heartily sorry for your sins for your penance say the rosary daily for one week and remember it is the law of the Church that you attend Mass on Sundays and holy days and receive the sacraments at least once a year. It's better to receive them often. Ask your pastor about birth control if it's still not clear to you. Or read a Catholic book on the subject. And now make a good act of contrition. . . ."

* * *

Father Burner climbed the three flights of narrow stairs. He waited a moment in silence, catching his breath. He knocked on the door and was suddenly afraid its density prevented him from being heard and that he might be found standing there like a fool or a spy. But to knock again, if heard the first time, would seem importunate.

"Come in, Father."

At the other end of the long study the Archbishop sat behind an ebony desk. Father Burner waited before him as though expecting not to be asked to sit down. The only light in the room, a lamp on the desk, was so set that it kept the Archbishop's face in the dark, fell with a gentle sparkle upon his pectoral cross, and was absorbed all around by the fabric of the piped cloth he wore. Father Burner's eyes came to rest upon the Archbishop's freckled hand—ringed, square, and healthy.

"Be seated, Father."

"Thank you, Your Excellency."

"Oh, sit in this chair, Father." There were two chairs. Father Burner changed to the soft one. He had a suspicion that in choosing the other one he had fallen into a silly trap, that it was a game the Archbishop played with his visitors: the innocent ones, seeing no issue, would take the soft chair, because handier; the guilty would go a step out of their way to take the hard one. "I called Saint Patrick's this morning, Father, but you were . . . out."

"I was visiting Father Desmond, Your Excellency."

"Father Desmond . . ."

"He's in the hospital."

"I know. Friend of his, are you, Father?"

"No, Your Excellency. Well"—Father Burner waited for the cock to crow the third time—"yes, I *know* the man." At once he regretted the scriptural complexion of the words and wondered if it were possible for the Archbishop not to be thinking of the earlier betrayal.

"It was good of you to visit Father Desmond, especially since you are not close to him. I hope he is better, Father."

"He is, Your Excellency."

The Archbishop got up and went across the room to a cabinet. "Will you have a little glass of wine, Father?"

"No. No, thanks, Your Excellency." Immediately he realized it could be another trap and, if so, he was caught again.

"Then I'll have a drop . . . *solus*." The Archbishop poured a glass and brought it back to the desk. "A little wine for the stomach's sake, Father."

Father Burner, not sure what he was expected to say to that, nodded gravely and said, "Yes, Your Excellency." He had seen that the Archbishop wore carpet slippers and that they had holes in both toes.

"But perhaps you've read Saint Bernard, Father, and recall where he says we priests remember well enough the apostolic counsel to use wine, but overlook the adjective 'little.' "

"I must confess I haven't read Saint Bernard lately, Your Excellency." Father Burner believed this was somehow in his favor. "Since seminary, in fact."

"Not all priests, Father, have need of him. A hard saint . . . for hardened sinners. What is your estimate of Saint Paul?"

Father Burner felt familiar ground under his feet at last. There were the Pauline and Petrine factions—a futile business, he thought—but he knew where the Archbishop stood and exclaimed, "One of the greatest—"

"Really! So many young men today consider him . . . a bore. It's always the deep-breathing ones, I notice. They say he cuts it too fine."

"I've never thought so, Your Excellency."

"Indeed? Well, it's a question I like to ask my priests. Perhaps you knew that."

"No, I didn't, Your Excellency."

"So much the better then . . . but I see you appraising the melodeon, Father. Are you musical?"

"Not at all, Your Excellency. Violin lessons as a child." Father Burner laughed quickly, as though it were nothing.

"But you didn't go on with them?"

"No, Your Excellency." He did not mean it to sound as sad as it came out.

"What a pity."

"No great loss, Your Excellency."

"You are too . . . modest, Father. But perhaps the violin was not your instrument."

"I guess it wasn't, Your Excellency." Father Burner laughed out too loud.

"And you have the choir at Saint Patrick's, Father?"

"Not this year, Your Excellency. Father Quinlan has it."

"Now I recall . . ."

"Yes." So far as he was concerned—and there were plenty of others who thought so, too—Quinlan had played hell with the choir, canning all the women, some of them members for fifteen and twenty years, a couple even longer and practically living for it, and none of them as bad as Quinlan said. The liturgical stuff that Quinlan tried to pull off was all right in monasteries, where they had the time to train for it, but in a parish it sounded stodgy to ears used to the radio and split up the activity along sexual lines, which was really old hat in the modern world. The Dean liked it though. He called it "honest" and eulogized the men from the pulpit—not a sign that he heard how they brayed and whinnied and just gave out or failed to start—and each time it happened ladies in the congregation were sick and upset for days afterward, for he inevitably ended by attacking women, pants, cocktails, communism, cigarettes, and running around half naked. The women looked at the men in the choir, all pretty in surplices, and said to themselves they knew plenty about some of them and what they had done to some women.

"He's tried a little Gregorian, hasn't he—Father Quinlan?"

"Yes, Your Excellency," Father Burner said. "He has."

"Would you say it's been a success—or perhaps I should ask you first if you care for Gregorian, Father."

"Oh, yes, Your Excellency. Very much."

"Many, I know, don't. . . . I've been told our chant sounds like a wild bull in a red barn or consumptives coughing into a bottle, but I will have it in the Cathedral, Father. Other places, I am aware, have done well with . . . light opera."

Father Burner frowned.

"We are told the people prefer and understand it. But at the risk of seeming reactionary, a fate my office prevents me from escaping in any event, I say we spend more time listening to the voice of the people than is good for either it or us. We have been too generous with our ears, Father. We have handed over our tongues also. When they are restored to us I wonder if we shall not find our ears more itching than before and our tongues more tied than ever."

Father Burner nodded in the affirmative.

"We are now entering the whale's tail, Father. We must go back the way we came in." The Archbishop lifted the lid of the humidor on the desk. "Will you smoke, Father?"

"No, thanks, Your Excellency."

The Archbishop let the lid drop. "Today there are few saints, fewer sinners, and everybody is already saved. We are all heroes in search of an underdog. As for villains, the classic kind with no illusions about themselves, they are . . . extinct. The very devil, for instance—where the devil is the devil today, Father?"

Father Burner, as the Archbishop continued to look at him, bit his lips for the answer, secretly injured that he should be expected to know, bewildered even as the children he toyed with in catechism.

The Archbishop smiled, but Father Burner was not sure at what—whether at him or what had been said. "Did you see, Father, where our brother Bishop Buckles said Hitler remains the one power on earth against the Church?"

Yes, Father Burner remembered seeing it in the paper; it was the sort of thing that kept Quinlan talking for days. "I did, Your Excellency."

"Alas, poor Buckles! He's a better croquet player than that." The Archbishop's hands unclasped suddenly and fell upon his memo pad. He tore off about a week and seemed to feel better for it. His hands, with no hint of violence about them now, came together again. "We look hard to the right and left, Father. It is rather to the center, I think, we should look—to ourselves, the devil in us."

Father Burner knew the cue for humility when he heard it. "Yes, Your Excellency."

With his chubby fingers the Archbishop made a steeple that was more like a dome. His eyes were reading the memo. "For instance, Father, I sometimes appear at banquets—when they can't line up a good foreign correspondent—banquets at which the poor are never present and at which I am unfailingly confronted by someone exceedingly well off who is moved to inform me that 'religion' is a great consolation to him. Opium, rather, I always think, perhaps wrongfully and borrowing a word from one of our late competitors, which is most imprudent of me, a bishop."

The Archbishop opened a drawer and drew out a sheet of paper and an envelope. "Yes, the rich have souls," he said softly, answering an imaginary objection which happened to be Father Burner's. "But if Christ were really with them they would not be themselves—that is to say, rich."

"Very true, Your Excellency," Father Burner said.

The Archbishop faced sideways to use an old typewriter. "And likewise, lest we forget, we would not be ourselves, that is to say—what? For we square the circle beautifully in almost every country on earth. We bring neither peace nor a sword. The rich give us money. We give them consolation and make of the eye of the needle a gate. Together we try to reduce the Church, the Bride of Christ, to a street-walker." The Archbishop rattled the paper, Father Burner's future, into place and rolled it crookedly into the typewriter. "Unfortunately for us, it doesn't end there. The penance will not be shared so equitably. Your Christian name, Father, is—?"

"Ernest, Your Excellency."

The Archbishop typed several words and stopped, looking over at Father Burner. "I can't call to mind a single Saint Ernest, Father. Can you help me?"

"There were two, I believe, Your Excellency, but Butler leaves them out of his *Lives.*"

"They would be German saints, Father?"

"Yes, Your Excellency. There was one an abbot and the other an archbishop."

"If Butler had been Irish, as the name has come to indicate, I'd say that's an Irishman for you, Father. He does not forget to include a power of Irish saints." The Archbishop was Irish himself. Father Burner begged to differ with him, believing here was a wrong deliberately set up for him to right. "I am not Irish myself, Your Excellency, but some of my best friends are."

"Tut, tut, Father. Such tolerance will be the death of you." The Archbishop, typing a few words, removed the paper, signed it and placed it in the envelope. He got up and took down a book from the shelves. He flipped it open, glanced through several pages and returned it to its place. "No Ernests in Baring-Gould either. Well, Father, it looks as if you have a clear field."

The Archbishop came from behind the desk and Father Burner, knowing the interview was over, rose. The Archbishop handed him the envelope. Father Burner stuffed it hastily in his pocket and knelt, the really important thing, to kiss the Archbishop's ring and receive his blessing. They walked together toward the door.

"Do you care for pictures, Father?"

"Oh, yes, Your Excellency."

The Archbishop, touching him lightly on the arm, stopped before a reproduction of Raphael's Sistine Madonna. "There is a good peasant woman, Father, and a nice fat baby." Father Burner nodded his appreciation. "She could be Our Blessed Mother, Father, though I doubt it. There is no question about the baby. He is not Christ." The Archbishop moved to another picture. "Rembrandt had the right idea, Father. See the gentleman pushing Christ up on the cross? That is Rembrandt, a self-portrait." Father Burner thought of some of the stories about the Archbishop, that he slept on a cot, stood in line with the people sometimes to go to confession, that he fasted on alternate days the year round. Father Burner was thankful for such men as the Archbishop. "But here is Christ, Father." This time it was a glassy-eyed Christ whose head lay against the rough wood of the cross he was carrying. "That is Christ, Father. The Greek painted Our Saviour."

The Archbishop opened the door for Father Burner, saying, "And, Father, you will please not open the envelope until after your Mass tomorrow."

Father Burner went swiftly down the stairs. Before he got into his car he looked up at the Cathedral. He could scarcely see the cross glowing on the dome. It seemed as far away as the stars. The cross needed a brighter light or the dome ought to be painted gold and lit up like the state capitol, so people would see it. He drove a couple of blocks down the street, pulled up to the curb, opened the envelope, which had not been sealed, and read: "You will report on August 8 to the Reverend Michael Furlong, to begin your duties on that day as his assistant. I trust that in your new appointment you will find not peace but a sword."

# JAMES PURDY
## (1923– )

Nathaniel Hawthorne once remarked that his fiction was like a "peephole" through which he explored the unlighted vistas of human life, the secret and hidden depths. The fiction of James Purdy is like that as well—gothic, intense, angular, dark. Perhaps this explains the fate of his literary reputation—it rose from the late 1950s through the late 1960s only to decline in the decades since, though his work has not diminished in quality or quantity. Hailed by most critics, his work lacks a wide following.

Purdy was born in Ohio and received his education at the University of Chicago and the University of Puebla in Mexico. Along with writing, Purdy worked as an interpreter in Latin America, France, and Spain. He also served as a lecturer with the U.S. Information Agency in 1982. He now lives in Brooklyn and teaches at New York University.

From the beginning, Purdy had difficulty getting his work published, and he received a lot of early rejections. He published his first two books, *63: Dream Palace* and *Don't Call Me by My Right Name, and Other Stories,* privately in 1956. The English poet Edith Sitwell liked Purdy's work and helped him get published in England. His first two books were republished in the United States a year later under the title *Color of Darkness: Eleven Stories and a Novella* (1957). Among his eighteen novels are *Malcolm* (1957), *Cabot Wright Begins* (1964), *I Am Elijah Thrush* (1972), *On Glory's Course* (1984), *Candles of Your Eyes* (1986), and *Out with the Stars* (1992). His 1976 novel *In a Shallow Grave* was made into a film in 1988.

Purdy has also published poetry, short stories, and plays, some of which were produced off-Broadway. Despite his fairly small audience, he has won awards and recognition—a National Institute of Arts and Letters grant in 1958, Guggenheim fellowships in 1958 and 1962, a Rockefeller grant, a Ford Foundation grant, and a Morten Dauwen Zabel Fiction Award from the Academy of Arts and Letters in 1993.

If Purdy's fiction is disturbing and disorienting, it is because he knows the power of language to alter consciousness, provoke reflection, and perhaps to illumine ways of deliverance.

## Don't Call Me by My Right Name

HER NEW name was Mrs. Klein. There was something in the meaning that irritated her. She liked everything about her husband except his name and that had never pleased her. She had fallen in love with him before she found out what his name was. Once she knew he was Klein, her disappointment had been strong. Names do make a great difference, and after six months of marriage she found herself still not liking her name. She began using more and more her maiden name. Then she always called herself on her letters Lois McBane. Her husband seldom saw the mail arrive so perhaps he did not know, and had he known she went by her old name he might not have cared enough to feel any particular hurt.

Lois Klein, she often thought as she lay next to her husband in bed. It is not the name of a woman like myself. It does not reflect my character.

One evening at a party when there had been more drinking for her than usual, she said offhand to him in the midst of some revelry: "I would like you to change your name."

He did not understand. He thought that it was a remark she was making in drink which did not refer to anything concrete, just as once she had said to him, "I want you to begin by taking your head off regularly." The remark had meant nothing, and he let it pass.

"Frank," she said, "you must change your name, do you hear? I cannot go on being Mrs. Klein."

Several people heard what it was she said, and they laughed loudly so that Lois and Frank would hear them appreciating the remark.

"If you were all called Mrs. Klein," she said turning to the men who were laughing, "you would not like to be Mrs. Klein either."

Being all men, they laughed harder.

"Well, you married him, didn't you," a man said, "and we guess you will have to keep his name."

"If he changed his name," another of the men said, "what name would you have him change it to?"

Frank put his hand on her glass, as though to tell her they must go home, but she seized the glass with his hand on it and drank quickly out of it.

"I hadn't thought what name I did want," she said, puzzled.

"Well, you aren't going to change your name," Frank said. "The gentlemen know that."

"The gentlemen do?" she asked him. "Well, I don't know what name I would like it changed to," she admitted to the men.

"You don't look much like Mrs. Klein," one of the men said and began to laugh again.

"You're not friends!" she called back at them.

"What are we, then?" they asked.

"Why don't I look like Mrs. Klein?" she wanted to know.

"Don't you ever look in the mirror?" one of the men replied.

"We ought to go, Lois," her husband said.

She sat there as though she had heard the last of the many possible truths she could hear about herself.

"I wonder how I will get out of here, Frank," she said.

"Out of where, dear?" he wondered. He was suddenly sad enough himself to be dead, but he managed to say something to her at this point.

"Out of where I seem to have got into," she told him.

The men had moved off now and were laughing among themselves. Frank and Lois did not notice this laughter.

"I'm not going to change my name," he said, as though to himself. Then turning to her: "I know it's supposed to be wrong to tell people when they're drunk the insane whim they're having is insane, but I am telling you now and I may tell the whole room of men."

"I have to have my name changed, Frank," she said. "You know I can't stand to be tortured. It is too painful and I am not young anymore. I am getting old and fat."

"No wife of mine would ever be old or fat," he said.

"I just cannot be Mrs. Klein and face the world."

"Anytime you want me to pull out is all right," he said. "Do you want me to pull out?"

"What are you saying?" she wanted to know. "What did you say about pulling out?"

"I don't want any more talk about your changing your name or I intend to pull up stakes."

"I don't know what you're talking about. You know you can't leave me. What would I do, Frank, at my age?"

"I told you no wife of mine is old."

"I couldn't find anybody now, Frank, if you went."

"Then quit talking about changing our name."

"*Our* name? I don't know what you mean by *our* name."

He took her drink out of her hand and when she coaxed and whined he struck her not too gently over the mouth.

"What was the meaning of that?" she wanted to know.

"Are you coming home, Mrs. Klein?" he said, and he hit her again. Her lip was cut against her teeth so that you could see it beginning to bleed.

"Frank, you're abusing me," she said, white and wide-eyed now, and as though tasting the blood slightly with the gin and soda mix.

"Mrs. Klein," he said idiotically.

It was one of those fake dead long parties where nobody actually knows anybody and where people could be pushed out of windows without anybody's being sure until the morrow.

"I'm not going home as Mrs. Klein," she said.

He hit her again.

"Frank, you have no right to hit me just because I hate your name."

"If you hate my name what do you feel then for me? Are you going to act like my wife or not."

"I don't want to have babies, Frank. I will not go through that at my age. Categorically not."

He hit her again so that she fell on the floor, but this did not seem to surprise either her or him because they both continued the conversation.

"I can't make up my mind what to do," she said, weeping a little. "I know of course what the safe thing is to do."

"Either you come out of here with me as Mrs. Klein, or I go to a hotel room alone. Here's the key to the house," he said, and he threw it on the floor at her.

Several of the men at the party had begun to notice what was really going on now. They thought that it was married clowning at first and they began to gather around in a circle, but what they saw had something empty and stiff about it that did not interest and yet kept one somehow watching. For one thing, Mrs. Klein's dress had come up and exposed her legs, which were not beautiful.

"I can't decide if I can go on with his name," she explained from the floor position to the men.

"Well, it's a little late, isn't it, Mrs. Klein," one of the men said in a sleepy voice.

"It's never too late, I don't suppose, is it?" she inquired. "Oh, I can't believe it is even though I feel old."

"Well, you're not young," the same man ventured. "You're too old to be lying there."

"My husband can't see my point of view," she explained. "And that is why he can't understand why his name doesn't fit me. I was unmarried too long, I suppose, to suddenly surrender my own name. I have always been known professionally and socially under my own name and it is hard to change now, I can tell you. I don't think I can go home with him unless he lets me change my name."

"I will give you just two minutes," Mr. Klein said.

"For what? Only two minutes for what?" she cried.

"To make up your mind what name you are going out of here with."

"I know, men," she said, "what the sensible decision is, and tomorrow, of course, when I'm sober I will wish I had taken it."

Turning to Frank Klein, she said simply, "You will have to go your way without me."

He looked hurriedly around as though looking for an exit to leave by, and then he looked back to her on the floor as though he could not come to a decision.

"Come to your senses," Frank Klein said unemphatically.

"There were hundreds of Kleins in the telephone directory," she went on, "but when people used to come to my name they recognized at once that I was the only woman going under my own special name."

"For Jesus Christ's sake, Lois," he said, turning a peculiar green color.

"I can't go with you as Mrs. Klein," she said.

"Well, let me help you up," he said.

She managed to let him help her up.

"I'm not going home with you, but I will send you in a cab," he informed her.

"Are you leaving me?" she wanted to know.

He did not know what to say. He felt anything he said might destroy his mind. He stood there with an insane emptiness on his eyes and lips.

Everyone had moved off from them. There was a silence from the phonograph and from the TV set which had both been going at the same time. The party was over and people were calling down to cabs from all the windows.

"Why won't you come home with me?" she said in a whisper.

Suddenly he hurried out the door without waiting for her.

"Frank!" she called after him, and a few of the men from the earlier group came over and joked with her.

"He went out just like a boy, without any sense of responsibility," she said to them without any expression in her voice.

She hurried on out too, not waiting to put her coat on straight.

She stood outside in the fall cold and shivered. Some children went by dressed in Hallowe'en costumes.

"Is she dressed as anybody?" one of the children said pointlessly.

"Frank!" she began calling. "I don't know what is happening really," she said to herself.

Suddenly he came up to her from behind a hedge next to where she was standing.

"I couldn't quite bring myself to go off," he said.

She thought for a minute of hitting him with her purse which she had remembered to bring, but she did nothing now but watch him.

"Will you change your name?" she said.

"We will live together the way we have been," he said not looking at her.

"We can't be married, Frank, with that name between us."

Suddenly he hit her and knocked her down to the pavement.

She lay there for a minute before anything was said.

"Are you conscious?" he said crouching down beside her. "Tell me if you are suffering," he wanted to know.

"You have hurt something in my head, I think," she said, getting up slightly on one elbow.

"You have nearly driven me out of my mind," he said, and he was making funny sounds in his mouth. "You don't know what it means to have one's name held up to ridicule like this. You are such a cruel person, Lois."

"We will both change our names, if you like," she said.

"Why do you torture me?" he said. "Why is it you can't control your power to torture?"

"Then we won't think about it, we will go home," she said, in a cold comforting voice. "Only I think I am going to be sick," she warned.

"We will go home," he said in a stupid voice.

"I will let you call me Mrs. Klein this one evening, then tomorrow we will have a good talk." At the same moment she fell back on the walk.

Some young men from the delicatessen who had been doing inventory came by and asked if there was anything they could do.

"My wife fell on the walk," he said. "I thought she was all right. She was talking to me just a moment ago."

"Was it your wife, did you say?" the younger man leaned down to look at her.

"Mrs. Klein," Frank replied.

"You are Mr. Klein, then?"

"I don't understand," the older of the two young men said. "You don't look somehow like her husband."

"We have been married six months."

"I think you ought to call a doctor," the younger man said. "She is bleeding at the mouth."

"I hit her at a party," Frank said.

"What did you say your name was?" the older man asked.

"Mr. Klein. She is Mrs. Klein," Frank told them.

The two men from the delicatessen exchanged looks.

"Did you push her?" the one man asked.

"Yes," Frank said. "I hit her. She didn't want to be Mrs. Klein."

"You're drunk," the one man ventured an opinion.

Lois suddenly came to. "Frank, you will have to take me home," she said. "There is something wrong with my head. My God," she began to scream, "I am in awful pain."

Frank helped her up again.

"Is this your husband?" the one man asked.

She nodded.

"What is your name?" he wanted to know.

"It's none of your business," she said.

"Are you Mrs. Klein?" he asked.

"No," Lois replied, "I don't happen to be Mrs. Klein."

"Come on, J. D., we can't get mixed up in this," the younger man said. "Whatever the hell their names are."

"Well, I'm not Mrs. Klein, whoever you are," she said.

Immediately then she struck Frank with the purse and he fell back in surprise against the building wall.

"Call me a cab, you cheap son of a bitch," she said. "Can't you see I'm bleeding?"

# ⁂ BERNARD MALAMUD
## (1914–1986)

After the Second World War, Jewishness became emblematic of the human predicament—a sense of exile, helplessness, vulnerability, and dislocation. Bernard Malamud, along with Saul Bellow and later Philip Roth, emerged as a major contemporary Jewish writer. Most of his characters are Jewish, and he writes about them in very realistic terms, often delightfully capturing the cadence and flavor of a translated Yiddish speech, but his Jews are also, perhaps mostly, symbolic. His stories often combine and mingle the real and the mythic into fables of moral compassion. While many of his stories tell of failure snatched from the jaws of success, defeat in Malamud's fiction is never final; hope is a function of grace and will.

Born in Brooklyn, New York, of Russian immigrant parents who ran a small grocery store, Malamud received his B.A. from City College of New York in 1936. He received his M.A. from Columbia University in 1942, completing a thesis on the work of Thomas Hardy. After trying various jobs—a factory hand, a Census Bureau clerk—he taught night classes at Erasmus High School from 1941 to 1949. From 1949 to 1961 he taught in the English Department at Oregon State University, except for a year spent in Italy on a writing grant. In 1961 he joined the English faculty at Bennington College in Vermont.

Malamud published short stories and novels, and won awards for both. His first two books were the novels *The Natural* (1952) and *The Assistant* (1957). His first story collection, *The Magic Barrel,* appeared in 1958 and won a National Book Award. Other story collections include *Idiots First* (1963), *Pictures of Fidelman* (1969), and *Rembrandt's Hat* (1973); *The Complete Stories* was issued in 1997. His novels include *A New Life* (1961); *The Fixer* (1963), which won the Pulitzer Prize; *The Tenants* (1971); *Dubin's Lives* (1978); and *God's Grace* (1982).

# The Jewbird

THE WINDOW was open so the skinny bird flew in. Flappity-flap with its frazzled black wings. That's how it goes. It's open, you're in. Closed, you're out and that's your fate. The bird wearily flapped through the open kitchen window of Harry Cohen's top-floor apartment on First Avenue near the lower East River. On a rod on the wall hung an escaped canary cage, its door wide open, but this black-type longbeaked bird—its ruffled head and small dull eyes, crossed a little, making it look like a dissipated crow—landed if not smack on Cohen's thick lamb chop, at least on the table, close by. The frozen foods salesman was sitting at supper with his wife and young son on a hot August evening a year ago. Cohen, a heavy man with hairy chest and beefy shorts; Edie, in skinny yellow shorts and red halter; and their ten-year-old Morris (after her father)—Maurie, they called him, a nice kid though not overly bright—were all in the city after two weeks out, because Cohen's mother was dying. They had been enjoying Kingston, New York, but drove back when Mama got sick in her flat in the Bronx.

"Right on the table," said Cohen, putting down his beer glass and swatting at the bird. "Son of a bitch."

"Harry, take care with your language," Edie said, looking at Maurie, who watched every move.

The bird cawed hoarsely and with a flap of its bedraggled wings—feathers tufted this way and that—rose heavily to the top of the open kitchen door, where it perched staring down.

"Gevalt, a pogrom!"

"It's a talking bird," said Edie in astonishment.

"In Jewish," said Maurie.

"Wise guy," muttered Cohen. He gnawed on his chop, then put down the bone. "So if you can talk, say what's your business. What do you want here?"

"If you can't spare a lamb chop," said the bird, "I'll settle for a piece of herring with a crust of bread. You can't live on your nerve forever."

"This ain't a restaurant," Cohen replied. "All I'm asking is what brings you to this address?"

"The window was open," the bird sighed; adding after a moment, "I'm running. I'm flying but I'm also running."

"From whom?" asked Edie with interest.

"Anti-Semeets."

"Anti-Semites?" they all said.

"That's from who."

"What kind of anti-Semites bother a bird?" Edie asked.

"Any kind," said the bird, "also including eagles, vultures, and hawks. And once in a while some crows will take your eyes out."

"But aren't you a crow?"

"Me? I'm a Jewbird."

Cohen laughed heartily. "What do you mean by that?"

The bird began dovening. He prayed without Book or tallith, but with passion. Edie bowed her head though not Cohen. And Maurie rocked back and forth with the prayer, looking up with one wide-open eye.

When the prayer was done Cohen remarked, "No hat, no phylacteries?"

"I'm an old radical."

"You're sure you're not some kind of a ghost or dybbuk?"

"Not a dybbukk," answered the bird, "though one of my relatives had such an experience once. It's all over now, thanks God. They freed her from a former lover, a crazy jealous man. She's now the mother of two wonderful children."

"Birds?" Cohen asked slyly.

"Why not?"

"What kind of birds?"

"Like me. Jewbirds."

Cohen tipped back in his chair and guffawed. "That's a big laugh. I've heard of a Jewfish but not a Jewbird."

"We're once removed." The bird rested on one skinny leg, then on the other. "Please, could you spare maybe a piece of herring with a small crust of bread?"

Edie got up from the table.

"What are you doing?" Cohen asked her.

"I'll clear the dishes."

Cohen turned to the bird. "So what's your name, if you don't mind saying?"

"Call me Schwartz."

"He might be an old Jew changed into a bird by somebody," said Edie, removing a plate.

"Are you?" asked Harry, lighting a cigar.

"Who knows?" answered Schwartz. "Does God tell us everything?"

Maurie got up on his chair. "What kind of herring?" he asked the bird in excitement.

"Get down, Maurie, or you'll fall," ordered Cohen.

"If you haven't got matjes, I'll take schmaltz," said Schwartz.

"All we have is marinated, with slices of onion—in a jar," said Edie.

"If you'll open for me the jar I'll eat marinated. Do you have also, if you don't mind, a piece of rye bread—the spitz?"

Edie thought she had.

"Feed him out on the balcony," Cohen said. He spoke to the bird. "After that take off."

Schwartz closed both bird eyes. "I'm tired and it's a long way."

"Which direction are you headed, north or south?"

Schwartz, barely lifting his wings, shrugged.

"You don't know where you're going?"

"Where there's charity I'll go."

"Let him stay, papa," said Maurie. "He's only a bird."

"So stay the night," Cohen said, "but no longer."

In the morning Cohen ordered the bird out of the house but Maurie cried, so Schwartz stayed for a while. Maurie was still on vacation from school and his friends were away. He was lonely and Edie enjoyed the fun he had, playing with the bird.

"He's no trouble at all," she told Cohen, "and besides his appetite is very small."

"What'll you do when he makes dirty?"

"He flies across the street in a tree when he makes dirty, and if nobody passes below, who notices?"

"So all right," said Cohen, "but I'm dead set against it. I warn you he ain't gonna stay here long."

"What have you got against the poor bird?"

"Poor bird, my ass. He's a foxy bastard. He thinks he's a Jew."

"What difference does it make what he thinks?"

"A Jewbird, what a chuzpah. One false move and he's out on his drumsticks."

At Cohen's insistence Schwartz lived out on the balcony in a new wooden birdhouse Edie had bought him.

"With many thanks," said Schwartz, "though I would rather have a human roof over my head. You know how it is at my age. I like the warm, the windows, the smell of cooking. I would also be glad to see once in a while the *Jewish Morning Journal* and have now and then a schnapps because it helps my breathing, thanks God. But whatever you give me, you won't hear complaints."

However, when Cohen brought home a bird feeder full of dried corn, Schwartz said, "Impossible."

Cohen was annoyed. "What's the matter, crosseyes, is your life getting too good for you? Are you forgetting what it means to be migratory? I'll bet a helluva lot of crows you happen to be acquainted with, Jews or otherwise, would give their eyeteeth to eat this corn."

Schwartz did not answer. What can you say to a grubber yung?

"Not for my digestion," he later explained to Edie. "Cramps. Herring is better even if it makes you thirsty. At least rainwater don't cost anything." He laughed sadly in breathy caws.

And herring, thanks to Edie, who knew where to shop, was what Schwartz got, with an occasional piece of potato pancake, and even a bit of soupmeat when Cohen wasn't looking.

When school began in September, before Cohen would once again suggest giving the bird the boot, Edie prevailed on him to wait a little while until Maurie adjusted.

"To deprive him right now might hurt his school work, and you know what trouble we had last year."

"So okay, but sooner or later the bird goes. That I promise you."

Schwartz, though nobody had asked him, took on full responsibility for Maurie's performance in school. In return for favors granted, when he was let in for an hour or two at night, he spent most of his time overseeing the boy's lessons. He sat on top of the dresser near Maurie's desk as he laboriously wrote out his homework. Maurie was a restless type and Schwartz gently kept him to his studies. He also listened to him practice his screechy violin, taking a few minutes off now and then to rest his ears in the bathroom. And they afterwards played dominoes. The boy was an indifferent checker player and it was impossible to teach him chess. When he was sick, Schwartz read him comic books though he personally disliked them. But Maurie's work improved in school and even his violin teacher admitted his playing was better. Edie gave Schwartz credit for these improvements though the bird pooh-poohed them.

Yet he was proud there was nothing lower then C minuses on Maurie's report card, and on Edie's insistence celebrated with a little schnapps.

"If he keeps up like this," Cohen said, "I'll get him in an Ivy League college for sure."

"Oh I hope so," sighed Edie.

But Schwartz shook his head. "He's a good boy—you don't have to worry. He won't be a shicker or a wifebeater, God forbid, but a scholar he'll never be, if you know what I mean, although maybe a good mechanic. It's no disgrace in these times."

"If I were you," Cohen said, angered, "I'd keep my big snoot out of other people's private business."

"Harry, please," said Edie.

"My goddamn patience is wearing out. That crosseyes butts into everything."

Though he wasn't exactly a welcome guest in the house, Schwartz gained a few ounces although he did not improve in appearance. He looked bedraggled as ever, his feathers unkempt, as though he had just flown out of a snowstorm. He spent, he admitted, little time taking care of himself. Too much to think about. "Also outside plumbing," he told Edie. Still there was more glow to his eyes so that though Cohen went on calling him crosseyes he said it less emphatically.

Liking his situation, Schwartz tried tactfully to stay out of Cohen's way, but one night when Edie was at the movies and Maurie was taking a hot shower, the frozen foods salesman began a quarrel with the bird.

"For Christ sake, why don't you wash yourself sometimes? Why must you always stink like a dead fish?"

"Mr. Cohen, if you'll pardon me, if somebody eats garlic he will smell from garlic. I eat herring three times a day. Feed me flowers and I will smell like flowers."

"Who's obligated to feed you anything at all? You're lucky to get herring."

"Excuse me, I'm not complaining," said the bird. "You're complaining."

"What's more," said Cohen, "even from out on the balcony I can hear you snoring away like a pig. It keeps me awake at night."

"Snoring," said Schwartz, "isn't a crime, thanks God."

"All in all you are a goddamn pest and free loader. Next thing you'll want to sleep in bed next to my wife."

"Mr. Cohen," said Schwartz, "on this rest assured. A bird is a bird."

"So you say, but how do I know you're a bird and not some kind of a goddamn devil?"

"If I was a devil you would know already. And I don't mean because your son's good marks."

"Shut up, you bastard bird," shouted Cohen.

"Grubber yung," cawed Schwartz, rising to the tips of his talons, his long wings outstretched.

Cohen was about to lunge for the bird's scrawny neck but Maurie came out of the bathroom, and for the rest of the evening until Schwartz's bedtime on the balcony, there was pretended peace.

But the quarrel had deeply disturbed Schwartz and he slept badly. His snoring woke him, and awake, he was fearful of what would become of him. Wanting to stay out of Cohen's way, he kept to the birdhouse as much as possible. Cramped by it, he paced back and forth on the balcony ledge, or sat on the birdhouse roof, staring into space. In the evenings, while overseeing Maurie's lessons, he often fell asleep. Awakening, he nervously hopped around exploring the four corners of the room. He spent much time in Maurie's closet, and carefully examined his bureau drawers when they were left open. And once when he found a large paper bag on the floor, Schwartz poked his way into it to investigate what possibilities were. The boy was amused to see the bird in the paper bag.

"He wants to build a nest," he said to his mother.

Edie, sensing Schwartz's unhappiness, spoke to him quietly.

"Maybe if you did some of the things my husband wants you, you would get along better with him."

"Give me a for instance," Schwartz said.

"Like take a bath, for instance."

"I'm too old for baths," said the bird. "My feathers fall out without baths."

"He says you have a bad smell."

"Everybody smells. Some people smell because of their thoughts or because who they are. My bad smell comes from the food I eat. What does his come from?"

"I better not ask him or it might make him mad," said Edie.

In late November Schwartz froze on the balcony in the fog and cold, and especially on rainy days he woke with stiff joints and could barely move his wings. Already he felt twinges of rheumatism. He would have liked to spend more time in the warm house, particularly when Maurie was in school and Cohen at work. But though Edie was good-hearted and might have sneaked him in in the morning, just to thaw out, he was afraid to ask her. In the meantime Cohen, who had been reading articles about the migration of birds, came out on the balcony one night after work when Edie was in the kitchen preparing pot roast, and peeking into the birdhouse, warned Schwartz to be on his way soon if he knew what was good for him. "Time to hit the flyways."

"Mr. Cohen, why do you hate me so much?" asked the bird. "What did I do to you?"

"Because you're an A-number-one trouble maker, that's why. What's more, who-ever heard of a Jewbird? Now scat or it's open war."

But Schwartz stubbornly refused to depart so Cohen embarked on a campaign of harassing him, meanwhile hiding it from Edie and Maurie. Maurie hated violence and Cohen didn't want to leave a bad impression. He thought maybe if he played dirty tricks on the bird he would fly off without being physically kicked out. The vacation was over, let him make his easy living off the fat of somebody else's land. Cohen worried about the effect of the bird's departure on Maurie's schooling but decided to take the chance, first, because the boy now seemed to have the knack of studying—give the black bird-bastard credit—and second, because Schwartz was driving him bats by being there always, even in his dreams.

The frozen foods salesman began his campaign against the bird by mixing watery cat food with the herring slices in Schwartz's dish. He also blew up and popped numerous paper bags outside the birdhouse as the bird slept, and when he had got Schwartz good and nervous, though not enough to leave, he brought a full-grown cat into the house, supposedly a gift for little Maurie, who had always wanted a pussy. The cat never stopped springing up at Schwartz whenever he saw him, one day managing to claw out several of his tailfeathers. And even at lesson time, when the cat was usually excluded from Maurie's room, though somehow or other he quickly found his way in at the end of the lesson, Schwartz was desperately fearful of his life and flew from pinnacle to pinnacle—light fixture to clothestree to door-top—in order to elude the beast's wet jaws.

Once when the bird complained to Edie how hazardous his existence was, she said, "Be patient, Mr. Schwartz. When the cat gets to know you better he won't try to catch you any more."

"When he stops trying we will both be in Paradise," Schwartz answered. "Do me a favor and get rid of him. He makes my whole life worry. I'm losing feathers like a tree loses leaves."

"I'm awfully sorry but Maurie likes the pussy and sleeps with it."

What could Schwartz do? He worried but came to no decision, being afraid to leave. So he ate the herring garnished with cat food, tried hard not to hear the paper bags bursting like fire crackers outside the birdhouse at night, and lived terror-stricken closer to the ceiling than the floor, as the cat, his tail flicking, endlessly watched him.

Weeks went by. Then on the day after Cohen's mother had died in her flat in the Bronx, when Maurie came home with a zero on an arithmetic test, Cohen, enraged, waited until Edie had taken the boy to his violin lesson, then openly attacked the bird. He chased him with a broom on the balcony and Schwartz frantically flew back and forth, finally escaping into his birdhouse. Cohen triumphantly reached in, and grabbing both skinny legs, dragged the bird out, cawing loudly, his wings wildly beating. He whirled the bird around and around his head. But Schwartz, as he moved in circles, managed to swoop down and catch Cohen's nose in his beak, and hung on for dear life. Cohen cried out in great pain, punched the bird with his fist, and tugging at its legs with all his might, pulled his nose free. Again he swung the yawking Schwartz around until the bird grew dizzy, then with a furious heave, flung him into the night. Schwartz sank like stone into the street. Cohen then tossed the birdhouse and feeder after him, listening at the ledge until they crashed on the sidewalk below. For a full hour, broom in hand, his heart palpitating and nose throbbing with pain, Cohen waited for Schwartz to return but the broken-hearted bird didn't.

That's the end of that dirty bastard, the salesman thought and went in. Edie and Maurie had come home.

"Look," said Cohen, pointing to his bloody nose swollen three times its normal size, "what that sonofabitchy bird did. It's a permanent scar."

"Where is he now?" Edie asked, frightened.

"I threw him out and he flew away. Good riddance."

Nobody said no, though Edie touched a handkerchief to her eyes and Maurie rapidly tried the nine times table and found he knew approximately half.

In the spring when the winter's snow had melted, the boy, moved by a memory, wandered in the neighborhood, looking for Schwartz. He found a dead black bird in a small lot near the river, his two wings broken, neck twisted, and both bird-eyes plucked clean.

"Who did it to you, Mr. Schwartz?" Maurie wept.

"Anti-Semeets," Edie said later.

# ⁂ PETER TAYLOR
## (1917–1994)

Peter Taylor was born in Trenton, Tennessee. His maternal grandfather was a governor of Tennessee and a U.S. senator. His father was the president of an insurance company in St. Louis. After growing up in Nashville, St. Louis, and Memphis, Taylor studied at Vanderbilt University and Kenyon College, where he was encouraged in his writing by his teacher John Crowe Ransom. Taylor served in the army from 1941 to 1945, and then began teaching creative writing at various colleges. As one of Taylor's teachers, the novelist Robert Penn Warren, once commented, Taylor's subject is the contemporary, urban, middle-class world of the upper South after the Second World War. Taylor's first story collection was *A Long Fourth, and Other Stories,* published in 1948. This was followed by *The Widows of Thornton* (1954), *Happy Families Are All Alike* (1959), and *Miss Leonora When Last Seen, and Fifteen Other Stories* (1963). In 1954 he published the novel *A Woman of Means,* and his 1986 novel, *A Summons to Memphis,* was awarded the Pulitzer Prize. Two other story collections have been published, *In the Miro District* (1977) and *The Old Forest* (1985), which won the PEN/Faulkner Award. His *Collected Stories* appeared in 1986. He taught for many years at the University of Virginia.

# The Old Forest

I WAS already formally engaged, as we used to say, to the girl I was going to marry. But still I sometimes went out on the town with girls of a different sort. And during the very week before the date set for the wedding, in December, I was in an automobile accident at a time when one of those girls was with me. It was a calamitous thing to have happen—not the accident itself, which caused no serious injury to anyone, but the accident plus the presence of that girl.

As a matter of fact, it was not unusual in those days—forty years ago and a little more—for a well-brought-up young man like me to keep up his acquaintance, until the very eve of his wedding, with some member of what we facetiously and somewhat arrogantly referred to as the Memphis demimonde. (That was merely to say with a girl who was not in the Memphis debutante set.) I am not even sure how many of us knew what the word "demimonde" meant or implied. But once it had been applied to such girls, it was hard for us to give it up. We even learned to speak of them individually as demimondaines—and later corrupted that to demimondames. The girls were of course a considerably less sophisticated lot than any of this sounds, though they were bright girls certainly and some of them even highly intelligent. They read books, they looked at pictures, and they were apt to attend any concert or play that came to Memphis. When the old San Carlo Opera Company turned up in town, you could count on certain girls of the demimonde being present in their block of seats, and often with a score of the opera in hand. From that you will understand that they certainly weren't the innocent, untutored types that we generally took to dances at the Memphis Country Club and whom we eventually looked forward to marrying.

These girls I refer to would, in fact, very frequently and very frankly say to us that the MCC (that's how we always spoke of the Club) was the last place they wanted to be taken. There was one girl in particular, not so smart as some of the others perhaps and certainly less restrained in the humor she sometimes poked at the world we boys lived in, an outspoken girl, who was the most vociferous of all in her disdain for the Country Club. I remember one night, in one of those beer gardens that became popular in Memphis in the late thirties, when this girl suddenly announced to a group of us, "*I* haven't lost anything at the MCC. That's something you boys can bet your daddy's bottom dollar on." We were gathered—four or five couples—about one of the big wooden beer-garden tables with an umbrella in its center, and when she said that, all the other girls in the party went into a fit of laughter. It was a kind of giggling that was unusual for them. The boys in the party laughed, too, of course, but we were surprised by the way the girls continued to giggle among themselves for such a long time. We were out of college by then and thought we knew the world pretty well; most of us had been working for two or three years in our fathers' business firms. But we didn't see why this joke was so very funny. I suppose it was too broad for us in its reference. There is no way of knowing, after all these years, if it was too broad for our sheltered minds or if the rest of the girls were laughing at the vulgar tone of the girl who had spoken. She was, you see, a little bit coarser than the rest, and I suspect they were laughing at the way she had phrased what she said. For us boys, anyhow, it was pleasant that the demimondaines took the lighthearted view they did about not going to the MCC, because it was the last place most of us would have wished to take them. Our *other* girls would have known too readily who they were and would not willingly or gracefully have endured their presence. To have brought one of those girls to the Club would have required, at any rate, a boy who was a much bolder and freer spirit than I was at twenty-three.

To the liberated young people of today all this may seem a corrupting factor in our old way of life—not our snobbery so much as our continuing to see those demimonde girls right up until the time of marriage. And yet I suspect that in the Memphis of today customs concerning serious courtship and customs concerning unacknowledged love affairs have not been entirely altered. Automobile accidents occur there still, for instance, the reports of which in the newspaper do not mention the name of the driver's "female companion," just as the report of my accident did not. If the driver is a "scion of a prominent local family" with his engagement to be married already announced at an MCC party, as well as in the Sunday newspaper, then the account of his automobile collision is likely to refer to the girl in the car with him only as his "female companion." Some newspaper readers might, I know, assume this to be a reference to the young man's fiancée. That is what is intended, I suppose—*for* the general reader. But it would almost certainly not have been the case—not in the Memphis, Tennessee, of 1937.

The girl with me in my accident was a girl whose origins nobody knew anything about. But she was a perfectly decent sort of girl, living independently in a respectable rooming house and working at a respectable job. That was the sort of girl about whom the Memphis newspapers felt obliged to exercise the greatest care when making any reference to her in their columns. It was as though she were their special ward. Such a girl must be protected from any blaze of publicity. Such a girl must not suffer from the misconduct of any Memphis man or group of men—even newspaper publishers. That was fine for the girl, of course, and who could possibly resent it? It was splendid for her, but I, the driver of the car, had to suffer considerable anguish just because of such a girl's presence in the car and suffer still more because of her behavior afterward. Moreover, the response of certain older men in town to her subsequent behavior would cause me still further anguish and prolong my suffering by several days. Those men were the editors of the city's two newspapers, along with the lawyers called in by my father to represent me if I should be taken into court. There was also my father himself, and the father of my fiancée, *his* lawyer (for some reason or other), and, finally, no less a person than the mayor of Memphis, all of whom one would ordinarily have supposed to be indifferent to the caprices of such a girl. They were the civic leaders and merchant princes of the city. They had great matters on their minds. They were, to say the least, an imposing group in the eyes of a young man who had just the previous year entered his father's cotton-brokerage firm, a young man who was still learning how to operate under the pecking order of Memphis's male establishment.

The girl in question was named Lee Ann Deehart. She was a quite beautiful, fair-haired, hazel-eyed girl with a lively manner, and surely she was far from stupid. The thing she did which drew attention from the city fathers came very near, also, to changing the course of my entire life. I had known Lee Ann for perhaps two years at the time, and knew her to be more level-headed and more reserved and self-possessed than most of her friends among the demimondaines. It would have been impossible for me to predict the behavior she was guilty of that winter afternoon. Immediately after the collision, she threw open the door on her side of the car, stepped out onto the roadside, and fled into the woods of Overton Park, which is where the accident took place. And from that time, and during the next four days, she was unheard from by people who wished to question her and protect her. During that endless-seeming period of four days no one could be certain of Lee Ann Deehart's whereabouts.

* * *

The circumstances of the accident were rather complicated. The collision occurred just after three o'clock on a very cold Saturday afternoon—the fourth of December. Although at that time in my life I was already a member of my father's cotton firm, I was nevertheless—and strange as it may seem—enrolled in a Latin class out at Southwestern College, which is on the north side of Overton Park. (We were reading Horace's *Odes!*) The class was not held on Saturday afternoon, but I was on my way out to the college to study for a test that had been scheduled for Monday. My interest in Latin was regarded by my father and mother as one of my "anomalies"—a remnant of many "anomalies" I had annoyed them with when I was in my teens and was showing some signs of "not turning out well." It seemed now of course that I had "turned out well" after all, except that nobody in the family and nobody among my friends could understand why I went on showing this interest in Latin. I was not able to explain to them why. Any more than I was able to explain why to myself. It clearly had nothing to do with anything else in my life at that period. Furthermore, in the classroom and under the strict eye of our classics professor, a rotund, mustachioed little man hardly four feet in height (he had to sit on a large Latin dictionary in order to be comfortable at his desk), I didn't excel. I was often embarrassed by having to own up to Professor Bartlett's accusation that I had not so much as glanced at the assigned odes before coming to class. Sometimes other members of the class would be caught helping me with the translation, out in the hallway, when Professor Bartlett opened his classroom door to us. My real excuse for neglecting the assignments made by that earnest and admirable little scholar was that too many hours of my life were consumed by my job, by my courtship of the society girl I was going to marry, and by my old, bad habits of knocking about town with my boyhood cronies and keeping company with girls like Lee Ann Deehart.

Yet I had persisted with my Horace class throughout that fall (against the advice of nearly everyone, including Professor Bartlett). On that frigid December afternoon I had resolved to mend my ways as a student. I decided I would take my Horace and go out to Professor Bartlett's classroom at the college and make use of his big dictionary in preparing for Monday's test. It was something we had all been urged to do, with the promise that we would always find the door unlocked. As it turned out, of course, I was destined not to take the test on Monday and never to enter Professor Bartlett's classroom again.

It happened that just before I was setting out from home that afternoon I was filled suddenly with a dread of the silence and the peculiar isolation of a college classroom building on a weekend afternoon. I telephoned my fiancée and asked her to go along with me. At the other end of the telephone line, Caroline Braxley broke into laughter. She said that I clearly had no conception of all the things she had to do within the next seven days before we were to be married. I said I supposed I ought to be helping in some way, though until now she had not asked me so much as to help address invitations to the wedding. "No indeed," said my bride-to-be, "I want to do everything myself. I wouldn't have it any other way."

Caroline Braxley, this capable and handsome bride-to-be of mine, was a very remarkable girl, just as today, as my wife, she seems to me a very remarkable woman of sixty. She and I have been married for forty-one years now, and her good judgment in all matters relating to our marriage has never failed her—or us. She had already said to me before that Saturday afternoon that a successful marriage depended in part on the two persons' developing and maintaining a certain number of separate interests in life. She was all for my keeping up my golf, my hunting, my fishing. And, unlike my own family, she saw no reason that I shouldn't keep up my peculiar interest in Latin, though she had to confess that she thought it almost the funniest thing she had ever heard of a man of my sort going in for.

Caroline liked any sort of individualism in men. But I already knew her ways sufficiently well to understand that there was no use trying to persuade her to come along with me to the college. I wished she would come with me, or maybe I wished even more she would try to persuade me to come over to her house and help her with something in preparation for the wedding. After I had put down the telephone, it even occurred to me that I might simply drive over to her house and present myself at her front door. But I knew what the expression on her face would be, and I could even imagine the sort of thing she would say: "No man is going to set foot in my house this afternoon, Nat Ramsey! *I'm* getting married next Saturday, in case the fact has slipped your mind. Besides, you're coming here for dinner tonight, aren't you? And there are parties every night next week!"

This Caroline Braxley of mine was a very tall girl. (Actually taller than she is nowadays. We have recently measured ourselves and found that each of us is an inch shorter than we used to be.) One often had the feeling that one was looking up at her, though of course she wasn't really so tall as that. Caroline's height and the splendid way she carried herself were one of her first attractions for me. It seems to me now that I was ever attracted to tall girls—that is, when there was the possibility of falling in love. And I think this was due in part to the fact that even as a boy I was half in love with my father's two spinster sisters, who were nearly six feet in height and were always more attentive to me than to the other children in the family.

Anyhow, only moments after I had put down the telephone that Saturday, when I still sat with my hand on the instrument and was thinking vaguely of rushing over to Caroline's house, the telephone underneath my hand began ringing. Perhaps, I thought, it was Caroline calling back to say that she had changed her mind. Instead, it was Lee Ann Deehart. As soon as she heard my voice, she began telling me that she was bored to death. Couldn't I think of something fun she and I could do on this dreary winter afternoon? I laughed aloud at her. "What a shameless wench you are, Lee Ann!" I said.

"Shameless? How so?" she said with pretended innocence.

"As if you weren't fully aware," I lectured her, "that I'm getting married a week from today!"

"What's that got to do with the price of eggs in Arkansas?" She laughed. "Do you think, old Nat, *I* want to marry you?"

"Well," I explained, "I happen to be going out to the college to cram for a Latin test on Monday."

I could hear her laughter at the other end. "Is your daddy going to let you off work long enough to take your Latin test?" she asked with heavy irony in her voice. It was the usual way those girls had of making fun of our dependence on our fathers.

"Ah, yes," I said tolerantly.

"And is he going to let you off next Saturday, too," she went on, "long enough to get married?"

"Listen," I said, "I've just had an idea. Why don't you ride out to the college with me, and fool around some while I do my Latin?" I suppose I didn't really imagine she would go, but suddenly I had thought again of the lonely isolation of Dr. Bartlett's classroom on a Saturday afternoon. I honestly wanted to go ahead out there. It was something I somehow felt I had to do. My preoccupation with the study of Latin poetry, ineffectual student though I was, may have represented a perverse wish to experience the isolation I was at the same time dreading or may have represented a taste for morbidity left over from my adolescence. I can allow myself to speculate on all that now, though it would not have occurred to me to do so at the time.

"Well," said Lee Ann Deehart presently, to my surprise and delight, "it couldn't be more boring out there than sitting here in my room is."

"I'll pick you up in fifteen minutes," I said quickly. And I hung up the telephone before she could possibly change her mind. Thirty minutes later, we were driving through Overton Park on our way to the college. We had passed the Art Gallery and were headed down the hill toward the low ground where the Park Pond is. Ahead of us, on the left, were the gates to the Zoo. And on beyond was the point where the road crossed the street-car tracks and entered a densely wooded area which is actually the last surviving bit of the primeval forest that once grew right up to the bluffs above the Mississippi River. Here are giant oak and yellow poplar trees older than the memory of the earliest white settler. Some of them surely may have been mature trees when Hernando de Soto passed this way, and were very old trees indeed when General Jackson, General Winchester, and Judge John Overton purchased this land and laid out the city of Memphis. Between the Art Gallery and the pond there used to be, in my day, a little spinney of woods which ran nearly all the way back to what was left of the old forest. It was just when I reached this spinney, with Lee Ann beside me, that I saw a truck approaching us on the wrong side of the icy road. There was a moderately deep snow on the ground, and the park roads had, to say the least, been imperfectly cleared. On the ice and the packed snow, the driver of the truck had clearly lost control of his vehicle. When he was within about seventy-five feet of us, Lee Ann said, "Pull off the road, Nat!"

Lee Ann Deehart's beauty was of the most feminine sort. She was a tiny, delicate-looking girl, and I had noticed, when I went to fetch her that day, in her fur-collared coat and knitted cap and gutta-percha boots she somehow seemed smaller than usual. And I was now struck by the tone of authority coming from this small person whose diminutive size and whose role in my life were such that it wouldn't have occurred to me to heed her advice about driving a car—or about anything else, I suppose. I remember feeling something like: This is an ordeal that I must, and that I want, to face in my own way. It was as though Professor Bartlett himself were in the approaching truck. It seemed my duty not to admit any weakness in my own position. At least I *thought* that was what I felt.

"Pull off the road, Nat!" Lee Ann urged again. And my incredible reply to her was "He's on *my* side of the road! Besides, trucks are not allowed in the park!" And in reply to this Lee Ann gave only a loud snicker.

I believe I did, in the last seconds, try to swing the car off onto the shoulder of the road. But the next thing I really remember is the fierce impact of the two vehicles' meeting.

It was a relatively minor sort of collision, or seemed so at the moment. Since the driver of the truck, which was actually a converted Oldsmobile sedan—and a rather ancient one at that—had the good sense not to put on his brakes and to turn off her motor, the crash was less severe than it might have been. Moreover, since I *had* pulled a little to the right it was not a head-on meeting. It is worth mentioning, though, that it was sufficiently bad to put permanently out of commission the car I was driving, which was not my own car (my car was in the shop, being refurbished for the honeymoon trip) but an aging Packard limousine of my mother's, which I knew she would actually be happy to see retired. I don't remember getting out of the car at all and I don't remember Lee Ann's getting out. The police were told by the driver of the truck, however, that within a second after the impact Lee Ann had thrown open her door, leaped out onto the snow-covered shoulder, jumped the ditch beyond, and run up the incline and into the spinney. The truck driver's account was corroborated by two ice skaters on the pond, who also saw her run through the leafless trees of the spinney and on across a narrow stretch of the public golf course which divides the spinney from the old forest. They agreed that, considering there was a deep snow on the ground and that she was wearing those gutta-percha boots, she traveled at a remarkable speed.

I didn't even know she was out of the car until I got around on the other side and saw the door there standing open and saw her tracks in the snow, going down the bank. I suppose I was too dazed even to follow the tracks with my eyes down the bank and up the other side of the ditch. I must have stood there for several seconds, looking down blankly at the tracks she had left just outside the car door. Presently I looked up at the truck driver, who was standing before me. I know now his eyes must have been following Lee Ann's progress. Finally he turned his eyes to me, and I could tell from his expression that I wasn't a pleasant sight. "Is your head hurt bad?" he asked. I put my hand up to my forehead and when I brought it down it was covered with blood. That was when I passed out. When I came to, they wouldn't let me get up. Besides the truck driver, there were two policemen and the two ice skaters standing over me. They told me that an ambulance was on the way.

At the hospital, the doctor took four stitches in my forehead; and that was it. I went home and lay down for a couple of hours, as I had been told to do. My parents and my two brothers and my little sister and even the servants were very much concerned about me. They hovered around in a way I had never before seen them do—not even when somebody was desperately sick. I suppose it was because a piece of violence like this accident was a very extraordinary thing in our quiet Memphis life in those years. They were disturbed, too, I soon realized, by my silence as I lay there on the daybed in the upstairs sitting room and particularly by my being reticent to talk about the collision. I had other things on my mind. Every so often I would remember Lee Ann's boot tracks in the snow. And I would begin to wonder where she was now. Since I had not found an opportunity to telephone her, I could only surmise that she had somehow managed to get back to the rooming house where she lived. I had not told anyone about her presence in the car with me. And as I lay there on the daybed, with the family and servants coming and going and making inquiries about how I felt, I would find myself wondering sometimes how and whether or not I could tell Caroline Braxley about Lee Ann's being with me that afternoon. It turned out the next day—or, rather, on Monday morning—that the truck driver had told the two policemen and then, later, repeated to someone who called from one of the newspapers that there had been a girl with me in the car. As a matter of fact, I learned that this was the case on the night of the accident, but as I lay there in the upstairs sitting room during the afternoon I didn't yet know it.

Shortly before five o'clock Caroline Braxley arrived at our house, making a proper sick call but also with the intention of taking me back to dinner with her parents and her two younger sisters. Immediately after she entered the upstairs sitting room, and almost before she and I had greeted each other, my mother's houseboy and sometime chauffeur came in, bringing my volume of Horace. Because Mother had thought it might raise my spirits, she had sent him down to the service garage where the wrecked car had been taken to fetch it for me. Smiling sympathetically, he placed it on a table near the daybed and left the room. Looking at the book, Caroline said to me with a smile that expressed a mixture of sympathy and reproach, "I hope you see now what folly your pursuit of Latin poetry is." And suddenly, then, the book on the table appeared to me as an alien object. In retrospect it seems to me that I really knew then that I would never open it again.

I went to dinner that night at Caroline's house, my head still in bandages. The Braxley family treated me with a tenderness equal to that I had received at home. At table, the servingman offered to help my plate for me, as though I were a sick child. I could have enjoyed all this immensely, I think, since I have always been one to relish loving, domestic care, if only I had not been worrying and speculating all the while about Lee Ann. As I talked genially with Caroline's family during the meal and immediately afterward before the briskly burning fire at the end of the Braxleys' long living room, I kept seeing Lee Ann's boot tracks in the snow. And then I would see my own bloody hand as I took it down from my face before I fainted. I remember still having the distinct feeling, as I sat there in the bosom of the Braxley family, that it had not been merely my bloody hand that had made me faint but my bloody hand plus the tracks in the deep snow. In a way, it is strange that I remember all these impressions so vividly after forty years, because it is not as though I have lived an uneventful life during the years since. My Second World War experiences are what I perhaps ought to remember best—those, along with the deaths of my two younger brothers in the Korean War. Even worse, really, were the deaths of my two parents in a terrible fire that destroyed our house on Central Avenue when they had got to be quite old, my mother leaping from a second-story window, my father asphyxiated inside the house. And I can hardly mention without being overcome with emotion the accidental deaths that took two of my and Caroline's children when they were in their early teens. It would seem that with all these disasters to remember, along with the various business and professional crises I have had, I might hardly be able to recall that earlier episode. But I think that, besides its coming at that impressionable period of my life and the fact that one just does remember things better from one's youth, there is the undeniable fact that life *was* different in those times. What I mean to say is that all these later, terrible events took place in a world where acts of terror are, so to speak, all around us—everyday occurrences—and are brought home to us audibly and pictorially on radio and television almost every hour. I am not saying that some of these ugly acts of terror did not need to take place or were not brought on by what our world was like in those days. But I am saying that the context was different. Our tranquil, upper-middle-class world of 1937 did not have the rest of the world crowding in on it so much. And thus when something only a little ugly did crowd in or when we, often unconsciously, reached out for it, the contrasts seemed sharper. It was not just in the Braxleys' household or in my own family's that everything seemed quiet and well ordered and unchanging. The households were in a context like themselves. Suffice it to say that though the Braxleys' house in Memphis was situated on East Parkway and our house on Central Avenue, at least two miles across town from each other, I could in those days feel perfectly safe, and *was* relatively safe, in walking home many a night from Caroline's house to our house at two in the morning. It was when we young men in Memphis ventured out with the more adventurous girls of the demimonde that we touched on the unsafe zones of Memphis. And there were girls still more adventurous, of course, with whom some of my contemporaries found their way into the very most dangerous zones. But we did think of it that way, you see, thought of it in terms of the girls' being the adventurous ones, whom we followed or didn't follow.

Anyhow, while we were sitting there before the fire, with the portrait of Caroline's paternal grandfather peering down at us from above the mantel and with her father in his broad-lapelled, double-breasted suit standing on the marble hearth, occasionally poking at the logs with the brass poker or sometimes kicking a log with the toe of his wing-tipped shoes, suddenly I was called to the telephone by the Negro servingman who had wanted to help my plate for me. As he preceded me the length of the living room and then gently guided me across the hall to the telephone in the library, I believe he would have put his hand under my elbow to help me—as if a real invalid—if I had allowed him to. As we passed through the hall, I glanced through one of the broad, etched sidelights beside the front door and caught a glimpse of the snow on the ground outside. The weather had turned even colder. There had been no additional snowfall, but even at a glance you could tell how crisply frozen the old snow was on its surface. The servingman at my elbow was saying, "It's your daddy on the phone. I'd suppose he just wants to know how you'd be feeling by now."

But I knew in my heart it wasn't that. It was as if that glimpse of the crisp snow through the front-door sidelight had told me what it was. When I took up the telephone and heard my father's voice pronouncing my name, I knew almost exactly what he was going to say. He said that his friend the editor of the morning paper had called him and reported that there had been a girl in the car with me, and though they didn't of course plan to use her name, probably wouldn't even run the story until Monday, they would have to *know* her name. And would have to assure themselves she wasn't hurt in the crash. And that she was unharmed after leaving the scene. Without hesitation I gave my father Lee Ann Deehart's name, as well as her address and telephone number. But I made no further explanation to Father, and he asked me for none. The only other thing I said was that I'd be home in a little while. Father was silent a moment after that. Then he said, "Are you all right?"

I said, "I'm fine."

And he said, "Good. I'll be waiting up for you."

I hung up the telephone, and my first thought was that before I left Caroline tonight I'd have to tell her that Lee Ann had been in the car with me. Then, without thinking almost, I dialed Lee Ann's rooming-house number. It felt very strange to be doing this in the Braxleys' library. The woman who ran the rooming house said that Lee Ann had not been in since she left with me in the afternoon.

As I passed back across the wide hallway and caught another glimpse of the snow outside, the question arose in my mind for the first time: *Had* Lee Ann come to some harm in those woods? More than the density of the underbrush, more than its proximity to the Zoo, where certain unsavory characters often hung out, it was the great size and antiquity of the forest trees somehow and the old rumors that white settlers had once been ambushed there by Chickasaw Indians that made me feel that if anything had happened to the girl, it had happened there. And on the heels of such thoughts I found myself wondering for the first time if all this might actually lead to my beautiful, willowy Caroline Braxley's breaking off our engagement. I returned to the living room, and at the sight of Caroline's tall figure at the far end of the room, placed between that of her mother and that of her father, the conviction became firm in me that I would have to tell her about Lee Ann before she and I parted that night. And as I drew nearer to her, still wondering if something ghastly had happened to Lee Ann there in the old forest, I saw the perplexed and even suspicious expression on Caroline's face and presently observed similar expressions on the faces of her two parents. And from that moment began the gnawing wonder which would be with me for several days ahead: What precisely would Caroline consider sufficient provocation for breaking off our engagement to be married? I had no idea, really. Would it be sufficient that I had had one of those unnamed "female companions" in the car with me at the time of the accident? I knew of engagements like ours which had been broken with apparently less provocation. Or would it be the suspicious-seeming circumstances of Lee Ann's leaping out of the car and running off through the snow? Or might it be the final, worst possibility—that of delicate little Lee Ann Deehart's having actually met with foul play in that infrequently entered area of underbrush and towering forest trees?

* * *

Broken engagements were a subject of common and considerable interest to girls like Caroline Braxley. Whereas a generation earlier a broken engagement had been somewhat of a scandal—an engagement that had been formally announced at a party and in the newspaper, that is—it did not necessarily represent that in our day. Even in our day, you see, it meant something quite different from what it had once meant. There was, after all, no written contract and it was in no sense so unalterably binding as it had been in our parents' day. For us it was not considered absolutely dishonorable for either party to break off the plans merely because he or she had had a change of heart. Since the boy was no longer expected literally to ask the father for the girl's hand (though he would probably be expected to go through the form, as I had done with Mr. Braxley), it was no longer a breach of contract between families. There was certainly nothing like a dowry any longer—not in Memphis—and there was only rarely any kind of property settlement involved, except in cases where both families were extraordinarily rich. The thought pleased me—that is, the ease with which an engagement might be ended. I suppose in part I was simply preparing myself for such an eventuality. And there in the Braxleys' long living room in the very presence of Caroline and Mr. and Mrs. Braxley themselves, I found myself indulging in a perverse fantasy, a fantasy in which Caroline had broken off our engagement and I was standing up pretty well, was even seeking consolation in the arms, so to speak, of a safely returned Lee Ann Deehart.

But all at once I felt so guilty for my private indiscretion that actually for the first time in the presence of my prospective in-laws I put my arm about Caroline Braxley's waist. And I told her that I felt so fatigued by events of the afternoon that probably I ought now to go ahead home. She and her parents agreed at once. And they agreed among themselves that they each had just now been reflecting privately that I looked exhausted. Mrs. Braxley suggested that under the circumstances she ought to ask Robert to drive me home. I accepted. No other suggestion could have seemed so welcome. Robert was the same servingman who had offered to help my plate at dinner and who had so gently guided me to the telephone when my father called. Almost at once, after I got into the front seat of the car beside him—in his dark chauffeur's uniform and cap—I fell asleep. He had to wake me when we pulled up to the side door of my father's house. I remember how warmly I thanked him for bringing me home, even shaking his hand, which was a rather unusual thing to do in those days. I felt greatly refreshed and restored and personally grateful to Robert for it. There was not, in those days in Memphis, any time or occasion when one felt more secure and relaxed than when one had given oneself over completely to the care and protection of the black servants who surrounded us and who created and sustained for the most part the luxury which distinguished the lives we lived then from the lives we live now. They did so for us, whatever their motives and however degrading our demands and our acceptance of their attentions may have been to them.

At any rate, after my slumber in the front seat beside Robert I felt sufficiently restored to face my father (and his awareness of Lee Ann's having been in the car) with some degree of equanimity. And before leaving the Braxleys' house I had found a moment in the hallway to break the news to Caroline that I had not been alone in the car that afternoon. To my considerable surprise she revealed, after a moment's hesitation, that she already knew that had been the case. Her father, like my father, had learned it from one of the newspaper editors—only he had learned it several hours earlier than my father had. I was obliged to realize as we were saying good night to each other that she, along with her two parents, had known all evening that Lee Ann had been with me and had fled into the woods of Overton Park—that she, Caroline, had as a matter of fact known the full story when she came to my house to fetch me back to her house to dinner. "Where is Lee Ann now?" she asked me presently, holding my two hands in her own and looking me directly in the eye. "I don't know," I said. Knowing how much she knew, I decided I must tell her the rest of it, holding nothing back. I felt that I was seeing a new side to my fiancée and that unless I told her the whole truth there might be something of this other side of her that wouldn't be revealed to me. "I tried to telephone her after I answered my father's call tonight. But she was not in her room and had not been in since I picked her up at two o'clock." And I told Caroline about Lee Ann's telephoning me (after Caroline and I had talked in the early afternoon) and about my inviting her to go out to the college with me. Then I gave her my uncensored version of the accident, including the sight of Lee Ann's footprints in the snow.

"How did she sound on the telephone?" she asked.

"What do you mean by that?" I said impatiently. "I just told you she wasn't home when I called."

"I mean earlier—when she called you."

"But why do you want to know that? It doesn't matter, does it?"

"I mean, did she sound depressed? But it doesn't matter for the moment." She still held my hands in hers. "You do know, don't you," she went on after a moment, "that you are going to have to *find* Lee Ann? And you probably are going to need help."

Suddenly I had the feeling that Caroline Braxley was someone twenty years older than I; but, rather than sounding like my parents or her parents, she sounded like one or another of the college teachers I had had—even like Dr. Bartlett, who once had told me that I was going to need outside help if I was going to keep up with the class. To reassure myself, I suppose, I put my arm about Caroline's waist again and drew her to me. But in our good-night kiss there was a reticence on her part, or a quality that I could only define as conditional or possibly probational. Still, I knew now that she knew everything, and I suppose that was why I was able to catch such a good nap in the car on the way home.

Girls who had been brought up the way Caroline had, in the Memphis of forty years ago, knew not only what was going to be expected of them in making a marriage and bringing up a family there in Memphis—a marriage and a family of the kind their parents had had—they knew also from a fairly early time that they would have to contend with girls and women of certain sorts before and frequently after they were married: with girls, that is, who had no conception of what it was to have a certain type of performance expected of them, or girls of another kind (and more like themselves) who came visiting in Memphis from Mississippi or Arkansas—pretty little plantation girls, my mother called them—or from Nashville or from the old towns of West Tennessee. Oftentimes these other girls were their cousins, but that made them no less dangerous. Not being on their home ground—in their own country, so to speak—these Nashville or Mississippi or West Tennessee or Arkansas girls did not bother to abide by the usual rules of civilized warfare. They were marauders. But girls like Lee Ann Deehart were something else again. They were the Trojan horse, more or less, established in the very citadel. They were the fifth column, and were perhaps the most dangerous of all. At the end of a brilliant debutante season, sometimes the most eligible bachelor of all those on the list would still remain uncommitted, or even secretly committed to someone who had never seen the inside of the Memphis Country Club. This kind of thing, girls like Caroline Braxley understood, was not to be tolerated—not if the power of moral woman included the power to divine the nature of any man's commitment and the power to test the strength and nature of another kind of woman's power. Young people today may say that that old-fashioned behavior on the part of girls doesn't matter today, that girls don't have those problems anymore. But I suspect that in Memphis, if not everywhere, there must be something equivalent even nowadays in the struggle of women for power among themselves.

Perhaps, though, to the present generation these distinctions I am making won't seem significant, after all, or worth my bothering so much about—especially the present generation outside of Memphis and the Deep South. Even in Memphis the great majority of people might say, Why is this little band of spoiled rich girls who lived here forty years ago so important as to deserve our attention? In fact, during the very period I am writing about it is likely that the majority of people in Memphis felt that way. I think the significant point is that those girls took themselves seriously—girls like Caroline—and took seriously the forms of the life they lived. They imagined they knew quite well who they were and they imagined that that was important. They were what, at any rate, those girls like Lee Ann were not. Or they claimed to be what those girls like Lee Ann didn't claim to be and what very few people nowadays claim to be. They considered themselves the heirs to something, though most likely they could not have said what: something their forebears had brought to Memphis with them from somewhere else—from the country around Memphis and from other places, from the country towns of West Tennessee, from Middle Tennessee and East Tennessee, from the Valley of Virginia, from the Piedmont, even from the Tidewater. Girls like Caroline thought they were the heirs to something, and that's what the other girls didn't think about themselves, though probably they were, and probably the present generation, in and out of Memphis—even the sad generation of the sixties and seventies—is heir to more than it thinks it is, in the matter of manners, I mean to say, and of general behavior. And it is of course because these girls like Caroline are regarded as mere old-fashioned society girls that the present generation tends to dismiss them, whereas if it were their fathers we were writing about, the story would, shocking though it is to say, be taken more seriously by everyone. Everyone would recognize now that the fathers and grandfathers of these girls were the sons of the old plantation South come to town and converted or half-converted into modern Memphis businessmen, only with a certain something held over from the old order that made them both better and worse than businessmen elsewhere. They are the authors of much good and much bad in modern Memphis—and modern Nashville and modern Birmingham and modern Atlanta, too. The good they mostly brought with them from life in cities elsewhere in the nation, the thing they were imitating when they constructed the new life in Memphis. And why not judge their daughters and wives in much the same way? Isn't there a need to know what they were like, too? One thing those girls did know they were heirs to was the old, country manners and the insistence upon old, country connections. The first evidence of this that comes to mind is the fact that they often spoke of girls like Lee Ann as "city girls," by which they meant that such girls didn't usually have the old family connections back in the country on the cotton farms in West Tennessee, in Mississippi, in Arkansas, or back in Nashville or in Jonesboro or in Virginia.

When Robert had let me out at our side door that night and I came into the house, my father and mother both were downstairs. It was still early of course, but I had the sense of their having waited up for me to come in. They greeted me as though I were returning from some dangerous mission. Each of them asked me how the Braxleys "seemed." Finally Mother insisted upon examining the stitches underneath the bandage on my forehead. After that, I said that I thought I would hit the hay. They responded to that with the same enthusiasm that Mr. and Mrs. Braxley had evidenced when I told them I thought I should go ahead home. Nothing would do me more good than a good night's sleep, my parents agreed. It was a day everybody was glad to have come to an end.

After I got upstairs and in my room, it occurred to me that my parents both suddenly looked very old. That seems laughable to me now almost, because my parents were then ten or fifteen years younger than I am today. I look back on them now as a youngish couple in their early middle age, whose first son was about to be married and about whose possible infidelity they were concerned. But indeed what an old-fashioned pair they seem to me in the present day, waiting up for their children to come in. Because actually they stayed downstairs a long while after I went up to bed, waiting there for my younger brothers and my little sister to come in, all of whom were out on their separate dates. In my mind's eye I can see them there, waiting as parents had waited for hundreds of years for their grown-up children to come home at night. They would seem now to be violating the rights of young individuals and even interfering with the maturing process. But in those times it seemed only natural for parents to be watchful and concerned about their children's first flight away from the nest. I am referring mainly to my parents' waiting up for my brothers and my sister, who were in their middle teens, but also as I lay in my bed I felt, myself, more relaxed knowing that they were downstairs in the front room speculating upon what Lee Ann's disappearance meant and alert to whatever new development there might be. After a while, my father came up and opened the door to my room. I don't know how much later it was. I don't think I had been to sleep, but I could not tell for sure even at the time—my waking and sleeping thoughts were so much alike that night. At any rate, Father stepped inside the room and came over to my bed.

"I have just called down to the police station," he said, "and they say they have checked and that Lee Ann has still not come back to her rooming house. She seems to have gone into some sort of hiding." He said this with wonderment and with just the slightest trace of irritation in his voice. "Have you any notion, Nat, why she *might* want to go into hiding?"

* * *

The next day was Sunday, December 5. During the night it had turned bitterly cold, the snow had frozen into a crisp sheet that covered most of the ground. At about nine o'clock in the morning another snow began falling. I had breakfast with the family, still wearing the bandage on my forehead. I sat around in my bathrobe all morning, pretending to read the newspaper. I didn't see any report of my accident, and my father said it wouldn't appear till Monday. At ten o'clock, I dialed Lee Ann's telephone number. One of the other girls who roomed in the house answered. She said she thought Lee Ann hadn't come in last night and she giggled. I asked her if she would make sure about it. She left the phone and came back presently to say in a whisper that there was no doubt about it: Lee Ann had not slept in her bed. I knew she was whispering so that the landlady wouldn't hear. . . . And then I had a call from Caroline, who wanted to know how my head was this morning and whether or not there had been any word about Lee Ann. After I told her what I had just learned, we were both silent for a time. Finally she said she had intended to come over and see how I was feeling but her father had decreed that nobody should go out in such bad weather. It would just be inviting another automobile wreck, he said. She reported that her parents were not going to church, and I said that mine weren't either. We agreed to talk later and to see each other after lunch if the weather improved. Then I could hear her father's voice in the background, and she said that he wanted to use the telephone.

At noon the snow was still falling. My father stood at a front window in the living room, wearing his dark smoking jacket. He predicted that it might be the deepest snowfall we had ever had in Memphis. He said that people in other parts of the country didn't realize how much cold weather came all the way down the Mississippi Valley from Minneapolis to Memphis. I had never heard him pay so much attention to the weather and talk so much about it. I wondered if, like me, he was really thinking about the old forest out in Overton Park and wishing he were free to go out there and make sure there was no sign of Lee Ann Deehart's having come to grief in those ancient woods. I wonder now if there weren't others besides us who were thinking of the old forest all day that day. I knew that my father, too, had been on the telephone that morning—and he was on it again during a good part of the afternoon. In retrospect, I am certain that all day that day he was in touch with a whole circle of friends and colleagues who were concerned about Lee Ann's safety. It was not only the heavy snow that checked his freedom—and mine, too, of course—to go out and search those woods and put his mind at rest on the possibility at least. It was more than just this snow, which the radio reported as snarling up and halting all traffic. What prevented him was his own unwillingness to admit fully to himself and to others that this particular danger was really there; what prevented him and perhaps all the rest of us was the fear that the answer to the gnawing question of Lee Ann's whereabouts might really be out there within that immemorial grove of snow-laden oaks and yellow poplars and hickory trees. It is a grove, I believe, that men in Memphis have feared and wanted to destroy for a long time and whose destruction they are still working at even in this latter day. It has only recently been saved by a very narrow margin from a great highway that men wished to put through there—saved by groups of women determined to save this last bit of the old forest from the axes of modern men. Perhaps in old pioneer days, before the plantation and the neoclassic towns were made, the great forests seemed woman's last refuge from the brute she lived alone with in the wilderness. Perhaps all men in Memphis who had any sense of their past felt this, though they felt more keenly (or perhaps it amounts to the same feeling) that the forest was woman's greatest danger. Men remembered mad pioneer women, driven mad by their loneliness and isolation, who ran off into the forest, never to be seen again, or incautious women who allowed themselves to be captured by Indians and returned at last so mutilated that they were unrecognizable to their husbands or who at their own wish lived out their lives among their savage captors. I think that if I had said to my father (or to myself), "What is it that's so scary about the old forest?," he (or I) would have answered, "There's nothing at all scary about it. But we can't do anything today because of the snow. It's the worst snow in history!" I think that all day long my father—like me—was busily not letting himself believe that anything awful had happened to Lee Ann Deehart, or that if it had it certainly hadn't happened in those woods. Not just my father and me, though. Caroline's father, too, and all their friends—their peers. And the newspapermen and the police. If they waited long enough, it would come out all right and there would be no need to search the woods even. And it turned out, in the most literal sense, that they—we—were right. Yet what guilty feelings must not everyone have lived with—lived with in silence—all that snowbound day.

At two o'clock, Caroline called again to say that because of the snow, her aunt was canceling the dinner party she had planned that night in honor of the bride and groom. I remember as well as anything else that terrible day how my mother and father looked at each other when they received this news. Surely they were wondering, as I had to also, if this was but the first gesture of withdrawal. There was no knowing what their behavior or the behavior of any of us that day meant. The day simply dragged on until the hour when we could decently go to bed. It was December, and we were near the shortest day of the year, but that day had seemed the longest day of my life.

* * *

On Monday morning, two uniformed policemen were at our house before I had finished my breakfast. When I learned they were waiting in the living room to see me, I got up from the table at once. I wouldn't let my father go in with me to see them. Mother tried to make me finish my eggs before going in, but I only laughed at her and kissed her on the top of the head as I left the breakfast room. The two policemen were sitting in the very chairs my parents had sat in the night before. This somehow made the interview easier from the outset. I felt initially that they were there to help me, not to harass me in any way. They had already, at the break of dawn, been out to Overton Park. (The whole case—if case it was—had of course been allowed to rest on Sunday.) And along with four other policemen they had conducted a full-scale search of the old forest. There was no trace of Lee Ann Deehart there. They had also been to her rooming house on Tutwiler Avenue and questioned Mrs. Troxler, whose house it was, about all of Lee Ann's friends and acquaintances and about the habits of her daily life. They said that they were sure the girl would turn up but that the newspapers were putting pressure on them to explain her disappearance and—more particularly—to explain her precipitate flight from the scene of the accident.

I spent that day with the police, leaving them only for an hour at lunchtime, when they dropped me off at my father's office on Front Street, where I worked. There I made a small pretense of attending to some business for the firm while I consumed a club sandwich and milk shake that my father or one of my uncles in the firm had had sent up for me. At the end of the hour, I jogged down the two flights of steep wooden stairs and found the police car waiting for me at the curb, just outside the entrance. At some time during the morning, one of the policemen had suggested that they might have a bulldozer or some other piece of machinery brought in to crack the ice on the Overton Park Pond and then drag the pond for Lee Ann's body. But I had pointed out that the two skaters had returned to the pond after the accident and skated there until dark. There was no hole in the ice anywhere. Moreover, the skaters had reported that when the girl left the scene she did not go by way of the pond but went up the rise and into the wooded area. There was every indication that she had gone that way, and so the suggestion that the pond be dragged was dismissed. And we continued during the rest of the morning to make the rounds of the rooming houses and apartments of Lee Ann's friends and acquaintances, as well as the houses of the parents with whom some of them lived. In the afternoon we planned to go to the shops and offices in which some of the girls worked and to interview them there concerning Lee Ann's whereabouts and where it was they last had seen her. It seemed a futile procedure to me. But while I was eating my club sandwich alone in our third-floor walkup office I received a shocking telephone call.

Our offices, like most of the other cotton factors' offices, were in one of the plain-faced, three- and four-story buildings put up on Front Street during the middle years of the last century, just before the Civil War. Cotton men were very fond of those offices, and the offices did possess a certain rough beauty that anyone could see. Apparently there had been few, if any, improvements or alterations since the time they were built. All the electrical wiring and all the plumbing, such as they were, were "exposed." The wooden stairsteps and the floors were rough and splintery and extremely worn down. The walls were whitewashed and the ceilings were twelve or fourteen feet in height. But the chief charm of the rooms was the tall windows across the front of the buildings—wide sash windows with small windowlights, windows looking down onto Front Street and from which you could catch glimpses of the brown Mississippi River at the foot of the bluff, and even of the Arkansas shoreline on the other side. I was sitting on a cotton trough beside one of those windows, eating my club sandwich, when I heard the telephone ring back in the inner office. I remember that when it rang my eyes were on a little stretch of the Arkansas shoreline roughly delineated by its scrubby trees and my thoughts were on the Arkansas roadhouses where we often went with the demimonde girls on a Saturday night. At first I thought I wouldn't answer the phone. I let it ring for a minute or two. It went on ringing—persistently. Suddenly I realized that a normal business call would have stopped ringing before now. I jumped down from my perch by the window and ran back between the cotton troughs to the office. When I picked up the receiver, a girl's voice called my name before I spoke.

"Yes," I said. The voice had sounded familiar, but I knew it wasn't Caroline's. And it wasn't Lee Ann's. I couldn't identify it exactly, though I did say to myself right away that it was one of the city girls.

"Nat," the voice said, "Lee Ann wants you to stop trying to trail her."

"Who is this?" I said. "Where is Lee Ann?"

"Never mind," the girl on the other end of the line said. "We're not going to let you find her, and you're making her very uncomfortable with your going around with the police after her and all that."

"The police aren't 'after her,' " I said. "They just want to be sure she's all right."

"She'll be all right," the voice said, "if you'll lay off and stop chasing her. Don't you have any decency at all? Don't you have a brain in your head? Don't you know what this is like for Lee Ann? We all thought you were her friend."

"I am," I said. "Just let me speak to Lee Ann."

But there was a click in the telephone, and no one was there any longer.

I turned back into the room where the cotton troughs were. When I saw my milk-shake carton and the sandwich paper up by the window, and remembered how the girl had called my name as soon as I picked up the telephone, I felt sure that someone had been watching me from down in the street or from a window across the way. Without going back to my lunch, I turned quickly and started down the stairs toward the street. But when I looked at my watch, I realized it was time for the policemen to pick me up again. And there they were, of course, waiting at the entrance to our building. When I got into the police car, I didn't tell them about my call. And we began our rounds again, going to the addresses where some of Lee Ann's friends worked.

Lee Ann Deehart and other girls like her that we went about with, as I have indicated, were not literally ladies of any Memphis demimonde. Possibly they got called that first by the only member of our generation in Memphis who had read Marcel Proust, a literary boy who later became a college professor and who wanted to make his own life in Memphis—and ours—seem more interesting than it was. Actually, they were girls who had gone to the public high schools, and more often than not to some school other than Central High, which during those Depression years had a degree of acceptance in Memphis society. As anyone could have observed on that morning when I rode about town with the policemen, those girls came from a variety of backgrounds. We went to the houses of some of their parents, some of whom were day laborers who spoke in accents of the old Memphis Irish, descendants of the Irish who were imported to build the railroads to Texas. Today some of the girls would inevitably have been black. But they were the daughters also of bank clerks and salesmen and of professional men, too, because they made no distinction among themselves. The parents of some of them had moved to Memphis from cities in other sections of the country or even from Southern small towns. The girls were not interested in such distinctions of origin, were not conscious of them, had not been made aware of them by their parents. They would have been highly approved of by the present generation of young people. Like the present generation in general, these girls—Lee Ann included—tended to be bookish and artistic in a middlebrow sort of way, and some of them had real intellectual aspirations. They did not care who each other's families were or where they had gone to school. They met and got to know each other in roadhouses, on double dates, and in the offices and stores where they worked. As I have said, they tended to be bookish and artistic. If they had found themselves in Proust's Paris, instead of in our Memphis of the 1930s, possibly they would have played some role in the intellectual life of the place. But of course this is only my ignorant speculation. It is always impossible to know what changes might have been wrought in people under circumstances of the greatest or slightest degree of difference from the actual.

The girls we saw that afternoon at their places of work were generally more responsive to the policemen's questions than to my own. And I became aware that the two policemen—youngish men in their late thirties, for whom this special assignment was somehow distasteful—were more interested in protecting these girls from any embarrassment than in obtaining information about Lee Ann. With all but one of the half-dozen girls we sought out, the policemen sent me in to see the girl first, to ask her if she would rather be questioned by them in her place of business or in the police car. In each case the girl treated my question concerning this as an affront, but always she finally sent word back to the policemen to come inside. And in each case I found myself admiring the girl not only for her boldness in dealing with the situation (they seemed fearless in their talk with the police and refused absolutely to acknowledge close friendship with Lee Ann, insisting—all of them—that they saw her only occasionally at night spots, sometimes with me, sometimes with other young men, that they had no idea who her parents were or where she came to Memphis from) but also for a personal, feminine beauty that I had never before been fully aware of. Perhaps I saw or sensed it now for the first time because I had not before seen them threatened or in danger. It is true, I know, that the effect of all this questioning seemed somehow to put them in jeopardy. Perhaps I saw now how much more vulnerable they were than were the girls in the set my parents more or less intended me to travel in. There was a delicacy about them, a frailty even, that didn't seem to exist in other girls I knew and that contrasted strangely—and disturbingly—with the rough surroundings of the roadhouses they frequented at night and the harsh, businesslike atmosphere of the places where they worked. Within each of them, moreover, there seemed a contrast between the delicate beauty of their bodies, their prettily formed arms and legs, their breasts and hips, their small feet and hands, their soft natural hair—hair worn so becomingly, groomed, in each case, on their pretty little heads to direct one's eyes first of all to the fair or olive complexion and the nicely proportioned features of the face—a contrast, that is to say, between this physical beauty and a bookishness and a certain toughness of mind and a boldness of spirit which were unmistakable in all of them.

The last girl we paid a call on that afternoon was one Nancy Minnifee, who happened to be the girl who was always frankest and crudest in making jokes about families like my own and who had made the crack that the other girls had laughed at so irrepressibly in the beer garden: "I haven't lost anything at the MCC." Or it may not have been that she just happened to be the last we called on. Perhaps out of dread of her jokes I guided the police last of all to the farm-implement warehouse where Nancy was a secretary. Or perhaps it wasn't so much because of her personality as because I knew she was Lee Ann's closest friend and I somehow dreaded facing her for that reason. Anyway, at the warehouse she was out on the loading platform with a clipboard and pencil in her hands when we drove up.

"That's Nancy Minnifee up there," I said to the two policemen in the front seat. I was sitting in the backseat alone. I saw them shake their heads. I knew that it was with a certain sadness and a personal admiration that they did so. Nancy was a very pretty girl, and they hated the thought of bothering this lovely creature with the kind of questions they were going to ask. They hated it without even knowing she was Lee Ann's closest friend. Suddenly I began seeing all those girls through the policemen's eyes, just as next day, when I would make a similar expedition in the company of my father and the newspaper editor, I'd see the girls through their eyes. The worst of it, somehow, for the policemen, was that the investigation wasn't really an official investigation but was something the newspapers had forced upon the police in case something had happened which they hadn't reported. The girl hadn't been missing long enough for anyone to declare her "officially" missing. Yet the police, along with the mayor's office and the newspaper editor, didn't want to risk something's having happened to a girl like Lee

Ann. They—all of them—thought of such girls, in a sense, as their special wards. It would be hard to say why they did. At any rate, before the police car had fully stopped I saw Nancy Minnifee up there on the platform. She was wearing a fur-collared overcoat but no hat or gloves. Immediately she began moving along the loading platform toward us, holding the clipboard up to shield her eyes from the late-afternoon winter sun. She came down the steps to the graveled area where we were stopped, and when the policeman at the wheel of the car ran down his window she bent forward and put her arm on his door. The casual way she did it seemed almost familiar—indeed, almost provocative. I found myself resenting her manner, because I was afraid she would give the wrong impression. The way she leaned on the door reminded me of the prostitutes down on Pontotoc Street when we, as teenage boys, used to stop in front of their houses and leave the motor running because we were afraid of them.

"I've been expecting you two gentlemen," Nancy said, smiling amiably at the two policemen and pointedly ignoring my presence in the backseat. The policemen broke into laughter.

"I suppose your friends have been calling ahead," the driver said. Then Nancy laughed as though he had said something very funny.

"I could draw you a map of the route you've taken this afternoon," she said. She was awfully polite in her tone, and the two policemen were awfully polite, too. But before they could really begin asking her their questions she began giving them her answers. She hadn't seen Lee Ann since several days before the accident. She didn't know anything about where she might be. She didn't know anything about her family. She had always understood that Lee Ann came from Texas.

"That's a big state," the policeman who wasn't driving said.

"Well, I've never been there," she said, "but I'm told it's a mighty big state."

The three of them burst into laughter again. Then the driver said quite seriously, "But we understand you're her best friend."

"I don't know her any better than most of the other girls do," she said. "I can't imagine who told you that." Now for the first time she looked at me in the backseat. "Hello, Nat," she said. I nodded to her. I couldn't imagine why she was lying to them. But I didn't tell her, as I hadn't told the other girls or the police, about the call I had had in the cotton office. I knew that she must know all about it, but I said nothing.

When we had pulled away, the policeman who was driving the car said, "This Lee Ann must be all right or these girls wouldn't be closing ranks so. They've got too much sense for that. They're smart girls."

Presently the other policeman turned his head halfway around, though not looking directly at me, and asked, "She wouldn't be pregnant by any chance, would she?"

"Uh-uh," I said. It was all the answer it seemed to me he deserved. But then I couldn't resist echoing what he had said. "They've got too much sense for that. They're smart girls." He looked all the way around at me now and gave me what I am sure he thought was a straight look.

"Damn right they are," said the driver, glancing at his colleague with a frown on his forehead and speaking with a curled lip. "Get your mind out of the gutter, Fred. After all, they're just kids, all of them."

We rode on in silence after that. For the first time in several hours, I thought of Caroline Braxley, and I wondered again whether or not she would break our engagement.

When the policemen let me off at my office at five o'clock, I went to my car and drove straight to the apartment house at Crosstown where Nancy Minnifee lived. I was waiting for Nancy in the parking lot when she got home. She invited me inside, but without a smile.

"I want to know where Lee Ann is," I said as soon as she had closed the door.

"Do you imagine I'd tell you if I knew?" she said.

I sat myself down in an upholstered chair as if I were going to stay there till she told me. "I want to know what the hell's going on," I said with what I thought was considerable force, "and why you told such lies to those policemen."

"If you don't know that now, Nat," she said, sitting down opposite me, "you probably won't ever know."

"She wouldn't be pregnant by any chance, would she?" I said, without really having known I was going to say it.

Nancy's mouth dropped open. Then she laughed aloud. Presently she said, "Well, one thing's certain, Nat. It wouldn't be any concern of yours if she were."

I pulled myself up out of the big chair and left without another word's passing between us.

* * *

Lee Ann Deehart and Nancy Minnifee and that whole band of girls that we liked to refer to as the girls of the Memphis demimonde were of course no more like the ladies of the demimonde as they appear in French literature than *they* were like some band of angels. And I hardly need say—though it does somehow occur to me to say—their manners and morals bore no resemblance whatsoever to those of the mercenary, filthy-mouthed whores on Pontotoc Street. I might even say that their manners were practically indistinguishable from those of the girls we knew who had attended Miss Hutchison's School and St. Mary's and Lausanne and were now members of the debutante set. The fact is that some of them—only a few perhaps—were from families that were related by blood, and rather closely related, to the families of the debutante set, but families that, for one reason or another, now found themselves economically in another class from their relatives. At any rate, they were all freed from old restraints put upon them by family and community, liberated in each case, so it seems to me, by sheer strength of character, liberated in many respects, but above all else—and I cannot say how it came about—liberated sexually. The most precise thing I can say about them is that they, in their little band, were like hordes of young girls today. It seems to me that in their attitude toward sex they were at least forty years ahead of their time. But I cannot say how it came about. Perhaps it was an individual thing with each of them—or partly so. Perhaps it was because they were the second or third generation of women in Memphis who were working in offices. They were not promiscuous—not most of them—but they slept with the men they were in love with and they did not conceal the fact. The men they were in love with were usually older than we were. Generally speaking, the girls merely amused themselves with us, just as we amused ourselves with them. There was a wonderful freedom in our relations which I have never known anything else quite like. And though I may not have had the most realistic sense of what their lives were, I came to know what I did know through my friendship with Lee Ann Deehart.

She and I first met, I think, at one of those dives where we all hung out. Or it may have been at some girl's apartment. I suspect we both would have been hard put to it to say where it was or exactly when. She was simply one of the good-looking girls we ran around with. I remember dancing with her on several occasions before I had any idea what her name was. We drifted into our special kind of friendship because, as a matter of fact, she was the good friend of Nancy Minnifee, whom my own close friend Bob Childress got very serious about for a time. Bob and Nancy may even have been living together for a while in Nancy's apartment. I think Bob, who was one of six or eight boys of approximately my background who used to go about with these girls, would have married Nancy if she'd consented to have him. Possibly it was at Nancy's apartment that I met Lee Ann. Anyway, we did a lot of double dating, the four of us, and had some wonderful times going to the sort of rough night spots that we all liked and found sufficiently exciting to return to again and again. We would be dancing and drinking at one of those places until about two in the morning, when most of them closed. At that hour most of us would take our girls home, because we nearly all of us had jobs—the girls and the boys, too—which we had to report to by eight or nine in the morning.

Between Lee Ann and me, as between most of the boys and their girls, I think, there was never a serious affair. That is, we never actually—as the young people today say—"had sex." But in the car on the way home or in the car parked outside her rooming house or even outside the night spot, as soon as we came out, we would regularly indulge in what used to be known as "heavy necking." Our stopping at that I must attribute first of all to Lee Ann's resistance, though also, in part, to a hesitation I felt about insisting with such a girl. You see, she was in all respects like the girls we called "nice girls," by which I suppose we really meant society girls. And most of us accepted the restriction that we were not to "go to bed" with society girls. They were the girls we were going to marry. These girls were not what those society girls would have termed shopgirls. They had much better taste in their clothes and in their general demeanor. And, as I have said, in the particular group I speak of there was at least an intellectual strain. Some of them had been to college for as much as a year or two, whereas others seemed hardly to have finished high school. Nearly all of them read magazines and books that most of us had never heard of. And they found my odd addiction to Latin poetry the most interesting thing about me. Most of them belonged to a national book club, from which they received a new book each month, and they nearly all bought records and listened to classical music. You would see them sometimes in groups at the Art Gallery. Or whenever there was an opera or a good play at the city auditorium they were all likely to be there in a group—almost never with dates. If you hadn't known who they were, you might easily have mistaken them for some committee from the Junior League or for an exceptionally pretty group of schoolteachers—from some fashionable girls' school probably.

But mostly, of course, one saw them with their dates at one of the roadhouses, over in Arkansas or down in Mississippi or out east on the Bristol Highway, or yet again at one of the places we called the "town joints." They preferred going to those road-houses and town joints to going to the Peabody Hotel Roof or the Claridge—as I suppose nearly everyone else did, really, including society girls like Caroline. You would, as a matter of fact, frequently see girls like Caroline at such places. At her request, I had more than once taken Caroline to a town joint down on Adams Street called The Cellar and once to a roadhouse called The Jungle, over in Arkansas. She had met some of the city girls there and said she found them "dead attractive." And she once recognized them at a play I took her to see and afterward expressed interest in them and asked me to tell her what they were like.

The fact may be that neither the roadhouses nor the town joints were quite as tough as they seemed. Or they weren't as tough as for the demimonde girls, anyway. Because the proprietors clearly had protective feelings about them. At The Jungle, for instance, the middle-aged couple who operated the place, an extremely obese couple who were forever grinning in our direction and who were usually barefoot (we called them Ma and Pa), would often come and stand by our table—one or the other of them—and sing the words to whatever was playing on the jukebox. Often as not, one of them would be standing there during the entire evening. Sometimes Ma would talk to us about her two little daughters, whom she kept in a private school in Memphis, and Pa, who was a practicing taxidermist, would talk to us about the dogs whose mounted heads adorned the walls on every side of the dimly lit room. All this afforded us great privacy and safety. No drunk or roughneck would come near our table while either Ma or Pa was close by. We had similar protection at other places. At The Cellar, for instance, old Mrs. Power was the sole proprietor. She had a huge goiter on her neck and was never known to smile. Not even in our direction. But it was easy to see that she watched our table like a hawk, and if any other patron lingered near us even momentarily she would begin moving slowly toward us. And whoever it was would catch one glimpse of her and move on. We went to these places quite regularly, though some of the girls had their favorites and dislikes among them. Lee Ann would never be taken to The Cellar. She would say only that the place depressed her. And Caroline, when I took her there, felt an instant dislike for The Jungle. She would shake her head afterward and say she would never go back and have those dogs' eyes staring down through the darkness at her.

* * *

On the day after I made the rounds with the policemen, I found myself following almost the same routine in the company of my father and the editor of the morning paper, and, as a matter of fact, the mayor of Memphis himself. The investigation or search was, you see, still entirely unofficial. And men like my father and the mayor and the editor wanted to keep it so. That's why after that routine and off-the-record series of questionings by the police they preferred to do a bit of investigation themselves rather than entrust the matter to someone else. As I have said, that generation of men in Memphis evidenced feelings of responsibility for such girls—for "working girls of a superior kind," as they phrased it—which I find somewhat difficult to explain. For it wasn't just the men I drove about town with that day. Or the dozen or so men who gathered for conference in our driveway before we set out—that is, Caroline's father, his lawyer, the driver of the other vehicle, his lawyer, my father's lawyer, ministers from three church denominations, the editor of the afternoon newspaper, and still others. That day, when I rode about town with my father and the two other men in our car, I came as near as I ever had or ever would to receiving a satisfactory explanation of the phenomenon. They were a generation of American men who were perhaps the last to grow up in a world where women were absolutely subjected and under the absolute protection of men.

While my father wheeled his big Cadillac through the side streets on which some of the girls lived and then along the wide boulevards of Memphis, they spoke of the changes they had seen. In referring to the character of the life girls like Lee Ann led—of which they showed a far greater awareness than I would have supposed they possessed—they agreed that this was the second or third generation there of women who had lived as independently, as freely as these girls did. I felt that what they said was in no sense as derogatory or critical as it would have been in the presence of their wives or daughters. They spoke almost affectionately and with a certain sadness of such girls. They spoke as if these were daughters of dead brothers of their own or of dead companions-in-arms during the First World War. And it seemed to me that they thought of these girls as the daughters of men who had abdicated their authority and responsibility as fathers, men who were not strangers or foreign to them, though they were perhaps of a different economic class. The family names of the girls were familiar to them. The fathers of these girls were Americans of the great hinterland like themselves, even Southerners like themselves. I felt that they were actually cousins of ours who had failed as fathers somehow, had been destined to fail, even required to do so in a changing world. And so these men of position and power had to act as surrogate fathers during a transitional period. It was a sort of communal fatherhood they were acting out. Eventually, they seemed to say, fathers might not be required. I actually heard my father saying, "That's what the whole world is going to be like someday." He meant like the life such girls as Lee Ann were making for themselves. I often think nowadays of Father's saying that whenever I see his prediction being fulfilled by the students in the university where I have been teaching for twenty years now, and I wonder if Father did really believe his prediction would come true.

Yet while he and the other two men talked their rather sanguine talk that day, I was thinking of a call I had had the night before after I came back from seeing Nancy Minnifee. One of the servants answered the telephone downstairs in the back part of the house, and she must have guessed it was something special. Because instead of buzzing the buzzer three times, which was the signal when a call was for me, the maid came up the backstairs and tapped gently on my door. "It's for you, Nat," she said softly. "Do you want to take it downstairs?"

There was nothing peculiar about her doing this, really. Since I didn't have an extension phone in my room, I had a tacit understanding with the servants that I preferred to take what I considered my private calls down in that quarter of the house. And so I followed the maid down the back stairway and shut myself in the little, servants' dining room that was behind the great white-tiled kitchen. I answered the call on the wall phone there.

A girl's voice, which wasn't the same voice I had heard on the office telephone at noon, said, "Lee Ann doesn't want another day like this one, Nat."

"Who is this?" I said, lowering my voice to be sure even the servants didn't hear me. "What the hell is going on?" I asked. "Where is Lee Ann?"

"She's been keeping just one apartment or one rooming house ahead of you all day."

"But why? Why is she hiding this way?"

"All I want to say is she's had about enough. You let up on pursuing her so."

"It's not me," I protested. "There's nothing I can do to stop them."

Over the phone there came a contemptuous laugh. "No. And you can't get married till they find her, can you?" Momentarily I thought I heard Lee Ann's voice in the background. "Anyhow," the same voice continued, "Lee Ann's had about as much as she can take of all this. She was depressed as it was when she called you in the first place. Why else do you think she would call you, Nat? She was desperate for some comic relief."

"Relief from what?"

"Relief from her depression, you idiot."

"But what's she depressed about?" I was listening carefully to the voice, thinking it was that of first one girl and then another.

"Nat, we don't always have to have something to be depressed about. But Lee Ann will be all right, if you'll let her alone."

"But what is she depressed about?" I persisted. I had begun to think maybe it was Lee Ann herself on the phone, disguising her voice.

"About life in general, you bastard! Isn't that enough?" Then I knew it wasn't Lee Ann, after all.

"Listen," I said, "let me speak to Lee Ann. I want to speak to Lee Ann."

And then I heard whoever it was I was talking with break off the connection. I quietly replaced the receiver and went upstairs again.

In those days I didn't know what it was to be depressed—not, anyway, about "life in general." Later on, you see, I did know. Later on, after years of being married, and having three children, and going to grown-up Memphis dinner parties three or four times a week, and working in the cotton office six days a week, I got so depressed about life in general that I sold my interest in the cotton firm to a cousin of mine (my father and uncles were dead by then) and managed to make Caroline understand that what I needed was to go back to school for a while so that we could start our life all over. I took degrees at three universities, which made it possible for me to become a college professor. That may be an awful revelation about myself—I mean to say, awful that what decided me to become a teacher was that I was so depressed about life in general. But I reasoned that being an English professor—even if I was relegated to teaching composition and simpleminded survey courses—would be something useful and would throw us in with a different kind of people. (Caroline tried to persuade me to go into the sciences, but I told her she was just lucky that I didn't take up classics again.) Anyway, teaching has made me see a lot of young people over the years, in addition to my own children, and I think it is why, in retrospect, those Memphis girls I'm writing about still seem interesting to me after all these many years.

But the fact is I was still so uneasy about the significance of both those calls from Lee Ann's friends that I was unwilling to mention them to Caroline that night. At first I thought I would tell her, but as soon as I saw her tall and graceful figure in her white, pleated evening dress and wearing the white corsage I had sent, I began worrying again about whether or not she might still break off the engagement. Besides, we had plenty of other matters to discuss, including the rounds I had made with the two policemen that day and her various activities in preparation for the wedding. We went to a dinner that one of my aunts gave for us at the Memphis Country Club that night. We came home early and spent twenty minutes or so in her living room, telling each other how much we loved each other and how we would let nothing on earth interfere with our getting married. I felt reassured, or I tried to feel so. It seemed to me, though, that Caroline still had not really made up her mind. It worried me that she didn't have more to say about Lee Ann. After I got home, I kept waking all night and wondering what if that had not been Lee Ann's voice I had heard in the background and what if she never surfaced again. The circumstances of her disappearance would have to be made public, and that would certainly be too embarrassing for Caroline and her parents to ignore.

Next day, I didn't tell my father and his two friends, the editor and the mayor, about either of the two telephone calls. I don't know why I didn't, unless it was because I feared they might begin monitoring all my calls. I could not tolerate the thought of having them hear the things that girl said to me.

In preference to interviewing the girls whose addresses I could give them, those three middle-aged men seemed much more interested in talking to the girls' rooming-house landladies, or their apartment landlords, or their mothers. They did talk to some of the girls themselves, though, and I observed that the girls were so impressed by having these older men want to talk to them that they could hardly look at them directly. What I think is that the girls were *afraid* they would tell them the truth. They would reply to their questions respectfully, if evasively, but they were apt to keep their eyes on me. This was not the case, however, with the mothers and the landlords and the landladies. There was an immediate rapport between these persons and the three men. There hardly needed to be any explanation required of the unofficial nature of the investigation or of the concern of these particular men about such a girl as Lee Ann. One woman who told them that Lee Ann had roomed with her for a time described her as being always a moody sort of girl. "But lots of these girls living on their own are moody," she said.

"Where did Miss Deehart come from?" my father asked. "Who were her people?"

"She always claimed she came from Texas," the woman said. "But she could never make it clear to me where it was in Texas."

Later the mayor asked Lee Ann's current landlady, Mrs. Troxler, where she supposed Lee Ann might have gone. "Well," Mrs. Troxler said, "a girl, a decent girl, even among these modern girls, generally goes to her mother when there's trouble. Women turn to women," she said, "when there's real trouble."

The three men found no trace of Lee Ann, got no real clue to where she might have gone. When finally we were leaving the editor at his newspaper office on Union Avenue, he hesitated a moment before opening the car door. "Well," he began, but he sat for a moment beating his leg thoughtfully with a newspaper he had rolled up in his hand. "I don't know," he said. "It's going to be a matter for the police, after all, if we can't do any better than this." I still didn't say anything about my telephone calls. But the calls were worrying me a good deal, and that night I told Caroline.

And when I had told her about the calls and told her how the police and my father and his friends had failed to get any information from the girls, Caroline, who was then sitting beside me on the couch in her living room, suddenly took my hand in hers and, putting her face close to mine and looking me directly in the eye, said, "Nat, I don't want you to go to work at all tomorrow. Don't make any explanation to your father or to anybody. Just get up early and come over here and get me. I want you to take me to meet some of those girls." Then she asked me which of the girls she might possibly have met on the rare occasions when I had taken her dancing at The Jungle or at The Cellar. And before I left that night she got me to tell her all I knew about "that whole tribe of city girls." I told her everything, including an account of my innocent friendship with Lee

Ann Deehart, as well as an account of my earlier relations, which were not innocent, with a girl named Fern Morris. When, next morning, I came to fetch Caroline for our expedition, there were only three girls that she wanted to be taken to see. One of the three was of course Fern Morris.

There was something that had happened to me the day before, when I was going about Memphis with my father and his two friends, that I could not tell Caroline about. You see, I had been imagining, each place we went, how as we came in the front door Lee Ann was hurriedly, quietly going out the back. This mental picture of her in flight I found not merely appealing but strangely exciting. And it seemed to me I was discovering what my true feelings toward Lee Ann had been during the past two years. I had never dared insist upon the occasional advances I had naturally made to her, because she had always seemed too delicate, too vulnerable, for me to think of suggesting a casual sexual relationship with her. She had seemed too clever and too intelligent for me to deceive her about my intentions or my worth as a person. And I imagined I relished the kind of restraint there was between us because it was so altogether personal and not one placed upon us by any element or segment of society, or by any outside circumstances whatever. It kept coming to my mind as we stood waiting for an answer to the pressure on each doorbell that she was the girl I ought and wanted to be marrying. I realized the absolute folly of such thoughts and the utter impossibility of any such conclusion to present events. But still such feelings and thoughts had kept swimming in and out of my head all that day. I kept seeing Lee Ann in my mind's eye and hearing her soft, somewhat husky voice. I kept imagining how her figure would appear in the doorway before us. I saw her slender ankles, her small breasts, her head of ash-blond hair, which had a way of seeming to fall about her face when she talked but which with one shake of her head she could throw back into perfect place. But of course when the door opened there was the inevitable landlady or mother or friend. And when the next day came and I saw Caroline rolling up her sleeves, so to speak, to pitch in and settle this matter once and for all, then my thoughts and fantasies of the day before seemed literally like something out of a dream that I might have had.

The first two girls Caroline had wanted to see were the two that she very definitely remembered having met when I had taken her—"on a lark"—to my favorite night spots. She caught them both before they went to work that morning, and I was asked to wait in the car. I felt like an idiot waiting out there in the car, because I knew I'd been seen from some window as I gingerly hopped out and opened the door for Caroline when she got out—and opened it again when she returned. But there was no way around it. I waited out there, playing the car radio even at the risk of running down the battery.

When she came back from seeing the first girl, whose name was Lucy Phelan, Caroline was very angry. She reported that Lucy Phelan had pretended not to remember ever having met her. Moreover, Lucy had pretended that she knew Lee Ann Deehart only slightly and had no idea where she could be or what her disappearance meant. As Caroline fumed and I started up the car, I was picturing Lee Ann quietly tiptoeing out the backdoor of Lucy's rooming house just as Lucy was telling Caroline she scarcely knew the girl or while she was insisting that she didn't remember Caroline. As Caroline came back down the walk from the big Victorian house to the car, Lucy, who had stepped out onto the narrow porch that ran across the front of the house and around one corner of it, squatted down on her haunches at the top of the wooden porch steps and waved to me from behind Caroline's back. Though I knew it was no good, I pretended not to see her there. As I put the car into second gear and we sped away down the block, I took a quick glance back at the house. Lucy was still standing on the porch and waving to me the way one waves to a little child. She knew I had seen her stooping and waving moments before. And knew I would be stealing a glance now.

For a short time Caroline seemed undecided about calling on the second girl. But she decided finally to press on. Lucy Phelan she remembered meeting at The Cellar. The next girl. Betsy Morehouse, she had met at The Jungle and at a considerably more recent time. Caroline was a dog fancier in those days and she recalled a conversation with Betsy about the mounted dogs heads that adorned the walls of The Jungle. They both had been outraged. When she mentioned this to me there in the car, I realized for the first time that by trying to make these girls acknowledge an acquaintance with her she had hoped to make them feel she was almost one of them and that they would thus be more likely to confide in her. But she failed with Betsy Morehouse, too. Betsy lived in an apartment house—an old residence, that is, converted into apartments—and when Caroline got inside the entrance-hall door she met Betsy, who was just then coming down the stairs. Betsy carried a purse and was wearing a fur coat and overshoes. When Caroline got back to the car and told me about it, I could not help feeling that Betsy had had a call from Lucy Phelan and even perhaps that Lee Ann was hiding in her apartment, having just arrived there from Lucy's. Because Betsy didn't offer to take Caroline back upstairs to her apartment for a talk. Instead, they sat down on two straight-backed chairs in the entrance hall and exchanged their few words there. Betsy at once denied the possibility of Caroline's ever having met her before. She denied that she had, herself, ever been to The Jungle. I knew this to be a lie, of course, but I didn't insist upon it to Caroline. I said that perhaps both she and I were mistaken about Betsy's being there on the night I had taken Caroline. As soon as Caroline saw she would learn nothing from Betsy, she got up and began to make motions of leaving. Betsy followed her to the door. But upon seeing my car out at the curb—so Caroline believed—she turned back, saying that she had remembered a telephone call she had to make. Caroline suspected that the girl didn't want to have to face me with her lie. That possibly was true. But my thought was that Betsy just might, also, have a telephone call she wanted to make.

There was now no question about Caroline's wanting to proceed to the third girl's house. This was the girl I had told her about having had a real affair with—the one I had gone with before Lee Ann and I had become friends. Caroline knew that she and Fern Morris had never met, but she counted on a different psychology with Fern. Most probably she had hoped it wouldn't be necessary for her to go to see Fern. She had been sure that one of those two other girls would give her the lead she needed. But as a last resort she was fully prepared to call on Fern Morris and to take me into the house with her.

Fern was a girl who still lived at home with her mother. She was in no sense a mama's girl or even a home-loving girl, since she was unhappy unless she went out on a date every night of her life. Perhaps she was not so clever and not so intellectual as most of her friends—if reading books, that is, on psychology and on China and every new volume of André Maurois indicated intellectuality. And though she was not home-loving, I suppose you would have to say she was more domestic than the other girls were. She had never "held down" a job. Rather, she stayed at home in the daytime and kept house for her mother, who was said to "hold down" a high-powered job under Boss Crump down at

City Hall. Mrs. Morris was a very sensible woman, who put no restrictions on her grown-up daughter and was glad to have her as a housekeeper. She used to tell me what a good cook and housekeeper Fern was and how well fixed she would leave her when she died. I really believe Mrs. Morris hoped our romance might end in matrimony, and, as a matter of fact, it was when I began to suspect that Fern, too, was entertaining such notions that I stopped seeing her and turned my attentions to Lee Ann Deehart.

Mrs. Morris still seemed glad to see me when I arrived at their bungalow that morning with Caroline and when I proceeded to introduce Caroline to her as my fiancée. Fern herself greeted me warmly. In fact, when I told her that Caroline and I were going to be married (though she must certainly have already read about it in the newspaper) she threw her arms about my neck and kissed me. "Oh, Natty," she said, "I'm so happy for you. Really I am. But poor Lee Ann." And in later life, especially in recent years, whenever Caroline has thought I was being silly about some other woman, usually a woman she considers her mental and social inferior, she has delighted in addressing me as "Natty." On more than one such occasion I have even had her say to me, "I am so happy for you, Natty. Really I am."

The fact is, Mrs. Morris was just leaving the house for work when we arrived. And so there was no delay in Caroline's interview with Fern. "I assume you know about Lee Ann's disappearance?" Caroline began as soon as we had seated ourselves in the little front parlor, with which I was very familiar.

"Of course I do," said Fern, looking at me and laughing gleefully.

"You think it's a laughing matter, then?" Caroline asked.

"I do indeed. It's all a big joke," Fern said at once. It was as though she had her answers all prepared. "And a very successful joke it is."

"Successful?" both Caroline and I asked. We looked at each other in dismay.

"It's only my opinion, of course. But I think she only wants to make you two suffer."

"Suffer?" I said. This time Caroline was silent.

Fern was now addressing me directly. "Everybody knows Caroline is not going to marry you until Lee Ann turns up safe."

"Everybody?" Both of us again.

"Everybody in the world practically," said Fern.

Caroline's face showed no expression. Neither, I believe, did mine.

"Fern, do you know where Lee Ann is?" Caroline asked gently.

Fern Morris, her eyes on me, shook her head, smiling.

"Do you know where her people are?" Caroline asked. "And whether she's with them or hiding with her friends?"

Fern shook her head again, but now she gazed directly at Caroline. "I'm not going to tell you anything!" she asserted. But after a moment she took a deep breath and said, still looking at Caroline, "You're a smart girl. I think you'll likely be going to Lee Ann's room in that place where she lives. If you do go there, and if you are a smart girl, you'll look in the left-hand drawer of Lee Ann's dressing table." Fern had an uneasy smile on her face after she had spoken, as if Caroline had got her to say something she hadn't really meant to say, as if she felt guilty for what she had just done.

Caroline had us out of there in only a minute or so and on our way to Lee Ann's rooming house.

It was a red-brick bungalow up in north Memphis. It looked very much like the one that Fern lived in but was used as a rooming house. When Mrs. Troxler opened the front door to us, Caroline said, "We're friends of Lee Ann's, and she wants us to pack a suitcase and bring it to her."

"You know where she is, then?" Mrs. Troxler asked. "Hello, Nat," she said, looking at me over Caroline's shoulder.

"Hello, Mrs. Troxler," I said. I was so stunned by what I had just heard Caroline say that I spoke in a whisper.

"She's with her mother—or with her family, at least," Caroline said. By now she had slipped into the hallway, and I had followed without Mrs. Troxler's really inviting us in.

"Where are her family?" Mrs. Troxler asked, giving way to Caroline's forward thrust. "She never volunteered to tell me anything about them. And I never think it's my business to ask."

Caroline nodded her head at me, indicating that I should lead the way to Lee Ann's room. I knew that her room was toward the back of the house and I headed in that direction.

"I'll have to unlock the room for you," said Mrs. Troxler. "There have been a number of people coming here and wanting to look about her room. And so I keep it locked."

"A number of people?" asked Caroline casually.

"Yes. Nat knows. There were the police. And then there were some other gentlemen. Nat knows about it, though he didn't come in. And there were two other girls. The girls just seemed idly curious, and so I've taken to locking the door. Where do her people live?"

"I don't know," said Caroline. "She's going to meet us down-town at the bus station and take a bus."

When Mrs. Troxler had unlocked the door she asked, "Is Lee Ann all right? Do you think she will be coming back here?"

"She's fine," Caroline said, "and I'm sure she'll be coming back. She just wants a few things."

"Yes, I've wondered how she's been getting along without a change of clothes. I'll fetch her suitcase. I keep my roomers' luggage in my storage closet down the hall." We waited till she came back with a piece of plaid luggage, and then we went into the room and closed the door. Caroline went to the oak dresser and began pulling things out and stuffing them in the bag. I stood by, watching, hardly able to believe what I saw Caroline doing. When she had closed the bag, she looked up at me as if to say, "What are you waiting for?" She had not gone near the little mahogany dressing table, and I had not realized that was going to be my part. I went over and opened the left-hand drawer. The only thing in the drawer was a small snapshot. I took it up and examined it carefully. I said nothing to Caroline, just handed her the picture. Finally I said, "Do you know who that is? And where the picture was taken?" She recognized the woman with the goiter who ran The Cellar. The picture had been taken with Mrs. Power standing in one of the flower beds against the side of the house. The big cut stones of the house were unmistakable. After bringing the snapshot up close to her face and peering into it for ten seconds or so, Caroline looked at me and said, "That's her family."

By the time we had stopped the car in front of The Cellar, I had told Caroline all that I knew about Lee Ann's schooling and about how it was that, though she had a "family" in Memphis, no one had known her when she was growing up. She had been to one boarding school in Shreveport, Louisiana, to one in East Texas, and to still another in St. Charles, Missouri. I had heard her make references to all of those schools. "They kept her away from home," Caroline speculated. "And so when she had finished school she wasn't prepared for the kind of 'family' she had. That's why she moved out on them and lived in a rooming house."

She reached that conclusion while I was parking the car at the curb, near the front entrance to the house. Meanwhile, I was preparing myself mentally to accompany Caroline to the door of the old woman's living quarters, which were on the main floor and above The Cellar. But Caroline rested her hand on the steering wheel beside mine and said, "This is something I have to do without you."

"But I'd like to see Lee Ann if she's here," I said.

"I know you would," said Caroline. "Of course you would."

"But, Caroline," I said, "I've made it clear that ours was an innocent—"

"I know," she said. "That's why I don't want you to see her again." Then she took Lee Ann's bag and went up to the front entrance of the house.

The main entrance to The Cellar was to the side of and underneath the high front stoop of the old house. Caroline had to climb a flight of ten or twelve stone steps to reach the door to the residence. From the car I saw a vague figure appear at one of the first-floor windows. I was relatively certain that it was Lee Ann I saw. I could barely restrain myself from jumping from the car and running up that flight of steps and forcing myself past Caroline and into the house. During the hundred hours or so since she had fled into the woods of Overton Park, Lee Ann Deehart had come to represent feelings of mine that I didn't try to comprehend. The notion I had had yesterday that I was in love with her and wanted to marry her didn't really adequately express the emotions that her disappearance had stirred in me. I felt that I had never looked at her really or had any conception of what sort of person she was or what her experience in life was like. Now it seemed I would never know. I suddenly realized—at that early age—that there was experience to be had in life that I might never know anything about except through hearsay and through books. I felt that this was my last moment to reach out and understand something of the world that was other than my own narrow circumstances and my own narrow nature. When, nearly fifteen years later, I came into a comfortable amount of money—after my father's death—I made my extraordinary decision to go back to the university and prepare myself to become a teacher. But I knew then, at thirty-seven, that I was only going to try to comprehend intellectually the world about me and beyond me and that I had failed somehow at some time to reach out and grasp direct experience of a larger life which no amount of intellectualizing could compensate for. It may be that the moment of my great failure was when I continued to sit there in the car and did not force my way into the house where the old woman with the goiter lived and where it now seemed Lee Ann had been hiding for four days.

I was scarcely aware of the moment when the big front door opened and Caroline was admitted to the house. She was in there for nearly an hour. During that time I don't know what thoughts I had. It was as though I ceased to exist for the time that Lee Ann Deehart and Caroline Braxley were closeted together. When Caroline reappeared on the high stone stoop of the house, I was surprised to see she was still carrying Lee Ann's suitcase. But she would soon make it all clear. It *was* Lee Ann who received her at the door. No doubt she had seen that Caroline was carrying her own piece of luggage. And no doubt Caroline had counted on just that mystification and its efficacy, because Caroline is an extremely clever psychologist when she sets her mind to it. At any rate, in that relatively brief interview between them Caroline learned that all she had surmised about Lee Ann was true. Moreover, she learned that Lee Ann had fled the scene of the accident because she feared that the publicity would reveal to everyone who her grandmother was.

Lee Ann had crossed the little strip of snow-covered golf course and had entered the part of the woods where the old-forest trees were. And something had made her want to remain there for a while. She didn't know what it was. She had leaned against one of the trees, feeling quite content. It had seemed to her that she was not alone in the woods. And whatever the other presences were, instead of interfering with her reflections they seemed to wish to help her clear her thoughts. She stood there for a long time—perhaps for an hour or more. At any rate, she remained there until all at once she realized how cold she had grown and realized that she had no choice but to go back to the real world. Yet she wasn't going back to her room or to her pretty possessions there. That wasn't the kind of freedom she wanted any longer. She was going back to her grandmother. But still she hoped to avoid the publicity that the accident might bring. She decided to go, first of all, and stay with some of her friends, so that her grandmother would not suppose she was only turning to her because she was in trouble. And while making this important change in her life she felt she must be protected by her friends. She wanted to have an interval of time to herself and she wanted, above all, not to be bothered during that time by the silly society boy in whose car she had been riding.

During the first days she had gone from one girl's house to another. Finally she went to her grandmother. In the beginning she had, it was true, been mightily depressed. That was why she had telephoned me to start with, and had wanted someone to cheer her up. But during these four days she had much time for thinking and had overcome all her depression and had no other thought but to follow through with the decision to go and live openly with her old grandmother in her quarters above The Cellar.

Caroline also, in that single interview, learned other things about Lee Ann which had been unknown to me. She learned that Lee Ann's own mother had abandoned her in infancy to her grandmother but had always through the years sent money back for her education. She had had—the mother—an extremely successful career as a buyer for a women's clothing store in Lincoln, Nebraska. But she had never tried to see her daughter and had never expressed a wish to see her. The only word she ever sent was that children were not her dish, but that she didn't want it on her conscience that, because of her, some little girl in Memphis, Tennessee, had got no education and was therefore the domestic slave of some man. When Caroline told me all of this about the mother's not caring to see the daughter, it brought from her her first emotional outburst with regard to the whole business. But that was at a later time. The first thing she had told me when she returned to the car was that once Lee Ann realized that her place of hiding could no longer be concealed, she was quickly and easily persuaded to speak to the newspaper editor on the telephone and to tell him that she was safe and well. But she did this only after Caroline had first spoken to the editor herself, and obtained a promise from him that there would be no embarrassing publicity for Lee Ann's grandmother.

The reason Caroline had returned with Lee Ann's suitcase was that Lee Ann had emptied it there in her grandmother's front parlor and had asked that we return to her rooming house and bring all of her possessions to her at her grandmother's. We obliged her in this, making appropriate, truthless explanations to her landlady, whom Lee Ann had meanwhile telephoned and given whatever little authority Mrs. Troxler required in order to let us remove her things. It seemed to me that the poor woman scarcely listened to the explanations we gave. Another girl was already moving into the room before we had well got Lee Ann's things out. When we returned to the grandmother's house with these possessions in the car, Caroline insisted upon making an endless number of trips into the house, carrying everything herself. She was firm in her stipulation that Lee Ann and I not see each other again.

The incident was closed then. I could be certain that there would be no broken engagement—not on Caroline's initiative. But from that point—from that afternoon—my real effort and my real concern would be to try to understand why Caroline had not been so terribly enraged or so sorely wounded upon first discovering that there had been another girl with me in the car at the time of the accident, and by the realization that I had not immediately disclosed her presence, that she had not at least once threatened to end the engagement. What her mental processes had been during the past four days, knowing now as I did that she was the person with whom I was going to spend the rest of my life, became of paramount interest to me.

But at that age I was so unquestioning of human behavior in general and so accepting of events as they came, and so without perception or reflection regarding the binding and molding effect upon people of the circumstances in which they are born, that I actually might not have found Caroline's thoughts of such profound interest and so vitally important to be understood had not Caroline, as soon as we were riding down Adams Street and were out of sight of The Cellar and of Mrs. Power's great stone house above it, suddenly requested that I drive her out to the Bristol Highway, and once we were on the Bristol Highway asked me to drive as fast and as far out of town as I could or would, to drive and drive until she should beg me to turn around and take her home; and had she not, as soon as we were out of town and beyond city speed limits, where I could press down on the accelerator and send us flying along the three-lane strip of concrete which cut through the endless expanse of cotton fields and swamps on either side, had she not then at last, after talking quietly about Lee Ann's mother's sending back the money for her education, burst into weeping that began with a kind of wailing and grinding of teeth that one ordinarily associates more with a very old person in very great physical pain, a wailing that became mixed almost immediately with a sort of hollow laughter in which there was no mirth. I commenced slowing the car at once. I was searching for a place where I could pull off to the side of the road. But through her tears and her harsh, dry laughter she hissed at me, "Don't stop! Don't stop! Go on. Go on. Go as far and as fast as you can, so that I can forget this day and put it forever behind me!" I obeyed her and sped on, reaching out my right hand to hold her two hands that were resting in her lap and were making no effort to wipe away her tears. I was not looking at her—only thinking thoughts of a kind I had never before had. It was the first time I had ever witnessed a victim of genuine hysteria. Indeed, I wasn't to hear such noises again until six or seven years later, during the Second World War. I heard them from men during days after a battle, men who had stood with great bravery against the enemy—particularly, as I remember now, men who had been brought back from the first onslaught of the Normandy invasion, physically whole but shaken in their souls. I think that during the stress of the four previous days Caroline Braxley had shed not a tear of self-pity or of shame and had not allowed herself a moment of genuine grief for my possible faithlessness to her. She had been far too busy with thinking—with thinking her thoughts of how to cope with Lee Ann's unexplained disappearance, with, that is, its possible effect upon her own life. But now the time had come when her checked emotions could be checked no longer.

The Bristol Highway, along which we were speeding as she wept hysterically, was a very straight and a very wide roadway for those days. It went northeast from Memphis. As its name implied, it was the old road that shot more or less diagonally across the long hinterland that is the state of Tennessee. It was the road along which many of our ancestors had first made their way from Virginia and the Carolinas to Memphis, to settle in the forest wilderness along the bluffs above the Mississippi River. And it occurred to me now that when Caroline said go as fast and as far as you can she really meant to take us all the way back into our past and begin the journey all over again, not merely from a point of four days ago or from the days of our childhood but from a point in our identity that would require a much deeper delving and a more radical return.

When we had got scarcely beyond the outskirts of Memphis, the most obvious signs of her hysteria had abated. Instead, however, she began to speak with a rapidity and in tones I was not accustomed to in her speech. This began after I had seen her give one long look over her shoulder and out the rear window of the car. Sensing some significance in that look and sensing some connection between it and the monologue she had now launched upon, I myself gave one glance into the rearview mirror. What met my eye was the skyline of modern Memphis beyond the snow-covered suburban rooftops—the modern Memphis of 1937, with its two or three high-rise office buildings. It was not clear to me immediately what there was in that skyline to inspire all that followed. She was speaking to me openly about Lee Ann and about her own feelings of jealousy and resentment of the girl—of *that* girl and of all those other girls, too, whose names and personalities and way of life had occupied our thoughts and had seemed to threaten our future during the four-day crisis that had followed my accident in the park.

"It isn't only Lee Ann that disturbs me," she said. "It began with her, of course. It began not with what she might be to you but with her freedom to jump out of your car, her freedom *from* you, her freedom to run off into the woods—with her capacity, which her special way of living provided her, simply to vanish, to remove herself from the eyes of the world, literally to disappear from the glaring light of day while the whole world, so to speak, looked on."

"*You* would like to be able to do that?" I interrupted. It seemed so unlike her role as I understood it.

"*Any*body would, wouldn't they?" she said, not looking at me but at the endless stretch of concrete that lay straight ahead. "*Men* have always been able to do it," she said. "In my own family, for as many generations back as our family stories go, there have been men who seemed to disappear from the face of the earth just because they wanted to. They used to write 'Gone to Texas' on the front door and leave the house and the farm to be sold for taxes. They walked out on dependent old parents and on sweethearts or even on wives and little children. And though they were considered black sheep for doing so, they were something of heroes, too. It seemed romantic to the rest of us that they had gone Out West somewhere and got a new start or had begun life over. But there was never a woman in our family who did that! There was no way it could happen. Or perhaps in some rare instance it did happen and the story hasn't come down to us. Her name simply isn't recorded in our family annals or reported in stories told around the fire. The assumption of course is that she is a streetwalker in Chicago or she resides in a red-plush whorehouse in Cheyenne. But with girls like Lee Ann and Lucy and Betsy it's all different. They have made their break with the past. Each of them had had the strength and intelligence to make the break for herself. But now they have formed a sort of league for their own protection. How I do admire and envy them! And how little you understand them, Nat. How little you understand Lee Ann's loneliness and depression and bravery. She and all the others are wonderful—even Fern. They occupy the real city of Memphis as none of the rest of us do. They treat men just as they please. And not the way men are treated in *our* circles. And men like them better for it. Those girls have learned to enjoy life together and to be mutually protective, but they enjoy a protection also, I hope you have observed, a kind of communal protection, from men who admire their very independence, from a league of men, mind you, not from individual men, from the police and from men like my father and your father, from men who would never say openly how much they admire them. Naturally we fear them. Those of us who are not like them in temperament—or in intelligence, because there is no use in denying it—we must fear them and find a means to give delaying action. And of course the only way we know is the age-old way!"

She became silent for a time now. But I knew I was going to hear what I had been waiting to hear. If I had been the least bit impatient with her explanation of Lee Ann and her friends, it was due in part to my impatience to see if she would explain *herself* to me. We were now speeding along the Bristol Highway at the very top speed the car would go. Except when we were passing through some crossroad or village I consciously kept the speed above ninety. In those days there was no speed limit in Tennessee. There were merely signs placed every so often along the roadside saying "Speed Limit: Please Drive Carefully." I felt somehow that, considering Caroline's emotional state and my own tension, it would be altogether unreasonable, it would constitute careless and unsafe driving, for me to reduce our speed to anything below the maximum capability of the car. And when we did of necessity slow down for some village or small town it was precisely as though we had arrived at some at once familiar and strange point in the past. And on each occasion I think we both experienced a sense of danger and disappointment. It was as though we expected to experience a satisfaction in having gone so far. But the satisfaction was not to be had. When we had passed that point, I felt only the need to press on at an even greater speed. And so we drove on and on, at first north and east through the wintry cotton land and cornland, past the old Orgill Plantation, the mansion house in plain view, its round brick columns on which the plaster was mostly gone, and now and then another white man's antebellum house, and always at the roadside or on the horizon, atop some distant ridge, a variety of black men's shacks and cabins, each with a little streamer of smoke rising from an improvised tin stovepipe or from an ill-made brick chimney bent away from the cabin at a precarious angle.

We went through the old villages of Arlington and Mason and the town of Brownsville—down streets of houses with columned porticoes and double galleries—and then we turned south to Bolivar, whose very name told you when it was built, and headed back to Memphis through Grand Junction and La Grange. (Mississippi towns really, though north of the Tennessee line.) I had slowed our speed after Bolivar, because that was where Caroline began her second monologue. The tone and pace of her speech were very different now. Her speech was slow and deliberate, her emotions more under control than usual, as she described what she had felt and thought in the time since the accident and explained how she came to reach the decision to take the action she had—that is, action toward searching out and finding Lee Ann Deehart. Though I had said nothing on the subject of what she had done about Lee Ann and not done about our engagement, expressed no request or demand for any explanation unless it was by my silence, when she spoke now it was almost as though Caroline were making a courtroom defense of accusations hurled at her by me. "I finally saw there was only one thing for me to do and saw why I had to do it. I saw that the only power in the world I had for saving myself lay in my saving you. And I saw that I could only save you by 'saving' Lee Ann Deehart. At first, of course, I thought I would have to break our engagement, or at least postpone the wedding for a year. That's what *every*body thought, of course—everybody in the family."

"Even your father and mother?" I could not help interjecting. It had seemed to me that Caroline's parents had—of all people—been most sympathetic to me.

"Yes, even my mother and father," she went on, rather serenely now. "They could not have been more sympathetic to you personally. Mother said that, after all, you were a mere man. Father said that, after all, you were only human. But circumstances were circumstances, and if some disaster had befallen Lee Ann, if she was murdered or if she was pregnant or if she was a suicide or whatever other horror you can conjure up, and it all came out, say, on our wedding day or came out afterward, for that matter—well, what then? *They* and *I* had to think of that. On the other hand, as I kept thinking, what if the wedding *was* called off? What then for me? The only power I had to save myself was to save you, and to save you by rescuing Lee Ann Deehart. It always came to that, and comes to that still. Don't you see, it was a question of how very much I had to lose and how little power I had to save myself. Because *I* had not set *my*self free the way those other girls have. One makes that choice at a much earlier age than this, I'm afraid. And so I knew already, Nat, and I know now what the only kind of power I can ever have must be."

She hesitated then. She was capable of phrasing what she said much more precisely. But it would have been indelicate, somehow, for her to have done so. And so I said it for her in my crude way: "You mean the power of a woman in a man's world."

She nodded and continued. "I had to protect *that.* Even if it had been *I* that broke our engagement, Nat, or even if you and I had been married before some second scandal broke, still I would have been a jilted, a rejected girl. And some part of my power to protect myself would be gone forever. Power, or strength, is what everybody must have some of if he—if she—is to survive in any kind of world. I have to protect and use whatever strength I have."

Caroline went on in that voice until we were back in Memphis and at her father's house on East Parkway. She kissed me before we got out of the car there, kissed me for my silence, I believe. I had said almost nothing during the whole of the long ride. And I think she has ever since been grateful to me for the silence I kept. Perhaps she mistook it for more understanding than I was capable of at the time. At any rate, I cannot help believing that it has much to do with the support and understanding—rather silent though it was—which she gave me when I made the great break in my life in my late thirties. Though it clearly meant that we must live on a somewhat more modest scale and live among people of a sort she was not used to, and even meant leaving Memphis forever behind us, the firmness with which she supported my decision, and the look in her eyes whenever I spoke of feeling I must make the change, seemed to say to me that she would dedicate her pride of power to the power of freedom I sought.

# ⁑ FLANNERY O'CONNOR

## (1925–1964)

For Flannery O'Connor, the modern secular age is Promethean and Faustian—we have taken our lives and the world into our own hands and we have given up our souls and spirits for worldly payoffs. Consequently, we have relinquished the old doctrines of sin, evil, and salvation and replaced them with the various therapies of medical science and psychology. As a devout Roman Catholic, O'Connor saw her fiction as an opportunity to assault the sensibilities of this age with intense, searing, often violent and grotesque, images of human spiritual distortion. Her stories are parables of spiritual crisis aimed at our blindness and deafness to the ultimate truths we have abandoned.

O'Connor was born in Savannah, Georgia, the only child of Roman Catholic parents. In 1938 the family moved to the town of Milledgeville, near Macon. In high school O'Connor wrote stories, drew cartoons, and made lithographs for the literary magazine and yearbook. In 1941 her father died of lupus, the disease that would take her own life in 1964.

O'Connor earned a bachelor's degree from the Georgia State College for Women in 1945. She earned an M.F.A. in 1947 from the prestigious Writer's Workshop of the University of Iowa. She then lived in New York City and Connecticut for several years. After being diagnosed with lupus in 1950, O'Connor returned to Milledgeville to live on her mother's dairy farm, where she wrote every day, and raised peacocks. When her health permitted it, she traveled and gave lectures at colleges.

O'Connor's stories appeared in many periodicals beginning in the late 1940s. Her first book was the novel *Wise Blood,* published in 1952. Her first collection of stories, *A Good Man Is Hard to Find,* came out in 1955. Her second collection, *Everything That Rises Must Converge,* appeared in 1965. Her *Complete Stories,* published in 1971, won the National Book Award for fiction in 1972. O'Connor's letters were published in 1979 under the title *The Habit of Being,* and her essays and lectures, entitled *Mystery and Manners,* appeared in 1969, edited by Sally and Robert Fitzgerald.

# A Good Man Is Hard to Find

> The dragon is by the side of the road, watching those who pass. Beware lest he devour you. We go to the Father of Souls, but it is necessary to pass by the dragon.
>
> —ST. CYRIL OF JERUSALEM

THE GRANDMOTHER didn't want to go to Florida. She wanted to visit some of her connections in east Tennessee and she was seizing at every chance to change Bailey's *train wreck waiting to happen

• lots of forshaddowing - clues everywhere



mind. Bailey was the son she lived with, her only boy. He was sitting on the edge of his chair at the table, bent over the orange sports section of the *Journal.* "Now look here, Bailey," she said, "see here, read this," and she stood with one hand on her thin hip and the other rattling the newspaper at his bald head. "Here this fellow that calls himself The Misfit is aloose from the Federal Pen and headed toward Florida and you read here what it says he did to these people. Just you read it. I wouldn't take my children in any direction with a criminal like that aloose in it. I couldn't answer to my conscience if I did."

Bailey didn't look up from his reading so she wheeled around then and faced the children's mother, a young woman in slacks, whose face was as broad and innocent as a cabbage and was tied around with a green headkerchief that had two points on the top like a rabbit's ears. She was sitting on the sofa, feeding the baby his apricots out of a jar. "The children have been to Florida before," the old lady said. "You all ought to take them somewhere else for a change so they would see different parts of the world and be broad. They never have been to east Tennessee."

The children's mother didn't seem to hear her but the eight-year-old boy, John Wesley, a stocky child with glasses, said, "If you don't want to go to Florida, why dontcha stay at home?" He and the little girl, June Star, were reading the funny papers on the floor.

"She wouldn't stay at home to be queen for a day," June Star said without raising her yellow head.

"Yes and what would you do if this fellow, The Misfit, caught you?" the grandmother asked.

"I'd smack his face," John Wesley said.

"She wouldn't stay at home for a million bucks," June Star said. "Afraid she'd miss something. She has to go everywhere we go."

"All right, Miss," the grandmother said. "Just remember that the next time you want me to curl your hair."

June Star said her hair was naturally curly.

The next morning the grandmother was the first one in the car, ready to go. She had her big black valise that looked like the head of a hippopotamus in one corner, and underneath it she was hiding a basket with Pitty Sing, the cat, in it. She didn't intend for the cat to be left alone in the house for three days because he would miss her too much and she was afraid he might brush against one of the gas burners and accidentally asphyxiate himself. Her son, Bailey, didn't like to arrive at a motel with a cat.

She sat in the middle of the back seat with John Wesley and June Star on either side of her. Bailey and the children's mother and the baby sat in front and they left Atlanta at eight forty-five with the mileage on the car at 55890. The grandmother wrote this down because she thought it would be interesting to say how many miles they had been when they got back. It took them twenty minutes to reach the outskirts of the city.

The old lady settled herself comfortably, removing her white cotton gloves and putting them up with her purse on the shelf in front of the back window. The children's mother still had on slacks and still had her head tied up in a green kerchief, but the grandmother had on a navy blue straw sailor hat with a bunch of white violets on the brim and a navy blue dress with a small white dot in the print. Her collars and cuffs were white organdy trimmed with lace and at her neckline she had pinned a purple spray of cloth violets containing a sachet. In case of an accident, anyone seeing her dead on the highway would know at once that she was a lady.

She said she thought it was going to be a good day for driving, neither too hot nor too cold, and she cautioned Bailey that the speed limit was fifty-five miles an hour and that the patrolmen hid themselves behind billboards and small clumps of trees and sped out after you before you had a chance to slow down. She pointed out interesting details of the scenery: Stone Mountain; the blue granite that in some places came up to both sides of the highway; the brilliant red clay banks slightly streaked with purple; and the various crops that made rows of green lace-work on the ground. The trees were full of silver-white sunlight and the meanest of them sparkled. The children were reading comic magazines and their mother had gone back to sleep.

"Let's go through Georgia fast so we won't have to look at it much," John Wesley said.

"If I were a little boy," said the grandmother, "I wouldn't talk about my native state that way. Tennessee has the mountains and Georgia has the hills."

"Tennessee is just a hillbilly dumping ground," John Wesley said, "and Georgia is a lousy state too."

"You said it," June Star said.

"In my time," said the grandmother, folding her thin veined fingers, "children were more respectful of their native states and their parents and everything else. People did right then. Oh look at the cute little pickaninny!" she said and pointed to a Negro child standing in the door of a shack. "Wouldn't that make a picture, now?" she asked and they all turned and looked at the little Negro out of the back window. He waved.

"He didn't have any britches on," June Star said.

"He probably didn't have any," the grandmother explained. "Little niggers in the country don't have things like we do. If I could paint, I'd paint that picture," she said.

The children exchanged comic books.

The grandmother offered to hold the baby and the children's mother passed him over the front seat to her. She set him on her knee and bounced him and told him about the things they were passing. She rolled her eyes and screwed up her mouth and stuck her leathery thin face into his smooth bland one. Occasionally he gave her a faraway smile. They passed a large cotton field with five or six graves fenced in the middle of it, like a small island. "Look at the graveyard!" the grandmother said, pointing it out. "That was the old family burying ground. That belonged to the plantation."

"Where's the plantation?" John Wesley asked.

"Gone with the Wind," said the grandmother. "Ha. Ha."

When the children finished all the comic books they had brought, they opened the lunch and ate it. The grandmother ate a peanut butter sandwich and an olive and would not let the children throw the box and the paper napkins out the window. When there was nothing else to do they played a game by choosing a cloud and making the other two guess what shape it suggested. John Wesley took one the shape of a cow and June Star guessed a cow and John Wesley said, no, an automobile, and June Star said he didn't play fair, and they began to slap each other over the grandmother.

The grandmother said she would tell them a story if they would keep quiet. When she told a story, she rolled her eyes and waved her head and was very dramatic. She said once when she was a maiden lady she had been courted by a Mr. Edgar Atkins Teagarden from Jasper, Georgia. She said he was a very good-looking man and a gentleman and that he brought her a watermelon every Saturday afternoon with his initials cut in it, E. A. T. Well, one Saturday, she said, Mr. Teagarden brought the watermelon and there was nobody at home and he left it on the front porch and returned in his buggy to Jasper, but she never got the watermelon, she said, because a nigger boy ate it when he saw the initials, E. A. T.! This story tickled John Wesley's funny bone and he giggled and giggled but June Star didn't think it was any good. She said she wouldn't marry a man that just brought her a watermelon on Saturday. The grandmother said she would have done well to marry Mr. Teagarden because he was a gentleman and had bought Coca-Cola stock when it first came out and that he had died only a few years ago, a very wealthy man.

They stopped at The Tower for barbecued sandwiches. The Tower was a part stucco and part wood filling station and dance hall set in a clearing outside of Timothy. A fat man named Red Sammy Butts ran it and there were signs stuck here and there on the building and for miles up and down the highway saying, TRY RED SAMMY'S FAMOUS BARBECUE. NONE LIKE FAMOUS RED SAMMY'S! RED SAM! THE FAT BOY WITH THE HAPPY LAUGH. A VETERAN! RED SAMMY'S YOUR MAN!

Red Sammy was lying on the bare ground outside The Tower with his head under a truck while a gray monkey about a foot high, chained to a small chinaberry tree, chattered nearby. The monkey sprang back into the tree and got on the highest limb as soon as he saw the children jump out of the car and run toward him.

Inside, The Tower was a long dark room with a counter at one end and tables at the other and dancing space in the middle. They all sat down at a board table next to the nickelodeon and Red Sam's wife, a tall burnt-brown woman with hair and eyes lighter than her skin, came and took their order. The children's mother put a dime in the machine and played "The Tennessee Waltz," and the grandmother said that tune always made her want to dance. She asked Bailey if he would like to dance but he only glared at her. He didn't have a naturally sunny disposition like she did and trips made him nervous. The grandmother's brown eyes were very bright. She swayed her head from side to side and pretended she was dancing in her chair. June Star said play something she could tap to so the children's mother put in another dime and played a fast number and June Star stepped out onto the dance floor and did her tap routine.

"Ain't she cute?" Red Sam's wife said, leaning over the counter. "Would you like to come be my little girl?"

"No I certainly wouldn't," June Star said. "I wouldn't live in a broken-down place like this for a million bucks!" and she ran back to the table.

"Ain't she cute?" the woman repeated, stretching her mouth politely.

"Aren't you ashamed?" hissed the grandmother.

Red Sam came in and told his wife to quit lounging on the counter and hurry up with these people's order. His khaki trousers reached just to his hip bones and his stomach hung over them like a sack of meal swaying under his shirt. He came over and sat down at a table nearby and let out a combination sigh and yodel. "You can't win," he said. "You can't win," and he wiped his sweating red face off with a gray handkerchief. "These days you don't know who to trust," he said. "Ain't that the truth?"

"People are certainly not nice like they used to be," said the grandmother.

"Two fellers come in here last week," Red Sammy said, "driving a Chrysler. It was a old beat-up car but it was a good one and these boys looked all right to me. Said they worked at the mill and you know I let them fellers charge the gas they bought? Now why did I do that?"

"Because you're a good man!" the grandmother said at once.

"Yes'm, I suppose so," Red Sam said as if he were struck with this answer.

His wife brought the orders, carrying the five plates all at once without a tray, two in each hand and one balanced on her arm. "It isn't a soul in this green world of God's that you can trust," she said. "And I don't count nobody out of that, not nobody," she repeated, looking at Red Sammy.

"Did you read about that criminal, The Misfit, that's escaped?" asked the grandmother.

"I wouldn't be a bit surprised if he didn't attack this place right here," said the woman. "If he hears about it being here, I wouldn't be none surprised to see him. If he hears it's two cent in the cash register, I wouldn't be a tall surprised if he. . . ."

"That'll do," Red Sam said. "Go bring these people their Co'-Colas," and the woman went off to get the rest of the order.

"A good man is hard to find," Red Sammy said. "Everything is getting terrible. I remember the day you could go off and leave your screen door unlatched. Not no more."

He and the grandmother discussed better times. The old lady said that in her opinion Europe was entirely to blame for the way things were now. She said the way Europe acted you would think we were made of money and Red Sam said it was no use talking about it, she was exactly right. The children ran outside into the white sunlight and looked at the monkey in the lacy chinaberry tree. He was busy catching fleas on himself and biting each one carefully between his teeth as if it were a delicacy.

They drove off again into the hot afternoon. The grandmother took cat naps and woke up every few minutes with her own snoring. Outside of Toombsboro she woke up and recalled an old plantation that she had visited in this neighborhood once when she was a young lady. She said the house had six white columns across the front and that there was an avenue of oaks leading up to it and two little wooden trellis arbors on either side in front where you sat down with your suitor after a stroll in the garden. She recalled exactly which road to turn off to get to it. She knew that Bailey would not be willing to lose any time looking at an old house, but the more she talked about it, the more she wanted to see it once again and find out if the little twin arbors were still standing. "There was a secret panel in this house," she said craftily, not telling the truth but wishing that she were, "and the story went that all the family silver was hidden in it when Sherman came through but it was never found. . . ."

"Hey!" John Wesley said. "Let's go see it! We'll find it! We'll poke all the woodwork and find it! Who lives there? Where do you turn off at? Hey Pop, can't we turn off there?"

"We never have seen a house with a secret panel!" June Star shrieked. "Let's go to the house with the secret panel! Hey Pop, can't we go see the house with the secret panel!"

"It's not far from here, I know," the grandmother said. "It won't take over twenty minutes."

Bailey was looking straight ahead. His jaw was as rigid as a horseshoe. "No." he said.

The children began to yell and scream that they wanted to see the house with the secret panel. John Wesley kicked the back of the front seat and June Star hung over her mother's shoulder and whined desperately into her ear that they never had any fun even on their vacation, that they could never do what THEY wanted to do. The baby began to scream and John Wesley kicked the back of the seat so hard that his father could feel the blows in his kidney.

"All right!" he shouted and drew the car to a stop at the side of the road. "Will you all shut up? Will you all just shut up for one second? If you don't shut up, we won't go anywhere."

"It would be very educational for them," the grandmother murmured.

"All right," Bailey said, "but get this: this is the only time we're going to stop for anything like this. This is the one and only time."

"The dirt road that you have to turn down is about a mile back," the grandmother directed. "I marked it when we passed."

"A dirt road," Bailey groaned.

After they had turned around and were headed toward the dirt road, the grandmother recalled other points about the house, the beautiful glass over the front doorway and the candle-lamp in the hall. John Wesley said that the secret panel was probably in the fireplace.

"You can't go inside this house," Bailey said. "You don't know who lives there."

"While you all talk to the people in front, I'll run around behind and get in a window," John Wesley suggested.

"We'll all stay in the car," his mother said.

They turned onto the dirt road and the car raced roughly along in a swirl of pink dust. The grandmother recalled the times when there were no paved roads and thirty miles was a day's journey. The dirt road was hilly and there were sudden washes in it and sharp curves on dangerous embankments. All at once they would be on a hill, looking down over the blue tops of trees for miles around, then the next minute, they would be in a red depression with the dust-coated trees looking down on them.

"This place had better turn up in a minute," Bailey said, "or I'm going to turn around."

The road looked as if no one had traveled on it for months.

"It's not much farther," the grandmother said and just as she said it, a horrible thought came to her. The thought was so embarrassing that she turned red in the face and her eyes dilated and her feet jumped up, upsetting her valise in the corner. The instant the valise moved, the newspaper top she had over the basket under it rose with a snarl and Pitty Sing, the cat, sprang onto Bailey's shoulder.

The children were thrown to the floor and their mother, clutching the baby, was thrown out the door onto the ground; the old lady was thrown into the front seat. The car turned over once and landed right-side-up in a gulch off the side of the road. Bailey remained in the driver's seat with the cat—gray-striped with a broad white face and an orange nose—clinging to his neck like a caterpillar.

As soon as the children saw they could move their arms and legs, they scrambled out of the car, shouting, "We've had an ACCIDENT!" The grandmother was curled up under the dashboard, hoping she was injured so that Bailey's wrath would not come down on her all at once. The horrible thought she had before the accident was that the house she had remembered so vividly was not in Georgia but in Tennessee.

Bailey removed the cat from his neck with both hands and flung it out the window against the side of a pine tree. Then he got out of the car and started looking for the children's mother. She was sitting against the side of the red gutted ditch, holding the screaming baby, but she only had a cut down her face and a broken shoulder. "We've had an ACCIDENT!" the children screamed in a frenzy of delight.

"But nobody's killed," June Star said with disappointment as the grandmother limped out of the car, her hat still pinned to her head but the broken front brim standing up at a jaunty angle and the violet spray hanging off the side. They all sat down in the ditch, except the children, to recover from the shock. They were all shaking.

"Maybe a car will come along," said the children's mother hoarsely.

"I believe I have injured an organ," said the grandmother, pressing her side, but no one answered her. Bailey's teeth were clattering. He had on a yellow sport shirt with bright blue parrots designed in it and his face was as yellow as the shirt. The grandmother decided that she would not mention that the house was in Tennessee.

The road was about ten feet above and they could only see the tops of the trees on the other side of it. Behind the ditch they were sitting in there were more woods, tall and dark and deep. In a few minutes they saw a car some distance away on top of a hill, coming slowly as if the occupants were watching them. The grandmother stood up and waved both arms dramatically to attract their attention. The car continued to come on slowly, disappeared around a bend and appeared again, moving even slower, on top of the hill they had gone over. It was a big black battered hearse-like automobile. There were three men in it.

It came to a stop just over them and for some minutes, the driver looked down with a steady expressionless gaze to where they were sitting, and didn't speak. Then he turned his head and muttered something to the other two and they got out. One was a fat boy in black trousers and a red sweat shirt with a silver stallion embossed on the front of it. He moved around on the right side of them and stood staring, his mouth partly open in a kind of loose grin. The other had on khaki pants and a blue striped coat and a gray hat pulled very low, hiding most of his face. He came around slowly on the left side. Neither spoke.

The driver got out of the car and stood by the side of it, looking down at them. He was an older man than the other two. His hair was just beginning to gray and he wore silver-rimmed spectacles that gave him a scholarly look. He had a long creased face and didn't have on any shirt or undershirt. He had on blue jeans that were too tight for him and was holding a black hat and a gun. The two boys also had guns.

"We've had an ACCIDENT!" the children screamed.

The grandmother had the peculiar feeling that the bespectacled man was someone she knew. His face was as familiar to her as if she had known him all her life but she could not recall who he was. He moved away from the car and began to come down the embankment, placing his feet carefully so that he wouldn't slip. He had on tan and white shoes and no socks, and his ankles were red and thin. "Good afternoon," he said. "I see you all had you a little spill."

"We turned over twice!" said the grandmother.

"Oncet," he corrected. "We seen it happen. Try their car and see will it run, Hiram," he said quietly to the boy with the gray hat.

"What you got that gun for?" John Wesley asked. "Whatcha gonna do with that gun?"

"Lady," the man said to the children's mother, "would you mind calling them children to sit down by you? Children make me nervous. I want all you all to sit down right together there where you're at."

"What are you telling US what to do for?" June Star asked.

Behind them the line of woods gaped like a dark open mouth. "Come here," said the mother.

"Look here now," Bailey said suddenly, "we're in a predicament! We're in. . . ."

The grandmother shrieked. She scrambled to her feet and stood staring. "You're The Misfit!" she said. "I recognized you at once!"

"Yes'm," the man said, smiling slightly as if he were pleased in spite of himself to be known, "but it would have been better for all of you, lady, if you hadn't of reckernized me."

Bailey turned his head sharply and said something to his mother that shocked even the children. The old lady began to cry and The Misfit reddened.

"Lady," he said, "don't you get upset. Sometimes a man says things he don't mean. I don't reckon he meant to talk to you thataway."

"You wouldn't shoot a lady, would you?" the grandmother said and removed a clean handkerchief from her cuff and began to slap at her eyes with it.

The Misfit pointed the toe of his shoe into the ground and made a little hole and then covered it up again. "I would hate to have to," he said.

"Listen," the grandmother almost screamed, "I know you're a good man. You don't look a bit like you have common blood. I know you must come from nice people!"

"Yes mam," he said, "finest people in the world." When he smiled he showed a row of strong white teeth. "God never made a finer woman than my mother and my daddy's heart was pure gold," he said. The boy with the red sweat shirt had come around behind them and was standing with his gun at his hip. The Misfit squatted down on the ground. "Watch them children, Bobby Lee," he said. "You know they make me nervous." He looked at the six of them huddled together in front of him and he seemed to be embarrassed as if he couldn't think of anything to say. "Ain't a cloud in the sky," he remarked, looking up at it. "Don't see no sun but don't see no cloud neither."

"Yes, it's a beautiful day," said the grandmother. "Listen," she said, "You shouldn't call yourself The Misfit because I know you're a good man at heart. I can just look at you and tell."

"Hush!" Bailey yelled. "Hush! Everybody shut up and let me handle this!" He was squatting in the position of a runner about to sprint forward but he didn't move.

"I pre-chate that, lady," The Misfit said and drew a little circle in the ground with the butt of his gun.

"It'll take a half a hour to fix this here car," Hiram called, looking over the raised hood of it.

"Well, first you and Bobby Lee get him and that little boy to step over yonder with you." The Misfit said, pointing to Bailey and John Wesley, "The boys want to ast you something," he said to Bailey. "Would you mind stepping back in them woods there with them?"

"Listen," Bailey began, "we're in a terrible predicament! Nobody realizes what this is," and his voice cracked. His eyes were as blue and intense as the parrots in his shirt and he remained perfectly still.

The grandmother reached up to adjust her hat brim as if she were going to the woods with him but it came off in her hand. She stood staring at it and after a second she let it fall to the ground. Hiram pulled Bailey up by the arm as if he were assisting an old man. John Wesley caught hold of his father's hand and Bobby Lee followed. They went off toward the woods and just as they reached the dark edge, Bailey turned and supporting himself against a gray naked pine trunk, he shouted, "I'll be back in a minute, Mamma, wait on me!"

"Come back this instant!" his mother shrilled but they all disappeared into the woods.

"Bailey Boy!" the grandmother called in a tragic voice but she found she was looking at The Misfit squatting on the ground in front of her. "I just know you're a good man," she said desperately. "You're not a bit common!"

"Nome, I ain't a good man," The Misfit said after a second as if he had considered her statement carefully, "but I ain't the worst in the world neither. My daddy said I was a different breed of dog from my brothers and sisters. 'You know,' Daddy said, 'it's some that can live their whole life out without asking about it and it's others has to know why it is, and this boy is one of the latters. He's going to be into everything!' " He put on his black hat and looked up suddenly and then away deep into the woods as if he were embarrassed again. "I'm sorry I don't have on a shirt before you ladies," he said, hunching his shoulders slightly. "We buried our clothes that we had on when we escaped and we're just making do until we can get better. We borrowed these from some folks we met," he explained.

"That's perfectly all right," the grandmother said. "Maybe Bailey has an extra shirt in his suitcase."

"I'll look and see terrectly," The Misfit said.

"Where are they taking him?" the children's mother screamed.

"Daddy was a card himself," The Misfit said. "You couldn't put anything over on him. He never got in trouble with the Authorities though. Just had the knack of handling them."

"You could be honest too if you'd only try," said the grandmother. "Think how wonderful it would be to settle down and live a comfortable life and not have to think about somebody chasing you all the time."

The Misfit kept scratching in the ground with the butt of his gun as if he were thinking about it. "Yes'm, somebody is always after you," he murmured.

The grandmother noticed how thin his shoulder blades were just behind his hat because she was standing up looking down at him. "Do you ever pray?" she asked.

He shook his head. All she saw was the black hat wiggle between his shoulder blades. "Nome," he said.

There was a pistol shot from the woods, followed closely by another. Then silence. The old lady's head jerked around. She could hear the wind move through the tree tops like a long satisfied insuck of breath. "Bailey Boy!" she called.

"I was a gospel singer for a while," The Misfit said. "I been most everything. Been in the arm service, both land and sea, at home and abroad, been twict married, been an undertaker, been with the railroads, plowed Mother Earth, been in a tornado, seen a man burnt alive oncet," and he looked up at the children's mother and the little girl who were sitting close together, their faces white and their eyes glassy; "I even seen a woman flogged," he said.

"Pray, pray," the grandmother began, "pray, pray. . . ."

"I never was a bad boy that I remember of," The Misfit said in an almost dreamy voice, "but somewheres along the line I done something wrong and got sent to the penitentiary. I was buried alive," and he looked up and held her attention to him by a steady stare.

"That's when you should have started to pray," she said. "What did you do to get sent to the penitentiary, that first time?"

"Turn to the right, it was a wall," The Misfit said, looking up again at the cloudless sky. "Turn to the left, it was a wall. Look up it was a ceiling, look down it was a floor. I forgot what I done, lady. I set there and set there, trying to remember what it was I done and I ain't recalled it to this day. Oncet in a while, I would think it was coming to me, but it never come."

"Maybe they put you in by mistake," the old lady said vaguely.

"Nome," he said. "It wasn't no mistake. They had the papers on me."

"You must have stolen something," she said.

The Misfit sneered slightly. "Nobody had nothing I wanted," he said. "It was a head-doctor at the penitentiary said what I had done was kill my daddy but I known that for a lie. My daddy died in nineteen ought nineteen of the epidemic flu and I never had a thing to do with it. He was buried in the Mount Hopewell Baptist churchyard and you can see for yourself."

"If you would pray," the old lady said, "Jesus would help you."

"That's right," The Misfit said.

"Well then, why don't you pray?" she asked trembling with delight suddenly.

"I don't want no hep," he said. "I'm doing all right by myself."

Bobby Lee and Hiram came ambling back from the woods. Bobby Lee was dragging a yellow shirt with bright blue parrots in it.

"Throw me that shirt, Bobby Lee," The Misfit said. The shirt came flying at him and landed on his shoulder and he put it on. The grandmother couldn't name what the shirt reminded her of. "No, lady," The Misfit said while he was buttoning it up, "I found out the crime don't matter. You can do one thing or you can do another, kill a man or take a tire off his car, because sooner or later you're going to forget what it was you done and just be punished for it."

The children's mother had begun to make heaving noises as if she couldn't get her breath. "Lady," he asked, "would you and that little girl like to step off yonder with Bobby Lee and Hiram and join your husband?"

"Yes, thank you," the mother said faintly. Her left arm dangled helplessly and she was holding the baby, who had gone to sleep, in the other. "Hep that lady up, Hiram," The Misfit said as she struggled to climb out of the ditch, "and Bobby Lee, you hold onto that little girl's hand."

"I don't want to hold hands with him," June Star said. "He reminds me of a pig."

The fat boy blushed and laughed and caught her by the arm and pulled her off into the woods after Hiram and her mother.

Alone with The Misfit, the grandmother found that she had lost her voice. There was not a cloud in the sky nor any sun. There was nothing around her but woods. She wanted to tell him that he must pray. She opened and closed her mouth several times before anything came out. Finally she found herself saying, "Jesus, Jesus," meaning, Jesus will help you, but the way she was saying it, it sounded as if she might be cursing.

"Yes'm," The Misfit said as if he agreed. "Jesus thown everything off balance. It was the same case with Him as with me except He hadn't committed any crime and they could prove I had committed one because they had the papers on me. Of course," he said, "they never shown me my papers. That's why I sign myself now. I said long ago, you get your signature and sign everything you do and keep a copy of it. Then you'll know what you done and you can hold up the crime to the punishment and see do they match and in the end you'll have something to prove you ain't been treated right. I call myself The Misfit," he said, "because I can't make what all I done wrong fit what all I gone through in punishment."

There was a piercing scream from the woods, followed closely by a pistol report. "Does it seem right to you, lady, that one is punished a heap and another ain't punished at all?"

"Jesus!" the old lady cried. "You've got good blood! I know you wouldn't shoot a lady! I know you come from nice people! Pray! Jesus, you ought not to shoot a lady. I'll give you all the money I've got!"

"Lady," The Misfit said, looking beyond her far into the woods, "there never was a body that give the undertaker a tip."

There were two more pistol reports and the grandmother raised her head like a parched old turkey hen crying for water and called, "Bailey Boy, Bailey Boy!" as if her heart would break.

"Jesus was the only One that ever raised the dead," The Misfit continued, "and He shouldn't have done it. He thrown everything off balance. If He did what He said, then it's nothing for you to do but throw away everything and follow Him, and if He didn't, then it's nothing for you to do but enjoy the few minutes you got left the best you can by killing somebody or burning down his house or doing some other meanness to him. No pleasure but meanness," he said and his voice had become almost a snarl.

"Maybe He didn't raise the dead," the old lady mumbled, not knowing what she was saying and feeling so dizzy that she sank down in the ditch with her legs twisted under her.

"I wasn't there so I can't say He didn't," The Misfit said. "I wisht I had of been there," he said, hitting the ground with his fist. "It ain't right I wasn't there because if I had of been there I would of known. Listen lady," he said in a high voice, "if I had of been there I would of known and I wouldn't be like I am now." His voice seemed about to crack and the grandmother's head cleared for an instant. She saw the man's face twisted close to her own as if he were going to cry and she murmured, "Why you're one of my babies. You're one of my own children!" She reached out and touched him on the shoulder. The Misfit sprang back as if a snake had bitten him and shot her three times through the chest. Then he put his gun down on the ground and took off his glasses and began to clean them.

Hiram and Bobby Lee returned from the woods and stood over the ditch, looking down at the grandmother who half sat and half lay in a puddle of blood with her legs crossed under her like a child's and her face smiling up at the cloudless sky.

Without his glasses, The Misfit's eyes were red-rimmed and pale and defenseless-looking. "Take her off and throw her where you thrown the others," he said, picking up the cat that was rubbing itself against his leg.

"She was a talker, wasn't she?" Bobby Lee said, sliding down the ditch with a yodel.

"She would of been a good woman," The Misfit said, "if it had been somebody there to shoot her every minute of her life." →

"Some fun!" Bobby Lee said.

"Shut up, Bobby Lee," The Misfit said. "It's no real pleasure in life."

the grandmother became honest at last. Started to think of others not just herself.

## Revelation

"or" she was just trying to manipulate the Misfit.

THE DOCTOR'S waiting room, which was very small, was almost full when the Turpins entered and Mrs. Turpin, who was very large, made it look even smaller by her presence. She stood looming at the head of the magazine table set in the center of it, a living demonstration that the room was inadequate and ridiculous. Her little bright black eyes took in all the patients as she sized up the seating situation. There was one vacant chair and a place on the sofa occupied by a blond child in a dirty blue romper who should have been told to move over and make room for the lady. He was five or six, but Mrs. Turpin saw at once that no one was going to tell him to move over. He was slumped down in the seat, his arms idle at his sides and his eyes idle in his head; his nose ran unchecked.

Mrs. Turpin put a firm hand on Claud's shoulder and said in a voice that included anyone who wanted to listen, "Claud, you sit in that chair there," and gave him a push down into the vacant one. Claud was florid and bald and sturdy, somewhat shorter than Mrs. Turpin, but he sat down as if he were accustomed to doing what she told him to.

Mrs. Turpin remained standing. The only man in the room besides Claud was a lean stringy old fellow with a rusty hand spread out on each knee, whose eyes were closed as if he were asleep or dead or pretending to be so as not to get up and offer her his seat. Her gaze settled agreeably on a well-dressed grey-haired lady whose eyes met hers and whose expression said: if that child belonged to me, he would have some manners and move over—there's plenty of room there for you and him too.

Claud looked up with a sigh and made as if to rise.

"Sit down," Mrs. Turpin said. "You know you're not supposed to stand on that leg. He has an ulcer on his leg," she explained.

Claud lifted his foot onto the magazine table and rolled his trouser leg up to reveal a purple swelling on a plump marble-white calf.

"My!" the pleasant lady said. "How did you do that?"

"A cow kicked him," Mrs. Turpin said.

"Goodness!" said the lady.

Claud rolled his trouser leg down.

"Maybe the little boy would move over," the lady suggested, but the child did not stir.

"Somebody will be leaving in a minute," Mrs. Turpin said. She could not understand why a doctor—with as much money as they made charging five dollars a day to just stick their head in the hospital door and look at you—couldn't afford a decent-sized waiting room. This one was hardly bigger than a garage. The table was cluttered with limp-looking magazines and at one end of it there was a big green glass ash tray full of cigaret butts and cotton wads with little blood spots on them. If she had had anything to do with the running of the place, that would have been emptied every so often. There were no chairs against the wall at the head of the room. It had a rectangular-shaped panel in it that permitted a view of the office where the nurse came and went and the secretary listened to the radio. A plastic fern in a gold pot sat in the opening and trailed its fronds down almost to the floor. The radio was softly playing gospel music.

Just then the inner door opened and a nurse with the highest stack of yellow hair Mrs. Turpin had ever seen put her face in the crack and called for the next patient. The woman sitting beside Claud grasped the two arms of her chair and hoisted herself up; she pulled her dress free from her legs and lumbered through the door where the nurse had disappeared.

Mrs. Turpin eased into the vacant chair, which held her tight as a corset. "I wish I could reduce," she said, and rolled her eyes and gave a comic sigh.

"Oh, *you* aren't fat," the stylish lady said.

"Ooooo I am too," Mrs. Turpin said. "Claud he eats all he wants to and never weighs over one hundred and seventy-five pounds, but me I just look at something good to eat and I gain some weight," and her stomach and shoulders shook with laughter. "You can eat all you want to, can't you, Claud?" she asked, turning to him.

Claud only grinned.

"Well, as long as you have such a good disposition," the stylish lady said, "I don't think it makes a bit of difference what size you are. You just can't beat a good disposition."

Next to her was a fat girl of eighteen or nineteen, scowling into a thick blue book which Mrs. Turpin saw was entitled *Human Development.* The girl raised her head and directed her scowl at Mrs. Turpin as if she did not like her looks. She appeared annoyed that anyone should speak while she tried to read. The poor girl's face was blue with acne and Mrs. Turpin thought how pitiful it was to have a face like that at that age. She gave the girl a friendly smile but the girl only scowled the harder. Mrs. Turpin herself was fat but she had always had good skin, and, though she was forty-seven years old, there was not a wrinkle in her face except around her eyes from laughing too much.

Next to the ugly girl was the child, still in exactly the same position, and next to him was a thin leathery old woman in a cotton print dress. She and Claud had three sacks of chicken feed in their pump house that was in the same print. She had seen from the first that the child belonged with the old woman. She could tell by the way they sat—kind of vacant and white-trashy, as if they would sit there until Doomsday if nobody called and told them to get up. And at right angles but next to the well-dressed pleasant lady was a lank-faced woman who was certainly the child's mother. She had on a yellow sweat shirt and wine-colored slacks, both gritty-looking, and the rims of her lips were stained with snuff. Her dirty yellow hair was tied behind with a little piece of red paper ribbon. Worse than niggers any day, Mrs. Turpin thought.

The gospel hymn playing was, "When I looked up and He looked down," and Mrs. Turpin, who knew it, supplied the last line mentally, "And wona these days I know I'll we-eara crown."

Without appearing to, Mrs. Turpin always noticed people's feet. The well-dressed lady had on red and grey suede shoes to match her dress. Mrs. Turpin had on her good black patent leather pumps. The ugly girl had on Girl Scout shoes and heavy socks. The old woman had on tennis shoes and the white-trashy mother had on what appeared to be bedroom slippers, black straw with gold braid threaded through them—exactly what you would have expected her to have on.

Sometimes at night when she couldn't go to sleep, Mrs. Turpin would occupy herself with the question of who she would have chosen to be if she couldn't have been herself. If Jesus had said to her before he made her, "There's only two places available for you. You can either be a nigger or white-trash," what would she have said? "Please, Jesus, please," she would have said, "just let me wait until there's another place available," and he would have said, "No, you have to go right now and I have only those two places so make up your mind." She would have wiggled and squirmed and begged and pleaded but it would have been no use and finally she would have said, "All right, make me a nigger then—but that don't mean a trashy one." And he would have made her a neat clean respectable Negro woman, herself but black.

Next to the child's mother was a red-headed youngish woman, reading one of the magazines and working a piece of chewing gum, hell for leather, as Claud would say. Mrs. Turpin could not see the woman's feet. She was not white-trash, just common. Sometimes Mrs. Turpin occupied herself at night naming the classes of people. On the bottom of the heap were most colored people, not the kind she would have been if she had been one, but most of them; then next to them—not above, just away from—were the white-trash; then above them were the home-owners, and above them the home-and-land owners, to which she and Claud belonged. Above she and Claud were people with a lot of money and much bigger houses and much more land. But here the complexity of it would begin to bear in on her, for some of the people with a lot of money were common and ought to be below she and Claud and some of the people who had good blood had lost their money and had to rent and then there were colored people who owned their homes and land as well. There was a colored dentist in town who had two red Lincolns and a swimming pool and a farm with registered white-face cattle on it. Usually by the time she had fallen asleep all the classes of people were moiling and roiling around in her head, and she would dream they were all crammed in together in a box car, being ridden off to be put in a gas oven.

"That's a beautiful clock," she said and nodded to her right. It was a big wall clock, the face encased in a brass sunburst.

"Yes, it's very pretty," the stylish lady said agreeably. "And right on the dot too," she added, glancing at her watch.

The ugly girl beside her cast an eye upward at the clock, smirked, then looked directly at Mrs. Turpin and smirked again. Then she returned her eyes to her book. She was obviously the lady's daughter because, although they didn't look anything alike as to disposition, they both had the same shape of face and the same blue eyes. On the lady they sparkled pleasantly but in the girl's seared face they appeared alternately to smolder and to blaze.

What if Jesus had said, "All right, you can be white-trash or a nigger or ugly"!

Mrs. Turpin felt an awful pity for the girl, though she thought it was one thing to be ugly and another to act ugly.

The woman with the snuff-stained lips turned around in her chair and looked up at the clock. Then she turned back and appeared to look a little to the side of Mrs. Turpin. There was a cast in one of her eyes. "You want to know wher you can get you one of themther clocks?" she asked in a loud voice.

"No, I already have a nice clock," Mrs. Turpin said. Once somebody like her got a leg in the conversation, she would be all over it.

"You can get you one with green stamps," the woman said. "That's most likely wher he got hisn. Save you up enough, you can get you most anythang. I got me some joo'ry."

Ought to have got you a wash rag and some soap, Mrs. Turpin thought.

"I get contour sheets with mine," the pleasant lady said.

The daughter slammed her book shut. She looked straight in front of her, directly through Mrs. Turpin and on through the yellow curtain and the plate glass window which made the wall behind her. The girl's eyes seemed lit all of a sudden with a peculiar light, an unnatural light like night road signs give. Mrs. Turpin turned her head to see if there was anything going on outside that she should see, but she could not see anything. Figures passing cast only a pale shadow through the curtain. There was no reason the girl should single her out for her ugly looks.

"Miss Finley," the nurse said, cracking the door. The gum-chewing woman got up and passed in front of her and Claud and went into the office. She had on red high-heeled shoes.

Directly across the table, the ugly girl's eyes were fixed on Mrs. Turpin as if she had some very special reason for disliking her.

"This is wonderful weather, isn't it?" the girl's mother said.

"It's good weather for cotton if you can get the niggers to pick it," Mrs. Turpin said, "but niggers don't want to pick cotton any more. You can't get the white folks to pick it and now you can't get the niggers—because they got to be right up there with the white folks."

"They gonna *try* anyways," the white-trash woman said, leaning forward.

"Do you have one of those cotton-picking machines?" the pleasant lady asked.

"No," Mrs. Turpin said, "they leave half the cotton in the field. We don't have much cotton anyway. If you want to make it farming now, you have to have a little of everything. We got a couple of acres of cotton and a few hogs and chickens and just enough white-face that Claud can look after them himself."

"One thang I don't want," the white-trash woman said, wiping her mouth with the back of her hand. "Hogs. Nasty stinking things, a-gruntin and a-rootin all over the place."

Mrs. Turpin gave her the merest edge of her attention. "Our hogs are not dirty and they don't stink," she said. "They're cleaner than some children I've seen. Their feet never touch the ground. We have a pig-parlor—that's where you raise them on concrete," she explained to the pleasant lady, "and Claud scoots them down with the hose every afternoon and washes off the floor." Cleaner by far than that child right there, she thought. Poor nasty little thing. He had not moved except to put the thumb of his dirty hand into his mouth.

The woman turned her face away from Mrs. Turpin. "I know I wouldn't scoot down no hog with no hose," she said to the wall.

You wouldn't have no hog to scoot down, Mrs. Turpin said to herself.

"A-gruntin and a-rootin and a-groanin," the woman muttered.

"We got a little of everything," Mrs. Turpin said to the pleasant lady. "It's no use in having more than you can handle yourself with help like it is. We found enough niggers to pick our cotton this year but Claud he has to go after them and take them home again in the evening. They can't walk that half a mile. No they can't. I tell you," she said and laughed merrily, "I sure am tired of buttering up niggers, but you got to love em if you want em to work for you. When they come in the morning, I run out and I say, 'Hi yawl this morning?' and when Claud drives them off to the field I just wave to beat the band and they just wave back." And she waved her hand rapidly to illustrate.

"Like you read out of the same book," the lady said, showing she understood perfectly.

"Child, yes," Mrs. Turpin said. "And when they come in from the field, I run out with a bucket of icewater. That's the way it's going to be from now on," she said. "You may as well face it."

"One thang I know," the white-trash woman said. "Two thangs I ain't going to do: love no niggers or scoot down no hog with no hose." And she let out a bark of contempt.

The look that Mrs. Turpin and the pleasant lady exchanged indicated they both understood that you had to *have* certain things before you could *know* certain things. But every time Mrs. Turpin exchanged a look with the lady, she was aware that the ugly girl's peculiar eyes were still on her, and she had trouble bringing her attention back to the conversation.

"When you got something," she said, "you got to look after it." And when you ain't got a thing but breath and britches, she added to herself, you can afford to come to town every morning and just sit on the Court House coping and spit.

A grotesque revolving shadow passed across the curtain behind her and was thrown palely on the opposite wall. Then a bicycle clattered down against the outside of the building. The door opened and a colored boy glided in with a tray from the drug store. It had two large red and white paper cups on it with tops on them. He was a tall, very black boy in discolored white pants and a green nylon shirt. He was chewing gum slowly, as if to music. He set the tray down in the office opening next to the fern and stuck his head through to look for the secretary. She was not in there. He rested his arms on the ledge and waited, his narrow bottom stuck out, swaying slowly to the left and right. He raised a hand over his head and scratched the base of his skull.

"You see that button there, boy?" Mrs. Turpin said. "You can punch that and she'll come. She's probably in the back somewhere."

"Is thas right?" the boy said agreeably, as if he had never seen the button before. He leaned to the right and put his finger on it. "She sometime out," he said and twisted around to face his audience, his elbows behind him on the counter. The nurse appeared and he twisted back again. She handed him a dollar and he rooted in his pocket and made the change and counted it out to her. She gave him fifteen cents for a tip and he went out with the empty tray. The heavy door swung to slowly and closed at length with the sound of suction. For a moment no one spoke.

"They ought to send all them niggers back to Africa," the white-trash woman said. "That's wher they come from in the first place."

"Oh, I couldn't do without my good colored friends," the pleasant lady said.

"There's a heap of things worse than a nigger," Mrs. Turpin agreed. "It's all kinds of them just like it's all kinds of us."

"Yes, and it takes all kinds to make the world go round," the lady said in her musical voice.

As she said it, the raw-complexioned girl snapped her teeth together. Her lower lip turned downwards and inside out, revealing the pale pink inside of her mouth. After a second it rolled back up. It was the ugliest face Mrs. Turpin had ever seen anyone make and for a moment she was certain that the girl had made it at her. She was looking at her as if she had known and disliked her all her life—all of Mrs. Turpin's life, it seemed too, not just all the girl's life. Why, girl, I don't even know you, Mrs. Turpin said silently.

She forced her attention back to the discussion. "It wouldn't be practical to send them back to Africa," she said. "They wouldn't want to go. They got it too good here."

"Wouldn't be what they wanted—if I had anythang to do with it," the woman said.

"It wouldn't be a way in the world you could get all the niggers back over there," Mrs. Turpin said. "They'd be hiding out and lying down and turning sick on you and wailing and hollering and raring and pitching. It wouldn't be a way in the world to get them over there."

"They got over here," the trashy woman said. "Get back like they got over."

"It wasn't so many of them then," Mrs. Turpin explained.

The woman looked at Mrs. Turpin as if here was an idiot indeed but Mrs. Turpin was not bothered by the look, considering where it came from.

"Nooo," she said, "they're going to stay here where they can go to New York and marry white folks and improve their color. That's what they all want to do, every one of them, improve their color."

"You know what comes of that, don't you?" Claud asked.

"No, Claud, what?" Mrs. Turpin said.

Claud's eyes twinkled. "White-faced niggers," he said with never a smile.

Everybody in the office laughed except the white-trash and the ugly girl. The girl gripped the book in her lap with white fingers. The trashy woman looked around her from face to face as if she thought they were all idiots. The old woman in the feed sack dress continued to gaze expressionless across the floor at the high-top shoes of the man opposite her, the one who had been pretending to be asleep when the Turpins came in. He was laughing heartily, his hands still spread out on his knees. The child had fallen to the side and was lying now almost face down in the old woman's lap.

While they recovered from their laughter, the nasal chorus on the radio kept the room from silence.

You go to blank blank
And I'll go to mine
But we'll all blank along
To-geth-ther,

And all along the blank
We'll hep eachother out
Smile-ling in any kind of
Weath-ther!

Mrs. Turpin didn't catch every word but she caught enough to agree with the spirit of the song and it turned her thoughts sober. To help anybody out that needed it was her philosophy of life. She never spared herself when she found somebody in need, whether they were white or black, trash or decent. And of all she had to be thankful for, she was most thankful that this was so. If Jesus had said, "You can be high society and have all the money you want and be thin and svelte-like, but you can't be a good woman with it," she would have had to say, "Well don't make me that then. Make me a good woman and it don't matter what else, how fat or how ugly or how poor!" Her heart rose. He had not made her a nigger or white-trash or ugly! He had made her herself and given her a little of everything. Jesus, thank you! she said. Thank you thank you thank you! Whenever she counted her blessings she felt as buoyant as if she weighed one hundred and twenty-five pounds instead of one hundred and eighty.

"What's wrong with your little boy?" the pleasant lady asked the white-trashy woman.

"He has a ulcer," the woman said proudly. "He ain't give me a minute's peace since he was born. Him and her are just alike," she said, nodding at the old woman, who was running her leathery fingers through the child's pale hair. "Look like I can't get nothing down them two but Co' Cola and candy."

That's all you try to get down em, Mrs. Turpin said to herself. Too lazy to light the fire. There was nothing you could tell her about people like them that she didn't know already. And it was not just that they didn't have anything. Because if you gave them everything, in two weeks it would all be broken or filthy or they would have chopped it up for lightwood. She knew all this from her own experience. Help them you must, but help them you couldn't.

All at once the ugly girl turned her lips inside out again. Her eyes were fixed like two drills on Mrs. Turpin. This time there was no mistaking that there was something urgent behind them.

Girl, Mrs. Turpin exclaimed silently, I haven't done a thing to you! The girl might be confusing her with somebody else. There was no need to sit by and let herself be intimidated. "You must be in college," she said boldly, looking directly at the girl. "I see you reading a book there."

The girl continued to stare and pointedly did not answer.

Her mother blushed at this rudeness. "The lady asked you a question, Mary Grace," she said under her breath.

"I have ears," Mary Grace said.

The poor mother blushed again. "Mary Grace goes to Wellesley College," she explained. She twisted one of the buttons on her dress. "In Massachusetts," she added with a grimace. "And in the summer she just keeps right on studying. Just reads all the time, a real book worm. She's done real well at Wellesley; she's taking English and Math and History and Psychology and Social Studies," she rattled on, "and I think it's too much. I think she ought to get out and have fun."

The girl looked as if she would like to hurl them all through the plate glass window.

"Way up north," Mrs. Turpin murmured and thought, well, it hasn't done much for her manners.

"I'd almost rather to have him sick," the white-trash woman said, wrenching the attention back to herself. "He's so mean when he ain't. Look like some children just take natural to meanness. It's some gets bad when they get sick but he was the opposite. Took sick and turned good. He don't give me no trouble now. It's me waitin to see the doctor," she said.

If I was going to send anybody back to Africa, Mrs. Turpin thought, it would be your kind, woman. "Yes, indeed," she said aloud, but looking up at the ceiling, "it's a heap of things worse than a nigger." And dirtier than a hog, she added to herself.

"I think people with bad dispositions are more to be pitied than anyone on earth," the pleasant lady said in a voice that was decidedly thin.

"I thank the Lord he has blessed me with a good one," Mrs. Turpin said. "The day has never dawned that I couldn't find something to laugh at."

"Not since she married me anyways," Claud said with a comical straight face.

Everybody laughed except the girl and the white-trash.

Mrs. Turpin's stomach shook. "He's such a caution," she said, "that I can't help but laugh at him."

The girl made a loud ugly noise through her teeth.

Her mother's mouth grew thin and tight. "I think the worst thing in the world," she said, "is an ungrateful person. To have everything and not appreciate it. I know a girl," she said, "who has parents who would give her anything, a little brother who loves her dearly, who is getting a good education, who wears the best clothes, but who can never say a kind word to anyone, who never smiles, who just criticizes and complains all day long."

"Is she too old to paddle?" Claud asked.

The girl's face was almost purple.

"Yes," the lady said, "I'm afraid there's nothing to do but leave her to her folly. Some day she'll wake up and it'll be too late."

"It never hurt anyone to smile," Mrs. Turpin said. "It just makes you feel better all over."

"Of course," the lady said sadly, "but there are just some people you can't tell anything to. They can't take criticism."

"If it's one thing I am," Mrs. Turpin said with feeling, "it's grateful. When I think who all I could have been besides myself and what all I got, a little of everything, and a good disposition besides, I just feel like shouting, 'Thank you, Jesus, for making everything the way it is!' It could have been different!" For one thing, somebody else could have got Claud. At the thought of this, she was flooded with gratitude and a terrible pang of joy ran through her. "Oh thank you, Jesus, Jesus, thank you!" she cried aloud.

The book struck her directly over her left eye. It struck almost at the same instant that she realized the girl was about to hurl it. Before she could utter a sound, the raw face came crashing across the table toward her, howling. The girl's fingers sank like clamps into the soft flesh of her neck. She heard the mother cry out and Claud shout, "Whoa!" There was an instant when she was certain that she was about to be in an earthquake.

All at once her vision narrowed and she saw everything as if it were happening in a small room far away, or as if she were looking at it through the wrong end of a telescope. Claud's face crumpled and fell out of sight. The nurse ran in, then out, then in again. Then the gangling figure of the doctor rushed out of the inner door. Magazines flew this way and that as the table turned over. The girl fell with a thud and Mrs. Turpin's vision suddenly reversed itself and she saw everything large instead of small. The eyes of the white-trashy woman were staring hugely at the floor. There the girl, held down on one side by the nurse and on the other by her mother, was wrenching and turning in their grasp. The doctor was kneeling astride her, trying to hold her arm down. He managed after a second to sink a long needle into it.

Mrs. Turpin felt entirely hollow except for her heart which swung from side to side as if it were agitated in a great empty drum of flesh.

"Somebody that's not busy call for the ambulance," the doctor said in the off-hand voice young doctors adopt for terrible occasions.

Mrs. Turpin could not have moved a finger. The old man who had been sitting next to her skipped nimbly into the office and made the call, for the secretary still seemed to be gone.

"Claud!" Mrs. Turpin called.

He was not in his chair. She knew she must jump up and find him but she felt like some one trying to catch a train in a dream, when everything moves in slow motion and the faster you try to run the slower you go.

"Here I am," a suffocated voice, very unlike Claud's, said.

He was doubled up in the corner on the floor, pale as paper, holding his leg. She wanted to get up and go to him but she could not move. Instead, her gaze was drawn slowly downward to the churning face on the floor, which she could see over the doctor's shoulder.

The girl's eyes stopped rolling and focused on her. They seemed a much lighter blue than before, as if a door that had been tightly closed behind them was now open to admit light and air.

Mrs. Turpin's head cleared and her power of motion returned. She leaned forward until she was looking directly into the fierce brilliant eyes. There was no doubt in her mind that the girl did know her, knew her in some intense and personal way, beyond time and place and condition. "What you got to say to me?" she asked hoarsely and held her breath, waiting, as for a revelation.

The girl raised her head. Her gaze locked with Mrs. Turpin's. "Go back to hell where you came from, you old wart hog," she whispered. Her voice was low but clear. Her eyes burned for a moment as if she saw with pleasure that her message had struck its target.

Mrs. Turpin sank back in her chair.

After a moment the girl's eyes closed and she turned her head wearily to the side.

The doctor rose and handed the nurse the empty syringe. He leaned over and put both hands for a moment on the mother's shoulders, which were shaking. She was sitting on the floor, her lips pressed together, holding Mary Grace's hand in her lap. The girl's fingers were gripped like a baby's around her thumb. "Go on to the hospital," he said. "I'll call and make the arrangements."

"Now let's see that neck," he said in a jovial voice to Mrs. Turpin. He began to inspect her neck with his first two fingers. Two little moon-shaped lines like pink fish bones were indented over her windpipe. There was the beginning of an angry red swelling above her eye. His fingers passed over this also.

"Lea' me be," she said thickly and shook him off. "See about Claud. She kicked him."

"I'll see about him in a minute," he said and felt her pulse. He was a thin grey-haired man, given to pleasantries. "Go home and have yourself a vacation the rest of the day," he said and patted her on the shoulder.

Quit your pattin me, Mrs. Turpin growled to herself.

"And put an ice pack over that eye," he said. Then he went and squatted down beside Claud and looked at his leg. After a moment he pulled him up and Claud limped after him into the office.

Until the ambulance came, the only sounds in the room were the tremulous moans of the girl's mother, who continued to sit on the floor. The white-trash woman did not take her eyes off the girl. Mrs. Turpin looked straight ahead at nothing. Presently the ambulance drew up, a long dark shadow, behind the curtain. The attendants came in and set the stretcher down beside the girl and lifted her expertly onto it and carried her out. The nurse helped the mother gather up her things. The shadow of the ambulance moved silently away and the nurse came back in the office.

"That there girl is going to be a lunatic, ain't she?" the white-trash woman asked the nurse, but the nurse kept on to the back and never answered her.

"Yes, she's going to be a lunatic," the white-trash woman said to the rest of them.

"Po' critter," the old woman murmured. The child's face was still in her lap. His eyes looked idly out over her knees. He had not moved during the disturbance except to draw one leg up under him.

"I thank Gawd," the white-trash woman said fervently, "I ain't a lunatic."

Claud came limping out and the Turpins went home.

As their pick-up truck turned into their own dirt road and made the crest of the hill, Mrs. Turpin gripped the window ledge and looked out suspiciously. The land sloped gracefully down through a field dotted with lavender weeds and at the start of the rise their small yellow frame house, with its little flower beds spread out around it like a fancy apron, sat primly in its accustomed place between two giant hickory trees. She would not have been startled to see a burnt wound between two blackened chimneys.

Neither of them felt like eating so they put on their house clothes and lowered the shade in the bedroom and lay down, Claud with his leg on a pillow and herself with a damp washcloth over her eye. The instant she was flat on her back, the image of a razor-backed hog with warts on its face and horns coming out behind its ears snorted into her head. She moaned, a low quiet moan.

"I am not," she said tearfully, "a wart hog. From hell." But the denial had no force. The girl's eyes and her words, even the tone of her voice, low but clear, directed only to her, brooked no repudiation. She had been singled out for the message, though there was trash in the room to whom it might justly have been applied. The full force of this fact struck her only now. There was a woman there who was neglecting her own child but she had been overlooked. The message had been given to Ruby Turpin, a respectable, hard-working, church-going woman. The tears dried. Her eyes began to burn instead with wrath.

She rose on her elbow and the washcloth fell into her hand. Claud was lying on his back, snoring. She wanted to tell him what the girl had said. At the same time, she did not wish to put the image of herself as a wart hog from hell into his mind.

"Hey, Claud," she muttered and pushed his shoulder.

Claud opened one pale baby blue eye.

She looked into it warily. He did not think about anything. He just went his way.

"Wha, whasit?" he said and closed the eye again.

"Nothing," she said. "Does your leg pain you?"

"Hurts like hell," Claud said.

"It'll quit terreckly," she said and lay back down. In a moment Claud was snoring again. For the rest of the afternoon they lay there. Claud slept. She scowled at the ceiling. Occasionally she raised her fist and made a small stabbing motion over her chest as if she was defending her innocence to invisible guests who were like the comforters of Job, reasonable-seeming but wrong.

About five-thirty Claud stirred. "Got to go after those niggers," he sighed, not moving.

She was looking straight up as if there were unintelligible handwriting on the ceiling. The protuberance over her eye had turned a greenish-blue. "Listen here," she said.

"What?"

"Kiss me."

Claud leaned over and kissed her loudly on the mouth. He pinched her side and their hands interlocked. Her expression of ferocious concentration did not change. Claud got up, groaning and growling, and limped off. She continued to study the ceiling.

She did not get up until she heard the pick-up truck coming back with the Negroes. Then she rose and thrust her feet in her brown oxfords, which she did not bother to lace, and stumped out onto the back porch and got her red plastic bucket. She emptied a tray of ice cubes into it and filled it half full of water and went out into the back yard. Every afternoon after Claud brought the hands in, one of the boys helped him put out hay and the rest waited in the back of the truck until he was ready to take them home. The truck was parked in the shade under one of the hickory trees.

"Hi yawl this evening?" Mrs. Turpin asked grimly, appearing with the bucket and the dipper. There were three women and a boy in the truck.

"Us doin nicely," the oldest woman said. "Hi you doin?" and her gaze stuck immediately on the dark lump on Mrs. Turpin's forehead. "You done fell down, ain't you?" she asked in a solicitous voice. The old woman was dark and almost toothless. She had on an old felt hat of Claud's set back on her head. The other two women were younger and lighter and they both had new bright green sun hats. One of them had hers on her head; the other had taken hers off and the boy was grinning beneath it.

Mrs. Turpin set the bucket down on the floor of the truck. "Yawl hep yourselves," she said. She looked around to make sure Claud had gone. "No. I didn't fall down," she said, folding her arms. "It was something worse than that."

"Ain't nothing bad happen to you!" the old woman said. She said it as if they all knew that Mrs. Turpin was protected in some special way by Divine Providence. "You just had you a little fall."

"We were in town at the doctor's office for where the cow kicked Mr. Turpin," Mrs. Turpin said in a flat tone that indicated they could leave off their foolishness. "And there was this girl there. A big fat girl with her face all broke out. I could look at that girl and tell she was peculiar but I couldn't tell how. And me and her mama were just talking and going along and all of a sudden WHAM! She throws this big book she was reading at me and . . ."

"Naw!" the old woman cried out.

"And then she jumps over the table and commences to choke me."

"Naw!" they all exclaimed, "naw!"

"Hi come she do that?" the old woman asked. "What ail her?"

Mrs. Turpin only glared in front of her.

"Somethin ail her," the old woman said.

"They carried her off in an ambulance," Mrs. Turpin continued, "but before she went she was rolling on the floor and they were trying to hold her down to give her a shot and she said something to me." She paused. "You know what she said to me?"

"What she say?" they asked.

"She said," Mrs. Turpin began, and stopped, her face very dark and heavy. The sun was getting whiter and whiter, blanching the sky overhead so that the leaves of the hickory tree were black in the face of it. She could not bring forth the words. "Something real ugly," she muttered.

"She sho shouldn't said nothin ugly to you," the old woman said. "You so sweet. You the sweetest lady I know."

"She pretty too," the one with the hat on said.

"And stout," the other one said. "I never knowed no sweeter white lady."

"That's the truth befo' Jesus," the old woman said. "Amen! You des as sweet and pretty as you can be."

Mrs. Turpin knew just exactly how much Negro flattery was worth and it added to her rage. "She said," she began again and finished this time with a fierce rush of breath, "that I was an old wart hog from hell."

There was an astounded silence.

"Where she at?" the youngest woman cried in a piercing voice.

"Lemme see her. I'll kill her!"

"I'll kill her with you!" the other one cried.

"She b'long in the sylum," the old woman said emphatically. "You the sweetest white lady I know."

"She pretty too," the other two said. "Stout as she can be and sweet. Jesus satisfied with her!"

"Deed he is," the old woman declared.

Idiots! Mrs. Turpin growled to herself. You could never say anything intelligent to a nigger. You could talk at them but not with them. "Yawl ain't drunk your water," she said shortly. "Leave the bucket in the truck when you're finished with it. I got more to do than just stand around and pass the time of day," and she moved off and into the house.

She stood for a moment in the middle of the kitchen. The dark protuberance over her eye looked like a miniature tornado cloud which might any moment sweep across the horizon of her brow. Her lower lip protruded dangerously. She squared her massive shoulders. Then she marched into the front of the house and out the side door and started down the road to the pig parlor. She had the look of a woman going single-handed, weaponless, into battle.

The sun was a deep yellow now like a harvest moon and was riding westward very fast over the far tree line as if it meant to reach the hogs before she did. The road was rutted and she kicked several good-sized stones out of her path as she strode along. The pig parlor was on a little knoll at the end of a lane that ran off from the side of the barn.

It was a square of concrete as large as a small room, with a board fence about four feet high around it. The concrete floor sloped slightly so that the hog wash could drain off into a trench where it was carried to the field for fertilizer. Claud was standing on the outside, on the edge of the concrete, hanging onto the top board, hosing down the floor inside. The hose was connected to the faucet of a water trough nearby.

Mrs. Turpin climbed up beside him and glowered down at the hogs inside. There were seven long-snouted bristly shoats in it—tan with liver-colored spots—and an old sow a few weeks off from farrowing. She was lying on her side grunting. The shoats were running about shaking themselves like idiot children, their little slit pig eyes searching the floor for anything left. She had read that pigs were the most intelligent animal. She doubted it. They were supposed to be smarter than dogs. There had even been a pig astronaut. He had performed his assignment perfectly but died of a heart attack afterwards because they left him in his electric suit, sitting upright throughout his examination when naturally a hog should be on all fours.

A-gruntin and a-rootin and a-groanin.

"Gimme that hose," she said, yanking it away from Claud. "Go on and carry them niggers home and then get off that leg."

"You look like you might have swallowed a mad dog," Claud observed, but he got down and limped off. He paid no attention to her humors.

Until he was out of earshot, Mrs. Turpin stood on the side of the pen, holding the hose and pointing the stream of water at the hind quarters of any shoat that looked as if it might try to lie down. When he had had time to get over the hill, she turned her head slightly and her wrathful eyes scanned the path. He was nowhere in sight. She turned back again and seemed to gather herself up. Her shoulders rose and she drew in her breath.

"What do you send me a message like that for?" she said in a low fierce voice, barely above a whisper but with the force of a shout in its concentrated fury. "How am I a hog and me both? How am I saved and from hell too?" Her free fist was knotted and with the other she gripped the hose, blindly pointing the stream of water in and out of the eye of the old sow whose outraged squeal she did not hear.

The pig parlor commanded a view of the back pasture where their twenty beef cows were gathered around the haybales Claud and the boy had put out. The freshly cut pasture sloped down to the highway. Across it was their cotton field and beyond that a dark green dusty wood which they owned as well. The sun was behind the wood, very red, looking over the paling of trees like a farmer inspecting his own hogs.

"Why me?" she rumbled. "It's no trash around here, black or white, that I haven't given to. And break my back to the bone every day working. And do for the church."

She appeared to be the right size woman to command the arena before her. "How am I a hog?" she demanded. "Exactly how am I like them?" and she jabbed the stream of water at the shoats. "There was plenty of trash there. It didn't have to be me.

"If you like trash better, go get yourself some trash then," she railed. "You could have made me trash. Or a nigger. If trash is what you wanted why didn't you make me trash?" She shook her fist with the hose in it and a watery snake appeared momentarily in the air. "I could quit working and take it easy and be filthy," she growled. "Lounge about the sidewalks all day drinking root beer. Dip snuff and spit in every puddle and have it all over my face. I could be nasty.

"Or you could have made me a nigger. It's too late for me to be a nigger," she said with deep sarcasm, "but I could act like one. Lay down in the middle of the road and stop traffic. Roll on the ground."

In the deepening light everything was taking on a mysterious hue. The pasture was growing a peculiar glassy green and the streak of highway had turned lavender. She braced herself for a final assault and this time her voice rolled out over the pasture. "Go on," she yelled, "call me a hog! Call me a hog again. From hell. Call me a wart hog from hell. Put that bottom rail on top. There'll still be a top and bottom!"

A garbled echo returned to her.

A final surge of fury shook her and she roared, "Who do you think you are?"

The color of everything, field and crimson sky, burned for a moment with a transparent intensity. The question carried over the pasture and across the highway and the cotton field and returned to her clearly like an answer from beyond the wood.

She opened her mouth but no sound came out of it.

A tiny truck, Claud's, appeared on the highway, heading rapidly out of sight. Its gears scraped thinly. It looked like a child's toy. At any moment a bigger truck might smash into it and scatter Claud's and the niggers' brains all over the road.

Mrs. Turpin stood there, her gaze fixed on the highway, all her muscles rigid, until in five or six minutes the truck reappeared, returning. She waited until it had had time to turn into their own road. Then like a monumental statue coming to life, she bent her head slowly and gazed, as if through the very heart of mystery, down into the pig parlor at the hogs. They had settled all in one corner around the old sow who was grunting softly. A red glow suffused them. They appeared to pant with a secret life.

Until the sun slipped finally behind the tree line, Mrs. Turpin remained there with her gaze bent to them as if she were absorbing some abysmal life-giving knowledge. At last she lifted her head. There was only a purple streak in the sky, cutting through a field of crimson and leading, like an extension of the highway, into the descending dusk. She raised her hands from the side of the pen in a gesture hieratic and profound. A visionary light settled in her eyes. She saw the streak as a vast swinging bridge extending upward from the earth through a field of living fire. Upon it a vast horde of souls were rumbling toward heaven. There were whole companies of white-trash, clean for the first time in their lives, and bands of black niggers in white robes, and battalions of freaks and lunatics shouting and clapping and leaping like frogs. And bringing up the end of the procession was a tribe of people whom she recognized at once as those who, like herself and Claud, had always had a little of everything and the God-given wit to use it right. She leaned forward to observe them closer. They were marching behind the others with great dignity, accountable as they had always been for good order and common sense and respectable behavior. They alone were on key. Yet she could see by their shocked and altered faces that even their virtues were being burned away. She lowered her hands and gripped the rail of the hog pen, her eyes small but fixed unblinkingly on what lay ahead. In a moment the vision faded but she remained where she was, immobile.

At length she got down and turned off the faucet and made her slow way on the darkening path to the house. In the woods around her the invisible cricket choruses had struck up, but what she heard were the voices of the souls climbing upward into the starry field and shouting hallelujah.

# ⁜ WRIGHT MORRIS
## (1910–1998)

Born in Central City, Nebraska, Wright Morris referred to himself as "half an orphan"—his mother died a few days after his birth and his father liked to wander and often left him in the care of neighbors. From 1919 to 1924, Morris lived in Omaha, and from 1924 to 1927 in Chicago. Going on long trips with his father gave Morris an avid interest in travel, which he indulged throughout his life. He attended Pomona College in California from 1930 to 1933, when he took off to wander about Europe for a year.

In the mid-1930s Morris began taking photographs and experimenting with phototexts, books that combined photographs with short prose passages. His photographs are highly esteemed for their clarity and honesty, and have been shown widely. In 1940 he published a phototext entitled *The Inhabitants,* which he later expanded into a book. That same year he traveled fifteen thousand miles around the United States, an experience that fed into his first novel *My Uncle Dudley* (1942). While living in Pennsylvania with his first wife, Morris formed a close friendship with Loren Eiseley, whose writings influenced his use of scientific metaphors in his fiction.

After 1948, Morris concentrated mostly on fiction, and from 1948 to 1960 he produced the works that established his reputation: *The Works of Love* (1952); *The Deep Sleep* (1953); *The Field of Vision* (1956); an excellent Hollywood novel, *Love Among the Cannibals* (1959); *Ceremony in Lone Tree* (1960); and a book of criticism, *The Territory Ahead* (1958). A prolific writer, Morris published phototexts, essays and criticism, autobiography, six collections of stories, and twenty novels. From 1962 to 1975 Morris taught creative writing at California State University at San Francisco. In the 1970s and 1980s Morris continued to write on photography and to produce fiction. His photography won three Guggenheim fellowships, and his novels *The Field of Vision* (1956) and *Plains Song* (1980) won National Book awards.

Known perhaps as the most honored but least read author in America, Morris deserves continued attention. His fiction is a testimony to the possibilities of transformation in human life.

# The Ram in the Thicket

In this dream Mr. Ormsby stood in the yard—at the edge of the yard where the weeds began—and stared at a figure that appeared to be on a rise. This figure had the head of a bird with a crown of bright, exotic plumage, only partially concealed by a paint-daubed helmet. Mr. Ormsby felt the urgent need to identify this strange bird. Feathery wisps of plumage shot through the crown of the helmet like a pillow leaking sharp spears of yellow straw. The face beneath it was indescribably solemn, with eyes so pale they were like openings on the sky. Slung over the left arm, casually, was a gun, but the right arm, the palm upward, extended toward a cloud of hovering birds. They came and went, like bees after honey, and there were so many and all so friendly, that Mr. Ormsby extended his own hand toward them. No birds came, but in his upturned palm he felt the dull throb of the alarm clock, which he held tenderly, a living thing, until it ran down.

In the morning light the photograph at the foot of his bed seemed startling. The boy stood alone on a rise, and he held, very casually, a gun. The face beneath the helmet had no features, but Mr. Ormsby would have known him just by the stance, by the way he held the gun, like some women hold their arms when their hands are idle, parts of their body that for the moment are not much use. Without the gun it was as if some part of the boy had been amputated; the way he stood, even the way he walked was not quite right.

Mr. Ormsby had given the boy a gun because he had never had a gun himself, not because he wanted him to shoot anything. The boy didn't want to kill anything either, and during the first year he found it hard to: the rattle of the BBs in the barrel of the gun frightened the birds before he could shoot them. And that was what had made him a *hunter.* He had to stalk everything in order to hit it, and after all that trouble you naturally try to hit what you're shooting at. He didn't seem to realize that after he hit it it might be dead. It seemed natural for a boy like that to join the Navy, and let God strike Mr. Ormsby dead to hear him say so, nothing ever seemed more natural to him than the news that the boy had been killed. Mother had steeled herself for the worst, the moment the boy enlisted, but Mr. Ormsby had not been prepared to feel what he felt. Mother need never know it unless he slipped up and talked in his sleep.

He turned slowly on the bed, careful to keep the springs quiet, and as he lowered his feet he scooped his socks from the floor. As a precaution Mother had slept the first few months of their marriage in her corset—as a precaution and as an aid to self-control. In the fall they had ordered twin beds. Carrying his shoes—today, of all days, would be a trial for Mother—he tiptoed to the closet and picked up his shirt and pants. There was simply no reason, as he had explained to her twenty years ago, why she should get up when he could just as well get a bite for himself. He had made that suggestion when the boy was just a baby and she needed her strength. Even as it was she didn't come out of it any too well. The truth was, Mother was so thorough about everything she did that her breakfasts usually took an hour or more. When he did it himself he was out of the kitchen in ten, twelve minutes and without leaving any pile of dishes around. By himself he could quick-rinse them in a little hot water, but with Mother there was the dishpan and all of the suds. Mother had the idea that a meal simply wasn't a meal without setting the table and using half the dishes in the place. It was easier to do it himself, and except for Sunday, when they had brunch, he was out of the house an hour before she got up. He had a bite of lunch at the store and at four o'clock he did the day's shopping since he was right downtown anyway. There was a time he called her up and inquired as to what she thought she wanted, but since he did all the buying he knew that better himself. As secretary for the League of Women Voters she had enough on her mind in times like these without cluttering it up with food. Now that he left the store an hour early he usually got home in the midst of her nap or while she was taking her bath. As he had nothing else to do he prepared the vegetables and dressed the meat, as Mother had never shown much of a flair for meat. There had been a year—when the boy was small and before he had taken up that gun—when she had made several marvelous lemon meringue pies. But feeling as she did about the gun—and she told them both how she felt about it—she didn't see why she should slave in the kitchen for people like that. She always spoke to them as *they*—or as *you* plural—from the time he had given the boy the gun. Whether this was because they were both men, both culprits, or both something else, they were never entirely separate things again. When she called, *they* would both answer, and though the boy had been gone two years he still felt him *there,* right beside him, when Mother said *you.*

For some reason Mr. Ormsby could not understand—although the rest of the house was neat as a pin—the room they *lived* in was always a mess. Mother refused to let the cleaning woman set her foot in it. Whenever she left the house she locked the door. Long, long ago he had said something, and she had said something, and she had said she wanted one room in the house where she could relax and just let her hair down. That had sounded so wonderfully human, so unusual for Mother, that he had been completely taken with it. As a matter of fact he still didn't know what to say. It was the only room in the house—except for the screened-in porch in the summer—where he could take off his shoes and open his shirt on his underwear. If the room was *clean,* it would be clean like all of the others, and that would leave him nothing but the basement and the porch. The way the boy took to the out-of-doors—he stopped looking for his cuff links, began to look for pins—was partially because he couldn't find a place in the house to sit down. They had just redecorated the house—the boy at that time was just a little shaver—and Mother had spread newspapers over everything. There hadn't been a chair in the place—except the straight-backed ones at the table—that hadn't been, that *wasn't,* covered with a piece of newspaper. Anyone who had ever scrunched around on a paper knew what that was like. It was at that time that he had got the idea of having his pipe in the basement, reading in the bedroom, and the boy had taken to the out-of-doors. Because he had always wanted a gun himself, and because the boy was alone, with no kids around to play with, he had brought him home a thousand-shot BB gun by the name of Daisy—funny that he should remember the name—and five thousand BBs in a drawstring bag.

That gun had been a mistake—he began to shave himself in tepid, lukewarm water rather than let it run hot, which would bang the pipes and wake Mother up. When the telegram came that the boy had been killed Mother hadn't said a word, but she made it clear whose fault it was. There was never any doubt, *any* doubt, as to just whose fault it was.

He stopped thinking while he shaved, attentive to the mole at the edge of his mustache, and leaned to the mirror to avoid dropping suds on the rug. There had been a time when he had wondered about an Oriental throw rug in the bathroom, but over twenty years he had become accustomed to it. As a matter of fact he sort of missed it whenever they had guests with children and Mother remembered to take it up. Without the rug he always felt just a little uneasy in the bathroom; it led him to whistle or turn on the water and let it run. If it hadn't been for that he might not have noticed as soon as he did that

Mother did the same thing whenever anybody was in the house. She turned on the water and let it run until she was through with the toilet, then she would flush it before she turned the water off. If you happen to have old-fashioned plumbing, and have lived with a person for twenty years, you can't help noticing little things like that. He had got to be a little like that himself: since the boy had gone he used the one in the basement or waited until he got down to the store. As a matter of fact it was more convenient, didn't wake Mother up, and he could have his pipe while he was sitting there.

With his pants on, but carrying his shirt—for he might get it soiled preparing breakfast—he left the bathroom and tiptoed down the stairs.

Although the boy had gone, was gone, that is, Mother still liked to preserve her slipcovers and the kitchen linoleum. It was a good piece, well worth preserving, but unless there were guests in the house and the papers were taken up, Mr. Ormsby forgot it was there. Right now he couldn't tell you what color the linoleum was. Stooping to see what the color might be—it proved to be blue, Mother's favorite color—he felt the stirring in his bowels. Usually this occurred while he was rinsing the dishes after his second cup of coffee or after the first long draw on his pipe. He was not supposed to smoke in the morning, but it was more important to be regular that way than irregular with his pipe. Mother had been the first to realize this—not in so many words—but she would rather he did anything than not be able to do *that.*

He measured out a pint and a half of water, put it over a medium fire, and added just a pinch of salt. Then he walked to the top of the basement stairs, turned on the light, and at the bottom turned it off. He dipped his head to pass beneath a sagging line of wash, the sleeves dripping, and with his hands out, for the corner was dark, he entered the cell.

The basement toilet had been put in to accommodate the help, who had to use something, and Mother would not have them on her Oriental rug. Until the day he dropped some money out of his pants and had to strike a match to look for it, he had never noticed what kind of a stool it was. Mother had picked it up secondhand—she had never told him where—because she couldn't see buying something new for a place always in the dark. It was very old, with a chain pull, and operated on a principle that invariably produced quite a splash. But, in spite of that, he preferred it to the one at the store and very much more than the one upstairs. This was rather hard to explain since the seat was pretty cold in the winter and the water sometimes nearly froze. But it was private like no other place in the house. Considering that the house was as good as empty, that was a strange thing to say, but it was the only way to say how he felt. If he went off for a walk like the boy, Mother would miss him, somebody would see him, and he wouldn't feel right about it anyhow. All he wanted was a dark, quiet place and the feeling that for five minutes, just five minutes, nobody would be looking for him. Who would ever believe five minutes like that were so hard to come by? The closest he had ever been to the boy—after he had given him the gun—was the morning he had found him here on the stool. It was then that the boy had said, *et tu, Brutus,* and they had both laughed so hard they had had to hold their sides. The boy had put his head in a basket of wash so Mother wouldn't hear. Like everything the boy said there were two or three ways to take it, and in the dark Mr. Ormsby could not see his face. When he stopped laughing the boy said, *Well, Pop, I suppose one flush ought to do,* but Mr. Ormsby had not been able to say anything. To be called Pop made him so weak that he had to sit right down on the stool, just like he was, and support his head in his hands. Just as he had never had a name for the boy, the boy had never had a name for him—none, that is, that Mother would permit him to use. Of all the names Mother couldn't stand, Pop was the worst, and he agreed with her; it was vulgar, common, and used by strangers to intimidate old men. He agreed with her, completely—until he heard the word in the boy's mouth. It was only natural that the boy would use it if he ever had the chance—but he never dreamed that any word, especially *that* word, could mean what it did. It made him weak, he had to sit down and pretend he was going about his business, and what a blessing it was that the place was dark. Nothing more was said, ever, but it remained their most important conversation—so important they were afraid to try and improve on it. Days later he remembered what the boy had actually said, and how shocking it was but without any *sense* of shock. A blow so sharp that he had no sense of pain, only a knowing, as he had under gas, that he had been worked on. For two, maybe three minutes, there in the dark, they had been what Mother called them, they were *they*—and they were there in the basement because they were so much alike. When the telegram came, and when he knew what he would find, he had brought it there, had struck a match, and read what it said. The match filled the cell with light and he saw—he couldn't help seeing—piles of tinned goods in the space beneath the stairs. Several dozen cans of tuna fish and salmon, and since *he* was the one that had the points, bought the groceries, there was only one place Mother could have got such things. It had been a greater shock than the telegram—that was the honest-to-God's truth and anyone who knew Mother as well as he did would have felt the same. It was unthinkable, but there it was—and there were more on top of the water closet, where he peered while precariously balanced on the stool. Cans of pineapple, crabmeat, and tins of Argentine beef. He had been stunned, the match had burned down and actually scorched his fingers, and he nearly killed himself when he forgot and stepped off the seat. Only later in the morning—after he had sent flowers to ease the blow for Mother—did he realize how such a thing *must* have occurred. Mother knew so many influential people, and they gave her so much that they had very likely given her all of this stuff as well. Rather than turn it down and needlessly alienate people, influential people, Mother had done the next best thing. While the war was on she refused to serve it, or profiteer in any way—and at the same time not alienate people foolishly. It had been an odd thing, certainly, that he should discover all of that by the same match that he read the telegram. Naturally, he never breathed a word of it to Mother, as something like that, even though she was not superstitious, would really upset her. It was one of those things that he and the boy would keep to themselves.

It would be like Mother to think of putting it in here, the very last place that the cleaning woman would look for it. The new cleaning woman would neither go upstairs nor down, and did whatever she did somewhere else. Mr. Ormsby lit a match to see if everything was all right—hastily blew it out when he saw that the can pile had increased. He stood up, then hurried up the stairs without buttoning his pants as he could hear the water boiling. He added half a cup, then measured three heaping tablespoons of coffee into the bottom of the double boiler, buttoned his pants. Looking at his watch he saw that it was seven thirty-five. As it would be a hard day—sponsoring a boat was a man-size job—he would give Mother another ten minutes or so. He took two bowls from the cupboard, set them on blue pottery saucers, and with the grapefruit knife in his hand walked to the icebox.

As he put his head in the icebox door—in order to see he had to—Mr. Ormsby stopped breathing and closed his eyes. What had been dying for some time was now dead. He leaned back, inhaled, leaned in again. The floor of the icebox was covered with a fine assortment of jars full of leftovers Mother simply could not throw away. Some of the jars were covered with little oilskin hoods, some with saucers, and some with wax paper snapped on with a rubber band. It was impossible to tell, from the outside, which one it was. Seating himself on the floor he removed them one at a time, starting at the front and working toward the back. As he had done this many times before, he got well into the problem, near the middle, before troubling to sniff anything. A jar that might have been carrots—it was hard to tell without probing—was now a furry marvel of green mold. It smelled only mildly, however, and Mr. Ormsby remembered that this was penicillin, the life giver. A spoonful of cabbage—it had been three months since they had had cabbage—had a powerful stench but was still not the one he had in mind. There were two more jars of mold; the one screwed tight he left alone as it had a frosted look and the top of the lid bulged. The culprit, however, was not that at all, but in an open saucer on the next shelf—part of an egg—Mr. Ormsby had beaten the white himself. He placed the saucer on the sink and returned all but two of the jars to the icebox: the cabbage and the explosive-looking one. If it smelled he took it out, otherwise Mother had to see for herself as she refused to take *their* word for these things. When he was just a little shaver the boy had walked into the living room full of Mother's guests and showed them something in a jar. Mother had been horrified—but she naturally thought it a frog or something and not a bottle out of her own icebox. When one of the ladies asked the boy where in the world he had found it, he naturally said, *In the icebox.* Mother had never forgiven him. After that she forbade him to look in the box without permission, and the boy had not so much as peeked in it since. He would eat only what he found on the table, or ready to eat in the kitchen—or what he found at the end of those walks he took everywhere.

With the jar of cabbage and furry mold Mr. Ormsby made a trip to the garage, picked up the garden spade, walked around behind. At one time he had emptied the jars and merely buried the contents, but recently, since the war that is, he had buried it all. Part of it was a question of time—he had more work to do at the store—but the bigger part of it was to put an end to the jars. Not that it worked out that way—all Mother had to do was open a new one—but it gave him a real satisfaction to bury them. Now that the boy and his dogs were gone there was simply no one around the house to eat up all the food Mother saved.

There were worms in the fork of earth he had turned and he stood looking at them—*they* both had loved worms—when he remembered the water boiling on the stove. He dropped everything and ran, ran right into Emil Ludlow, the milkman, before he noticed him. Still on the run he went up the steps and through the screen door into the kitchen—he was clear to the stove before he remembered the door would slam. He started back, but too late, and in the silence that followed the BANG he stood with his eyes tightly closed, his fists clenched. Usually he remained in this condition until a sign from Mother—a thump on the floor or her voice at the top of the stairs. None came, however, only the sound of the milk bottles that Emil Ludlow was leaving on the porch. Mr. Ormsby gave him time to get away, waited until he heard the horse walking, then he went out and brought the milk in. At the icebox he remembered the water—why it was he had come running in the first place—and he left the door open and hurried to the stove. It was down to half a cup but not, thank heavens, dry. He added a full pint, then put the milk in the icebox; took out the butter, four eggs, and a Flori-gold grapefruit. Before he cut the grapefruit he looked at his watch and, seeing that it was ten minutes to eight, an hour before train time, he opened the stairway door.

"Ohhh, Mother!" he called, and then he returned to the grapefruit.

* * *

*"Ad astra per aspera,"* she said, and rose from the bed. In the darkness she felt about for her corset, then let herself go complete for the thirty-five seconds it required to get it on. This done, she pulled the cord to the light that hung in the attic, and as it snapped on, in a firm voice she said, *"Fiat lux."* Light having been made, Mother opened her eyes.

As the bulb hung in the attic, the closet remained in an after-glow, a twilight zone. It was not light, strictly speaking, but it was all Mother wanted to see. Seated on the attic stairs she trimmed her toenails with a pearl-handled knife that Mr. Ormsby had been missing for several years. The blade was not so good any longer and using it too freely had resulted in ingrown nails on both of her big toes. But Mother preferred it to scissors, which were proven, along with bathtubs, to be one of the most dangerous things in the home. *Even more than the battlefield, the most dangerous place in the world. Dry feet and hands before turning on lights, dry between toes.*

Without stooping she slipped into her sabots and left the closet, the light burning, and with her eyes dimmed, but not closed, went down the hall. Locking the bathroom door she stepped to the basin and turned on the cold water, then she removed several feet of paper from the toilet-paper roll. This took time, as in order to keep the roller from squeaking it had to be removed from its socket in the wall, then returned. One piece she put in the pocket of her kimono, the other she folded into a wad and used as a blotter to dab up spots on the floor. Turning up the water she sat down on the stool—then she got up to get a pencil and pad from the table near the window. On the first sheet she wrote—

*Ars longa, vita brevis*
Wildflower club, sun. 4 P.M.

She tore this off and filed it, tip showing, right at the front of her corset. On the next page—

ROGER—
Ivory Snow
Sani-Flush on thurs.

As she placed this on top of the toilet-paper roll she heard him call "First for breakfast." She waited until he closed the stairway door, then she stood up and turned on the shower. As it rained into the tub and splashed behind her in the basin, she lowered the lid, flushed the toilet. Until the water closet had filled, stopped gurgling, she stood at the window watching a squirrel cross the yard from tree to tree. Then she turned the shower off and noisily dragged the shower curtain, on its metal rings, back to the wall. She dampened her shower cap in the basin and hung it on the towel rack to dry, dropping the towel that was there down the laundry chute. This done, she returned to the basin and held her hands under the running water, now cold, until she was awake. With her index finger she massaged her gums—*there is no pyorrhea among the Indians*—and then, with the tips of her fingers, she dampened her eyes.

She drew the blind, and in the half-light the room seemed to be full of lukewarm water, greenish in color. With a piece of Kleenex, she dried her eyes, then turned it to gently blow her nose, first the left side, then with a little more blow on the right. There was nothing to speak of, nothing, so she folded the tissue, slipped it into her pocket. Raising the blind, she faced the morning with her eyes softly closed, letting the light come in as prescribed—gradually. Eyes wide, she then stared for a full minute at the yard full of grackles, covered with grackles, before she actually saw them. Running to the door, her head in the hall, her arm in the bathroom wildly pointing, she tried to whisper, loud-whisper to him, but her voice cracked.

"Roger," she called, a little hoarsely. "The window—run!"

She heard him turn from the stove and skid on the newspapers, bump into the sink, curse, then get on again.

"Blackbirds?" he whispered.

"Grackles!" she said, for the thousandth time she said *Grackles.*

"They're pretty!" he said.

"Family—" she said, ignoring him, "family *Icteridae* American."

"Well—" he said.

"Roger!" she said. "Something's burning."

She heard him leave the window and on his way back to the stove, on the same turn, skid on the papers again. She left him there and went down the hall to the bedroom, closed the door and passed between the mirrors once more to the closet. From five dresses—*any woman with more than five dresses, at this time, should have the vote taken away from her*—she selected the navy blue sheer with pink lace yoke and kerchief, short bolero. At the back of the closet—but in order to see she had to return to the bathroom, look for the flashlight in the drawer full of rags and old tins of shoe polish—were three shelves, each supporting ten to twelve pairs of shoes, and a large selection of slippers were piled on the floor. On the second shelf were the navy blue pumps—*we all have one weakness, but between men and shoes you can give me shoes*—navy blue pumps with a Cuban heel and a small bow. She hung the dress from the neck of the floor lamp, placed the shoes on the bed. From beneath the bed she pulled a hat box—the hat was new. Navy straw with shasta daisies, pink geraniums, and a navy blue veil with pink and white fuzzy dots. She held it out where it could be seen in the mirror, front and side, without seeing herself—*it's not every day that one sponsors a boat.* Not every day, and she turned to the calendar on her night table, a bird calendar featuring the natural-color male goldfinch for the month of June. Under the date of June 23 she printed the words, FAMILY ICTERIDAE—YARDFUL, and beneath it—

Met Captain Sudcliffe and gave him U.S.S. *Ormsby*

When he heard Mother's feet on the stairs Mr. Ormsby cracked her soft-boiled eggs and spooned them carefully into her heated cup. He had spilled his own on the floor when he had run to look at the black—or whatever color they were—birds. As they were very, very soft he had merely wiped them up. As he buttered the toast—the four burned slices were on the back porch airing—Mother entered the kitchen and said, "Roger—*more* toast?"

"I was watching blackbirds," he said.

"Grack-les," she said. "Any bird is a *black*bird if the males are largely or entirely black."

Talk about male and female birds really bothered Mr. Ormsby. Although she was a girl of the old school Mother never hesitated, *anywhere,* to speak right out about male and female birds. A cow was a cow, a bull was a bull, but to Mr. Ormsby a bird was a bird.

"Among the birdfolk," said Mother, "the menfolk, so to speak, wear the feathers. The female has more serious work to do."

"How does that fit the blackbirds?" said Mr. Ormsby.

"Every rule," said Mother, "has an exception."

There was no denying the fact that the older Mother got the more distinguished she appeared. As for himself, what he saw in the mirror looked very much like the Roger Ormsby that had married Violet Ames twenty years ago. As the top of his head got hard the bottom tended to get a little soft, but otherwise there wasn't much change. But it was hard to believe that Mother was the pretty little pop-eyed girl—he had thought it was her corset that popped them—whose nipples had been like buttons on her dress. Any other girl would have looked like a you-know—but there wasn't a man in Media County, or anywhere else, who ever mentioned it. A man could think what he would think, but he was the only man who really knew what Mother was like. And how little she was like *that.*

"Three-seven-four East One-One-Six," said Mother.

That was the way her mind worked, all over the place on one cup of coffee—birds one moment, Mrs. Dinardo the next.

He got up from the table and went after Mrs. Dinardo's letter—Mother seldom had time to read them unless he read them to her. Returning, he divided the rest of the coffee between them, unequally: three-quarters for Mother, a swallow of grounds for himself. He waited a moment, wiping his glasses, while Mother looked through the window at another blackbird. "Cowbird," she said, *"Molothrus ater."*

" 'Dear Mrs. Ormsby,' " Mr. Ormsby began. Then he stopped to scan the page, as Mrs. Dinardo had a strange style and was not much given to writing letters. " 'Dear Mrs. Ormsby,' " he repeated, " 'I received your letter and I Sure was glad to know that you are both well and I know you often think of me I often think of you too—' " He paused to get his breath—Mrs. Dinardo's style was not much for pauses—and to look at Mother. But Mother was still with the cowbird. " 'Well, Mrs. Ormsby,' " he continued, " 'I haven't a thing in a room that I know of the people that will be away from the room will be only a week next month. But come to See me I may have Something if you don't get Something.' " Mrs. Dinardo, for some reason, always capitalized the letter S which along with everything else didn't make it easier to read. " 'We are both well and he is Still in the Navy Yard. My I do wish the war was over it is So long. We are So tired of it do come and See us when you give them your boat. Wouldn't a Street be better than a boat? If you are going to name Something why not a Street? Here in my hand is news of a boat Sunk what is wrong with Ormsby on a Street? Well 116 is about the Same we have the river and its nice. If you don't find Something See me I may have Something. Best Love, Mrs. Myrtle Dinardo.' "

It was quite a letter to get from a woman that Mother had known, known Mother, that is, for nearly eighteen years. Brought in to nurse the boy—he could never understand why a woman like Mother, with her figure—but anyhow, Mrs. Dinardo was brought in. Something in her milk, Dr. Paige said, when it was as plain as the nose on your face it was nothing in the milk, but something in the boy. He just refused, plain refused, to nurse with Mother. The way the little rascal would look at her, but not a sound out of him but gurgling when Mrs. Dinardo would scoop him up and go upstairs to their room—the only woman—other woman, that is, that Mother ever let step inside of it. She had answered an ad that Mother had run, on Dr. Paige's suggestion, and they had been like *that* from the first time he saw them together.

"I'll telephone," said Mother.

On the slightest provocation Mother would call Mrs. Dinardo by long distance—she had to come down four flights of stairs to answer—and tell her she was going to broadcast over the radio or something. Although Mrs. Dinardo hardly knew one kind of bird from another, Mother sent her printed copies of every single one of her bird-lore lectures. She also sent her hand-pressed flowers from the garden.

"I'll telephone," repeated Mother.

"My own opinion—" began Mr. Ormsby, but stopped when Mother picked up her egg cup, made a pile of her plates, and started toward the sink. "I'll take care of that," he said. "Now you run along and telephone." But Mother walked right by him and took her stand at the sink. With one hand—with the other she held her kimono close about her—she let the water run into a large dish pan. Mr. Ormsby had hoped to avoid this; now he would have to first rinse, then dry, every piece of silver and every dish they had used. As Mother could only use one hand it would be even slower than usual.

"We don't want to miss our local," he said. "You better run along and let me do it."

"Cold water," she said, "for the eggs." He had long ago learned not to argue with Mother about the fine points of washing pots, pans, or dishes with bits of egg. He stood at the sink with the towel while she went about trying to make suds with a piece of stale soap in a little wire cage. As Mother refused to use a fresh piece of soap, nothing remotely like suds ever appeared. For this purpose, he kept a box of Gold Dust Twins concealed beneath the sink, and when Mother turned her back he slipped some in.

"There now," Mother said, and placed the rest of the dishes in the water, rinsed her fingers under the tap, paused to sniff at them.

"My own opinion—" Mr. Ormsby began, but stopped when Mother raised her finger, the index finger with the scar from the wart she once had. They stood quiet, and Mr. Ormsby listened to the water drip in the sink—the night before he had come down in his bare feet to shut it off. All of the taps dripped now and there was just nothing to do about it but put a rag or something beneath it to break the ping.

"Thrush!" said Mother. "Next to the nightingale the most popular of European songbirds."

"Very pretty," he said, although he simply couldn't hear a thing. Mother walked to the window, folding the collar of her kimono over her bosom and drawing the tails into a hammock beneath her behind. Mr. Ormsby modestly turned away. He quick-dipped one hand into the Gold Dust—drawing it out as he slipped it into the dishpan and worked up a suds.

As he finished wiping the dishes she came in with a bouquet for Mrs. Dinardo and arranged it, for the moment, in a tall glass.

"According to her letter," Mrs. Ormsby said, "she isn't too sure of having something—Roger!" she said. "You're dripping."

Mr. Ormsby put his hands over the sink and said, "If we're going to be met right at the station I don't see where you're going to see Mrs. Dinardo. You're going to be met at the station and then you're going to sponsor the boat. My own opinion is that after the boat we come on home."

"I know that street of hers," said Mother. "There isn't a wild-flower on it!"

On the wall above the icebox was a pad of paper and a blue pencil hanging by a string. As Mother started to write the point broke off, fell behind the icebox.

"Mother," he said, "you ever see my knife?"

"Milkman," said Mother. "If we're staying overnight we won't need milk in the morning."

In jovial tones Mr. Ormsby said, "I'll bet we're right back here before dark." That was all, that was *all* that he said. He had merely meant to call her attention to the fact that Mrs. Dinardo said—all but said—that she didn't have a room for them. But when Mother turned he saw that her mustache was showing, a sure sign that she was mad.

"Well—now," Mother said and lifting the skirt of her kimono swished around the cabinet, and then he heard her on the stairs. From the landing at the top of the stairs she said, "In that case I'm sure there's no need for *my* going. I'm sure the Navy would just as soon have you. After all," she said, "it's *your* name on the boat!"

"Now, Mother," he said, just as she closed the door, *not* slammed it, just closed it as quiet and nice as you'd please. Although he had been through this a thousand times it seemed he was never ready for it, never knew when it would happen, never felt anything but nearly sick. He went into the front room and sat down on the chair near the piano—then got up to arrange the doily at the back of his head. Ordinarily he could leave the house and after three or four days it would blow over, but in all his life—their life—there had been nothing like this. The government of the United States—he got up again and called, "OHHhhhh, Mother!"

No answer.

He could hear her moving around upstairs, but as she often went back to bed after a spat, just moving around didn't mean much of anything. He came back into the front room and sat down on the milk stool near the fireplace. It was the only seat in the room not protected with newspapers. The only thing the boy ever sat on when he had to sit on something. Somehow, thinking about that made him stand up. He could sit in the lawn swing, in the front yard, if Mother hadn't told everybody in town why it was that he, Roger Ormsby, would have to take the day off—not to sit in the lawn swing, not by a long shot. Everybody knew—Captain Sudcliffe's nice letter had appeared on the first page of the *Graphic,* under a picture of Mother leading a bird-lore hike in the Poconos. This picture bore the title LOCAL WOMAN HEADS DAWN BUSTERS, and marked Mother's appearance on the national bird-lore scene. But it was not one of her best pictures—it dated from way back in the twenties and those hipless dresses and round, bucket hats were not Mother's type. Until they saw that picture, and the letter beneath it, some people had forgotten that Virgil was missing, and most of them seemed to think it was a good idea to swap him for a boat. The U.S.S. *Ormsby* was a permanent sort of thing. Although he was born and raised in the town hardly anybody knew very much about Virgil, but they all were pretty familiar with his boat. "How's that boat of yours coming along?" they would say, but in more than twenty years nobody had ever asked him about *his* boy. Whose boy? Well, that was just the point. Everyone agreed Ormsby was a fine name for a boat.

It would be impossible to explain to Mother, maybe to anybody for that matter, what this U.S.S. *Ormsby* business meant to him. "The" boy and "the" *Ormsby*—it was a pretty strange thing that they both had the definite article, and gave him the feeling he was facing a monument.

"Oh Rog-gerrr!" Mother called.

"Coming," he said, and made for the stairs.

From the bedroom Mother said, "However I might feel personally, I do have my *own* name to think of. I am not one of these people who can do as they please—Roger, are you listening?"

"Yes, Mother," he said.

"—with their life."

As he went around the corner he found a note pinned to the door.

> Bathroom window up
> Cellar door down
> Is it blue or brown for Navy?

He stopped on the landing and looked up the stairs.

"Did you say something?" she said.

"No, Mother—" he said, then he added, "it's blue. For the Navy, Mother, it's blue."

# JOHN CHEEVER

## (1912–1982)

For John Cheever, fiction was a way of sounding an alarm—in particular about the dearth and failure of moral purpose in the lives of the upper middle class in New York City and its wealthy suburbs. Cheever's fiction chronicled and satirized the sad lives of successful people—spiritual derelicts, who on occasion recover a glimpse of grace. But his writing is more than the epitome of the urbane, sophisticated *New Yorker* style; its realism and satire are often infused with Cheever's special brand of magic and fantasy, as seen in such stories as "The Enormous Radio" and "The Swimmer."

Cheever was born in Quincy, Massachusetts, and was raised by prosperous and literature-loving parents. His father left the family after the 1929 market crash, however, and Cheever's mother kept the family going by running a gift shop. Intending to prep for Harvard, Cheever managed to get himself expelled from the exclusive Thayer Academy of South Braintree. At age 17 he turned this experience into his first story, "Expelled," which Malcolm Cowley accepted for publication in *The New Republic* in 1930. Six years later Cheever published his first story in *The New Yorker.*

After serving in the army from 1941 to 1945, Cheever wrote television scripts for a few years, but soon returned to writing fiction full-time. His short-story collections include *The Way Some People Live* (1943), *The Enormous Radio* (1953), *The Housebreaker of Shady Hill* (1958), *Some People, Places, and Things That Will Not Appear in My Next Novel* (1961), *The Brigadier and the Golf Widow* (1964), *The World of Apples* (1973), and *The Stories of John Cheever* (1978). The last won both the Pulitzer Prize and the National Book Critics Circle Award. Cheever's novel *The Wapshot Chronicle* (1957) won the National Book Award. It was followed by *The Wapshot Scandal* (1964), *Bullet Park* (1969), *Falconer* (1977), and *Oh, What a Paradise It Seems* (1982). Cheever's *Journals* appeared in 1991.

# The Country Husband

To begin at the beginning, the airplane from Minneapolis in which Francis Weed was traveling East ran into heavy weather. The sky had been a hazy blue, with the clouds below the plane lying so close together that nothing could be seen of the earth. Then mist began to form outside the windows, and they flew into a white cloud of such density that it reflected the exhaust fires. The color of the cloud darkened to gray, and the plane began to rock. Francis had been in heavy weather before, but he had never been shaken up so much. The man in the seat beside him pulled a flask out of his pocket and took a drink. Francis smiled at his neighbor, but the man looked away; he wasn't sharing his painkiller with anyone. The plane had begun to drop and flounder wildly. A child was crying. The air in the cabin was overheated and stale, and Francis' left foot went to sleep. He read a little from a paper book that he had bought at the airport, but the violence of the storm divided his attention. It was black outside the ports. The exhaust fires blazed and shed sparks in the dark, and, inside, the shaded lights, the stuffiness, and the window curtains gave the cabin an atmosphere of intense and misplaced domesticity. Then the lights flickered and went out. "You know what I've always wanted to do?" the man beside Francis said suddenly. "I've always wanted to buy a farm in New Hampshire and raise beef cattle." The stewardess announced that they were going to make an emergency landing. All but the child saw in their minds the spreading wings of the Angel of Death. The pilot could be heard singing faintly, "I've got sixpence, jolly, jolly sixpence. I've got sixpence to last me all my life. . . ." There was no other sound.

The loud groaning of the hydraulic valves swallowed up the pilot's song, and there was a shrieking high in the air, like automobile brakes, and the plane hit flat on its belly in a cornfield and shook them so violently that an old man up forward howled, "Me kidneys! Me kidneys!" The stewardess flung open the door, and someone opened an emergency door at the back, letting in the sweet noise of their continuing mortality—the idle splash and smell of a heavy rain. Anxious for their lives, they filed out of the doors and scattered over the cornfield in all directions, praying that the thread would hold. It did. Nothing happened. When it was clear that the plane would not burn or explode, the crew and the stewardess gathered the passengers together and led them to the shelter of a barn. They were not far from Philadelphia, and in a little while a string of taxis took them into the city. "It's just like the Marne," someone said, but there was surprisingly little relaxation of that suspiciousness with which many Americans regard their fellow-travelers.

In Philadelphia, Francis Weed got a train to New York. At the end of that journey, he crossed the city and caught just as it was about to pull out, the commuting train that he took five nights a week to his home in Shady Hill.

He sat with Trace Bearden. "You know, I was in that plane that just crashed outside Philadelphia," he said. "We came down in a field. . . ." He had traveled faster than the newspapers or the rain, and the weather in New York was sunny and mild. It was a day in late September, as fragrant and shapely as an apple. Trace listened to the story, but how could he get excited? Francis had no powers that would let him re-create a brush with death—particularly in the atmosphere of a commuting train, journeying through a sunny countryside where already, in the slum gardens, there were signs of harvest. Trace picked up his newspaper, and Francis was left alone with his thoughts. He said good night to Trace on the platform at Shady Hill and drove in his secondhand Volkswagen up to the Blenhollow neighborhood, where he lived.

* * *

The Weeds' Dutch Colonial house was larger than it appeared to be from the driveway. The living room was spacious and divided like Gaul into three parts. Around an ell to the left as one entered from the vestibule was the long table, laid for six, with candles and a bowl of fruit in the center. The sounds and smells that came from the open kitchen door were appetizing, for Julia Weed was a good cook. The largest part of the living room centered around a fireplace. On the right were some bookshelves and a piano. The room was polished and tranquil, and from the windows that opened to the west there was some late-summer sunlight, brilliant and as clear as water. Nothing here was neglected; nothing had not been burnished. It was not the kind of household where, after prying open a stuck cigarette box, you would find an old shirt button and a tarnished nickel. The hearth was swept, the roses on the piano were reflected in the polish of the broad top, and there was an album of Schubert waltzes on the rack. Louisa Weed, a pretty girl of nine, was looking out the western windows. Her younger brother Henry was standing beside her. Her still younger brother, Toby, was studying the figures of some tonsured monks drinking beer on the polished brass of the wood box. Francis, taking off his hat and putting down his paper, was not consciously pleased with the scene; he was not that reflective. It was his element, his creation, and he returned to it with that sense of lightness and strength with which any creature returns to its home. "Hi, everybody," he said. "The plane from Minneapolis . . ."

Nine times out of ten, Francis would be greeted with affection, but tonight the children are absorbed in their own antagonisms. Francis has not finished his sentence about the plane crash before Henry plants a kick in Louisa's behind. Louisa swings around, saying, "*Damn* you!" Francis makes the mistake of scolding Louisa for bad language before he punishes Henry. Now Louisa turns on her father and accuses him of favoritism. Henry is always right; she is persecuted and lonely; her lot is hopeless. Francis turns to his son, but the boy has justification for the kick—she hit him first; she hit him on the ear, which is dangerous. Louisa agrees with this passionately. She hit him on the ear, and she *meant* to hit him on the ear, because he messed up her china collection. Henry says that this is a lie. Little Toby turns away from the wood box to throw in some evidence for Louisa. Henry claps his hand over little Toby's mouth. Francis separates the two boys but accidentally pushes Toby into the wood box. Toby begins to cry. Louisa is already crying. Just then, Julia Weed comes into that part of the room where the table is laid. She is a pretty, intelligent woman, and the white in her hair is premature. She does not seem to notice the fracas. "Hello, darling," she says serenely to Francis. "Wash your hands, everyone. Dinner is ready." She strikes a match and lights the six candles in this vale of tears.

This simple announcement, like the war cries of the Scottish chieftains, only refreshes the ferocity of the combatants. Louisa gives Henry a blow on the shoulder. Henry, although he seldom cries, has pitched nine innings and is tired. He bursts into tears. Little Toby discovers a splinter in his hand and begins to howl. Francis says loudly that he has been in a plane crash and that he is tired. Julia appears again, from the kitchen, and, still ignoring the chaos, asks Francis to go upstairs and tell Helen that everything is ready. Francis is happy to go; it is like getting back to headquarters company. He is planning to tell his oldest daughter about the airplane crash, but Helen is lying on her bed reading a *True Romance* magazine, and the first thing Francis does is to take the magazine from her hand and remind Helen that he has forbidden her to buy it. She did not buy it, Helen replies. It was given to her by her best friend, Bessie Black. Everybody reads *True Romance.* Bessie Black's father reads *True Romance.* There isn't a girl in Helen's class who doesn't read *True Romance.* Francis expresses his detestation of the magazine and then tells her that dinner is ready—although from the sounds downstairs it doesn't seem so. Helen follows him down the stairs. Julia has seated herself in the candlelight and spread a napkin over her lap. Neither Louisa nor Henry has come to the table. Little Toby is still howling, lying face down on the floor. Francis speaks to him gently: "Daddy was in a plane crash this afternoon, Toby. Don't you want to hear about it?" Toby goes on crying. "If you don't come to the table now, Toby," Francis says, "I'll have to send you to bed without any supper." The little boy rises, gives him a cutting look, flies up the stairs to his bedroom, and slams the door. "Oh dear," Julia says, and starts to go after him. Francis says that she will spoil him. Julia says that Toby is ten pounds underweight and has to be encouraged to eat. Winter is coming, and he will spend the cold months in bed unless he has his dinner. Julia goes upstairs. Francis sits down at the table with Helen. Helen is suffering from the dismal feeling of having read too intently on a fine day, and she gives her father and the room a jaded look. She doesn't understand about the plane crash, because there wasn't a drop of rain in Shady Hill.

Julia returns with Toby, and they all sit down and are served. "Do I have to look at that big, fat slob?" Henry says of Louisa. Everybody but Toby enters into this skirmish, and it rages up and down the table for five minutes. Toward the end, Henry puts his napkin over his head and, trying to eat that way, spills spinach all over his shirt. Francis asks Julia if the children couldn't have their dinner earlier. Julia's guns are loaded for this. She can't cook two dinners and lay two tables. She paints with lightning strokes that panorama of drudgery in which her youth, her beauty, and her wit have been lost. Francis says that he must be understood; he was nearly killed in an airplane crash, and he doesn't like to come home every night to a battlefield. Now Julia is deeply committed. Her voice trembles. He doesn't come home every night to a battlefield. The accusation is stupid and mean. Everything was tranquil until he arrived. She stops speaking, puts down her knife and fork, and looks into her plate as if it is a gulf. She begins to cry. "Poor Mummy!" Toby says, and when Julia gets up from the table, drying her tears with a napkin, Toby goes to her side. "Poor Mummy," he says. "Poor Mummy!" And they climb the stairs together. The other children drift away from the battlefield, and Francis goes into the back garden for a cigarette and some air.

* * *

It was a pleasant garden, with walks and flower beds and places to sit. The sunset had nearly burned out, but there was still plenty of light. Put into a thoughtful mood by the crash and the battle, Francis listened to the evening sounds of Shady Hill. "Varmints! Rascals!" old Mr. Nixon shouted to the squirrels in his bird-feeding station. "Avaunt and quit my sight!" A door slammed. Someone was playing tennis on the Babcocks' court; someone was cutting grass. Then Donald Goslin, who lived at the corner, began to play the "Moonlight Sonata." He did this nearly every night. He threw the tempo out the window and played it *rubato* from beginning to end, like an outpouring of tearful petulance, lonesomeness, and self-pity—of everything it was Beethoven's greatness not to know. The music rang up and down the street beneath the trees like an appeal for love, for tenderness, aimed at some lonely housemaid—some fresh-faced, homesick girl from Galway, looking at old snapshots in her third-floor room. "Here, Jupiter, here, Jupiter," Francis called to the Mercers' retriever. Jupiter crashed through the tomato vines with the remains of a felt hat in his mouth.

Jupiter was an anomaly. His retrieving instincts and his high spirits were out of place in Shady Hill. He was as black as coal, with a long, alert, intelligent, rakehell face. His eyes gleamed with mischief, and he held his head high. It was the fierce, heavily collared dog's head that appears in heraldry, in tapestry, and that used to appear on umbrella handles and walking sticks. Jupiter went where he pleased ransacking wastebaskets, clotheslines, garbage pails, and shoe bags. He broke up garden parties and tennis matches and got mixed up in the processional at Christ Church on Sunday, barking at the men in red dresses. He crashed through old Mr. Nixon's rose garden two or three times a day cutting a wide swath through the Condesa de Sastagos, and as soon as Donald Goslin lighted his barbecue fire on Thursday nights, Jupiter would get the scent. Nothing the Goslins did could drive him away. Sticks and stones and rude command only moved him to the edge of the terrace, where he remained, with his gallant and heraldic muzzle, waiting for Donald Goslin to turn his back and reach for the salt. Then he would spring onto the terrace, lift the steak lightly off the fire, and run away with the Goslins' dinner. Jupiter's day were numbered. The Wrightsons' German gardener or the Farquarsons' cook would soon poison him. Even old Mr. Nixon might put some arsenic in the garbage that Jupiter loved. "Here, Jupiter, Jupiter!" Francis called, but the dog pranced off, shaking the hat in his white teeth. Looking in at the windows of his house, Francis saw that Julia had come down and was blowing out the candles.

* * *

Julia and Francis Weed went out a great deal. Julia was well liked and gregarious, and her love of parties sprang from a most natural dread of chaos and loneliness. She went through her morning mail with real anxiety, looking for invitations, and she usually found some, but she was insatiable, and if she had gone out seven nights a week, it would not have cured her of a reflective look—the look of someone who hears distant music—for she would always suppose that there was a more brilliant party somewhere else. Francis limited her to two week-night parties, putting a flexible interpretation on Friday, and rode through the weekend like a dory in a gale. The day after the airplane crash, the Weeds were to have dinner with the Farquarsons.

Francis got home late from town, and Julia got the sitter while he dressed, and then hurried him out of the house. The party was small and pleasant, and Francis settled down to enjoy himself. A new maid passed the drinks. Her hair was dark, and her face was round and pale and seemed familiar to Francis. He had not developed his memory as a sentimental faculty. Wood smoke, lilac, and other such perfumes did not stir him, and his memory was something like his appendix—a vestigial repository. It was not his limitation at all to be unable to escape the past; it was perhaps his limitation that he had escaped it so successfully. He might have seen the maid at other parties, he might have seen her taking a walk on Sunday afternoons, but in either case he would not be searching his memory now. Her face was, in a wonderful way, a moon face—Norman or Irish—but it was not beautiful enough to account for his feeling that he had seen her before, in circumstances that he ought to be able to remember. He asked Nellie Farquarson who she was. Nellie said that the maid had come through an agency, and that her home was Trénon, in Normandy—a small place with a church and a restaurant that Nellie had once visited. While Nellie talked on about her travels abroad, Francis realized where he had seen the woman before. It had been at the end of the war. He had left a replacement depot with some other men and taken a three-day pass in Trénon. On their second day, they had walked out to a crossroads to see the public chastisement of a young woman who had lived with the German commandant during the Occupation.

It was a cool morning in the fall. The sky was overcast, and poured down onto the dirt crossroads a very discouraging light. They were on high land and could see how like one another the shapes of the clouds and the hills were as they stretched off toward the sea. The prisoner arrived sitting on a three-legged stool in a farm cart. She stood by the cart while the mayor read the accusation and the sentence. Her head was bent and her face was set in that empty half smile behind which the whipped soul is suspended. When the mayor was finished, she undid her hair and let it fall across her back. A little man with a gray mustache cut off her hair with shears and dropped it on the ground. Then, with a bowl of soapy water and a straight razor, he shaved her skull clean. A woman approached and began to undo the fastenings of her clothes, but the prisoner pushed her aside and undressed herself. When she pulled her chemise over her head and threw it on the ground, she was naked. The women jeered; the men were still. There was no change in the falseness or the plaintiveness of the prisoner's smile. The cold wind made her white skin rough and hardened the nipples of her breasts. The jeering ended gradually, put down by the recognition of their common humanity. One woman spat on her, but some inviolable grandeur in her nakedness lasted through the ordeal. When the crowd was quiet, she turned—she had begun to cry—and, with nothing on but a pair of worn black shoes and stockings, walked down the dirt road alone away from the village. The round white face had aged a little, but there was no question but that the maid who passed his cocktails and later served Francis his dinner was the woman who had been punished at the crossroads.

The war seemed now so distant and that world where the cost of partisanship had been death or torture so long ago. Francis had lost track of the men who had been with him in Vésey. He could not count on Julia's discretion. He could not tell anyone. And if he had told the story now, at the dinner table, it would have been a social as well as a human error. The people in the Farquarsons' living room seemed united in their tacit claim that there had been no past, no war—that there was no danger or trouble in the world. In the recorded history of human arrangements, this extraordinary meeting would have fallen into place, but the atmosphere of Shady Hill made the memory unseemly and impolite. The prisoner withdrew after passing the coffee, but the encounter left Francis feeling languid; it had opened his memory and his senses, and left them dilated. He and Julia drove home when the party ended, and Julia went into the house. Francis stayed in the car to take the sitter home.

Expecting to see Mrs. Henlein, the old lady who usually stayed with the children, he was surprised when a young girl opened the door and came out onto the lighted stoop. She stayed in the light to count her textbooks. She was frowning and beautiful. Now, the world is full of beautiful young girls, but Francis saw here the difference between beauty and perfection. All those endearing flaws, moles, birthmarks, and healed wounds were missing, and he experienced in his consciousness that moment when music breaks glass, and felt a pang of recognition as strange, deep, and wonderful as anything in his life. It hung from her frown, from an impalpable darkness in her face—a look that impressed him as a direct appeal for love. When she had counted her books, she came down the steps and opened the car door. In the light, he saw that her cheeks were wet. She got in and shut the door.

"You're new," Francis said.

"Yes. Mrs. Henlein is sick. I'm Anne Murchison."

"Did the children give you any trouble?"

"Oh, no, no." She turned and smiled at him unhappily in the dim dashboard light. Her light hair caught on the collar of her jacket, and she shook her head to set it loose.

"You've been crying."

"Yes."

"I hope it was nothing that happened in our house."

"No, no, it was nothing that happened in your house." Her voice was bleak. "It's no secret. Everybody in the village knows. Daddy's an alcoholic, and he just called me from some saloon and gave me a piece of his mind. He thinks I'm immoral. He called just before Mrs. Weed came back."

"I'm sorry."

"Oh, *Lord!*" She gasped and began to cry. She turned toward Francis, and he took her in his arms and let her cry on his shoulder. She shook in his embrace, and this movement accentuated his sense of the fineness of her flesh and bone. The layers of their clothing felt thin, and when her shuddering began to diminish, it was so much like a paroxysm of love that Francis lost his head and pulled her roughly against him. She drew away. "I live on Belleview Avenue," she said. "You go down Lansing Street to the railroad bridge."

"All right." He started the car.

"You turn left at that traffic light. . . . Now you turn right here and go straight on toward the tracks."

The road Francis took brought him out of his own neighborhood, across the tracks, and toward the river, to a street where the near-poor lived, in houses whose peaked gables and trimmings of wooden lace conveyed the purest feelings of pride and romance, although the houses themselves could not have offered much privacy or comfort, they were all so small. The street was dark, and, stirred by the grace and beauty of the troubled girl, he seemed, in turning in to it, to have come into the deepest part of some submerged memory. In the distance, he saw a porch light burning. It was the only one, and she said that the house with the light was where she lived. When he stopped the car, he could see beyond the porch light into a dimly lighted hallway with an old-fashioned clothes tree. "Well, here we are," he said, conscious that a young man would have said something different.

She did not move her hands from the books, where they were folded, and she turned and faced him. There were tears of lust in his eyes. Determinedly—not sadly—he opened the door on his side and walked around to open hers. He took her free hand, letting his fingers in between hers, climbed at her side the two concrete steps, and went up a narrow walk through a front garden where dahlias, marigolds, and roses—things that had withstood the light frosts—still bloomed, and made a bittersweet smell in the night air. At the steps, she freed her hand and then turned and kissed him swiftly. Then she crossed the porch and shut the door. The porch light went out, then the light in the hall. A second later, a light went on upstairs at the side of the house, shining into a tree that was still covered with leaves. It took her only a few minutes to undress and get into bed, and then the house was dark.

Julia was asleep when Francis got home. He opened a second window and got into bed to shut his eyes on that night, but as soon as they were shut—as soon as he had dropped off to sleep—the girl entered his mind, moving with perfect freedom through its shut doors and filling chamber after chamber with her light, her perfume, and the music of her voice. He was crossing the Atlantic with her on the old *Mauretania* and, later, living with her in Paris. When he woke from his dream, he got up and smoked a cigarette at the open window. Getting back into bed, he cast around in his mind for something he desired to do that would injure no one, and he thought of skiing. Up through the dimness in his mind rose the image of a mountain deep in snow. It was late in the day. Wherever his eyes looked, he saw broad and heartening things. Over his shoulder, there was a snow-filled valley, rising into wooded hills where the trees dimmed the whiteness like a sparse coat of hair. The cold deadened all sound but the loud, iron clanking of the lift machinery. The light on the trails was blue, and it was harder than it had been a minute or two earlier to pick the turns, harder to judge—now that the snow was all deep blue—the crust, the ice, the bare spots, and the deep piles of dry powder. Down the mountain he swung, matching his speed against the contours of a slope that had been formed in the first ice age, seeking with ardor some simplicity of feeling and circumstance. Night fell then, and he drank a Martini with some old friend in a dirty country bar.

In the morning, Francis' snow-covered mountain was gone, and he was left with his vivid memories of Paris and the *Mauretania.* He had been bitten gravely. He washed his body, shaved his jaws, drank his coffee, and missed the seven-thirty-one. The train pulled out just as he brought his car to the station, and the longing he felt for the coaches as they drew stubbornly away from him reminded him of the humors of love. He waited for the eight-two, on what was now an empty platform. It was a clear morning; the morning seemed thrown like a gleaming bridge of light over his mixed affairs. His spirits were feverish and high. The image of the girl seemed to put him into a relationship to the world that was mysterious and enthralling. Cars were beginning to fill up the parking lot, and he noticed that those that had driven down from the high land above Shady Hill were white with hoarfrost. This first clear sign of autumn thrilled him. An express train—a night train from Buffalo or Albany—came down the tracks between the platforms, and he saw that the roofs of the foremost cars were covered with a skin of ice. Struck by the miraculous physicalness of everything, he smiled at the passengers in the dining car, who could be seen eating eggs and wiping their mouths with napkins as they traveled. The sleeping-car compartments, with their soiled bed linen, trailed through the fresh morning like a string of rooming-house windows. Then he saw an extraordinary thing; at one of the bedroom windows sat an unclothed woman of exceptional beauty, combing her golden hair. She passed like an apparition through Shady Hill, combing and combing her hair, and Francis followed her with his eyes until she was out of sight. Then old Mrs. Wrightson joined him on the platform and began to talk.

"Well, I guess you must be surprised to see me here the third morning in a row," she said, "but because of my window curtains I'm becoming a regular commuter. The curtains I bought on Monday I returned on Tuesday, and the curtains I bought Tuesday I'm returning today. On Monday, I got exactly what I wanted—it's a wool tapestry with roses and birds—but when I got them home, I found they were the wrong length. Well, I exchanged them yesterday, and when I got them home, I found they were still the wrong length. Now I'm praying to high Heaven that the decorator will have them in the right length, because you know my house, you *know* my living-room windows, and you can imagine what a problem they present. I don't know what to do with them."

"I know what to do with them," Francis said.

"What?"

"Paint them black on the inside, and shut up."

There was a gasp from Mrs. Wrightson, and Francis looked down at her to be sure that she knew he meant to be rude. She turned and walked away from him, so damaged in spirit that she limped. A wonderful feeling enveloped him, as if light were being shaken about him, and he thought again of Venus combing and combing her hair as she drifted through the Bronx. The realization of how many years had passed since he had enjoyed being deliberately impolite sobered him. Among his friends and neighbors, there were brilliant and gifted people—he saw that—but many of them, also, were bores and fools, and he had made the mistake of listening to them all with equal attention. He had confused a lack of discrimination with Christian love, and the confusion seemed general and destructive. He was grateful to the girl for this bracing sensation of independence. Birds were singing—cardinals and the last of the robins. The sky shone like enamel. Even the smell of ink from his morning paper honed his appetite for life, and the world that was spread out around him was plainly a paradise.

If Francis had believed in some hierarchy of love—in spirits armed with hunting bows, in the capriciousness of Venus and Eros—or even in magical potions, philters, and stews, in scapulae and quarters of the moon, it might have explained his susceptibility and his feverish high spirits. The autumnal loves of middle age are well publicized, and he guessed that he was face to face with one of these, but there was not a trace of autumn in what he felt. He wanted to sport in the green woods, scratch where he itched, and drink from the same cup.

His secretary, Miss Rainey, was late that morning—she went to a psychiatrist three mornings a week—and when she came in, Francis wondered what advice a psychiatrist would have for him. But the girl promised to bring back into his life something like the sound of music. The realization that this music might lead him straight to a trial for statutory rape at the county courthouse collapsed his happiness. The photograph of his four children laughing into the camera on the beach at Gay Head reproached him. On the letterhead of his firm there was a drawing of the Laocoön, and the figure of the priest and his sons in the coils of the snake appeared to him to have the deepest meaning.

He had lunch with Pinky Trabert. At a conversational level, the mores of his friends were robust and elastic, but he knew that the moral card house would come down on them all—on Julia and the children as well—if he got caught taking advantage of a babysitter. Looking back over the recent history of Shady Hill for some precedent, he found there was none. There was no turpitude; there had not been a divorce since he lived there; there had not even been a breath of scandal. Things seemed arranged with more propriety even than in the Kingdom of Heaven. After leaving Pinky, Francis went to a jeweler's and bought the girl a bracelet. How happy this clandestine purchase made him, how stuffy and comical the jeweler's clerks seemed, how sweet the women who passed at his back smelled! On Fifth Avenue, passing Atlas with his shoulders bent under the weight of the world, Francis thought of the strenuousness of containing his physicalness within the patterns he had chosen.

He did not know when he would see the girl next. He had the bracelet in his inside pocket when he got home. Opening the door of his house, he found her in the hall. Her back was to him, and she turned when she heard the door close. Her smile was open and loving. Her perfection stunned him like a fine day—a day after a thunderstorm. He seized her and covered her lips with his, and she struggled but she did not have to struggle for long, because just then little Gertrude Flannery appeared from somewhere and said, "Oh, Mr. Weed . . ."

Gertrude was a stray. She had been born with a taste for exploration, and she did not have it in her to center her life with her affectionate parents. People who did not know the Flannerys concluded from Gertrude's behavior that she was the child of a bitterly divided family, where drunken quarrels were the rule. This was not true. The fact that little Gertrude's clothing was ragged and thin was her own triumph over her mother's struggle to dress her warmly and neatly. Garrulous, skinny, and unwashed, she drifted from house to house around the Blenhollow neighborhood, forming and breaking alliances based on an attachment to babies, animals, children her own age, adolescents, and sometimes adults. Opening your front door in the morning, you would find Gertrude sitting on your stoop. Going into the bathroom to shave, you would find Gertrude using the toilet. Looking into your son's crib, you would find it empty, and, looking further, you would find that Gertrude had pushed him in his baby carriage into the next village. She was helpful, pervasive, honest, hungry, and loyal. She never went home of her own choice. When the time to go arrived, she was indifferent to all its signs. "Go home, Gertrude," people could be heard saying in one house or another, night after night. "Go home, Gertrude. It's time for you to go home now, Gertrude." "You had better go home and get your supper, Gertrude." "I told you to go home twenty minutes ago, Gertrude." "Your mother will be worrying about you, Gertrude." "Go home, Gertrude, go home."

There are times when the lines around the human eye seem like shelves of eroded stone and when the staring eye itself strikes us with such a wilderness of animal feeling that we are at a loss. The look Francis gave the little girl was ugly and queer, and it frightened her. He reached into his pocket—his hands were shaking—and took out a quarter. "Go home, Gertrude, go home, and don't tell anyone, Gertrude. Don't—" He choked and ran into the living room as Julia called down to him from upstairs to hurry and dress.

The thought that he would drive Anne Murchison home later that night ran like a golden thread through the events of the party that Francis and Julia went to, and he laughed uproariously at dull jokes, dried a tear when Mabel Mercer told him about the death of her kitten, and stretched, yawned, sighed, and grunted like any other man with a rendezvous at the back of his mind. The bracelet was in his pocket. As he sat talking, the smell of grass was in his nose, and he was wondering where he would park the car. Nobody lived in the old Parker mansion, and the driveway was used as a lovers' lane. Townsend Street was a dead end, and he could park there, beyond the last house. The old lane that used to connect Elm Street to the riverbanks was overgrown, but he had walked there with his children, and he could drive his car deep enough into the brushwoods to be concealed.

The Weeds were the last to leave the party, and their host and hostess spoke of their own married happiness while they all four stood in the hallway saying good night. "She's my girl," their host said, squeezing his wife. "She's my blue sky. After sixteen years, I still bite her shoulders. She makes me feel like Hannibal crossing the Alps."

The Weeds drove home in silence. Francis brought the car up the driveway and sat still, with the motor running. "You can put the car in the garage," Julia said as she got out. "I told the Murchison girl she could leave at eleven. Someone drove her home." She shut the door, and Francis sat in the dark. He would be spared nothing then, it seemed, that a fool was not spared: ravening lewdness, jealousy, this hurt to his feelings that put tears in his eyes, even scorn—for he could see clearly the image he now presented, his arms spread over the steering wheel and his head buried in them for love.

* * *

Francis had been a dedicated Boy Scout when he was young, and, remembering the precepts of his youth, he left his office early the next afternoon and played some round-robin squash, but, with his body toned up by exercise and a shower, he realized that he might better have stayed at his desk. It was a frosty night when he got home. The air smelled sharply of change. When he stepped into the house, he sensed an unusual stir. The children were in their best clothes, and when Julia came down, she was wearing a lavender dress and her diamond sunburst. She explained the stir: Mr. Hubber was coming at seven to take their photograph for the Christmas card. She had put out Francis' blue suit and a tie with some color in it, because the picture was going to be in color this year. Julia was lighthearted at the thought of being photographed for Christmas. It was the kind of ceremony she enjoyed.

Francis went upstairs to change his clothes. He was tired from the day's work and tired with longing, and sitting on the edge of the bed had the effect of deepening his weariness. He thought of Anne Murchison, and the physical need to express himself, instead of being restrained by the pink lamps on Julia's dressing table, engulfed him. He went to Julia's desk, took a piece of writing paper, and began to write on it. "Dear Anne, I love you, I love you, I love you . . ." No one would see the letter, and he used no restraint. He used phrases like "heavenly bliss," and "love nest." He salivated, sighed, and trembled. When Julia called him to come down, the abyss between his fantasy and the practical world opened so wide that he felt it affect the muscles of his heart.

Julia and the children were on the stoop, and the photographer and his assistant had set up a double battery of floodlights to show the family and the architectural beauty of the entrance to their house. People who had come home on a late train slowed their cars to see the Weeds being photographed for their Christmas card. A few waved and called to the family. It took half an hour of smiling and wetting their lips before Mr. Hubber was satisfied. The heat of the lights made an unfresh smell in the frosty air, and when they were turned off, they lingered on the retina of Francis' eyes.

Later that night, while Francis and Julia were drinking their coffee in the living room, the doorbell rang. Julia answered the door and let in Clayton Thomas. He had come to pay her for some theater tickets that she had given his mother some time ago, and that Helen Thomas had scrupulously insisted on paying for, though Julia had asked her not to. Julia invited him in to have a cup of coffee. "I won't have any coffee," Clayton said, "but I will come in for a minute." He followed her into the living room, said good evening to Francis, and sat awkwardly in a chair.

Clayton's father had been killed in the war, and the young man's fatherlessness surrounded him like an element. This may have been conspicuous in Shady Hill because the Thomases were the only family that lacked a piece; all the other marriages were intact and productive. Clayton was in his second or third year of college, and he and his mother lived alone in a large house, which she hoped to sell. Clayton had once made some trouble. Years ago, he had stolen some money and run away; he had got to California before they caught up with him. He was tall and homely, wore horn-rimmed glasses, and spoke in a deep voice.

"When do you go back to college, Clayton?" Francis asked.

"I'm not going back," Clayton said. "Mother doesn't have the money, and there's no sense in all this pretense. I'm going to get a job, and if we sell the house, we'll take an apartment in New York."

"Won't you miss Shady Hill?" Julia asked.

"No," Clayton said. "I don't like it."

"Why not?" Francis asked.

"Well, there's a lot here I don't approve of," Clayton said gravely. "Things like the club dances. Last Saturday night, I looked in toward the end and saw Mr. Granner trying to put Mrs. Minot into the trophy case. They were both drunk. I disapprove of so much drinking."

"It was Saturday night," Francis said.

"And all the dovecotes are phony," Clayton said. "And the way people clutter up their lives. I've thought about it a lot, and what seems to me to be really wrong with Shady Hill is that it doesn't have any future. So much energy is spent in perpetuating the place—in keeping out undesirables, and so forth—that the only idea of the future anyone has is just more and more commuting trains and more parties. I don't think that's healthy. I think people ought to be able to dream big dreams about the future. I think people ought to be able to dream great dreams."

"It's too bad you couldn't continue with college," Julia said.

"I wanted to go to divinity school," Clayton said.

"What's your church?" Francis asked.

"Unitarian, Theosophist, Transcendentalist, Humanist," Clayton said.

"Wasn't Emerson a transcendentalist?" Julia asked.

"I mean the English transcendentalists," Clayton said. "All the American transcendentalists were goops."

"What kind of a job do you expect to get?" Francis asked.

"Well, I'd like to work for a publisher," Clayton said, "but everyone tells me there's nothing doing. But it's the kind of thing I'm interested in. I'm writing a long verse play about good and evil. Uncle Charlie might get me into a bank, and that would be good for me. I need the discipline. I have a long way to go in forming my character. I have some terrible habits. I talk too much. I think I ought to take vows of silence. I ought to try not to speak for a week, and discipline myself. I've thought of making a retreat at one of the Episcopalian monasteries, but I don't like Trinitarianism."

"Do you have any girl friends?" Francis asked.

"I'm engaged to be married," Clayton said. "Of course, I'm not old enough or rich enough to have my engagement observed or respected or anything, but I bought a simulated emerald for Anne Murchison with the money I made cutting lawns this summer. We're going to be married as soon as she finishes school."

Francis recoiled at the mention of the girl's name. Then a dingy light seemed to emanate from his spirit, showing everything—Julia, the boy, the chairs—in their true colorlessness. It was like a bitter turn of the weather.

"We're going to have a large family," Clayton said. "Her father's a terrible rummy, and I've had my hard times, and we want to have lots of children. Oh, she's wonderful, Mr. and Mrs. Weed, and we have so much in common. We like all the same things. We sent out the same Christmas card last year without planning it, and we both have an allergy to tomatoes, and our eyebrows grow together in the middle. Well, good night."

Julia went to the door with him. When she returned, Francis said that Clayton was lazy, irresponsible, affected, and smelly. Julia said that Francis seemed to be getting intolerant; the Thomas boy was young and should be given a chance. Julia had noticed other cases where Francis had been short-tempered. "Mrs. Wrightson has asked everyone in Shady Hill to her anniversary party but us," she said.

"I'm sorry, Julia."

"Do you know why they didn't ask us?"

"Why?"

"Because you insulted Mrs. Wrightson."

"Then you know about it?"

"June Masterson told me. She was standing behind you."

Julia walked in front of the sofa with a small step that expressed, Francis knew, a feeling of anger.

"I did insult Mrs. Wrightson, Julia, and I meant to. I've never liked her parties, and I'm glad she's dropped us."

"What about Helen?"

"How does Helen come into this?"

"Mrs. Wrightson's the one who decides who goes to the assemblies."

"You mean she can keep Helen from going to the dances?"

"Yes."

"I hadn't thought of that."

"Oh, I knew you hadn't thought of it," Julia cried, thrusting hilt-deep into this chink of his armor. "And it makes me furious to see this kind of stupid thoughtlessness wreck everyone's happiness."

"I don't think I've wrecked anyone's happiness."

"Mrs. Wrightson runs Shady Hill and has run it for the last forty years. I don't know what makes you think that in a community like this you can indulge every impulse you have to be insulting, vulgar, and offensive."

"I have very good manners," Francis said, trying to give the evening a turn toward the light.

"Damn you, Francis Weed!" Julia cried, and the spit of her words struck him in the face. "I've worked hard for the social position we enjoy in this place, and I won't stand by and see you wreck it. You must have understood when you settled here that you couldn't expect to live like a bear in a cave."

"I've got to express my likes and dislikes."

"You can conceal your dislikes. You don't have to meet everything head-on, like a child. Unless you're anxious to be a social leper. It's no accident that we get asked out a great deal. It's no accident that Helen has so many friends. How would you like to spend your Saturday nights at the movies? How would you like to spend your Sundays raking up dead leaves? How would you like it if your daughter spent the assembly nights sitting at her window, listening to the music from the club? How would you like it—" He did something then that was, after all, not so unaccountable, since her words seemed to raise up between them a wall so deadening that he gagged: He struck her full in the face. She staggered and then, a moment later, seemed composed. She went up the stairs to their room. She didn't slam the door. When Francis followed, a few minutes later, he found her packing a suitcase.

"Julia, I'm very sorry."

"It doesn't matter," she said. She was crying.

"Where do you think you're going?"

"I don't know. I just looked at a timetable. There's an eleven-sixteen into New York. I'll take that."

"You can't go, Julia."

"I can't stay. I know that."

"I'm sorry about Mrs. Wrightson, Julia, and I'm—"

"It doesn't matter about Mrs. Wrightson. That isn't the trouble."

"What is the trouble?"

"You don't love me."

"I do love you, Julia."

"No, you don't."

"Julia, I do love you, and I would like to be as we were—sweet and bawdy and dark—but now there are so many people."

"You hate me."

"I don't hate you, Julia."

"You have no idea of how much you hate me. I think it's subconscious. You don't realize the cruel things you've done."

"What cruel things, Julia?"

"The cruel acts your subconscious drives you to in order to express your hatred of me."

"What, Julia?"

"I've never complained."

"Tell me."

"You don't know what you're doing."

"Tell me."

"Your clothes."

"What do you mean?"

"I mean the way you leave your dirty clothes around in order to express your subconscious hatred of me."

"I don't understand."

"I mean your dirty socks and your dirty pajamas and your dirty underwear and your dirty shirts!" She rose from kneeling by the suitcase and faced him, her eyes blazing and her voice ringing with emotion. "I'm talking about the fact that you've never learned to hang up anything. You just leave your clothes all over the floor where they drop, in order to humiliate me. You do it on purpose!" She fell on the bed, sobbing.

"Julia, darling!" he said, but when she felt his hand on her shoulder she got up.

"Leave me alone," she said. "I have to go." She brushed past him to the closet and came back with a dress. "I'm not taking any of the things you've given me," she said. "I'm leaving my pearls and the fur jacket."

"Oh, Julia!" Her figure, so helpless in its self-deceptions, bent over the suitcase made him nearly sick with pity. She did not understand how desolate her life would be without him. She didn't understand the hours that working women have to keep. She didn't understand that most of her friendships existed within the framework of their marriage, and that without this she would find herself alone. She didn't understand about travel, about hotels, about money. "Julia, I can't let you go! What you don't understand, Julia, is that you've come to be dependent on me."

She tossed her head back and covered her face with her hands. "Did you say that *I* was dependent on *you?*" she asked. "Is that what you said? And who is it that tells you what time to get up in the morning and when to go to bed at night? Who is it that prepares your meals and picks up your dirty clothes and invites your friends to dinner? If it weren't for me, your neckties would be greasy and your clothing would be full of moth holes. You were alone when I met you, Francis Weed, and you'll be alone when I leave. When Mother asked you for a list to send out invitations to our wedding, how many names did you have to give her? Fourteen!"

"Cleveland wasn't my home, Julia."

"And how many of your friends came to the church? Two!"

"Cleveland wasn't my home, Julia."

"Since I'm not taking the fur jacket," she said quietly, "you'd better put it back into storage. There's an insurance policy on the pearls that comes due in January. The name of the laundry and the maid's telephone number—all those things are in my desk. I hope you won't drink too much, Francis. I hope that nothing bad will happen to you. If you do get into serious trouble, you can call me."

"Oh, my darling, I can't let you go!" Francis said. "I can't let you go, Julia!" He took her in his arms.

"I guess I'd better stay and take care of you for a little while longer," she said.

* * *

Riding to work in the morning, Francis saw the girl walk down the aisle of the coach. He was surprised; he hadn't realized that the school she went to was in the city, but she was carrying books, she seemed to be going to school. His surprise delayed his reaction, but then he got up clumsily and stepped into the aisle. Several people had come between them, but he could see her ahead of him, waiting for someone to open the car door, and then, as the train swerved, putting out her hand to support herself as she crossed the platform into the next car. He followed her through that car and halfway through another before calling her name—"Anne! Anne!"—but she didn't turn. He followed her into still another car, and she sat down in an aisle seat. Coming up to her, all his feelings warm and bent in her direction, he put his hand on the back of her seat—even this touch warmed him—and, leaning down to speak to her, he saw that it was not Anne. It was an older woman wearing glasses. He went on deliberately into another car, his face red with embarrassment and the much deeper feeling of having his good sense challenged; for if he couldn't tell one person from another, what evidence was there that his life with Julia and the children had as much reality as his dreams of iniquity in Paris or the litter, the grass smell, and the cave-shaped trees in Lovers' Lane.

Late that afternoon, Julia called to remind Francis that they were going out for dinner. A few minutes later, Trace Bearden called. "Look, fellar," Trace said. "I'm calling for Mrs. Thomas. You know? Clayton, that boy of hers, doesn't seem able to get a job, and I wondered if you could help. If you'd call Charlie Bell—I know he's indebted to you—and say a good word for the kid, I think Charlie would—"

"Trace, I hate to say this," Francis said, "but I don't feel that I can do anything for that boy. The kid's worthless. I know it's a harsh thing to say, but it's a fact. Any kindness done for him would backfire in everybody's face. He's just a worthless kid, Trace, and there's nothing to be done about it. Even if we got him a job, he wouldn't be able to keep it for a week. I know that to be a fact. It's an awful thing, Trace, and I know it is, but instead of recommending that kid, I'd feel obliged to warn people against him—people who knew his father and would naturally want to step in and do something. I'd feel obliged to warn them. He's a thief . . ."

The moment this conversation was finished, Miss Rainey came in and stood by his desk. "I'm not going to be able to work for you any more, Mr. Weed," she said. "I can stay until the seventeenth if you need me, but I've been offered a whirlwind of a job, and I'd like to leave as soon as possible."

She went out, leaving him to face alone the wickedness of what he had done to the Thomas boy. His children in their photograph laughed and laughed, glazed with all the bright colors of summer, and he remembered that they had met a bagpiper on the beach that day and he had paid the piper a dollar to play them a battle song of the Black Watch. The girl would be at the house when he got home. He would spend another evening among his kind neighbors, picking and choosing dead-end streets, cart tracks, and the driveways of abandoned houses. There was nothing to mitigate his feeling—nothing that laughter or a game of softball with the children would change—and, thinking back over the plane crash, the Farquarsons' new maid, and Anne Murchison's difficulties with her drunken father, he wondered how he could have avoided arriving at just where he was. He was in trouble. He had been lost once in his life, coming back from a trout stream in the north woods, and he had now the same bleak realization that no amount of cheerfulness or hopefulness or valor or perseverance could help him find, in the gathering dark, the path that he'd lost. He smelled the forest. The feeling of bleakness was intolerable, and he saw clearly that he had reached the point where he would have to make a choice.

He could go to a psychiatrist, like Miss Rainey; he could go to church and confess his lusts; he could go to a Danish massage parlor in the West Seventies that had been recommended by a salesman; he could rape the girl or trust that he would somehow be prevented from doing this; or he could get drunk. It was his life, his boat, and, like every other man, he was made to be the father of thousands, and what harm could there be in a tryst that would make them both feel more kindly toward the world? This was the wrong train of thought, and he came back to the first, the psychiatrist. He had the telephone number of Miss Rainey's doctor, and he called and asked for an immediate appointment. He was insistent with the doctor's secretary—it was his manner in business—and when she said that the doctor's schedule was full for the next few weeks, Francis demanded an appointment that day and was told to come at five.

The psychiatrist's office was in a building that was used mostly by doctors and dentists, and the hallways were filled with the candy smell of mouthwash and memories of pain. Francis' character had been formed upon a series of private resolves—resolves about cleanliness, about going off the high diving board or repeating any other feat that challenged his courage, about punctuality, honesty, and virtue. To abdicate the perfect loneliness in which he had made his most vital decisions shattered his concept of character and left him now in a condition that felt like shock. He was stupefied. The scene for his *miserere mei Deus* was, like the waiting room of so many doctors' offices, a crude token gesture toward the sweets of domestic bliss: a place arranged with antiques, coffee tables, potted plants, and etchings of snow-covered bridges and geese in flight, although there were no children, no marriage bed, no stove, even, in this travesty of a house, where no one had ever spent the night and where the curtained windows looked straight onto a dark air shaft. Francis gave his name and address to a secretary and then saw, at the side of the room, a policeman moving toward him. "Hold it, hold it," the policeman said. "Don't move. Keep your hands where they are."

"I think it's all right, officer," the secretary began. "I think it will be—"

"Let's make sure," the policeman said, and he began to slap Francis' clothes, looking for what—pistols, knives, an icepick? Finding nothing, he went off, and the secretary began a nervous apology: "When you called on the telephone, Mr. Weed, you seemed very excited, and one of the doctor's patients has been threatening his life, and we have to be careful. If you want to go in now?" Francis pushed open a door connected to an electrical chime, and in the doctor's lair sat down heavily, blew his nose into a handkerchief, searched in his pockets for cigarettes, for matches, for something, and said hoarsely, with tears in his eyes, "I'm in love, Dr. Herzog."

* * *

It is a week or ten days later in Shady Hill. The seven-fourteen has come and gone, and here and there dinner is finished and the dishes are in the dish-washing machine. The village hangs, morally and economically, from a thread; but it hangs by its thread in the evening light. Donald Goslin has begun to worry the "Moonlight Sonata" again. *Marcato ma sempre pianissimo!* He seems to be wringing out a wet bath towel, but the housemaid does not heed him. She is writing a letter to Arthur Godfrey. In the cellar of his house, Francis Weed is building a coffee table. Dr. Herzog recommended woodwork as a therapy, and Francis finds some true consolation in the simple arithmetic involved and in the holy smell of new wood. Francis is happy. Upstairs, little Toby is crying, because he is tired. He puts off his cowboy hat, gloves, and fringed jacket, unbuckles the belt studded with gold and rubies, the silver bullets and holsters, slips off his suspenders, his checked shirt, and Levis, and sits on the edge of his bed to pull off his high boots. Leaving this equipment in a heap, he goes to the closet and takes his space suit off a nail. It is a struggle for him to get into the long tights, but he succeeds. He loops the magic cape over his shoulders and, climbing onto the footboard of his bed, he spreads his arms and flies the short distance to the floor, landing with a thump that is audible to everyone in the house but himself.

"Go home, Gertrude, go home," Mrs. Masterson says. "I told you to go home an hour ago, Gertrude. It's way past your suppertime, and your mother will be worried. Go home!" A door on the Babcocks' terrace flies open, and out comes Mrs. Babcock without any clothes on, pursued by her naked husband. (Their children are away at boarding school, and their terrace is screened by a hedge.) Over the terrace they go and in at the kitchen door, as passionate and handsome a nymph and satyr as you will find on any wall in Venice. Cutting the last of the roses in her garden, Julia hears old Mr. Nixon shouting at the squirrels in his bird-feeding station. "Rapscallions! Varmints! Avaunt and quit my sight!" A miserable cat wanders into the garden, sunk in spiritual and physical discomfort. Tied to its head is a small straw hat—a doll's hat—and it is securely buttoned into a doll's dress, from the skirts of which protrudes its long, hairy tail. As it walks, it shakes its feet, as if it had fallen into water.

"Here, pussy, pussy, pussy!" Julia calls.

"Here, pussy, here, poor pussy!" But the cat gives her a skeptical look and stumbles away in its skirts. The last to come is Jupiter. He prances through the tomato vines, holding in his generous mouth the remains of an evening slipper. Then it is dark; it is a night where kings in golden suits ride elephants over the mountains.

# The Housebreaker of Shady Hill

My name is Johnny Hake. I'm thirty-six years old, stand five feet eleven in my socks, weigh one hundred and forty-two pounds stripped, and am, so to speak, naked at the moment and talking into the dark. I was conceived in the Hotel St. Regis, born in the Presbyterian Hospital, raised on Sutton Place, christened and confirmed in St. Bartholomew's, and I drilled with the Knickerbocker Greys, played football and baseball in Central Park, learned to chin myself on the framework of East Side apartment-house canopies, and met my wife (Christina Lewis) at one of those big cotillions at the Waldorf. I served four years in the Navy, have four kids now, and live in a *banlieue* called Shady Hill. We have a nice house with a garden and a place outside for cooking meat, and on summer nights, sitting there with the kids and looking into the front of Christina's dress as she bends over to salt the steaks, or just gazing at the lights in heaven, I am as thrilled as I am thrilled by more hardy and dangerous pursuits, and I guess this is what is meant by the pain and sweetness of life.

I went to work right after the war for a parablendeum manufacturer, and seemed on the way to making this my life. The firm was patriarchal; that is, the old man would start you on one thing and then switch you to another, and he had his finger in every pie—the Jersey mill and the processing plant in Nashville—and behaved as if he had wool-gathered the whole firm during a catnap. I stayed out of the old man's way as nimbly as I could, and behaved in his presence as if he had shaped me out of clay with his own hands and breathed the fire of life into me. He was the kind of despot who needed a front, and this was Gil Bucknam's job. He was the old man's right hand, front, and peacemaker, and he could garnish any deal with the humanity the old man lacked, but he started staying out of the office—at first for a day or two, then for two weeks, and then for longer. When he returned, he would complain about stomach trouble or eyestrain, although anyone could see that he was looped. This was not so strange, since hard drinking was one of the things he had to do for the firm. The old man stood it for a year and then came into my office one morning and told me to get up to Bucknam's apartment and give him the sack.

This was as devious and dirty as sending an office boy to can the chairman of the board. Bucknam was my superior and my senior by many years, a man who condescended to do so whenever he bought me a drink, but this was the way the old man operated, and I knew what I had to do. I called the Bucknam apartment, and Mrs. Bucknam said that I could see Gil that afternoon. I had lunch alone and hung around the office until about three, when I *walked* from our midtown office to the Bucknams' apartment, in the East Seventies. It was early in the fall—the World Series was being played—and a thunderstorm was entering the city. I could hear the noise of big guns and smell the rain when I got to the Bucknams' place. Mrs. Bucknam let me in, and all the troubles of that past year seemed to be in her face, hastily concealed by a thick coat of powder. I've never seen such burned-out eyes, and she was wearing one of those old-fashioned garden-party dresses with big flowers on it. (They had three kids in college, I knew, and a schooner with a hired hand, and many other expenses.) Gil was in bed, and Mrs. Bucknam let me into the bedroom. The storm was about to break now, and everything stood in a gentle half darkness so much like dawn that it seemed as if we should be sleeping and dreaming, and not bringing one another bad news.

Gil was jolly and lovable and condescending, and said that he was *so* glad to see me; he had bought a lot of presents for my children when he was last in Bermuda and had forgotten to mail them. "Would you get those things, darling?" he asked. "Do you remember where we put them?" Then she came back into the room with five or six large and expensive-looking packages and unloaded them into my lap.

I think of my children mostly with delight, and I love to give them presents. I was charmed. It was a ruse, of course—hers, I guessed—and one of many that she must have thought up over the last year to hold their world together. (The wrappings were not fresh, I could see, and when I got home and found in them some old cashmere sweaters that Gil's daughters had not taken to college and a Scotch cap with a soiled sweatband, it only deepened my feeling of sympathy for the Bucknams in their trouble.) With a lap full of presents for my kiddies and sympathy leaking out of every joint, I couldn't give him the ax. We talked about the World Series and about some small matters at the office, and when the rain and the wind began, I helped Mrs. Bucknam shut the windows in the apartment, and then I left and took an early train home through the storm. Five days later, Gil Bucknam went on the wagon for good, and came back to the office to sit again at the right hand of the old man, and my skin was one of the first he went after. It seemed to me that if it had been my destiny to be a Russian ballet dancer, or to make art jewelry, or to paint *Schuhplattler* dancers on bureau drawers and landscapes on clamshells and live in some very low-tide place like Provincetown, I wouldn't have known a queerer bunch of men and women than I knew in the parablendeum industry, and I decided to strike out on my own.

* * *

My mother taught me never to speak about money when there was a shirtful, and I've always been very reluctant to speak about it when there was any scarcity, so I cannot paint much of a picture of what ensued in the next six months. I rented office space—a cubicle with a desk and a phone was what it amounted to—and sent out letters, but the letters were seldom answered and the telephone might just as well have been disconnected, and when it came time to borrow money, I had nowhere to turn. My mother hated Christina, and I don't think she can have much money, in any case, because she never bought me an overcoat or a cheese sandwich when I was a kid without telling me that it came out of her principal. I had plenty of friends, but if my life depended on it I couldn't ask a man for a drink and touch him for five hundred—and I needed more. The worst of it was that I hadn't painted anything like an adequate picture to my wife.

I thought about this one night when we were dressing to go to dinner up the road at the Warburtons'. Christina was sitting at her dressing table putting on earrings. She is a pretty woman in the prime of life, and her ignorance of financial necessity is complete. Her neck is graceful, her breasts gleamed as they rose in the cloth of her dress, and, seeing the decent and healthy delight she took in her own image, I could not tell her that we were broke. She had sweetened much of my life, and to watch her seemed to freshen the wellsprings of some clear energy in me that made the room and the pictures on the wall and the moon that I could see outside the window all vivid and cheerful. The truth would make her cry and ruin her make-up and the Warburtons' dinner party for her, and she would sleep in the guest room. There seemed to be as much truth in her beauty and the power she exerted over my senses as there was in the fact that we were overdrawn at the bank.

The Warburtons are rich, but they don't mix; they may not even care. She is an aging mouse, and he is the kind of man that you wouldn't have liked at school. He has a bad skin and rasping voice and a fixed idea—lechery. The Warburtons are always spending money, and that's what you talk about with them. The floor of their front hall is black-and-white marble from the old Ritz, and their cabañas at Sea Island are being winterized, and they are flying to Davos for ten days, and buying a pair of saddle horses, and building a new wing. We were late that night, and the Meserves and the Chesneys were already there, but Carl Warburton hadn't come home, and Sheila was worried. "Carl has to walk through a terrible slum to get to the station," she said, "and he carries thousands of dollars on him, and I'm so afraid he'll be *victimized. . . .*" Then Carl came home and told a dirty story to the mixed company, and we went in to dinner. It was the kind of party where everybody has taken a shower and put on their best clothes, and where some old cook has been peeling mushrooms or picking the meat out of crab shells since daybreak. I wanted to have a good time. That was my wish, but my wishes could not get me off the ground that night. I felt as if I was at some god-awful birthday party of my childhood that my mother had brought me to with threats and promises. The party broke up at about half past eleven, and we went home. I stayed out in the garden finishing one of Carl Warburton's cigars. It was a Thursday night, and my checks wouldn't bounce until Tuesday, but I had to do something soon. When I went upstairs, Christina was asleep, and I fell asleep myself, but I woke again at about three.

I had been dreaming about wrapping bread in colored parablendeum. Filmex. I had dreamed a full-page spread in a national magazine: BRING SOME COLOR INTO YOUR BREADBOX! The page was covered with jewel-toned loaves of bread—turquoise bread, ruby bread, and bread the color of emeralds. In my sleep the idea had seemed to me like a good one; it had cheered me, and it was a letdown to find myself in the dark bedroom. Feeling sad then, I thought about all the loose ends of my life, and this brought me around to my old mother, who lives alone in a hotel in Cleveland. I saw her getting dressed to go down and have dinner in the hotel dining room. She seemed pitiable, as I imagined her—lonely and among strangers. And yet, when she turned her head, I saw that she still had some biting teeth left in her gums.

She sent me through college, arranged for me to spend my vacations in pleasant landscapes, and fired my ambitions, such as they are, but she bitterly opposed my marriage, and our relations have been strained ever since. I've often invited her to come and live with us, but she always refuses, and always with bad feeling. I send her flowers and presents, and write her every week, but these attentions only seem to fortify her conviction that my marriage was a disaster for her and for me. Then I thought about her apron strings, for when I was a kid, she seemed to be a woman whose apron strings were thrown across the Atlantic and the Pacific oceans; they seemed to be looped, like vapor trails, across the very drum of heaven. I thought of her now without rebellion or anxiety—only with sorrow that all our exertions should have been rewarded with so little clear emotion, and that we could not drink a cup of tea together without stirring up all kinds of bitter feeling. I longed to correct this, to re-enact the whole relationship with my mother against a more simple and human background, where the cost of my education would not have come so high in morbid emotion. I wanted to do it all over again in some emotional Arcadia, and have us both behave differently, so that I could think of her at three in the morning without guilt, and so that she would be spared loneliness and neglect in her old age.

I moved a little closer to Christina and, coming into the area of her warmth, suddenly felt all kindly and delighted with everything, but she moved in her sleep, away from me. Then I coughed. I coughed again. I coughed loudly. I couldn't stop coughing, and I got out of bed and went into the dark bathroom and drank a glass of water. I stood at the bathroom window and looked down into the garden. There was a little wind. It seemed to be changing its quarter. It sounded like a dawn wind—the air was filled with a showery sound—and felt good on my face. There were some cigarettes on the back of the toilet, and I lit one in order to get back to sleep. But when I inhaled the smoke, it hurt my lungs, and I was suddenly convinced that I was dying of bronchial cancer.

I have experienced all kinds of foolish melancholy—I've been homesick for countries I've never seen, and longed to be what I couldn't be—but all these moods were trivial compared to my premonition of death. I tossed my cigarette into the toilet (ping) and straightened my back, but the pain in my chest was only sharper, and I was convinced that the corruption had begun. I had friends who would think of me kindly, I knew, and Christina and the children would surely keep alive an affectionate memory. But then I thought about money again, and the Warburtons, and my rubber checks approaching the clearinghouse, and it seemed to me that money had it all over love. I had yearned for some women—turned green, in fact—but it seemed to me that I had never yearned for anyone the way I yearned that night for money. I went to the closet in our bedroom and put on some old blue sneakers and a pair of pants and a dark pullover. Then I went downstairs and out of the house. The moon had set, and there were not many stars, but the air above the trees and hedges was full of dim light. I went around the Trenholmes' garden then, gumshoeing over the grass, and down the lawn to the Warburtons' house. I listened for sounds from the open windows, and all I heard was the ticking of a clock. I went up the front steps and opened the screen door and started across the floor from the old Ritz. In the dim night light that came in at the windows, the house looked like a shell, a nautilus, shaped to contain itself.

I heard the noise of a dog's license tag, and Sheila's old cocker came trotting down the hall. I rubbed him behind the ears, and then he went back to wherever his bed was, grunted, and fell asleep. I knew the plan of the Warburtons' house as well as I knew the plan of my own. The staircase was carpeted, but I first put my foot on one of the treads to see if it creaked. Then I started up the stairs. All the bedroom doors stood open, and from Carl and Sheila's bedroom, where I had often left my coat at big cocktail parties, I could hear the sound of deep breathing. I stood in the doorway for a second to take my bearings. In the dimness I could see the bed, and a pair of pants and a jacket hung over the back of a chair. Moving swiftly, I stepped into the room and took a big billfold from the inside pocket of the coat and started back to the hall. The violence of my emotions may have made me clumsy, because Sheila woke. I heard her say, "Did you hear that noise, darling?" "S'wind," he mumbled, and then they were quiet again. I was safe in the hall—safe from everything but myself. I seemed to be having a nervous breakdown out there. All my saliva was gone, the lubricants seemed to drain out of my heart, and whatever the juices were that kept my legs upright were going. It was only by holding on to the wall that I could make any progress at all. I clung to the banister on my way down the stairs, and staggered out of the house.

* * *

Back in my own dark kitchen, I drank three or four glasses of water. I must have stood by the kitchen sink for a half hour or longer before I thought of looking in Carl's wallet. I went into the cellarway and shut the cellar door before I turned the light on. There was a little over nine hundred dollars. I turned the light off and went back into the dark kitchen. Oh, I never knew that a man could be so miserable and that the mind could open up so many chambers and fill them with self-reproach! Where were the trout streams of my youth, and other innocent pleasures? The wet-leather smell of the loud waters and the keen woods after a smashing rain; or at opening day the summer breezes smelling like the grassy breath of Holsteins—your head would swim—and all the brooks full then (or so I imagined, in the dark kitchen) of trout, our sunken treasure. I was crying.

Shady Hill, as I say, a *banlieue* and open to criticism by city planners, adventurers, and lyric poets, but if you work in the city and have children to raise, I can't think of a better place. My neighbors are rich, it is true, but riches in this case mean leisure, and they use their time wisely. They travel around the world, listen to good music, and given a choice of paper books at an airport, will pick Thucydides, and sometimes Aquinas. Urged to build bomb shelters, they plant trees and roses, and their gardens are splendid and bright. Had I looked, the next morning, from my bathroom window into the evil-smelling ruin of some great city, the shock of recalling what I had done might not have been so violent, but the moral bottom had dropped out of my world without changing a mote of sunlight. I dressed stealthily—for what child of darkness would want to hear the merry voices of his family?—and caught an early train. My gabardine suit was meant to express cleanliness and probity, but I was a miserable creature whose footsteps had been mistaken for the noise of the wind. I looked at the paper. There had been a thirty-thousand-dollar payroll robbery in the Bronx. A White Plains matron had come home from a party to find her furs and jewelry gone. Sixty thousand dollars' worth of medicine had been taken from a warehouse in Brooklyn. I felt better at discovering how common the thing I had done was. But only a little better, and only for a short while. Then I was faced once more with the realization that I was a common thief and an impostor, and that I had done something so reprehensible that it violated the tenets of every known religion. I had stolen, and what's more, I had criminally entered the house of a friend and broken all the unwritten laws that held the community together. My conscience worked so on my spirits—like the hard beak of a carnivorous bird—that my left eye began to twitch, and again I seemed on the brink of a general nervous collapse. When the train reached the city, I went to the bank. Leaving the bank, I was nearly hit by a taxi. My anxiety was not for my bones but for the fact that Carl Warburton's wallet might be found in my pocket. When I thought no one was looking, I wiped the wallet on my trousers (to remove the fingerprints) and dropped it into the ash can.

I thought that coffee might make me feel better, and went into a restaurant, and sat down at a table with a stranger. The soiled lace-paper doilies and half-empty glasses of water had not been taken away, and at the stranger's place there was a thirty-five-cent tip, left by an earlier customer. I looked at the menu, but out of the corner of my eye I saw the stranger pocket the thirty-five-cent tip. What a crook! I got up and left the restaurant.

I walked into my cubicle, hung up my hat and coat, sat down at my desk, shot my cuffs, sighed, and looked into space, as if a day full of challenge and decision were about to begin. I hadn't turned on the light. In a little while, the office beside mine was occupied, and I heard my neighbor clear his throat, cough, scratch a match, and settle down to attack the day's business.

The walls were flimsy—part frosted glass and part plywood—and there was no acoustical privacy in these offices. I reached into my pocket for a cigarette with as much stealth as I had exercised at the Warburtons', and waited for the noise of a truck passing on the street outside before I lit a match. The excitement of eavesdropping took hold of me. My neighbor was trying to sell uranium stock over the telephone. His line went like this: First he was courteous. Then he was nasty. "What's the matter, Mr. X? Don't you want to make any money?" Then he was *very* scornful. "I'm sorry to have bothered you, Mr. X. I thought you *had* sixty-five dollars to invest." He called twelve numbers without any takers. I was as quiet as a mouse. Then he telephoned the information desk at Idlewild, checking the arrival of planes from Europe. London was on time. Rome and Paris were late. "No, he ain't in yet," I heard him say to someone over the phone. "It's dark in there." My heart was beating fast. Then my telephone began to ring, and I counted twelve rings before it stopped. "I'm positive, I'm positive," the man in the next office said. "I can hear his telephone ringing, and he ain't answering it, and he's just a lonely son of a bitch looking for a job. Go ahead, go ahead, I tell you. I ain't got time to get over there. Go ahead. . . . Seven, eight, three, five, seven, seven. . . ." When he hung up, I went to the door, opened and closed it, turned the light on, rattled the coat hangers, whistled a tune, sat down heavily at my desk chair, and dialed the first telephone number that came to my mind. It was an old friend—Burt Howe—and he exclaimed when he heard my voice. "Hakie, I been looking for you everywhere! You sure folded up your tents and stole away."

"Yes," I said.

"Stole away," Howe repeated. "Just stole away. But what I wanted to talk with you about is this deal I thought you might be interested in. It's a one-shot, but it won't take you more than three weeks. It's a steal. They're green, and they're dumb, and they're loaded, and it's just like stealing."

"Yes," I said.

"Well, then, can you meet me for lunch at Cardin's at twelve-thirty, and I'll give you the details?" Howe asked.

"O.K.," I said hoarsely. "Thanks a lot, Burt."

"We went out to the shack on Sunday," the man in the next office was saying as I hung up. "Louise got bit by a poisonous spider. The doctor gave her some kind of injection. She'll be all right." He dialed another number and began, "We went out to the shack on Sunday. Louise got bit by a poisonous spider . . ."

It was possible that a man whose wife had been bitten by a spider and who found some time on his hands might call three or four friends and tell them about it, and it was equally possible that the spider might be a code of warning or of assent to some unlawful traffic. What frightened me was that by becoming a thief I seemed to have surrounded myself with thieves and operators. My left eye had begun to twitch again, and the inability of one part of my consciousness to stand up under the reproach that was being heaped into it by another part made me cast around desperately for someone else who could be blamed. I had read often enough in the papers that divorce sometimes led to crime. My parents were divorced when I was about five. This was a good clue and quickly led me on to something better.

My father went to live in France after the divorce, and I didn't see him for ten years. Then he wrote Mother for permission to see me, and she prepared me for this reunion by telling me how drunken, cruel, and lewd the old man was. It was in the summer, and we were on Nantucket, and I took the steamer alone, and went to New York on the train. I met my father at the Plaza early in the evening, but not so early that he hadn't begun to drink. With the long, sensitive nose of an adolescent I smelled the gin on his breath, and I noticed that he bumped into a table and sometimes repeated himself. I realized later that this reunion must have been strenuous for a man of sixty, which he was. We had dinner and then went to see *The Roses of Picardy.* As soon as the chorus came on, Father said that I could have any one of them that I wanted; the arrangements were all made. I could even have one of the specialty dancers. Now, if I'd felt that he had crossed the Atlantic to perform this service for me, it might have been different, but I felt he'd made the trip in order to do a disservice to my mother. I was scared. The show was in one of those old-fashioned theatres that appear to be held together with angels. Brown-gold angels held up the ceiling; they held up the boxes; they even seemed to hold up the balcony with about four hundred people in it. I spent a lot of time looking at those dusty gold angels. If the ceiling of the theatre had fallen on my head, I would have been relieved. After the show, we went back to the hotel to wash before meeting the girls, and the old man stretched out on the bed for a minute and began to snore. I picked his wallet of fifty dollars, spent the night at Grand Central, and took an early morning train to Woods Hole. So the whole thing was explained, including the violence of the emotion I had experienced in the Warburtons' upstairs hall; I had been reliving that scene at the Plaza. It had not been my fault that I had stolen then, and it had not been my fault when I went to the Warburtons'. It was my father's fault! Then I remembered that my father was buried in Fontainebleau fifteen years ago, and could be nothing much more now than dust.

I went into the men's room and washed my hands and face, and combed my hair down with a lot of water. It was time to go out for lunch. I thought anxiously of the lunch ahead of me, and, wondering why, was astonished to realize that it was Burt Howe's free use of the word "steal." I hoped he wouldn't keep on saying it.

Even as the thought floated across my mind in the men's room, the twitching in my eye seemed to spread over my cheek; it seemed as if this verb were embedded in the English language like a poisoned fishhook. I had committed adultery, and the word "adultery" had no force for me; I had been drunk, and the word "drunkenness" had no extraordinary power. It was only "steal" and all its allied nouns, verbs, and adverbs that had the power to tyrannize over my nervous system, as if I had evolved, unconsciously, some doctrine wherein the act of theft took precedence over all the other sins in the Decalogue and was a sign of moral death.

The sky was dark when I came out on the street. Lights were burning everywhere. I looked into the faces of the people that I passed for some encouraging signs of honesty in such a crooked world, and on Third Avenue I saw a young man with a tin cup, holding his eyes shut to impersonate blindness. That seal of blindness, the striking innocence of the upper face, was betrayed by the frown and the crow's-feet of a man who could see his drinks on the bar. There was another blind beggar on Forty-first Street, but I didn't examine his eye sockets, realizing that I couldn't assess the legitimacy of every beggar in the city.

Cardin's is a men's restaurant in the Forties. The stir and bustle in the vestibule only made me feel retiring, and the hat-check girl, noticing, I suppose, the twitch in my eye, gave me a very jaded look.

Burt was at the bar, and when we had ordered our drinks, we got down to business. "For a deal like this, we ought to meet in some back alley," he said, "but a fool and his money *and* so forth. It's three kids. P. J. Burdette is one of them, and they've got a cool million between them to throw away. Someone's bound to steal from them, so it may as well be you." I put my hand over the left side of my face to cover the tic. When I tried to raise my glass to my mouth, I spilled gin all over my suit. "They're all three of them just out of college," Burt said. "And they've all three of them got so much in the kitty that even if you picked them clean they wouldn't feel any pain. Now, in order to participate in this burglary, all you have to do . . ."

The toilet was at the other end of the restaurant, but I got there. Then I drew a basin of cold water and stuck my head and face into it. Burt had followed me to the washroom. As I was drying myself with a paper towel, he said, "You know, Hakie, I wasn't going to mention it, but now that you've been sick, I may as well tell you that you look awful. I mean, from the minute I saw you I knew something was wrong. I just want to tell you that whatever it is—sauce or dope or trouble at home—it's a lot later than you think, and maybe you should be doing something about it. No hard feelings?" I said that I was sick, and waited in the toilet long enough for Burt to make a getaway. Then I got my hat and another jaded look from the hat-check girl, and saw in the afternoon paper on a chair by the checkroom that some bank robbers in Brooklyn had got away with eighteen thousand dollars.

I walked around the streets, wondering how I would shape up as a pickpocket and bag snatcher, and all the arches and spires of St. Patrick's only reminded me of poor boxes. I took the regular train home, looking out of the window at a peaceable landscape and a spring evening, and it seemed to me fishermen and lone bathers and grade-crossing watchmen and sand-lot ball players and lovers unashamed of their sport and the owners of small sailing craft and old men playing pinochle in firehouses were the people who stitched up the big holes in the world that were made by men like me.

* * *

Now Christina is the kind of woman who, when she is asked by the alumnae secretary of her college to describe her status, gets dizzy thinking about the variety of her activities and interests. And what, on a given day, stretching a point here and there, does she have to do? Drive me to the train. Have the skis repaired. Book a tennis court. Buy the wine and groceries for the monthly dinner of the Société Gastronomique du Westchester Nord. Look up some definitions in Larousse. Attend a League of Women Voters symposium on sewers. Go to a full-dress lunch for Bobsie Neil's aunt. Weed the garden. Iron a uniform for the part-time maid. Type two and a half pages of her paper on the early novels of Henry James. Empty the wastebaskets. Help Tabitha prepare the children's supper. Give Ronnie some batting practice. Put her hair in pin curls. Get the cook. Meet the train. Bathe. Dress. Greet her guests in French at half past seven. Say *bon soir* at eleven. Lie in my arms until twelve. Eureka! You might say that she is prideful, but I think only that she is a woman enjoying herself in a country that is prosperous and young. Still, when she met me at the train that night, it was difficult for me to rise to all this vitality.

It was my bad luck to have to take the collection at early Communion on Sunday, although I was in no condition. I answered the pious looks of my friends with a very crooked smile and then knelt by a lancet-shaped stained-glass window that seemed to be made from the butts of vermouth and Burgundy bottles. I knelt on an imitation-leather hassock that had been given by some guild or auxiliary to replace one of the old, snuff-colored hassocks, which had begun to split at the seams and show bits of straw, and made the whole place smell like an old manger. The smell of straw and flowers, and the vigil light, and the candles flickering in the rector's breath, and the damp of this poorly heated stone building were all as familiar to me and belonged as much to my early life as the sounds and smells of a kitchen or a nursery, and yet they seemed, that morning, to be so potent that I felt dizzy. Then I heard, in the baseboard on my right, a rat's tooth working like an auger in the hard oak. "Holy, Holy, Holy," I said very loudly, hoping to frighten the rat. "Lord God of hosts, Heaven and earth are FULL of Thy Glory!" The small congregation muttered its amens with a sound like a footstep, and the rat went on scraping away at the baseboard. And then—perhaps because I was absorbed in the noise of the rat's tooth, or because the smell of dampness and straw was soporific—when I looked up from the shelter I had made of my hands, I saw the rector drinking from the chalice and realized that I had missed Communion.

At home, I looked through the Sunday paper for other thefts, and there were plenty. Banks had been looted, hotel safes had been emptied of jewelry, maids and butlers had been tied to kitchen chairs, furs and industrial diamonds had been stolen in job lots, delicatessens, cigar stores, and pawnshops had been broken into, and someone had stolen a painting from the Cleveland Institute of Art. Late in the afternoon, I raked leaves. What could be more contrite than cleaning the lawn of the autumn's dark rubbish under the streaked, pale skies of spring?

While I was raking leaves, my sons walked by. "The Toblers are having a softball game," Ronnie said. "*Everybody's* there."

"Why don't you play?" I asked.

"You can't play unless you've been invited," Ronnie said over his shoulder, and then they were gone. Then I noticed that I could hear the cheering from the softball game to which we had not been invited. The Toblers lived down the block. The spirited voices seemed to sound clearer and clearer as the night came on; I could even hear the noise of ice in glasses, and the voices of the ladies raised in a feeble cheer.

Why hadn't I been asked to play softball at the Toblers'? I wondered. Why had we been excluded from these simple pleasures, this lighthearted gathering, the fading laughter and voices and slammed doors of which seemed to gleam in the darkness as they were withdrawn from my possession? Why wasn't *I* asked to play softball at the Toblers'? Why should social aggrandizement—*climbing,* really—exclude a nice guy like me from a softball game? What kind of a world was that? Why should I be left alone with my dead leaves in the twilight—as I was—feeling so forsaken, lonely, and forlorn that I was chilled?

If there is anybody I detest, it is weak-minded sentimentalists—all those melancholy people who, out of an excess of sympathy for others, miss the thrill of their own essence and drift through life without identity, like a human fog, feeling sorry for everyone. The legless beggar in Times Square with his poor display of pencils, the rouged old lady in the subway who talks to herself, the exhibitionist in the public toilet, the drunk who has dropped on the subway stairs, do more than excite their pity; they are at a glance transformed into these unfortunates. Derelict humanity seems to trample over their unrealized souls, leaving them at twilight in a condition closely resembling the scene of a prison riot. Disappointed in themselves, they are always ready to be disappointed for the rest of us, and they will build whole cities, whole creations, firmaments and principalities, of tear-wet disappointment. Lying in bed at night, they will think tenderly of the big winner who lost his pari-mutuel ticket, of the great novelist whose magnum opus was burned mistakenly for trash, and of Samuel Tilden, who lost the Presidency of the United States through the shenanigans of the electoral college. Detesting this company, then, it was doubly painful for me to find myself in it. And, seeing a bare dogwood tree in the starlight, I thought, How sad everything is!

* * *

Wednesday was my birthday. I recalled this fact in the middle of the afternoon, at the office, and the thought that Christina might be planning a surprise party brought me in one second from a sitting to a standing position, breathless. Then I decided that she wouldn't. But just the preparations the children would make presented an emotional problem; I didn't see how I could face it.

I left the office early and had two drinks before I took the train. Christina looked pleased with everything when she met me at the station, and I put a very good face on my anxiety. The children had changed into clean clothes, and wished me a happy birthday so fervently that I felt awful. At the table there was a pile of small presents, mostly things the children had made—cuff links out of buttons, and a memo pad, and so forth. I thought I was very bright, considering the circumstances, and pulled my snapper, put on my silly hat, blew out the candles on the cake, and thanked them all, but then it seemed that there was another present—my *big* present—and after dinner I was made to stay inside while Christina and the children went outside, and then Juney came in and led me outdoors and around in back of the house, where they all were. Leaning against the house was an aluminum extension ladder with a card and a ribbon tied to it, and I said, as if I'd been hit, "What in *hell* is the meaning of this?"

"We thought you'd need it, Daddy," Juney said.

"What would I ever need a ladder for? What do you think I am—a second-story worker?"

"Storm windows," Juney said. "Screens—"

I turned to Christina. "Have I been talking in my sleep?"

"No," Christina said. "You haven't been talking in your sleep."

Juney began to cry.

"You could take the leaves out of the rain gutters," Ronnie said. Both of the boys were looking at me with long faces.

"Well, you must admit it's a very unusual present," I said to Christina.

*"God!"* Christina said. "Come on, children. Come on." She herded them in at the terrace door.

I kicked around the garden until after dark. The lights went on upstairs. Juney was still crying, and Christina was singing to her. Then she was quiet. I waited until the lights went on in our bedroom, and after a little while I climbed the stairs. Christina was in a nightgown, sitting at her dressing table, and there were heavy tears in her eyes.

"You'll have to try and understand," I said.

"I couldn't possibly. The children have been saving for months to buy you that damned-fool contraption."

"You don't know what I've been through," I said.

"If you'd been through hell, I wouldn't forgive you," she said. "You haven't been through anything that would justify your behavior. They've had it hidden in the garage for a week. They're so *sweet.*"

"I haven't felt like myself," I said.

"Don't tell *me* that you haven't felt like yourself," she said. "I've looked forward to having you leave in the morning, and I've dreaded having you come home at night."

"I can't have been all that bad," I said.

"It's been hell," she said. "You've been sharp with the children, nasty to me, rude to your friends, and malicious behind their backs. It's been hideous."

"Would you like me to go?"

"Oh, Lord, would I like you to go! Then I could breathe."

"What about the children?"

"Ask my lawyer."

"I'll go, then."

I went down the hall to the closet where we keep the bags. When I took out my suitcase, I found that the children's puppy had chewed the leather binding loose all along one side. Trying to find another suitcase, I brought the whole pile down on top of me, boxing my ears. I carried my bag with this long strip of leather trailing behind me back into our bedroom. *"Look,"* I said. "Look at this, Christina. The dog has chewed the binding off my suitcase." She didn't even raise her head. "I've poured twenty thousand dollars a year into this establishment for ten years," I shouted, "and when the time comes for me to go, I don't even have a decent suitcase! Everybody else has a suitcase. Even the cat has a nice traveling bag." I threw open my shirt drawer, and there were only four clean shirts. "I don't have enough clean shirts to last a week!" I shouted. Then I got a few things together, clapped my hat on my head, and marched out. I even thought, for a minute, of taking the car, and I went into the garage and looked it over. Then I saw the FOR SALE sign that had been hanging on the house when we bought it long, long ago. I wiped the dirt off the sign and got a nail and a rock and went around to the front of the house and nailed the FOR SALE sign onto a maple tree. Then I walked to the station. It's about a mile. The long strip of leather was trailing along behind me, and I stopped and tried to rip it off the suitcase, but it wouldn't come. When I got down to the station, I found there wasn't another train until four in the morning. I decided I would wait. I sat down on my suitcase and waited five minutes. Then I marched home again. Halfway there I saw Christina coming down the street, in a sweater and a skirt and sneakers—the quickest things to put on, but summery things—and we walked home together and went to bed.

On Saturday, I played golf, and although the game finished late, I wanted to take a swim in the club pool before I went home. There was no one at the pool but Tom Maitland. He is a dark-skinned and nice-looking man, very rich, but quiet. He seems withdrawn. His wife is the fattest woman in Shady Hill, and nobody much likes his children, and I think he is the kind of man whose parties and friendship and affairs in love and business all rest like an intricate superstructure—a tower of matchsticks—on the melancholy of his early youth. A breath could bring the whole thing down. It was nearly dark when I had finished swimming; the club-house was lighted and you could hear the sounds of dinner on the porch. Maitland was sitting at the edge of the pool dabbling his feet in the bright-blue water, with its Dead Sea smell of chlorine. I was drying myself off, and as I passed him, I asked if he wasn't going in. "I don't know how to swim," he said. He smiled and looked away from me then to the still, polished water of the pool, in the dark landscape. "We used to have a pool at home," he said, "but I never got a chance to swim in it. I was always studying the violin." There he was, forty-five years old and at least a millionaire, and he couldn't even float, and I don't suppose he had many occasions to speak as honestly as he had just spoken. While I was getting dressed, the idea settled in my head—with no help from me—that the Maitlands would be my next victims.

A few nights later, I woke up at three. I thought over the loose ends in my life—Mother in Cleveland, and parablendeum—and then I went into the bathroom to light a cigarette before I remembered that I was dying of bronchial cancer and leaving my widow and orphans penniless. I put on my blue sneakers and the rest of the outfit, looked in at the open doors of the children's rooms, and then went out. It was cloudy. I walked through back gardens to the corner. Then I crossed the street and turned up the Maitlands' driveway, walking on the grass at the edge of the gravel. The door was open, and I went in, just as excited and frightened as I had been at the Warburtons' and feeling insubstantial in the dim light—a ghost. I followed my nose up the stairs to where I knew their bedroom was, and, hearing heavy breathing and seeing a jacket and some pants on a chair, I reached for the pocket of the jacket, but there wasn't one. It wasn't a suit coat at all; it was one of those bright satin jackets that kids wear. There was no sense in looking for a wallet in *his* trousers. He couldn't make that much cutting the Maitlands' grass. I got out of there in a hurry.

I did not sleep any more that night but sat in the dark thinking about Tom Maitland, and Gracie Maitland, and the Warburtons, and Christina, and my own sordid destiny, and how different Shady Hill looked at night than in the light of day.

But I went out the next night—this time to the Pewters', who were not only rich but booze fighters, and who drank so much that I didn't see how they could hear thunder after the lights were turned out. I left, as usual, a little after three.

I was thinking sadly about my beginnings—about how I was made by a riggish couple in a midtown hotel after a six-course dinner with wines, and my mother had told me so many times that if she hadn't drunk so many Old-Fashioneds before that famous dinner I would still be unborn on a star. And I thought about my old man and that night at the Plaza and the bruised thighs of the peasant women of Picardy and all the brown-gold angels that held the theatre together and my terrible destiny. While I was walking toward the Pewters', there was a harsh stirring in all the trees and gardens, like a draft on a bed of fire, and I wondered what it was until I felt the rain on my hands and face, and then I began to laugh.

I wish I could say that a kindly lion had set me straight, or an innocent child, or the strains of distant music from some church, but it was no more than the rain on my head—the smell of it flying up to my nose—that showed me the extent of my freedom from the bones in Fontainebleau and the works of a thief. There were ways out of my trouble if I cared to make use of them. I was not trapped. I was here on earth because I chose to be. And it was no skin off my elbow how I had been given the gifts of life so long as I possessed them, and I possessed them then—the tie between the wet grass roots and the hair that grew out of my body, the thrill of my mortality that I had known on summer nights, loving the children, and looking down the front of Christina's dress. I was standing in front of the Pewters' by this time, and I looked up at the dark house and then turned and walked away. I went back to bed and had pleasant dreams. I dreamed I was sailing a boat on the Mediterranean. I saw some worn marble steps leading down into the water, and the water itself—blue, saline, and dirty. I stepped the mast, hoisted the sail, and put my hand on the tiller. But why, I wondered as I sailed away, should I seem to be only seventeen years old? But you can't have everything.

It is not, as somebody once wrote, the smell of corn bread that calls us back from death; it is the lights and signs of love and friendship. Gil Bucknam called me the next day and said that the old man was dying and would I come back to work? I went to see him, and he explained that it was the old man who was after my skin, and, of course, I was glad to come home to parablendeum.

What I did not understand, as I walked down Fifth Avenue that afternoon, was how a world that had seemed so dark could, in a few minutes, become so sweet. The sidewalks seemed to shine, and, going home on the train, I beamed at those foolish girls who advertise girdles on the signboards in the Bronx. I got an advance on my salary the next morning, and, taking some precautions about fingerprints, I put nine hundred dollars into an envelope and walked over to the Warburtons' when the last lights in the neighborhood had been put out. It had been raining, but the rain had let up. The stars were beginning to show. There was no sense in overdoing prudence, and I went around to the back of their house, found the kitchen door open, and put the envelope on a table in the dark room. As I was walking away from the house, a police car drew up beside me, and a patrolman I know cranked down the window and asked, "What are you doing out at this time of night, Mr. Hake?"

"I'm walking the dog," I said cheerfully. There was no dog in sight, but they didn't look. "Here, Toby! Here, Toby! Here, Toby! *Good* dog!" I called, and off I went, whistling merrily in the dark.

# PHILIP ROTH
## (1933– )

Philip Roth's career began in controversy in 1959 with the publication of his first book, *Goodbye, Columbus, and Five Short Stories.* For many Jewish readers the book smacked of anti-Semitism; nevertheless it won the National Book Award. For Roth, being Jewish suggests a condition of uncertainty, of doubleness, of identity-anxiety, and a blurring of boundaries between the real and fantasy or the irrational. His fiction ranges from realism to surrealism to postmodern experiments in self-reflexivity. Controversy raged again with the publication of his *Portnoy's Complaint* (1969). This comic, psychoanalytic monologue also won a National Book Award.

Roth was born in Newark, New Jersey, of a middle-class Jewish family. He attended the Newark branch of Rutgers University for one year, and then transferred to Bucknell University, from which he graduated with honors in 1954. He earned an M.A. in English at the University of Chicago in 1955. After army service he returned to Chicago to study for a Ph.D. and to teach. His success with his writing enabled him to give up teaching, except for brief visiting appointments at various colleges. He married in 1958; his wife died ten years later. In 1990 he married actress Claire Bloom, but this marriage ended in divorce.

Roth's many novels include *Letting Go* (1962); *When She Was Good* (1967); *Our Gang,* a satire of the Nixon years (1971); *The Great American Novel* (1973); *The Breast* (1972), his overtly Kafkaesque novel; *The Professor of Desire* (1977); the Zuckerman novels *The Ghost Writer* (1979), *Zuckerman Unbound* (1981), *The Anatomy Lesson* (1983), and *The Prague Orgy* (1985); *Operation Shylock: A Confession* (1993); and *Sabbath's Theater* (1995). His 1997 novel *American Pastoral* won the Pulitzer Prize. His latest novel is *Human Stain,* published in 2000.

# Defender of the Faith

In May of 1945, only a few weeks after the fighting had ended in Europe, I was rotated back to the States, where I spent the remainder of the war with a training company at Camp Crowder, Missouri. Along with the rest of the Ninth Army, I had been racing across Germany so swiftly during the late winter and spring that when I boarded the plane, I couldn't believe its destination lay to the west. My mind might inform me otherwise, but there was an inertia of the spirit that told me we were flying to a new front, where we would disembark and continue our push eastward—eastward until we'd circled the globe, marching through villages along whose twisting, cobbled streets crowds of the enemy would watch us take possession of what, up till then, they'd considered their own. I had changed enough in two years not to mind the trembling of the old people, the crying of the very young, the uncertainty and fear in the eyes of the once arrogant. I had been fortunate enough to develop an infantryman's heart, which, like his feet, at first aches and swells but finally grows horny enough for him to travel the weirdest paths without feeling a thing.

Captain Paul Barrett was my C.O. in Camp Crowder. The day I reported for duty, he came out of his office to shake my hand. He was short, gruff, and fiery, and—indoors or out—he wore his polished helmet liner pulled down to his little eyes. In Europe, he had received a battlefield commission and a serious chest wound, and he'd been returned to the States only a few months before. He spoke easily to me, and at the evening formation he introduced me to the troops. "Gentlemen," he said, "Sergeant Thurston, as you know, is no longer with this company. Your new first sergeant is Sergeant Nathan Marx, here. He is a veteran of the European theater, and consequently will expect to find a company of soldiers here, and not a company of *boys.*"

I sat up late in the orderly room that evening, trying half-heartedly to solve the riddle of duty rosters, personnel forms, and morning reports. The Charge of Quarters slept with his mouth open on a mattress on the floor. A trainee stood reading the next day's duty roster, which was posted on the bulletin board just inside the screen door. It was a warm evening, and I could hear radios playing dance music over in the barracks. The trainee, who had been staring at me whenever he thought I wouldn't notice, finally took a step in my direction.

"Hey, Sarge—we having a G.I. party tomorrow night?" he asked. A G.I. party is a barracks cleaning.

"You usually have them on Friday nights?" I asked him.

"Yes," he said, and then he added, mysteriously, "that's the whole thing."

"Then you'll have a G.I. party."

He turned away, and I heard him mumbling. His shoulders were moving, and I wondered if he was crying.

"What's your name, soldier?" I asked.

He turned, not crying at all. Instead, his green-speckled eyes, long and narrow, flashed like fish in the sun. He walked over to me and sat on the edge of my desk. He reached out a hand. "Sheldon," he said.

"Stand on your feet, Sheldon."

Getting off the desk, he said, "Sheldon Grossbart." He smiled at the familiarity into which he'd led me.

"You against cleaning the barracks Friday night, Grossbart?" I said. "Maybe we shouldn't have G.I. parties. Maybe we should get a maid." My tone startled me. I felt I sounded like every top sergeant I had ever known.

"No, Sergeant." He grew serious, but with a seriousness that seemed to be only the stifling of a smile. "It's just—G.I. parties on Friday night, of all nights."

He slipped up onto the corner of the desk again—not quite sitting, but not quite standing, either. He looked at me with those speckled eyes flashing, and then made a gesture with his hand. It was very slight—no more than a movement back and forth of the wrist—and yet it managed to exclude from our affairs everything else in the orderly room, to make the two of us the center of the world. It seemed, in fact, to exclude everything even about the two of us except our hearts.

"Sergeant Thurston was one thing," he whispered, glancing at the sleeping C.Q., "but we thought that with you here things might be a little different."

"We?"

"The Jewish personnel."

"Why?" I asked, harshly. "What's on your mind?"

Whether I was still angry at the "Sheldon" business, or now at something else, I hadn't time to tell, but clearly I was angry.

"We thought you—Marx, you know, like Karl Marx. The Marx Brothers. Those guys are all—M-a-r-x. Isn't that how *you* spell it, Sergeant?"

"M-a-r-x."

"Fishbein said—" He stopped. "What I mean to say, Sergeant—" His face and neck were red, and his mouth moved but no words came out. In a moment, he raised himself to attention, gazing down at me. It was as though he had suddenly decided he could expect no more sympathy from me than from Thurston, the reason being that I was of Thurston's faith, and not his. The young man had managed to confuse himself as to what my faith really was, but I felt no desire to straighten him out. Very simply, I didn't like him.

When I did nothing but return his gaze, he spoke, in an altered tone. "You see, Sergeant," he explained to me, "Friday nights, Jews are supposed to go to services."

"Did Sergeant Thurston tell you you couldn't go to them when there was a G.I. party?"

"No."

"Did he say you had to stay and scrub the floors?"

"No, Sergeant."

"Did the Captain say you had to stay and scrub the floors?"

"That isn't it, Sergeant. It's the other guys in the barracks." He leaned toward me. "They think we're goofing off. But we're not. That's when Jews go to services, Friday night. We have to."

"Then go."

"But the other guys make accusations. They have no right."

"That's not the Army's problem, Grossbart. It's a personal problem you'll have to work out yourself."

"But it's un*fair.*"

I got up to leave. "There's nothing I can do about it," I said.

Grossbart stiffened and stood in front of me. "But this is a matter of *religion,* sir."

"Sergeant," I said.

"I mean 'Sergeant,' " he said, almost snarling.

"Look, go see the chaplain. You want to see Captain Barrett, I'll arrange an appointment."

"No, no. I don't want to make trouble, Sergeant. That's the first thing they throw up to you. I just want my rights!"

"Damn it, Grossbart, stop whining. You have your rights. You can stay and scrub floors or you can go to shul—"

The smile swam in again. Spittle gleamed at the corners of his mouth. "You mean church, Sergeant."

"I mean shul, Grossbart!"

I walked past him and went outside. Near me, I heard the scrunching of a guard's boots on gravel. Beyond the lighted windows of the barracks, young men in T shirts and fatigue pants were sitting on their bunks, polishing their rifles. Suddenly there was a light rustling behind me. I turned and saw Grossbart's dark frame fleeing back to the barracks, racing to tell his Jewish friends that they were right—that, like Karl and Harpo, I was one of them.

* * *

The next morning, while chatting with Captain Barrett, I recounted the incident of the previous evening. Somehow, in the telling, it must have seemed to the Captain that I was not so much explaining Grossbart's position as defending it. "Marx, I'd fight side by side with a nigger if the fella proved to me he was a man. I pride myself," he said, looking out the window, "that I've got an open mind. Consequently, Sergeant, nobody gets special treatment here, for the good *or* the bad. All a man's got to do is prove himself. A man fires well on the range, I give him a weekend pass. He scores high in P.T., he gets a weekend pass. He *earns* it." He turned from the window and pointed a finger at me. "You're a Jewish fella, am I right, Marx?"

"Yes, sir."

"And I admire you. I admire you because of the ribbons on your chest. I judge a man by what he shows me on the field of battle, Sergeant. It's what he's got *here,*" he said, and then, though I expected he would point to his chest, he jerked a thumb toward the buttons straining to hold his blouse across his belly. "Guts," he said.

"O.K., sir. I only wanted to pass on to you how the men felt."

"Mr. Marx, you're going to be old before your time if you worry about how the men feel. Leave that stuff to the chaplain—that's his business, not yours. Let's us train these fellas to shoot straight. If the Jewish personnel feels the other men are accusing them of goldbricking—well, I just don't know. Seems awful funny that suddenly the Lord is calling so loud in Private Grossman's ear he's just got to run to church."

"Synagogue," I said.

"Synagogue is right, Sergeant. I'll write that down for handy reference. Thank you for stopping by."

That evening, a few minutes before the company gathered outside the orderly room for the chow formation, I called the C.Q., Corporal Robert LaHill, in to see me. LaHill was a dark, burly fellow whose hair curled out of his clothes wherever it could. He had a glaze in his eyes that made one think of caves and dinosaurs. "LaHill," I said, "when you take the formation, remind the men that they're free to attend church services *whenever* they are held, provided they report to the orderly room before they leave the area."

LaHill scratched his wrist, but gave no indication that he'd heard or understood.

"LaHill," I said, "*church.* You remember? Church, priest, Mass, confession."

He curled one lip into a kind of smile; I took it for a signal that for a second he had flickered back up into the human race.

"Jewish personnel who want to attend services this evening are to fall out in front of the orderly room at 1900," I said. Then, as an afterthought, I added, "By order of Captain Barrett."

A little while later, as the day's last light—softer than any I had seen that year—began to drop over Camp Crowder, I heard LaHill's thick, inflectionless voice outside my window: "Give me your ears, troopers. Toppie says for me to tell you that at 1900 hours all Jewish personnel is to fall out in front, here, if they want to attend the Jewish Mass."

* * *

At seven o'clock, I looked out the orderly-room window and saw three soldiers in starched khakis standing on the dusty quadrangle. They looked at their watches and fidgeted while they whispered back and forth. It was getting dimmer, and, alone on the otherwise deserted field, they looked tiny. When I opened the door, I heard the noises of the G.I. party coming from the surrounding barracks—bunks being pushed to the walls, faucets pounding water into buckets, brooms whisking at the wooden floors, cleaning the dirt away for Saturday's inspection. Big puffs of cloth moved round and round on the windowpanes. I walked outside, and the moment my foot hit the ground I thought I heard Grossbart call to the others, " 'Ten-*hut!*" Or maybe, when they all three jumped to attention, I imagined I heard the command.

Grossbart stepped forward. "Thank you, sir," he said.

" 'Sergeant,' Grossbart," I reminded him. "You call officers 'sir.' I'm not an officer. You've been in the Army three weeks—you know that."

He turned his palms out at his sides to indicate that, in truth, he and I lived beyond convention. "Thank you, anyway," he said.

"Yes," a tall boy behind him said. "Thanks a lot."

And the third boy whispered, "Thank you," but his mouth barely fluttered, so that he did not alter by more than a lip's movement his posture of attention.

"For what?" I asked.

Grossbart snorted happily. "For the announcement. The Corporal's announcement. It helped. It made it—"

"Fancier." The tall boy finished Grossbart's sentence.

Grossbart smiled. "He means formal, sir. Public," he said to me. "Now it won't seem as though we're just taking off—goldbricking because the work has begun."

"It was by order of Captain Barrett," I said.

"Aaah, but you pull a little weight," Grossbart said. "So we thank you." Then he turned to his companions. "Sergeant Marx, I want you to meet Larry Fishbein."

The tall boy stepped forward and extended his hand. I shook it. "You from New York?" he asked.

"Yes."

"Me, too." He had a cadaverous face that collapsed inward from his cheekbone to his jaw, and when he smiled—as he did at the news of our communal attachment—revealed a mouthful of bad teeth. He was blinking his eyes a good deal, as though he were fighting back tears. "What borough?" he asked.

I turned to Grossbart. "It's five after seven. What time are services?"

"Shul," he said, smiling, "is in ten minutes. I want you to meet Mickey Halpern. This is Nathan Marx, our sergeant."

The third boy hopped forward. "Private Michael Halpern." He saluted.

"Salute officers, Halpern," I said. The boy dropped his hand, and, on its way down, in his nervousness, checked to see if his shirt pockets were buttoned.

"Shall I march them over, sir?" Grossbart asked. "Or are you coming along?"

From behind Grossbart, Fishbein piped up. "Afterward, they're having refreshments. A ladies' auxiliary from St. Louis, the rabbi told us last week."

"The chaplain," Halpern whispered.

"You're welcome to come along," Grossbart said.

To avoid his plea, I looked away, and saw, in the windows of the barracks, a cloud of faces staring out at the four of us. "Hurry along, Grossbart," I said.

"O.K., then," he said. He turned to the others. "Double time, *march!*"

They started off, but ten feet away Grossbart spun around and, running backward, called to me, "Good *shabbus,* sir!" And then the three of them were swallowed into the alien Missouri dusk.

Even after they had disappeared over the parade ground, whose green was now a deep blue, I could hear Grossbart singing the double-time cadence, and as it grew dimmer and dimmer, it suddenly touched a deep memory—as did the slant of the light—and I was remembering the shrill sounds of a Bronx playground where, years ago, beside the Grand Concourse, I had played on long spring evenings such as this. It was a pleasant memory for a young man so far from peace and home, and it brought so many recollections with it that I began to grow exceedingly tender about myself. In fact, I indulged myself in a reverie so strong that I felt as though a hand were reaching down inside me. It had to reach so very far to touch me! It had to reach past those days in the forests of Belgium, and past the dying I'd refused to weep over; past the nights in German farmhouses whose books we'd burned to warm us; past endless stretches when I had shut off all softness I might feel for my fellows, and had managed even to deny myself the posture of a conqueror—the swagger that I, as a Jew, might well have worn as my boots whacked against the rubble of Wesel, Münster, and Braunschweig.

But now one night noise, one rumor of home and time past, and memory plunged down through all I had anesthetized, and came to what I suddenly remembered was myself. So it was not altogether curious that, in search of more of me, I found myself following Grossbart's tracks to Chapel No. 3, where the Jewish services were being held.

I took a seat in the last row, which was empty. Two rows in front of me sat Grossbart, Fishbein, and Halpern, holding little white Dixie cups. Each row of seats was raised higher than the one in front of it, and I could see clearly what was going on. Fishbein was pouring the contents of his cup into Grossbart's, and Grossbart looked mirthful as the liquid made a purple arc between Fishbein's hand and his. In the glaring yellow light, I saw the chaplain standing on the platform at the front; he was chanting the first line of the responsive reading. Grossbart's prayer book remained closed on his lap; he was swishing the cup around. Only Halpern responded to the chant by praying. The fingers of his right hand were spread wide across the cover of his open book. His cap was pulled down low onto his brow, which made it round, like a yarmulke. From time to time, Grossbart wet his lips at the cup's edge; Fishbein, his long yellow face a dying light bulb, looked from here to there, craning forward to catch sight of the faces down the row, then of those in front of him, then behind. He saw me, and his eyelids beat a tattoo. His elbow slid into Grossbart's side, his neck inclined toward his friend, he whispered something, and then, when the congregation next responded to the chant, Grossbart's voice was among the others. Fishbein looked into his book now, too; his lips, however, didn't move.

Finally, it was time to drink the wine. The chaplain smiled down at them as Grossbart swigged his in one long gulp, Halpern sipped, meditating, and Fishbein faked devotion with an empty cup. "As I look down amongst the congregation"—the chaplain grinned at the word—"this night, I see many new faces, and I want to welcome you to Friday-night services here at Camp Crowder. I am Major Leo Ben Ezra, your chaplain." Though an American, the chaplain spoke deliberately—syllable by syllable, almost—as though to communicate, above all, with the lip readers in his audience. "I have only a few words to say before we adjourn to the refreshment room, where the kind ladies of the Temple Sinai, St. Louis, Missouri, have a nice setting for you."

Applause and whistling broke out. After another momentary grin, the chaplain raised his hands, palms out, his eyes flicking upward a moment, as if to remind the troops where they were and Who Else might be in attendance. In the sudden silence that followed, I thought I heard Grossbart cackle, "Let the goyim clean the floors!" Were those the words? I wasn't sure, but Fishbein, grinning, nudged Halpern. Halpern looked dumbly at him, then went back to his prayer book, which had been occupying him all through the rabbi's talk. One hand tugged at the black kinky hair that stuck out under his cap. His lips moved.

The rabbi continued. "It is about the food that I want to speak to you for a moment. I know, I know, I know," he intoned, wearily, "how in the mouths of most of you the *trafe* food tastes like ashes. I know how you gag, some of you, and how your parents suffer to think of their children eating foods unclean and offensive to the palate. What can I tell you? I can only say, close your eyes and swallow as best you can. Eat what you must to live, and throw away the rest. I wish I could help more. For those of you who find this impossible, may I ask that you try and try, but then come to see me in private. If your revulsion is so great, we will have to seek aid from those higher up."

A round of chatter rose and subsided. Then everyone sang "Ain Kelohainu"; after all those years, I discovered I still knew the words. Then, suddenly, the service over, Grossbart was upon me. "Higher up? He means the General?"

"Hey, Shelly," Fishbein said, "he means God." He smacked his face and looked at Halpern. "How high can you go!"

"Sh-h-h!" Grossbart said. "What do you think, Sergeant?"

"I don't know," I said. "You better ask the chaplain."

"I'm going to. I'm making an appointment to see him in private. So is Mickey."

Halpern shook his head. "No, no, Sheldon—"

"You have rights, Mickey," Grossbart said. "They can't push us around."

"It's O.K.," said Halpern. "It bothers my mother, not me."

Grossbart looked at me. "Yesterday he threw up. From the hash. It was all ham and God knows what else."

"I have a cold—that was why," Halpern said. He pushed his yarmulke back into a cap.

"What about you, Fishbein?" I asked. "You kosher, too?"

He flushed. "A little. But I'll let it ride. I have a very strong stomach, and I don't eat a lot anyway." I continued to look at him, and he held up his wrist to reinforce what he'd just said; his watch strap was tightened to the last hole, and he pointed that out to me.

"But services are important to you?" I asked him.

He looked at Grossbart. "Sure, sir."

" 'Sergeant.' "

"Not so much at home," said Grossbart, stepping between us, "but away from home it gives one a sense of his Jewishness."

"We have to stick together," Fishbein said.

I started to walk toward the door; Halpern stepped back to make way for me.

"That's what happened in Germany," Grossbart was saying, loud enough for me to hear. "They didn't stick together. They let themselves get pushed around."

I turned. "Look, Grossbart. This is the Army, not summer camp."

He smiled. "So?"

Halpern tried to sneak off, but Grossbart held his arm.

"Grossbart, how old are you?" I asked.

"Nineteen."

"And you?" I said to Fishbein.

"The same. The same month, even."

"And what about him?" I pointed to Halpern, who had by now made it safely to the door.

"Eighteen," Grossbart whispered. "But like he can't tie his shoes or brush his teeth himself. I feel sorry for him."

"I feel sorry for all of us, Grossbart," I said, "but just act like a man. Just don't overdo it."

"Overdo what, sir?"

"The 'sir' business, for one thing. Don't overdo that," I said.

I left him standing there. I passed by Halpern, but he did not look at me. Then I was outside, but, behind, I heard Grossbart call, "Hey, Mickey, my *leben,* come on back. Refreshments!"

*"Leben!"* My grandmother's word for me!

* * *

One morning a week later, while I was working at my desk, Captain Barrett shouted for me to come into his office. When I entered, he had his helmet liner squashed down so far on his head that I couldn't even see his eyes. He was on the phone, and when he spoke to me, he cupped one hand over the mouthpiece. "Who the hell is Grossbart?"

"Third platoon, Captain," I said. "A trainee."

"What's all this stink about food? His mother called a goddam congressman about the food." He uncovered the mouthpiece and slid his helmet up until I could see his bottom eyelashes. "Yes, sir," he said into the phone. "Yes, sir. I'm still here, sir. I'm asking Marx, here, right now—"

He covered the mouthpiece again and turned his head back toward me. "Lightfoot Harry's on the phone," he said, between his teeth. "This congressman calls General Lyman, who calls Colonel Sousa, who calls the Major, who calls me. They're just dying to stick this thing on me. Whatsa matter?" He shook the phone at me. "I don't feed the troops? What is this?"

"Sir, Grossbart is strange—" Barrett greeted that with a mockingly indulgent smile. I altered my approach. "Captain, he's a very orthodox Jew, and so he's only allowed to eat certain foods."

"He throws up, the congressman said. Every time he eats something, his mother says, he throws up!"

"He's accustomed to observing the dietary laws, Captain."

"So why's his old lady have to call the White House?"

"Jewish parents, sir—they're apt to be more protective than you expect. I mean, Jews have a very close family life. A boy goes away from home, sometimes the mother is liable to get very upset. Probably the boy mentioned something in a letter, and his mother misinterpreted."

"I'd like to punch him one right in the mouth," the Captain said. "There's a war on, and he wants a silver platter!"

"I don't think the boy's to blame, sir. I'm sure we can straighten it out by just asking him. Jewish parents worry—"

"*All* parents worry, for Christ's sake. But they don't get on their high horse and start pulling strings—"

I interrupted, my voice higher, tighter than before. "The home life, Captain, is very important—but you're right, it may sometimes get out of hand. It's a very wonderful thing, Captain, but because it's so close, this kind of thing . . ."

He didn't listen any longer to my attempt to present both myself and Lightfoot Harry with an explanation for the letter. He turned back to the phone. "Sir?" he said. "Sir—Marx, here, tells me Jews have a tendency to be pushy. He says he thinks we can settle it right here in the company. . . . Yes, sir. . . . I *will* call back, sir, soon as I can." He hung up. "Where are the men, Sergeant?"

"On the range."

With a whack on the top of his helmet, he crushed it down over his eyes again, and charged out of his chair. "We're going for a ride," he said.

* * *

The Captain drove, and I sat beside him. It was a hot spring day, and under my newly starched fatigues I felt as though my armpits were melting down onto my sides and chest. The roads were dry, and by the time we reached the firing range, my teeth felt gritty with dust, though my mouth had been shut the whole trip. The Captain slammed the brakes on and told me to get the hell out and find Grossbart.

I found him on his belly, firing wildly at the five-hundred-feet target. Waiting their turns behind him were Halpern and Fishbein. Fishbein, wearing a pair of steel-rimmed G.I. glasses I hadn't seen on him before, had the appearance of an old peddler who would gladly have sold you his rifle and the cartridges that were slung all over him. I stood back by the ammo boxes, waiting for Grossbart to finish spraying the distant targets. Fishbein straggled back to stand near me.

"Hello, Sergeant Marx," he said.

"How are you?" I mumbled.

"Fine, thank you. Sheldon's really a good shot."

"I didn't notice."

"I'm not so good, but I think I'm getting the hang of it now. Sergeant, I don't mean to, you know, ask what I shouldn't—" The boy stopped. He was trying to speak intimately, but the noise of the shooting forced him to shout at me.

"What is it?" I asked. Down the range, I saw Captain Barrett standing up in the jeep, scanning the line for me and Grossbart.

"My parents keep asking and asking where we're going," Fishbein said. "Everybody says the Pacific. I don't care, but my parents—If I could relieve their minds, I think I could concentrate more on my shooting."

"I don't know where, Fishbein. Try to concentrate anyway."

"Sheldon says you might be able to find out."

"I don't know a thing, Fishbein. You just take it easy, and don't let Sheldon—"

"*I'm* taking it easy, Sergeant. It's at home—"

Grossbart had finished on the line, and was dusting his fatigues with one hand. I called to him. "Grossbart, the Captain wants to see you."

He came toward us. His eyes blazed and twinkled. "Hi!"

"Don't point that rifle!" I said.

"I wouldn't shoot you, Sarge." He gave me a smile as wide as a pumpkin, and turned the barrel aside.

"Damn you, Grossbart, this is no joke! Follow me."

I walked ahead of him, and had the awful suspicion that, behind me, Grossbart was *marching,* his rifle on his shoulder, as though he were a one-man detachment. At the jeep, he gave the Captain a rifle salute. "Private Sheldon Grossbart, sir."

"At ease, Grossman." The Captain sat down, slid over into the empty seat, and, crooking a finger, invited Grossbart closer.

"Bart, sir. Sheldon Gross*bart.* It's a common error." Grossbart nodded at me; *I* understood, he indicated. I looked away just as the mess truck pulled up to the range, disgorging a half-dozen K.P.s with rolled-up sleeves. The mess sergeant screamed at them while they set up the chowline equipment.

"Grossbart, your mama wrote some congressman that we don't feed you right. Do you know that?" the Captain said.

"It was my father, sir. He wrote to Representative Franconi that my religion forbids me to eat certain foods."

"What religion is that, Grossbart?"

"Jewish."

" 'Jewish, *sir,*' " I said to Grossbart.

"Excuse me, sir. Jewish, sir."

"What have you been living on?" the Captain asked.

"You've been in the Army a month already. You don't look to me like you're falling to pieces."

"I eat because I have to, sir. But Sergeant Marx will testify to the fact that I don't eat one mouthful more than I need to in order to survive."

"Is that so, Marx?" Barrett asked.

"I've never seen Grossbart eat, sir," I said.

"But you heard the rabbi," Grossbart said. "He told us what to do, and I listened."

The Captain looked at me. "Well, Marx?"

"I still don't know what he eats and doesn't eat, sir."

Grossbart raised his arms to plead with me, and it looked for a moment as though he were going to hand me his weapon to hold. "But, Sergeant—"

"Look, Grossbart, just answer the Captain's questions," I said sharply.

Barrett smiled at me, and I resented it. "All right, Grossbart," he said. "What is it you want? The little piece of paper? You want out?"

"No, sir. Only to be allowed to live as a Jew. And for the others, too."

"What others?"

"Fishbein, sir, and Halpern."

"They don't like the way we serve, either?"

"Halpern throws up, sir. I've seen it."

"I thought *you* throw up."

"Just once, sir. I didn't know the sausage was sausage."

"We'll give menus, Grossbart. We'll show training films about the food, so you can identify when we're trying to poison you."

Grossbart did not answer. The men had been organized into two long chow lines. At the tail end of one, I spotted Fishbein—or, rather, his glasses spotted me. They winked sunlight back at me. Halpern stood next to him, patting the inside of his collar with a khaki handkerchief. They moved with the line as it began to edge up toward the food. The mess sergeant was still screaming at the K.P.s. For a moment, I was actually terrified by the thought that somehow the mess sergeant was going to become involved in Grossbart's problem.

"Marx," the Captain said, "you're a Jewish fella—am I right?"

I played straight man. "Yes, sir."

"How long you been in the Army? Tell this boy."

"Three years and two months."

"A year in combat, Grossbart. Twelve goddam months in combat all through Europe. I admire this man." The Captain snapped a wrist against my chest. "Do you hear him peeping about the food? Do you? I want an answer, Grossbart. Yes or no."

"No, sir."

"And why not? He's a Jewish fella."

"Some things are more important to some Jews than other things to other Jews."

Barrett blew up. "Look, Grossbart. Mark, here, is a good man—a goddam hero. When you were in high school, Sergeant Marx was killing Germans. Who does more for the Jews—you, by throwing up over a lousy piece of sausage, a piece of first-cut meat, or Marx, by killing those Nazi bastards? If I was a Jew, Grossbart, I'd kiss this man's feet. He's a goddam hero, and *he* eats what we give him. Why do you have to cause trouble is what I want to know! What is it you're buckin' for—a discharge?"

"No, sir."

"I'm talking to a wall! Sergeant, get him out of my way." Barrett swung himself back into the driver's seat. "I'm going to see the chaplain." The engine roared, the jeep spun around in a whirl of dust, and the Captain was headed back to camp.

For a moment, Grossbart and I stood side by side, watching the jeep. Then he looked at me and said, "I don't want to start trouble. That's the first thing they toss up to us."

When he spoke, I saw that his teeth were white and straight, and the sight of them suddenly made me understand that Grossbart actually did have parents—that once upon a time someone had taken little Sheldon to the dentist. He was their son. Despite all the talk about his parents, it was hard to believe in Grossbart as a child, an heir—as related by blood to anyone, mother, father, or, above all, to me. This realization led me to another.

"What does your father do, Grossbart?" I asked as we started to walk back toward the chow line.

"He's a tailor."

"An American?"

"Now, yes. A son in the Army," he said, jokingly.

"And your mother?" I asked.

He winked. "A *ballabusta.* She practically sleeps with a dustcloth in her hand."

"She's also an immigrant?"

"All she talks is Yiddish, still."

"And your father, too?"

"A little English. 'Clean,' 'Press,' 'Take the pants in.' That's the extent of it. But they're good to me."

"Then, Grossbart—" I reached out and stopped him. He turned toward me, and when our eyes met, his seemed to jump back, to shiver in their sockets. "Grossbart—you were the one who wrote that letter, weren't you?"

It took only a second or two for his eyes to flash happy again. "Yes." He walked on, and I kept pace. "It's what my father *would* have written if he had known how. It was his name, though. *He* signed it. He even mailed it. I sent it home. For the New York postmark."

I was astonished, and he saw it. With complete seriousness, he thrust his right arm in front of me. "Blood is blood, Sergeant," he said, pinching the blue vein in his wrist.

"What the hell *are* you trying to do, Grossbart?" I asked. "I've seen you eat. Do you know that? I told the Captain I don't know what you eat, but I've seen you eat like a hound at chow."

"We work hard, Sergeant. We're in training. For a furnace to work, you've got to feed it coal."

"Why did you say in the letter that you threw up all the time?"

"I was really talking about Mickey there. I was talking *for* him. He would never write, Sergeant, though I pleaded with him. He'll waste away to nothing if I don't help. Sergeant, I used my name—my father's name—but it's Mickey, and Fishbein, too, I'm watching out for."

"You're a regular Messiah, aren't you?"

We were at the chow line now.

"That's a good one, Sergeant," he said, smiling. "But who knows? Who can tell? Maybe you're the Messiah—a little bit. What Mickey says is the Messiah is a collective idea. He went to Yeshiva, Mickey, for a while. He says *together* we're the Messiah. Me a little bit, you a little bit. You should hear that kid talk, Sergeant, when he gets going."

"Me a little bit, you a little bit," I said. "You'd like to believe that, wouldn't you, Grossbart? That would make everything so clean for you."

"It doesn't seem too bad a thing to believe, Sergeant. It only means we should all *give* a little, is all."

I walked off to eat my rations with the other noncoms.

* * *

Two days later, a letter addressed to Captain Barrett passed over my desk. It had come through the chain of command—from the office of Congressman Franconi, where it had been received, to General Lyman, to Colonel Sousa, to Major Lamont, now to Captain Barrett. I read it over twice. It was dated May 14, the day Barrett had spoken with Grossbart on the rifle range.

*Dear Congressman:*

*First let me thank you for your interest in behalf of my son, Private Sheldon Grossbart. Fortunately, I was able to speak with Sheldon on the phone the other night, and I think I've been able to solve our problem. He is, as I mentioned in my last letter, a very religious boy, and it was only with the greatest difficulty that I could persuade him that the religious thing to do—what God Himself would want Sheldon to do—would be to suffer the pangs of religious remorse for the good of his country and all mankind. It took some doing, Congressman, but finally he saw the light. In fact, what he said (and I wrote down the words on a scratch pad so as never to forget), what he said was "I guess you're right, Dad. So many millions of my fellow-Jews gave up their lives to the enemy, the least I can do is live for a while minus a bit of my heritage so as to help end this struggle and regain for all the children of God dignity and humanity." That, Congressman, would make any father proud.*

*By the way, Sheldon wanted me to know—and to pass on to you—the name of a soldier who helped him reach this decision: SERGEANT NATHAN MARX. Sergeant Marx is a combat veteran who is Sheldon's first sergeant. This man has helped Sheldon over some of the first hurdles he's had to face in the Army, and is in part responsible for Sheldon's changing his mind about the dietary laws. I know Sheldon would appreciate any recognition Marx could receive.*

*Thank you and good luck. I look forward to seeing your name on the next election ballot.*

*Respectfully,*
*Samuel E. Grossbart*

Attached to the Grossbart communiqué was another, addressed to General Marshall Lyman, the post commander, and signed by Representative Charles E. Franconi, of the House of Representatives. The communiqué informed General Lyman that Sergeant Nathan Marx was a credit to the U.S. Army and the Jewish people.

What was Grossbart's motive in recanting? Did he feel he'd gone too far? Was the letter a strategic retreat—a crafty attempt to strengthen what he considered our alliance? Or had he actually changed his mind, via an imaginary dialogue between Grossbart *père* and Grossbart *fils?* I was puzzled, but only for a few days—that is, only until I realized that, whatever his reasons, he had actually decided to disappear from my life; he was going to allow himself to become just another trainee. I saw him at inspection, but he never winked; at chow formations, but he never flashed me a sign. On Sundays, with the other trainees, he would sit around watching the noncoms' softball team, for which I pitched, but not once did he speak an unnecessary word to me. Fishbein and Halpern retreated, too—at Grossbart's command, I was sure. Apparently he had seen that wisdom lay in turning back before he plunged over into the ugliness of privilege undeserved. Our separation allowed me to forgive him our past encounters, and, finally, to admire him for his good sense.

* * *

Meanwhile, free of Grossbart, I grew used to my job and my administrative tasks. I stepped on a scale one day, and discovered I had truly become a noncombatant; I had gained seven pounds. I found patience to get past the first three pages of a book. I thought about the future more and more, and wrote letters to girls I'd known before the war. I even got a few answers. I sent away to Columbia for a Law School catalogue. I continued to follow the war in the Pacific, but it was not my war. I thought I could see the end, and sometimes, at night, I dreamed that I was walking on the streets of Manhattan—Broadway, Third Avenue, 116th Street, where I had lived the three years I attended Columbia. I curled myself around these dreams and I began to be happy.

And then, one Sunday, when everybody was away and I was alone in the orderly room reading a month-old copy of the *Sporting News,* Grossbart reappeared.

"You a baseball fan, Sergeant?"

I looked up. "How are you?"

"Fine," Grossbart said. "They're making a soldier out of me."

"How are Fishbein and Halpern?"

"Coming along," he said. "We've got no training this afternoon. They're at the movies."

"How come you're not with them?"

"I wanted to come over and say hello."

He smiled—a shy, regular-guy smile, as though he and I well knew that our friendship drew its sustenance from unexpected visits, remembered birthdays, and borrowed lawnmowers. At first it offended me, and then the feeling was swallowed by the general uneasiness I felt at the thought that everyone on the post was locked away in a dark movie theater and I was here alone with Grossbart. I folded up my paper.

"Sergeant," he said, "I'd like to ask a favor. It is a favor, and I'm making no bones about it."

He stopped, allowing me to refuse him a hearing—which, of course, forced me into a courtesy I did not intend. "Go ahead."

"Well, actually it's two favors."

I said nothing.

"The first one's about these rumors. Everybody says we're going to the Pacific."

"As I told your friend Fishbein, I don't know," I said. "You'll just have to wait to find out. Like everybody else."

"You think there's a chance of any of us going East?"

"Germany?" I said. "Maybe."

"I meant New York."

"I don't think so, Grossbart. Offhand."

"Thanks for the information, Sergeant," he said.

"It's not information, Grossbart. Just what I surmise."

"It certainly would be good to be near home. My parents—you know." He took a step toward the door and then turned back. "Oh, the other thing. May I ask the other?"

"What is it?"

"The other thing is—I've got relatives in St. Louis, and they say they'll give me a whole Passover dinner if I can get down there. God, Sergeant, that'd mean an awful lot to me."

I stood up. "No passes during basic, Grossbart."

"But we're off from now till Monday morning, Sergeant. I could leave the post and no one would even know."

"I'd know. You'd know."

"But that's all. Just the two of us. Last night, I called my aunt, and you should have heard her. 'Come—come,' she said. 'I got gefilte fish, *chrain*—the works!' Just a day, Sergeant. I'd take the blame if anything happened."

"The Captain isn't here to sign a pass."

"You could sign."

"Look, Grossbart—"

"Sergeant, for two months, practically, I've been eating *trafe* till I want to die."

"I thought you'd made up your mind to live with it. To be minus a little bit of heritage."

He pointed a finger at me. "You!" he said. "That wasn't for you to read."

"I read it. So what?"

"That letter was addressed to a congressman."

"Grossbart, don't feed me any baloney. You *wanted* me to read it."

"Why are you persecuting me, Sergeant?"

"Are you kidding!"

"I've run into this before," he said, "but never from my own!"

"Get out of here, Grossbart! Get the hell out of my sight!"

He did not move. "Ashamed, that's what you are," he said. "So you take it out on the rest of us. They say Hitler himself was half a Jew. Hearing you, I wouldn't doubt it."

"What are you trying to do with me, Grossbart?" I asked him. "What are you after? You want me to give you special privileges, to change the food, to find out about your orders, to give you weekend passes."

"You even talk like a goy!" Grossbart shook his fist. "Is this just a weekend pass I'm asking for? Is a Seder sacred, or not?"

Seder! It suddenly occurred to me that Passover had been celebrated weeks before. I said so.

"That's right," he replied. "Who says no? A month ago—and I was in the field eating hash! And now all I ask is a simple favor. A Jewish boy I thought would understand. My aunt's willing to go out of her way—to make a Seder a month later. . . ." He turned to go, mumbling.

"Come back here!" I called. He stopped and looked at me. "Grossbart, why can't you be like the rest? Why do you have to stick out like a sore thumb?"

"Because I'm a Jew, Sergeant. I *am* different. Better, maybe not. But different."

"This is a war, Grossbart. For the time being *be* the same."

"I refuse."

"What?"

"I refuse. I can't stop being me, that's all there is to it." Tears came to his eyes. "It's a hard thing to be a Jew. But now I understand what Mickey says—it's a harder thing to stay one." He raised a hand sadly toward me. "Look at *you*."

"Stop crying!"

"Stop this, stop that, stop the other thing! *You* stop, Sergeant. Stop closing your heart to your own!" And, wiping his face with his sleeve, he ran out the door. "The least we can do for one another—the least . . ."

An hour later, looking out of the window, I saw Grossbart headed across the field. He wore a pair of starched khakis and carried a little leather ditty bag. I went out into the heat of the day. It was quiet; not a soul was in sight except, over by the mess hall, four K.P.s sitting around a pan, sloped forward from their waists, gabbing and peeling potatoes in the sun.

"Grossbart!" I called.

He looked toward me and continued walking.

"Grossbart, get over here!"

He turned and came across the field. Finally, he stood before me.

"Where are you going?" I asked.

"St. Louis. I don't care."

"You'll get caught without a pass."

"So I'll get caught without a pass."

"You'll go to the stockade."

"I'm *in* the stockade." He made an about-face and headed off.

I let him go only a step or two. "Come back here," I said, and he followed me into the office, where I typed out a pass and signed the Captain's name, and my own initials after it.

He took the pass and then, a moment later, reached out and grabbed my hand. "Sergeant, you don't know how much this means to me."

"O.K.," I said. "Don't get in any trouble."

"I wish I could show you how much this means to me."

"Don't do me any favors. Don't write any more congressmen for citations."

He smiled. "You're right. I won't. But let me do something."

"Bring me a piece of that gefilte fish. Just get out of here."

"I will!" he said. "With a slice of carrot and a little horseradish. I won't forget."

"All right. Just show your pass at the gate. And don't tell *anybody*."

"I won't. It's a month late, but a good Yom Tov to you."

"Good Yom Tov, Grossbart," I said.

"You're a good Jew, Sergeant. You like to think you have a hard heart, but underneath you're a fine, decent man. I mean that."

Those last three words touched me more than any words from Grossbart's mouth had the right to. "All right, Grossbart," I said. "Now call me 'sir,' and get the hell out of here."

He ran out the door and was gone. I felt very pleased with myself; it was a great relief to stop fighting Grossbart, and it had cost me nothing. Barrett would never find out, and if he did, I could manage to invent some excuse. For a while, I sat at my desk, comfortable in my decision. Then the screen door flew back and Grossbart burst in again. "Sergeant!" he said. Behind him I saw Fishbein and Halpern, both in starched khakis, both carrying ditty bags like Grossbart's.

"Sergeant, I caught Mickey and Larry coming out of the movies. I almost missed them."

"Grossbart—did I say tell no one?" I said.

"But my aunt said I could bring friends. That I should, in fact."

"*I'm* the Sergeant, Grossbart—not your aunt!"

Grossbart looked at me in disbelief. He pulled Halpern up by his sleeve. "Mickey, tell the Sergeant what this would mean to you."

Halpern looked at me and, shrugging, said, "A lot."

Fishbein stepped forward without prompting. "This would mean a great deal to me and my parents, Sergeant Marx."

"No!" I shouted.

Grossbart was shaking his head. "Sergeant, I could see you denying me, but how you can deny Mickey, a Yeshiva boy—that's beyond me."

"I'm not denying Mickey anything," I said. "You just pushed a little too hard, Grossbart. *You* denied him."

"I'll give him my pass, then," Grossbart said. "I'll give him my aunt's address and a little note. At least let him go."

In a second, he had crammed the pass into Halpern's pants pocket. Halpern looked at me, and so did Fishbein. Grossbart was at the door, pushing it open. "Mickey, bring me a piece of gelfilte fish, at least," he said, and then he was outside again.

The three of us looked at one another, and then I said, "Halpern, hand that pass over."

He took it from his pocket and gave it to me. Fishbein had now moved to the doorway, where he lingered. He stood there for a moment with his mouth slightly open, and then he pointed to himself. "And me?" he asked.

His utter ridiculousness exhausted me. I slumped down in my seat and felt pulses knocking at the back of my eyes. "Fishbein," I said, "you understand I'm not trying to deny you anything, don't you? If it was my Army, I'd serve gefilte fish in the mess hall. I'd sell *kugel* in the PX, honest to God."

Halpern smiled.

"You understand, don't you, Halpern?"

"Yes, Sergeant."

"And you, Fishbein? I don't want enemies. I'm just like you—I want to serve my time and go home. I miss the same things you miss."

"Then, Sergeant," Fishbein said, "why don't you come, too?"

"Where?"

"To St. Louis. To Shelly's aunt. We'll have a regular Seder. Play hide-the-matzoh." He gave me a broad, black-toothed smile.

I saw Grossbart again, on the other side of the screen.

"Pst!" He waved a piece of paper. "Mickey, here's the address. Tell her I couldn't get away."

Halpern did not move. He looked at me, and I saw the shrug moving up his arms into his shoulders again. I took the cover off my typewriter and made out passes for him and Fishbein. "Go," I said. "The three of you."

I thought Halpern was going to kiss my hand.

* * *

That afternoon, in a bar in Joplin, I drank beer and listened with half an ear to the Cardinal game. I tried to look squarely at what I'd become involved in, and began to wonder if perhaps the struggle with Grossbart wasn't as much my fault as his. What was I that I had to *muster* generous feelings? Who was I to have been feeling so grudging, so tight-hearted? After all, I wasn't being asked to move the world. Had I a right, then, or a reason, to clamp down on Grossbart, when that meant clamping down on Halpern, too? And Fishbein—that ugly, agreeable soul? Out of the many recollections of my childhood that had tumbled over me these past few days I heard my grandmother's voice: "What are you making a *tsimmes?*" It was what she would ask my mother when, say, I had cut myself while doing something I shouldn't have done, and her daughter was busy bawling me out. I needed a hug and a kiss, and my mother would moralize. But my grandmother knew—mercy overrides justice. I should have known it, too. Who was Nathan Marx to be such a penny pincher with kindness? Surely, I thought, the Messiah himself—if He should ever come—won't niggle over nickels and dimes. God willing, he'll hug and kiss.

The next day, while I was playing softball over on the parade ground, I decided to ask Bob Wright, who was noncom in charge of Classification and Assignment, where he thought our trainees would be sent when their cycle ended, in two weeks. I asked casually, between innings, and he said, "They're pushing them all into the Pacific. Shulman cut the orders on your boys the other day."

The news shocked me, as though I were the father of Halpern, Fishbein, and Grossbart.

* * *

That night, I was just sliding into sleep when someone tapped on my door. "Who is it?" I asked.

"Sheldon."

He opened the door and came in. For a moment, I felt his presence without being able to see him. "How was it?" I asked.

He popped into sight in the near-darkness before me. "Great, Sergeant." Then he was sitting on the edge of the bed. I sat up.

"How about you?" he asked. "Have a nice weekend?"

"Yes."

"The others went to sleep." He took a deep, paternal breath. We sat silent for a while, and a homey feeling invaded my ugly little cubicle; the door was locked, the cat was out, the children were safely in bed.

"Sergeant, can I tell you something? Personal?"

I did not answer, and he seemed to know why. "Not about me. About Mickey. Sergeant, I never felt for anybody like I feel for him. Last night I heard Mickey in the bed next to me. He was crying so, it could have broken your heart. Real sobs."

"I'm sorry to hear that."

"I had to talk to him to stop him. He held my hand, Sergeant—he wouldn't let it go. He was almost hysterical. He kept saying if he only knew where we were going. Even if he knew it *was* the Pacific, that would be better than nothing. Just to know."

Long ago, someone had taught Grossbart the sad rule that only lies can get the truth. Not that I couldn't believe in the fact of Halpern's crying; his eyes *always* seemed red-rimmed. But, fact or not, it became a lie when Grossbart uttered it. He was entirely strategic. But then—it came with the force of indictment—so was I! There are strategies of aggression, but there are strategies of retreat as well. And so, recognizing that I myself had not been without craft and guile, I told him what I knew. "It is the Pacific."

He let out a small gasp, which was not a lie. "I'll tell him. I wish it was otherwise."

"So do I."

He jumped on my words. "You mean you think you could do something? A change, maybe?"

"No, I couldn't do a thing."

"Don't you know anybody over at C. and A.?"

"Grossbart, there's nothing I can do," I said. "If your orders are for the Pacific, then it's the Pacific."

"But Mickey—"

"Mickey, you, me—everybody, Grossbart. There's nothing to be done. Maybe the war'll end before you go. Pray for a miracle."

"But—"

"Good night, Grossbart." I settled back, and was relieved to feel the springs unbend as Grossbart rose to leave. I could see him clearly now; his jaw had dropped, and he looked like a dazed prizefighter. I noticed for the first time a little paper bag in his hand.

"Grossbart." I smiled. "My gift?"

"Oh, yes, Sergeant. Here—from all of us." He handed me the bag. "It's egg roll."

"Egg roll?" I accepted the bag and felt a damp grease spot on the bottom. I opened it, sure that Grossbart was joking.

"We thought you'd probably like it. You know—Chinese egg roll. We thought you'd probably have a taste for—"

"Your aunt served egg roll?"

"She wasn't home."

"Grossbart, she invited you. You told me she invited you and your friends."

"I know," he said. "I just reread the letter. *Next* week."

I got out of bed and walked to the window. "Grossbart," I said. But I was not calling to him.

"What?"

"What are you, Grossbart? Honest to God, what are you?"

I think it was the first time I'd asked him a question for which he didn't have an immediate answer.

"How can you do this to people?" I went on.

"Sergeant, the day away did us all a world of good. Fishbein, you should see him, he *loves* Chinese food."

"But the Seder," I said.

"We took second best, Sergeant."

Rage came charging at me. I didn't sidestep. "Grossbart, you're a liar!" I said. "You're a schemer and a crook. You've got no respect for anything. Nothing at all. Not for me, for the truth—not even for poor Halpern! You use us all—"

"Sergeant, Sergeant, I feel for Mickey. Honest to God, I do. I *love* Mickey. I try—"

"You try! You feel!" I lurched toward him and grabbed his shirt front. I shook him furiously. "Grossbart, get out! Get out and stay the hell away from me. Because if I see you, I'll make your life miserable. You *understand that?*"

"Yes."

I let him free, and when he walked from the room, I wanted to spit on the floor where he had stood. I couldn't stop the fury. It engulfed me, owned me, till it seemed I could only rid myself of it with tears or an act of violence. I snatched from the bed the bag Grossbart had given me and, with all my strength, threw it out the window. And the next morning, as the men policed the area around the barracks, I heard a great cry go up from one of the trainees, who had been anticipating only his morning handful of cigarette butts and candy wrappers. "Egg roll!" he shouted. "Holy Christ, Chinese goddam egg roll!"

* * *

A week later, when I read the orders that had come down from C. and A., I couldn't believe my eyes. Every single trainee was to be shipped to Camp Stoneman, California, and from there to the Pacific—every trainee but one. Private Sheldon Grossbart. He was to be sent to Fort Monmouth, New Jersey. I read the mimeographed sheet several times. Dee, Farrell, Fishbein, Fuselli, Fylypowycz, Glinicki, Gromke, Gucwa, Halpern, Hardy, Helebrandt, right down to Anton Zygadlo—all were to be headed West before the month was out. All except Grossbart. He had pulled a string, and I wasn't it.

I lifted the phone and called C. and A.

The voice on the other end said smartly, "Corporal Shulman, sir."

"Let me speak to Sergeant Wright."

"Who is this calling, sir?"

"Sergeant Marx."

And, to my surprise, the voice said, *"Oh!"* Then, "Just a minute, Sergeant."

Shulman's *"Oh!"* stayed with me while I waited for Wright to come to the phone. Why *"Oh!"*? Who was Shulman? And then, so simply, I knew I'd discovered the string that Grossbart had pulled. In fact, I could hear Grossbart the day he'd discovered Shulman in the PX, or in the bowling alley, or maybe even at services. "Glad to meet you. Where you from? Bronx? Me, too. Do you know So-and-So? And So-and-So? Me, too! You work at C. and A.? Really? Hey, how's chances of getting East? Could you do something? Change something? Swindle, cheat, lie? We gotta help each other, you know. If the Jews in Germany . . ."

Bob Wright answered the phone. "How are you, Nate? How's the pitching arm?"

"Good. Bob, I wonder if you could do me a favor." I heard clearly my own words, and they so reminded me of Grossbart that I dropped more easily than I could have imagined into what I had planned. "This may sound crazy, Bob, but I got a kid here on orders to Monmouth who wants them changed. He had a brother killed in Europe, and he's hot to go to the Pacific. Says he'd feel like a coward if he wound up Stateside. I don't know, Bob—can anything be done? Put somebody else in the Monmouth slot?"

"Who?" he asked cagily.

"Anybody. First guy in the alphabet. I don't care. The kid just asked if something could be done."

"What's his name?"

"Grossbart, Sheldon."

Wright didn't answer.

"Yeah," I said. "He's a Jewish kid, so he thought I could help him out. You know."

"I guess I can do something," he finally said. "The Major hasn't been around here for weeks. Temporary duty to the golf course. I'll try, Nate, that's all I can say."

"I'd appreciate it, Bob. See you Sunday." And I hung up, perspiring.

The following day, the corrected orders appeared: Fishbein, Fuselli, Fylypowycz, Glinicki, Gromke, Grossbart, Gucwa, Halpern, Hardy . . . Lucky Private Harley Alton was to go to Fort Monmouth, New Jersey, where, for some reason or other, they wanted an enlisted man with infantry training.

After chow that night, I stopped back at the orderly room to straighten out the guard-duty roster. Grossbart was waiting for me. He spoke first.

"You son of a bitch!"

I sat down at my desk, and while he glared at me, I began to make the necessary alterations in the duty roster.

"What do you have against me?" he cried. "Against my family? Would it kill you for me to be near my father, God knows how many months he has left to him?"

"Why so?"

"His heart," Grossbart said. "He hasn't had enough troubles in a lifetime, you've got to add to them. I curse the day I ever met you, Marx! Shulman told me what happened over there. There's no limit to your anti-Semitism, is there? The damage you've done here isn't enough. You have to make a special phone call! You really want me dead!"

I made the last few notations in the duty roster and got up to leave. "Good night, Grossbart."

"You owe me an explanation!" He stood in my path.

"Sheldon, you're the one who owes explanations."

He scowled. "To *you?*"

"To me, I think so—yes. Mostly to Fishbein and Halpern."

"That's right, twist things around. I owe nobody nothing, I've done all I could do for them. Now I think I've got the right to watch out for myself."

"For each other we have to learn to watch out, Sheldon. You told me yourself."

"You call this watching out for me—what you did?"

"No. For all of us."

I pushed him aside and started for the door. I heard his furious breathing behind me, and it sounded like steam rushing from an engine of terrible strength.

"*You'll* be all right," I said from the door. And, I thought, so would Fishbein and Halpern be all right, even in the Pacific, if only Grossbart continued to see—in the obsequiousness of the one, the soft spirituality of the other—some profit for himself.

I stood outside the orderly room, and I heard Grossbart weeping behind me. Over in the barracks, in the lighted windows, I could see the boys in their T shirts sitting on their bunks talking about their orders, as they'd been doing for the past two days. With a kind of quiet nervousness, they polished shoes, shined belt buckles, squared away underwear, trying as best they could to accept their fate. Behind me, Grossbart swallowed hard, accepting his. And then, resisting with all my will an impulse to turn and seek pardon for my vindictiveness, I accepted my own.

# JAMES BALDWIN
## (1924–1987)

The oldest of nine children, James Baldwin was born, raised, and schooled in Harlem. His stepfather, a factory worker and lay preacher, loomed as a tyrannical figure in his life. At age 14, Baldwin began a brief career as an evangelist, preaching in a storefront Harlem church. Three years later he renounced the church and then worked at a number of jobs while beginning to write. He wrote book reviews and essays for such journals as *Commentary* and *Partisan Review,* establishing himself early as a powerful essayist. His friendship with Richard Wright led to his move to France in 1948, where he lived until 1957. After that he lived some time in the United States and some time in France.

Baldwin was actively involved in the intellectual controversies of the civil rights movement. His highly acclaimed first novel, the semiautobiographical *Go Tell It on the Mountain,* published in 1953, explores the torturous quest for racial identity and dignity. The controversial *Giovanni's Room* (1956) added the issue of homosexuality to the social struggle. Baldwin continued this exploration in the novel *Another Country* (1962). Other novels include *Tell Me How Long the Train's Been Gone* (1968), *If Beale Street Could Talk* (1974), and *Just Above My Head* (1979). Baldwin's essays were published under the titles *Notes of a Native Son* (1955), *Nobody Knows My Name* (1961), *The Fire Next Time* (1963), *No Name in the Street* (1972), *The Devil Finds Work* (1976), and *Collected Nonfiction, 1948–1985* (1985). Baldwin also wrote two plays, *Blues for Mister Charlie* (1964) and *The Amen Corner* (1958). The selection here, "Sonny's Blues," comes from his collection of stories *Going to Meet the Man* (1965). The affirmations that Baldwin's fiction makes do not come cheaply, for human suffering, leavened and illumined by love, can lead to brotherhood and a genuine joy in living.

## Sonny's Blues

I READ about it in the paper, in the subway, on my way to work. I read it, and I couldn't believe it, and I read it again. Then perhaps I just stared at it, at the newsprint spelling out his name, spelling out the story. I stared at it in the swinging lights of the subway car, and in the faces and bodies of the people, and in my own face, trapped in the darkness which roared outside.

It was not to be believed and I kept telling myself that, as I walked from the subway station to the high school. And at the same time I couldn't doubt it. I was scared, scared for Sonny. He became real to me again. A great block of ice got settled in my belly and kept melting there slowly all day long, while I taught my classes algebra. It was a special kind of ice. It kept melting, sending trickles of ice water all up and down my veins, but it never got less. Sometimes it hardened and seemed to expand until I felt my guts were going to come spilling out or that I was going to choke or scream. This would always be at a moment when I was remembering some specific thing Sonny had once said or done.

When he was about as old as the boys in my class his face had been bright and open, there was a lot of copper in it; and he'd had wonderfully direct brown eyes, and great gentleness and privacy. I wondered what he looked like now. He had been picked up, the evening before, in a raid on an apartment downtown, for peddling and using heroin.

I couldn't believe it: but what I mean by that is that I couldn't find any room for it anywhere inside me. I had kept it outside me for a long time. I hadn't wanted to know. I had had suspicions, but I didn't name them, I kept putting them away. I told myself that Sonny was wild, but he wasn't crazy. And he'd always been a good boy, he hadn't ever turned hard or evil or disrespectful, the way kids can, so quick, so quick especially in Harlem. I didn't want to believe that I'd ever see my brother going down, coming to nothing, all that light in his face gone out, in the condition I'd already seen so many others. Yet it had happened and here I was, talking about algebra to a lot of boys who might, every one of them for all I knew, be popping off needles every time they went to the head. Maybe it did more for them than algebra could.

I was sure that the first time Sonny had ever had horse, he couldn't have been much older than these boys were now. These boys, now, were living as we'd been living then, they were growing up with a rush and their heads bumped abruptly against the low ceiling of their actual possibilities. They were filled with rage. All they really knew were two darknesses, the darkness of their lives, which was now closing in on them, and the darkness of the movies, which had blinded them to that other darkness, and in which they now, vindictively, dreamed, at once more together than they were at any other time, and more alone.

When the last bell rang, the last class ended, I let out my breath. It seemed I'd been holding it for all that time. My clothes were wet—I may have looked as though I'd been sitting in a steam bath, all dressed up, all afternoon. I sat alone in the classroom a long time. I listened to the boys outside, downstairs, shouting and cursing and laughing.

conflict two brothers one wanted to settle & Sonny wanted to escape & live



Their laughter struck me for perhaps the first time. It was not the joyous laughter which—God knows why—one associates with children. It was mocking and insular, its intent was to denigrate. It was disenchanted, and in this, also, lay the authority of their curses. Perhaps I was listening to them because I was thinking about my brother and in them I heard my brother. And myself.

One boy was whistling a tune, at once very complicated and very simple, it seemed to be pouring out of him as though he were a bird, and it sounded very cool and moving through all that harsh, bright air, only just holding its own through all those other sounds.

I stood up and walked over to the window and looked down into the courtyard. It was the beginning of the spring and the sap was rising in the boys. A teacher passed through them every now and again, quickly, as though he or she couldn't wait to get out of that courtyard, to get those boys out of their sight and off their minds. I started collecting my stuff. I thought I'd better get home and talk to Isabel.

The courtyard was almost deserted by the time I got downstairs. I saw this boy standing in the shadow of a doorway, looking just like Sonny. I almost called his name. Then I saw that it wasn't Sonny, but somebody we used to know, a boy from around our block. He'd been Sonny's friend. He'd never been mine, having been too young for me, and, anyway, I'd never liked him. And now, even though he was a grown-up man, he still hung around that block, still spent hours on the street corners, was always high and raggy. I used to run into him from time to time and he'd often work around to asking me for a quarter or fifty cents. He always had some real good excuse, too, and I always gave it to him, I don't know why.

But now, abruptly, I hated him. I couldn't stand the way he looked at me, partly like a dog, partly like a cunning child. I wanted to ask him what the hell he was doing in the school courtyard.

He sort of shuffled over to me, and he said, "I see you got the papers. So you already know about it."

"You mean about Sonny! Yes, I already know about it. How come they didn't get you?"

He grinned. It made him repulsive and it also brought to mind what he'd looked like as a kid. "I wasn't there. I stay away from them people."

"Good for you." I offered him a cigarette and I watched him through the smoke. "You come all the way down here just to tell me about Sonny?"

"That's right." He was sort of shaking his head and his eyes looked strange, as though they were about to cross. The bright sun deadened his damp dark brown skin and it made his eyes look yellow and showed up the dirt in his kinked hair. He smelled funky. I moved a little away from him and I said, "Well, thanks. But I already know about it and I got to get home."

"I'll walk you a little ways," he said. We started walking. There were a couple of kids still loitering in the courtyard and one of them said goodnight to me and looked strangely at the boy beside me.

"What're you going to do?" he asked me. "I mean, about Sonny?"

"Look. I haven't seen Sonny for over a year, I'm not sure I'm going to do anything. Anyway, what the hell can I do?"

"That's right," he said quickly, "ain't nothing you can do: Can't much help old Sonny no more, I guess."

It was what I was thinking and so it seemed to me he had no right to say it.

"I'm surprised at Sonny, though," he went on—he had a funny way of talking, he looked straight ahead as though he were talking to himself—"I thought Sonny was a smart boy, I thought he was too smart to get hung."

"I guess he thought so too," I said sharply, "and that's how he got hung. And how about you? You're pretty goddamn smart, I bet."

Then he looked directly at me, just for a minute. "I ain't smart," he said. "If I was smart, I'd have reached for a pistol a long time ago."

"Look. Don't tell *me* your sad story, if it was up to me, I'd give you one." Then I felt guilty—guilty, probably, for never having supposed that the poor bastard *had* a story of his own, much less a sad one, and I asked quickly, "What's going to happen to him now?"

He didn't answer this. He was off by himself some place. "Funny thing," he said, and from his tone we might have been discussing the quickest way to get to Brooklyn, "when I saw the papers this morning, the first thing I asked myself was if I had anything to do with it. I felt sort of responsible."

I began to listen more carefully. The subway station was on the corner, just before us, and I stopped. He stopped, too. We were in front of a bar and he ducked slightly, peering in, but whoever he was looking for didn't seem to be there. The juke box was blasting away with something black and bouncy and I half watched the barmaid as she danced her way from the juke box to her place behind the bar. And I watched her face as she laughingly responded to something someone said to her, still keeping time to the music. When she smiled one saw the little girl, one sensed the doomed, still-struggling woman beneath the battered face of the semi-whore.

"I never *give* Sonny nothing," the boy said finally, "but a long time ago I come to school high and Sonny asked me how it felt." He paused, I couldn't bear to watch him, I watched the barmaid, and I listened to the music which seemed to be causing the pavement to shake. "I told him it felt great." The music stopped, the barmaid paused and watched the juke box until the music began again. "It did."

All this was carrying me some place I didn't want to go. I certainly didn't want to know how it felt. It filled everything, the people, the houses, the music, the dark, quicksilver barmaid, with menace; and this menace was their reality.

"What's going to happen to him now?" I asked again.

"They'll send him away some place and they'll try to cure him." He shook his head. "Maybe he'll even think he's kicked the habit. Then they'll let him loose"—he gestured, throwing his cigarette into the gutter. "That's all."

"What do you mean, that's *all.*"

But I knew what he meant.

"I *mean,* that's all." He turned his head and looked at me, pulling down the corners of his mouth. "Don't you know what I mean?" he asked, softly.

"How the hell *would* I know what you mean?" I almost whispered it, I don't know why.

"That's right," he said to the air, "how would *he* know what I mean?" He turned toward me again, patient and calm, and yet I somehow felt him shaking, shaking as though he were going to fall apart. I felt that ice in my guts again, the dread I'd felt all afternoon; and again I watched the barmaid, moving about the bar, washing glasses, and singing. "Listen. They'll let him out and then it'll just start all over again. That's what I mean."

"You mean—they'll let him out. And then he'll just start working his way back in again. You mean he'll never kick the habit. Is that what you mean?"

"That's right," he said, cheerfully. "*You* see what I mean."

"Tell me," I said at last, "why does he want to die? He must want to die, he's killing himself, why does he want to die?"

He looked at me in surprise. He licked his lips, "He don't want to die. He wants to live. Don't nobody want to die, ever."

Then I wanted to ask him—too many things. He could not have answered, or if he had, I could not have borne the answers. I started walking. "Well, I guess it's none of my business."

"It's going to be rough on old Sonny," he said. We reached the subway station. "This is your station?" he asked. I nodded. I took one step down. "Damn!" he said suddenly. I looked up at him. He grinned again. "Damn if I didn't leave all my money home. You ain't got a dollar on you, have you? Just for a couple of days is all."

All at once something inside gave and threatened to come pouring out of me. I didn't hate him any more. I felt that in another moment I'd start crying like a child.

"Sure," I said. "Don't sweat." I looked in my wallet and didn't have a dollar, I only had a five. "Here," I said, "That hold you?"

He didn't look at it—he didn't want to look at it. A terrible, closed look came over his face, as though he were keeping the number on the bill a secret from him and me. "Thanks," he said, and now he was dying to see me go. "Don't worry about Sonny. Maybe I'll write him or something."

"Sure," I said. "You do that. So long."

"Be seeing you," he said. I went on down the steps.

* * *

And I didn't write Sonny or send him anything for a long time. When I finally did, it was just after my little girl died, he wrote me back a letter which made me feel like a bastard.

Here's what he said:

*Dear brother,*

*You don't know how much I needed to hear from you. I wanted to write you many a time but I dug how much I must have hurt you and so I didn't write. But now I feel like a man who's been trying to climb up out of some deep, real deep and funky hole and just the sun up there, outside. I got to get outside.*

*I can't tell you much about how I got here. I mean I don't know how to tell you. I guess I was afraid of something or I was trying to escape from something and you know I have never been very strong in the head (smile). I'm glad Mama and Daddy are dead and can't see what's happened to their son and I swear if I'd known what I was doing I would never have hurt you so, you and a lot of other fine people who were nice to me and who believed in me.*

*I don't want you to think it had anything to do with me being a musician. It's more than that. Or maybe less than that. I can't get anything straight in my head down here and I try not to think about what's going to happen to me when I get outside again. Sometime I think I'm going to flip and never get outside and sometime I think I'll come straight back. I tell you one thing, though, I'd rather blow my brains out than go through this again. But that's what they all say, so they tell me. If I tell you when I'm coming to New York and if you could meet me, I sure would appreciate it. Give my love to Isabel and the kids and I was sure sorry to hear about little Gracie. I wish I could be like Mama and say the Lord's will be done, but I don't know it seems to me that trouble is the one thing that never does get stopped and I don't know what good it does to blame it on the Lord. But maybe it does some good if you believe it.*

*Your brother,*
*Sonny*

Then I kept in constant touch with him and I sent him whatever I could and I went to meet him when he came back to New York. When I saw him many things I thought I had forgotten came flooding back to me. This was because I had begun, finally, to wonder about Sonny, about the life that Sonny lived inside. This life, whatever it was, had made him older and thinner and it had deepened the distant stillness in which he had always moved. He looked very unlike my baby brother. Yet, when he smiled, when we shook hands, the baby brother I'd never known looked out from the depths of his private life, like an animal waiting to be coaxed into the light.

"How you been keeping?" he asked me.

"All right. And you?"

"Just fine." He was smiling all over his face. "It's good to see you again."

"It's good to see you."

The seven years' difference in our ages lay between us like a chasm: I wondered if these years would ever operate between us as a bridge. I was remembering, and it made it hard to catch my breath, that I had been there when he was born; and I had heard the first words he had ever spoken. When he started to walk, he walked from our mother straight to me. I caught him just before he fell when he took the first steps he ever took in this world.

"How's Isabel?"

"Just fine. She's dying to see you."

"And the boys?"

"They're fine, too. They're anxious to see their uncle."

"Oh, come on. You know they don't remember me."

"Are you kidding? Of course they remember you."

He grinned again. We got into a taxi. We had a lot to say to each other, far too much to know how to begin.

As the taxi began to move, I asked, "You still want to go to India?"

He laughed. "You still remember that. Hell, no. This place is Indian enough for me."

"It used to belong to them," I said.

And he laughed again. "They damn sure knew what they were doing when they got rid of it."

Years ago, when he was around fourteen, he'd been all hipped on the idea of going to India. He read books about people sitting on rocks, naked, in all kinds of weather, but mostly bad, naturally, and walking barefoot through hot coals and arriving at wisdom.

I used to say that it sounded to me as though they were getting away from wisdom as fast as they could. I think he sort of looked down on me for that.

"Do you mind," he asked, "if we have the driver drive alongside the park? On the west side—I haven't seen the city in so long."

"Of course not," I said. I was afraid that I might sound as though I were humoring him, but I hoped he wouldn't take it that way.

So we drove along, between the green of the park and the stony, lifeless elegance of hotels and apartment buildings, toward the vivid, killing streets of our childhood. These streets hadn't changed, though housing projects jutted up out of them now like rocks in the middle of a boiling sea. Most of the houses in which we had grown up had vanished, as had the stores from which we had stolen, the basements in which we had first tried sex, the rooftops from which we had hurled tin cans and bricks. But houses exactly like the houses of our past yet dominated the landscape, boys exactly like the boys we once had been found themselves smothering in these houses, came down into the streets for light and air and found themselves encircled by disaster. Some escaped the trap, most didn't. Those who got out always left something of themselves behind, as some animals amputate a leg and leave it in the trap. It might be said, perhaps, that I had escaped, after all, I was a school teacher, or that Sonny had, he hadn't lived in Harlem for years. Yet, as the cab moved uptown through streets which seemed, with a rush, to darken with dark people, and as I covertly studied Sonny's face, it came to me that what we both were seeking through our separate cab windows was that part of ourselves which had been left behind. It's always at the hour of trouble and confrontation that the missing member aches. ?

We hit 110th Street and started rolling up Lenox Avenue. And I'd known this avenue all my life, but it seemed to me again, as it had seemed on the day I'd first heard about Sonny's trouble, filled with a hidden menace which was its very breath of life.

"We almost there," said Sonny.

"Almost." We were both too nervous to say anything more.

We live in a housing project. It hasn't been up long. A few days after it was up it seemed uninhabitably new, now, of course, it's already rundown. It looks like a parody of the good, clean, faceless life—God knows the people who live in it do their best to make it a parody. The beat-looking grass lying around isn't enough to make their lives green, the hedges will never hold out the streets, and they know it. The big windows fool no one, they aren't big enough to make space out of no space. They don't bother with the windows, they watch the TV screen instead. The playground is most popular with the children who don't play at jacks, or skip rope, or roller skate, or swing, and they can be found in it after dark. We moved in partly because it's not too far from where I teach, and partly for the kids; but it's really just like the houses in which Sonny and I grew up. The same things happen, they'll have the same things to remember. The moment Sonny and I started into the house I had the feeling that I was simply bringing him back into the danger he had almost died trying to escape.

Sonny has never been talkative. So I don't know why I was sure he'd be dying to talk to me when supper was over the first night. Everything went fine, the oldest boy remembered him, and the youngest boy liked him, and Sonny had remembered to bring something for each of them; and Isabel, who is really much nicer than I am, more open and giving, had gone to a lot of trouble about dinner and was genuinely glad to see him.

And she's always been able to tease Sonny in a way that I haven't. It was nice to see her face so vivid again and to hear her laugh and watch her make Sonny laugh. She wasn't, or, anyway, she didn't seem to be, at all uneasy or embarrassed. She chatted as though there were no subject which had to be avoided and she got Sonny past his first, faint stiffness. And thank God she was there, for I was filled with that icy dread again. Everything I did seemed awkward to me, and everything I said sounded freighted with hidden meaning. I was trying to remember everything I'd heard about dope addiction and I couldn't help watching Sonny for signs. I wasn't doing it out of malice. I was trying to find out something about my brother. I was dying to hear him tell me he was safe.

"Safe!" my father grunted, whenever Mama suggested trying to move to a neighborhood which might be safer for children. "Safe, hell! Ain't no place safe for kids, nor nobody."

He always went on like this, but he wasn't ever, really as bad as he sounded, not even on weekends, when he got drunk. As a matter of fact, he was always on the lookout for "something a little better," but he died before he found it. He died suddenly, during a drunken weekend in the middle of the war, when Sonny was fifteen. He and Sonny hadn't ever got on too well. And this was partly because Sonny was the apple of his father's eye. It was because he loved Sonny so much and was frightened for him, that he was always fighting with him. It doesn't do any good to fight with Sonny. Sonny just moves back, inside himself, where he can't be reached. But the principal reason that they never hit it off is that they were so much alike. Daddy was big and rough and loud talking, just the opposite of Sonny, but they both had—that same privacy.

Mama tried to tell me something about this, just after Daddy died. I was home on leave from the army.

This was the last time I ever saw my mother alive. Just the same, this picture gets all mixed up in my mind with pictures I had of her when she was younger. The way I always see her is the way she used to be on a Sunday afternoon, say, when the old folks were talking after the big Sunday dinner. I always see her wearing pale blue. She'd be sitting on the sofa. And my father would be sitting in the easy chair, not far from her. And the living room would be full of church folks and relatives. There they sit, in chairs all around the living room, and the night is creeping up outside, but nobody knows it yet. You can see the darkness growing against the windowpanes and you hear the street noises every now and again, or maybe the jangling beat of a tambourine from one of the churches close by, but it's real quiet in the room. For a moment nobody's talking, but every face looks darkening, like the sky outside. And my mother rocks a little from the waist, and my father's eyes are closed. Everyone is looking at something a child can't see. For a minute they've forgotten the children. Maybe a kid is lying on the rug, half asleep. Maybe somebody's got a kid in his lap and is absent-mindedly stroking the kid's head. Maybe there's a kid, quiet and big-eyed, curled up in a big chair in the corner. The silence, the darkness coming, and the darkness in the faces frightens the child obscurely. He hopes that the hand which strokes his forehead will never stop—will never die. He hopes that there will never come a time when the old folks won't be sitting around the living room, talking about where they've come from, and what they've seen, and what's happened to them and their kinfolk.

But something deep and watchful in the child knows that this is bound to end, is already ending. In a moment someone will get up and turn on the light. Then the old folks will remember the children and they won't talk any more that day. And when light fills the room, the child is filled with darkness. He knows that every time this happens he's moved just a little closer to that darkness outside. The darkness outside is what the old folks have been talking about. It's what they've come from. It's what they endure. The child knows that they won't talk any more because if he knows too much about what's happened to *them,* he'll know too much too soon, about what's going to happen to *him.*

The last time I talked to my mother, I remembered I was restless. I wanted to get out and see Isabel. We weren't married then and we had a lot to straighten out between us.

There Mama sat, in black, by the window. She was humming an old church song, *Lord, you brought me from a long ways off.* Sonny was out somewhere. Mama kept watching the streets.

"I don't know," she said, "if I'll ever see you again, after you go off from here. But I hope you'll remember the things I tried to teach you."

"Don't talk like that," I said, and smiled. "You'll be here a long time yet." She smiled, too, but she said nothing. She was quiet for a long time. And I said, "Mama, don't you worry about nothing. I'll be writing all the time, and you be getting the checks. . . ."

"I want to talk to you about your brother," she said, suddenly. "If anything happens to me he ain't going to have nobody to look out for him."

"Mama," I said, "ain't nothing going to happen to you *or* Sonny. Sonny's all right. He's a good boy and he's got good sense."

"It ain't a question of his being a good boy," Mama said, "nor of his having good sense. It ain't only the bad ones, nor yet the dumb ones that gets sucked under." She stopped, looking at me. "Your Daddy once had a brother," she said, and she smiled in a way that made me feel she was in pain. "You didn't never know that, did you?"

"No," I said, "I never knew that," and I watched her face.

"Oh, yes," she said, "your Daddy had a brother." She looked out of the window again. "I know you never saw your Daddy cry. But *I* did—many a time, through all these years."

I asked her, "What happened to his brother? How come nobody's ever talked about him?"

This was the first time I ever saw my mother look old.

"His brother got killed," she said, "when he was just a little younger than you are now. I knew him. He was a fine boy. He was maybe a little full of the devil, but he didn't mean nobody no harm."

Then she stopped and the room was silent, exactly as it had sometimes been on those Sunday afternoons. Mama kept looking out into the streets.

"He used to have a job in the mill," she said, "and, like all young folks, he just liked to perform on Saturday nights. Saturday nights, him and your father would drift around to different places, go to dances and things like that, or just sit around with people they knew, and your father's brother would sing, he had a fine voice, and play along with himself on his guitar. Well, this particular Saturday night, him and your father was coming home from some place, and they were both a little drunk and there was a moon that night, it was bright like day. Your father's brother was feeling kind of good, and he was whistling to himself, and he had his guitar slung over his shoulder. They was coming down a hill and beneath them was a road that turned off from the highway. Well, your father's brother, being always kind of frisky, decided to run down this hill; and he did, with that guitar banging and clanging behind him, and he ran across the road, and he was making water behind a tree. And your father was sort of amused at him and he was still coming down the hill, kind of slow. Then he heard a car motor and that same minute his brother stepped from behind the tree, into the road, in the moonlight. And he started to cross the road. And your father started to run down the hill, he says he don't know why. This car was full of white men. They was all drunk, and when they seen your father's brother they let out a great whoop and holler and they aimed the car straight at him. They was having fun, they just wanted to scare him, the way they do sometimes, you know. But they was drunk. And I guess the boy, being drunk, too, and scared, kind of lost his head. By the time he jumped it was too late. Your father says he heard his brother scream when the car rolled over him, and he heard the wood of that guitar when it give, and he heard them strings go flying, and he heard them white men shouting, and the car kept on a-going and it ain't stopped till this day. And, time your father got down the hill, his brother weren't nothing but blood and pulp."

Tears were gleaming on my mother's face. There wasn't anything I could say.

"He never mentioned it," she said, "because I never let him mention it before you children. Your Daddy was like a crazy man that night and for many a night thereafter. He says he never in his life seen anything as dark as that road after the lights of that car had gone away. Weren't nothing, weren't nobody on that road, just your Daddy and his brother and that busted guitar. Oh, yes. Your Daddy never did really get right again. Till the day he died he weren't sure but that every white man he saw was the man that killed his brother."

She stopped and took out her handkerchief and dried her eyes and looked at me.

"I ain't telling you all this," she said, "to make you scared or bitter or to make you hate nobody. I'm telling you this because you got a brother. And the world ain't changed."

I guess I didn't want to believe this. I guess she saw this in my face. She turned away from me, toward the window again, searching those streets.

"But I praise my Redeemer," she said at last, "that He called your Daddy home before me. I ain't saying it to throw no flowers at myself, but, I declare, it keeps me from feeling too cast down to know I helped your father get safely through this world. Your father always acted like he was the roughest, strongest man on earth. And everybody took him to be like that. But if he hadn't had me there to see his tears!"

She was crying again. Still, I couldn't move. I said, "Lord, Lord, Mama, I didn't know it was like that."

"Oh, honey," she said, "there's a lot that you don't know. But you are going to find out." She stood up from the window and came over to me. "You got to hold on to your brother," she said, "and don't let him fall, no matter what it looks like is happening to him and no matter how evil you gets with him. You going to be evil with him many a time. But don't you forget what I told you, you hear?"

"I won't forget," I said. "Don't you worry, I won't forget. I won't let nothing happen to Sonny."

My mother smiled as though she were amused at something she saw in my face. Then, "You may not be able to stop nothing from happening. But you got to let him know you's *there*."

* * *

Two days later I was married, and then I was gone. And I had a lot of things on my mind and I pretty well forgot my promise to Mama until I got shipped home on a special furlough for her funeral.

And, after the funeral, with just Sonny and me alone in the empty kitchen, I tried to find out something about him.

"What do you want to do?" I asked him.

"I'm going to be a musician," he said.

For he had graduated, in the time I had been away, from dancing to the juke box to finding out who was playing what, and what they were doing with it, and he bought himself a set of drums.

"You mean, you want to be a drummer?" I somehow had the feeling that being a drummer might be all right for other people but not for my brother Sonny.

"I don't think," he said, looking at me very gravely, "that I'll ever be a good drummer. But I think I can play a piano."

I frowned. I'd never played the role of the older brother quite so seriously before, had scarcely ever, in fact, *asked* Sonny a damn thing. I sensed myself in the presence of something I didn't really know how to handle, didn't understand. So I made my frown a little deeper as I asked: "What kind of musician do you want to be?"

He grinned. "How many kinds do you think there are?"

"Be *serious,*" I said.

He laughed, throwing his head back, and then looked at me. "I *am* serious."

"Well, then, for Christ's sake, stop kidding around and answer a serious question. I mean, do you want to be a concert pianist, you want to play classical music and all that, or—or what?" Long before I finished he was laughing again. "For Christ's *sake,* Sonny!"

He sobered, but with difficulty. "I'm sorry. But you sound so—*scared!*" and he was off again.

"Well, you may think it's funny now, baby, but it's not going to be so funny when you have to make your living at it, let me tell you *that.*" I was furious because I knew he was laughing at me and I didn't know why.

"No," he said, very sober now, and afraid, perhaps, that he'd hurt me, "I don't want to be a classical pianist. That isn't what interests me. I mean"—he paused, looking hard at me, as though his eyes would help me to understand, and then gestured helplessly, as though perhaps his hand would help—"I mean, I'll have a lot of studying to do, and I'll have to study *everything,* but, I mean, I want to play *with*—jazz musicians," He stopped. "I want to play jazz," he said.

Well, the word had never before sounded as heavy, as real, as it sounded that afternoon in Sonny's mouth. I just looked at him and I was probably frowning a real frown by this time. I simply couldn't see why on earth he'd want to spend his time hanging around nightclubs, clowning around on bandstands, while people pushed each other around a dance floor. It seemed—beneath him, somehow. I had never thought about it before, had never been forced to, but I suppose I had always put jazz musicians in a class with what Daddy called "good-time people."

"Are you *serious?*"

"Hell, *yes,* I'm serious."

He looked more helpless than ever, and annoyed, and deeply hurt.

I suggested, helpfully: "You mean—like Louis Armstrong?"

His face closed as though I'd struck him. "No. I'm not talking about none of that old-time, down home crap."

"Well, look, Sonny, I'm sorry, don't get mad. I just don't altogether get it, that's all. Name somebody—you know, a jazz musician you admire."

"Bird."

"Who?"

"Bird! Charlie Parker! Don't they teach you nothing in the goddamn army?"

I lit a cigarette. I was surprised and then a little amused to discover that I was trembling. "I've been out of touch," I said. "You'll have to be patient with me. Now. Who's this Parker character?"

"He's just one of the greatest jazz musicians alive," said Sonny, sullenly, his hands in his pockets, his back to me. "Maybe *the* greatest," he added, bitterly, "that's probably why *you* never heard of him."

"All right," I said, "I'm ignorant. I'm sorry. I'll go out and buy all the cat's records right away, all right?"

"It don't," said Sonny, with dignity, "make any difference to me. I don't care what you listen to. Don't do me no favors."

I was beginning to realize that I'd never seen him so upset before. With another part of my mind I was thinking that this would probably turn out to be one of those things kids go through and that I shouldn't make it seem important by pushing it too hard. Still, I didn't think it would do any harm to ask: "Doesn't all this take a lot of time? Can you make a living at it?"

He turned back to me and half leaned, half sat, on the kitchen table. "Everything takes time," he said, "and—well, yes, sure, I can make a living at it. But what I don't seem to be able to make you understand is that it's the only thing I want to do."

"Well, Sonny," I said, gently, "you know people can't always do exactly what they *want* to do—"

"*No,* I don't know that," said Sonny, surprising me. "I think people *ought* to do what they want to do, what else are they alive for?"

"You getting to be a big boy," I said desperately, "it's time you started thinking about your future."

"I'm thinking about my future," said Sonny, grimly. "I think about it all the time."

I gave up. I decided, if he didn't change his mind, that we could always talk about it later. "In the meantime," I said, "you got to finish school." We had already decided that he'd have to move in with Isabel and her folks. I knew this wasn't the ideal arrangement because Isabel's folks are inclined to be dicty and they hadn't especially wanted Isabel to marry me. But I didn't know what else to do. "And we have to get you fixed up at Isabel's."

There was a long silence. He moved from the kitchen table to the window. "That's a terrible idea. You know it yourself."

"Do you have a *better* idea?"

He just walked up and down the kitchen for a minute. He was as tall as I was. He had started to shave. I suddenly had the feeling that I didn't know him at all.

He stopped at the kitchen table and picked up my cigarettes. Looking at me with a kind of mocking, amused defiance, he put one between his lips. "You mind?"

"You smoking already?"

He lit the cigarette and nodded, watching me through the smoke. "I just wanted to see if I'd have the courage to smoke in front of you." He grinned and blew a great cloud of smoke to the ceiling. "It was easy." He looked at my face. "Come on, now. I bet you was smoking at my age, tell the truth."

I didn't say anything but the truth was on my face, and he laughed. But now there was something very strained in his laugh. "Sure. And I bet that ain't all you was doing."

He was frightening me a little. "Cut the crap," I said. "We already decided that you was going to go and live at Isabel's. Now what's got into you all of a sudden?"

"*You* decided it," he pointed out. "*I* didn't decide nothing." He stopped in front of me, leaning against the stove, arms loosely folded. "Look, brother. I don't want to stay in Harlem no more, I really don't." He was very earnest. He looked at me, then over toward the kitchen window. There was something in his eyes I'd never seen before, some thoughtfulness, some worry all his own. He rubbed the muscle of one arm—"It's time I was getting out of here."

"Where do you want to *go,* Sonny?"

"I want to join the army. Or the navy, I don't care. If I say I'm old enough, they'll believe me."

Then I got mad. It was because I was so scared. "You must be crazy. You goddamn fool, what the hell do you want to go and join the *army* for?"

"I just told you. To get out of Harlem."

"Sonny, you haven't even finished *school.* And if you really want to be a musician, how do you expect to study if you're in the *army?*"

He looked at me, trapped, and in anguish. "There's ways. I might be able to work out some kind of deal. Anyway, I'll have the G.I. Bill when I come out."

"*If* you come out." We stared at each other. "Sonny, please. Be reasonable. I know the setup is far from perfect. But we got to do the best we can."

"I ain't learning nothing in school," he said. "Even when I go." He turned away from me and opened the window and threw his cigarette out into the narrow alley. I watched his back. "At least, I ain't learning nothing you'd want me to learn." He slammed the window so hard I thought the glass would fly out, and turned back to me. "And I'm sick of the stink of these garbage cans!"

"Sonny," I said, "I know how you feel. But if you don't finish school now, you're going to be sorry later that you didn't." I grabbed him by the shoulders. "And you only got another year. It ain't so bad. And I'll come back and I swear I'll help you do *whatever* you want to do. Just try to put up with it till I come back. Will you please do that? For me?"

He didn't answer and he wouldn't look at me.

"Sonny, You hear me?"

He pulled away. "I hear you. But you never hear anything I say."

I didn't know what to say to that. He looked out of the window and then back to me. "OK," he said, and sighed. "I'll try."

Then I said, trying to cheer him up a little, "They got a piano at Isabel's. You can practice on it."

And as a matter of fact, it did cheer him up for a minute. "That's right," he said to himself. "I forgot that." His face relaxed a little. But the worry, the thoughtfulness, played on it still: the way shadows play on a face which is staring into the fire.

But I thought I'd never hear the end of that piano. At first, Isabel would write me, saying how nice it was that Sonny was so serious about his music and how, as soon as he came in from school, or wherever he had been when he was supposed to be at school, he went straight to that piano and stayed there until suppertime. And, after supper, he went back to that piano and stayed there until everybody went to bed. He was at the piano all day Saturday and all day Sunday. Then he bought a record player and started playing records. He'd play one record over and over again, all day long sometimes, and he'd improvise along with it on the piano. Or he'd play one section of the record, one chord, one change, one progression, then he'd do it on the piano. Then back to the record. Then back to the piano.

Well, I really don't know how they stood it. Isabel finally confessed that it wasn't like living with a person at all, it was like living with sound. And the sound didn't make any sense to her, didn't make any sense to any of them—naturally. They began, in a way, to be afflicted by this presence that was living in their home. It was as though Sonny were some sort of god, or monster. He moved in an atmosphere which wasn't like theirs at all. They fed him and he ate, he washed himself, he walked in and out of their door; he certainly wasn't nasty or unpleasant or rude, Sonny isn't any of those things; but it was as though he were all wrapped up in some cloud, some fire, some vision all his own; and there wasn't any way to reach him.

At the same time, he wasn't really a man yet, he was still a child, and they had to watch out for him in all kinds of ways. They certainly couldn't throw him out. Neither did they dare to make a great scene about that piano because even they dimly sensed; as I sensed, from so many thousands of miles away, that Sonny was at that piano playing for his life.

But he hadn't been going to school. One day a letter came from the school board and Isabel's mother got it—there had, apparently, been other letters but Sonny had torn them up. This day, when Sonny came in, Isabel's mother showed him the letter and asked where he'd been spending his time. And she finally got it out of him that he'd been down in Greenwich Village, with musicians and other characters, in a white girl's apartment. And this scared her and she started to scream at him and what came up, once she began—though she denies it to this day was what sacrifices they were making to give Sonny a decent home and how little he appreciated it.

Sonny didn't play the piano that day. By evening, Isabel's mother had calmed down but then there was the old man to deal with, and Isabel herself. Isabel says she did her best to be calm but she broke down and started crying. She says she just watched Sonny's face. She could tell, by watching him, what was happening with him. And what was happening was that they penetrated his cloud, they had reached him. Even if their fingers had been a thousand times more gentle than human fingers ever are, he could hardly help feeling that they had stripped him naked and were spitting on that nakedness. For he also had to see that his presence, that music, which was life or death to him, had been torture for them and that they had endured it, not at all for his sake, but only for mine. And Sonny couldn't take that. He can take it a little better today than he could then but he's still not very good at it and, frankly, I don't know anybody who is.

The silence of the next few days must have been louder than the sound of all the music ever played since time began. One morning, before she went to work, Isabel was in his room for something and she suddenly realized that all of his records were gone. And she knew for certain that he was gone. And he was. He went as far as the navy would carry him. He finally sent me a postcard from some place in Greece and that was the first I knew that Sonny was still alive. I didn't see him any more until we were both back in New York and the war had long been over.

He was a man by then, of course, but I wasn't willing to see it. He came by the house from time to time, but we fought almost every time we met. I didn't like the way he carried himself, loose and dreamlike all the time, and I didn't like his friends, and his music seemed to be merely an excuse for the life he led. It sounded just that weird and disordered.

Then we had a fight, a pretty awful fight, and I didn't see him for months. By and by I looked him up, where he was living, in a furnished room in the Village, and I tried to make it up. But there were lots of other people in the room and Sonny just lay on his bed, and he wouldn't come downstairs with me, and he treated these other people as though they were his family and I weren't. So I got mad and then he got mad, and then I told him that he might just as well be dead as live the way he was living. Then he stood up and he told me not to worry about him any more in life, that he was dead as far as I was concerned. Then he pushed me to the door and the other people looked on as though nothing were happening, and he slammed the door behind me. I stood in the hallway, staring at the door. I heard somebody laugh in the room and then the tears came to my eyes. I started down the steps, whistling to keep from crying, I kept whistling to myself, *You going to need me, baby, one of these cold, rainy days.*

* * *

I read about Sonny's trouble in the spring. Little Grace died in the fall. She was a beautiful little girl. But she only lived a little over two years. She died of polio and she suffered. She had a slight fever for a couple of days, but it didn't seem like anything and we just kept her in bed. And we would certainly have called the doctor, but the fever dropped, she seemed to be all right. So we thought it had just been a cold. Then, one day, she was up, playing, Isabel was in the kitchen fixing lunch for the two boys when they'd come in from school, and she heard Grace fall down in the living room. When you have a lot of children you don't always start running when one of them falls, unless they start screaming or something. And, this time, Grace was quiet. Yet, Isabel says that when she heard that *thump* and then that silence, something happened in her to make her afraid. And she ran to the living room and there was little Grace on the floor, all twisted-up, and the reason she hadn't screamed was that she couldn't get her breath. And when she did scream, it was the worst sound, Isabel says, that she'd ever heard in all her life, and she still hears it sometimes in her dreams. Isabel will sometimes wake me up with a low, moaning, strangled sound and I have to be quick to awaken her and hold her to me and where Isabel is weeping against me seems a mortal wound.

I think I may have written Sonny the very day that little Grace was buried. I was sitting in the living room in the dark, by myself, and I suddenly thought of Sonny. My trouble made his real.

One Saturday afternoon, when Sonny had been living with us, or, anyway, been in our house, for nearly two weeks, I found myself wandering aimlessly about the living room, drinking from a can of beer, and trying to work up the courage to search Sonny's room. He was out, he was usually out whenever I was home, and Isabel had taken the children to see their grandparents. Suddenly I was standing still in front of the living room window, watching Seventh Avenue. The idea of searching Sonny's room made me still. I scarcely dared to admit to myself what I'd been searching for. I didn't know what I'd do if I found it. Or if I didn't.

On the sidewalk across from me, near the entrance to a barbecue joint, some people were holding an old-fashioned revival meeting. The barbecue cook, wearing a dirty white apron, his conked hair reddish and metallic in the pale sun, and a cigarette between his lips, stood in the doorway, watching them. Kids and older people paused in their errands and stood there, along with some older men and a couple of very tough looking women who watched everything that happened on the avenue, as though they owned it, or were maybe owned by it. Well, they were watching this, too. The revival was being carried on by three sisters in black, and a brother. All they had were their voices and their Bibles and a tambourine. The brother was testifying and while he testified two of the sisters stood together, seeming to say, amen, and the third sister walked around with the tambourine outstretched and a couple of people dropped coins into it. Then the brother's testimony ended and the sister who had been taking up the collection dumped the coins into her palm and transferred them to the pocket of her long black robe. Then she raised both hands, striking the tambourine against the air, and then against one hand, and she started to sing. And the two other sisters and the brother joined in.

It was strange, suddenly, to watch, though I had been seeing these street meetings all my life. So, of course, had everybody else down there. Yet, they paused and watched and listened and I stood still at the window. *"Tis the old ship of Zion,"* they sang, and the sister with the tambourine kept a steady, jangling beat, *"it has rescued many a thousand!"* Not a soul under the sound of their voices was hearing this song for the first time, not one of them had been rescued. Nor had they seen much in the way of rescue work being done around them. Neither did they especially believe in the holiness of the three sisters and the brother, they knew too much about them, knew where they lived, and how. The woman with the tambourine, whose voice dominated the air, whose face was bright with joy, was divided by very little from the woman who stood watching her, a cigarette between her heavy, chapped lips, her hair a cuckoo's nest, her face scarred and swollen from many beatings, and her black eyes glittering like coal. Perhaps they both knew this, which was why, when, as rarely, they addressed each other, they addressed each other as Sister. As the singing filled the air the watching, listening faces underwent a change, the eyes focusing on something within; the music seemed to soothe a poison out of them; and time seemed, nearly, to fall away from the sullen, belligerent, battered faces, as though they were fleeing back to their first condition, while dreaming of their last. The barbecue cook half shook his head and smiled, and dropped his cigarette and disappeared into his joint. A man fumbled in his pockets for change and stood holding it in his hand impatiently, as though he had just remembered a pressing appointment further up the avenue. He looked furious. Then I saw Sonny, standing on the edge of the crowd. He was carrying a wide, flat notebook with a green cover, and it made him look, from where I was standing, almost like a schoolboy. The coppery sun brought out the copper in his skin, he was very faintly smiling, standing very still. Then the singing stopped, the tambourine turned into a collection plate again. The furious man dropped in his coins and vanished, so did a couple of the women, and Sonny dropped some change in the plate, looking directly at the woman with a little smile. He started across the avenue, toward the house. He has a slow, loping walk, something like the way Harlem hipsters walk, only he's imposed on this his own half-beat. I had never really noticed it before.

I stayed at the window, both relieved and apprehensive. As Sonny disappeared from my sight, they began singing again. And they were still singing when his key turned in the lock.

"Hey," he said.

"Hey, yourself. You want some beer?"

"No. Well, maybe." But he came up to the window and stood beside me, looking out. "What a warm voice," he said.

They were singing *If I could only hear my mother pray again!*

"Yes," I said, "and she can sure beat that tambourine."

"But what a terrible song," he said, and laughed. He dropped his notebook on the sofa and disappeared into the kitchen. "Where's Isabel and the kids?" "I think they went to see their grandparents. You hungry?"

"No." He came back into the living room with his can of beer. "You want to come some place with me tonight?"

I sensed, I don't know how, that I couldn't possibly say no. "Sure. Where?"

He sat down on the sofa and picked up his notebook and started leafing through it. "I'm going to sit in with some fellows in a joint in the Village."

"You mean, you're going to play, tonight?"

"That's right." He took a swallow of his beer and moved back to the window. He gave me a sidelong look. "If you can stand it."

"I'll try," I said.

He smiled to himself and we both watched as the meeting across the way broke up. The three sisters and the brother, heads bowed, were singing *God be with you till we meet again.* The faces around them were very quiet. Then the song ended. The small crowd dispersed. We watched the three women and the lone man walk slowly up the avenue.

"When she was singing before," said Sonny, abruptly, "her voice reminded me for a minute of what heroin feels like sometimes—when it's in your veins. It makes you feel sort of warm and cool at the same time. And distant. And—and sure." He sipped his beer, very deliberately not looking at me. I watched his face. "It makes you feel—in control. Sometimes you've got to have that feeling."

"Do you?" I sat down slowly in the easy chair.

"Sometimes." He went to the sofa and picked up his notebook again. "Some people do."

"In order," I asked, "to play?" And my voice was very ugly, full of contempt and anger.

"Well" he looked at me with great, troubled eyes, as though, in fact, he hoped his eyes would tell me things he could never otherwise say—"they *think so.* And *if* they think so—!"

"And what do *you* think?" I asked.

He sat on the sofa and put his can of beer on the floor. "I don't know," he said, and I couldn't be sure if he were answering my question or pursuing his thoughts. His face didn't tell me. "It's not so much to *play.* It's to *stand* it, to be able to make it at all. On any level." He frowned and smiled: "In order to keep from shaking to pieces."

"But these friends of yours," I said, "they seem to shake themselves to pieces pretty goddamn fast."

"Maybe." He played with the notebook. And something told me that I should curb my tongue, that Sonny was doing his best to talk, that I should listen. "But of course you only know the ones that've gone to pieces. Some don't—or at least they haven't *yet* and that's just about all *any* of us can say." He paused. "And then there are some who just live, really, in hell, and they know it and they see what's happening and they go right on. I don't know." He sighed, dropped the notebook, folded his arms. "Some guys, you can tell from the way they play, they on something *all* the time. And you can see that, well, it makes something real for them. But of course," he picked up his beer from the floor and sipped it and put the can down again, "they *want* to, too, you've got to see that. Even some of them that say they don't—*some,* not all."

"And what about you?" I asked—I couldn't help it. "What about you? Do *you* want to?"

He stood up and walked to the window and remained silent for a long time. Then he sighed. "Me," he said. Then: "While I was downstairs before, on my way here, listening to that woman sing, it struck me all of a sudden how much suffering she must have had to go through—to sing like that. It's *repulsive* to think you have to suffer that much."

I said: "But there's no way not to suffer—is there, Sonny?"

"I believe not," he said and smiled, "but that's never stopped anyone from trying." He looked at me. "Has it?" I realized, with this mocking look, that there stood between us, forever, beyond the power of time or forgiveness, the fact that I had held silence—so long!—when he had needed human speech to help him. He turned back to the window. "No, there's no way not to suffer. But you try all kinds of ways to keep from drowning in it, to keep on top of it, and to make it seem—well, like *you.* Like you did something, all right, and now you're suffering for it. You know?" I said nothing. "Well you know," he said, impatiently, "why *do* people suffer? Maybe it's better to do something to give it a reason, *any* reason."

"But we just agreed," I said, "that there's no way not to suffer. Isn't it better, then, just to—take it?"

"But nobody just takes it," Sonny cried, "that's what I'm telling you! *Everybody* tries not to. You're just hung up on the *way* some people try—it's not *your* way!"

The hair on my face began to itch, my face felt wet. "That's not true," I said, "that's not true. I don't give a damn what other people do, I don't even care how they suffer. I just care how *you* suffer." And he looked at me. "Please believe me," I said, "I don't want to see you—die—trying not to suffer."

"I won't," he said, flatly, "die trying not to suffer. At least, not any faster than anybody else."

"But there's no need," I said, trying to laugh, "is there? in killing yourself."

I wanted to say more, but I couldn't. I wanted to talk about will power and how life could be—well, beautiful. I wanted to say that it was all within; but was it? or, rather, wasn't that exactly the trouble? And I wanted to promise that I would never fail him again. But it would all have sounded—empty words and lies.

So I made the promise to myself and prayed that I would keep it.

"It's terrible sometimes, inside," he said, "that's what's the trouble. You walk these streets, black and funky and cold, and there's not really a living ass to talk to, and there's nothing shaking, and there's no way of getting it out—that storm inside. You can't talk it and you can't make love with it, and when you finally try to get with it and play it, you realize *nobody's* listening. So *you've* got to listen. You got to find a way to listen."

And then he walked away from the window and sat on the sofa again, as though all the wind had suddenly been knocked out of him. "Sometimes you'll do *anything* to play, even cut your mother's throat." He laughed and looked at me. "Or your brother's." Then he sobered. "Or your own." Then: "Don't worry. I'm all right now and I think I'll *be* all right. But I can't forget—where I've been. I don't mean just the physical place I've been, I mean where I've *been.* And *what* I've been."

"What have you been, Sonny?" I asked.

He smiled—but sat sideways on the sofa, his elbow resting on the back, his fingers playing with his mouth and chin, not looking at me. "I've been something I didn't realize, didn't know I could be. Didn't know anybody could be." He stopped, looking inward, looking helplessly young, looking old. "I'm not talking about it now because I feel *guilty* or anything like that—maybe it would be better if I did, I don't know. Anyway, I can't really talk about it. Not to you, not to anybody," and now he turned and faced me. "Sometimes, you know, and it was actually when I was most *out* of the world, I felt that I was in it, that I was *with* it, really, and I could play or I didn't really have to *play,* it just came out of me, it was there. And I don't know how I played, thinking about it now, but I know I did awful things, those times, sometimes, to people. Or it wasn't that I *did* anything to them—it was that they weren't real." He picked up the beer can; it was empty; he rolled it between his palms: "And other times—well, I needed a fix, I needed to find a place to lean, I needed to clear a space to *listen*—and I couldn't find it, and I—went crazy, I did terrible things to *me,* I was terrible *for* me." He began pressing the beer can between his hands, I watched the metal begin to give. It glittered, as he played with it, like a knife, and I was afraid he could cut himself, but I said nothing. "Oh well. I can never tell you. I was all by myself at the bottom of something, stinking and sweating and crying and shaking, and I smelled it, you know? *my* stink, and I thought I'd die if I couldn't get away from it and yet, all the same, I knew that everything I was doing was just locking me in with it. And I didn't know," he paused, still flattening the beer can, "I didn't know, I still *don't* know, something kept telling me that maybe it was good to smell your own stink, but I didn't think that *that* was what I'd been trying to do—and—who can stand it?" and he abruptly dropped the ruined beer can, looking at me with a small, still smile, and then rose, walking to the window as though it were the lodestone rock. I watched his face, he watched the avenue. "I couldn't tell you when Mama died—but the reason I wanted to leave Harlem so bad was to get away from drugs. And then, when I ran away, that's what I was running from—really. When I came back, nothing had changed, I hadn't changed, I was just—older." And he stopped, drumming with his fingers on the windowpane. The sun had vanished, soon darkness would fall. I watched his face. "It can come again," he said, almost as though speaking to himself. Then he turned to me. "It can come again," he repeated." I just want you to know that."

"All right," I said, at last. "So it can come again. All right?"

He smiled, but the smile was sorrowful. "I had to try to tell you," he said.

"Yes," I said. "I understood that."

"You're my brother," he said, looking straight at me, and not smiling at all.

"Yes," I repeated, "yes. I understand that."

He turned back to the window, looking out. "All that hatred down there," he said, "all that hatred and misery and love. It's a wonder it doesn't blow the avenue apart."

We went to the only nightclub on a short, dark street; downtown. We squeezed through the narrow, chattering, jampacked bar to the entrance of the big room, where the bandstand was. And we stood there for a moment, for the lights were very dim in this room and we couldn't see. Then, "Hello, boy," said a voice and an enormous black man, much older than Sonny or myself, erupted out of all that atmospheric lighting and put an arm around Sonny's shoulder. "I been sitting right here," he said, "waiting for you."

He had a big voice, too, and heads in the darkness turned toward us.

Sonny grinned and pulled a little away, and said, "Creole, this is my brother. I told you about him."

Creole shook my hand. "I'm glad to meet you, son," he said, and it was clear that he was glad to meet me *there,* for Sonny's sake. And he smiled, "You got a real musician in *your* family," and he took his arm from Sonny's shoulder and slapped him, lightly, affectionately, with the back of his hand.

"Well. Now I've heard it all," said a voice behind us. This was another musician, and a friend of Sonny's, a coal-black, cheerful-looking man, built close to the ground. He immediately began confiding to me, at the top of his lungs, the most terrible things about Sonny, his teeth gleaming like a lighthouse and his laugh coming up out of him like the beginning of an earthquake. And it turned out that everyone at the bar knew Sonny, or almost everyone; some were musicians, working there, or nearby, or not working, some were simply hangers-on, and some were there to hear Sonny play. I was introduced to all of them and they were all very polite to me. Yet, it was clear that, for them, I was only Sonny's brother. Here, I was in Sonny's world. Or, rather his kingdom. Here, it was not even a question that his veins bore royal blood.

They were going to play soon and Creole installed me, by myself, at a table in a dark corner. Then I watched them, Creole, and the little black man, and Sonny, and the others, while they horsed around; standing just below the bandstand. The light from the bandstand spilled just a little short of them and, watching them laughing and gesturing and moving about, I had the feeling that they, nevertheless, were being most careful not to step into that circle of light too suddenly: that if they moved into the light too suddenly, without thinking, they would perish in flame. Then, while I watched, one of them, the small, black man, moved into the light and crossed the bandstand and started fooling around with his drums. Then—being funny and being, also, extremely ceremonious—Creole took Sonny by the arm and led him to the piano. A woman's voice called Sonny's name and a few hands started clapping. And Sonny, also being funny and being ceremonious, and so touched, I think, that he could have cried, but neither hiding it nor showing it, riding it like a man, grinned, and put both hands to his heart and bowed from the waist.

Creole then went to the bass fiddle and a lean, very bright-skinned brown man jumped up on the bandstand and picked up his horn. So there they were, and the atmosphere on the bandstand and in the room began to change and tighten. Someone stepped up to the microphone and announced them. Then there were all kinds of murmurs. Some people at the bar shushed others. The waitress ran around, frantically getting in the last orders, guys and chicks got closer to each other, and the lights on the bandstand, on the quartet, turned to a kind of indigo. Then they all looked different there. Creole looked about him for the last time, as though he were making certain that all his chickens were in the coop, and then he—jumped and struck the fiddle. And there they were.

All I know about music is that not many people ever really hear it. And even then, on the rare occasions when something opens within, and the music enters, what we mainly hear, or hear corroborated, are personal, private, vanishing evocations. But the man who creates the music is hearing something else, is dealing with the roar rising from the void and imposing order on it as it hits the air. What is evoked in him, then, is

* narrator is now in Sonny environment he starts to understand Sonny –

of another order, more terrible because it has no words, and triumphant, too, for that same reason. And his triumph, when he triumphs, is ours. I just watched Sonny's face. His face was troubled, he was working hard, but he wasn't with it. And I had the feeling that, in a way, everyone on the bandstand was waiting for him, both waiting for him and pushing him along. But as I began to watch Creole, I realized that it was Creole who held them all back. He had them on a short rein. Up there, keeping the beat with his whole body, waiting on the fiddle, with his eyes half closed, he was listening to everything, but he was listening to Sonny. He was having a dialogue with Sonny. He wanted Sonny to leave the shoreline and strike out for the deep water. He was Sonny's witness that deep water and drowning were not the same thing—he had been there, and he knew. And he wanted Sonny to know. He was waiting for Sonny to do the things on the keys which would let Creole know that Sonny was in the water.

And while Creole listened, Sonny moved, deep within, exactly like someone in torment. I had never before thought of how awful the relationship must be between the musician and his instrument. He has to fill it, this instrument, with the breath of life, his own. He has to make it do what he wants it to do. And a piano is just a piano. It's made out of so much wood and wires and little hammers and big ones, and ivory. While there's only so much you can do with it, the only way to find this out is to try; to try and make it do everything.

And Sonny hadn't been near a piano for over a year. And he wasn't on much better terms with his life, not the life that stretched before him now. He and the piano stammered, started one way, got scared, stopped; started another way, panicked, marked time, started again; then seemed to have found a direction, panicked again, got stuck. And the face I saw on Sonny I'd never seen before. Everything had been burned out of it, and, at the same time, things usually hidden were being burned in, by the fire and fury of the battle which was occurring in him up there.

Yet, watching Creole's face as they neared the end of the first set, I had the feeling that something had happened, something I hadn't heard. Then they finished, there was scattered applause, and then, without an instant's warning, Creole started into something else, it was almost sardonic, it was *Am I Blue*. And, as though he commanded, Sonny began to play. Something began to happen. And Creole let out the reins. The dry, low, black man said something awful on the drums, Creole answered, and the drums talked back. Then the horn insisted, sweet and high, slightly detached perhaps, and Creole listened, commenting now and then, dry, and driving, beautiful and calm and old. Then they all came together again, and Sonny was part of the family again. I could tell this from his face. He seemed to have found, right there beneath his fingers, a damn brand-new piano. It seemed that he couldn't get over it. Then, for awhile, just being happy with Sonny, they seemed to be agreeing with him that brand-new pianos certainly were a gas.

Then Creole stepped forward to remind them that what they were playing was the blues. He hit something in all of them, he hit something in me, myself, and the music tightened and deepened, apprehension began to beat the air. Creole began to tell us what the blues were all about. They were not about anything very new. He and his boys up there were keeping it new, at the risk of ruin, destruction, madness, and death, in order to find new ways to make us listen. For, while the tale of how we suffer, and how we are delighted, and how we may triumph is never new, it always must be heard. There isn't any other tale to tell, it's the only light we've got in all this darkness.

And this tale, according to that face, that body, those strong hands on those strings, has another aspect in every country, and a new depth in every generation. Listen, Creole seemed to be saying, listen. Now these are Sonny's blues. He made the little black man on the drums know it, and the bright, brown man on the horn. Creole wasn't trying any longer to get Sonny in the water. He was wishing him Godspeed. Then he stepped back, very slowly, filling the air with the immense suggestion that Sonny speak for himself.

Then they all gathered around Sonny and Sonny played. Every now and again one of them seemed to say, amen. Sonny's fingers filled the air with life, his life. But that life contained so many others. And Sonny went all the way back, he really began with the spare, flat statement of the opening phrase of the song. Then he began to make it his. It was very beautiful because it wasn't hurried and it was no longer a lament. I seemed to hear with what burning he had made it his, with what burning we had yet to make it ours, how we could cease lamenting. Freedom lurked around us and I understood, at last, that he could help us to be free if we would listen, that he would never be free until we did. Yet, there was no battle in his face now. I heard what he had gone through, and would continue to go through until he came to rest in earth. He had made it his: that long line, of which we knew only Mama and Daddy. And he was giving it back, as everything must be given back, so that, passing through death, it can live forever. I saw my mother's face again, and felt, for the first time, how the stones of the road she had walked on must have bruised her feet. I saw the moonlit road where my father's brother died. And it brought something else back to me, and carried me past it, I saw my little girl again and felt Isabel's tears again, and I felt my own tears begin to rise. And I was yet aware that this was only a moment, that the world waited outside, as hungry as a tiger, and that trouble stretched above us, longer than the sky.

Surreal?

Then it was over. Creole and Sonny let out their breath, both soaking wet, and grinning. There was a lot of applause and some of it was real. In the dark, the girl came by and I asked her to take drinks to the bandstand. There was a long pause, while they talked up there in the indigo light and after awhile I saw the girl put a Scotch and milk on top of the piano for Sonny. He didn't seem to notice it, but just before they started playing again, he sipped from it and looked toward me, and nodded. Then he put it back on top of the piano. For me, then, as they began to play again, it glowed and shook above my brother's head like the very cup of trembling.

# ⁜ HISAYE YAMAMOTO

## (1921– )

Hisaye Yamamoto was born in Redondo Beach, California, to immigrant parents. In 1941, after the Japanese attack on Pearl Harbor, the family was relocated to an internment camp in Poston, Arizona. Yamamoto developed and nurtured an interest in writing by publishing stories in the camp newspapers.

After the family's release from the camps in 1945, Yamamoto worked for an African-American newspaper, the *Los Angeles Tribune,* for three years. By

1948, she was publishing stories in such journals as the *Kenyon Review, Arizona Quarterly,* and *Partisan Review.* In 1948 also she adopted a son who was five months old. In 1950–1951, she received a John Hay Whitney Foundation Opportunity Fellowship. In 1953 she turned down a Stanford writing fellowship. Yamamoto was inspired by Dorothy Day, founder of the *Catholic Worker* magazine, to work as a volunteer in a Catholic Worker's rehabilitation center on Staten Island, New York, from 1953 to 1955. After her marriage to Anthony DeSoto, the couple returned to Los Angeles. Together they had four children.

As a nisei or second-generation Japanese American, Yamamoto sensitively explores the complex relationships between first- and second-generation Japanese-American men and women and between immigrant parents and their American-born children. Her stories won her the Before Columbus Foundation Lifetime Achievement Award in 1986. While Yamamoto has published nearly sixty stories in various journals and magazines, some of her finest were collected and published as *Seventeen Syllables, and Other Stories* in 1988.

# Seventeen Syllables

THE FIRST Rosie knew that her mother had taken to writing poems was one evening when she finished one and read it aloud for her daughter's approval. It was about cats, and Rosie pretended to understand it thoroughly and appreciate it no end, partly because she hesitated to disillusion her mother about the quantity and quality of Japanese she had learned in all the years now that she had been going to Japanese school every Saturday (and Wednesday, too, in the summer). Even so, her mother must have been skeptical about the depth of Rosie's understanding, because she explained afterwards about the kind of poem she was trying to write.

See, Rosie, she said, it was a *haiku,* a poem in which she must pack all her meaning into seventeen syllables only, which were divided into three lines of five, seven, and five syllables. In the one she had just read, she had tried to capture the charm of a kitten, as well as comment on the superstition that owning a cat of three colors meant good luck.

"Yes, yes, I understand. How utterly lovely," Rosie said, and her mother, either satisfied or seeing through the deception and resigned, went back to composing.

The truth was that Rosie was lazy; English lay ready on the tongue but Japanese had to be searched for and examined, and even then put forth tentatively (probably to meet with laughter). It was so much easier to say yes, yes, even when one meant no, no. Besides, this was what was in her mind to say: I was looking through one of your magazines from Japan last night, Mother, and towards the back I found some *haiku* in English that delighted me. There was one that made me giggle off and on until I fell asleep—

It is morning, and lo!<br>
I lie awake, comme il faut,<br>
sighing for some dough.

Now, how to reach her mother, how to communicate the melancholy song? Rosie knew formal Japanese by fits and starts, her mother had even less English, no French. It was much more possible to say yes, yes.

* * *

It developed that her mother was writing the *haiku* for a daily newspaper, the *Mainichi Shimbun,* that was published in San Francisco. Los Angeles, to be sure, was closer to the farming community in which the Hayashi family lived and several Japanese vernaculars were printed there, but Rosie's parents said they preferred the tone of the northern paper. Once a week, the *Mainichi* would have a section devoted to *haiku,* and her mother became an extravagant contributor, taking for herself the blossoming pen name, Ume Hanazono.

So Rosie and her father lived for awhile with two women, her mother and Ume Hanazono. Her mother (Tome Hayashi by name) kept house, cooked, washed, and, along with her husband and the Carrascos, the Mexican family hired for the harvest, did her ample share of picking tomatoes out in the sweltering fields and boxing them in tidy strata in the cool packing shed. Ume Hanazono, who came to life after the dinner dishes were done, was an earnest, muttering stranger who often neglected speaking when spoken to and stayed busy at the parlor table as late as midnight scribbling with pencil on scratch paper or carefully copying characters on good paper with her fat, pale green Parker.

The new interest had some repercussions on the household routine. Before, Rosie had been accustomed to her parents and herself taking their hot baths early and going to bed almost immediately afterwards, unless her parents challenged each other to a game of flower cards or unless company dropped in. Now if her father wanted to play cards, he had to resort to solitaire (at which he always cheated fearlessly), and if a group of friends came over, it was bound to contain someone who was also writing *haiku,* and the small assemblage would be split in two, her father entertaining the nonliterary members and her mother comparing ecstatic notes with the visiting poet.

If they went out, it was more of the same thing. But Ume Hanazono's life span, even for a poet's, was very brief—perhaps three months at most.

* * *

One night they went over to see the Hayano family in the neighboring town to the west, an adventure both painful and attractive to Rosie. It was attractive because there were four Hayano girls, all lovely and each one named after a season of the year (Haru, Natsu, Aki, Fuyu), painful because something had been wrong with Mrs. Hayano ever since the birth of her first child. Rosie would sometimes watch Mrs. Hayano, reputed to have been the belle of her native village, making her way about a room, stooped, slowly shuffling, violently trembling (*always* trembling), and she would be reminded that this woman, in this same condition, had carried and given issue to three babies. She would look wonderingly at Mr. Hayano, handsome, tall, and strong, and she would look at her four pretty friends. But it was not a matter she could come to any decision about.

On this visit, however, Mrs. Hayano sat all evening in the rocker, as motionless and unobtrusive as it was possible for her to be, and Rosie found the greater part of the evening practically anaesthetic. Too, Rosie spent most of it in the girls' room, because

Haru, the garrulous one, said almost as soon as the bows and other greetings were over, "Oh, you must see my new coat!"

It was a pale plaid of grey, sand, and blue, with an enormous collar, and Rosie, seeing nothing special in it, said, "Gee, how nice."

"Nice?" said Haru, indignantly. "Is that all you can say about it? It's gorgeous! And so cheap, too. Only seventeen-ninety eight, because it was a sale. The saleslady said it was twenty-five dollars regular."

"Gee," said Rosie. Natsu, who never said much and when she said anything said it shyly, fingered the coat covetously and Haru pulled it away.

"Mine," she said, putting it on. She minced in the aisle between the two large beds and smiled happily. "Let's see how your mother likes it."

She broke into the front room and the adult conversation and went to stand in front of Rosie's mother, while the rest watched from the door. Rosie's mother was properly envious. "May I inherit it when you're through with it?"

Haru, pleased, giggled and said yes, she could, but Natsu reminded gravely from the door, "You promised me, Haru."

Everyone laughed but Natsu, who shamefacedly retreated into the bedroom. Haru came in laughing, taking off the coat. "We were only kidding, Natsu," she said. "Here, you try it on now."

After Natsu buttoned herself into the coat, inspected herself solemnly in the bureau mirror, and reluctantly shed it, Rosie, Aki, and Fuyu got their turns, and Fuyu, who was eight, drowned in it while her sisters and Rosie doubled up in amusement. They all went into the front room later, because Haru's mother quaveringly called to her to fix the tea and rice cakes and open a can of sliced peaches for everybody. Rosie noticed that her mother and Mr. Hayano were talking together at the little table—they were discussing a *haiku* that Mr. Hayano was planning to send to the *Mainichi,* while her father was sitting at one end of the sofa looking through a copy of *Life,* the new picture magazine. Occasionally, her father would comment on a photograph, holding it toward Mrs. Hayano and speaking to her as he always did—loudly, as though he thought someone such as she must surely be at least a trifle deaf also.

The five girls had their refreshments at the kitchen table, and it was while Rosie was showing the sisters her trick of swallowing peach slices without chewing (she chased each slippery crescent down with a swig of tea) that her father brought his empty teacup and untouched saucer to the sink and said, "Come on, Rosie, we're going home now."

"Already?" asked Rosie.

"Work tomorrow," he said.

He sounded irritated, and Rosie, puzzled, gulped one last yellow slice and stood up to go, while the sisters began protesting, as was their wont.

"We have to get up at five-thirty," he told them, going into the front room quickly, so that they did not have their usual chance to hang onto his hands and plead for an extension of time.

Rosie, following, saw that her mother and Mr. Hayano were sipping tea and still talking together, while Mrs. Hayano concentrated, quivering, on raising the handleless Japanese cup to her lips with both her hands and lowering it back to her lap. Her father, saying nothing, went out the door, onto the bright porch, and down the steps. Her mother looked up and asked, "Where is he going?"

"Where is he going?" Rosie said. "He said we were going home now."

"Going home?" Her mother looked with embarrassment at Mr. Hayano and his absorbed wife and then forced a smile. "He must be tired," she said.

Haru was not giving up yet. "May Rosie stay overnight?" she asked, and Natsu, Aki, and Fuyu came to reinforce their sister's plea by helping her make a circle around Rosie's mother. Rosie, for once having no desire to stay, was relieved when her mother, apologizing to the perturbed Mr. and Mrs. Hayano for her father's abruptness at the same time, managed to shake her head no at the quartet, kindly but adamant, so that they broke their circle and let her go.

Rosie's father looked ahead into the windshield as the two joined him. "I'm sorry," her mother said. "You must be tired." Her father, stepping on the starter, said nothing. "You know how I get when it's *haiku,*" she continued, "I forget what time it is." He only grunted.

As they rode homeward silently, Rosie, sitting between, felt a rush of hate for both—for her mother for begging, for her father for denying her mother. I wish this old Ford would crash, right now, she thought, then immediately, no, no, I wish my father would laugh, but it was too late: already the vision had passed through her mind of the green pick-up crumpled in the dark against one of the mighty eucalyptus trees they were just riding past, of the three contorted, bleeding bodies, one of them hers.

* * *

Rosie ran between two patches of tomatoes, her heart working more rambunctiously than she had ever known it to. How lucky it was that Aunt Taka and Uncle Gimpachi had come tonight, though, how very lucky. Otherwise she might not have really kept her half-promise to meet Jesus Carrasco. Jesus was going to be a senior in September at the same school she went to, and his parents were the ones helping with the tomatoes this year. She and Jesus, who hardly remembered seeing each other at Cleveland High where there were so many other people and two whole grades between them, had become great friends this summer—he always had a joke for her when he periodically drove the loaded pick-up up from the fields to the shed where she was usually sorting while her mother and father did the packing, and they laughed a great deal together over infinitesimal repartee during the afternoon break for chilled watermelon or ice cream in the shade of the shed.

* * *

What she enjoyed most was racing him to see who could finish picking a double row first. He, who could work faster, would tease her by slowing down until she thought she would surely pass him this time, then speeding up furiously to leave her several sprawling vines behind. Once he had made her screech hideously by crossing over, while her back was turned, to place atop the tomatoes in her green-stained bucket a truly monstrous, pale green worm (it had looked more like an infant snake). And it was when they had finished a contest this morning, after she had pantingly pointed a green finger at the immature tomatoes evident in the lugs at the end of his row and he had returned the accusation (with justice), that he had startlingly brought up the matter of their possibly meeting outside the range of both their parents' dubious eyes.

"What for?" she had asked.

"I've got a secret I want to tell you," he said.

"Tell me now," she demanded.

"It won't be ready till tonight," he said.

She laughed. "Tell me tomorrow then."

"It'll be gone tomorrow," he threatened.

"Well, for seven hakes, what is it?" she had asked, more than twice, and when he had suggested that the packing shed would be an appropriate place to find out, she had cautiously answered maybe. She had not been certain she was going to keep the appointment until the arrival of mother's sister and her husband. Their coming seemed a sort of signal of permission, of grace, and she had definitely made up her mind to lie and leave as she was bowing them welcome.

So as soon as everyone appeared settled back for the evening, she announced loudly that she was going to the privy outside, "I'm going to the *benjo!*" and slipped out the door. And now that she was actually on her way, her heart pumped in such an undisciplined way that she could hear it with her ears. It's because I'm running, she told herself, slowing to a walk. The shed was up ahead, one more patch away, in the middle of the fields. Its bulk, looming in the dimness, took on a sinisterness that was funny when Rosie reminded herself that it was only a wooden frame with a canvas roof and three canvas walls that made a slapping noise on breezy days.

* * *

Jesus was sitting on the narrow plank that was the sorting platform and she went around to the other side and jumped backwards to seat herself on the rim of a packing stand. "Well, tell me," she said without greeting, thinking her voice sounded reassuringly familiar.

"I saw you coming out the door," Jesus said. "I heard you running part of the way, too."

"Uh-huh," Rosie said. "Now tell me the secret."

"I was afraid you wouldn't come," he said.

Rosie delved around on the chicken-wire bottom of the stall for number two tomatoes, ripe, which she was sitting beside, and came up with a left-over that felt edible. She bit into it and began sucking out the pulp and seeds. "I'm here," she pointed out.

"Rosie, are you sorry you came?"

"Sorry? What for?" she said. "You said you were going to tell me something."

"I will, I will," Jesus said, but his voice contained disappointment, and Rosie fleetingly felt the older of the two, realizing a brand-new power which vanished without category under her recognition.

"I have to go back in a minute," she said. "My aunt and uncle are here from Wintersburg. I told them I was going to the privy."

Jesus laughed. "You funny thing," he said. "You slay me!"

"Just because you have a bathroom *inside,*" Rosie said. "Come on, tell me."

Chuckling, Jesus came around to lean on the stand facing her. They still could not see each other very clearly, but Rosie noticed that Jesus became very sober again as he took the hollow tomato from her hand and dropped it back into the stall. When he took hold of her empty hand, she could find no words to protest; her vocabulary had become distressingly constricted and she thought desperately that all that remained intact now was yes and no and oh, and even these few sounds would not easily out. Thus, kissed by Jesus, Rosie fell for the first time entirely victim to a helplessness delectable beyond speech. But the terrible, beautiful sensation lasted no more than a second, and the reality of Jesus' lips and tongue and teeth and hands made her pull away with such strength that she nearly tumbled.

Rosie stopped running as she approached the lights from the windows of home. How long since she had left? She could not guess, but gasping yet, she went to the privy in back and locked herself in. Her own breathing deafened her in the dark, close space, and she sat and waited until she could hear at last the nightly calling of the frogs and crickets. Even then, all she could think to say was oh, my, and the pressure of Jesus' face against her face would not leave.

* * *

No one had missed her in the parlor, however, and Rosie walked in and through quickly, announcing that she was next going to take a bath. "Your father's in the bathhouse," her mother said, and Rosie, in her room, recalled that she had not seen him when she entered. There had been only Aunt Taka and Uncle Gimpachi with her mother at the table, drinking tea. She got her robe and straw sandals and crossed the parlor again to go outside. Her mother was telling them about the *haiku* competition in the *Mainichi* and the poem she had entered.

Rosie met her father coming out of the bathhouse. "Are you through, Father?" she asked. "I was going to ask you to scrub my back."

"Scrub your own back," he said shortly, going toward the main house.

"What have I done now?" she yelled after him. She suddenly felt like doing a lot of yelling. But he did not answer, and she went into the bathhouse. Turning on the dangling light, she removed her denims and T-shirt and threw them in the big carton for dirty clothes standing next to the washing machine. Her other things she took with her into the bath compartment to wash after her bath. After she had scooped a basin of hot water from the square wooden tub, she sat on the grey cement of the floor and soaped herself at exaggerated leisure, singing "Red Sails in the Sunset" at the top of her voice and using da-da-da where she suspected her words. Then, standing up, still singing, for she was possessed by the notion that any attempt now to analyze would result in spoilage and she believed that the larger her volume the less she would be able to hear herself think, she obtained more hot water and poured it on until she was free of lather. Only then did she allow herself to step into the steaming vat, one leg first, then the remainder of her body inch by inch until the water no longer stung and she could move around at will.

She took a long time soaking, afterwards remembering to go around outside to stoke the embers of the tin-lined fireplace beneath the tub and to throw on a few more sticks so that the water might keep its heat for her mother, and when she finally returned to the parlor, she found her mother still talking *haiku* with her aunt and uncle, the three of them on another round of tea. Her father was nowhere in sight.

* * *

At Japanese school the next day (Wednesday, it was), Rosie was grave and giddy by turns. Preoccupied at her desk in the row for students on Book Eight, she made up for it at recess by performing wild mimicry for the benefit of her friend Chizuko. She held her nose and whined a witticism or two in what she considered was the manner of Fred Allen; she assumed intoxication and a British accent to go over the climax of the Rudy Vallee recording of the pub conversation about William Ewart Gladstone; she was the child Shirley Temple piping, "On the Good Ship Lollipop"; she was the gentleman soprano of the Four Inkspots trilling, "If I Didn't Care." And she felt reasonably satisfied when Chizuko wept and gasped, "Oh, Rosie, you ought to be in the movies!"

Her father came after her at noon, bringing her sandwiches of minced ham and two nectarines to eat while she rode, so that she could pitch right into the sorting when they got home. The lugs were piling up, he said, and the ripe tomatoes in them would probably have to be taken to the cannery tomorrow if they were not ready for the produce haulers tonight. "This heat's not doing them any good. And we've got no time for a break today."

It *was* hot, probably the hottest day of the year, and Rosie's blouse stuck damply to her back even under the protection of the canvas. But she worked as efficiently as a flawless machine and kept the stalls heaped, with one part of her mind listening in to the parental murmuring about the heat and the tomatoes and with another part planning the exact words she would say to Jesus when he drove up with the first load of the afternoon. But when at last she saw that the pick-up was coming, her hands went berserk and the tomatoes started falling in the wrong stalls, and her father said, "Hey, hey! Rosie, watch what you're doing!"

"Well, I have to go to the *benjo,*" she said, hiding panic.

"Go in the weeds over there," he said, only half-joking.

"Oh, Father!" she protested.

"Oh, go on home," her mother said. "We'll make out for awhile."

In the privy Rosie peered through a knothole toward the fields, watching as much as she could of Jesus. Happily she thought she saw him look in the direction of the house from time to time before he finished unloading and went back toward the patch where his mother and father worked. As she was heading for the shed, a very presentable black car purred up the dirt driveway to the house and its driver motioned to her. Was this the Hayashi home, he wanted to know. She nodded. Was she a Hayashi? Yes, she said, thinking that he was a good-looking man. He got out of the car with a huge, flat package and she saw that he warmly wore a business suit. "I have something here for your mother then," he said, in a more elegant Japanese than she was used to.

She told him where her mother was and he came along with her, patting his face with an immaculate white handkerchief and saying something about the coolness of San Francisco. To her surprised mother and father, he bowed and introduced himself as, among other things, the *haiku* editor of the *Mainichi Shimbun,* saying that since he had been coming as far as Los Angeles anyway, he had decided to bring her the first prize she had won in the recent contest.

"First prize?" her mother echoed, believing and not believing, pleased and overwhelmed. Handed the package with a bow, she bobbed her head up and down numerous times to express her utter gratitude.

"It is nothing much," he added, "but I hope it will serve as a token of our great appreciation for your contributions and our great admiration of your considerable talent."

"I am not worthy," she said, falling easily into his style. "It is I who should make some sign of my humble thanks for being permitted to contribute."

"No, no, to the contrary," he said, bowing again.

But Rosie's mother insisted, and then saying that she knew she was being unorthodox, she asked if she might open the package because her curiosity was so great. Certainly she might. In fact, he would like her reaction to it, for personally, it was one of his favorite *Hiroshiges*.

Rosie thought it was a pleasant picture, which looked to have been sketched with delicate quickness. There were pink clouds, containing some graceful calligraphy, and a sea that was a pale blue except at the edges, containing four sampans with indications of people in them. Pines edged the water and on the far-off beach there was a cluster of thatched huts towered over by pine-dotted mountains of grey and blue. The frame was scalloped and gilt.

After Rosie's mother pronounced it without peer and somewhat prodded her father into nodding agreement, she said Mr. Kuroda must at least have a cup of tea after coming all this way, and although Mr. Kuroda did not want to impose, he soon agreed that a cup of tea would be refreshing and went along with her to the house, carrying the picture for her.

"Ha, your mother's crazy!" Rosie's father said, and Rosie laughed uneasily as she resumed judgment on the tomatoes. She had emptied six lugs when he broke into an imaginary conversation with Jesus to tell her to go and remind her mother of the tomatoes, and she went slowly.

Mr. Kuroda was in his shirtsleeves expounding some *haiku* theory as he munched a rice cake, and her mother was rapt. Abashed in the great man's presence, Rosie stood next to her mother's chair until her mother looked up inquiringly, and then she started to whisper the message, but her mother pushed her gently away and reproached, "You are not being very polite to our guest."

"Father says the tomatoes . . ." Rosie said aloud, smiling foolishly.

"Tell him I shall only be a minute," her mother said, speaking the language of Mr. Kuroda.

When Rosie carried the reply to her father, he did not seem to hear and she said again, "Mother says she'll be back in a minute."

"All right, all right," he nodded, and they worked again in silence. But suddenly, her father uttered an incredible noise, exactly like the cork of a bottle popping, and the next Rosie knew, he was stalking angrily toward the house, almost running in fact, and she chased after him crying, "Father! Father! What are you going to do?"

He stopped long enough to order her back to the shed. "Never mind!" he shouted. "Get on with the sorting!"

And from the place in the fields where she stood, frightened and vacillating, Rosie saw her father enter the house. Soon Mr. Kuroda came out alone, putting on his coat. Mr. Kuroda got into his car and backed out down the driveway onto the highway. Next her father emerged, also alone, something in his arms (it was the picture, she realized), and, going over to the bathhouse woodpile, he threw the picture on the ground and picked up the axe. Smashing the picture, glass and all (she heard the explosion faintly), he reached over for the kerosene that was used to encourage the bath fire and poured it over the wreckage. I am dreaming, Rosie said to herself, I am dreaming, but her father, having made sure that his act of cremation was irrevocable, was even then returning to the fields.

Rosie ran past him and toward the house. What had become of her mother? She burst into the parlor and found her mother at the back window watching the dying fire. They watched together until there remained only a feeble smoke under the blazing sun. Her mother was very calm.

"Do you know why I married your father?" she said without turning.

"No," said Rosie. It was the most frightening question she had ever been called upon to answer. Don't tell me now, she wanted to say, tell me tomorrow, tell me next week, don't tell me today. But she knew she would be told now, that the telling would combine with the other violence of the hot afternoon to level her life, her world to the very ground.

It was like a story out of the magazines illustrated in sepia, which she had consumed so greedily for a period until the information had somehow reached her that those wretchedly unhappy autobiographies, offered to her as the testimonials of living men and women, were largely inventions: Her mother, at nineteen, had come to America and married her father as an alternative to suicide.

At eighteen she had been in love with the first son of one of the well-to-do families in her village. The two had met whenever and wherever they could, secretly, because it would not have done for his family to see him favor her—her father had no money; he was a drunkard and a gambler besides. She had learned she was with child; an excellent match had already been arranged for her lover. Despised by her family, she had given premature birth to a stillborn son, who would be seventeen now. Her family did not turn her out, but she could no longer project herself in any direction without refreshing in them the memory of her indiscretion. She wrote to Aunt Taka, her favorite sister in America, threatening to kill herself if Aunt Taka would not send for her. Aunt Taka hastily arranged a marriage with a young man of whom she knew, but lately arrived from Japan, a young man of simple mind, it was said, but of kindly heart. The young man was never told why his unseen betrothed was so eager to hasten the day of meeting.

The story was told perfectly, with neither groping for words nor untoward passion. It was as though her mother had memorized it by heart, reciting it to herself so many times over that its nagging vileness had long since gone.

"I had a brother then?" Rosie asked, for this was what seemed to matter now; she would think about the other later, she assured herself, pushing back the illumination which threatened all that darkness that had hitherto been merely mysterious or even glamorous. "A half-brother?"

"Yes."

"I would have liked a brother," she said.

Suddenly, her mother knelt on the floor and took her by the wrists. "Rosie," she said urgently, "Promise me you will never marry!" Shocked more by the request than the revelation, Rosie stared at her mother's face. Jesus, Jesus, she called silently, not certain whether she was invoking the help of the son of the Carrascos or of God, until there returned sweetly the memory of Jesus' hand, how it had touched her and where. Still her mother waited for an answer, holding her wrists so tightly that her hands were going numb. She tried to pull free. Promise, her mother whispered fiercely, promise. Yes, yes, I promise, Rosie said. But for an instant she turned away, and her mother, hearing the familiar glib agreement, released her. Oh, you, you, you, her eyes and twisted mouth said, you fool. Rosie, covering her face, began at last to cry, and the embrace and consoling hand came much later than she expected.

# 2

# 1960s AND 1970s

## *Breakdowns and Breakthroughs*

# SAUL BELLOW

## (1915– )

Saul Bellow was born in Quebec of immigrant parents from Russia, and he grew up speaking or learning Yiddish, Hebrew, English, and French. In 1924 the family moved to Chicago, where he attended public schools and the University of Chicago. He graduated from Northwestern University in 1937 and began a graduate program in anthropology at the University of Wisconsin, but left to become a writer.

Bellow worked briefly with the Works Progress Administration writers project and then served in the Merchant Marine in World War II. After the war he taught at various schools and lived briefly in Paris. In 1962 he began a long association with the University of Chicago, where he taught and chaired the Committee on Social Thought, an interdisciplinary program. In more recent years he taught at Boston University. In 2000, at 85 years of age, he became a father and the author of a new novel, *Ravelstein.*

Bellow's first two works, *Dangling Man* (1944) and *The Victim* (1947), are somber and tightly composed novels. With *The Adventures of Augie March* (1953), Bellow produced a picaresque novel in an open, free, and exuberant style, a comedy of coming of age in the modern city. Other major works include *Seize the Day* (1956), *Henderson, the Rain King* (1959), *Herzog* (1964), *Mr. Sammler's Planet* (1970), *Humboldt's Gift* (1975), *The Dean's December* (1982), and *More Die of Heartbreak* (1987). In addition to several plays, he wrote a nonfiction memoir *To Jerusalem and Back* (1976). His stories are collected in *Mosby's Memoirs, and Other Stories* (1968) and *Him with His Foot in His Mouth, and Other Stories* (1984). In addition to the Nobel Prize for literature, won in 1976, Bellow's fiction has won National Book awards and the Pulitzer Prize.

Bellow's fiction is noted for finely imagined characters in quest of what Augie March calls "a worthwhile fate." Bellow does not shirk from depicting the often harsh and evil realities of life, but refuses to find any satisfaction in nihilism or relativism. He affirms the spiritual potential of the individual despite the often overwhelming odds against him.

# Looking for Mr. Green

Whatsoever thy hand findeth to do, do it with thy might. . . .[1]

HARD WORK? No, it wasn't really so hard. He wasn't used to walking and stair-climbing, but the physical difficulty of his new job was not what George Grebe felt most. He was delivering relief checks in the Negro district, and although he was a native Chicagoan this was not a part of the city he knew much about—it needed a depression to introduce him to it. No, it wasn't literally hard work, not as reckoned in foot-pounds, but yet he was beginning to feel the strain of it, to grow aware of its peculiar difficulty. He could find the streets and numbers, but the clients were not where they were supposed to be, and he felt like a hunter inexperienced in the camouflage of his game. It was an unfavorable day, too—fall, and cold, dark weather, windy. But, anyway, instead of shells in his deep trenchcoat pocket he had the cardboard of checks, punctured for the spindles of the file, the holes reminding him of the holes in player-piano paper. And he didn't look much like a hunter, either; his was a city figure entirely, belted up in this Irish conspirator's coat. He was slender without being tall, stiff in the back, his legs looking shabby in a pair of old tweed pants gone through and fringy at the cuffs. With this stiffness, he kept his head forward, so that his face was red from the sharpness of the weather; and it was an indoors sort of face with gray eyes that persisted in some kind of thought and yet seemed to avoid definiteness of conclusion. He wore sideburns that surprised you somewhat by the tough curl of the blond hair and the effect of assertion in their length. He was not so mild as he looked, nor so youthful; and nevertheless there was no effort on his part to seem what he was not. He was an educated man; he was a bachelor; he was in some ways simple; without lushing, he liked a drink; his luck had not been good. Nothing was deliberately hidden.

He felt that his luck was better than usual today. When he had reported for work that morning he had expected to be shut up in the relief office at a clerk's job, for he had been hired downtown as a clerk, and he was glad to have, instead, the freedom of the streets and welcomed, at least at first, the vigor of the cold and even the blowing of the hard wind. But on the other hand he was not getting on with the distribution of the checks. It was true that it was a city job; nobody expected you to push too hard at a city job. His supervisor, that young Mr. Raynor, had practically told him that. Still, he wanted to do well at it. For one thing, when he knew how quickly he could deliver a batch of checks, he would know also how much time he could expect to clip for himself. And then, too, the clients would be waiting for their money. That was not the most important consideration, though it certainly mattered to him. No, but he wanted to do well, simply for doing-well's sake, to acquit himself decently of a job because he so rarely had a job to do that required just this sort of energy. Of this peculiar energy he now had a superabundance; once it had started to flow, it flowed all too heavily. And, for the time being anyway, he was balked. He could not find Mr. Green.

1. Ecclesiastes 9:10.

So he stood in his big-skirted trenchcoat with a large envelope in his hand and papers showing from his pocket, wondering why people should be so hard to locate who were too feeble or sick to come to the station to collect their own checks. But Raynor had told him that tracking them down was not easy at first and had offered him some advice on how to proceed. "If you can see the postman, he's your first man to ask, and your best bet. If you can't connect with him, try the stores and tradespeople around. Then the janitor and the neighbors. But you'll find the closer you come to your man the less people will tell you. They don't want to tell you anything."

"Because I'm a stranger."

"Because you're white. We ought to have a Negro doing this, but we don't at the moment, and of course you've got to eat, too, and this is public employment. Jobs have to be made. Oh, that holds for me too. Mind you, I'm not letting myself out. I've got three years of seniority on you, that's all. And a law degree. Otherwise, you might be back of the desk and I might be going out into the field this cold day. The same dough pays us both and for the same, exact, identical reason. What's my law degree got to do with it? But you have to pass out these checks, Mr. Grebe, and it'll help if you're stubborn, so I hope you are."

"Yes, I'm fairly stubborn."

Raynor sketched hard with an eraser in the old dirt of his desk, left-handed, and said, "Sure; what else can you answer to such a question. Anyhow, the trouble you're going to have is that they don't like to give information about anybody. They think you're a plain-clothes dick or an installment collector, or summons-server or something like that. Till you've been seen around the neighborhood for a few months and people know you're only from the relief."

It was dark, ground-freezing, pre-Thanksgiving weather, the wind played hob with the smoke, rushing it down, and Grebe missed his gloves, which he had left in Raynor's office. And no one would admit knowing Green. It was past three o'clock and the postman had made his last delivery. The nearest grocer, himself a Negro, had never heard the name Tulliver Green, or said he hadn't. Grebe was inclined to think that it was true, that he had in the end convinced the man that he wanted only to deliver a check. But he wasn't sure. He needed experience in interpreting looks and signs and, even more, the will not to be put off or denied and even the force to bully if need be. If the grocer did know, he had got rid of him easily. But since most of his trade was with reliefers, why should he prevent the delivery of a check? Maybe Green, or Mrs. Green, if there was a Mrs. Green, patronized another grocer. And was there a Mrs. Green? It was one of Grebe's great handicaps that he hadn't looked at any of the case records. Raynor should have let him read files for a few hours. But he apparently saw no need for that, probably considering the job unimportant. Why prepare systematically to deliver a few checks?

But now it was time to look for the janitor. Grebe took in the building in the wind and gloom of the late November day—trampled, frost-hardened lots on one side; on the other, an automobile junk yard and then the infinite work of Elevated frames, weak-looking, gaping with rubbish fires; two sets of leaning brick porches three stories high and a flight of cement stairs to the cellar. Descending, he entered the underground passage, where he tried the doors until one opened and he found himself in the furnace room. There someone rose toward him and approached, scraping on the coal grit and bending under the canvas-jacketed pipes.

"Are you the janitor?"

"What do you want?"

"I'm looking for a man who's supposed to be living here. Green."

"What Green?"

"Oh, you maybe have more than one Green?" said Grebe with new, pleasant hope: "This is Tulliver Green."

"I don't think I c'n help you, mister. I don't know any."

"A crippled man."

The janitor stood bent before him. Could it be that he was crippled? Oh, God! what if he was. Grebe's gray eyes sought with excited difficulty to see. But no, he was only very short and stooped. A head awakened from meditation, a strong-haired beard, low, wide shoulders. A staleness of sweat and coal rose from his black shirt and the burlap sack he wore as an apron.

"Crippled how?"

Grebe thought and then answered with the light voice of unmixed candor, "I don't know. I've never seen him." This was damaging, but his only other choice was to make a lying guess, and he was not up to it. "I'm delivering checks for the relief to shut-in cases. If he weren't crippled he'd come to collect himself. That's why I said crippled. Bedridden, chair-ridden—is there anybody like that?"

This sort of frankness was one of Grebe's oldest talents, going back to childhood. But it gained him nothing here.

"No suh. I've got four buildin's same as this that I take care of. I don't know all the tenants, leave alone the tenants' tenants. The rooms turn over so fast, people movin' in and out every day. I can't tell you."

The janitor opened his grimy lips but Grebe did not hear him in the piping of the valves and the consuming pull of air to flame in the body of the furnace. He knew, however, what he had said.

"Well, all the same, thanks. Sorry I bothered you. I'll prowl around upstairs again and see if I can turn up someone who knows him."

Once more in the cold air and early darkness he made the short circle from the cellarway to the entrance crowded between the brickwork pillars and began to climb to the third floor. Pieces of plaster ground under his feet; strips of brass tape from which the carpeting had been torn away marked old boundaries at the sides. In the passage, the cold reached him worse than in the street; it touched him to the bone. The hall toilets ran like springs. He thought grimly as he heard the wind burning around the building with a sound like that of the furnace, that this was a great piece of constructed shelter. Then he struck a match in the gloom and searched for names and numbers among the writings and scribbles on the walls. He saw whoody-doody go to jesus, and zigzags, caricatures, sexual scrawls, and curses. So the sealed rooms of pyramids were also decorated, and the caves of human dawn.

The information on his card was, TULLIVER GREEN—apt 3d. There were no names, however, and no numbers: His shoulders drawn up, tears of cold in his eyes, breathing vapor, he went the length of the corridor and told himself that if he had been lucky enough to have the temperament for it he would bang on one of the doors and bawl out "Tulliver Green!" until he got results. But it wasn't in him to make an uproar and he continued to burn matches, passing the light over the walls. At the rear, in a corner off the hall, he discovered a door he had not seen before and he thought it best to investigate. It sounded empty when he knocked, but a young Negress answered, hardly more than a girl. She opened only a bit, to guard the warmth of the room.

"Yes suh?"

"I'm from the district relief station on Prairie Avenue. I'm looking for a man named Tulliver Green to give him his check. Do you know him?"

No, she didn't; but he thought she had not understood anything of what he had said. She had a dream-bound, dream-blind face, very soft and black, shut off. She wore a man's jacket and pulled the ends together at her throat. Her hair was parted in three directions, at the sides and transversely, standing up at the front in a dull puff.

"Is there somebody around here who might know?"

"I jus' taken this room las' week."

He observed that she shivered, but even her shiver was somnambulistic and there was no sharp consciousness of cold in the big smooth eyes of her handsome face.

"All right, miss, thank you. Thanks," he said, and went to try another place.

Here he was admitted. He was grateful, for the room was warm. It was full of people, and they were silent as he entered—ten people, or a dozen, perhaps more, sitting on benches like a parliament. There was no light, properly speaking, but a tempered darkness that the window gave, and everyone seemed to him enormous, the men padded out in heavy work clothes and winter coats, and the women huge, too, in their sweaters, hats, and old furs. And, besides, bed and bedding, a black cooking range, a piano piled towering to the ceiling with papers, a dining-room table of the old style of prosperous Chicago. Among these people Grebe, with his cold-heightened fresh color and his smaller stature, entered like a school-boy. Even though he was met with smiles and good will, he knew, before a single word was spoken, that all the currents ran against him and that he would make no headway. Nevertheless he began. "Does anybody here know how I can deliver a check to Mr. Tulliver Green?"

"Green?" It was the man that had let him in who answered. He was in short sleeves, in a checkered shirt, and had a queer, high head, profusely overgrown and long as a shako,[2] the veins entered it strongly from his forehead. "I never heard mention of him. Is this where he live?"

"This is the address they gave me at the station. He's a sick man, and he'll need his check. Can't anybody tell me where to find him?"

He stood his ground and waited for a reply, his crimson wool scarf wound about his neck and drooping outside his trenchcoat, pockets weighted with the block of checks and official forms. They must have realized that he was not a college boy employed afternoons by a bill collector, trying foxily to pass for a relief clerk, recognized that he was an older man who knew himself what need was, who had more than an average seasoning in hardship. It was evident enough if you looked at the marks under his eyes and at the sides of his mouth.

"Anybody know this sick man?"

"No suh." On all sides he saw heads shaken and smiles of denial. No one knew.

2. A stiff military cap with a high crown.

And maybe it was true, he considered, standing silent in the earthen, musky human gloom of the place as the rumble continued. But he could never really be sure.

"What's the matter with this man?" said shako-head.

"I've never seen him. All I can tell you is that he can't come in person for his money. It's my first day in this district."

"Maybe they given you the wrong number?"

"I don't believe so. But where else can I ask about him?" He felt that this persistence amused them deeply, and in a way he shared their amusement that he should stand up so tenaciously to them. Though smaller, though slight, he was his own man, he retracted nothing about himself, and he looked back at them, gray-eyed, with amusement and also with a sort of courage. On the bench some man spoke in his throat, the words impossible to catch, and a woman answered with a wild, shrieking laugh, which was quickly cut off.

"Well, so nobody will tell me?"

"Ain't nobody who knows."

"At least, if he lives here, he pays rent to someone. Who manages the building?"

"Greatham Company. That's on Thirty-ninth Street."

Grebe wrote it in his pad. But, in the street again, a sheet of wind-driven paper clinging to his leg while he deliberated what direction to take next, it seemed a feeble lead to follow. Probably this Green didn't rent a flat, but a room. Sometimes there were as many as twenty people in an apartment; the real-estate agent would know only the lessee. And not even the agent could tell you who the renters were. In some places the beds were even used in shifts, watchmen or jitney drivers or short-order cooks in night joints turning out after a day's sleep and surrendering their beds to a sister, a nephew, or perhaps a stranger, just off the bus. There were large numbers of newcomers in this terrific, blight-bitten portion of the city between Cottage Grove and Ashland, wandering from house to house and room to room. When you saw them, how could you know them? They didn't carry bundles on their backs or look picturesque. You only saw a man, a Negro, walking in the street or riding in the car, like everyone else, with his thumb closed on a transfer. And therefore how were you supposed to tell? Grebe thought the Greatham agent would only laugh at his question.

But how much it would have simplified the job to be able to say that Green was old, or blind, or consumptive. An hour in the files, taking a few notes, and he needn't have been at such a disadvantage. When Raynor gave him the block of checks he asked, "How much should I know about these people?" Then Raynor had looked as though he were preparing to accuse him of trying to make the job more important than it was. He smiled, because by then they were on fine terms, but nevertheless he had been getting ready to say something like that when the confusion began in the station over Staika and her children.

Grebe had waited a long time for this job. It came to him through the pull of an old schoolmate in the Corporation Counsel's office, never a close friend, but suddenly sympathetic and interested—pleased to show, moreover, how well he had done, how strongly he was coming on even in these miserable times. Well, he was coming through strongly, along with the Democratic administration itself. Grebe had gone to see him in City Hall, and they had had a counter lunch or beers at least once a month for a year, and finally it had been possible to swing the job. He didn't mind being assigned the lowest clerical grade, nor even being a messenger, though Raynor thought he did.

This Raynor was an original sort of guy and Grebe had taken to him immediately. As was proper on the first day, Grebe had come early, but he waited long, for Raynor was late. At last he darted into his cubicle of an office as though he had just jumped from one of those hurtling huge red Indian Avenue cars. His thin, rough face was wind-stung and he was grinning and saying something breathlessly to himself. In his hat, a small fedora, and his coat, the velvet collar a neat fit about his neck, and his silk muffler that set off the nervous twist of his chin, he swayed and turned himself in his swivel chair, feet leaving the ground, so that he pranced a little as he sat. Meanwhile he took Grebe's measure out of his eyes, eyes of an unusual vertical length and slightly sardonic. So the two men sat for a while, saying nothing, while the supervisor raised his hat from his miscombed hair and put it in his lap. His cold-darkened hands were not clean. A steel beam passed through the little makeshift room, from which machine belts once had hung. The building was an old factory.

"I'm younger than you; I hope you won't find it hard taking orders from me," said Raynor. "But I don't make them up, either. You're how old, about?"

"Thirty-five."

"And you thought you'd be inside doing paper work. But it so happens I have to send you out."

"I don't mind."

"And it's mostly a Negro load we have in this district."

"So I thought it would be."

"Fine. You'll get along. *C'est un bon boulot.*[3] Do you know French?"

"Some."

"I thought you'd be a university man."

"Have you been in France?" said Grebe.

"No, that's the French of the Berlitz School. I've been at it for more than a year, just as I'm sure people have been, all over the world, office boys in China and braves in Tanganyika. In fact, I damn well know it. Such is the attractive power of civilization. It's overrated, but what do you want? *Que voulez-vous?*[4] I get *Le Rire*[5] and all the spicy-papers, just like in Tanganyika. It must be mystifying, out there. But my reason is that I'm aiming at the diplomatic service. I have a cousin who's a courier, and the way he describes it is awfully attractive. He rides in the *wagon-lits*[6] and reads books. While we—What did you do before?"

"I sold."

"Where?"

"Ganned meat at Stop and Shop. In the basement."

"And before that?"

"Window shades, at Goldblatt's."

"Steady work?"

"No, Thursdays and Saturdays. I also sold shoes."

3. "It's a good job."

4. "What do you want?"

5. A humorous French periodical.

6. Railroad sleeping cars.

"You've been a shoe-dog too. Well. And prior to that? Here it is in your folder." He opened the record. "Saint Olaf's College, instructor in classical languages. Fellow, University of Chicago, 1926–27. I've had Latin, too. Let's trade quotations—'*Dum spiro spero.*' "[7]

" '*Da dextram misero.*' "[8]

" '*Alea jacta est.*' "[9]

" '*Excelsior.*' "[10]

Raynor shouted with laughter, and other workers came to look at him over the partition. Grebe also laughed, feeling pleased and easy. The luxury of fun on a nervous morning.

When they were done and no one was watching or listening, Raynor said rather seriously, "What made you study Latin in the first place? Was it for the priesthood?"

"No."

"Just for the hell of it? For the culture? Oh, the things people think they can pull!" He made his cry hilarious and tragic. "I ran my pants off so I could study for the bar, and I've passed the bar, so I get twelve dollars a week more than you as a bonus for having seen life straight and whole. I'll tell you, as a man of culture, that even though nothing looks to be real, and everything stands for something else, and that thing for another thing; and that thing for a still further one—there ain't any comparison between twenty-five and thirty-seven dollars a week, regardless of the last reality. Don't you think that was clear to your Greeks? They were a thoughtful people, but they didn't part with their slaves."

This was a great deal more than Grebe had looked for in his first interview with his supervisor. He was too shy to show all the astonishment he felt. He laughed a little, aroused, and brushed at the sunbeam that covered his head with its dust. "Do you think my mistake was so terrible?"

"Damn right it was terrible, and you know it now that you've had the whip of hard times laid on your back. You should have been preparing yourself for trouble. Your people must have been well off to send you to the university. Stop me, if I'm stepping on your toes. Did your mother pamper you? Did your father give in to you? Were you brought up tenderly, with permission to go and find out what were the last things that everything else stands for while everybody else labored in the fallen world of appearances?"

"Well, no, it wasn't exactly like that." Grebe smiled. *The fallen world of appearances!* no less. But now it was his turn to deliver a surprise. "We weren't rich. My father was the last genuine English butler in Chicago—"

"Are you kidding?"

"Why should I be?"

"In a livery?"

"In livery. Up on the Gold Coast."[11]

"And he wanted you to be educated like a gentleman?"

7. "While I breathe, I hope."

8. "Give your right hand to the wretched."

9. "The die is cast."

10. "Higher."

11. A fashionable residential area on Chicago's north side.

"He did not. He sent me to the Armour Institute to study chemical engineering. But when he died I changed schools."

He stopped himself, and considered how quickly Raynor had reached him. In no time he had your valise on the table and all your stuff unpacked. And afterward, in the streets, he was still reviewing how far he might have gone, and how much he might have been led to tell if they had not been interrupted by Mrs. Staika's great noise.

But just then a young woman, one of Raynor's workers, ran into the cubicle exclaiming, "Haven't you heard all the fuss?"

"We haven't heard anything."

"It's Staika, giving out with all her might. The reporters are coming. She said she phoned the papers, and you know she did."

"But what is she up to?" said Raynor.

"She brought her wash and she's ironing it here, with our current, because the relief won't pay her electric bill. She has her ironing board set up by the admitting desk, and her kids are with her, all six. They never are in school more than once a week. She's always dragging them around with her because of her reputation."

"I don't want to miss any of this," said Raynor, jumping up. Grebe, as he followed with the secretary, said, "Who is this Staika?"

"They call her the 'Blood Mother of Federal Street.' She's a professional donor at the hospitals. I think they pay ten dollars a pint. Of course it's no joke, but she makes a very big thing out of it and she and the kids are in the papers all the time."

A small crowd, staff and clients divided by a plywood barrier, stood in the narrow space of the entrance, and Staika was shouting in a gruff, mannish voice, plunging the iron on the board and slamming it on the metal rest.

"My father and mother came in a steerage, and I was born in our house, Robey by Huron. I'm no dirty immigrant. I'm no dirty immigrant. I'm a U.S. citizen. My husband is a gassed veteran from France with lungs weaker'n paper, that hardly can he go to the toilet by himself. These six children of mine, I have to buy the shoes for their feet with my own blood. Even a lousy little white Communion necktie, that's a couple of drops of blood; a little piece of mosquito veil for my Vadja so she won't be ashamed in church for the other girls, they take my blood for it by Goldblatt. That's how I keep goin.' A fine thing if I had to depend on the relief. And there's plenty of people on the rolls—fakes! There's nothin' *they* can't get, that can go and wrap bacon at Swift and Armour any time. They're lookin' for them by the Yards. They never have to be out of work. Only they rather lay in their lousy beds and eat the public's money." She was not afraid, in a predominantly Negro station, to shout this way about Negroes.

Grebe and Raynor worked themselves forward to get a closer view of the woman. She was flaming with anger and with pleasure at herself, broad and huge, a golden-headed woman who wore a cotton cap laced with pink ribbon. She was barelegged and had on black gym shoes, her Hoover apron was open and her great breasts, not much restrained by a man's undershirt, hampered her arms as she worked at the kid's dress on the ironing board. And the children, silent and white, with a kind of locked obstinacy, in sheepskins and lumberjackets, stood behind her. She had captured the station, and the pleasure this gave her was enormous. Yet her grievances were true grievances. She was telling the truth. But she behaved like a liar. The look of her small eyes was hidden, and while she raged she also seemed to be spinning and planning.

"They send me out college case workers in silk pants to talk me out of what I got comin'. Are they better'n me? Who told them? Fire them. Let 'em go and get married and then you won't have to cut electric from people's budget."

The chief supervisor, Mr. Ewing, couldn't silence her and he stood with folded arms at the head of his staff, bald, bald-headed, saying to his subordinates like the ex-school principal he was, "Pretty soon she'll be tired and go."

"No she won't," said Raynor to Grebe. "She'll get what she wants. She knows more about the relief even then Ewing. She's been on the rolls for years, and she always gets what she wants because she puts on a noisy show. Ewing knows it. He'll give in soon. He's only saving face. If he gets bad publicity, the Commissioner'll have him on the carpet, downtown. She's got him submerged; she'll submerge everybody in time, and that includes nations and governments."

Grebe replied with his characteristic smile, disagreeing completely. Who would take Staika's orders, and what changes could her yelling ever bring about?

No, what Grebe saw in her, the power that made people listen, was that her cry expressed the war of flesh and blood, perhaps turned a little crazy and certainly ugly, on this place and this condition. And at first, when he went out, the spirit of Staika somehow presided over the whole district for him, and it took color from her; he saw her color, in the spotty curb fires, and the fires under the El, the straight alley of flamy gloom. Later, too, when he went into a tavern for a shot of rye, the sweat of beer, association with West Side Polish streets, made him think of her again.

He wiped the corners of his mouth with his muffler, his handkerchief being inconvenient to reach for, and went out again to get on with the delivery of his checks. The air bit cold and hard and a few flakes of snow formed near him. A train struck by and left a quiver in the frames and a bristling icy hiss over the rails.

Crossing the street, he descended a flight of board steps into a basement grocery, setting off a little bell. It was a dark, long store and it caught you with its stinks of smoked meat, soap, dried peaches, and fish. There was a fire wrinkling and flapping in the little stove, and the proprietor was waiting, an Italian with a long, hollow face and stubborn bristles. He kept his hands warm under his apron.

No, he didn't know Green. You knew people but not names. The same man might not have the same name twice. The police didn't know, either, and mostly didn't care. When somebody was shot or knifed they took the body away and didn't look for the murderer. In the first place, nobody would tell them anything. So they made up a name for the coroner and called it quits. And in the second place, they didn't give a goddamn anyhow. But they couldn't get to the bottom of a thing even if they wanted to. Nobody would get to know even a tenth of what went on among these people. They stabbed and stole, they did every crime and abomination you ever heard of, men and men, women and women, parents and children, worse than the animals. They carried on their own way, and the horrors passed off like a smoke. There was never anything like it in the history of the whole world.

It was a long speech, deepening with every word in its fantasy and passion and becoming increasingly senseless and terrible: a swarm amassed by suggestion and invention, a huge, hugging, despairing knot, a human wheel of heads, legs, bellies, arms, rolling through his shop.

Grebe felt that he must interrupt him. He said sharply, "What are you talking about! All I asked was whether you knew this man."

"That isn't even the half of it. I been here six years. You probably don't want to believe this. But suppose it's true?"

"All the same," said Grebe, "there must be a way to find a person."

The Italian's close-spaced eyes had been queerly concentrated, as were his muscles, while he leaned across the counter trying to convince Grebe. Now he gave up the effort and sat down on his stool. "Oh—I suppose. Once in a while. But I been telling you, even the cops don't get anywhere."

"They're always after somebody. It's not the same thing."

"Well, keep trying if you want. I can't help you."

But he didn't keep trying. He had no more time to spend on Green. He slipped Green's check to the back of the block. The next name on the list was field, winston.

He found the backyard bungalow without the least trouble; it shared a lot with another house, a few feet of yard between. Grebe knew these two-shack arrangements. They had been built in vast numbers in the days before the swamps were filled and the streets raised, and they were all the same—a boardwalk along the fence, well under street level, three or four ball-headed posts for clotheslines, greening wood, dead shingles, and a long, long flight of stairs to the rear door.

A twelve-year-old boy let him into the kitchen, and there the old man was, sitting by the table in a wheel chair.

"Oh, it's d' Government man," he said to the boy when Grebe drew out his checks. "Go bring me my box of papers." He cleared a space on the table.

"Oh, you don't have to go to all that trouble," said Grebe. But Field laid out his papers: Social Security card, relief certification, letters from the state hospital in Manteno, and a naval discharge dated San Diego, 1920.

"That's plenty," Grebe said. "Just sign."

"You got to know who I am," the old man said. "You're from the Government. It's not your check, it's a Government check and you got no business to hand it over till everything is proved."

He loved the ceremony of it, and Grebe made no more objections. Field emptied his box and finished out the circle of cards and letters.

"There's everything I done and been. Just the death certificate and they can close book on me." He said this with a certain happy pride and magnificence. Still he did not sign, he merely held the little pen upright on the golden-green corduroy of his thigh. Grebe did not hurry him. He felt the old man's hunger for conversation.

"I got to get better coal," he said. "I send my little gran'son to the yard with my order and they fill his wagon with screening. The stove ain't made for it. It fall through the grate. The order says Franklin County egg-size coal."

"I'll report it and see what can be done."

"Nothing can be done, I expect. You know and I know. There ain't no little ways to make things better, and the only big thing is money. That's the only sunbeams, money. Nothing is black where it shines, and the only place you see black is where it ain't shining. What we colored have to have is our own rich. There ain't no other way."

Grebe sat, his reddened forehead bridged levelly by his close-cut hair and his cheeks, lowered in the wings of his collar—the caked fire shone hard within the isinglass-and-iron frames but the room was not comfortable—sat and listened while the old man unfolded his scheme. This was to create one Negro millionaire a month by subscription. One clever, good-hearted young fellow elected every month would sign a contract to use the money to start a business employing Negroes. This would be advertised by chain letters and word of mouth, and every Negro wage earner would contribute a dollar a month. Within five years there would be sixty millionaires.

"That'll fetch respect," he said with a throat-stopped sound that came out like a foreign syllable. "You got to take and organize all the money that gets thrown away on the policy wheel and horse race. As long as they can take it away from you, they got no respect for you. Money, that's d' sun of human kind!" Field was a Negro of mixed blood, perhaps Cherokee, or Natchez; his skin was reddish. And he sounded, speaking about a golden sun in this dark room, and looked, shaggy and slab-headed, with the mingled blood of his face and broad lips, the little pen still upright in his hand, like one of the underground kings of mythology, old judge Minos[12] himself.

And now he accepted the check and signed. Not to soil the slip, he held it down with his knuckles. The table budged and creaked, the center of the gloomy, heathen midden[13] of the kitchen covered with bread, meat, and cans, and the scramble of papers.

"Don't you think my scheme'd work?"

"It's worth thinking about. Something ought to be done, I agree."

"It'll work if people will do it. That's all. That's the only thing, any time. When they understand it in the same way, all of them."

"That's true," said Grebe, rising. His glance met the old man's.

"I know you got to go," he said. "Well, God bless you, boy, you ain't been sly with me. I can tell it in a minute."

He went back through the buried yard. Someone nursed a candle in a shed, where a man unloaded kindling wood from a sprawl-wheeled baby buggy and two voices carried on a high conversation. As he came up the sheltered passage he heard the hard boost of the wind in the branches and against the house fronts, and then, reaching the sidewalk, he saw the needle-eye red of cable towers in the open icy height hundreds of feet above the river and the factories—those keen points. From here, his view was obstructed all the way to the South Branch and its timber banks, and the cranes beside the water. Rebuilt after the Great Fire, this part of the city was, not fifty years later, in ruins again, factories boarded up, buildings deserted or fallen, gaps of prairie between. But it wasn't desolation that this made you feel, but rather a faltering of organization that set free a huge energy, an escaped, unattached, unregulated power from the giant raw place. Not only must people feel it but, it seemed to Grebe, they were compelled to match it. In their very bodies. He no less than others, he realized. Say that his parents had been servants in their time, whereas he was not supposed to be one. He thought that they had never done any service like this, which no one visible asked for, and probably flesh and blood could not even perform. Nor could anyone show why it should be performed; or see where the performance would lead. That did not mean that he wanted to be released from it, he realized with a grimly pensive face. On the contrary. He had something to do. To be compelled to feel this energy and yet have no task to do—that was horrible; that was suffering; he knew what that was. It was now quitting time. Six o'clock. He could go home if he liked, to his room, that is, to wash in hot water, to pour

12. The mythical king and lawgiver of Crete who had the Labyrinth built.

13. Refuse pile.

a drink, lie down on his quilt, read the paper, eat some liver paste on crackers before going out to dinner. But to think of this actually made him feel a little sick, as though he had swallowed hard air. He had six checks left, and he was determined to deliver at least one of these: Mr. Green's check.

So he started again. He had four or five dark blocks to go, past open lots, condemned houses, old foundations, closed schools, black churches, mounds, and he reflected that there must be many people alive who had once seen the neighborhood rebuilt and new. Now there was a second layer of ruins; centuries of history accomplished through human massing. Numbers had given the place forced growth; enormous numbers had also broken it down. Objects once so new, so concrete that it could have occurred to anyone they stood for other things, had crumbled. Therefore, reflected Grebe, the secret of them was out. It was that they stood for themselves by agreement, and were natural and not unnatural by agreement, and when the things themselves collapsed the agreement became visible. What was it, otherwise, that kept cities from looking peculiar? Rome, that was almost permanent, did not give rise to thoughts like these. And was it abidingly real? But in Chicago, where the cycles were so fast and the familiar died out, and again rose changed, and died again in thirty years, you saw the common agreement or covenant, and you were forced to think about appearances and realities. (He remembered Raynor and he smiled. Raynor was a clever boy.) Once you had grasped this, a great many things became intelligible. For instance, why Mr. Field should conceive such a scheme. Of course, if people were to agree to create a millionaire, a real millionaire would come into existence. And if you wanted to know how Mr. Field was inspired to think of this, why, he had within sight of his kitchen window the chart, the very bones of a successful scheme—the El with its blue and green confetti of signals. People consented to pay dimes and ride the crash-box cars, and so it was a success. Yet how absurd it looked; how little reality there was to start with. And yet Yerkes,[14] the great financier who built it, had known that he could get people to agree to do it. Viewed as itself, what a scheme of a scheme it seemed, how close to an appearance. Then why wonder at Mr. Field's idea? He had grasped a principle. And then Grebe remembered, too, that Mr. Yerkes had established the Yerkes Observatory and endowed it with millions. Now how did the notion come to him in his New York museum of a palace or his Aegean-bound yacht to give money to astronomers? Was he awed by the success of his bizarre enterprise and therefore ready to spend money to find out where in the universe being and seeming were identical? Yes, he wanted to know what abides; and whether flesh is Bible grass;[15] and he offered money to be burned in the fire of suns. Okay, then, Grebe thought further, these things exist because people consent to exist with them—we have got so far and also there is a reality which doesn't depend on consent but within which consent is a game. But what about need, the need that keeps so many vast thousands in position? You tell me that, you *private* little gentleman and *decent* soul—he used these words against himself scornfully. Why is the consent given to misery? And why so painfully ugly? Because there is *something* that is dismal and permanently ugly? Here he sighed and gave it up, and thought it was enough for the present moment that he had a real check in his pocket

14. Charles T. Yerkes (1837–1905), the financier who built the Chicago railway system.

15. See Isaiah 40:6

for a Mr. Green who must be real beyond question. If only his neighbors didn't think they had to conceal him.

This time he stopped at the second floor. He struck a match and found a door. Presently a man answered his knock and Grebe had the check ready and showed it even before he began. "Does Tulliver Green live here? I'm from the relief."

The man narrowed the opening and spoke to someone at his back.

"Does he live here?"

"Uh-uh. No."

"Or anywhere in this building? He's a sick man and he can't come for his dough." He exhibited the check in the light, which was smoky—the air smelled of charred lard—and the man held off the brim of his cap to study it.

"Uh-uh. Never seen the name."

"There's nobody around here that uses crutches?"

He seemed to think, but it was Grebe's impression that he was simply waiting for a decent interval to pass.

"No, suh. Nobody I ever see."

"I've been looking for this man all afternoon"—Grebe spoke out with sudden force—"and I'm going to have to carry this check back to the station. It seems strange not to be able to find a person to give him something when you're looking for him for a good reason. I suppose if I had bad news for him I'd find him quick enough."

There was a responsive motion in the other man's face. "That's right, I reckon."

"It almost doesn't do any good to have a name if you can't be found by it. It doesn't stand for anything. He might as well not have any," he went on, smiling. It was as much of a concession as he could make to his desire to laugh.

"Well, now, there's a little old knot-back man I see once in a while. He might be the one you lookin' for Downstairs."

"Where? Right side or left? Which door?"

"I don't know which. Thin-face little knot-back with a stick."

But no one answered at any of the doors on the first floor. He went to the end of the corridor, searching by match-light, and found only a stairless exit to the yard, a drop of about six feet. But there was a bungalow near the alley, an old house like Mr. Fields. To jump was unsafe. He ran from the front door, through the underground passage and into the yard. The place was occupied. There was a light through the curtains, upstairs. The name on the ticket under the broken, scoop-shaped mailbox was Green! He exultantly rang the bell and pressed against the locked door. Then the lock clicked faintly and a long staircase opened before him. Someone was slowly coming down—a woman. He had the impression in the weak light that she was shaping her hair as she came, making herself presentable, for he saw her arms raised. But it was for support that they were raised; she was feeling her way downward, down the wall, stumbling. Next he wondered about the pressure of her feet on the treads; she did not seem to be wearing shoes. And it was a freezing stairway. His ring had got her out of bed, perhaps, and she had forgotten to put them on. And then he saw that she was not only shoeless but naked; she was entirely naked, climbing down while she talked to herself, a heavy woman, naked and drunk. She blundered into him. The contact of her breasts, though they touched only his coat, made him go back against the door with a blind shock. See what he had tracked down, in his hunting game!

The woman was saying to herself, furious with insult, "So I cain't—k, huh? I'll show that son-of-a-bitch kin I, cain't I."

What should he do now? Grebe asked himself. Why, he should go. He should turn away and go. He couldn't talk to this woman. He couldn't keep her standing naked in the cold. But when he tried he found himself unable to turn away.

He said, "Is this where Mr. Green lives?"

But she was still talking to herself and did not hear him.

"Is this Mr. Green's house?"

At last she turned her furious drunken glance on him. "What do you want?"

Again her eyes wandered from him; there was a dot of blood in their enraged brilliance. He wondered why she didn't feel the cold.

"I'm from the relief"

"Awright, what?"

"I've got a check for Tulliver Green."

This time she heard him and put out her hand.

"No, no, for Mr. Green. He's got to sign," he said. How was he going to get Green's signature tonight!

"I'll take it. He cain't."

He desperately shook his head, thinking of Mr. Field's precautions about identification. "I can't let you have it. It's for him. Are you Mrs. Green?"

"Maybe I is, and maybe I ain't. Who want to know?"

"Is he upstairs?"

"Awright. Take it up yourself, you goddamn fool."

Sure, he was a goddamn fool. Of course he could not go up because Green would probably be drunk and naked, too. And perhaps he would appear on the landing soon. He looked eagerly upward. Under the light was a high narrow brown wall. Empty! It remained empty!

"Hell with you, then!" he heard her cry. To deliver a check for coal and clothes, he was keeping her in the cold. She did not feel it, but his face was burning with frost and self-ridicule. He backed away from her.

"I'll come tomorrow, tell him."

"Ah, hell with you. Don' never come. What you doin' here in the nighttime? Don' come back." She yelled so that he saw the breadth of her tongue. She stood astride in the long cold box of the hall and held on to the banister and the wall. The bungalow itself was shaped something like a box, a clumsy, high box pointing into the freezing air with its sharp, wintry lights.

"If you are Mrs. Green, I'll give you the check," he said, changing his mind.

"Give here, then." She took it, took the pen offered with it in her left hand, and tried to sign the receipt on the wall. He looked around, almost as though to see whether his madness was being observed, and came near believing that someone was standing on a mountain of used tires in the auto-junking shop next door.

"But are you Mrs. Green?" he now thought to ask. But she was already climbing the stairs with the check, and it was too late, if he had made an error, if he was now in trouble, to undo the thing. But he wasn't going to worry about it. Though she might not be Mrs. Green, he was convinced that Mr. Green was upstairs. Whoever she was, the woman stood for Green, whom he was not to see this time. Well, you silly bastard, he said to himself, so you think you found him. So what? Maybe you really did find him—what of it? But it was important that there was a real Mr. Green whom they could not keep him from reaching because he seemed to come as an emissary from hostile appearances. And though the self-ridicule was slow to diminish, and his face still blazed with it, he had, nevertheless, a feeling of elation, too. "For after all," he said. "he *could* be found!"

# WILLIAM H. GASS
## (1924– )

Considered by critics an early practitioner of postmodernism, William H. Gass wrote fiction that is often highly foregrounded, calling attention to narrative form and linguistic referentiality. It also shows the influence of Gertrude Stein. Gass' work challenges narrative and generic boundaries as it explores the theme of human isolation and the difficulty of love.

Gass was born in Fargo, North Dakota, but was raised in Warren, Ohio. After serving in the navy during World War II, he graduated from Kenyon College. He earned a Ph.D. in philosophy from Cornell University in 1954. He has taught for many years at Washington University in St. Louis, where he is David May Distinguished University Professor in the Humanities and director of the International Writers' Center.

Gass began publishing stories in the 1950s, some of which appeared in the annuals *The Best American Stories.* His fiction includes *Omensetter's Luck* (1966), *Willie Masters' Lonesome Wife* (1971), *The Tunnel* (1995), and the story collection *In the Heart of the Heart of the Country* (1968). His nonfiction works include *Fiction and the Figures of Life* (1970), *On Being Blue: A Philosophical Inquiry* (1975), *The Habitations of the Word: Essays* (1984), and *Finding a Form: Essays* (1996).

# In the Heart of the Heart of the Country

### A Place

O I have sailed the seas and come . . .
to B . . .

a small town fastened to a field in Indiana. Twice there have been twelve hundred people here to answer to the census. The town is outstandingly neat and shady, and always puts its best side to the highway. On one lawn there's even a wood or plastic iron deer.

You can reach us by crossing a creek. In the spring the lawns are green, the forsythia is singing, and even the railroad that guts the town has straight bright rails which hum when the train is coming, and the train itself has a welcome horning sound.

Down the back streets the asphalt crumbles into gravel. There's Westbrook's, with the geraniums, Horsefall's, Mott's. The sidewalk shatters. Gravel dust rises like breath behind the wagons. And I am in retirement from love.

## Weather

In the Midwest, around the lower Lakes, the sky in the winter is heavy and close, and it is a rare day, a day to remark on, when the sky lifts and allows the heart up. I am keeping count, and as I write this page, it is eleven days since I have seen the sun.

## My House

There's a row of headless maples behind my house, cut to free the passage of electric wires. High stumps, ten feet tall, remain, and I climb these like a boy to watch the country sail away from me. They are ordinary fields, a little more uneven than they should be, since in the spring they puddle. The topsoil's thin, but only moderately stony. Corn is grown one year, soybeans another. At dusk starlings darken the single tree—a larch—which stands in the middle. When the sky moves, fields move under it. I feel, on my perch, that I've lost my years. It's as though I were living at last in my eyes, as I have always dreamed of doing, and I think then I know why I've come here: to see, and so to go out against new things—oh god how easily—like air in a breeze. It's true there are moments—foolish moments, ecstasy on a tree stump—when I'm all but gone, scattered I like to think like seed, for I'm the sort now in the fool's position of having love left over which I'd like to lose; what good is it now to me, candy ungiven after Halloween?

## A Person

There are vacant lots on either side of Billy Holsclaw's house. As the weather improves, they fill with hollyhocks. From spring through fall, Billy collects coal and wood and puts the lumps and pieces in piles near his door, for keeping warm is his one work. I see him most often on mild days sitting on his doorsill in the sun. I notice he's squinting a little, which is perhaps the reason he doesn't cackle as I pass. His house is the size of a single garage, and very old. It shed its paint with its youth, and its boards are a warped and weathered gray. So is Billy. He wears a short lumpy faded black coat when it's cold, otherwise he always goes about in the same loose, grease-spotted shirt and trousers. I suspect his galluses were yellow once, when they were new.

## Wires

These wires offend me. Three trees were maimed on their account, and now these wires deface the sky. They cross like a fence in front of me, enclosing the crows with the clouds. I can't reach in, but like a stick, I throw my feelings over. What is it that offends me? I am on my stump, I've built a platform there and the wires prevent my going out.

The cut trees, the black wires, all the beyond birds therefore anger me. When I've wormed through a fence to reach a meadow, do I ever feel the same about the field?

## The Church

The church has a steeple like the hat of a witch, and five birds, all doves, perch in its gutters.

## My House

Leaves move in the windows. I cannot tell you yet how beautiful it is, what it means. But they do move. They move in the glass.

## Politics

. . . for all those not in love.

I've heard Batista described as a Mason. A farmer who'd seen him in Miami made this claim. He's as nice a fellow as you'd ever want to meet. Of Castro, of course, no one speaks.

For all those not in love there's law: to rule . . . to regulate . . . to rectify. I cannot write the poetry of such proposals, the poetry of politics, though sometimes—often—always now—I am in that uneasy peace of equal powers which makes a State; then I communicate by passing papers, proclamations, orders, through my bowels. Yet I was not a State with you, nor were we both together any Indiana. A squad of Pershing Rifles at the moment, I make myself Right Face! Legislation packs the screw of my intestines. Well, king of the classroom's king of the hill. You used to waddle when you walked because my sperm between your legs was draining to a towel. Teacher, poet, folded lover—like the politician, like those drunkards, ill, or those who faucet-off while pissing heartily to preach upon the force and fullness of that stream, or pause from vomiting to praise the purity and passion of their puke—I chant, I beg, I orate, I command, I sing—

Come back to Indiana—not too late!
        (Or will you be a ranger to the end?)
Good-bye . . . Good-bye . . . oh, I shall always wait
        You, Larry, traveler—
                                stranger,
                                        son,
                                            —my friend—

my little girl, my poem by heart, my self, my childhood.

But I've heard Batista described as a Mason. That dries up my pity, melts my hate. Back from the garage where I have overheard it, I slap the mended fender of my car to laugh, and listen to the metal stinging tartly in my hand.

## People

Their hair in curlers and their heads wrapped in loud scarves, young mothers, fattish in trousers, lounge about in the speedwash, smoking cigarettes, eating candy, drinking pop, thumbing magazines, and screaming at their children above the whir and rumble of the machines.

At the bank a young man freshly pressed is letting himself in with a key. Along the street, delicately teetering, many grandfathers move in a dream. During the murderous heat of summer, they perch on window ledges, their feet dangling just inside the narrow shelf of shade the store has made, staring steadily into the street. Where their consciousness has gone I can't say. It's not in the eyes. Perhaps it's diffuse, all temperature and skin, like an infant's though more mild. Near the corner there are several large overalled men employed in standing. A truck turns to be weighed on the scales at the Feed and Grain. Images drift on the drugstore window. The wind has blown the smell of cattle into town. Our eyes have been driven in like the eyes of the old men. And there's no one to have mercy on us.

## Vital Data

There are two restaurants here and a tearoom. two bars. one bank, three barbers, one with a green shade with which he blinds his window. two groceries. a dealer in Fords. one drug, one hardware, and one appliance store. several that sell feed, grain, and farm equipment. an antique shop. a pool-room. a laundromat. three doctors. a dentist. a plumber. a vet. a funeral home in elegant repair the color of a buttercup. numerous beauty parlors which open and shut like night-blooming plants. a tiny dime and department store of no width but several floors. a hutch, homemade, where you can order, after lying down or squirming in, furniture that's been fashioned from bent lengths of stainless tubing, glowing plastic, metallic thread, and clear shellac. an American Legion Post and a root beer stand. little agencies for this and that: cosmetics, brushes, insurance, greeting cards and garden produce—anything—sample shoes—which do their business out of hats and satchels, over coffee cups and dissolving sugar. a factory for making paper sacks and pasteboard boxes that's lodged in an old brick building bearing the legend OPERA HOUSE, still faintly golden, on its roof. a library given by Carnegie. a post office. a school. a railroad station. fire station. lumberyard. telephone company. welding shop. garage . . . and spotted through the town from one end to the other in a line along the highway, gas stations to the number five.

## Education

In 1833, Colin Goodykoontz, an itinerant preacher with a name from a fairytale, summed up the situation in one Indiana town this way:

> Ignorance and her squalid brood. A universal dearth of intellect. Total abstinence from literature is very generally practiced. . . . There is not a scholar in grammar or geography, or a *teacher capable* of *instructing* in them, to my knowledge. . . . Others are sup-

> plied a few months of the year with the most antiquated & unreasonable forms of teaching reading, writing & cyphering. . . . Need I stop to remind you of the host of loathsome reptiles such a stagnant pool is fitted to breed! Croaking jealousy; bloated bigotry; coiling suspicion; wormish blindness; crocodile malice!

Things have changed since then, but in none of the respects mentioned.

## Business

One side section of street is blocked off with sawhorses. Hard, thin, bitter men in blue jeans, cowboy boots and hats, untruck a dinky carnival. The merchants are promoting themselves. There will be free rides, raucous music, parades and coneys, pop, popcorn, candy, cones, awards and drawings, with all you can endure of pinch, push, bawl, shove, shout, scream, shriek, and bellow. Children pedal past on decorated bicycles, their wheels a blur of color, streaming crinkled paper and excited dogs. A little later there's a pet show for a prize—dogs, cats, birds, sheep, ponies, goats—none of which wins. The whirlabouts whirl about. The Ferris wheel climbs dizzily into the sky as far as a tall man on tiptoe might be persuaded to reach, and the irritated operators measure the height and width of every child with sour eyes to see if they are safe for the machines. An electrical megaphone repeatedly trumpets the names of the generous sponsors. The following day they do not allow the refuse to remain long in the street.

## My House, This Place and Body

I have met with some mischance, wings withering, as Plato says obscurely, and across the breadth of Ohio, like heaven on a table, I've fallen as far as the poet, to the sixth sort of body, this house in B, in Indiana, with its blue and gray bewitching windows, holy magical insides. Great thick evergreens protect its entry. And I live *in.*

Lost in the corn rows, I remember feeling just another stalk, and thus this country takes me over in the way I occupy myself when I am well . . . completely—to the edge of both my house and body. No one notices, when they walk by, that I am brimming in the doorways. My house, this place and body, I've come in mourning to be born in. To anybody else it's pretty silly: love. Why should I feel a loss? How am I bereft? She was never mine; she was a fiction, always a golden tomgirl, barefoot, with an adolescent's slouch and a boy's taste for sports and fishing, a figure out of Twain, or worse, in Riley. Age cannot be kind.

There's little hand-in-hand here . . . not in B. No one touches except in rage. Occasionally girls will twine their arms about each other and lurch along, school out, toward home and play. I dreamed my lips would drift down your back, like a skiff on a river. I'd follow a vein with the point of my finger, hold your bare feet in my naked hands.

## The Same Person

Billy Holsclaw lives alone—how alone it is impossible to fathom. In the post office he talks greedily to me about the weather. His head bobs on a wild flood of words, and I take this violence to be a measure of his eagerness for speech. He badly needs a shave, coal dust has layered his face, he spits when he speaks, and his fingers pick at his tatters. He wobbles out in the wind when I leave him, a paper sack mashed in the fold of his arm, the leaves blowing past him, and our encounter drives me sadly home to poetry—where there's no answer. Billy closes his door and carries coal or wood to his fire and closes his eyes, and there's simply no way of knowing how lonely and empty he is or whether he's as vacant and barren and loveless as the rest of us are—here in the heart of the country.

## Weather

For we're always out of luck here. That's just how it is—for instance in the winter. The sides of the buildings, the roofs, the limbs of the trees are gray. Streets, sidewalks, faces, feelings—they are gray. Speech is gray, and the grass when it shows. Every flank and front, each top is gray. Everything is gray: hair, eyes, window glass, the hawkers' bills and touters' posters, lips, teeth, poles and metal signs—they're gray, quite gray. Horses, sheep, and cows, cats killed in the road, squirrels in the same way, sparrows, doves, and pigeons, all are gray, everything is gray, and everyone is out of luck who lives here.

A similar haze turns the summer sky milky, and the air muffles your head and shoulders like a sweater you've got caught in. In the summer light, too, the sky darkens a moment when you open your eyes. The heat is pure distraction. Steeped in our fluids, miserable in the folds of our bodies, we can scarcely think of anything but our sticky parts. Hot cyclonic winds and storms of dust crisscross the country. In many places, given an indifferent push, the wind will still coast for miles, gathering resource and edge as it goes, cunning and force. According to the season, paper, leaves, field litter, seeds, snow, fill up the fences. Sometimes I think the land is flat because the winds have leveled it, they blow so constantly. In any case, a gale can grow in a field of corn that's as hot as a draft from hell, and to receive it is one of the most dismaying experiences of this life, though the smart of the same wind in winter is more humiliating, and in that sense even worse. But in the spring it rains as well, and the trees fill with ice.

## Place

Many small Midwestern towns are nothing more than rural slums, and this community could easily become one. Principally during the first decade of the century, though there were many earlier instances, well-to-do farmers moved to town and built fine homes to contain them in their retirement. Others desired a more social life, and so lived in, driving to their fields like storekeepers to their businesses. These houses are now dying like the bereaved who inhabit them; they are slowly losing their senses—deafness, blindness, forgetfulness, mumbling, an insecure gait, an uncontrollable trembling has overcome them. Some kind of Northern Snopes will occupy them next: large-familied, Catholic, Democratic, scrambling, vigorous, poor; and since the parents will work in larger, nearby towns, the children will be loosed upon themselves and upon the hapless neighbors much as the fabulous Khan loosed his legendary horde. These Snopes will undertake makeshift repairs with materials that other people have thrown away; paint halfway round their house, then quit; almost certainly maintain an ugly loud cantankerous dog and underfeed a pair of cats to keep the rodents down. They will collect piles of possibly useful junk in the back yard, park their cars in the front, live largely leaning over engines, give not a hoot for the land, the old community, the hallowed ways, the established clans. Weakening widow ladies have already begun to hire large rude youths from families such as these to rake and mow and tidy the grounds they will inherit.

## People

In the cinders at the station boys sit smoking steadily in darkened cars, their arms bent out the windows, white shirts glowing behind the glass. Nine o'clock is the best time. They sit in a line facing the highway—two or three or four of them—idling their engines. As you walk by a machine may growl at you or a pair of headlights flare up briefly. In a moment one will pull out, spinning cinders behind it, to stalk impatiently up and down the dark streets or roar half a mile into the country before returning to its place in line and pulling up.

## My House, My Cat, My Company

I must organize myself. I must, as they say, pull myself together, dump this cat from my lap, stir—yes, resolve, move, do. But do what? My will is like the rosy dustlike light in this room: soft, diffuse, and gently comforting. It lets me do . . . anything . . . nothing. My ears hear what they happen to; I eat what's put before me; my eyes see what blunders into them; my thoughts are not thoughts, they are dreams. I'm empty or I'm full . . . depending; and I cannot choose. I sink my claws in Tick's fur and scratch the bones of his back until his rear rises amorously. Mr. Tick, I murmur, I must organize myself. I must pull myself together. And Mr. Tick rolls over on his belly, all ooze.

I spill Mr. Tick when I've rubbed his stomach. Shoo. He steps away slowly, his long tail rhyming with his paws. How beautifully he moves, I think; how beautifully, like you, he commands his loving, how beautifully he accepts. So I rise and wander from room to room, up and down, gazing through most of my forty-one windows. How well this house receives its loving too. Let out like Mr. Tick, my eyes sink in the shrubbery. I am not here; I've passed the glass, passed second-story spaces, flown by branches, brilliant berries, to the ground, grass high in seed and leafage every season; and it is the same as when I passed above you in my aged, ardent body; it's, in short, a kind of love; and I am learning to restore myself, my house, my body, by paying court to gardens, cats, and running water, and with neighbors keeping company.

Mrs. Desmond is my right-hand friend; she's eighty-five. A thin white mist of hair, fine and tangled, manifests the climate of her mind. She is habitually suspicious, fretful, nervous. Burglars break in at noon. Children trespass. Even now they are shaking the pear tree, stealing rhubarb, denting lawn. Flies caught in the screens and numbed by frost awake in the heat to buzz and scrape the metal cloth and frighten her, though she is deaf to me, and consequently cannot hear them. Boards creak, the wind whistles across the chimney mouth, drafts cruise like fish through the hollow rooms. It is herself she hears, her own flesh failing, for only death will preserve her from those daily chores she climbs like stairs, and all that anxious waiting. Is it now, she wonders. No? Then: is it now?

We do not converse. She visits me to talk. My task to murmur. She talks about her grandsons, her daughter who lives in Delphi, her sister or her husband—both gone—

obscure friends—dead—obscurer aunts and uncles—lost—ancient neighbors, members of her church or of her clubs—passed or passing on; and in this way she brings the ends of her life together with a terrifying rush: she is a girl, a wife, a mother, widow, all at once. All at once—appalling—but I believe it; I wince in expectation of the clap. Her talk's a fence—a shade drawn, window fastened, door that's locked—for no one dies taking tea in a kitchen; and as her years compress and begin to jumble, I really believe in the brevity of life; I sweat in my wonder; death is the dog down the street, the angry gander, bedroom spider, goblin who's come to get her; and it occurs to me that in my listening posture I'm the boy who suffered the winds of my grandfather with an exactly similar politeness, that I am, right now, all my ages, out in elbows, as angular as badly stacked cards. Thus was I, when I loved you, every man I could be, youth and child—far from enough—and you, so strangely ambiguous a being, met me, heart for spade, play after play, the whole run of our suits.

Mr. Tick, you do me honor. You not only lie in my lap, but you remain alive there, coiled like a fetus. Through your deep nap, I feel you hum. You are, and are not, a machine. You are alive, alive exactly, and it means nothing to you—much to me. You are a cat—you cannot understand—you are a cat so easily. Your nature is not something you must rise to. You, not I, live in: in house, in skin, in shrubbery. Yes. I think I shall hat my head with a steeple; turn church; devour people. Mr. Tick, though, has a tail he can twitch, he need not fly his Fancy. Claws, not metrical schema, poetry his paws; while smoothing . . . smoothing . . . smoothing roughly, his tongue laps its neatness. O Mr. Tick, I know you; you are an electrical penis. Go on now, shoo. Mrs. Desmond doesn't like you. She thinks you will tangle yourself in her legs and she will fall. You murder her birds, she knows, and walk upon her roof with death in your jaws. I must gather myself together for a bound. What age is it I'm at right now, I wonder. The heart, don't they always say, keeps the true time. Mrs. Desmond is knocking. Faintly, you'd think, but she pounds. She's brought me a cucumber. I believe she believes I'm a woman. Come in, Mrs. Desmond, thank you, be my company, it looks lovely, and have tea. I'll slice it, crisp, with cream, for luncheon, each slice as thin as me.

## Politics

O all ye isolate and separate powers, Sing! Sing, and sing in such a way that from a distance it will seem a harmony, a Strindberg play, a friendship ring . . . so happy—happy, happy, happy—as here we go hand in handling, up and down. Our union was a singing, though we were silent in the songs we sang like single notes are silent in a symphony. In no sense sober, we barbershopped together and never heard the discords in our music or saw ourselves as dirty, cheap, or silly. Yet cats have worn out better shoes than those thrown through our love songs at us. Hush. Be patient—prudent—politic. Still, Cleveland killed you, Mr. Crane. Were you not politic enough and fond of being beaten? Like a piece of sewage, the city shat you from its stern three hundred miles from history—beyond the loving reach of sailors. Well, I'm not a poet who puts Paris to his temple in his youth to blow himself from Idaho, or—fancy that—Missouri. My god, I said, this is my country, but must my country go so far as Terre Haute or Whiting, go so far as Gary?

When the Russians first announced the launching of their satellite, many people naturally refused to believe them. Later others were outraged that they had sent a dog around the earth. I wouldn't want to take that mutt from out that metal flying thing if he's still living when he lands, our own dog catcher said; anybody knows you shut a dog up by himself to toss around the first thing he'll be setting on to do you let him out is bite somebody.

This Midwest. A dissonance of parts and people, we are a consonance of Towns. Like a man grown fat in everything but heart, we overlabor; our outlook never really urban, never rural either, we enlarge and linger at the same time, as Alice both changed and remained in her story. You are blond. I put my hand upon your belly; feel it tremble from my trembling. We always drive large cars in my section of the country. How could you be a comfort to me now?

## More Vital Data

The town is exactly fifty houses, trailer, stores, and miscellaneous buildings long, but in places no streets deep. It takes on width as you drive south, always adding to the east. Most of the dwellings are fairly spacious farm houses in the customary white, with wide wraparound porches and tall narrow windows, though there are many of the grander kind—fretted, scalloped, turreted, and decorated with clapboards set at angles or on end, with stained-glass windows at the stair landings and lots of wrought iron full of fancy curls—and a few of these look like castles in their rarer brick. Old stables serve as garages now, and the lots are large to contain them and the vegetable and flower gardens which, ultimately, widows plant and weed and then entirely disappear in. The shade is ample, the grass is good, the sky a glorious fall violet; the apple trees are heavy and red, the roads are calm and empty; corn has sifted from the chains of tractored wagons to speckle the streets with gold and with the russet fragments of the cob, and a man would be a fool who wanted, blessed with this, to live anywhere else in the world.

## Education

Buses like great orange animals move through the early light to school. There the children will be taught to read and warned against Communism. By Miss Janet Jakes. That's not her name. Her name is Helen something—Scott or James. A teacher twenty years. She's now worn fine and smooth, and has a face, Wilfred says, like a mail-order ax. Her voice is hoarse, and she has a cough. For she screams abuse. The children stare, their faces blank. This is the thirteenth week. They are used to it. You will all, she shouts, you will all draw pictures of me. No. She is a Mrs.—someone's missus. And in silence they set to work while Miss Jakes jabs hairpins in her hair. Wilfred says an ax, but she has those rimless tinted glasses, graying hair, an almost dimpled chin. I must concentrate. I must stop making up things. I must give myself to life; let it mold me: that's what they say in *Wisdom's Monthly Digest* every day. Enough, enough—you've been at it long enough; and the children rise formally a row at a time to present their work to her desk. No, she wears rims; it's her chin that's dimpleless. Well, it will take more than a tablespoon of features to sweeten that face. So she grimly shuffles their sheets, examines her reflection crayoned on them. I would not dare . . . allow a child . . . to put a line around me. Though now and then she smiles like a nick in the blade, in the end these drawings depress her. I could not bear it—how can she ask?—that anyone . . . draw me. Her anger's lit. That's why she does it: flame. There go her eyes; the pink in her glasses brightens, dims. She is a pumpkin, and her rage is breathing like the candle in. No, she shouts, no—the cartoon trembling—no, John Mauck, John Stewart Mauck, this will not do. The picture flutters from her fingers. You've made me too muscular.

I work on my poetry. I remember my friends, associates, my students, by their names. Their names are Maypop, Dormouse, Upsydaisy. Their names are Gladiolus, Callow Bladder, Prince and Princess Oleo, Hieronymus, Cardinal Mummum, Mr. Fitchew, The Silken Howdah, Spot. Sometimes you're Tom Sawyer, Huckleberry Finn; it is perpetually summer; your buttocks are my pillow; we are adrift on a raft; your back is our river. Sometimes you are Major Barbara, sometimes a goddess who kills men in battle, sometimes you are soft like a shower of water; you are bread in my mouth.

I do not work on my poetry. I forget my friends, associates, my students, and their names: Gramophone, Blowgun, Pickle, Serenade . . . Marge the Barge, Arena, Uberhaupt . . . Doctor Dildoe, The Fog Machine. For I am now in B, in Indiana: out of job and out of patience, out of love and time and money, out of bread and out of body, in a temper, Mrs. Desmond, out of tea. So shut your fist up, bitch, you bag of death; go bang another door; go die, my dearie. Die, life-deaf old lady. Spill your breath. Fall over like a frozen board. Gray hair grown from the nose of your mind. You are a skull already—*memento mori*—the foreskin retracts from your teeth. Will your plastic gums last longer than your bones, and color their grinning? And is your twot still hazel-hairy, or are you bald as a ditch? . . . bitch. . . . . . bitch . . . . . . . . . bitch. I wanted to be famous, but you bring me age—my emptiness. Was it *that* which I thought would balloon me above the rest? Love? where are you? . . . love me. I want to rise so high, I said, that when I shit I won't miss anybody.

## Business

For most people, business is poor. Nearby cities have siphoned off all but a neighborhood trade. Except for feed and grain and farm supplies, you stand a chance to sell only what one runs out to buy. Chevrolet has quit, and Frigidaire. A locker plant has left its afterimage. The lumberyard has been, so far, six months about its going. Gas stations change hands clumsily, a restaurant becomes available, a grocery closes. One day they came and knocked the cornices from the watch repair and pasted campaign posters on the windows. Torn across, by now, by boys, they urge you still to vote for half an orange beblazoned man who as a whole one failed two years ago to win at his election. Everywhere, in this manner, the past speaks, and it mostly speaks of failure. The empty stores, the old signs and dusty fixtures, the debris in alleys, the flaking paint and rusty gutters, the heavy locks and sagging boards: they say the same disagreeable things. What do the sightless windows see, I wonder, when the sun throws a passerby against them? Here a stair unfolds toward the street—dark, rickety, and treacherous—and I always feel, as I pass it, that if I just went carefully up and turned the corner at the landing, I would find myself out of the world. But I've never had the courage.

## That Same Person

The weeds catch up with Billy. In pursuit of the hollyhocks, they rise in coarse clumps all around the front of his house. Billy has to stamp down a circle by his door like a dog or cat does turning round to nest up, they're so thick. What particularly troubles me is that winter will find the weeds still standing stiff and tindery to take the sparks which Billy's little mortarless chimney spouts. It's true that fires are fun here. The town whistle, which otherwise only blows for noon (and there's no noon on Sunday), signals the direction of the fire by the length and number of its blasts, the volunteer firemen rush past in their cars and trucks, houses empty their owners along the street every time like an illustration in a children's book. There are many bikes, too, and barking dogs, and sometimes—halleluiah—the fire's right here in town—a vacant lot of weeds and stubble flaming up. But I'd rather it weren't Billy or Billy's lot or house. Quite selfishly I want him to remain the way he is—counting his sticks and logs, sitting on his sill in the soft early sun—though I'm not sure what his presence means to me . . . or to anyone. Nevertheless, I keep wondering whether, given time, I might not someday find a figure in our language which would serve him faithfully, and furnish his poverty and loneliness richly out.

## Wires

Where sparrows sit like fists. Doves fly the steeple. In mist the wires change perspective, rise and twist. If they led to you, I would know what they were. Thoughts passing often, like the starlings who flock these fields at evening to sleep in the trees beyond, would form a family of paths like this; they'd foot down the natural height of air to just about a bird's perch. But they do not lead to you.

> Of whose beauty it was sung
> She shall make the old man young.

They fasten me.

If I walked straight on, in my present mood, I would reach the Wabash. It's not a mood in which I'd choose to conjure you. Similes dangle like baubles from me. This time of year the river is slow and shallow, the clay banks crack in the sun, weeds surprise the sandbars. The air is moist and I am sweating. It's impossible to rhyme in this dust. Everything—sky, the cornfield, stump, wild daisies, my old clothes and pressless feelings—seem fabricated for installment purchase. Yes. Christ. I am suffering a summer Christmas; and I cannot walk under the wires. The sparrows scatter like handfuls of gravel. Really, wires are voices in thin strips. They are words wound in cables. Bars of connection.

## Weather

I would rather it were the weather that was to blame for what I am and what my friends and neighbors are—we who live here in the heart of the country. Better the weather, the wind, the pale dying snow . . . the snow—why not the snow? There's never much really, not around the lower Lakes anyway, not enough to boast about, not enough to be useful. My father tells how the snow in the Dakotas would sweep to the roofs of the barns in the old days, and he and his friends could sled on the crust that would form because the snow was so fiercely driven. In Bemidji trees have been known to explode.

That would be something—if the trees in Davenport or Francisville or Carbondale or Niles were to go blam some winter—blam! blam! blam! all the way down the gray, cindery, snow-sick streets.

A cold fall rain is blackening the trees or the air is like lilac and full of parachuting seeds. Who cares to live in any season but his own? Still I suspect the secret's in this snow, the secret of our sickness, if we could only diagnose it, for we are all dying like the elms in Urbana. This snow—like our skin it covers the country. Later dust will do it. Right now—snow. Mud presently. But it is snow without any laughter in it, a pale gray pudding thinly spread on stiff toast, and if that seems a strange description, it's accurate all the same. Of course soot blackens everything, but apart from that, we are never sufficiently cold here. The flakes as they come, alive and burning, we cannot retain, for if our temperatures fall, they rise promptly again, just as, in the summer, they bob about in the same feckless way. Suppose though . . . suppose they were to rise some August, climb and rise, and then hang in the hundreds like a hawk through December, what a desert we could make of ourselves—from Chicago to Cairo, from Hammond to Columbus—what beautiful Death Valleys.

## Place

I would rather it were the weather. It drives us in upon ourselves—an unlucky fate. Of course there is enough to stir our wonder anywhere; there's enough to love, anywhere, if one is strong enough, if one is diligent enough, if one is perceptive, patient, kind enough—whatever it takes; and surely it's better to live in the country, to live on a prairie by a drawing of rivers, in Iowa or Illinois or Indiana, say, than in any city, in any stinking fog of human beings, in any blooming orchard of machines. It ought to be. The cities are swollen and poisonous with people. It ought to be better. Man has never been a fit environment for man—for rats, maybe, rats do nicely, or for dogs or cats and the household beetle.

And how long the street is, nowadays. These endless walls are fallen to keep back the tides of earth. Brick could be beautiful but we have covered it gradually with gray industrial vomits. Age does not make concrete genial, and asphalt is always—like America—twenty-one, until it breaks up in crumbs like stale cake. The brick, the asphalt, the concrete, the dancing signs and garish posters, the feed and excrement of the automobile, the litter of its inhabitants: they compose, they decorate, they line our streets, and there is nowhere, nowadays, our streets can't reach.

A man in the city has no natural thing by which to measure himself. His parks are potted plants. Nothing can live and remain free where he resides but the pigeon, starling, sparrow, spider, cockroach, mouse, moth, fly and weed, and he laments the existence of even these and makes his plans to poison them. The zoo? There *is* the zoo. Through its bars the city man stares at the great cats and dully sucks his ice. Living, alas, among men and their marvels, the city man supposes that his happiness depends on establishing, somehow, a special kind of harmonious accord with others. The novelists of the city, of slums and crowds, they call it love—and break their pens.

Wordsworth feared the accumulation of men in cities. He foresaw their "degrading thirst after outrageous stimulation," and some of their hunger for love. Living in a city, among so many, dwelling in the heat and tumult of incessant movement, a man's affairs are touch and go—that's all. It's not surprising that the novelists of the slums, the cities, and the crowds, should find that sex is but a scratch to ease a tickle, that we're most human when we're sitting on the john, and that the justest image of our life is in full passage through the plumbing.

> That man, immur'd in cities, still retains
> His inborn inextinguishable thirst
> Of rural scenes, compensating his loss
> By supplemental shifts, the best he may.

Come into the country, then. The air nimbly and sweetly recommends itself unto our gentle senses. Here, growling tractors tear the earth. Dust roils up behind them. Drivers sit jouncing under bright umbrellas. They wear refrigerated hats and steer by looking at the tracks they've cut behind them, their transistors blaring. Close to the land, are they? good companions to the soil? Tell me: do they live in harmony with the alternating seasons?

It's a lie of old poetry. The modern husbandman uses chemicals from cylinders and sacks, spike-ball-and-claw machines, metal sheds, and cost accounting. Nature in the old sense does not matter. It does not exist. Our farmer's only mystical attachment is to parity. And if he does not realize that cows and corn are simply different kinds of chemical engine, he cannot expect to make a go of it.

It isn't necessary to suppose our cows have feelings; our neighbor hasn't as many as he used to have either; but think of it this way a moment, you can correct for the human imputations later: how would it feel to nurse those strange tentacled calves with their rubber, glass, and metal lips, their stainless eyes?

### People

Aunt Pet's still able to drive her car—a high square Ford—even though she walks with difficulty and a stout stick. She has a watery gaze, a smooth plump face despite her age, and jet black hair in a bun. She has the slowest smile of anyone I ever saw, but she hates dogs, and not very long ago cracked the back of one she cornered in her garden. To prove her vigor she will tell you this, her smile breaking gently while she raises the knob of her stick to the level of your eyes.

### House, My Breath and Window

My window is a grave, and all that lies within it's dead. No snow is falling. There's no haze. It is not still, not silent. Its images are not an animal that waits, for movement is no demonstration. I have seen the sea slack, life bubble through a body without a trace, its spheres impervious as soda's. Downwound, the whore at wagtag clicks and clacks. Leaves wiggle. Grass sways. A bird chirps, pecks the ground. An auto wheel in penning circles keeps its rigid spokes. These images are stones; they are memorials. Beneath this sea lies sea: god rest it . . . rest the world beyond my window, me in front of my reflection, above this page, my shade. Death is not so still, so silent, since silence implies a falling quiet, stillness a stopping, containing, holding in; for death is time in a clock, like

Mr. Tick, electric . . . like wind through a windup poet. And my blear floats out to visible against the glass, befog its country and bespill myself. The mist lifts slowly from the fields in the morning. No one now would say: the Earth throws back its covers; it is rising from sleep. Why is the feeling foolish? The image is too Greek. I used to gaze at you so wantonly your body blushed. Imagine: wonder: that my eyes could cause such flowering. Ah, my friend, your face is pale, the weather cloudy; a street has been felled through your chin, bare trees do nothing, houses take root in their rectangles, a steeple stands up in your head. You speak of loving; then give me a kiss. The pane is cold. On icy mornings the fog rises to greet me (as you always did); the barns and other buildings, rather than ghostly, seem all the more substantial for looming, as if they grew in themselves while I watched (as you always did). Oh my approach, I suppose, was like breath in a rubber monkey. Nevertheless, on the road along the Wabash in the morning, though the trees are sometimes obscured by fog, their reflection floats serenely on the river, reasoning the banks, the sycamores in French rows. Magically, the world tips. I'm led to think that only those who grow down live (which will scarcely win me twenty-five from *Wisdom's Monthly Digest*), but I find I write that only those who live down grow; and what I write, I hold, whatever I really know. My every word's inverted, or reversed—or I am. I held you, too, that way. You were so utterly provisional, subject to my change. I could inflate your bosom with a kiss, disperse your skin with gentleness, enter your vagina from within, and make my love emerge like a fresh sex. The pane is cold. Honesty is cold, my inside lover. The sun looks, through the mist, like a plum on the tree of heaven, or a bruise on the slope of your belly. Which? The grass crawls with frost. We meet on this window, the world and I, inelegantly, swimmers of the glass; and swung wrong way round to one another, the world seems in. The world—how grand, how monumental, grave and deadly, that word is: the world, my house and poetry. All poets have their inside lovers. Wee penis does not belong to me, or any of this foggery. It is *his* property which he's thrust through what's womanly of me to set down this. These wooden houses in their squares, gray streets and fallen sidewalks, standing trees, your name I've written sentimentally across my breath into the whitening air, pale birds: they exist in me now because of him. I gazed with what intensity . . . A bush in the excitement of its roses could not have bloomed so beautifully as you did then. It was a look I'd like to give this page. For that is poetry: to bring within about, to change.

## Politics

Sports, politics, and religion are the three passions of the badly educated. They are the Midwest's open sores. Ugly to see, a source of constant discontent, they sap the body's strength. Appalling quantities of money, time, and energy are wasted on them. The rural mind is narrow, passionate, and reckless on these matters. Greed, however shortsighted and direct, will not alone account for it. I have known men, for instance, who for years have voted squarely against their interests. Nor have I ever noticed that their surly Christian views prevented them from urging forward the smithereening, say, of Russia, China, Cuba, or Korea. And they tend to back their country like they back their local team: they have a fanatical desire to win; yelling is their forte; and if things go badly, they are inclined to sack the coach. All in all, then, Birch is a good name. It stands for the bigot's stick, the wild-child-tamer's cane.

Forgetfulness—is that their object?

Oh, I was new, I thought. A fresh start: new cunt, new climate, and new country—there you were, and I was pioneer, and had no history. That language hurts me, too, my dear. You'll never hear it.

## Final Vital Data

The Modern Homemaker's Demonstration Club. The Prairie Home Demonstration Club. The Night-outers' Home Demonstration Club. The IOOF, FFF, VFW, WCTU, WSCS, 4-H, 40 and 8, Psi Iota Chi, and PTA. The Boy and Girl Scouts, Rainbows, Masons, Indians and Rebekah Lodge. Also the Past Noble Grand Club of the Rebekah Lodge. As well as the Moose and the Ladies of the Moose. The Elks, the Eagles, the Jaynettes and the Eastern Star. The Women's Literary Club, the Hobby Club, the Art Club, the Sunshine Society, the Dorcas Society, the Pythian Sisters, the Pilgrim Youth Fellowship, the American Legion, the American Legion Auxiliary, the American Legion Junior Auxiliary, the Garden Club, the Bridge for Fun Club, the What-can-you-do? Club, the Get Together Club, the Coterie Club, the Worthwhile Club, the Let's Help Our Town Club, the No Name Club, the Forget-me-not Club, the Merry-go-round Club . . .

## Education

Had a quarter disappeared from Paula Frosty's pocket book? Imagine the landscape of that face: no crayon could engender it; soft wax is wrong; thin wire in trifling snips might do the trick. Paula Frosty and Christopher Roger accuse the pale and splotchy Cheryl Pipes. But Miss Jakes, I *saw* her. Miss Jakes is so extremely vexed she snaps her pencil. What else is missing? I appoint you a detective, John: search her desk. Gum, candy, paper, pencils, marble, round eraser—whose? A thief. I can't watch her all the time, I'm here to teach. Poor pale fossetted Cheryl, it's determined, can't return the money because she took it home and spent it. Cindy, Janice, John, and Pete—you four who sit around her—you will be detectives this whole term to watch her. A thief. In all my time. Miss Jakes turns, unfists, and turns again. I'll handle you, she cries. To think. A thief. In all my years. Then she writes on the blackboard the name of Cheryl Pipes and beneath that the figure twenty-five with a large sign for cents. Now Cheryl, she says, this won't be taken off until you bring that money out of home, out of home straight up to here, Miss Jakes says, tapping her desk.

Which is three days.

## Another Person

I was raking leaves when Uncle Halley introduced himself to me. He said his name came from the comet, and that his mother had borne him prematurely in her fright of it. I thought of Hobbes, whom fear of the Spanish Armada had hurried into birth, and so I believed Uncle Halley to honor the philosopher, though Uncle Halley is a liar, and neither the one hundred twenty-nine nor the fifty-three he ought to be. That fall the leaves had burned themselves out on the trees, the leaf lobes had curled, and now they flocked noisily down the street and were broken in the wires of my rake. Uncle Halley was himself (like Mrs. Desmond and history generally) both deaf and implacable, and he shooed me down his basement stairs to a room set aside there for stacks of newspapers reaching to the ceiling, boxes of leaflets and letters and programs, racks of photo albums, scrapbooks, bundles of rolled-up posters and maps, flags and pennants and slanting piles of dusty magazines devoted mostly to motoring and the Christian ethic. I saw a bird cage, a tray of butterflies, a bugle, a stiff straw boater, and all kinds of tassels tied to a coat tree. He still possessed and had on display the steering lever from his first car, a linen duster, driving gloves and goggles, photographs along the wall of himself, his friend, and his various machines, a shell from the first war, a record of "Ramona" nailed through its hole to a post, walking sticks and fanciful umbrellas, shoes of all sorts (his baby shoes, their counters broken, were held in sorrow beneath my nose—they had not been bronzed, but he might have them done someday before he died, he said), countless boxes of medals, pins, beads, trinkets, toys, and keys (I scarcely saw—they flowed like jewels from his palms), pictures of downtown when it was only a path by the rail-road station, a brightly colored globe of the world with a dent in Poland, antique guns, belt buckles, buttons, souvenir plates and cups and saucers (I can't remember all of it—I won't), but I recall how shamefully, how rudely, how abruptly, I fled, a good story in my mouth but death in my nostrils; and how afterward I busily, righteously, burned my leaves as if I were purging the world of its years. I still wonder if this town—its life, and mine now—isn't really a record like the one of "Ramona" that I used to crank around on my grandmother's mahogany Victrola through lonely rainy days as a kid.

## The First Person

Billy's like the coal he's found: spilled, mislaid, discarded. The sky's no comfort. His house and his body are dying together. His windows are boarded. And now he's reduced to his hands. I suspect he has glaucoma. At any rate he can scarcely see, and weeds his yard of rubble on his hands and knees. Perhaps he's a surgeon cleansing a wound or an ardent and tactile lover. I watch, I must say, apprehensively. Like mine-war detectors, his hands graze in circles ahead of him. Your nipples were the color of your eyes. Pebble. Snarl of paper. Length of twine. He leans down closely, picks up something silvery, holds it near his nose. Foil? cap? coin? He has within him—what, I wonder? Does he know more now because he fingers everything and has to sniff to see? It would be romantic cruelty to think so. He bends the down on your arms like a breeze. You wrote me: something is strange when we don't understand. I write in return: I think when I loved you I fell to my death.

Billy, I could read to you from Beddoes; he's your man perhaps; he held with dying, freed his blood of its arteries; and he said that there were many wretched love-ill fools like me lying alongside the last bone of their former selves, as full of spirit and speech, nonetheless, as Mrs. Desmond, Uncle Halley and the Ferris wheel, Aunt Pet, Miss Jakes, Ramona or the megaphone; yet I reverse him finally, Billy, on no evidence but braggadocio, and I declare that though my inner organs were devoured long ago, the worm which swallowed down my parts still throbs and glows like a crystal palace.

Yes, you were younger. I was Uncle Halley, the museum man and infrequent meteor. Here is my first piece of ass. They weren't so flat in those days, had more round, more juice. And over here's the sperm I've spilled, nicely jarred and clearly labeled.

Look at this tape like lengths of intestine where I've stored my spew, the endless worm of words I've written, a hundred million emissions or more: oh I was quite a man right from the start; even when unconscious in my cradle, from crotch to cranium, I was erectile tissue; though mostly, after the manner approved by Plato, I had intercourse by eye. Never mind, old Holsclaw, you are blind. We pull down darkness when we go to bed; put out like Oedipus the actually offending organ, and train our touch to lies. All cats are gray, says Mr. Tick; so under cover of glaucoma you are sack gray too, and cannot be distinguished from a stallion.

I must pull myself together, get a grip, just as they say, but I feel spilled, bewildered, quite mislaid. I did not restore my house to its youth, but to its age. Hunting, you hitch through the hollyhocks. I'm inclined to say you aren't half the cripple I am, for there is nothing left of me but mouth. However, I resist the impulse. It is another lie of poetry. My organs are all there, though it's there where I fail—at the roots of my experience. Poet of the spiritual, Rilke, weren't you? yet that's what you said. Poetry, like love, is—in and out—a physical caress. I can't tolerate any more of my sophistries about spirit, mind, and breath. Body equals being, and if your weight goes down, you are the less.

## Household Apples

I knew nothing about apples. Why should I? My country came in my childhood, and I dreamed of sitting among the blooms like the bees. I failed to spray the pear tree too. I doubled up under them at first, admiring the sturdy low branches I should have pruned, and later I acclaimed the blossoms. Shortly after the fruit formed there were falls—not many—apples the size of goodish stones which made me wobble on my ankles when I walked about the yard. Sometimes a piece crushed by a heel would cling on the shoe to track the house. I gathered a few and heaved them over the wires. A slingshot would have been splendid. Hard, an unattractive green, the worms had them. Before long I realized the worms had them all. Even as the apples reddened, lit their tree, they were being swallowed. The birds preferred the pears, which were small—sugar pears I think they're called—with thick skins of graying green that ripen on toward violet. So the fruit fell, and once I made some applesauce by quartering and paring hundreds; but mostly I did nothing, left them, until suddenly, overnight it seemed, in that ugly late September heat we often have in Indiana, my problem was upon me.

My childhood came in the country. I remember, now, the flies on our snowy luncheon table. As we cleared away they would settle, fastidiously scrub themselves and stroll to the crumbs to feed where I would kill them in crowds with a swatter. It was quite a game to catch them taking off. I struck heavily since I didn't mind a few stains; they'd wash. The swatter was a square of screen bound down in red cloth. It drove no air ahead of it to give them warning. They might have thought they'd flown headlong into a summered window. The faint pink dot where they had died did not rub out as I'd supposed, and after years of use our luncheon linen would faintly, pinkly, speckle.

The country became my childhood. Flies braided themselves on the flypaper in my grandmother's house. I can smell the bakery and the grocery and the stables and the dairy in that small Dakota town I knew as a kid; knew as I dreamed I'd know your body, as I've known nothing, before or since; knew as the flies knew, in the honest, unchaste sense: the burned house, hose-wet, which drew a mist of insects like the blue smoke of its smolder, and gangs of boys, moist-lipped, destructive as its burning. Flies have always impressed me; they are so persistently alive. Now they were coating the ground beneath my trees. Some were ordinary flies; there were the large blue-green ones; there were swarms of fruit flies too, and the red-spotted scavenger beetle; there were a few wasps, several sorts of bees and butterflies—checkers, sulphurs, monarchs, commas, question marks—and delicate dragonflies . . . but principally houseflies and horseflies and bottleflies, flies and more flies in clusters around the rotting fruit. They loved the pears. Inside, they fed. If you picked up a pear, they flew, and the pear became skin and stem. They were everywhere the fruit was: in the tree still—apples like a hive for them—or where the fruit littered the ground, squashing itself as you stepped . . . there was no help for it. The flies droned, feasting on the sweet juice. No one could go near the trees; I could not climb; so I determined at last to labor like Hercules. There were fruit baskets in the barn. Collecting them and kneeling under the branches, I began to gather remains. Deep in the strong rich smell of the fruit, I began to hum myself. The fruit caved in at the touch. Glistening red apples, my lifting disclosed, had families of beetles, flies, and bugs, devouring their rotten undersides. There were streams of flies; there were lakes and cataracts and rivers of flies, seas and oceans. The hum was heavier, higher, than the hum of the bees when they came to the blooms in the spring, though the bees were there, among the flies, ignoring me—ignoring everyone. As my work went on and juice covered my hands and arms, they would form a sleeve, black and moving, like knotty wool. No caress could have been more indifferently complete. Still I rose fearfully, ramming my head in the branches, apples bumping against me before falling, bursting with bugs. I'd snap my hand sharply but the flies would cling to the sweet. I could toss a whole cluster into a basket from several feet. As the pear or apple lit, they would explosively rise, like monads for a moment, windowless, certainly, with respect to one another, sugar their harmony. I had to admit, though, despite my distaste, that my arm had never been more alive, oftener or more gently kissed. Those hundreds of feet were light. In washing them off, I pretended the hose was a pump. What have I missed? Childhood is a lie of poetry.

### The Church

Friday night. Girls in dark skirts and white blouses sit in ranks and scream in concert. They carry funnels loosely stuffed with orange and black paper which they shake wildly, and small megaphones through which, as drilled, they direct and magnify their shouting. Their leaders, barely pubescent girls, prance and shake and whirl their skirts above their bloomers. The young men, leaping, extend their arms and race through puddles of amber light, their bodies glistening. In a lull, though it rarely occurs, you can hear the squeak of tennis shoes against the floor. Then the yelling begins again, and then continues; fathers, mothers, neighbors joining in to form a single pulsing ululation—a cry of the whole community—for in this gymnasium each body becomes the bodies beside it, pressed as they are together, thigh to thigh, and the same shudder runs through all of them, and runs toward the same release. Only the ball moves serenely through this dazzling din. Obedient to law it scarcely speaks but caroms quietly and lives at peace.

### Business

It is the week of Christmas and the stores, to accommodate the rush they hope for, are remaining open in the evening. You can see snow falling in the cones of the street lamps. The roads are filling—undisturbed. Strings of red and green lights droop over the principal highway, and the water tower wears a star. The windows of the stores have been bedizened. Shamelessly they beckon. But I am alone, leaning against a pole—no . . . there is no one in sight. They're all at home, perhaps by their instruments, tuning in on their evenings, and like Ramona, tirelessly playing and replaying themselves. There's a speaker perched in the tower, and through the boughs of falling snow and over the vacant streets, it drapes the twisted and metallic strains of a tune that can barely be distinguished—yes, I believe it's one of the jolly ones, it's "Joy to the World." There's no one to hear the music but myself, and though I'm listening, I'm no longer certain. Perhaps the record's playing something else.

# ERNEST J. GAINES

(1933– )

Exploring the theme of the struggle for dignity and manhood amidst the old but changing racial structures of Louisiana, Ernest J. Gaines is one of the most important black authors writing today. He was born to sharecropper parents near Oscar, Louisiana, where he remembers digging for potatoes for fifty cents a day. His father left when Gaines was eight, and the boy was often left in the care of and to care for his paraplegic aunt, who was a model for him of the strong black woman triumphing over adversity.

In 1948 Gaines moved to Vallejo, California, to join his mother and stepfather and to attend high school. After attending junior college and serving two years in the army, he graduated from San Francisco State College in 1957. In 1958 he was awarded a Wallace Stegner fellowship in creative writing at Stanford University. In 1959 he received the Joseph Henry Jackson Literary Award.

Gaines' early stories are collected in *Bloodline* (1968). He has published six novels: *Catherine Carmier* (1964), *Of Love and Dust* (1967), *Autobiography of Miss Jane Pittman* (1971), *In My Father's House* (1978), *A Gathering of Old Men* (1983), and *A Lesson Before Dying* (1993).

## The Sky Is Gray

I

Go'n be coming in a few minutes. Coming round that bend down there full speed. And I'm go'n get out my handkerchief and wave it down, and we go'n get on it and go.

I keep looking for it, but Mama don't look that way no more. She's looking down the road where we just come from. It's a long old road, and far's you can see you don't see nothing but gravel. You got dry weeds on both sides, and you got trees on both sides, and fences on both sides, too. And you got cows in the pastures and they standing close together. And when we was coming out here to catch the bus I seen the smoke coming out of the cows's noses.

I look at my mama and I know what she's thinking. I been with Mama so much, just me and her, I know what she's thinking all the time. Right now it's home—Auntie and them. She's thinking if they got enough wood—if she left enough there to keep them warm till we get back. She's thinking if it go'n rain and if any of them go'n have to go out in the rain. She's thinking 'bout the hog—if he go'n get out, and if Ty and Val be able to get him back in. She always worry like that when she leaves the house. She don't worry too much if she leave me there with the smaller ones, 'cause she know I'm go'n look after them and look after Auntie and everything else. I'm the oldest and she say I'm the man.

I look at my mama and I love my mama. She's wearing that black coat and that black hat and she's looking sad. I love my mama and I want put my arm round her and tell her. But I'm not supposed to do that. She say that's weakness and that's crybaby stuff, and she don't want no crybaby round her. She don't want you to be scared, either. 'Cause Ty's scared of ghosts and she's always whipping him. I'm scared of the dark, too, but I make 'tend I ain't. I make 'tend I ain't 'cause I'm the oldest, and I got to set a good sample for the rest. I can't ever be scared and I can't ever cry. And that's why I never said nothing 'bout my teeth. It's been hurting me and hurting me close to a month now, but I never said it. I didn't say it 'cause I didn't want to act like a crybaby, and 'cause we didn't have enough money to go have it pulled. But, Lord, it been hurting me. And look like it wouldn't start till at night when you was trying to get yourself little sleep. Then soon's you shut your eyes—ummm-ummm, Lord, look like it go right down to your heartstring.

"Hurting, hanh?" Ty'd say.

I'd shake my head, but I wouldn't open my mouth for nothing. You open your mouth and let that wind in, and it almost kill you.

I'd just lay there and listen to them snore. Ty there, right 'side me, and Auntie and Val over by the fireplace. Val younger than me and Ty, and he sleeps with Auntie. Mama sleeps round the other side with Louis and Walker.

I'd just lay there and listen to them, and listen to that wind out there, and listen to that fire in the fireplace. Sometimes it'd stop long enough to let me get little rest. Sometimes it just hurt, hurt, hurt. Lord, have mercy.

## 2

Auntie knowed it was hurting me. I didn't tell anybody but Ty, 'cause we buddies and he ain't go'n tell nobody. But some kind of way Auntie found out. When she asked me, I told her no, nothing was wrong. But she knowed it all the time. She told me to mash up a piece of aspirin and wrap it in some cotton and jugg it down in that hole. I did it, but it didn't do no good. It stopped for a little while, and started right back again. Auntie wanted to tell Mama, but I told her, "Uh-uh." 'Cause I knowed we didn't have any money, and it just was go'n make her mad again. So Auntie told Monsieur Bayonne, and Monsieur Bayonne came over to the house and told me to kneel down 'side him on the fireplace. He put his finger in his mouth and made the Sign of the Cross on my jaw. The tip of Monsieur Bayonne's finger is some hard, 'cause he's always playing on that guitar. If we sit outside at night we can always hear Monsieur Bayonne playing on his guitar. Sometimes we leave him out there playing on the guitar.

Monsieur Bayonne made the Sign of the Cross over and over on my jaw, but that didn't do no good. Even when he prayed and told me to pray some, too, that tooth still hurt me.

"How you feeling?" he say.

"Same," I say.

He kept on praying and making the Sign of the Cross and I kept on praying, too.

"Still hurting?" he say.

"Yes, sir."

Monsieur Bayonne mashed harder and harder on my jaw. He mashed so hard he almost pushed me over on Ty. But then he stopped.

"What kind of prayers you praying, boy?" he say.

"Baptist," I say.

"Well, I'll be—no wonder that tooth killing him. I'm going one way and he pulling the other. Boy, don't you know any Catholic prayers?"

"I know 'Hail Mary,' " I say.

"Then you better start saying it."

"Yes, sir."

He started mashing on my jaw again, and I could hear him praying at the same time. And, sure enough, after while it stopped hurting me.

Me and Ty went outside where Monsieur Bayonne's two hounds was and we started playing with them. "Let's go hunting," Ty say. "All right," I say; and we went on back in the pasture. Soon the hounds got on a trail, and me and Ty followed them all 'cross the pasture and then back in the woods, too. And then they cornered this little old rabbit and killed him, and me and Ty made them get back, and we picked up the rabbit and started back home. But my tooth had started hurting me again. It was hurting me plenty now, but I wouldn't tell Monsieur Bayonne. That night I didn't sleep a bit, and first thing in the morning Auntie told me to go back and let Monsieur Bayonne pray over me some more. Monsieur Bayonne was in his kitchen making coffee when I got there. Soon's he seen me he knowed what was wrong.

"All right, kneel down there 'side that stove," he say. "And this time make sure you pray Catholic. I don't know nothing 'bout that Baptist, and I don't want know nothing 'bout him."

## 3

Last night Mama say, "Tomorrow we going to town."

"It ain't hurting me no more," I say. "I can eat anything on it."

"Tomorrow we going to town," she say.

And after she finished eating, she got up and went to bed. She always go to bed early now. 'Fore Daddy went in the Army, she used to stay up late. All of us sitting out on the gallery or round the fire. But now, look like soon's she finish eating she go to bed.

This morning when I woke up, her and Auntie was standing 'fore the fireplace. She say: "Enough to get there and get back. Dollar an a half to have it pulled. Twenty-five for me to go, twenty-five for him. Twenty-five for me to come back, twenty-five for him. Fifty cents left. Guess I get a little piece of salt meat with that."

"Sure can use it," Auntie say. "White beans and no salt meat ain't white beans."

"I do the best I can," Mama say.

They was quiet after that, and I made 'tend I was still sleep.

"James, hit the floor," Auntie say.

I still made 'tend I was asleep. I didn't want them to know I was listening.

"All right," Auntie say, shaking me by the shoulder. "Come on. Today's the day."

I pushed the cover down to get out, and Ty grabbed it and pulled it back.

"You, too, Ty," Auntie say.

"I ain't getting no teef pulled," Ty say.

"Don't mean it ain't time to get up." Auntie say. "Hit it, Ty."

Ty got up grumbling.

"James, you hurry up and get in your clothes and eat your food," Auntie say. "What time y'all coming back?" she said to Mama.

"That 'leven o'clock bus," Mama say. "Got to get back in that field this evening."

"Get a move on you, James," Auntie say.

I went in the kitchen and washed my face, then I ate my breakfast, I was having bread and syrup. The bread was warm and hard and tasted good. And I tried to make it last a long time.

Ty came back there grumbling and mad at me.

"Got to get up," he say. "I ain't having no teefes pulled. What I got to be getting up for?"

Ty poured some syrup in his pan and got a piece of bread. He didn't wash his hands, neither his face, and I could see that white stuff in his eyes.

"You the one getting your teef pulled," he say. "What I got to get up for. I bet if I was getting a teef pulled, you wouldn't be getting up. Shucks; syrup again. I'm getting tired of this old syrup. Syrup, syrup, syrup. I'm go'n take with the sugar diabetes. I want some bacon sometime."

"Go out in the field and work and you can have your bacon," Auntie say. She stood in the middle door looking at Ty. "You better be glad you got syrup. Some people ain't got that—hard's time is."

"Shucks," Ty say. "How can I be strong?"

"I don't know too much 'bout your strength," Auntie say; "but I know where you go'n be hot at, you keep that grumbling up. James, get a move on you; your mama waiting."

I ate my last piece of bread and went in the front room. Mama was standing 'fore the fireplace warming her hands. I put on my coat and my cap, and we left the house.

## 4

I look down there again, but it still ain't coming. I almost say, "It ain't coming yet," but I keep my mouth shut. 'Cause that's something else she don't like. She don't like for you to say something just for nothing. She can see it ain't coming, I can see it ain't coming, so why say it ain't coming. I don't say it, I turn and look at the river that's back of us. It's so cold the smoke's just raising up from the water. I see a bunch of pool-doos not too far out—just on the other side the lilies. I'm wondering if you can eat pool-doos. I ain't too sure, 'cause I ain't never ate none. But I done ate owls and blackbirds, and I done ate redbirds, too. I didn't want to kill the redbirds, but she made me kill them. They had two of them back there. One in my trap, one in Ty's trap. Me and Ty was go'n play with them and let them go, but she made me kill them 'cause we needed the food.

"I can't," I say. "I can't."

"Here," she say. "Take it."

"I can't," I say. "I can't. I can't kill him, Mama, please."

"Here," she say. "Take this fork, James."

"Please, Mama, I can't kill him," I say.

I could tell she was go'n hit me. I jerked back, but I didn't jerk back soon enough.

"Take it," she say.

I took it and reached in for him, but he kept on hopping to the back.

"I can't, Mama," I say. The water just kept on running down my face. "I can't," I say.

"Get him out of there," she say.

I reached in for him and he kept on hopping to the back. Then I reached in farther, and he pecked me on the hand.

"I can't, Mama," I say.

She slapped me again.

I reached in again, but he kept on hopping out my way. Then he hopped to one side and I reached there. The fork got him on the leg and I heard his leg pop. I pulled my hand out 'cause I had hurt him.

"Give it here," she say, and jerked the fork out of my hand.

She reached in and got the little bird right in the neck. I heard the fork go in his neck, and I heard it go in the ground. She brought him out and helt him right in front of me.

"That's one," she say. She shook him off and gived me the fork. "Get the other one."

"I can't, Mama," I say. "I'll do anything, but don't make me do that."

She went to the corner of the fence and broke the biggest switch over there she could find. I knelt 'side the trap, crying.

"Get him out of there," she say.

"I can't, Mama."

She started hitting me 'cross the back. I went down on the ground, crying.

"Get him," she say.

"Octavia?" Auntie say.

'Cause she had come out of the house and she was standing by the tree looking at us.

"Get him out of there," Mama say.

"Octavia," Auntie say, "explain to him. Explain to him. Just don't beat him. Explain to him."

But she hit me and hit me and hit me.

I'm still young—I ain't no more than eight; but I know now; I know why I had to do it. (They was so little, though. They was so little. I 'member how I picked the feathers off them and cleaned them and helt them over the fire. Then we all ate them. Ain't had but a little bitty piece each, but we all had a little bitty piece, and everybody just looked at me 'cause they was so proud.) Suppose she had to go away? That's why I had to do it. Suppose she had to go away like Daddy went away? Then who was go'n look after us? They had to be somebody left to carry on. I didn't know it then, but I know it now. Auntie and Monsieur Bayonne talked to me and made me see.

## 5

Time I see it I get out my handkerchief and start waving. It's still 'way down there, but I keep waving anyhow. Then it come up and stop and me and Mama get on. Mama tell me go sit in the back while she pay. I do like she say, and the people look at me. When I pass the little sign that say "White" and "Colored," I start looking for a seat. I just see one of them back there, but I don't take it, 'cause I want my mama to sit down herself. She comes in the back and sit down, and I lean on the seat. They got seats in the front, but I know I can't sit there, 'cause I have to sit back of the sign. Anyhow, I don't want sit there if my mama go'n sit back here.

They got a lady sitting 'side my mama and she looks at me and smiles little bit. I smile back, but I don't open my mouth, 'cause the wind'll get in and make that tooth ache. The lady take out a pack of gum and reach me a slice, but I shake my head. The lady just can't understand why a little boy'll turn down gum, and she reach me a slice again. This time I point to my jaw. The lady understands and smiles little bit, and I smile little bit, but I don't open my mouth, though.

They got a girl sitting 'cross from me. She got on a red overcoat and her hair's plaited in one big plait. First, I make 'tend I don't see her over there, but then I start looking at her little bit. She make 'tend she don't see me, either, but I catch her looking that way. She got a cold, and every now and then she h'ist that little handkerchief to her nose. She ought to blow it, but she don't. Must think she's too much a lady or something.

Every time she h'ist that little handkerchief, the lady side her say something in her ear. She shakes her head and lays her hands in her lap again. Then I catch her kind of looking where I'm at. I smile at her little bit. But think she'll smile back? Uh-uh. She just turn up her little old nose and turn her head. Well, I show her both of us can turn us head. I turn mine too and look out at the river.

The river is gray. The sky is gray. They have pool-doos on the water. The water is wavy, and the pool-doos go up and down. The bus go round a turn, and you got plenty trees hiding the river. Then the bus go round another turn, and I can see the river again.

I look toward the front where all the white people sitting. Then I look at that little old gal again. I don't look right at her, 'cause I don't want all them people to know I love her. I just look at her little bit, like I'm looking out that window over there. But she knows I'm looking that way, and she kind of look at me, too. The lady sitting 'side her catch her this time, and she leans over and says something in her ear.

"I don't love him nothing," that little old gal says out loud.

Everybody back there hear her mouth, and all of them look at us and laugh.

"I don't love you, either," I say. "So you don't have to turn up your nose, Miss."

"You the one looking," she say.

"I wasn't looking at you," I say. "I was looking out that window, there."

"Out that window my foot," she say. "I seen you. Everytime I turned round you was looking at me."

"You must of been looking yourself if you seen me all them times," I say.

"Shucks," she say, "I got me all kind of boyfriends."

"I got girlfriends, too," I say.

"Well, I just don't want you getting your hopes up," she say.

I don't say no more to that little old gal 'cause I don't want have to bust her in the mouth. I lean on the seat where Mama sitting, and I don't even look that way no more. When we get to Bayonne, she jugg her little old tongue out at me. I make 'tend I'm go'n hit her, and she duck down 'side her mama. And all the people laugh at us again.

## 6

Me and Mama get off and start walking in town. Bayonne is a little bitty town. Baton Rouge is a hundred times bigger than Bayonne. I went to Baton Rouge once—me, Ty, Mama, and Daddy. But that was 'way back yonder, 'fore Daddy went in the Army. I wonder when we go'n see him again. I wonder when. Look like he ain't ever coming back home. . . . Even the pavement all cracked in Bayonne. Got grass shooting right out in the sidewalk. Got weeds in the ditch, too; just like they got at home.

It's some cold in Bayonne. Look like it's colder than it is home. The wind blows in my face, and I feel that stuff running down my nose. I sniff. Mama says use that handkerchief. I blow my nose and put it back.

We pass a school and see them white children playing in the yard. Big old red school, and them children just running and playing. Then we pass a café, and I see a bunch of people in there eating. I wish I was in there 'cause I'm cold. Mama tells me keep my eyes in front where they belong.

We pass stores that's got dummies, and we pass another café, and then we pass a shoe shop, and that bald-head man in there fixing on a shoe. I look at him and I butt into that white lady, and Mama jerks me in front and tells me stay there.

We come up to the courthouse, and I see the flag waving there. This flag ain't like the one we got at school. This one here ain't got but a handful of stars. One at the school got a big pile of stars—one for every state. We pass it and we turn and there it is—the dentist office. Me and Mama go in, and they got people sitting everywhere you look. They even got a little boy in there younger than me.

Me and Mama sit on that bench, and a white lady come in there and ask me what my name is. Mama tells her and the white lady goes on back. Then I hear somebody hollering in there. Soon's that little boy hear him hollering, he starts hollering, too. His mama pats him and pats him, trying to make him hushup, but he ain't thinking 'bout his mama.

The man that was hollering in there comes out holding his jaw. He is a big old man and he's wearing overalls and a jumper.

"Got it, hanh?" another man asks him.

The man shakes his head—don't want to open his mouth.

"Man, I thought they was killing you in there," the other man says. "Hollering like a pig under a gate."

The man don't say nothing. He just heads for the door, and the other man follows him.

"John Lee," the white lady says. "John Lee Williams."

The little boy juggs his head down in his mama's lap and holler more now. His mama tells him go with the nurse, but he ain't thinking 'bout his mama. His mama tells him again, but he don't even hear her. His mama picks him up and takes him in there, and even when the white lady shuts the door I can still hear little old John Lee.

"I often wonder why the Lord let a child like that suffer," a lady says to my mama. The lady's sitting right in front of us on another bench. She's got on a white dress and a black sweater. She must be a nurse or something herself, I reckon.

"Not us to question," a man says.

"Sometimes I don't know if we shouldn't," the lady says.

"I know definitely we shouldn't," the man says. The man looks like a preacher. He's big and fat and he's got on a black suit. He's got a gold chain, too.

"Why?" the lady said.

"Why anything?" the preacher says.

"Yes," the lady says. "Why anything?"

"Not us to question," the preacher says.

The lady looks at the preacher a little while and looks at Mama again.

"And look like it's the poor who suffers the most," she says. "I don't understand it."

"Best not to even try," the preacher says. "He works in mysterious ways—wonders to perform."

Right then little John Lee bust out hollering, and everybody turn their head to listen.

"He's not a good dentist," the lady says. "Dr. Robillard is much better. But more expensive. That's why most of the colored people come here. The white people go to Dr. Robillard. Y'all from Bayonne?"

"Down the river," my mama says. And that's all she go'n say, 'cause she don't talk much. But the lady keeps on looking at her, and so she says, "Near Morgan."

"I see," the lady says.

## 7

"That's the trouble with the black people in this country today," somebody else says. This one here's sitting on the same side me and Mama's sitting, and he is kind of sitting in front of that preacher. He looks like a teacher or somebody that goes to college. He's got on a suit, and he's got a book that he's been reading. "We don't question is exactly our problem," he says. "We should question and question and question—question everything."

The preacher just looks at him a long time. He done put a toothpick or something in his mouth, and he just keeps turning it and turning it. You can see he don't like that boy with that book.

"Maybe you can explain to me what you mean," he says.

"I said what I meant," the boy says. "Question everything. Every stripe, every star, every word spoken. Everything."

"It 'pears to me that this young lady and I was talking 'bout God, young man," the preacher says.

"Question Him, too," the boy says.

"Wait," the preacher says. "Wait now."

"You heard me right," the boy says. "His existence as well as everything else. Everything."

The preacher just looks across the room at the boy. You can see he's getting madder and madder. But mad or no mad, the boy ain't thinking 'bout him. He looks at that preacher just 's hard 's the preacher looks at him.

"Is this what they coming to?" the preacher says. "Is this what we educating them for?"

"You're not educating me," the boy says. "I wash dishes at night so that I can go to school in the day. So even the words you spoke need questioning."

The preacher just looks at him and shakes his head.

"When I come in this room and seen you there with your book, I said to myself, 'There's an intelligent man.' How wrong a person can be."

"Show me one reason to believe in the existence of a God," the boy says.

"My heart tells me," the preacher says.

" 'My heart tells me,' " the boy says. " 'My heart tells me.' Sure. 'My heart tells me.' And as long as you listen to what your heart tells you, you will have only what the white man gives you and nothing more. Me, I don't listen to my heart. The purpose of the heart is to pump blood throughout the body, and nothing else."

"Who's your paw, boy?" the preacher says.

"Why?"

"Who is he?"

"He's dead."

"And your mom?"

"She's in Charity Hospital with pneumonia. Half killed herself, working for nothing."

"And 'cause he's dead and she's sick, you mad at the world?"

"I'm not mad at the world. I'm questioning it with cold logic, sir. What do words like Freedom, Liberty, God, White, Colored mean? I want to know. That's why *you* are sending us to school, to read and to ask questions. And because we ask these questions, you call us mad. No sir, it is not us who are mad."

"You keep saying 'us'?"

" 'Us.' Yes—us. I'm not alone."

The preacher just shakes his head. Then he looks at everybody in the room—everybody. Some of the people look down at the floor, keep from looking at him. I think of look 'way myself, but soon 's I know he done turn his head, I look that way again.

"I'm sorry for you," he says to the boy.

"Why?" the boy says. "Why not be sorry for yourself? Why are you so much better off than I am? Why aren't you sorry for these other people in here? Why not be sorry for the lady who had to drag her child into the dentist office? Why not be sorry for the lady sitting on that bench over there? Be sorry for them. Not for me. Some way or the other I'm going to make it."

"No, I'm sorry for you," the preacher says.

"Of course, of course," the boy says, nodding his head. "You're sorry for me because I rock that pillar you're leaning on."

"You can't never rock the pillar I'm leaning on, young man. It's stronger than anything man can ever do."

"You believe in God because a man told you to believe in God," the boy says. "A white man told you to believe in God. And why? To keep you ignorant so he can keep his feet on your neck."

"So now we the ignorant?" the preacher says.

"Yes," the boy says."Yes." And he opens his book again.

The preacher just looks at him sitting there. The boy done forgot all about him. Everybody else make 'tend they done forgot the squabble, too.

Then I see that preacher getting up real slow. Preacher's a great big old man and he got to brace himself to get up. He comes over where the boy is sitting. He just stands there a little while looking down at him, but the boy don't raise his head.

"Get up, boy," preacher says.

The boy looks up at him, then he shuts his book real slow and stands up. Preacher just hauls back and hit him in the face. The boy falls back 'gainst the wall, but he straightens himself up and looks right back at the preacher.

"You forgot the other cheek," he says.

The preacher hauls back and hit him again on the other side. But this time the boy braces himself and don't fall.

"That hasn't changed a thing," he says.

The preacher just looks at the boy. The preacher's breathing real hard like he just run up a big hill. The boy sits down and opens his book again.

"I feel sorry for you," the preacher says. "I never felt so sorry for a man before."

The boy makes 'tend he don't even hear that preacher. He keeps on reading his book. The preacher goes back and gets his hat off the chair.

"Excuse me," he says to us. "I'll come back some other time. Y'all, please excuse me."

And he looks at the boy and goes out the room. The boy h'ist his hand up to his mouth one time to wipe 'way some blood. All the rest of the time he keeps on reading. And nobody else in there say a word.

## 8

Little John Lee and his mama come out the dentist office, and the nurse calls somebody else in. Then little bit later they come out, and the nurse calls another name. But fast's she calls somebody in there, somebody else comes in the place where we sitting, and the room stays full.

The people coming in now, all of them wearing big coats. One of them says something 'bout sleeting, another one says he hope not. Another one says he think it ain't nothing but rain. 'Cause, he says, rain can get awful cold this time of year.

All round the room they talking. Some of them talking to people right by them, some of them talking to people clear 'cross the room, some of them talking to anybody'll listen. It's a little bitty room, no bigger than us kitchen, and I can see everybody in there. The little old room's full of smoke, 'cause you got two old men smoking pipes over by that side door. I think I feel my tooth thumping me some, and I hold my breath and wait. I wait and wait, but it don't thump me no more. Thank God for that.

I feel like going to sleep, and I lean 'gainst the wall. But I'm scared to go to sleep. Scared 'cause the nurse might call my name and I won't hear her. And Mama might go to sleep, too, and she'll be mad if neither one of us heard the nurse.

I look up at Mama. I love my mama. And when cotton come I'm go'n get her a new coat. And I ain't go'n get a black one, either. I think I'm go'n get her a red one.

"They got some books over there," I say. "Want read one of them?"

Mama looks at the books, but she don't answer me.

"You got yourself a little man there," the lady says.

Mama don't say nothing to the lady, but she must've smiled, 'cause I seen the lady smiling back. The lady looks at me a little while, like she's feeling sorry for me.

"You sure got that preacher out here in a hurry," she says to that boy.

The boy looks up at her and looks in his book again. When I grow up I want to be just like him. I want clothes like that and I want to keep a book with me, too.

"You really don't believe in God?" the lady says.

"No," he says.

"But why?" the lady says.

"Because the wind is pink," he says.

"What?" the lady says.

The boy don't answer her no more. He just reads in his book.

"Talking 'bout the wind is pink," that old lady says. She's sitting on the same bench with the boy and she's trying to look in his face. The boy makes 'tend the old lady ain't even there. He just keeps on reading. "Wind is pink," she says again. "Eh, Lord, what children go'n be saying next?"

The lady 'cross from us bust out laughing.

"That's a good one," she says. "The wind is pink. Yes sir, that's a good one."

"Don't you believe the wind is pink?" the boy says. He keeps his head down in the book.

"Course I believe it, honey," the lady says. "Course I do." She looks at us and winks her eye. "And what color is grass, honey?"

"Grass? Grass is black."

She bust out laughing again. The boy looks at her.

"Don't you believe grass is black?" he says.

The lady quits her laughing and looks at him. Everybody else looking at him, too. The place quiet, quiet.

"Grass is green, honey," the lady says. "It was green yesterday, it's green today, and it's go'n be green tomorrow."

"How do you know it's green?"

"I know because I know."

"You don't know it's green," the boy says. "You believe it's green because someone told you it was green. If someone had told you it was black you'd believe it was black."

"It's green," the lady says. "I know green when I see green."

"Prove it's green," the boy says.

"Sure, now," the lady says. "Don't tell me it's coming to that."

"It's coming to just that," the boy says. "Words mean nothing. One means no more than the other."

"That's what it all coming to?" the old lady says. That old lady got on a turban and she got on two sweaters. She got a green sweater under a black sweater. I can see the green sweater 'cause some of the buttons on the other sweater's missing.

"Yes ma'am," he says. "Words mean nothing. Action is the only thing. Doing. That's the only thing."

"Other words, you want the Lord to come down here and show Hisself to you?" she says.

"Exactly, ma'am," he says.

"You don't mean that, I'm sure?" she says.

"I do, ma'am," he says.

"Done, Jesus," the lady says, shaking her head.

"I didn't go 'long with that preacher at first," the other lady says; "but now—I don't know. When a person says the grass is black, he's either a lunatic or something's wrong."

"Prove to me that it's green," the boy says.

"It's green because the people say it's green."

"Those same people say we're citizens of these United States," the boy says.

"I think I'm a citizen," the lady says.

"Citizens have certain rights," the boy says. "Name me one right that you have. One right, granted by the Constitution, that you can exercise in Bayonne."

The lady don't answer him. She just looks at him like she don't know what he's talking 'bout. I know I don't.

"Things changing," she says.

"Things are changing because some black men have begun to think with their brains and not their hearts," the boy says.

"You trying to say these people don't believe in God?"

"I'm sure some of them do, Maybe most of them do. But they don't believe that God is going to touch these white people's hearts and change things tomorrow. Things change through action. By no other way."

Everybody sit quiet and look at the boy. Nobody says a thing. Then the lady 'cross the room from me and Mama just shakes her head.

"Let's hope that not all your generation feel the same way you do," she says.

"Think what you please, it doesn't matter," the boy says. "But it will be men who listen to their heads and not their hearts who will see that your children have a better chance than you had."

"Let's hope they ain't all like you, though," the old lady says. "Done forgot the heart absolutely."

"Yes ma'am, I hope they aren't all like me," the boy says. "Unfortunately, I was born too late to believe in your God. Let's hope that the ones who come after will have your faith—if not in your God, then in something else, something definitely that they can lean on. I haven't anything. For me, the wind is pink, the grass is black."

## 9

The nurse comes in the room where we are all sitting and waiting and says the doctor won't take no more patients till one o'clock this evening. My mama jumps up off the bench and goes up to the white lady.

"Nurse, I have to go back in the field this evening," she says.

"The doctor is treating his last patient now," the nurse says. "One o'clock this evening."

"Can I at least speak to the doctor?" my mama asks.

"I'm his nurse," the lady says.

"My little boy's sick," my mama says. "Right now his tooth almost killing him."

The nurse looks at me. She's trying to make up her mind if to let me come in. I look at her real pitiful. The tooth ain't hurting me at all, but Mama say it is, so I make 'tend for her sake.

"This evening," the nurse says, and goes on back in the office.

"Don't feel 'jected, honey," the lady says to Mama. "I been round them a long time—they take you when they want to. If you was white, that's something else; but we the wrong color."

Mama don't say nothing to the lady, and me and her go outside and stand 'gainst the wall. It's cold out there. I can feel that wind going through my coat. Some of the other people come out of the room and go up the street. Me and Mama stand there a little while and we start walking. I don't know where we going. When we come to the other street we just stand there.

"You don't have to make water, do you?" Mama says. "No, ma'am," I say.

We go on up the street. Walking real slow. I can tell Mama don't know where she's going. When we come to a store we stand there and look at the dummies. I look at a little boy wearing a brown overcoat. He's got on brown shoes, too. I look at my old shoes and look at his'n again. You wait till summer, I say.

Me and Mama walk away. We come up to another store and we stop and look at them dummies, too. Then we go on again. We pass a café where the white people in there eating. Mama tells me keep my eyes in front where they belong, but I can't help from seeing them people eat. My stomach starts to growling 'cause I'm hungry. When I see people eating, I get hungry; when I see a coat, I get cold.

A man whistles at my mama when we go by a filling station. She makes 'tend she don't even see him. I look back and I feel like hitting him in the mouth. If I was bigger, I say; if I was bigger, you'd see.

We keep on going. I'm getting colder and colder, but I don't say nothing. I feel that stuff running down my nose and I sniff.

"That rag," Mama says.

I get it out and wipe my nose. I'm getting cold all over now—my face, my hands, my feet, everything. We pass another little café, but this'n for white people, too, and we can't go in there, either. So we just walk. I'm so cold now I'm 'bout ready to say it. If I knowed where we was going I wouldn't be so cold, but I don't know where we going. We go, we go, we go. We walk clean out of Bayonne. Then we cross the street and we come back. Same thing I seen when I got off the bus this morning. Same old trees, same old walks, same old weeds, same old cracked pave—same old everything.

I sniff again.

"That rag," Mama says.

I wipe my nose real fast and jugg that handkerchief back in my pocket 'fore my hand gets too cold. I raise my head and I can see David's hardware store. When we come up to it, we go in. I don't know why, but I'm glad.

It's warm in there. It's so warm in there you don't ever want to leave. I look for the heater, and I see it over by them barrels. Three white men standing round the heater talking in Creole. One of them comes over to see what my mama want.

"Got any axe handles?" she says.

Me, Mama and the white man start to the back, but Mama stops me when we come up to the heater. She and the white man go on. I hold my hands over the heater and look at them. They go all the way to the back, and I see the white man pointing to the axe handles 'gainst the wall.

Mama takes one of them and shakes it like she's trying to figure how much it weighs. Then she rubs her hand over it from one end to the other end. She turns it over and looks at the other side, then she shakes it again, and shakes her head and puts it back. She gets another one and she does it just like she did the first one, then she shakes her head. Then she gets a brown one and do it that, too. But she don't like this one, either. Then she gets another one, but 'fore she shakes it or anything, she looks at me. Look like she's trying to say something to me, but I don't know what it is. All I know is I done got warm now and I'm feeling right smart better. Mama shakes this axe handle just like she did the others, and shakes her head and says something to the white man. The white man just looks at his pile of axe handles, and when Mama pass him to come to the front, the white man just scratch his head and follows her. She tells me to come on and we go on out and start walking again.

We walk and walk, and no time at all I'm cold again. Look like I'm colder now 'cause I can still remember how good it was back there. My stomach growls and I suck it in to keep Mama from hearing it. She's walking right 'side me, and it growls so loud you can hear it a mile. But Mama don't say a word.

## 10

When we come to the courthouse, I look at the clock. It's got quarter to twelve. Mean we got another hour and a quarter to be out here in the cold. We go and stand 'side a building. Something hits my cap and I look up at the sky. Sleet's falling.

I look at Mama standing there. I want stand close 'side her, but she don't like that. She say that's crybaby stuff. She say you got to stand for yourself, by yourself.

"Let's go back to that office," she says.

We cross the street. When we get to the dentist office I try to open the door, but I can't. I twist and twist, but I can't. Mama pushes me to the side and she twist the knob, but she can't open the door, either. She turns 'way from the door. I look at her, but I don't move and I don't say nothing. I done seen her like this before and I'm scared of her.

"You hungry?" she says. She says it like she's mad at me, like I'm the cause of everything.

"No, ma'am," I say.

"You want eat and walk back, or you rather don't eat and ride?"

"I ain't hungry," I say.

I ain't just hungry, but I'm cold, too. I'm so hungry and cold I want to cry. And look like I'm getting colder and colder. My feet done got numb. I try to work my toes, but I don't even feel them. Look like I'm go'n die. Look like I'm go'n stand right here and freeze to death. I think 'bout home. I think 'bout Val and Auntie and Ty and Louis and Walker. It's 'bout twelve o'clock and I know they eating dinner now. I can hear Ty making jokes. He done forgot 'bout getting up early this morning and right now he's probably making jokes. Always trying to make somebody laugh. I wish I was right there listening to him. Give anything in the world if I was home round the fire.

"Come on," Mama says.

We start walking again. My feet so numb I can't hardly feel them. We turn the corner and go on back up the street. The clock in the courthouse starting hitting for twelve.

The sleet's coming down plenty now. They hit the pave and bounce like rice. Oh, Lord; oh, Lord, I pray. Don't let me die, don't let me die, don't let me die, Lord.

II

Now I know where we going. We going back of town where the colored people eat. I don't care if I don't eat. I been hungry before. I can stand it. But I can't stand the cold.

I can see we go'n have a long walk. It's 'bout a mile down there. But I don't mind. I know when I get there I'm go'n warm myself. I think I can hold out. My hands numb in my pockets and my feet numb, too, but if I keep moving I can hold out. Just don't stop no more, that's all.

The sky's gray. The sleet keeps on falling. Falling like rain now—plenty, plenty. You can hear it hitting the pave. You can see it bouncing. Sometimes it bounces two times 'fore it settles.

We keep on going. We don't say nothing. We just keep on going, keep on going.

I wonder what Mama's thinking. I hope she ain't mad at me. When summer come I'm go'n pick plenty cotton and get her a coat. I'm go'n get her a red one.

I hope they'd make it summer all the time. I'd be glad if it was summer all the time—but it ain't. We got to have winter, too. Lord, I hate the winter. I guess everybody hate the winter.

I don't sniff this time, I get out my handkerchief and wipe my nose. My hands's so cold I can hardly hold the handkerchief.

I think we getting close, but we ain't there yet. I wonder where everybody is. Can't see a soul but us. Look like we the only two people moving round today. Must be too cold for the rest of the people to move round in.

I can hear my teeth. I hope they don't knock together too hard and make that bad one hurt. Lord, that's all I need, for that bad one to start off.

I hear a church bell somewhere. But today ain't Sunday. They must be ringing for a funeral or something.

I wonder what they doing at home. They must be eating. Monsieur Bayonne might be there with his guitar. One day Ty played with Monsieur Bayonne's guitar and broke one of the strings. Monsieur Bayonne was some mad with Ty. He say Ty wasn't go'n ever 'mount to nothing. Ty can go just like Monsieur Bayonne when he ain't there. Ty can make everybody laugh when he starts to mocking Monsieur Bayonne.

I used to like to be with Mama and Daddy. We used to be happy. But they took him in the Army. Now, nobody happy no more. . . . I be glad when Daddy comes home.

Monsieur Bayonne say it wasn't fair for them to take Daddy and give Mama nothing and give us nothing. Auntie say, "Shhh, Etienne. Don't let them hear you talk like that." Monsieur Bayonne say, "It's God truth. What they giving his children? They have to walk three and a half miles to school hot or cold. That's anything to give for a paw? She's got to work in the field rain or shine just to make ends meet. That's anything to give for a husband?" Auntie say, "Shhh, Etienne, shhh." "Yes, you right," Monsieur Bayonne say. "Best don't say it in front of them now. But one day they go'n find out.

One day." "Yes, I suppose so," Auntie say. "Then what, Rose Mary?" Monsieur Bayonne say. "I don't know, Etienne," Auntie say. "All we can do is us job, and leave everything else in His hand . . ."

We getting closer, now. We getting closer. I can even see the railroad tracks.

We cross the tracks, and now I see the café. Just to get in there, I say. Just to get in there. Already I'm starting to feel little better.

## 12

We go in. Ahh, it's good. I look for the heater; there 'gainst the wall. One of them little brown ones. I just stand there and hold my hands over it. I can't open my hands too wide 'cause they almost froze.

Mama's standing right 'side me. She done unbuttoned her coat. Smoke rises out of the coat, and the coat smells like a wet dog.

I move to the side so Mama can have more room. She opens out her hands and rubs them together. I rub mine together, too, 'cause this keep them from hurting. If you let them warm too fast, they hurt you sure. But if you let them warm just little bit at a time, and you keep rubbing them, they be all right every time.

They got just two more people in the café. A lady back of the counter, and a man on this side of the counter. They been watching us ever since we come in.

Mama gets out the handkerchief and count up the money. Both of us know how much money she's got there. Three dollars. No, she ain't got three dollars, 'cause she had to pay us way up here. She ain't got but two dollars and a half left. Dollar and half to get my tooth pulled, and fifty cents for us to go back on, and fifty cents worth of salt meat.

She stirs the money round with her finger. Most of the money is change 'cause I can hear it rubbing together. She stirs it and stirs it. Then she looks at the door. It's still sleeting. I can hear it hitting 'gainst the wall like rice.

"I ain't hungry, Mama," I say.

"Got to pay them something for they heat," she says.

She takes a quarter out the handkerchief and ties the handkerchief up again. She looks over her shoulder at the people, but she still don't move. I hope she don't spend the money. I don't want her spending it on me. I'm hungry, I'm almost starving I'm so hungry, but I don't want her spending the money on me.

She flips the quarter over like she's thinking. She's must be thinking 'bout us walking back home. Lord, I sure don't want walk home. If I thought it'd do any good to say something, I'd say it. But Mama makes up her own mind 'bout things.

She turns 'way from the heater right fast, like she better hurry up and spend the quarter 'fore she change her mind. I watch her go toward the counter. The man and the lady look at her, too. She tells the lady something and the lady walks away. The man keeps on looking at her. Her back's turned to the man, and she don't even know he's standing there.

The lady puts some cakes and a glass of milk on the counter. Then she pours up a cup of coffee and set it 'side the other stuff. She's looking real sad. I say to myself, I'm go'n make all this up one day. You see, one day, I'm go'n make all this up. I want say it now; I want tell her how I feel right now; but Mama don't like us to talk like that.

"I can't eat all this," I say.

They ain't got but just three little old cakes there. I'm so hungry right now, the Lord knows I can eat a hundred times three, but I want my mama to have one.

Mama don't even look my way. She knows I'm hungry, she knows I want it. I let it stay there a little while, then I get it and eat it. I eat just on my front teeth, though 'cause if cake touch that back tooth I know what'll happen. Thank God it ain't hurt me at all today.

After I finish eating I see the man go to the juke box. He drops a nickel in it, then he just stand there a little while looking at the record. Mama tells me keep my eyes in front where they belong. I turn my head like she say, but then I hear the man coming toward us.

"Dance, pretty?" he says.

Mama gets up to dance with him. But 'fore you know it, she done grabbed the little man in the collar and done heaved him 'side the wall. He hit the wall so hard he stop the juke box from playing.

"Some pimp," the lady back of the counter says. "Some pimp."

The little man jumps up off the floor and starts toward my mama. 'Fore you know it, Mama done sprung open her knife and she's waiting for him.

"Come on," she says. "Come on. I'll gut you from your neighbo to your throat. Come on."

I got up to the little man to hit him, but Mama makes me come and stand 'side her. The little man looks at me and Mama and goes on back to the counter.

"Some pimp," the lady back of the counter says. "Some pimp." She starts laughing and pointing at the little man. "Yes sir, you a pimp, all right. Yes sir-ree."

## 13

"Fasten that coat, let's go," Mama says.

"You don't have to leave," the lady says.

Mama don't answer the lady, and we right out in the cold again. I'm warm right now—my hands, my ears, my feet—but I know this ain't go'n last too long. It done sleet so much now you got ice everywhere you look.

We cross the railroad tracks, and soon's we do, I get cold. That wind goes through this little old coat like it ain't even there. I got on a shirt and a sweater under the coat, but that wind don't pay them no mind. I look up and I can see we got a long way to go. I wonder if we go'n make it 'fore I get too cold.

We cross over to walk on the sidewalk. They got just one sidewalk back here, and it's over there.

After we go just a little piece, I smell bread cooking. I look, then I see a baker shop. When we get closer, I can smell it more better, I shut my eyes and make 'tend I'm eating. But I keep them shut too long and I butt up 'gainst a telephone post. Mama grabs me and see if I'm hurt. I ain't bleeding or nothing and she turns me loose.

I can feel I'm getting colder and colder, and I look up to see how far we still got to go. Uptown is 'way up yonder. A half mile more, I reckon. I try to think of something. They say think and you won't get cold. I think of that poem, "Annabel Lee." I ain't been to school in so long—this bad weather—I reckon they done passed "Annabel Lee" by now. But passed it or not, I'm sure Miss Walker go'n make me recite it when I get there. That woman don't never forget nothing. I ain't never seen nobody like that in my life.

I'm still getting cold. "Annabel Lee" or no "Annabel Lee," I'm still getting cold. But I can see we getting closer. We getting there gradually.

Soon's we turn the corner, I see a little old white lady up in front of us. She's the only lady on the street. She's all in black and she's got a long black rag over her head.

"Stop," she says.

Me and Mama stop and look at her. She must be crazy to be out in all this bad weather. Ain't got but a few other people out there, and all of them's men.

"Y'all done ate?" she says.

"Just finish," Mama says.

"Y'all must be cold then?" she says.

"We headed for the dentist," Mama says. "We'll warm up when we get there."

"What dentist?" the old lady says. "Mr. Bassett?"

"Yes, Ma'am," Mama says.

"Come on in," the old lady says. "I'll telephone him and tell him y'all coming."

Me and Mama follow the old lady in the store. It's a little bitty store, and it don't have much in there. The old lady takes off her head rag and folds it up.

"Helena?" somebody calls from the back.

"Yes, Alnest?" the old lady says.

"Did you see them?"

"They're here. Standing beside me."

"Good. Now you can stay inside."

The old lady looks at Mama. Mama's waiting to hear what she brought us in here for. I'm waiting for that, too.

"I saw y'all each time you went by," she says. "I came out to catch you, but you were gone."

"We went back of town," Mama says.

"Did you eat?"

"Yes, ma'am."

The old lady looks at Mama a long time, like she's thinking Mama might be just saying that. Mama looks right back at her. The old lady looks at me to see what I have to say. I don't say nothing. I sure ain't going 'gainst my Mama.

"There's food in the kitchen," she says to Mama. "I've been keeping it warm."

Mama turns right around and starts for the door.

"Just a minute," the old lady says. Mama stops. "The boy'll have to work for it. It isn't free."

"We don't take no handout," Mama says.

"I'm not handing out anything," the old lady says. "I need my garbage moved to the front. Ernest has a bad cold and can't go out there."

"James'll move it for you," Mama says.

"Not unless you eat," the old lady says. "I'm old, but I have my pride, too, you know."

Mama can see she ain't go'n beat this old lady down, so she just shakes her head.

"All right," the old lady says. "Come into the kitchen."

She leads the way with that rag in her hand. The kitchen is a little bitty little old thing, too. The table and the stove just 'bout fill it up. They got a little room to the side. Somebody in there laying 'cross the bed—'cause I can see one of his feet. Must be the person she was talking to: Ernest or Alnest—something like that.

"Sit down," the old lady says to Mama. "Not you," she says to me. "You have to move the cans."

"Helena?" the man says in the other room.

"Yes, Alnest?" the old lady says.

"Are you going out there again?"

"I must show the boy where the garbage is, Alnest," the old lady says.

"Keep that shawl over you head," the old man says.

"You don't have to remind me, Alnest. Come, boy," the old lady says.

We go out in the yard. Little old back yard ain't no bigger than the store or the kitchen. But it can sleet here just like it can sleet in any big back yard. And 'fore you know it, I'm trembling.

"There," the old lady says, pointing to the cans. I pick up one of the cans and set it right back down. The can's so light, I'm go'n see what's inside of it.

"Here," the old lady says. "Leave that can alone."

I look back at her standing there in the door. She's got that black rag wrapped around her shoulders, and she's pointing one of her little old fingers at me.

"Pick it up and carry it to the front," she says. I go by her with the can, and she's looking at me all the time. I'm sure the can's empty. I'm sure she could've carried it herself—maybe both of them at the same time. "Set it on the sidewalk by the door and come back for the other one," she says.

I go and come back, and Mama looks at me when I pass her. I get the other can and take it to the front. It don't feel a bit heavier than that first one. I tell myself I ain't go'n be nobody's fool, and I'm go'n look inside this can to see just what I been hauling. First, I look up the street, then down the street. Nobody coming. Then I look over my shoulder toward the door. That little old lady done slipped up there quiet's mouse, watching me again. Look like she knowed what I was go'n do.

"Ehh, Lord," she says. "Children, children. Come in here, boy, and go wash your hands."

I follow her in the kitchen. She point toward the bathroom, and I go in there and wash up. Little bitty old bathroom, but it's clean, clean. I don't use any of her towels; I wipe my hands on my pants legs.

When I come back in the kitchen, the old lady done dished up the food. Rice, gravy, meat—and she even got some lettuce and tomato in a saucer. She even got a glass of milk and a piece of cake there, too. It looks so good, I almost start eating 'fore I say my blessing.

"Helena?" the old man says.

"Yes, Alnest?"

"Are they eating?"

"Yes," she says.

"Good," he says. "Now you'll stay inside."

The old lady goes in there where he is and I can hear them talking. I look at Mama. She's eating slow like she's thinking. I wonder what's the matter now. I reckon she's thinking 'bout home.

The old lady comes back in the kitchen.

"I talked to Dr. Bassett's nurse," she says. "Dr. Bassett will take you as soon as you get there."

"Thank you, ma'am," Mama says.

"Perfectly all right," the old lady says. "Which one is it?"

Mama nods toward me. The old lady looks at me real sad. I look sad, too.

"You're not afraid, are you?" she says.

"No ma'am," I say.

"That's a good boy," the old lady says. "Nothing to be afraid of. Dr. Bassett will not hurt you."

When me and Mama get through eating, we thank the old lady again.

"Helena, are they leaving?" the old man says.

"Yes, Alnest."

"Tell them I say good-bye."

"They can hear you, Alnest."

"Good-bye both mother and son," the old man says. "And may God be with you."

Me and Mama tell the old man good-bye, and we follow the old lady in the front room. Mama opens the door to go out, but she stops and comes back in the store.

"You sell salt meat?" she says.

"Yes."

"Give me two bits worth."

"That isn't very much salt meat," the old lady says.

"That's all I have," Mama says.

The old lady goes back of the counter and cuts a big piece off the chunk. Then she wraps it up and put it in a paper bag.

"Two bits," she says.

"That looks like awful lot of meat for a quarter," Mama says.

"Two bits," the old lady says. "I've been selling salt meat behind this counter twenty-five years. I think I know what I'm doing."

"You got a scale there," Mama says.

"What?" the old lady says.

"Weigh it," Mama says.

"What?" the old lady says. "Are you telling me how to run my business?"

"Thanks very much for the food," Mama says.

"Just a minute," the old lady says.

"James," Mama says to me. I move toward the door.

"Just one minute, I said," the old lady says.

Me and Mama stop again and look at her. The old lady takes the meat out of the bag and unwraps it and cuts 'bout half of it off. Then she wraps it up again and juggs it back in the bag and gives the bag to Mama. Mama lays the quarter on the counter.

"Your kindness will never be forgotten," she says. "James," she says to me.

We go out, and the old lady comes to the door to look at us. After we go a little piece I look back, and she's still there watching us.

The sleet's coming down heavy, heavy now, and I turn up my coat collar to keep my neck warm. My Mama tells me turn it right back down.

"You not a bum," she says. "You a man."

# ⁜ ROBERT COOVER
(1932– )

An innovator and metafictionist, Robert Coover writes a fiction that subverts realist conventions by foregrounding narrative forms and demythologizing the contents of history and culture. At times satirical, at times slapstick and farce, Coover's fiction never lets the reader forget the way narratives construct social reality, and the contingent status of truth and knowledge. His fiction blurs and dismantles distinctions between high, low, and popular forms of culture.

A product of the Midwest, Coover was born in Charles City, Iowa, and later moved with his family to Indiana, where his father was a newspaper reporter. He early showed an interest in writing, sometimes accompanying his father on journalistic assignments. He graduated from Indiana University in 1953, and then served four years in the navy. He also studied philosophy and history at the University of Chicago. He lived for a while in England and Spain, where he married a Spanish woman.

Coover has published over twenty works of fiction, including the novels *The Origin of the Brunists* (1966), *The Universal Baseball Association, Inc., J. Henry Waugh, Prop.* (1968), *The Public Burning* (1977), *Gerald's Party* (1987), *Spanking the Maid* (1982), and *John's Wife* (1996), and the story collections *Pricksongs & Descants* (1969) and *A Night at the Movies, or, You Must Remember This* (1987).

## The Babysitter

SHE ARRIVES at 7:40, ten minutes late, but the children, Jimmy and Bitsy, are still eating supper, and their parents are not ready to go yet. From other rooms come the sounds of a baby screaming, water running, a television musical (no words: probably a dance number—patterns of gliding figures come to mind). Mrs. Tucker sweeps into the kitchen, fussing with her hair, and snatches a baby bottle full of milk out of a pan of warm water, rushes out again. "Harry!" she calls. "The babysitter's here already!"

* * *

That's My Desire? I'll Be Around?[1] He smiles toothily, beckons faintly with his head, rubs his fast balding pate. Bewitched, maybe? Or, What's the Reason? He pulls on his

1. Titles of popular songs, as are *What's the Reason* and *Who's Sorry Now.*

shorts, gives his hips a slap. The baby goes silent in mid-scream. Isn't this the one who used their tub last time? Who's Sorry Now, that's it.

* * *

Jack is wandering around town, not knowing what to do. His girlfriend is babysitting at the Tuckers', and later, when she's got the kids in bed, maybe he'll drop over there. Sometimes he watches TV with her when she's babysitting, it's about the only chance he gets to make out a little since he doesn't own wheels, but they have to be careful because most people don't like their sitters to have boyfriends over. Just kissing her makes her nervous. She won't close her eyes because she has to be watching the door all the time. Married people really have it good, he thinks.

* * *

"Hi," the babysitter says to the children, and puts her books on top of the refrigerator. "What's for supper?" The little girl, Bitsy, only stares at her obliquely. She joins them at the end of the kitchen table. "I don't have to go to bed until nine," the boy announces flatly, and stuffs his mouth full of potato chips. The babysitter catches a glimpse of Mr. Tucker hurrying out of the bathroom in his underwear.

* * *

Her tummy. Under her arms. And her feet. Those are the best places. She'll spank him, she says sometimes. Let her.

* * *

That sweet odor that girls have. The softness of her blouse. He catches a glimpse of the gentle shadows amid her thighs, as she curls her legs up under her. He stares hard at her. He has a lot of meaning packed into that stare, but she's not even looking. She's popping her gum and watching television. She's sitting right there, inches away, soft, fragrant, and ready: but what's his next move? He notices his buddy Mark in the drugstore, playing the pinball machine, and joins him. "Hey, this mama's cold, Jack baby! She needs your touch!"

* * *

Mrs. Tucker appears at the kitchen doorway, holding a rolled-up diaper. "Now, don't just eat potato chips, Jimmy! See that he eats his hamburger, dear." She hurried away to the bathroom. The boy glares sullenly at the babysitter, silently daring her to carry out the order. "How about a little of that good hamburger now, Jimmy?" she says perfunctorily. He lets half of it drop to the floor. The baby is silent and a man is singing a love song on the TV. The children crunch chips.

* * *

He loves her. She loves him. They whirl airily, stirring a light breeze, through a magical landscape of rose and emerald and deep blue. Her light brown hair coils and wisps softly in the breeze, and the soft folds of her white gown tug at her body and then float away. He smiles in a pulsing crescendo of sincerity and song.

* * *

"You mean she's alone?" Mark asks. "Well, there's two or three kids," Jack says. He slides the coin in. There's a rumble of steel balls tumbling, lining up. He pushes a plunger with his thumb, and one ball pops up in place, hard and glittering with promise. His stare? to say he loves her. That he cares for her and would protect her, would shield her, if need be, with his own body. Grinning, he bends over the ball to take careful aim: he and Mark have studied this machine and have it figured out, but still it's not that easy to beat.

* * *

On the drive to the party, his mind is partly on the girl, partly on his own high-school days, long past. Sitting at the end of the kitchen table there with his children, she had seemed to be self-consciously arching her back, jutting her pert breasts, twitching her thighs: and for whom if not for him? So she'd seen him coming out of there, after all. He smiles. Yet what could he ever do about it? Those good times are gone, old man. He glances over at his wife, who, readjusting a garter, asks: "What do you think of our babysitter?"

* * *

He loves her. She loves him. And then the babies come. And dirty diapers and one goddamn meal after another. Dishes. Noise. Clutter. And fat. Not just tight, her girdle actually hurts. Somewhere recently she's read about women getting heart attacks or cancer or something from too-tight girdles. Dolly pulls the car door shut with a grunt, strangely irritated, not knowing why. Party mood. Why is her husband humming, "Who's Sorry Now?" Pulling out of the drive, she glances back at the lighted kitchen window. "What do you think of our babysitter?" she asks. While her husband stumbles all over himself trying to answer, she pulls a stocking tight, biting deeper with the garters.

* * *

"Stop it!" she laughs. Bitsy is pulling on her skirt and he is tickling her in the ribs. "Jimmy! Don't!" But she is laughing too much to stop him. He leaps on her, wrapping his legs around her waist, and they all fall to the carpet in front of the TV, where just now a man in a tuxedo and a little girl in a flouncy white dress are doing a tapdance together. The babysitter's blouse is pulling out of her skirt, showing a patch of bare tummy: the target. "I'll spank!"

* * *

Jack pushes the plunger, thrusting up a steel ball, and bends studiously over the machine. "You getting any off her?" Mark asks, and clears his throat, flicks ash from his cigarette. "Well, not exactly, not yet," Jack says, grinning awkwardly, but trying to suggest more than he admits to, and fires. He heaves his weight gently against the machine as the ball bounds off a rubber bumper. He can feel her warming up under his hands, the flippers suddenly coming alive, delicate rapid-fire patterns emerging in the flashing of the lights. 1000 WHEN LIT: *now!* "Got my hand on it, that's about all." Mark glances up from the machine, cigarette dangling from his lip. "Maybe you need some help," he suggests with a wry one-sided grin. "Like maybe together, man, we could do it."

* * *

She likes the big tub. She uses the Tuckers' bath salts, and loves to sink into the hot fragrant suds. She can stretch out, submerged, up to her chin. It gives her a good sleepy tingly feeling.

* * *

"What do you think of our babysitter?" Dolly asks, adjusting a garter. "Oh, I hardly noticed," he says "Cute girl. She seems to get along fine with the kids. Why?" "I don't know." His wife tugs her skirt down, glances at a lighted window they are passing, adding: "I'm not sure I trust her completely, that's all. With the baby, I mean. She seems a little careless. And the other time, I'm almost sure she had a boyfriend over." He grins, claps one hand on his wife's broad gartered thigh. "What's wrong with that?" he asks. Still in anklets, too. Bare thighs, no girdles, nothing up there but a flimsy pair of panties and soft adolescent flesh. He's flooded with vague remembrances of football rallies and movie balconies.

* * *

How tiny and rubbery it is! she thinks, soaping between the boy's legs, giving him his bath. Just a funny jiggly little thing that looks like it shouldn't even be there at all. Is that what all the songs are about?

* * *

Jack watches Mark lunge and twist against the machine. Got her running now, racked them up. He's not too excited about the idea of Mark fooling around with his girlfriend, but Mark's a cooler operator than he is, and maybe, doing it together this once, he'd get over his own timidity. And if she didn't like it, there were other girls around. If Mark went too far, he could cut him off too. He feels his shoulders tense: enough's enough, man . . . but sees the flesh, too. "Maybe I'll call her later," he says.

* * *

"Hey, Harry! Dolly! Glad you could make it!" "I hope we're not late." "No, no, you're one of the first, come on in! By golly, Dolly, you're looking younger every day! How do you do it? Give my wife your secret, will you?" He pats her on her girdled bottom behind Mr. Tucker's back, leads them in for drinks.

* * *

8:00. The babysitter runs water in the tub, combs her hair in front of the bathroom mirror. There's a western on television, so she lets Jimmy watch it while she gives Bitsy her bath. But Bitsy doesn't want a bath. She's angry and crying because she has to be first. The babysitter tells her if she'll take her bath quickly, she'll let her watch television while Jimmy takes his bath, but it does no good. The little girl fights to get out of the bathroom, and the babysitter has to squat with her back against the door and forcibly undress the child. There are better places to babysit. Both children mind badly, and then, sooner or later, the baby is sure to wake up for a diaper change and more bottle. The Tuckers do have a good color TV, though, and she hopes things will be settled down enough to catch the 8:30 program. She thrusts the child into the tub, but she's still screaming and thrashing around. "Stop it now, Bitsy, or you'll wake the baby!" "I have to go potty!" the child wails, switching tactics. The babysitter sighs, lifts the girl out of the tub and onto the toilet, getting her skirt and blouse all wet in the process. She glances at herself in the mirror. Before she knows it, the girl is off the seat and out of the bathroom. "Bitsy! Come back here!"

* * *

"Okay, that's enough!" Her skirt is ripped and she's flushed and crying. "Who says?" "I do, man!" The bastard goes for her, but she tackles him. They roll and tumble. Tables tip, lights topple, the TV crashes to the floor. He slams a hard right to the guy's gut, clips his chin with a rolling left.

* * *

"We hope it's a girl." That's hardly surprising, since they already have four boys. Dolly congratulates the woman like everybody else, but she doesn't envy her, not a bit. That's all she needs about now. She stares across the room at Harry, who is slapping backs and getting loud, as usual. He's spreading out through the middle, so why the hell does he have to complain about her all the time? "Dolly, you're looking younger every day!" was the nice greeting she got tonight. "What's your secret?" And Harry: "It's all those calories. She's getting back her baby fat." "Haw haw! Harry, have a heart!"

* * *

"Get her feet" he hollers at Bitsy, his fingers in her ribs, running over her naked tummy, tangling in the underbrush of straps and strange clothing. "Get her shoes off!" He holds her pinned by pressing his head against her soft chest. "No! No, Jimmy! Bitsy, stop!" But though she kicks and twists and rolls around, she doesn't get up, she can't get up, she's laughing too hard, and the shoes come off, and he grabs a stockinged foot and scratches the sole ruthlessly, and she raises up her legs, trying to pitch him off, she's wild, boy, but he hangs on, and she's laughing, and on the screen there's a rattle of hooves, and he and Bitsy are rolling around and around on the floor in a crazy rodeo of long bucking legs.

* * *

He slips the coin in. There's a metallic fall and a sharp click as the dial tone begins. "I hope the Tuckers have gone," he says. "Don't worry, they're at our place," Mark says. "They're always the first ones to come and the last ones to go home. My old man's always bitching about them." Jack laughs nervously and dials the number. "Tell her we're coming over to protect her from getting raped," Mark suggests, and lights a cigarette. Jack grins, leaning casually against the door jamb of the phonebooth, chewing gum, one hand in his pocket. He's really pretty uneasy, though. He has the feeling he's somehow messing up a good thing.

* * *

Bitsy runs naked into the livingroom, keeping a hassock between herself and the babysitter. "Bitsy . . . !" the babysitter threatens. Artificial reds and greens and purples flicker over the child's wet body, as hooves clatter, guns crackle, and stagecoach wheels thunder over rutted terrain. "Get outa the way, Bitsy!" the boy complains. "I can't see!" Bitsy streaks past and the babysitter chases, cornering the girl in the back bedroom.

Bitsy throws something that hits her softly in the face: a pair of men's undershorts. She grabs the girl scampering by, carries her struggling to the bathroom, and with a smart crack on her glistening bottom, pops her back into the tub. In spite, Bitsy peepees in the bath-water.

* * *

Mr. Tucker stirs a little water into his bourbon and kids with his host and another man, just arrived, about their golf games. They set up a match for the weekend, a threesome looking for a fourth. Holding his drink in his right hand, Mr. Tucker swings his left through the motion of a tee-shot. "You'll have to give me a stroke a hole," he says. "I'll give you a stroke!" says his host: "Bend over!" Laughing, the other man asks. "Where's your boy Mark tonight?" "I don't know," replies the host, gathering up a trayful of drinks. Then he adds in a low growl: "Out chasing tail probably." They chuckle loosely at that, then shrug in commiseration and return to the living room to join their women.

* * *

Shades pulled. Door locked. Watching the TV. Under a blanket maybe. Yes, that's right, under a blanket. Her eyes close when he kisses her. Her breasts, under both their hands, are soft and yielding.

* * *

A hard blow to the belly. The face. The dark beardy one staggers, the lean-jawed sheriff moves in, but gets a spurred boot in his face. The dark one hurls himself forward, drives his shoulder into the sheriff's hard midriff, her own tummy tightens, withstands, as the sheriff smashes the dark man's nose, slams him up against a wall, slugs him again! and again! The dark man grunts rhythmically, backs off, then plunges suicidally forward—her own knees draw up protectively—the sheriff staggers! caught low! but instead of following through, the other man steps back—a pistol! the dark one has a pistol! the sheriff draws! shoots from the hip! explosions! she clutches her hands between her thighs—no! the sheriff spins! wounded! the dark man hesitates, aims, her legs stiffen toward the set, the sheriff rolls desperately in the straw, fires: dead! the dark man is dead! groans, crumples, his pistol drooping in his collapsing hand, dropping, he drops. The sheriff, spent, nicked, watches weakly from the floor where he lies. Oh, to be whole! to be good and strong and right! to embrace and be embraced by harmony and wholeness! The sheriff, drawing himself painfully up on one elbow, rubs his bruised mouth with the back of his other hand.

* * *

"Well, we just sorta thought we'd drop over," he says, and winks broadly at Mark. "Who's we?" "Oh, me and Mark here." "Tell her, good thing like her, gotta pass it around," whispers Mark, dragging on his smoke, then flicking the butt over under the pinball machine. "What's that?" she asks. "Oh, Mark and I were just saying, like two's company, three's an orgy," Jack says, and winks again. She giggles. "Oh Jack!" Behind her, he can hear shouts and gunfire. "Well, okay, for just a little while, if you'll both be good." Way to go, man.

* * *

Probably some damn kid over there right now. Wrestling around on the couch in front of his TV. Maybe he should drop back to the house. Just to check. None of that stuff, she was there to do a job! Park the car a couple doors down, slip in the front door before she knows it. He sees the disarray of clothing, the young thighs exposed to the flickering television light, hears his baby crying. "Hey, what's going on here! Get outa here, son, before I call the police!" Of course, they haven't really been doing anything. They probably don't even know how. He stares benignly down upon the girl, her skirt rumpled loosely around her thighs. Flushed, frightened, yet excited, she stares back at him. He smiles. His finger touches a knee, approaches the hem. Another couple arrives. Filling up here with people. He wouldn't be missed. Just slip out, stop back casually to pick up something or other he forgot, never mind what. He remembers that the other time they had this babysitter, she took a bath in their house. She had a date afterwards, and she'd come from cheerleading practice or something. Aspirin maybe. Just drop quietly and casually into the bathroom to pick up some aspirin. "Oh, excuse me, dear! I only . . . !" She gazes back at him, astonished, yet strangely moved. Her soft wet breasts rise and fall in the water, and her tummy looks pale and ripply. He recalls that her pubic hairs, left in the tub, were brown. Light brown.

* * *

She's no more than stepped into the tub for a quick bath, when Jimmy announces from outside the door that he has to go to the bathroom. She sighs: just an excuse, she knows. "You'll have to wait." The little nuisance. "I can't wait." "Okay, then come ahead, but I'm taking a bath." She supposes that will stop him, but it doesn't. In he comes. She slides down into the suds until she's eye-level with the edge of the tub. He hesitates. "Go ahead, if you have to," she says, a little awkwardly, "but I'm not getting out." "Don't look," he says. She: "I will if I want to."

* * *

She's crying. Mark is rubbing his jaw where he's just slugged him. A lamp lies shattered. "Enough's enough, Mark! Now get outa here!" Her skirt is ripped to the waist, her bare hip bruised. Her panties lie on the floor like a broken balloon. Later, he'll wash her wounds, help her dress, he'll take care of her. Pity washes through him, giving him a sudden hard-on. Mark laughs at it, pointing. Jack crouches, waiting, ready for anything.

* * *

Laughing, they roll and tumble. Their little hands are all over her, digging and pinching. She struggles to her hands and knees, but Bitsy leaps astride her neck, bowing her head to the carpet. "Spank her, Jimmy!" His swats sting: is her skirt up? The phone rings. "The cavalry to the rescue!" she laughs, and throws them off to go answer.

* * *

Kissing Mark, her eyes closed, her hips nudge toward Jack. He stares at the TV screen, unsure of himself, one hand slipping cautiously under her skirt. Her hand touches his arm as though to resist, then brushes on by to rub his leg. This blanket they're under was a good idea. "Hi! This is Jack!"

* * *

Bitsy's out and the water's running. "Come on, Jimmy, your turn!" Last time, he told her he took his own baths, but she came in anyway. "I'm not gonna take a bath," he announces, eyes glued on the set. He readies for the struggle. "But I've already run your water. Come on, Jimmy, please!" He shakes his head. She can't make him, he's sure he's as strong as she is. She sighs. "Well, it's up to you. I'll use the water myself then," she says. He waits until he's pretty sure she's not going to change her mind, then sneaks in and peeks through the keyhole in the bathroom door: just in time to see her big bottom as she bends over to stir in the bubblebath. Then she disappears. Trying to see as far down as the keyhole will allow, he bumps his head on the knob. "Jimmy, is that you?" "I—I have to go to the bathroom!" he stammers.

* * *

Not actually in the tub, just getting in. One foot on the mat, the other in the water. Bent over slightly, buttocks flexed, teats swaying, holding on to the edge of the tub. "Oh, excuse me! I only wanted . . . !" He passes over her astonishment, the awkward excuses, moves quickly to the part where he reaches out to—"What on earth are you doing, Harry?" his wife asks, staring at his hand. His host, passing, laughs. "He's practicing his swing for Sunday, Dolly, but it's not going to do him a damn bit of good!" Mr. Tucker laughs, sweeps his right hand on through the air as though lifting a seven-iron shot onto the green. He makes a *dok!* sound with his tongue. "In there!"

* * *

"No, Jack, I don't think you'd better." "Well, we just called, we just, uh, thought we'd, you know, stop by for a minute, watch television for thirty minutes, or, or something." "Who's we?" "Well, Mark's here, I'm with him, and he said he'd like to, you know, like if it's all right, just—" "Well, it's *not* all right. The Tuckers said no." "Yeah, but if we only—" "And they seemed awfully suspicious about last time." "Why? We didn't—I mean, I just thought—" "No, Jack, and that's period." She hangs up. She returns to the TV, but the commercial is on. Anyway, she's missed most of the show. She decides maybe she'll take a quick bath. Jack might come by anyway, it'd make her mad, that'd be the end as far as he was concerned, but if he should, she doesn't want to be all sweaty. And besides, she likes the big tub the Tuckers have.

* * *

He is self-conscious and stands with his back to her, his little neck flushed. It takes him forever to get started, and when it finally does come, it's just a tiny trickle. "See, it was just an excuse," she scolds, but she's giggling inwardly at the boy's embarrassment. "You're just a nuisance, Jimmy." At the door, his hand on the knob, he hesitates, staring timidly down on his shoes. "Jimmy?" She peeks at him over the edge of the tub, trying to keep a straight face, as he sneaks a nervous glance back over his shoulder. "As long as you bothered me," she says, "you might as well soap my back."

* * *

"The aspirin . . ." They embrace. She huddles in his arms like a child. Lovingly, paternally, knowledgeably, he wraps her nakedness. How compact, how tight and small her body is! Kissing her ear, he stares down past her rump at the still clear water. "I'll join you," he whispers hoarsely.

* * *

She picks up the shorts Bitsy threw at her. Men's underwear. She holds them in front of her, looks at herself in the bedroom mirror. About twenty sizes too big for her, of course. She runs her hand inside the opening in front, pulls out her thumb. How funny it must feel!

* * *

"Well, man, I say we just go rape her," Mark says flatly, and swings his weight against the pinball machine. "Uff! Ahh! Get in there, you mother! Look at that! Hah! Man, I'm gonna turn this baby over!" Jack is embarrassed about the phone conversation. Mark just snorted in disgust when he hung up. He cracks down hard on his gum, angry that he's such a chicken. "Well, I'm game if you are," he says coldly.

* * *

8:30 "Okay, come on, Jimmy, it's time." He ignores her. The western gives way to a spy show. Bitsy, in pajamas, pads into the living room. "No, Bitsy, it's time to go to bed." "You said I could watch!" the girl whines, and starts to throw another tantrum. "But you were too slow and it's late. Jimmy, you get in that bathroom, and right now!" Jimmy stares sullenly at the set, unmoving. The babysitter tries to catch the opening scene of the television program so she can follow it later, since Jimmy gives himself his own baths. When the commercial interrupts, she turns off the sound, stands in front of the screen. "Okay, into the tub, Jimmy Tucker, or I'll take you in there and give you your bath myself!" "Just try it," he says, "and see what happens."

* * *

They stand outside, in the dark, crouched in the bushes, peeking in. She's on the floor, playing with the kids. Too early. They seem to be tickling her. She gets to her hands and knees, but the little girl leaps on her head, pressing her face to the floor. There's an obvious target, and the little boy proceeds to beat on it. "Hey, look at that kid go!" whispers Mark, laughing and snapping his fingers softly. Jack feels uneasy out here. Too many neighbors, too many cars going by, too many people in the world. That little boy in there is one up on him, though: he's never thought about tickling her as a starter.

* * *

His little hand, clutching the bar of soap, lathers shyly a narrow space between her shoulderblades. She is doubled forward against her knees, buried in rich suds, pecking at him over the edge of her shoulder. The soap slithers out of his grip and plunks into the water. "I . . . I dropped the soap," he whispers. She: "Find it."

* * *

"I dream of Jeannie with the light brown pubic hair!" "Harry! Stop that! You're drunk!" But they're laughing, they're all laughing, damn! he's feeling pretty goddamn good at that, and now he just knows he needs that aspirin. Watching her there, her thighs spread for him, on the couch, in the tub, hell, on the kitchen table for that matter, he tees off on Number Nine, and—*whap!*—swats his host's wife on the bottom. "Hole in one!" he shouts. "Harry!" Why can't his goddamn wife Dolly ever get happy-drunk instead of sour-drunk all the time? "Gonna be tough Sunday, old buddy!" "You're pretty tough right now, Harry," says his host.

* * *

The babysitter lunges forward, grabs the boy by the arms and hauls him off the couch, pulling two cushions with him, and drags him toward the bathroom. He lashes out, knocking over an endtable full of magazines and ashtrays. "You leave my brother alone!" Bitsy cries and grabs the sitter around the waist. Jimmy jumps on her and down they all go. On the silent screen, there's a fade-in to a dark passageway in an old apartment building in some foreign country. She kicks out and somebody falls between her legs. Somebody else is sitting on her face. "Jimmy! Stop that!" the babysitter laughs, her voice muffled.

* * *

She's watching television. All alone. It seems like a good time to go in. Just remember: really, no matter what she says, she wants it. They're standing in the bushes, trying to get up the nerve. "We'll tell her to be good," Mark whispers, "and if she's not good, we'll spank her." Jack giggles softly, but his knees are weak. She stands. They freeze. She looks right at them. "She can't see us." Mark whispers tensely. "Is she coming out?" "No," says Mark, "She's going into—that must be the bathroom!" Jack takes a deep breath, his heart pounding. "Hey, is there a window back there?" Mark asks.

* * *

The phone rings. She leaves the tub, wrapped in a towel. Bitsy gives a tug on the towel. "Hey, Jimmy, get the towel!" she squeals. "Now stop that, Bitsy!" the babysitter hisses, but too late: with one hand on the phone, the other isn't enough to hang on to the towel. Her sudden nakedness awes them and it takes them a moment to remember about tickling her. By then, she's in the towel again. "I hope you got a good look," she says angrily. She feels chilled and oddly a little frightened. "Hello?" No answer. She glances at the window—is somebody out there? Something, she saw something, and a rustling—footsteps?

* * *

"Okay, I don't care, Jimmy, don't take a bath," she says irritably. Her blouse is pulled out and wrinkled, her hair is all mussed, and she feels sweaty. There's about a million things she'd rather be doing than babysitting with these two. Three: at least the baby's sleeping. She knocks on the overturned endtable for luck, rights it, replaces the magazines and ashtrays. The one thing that really makes her sick is a dirty diaper. "Just go on to bed." "I don't have to go to bed until nine," he reminds her. Really, she couldn't care less. She turns up the volume on the TV, settles down on the couch, poking her blouse back into her skirt, pushing her hair out of her eyes. Jimmy and Bitsy watch from the floor. Maybe, once they're in bed, she'll take a quick bath. She wishes Jack would come by. The man, no doubt the spy, is following a woman, but she doesn't know why. The woman passes another man. Something seems to happen, but it's not clear what. She's probably already missed too much. The phone rings.

* * *

Mark is kissing her. Jack is under the blanket, easing her panties down over her squirming hips. Her hand is in his pants, pulling it out, pulling it toward her, pulling it hard. She knew just where it was! Mark is stripping, too. God, it's really happening! he thinks with a kind of pious joy, and notices the open door. "Hey! What's going on here?"

* * *

He soaps her back, smooth and slippery under his hand. She is doubled over, against her knees, between his legs. Her light brown hair, reaching to her gleaming shoulders, is wet at the edges. The soap slips, falls between his legs. He fishes for it, finds it, slips it behind him. "Help me find it," he whispers in her ear. "Sure Harry," says his host, going around behind him. "What'd you lose?"

* * *

Soon be nine, time to pack the kids off to bed. She clears the table, dumps paper plates and leftover hamburgers into the garbage, puts glasses and silverware into the sink, and the mayonnaise, mustard, and ketchup in the refrigerator. Neither child has eaten much supper finally, mostly potato chips and ice cream, but it's really not her problem. She glances at the books on the refrigerator. Not much chance she'll get to them, she's already pretty worn out. Maybe she'd feel better if she had a quick bath. She runs water into the tub, tosses in bubblebath salts, undresses. Before pushing down her panties, she stares for a moment at the smooth silken panel across her tummy, fingers the place where the opening would be if there were one. Then she steps quickly out of them, feeling somehow ashamed, unhooks her brassiere. She weighs her breasts in the palms of her hands, watching herself in the bathroom mirror, where, in the open window behind her, she sees a face. She screams.

* * *

She screams: "Jimmy! Give me that!" "What's the matter?" asks Jack on the other end. "Jimmy! Give me my towel! Right now!" "Hello? Hey, are you still there?" "I'm sorry, Jack," she says, panting. "You caught me in the tub. I'm just wrapped in a towel and these silly kids grabbed it away!" "Gee, I wish I'd been there!" "Jack—!" "To protect you, I mean." "Oh, sure," she says, giggling. "Well, what do you think, can I come over and watch TV with you?" "Well, not right this minute," she says. He laughs lightly. He feels very cool. "Jack?" "Yeah?" "Jack, I . . . I think there's somebody outside the window!"

* * *

She carries him, fighting all the way, to the tub, Bitsy pummeling her in the back and kicking her ankles. She can't hang on to him and undress him at the same time. "I'll throw you in, clothes and all, Jimmy Tucker!" she gasps. "You better not!" he cries. She sits on the toilet seat, locks her legs around him, whips his shirt up over his head before he knows what's happening. The pants are easier. Like all little boys his age, he has almost no hips at all. He hangs on desperately to his underpants, but when she succeeds in snapping these down out of his grip, too, he gives up, starts to bawl, and beats her wildly in the face with his fists. She ducks her head, laughing hysterically, oddly entranced by the spectacle of that pale little thing down there, bobbing and bouncing rubberlike about the boy's helpless fury and anguish.

* * *

"Aspirin? Whaddaya want aspirin for, Harry? I'm sure they got aspirin here, if you—" "Did I say aspirin? I meant uh, my glasses. And, you know, I thought, well, I'd sorta check to see if everything was okay at home." Why the hell is it his mouth feels like it's got about six sets of teeth packed in there, and a tongue the size of that liverwurst his host's wife is passing around? "Whaddaya want your glasses for, Harry? I don't understand you at all!" "Aw, well, honey, I was feeling kind of dizzy or something, and I thought—" "Dizzy is right. If you want to check on the kids, why don't you just call on the phone?"

* * *

They can tell she's naked and about to get into the tub, but the bathroom window is frosted glass, and they can't see anything clearly. "I got an idea," Mark whispers. "One of us goes and calls her on the phone, and the other watches when she comes out." "Okay, but who calls?" "Both of us, we'll do it twice. Or more."

* * *

Down forbidden alleys. Into secret passageways. Unlocking the world's terrible secrets. Sudden shocks: a trapdoor! a fall! or the stunning report of a rifle shot, the *whaaii-ii-ing!* of the bullet biting concrete by your ear! Careful! Then edge forward once more, avoiding the light, inch at a time, now a quick dash for an open doorway—*look out!* there's a knife! a struggle! no! the long blade glistens! jerks! thrusts! *stabbed!* No, no, it missed! The assailant's down, yes! the spy's on top, pinning him, a terrific thrashing about, the spy rips off the assailant's mask: *a woman!*

* * *

Fumbling behind her, she finds it, wraps her hand around it, tugs. "Oh!" she gasps, pulling her hand back quickly, her ears turning crimson. "I . . . I thought it was the soap!" He squeezes her close between his thighs, pulls her back toward him, one hand sliding down her tummy between her legs. I Dream of Jeannie—"I have to go to the bathroom!" says someone outside the door.

* * *

She's combing her hair in the bathroom when the phone rings. She hurries to answer it before it wakes the baby. "Hello, Tuckers." There's no answer. "Hello?" A soft click.

Strange. She feels suddenly alone in the big house, and goes in to watch TV with the children.

* * *

"Stop it!" she screams, "Please stop!" She's on her hands and knees, trying to get up, but they're too strong for her. Mark holds her head down. "Now, baby, we're gonna teach you how to be a nice girl," he says coldly, and nods at Jack. When she's doubled over like that, her skirt rides up her thighs to the leg bands of her panties. "C'mon, man, go! This baby's cold! She needs your touch!"

* * *

Parks the car a couple blocks away. Slips up to the house, glances in his window. Just like he's expected. Her blouse is off and the kid's shirt is unbuttoned. He watches, while slowly, clumsily, childishly, they fumble with each other's clothes. My God, it takes them forever. "Some party!" "You said it!" When they're more or less naked, he walks in. "Hey! What's going on here?" They go white as bleu cheese. Haw haw! "What's the little thing you got sticking out there, boy?" "Harry, behave yourself!" No, he doesn't let the kid get dressed, he sends him home bareassed. "Bareassed!" He drinks to that. "Promises, promises," says his host's wife. "I'll mail you your clothes, son!" He gazes down on the naked little girl on his couch. "Looks like you and me, we got a little secret to keep, honey," he says coolly. "Less you wanna go home the same way your boyfriend did!" He chuckles at his easy wit, leans down over her, and unbuckles his belt. "Might as well make it two secrets, right?" "What in God's name are you talking about, Harry?" He staggers out of there, drink in hand, and goes to look for his car.

* * *

"Hey! What's going on here?" They huddle half-naked under the blanket, caught utterly unawares. On television: the clickety-click of frightened running feet on foreign pavements. Jack is fumbling for his shorts, tangled somehow around his ankles. The blanket is snatched away. "On your feet there!" Mr. Tucker, Mrs. Tucker, and Mark's mom and dad, the police, the neighbors, everybody comes crowding in. Hopelessly, he has a terrific erection. So hard it hurts. Everybody stares down at it.

* * *

Bitsy's sleeping on the floor. The babysitter is taking a bath. For more than an hour now, he'd had to use the bathroom. He doesn't know how much longer he can wait. Finally, he goes to knock on the bathroom door. "I have to use the bathroom." "Well, come ahead, if you have to." "Not while you're in there." She sighs loudly. "Okay, okay, just a minute," she says, "but you're a real nuisance, Jimmy!" He's holding on, pinching it as tight as he can. *"Hurry!"* He holds his breath, squeezing shut his eyes. No. Too late. At last, she opens the door. "Jimmy!" "I *told* you to hurry!" he sobs. She drags him into the bathroom and pulls his pants down.

* * *

He arrives just in time to see her emerge from the bathroom, wrapped in a towel, to answer the phone. His two kids sneak up behind her and pull the towel away. She's trying to hang onto the phone and get the towel back at the same time. It's quite a picture.

She's got a sweet ass. Standing there in the bushes, pawing himself with one hand, he lifts his glass with the other and toasts her sweet ass, which his son now swats. Haw haw, maybe that boy's gonna shape up, after all.

* * *

They're in the bushes, arguing about their next move, when she comes out of the bathroom, wrapped in a towel. They can hear the baby crying. Then it stops. They see her running, naked, back to the bathroom like she's scared or something. "I'm going in after her, man, whether you're with me or not!" Mark whispers, and he starts out of the bushes. But just then, a light comes sweeping up through the yard, as a car swings in the drive. They hit the dirt, hearts pounding. "Is it the cops?" "I don't know!" "Do you think they saw us?" "Sshh!" A man comes staggering up the walk from the drive, a drink in his hand, stumbles on in the kitchen door and then straight into the bathroom. "It's Mr. Tucker!" Mark whispers. A scream. "Let's get outa here, man!" 9:00. Having missed most of the spy show anyway and having little else to do, the babysitter has washed the dishes and cleaned the kitchen up a little. The books on the refrigerator remind her of her better intentions, but she decides that first she'll see what's next on TV. In the living room, she finds little Bitsy sound asleep on the floor. She lifts her gently, carries her into her bed, and tucks her in. "Okay, Jimmy, it's nine o'clock, I've let you stay up, now be a good boy." Sullenly, his sleepy eyes glued still to the set, the boy backs out of the room toward his bedroom. A drama comes on. She switches channels. A ballgame and a murder mystery. She switches back to the drama. It's a love story of some kind. A man married to an aging invalid wife, but in love with a younger girl. "Use the bathroom and brush your teeth before going to bed, Jimmy!" she calls, but as quickly regrets it, for she hears the baby stir in its crib.

* * *

Two of them are talking about mothers they've salted away in rest homes. Oh boy, that's just wonderful, this is one helluva party. She leaves them to use the john, takes advantage of the retreat to ease her girdle down awhile, get a few good deep breaths. She has this picture of her three kids carting her off to a rest home. In a wheelbarrow. That sure is something to look forward to, all right. When she pulls her girdle back up, she can't seem to squeeze into it. The host looks in. "Hey, Dolly, are you all right?" "Yeah, I just can't get into my damn girdle, that's all." "Here, let me help."

* * *

She pulls them on, over her own, standing in front of the bedroom mirror, holding her skirt bundled up around the waist. About twenty sizes too big for her, of course. She pulls them tight from behind, runs her hand inside the opening in front, pulls out her thumb. "And what a good boy am I!" She giggles: how funny it must feel! Then, in the mirror, she sees him: in the doorway behind her, sullenly watching. "Jimmy! You're supposed to be in bed!" "Those are my daddy's!" the boys says. "I'm gonna tell!"

* * *

"Jimmy!" She drags him into the bathroom and pulls his pants down. "Even your shoes are wet! Get them off!" She soaps up a warm washcloth she's had with her in the bathtub, scrubs him from the waist down with it. Bitsy stands in the doorway, staring. "Get out! Get out!" the boy screams at his sister. "Go back to bed, Bitsy. It's just an accident." "Get out!" The baby wakes and starts to howl.

* * *

The young lover feels sorry for her rival, the invalid wife; she believes the man has a duty toward the poor woman and and insists she is willing to wait. But the man argues that he also has a duty toward himself: his life, too, is short, and he could not love his wife now even were she well. He embraces the young girl feverishly; she twists away in anguish. The door opens. They stand there grinning, looking devilish, but pretty silly at the same time. "Jack! I thought I told you not to come!" She's angry, but she's also glad in a way she was beginning to feel a little too alone in the big house, with the children all sleeping. She should have taken that bath, after all. "We just came by to see if you were being a good girl," Jack says and blushes. The boys glance at each other nervously.

* * *

She's just sunk down into the tubful of warm fragrant suds, ready for a nice long soaking, when the phone rings. Wrapping a towel around her, she goes to answer: no one there. But now the baby's awake and bawling. She wonders if that's Jack bothering her all the time. If it is, brother, that's the end. Maybe it's the end anyway. She tries to calm the baby with the half-empty bottle, not wanting to change it until she's finished her bath. The bathroom's where the diapers go dirty, and they make it stink to high heaven. "Shush, shush!" she whispers, rocking the crib. The towel slips away, leaving an airy empty tingle up and down her backside. Even before she stoops for the towel, even before she turns around, she knows there's somebody behind her.

* * *

"We just came by to see if you were being a good girl," Jack says, grinning down at her. She's flushed and silent, her mouth half open. "Lean over," says Mark amiably. "We'll soap your back, as long as we're here." But she just huddles there, down in the suds, staring up at them with big eyes.

* * *

"Hey! What's going on here?" It's Mr. Tucker, stumbling through the door with a drink in his hand. She looks up from the TV. "What's the matter, Mr. Tucker?" "Oh, uh, I'm sorry, I got lost—no, I mean, I had to get some aspirin. Excuse me!" And he rushes past her into the bathroom, caroming off the living room door jamb on the way. The baby awakes.

* * *

"Okay, get off her, Mr. Tucker!" "Jack!" she cries, "what are *you* doing here?" He stares hard at them a moment: so that's where it goes. Then, as Mr. Tucker swings heavily off, he leans into the bastard with a hard right to the belly. Next thing he knows, though, he's got a face full of an old man's fist. He's not sure, as the lights go out, if that's his girlfriend screaming or the baby . . .

* * *

Her host pushes down on her fat fanny and tugs with all his might on her girdle, while she bawls on his shoulder: "I don't *wanna* go to a rest home!" "Now, now, take it easy, Dolly, nobody's gonna make you—" "Ouch! Hey, you're hurting!" "You should buy a bigger girdle, Dolly." "You're telling me?" Some other guy pokes his head in. "Whatsamatter? Dolly fall in?" "No, she fell out. Give me a hand."

* * *

By the time she's chased Jack and Mark out of there, she's lost track of the program she's been watching on television. There's another woman in the story now for some reason. That guy lives a very complicated life. Impatiently, she switches channels. She hates ballgames, so she settles for the murder mystery. She switches just in time, too: there's a dead man sprawled out on the floor of what looks like an office or a study or something. A heavyset detective gazes up from his crouch over the body. "He's been strangled." Maybe she'll take that bath, after all.

* * *

She drags him into the bathroom and pulls his pants down. She soaps up a warm washcloth she's had in the tub with her, but just as she reaches between his legs, it starts to spurt, spraying her arms and hands. "Oh, Jimmy! I thought you were done!" she cries, pulling him toward the toilet and aiming it into the bowl. How moist and rubbery it is! And you can turn it every which way. How funny it must feel!

* * *

"Stop it!" she screams. "Please stop!" She's on her hands and knees and Jack is holding her head down. "Now we're gonna teach you how to be a nice girl," Mark says and lifts her skirt. "Well, I'll be damned!" "What's the matter?" asks Jack, his heart pounding. "Look at this big pair of men's underpants she's got on!" "Those are my daddy's!" Jimmy, watching them from the doorway. "I'm gonna tell!"

* * *

People are shooting at each other in the murder mystery, but she's so mixed up, she doesn't know which ones are the good guys. She switches back to the love story. Something seems to have happened, because now the man is kissing his invalid wife tenderly. Maybe she's finally dying. The baby wakes, begins to scream. Let it. She turns up the volume on the TV.

* * *

Leaning down over her, unbuckling his belt. It's all happening just like he's known it would. Beautiful! The kid is gone, though his pants, poor lad, remain. "Looks like you and me, we got a secret to keep, child!" But he's cramped on the couch and everything is too slippery and small. "Lift your legs up, honey. Put them around my back." But instead, she screams. He rolls off, crashing to the floor. There they all come, through the front door. On television, somebody is saying: "Am I a burden to you, darling?" "Dolly! My God! Dolly, I can explain . . . !"

* * *

The game of the night is Get Dolly Tucker Back in Her Girdle Again. They've got her down on her belly in the living room and the whole damn crowd is working on her. Several of them are stretching the girdle, while others try to jam the fat inside. "I think we made a couple inches on this side! Roll her over!" Harry?

* * *

She's just stepped into the tub, when the phone rings, waking the baby. She sinks down in the suds, trying not to hear. But that baby doesn't cry, it screams. Angrily, she wraps a towel around herself, stamps peevishly into the baby's room, just letting the phone jangle. She tosses the baby down on its back, unpins its diapers hastily, and gets yellowish baby stool all over her hands. Her towel drops away. She turns to find Jimmy staring at her like a little idiot. She slaps him in the face with her dirty hand, while the baby screams, the phone rings, and nagging voices argue on the TV. There are better things she might be doing.

* * *

What's happening? Now there's a young guy in it. Is he after the young girl or the old invalid? To tell the truth, it looks like he's after the same man the women are. In disgust, she switches channels. "The strangler again," growls the fat detective, hands on hips, staring down at the body of a half-naked girl. She's considering either switching back to the love story or taking a quick bath, when a hand suddenly clutches her mouth.

* * *

"You're both chicken," she says, staring up at them. "But what if Mr. Tucker comes home?" Mark asks nervously.

* * *

How did he get here? He's standing pissing in his own goddamn bathroom, his wife is still back at the party, the three of them are, like good kids, sitting in there in the living room watching TV. One of them is his host's boy Mark. "It's a good murder mystery, Mr. Tucker," Mark said, when he came staggering in on them a minute ago. "Sit still!" he shouted, "I am just home for a moment!" Then whump thump on into the bathroom. Long hike for a wee-wee, Mister. But something keeps bothering him. Then it hits him: the girl's panties hanging like a broken balloon from the rabbit-ear antennae on the TV! He barges back in there, giving his shoulder a helluva crack on the living room door jamb on the way—but they're not hanging there any more. Maybe he's only imagined it. "Hey, Mr. Tucker," Mark says flatly. "Your fly's open."

* * *

The baby's dirty. Stinks to high heaven. She hurries back to the living room, hearing sirens and gunshots. The detective is crouched peering in. Already, she's completely lost. The baby screams at the top of its lungs. She turns up the volume. But it's all confused. she hurries back in there, claps an angry hand to the baby's mouth. "Shut up!" she cries. She throws the baby down on its back, starts to unpin the diaper, as the baby tunes up again. The phone rings. She answers it, one eye on the TV. *"What?"* The baby cries so hard it starts to choke. Let it. "I said, hi, this is Jack!" Then it hits her: oh no! The diaper pin!

* * *

"The aspirin . . ." But she's already in the tub. Way down in the tub. Staring at him through the water. Her tummy looks pale and ripply. He hears sirens, people on the porch.

* * *

Jimmy gets up to the bathroom and gets his face slapped and smeared with baby poop. Then she hauls him off to the bathroom, yanks off his pajamas, and throws him into the tub. That's okay, but next she gets naked and acts like she's gonna get in the tub, too. The baby's screaming and the phone's ringing like crazy and in walks his dad. Saved! he thinks, but, no, his dad grabs him right back out of the tub and whales the dickens out of him no questions asked, while she watches, then sends him—*whack!*—back to bed. So he's lying there, wet and dirty and naked and sore, and he still has to go to the bathroom, and outside his window he hears two older guys talking. "Listen, you know where to do it if we get her pinned?" "No! Don't you?"

* * *

"Yo ho heave ho! *Ugh!*" Dolly's on her back and they're working on the belly side. Somebody got the great idea of buttering her down first. Not to lose the ground they've gained, they've shot it inside with a basting syringe. But now suddenly there's this big tug-of-war under way between those who want to stuff her in and those who want to let her out. Something rips, but she feels better. The odor of hot butter makes her think of movie theaters and popcorn. "Hey, has anybody seen Harry?" she asks. "Where's Harry?"

* * *

Somebody's getting chased. She switches back to the love story, and now the man's back kissing the young lover again. What's going on? She gives it up, decides to take a quick bath. She's just stepping into the tub, one foot in, one foot out, when Mr. Tucker walks in. "Oh, excuse me! I only wanted some aspirin . . ." She grabs for a towel, but he yanks it away. "Now, that's not how it's supposed to happen, child," he scolds. "Please! Mr. Tucker . . . !" He embraces her savagely, his calloused old hands clutching roughly at her backside. "Mr. Tucker!" she cries, squirming. "Your wife called—!" He's pushing something between her legs, hurting her. She slips, they both slip—something cold and hard slams her in the back, cracks her skull, she seems to be sinking into a sea . . .

* * *

They've got her over the hassock, skirt up and pants down. "Give her a little lesson there, Jack baby!" The television lights flicker and flash over her glossy flesh, 1000 WHEN LIT. Whack! Slap! Bumper to bumper! He leans into her, feeling her come alive.

* * *

The phone rings, waking the baby. "Jack, is that you? Now, you listen to me—" "No, dear, this is Mrs. Tucker. Isn't the TV awfully loud?" "Oh, I'm sorry, Mrs. Tucker! I've been getting—" "I tried to call you before, but I couldn't hang on. To the phone, I mean. I'm sorry, dear." "Just a minute, Mrs. Tucker, the baby's—" "Honey, listen! Is Harry there? Is Mr. Tucker there, dear?"

* * *

"Stop it!" she screams and claps a hand over the baby's mouth. "Stop it! Stop it! *Stop it!*" Her other hand is full of baby stool and she's afraid she's going to be sick. The phone rings. "No!" she cries. She's hanging on to the baby, leaning woozily away, listening to the phone ring. "Okay, okay," she sighs, getting ahold of herself. But when she lets go of the baby, it isn't screaming any more. She shakes it. Oh no . . .

* * *

"Hello?" No answer. Strange. She hangs up and, wrapped only in a towel, stares out the window at the cold face staring in—she screams!

* * *

She screams, scaring the hell out of him. He leaps out of the tub, glances up at the window she's gaping at just in time to see two faces duck away, then slips on the bathroom tiles, and crashes to his ass, whacking his head on the sink on the way down. She stares down at him, trembling, a towel over her narrow shoulders. "Mr. Tucker! Mr. Tucker, are you all right . . . ?" Who's Sorry Now? Yessir, who's back is breaking with each . . . He stares up at the little tufted locus of all his woes, and passes out, dreaming of Jeannie . . .

* * *

The phone rings. "Dolly! It's for you!" "Hello?" "Hello, Mrs. Tucker?" "Yes, speaking." "Mrs. Tucker, this is the police calling . . ."

* * *

It's cramped and awkward and slippery, but he's pretty sure he got it in her, once anyway. When he gets the suds out of his eyes, he sees her staring up at them. Through the water. "Hey, Mark! Let her up!"

* * *

Down in the suds. Feeling sleepy. The phone rings, startling her. Wrapped in a towel, she goes to answer. "No, he's not here, Mrs. Tucker." Strange. Married people act pretty funny sometimes. The baby is awake and screaming. Dirty, a real mess. Oh boy, there's a lot of things she'd rather be doing than babysitting in this madhouse. She decides to wash the baby off in her own bathwater. She removes her towel, unplugs the tub, lowers the water level so the baby can sit. Glancing back over her shoulder, she sees Jimmy staring at her. "Go back to bed, Jimmy." "I have to go to the bathroom." "Good grief, Jimmy! It looks like you already have!" The phone rings. She doesn't bother with the towel—what can Jimmy see he hasn't already seen?—and goes to answer. "No, Jack, and that's final." Sirens, on the TV, as the police move in. But wasn't that the channel with the love story? Ambulance maybe. Get this over with so she can at least catch the news. "Get those wet pajamas off, Jimmy, and I'll find clean ones. Maybe you better get in the tub, too." "I think something's wrong with the baby," he says. "It's down in the water and it's not swimming or anything."

* * *

She's staring up at them from the rug. They slap her. Nothing happens. "You just tilted her, man!" Mark says softly. "We gotta get outa here!" Two little kids are standing wideeyed in the doorway. Mark looks hard at Jack. "No, Mark, they're just little kids . . . !" "We gotta, man, or we're dead."

* * *

"Dolly! My God! Dolly, I can explain!" She glowers down at them, her ripped girdle around her ankles. "What the four of you are doing in the bathtub with *my* babysitter?" she says sourly. "I can hardly wait!"

* * *

Police sirens wail, lights flash. "I heard the scream!" somebody shouts. "There were two boys!" "I saw a man!" "She was running with the baby!" "My God!" somebody screams "they're *all* dead!" Crowds come running. Spotlights probe the bushes.

* * *

"Harry, where the hell you been?" his wife whines, glaring blearily up at him from the carpet. "I can explain," he says. "Hey, whatsamatter, Harry?" his host asks, smeared with butter for some goddamn reason. "You look like you just seen a ghost!" Where did he leave his drink? Everybody's laughing, everybody except Dolly, whose cheeks are streaked with tears. "Hey, Harry, you won't let them take me to a rest home, will you, Harry?"

* * *

10:00. The dishes done, children to bed, her books read, she watches the news on television. Sleepy. The man's voice is gentle, soothing. She dozes—awakes with a start: a babysitter? Did the announcer say something about a babysitter?

* * *

"Just want to catch the weather," the host says, switching on the TV. Most of the guests are leaving, but the Tuckers stay to watch the news. As it comes on, the announcer is saying something about a babysitter. The host switches channels. "They got a better weatherman on four," he explains. "Wait!" says Mrs. Tucker. "There was something about a babysitter . . . !" The host switches back. "Details have not yet been released by the police," the announcer says. "Harry, maybe we'd better go . . ."

* * *

They stroll casually out of the drugstore, run into a buddy of theirs. "Hey! Did you hear about the babysitter?" the guy asks. Mark grunts, glances at Jack. "Got a smoke?" he asks the guy.

* * *

"I think I hear the baby screaming!" Mrs. Tucker cries, running across the lawn from the drive.

* * *

She wakes, startled, to find Mr. Tucker hovering over her. "I must have dozed off!" she exclaims. "Did you hear the news about the babysitter?" Mr. Tucker asks. "Part of it," she says, rising. "Too bad, wasn't it?" Mr. Tucker is watching the report of the ball scores and golf tournaments. "I'll drive you home in just a minute, dear," he says. "Why, how nice!" Mrs. Tucker exclaims from the kitchen. "The dishes are all done!"

* * *

"What can I say, Dolly?" the host says with a sigh, twisting the buttered strands of her ripped girdle between his fingers. "Your children are murdered, your husband gone, a corpse in your bathtub, and your house is wrecked. I'm sorry. But what can I say?" On the TV, the news is over, and they're selling aspirin. "Hell, I don't know," she says. "Let's see what's on the late late movie."

# JOHN BARTH
## (1930– )

Few writers have gone as far as John Barth has in self-reflexivity—a highly self-conscious foregrounding of fiction-making as it is going on. In his 1967 essay "The Literature of Exhaustion," Barth ponders whether, after James Joyce, contemporary writers can really do anything new. The traditional modes of fiction are tired, but they do present opportunities to innovative authors in the form of parody, irony, and self-conscious reflexiveness, a fiction about fiction. Essentially antirealist, Barth has produced a large body of fiction on the enterprise of making fiction itself, showing the influence of the writers Jorge Luis Borges and Vladimir Nabokov.

Barth was born in Cambridge, Maryland, on the eastern shore of the Chesapeake, the locale of much of his fiction. His first love was music, and he studied at the Juilliard School for a year, intending to prepare for a career in jazz music. He enrolled at Johns Hopkins where he earned a B.A. in 1951 and an M.A. in 1952 in English. He taught many years at Pennsylvania State University and at the State University of New York at Buffalo. In 1973 he returned to Johns Hopkins to teach until his retirement in the mid-1990s.

Barth has written over a dozen works of fiction, including the novels *The Floating Opera* (1956); *The End of the Road* (1958); *The Sot-Weed Factor* (1960); *Giles Goat-Boy* (1966); *Chimera* (1972), which won the National Book Award; *Letters* (1979); *Tidewater Tales* (1987); and *Last Voyage of Somebody the Sailor* (1991), and the story collections *Lost in the Funhouse* (1968) and *On with the Story* (1996).

# Night-Sea Journey

"One way or another, no matter which theory of our journey is correct, it's myself I address; to whom I rehearse as to a stranger our history and condition, and will disclose my secret hope though I sink for it.

"Is the journey my invention? Do the night, the sea, exist at all, I ask myself, apart from my experience of them? Do I myself exist, or is this a dream? Sometimes I wonder. And if I am, who am I? The Heritage I supposedly transport? But how can I be both vessel and contents? Such are the questions that beset my intervals of rest.

"My trouble is, I lack conviction. Many accounts of our situation seem plausible to me—where and what we are, why we swim and whither. But implausible ones as well, perhaps especially those, I must admit as possibly correct. Even likely. If at times, in certain humors—stroking in unison, say, with my neighbors and chanting with them 'Onward! Upward!'—I have supposed that we have after all a common Maker, Whose nature and motives we may not know, but Who engendered us in some mysterious wise and launched us forth toward some end known but to Him—if (for a moodslength only) I have been able to entertain such notions, very popular in certain quarters, it is because our night-sea journey partakes of their absurdity. One might even say: I can believe them *because* they are absurd.

"Has that been said before?

"Another paradox: it appears to be these recesses from swimming that sustain me in the swim. Two measures onward and upward, flailing with the rest, then I float exhausted and dispirited, brood upon the night, the sea, the journey, while the flood bears me a measure back and down: slow progress, but I live, I live, and make my way, aye, past many a drownèd comrade in the end, stronger, worthier than I, victims of their unremitting *joie de nager.* I have seen the best swimmers of my generation go under. Numberless the number of the dead! Thousands drown as I think this thought, millions as I rest before returning to the swim. And scores, hundreds of millions have expired since we surged forth, brave in our innocence, upon our dreadful way. 'Love! Love!' we sang then, a quarter-billion strong, and churned the warm sea white with joy of swimming! Now all are gone down—the buoyant, the sodden, leaders and followers, all gone under, while wretched I swim on. Yet these same reflective intervals that keep me afloat have led me into wonder, doubt, despair—strange emotions for a swimmer!—have led me, even, to suspect . . . that our night-sea journey is without meaning.

"Indeed, if I have yet to join the hosts of the suicides, it is because (fatigue apart) I find it no meaningfuller to drown myself than to go on swimming.

"I know that there are those who seem actually to enjoy the night-sea; who claim to love swimming for its own sake, or sincerely believe that 'reaching the Shore,' 'transmitting the Heritage' (*Whose* Heritage, I'd like to know? And to whom?) is worth the staggering cost. I do not. Swimming itself I find at best not actively unpleasant, more often tiresome, not infrequently a torment. Arguments from function and design don't impress me: granted that we can and do swim, that in a manner of speaking our long tails and streamlined heads are 'meant for' swimming; it by no means follows—for me, at least—that we *should* swim, or otherwise endeavor to 'fulfill our destiny.' Which is to say, Someone Else's destiny, since ours, so far as I can see, is merely to perish, one way or another, soon or late. The heartless zeal of our (departed) leaders, like the blind ambition and good cheer of my own youth, appalls me now; for the death of my comrades I am inconsolable. If the night-sea journey has justification, it is not for us swimmers ever to discover it.

"Oh, to be sure, 'Love!' one heard on every side: 'Love it is that drives and sustains us!' I translate: we don't know *what* drives and sustains us, only that we are most miserably driven and, imperfectly, sustained. *Love* is how we call our ignorance of what whips us. 'To reach the Shore,' then: but what if the Shore exists in the fancies of us swimmers merely, who dream it to account for the dreadful fact that we swim, have always and only swum, and continue swimming without respite (myself excepted) until we die? Supposing even that there *were* a Shore—that, as a cynical companion of mine once imagined, we rise from the drowned to discover all those vulgar superstitions and exalted metaphors to be literal truth: the giant Maker of us all, the Shores of Light beyond our night-sea journey!—whatever would a swimmer do there? The fact is, when we imagine the Shore, what comes to mind is just the opposite of our condition: no more night, no more sea, no more journeying. In short, the blissful estate of the drowned.

" 'Ours not to stop and think; ours but to swim and sink. . . .' Because a moment's thought reveals the pointlessness of swimming. 'No matter,' I've heard some say, even as they gulped their last: 'The night-sea journey may be absurd, but here we swim, will-we nill-we, against the flood, onward and upward, toward a Shore that may not exist and couldn't be reached if it did.' The thoughtful swimmer's choices, then, they say, are two: give over thrashing and go under for good, or embrace the absurdity; affirm in and for itself the night-sea journey; swim on with neither motive nor destination, for the sake of swimming, and compassionate moreover with your fellow swimmer, we being all at sea and equally in the dark. I find neither course acceptable. If not even the hypothetical Shore can justify a sea-full of drownèd comrades, to speak of the swim-in-itself as somehow doing so strikes me as obscene. I continue to swim—but only because blind habit, blind instinct, blind fear of drowning are still more strong than the horror of our journey. And if on occasion I have assisted a fellow-thrasher, joined in the cheers and songs, even passed along to others strokes of genius from the drownèd great, it's that I shrink by temperament from making myself conspicuous. To paddle off in one's own direction, assert one's independent right-of-way, overrun one's fellows without compunction, or dedicate oneself entirely to pleasures and diversions without regard for conscience—I can't finally condemn those who journey in this wise; in half my moods I envy them and despise the weak vitality that keeps me from following their example. But in reasonabler moments I remind myself that it's their very freedom and self-responsibility I reject, as more dramatically absurd, in our senseless circumstances, than tailing along in conventional fashion. Suicides, rebels, affirmers of the paradox—nay-sayers and yea-sayers alike to our fatal journey—I finally shake my head at them. And splash sighing past their corpses, one by one, as past a hundred sorts of others: friends, enemies, brothers; fools, sages, brutes—and nobodies, million upon million. I envy them all.

"A poor irony: that I, who find abhorrent and tautological the doctrine of survival of the fittest (*fitness* meaning, in my experience, nothing more than survival-ability, a talent whose only demonstration is the fact of survival, but whose chief ingredients seem to be strength, guile, callousness), may be the sole remaining swimmer! But the doctrine is false as well as repellent: Chance drowns the worthy with the unworthy, bears up the unfit with the fit by whatever definition, and makes the night-sea journey essentially *haphazard* as well as murderous and unjustified.

" 'You only swim once.' Why bother, then?

" 'Except ye drown, ye shall not reach the Shore of Life.' Poppycock.

"One of my late companions—that same cynic with the curious fancy, among the first to drown—entertained us with odd conjectures while we waited to begin our journey. A favorite theory of his was that the Father does exist, and did indeed make us and the sea we swim—but not a-purpose or even consciously; He made us, as it were, despite Himself, as we make waves with every tail-thrash, and may be unaware of our existence. Another was that He knows we're here but doesn't care what happens to us, inasmuch as He creates (voluntarily or not) other seas and swimmers at more or less regular intervals. In bitterer moments, such as just before he drowned, my friend even supposed that our Maker wished us unmade; there was indeed a Shore, he'd argue, which could save at least some of us from drowning and toward which it was our function to struggle—but for reasons unknowable to us He wanted desperately to prevent our reaching that happy place and fulfilling our destiny. Our 'Father,' in short, was our adversary and would-be killer! No less outrageous, and offensive to traditional opinion, were the fellow's speculations on the nature of our Maker: that He might well be no swimmer Himself at all, but some sort of monstrosity, perhaps even tailless; that He might be stupid, malicious, insensible, perverse, or asleep and dreaming; that the end for which He created and launched us forth, and which we flagellate ourselves to fathom, was perhaps immoral, even obscene. Et cetera, et cetera: there was no end to the chap's conjectures, or the impoliteness of his fancy; I have reason to suspect that his early demise, whether planned by 'our Maker' or not, was expedited by certain fellow-swimmers indignant at his blasphemies.

"In other moods, however (he was as given to moods as I), his theorizing would become half-serious, so it seemed to me, especially upon the subjects of Fate and Immortality, to which our youthful conversations often turned. Then his harangues, if no less fantastical, grew solemn and obscure, and if he was still baiting us, his passion undid the joke. His objection to popular opinions of the hereafter, he would declare, was their claim to general validity. Why need believers hold that *all* the drownèd rise to be judged at journey's end, and non-believers that drowning is final without exception? In *his* opinion (so he'd vow at least), nearly everyone's fate was permanent death; indeed he took a sour pleasure in supposing that every 'Maker' made thousands of separate seas in His creative lifetime, each populated like ours with millions of swimmers, and that in almost every instance both sea and swimmers were utterly annihilated, whether accidentally or by malevolent design. (Nothing if not pluralistical, he imagined there might be millions and billions of 'Fathers,' perhaps in some 'night-sea' of their own!) However—and here he turned infidels against him with the faithful—he professed to believe that in possibly a single night-sea per thousand, say, one of its quarter-billion swimmers (that is, one swimmer in two hundred fifty billions) achieved a qualified immortality. In some cases the rate might be slightly higher; in others it was vastly lower, for just as there are swimmers of every degree of proficiency, including some who drown before the journey starts, unable to swim at all, and others created drowned, as it were, so he imagined what can only be termed impotent Creators, Makers unable to Make, as well as uncommonly fertile ones and all grades between. And it pleased him to deny any necessary relation between a Maker's productivity and His other virtues—including, even, the quality of His creatures.

"I could go on (*he* surely did) with his elaboration of these mad notions—such as that swimmers in other night-seas needn't be of our kind; that Makers themselves might belong to different *species,* so to speak; that our particular Maker mightn't Himself be immortal, or that we might be not only His emissaries but His 'immortality,' continuing His life and our own, transmogrified, beyond our individual deaths. Even this modified immortality (meaningless to me) he conceived as relative and contingent, subject to accidental or deliberate termination: his pet hypothesis was that Makers and swimmers *each generate the other*—against all odds, their number being so great—and that any given 'immortality-chain' could terminate after any number of cycles, so that what was 'immortal' (still speaking relatively) was only the cyclic process of incarnation, which itself might have a beginning and an end. Alternatively he liked to imagine cycles within cycles, either finite or infinite: for example, the 'night-sea,' as it were, in which Makers 'swam' and created night-seas and swimmers like ourselves, might be the creation of a larger Maker, Himself one of many, Who in turn et cetera. Time itself he regarded as relative to our experience, like magnitude: who knew but what, with each thrash of our tails, minuscule seas and swimmers, whole eternities, came to pass—as ours, perhaps, and our Maker's Maker's, was elapsing between the strokes of some supertail, in a slower order of time?

"Naturally I hooted with the others at this nonsense. We were young then, and had only the dimmest notion of what lay ahead; in our ignorance we imagined night-sea journeying to be a positively heroic enterprise. Its meaning and value we never questioned; to be sure, some must go down by the way, a pity no doubt, but to win a race requires that others lose, and like all my fellows I took for granted that I would be the winner. We milled and swarmed, impatient to be off, never mind where or why, only to try our youth against the realities of night and sea; if we indulged the skeptic at all, it was as a droll, half-contemptible mascot. When he died in the initial slaughter, no one cared.

"And even now I don't subscribe to all his views—but I no longer scoff. The horror of our history has purged me of opinions, as of vanity, confidence, spirit, charity, hope, vitality, everything—except dull dread and a kind of melancholy, stunned persistence. What leads me to recall his fancies is my growing suspicion that I, of all swimmers, may be the sole survivor of this fell journey, tale-bearer of a generation. This suspicion, together with the recent sea-change, suggests to me now that nothing is impossible, not even my late companion's wildest visions, and brings me to a certain desperate resolve, the point of my chronicling.

"Very likely I have lost my senses. The carnage at our setting out; our decimation by whirlpool, poisoned cataract, sea-convulsion; the panic stampedes, mutinies, slaughters, mass suicides; the mounting evidence that none will survive the journey—add to these anguish and fatigue; it were a miracle if sanity stayed afloat. Thus I admit, with the other possibilities, that the present sweetening and calming of the sea, and what seems to be a kind of vasty presence, song, or summons from the near upstream, may be hallucinations of disordered sensibility. . . .

"Perhaps, even, I am drowned already. Surely I was never meant for the rough-and-tumble of the swim; not impossibly I perished at the outset and have only imaged the night-sea journey from some final deep. In any case, I'm no longer young, and it is we spent old swimmers, disabused of every illusion, who are most vulnerable to dreams.

"Sometimes I think I am my drownèd friend.

"Out with it: I've begun to believe, not only that *She* exists, but that She lies not far ahead, and stills the sea, and draws me Herward! Aghast, I recollect his maddest notion: that our destination (which existed, mind, in but one night-sea out of hundreds and thousands) was no Shore, as commonly conceived, but a mysterious being, indescribable except by paradox and vaguest figure: wholly different from us swimmers, yet our complement; the death of us, yet our salvation and resurrection; simultaneously our journey's end, mid-point, and commencement; not membered and thrashing like us, but a motionless or hugely gliding sphere of unimaginable dimension; self-contained, yet dependent absolutely, in some wise, upon the chance (always monstrously improbable) that one of us will survive the night-sea journey and reach . . . Her! *Her,* he called it, or *She,* which is to say, Other-than-a-he. I shake my head; the thing is too preposterous; it is myself I talk to, to keep my reason in this awful darkness. There is no She! There is no You! I rave to myself; it's Death alone that hears and summons. To the drowned, all seas are calm. . . .

"Listen: my friend maintained that in every order of creation there are two sorts of creators, contrary yet complementary, one of which gives rise to seas and swimmers, the other to the Night-which-contains-the-sea and to What-waits-at-the-journey's-end: the former, in short, to destiny, the latter to destination (and both profligately, involuntarily, perhaps indifferently or unwittingly). The 'purpose' of the night-sea journey—but not necessarily of the journeyer or of either Maker!—my friend could describe only in abstractions: *consummation, transfiguration, union of contraries, transcension of categories.* When we laughed, he would shrug and admit that he understood the business no better than we, and thought it ridiculous, dreary, possibly obscene. 'But one of you,' he'd add with his wry smile, 'may be the Hero destined to complete the night-sea journey and be one with Her. Chances are, of course, you won't make it.' He himself, he declared, was not even going to try; the whole idea repelled him; if we chose to dismiss it as an ugly fiction, so much the better for us; thrash, splash, and be merry, we were soon enough drowned. But there it was, he could not say how he knew or why he bothered to tell us, any more than he could say what would happen after She and Hero, Shore and Swimmer, 'merged identities' to become something both and neither. He quite agreed with me that if the issue of that magical union had no memory of the night-sea journey, for example, it enjoyed a poor sort of immortality; even poorer if, as he rather imagined, a swimmer-hero plus a She equaled or became merely another Maker of future night-seas and the rest, at such incredible expense of life. This being the case—he was persuaded it was—the merciful thing to do was refuse to participate; the genuine heroes, in his opinion, were the suicides, and the hero of heroes would be the swimmer who, in the very presence of the Other, refused Her proffered 'immortality' and thus put an end to at least one cycle of catastrophes.

"How we mocked him! Our moment came, we hurtled forth, pretending to glory in the adventure, thrashing, singing, cursing, strangling, rationalizing, rescuing, killing, inventing rules and stories and relationships, giving up, struggling on, but dying all, and still in darkness, until only a battered remnant was left to croak 'Onward, upward,' like a bitter echo. Then they too fell silent—victims, I can only presume, of the last frightful wave—and the moment came when I also, utterly desolate and spent, thrashed my last and gave myself over to the current, to sink or float as might be, but swim no more. Whereupon, marvelous to tell, in an instant the sea grew still! Then warmly, gently, the great tide turned, began to bear me, as it does now, onward and upward will-I nill-I, like a flood of joy—and I recalled with dismay my dead friend's teaching.

"I am not deceived. This new emotion is Her doing; the desire that possesses me is Her bewitchment. Lucidity passes from me; in a moment I'll cry 'Love!' bury myself in Her side, and be 'transfigured.' Which is to say, I die already; this fellow transported by passion is not I; *I am he who abjures and rejects the night-sea journey!* I. . . .

"I am all love. 'Come!' She whispers, and I have no will.

"You who I may be about to become, whatever You are: with the last twitch of my real self I beg You to listen. It is *not* love that sustains me! No; though Her magic makes me burn to sing the contrary, and though I drown even now for the blasphemy, I will say truth. What has fetched me across this dreadful sea is a single hope, gift of my poor dead comrade: that You may be stronger-willed than I, and that by sheer force of concentration I may transmit to You, along with Your official Heritage, a private legacy of awful recollection and negative resolve. Mad as it may be, my dream is that some unimaginable embodiment of myself (or myself plus Her if that's how it must be) will come to find itself expressing, in however garbled or radical a translation, some reflection of these reflections. If against all odds this comes to pass, may You to whom, through whom I speak, do what I cannot: terminate this aimless, brutal business! Stop Your hearing against Her song! Hate love!

"Still alive, afloat, afire. Farewell then my penultimate hope: that one may be sunk for direst blasphemy on the very shore of the Shore. Can it be (my old friend would smile) that only utterest nay-sayers survive the night? But even that were Sense, and there is no sense, only senseless love, senseless death. Whoever echoes these reflections: be more courageous than their author! An end to night-sea journeys! Make no more! And forswear me when I shall forswear myself, deny myself, plunge into Her who summons, singing . . .

" '! Love! Love! Love!' "

# DONALD BARTHELME

## (1931–1989)

Often labeled a minimalist, Donald Barthelme did indeed make a lot out of very little. If, as many postmodernists aver, all Grand Narratives and Ultimate Discourses have been exploded or abandoned, the artist's problem is what to make from diminished things. Principles of linearity, unity, wholeness, coherence, and rationality have been replaced by their opposites. One of Barthelme's characters says, "Fragments are the only forms I trust." Although Barthelme later repudiated this as a statement of his aesthetic, it does give a clue to the contemporary writer's situation. In the wreckage of the old, from the ever-mounting debris of contemporary life, Barthelme fashioned verbal collages that challenge a reader's participation in the creation of something new. Parodic, satiric, ironic, playful, Barthelme's fiction, though lacking subjective interiority, makes a fitting commentary on an age of ever-shifting surfaces and moral forgetfulness.

Barthelme was born in Philadelphia, Pennsylvania, but grew up in Houston, Texas, where his father was an architect. After graduating from the University of Houston he worked as a reporter and museum director, and helped edit *Location,* a journal of art and literature. From 1962 until his death from cancer in 1989, Barthelme lived in New York City, with occasional stints of teaching at the University of Houston.

Barthelme's stories began appearing in *The New Yorker* in the early 1960s. They were collected under the titles *Come Back, Dr. Caligari* (1964), *Unspeakable Practices, Unnatural Acts* (1968), *City Life* (1970), *Sadness* (1973), *Guilty Pleasures* (1974), *Amateurs* (1976), *Great Days* (1979), *Sixty Stories* (1981), *Overnight to Many Distant Cities* (1983), and *Forty Stories* (1987). He wrote four novels, *Snow White* (1967), *The Dead Father* (1975), *Paradise* (1986), and *The King* (1990).

# Views of My Father Weeping

AN ARISTOCRAT was riding down the street in his carriage. He ran over my father.

* * *

After the ceremony I walked back to the city. I was trying to think of the reason my father had died. Then I remembered: he was run over by a carriage.

* * *

I telephoned my mother and told her of my father's death. She said she supposed it was the best thing. I too supposed it was the best thing. His enjoyment was diminishing. I wondered if I should attempt to trace the aristocrat whose carriage had run him down. There were said to have been one or two witnesses.

* * *

Yes it is possible that it is not my father who sits there in the center of the bed weeping. It may be someone else, the mailman, the man who delivers the groceries, an insurance salesman or tax collector, who knows. However, I must say, it resembles my father. The resemblance is very strong. He is not smiling through his tears but frowning through them. I remember once we were out on the ranch shooting peccadillos (result of a meeting, on the plains of the West, of the collared peccary and the nine-banded armadillo). My father shot and missed. He wept. This weeping resembles that weeping.

* * *

"Did you see it?" "Yes but only part of it. Part of the time I had my back turned." The witness was a little girl, eleven or twelve. She lived in a very poor quarter and I could not imagine that, were she to testify, anyone would credit her. "Can you recall what the man in the carriage looked like?" "Like an aristocrat," she said.

* * *

The first witness declares that the man in the carriage looked "like an aristocrat." But that might be simply the carriage itself. Any man sitting in a handsome carriage with a driver on the box and perhaps one or two footmen up behind tends to look like an aristocrat. I wrote down her name and asked her to call me if she remembered anything else. I gave her some candy.

* * *

I stood in the square where my father was killed and asked people passing by if they had seen, or knew of anyone who had seen, the incident. At the same time I felt the effort was wasted. Even if I found the man whose carriage had done the job, what would I say to him? "You killed my father." "Yes," the aristocrat would say, "but he ran right in under the legs of the horses. My man tried to stop but it happened too quickly. There was nothing anyone could do." Then perhaps he would offer me a purse full of money.

* * *

The man sitting in the center of the bed looks very much like my father. He is weeping, tears coursing down his cheeks. One can see that he is upset about something. Looking at him I see that something is wrong. He is spewing like a fire hydrant with its lock knocked off. His yammer darts in and out of all the rooms. In a melting mood I lay my paw on my breast and say, "Father." This does not distract him from his plaint, which rises to a shriek, sinks to a pule. His range is great, his ambition commensurate. I say again, "Father," but he ignores me. I don't know whether it is time to flee or will not be time to flee until later. He may suddenly stop, assume a sternness. I have kept the door open and nothing between me and the door, and moreover the screen unlatched, and on top of that the motor running, in the Mustang. But perhaps it is not my father weeping there, but another father: Tom's father, Phil's father, Pat's father, Pete's father, Paul's father. Apply some sort of test, voiceprint reading or

* * *

My father throws his ball of knitting up in the air. The orange wool hangs there.

* * *

My father regards the tray of pink cupcakes. Then he jams his thumb into each cupcake, into the top. Cupcake by cupcake. A thick smile spreads over the face of each cupcake.

* * *

Then a man volunteered that he had heard two other men talking about the accident in a shop. "What shop?" The man pointed it out to me, a draper's shop on the south side of the square. I entered the shop and made inquiries. "It was your father, eh? He was bloody clumsy if you ask me." This was the clerk behind the counter. But another man standing nearby, well-dressed, even elegant, a gold watchchain stretched across his vest, disagreed. "It was the fault of the driver," the second man said. "He could have stopped them if he had cared to." "Nonsense," the clerk said, "not a chance in the world. If your father hadn't been drunk—" "He wasn't drunk," I said. "I arrived on the scene soon after it happened and I smelled no liquor."

* * *

This was true. I had been notified by the police, who came to my room and fetched me to the scene of the accident. I bent over my father, whose chest was crushed, and laid my cheek against his. His cheek was cold. I smelled no liquor but blood from his mouth stained the collar of my coat. I asked the people standing there how it had happened. "Run down by a carriage," they said. "Did the driver stop?" "No, he whipped up the horses and went off down the street and then around the corner at the end of the street, toward King's New Square." "You have no idea as to whose carriage . . ." "None." Then I made the arrangements for the burial. It was not until several days later that the idea of seeking the aristocrat in the carriage came to me.

* * *

I had had in my life nothing to do with aristocrats, did not even know in what part of the city they lived, in their great houses. So that even if I located someone who had seen the incident and could identify the particular aristocrat involved, I would be faced with the further task of finding his house and gaining admittance (and even then, might he not be abroad?). "No, the driver was at fault," the man with the gold watchchain said. "Even if your father was drunk—and I can't say about that, one way or another, I have no opinion—even if your father was drunk, the driver could have done more to avoid the accident. He was dragged, you know. The carriage dragged him about forty feet." I had noticed that my father's clothes were torn in a peculiar way. "There was one thing," the clerk said, "don't tell anyone I told you, but I can give you one hint. The driver's livery was blue and green."

* * *

It is someone's father. That much is clear. He is fatherly. The gray in the head. The puff in the face. The droop in the shoulders. The flab on the gut. Tears falling. Tears falling. Tears falling. Tears falling. More tears. It seems that he intends to go further along this salty path. The facts suggest that this is his program, weeping. He has something in mind, more weeping. O lud lud! But why remain? Why watch it? Why tarry? Why not fly? Why subject myself? I could be somewhere else, reading a book, watching the telly, stuffing a big ship into a little bottle, dancing the Pig. I could be out in the streets feeling up eleven-year-old girls in their soldier drag, there are thousands, as alike as pennies, and I could be—Why doesn't he stand up, arrange his clothes, dry his face? He's trying to embarrass us. He wants attention. He's trying to make himself interesting. He wants his brow wrapped in cold cloths perhaps, his hands held perhaps, his back rubbed, his neck kneaded, his wrists patted, his elbows anointed with rare oils, his toenails painted with tiny scenes representing God blessing America. I won't do it.

* * *

My father has a red bandana tied around his face covering the nose and mouth. He extends his right hand in which there is a water pistol. "Stick 'em up!" he says.

* * *

But blue and green livery is not unusual. A blue coat with green trousers, or the reverse, if I saw a coachman wearing such livery I would take no particular notice. It is true that most livery tends to be blue and buff, or blue and white, or blue and a sort of darker blue (for the trousers). But in these days one often finds a servant aping the more exquisite color combinations affected by his masters. I have even seen them in red trousers although red trousers used to be reserved, by unspoken agreement, for the aristocracy. So that the colors of the driver's livery were not of much consequence. Still it was something. I could now go about in the city, especially in stables and gin shops and such places, keeping a weather eye for the livery of the lackeys who gathered there. It was possible that more than one of the gentry dressed his servants in this blue and green livery, but on the other hand, unlikely that there were as many as half a dozen. So that in fact the draper's clerk had offered a very good clue indeed, had one the energy to pursue it vigorously.

* * *

There is my father, standing alongside an extremely large dog, a dog ten hands high at the very least. My father leaps on the dog's back, straddles him. My father kicks the large dog in the ribs with his heels. "Giddyap!"

* * *

My father has written on the white wall with his crayons.

* * *

I was stretched out on my bed when someone knocked at the door. It was the small girl to whom I had given candy when I had first begun searching for the aristocrat. She looked frightened, yet resolute; I could see that she had some information for me. "I know who it was," she said. "I know his name." "What is it?" "First you must give me five crowns." Luckily I had five crowns in my pocket, had she come later in the day, after I had eaten, I would have had nothing to give her. I handed over the money and she said, "Lars Bang." I looked at her in some surprise. "What sort of name is that for an aristocrat?" "His coachman," she said. "The coachman's name is Lars Bang." Then she fled.

* * *

When I heard this name, which in its sound and appearance is rude, vulgar, not unlike my own name, I was seized with repugnance, thought of dropping the whole business, although the piece of information she had brought had just cost me five crowns. When I was seeking him and he was yet nameless, the aristocrat and, by extension, his servants, seemed vulnerable: they had, after all, been responsible for a crime, or a sort of crime. My father was dead and they were responsible, or at least involved; and even though they were of the aristocracy or servants of the aristocracy, still common justice might be sought for; they might be required to make reparation, in some measure, for what they had done. Now, having the name of the coachman, and being thus much closer to his master than when I merely had the clue of the blue and green livery, I became afraid. For, after all, the unknown aristocrat must be a very powerful man, not at all accustomed to being called to account by people like me; indeed, his contempt for people like me was so great that, when one of us was so foolish as to stray into the path of his carriage, the aristocrat dashed him down, or permitted his coachman to do so, dragged him along the cobblestones for as much as forty feet, and then went gaily on his way, toward King's New Square. Such a man, I reasoned, was not very likely to take kindly to what I had to say to him. Very possibly there would be no purse of money at all, not a crown, not an öre, but rather he would, with an abrupt, impatient nod of his head, set his servants upon me. I would be beaten, perhaps killed. Like my father.

* * *

But if it is not my father sitting there in the bed weeping, why am I standing before the bed, in an attitude of supplication? Why do I desire with all my heart that this man, my father, cease what he is doing, which is so painful to me? Is it only that my position is a familiar one? That I remember, before, desiring with all my heart that this man, my father, cease what he is doing?

* * *

Why! . . . there's my father! . . . sitting in the bed there! . . . and he's *weeping!* . . . as though his heart would burst! . . . Father! . . . how is this? . . . who has wounded you? . . . name the man! . . . why I'll . . . I'll . . . here, Father, take this handkerchief! . . . and this handkerchief! . . . and this handkerchief! . . . I'll run for a towel . . . for a doctor . . . for a priest . . . for a good fairy . . . is there . . . can you . . . can I . . . a cup of hot tea? . . . bowl of steaming soup? . . . shot of Calvados? . . . a joint? . . . a red jacket? . . . a blue jacket? . . . Father, please! . . . look at me, Father . . . who has insulted you? . . . are you, then, compromised? . . . ruined? . . . a slander is going around? . . . an obloquy? . . . a traducement? . . . 'sdeath! . . . I won't permit it! . . . I won't abide it! . . . I'll . . . move every mountain . . . climb every river . . . etc.

* * *

My father is playing with the salt and pepper shakers, and with the sugar bowl. He lifts the cover off the sugar bowl, and shakes pepper into it.

* * *

Or: My father thrusts his hand through a window of the doll's house. His hand knocks over the doll's chair, knocks over the doll's chest of drawers, knocks over the doll's bed.

* * *

The next day, just before noon, Lars Bang himself came to my room. "I understand that you are looking for me." He was very much of a surprise. I had expected a rather burly, heavy man, of a piece with all of the other coachmen one saw sitting up on the box; Lars Bang was, instead, slight, almost feminine-looking, more the type of the secretary or valet than the coachman. He was not threatening at all, contrary to my fears; he was almost helpful, albeit with the slightest hint of malice in his helpfulness. I stammeringly explained that my father, a good man although subject to certain weaknesses, including a love of the bottle, had been run down by an aristocrat's coach, in the vicinity of King's New Square, not very many days previously; that I had information that the coach had dragged him some forty feet; and that I was eager to establish certain facts about the case. "Well then," Lars Bang said, with a helpful nod, "I'm your man, for it was my coach that was involved. A sorry business! Unfortunately I haven't the time right now to give you the full particulars, but if you will call round at the address written on this card, at six o'clock in the evening, I believe I will be able to satisfy you." So saying, he took himself off, leaving me with the card in my hand.

* * *

I spoke to Miranda, quickly sketching what had happened. She asked to see the white card; I gave it to her, for the address meant nothing to me. "Oh my," she said. "17 rue du Bac, that's over by the Vixen Gate—a very special quarter. Only aristocrats of the highest rank live there, and common people are not even allowed into the great park that lies between the houses and the river. If you are found wandering about there at night, you are apt to earn yourself a very severe beating." "But I have an appointment," I said. "An appointment with a coachman!" Miranda cried, "how foolish you are! Do you think the men of the watch will believe that, or even if they believe it (you have an honest enough face) will allow you to prowl that rich quarter, where so many thieves would dearly love to be set free for an hour or so, after dark? Go to!" Then she advised me that I must carry something with me, a pannier of beef or some dozen bottles of wine, so that if apprehended by the watch, I could say that I was delivering to such and such a house, and thus be judged an honest man on an honest errand, and escape a beating. I saw that she was right; and going out, I purchased at the wine merchant's a dozen bottles of a rather good claret (for it would never do to be delivering wine no aristocrat would drink); this cost me thirty crowns, which I had borrowed from Miranda. The bottles we wrapped round with straw, to prevent them banging into one another, and the whole we arranged in a sack, which I could carry on my back. I remember thinking, how they rhymed, fitted together, *sack* and *back*. In this fashion I set off across the city.

* * *

There is my father's bed. In it, my father. Attitude of dejection. Graceful as a mule deer once, the same large ears. For a nanosecond, there is a nanosmile. Is he having me on? I remember once we went out on the ups and downs of the West (out past Vulture's Roost) to shoot. First we shot up a lot of old beer cans, then we shot up a lot of old whiskey bottles, better because they shattered. Then we shot up some mesquite bushes and some parts of a Ford pickup somebody'd left lying around. But no animals came to our party (it was noisy, I admit it). A long list of animals failed to arrive, no deer, quail, rabbit, seals, sea lions, condylarths. It was pretty boring shooting up mesquite bushes, so we hunkered down behind some rocks, Father and I, he hunkered down behind his rocks and I hunkered down behind my rocks, and we commenced to shooting at each other. That was interesting.

* * *

My father is looking at himself in a mirror. He is wearing a large hat (straw) on which there are a number of blue and yellow plastic jonquils. He says: "How do I look?"

* * *

Lars Bang took the sack from me and without asking permission reached inside, withdrawing one of the straw-wrapped bottles of claret. "Here's something!" he exclaimed, reading the label. "A gift for the master, I don't doubt!" Then, regarding me steadily all the while, he took up an awl and lifted the cork. There were two other men seated at the pantry table, dressed in the blue-and-green livery, and with them a dark-haired, beautiful girl, quite young, who said nothing and looked at no one. Lars Bang obtained glasses, kicked a chair in my direction, and poured drinks all round. "To your health!" he said (with what I thought an ironical overtone) and we drank. "This young man," Lars Bang said, nodding at me, "is here seeking our advice on a very complicated business. A murder, I believe you said?" "I said nothing of the kind. I seek information about an accident." The claret was soon exhausted. Without looking at me, Lars Bang opened a second bottle and set it in the center of the table. The beautiful dark-haired girl ignored me along with all the others. For my part, I felt I had conducted myself rather well thus far. I had not protested when the wine was made free of (after all, they would be accustomed to levying a sort of tax on anything entering through the back door). But also I had not permitted his word "murder" to be used, but instead specified the use of the word "accident." Therefore I was, in general, comfortable sitting at the table drinking the wine, for which I have no better head than had my father. "Well," said Lars Bang at length, "I will relate the circumstances of the accident, and you may judge for yourself as to whether myself and my master, the Lensgreve Aklefeldt, were at fault." I absorbed this news with a slight shock. A count! I had selected a man of very high rank indeed to put my question to. In a moment my accumulated self-confidence drained away. A count! Mother of God, have mercy on me.

* * *

There is my father, peering through an open door into an empty house. He is accompanied by a dog (small dog; not the same dog as before). He looks into the empty room. He says: "Anybody home?"

* * *

There is my father, sitting in his bed, weeping.

* * *

"It was a Friday," Lars Bang began, as if he were telling a tavern story. "The hour was close upon noon and my master directed me to drive him to King's New Square, where he had some business. We were proceeding there at a modest easy pace, for he was in no great hurry. Judge of my astonishment when, passing through the draper's quarter, we found ourselves set upon by an elderly man, thoroughly drunk, who flung himself at my lead pair and began cutting at their legs with a switch, in the most vicious manner imaginable. The poor dumb brutes reared, of course, in fright and fear, for," Lars Bang said piously, "they are accustomed to the best of care, and never a blow do they receive from me, or from the other coachman, Rik, for the count is especially severe upon this point, that his animals be well-treated. The horses, then, were rearing and plunging; it was all I could do to hold them; I shouted at the man, who fell back for an instant. The count stuck his head out of the window, to inquire as to the nature of the trouble, and I told him that a drunken man had attacked our horses. Your father, in his blindness, being not content with the mischief he had already worked, ran back in again, close to the animals, and began madly cutting at their legs with his stick. At this renewed attack the horses, frightened out of their wits, jerked the reins from my hands, and ran headlong over your father, who fell beneath their hooves. The heavy wheels of the carriage passed over him (I felt two quite distinct thumps), his body caught upon a projection under the boot, and he was dragged some forty feet, over the cobblestones. I was attempting, with all my might, merely to hang on to the box, for, having taken the bit between their teeth, the horses were in no mood to tarry; nor could any human agency have stopped them. We flew down the street . . ."

* * *

My father is attending a class in good behavior.

"Do the men rise when friends greet us while we are sitting in a booth?"

"The men do not rise when they are seated in a booth," he answers, "although they may half-rise and make apologies for not fully rising."

* * *

". . . the horses turning into the way that leads to King's New Square; and it was not until we reached that place that they stopped and allowed me to quiet them. I wanted to go back and see what had become of the madman, your father, who had attacked us; but my master, vastly angry and shaken up, forbade it. I have never seen him in so fearful a temper as that day; if your father had survived, and my master got his hands on him, it would have gone ill with your father, that's a certainty. And so, you are now in possession of all the facts. I trust you are satisfied, and will drink another bottle of this quite fair claret you have brought us, and be on your way." Before I had time to frame a reply, the dark-haired girl spoke. "Bang is an absolute bloody liar," she said.

* * *

Etc.

# ⁜ URSULA K. LE GUIN

(1929– )

Born in Berkeley, California, Ursula Le Guin is the daughter of Theodora Kroeber, a writer, and Alfred Louis Kroeber, a well-known anthropologist at the University of California at Berkeley. Le Guin received a B.A. from Radcliffe College in 1951 and an M.A. from Columbia University in 1952. She spent a year in Paris on a Fulbright Fellowship, where she met her husband, the historian Charles Le Guin. They had three children. Le Guin currently lives in Portland, Oregon.

Le Guin is noted for her abundant and award-winning work in science fiction, fantasy, and children's stories. These labels, however, do not do justice to the scope and intent of her fiction. Her work expands and breaks generic boundaries to explore the imaginative possibilities of the self and human society. She has published more than thirty books, including novels, collections of short stories and poems, children's books, and essays. Some of her best-known works include the fantasy novels *Wizard of Earthsea* (1968), *The Tombs of Atuan* (1971), *The Farthest Shore* (1972), and *Tehanu* (1990), and the science fiction novels *Planet of Exile* (1966), *City of Illusions* (1967), *The Left Hand of Darkness* (1969), *The Lathe of Heaven* (1971), and *The Dispossessed* (1974). Her story collections include *The Wind's Twelve Quarters* (1975), *Orsinian Tales* (1976), *The Compass Rose* (1982), *Buffalo Gals and Other Animal Presences* (1987), and *Unlocking the Air* (1996). Her volumes of essays include *The Language of the Night: Essays on Fantasy and Science Fiction* (1979) and *Dancing at the Edge of the World: Thoughts on Words, Women, Places* (1989).

## The Ones Who Walk Away from Omelas

WITH A clamor of bells that set the swallows soaring, the Festival of Summer came to the city Omelas, bright-towered by the sea. The rigging of the boats in harbor sparkled with flags. In the streets between houses with red roofs and painted walls, between old moss-grown gardens and under avenues of trees, past great parks and public buildings, processions moved. Some were decorous: old people in long stiff robes of mauve and grey, grave master workmen, quiet, merry women carrying their babies and chatting as they walked. In other streets the music beat faster, a shimmering of gong and tambourine, and the people went dancing, the procession was a dance. Children dodged in and out, their high calls rising like the swallows' crossing flights over the music and the singing. All the processions wound towards the north side of the city, where on the great water-meadow called the Green Fields boys and girls, naked in the bright air, with mud-stained feet and ankles and long, lithe arms, exercised their restive horses before the race. The horses wore no gear at all but a halter without bit. Their manes were braided with streamers of silver, gold, and green. They flared their nostrils and pranced and boasted to one another; they were vastly excited, the horse being the only animal who has adopted our ceremonies as his own. Far off to the north and west the mountains stood up half encircling Omelas on her bay. The air of morning was so clear that the snow still crowning the Eighteen Peaks burned with white-gold fire across the miles of sunlit air, under the dark blue of the sky. There was just enough wind to make the banners that marked the racecourse snap and flutter now and then. In the silence of the broad green meadows one could hear the music winding through the city streets, farther and nearer and ever approaching, a cheerful faint sweetness of the air that from time to time trembled and gathered together and broke out into the great joyous clanging of the bells.

Joyous! How is one to tell about joy? How describe the citizens of Omelas?

They were not simple folk, you see, though they were happy. But we do not say the words of cheer much any more. All smiles have become archaic. Given a description such as this one tends to make certain assumptions. Given a description such as this one tends to look next for the King, mounted on a splendid stallion and surrounded by his noble knights, or perhaps in a golden litter borne by great-muscled slaves. But there was no king. They did not use swords, or keep slaves. They were not barbarians. I do not know the rules and laws of their society, but I suspect that they were singularly few. As they did without monarchy and slavery, so they also go on without the stock exchange, the advertisement, the secret police, and the bomb. Yet I repeat that these were not simple folk, not dulcet shepherds, noble savages, bland utopians. They were not less complex than us. The trouble is that we have a bad habit, encouraged by pedants and sophisticates, of considering happiness as something rather stupid. Only pain is intellectual, only evil interesting. This is the treason of the artist: a refusal to admit the banality of evil and the terrible boredom of pain. If you can't lick 'em, join 'em. If it hurts, repeat it. But to praise despair is to condemn delight, to embrace violence is to lose hold of everything else. We have almost lost hold; we can no longer describe a happy man, nor make any celebration of joy. How can I tell you about the people of Omelas? They were not naïve and happy children—though their children were, in fact, happy. They were mature, intelligent, passionate adults whose lives were not wretched. O miracle! but I wish I could describe it better. I wish I could convince you. Omelas sounds in my words like a city in a fairy tale, long ago and far away, once upon a time. Perhaps it would be best if you imagined it as your own fancy bids, assuming it will rise to the occasion, for certainly I cannot suit you all. For instance, how about technology? I think that there would be no cars or helicopters in and above the streets; this follows from the fact that the people of Omelas are happy people. Happiness is based on a just discrimination of what is necessary, what is neither necessary nor destructive, and what is destructive. In the middle category, however—that of the unnecessary but undestructive, that of comfort, luxury, exuberance, etc.—they could perfectly well have central heating, subway trains, washing machines, and all kinds of marvelous devices not yet invented here, floating light-sources, fuelless power, a cure for the common cold. Or they could have none of that: it doesn't matter. As you like it. I incline to think that people from towns up and down the coast have been coming in to Omelas during the last days before the Festival on very fast little trains and double-decker trams, and that the train station of Omelas is actually the handsomest building in town, though plainer than the magnificent Farmers' Market. But even granted trains, I fear that Omelas so far strikes some of you as goody-goody. Smiles, bells, parades, horses, bleh. If so, please add an orgy. If an orgy would help, don't hesitate. Let us not, however, have temples from which issue beautiful nude priests and priestesses already half in ecstasy and ready to copulate with any man or woman, lover or stranger, who desires union with the deep godhead of the blood, although that was my first idea. But really it would be better not to have any temples in Omelas—at least, not manned temples. Religion yes, clergy no. Surely the beautiful nudes can just wander about, offering themselves like divine soufflés to the hunger of the needy and the rapture of the flesh. Let them join the processions. Let tambourines be struck above the copulations, and the glory of desire be proclaimed upon the gongs, and (a not unimportant point) let the offspring of these delightful rituals be beloved and looked after by all. One thing I know there is none of in Omelas is guilt. But what else should there be? I thought at first there were no drugs, but that is puritanical. For those who like it, the faint insistent sweetness of *drooz* may perfume the ways of the city, *drooz* which first brings a great lightness and brilliance to the mind and limbs, and then after some hours a dreamy languor, and wonderful visions at last of the very arcana and inmost secrets of the Universe, as well as exciting the pleasure of sex beyond all belief; and it is not habit-forming. For more modest tastes I think there ought to be beer. What else, what else belongs in the joyous city? The sense of victory, surely, the celebration of courage. But as we did without clergy, let us do without soldiers. The joy built upon successful slaughter is not the right kind of joy; it will not do; it is fearful and it is trivial. A boundless and generous contentment, a magnanimous triumph felt not against some outer enemy but in communion with the finest and fairest in the souls of all men everywhere and the splendor of the world's summer: this is what swells the hearts of the people of Omelas, and the victory they celebrate is that of life. I really don't think many of them need to take *drooz.*

Most of the processions have reached the Green Fields by now. A marvelous smell of cooking goes forth from the red and blue tents of the provisioners. The faces of small children are amiably sticky; in the benign grey beard of a man a couple of crumbs of rich pastry are entangled. The youths and girls have mounted their horses and are beginning to group around the starting line of the course. An old woman, small, fat, and laughing, is passing out flowers from a basket, and tall young men wear her flowers in their shining hair. A child of nine or ten sits at the edge of the crowd, alone, playing on a wooden flute. People pause to listen, and they smile, but they do not speak to him, for he never ceases playing and never sees them, his dark eyes wholly rapt in the sweet, thin magic of the tune.

He finishes, and slowly lowers his hands holding the wooden flute.

As if that little private silence were the signal, all at once a trumpet sounds from the pavilion near the starting line: imperious, melancholy, piercing. The horses rear on their slender legs, and some of them neigh in answer. Sober-faced, the young riders stroke the horses' necks and soothe them, whispering, "Quiet, quiet, there my beauty, my hope. . . ." They begin to form in rank along the starting line. The crowds along the racecourse are like a field of grass and flowers in the wind. The Festival of Summer has begun.

Do you believe? Do you accept the festival, the city, the joy? No? Then let me describe one more thing.

In a basement under one of the beautiful public buildings of Omelas, or perhaps in the cellar of one of its spacious private homes, there is a room. It has one locked door, and no window. A little light seeps in dustily between cracks in the boards, secondhand from a cobwebbed window somewhere across the cellar. In one corner of the little room a couple of mops, with stiff, clotted, foul-smelling heads, stand near a rusty bucket. The floor is dirt, a little damp to the touch, as cellar dirt usually is. The room is about three paces long and two wide: a mere broom closet or disused too! room. In the room a child is sitting. It could be a boy or a girl. It looks about six, but actually is nearly ten. It is feeble-minded. Perhaps it was born defective, or perhaps it has become imbecile through fear, malnutrition, and neglect. It picks its nose and occasionally fumbles vaguely with its toes or genitals, as it sits hunched in the corner farthest from the bucket and the two mops. It is afraid of the mops. It finds them horrible. It shuts its eyes, but it knows the mops are still standing there; and the door is locked; and nobody will come. The door is always locked; and nobody ever comes, except that sometimes—the child has no understanding of time or interval—sometimes the door rattles terribly and opens, and a person, or several people, are there. One of them may come in and kick the child to make it stand up. The others never come close, but peer in at it with frightened, disgusted eyes. The food bowl and the water jug are hastily filled, the door is locked, the eyes disappear. The people at the door never say anything, but the child, who has not always lived in the tool room, and can remember sunlight and its mother's voice, sometimes speaks. "I will be good," it says. "Please let me out. I will be good!" They never answer. The child used to scream for help at night, and cry a good deal, but now it only makes a kind of whining, "eh-haa, eh-haa," and it speaks less and less often. It is so thin there are no calves to its legs; its belly protrudes; it lives on a half-bowl of corn meal and grease a day. It is naked. Its buttocks and thighs are a mass of festered sores, as it sits in its own excrement continually.

They all know it is there, all the people of Omelas. Some of them have come to see it, others are content merely to know it is there. They all know that it has to be there. Some of them understand why, and some do not, but all understand that their happiness, the beauty of their city, the tenderness of their friendships, the health of their children, the wisdom of their scholars, the skill of their makers, even the abundance of their harvest and the kindly weathers of their skies, depend wholly on this child's abominable misery.

This is usually explained to children when they are between eight and twelve, whenever they seem capable of understanding; and most of those who come to see the child are young people, though often enough an adult comes, or comes back, to see the child. No matter how well the matter has been explained to them, these young spectators are always shocked and sickened at the sight. They feel disgust, which they had thought themselves superior to. They feel anger, outrage, impotence, despite all the explanations. They would like to do something for the child. But there is nothing they can do. If the child were brought up into the sunlight out of that vile place, if it were cleaned and fed and comforted, that would be a good thing, indeed; but if it were done, in that day and hour all the prosperity and beauty and delight of Omelas would wither and be destroyed. Those are the terms. To exchange all the goodness and grace of every life in Omelas for that single, small improvement: to throw away the happiness of thousands for the chance of the happiness of one: that would be to let guilt within the walls indeed.

The terms are strict and absolute; there may not even be a kind word spoken to the child.

Often the young people go home in tears, or in a tearless rage, when they have seen the child and faced this terrible paradox. They may brood over it for weeks or years. But as time goes on they begin to realize that even if the child could be released, it would not get much good of its freedom: a little vague pleasure of warmth and food, no doubt, but little more. It is too degraded and imbecile to know any real joy. It has been afraid too long ever to be free of fear. Its habits are too uncouth for it to respond to humane treatment. Indeed, after so long it would probably be wretched without walls about it to protect it, and darkness for its eyes, and its own excrement to sit in. Their tears at the bitter injustice dry when they begin to perceive the terrible justice of reality, and to accept it. Yet it is their tears and anger, the trying of their generosity and the acceptance of their helplessness, which are perhaps the true source of the splendor of their lives. Theirs is no vapid, irresponsible happiness. They know that they, like the child, are not free. They know compassion. It is the existence of the child, and their knowledge of its existence, that makes possible the nobility of their architecture, the poignancy of their music, the profundity of their science. It is because of the child that they are so gentle with children. They know that if the wretched one were not there snivelling in the dark, the other one, the flute-player, could make no joyful music as the young riders line up in their beauty for the race in the sunlight of the first morning of summer.

Now do you believe in them? Are they not more credible? But there is one more thing to tell, and this is quite incredible.

At times one of the adolescent girls or boys who go to see the child does not go home to weep or rage, does not, in fact, go home at all. Sometimes also a man or woman much older falls silent for a day or two, and then leaves home. These people go out into the street, and walk down the street alone. They keep walking, and walk straight out of the city of Omelas, through the beautiful gates. They keep walking across the farmlands of Omelas. Each one goes alone, youth or girl, man or woman. Night falls; the traveler must pass down village streets, between the houses with yellow-lit windows, and on out into the darkness of the fields. Each alone, they go west or north, towards the mountains. They go on. They leave Omelas, they walk ahead into the darkness, and they do not come back. The place they go towards is a place even less imaginable to most of us than the city of happiness. I cannot describe it at all. It is possible that it does not exist. But they seem to know where they are going, the ones who walk away from Omelas.

# ⁂ CYNTHIA OZICK
(1928–    )

Cynthia Ozick was born and raised in New York City. She graduated from New York University and earned an M.A. from The Ohio State University. She has been a longtime resident of New Rochelle, New York.

Ozick wrote for a long time before she found significant publication. She has published novels, stories, poetry, criticism, and translations. For her, fiction must bear witness, not only to past evils like the Holocaust, but to traditional Jewish moral values of respect for limits and responsibility. Her often poetic prose at times makes use of postmodern techniques for decidedly unpostmodern ends: the affirmation of traditional moral values. Her books include the novel *Trust* (1966) and the story collections *The Pagan Rabbi* (1971), *Bloodshed* (1976), and *Levitation* (1982). Her essays are published under the titles *Art & Ardor* (1983), *Metaphor & Memory: Essays* (1989), *Fame & Folly: Essays* (1996), and *Quarrel & Quandary: Essays* (2000). More recent novels include *The Cannibal Galaxy* (1983), *The Messiah of Stockholm* (1987), and *The Puttermesser Papers* (1997). *The Shawl* (1989) consists of a story and a novella.

## The Shawl

STELLA, COLD, cold, the coldness of hell. How they walked on the roads together, Rosa with Magda curled up between sore breasts, Magda wound up in the shawl. Sometimes Stella carried Magda. But she was jealous of Magda. A thin girl of fourteen, too small, with thin breasts of her own, Stella wanted to be wrapped in a shawl, hidden away, asleep, rocked by the march, a baby, a round infant in arms. Magda took Rosa's nipple, and Rosa never stopped walking, a walking cradle. There was not enough milk; sometimes Magda sucked air; then she screamed. Stella was ravenous. Her knees were tumors on sticks, her elbows chicken bones.

Rosa did not feel hunger; she felt light, not like someone walking but like someone in a faint, in trance, arrested in a fit, someone who is already a floating angel, alert and seeing everything, but in the air, not there, not touching the road. As if teetering on the tips of her fingernails. She looked into Magda's face through a gap in the shawl: a squirrel in a nest, safe, no one could reach her inside the little house of the shawl's windings. The face, very round, a pocket mirror of a face; but it was not Rosa's bleak complexion, dark like cholera, it was another kind of face altogether, eyes blue as air, smooth feathers of hair nearly as yellow as the Star sewn into Rosa's coat. You could think she was one of *their* babies.

Rosa, floating, dreamed of giving Magda away in one of the villages. She could leave the line for a minute and push Magda into the hands of any woman on the side of the road. But if she moved out of line they might shoot. And even if she fled the line for half a second and pushed the shawl-bundle at a stranger, would the woman take it? She might be surprised, or afraid; she might drop the shawl, and Magda would fall out and strike her head and die. The little round head. Such a good child, she gave up screaming, and sucked now only for the taste of the drying nipple itself. The neat grip of the tiny gums. One mite of a tooth tip sticking up in the bottom gum, how shining, an elfin tombstone of white marble, gleaming there. Without complaining, Magda relinquished Rosa's teats, first the left, then the right; both were cracked, not a sniff of milk. The duct crevice extinct, a dead volcano, blind eye, chill hole, so Magda took the corner of the shawl and milked it instead. She sucked and sucked, flooding the threads with wetness. The shawl's good flavor, milk of linen.

It was a magic shawl, it could nourish an infant for three days and three nights. Magda lifted out of her mouth. She held her eyes open every moment, forgetting how to blink or nap, and Rosa and sometimes Stella studied their blueness. On the road they raised one burden of a leg after another and studied Magda's face. "Aryan," Stella said, in a voice grown as thin as a string; and Rosa thought how Stella gazed at Magda like a young cannibal. And the time that Stella said "Aryan," it sounded to Rosa as if Stella had really said "Let us devour her."

But Magda lived to walk. She lived that long, but she did not walk very well, partly because she was only fifteen months old, and partly because the spindles of her legs could not hold up her fat belly. It was fat with air, full and round. Rosa gave almost all her food to Magda. Stella gave nothing; Stella was ravenous, a growing child herself, but not growing much. Stella did not menstruate. Rosa did not menstruate. Rosa was ravenous, but also not; she learned from Magda how to drink the taste of a finger in one's mouth. They were in a place without pity, all pity was annihilated in Rosa, she looked at Stella's bones without pity. She was sure that Stella was waiting for Magda to die so she could put her teeth into the little thighs.

Rosa knew Magda was going to die very soon; she should have been dead already, but she had been buried away deep inside the magic shawl, mistaken there for the shivering mound of Rosa's breasts; Rosa clung to the shawl as if it covered only herself. No one took it away from her. Magda was mute. She never cried. Rosa hid her in the barracks, under the shawl, but she knew that one day someone would inform; or one day someone, not even Stella, would steal Magda to eat her. When Magda began to walk Rosa knew that Magda was going to die very soon, something would happen. She was afraid to fall asleep; she slept with the weight of her thigh on Magda's body; she was afraid she would smother Magda under her thigh. The weight of Rosa was becoming less and less; Rosa and Stella were slowly turning into air.

Magda was quiet, but her eyes were horribly alive, like blue tigers. She watched. Sometimes she laughed—it seemed a laugh, but how could it be? Magda had never seen anyone laugh. Still, Magda laughed at her shawl when the wind blew its corners, the bad wind with pieces of black in it, that made Stella's and Rosa's eyes tear. Magda's eyes were always clear and tearless. She watched like a tiger. She guarded her shawl. No one could touch it; only Rosa could touch it. Stella was not allowed. The shawl was Magda's own baby, her pet, her little sister. She tangled herself up in it and sucked on one of the corners when she wanted to be very still.

Then Stella took the shawl away and made Magda die.

Afterward Stella said: "I was cold."

And afterward she was always cold, always. The cold went into her heart: Rosa saw that Stella's heart was cold. Magda flopped onward with her little pencil legs scribbling this way and that, in search of the shawl; the pencils faltered at the barracks opening, where the light began. Rosa saw and pursued. But already Magda was in the square outside the barracks, in the jolly light. It was the roll-call arena. Every morning Rosa had to conceal Magda under the shawl against a wall of the barracks and go out and stand in the arena with Stella and hundreds of others, sometimes for hours, and Magda, deserted, was quiet under the shawl, sucking on her corner. Every day Magda was silent, and so she did not die. Rosa saw that today Magda was going to die, and at the same time a fearful joy ran in Rosa's two palms, her fingers were on fire, she was astonished, febrile: Magda, in the sunlight, swaying on her pencil legs, was howling. Ever since the drying up of Rosa's nipples, ever since Magda's last scream on the road, Magda had been devoid of any syllable; Magda was a mute. Rosa believed that something had gone wrong with her vocal cords, with her wind-pipe, with the cave of her larynx; Magda was defective, without a voice; perhaps she was deaf; there might be something amiss with her intelligence; Magda was dumb. Even the laugh that came when the ash-stippled wind made a clown out of Magda's shawl was only the air-blown showing of her teeth. Even when the lice, head lice and body lice, crazed her so that she became as wild as one of the big rats that plundered the barracks at daybreak looking for carrion, she rubbed and scratched and kicked and bit and rolled without a whimper. But now Magda's mouth was spilling a long viscous rope of clamor.

"Maaaa—"

It was the first noise Magda had ever sent out from her throat since the drying up of Rosa's nipples.

"Maaaa . . . aaa!"

Again! Magda was wavering in the perilous sunlight of the arena, scribbling on such pitiful little bent shins. Rosa saw. She saw that Magda was grieving for the loss of her shawl, she saw that Magda was going to die. A tide of commands hammered in Rosa's nipples: Fetch, get, bring! But she did not know which to go after first, Magda or the shawl. If she jumped out into the arena to snatch Magda up, the howling would not stop, because Magda would still not have the shawl; but if she ran back into the barracks to find the shawl, and if she found it, and if she came after Magda holding it and shaking it, then she would get Magda back, Magda would put the shawl in her mouth and turn dumb again.

Rosa entered the dark. It was easy to discover the shawl. Stella was heaped under it, asleep in her thin bones. Rosa tore the shawl free and flew—she could fly, she was only air—into the arena. The sunheat murmured of another life, of butterflies in summer. The light was placid, mellow. On the other side of the steel fence, far away, there were green meadows speckled with dandelions and deep-colored violets; beyond them, even farther, innocent tiger lilies, tall, lifting their orange bonnets. In the barracks they spoke of "flowers," of "rain": excrement, thick turd-braids, and the slow stinking maroon waterfall that slunk down from the upper bunks, the stink mixed with a bitter fatty floating smoke that greased Rosa's skin. She stood for an instant at the margin of the arena. Sometimes the electricity inside the fence would seem to hum; even Stella said it was only an imagining, but Rosa heard real sounds in the wire: grainy sad voices. The farther she was from the fence, the more clearly the voices crowded at her. The lamenting voices strummed so convincingly, so passionately, it was impossible to suspect them of being phantoms. The voices told her to hold up the shawl, high; the voices told her to shake it, to whip with it, to unfurl it like a flag. Rosa lifted, shook, whipped, unfurled. Far off, very far, Magda leaned across her air-fed belly, reaching out with the rods of her arms. She was high up, elevated, riding someone's shoulder. But the shoulder that carried Magda was not coming toward Rosa and the shawl, it was drifting away, the speck of Magda was moving more and more into the smoky distance. Above the shoulder a helmet glinted. The light tapped the helmet and sparkled it into a goblet. Below the helmet a black body like a domino and a pair of black boots hurled themselves in the direction of the electrified fence. The electric voices began to chatter wildly. "Maamaa, maaamaaa," they all hummed together. How far Magda was from Rosa now, across the whole square, past a dozen barracks, all the way on the other side! She was no bigger than a moth.

All at once Magda was swimming through the air. The whole of Magda traveled through loftiness. She looked like a butterfly touching a silver vine. And the moment Magda's feathered round head and her pencil legs and balloonish belly and zigzag arms splashed against the fence, the steel voices went mad in their growling, urging Rosa to run and run to the spot where Magda had fallen from her flight against the electrified fence; but of course Rosa did not obey them. She only stood, because if she ran they would shoot, and if she tried to pick up the sticks of Magda's body they would shoot, and if she let the wolf's screech ascending now through the ladder of her skeleton break out, they would shoot; so she took Magda's shawl and filled her own mouth with it, stuffed it in and stuffed it in, until she was swallowing up the wolf's screech and tasting the cinnamon and almond depth of Magda's saliva; and Rosa drank Magda's shawl until it dried.

# JOHN GARDNER
## (1933–1982)

The eldest of four children, John Gardner was born in Batavia, New York. His father was a farmer and lay preacher in the Presbyterian church; his mother was an English teacher. When Gardner was 11 years old, he accidentally killed his brother while driving a heavy farm machine. This tragic event appears in his short story "Redemption." After completing high school Gardner enrolled in De Pauw University. He married his second cousin, Joan, in 1953, and transferred to Washington University in St. Louis. He graduated with honors in 1955, and went on to the University of Iowa on a Woodrow Wilson Fellowship. He completed a Ph.D. there in 1958. He taught briefly at Oberlin College; at Chico State College, California; and then at San Francisco State College. In 1965 he took a teaching appointment at Southern Illinois University, and his first published novel, *The Resurrection,* appeared in 1966. He later taught at the Bread Loaf Writers' Conference, and at Bennington College.

Gardner wrote scholarly works on Chaucer and medieval literature as well as fiction. In 1978 he was accused of plagiarism for his work on Chaucer. His book *On Moral Fiction* (1978), containing his negative criticisms of his fellow writers, caused a stir among writers and critics, and hurt his career. He moved to the State University of New York at Binghamton, where he directed the creative writing program until his death in 1982 from a motorcycle accident.

Among Gardner's major publications are *The Wreckage of Agathon* (1970), *Grendel* (1971), *The Sunlight Dialogues* (1972), *Nickel Mountain* (1973), *October Light* (1976), *Freddy's Book* (1980), *The Art of Living, and Other Stories* (1981), and *Mickelsson's Ghosts* (1982). Gardner's fiction aspires to counter the various nihilisms of his age with visions of pastoral transformation and a deep appreciation for the fullness of life.

## Come on Back

FORTY-FIVE years ago, when Remsen, New York, was called "Jack" and nearly all the people who lived there were Welsh, my uncle, or, rather, my maternal great-uncle, E. L. Hughes, ran the feedmill. His name is no longer remembered in the village, and the feedmill is in ruins, set back behind houses and trees so that you have to know it's there to find it. There's a big sprawling Agway that already looks ancient, though it can't be more than fifteen or twenty years old, on the other side of town.

I seldom get up to that area anymore, but I used to visit often when I was a child living with my parents on their farm outside Batavia. My grandfather Hughes, whom I never knew except by the wooden chest of carpenter's tools he left my father and a few small, tattered Welsh hymnbooks he left my mother, had originally settled in the village of Remsen, or just outside it, and for years, even past the time of my uncle Ed's death, my parents made pilgrimages back to see old friends, attend the Cymanfa Ganu festivals, visit the white wooden church called Capel Ucca, and keep a casual eye on the mill's decline. At the time my grandfather and his brothers came over, Remsen was generally viewed, back in Wales, as a kind of New Jerusalem, a shining hope, a place of peace and prosperity. There was a story of a Welshman who landed in New York, and looking up bug-eyed at the towering buildings, said, "If this is New York, what must Remsen be!"

In those days it was a sleepy little hamlet beside a creek. Though the Depression was on in the rest of the country, you saw no signs of it in Remsen. On the tree-lined streets with tall houses set back from them, each with its roses, small vegetable garden, and grape arbor, there were shined-up square cars, mostly Model A Fords, and occasional buggies. (My uncle Ed, one of the richest men in town, had a black-and-green Buick.) Milk was still delivered in squarish glass bottles by an orange horse-drawn cart; coal for people's furnaces came on a huge, horse-drawn wagon, black with white lettering: W.B. PRICE & SONS, COAL & LUMBER. The horses were chestnut-colored Belgians, I remember, so immense and so beautiful they didn't seem real. At the end of almost every driveway, back behind the house, there was a two-storey garage with chickenwire on the upstairs windows. If you shouted from the driveway, one or two of the chickens would look out at you, indignant, like old ladies; but however you shouted, even if you threw pebbles, most of them just went about their business. The people were pretty much the same, unexcitable. There weren't many houses, maybe twenty or thirty, a couple of churches, a school, Price's lumberyard, and a combination gas-station and market.

As we entered, from the south, my uncle Ed's high gray mill reaching up past the trees into the sunlight was the first thing we'd see. The mill was to the left of the narrow dirt road, a three-towered, barnlike building set back beyond the lawn and flower garden that rose gradually toward the brown-shingled house where Uncle Ed had lived for years with his wife, my great-aunt Kate. I remember her only dimly, as an occasional bright presence, soft-spoken and shy, in my uncle Ed's kitchen or in his "camp," as they called it, on Black River. She wore thick glasses that made her eyes look unpleasantly large. They shared the house, or anyway the basement, with Uncle Ed's younger brother, my great-uncle Charley—Cholly, they called him—who helped out at the mill for room and board and a trifling wage. Across the road from the mill and Uncle Ed's house stood a blacksmith's shop, then still in operation, a dark, lively place full of coal smell, iron smell, and horse smell. All day long it rang like a musical instrument with the clanging of iron on iron, just far enough from the house and mill to sound like bells. The creek ran just behind the blacksmith's shop, a bright, noisy rattle. I used to catch tadpoles and minnows there, though it was deep in places, and if my grandmother found out I'd been playing in the creek I got spanked. The building's gone now, and the creek's fallen silent, grown up in weeds. I remember the building as small, made of stone burned black inside, crowded outside with burdocks whose leaves were always wet with the mist from the waterfall that rumbled day and night not far upstream.

I was five or six, still at that age when a day lasts for weeks and everything you see or hear or smell seems vividly alive, though later you can get only glimpses to serve as memories—or anyway so it seems until you start to write. This much comes at once: the large, grinning figure of my uncle Ed, Uncle Charley next to him, timidly smiling, dwarfed beside his brother, and standing not far from them Aunt Kate with a dishtowel and teapot. I get back, too, a little of the sunlit world they inhabited, seemingly without a care, as if forever. On one kitchen wall they had a large black pendulum clock on which the four was written IIII; I could never decide whether the thing was a mistake (I was already aware that the Welsh were prone to make curious mistakes) or something more mysterious, brought down from the ancient, unimaginable time when, according to Uncle Ed, the Welsh lived in caves and trees and couldn't talk yet, but had to get along by singing.

In those days everything was for me—for me more than for most children, perhaps—half real, half ethereal. It was not just the stories Uncle Ed liked to tell. In our farmhouse I slept with my grandmother, and every night before she turned off the bed-lamp she would read me something from the Bible or the *Christian Herald.* I don't remember what she read, but I remember seeing pictures of bright-winged angels playing harps and singing—beings she insisted were entirely real, as real as trees or hay wagons. She made my world mythic—her own as well. During the day she would sometimes go out in our front yard with a hoe and kill grass-snakes. It made my father, who was a practical man, furious. "Mother," he would ask, "what *harm* do they do?" "They bite," she would say. Sometimes my mother would try to defend her. Grandma Hughes had lived in Missouri for a time, where there were rattlesnakes, and she was too old now to change her ways. "Even a darn fool *mule* can be reasoned with," my father would say—he was a breeder and trainer of plough-horses—but he wouldn't pursue the argument. To me, though, steeped in her Bible and *Christian Herald* stories, nothing seemed more natural than that my grandmother in her righteousness should be out there in the dappled light below the maple trees, her bright blue eyes narrowed, her hoe-blade poised, every nerve on the look-out for serpents.

"Did you ever really *see* an angel?" I once asked her. Since there really were snakes, it seemed to me probable that there were angels.

"Not that I'm aware of," she said.

I thought it over. "Did my dad?"

"I doubt it," she said, then bit her lips together, trying not to smile.

So I knew on my grandmother's authority, to say nothing of Uncle Ed's, that there was more to the world than met the eye, or rather, knew that there were two worlds, and it came to seem to me that Remsen, like the valley where Jacob saw the ladder, was one of the places where they connected. Perhaps it was Remsen's peculiar, clear light, or the sense of peace my whole family seemed to feel there, gathering with relatives and friends to sing hymns in Capel Ucca those bright Sunday mornings; or perhaps it was simply the otherworldliness of a village that spoke Welsh. It was true that time had stopped there, or at very least had paused. We had no blacksmith's shops in Batavia. Mr. Culver, who shoed my father's horses, came with his equipment in a panel truck. And the mill where my father took his grain, the G.L.F., was like a factory—freightcars on one side of it, track on track of them, and inside, wherever you looked through the billowing white dust, big iron machines and men in goggles. My uncle Ed, when he worked in the old-fashioned mill in Remsen, wore a suit. It was gray with grain-dust, and it was a little dishevelled; but it was a suit. (Uncle Charley wore striped bib-overalls.) Uncle Ed's machinery was mostly made of wood and made very little noise, just a low, sweet humming sound, with rhythmical thumps.

I would sometimes be left over night with the two old men and Aunt Kate while my parents went off with younger relatives to some "sing." There was always a sing on somewhere around Remsen. "Every time three Welshmen meet," people said, "it's a choir." In those days it was more or less true. Everywhere my parents drove, they sang, almost always in a minor key and always in harmony; and every time relatives got together they sang, in almost as many parts as there were people.

I'd be alarmed when my parents began dressing for a sing, telling me in falsely sweet voices that I was to stay with my uncles and aunt and be a good boy. My grandmother, if she was there, would insist on going with them. Though she was nearly eighty, she had a voice like a bird, she claimed. The songfest wouldn't be the same without her. Uncle Charley would shake his head as if disgusted, though everyone said he'd had a wonderful tenor voice when he was younger. In those days, they said, he wouldn't have missed a Cymanfa Ganu or an Eisteddfod—the really big sing, where hundreds and hundreds of Welshmen came together—for all the tea in China. Uncle Charley would blush like a girl when they spoke of his singing days. "Well, a body gets old," he'd mutter. "Pride!" my grandmother would snap. "Sinful pride!"

She was a woman of temper; she'd been a red-head when she was young. But for all her sternness, she loved Uncle Charley as she loved nobody else—her husband's youngest brother, just a boy when she first knew him, all his life the one who'd been of no account. "That voice of his was his downfall," she said once to my mother, wiping dishes while my mother washed. "It gave him ideas."

To me, a child, it was a puzzling statement, though my mother, ruefully nodding, apparently understood. I tried to get my grandmother to explain it later, when she was sitting at her darning in our bedroom—more my bedroom than hers, she would say when a certain mood was on her. Another puzzling statement.

"Grandma," I asked, "how come Uncle Charley's voice gave him ideas?"

"Hush now," she said. That was always her answer to troublesome questions, and I knew how to deal with it. I just waited, watching her darn, making a nuisance of myself.

"Well," she said at last, then stopped to bite a thread. She looked at the end, twirled it between her fingers to make it pointed, then continued: "Singing's got its place. But a body can get to thinking, when he's singing with a choir, that that's how the whole blessed world should be, and then when he comes down out of the clouds it's a terrible disappointment."

I suppose I looked as puzzled as ever, tentatively considering the idea of people singing up in the clouds, like the angels in her pictures.

She leaned toward me and said, "Uncle Charley never found a good woman, *that's* what's wrong with him. Bills to pay, whippersnappers—*that'll* bring you down from your *la-la-la!*"

I gave up, as puzzled as before and slightly hurt. I knew well enough—she never let me forget—what a burden I was, not that she didn't kiss me and make a great to-do when I was dressed up for church or had done something nice for her, dust-mopping the bedrooms without being told to, or helping her find her brass thimble. (She was a great mislayer of things. It made my father sigh deeply and shake his head.) I was, in general, as good a child as I knew how to be, but it's true, I was sometimes a trouble. I justified her existence, I realize now: living with my parents, too old and poor to live alone, she didn't have to think herself a nuisance to the world. As my babysitter, she made it possible for my mother to teach school and for my father to work in the fields all day. All the same, I'm sure I ran her ragged, and there were times—especially when my parents had somewhere to go after dark—when I was as much trouble as I dared to be.

I hated those nights when my parents left me—for a Grange meeting, at home, or for a sing when we were in Remsen. I'd live through them, I knew—I might even enjoy myself, after a fashion—but the night would be darker than usual, outside the big old Remsen house when my parents and grandmother weren't somewhere within call, upstairs, or in the elegant, dimly lit livingroom. The mill, much as I loved it by day, looked ominous from Uncle Ed's kitchen window after dark. It would seem to have moved closer, blocking out the starlight like an immense black tombstone. I would hear the clock on the kitchen wall solemnly knocking the seconds off—*tock . . . tock*—the silence so deep I could also hear the clock on the desk in the livingroom, hurrying as if in panic—*tick-tick-tick-tick!* The sunflowers at the end of the garden would be gray now, staring back at me like motionless ghosts, and the blacksmith's shop across the road, a darker blot in the surrounding darkness—weeds all around it, hushed as if listening to the clatter of the creek—was transformed in my mind to a terrible place, the overgrown hovel of a cum-witch.

I would whine, hanging around, clinging to the white porcelain doorknob as my parents dressed. "Why can't I come with you?" I'd say. My mother's eyes would remain on the mirror, concentrating hard on the eyebrow pencil. Though she was fat, I thought she was amazingly beautiful. Her hair was dark red. "You can, when you're bigger," my father would say, standing behind my mother, chin lifted, putting on his tie. In the bathroom my grandmother would be singing, loosening up her voice. She *did* sound like a bird, I thought grimly. Like a chicken.

In the end, knowing I had no chance of winning, I would pretend to be seduced by Aunt Kate's molasses cookies and the promise that Uncle Ed would tell me stories. Sulking a little, to show them I didn't intend to forget this, I'd walk with my parents as far as the door, keeping an eye on their red, beaming faces and listening, full of disapproval, to their loud, cheerful talk as they took leave of my uncles and aunt and went down the wooden steps between the house and the big, dark mill to greet the relatives who'd come for them in their car. The inside lights of the car would go on as the car doors opened, and in that little, square-windowed island of light I'd see grown-up cousins and children cousins just a little more than my age squeezing over, climbing onto other cousins' laps. The alley between the mill and the house would fill up like a pool with laughter and shouts of "Watch your elbows!" and sometimes my father's voice, carefully patient, "That's all right, Mother. Take your time." Then the doors would close, leaving only the headlights, and the car would *chuff-chuff-chuff* past the mill and, listing like a carriage, would go around the corner at the end of the garden, then, listing again, taillights like two garnets, would veer out onto the road, briefly lighting up trees. When the taillights were out of sight I would turn, trying not to cry, to Uncle Ed, who would lift me and carry me on his shoulder like a feedsack to the kitchen. "*So,*" he would say, "I guess you didn't know I used to work for a bear!"

"I don't believe it," I would say, though I did, in fact.

"Big old black bear name of Herman. Used to live up by Blue Mountain Lake."

He often set his stories on Blue Mountain Lake, or on nearby Black River, where his camp was (he would take us there sometimes, to my grandmother's dismay)—an immense log-and-stone lodge filled with stuffed lynxes, wolves, and owls, Japanese lanterns overhead, and on the rustic tables a whole museum's worth of strange objects Aunt Kate had collected—little models of birch canoes, carved figures, a stereopticon with pictures of Paris long ago. The lodge was set in among trees, all but inaccessible, a wooden dock below it, where Uncle Ed's guideboat was tied during the day. The water on the river, shallow and clear as glass, seemed hardly to move, though when you dropped a leaf on it it quickly sped away. Fish poked thoughtfully in and out among the shadows of underwater weeds, and when you looked up you saw a world almost equally strange—pinewoods and mountains, large hurrying clouds of the kind I thought angels lived on, huge white mounds full of sunlight. Whenever Uncle Ed began to speak of the

Adirondacks, you knew that in a minute he'd be telling of his childhood in Wales, where people lived in cottages on dark green hills with their sheep and collie dogs, and nothing ever changed.

All through supper Uncle Ed would tell me stories, Aunt Kate tisk-tisking, moving back and forth between the table and the stove, patting my head sometimes, telling me not to believe a word of it. Uncle Charley would sit grinning as if sheepishly, sometimes throwing me a wink, sometimes saying a few words in a high-pitched voice, trying to make me think it was the parrot, Bobby Watson, who stood watching and pecking at lettuce in his cage in the corner. Uncle Charley was as small-boned as a sparrow and had startling eyes, one brown, one blue. Though he was almost as old as Uncle Ed, he had light brown hair and a brown moustache—a shiny, soft brown with hardly any gray in it. Perhaps it was partly the way he sat, head forward, eyes lowered, his hands on his knees except when he raised his fork or spoon: he seemed, even with all his wrinkles, just a boy, no bigger around than Uncle Ed's right arm. People who didn't know them thought Uncle Charley was Aunt Kate's brother, not Uncle Ed's. She too was, she liked to say, petite. After supper, while Aunt Kate washed dishes and the two old men went out to the mill to "catch up"—really to smoke cigars—I would bang on Aunt Kate's piano in the livingroom. The piano was a good one, a Storey & Clark upright. In the tiffanied dimness of the livingroom, its coal-black surfaces shone like mirrors, or like Black River at night, and everything I played on it sounded to me like real music. I would lose all track of time, closing my eyes and tipping my head to the piano sound, dark, sustained chords that in my mind made a shadowy place you could move around in, explore like an old-time Indian. When my uncles and aunt came together again, after the dishes and cigar smoking, they'd call me back and we'd play dominoes at the kitchen table. After an hour or so, Uncle Charley would say, grinning, not meeting anyone's eyes, "Well, time to turn in by gol, ant-it?" and he'd go down to his narrow, yellow-wallpapered room in the basement.

I'd sit a little longer with Uncle Ed and Aunt Kate. They must have known how I hated to go upstairs alone in that big, quiet house; but it was Aunt Kate's habit to listen to her records—some of them old, thick Edison records, most of them opera—and sew for a while before going up to bed, and it was Uncle Ed's habit to settle down across from her, heavy and comfortable as an old gray cat, draw on his steel-rimmed spectacles, and read. They were both too old to go climbing that narrow back stairway twice. (The front-hallway stairs were wide and glossy, with a runner down the steps; I don't remember anyone's ever using them much except my cousins and me, playing Chinese School.) Aunt Kate was brittle and climbed steps one at a time. As for Uncle Ed, he was huge, for a Welshman, with hair as white as snow. When I began to nod, he'd say, looking at me over the spectacle rims, "You run and put your pajamas on, Buddy. We'll be up in a jiffy." As I think back to it, it surprises me that I didn't make a fuss; but I obeyed without protest, knowing I'd be long asleep before they got there.

Once in a while I'd wake up for a minute when they came, and I'd see them in their white flannel nightgowns, kneeling beside the bed. Pretending to be asleep—I slept on a cot across the room from them—I'd watch them bow their heads, side by side, and press their hands together just below their chins, and I'd listen to their whisperings in Welsh. Uncle Ed had three stubbed fingers, cut off in a gristmill when he was young. His rounded shoulders were enormous. In my memory, no doubt inaccurate, they went a third the length of the bed. In the mill, during the day, Uncle Ed was like a king, lifting heavy feed-sacks as if they were nothing, chattering lightly past his dead cigar, mostly in that clicking, lilting gibberish he spoke; but now, for all his size, he was as subdued and meek as Uncle Charley, or Aunt Kate there beside him. The only light in the room was the dim one on the table beside the bed. It made his hair look soft, like a baby's. Aunt Kate's hair was like fine silver wire.

* * *

One time when we were visiting, Uncle Charley took what they all called later "a tumble." I'm not sure how much of it I actually saw. I was, as I've said, only five or six. A few sharp images have stayed with me all these years, but for the rest I must trust imagination and family stories. I remember sitting in the office at the mill—that time or some other time—drawing on one of the yellow, legal-sized notepads Uncle Ed used for figuring and keeping records, the pot-bellied stove unlit in the corner. It was August; I know because farmers were bringing their wheat in. All around the stove stood pale, bluish saltblocks, the slippery blue-white of bone in a butchershop, and stacked around the saltblocks there were bales of twine and barbed wire, kerosene lanterns, and zinc-coated buckets set one inside the other, the top bucket filled with nails. Outside the window I could see Aunt Kate's garden, aglow at that time of year with roses, zinnias, and sunflowers, vegetables down the middle, at one end a scarecrow in a washed-out, ragged coat and straw hat that had once been, no doubt, Uncle Charley's. There were farmers in the room with me, ritched back on their round-backed wooden chairs, talking and joking as they always did while they waited for Uncle Ed to grind their grist and then for Uncle Charley to load the bags on the two-wheeled feedtruck and roll them to the dock, then lift them down a foot or two onto the wagon. No doubt I'd been running back and forth with Uncle Charley for most of the morning, since that's what I usually did, neither of us talking—Uncle Charley almost never talked, except when he pretended to be the parrot in the kitchen—I, for my part, trying to be of help: snatching an empty feedsack from his path, though in fact there was plenty of room; trying to push a heavy door open further. But now I was in the office, weary of the game, half listening to the singing of the wooden walls as they resounded to the mill-wheels, and drawing rabbits so much like those my father drew (rabbits were all he knew how to draw) that if you'd asked him later, he couldn't have told you for sure which one of us had done them.

I heard no shout, no noise of any kind, but suddenly the farmers were up out of their chairs, running in their heavy boots from the office into the mill, and as fast as I could get down out of my chair I was after them. Where the wooden machinery thudded and sang, sending up white powder, nothing was wrong. Uncle Ed stood blinking as the farmers ran up to him and past him; then he pushed the worn-smooth wooden lever that made the rumbling stop, caught me up in his arms, and ran after the farmers. When we came into the sunlight beyond the open door, we found Uncle Charley climbing up from between the loading dock and one of the farmers' wagons, furiously shouting and wiping dirt from his mouth and moustache. The wagon had been carelessly parked, a three-foot gap between the dock and the wagonbed. On the wagon, where Uncle Charley had dropped it when he stepped into the gap and fell, a sack lay split open, slowly drizzling grist down through the slats onto the ground. He shouted louder than before, no doubt swearing in Welsh—an amazing sound from a man always so quiet—and with a look half enraged, half guilty, he tried to get up on his feet and save the grain. Then another look came over him—surprise, indignation—and one leg, cocked like a corn-knife, flipped out from under him. Uncle Ed set me down, almost threw me from him, and jumped onto the wagon, holding out his arms as if to pick up Uncle Charley, then thought better of it, or got confused. He just stood there, bent at the waist, arms thrown forward, like a child playing catch.

At the top of the stairs across the way, the back door of the house opened, and my grandmother came out in her knitted black shawl. "Land of Goshen!" she cried in a loud, angry voice. "*Now* look what you've done!" My father came out behind her, looking baffled and apologetic, as if if he hadn't been taking a nap he could have prevented it. "Now stop that," he said to my grandmother, almost absentmindedly, and instantly she stopped. Tears ran down the sides of Uncle Charley's moustache and he clung to his leg with both hands, not shouting now, clamping his lips together and whimpering. Then Aunt Kate was there with them, near-sightedly bending forward. "I'll call the doctor," she said, turning, and went back into the house.

"It's all my fault," one of the farmers said, shaking his head and working his jaw as if in a minute he meant to hit himself.

"Here now," Uncle Ed said, "let's get you inside," and carefully fitting his arms under Uncle Charley, taking pains to support the broken leg, he lifted him like a child or a newborn calf and carried him up onto the loading platform, over to the steps at the far end, then down and across the way and up the wooden stairs toward the kitchen.

"Mercy!" my grandmother said, unable to control herself, her eyes as bright as when she went out with a hoe to kill snakes. My mother took her arm and patted it.

I was of course not aware at the time that they all felt as guilty as I did. Even my grandmother, I realize now, must have felt guilty, shouting at us all as if she secretly believed she should have taken better care of us. But whatever they were feeling, they soon got over it, once Uncle Charley was inside, on the couch in the livingroom. I myself took longer. It was a matter of fact to me that if I'd been doing my job, running along with Uncle Charley and his feedtruck, keeping his way clear and watching out for trouble, he'd never have fallen down and broken his leg. The doctor, when he came, was professionally grave. Aunt Kate wrung her hands in her apron. I offered, bursting into tears as I did so, to pay Uncle Charley's doctor bills. Uncle Ed just looked at me, lips puckered in surprise. None of the others seemed to have noticed what I'd said. "I really will," I bawled, clinging to his leg.

"Here now," Uncle Ed said. "Katy, get this boy a cookie!" And then: "Go on, now. Away with you both!"

I went with her, looking over my shoulder at Uncle Charley, gray-faced on the couch, the doctor in his black suit bending down beside him. They were all smiling now, even Uncle Charley, all of them describing what had happened as "a tumble"—or all except my grandmother, who always took, according to my father, the darkest possible view of things. My mother and father had a fight that night, when they thought I was asleep. My father said my grandmother was an Angel of Death. (His anger may have made him unusually poetic—though now that I think of it, he said the phrase as if he'd used it against her many times.) "If you hate her so," my mother said, "why don't you just send her to the old folks' home?" Thus my mother won, as she always did. When it was clear to them both that she'd won, she said, "Oh, Bill, she's just worried. You know that. She's like a child." I lay in the darkness with my eyes open, trying to make sense of the queer idea.

* * *

It wasn't until the following summer that my family visited Remsen again. Letters passed back and forth two or three a week in the meantime, Aunt Kate telling us of, among other things, Uncle Charley's gradual recovery—not as quick as it should be, she let us know—my mother sending back our family's encouragement and sometimes inspirational poems from my grandmother's magazines. When we finally went to visit it was partly because a Cymanfa Ganu—a singing festival—was to be held nearby, in Utica. At Uncle Ed's I learned to my surprise and dismay—since I disliked change, hated to see any slightest hint that the universe might not be orderly to the core, as smooth in its operations as an immense old mill—that my uncles and aunt, though they'd never before shown much interest in such things, were planning to go to the festival with my parents and grandmother. I learned it by eavesdropping. When I was supposed to be asleep—as Uncle Charley was, down in his basement room, snoring with his mouth open (I'd sneaked down earlier and seen him there, lying with one arm hanging over the bedside)—I crept without a sound down the front-hallway stairs and settled near the bottom to listen to the voices in the livingroom, just to my left.

Aunt Kate was saying, speaking more softly than usual, "He could do with the lift."

"He's still down, isn't he," my mother said.

"Oh, Cholly'll be fine," Uncle Ed said, hearty as ever, and gave a laugh.

I listened, uneasy, for what my grandmother would say. When she said nothing, I let myself believe she'd fallen asleep over her sewing.

"He keeps in too much, that's all," Aunt Kate said, as if shyly, embarrassed that Uncle Ed hadn't agreed with her.

"So anyway, we'll all go," my father said, settling things. "Take Buddy too. He's never been to a Cymanfa Ganu yet. High time he went!"

"Heavens to Betsy!" my grandmother burst out. "You'd let that poor whippersnapper stay out till midnight with a bunch of wild lunatics howling their miserable heads off?"

A shiver went up my back. I was much too literal-minded a child to fit her description with any kind of singing I'd ever heard of, much less any I'd been in on. I remembered stories my uncle Ed had told me of how the Welsh were all witches in olden times—how they used to fly around like birds at night, and make magic circles among trees and stones.

The following day I was so filled with anxious anticipation I could hardly breathe. Out in the mill I kept close to Uncle Charley, trying to guess every move he was about to make and help with it. He seemed smaller all over, since the accident. Though he wore arm-elastics, his cuffs hung low, as did the crotch of his overalls. His hands trembled, and he no longer bothered to put his teeth in. In the past he'd pretended to appreciate my help. Now, as I gradually made out, it annoyed him. "I'll get that," he'd say, kicking a twine-bale from the aisle as I reached for it. Or as I ran to push a heavy door open further, he'd say, "Leave it be, boy. It's open far enough." In the end I did nothing for him, simply stayed with him because I was ashamed to leave him and go look for Uncle Ed.

He no longer did the kinds of work he'd done before. The hundred-pound sacks were too heavy for him—he wasn't much heavier than the sacks himself—and when he pushed the feedtruck, after Uncle Ed had loaded it, both Uncle Ed and I would watch him in distress, afraid it would tilt too far back, off balance, and fall on him. Mostly, Uncle Ed had taken over the pushing of the feedtruck. "Go ahead, then," Uncle Charley said crossly. "It's your mill." To keep busy, Uncle Charley set rat traps, wound wire around old ladder rungs, swiped down cobwebs, swept the floors. He still joked with farmers, as he'd always done, but it seemed to me the lightness was gone from his voice, and his eyes had a mean look, as if he didn't really think the jokes were funny or the farmers his friends. Sometimes in the office, when the farmers were alone with Uncle Ed and me, one of the farmers would say something like, "Cholly's gettin better every day, looks like," and I would know by their smiles that none of them believed it. I would stand by the heavy old desk full of pigeonholes and secret compartments—Uncle Charley had once shown me how to work them all—trying to guess what Uncle Ed might need: his pocket-sized notebook, one of his yellow pads, or one of the big white pencils that said "E. L. Hughes" in red—but I could never guess which object he'd want next, so I could serve no useful purpose except if he happened to look over and say, "Buddy, hand me that calendar there." Then I'd leap. Out in the mill Uncle Charley moved slowly back and forth with a pushbroom, needlessly sweeping white dust from the aisles, or hammered nails into loosened bin-boards, or mended burlap sacks not yet bad enough to leak. Now and then he'd poke his head in, the buttoned collar much too large for his neck, and would ask Uncle Ed if he'd gotten to Bill Williams' oats yet. "I'll get to it, Cholly," Uncle Ed would say, waving his cigar. Uncle Charley would frown, shaking his head, then disappear, going about his business.

Sometime after lunch I found Uncle Charley sitting on the floor beside one of the bins, nailing a round piece of tin—the top of a coffeecan—over a hole where bits of grain leaked out. I stood awhile watching him. His hand, when he reached to his mouth for a nail, shook badly. He pretended not to notice me. After a while I went over and hunkered down beside him, thinking I might hand him nails from the zinc-coated bucket beside his knee, though at the moment his mouth was as full as a pincushion. When he said nothing, I asked, "What's a Cymanfa Ganu, Uncle Charley?"

"Welsh word," he brought out through the nails, and carefully finished driving the nail between his fingers through the tin. Then he glanced at me guiltily, took the nails from his mouth and laid them on the floor between us. "Means 'Come on back,' " he said, then suddenly—his heart not in it—grinned. " 'Come on back to Wales,' that is. That's what all the Welshmen want, or so they think."

He tipped his head back, as if he were listening. The way the sunlight came slanting through the mill—great generous shafts full of floating white specks all whirling and swirling in patterns too complex for the eye to comprehend—it was like being in church. Even better than church. I thought of the trees where Uncle Ed had told me the Welshmen used to worship their peculiar bug-eyed gods—"River gods, tree gods, pig gods, Lord knows what," he'd said. (My grandmother wouldn't speak of it. "Your uncle Ed," she said, "has peculiar ideas.") Abruptly, Uncle Charley dropped his head back down, snatched up a nail, cocked it between two fingers over the tin, and started hammering. "Damn fools," he said, then glanced at me and frowned, then winked.

"Tell me something else in Welsh," I said.

He thought about it, placing another nail. At last he said, squinting, "You know what 'Buddy' means?" Before I could answer, he said, "Means 'the poet.' They used to set great store by poets, back in Wales. Only second to kings—maybe not even second. Same thing, kings and poets. Different kinds of liars." He looked solemn, his face ash-gray under the age-spots. I studied him, perturbed—no more perturbed than he was, I realize now; but at six I knew nothing of the confusion of adults. All I knew was that his eyes were screwed up tight, one brown, one blue, and his moustache half covered the black hole of his mouth like a sharp-gabled roof of old straw.

I asked, "Are we *all* going to the Cymanfa Ganu?"

His eyes slipped off axis, then abruptly he reached for another nail. "Course we are," he said. He lined up the nail and with two angry raps drove it home. "Don't worry," he said, "it don't hurt much."

I remember only the inside of the building where the songfest was held. It must have been a church, very large, with wooden walls, as yellow-gray as the walls of a new barn. It was brightly lighted, the walls and overhead beams high above us all glowing as if waxed. Everyone my parents had ever known was there, it looked like. The people milled around for what seemed to me hours, shouting and talking, pressing tightly together, my father moving behind my mother from group to group, carrying me on his shoulders. My grandmother, wearing a light black coat and helping herself along on two brown canes—it was only that winter that she'd begun to need them—went from one old white-haired Welshwoman to another, talking and nodding and laughing till she cried, sometimes pointing a bony, crooked finger across the room and gleefully shouting out a name, though no one could possibly have heard her in all that uproar.

Then somehow we got to seats, all of us together, me wedged in between my father and Uncle Charley. A man got up in the front of the room—he looked like a congressman or a well-to-do minister—and said something. Everyone laughed. He said something more, they laughed some more, and then from somewhere, booming around us, came organ music. Uncle Charley was jerking at my elbow, making me look down. He held a small Bible-like book with writing in it—no music, as in the hymnbooks in our church at home (I hadn't yet seen the ones my grandfather left my mother), just writing, and not a word anywhere that I could read. "You know your *do re mi?*" he asked, looking at me sternly, his face very bright. I shook my head, noticing only now that above the hymn words, all in Welsh, there were little words—*do, re, mi,* and so on—as meaningless to me at the time as all the others. Uncle Charley looked up at my father as if in alarm, then grinned, looking back at me. "Never mind," he said, "you sing what *I* sing." On every side of us people were standing up now, a few of them beginning to tap their feet, just barely moving the toes of their lumpy shoes. My father and Uncle Charley helped me stand up on my chair. Suddenly, like a shock of thunder that made the whole room shake, they began to sing.

Most of them seemed to have no need of the hymnbooks and couldn't have used them anyway, singing as they did with their heads lifted, mouths wide as fishmouths, proclaiming whatever it was they proclaimed not so much to the front of the hall as to the gleaming roof. They sang, as Welsh choruses always do, in numerous parts, each as clearly defined as cold, individual currents in a wide, bright river. There were no weak voices, though some, like Uncle Charley's, were reedy and harsh—not that it mattered; the river of sound could use it all. They sang as if the music were singing itself through them—sang out boldly, no uncertainties or hesitations; and I, as if by magic, sang with them, as sure of myself every note of the way as the wisest and heartiest in the room. Though I was astonished by my powers, I know, thinking back, that it was not as miraculous as I imagined. Borne along by those powerful voices, the music's ancient structure, only a very good musician could have sung off key. And yet it did seem miraculous. It seemed our bones and blood that sang, all heaven and earth singing harmony lines, and when the music broke off on the final chord, the echo that rang on the walls around us was like a roaring Amen.

Hymn after hymn we sang—old people, children, people my parents' age—ancient tunes invented before the major mode was thought of, tunes like hugely breathing creatures. We were outside ourselves, caught up in a *hwell,* as the Welsh say. It really did seem to me, once or twice, that I looked down on all the congregation from the beams above our heads. My father's hand was closed hard on mine; Uncle Charley held my other hand, squeezing it just as tightly. Tears streamed from his brown eye and blue eye, washing his cheeks, dripping from his moustache, making his whole face shine. Afterward, when we were leaving, I saw that Aunt Kate and my mother had been crying too, even my grandmother, though not my father or Uncle Ed. On the steps outside, lighting his cigar, Uncle Ed said, "Good sing." My father nodded and hitched up his pants, then turned to look back at the door as if sorry to leave. "Good turn-out." Uncle Charley, with his hands in his pockets, staring at the ground, said nothing.

* * *

The following night Uncle Charley didn't come in for supper, though they called and called. I watched through the kitchen window as Uncle Ed and my father, gray as ghosts in the moonlit garden, shouted toward the trees across the road, the glittering creek, the blacksmith's shop, then turned and moved heavily, as if gravity had changed and the air had grown thick, toward the mill. Later, Uncle Ed, in the wooden armchair in the kitchen, holding his cigar in the hand that had three fingers missing, stared into space and said, "Poor Cholly. I wonder what's got into him."

Aunt Kate stood over by the sink with her head bowed, thinking, folding the dishtowel, then unfolding it, then folding it again. "I guess we better phone the police," she said at last.

"No, don't do that!" Uncle Ed said suddenly, as if she'd startled him out of a daydream. He leaned his forearms on the arms of the chair and hefted himself up out of it. "I'll run out to the office and phone around among the neighbors a bit," he said, and at once went to the door.

"Why not phone from here?" Aunt Kate said, or began to say, then glanced at me and stopped.

"Here, let me give you a hand," my father said. The two of them went out, bent forward like shy boys, and closed the door quietly behind them.

"I'll give Buddy his supper," my mother said. "I suppose it won't hurt for the rest of us to wait."

"That's fine," Aunt Kate said, still folding and unfolding the dishtowel.

"We should never have taken him to the songfest," my grandmother said. "I *told* you it wouldn't be good for him!"

My mother, herding me over to my chair, said, "Mother, you never said any such thing!"

"Well, I meant to," my grandmother said, and firmly clamped her mouth shut.

Toward morning they found him, I learned much later, right across the road in the creek behind the blacksmith's shop. I still occasionally dream of it, though of course I never saw it, Uncle Charley lying face up below the moonlit, glass-clear surface, staring, emotionless, at the perfectly quiet stars.

Aunt Kate, it turned out, had known all along that he'd gone off to take his own life, though she'd refused to believe it and had therefore told no one. She'd found his clothes that afternoon, just a little after sunset, neatly folded and stacked on the chair beside his bed in the room they let him live in downstairs. He'd left them as a message, my grandmother said: for what they were worth, the world could have them back. ("Now that's enough of that," my father said sharply.) Aunt Kate had told herself one foolish lie after another, she explained to us, her hands over her eyes, her glasses on the table in front of her. Perhaps he'd found a lady-friend, she'd said to herself, and had gone out and bought himself new clothes, even new socks and shoes.

The following night, when everyone knew Uncle Charley was dead, though no one was admitting it was suicide (they never did admit that), Uncle Ed's livingroom was filled with people. All the chairs were occupied, even the arms of them, where boys or young women sat, most of them cousins, and there were people on the chairs my father had brought in from the diningroom and kitchen, too. The people were all talking in low voices and sniffling, their eyes wet and red. I sat on one of my father's legs, watching.

They talked of the singer Uncle Charley had been; the festivals would never be the same without him. They spoke of what a shame it was that he'd never had a wife and children; it would have made all the difference. Then for a while, since sad talk made them ill at ease, they talked about other things—crops and the weather, marriages, politics. Sometimes they talked now in groups of three or four, sometimes all as one group. Aunt Kate served tea. Some of the men had whiskey with them, which Aunt Kate didn't approve of, but she looked at the carpet and said nothing. The clock on the mahogany desk ticked on and on, but neither in the darkness outside nor in the dimly lit livingroom was anything changing. People stirred a little, now and then, shifting position, moving just an arm or a foot, sometimes blowing their noses, but no one got up yet, no one left for home. Slowly the whole conversation died out like embers in a fireplace, and as the stillness deepened, settling in like winter or an old magic spell, it began to seem that the silence was unbreakable, our final say.

Then an old farmer named Sy Thomas, sitting in the corner with his hands folded, twine around his pants cuffs, cleared his throat, pushed his chin out, face reddening, eyes evasive, and began to sing. Tentatively, then more boldly, others joined in with him. Aunt Kate, with an expression half timid, half cunning, went to the piano and, after a minute, sat down, took off her glasses, and began to play. They were singing in parts now, their heads slightly lifted. On the carpet, one after another, as if coming to life, their shoes began to move.

# ⁂ JOYCE CAROL OATES
(1938– )

In a multitude of works—in all genres—Joyce Carol Oates has been mapping the often menacing terrain of contemporary American life. Made vulnerable by the powerful and complex forces that make up their worlds, Oates' characters yearn and strive for comprehension and survival of the violence, both latent and overt, that threatens them. Called by one critic "the dark lady of American letters," Oates explores the dark realities of American life out of her concern for "the moral and social conditions of my generation," as she expressed it in an article in the *Chicago Tribune Book World.* Moreover, like Flannery O'Connor, she sees writing as essentially an optimistic act, "a gesture of sympathy."

Oates was born to a working-class family in Lockport, New York. Finishing high school in 1956, she went to Syracuse University on a scholarship, graduating in 1960. She earned her M.A. degree from the University of Wisconsin in 1961. She taught for five years at the University of Detroit and then ten years at the University of Windsor in Canada. Since 1978 she has been teaching at Princeton University, where she and her husband coedit the *Ontario Review and Press.* Among her many novels are *With Shuddering Fall* (1964); *Expensive People* (1968); *Them* (1969), winner of the National Book Award; *Do with Me What You Will* (1973); *Childworld* (1976); *Bellefleur* (1980); *Marya: A Life* (1986); *American Appetites* (1988); *Black Water* (1992); *Zombie* (1995); and *We Were the Mulvaneys* (1996). Her story collections include *By the North Gate* (1963), *The Wheel of Love* (1970), *The Goddess and Other Women* (1974), *Night-side* (1977), *Last Days* (1984), *Heat* (1991), *Haunted: Tales of the Grotesque* (1994), *Will You Always Love Me?* (1996), and *The Collector of Hearts* (1998). Many of her stories have received recognition and awards. In 1987 she published the nonfiction book, *On Boxing,* a serious look at a sport of which she confesses to being a fan.

## Where Are You Going, Where Have You Been?

FOR BOB DYLAN

HER NAME was Connie. She was fifteen and she had a quick, nervous giggling habit of craning her neck to glance into mirrors or checking other people's faces to make sure her own was all right. Her mother, who noticed everything and knew everything and who hadn't much reason any longer to look at her own face, always scolded Connie about it. "Stop gawking at yourself. Who are you? You think you're so pretty?" she would say. Connie would raise her eyebrows at these familiar old complaints and look right through her mother, into a shadowy vision of herself as she was right at that moment: she knew she was pretty and that was everything. Her mother had been pretty once too, if you could believe those old snapshots in the album, but now her looks were gone and that was why she was always after Connie.

"Why don't you keep your room clean like your sister? How've you got your hair fixed—what the hell stinks? Hair spray? You don't see your sister using that junk."

Her sister June was twenty-four and still lived at home. She was a secretary in the high school Connie attended, and if that wasn't bad enough—with her in the same building—she was so plain and chunky and steady that Connie had to hear her praised all the time by her mother and her mother's sisters. June did this, June did that, she saved money and helped clean the house and cooked and Connie couldn't do a thing, her mind was all filled with trashy daydreams. Their father was away at work most of the time and when he came home he wanted supper and he read the newspaper at supper and after supper he went to bed. He didn't bother talking much to them, but around his bent head Connie's mother kept picking at her until Connie wished her mother was dead and she herself was dead and it was all over. "She makes me want to throw up sometimes," she complained to her friends. She had a high, breathless, amused voice that made everything she said sound a little forced, whether it was sincere or not.

There was one good thing: June went places with girl friends of hers, girls who were just as plain and steady as she, and so when Connie wanted to do that her mother had no objections. The father of Connie's best girl friend drove the girls the three miles to town and left them at a shopping plaza so they could walk through the stores or go to a movie, and when he came to pick them up again at eleven he never bothered to ask what they had done.

They must have been familiar sights, walking around the shopping plaza in their shorts and flat ballerina slippers that always scuffed the sidewalk, with charm bracelets jingling on their thin wrists; they would lean together to whisper and laugh secretly if someone passed who amused or interested them. Connie had long dark blond hair that drew anyone's eye to it, and she wore part of it pulled up on her head and puffed out and the rest of it she let fall down her back. She wore a pull-over jersey blouse that looked one way when she was at home and another way when she was away from home. Everything about her had two sides to it, one for home and one for anywhere that was not home: her walk, which could be childlike and bobbing, or languid enough to make anyone think she was hearing music in her head; her mouth, which was pale and smirking most of the time, but bright and pink on these evenings out; her laugh, which was cynical and drawling at home—"Ha, ha, very funny,"—but high-pitched and nervous anywhere else, like the jingling of the charms on her bracelet.

Sometimes they did go shopping or to a movie, but sometimes they went across the highway, ducking fast across the busy road, to a drive-in restaurant where older kids hung out. The restaurant was shaped like a big bottle, though squatter than a real bottle, and on its cap was a revolving figure of a grinning boy holding a hamburger aloft. One night in midsummer they ran across, breathless with daring, and right away someone leaned out a car window and invited them over, but it was just a boy from high school they didn't like. It made them feel good to be able to ignore him. They went up through the maze of parked and cruising cars to the bright-lit, fly-infested restaurant, their faces pleased and expectant as if they were entering a sacred building that loomed up out of the night to give them what haven and blessing they yearned for. They sat at the counter and crossed their legs at the ankles, their thin shoulders rigid with excitement, and listened to the music that made everything so good: the music was always in the background, like music at a church service; it was something to depend upon.

A boy named Eddie came in to talk with them. He sat backwards on his stool, turning himself jerkily around in semi-circles and then stopping and turning back again, and after a while he asked Connie if she would like something to eat. She said she would and so she tapped her friend's arm on her way out—her friend pulled her face up into a brave, droll look—and Connie said she would meet her at eleven, across the way. "I just hate to leave her like that," Connie said earnestly, but the boy said that she wouldn't be alone for long. So they went out to his car, and on the way Connie couldn't help but let her eyes wander over the windshields and faces all around her, her face gleaming with a joy that had nothing to do with Eddie or even this place; it might have been the music. She drew her shoulders up and sucked in her breath with the pure pleasure of being alive, and just at that moment she happened to glance at a face just a few feet from hers. It was a boy with shaggy black hair, in a convertible jalopy painted gold. He stared at her and then his lips widened into a grin. Connie slit her eyes at him and turned away, but she couldn't help glancing back and there he was, still watching her. He wagged a finger and laughed and said, "Gonna get you, baby," and Connie turned away again without Eddie noticing anything.

She spent three hours with him, at the restaurant where they ate hamburgers and drank Cokes in wax cups that were always sweating, and then down an alley a mile or so away, and when he left her off at five to eleven only the movie house was still open at the plaza. Her girl friend was there, talking with a boy. When Connie came up, the two girls smiled at each other and Connie said, "How was the movie?" and the girl said, "*You* should know." They rode off with the girl's father, sleepy and pleased, and Connie couldn't help but look back at the darkened shopping plaza with its big empty parking lot and its signs that were faded and ghostly now, and over at the drive-in restaurant where cars were still circling tirelessly. She couldn't hear the music at this distance.

Next morning June asked her how the movie was and Connie said, "So-so."

She and that girl and occasionally another girl went out several times a week, and the rest of the time Connie spent around the house—it was summer vacation—getting in her mother's way and thinking, dreaming about the boys she met. But all the boys fell back and dissolved into a single face that was not even a face but an idea, a feeling, mixed up with the urgent insistent pounding of the music and the humid night air of July. Connie's mother kept dragging her back to the daylight by finding things for her to do or saying suddenly, "What's this about the Pettinger girl?"

And Connie would say nervously, "Oh, her. That dope." She always drew thick clear lines between herself and such girls, and her mother was simple and kind enough to believe it. Her mother was so simple, Connie thought, that it was maybe cruel to fool her so much. Her mother went scuffling around the house in old bedroom slippers and complained over the telephone to one sister about the other, then the other called up and the two of them complained about the third one. If June's name was mentioned her mother's tone was approving, and if Connie's name was mentioned it was disapproving. This did not really mean she disliked Connie, and actually Connie thought that her mother preferred her to June just because she was prettier, but the two of them kept up a pretense of exasperation, a sense that they were tugging and struggling over something of little value to either of them. Sometimes, over coffee, they were almost friends, but something would come up—some vexation that was like a fly buzzing suddenly around their heads—and their faces went hard with contempt.

One Sunday Connie got up at eleven—none of them bothered with church—and washed her hair so that it could dry all day long in the sun. Her parents and sister were going to a barbecue at an aunt's house and Connie said no, she wasn't interested, rolling her eyes to let her mother know just what she thought of it. "Stay home alone then," her mother said sharply. Connie sat out back in a lawn chair and watched them drive away, her father quiet and bald, hunched around so that he could back the car out, her mother with a look that was still angry and not at all softened through the windshield, and in the back seat poor old June, all dressed up as if she didn't know what a barbecue was; with all the running yelling kids and the flies. Connie sat with her eyes closed in the sun, dreaming and dazed with the warmth about her as if this were a kind of love, the caresses of love, and her mind slipped over onto thoughts of the boy she had been with the night before and how nice he had been, how sweet it always was, not the way someone like June would suppose but sweet, gentle, the way it was in movies and promised in songs; and when she opened her eyes she hardly knew where she was, the back yard ran off into weeds and a fence-like line of trees and behind it the sky was perfectly blue and still. The asbestos "ranch house" that was now three years old startled her—it looked small. She shook her head as if to get awake.

It was too hot. She went inside the house and turned on the radio to drown out the quiet. She sat on the edge of her bed, barefoot, and listened for an hour and a half to a program called XYZ Sunday Jamboree, record after record of hard, fast, shrieking songs she sang along with, interspersed by exclamations from "Bobby King": "An' look here, you girls at Napoleon's—Son and Charley want you to pay real close attention to this song coming up!"

And Connie paid close attention herself, bathed in a glow of slow-pulsed joy that seemed to rise mysteriously out of the music itself and lay languidly, about the airless little room, breathed in and breathed out with each gentle rise and fall of her chest.

After a while she heard a car coming up the drive. She sat up at once, startled, because it couldn't be her father so soon. The gravel kept crunching all the way in from the road—the driveway was long—and Connie ran to the window. It was a car she didn't know. It was an open jalopy, painted a bright gold that caught the sunlight opaquely. Her heart began to pound and her fingers snatched at her hair, checking it, and she whispered, "Christ. Christ," wondering how bad she looked. The car came to a stop at the side door and the horn sounded four short taps, as if this were a signal Connie knew.

She went into the kitchen and approached the door slowly, then hung out the screen door, her bare toes curling down off the step. There were two boys in the car and now she recognized the driver: he had shaggy, shabby black hair that looked crazy as a wig and he was grinning at her.

"I ain't late, am I?" he said.

"Who the hell do you think you are?" Connie said.

"Toldja I'd be out, didn't I?"

"I don't even know who you are."

She spoke sullenly, careful to show no interest or pleasure, and he spoke in a fast, bright monotone. Connie looked past him to the other boy, taking her time. He had fair brown hair, with a lock that fell onto his forehead. His sideburns gave him a fierce, embarrassed look, but so far he hadn't even bothered to glance at her. Both boys wore sunglasses. The driver's glasses were metallic and mirrored everything in miniature.

"You wanta come for a ride?" he said.

Connie smirked and let her hair fall loose over one shoulder.

"Don'tcha like my car? New paint job," he said. "Hey."

"What?"

"You're cute."

She pretended to fidget, chasing flies away from the door.

"Don'tcha believe me, or what?" he said.

"Look, I don't even know who you are," Connie said in disgust.

"Hey, Ellie's got a radio, see. Mine broke down." He lifted his friend's arm and showed her the little transistor radio the boy was holding, and now Connie began to hear the music. It was the same program that was playing inside the house.

"Bobby King?" she said.

"I listen to him all the time. I think he's great."

"He's kind of great," Connie said reluctantly.

"Listen, that guy's *great*. He knows where the action is."

Connie blushed a little, because the glasses made it impossible for her to see just what this boy was looking at. She couldn't decide if she liked him or if he was just a jerk, and so she dawdled in the doorway and wouldn't come down or go back inside. She said, "What's all that stuff painted on your car?"

"Can'tcha read it?" He opened the door very carefully, as if he were afraid it might fall off. He slid out just as carefully, planting his feet firmly on the ground, the tiny metallic world in his glasses slowing down like gelatine hardening, and in the midst of it Connie's bright green blouse. "This here is my name, to begin with," he said. ARNOLD FRIEND was written in tarlike black letters on the side, with a drawing of a round, grinning face that reminded Connie of a pumpkin, except it wore sunglasses. "I wanta introduce myself, I'm Arnold Friend and that's my real name and I'm gonna be your friend, honey, and inside the car's Ellie Oscar, he's kinda shy." Ellie brought his transistor radio up to his shoulder and balanced it there. "Now, these numbers are a secret code, honey," Arnold Friend explained. He read off the numbers 33, 19, 17 and raised his eyebrows at her to see what she thought of that, but she didn't think much of it. The left rear fender had been smashed and around it was written, on the gleaming gold background: done by crazy woman driver. Connie had to laugh at that. Arnold Friend was pleased at her laughter and looked up at her. "Around the other side's a lot more—you wanta come and see them?"

"No."

"Why not?"

"Why should I?"

"Don'tcha wanta see what's on the car? Don'tcha wanta go for a ride?"

"I don't know."

"Why not?"

"I got things to do."

"Like what?"

"Things."

He laughed as if she had said something funny. He slapped his thighs. He was standing in a strange way, leaning back against the car as if he were balancing himself. He wasn't tall, only an inch or so taller than she would be if she came down to him. Connie liked the way he was dressed, which was the way all of them dressed: tight faded jeans stuffed into black, scuffed boots, a belt that pulled his waist in and showed how lean he was, and a white pull-over shirt that was a little soiled and showed the hard small muscles of his arms and shoulders. He looked as if he probably did hard work, lifting and carrying things. Even his neck looked muscular. And his face was a familiar face, somehow: the jaw and chin and cheeks slightly darkened because he hadn't shaved for a day or two, and the nose long and hawklike, sniffing as if she were a treat he was going to gobble up and it was all a joke.

"Connie, you ain't telling the truth. This is your day set aside for a ride with me and you know it," he said, still laughing. The way he straightened and recovered from his fit of laughing showed that it had been all fake.

"How do you know what my name is?" she said suspiciously.

"It's Connie."

"Maybe and maybe not."

"I know my Connie," he said, wagging his finger. Now she remembered him even better, back at the restaurant, and her cheeks warmed at the thought of how she had sucked in her breath just at the moment she passed him—how she must have looked to him. And he had remembered her. "Ellie and I come out here especially for you," he said. "Ellie can sit in back. How about it?"

"Where?"

"Where what?"

"Where're we going?"

He looked at her. He took off the sunglasses and she saw how pale the skin around his eyes was, like holes that were not in shadow but instead in light. His eyes were like chips of broken glass that catch the light in an amiable way. He smiled. It was as if the idea of going for a ride somewhere, to someplace, was a new idea to him.

"Just for a ride, Connie sweetheart."

"I never said my name was Connie," she said.

"But I know what it is. I know your name and all about you, lots of things," Arnold Friend said. He had not moved yet but stood still leaning back against the side of his jalopy. "I took a special interest in you, such a pretty girl, and found out all about you—like I know your parents and sister are gone somewheres and I know where and how long they're going to be gone, and I know who you were with last night, and your best girl friend's name is Betty. Right?"

He spoke in a simple lilting voice, exactly as if he were reciting the words to a song. His smile assured her that everything was fine. In the car Ellie turned up the volume of his radio and did not bother to look around at them.

"Ellie can sit in the back seat," Arnold Friend said. He indicated his friend with a casual jerk of his chin, as if Ellie did not count and she should not bother with him.

"How'd you find out all that stuff?" Connie said.

"Listen: Betty Schultz and Tony Fitch and Jimmy Pettinger and Nancy Pettinger," he said in a chant. "Raymond Stanley and Bob Hutter—"

"Do you know all those kids?"

"I know everybody."

"Look, you're kidding. You're not from around here."

"Sure."

"But—how come we never saw you before?"

"Sure you saw me before," he said. He looked down at his boots, as if he were a little offended. "You just don't remember."

"I guess I'd remember you," Connie said.

"Yeah?" He looked up at this, beaming. He was pleased. He began to mark time with the music from Ellie's radio, tapping his fists lightly together. Connie looked away from his smile to the car, which was painted so bright it almost hurt her eyes to look at it. She looked at that name, ARNOLD FRIEND. And up at the front fender was an expression that was familiar—MAN THE FLYING SAUCERS. It was an expression kids had used the year before but didn't use this year. She looked at it for a while as if the words meant something to her that she did not yet know.

"What're you thinking about? Huh?" Arnold Friend demanded. "Not worried bout your hair blowing, around in the car, are you?"

"No."

"Think I maybe can't drive good?"

"How do I know?"

"You're a hard girl to handle. How come?" he said. "Don't you know I'm your friend? Didn't you see me put my sign in the air when you walked by?"

"What sign?"

"My sign." And he drew an X in the air, leaning out toward her. They were maybe ten feet apart. After his hand fell back to his side the X was still in the air, almost visible. Connie let the screen door close and stood perfectly still inside it, listening to the music from her radio and the boy's blend together. She stared at Arnold Friend. He stood there so stiffly relaxed, pretending to be relaxed, with one hand idly on the door handle as if he were keeping himself up that way and had no intention of ever moving again. She recognized most things about him, the tight jeans that showed his thighs and buttocks and the greasy leather boots and the tight shirt, and even that slippery friendly smile of his, that sleepy dreamy smile that all the boys used to get across ideas they didn't want to put into words. She recognized all this and also the sing-song way he talked, slightly mocking, kidding, but serious and a little melancholy, and she recognized the way he tapped one fist against the other in homage to the perpetual music behind him. But all these things did not come together.

She said suddenly, "Hey, how old are you?"

His smile faded. She could see then that he wasn't a kid, he was much older—thirty, maybe more. At this knowledge her heart began to pound faster.

"That's crazy thing to ask. Can'tcha see I'm your own age?"

"Like hell you are."

"Or maybe a coupla years older. I'm eighteen."

"Eighteen?" she said doubtfully.

He grinned to reassure her and lines appeared at the corners of his mouth. His teeth were big and white. He grinned so broadly his eyes became slits and she saw how thick the lashes were, thick and black as if painted with a black tarlike material. Then, abruptly, he seemed to become embarrassed and looked over his shoulder at Ellie. "*Him,* he's crazy," he said. "Ain't he a riot? He's a nut, a real character." Ellie was still listening to the music. His sunglasses told nothing about what he was thinking. He wore a bright orange shirt unbuttoned halfway to show his chest, which was a pale, bluish chest and not muscular like Arnold Friend's. His shirt collar was turned up all around and the very tips of the collar pointed out past his chin as if they were protecting him. He was pressing the transistor radio up against his ear and sat there in a kind of daze, right in the sun.

"He's kinda strange," Connie said.

"Hey, she says you're kinda strange! Kinda strange!" Arnold Friend cried. He pounded on the car to get Ellie's attention. Ellie turned for the first time and Connie saw with shock that he wasn't a kid either—he had a fair, hairless face, cheeks reddened slightly as if the veins grew too close to the surface of his skin, the face of a forty-year-old baby. Connie felt a wave of dizziness rise in her at this sight and she stared at him as if waiting for something to change the shock at the moment, make it all right again. Ellie's lips kept shaping words, mumbling along with the words blasting in his ear.

"Maybe you two better go away," Connie said faintly.

"What? How come?" Arnold Friend cried. "We come out here to take you for a ride. It's Sunday." He had the voice of the man on the radio now. It was the same voice, Connie thought. "Don'tcha know it's Sunday all day? And honey, no matter who you were with last night, today you're with Arnold Friend and don't you forget it! Maybe you better step out here," he said, and this last was in a different voice. It was a little flatter, as if the heat was finally getting to him.

"No. I got things to do."

"Hey."

"You two better leave."

"We ain't leaving until you come with us."

"Like hell I am—"

"Connie, don't fool around with me. I mean—I mean, don't fool *around,*" he said, shaking his head. He laughed incredulously. He placed his sunglasses on top of his head, carefully, as if he were indeed wearing a wig, and brought the stems down behind his ears. Connie stared at him, another wave of dizziness and fear rising in her so that for a moment he wasn't even in focus but was just a blur standing there against his gold car, and she had the idea that he had driven up the driveway all right but had come from nowhere before that and belonged nowhere and that everything about him and even about the music that was so familiar to her was only half real.

"If my father comes and sees you—"

"He ain't coming. He's at a barbecue."

"How do you know that?"

"Aunt Tillie's. Right now they're—uh—they're drinking. Sitting around," he said vaguely, squinting as if he were staring all the way to town and over to Aunt Tillie's back yard. Then the vision seemed to get clear and he nodded energetically. "Yeah. Sitting around. There's your sister in a blue dress, huh? And high heels, the poor sad bitch—nothing like you, sweetheart! And your mother's helping some fat woman with the corn, they're cleaning the corn—husking the corn—"

"What fat woman?" Connie cried.

"How do I know what fat woman, I don't know every goddamn fat woman in the world!" Arnold Friend laughed.

"Oh, that's Mrs. Hornsby. . . . Who invited her?" Connie said. She felt a little lightheaded. Her breath was coming quickly.

"She's too fat. I don't like them fat. I like them the way you are, honey," he said, smiling sleepily at her. They stared at each other for a while through the screen door. He said softly, "Now, what you're going to do is this: you're going to come out that door. You're going to sit up front with me and Ellie's going to sit in the back, the hell with Ellie, right? This isn't Ellie's date. You're my date. I'm your lover, honey."

"What? You're crazy—"

"Yes, I'm your lover. You don't know what that is but you will," he said. "I know that too. I know all about you. But look: it's real nice and you couldn't ask for nobody better than me, or more polite. I always keep my word. I'll tell you how it is, I'm always nice at first, the first time. I'll hold you so tight you won't think you have to try to get away or pretend anything because you'll know you can't. And I'll come inside you where it's all secret and you'll give in to me and you'll love me—"

"Shut up! You're crazy!" Connie said. She backed away from the door. She put her hands up against her ears as if she'd heard something terrible, something not meant for her. "People don't talk like that, you're crazy," she muttered. Her heart was almost too big for her chest and its pumping made sweat break out all over her. She looked out to see Arnold Friend pause and then take a step toward the porch, lurching. He almost fell. But, like a clever drunken man, he managed to catch his balance. He wobbled in his high boots and grabbed hold of one of the porch posts.

"Honey?" he said. "You still listening?"

"Get the hell out of here!"

"Be nice, honey. Listen."

"I'm going to call the police—"

He wobbled again and out of the side of his mouth came a fast spat curse, an aside not meant for her to hear. But even this "Christ!" sounded forced. Then he began to smile again. She watched this smile come, awkward as if he were smiling from inside a mask. His whole face was a mask, she thought wildly, tanned down to his throat but then running out as if he had plastered make-up on his face but had forgotten about his throat.

"Honey—? Listen, here's how it is. I always tell the truth and I promise you this: I ain't coming in that house after you."

"You better not! I'm going to call the police if you—if you don't—"

"Honey," he said, talking right through her voice, "honey, I'm not coming in there but you are coming out here. You know why?"

She was panting. The kitchen looked like a place she had never seen before, some room she had run inside but that wasn't good enough, wasn't going to help her. The kitchen window had never had a curtain, after three years, and there were dishes in the sink for her to do—probably—and if you ran your hand across the table you'd probably feel something sticky there.

"You listening honey? Hey?"

"—going to call the police—"

"Soon as you touch the phone I don't need to keep my promise and can come inside. You won't want that."

She rushed forward and tried to lock the door. Her fingers were shaking. "But why lock it," Arnold Friend said gently, talking right into her face. "It's just a screen door. It's just nothing." One of his boots was at a strange angle, as if his foot wasn't in it. It pointed out to the left, bent at the ankle. "I mean, anybody can break through a screen door and glass and wood and iron or anything else if he needs to, anybody at all, and especially Arnold Friend. If the place got lit up with a fire, honey, you'd come runnin' out into my arms, right into my arms an' safe at home—like you knew I was your lover and'd stopped fooling around. I don't mind a nice shy girl but I don't like no fooling around." Part of those words were spoken with a slight rhythmic lilt, and Connie somehow recognized them—the echo of a song from last year, about a girl rushing into her boy friend's arms and coming home again—Connie stood barefoot on the linoleum floor, staring at him. "What do you want?" she whispered.

"I want you," he said.

"What?"

"Seen you that night and thought, that's the one, yes sir. I never needed to look anymore."

"But my father's coming back. He's coming to get me. I had to wash my hair first—" She spoke in a dry, rapid voice, hardly raising it for him to hear.

"No, your daddy is not coming and yes, you had to wash your hair and you washed it for me. It's nice and shining and all for me. I thank you sweetheart," he said with a mock bow, but again he almost lost his balance. He had to bend and adjust his boots. Evidently his feet did not go all the way down; the boots must have been stuffed with something so that he would seem taller. Connie stared out at him and behind him at Ellie in the car, who seemed to be looking off toward Connie's right, into nothing. This Ellie said, pulling the words out of the air one after another as if he were just discovering them, "You want me to pull out the phone?"

"Shut your mouth and keep it shut," Arnold Friend said, his face red from bending over or maybe from embarrassment because Connie had seen his boots. "This ain't none of your business."

"What—what are you doing? What do you want?" Connie said. "If I call the police they'll get you, they'll arrest you—"

"Promise was not to come in unless you touch that phone, and I'll keep that promise," he said. He resumed his erect position and tried to force his shoulders back. He sounded like a hero in a movie, declaring something important. But he spoke too loudly and it was as if he were speaking to someone behind Connie. "I ain't made plans for coming in that house where I don't belong but just for you to come out to me, the way you should. Don't you know who I am?"

"You're crazy," she whispered. She backed away from the door but did not want to go into another part of the house, as if this would give him permission to come through the door. "What do you . . . you're crazy, you. . . ."

"Huh? What're you saying, honey?"

Her eyes darted everywhere in the kitchen. She could not remember what it was, this room.

"This is how it is, honey: you come out and we'll drive away, have a nice ride. But if you don't come out we're gonna wait till your people come home and then they're all going to get it."

"You want that telephone pulled out?" Ellie said. He held the radio away from his ear and grimaced, as if without the radio the air was too much for him.

"I toldja shut up, Ellie," Arnold Friend said, "you're deaf, get a hearing aid, right? Fix yourself up. This little girl's no trouble and's gonna be nice to me, so Ellie keep to yourself, this ain't your date—right? Don't hem in on me, don't hog, don't crush, don't bird dog, don't trail me," he said in a rapid, meaningless voice, as if he were running through all the expressions he'd learned but was no longer sure which of them was in style, then rushing on to new ones, making them up with his eyes closed. "Don't crawl under my fence, don't squeeze in my chipmunk hole, don't sniff my glue, suck my popsicle, keep your own greasy fingers on yourself!" He shaded his eyes and peered in at Connie, who was backed against the kitchen table. "Don't mind him, honey, he's just a creep. He's a dope. Right? I'm the boy for you and like I said, you come out here nice like a lady and give me your hand, and nobody else gets hurt, I mean, your nice old baldheaded daddy and your mummy and your sister in her high heels. Because listen: why bring them in this?"

"Leave me alone," Connie whispered.

"Hey, you know that old woman down the road, the one with the chickens and stuff—you know her?"

"She's dead!"

"Dead? What? You know her?" Arnold Friend said.

"She's dead—"

"Don't you like her?"

"She's dead—she's—she isn't here any more—"

"But don't you like her, I mean, you got something against her? Some grudge or something?" Then his voice dipped as if he were conscious of a rudeness. He touched the sunglasses perched up on top of his head as if to make sure they were still "Now, you be a good girl."

"What are you going to do?"

"Just two things, or maybe three," Arnold Friend said. "But I promise it won't last long and you'll like me the way you get to like people you're close to. You will. It's all over for you here, so come on out. You don't want your people in any trouble, do you?"

She turned and bumped against a chair or something, hurting her leg, but she ran into the back room and picked up the telephone. Something roared in her ear, a tiny roaring, and she was so sick with fear that she could do nothing but listen to it—the telephone was clammy and very heavy and her fingers groped down to the dial but were too weak to touch it. She began to scream into the phone, into the roaring. She cried out, she cried for her mother, she felt her breath start jerking back and forth in her lungs as if it were something Arnold Friend was stabbing her with again and again with no tenderness. A noisy sorrowful wailing rose all about her and she was locked inside it the way she was locked inside this house.

After a while she could hear again. She was sitting on the floor with her wet back against the wall.

Arnold Friend was saying from the door, "That's a good girl. Put the phone back."

She kicked the phone away from her.

"No, honey. Pick it up. Put it back right."

She picked it up and put it back. The dial tone stopped.

"That's a good girl. Now, you come outside."

She was hollow with what had been fear but what was now just an emptiness. All that screaming had blasted it out of her. She sat, one leg cramped under her, and deep inside her brain was something like a pinpoint of light that kept going and would not let her relax. She thought, I'm not going to see my mother again. She thought, I'm not going to sleep in my bed again. Her bright green blouse was all wet.

Arnold Friend said, in a gentle-loud voice that was like a stage voice, "The place where you came from ain't' there any more, and where you had in mind to go is cancelled out. This place you are now—inside your daddy's house—is nothing but a cardboard box I can knock down any time. You know that and always did know it. You hear me?"

She thought, I have got to think. I have got to know what to do.

"We'll go out to a nice field, out in the country here where it smells so nice and it's sunny," Arnold Friend said. "I'll have my arms tight around you so you won't need to try to get away and I'll show you what love is like, what it does. The hell with this house! It looks solid all right," he said. He ran a fingernail down the screen and the noise did not make Connie shiver, as it would have the day before. "Now, put your hand on your heart, honey. Feel that? That feels solid too but we know better. Be nice to me, be sweet like you can because what else is there for a girl like you but to be sweet and pretty and give in?—and get away before her people come back?"

She felt her pounding heart. Her hand seemed to enclose it. She thought for the first time in her life that it was nothing that was hers, that belonged to her, but just a pounding, living thing inside this body that wasn't really hers either.

"You don't want them to get hurt," Arnold Friend went on. "Now, get up, honey. Get up all by yourself."

She stood.

"Now, turn this way. That's right. Come over here to me—Ellie, put that away, didn't I tell you? You dope. You miserable creepy dope," Arnold Friend said. His words were not angry but only part of an incantation. The incantation was kindly. "Now, come out through the kitchen to me, honey, and let's see a smile, try it, you're a brave, sweet little girl and now they're eating corn and hot dogs cooked to bursting over an outdoor fire, and they don't know one thing about you and never did and honey, you're better than them because not a one of them would have done this for you."

Connie felt the linoleum under her feet; it was cool. She brushed her hair back out of her eyes. Arnold Friend let go of the post tentatively and opened his arms for her, his elbows pointing in toward each other and his wrists limp, to show that this was an embarrassed embrace and a little mocking, he didn't want to make her self-conscious.

She put out her hand against the screen. She watched herself push the door slowly open as if she were back safe somewhere in the other doorway, watching this body and this head of long hair moving out into the sunlight where Arnold Friend waited.

"My sweet little blue-eyed girl," he said in a half-sung sigh that had nothing to do with her brown eyes but was taken up just the same by the vast sunlit reaches of the land behind him and on all sides of him—so much land that Connie had never seen before and did not recognize except to know that she was going to it.

# ⁂ TONI CADE BAMBARA (1939–1995)

In graphic, vivid, and street-wise language, Toni Cade Bambara's stories lovingly capture the experience of poor, urban blacks, especially the black woman. Bambara was born in New York City and was raised in Harlem, Bedford-Stuyvesant, Queens, and Jersey City, New Jersey. She earned a B.A. from Queens College in 1959, then went abroad to study in Florence and Paris. In 1964 she completed an M.A. in English at City College of New York.

Bambara studied dance, mime, drama, and film. Her career was as varied as her interests. She was a social worker, a director and advisor to a black theater group, recreation director at a psychiatric hospital, anthologist, screenplay writer, and documentary filmmaker. She taught at a number of colleges and universities, including Rutgers University and Spelman College.

Bambara's stories have been collected in *Gorilla, My Love* (1970) and *The Sea Birds Are Still Alive* (1977). Her two novels are *The Salt Eaters* (1980), which won the American Book Award, and *If Blessing Comes* (1987). *Deep Sightings and Rescue Missions: Fiction, Essays, and Conversations* was published in 1996.

## The Lesson

Back in the days when everyone was old and stupid or young and foolish and me and Sugar were the only ones just right, this lady moved on our block with nappy hair and proper speech and no makeup. And quite naturally we laughed at her, laughed the way we did at the junk man who went about his business like he was some big-time president and his sorry ass horse his secretary. And we kinda hated her too, hated the way we did the winos who cluttered up our parks and pissed on our handball walls and stank up our hallways and stairs so you couldn't halfway play hide-and-seek without a goddamn gas mask. Miss Moore was her name. The only woman on the block with no first name. And she was black as hell, cept for her feet, which were fish-white and spooky. And she was always planning these boring-ass things for us to do, us being my cousin, mostly, who lived on the block cause we all moved North the same time and to the same apartment then spread out gradual to breathe. And our parents would yank our heads into some kinda shape and crisp up our clothes so we'd be presentable for travel with

Miss Moore, who always looked like she was going to church, though she never did. Which is just one of the things the grownups talked about when they talked behind her back like a dog. But when she came calling with some sachet she'd sewed up or some gingerbread she'd made or some book, why then they'd all be too embarrassed to turn her down and we'd get handed over all spruced up. She'd been to college and said it was only right that she should take responsibility for the young ones' education, and she not even related by marriage or blood. So they'd go for it. Specially Aunt Gretchen. She was the main gofer in the family. You got some ole dumb shit foolishness you want somebody to go for, you send for Aunt Gretchen. She been screwed into the go-along for so long, it's a blood-deep natural thing with her. Which is how she got saddled with me and Sugar and Junior in the first place while our mothers were in a la-de-da apartment up the block having a good ole time.

So this one day Miss Moore rounds us all up at the mailbox and it's puredee hot and she's knockin herself out about arithmetic. And school suppose to let up in summer I heard, but she don't never let up. And the starch in my pinafore scratching the shit outta me and I'm really hating this nappy-head bitch and her goddamn college degree. I'd much rather go to the pool or to the show where it's cool. So me and Sugar leaning on the mailbox being surly, which is a Miss Moore word. And Flyboy checking out what everybody brought for lunch. And Fat Butt already wasting his peanut-butter-and-jelly sandwich like the pig he is. And Junebug punchin on Q.T.'s arm for potato chips. And Rosie Giraffe shifting from one hip to the other waiting for somebody to step on her foot or ask her if she from Georgia so she can kick ass, preferably Mercedes'. And Miss Moore asking us do we know what money is, like we a bunch of retards. I mean real money, she say, like it's only poker chips or monopoly papers we lay on the grocer. So right away I'm tired of this and say so. And would much rather snatch Sugar and go to the Sunset and terrorize the West Indian kids and take their hair ribbons and their money too. And Miss Moore files that remark away for next week's lesson on brotherhood, I can tell. And finally I say we oughta get to the subway cause it's cooler and besides we might meet some cute boys. Sugar done swiped her mama's lipstick, so we ready.

So we heading down the street and she's boring us silly about what things cost and what our parents make and how much goes for rent and how money ain't divided up right in this country. And then she gets to the part about we all poor and live in the slums, which I don't feature. And I'm ready to speak on that, but she steps out in the street and hails two cabs just like that. Then she hustles half the crew in with her and hands me a five-dollar bill and tells me to calculate 10 percent tip for the driver. And we're off Me and Sugar and Junebug and Flyboy hangin out the window and hollering to everybody, putting lipstick on each other cause Flyboy a faggot anyway, and making farts with our sweaty armpits. But I'm mostly trying to figure how to spend this money. But they all fascinated with the meter ticking and Junebug starts laying bets as to how much it'll read when Flyboy can't hold his breath no more. Then Sugar lays bets as to how much it'll be when we get there. So I'm stuck. Don't nobody want to go for my plan, which is to jump out at the next light and run off the first bar-b-que we can find. Then the driver tells us to get the hell out cause we there already. And the meter reads eighty five cents. And I'm stalling to figure out the tip and Sugar say give him a dime.

And I decide he don't need it bad as I do, so later for him. But then he tries to take off with Junebug foot still in the door so we talk about his mama something ferocious. Then we check out that we on Fifth Avenue and everybody dressed up in stockings. One lady in a fur coat, hot as it is. White folks crazy.

"This is the place," Miss Moore say, presenting it to us in the voice she uses at the museum. "Let's look in the windows before we go in."

"Can we steal?" Sugar asks very serious like she's getting the ground rules squared away before she plays. "I beg your pardon," say Miss Moore, and we fall out. So she leads us around the windows of the toy store and me and Sugar screamin, "This is mine, that's mine, I gotta have that, that was made for me, I was born for that," till Big Butt drowns us out.

"Hey, I'm goin to buy that there."

"That there? You don't even know what it is, stupid."

"I do so," he say punchin on Rosie Giraffe. "It's a microscope."

"Whatcha gonna do with a microscope, fool?"

"Look at things."

"Like what, Ronald?" ask Miss Moore. And Big Butt ain't got the first notion. So here go Miss Moore gabbing about the thousands of bacteria in a drop of water and the somethinorother in a speck of blood and the million and one living things in the air around us is invisible to the naked eye. And what she say that for? Junebug go to town on that "naked" and we rolling. Then Miss Moore ask what it cost. So we all jam into the window smudgin it up and the price tag say $300. So then she ask how long'd take for Big Butt and Junebug to save up their allowances. "Too long," I say. "Yeh," adds Sugar, "outgrown it by that time." And Miss Moore say no, you never outgrow learning instruments. "Why, even medical students and interns and," blah, blah, blah. And we ready to choke Big Butt for bringing it up in the first damn place.

"This here costs four hundred eighty dollars," say Rosie Giraffe. So we pile up all over her to see what she pointin out. My eyes tell me it's a chunk of glass cracked with something heavy, and different-color inks dripped into the splits, then the whole thing put into a oven or something. But for $480 it don't make sense.

"That's a paperweight made of semi-precious stones fused together under tremendous pressure," she explains slowly, with her hands doing the mining and all the factory work.

"So what's a paperweight?" asks Rosie Giraffe.

"To weigh paper with, dumbbell," say Flyboy, the wise man from the East.

"Not exactly," say Miss Moore, which is what she say when you warm or way off too. "It's to weigh paper down so it won't scatter and make your desk untidy." So right away me and Sugar curtsy to each other and then to Mercedes who is more the tidy type.

"We don't keep paper on top of the desk in my class," say Junebug, figuring Miss Moore crazy or lyin one.

"At home, then," she say. "Don't you have a calendar and a pencil case and a blotter and a letter-opener on your desk at home where you do your homework?" And she know damn well what our homes look like cause she nosys around in them every chance she gets.

"I don't even have a desk," say Junebug. "Do we?"

"No. And I don't get no homework neither," says Big Butt.

"And I don't even have a home," say Flyboy like he do at school to keep the white folks off his back and sorry for him. Send this poor kid to camp posters, is his specialty.

"I do," says Mercedes. "I have a box of stationery on my desk and a picture of my cat. My godmother bought the stationery and the desk. There's a big rose on each sheet and the envelopes smell like roses."

"Who wants to know about your smelly-ass stationery," say Rosie Giraffe fore I can get my two cents in.

"It's important to have a work area all your own so that . . ."

"Will you look at this sailboat, please," say Flyboy, cuttin her off and pointin to the thing like it was his. So once again we tumble all over each other to gaze at this magnificent thing in the toy store which is just big enough to maybe sail two kittens across the pond if you strap them to the posts tight. We all start reciting the price tag like we in assembly. "Handcrafted sailboat of fiberglass at one thousand one hundred ninety-five dollars."

"Unbelievable," I hear myself say and am really stunned. I read it again for myself just in case the group recitation put me in a trance. Same thing. For some reason this pisses me off. We look at Miss Moore and she lookin at us, waiting for I dunno what.

"Who'd pay all that when you can buy a sailboat set for a quarter at Pop's, a tube of glue for a dime, and a ball of string for eight cents? It must have a motor and a whole lot else besides," I say. "My sailboat cost me about fifty cents."

"But will it take water?" say Mercedes with her smart ass.

"Took mine to Alley Pond Park once," say Flyboy. "String broke. Lost it. Pity."

"Sailed mine in Central Park and it keeled over and sank. Had to ask my father for another dollar."

"And you got the strap," laugh Big Butt. "The jerk didn't even have a string on it. My old man wailed on his behind."

Little Q.T. was staring hard at the sailboat and you could see he wanted it bad. But he too little and somebody'd just take it from him. So what the hell. "This boat for kids, Miss Moore?"

"Parents silly to buy something like that just to get all broke up," say Rosie Giraffe.

"That much money it should last forever," I figure.

"My father'd buy it for me if I wanted it."

"Your father, my ass," say Rosie Giraffe getting a chance to finally push Mercedes.

"Must be rich people shop here," say Q.T.

"You are a very bright boy," say Flyboy. "What was your first clue?" And he rap him on the head with the back of his knuckles, since Q.T. the only one he could get away with. Though Q.T. liable to come up behind you years later and get his licks in when you half expect it.

"What I want to know is," I says to Miss Moore though I never talk to her, I wouldn't give the bitch that satisfaction, "is how much a real boat costs? I figure a thousand'd get you a yacht any day."

"Why don't you check that out," she says, "and report back to the group?" Which really pains my ass. If you gonna mess up a perfectly good swim day least you could do is have some answers. "Let's go in," she say like she got something up her sleeve only she don't lead the way. So me and Sugar turn the corner to where the entrance is, but when we get there I kinda hang back. Not that I'm scared, what's there to be afraid of, just a toy store. But I feel funny, shame. But what I got to be shamed about? Got as much right to go in as anybody. But somehow I can't seem to get hold of the door, so I step away for Sugar to lead. But she hangs back too. And I look at her and she looks at me and this is ridiculous. I mean, damn, I have never ever been shy about doing nothing or going nowhere. But then Mercedes steps up and then Rosie Giraffe and Big Butt crowd in behind and shove, and next thing we all stuffed into the doorway with only Mercedes squeezing past us, smoothing out her jumper and walking right down the aisle. Then the rest of us tumble in like a glued together jigsaw done all wrong. And people lookin at us. And it's like the time me and Sugar crashed into the Catholic church on a dare. But once we got in there and everything so hushed and holy and the candles and the bowin and the handkerchiefs on all the drooping heads, I just couldn't go through with the plan. Which was for me to run up to the altar and do a tap dance while Sugar played the nose flute and messed around in the holy water. And Sugar kept givin me the elbow. Then later teased me so bad I tied her up in the shower and turned it on and locked her in. And she'd be there till this day if Aunt Gretchen hadn't finally figured I was lyin about the boarder takin a shower.

Same thing in the store. We all walkin on tiptoe and hardly touchin the games and puzzles and things. And I watched Miss Moore who is steady watchin us like she waitin for a sign. Like Mama Drewery watches the sky and sniffs the air and takes note of just how much slant is in the bird formation. Then me and Sugar bump smack into each other, so busy gazing at the toys, 'specially the sailboat. But we don't laugh and go into our fat-lady bump-stomach routine. We just stare at that price tag. Then Sugar run a finger over the whole boat. And I'm jealous and want to hit her. Maybe not her, but I sure want to punch somebody in the mouth.

"Watcha bring us here for, Miss Moore?"

"You sound angry, Sylvia. Are you mad about something?" Givin me one of them grins like she tellin a grown-up joke that never turns out to be funny. And she's lookin very closely at me like maybe she plannin to do my portrait from memory. I'm mad, but I won't give her that satisfaction. So I slouch around the store bein very bored and say, "Let's go."

Me and Sugar at the back of the train watchin the tracks whizzin by large then small then gettin gobbled up in the dark. I'm thinkin about this tricky toy I saw in the store. A clown that somersaults on a bar then does chin-ups just cause you yank lightly at his leg. Cost $35. I could see me askin my mother for a $35 birthday clown. "You wanna who that costs what?" she'd say, cocking her head to the side to get a better view of the hole in my head. Thirty-five dollars could buy new bunk beds for Junior and Gretchen's boy. Thirty-five dollars and the whole household could go visit Granddaddy Nelson in the country. Thirty-five dollars would pay for the rent and the piano bill too. Who are these people that spend that much for performing clowns and $1000 for toy sailboats? What kinda work they do and how they live and how come we ain't in on it? Where we are is who we are, Miss Moore always pointin out. But it don't necessarily have to be that way, she always adds then waits for somebody to say that poor people have to wake up and demand their share of the pie and don't none of us know what kind of pie she talkin about in the first damn place. But she ain't so smart cause I still got her four dollars from the taxi and she sure ain't gettin it. Messin up my day with this shit. Sugar nudges me in my pocket and winks.

Miss Moore lines us up in front of the mailbox where we started from, seem like years ago, and I got a headache for thinkin so hard. And we lean all over each other so we can hold up under the draggy-ass lecture she always finishes us off with at the end before we thank her for borin us to tears. But she just looks at us like she readin tea leaves. Finally she say, "Well, what did you think of F.A.O. Schwarz?"

Rosie Giraffe mumbles, "White folks crazy."

"I'd like to go there again when I get my birthday money," says Mercedes, and we shove her out the pack so she has to lean on the mailbox by herself.

"I'd like a shower. Tiring day," say Flyboy.

Then Sugar surprises me by saying, "You know, Miss Moore, I don't think all of us here put together eat in a year what that sailboat costs." And Miss Moore lights up like somebody goosed her. "And?" she say, urging Sugar on. Only I'm standin on her foot so she don't continue.

"Imagine for a minute what kind of society it is in which some people can spend on a toy what it would cost to feed a family of six or seven. What do you think?"

"I think," say Sugar pushing me off her feet like she never done before, cause I whip her ass in a minute, "that this is not much of a democracy if you ask me. Equal chance to pursue happiness means an equal crack at the dough, don't it?" Miss Moore is besides herself and I am disgusted with Sugar's treachery. So I stand on her foot one more time to see if she'll shove me. She shuts up, and Miss Moore looks at me, sorrowfully I'm thinkin. And somethin weird is going on, I can feel it in my chest.

"Anybody else learn anything today?" lookin dead at me. I walk away and Sugar has to run to catch up and don't even seem to notice when I shrug her arm off my shoulder.

"Well, we got four dollars anyway," she says.

"Uh hunh."

"We could go to Hascombs and get half a chocolate layer and then go to the Sunset and still have plenty money for potato chips and ice cream sodas."

"Uh hunh."

"Race you to Hascombs," she say.

We start down the block and she gets ahead which is O.K. by me cause I'm going to the West End and then over to the Drive to think this day through. She can run if she want to and even run faster. But ain't nobody gonna beat me at nuthin.

# ⁂ LEONARD MICHAELS
(1933– )

Leonard Michaels was born in New York City, the son of immigrant Polish Jews. He spoke only Yiddish until he was about five or six years old. His mother read Dickens to him in a heavily accented voice. He was initially drawn to painting, but enrolled in New York University as a premed student. While there he became a protegé of the critic Austin Warren, who encouraged his literary interests. He graduated with a B.A. in 1953. After a brief break to concentrate on writing, he enrolled at the University of Michigan and completed an M.A. in 1956 and a Ph.D. in 1966. He taught at several colleges before accepting an appointment to teach English at the University of California, Berkeley, where he currently makes his residence.

Generally regarded as a master of short fiction forms, Michaels writes fast-moving prose that captures well the nature of contemporary urban experience. His stories blend horror and humor; his characters cannot seem to help inflicting damage on one another even as they reach out for one another. His is a fiction attempting to rescue art from the horrors of our age. Michaels' story collections include *Going Places* (1969), *I Would Have Saved Them If I Could* (1975), and *A Girl with a Monkey: New and Selected Stories* (2000). *The Men's Club* (1981), a short novel, was well received but was made into a rather disappointing film in 1986. He has coedited, with Christopher Ricks, two books on language, *The State of the Language,* 1980 and 1989. A book of essays, *To Feel These Things: Essays,* appeared in 1993. He also coedited, with David Reid and Raquel Scherr, an excellent anthology on California fiction, *West of the West* (1995). In 1999 he published a book of personal meditations, *Time Out of Mind: The Diaries of Leonard Michaels.*

## I Would Have Saved Them If I Could

### Giving Notice

A few days prior to the event, my cousin said, "I'm not going through with it. Call off the bar mitzvah." My uncle said, "You're crazy." My aunt said, "I think so." He'd already reserved the banquet hall, said my uncle, with a big deposit; already paid the rabbis, the caterers, the orchestra. Flying in from everywhere in the Americas and Canada were relatives and friends. My aunt said, "Deposit. Relatives." My cousin said, "Do I know the meaning of even ten Hebrew words? Is the bar mitzvah a Jewish ceremony? Do I believe in God?" My aunt said, "Get serious." My uncle said, "Shut up. The crazy is talking to me." My aunt said, "You too must be crazy." My cousin said, "Call it off." My uncle said, "I listened. Now you listen. When the anti-Semites come to kill your mother, will it be nice to say you aren't a bar mitzvah? Don't you want to be counted?" My cousin pulled open his shirt. "Look," he cried. My aunt said, "I can't talk so I can't look." "Look," he screamed. Green, iridescent Stars of David had grown from his nipples. My uncle collapsed on the wall-to-wall carpet. Looking, my aunt said, "I can't talk so I refuse to look at your crazy tits." That night my uncle sent telegrams throughout the Western Hemisphere. He explained, with regrets, that his son didn't believe in God, so the bar mitzvah was canceled. Then he pulled my cousin's five-hundred-dollar racing bike into the driveway, mangled the handlebars, kicked out the spokes, and left it for the neighborhood to notice.

## A Suspected Jew

Jaromir Hladík is suspected of being a Jew, imprisoned by the Gestapo, sentenced to death. In his prison cell, despite terror and confusion, he becomes ecstatic, then indistinguishable from his ecstasy. He is, in short, an ecstasy—the incarnation of a metaphysical state. Borges wrote this story. He calls it "The Secret Miracle." Whatever you call it, says Gramsci, it exemplifies the ideological hegemony of the ruling class. In the mediating figure, Jaromir Hladík, absolute misery translates into the consolations of redemptive esthesis. It follows, then, the Gestapo, an organization of death, gives birth to "The Ecstatic Hladík"—or, to be precise, "The Secret Miracle." Borges, master of controlled estrangement, makes it impossible to feel that Jaromir Hladík—say, a suspected Jew of average height, with bad teeth, gray hair, nervous cough, tinted spectacles, delicate fingers, gentle musical voice—physically and exactly disintegrates (as intimated in the final sentences) between a hard stone wall and the impact of specific bullets.

## The Subject at the Vanishing Point

My grandfather—less than average height—had bad teeth, gray hair, nervous cough, tinted spectacles, delicate fingers, and a gentle musical voice. To appear confident and authentic, worthy of attention by clerks in the visa office, he memorized the required information—his mother's maiden name, the addresses of relatives in America—and, walking down the street, he felt constantly in his coat pockets to be sure that he had photos of himself, wife, daughter, enough money for the required bribes, and the necessary papers—documents from America, passports, birth certificates, and an essay by himself in praise of Poland—when a pogrom started. Doors and windows slammed shut. The robots were coming. Alone in a strange street, he couldn't tell which way to go. At every corner was death. Suddenly—for good or ill isn't known—somebody flung him into a cellar. Others died. He, bleeding and semiconscious, hidden in a cellar, survived the pogrom. That day he didn't get a visa to leave Poland. He was a tailor—short, thin-boned. Even in a winter coat, easy to fling. He crawled amid rats and dirt, collecting his papers. When night came and Poland lay snoring in the street, he climbed out of the cellar and ran home. Wife and daughter ministered to his wounds. All thanked God that he was alive. But it was too late to get a visa. The Nazis came with the meaning of history—what flings you into a cellar saves you for bullets. I don't say, in the historical dialectic, individual life reduces to hideous idiocy. I'm talking about my grandfather, my grandmother, and my aunt. It seems to me, in the dialectic, individual life reduces not even to hideous idiocy.

## Material Circumstances

His idea about labor power came to him while he strode back and forth in his room in Paris and smoked cigarettes. Indeed, striding back and forth, he smoked cigarettes, but striding, smoking, whistling, etc., are contingent activities. What *matters* is the stage of development in the class struggle when it is possible for a person to think seriously—to have an idea—about labor power. Certainly, in Paris, Karl Marx strode, for example, smoking cigarettes. Now and then, he strode to the window, pushed it open to free the room of smoke and listen for developments. But the precisely particular determinants of consciousness, within the class struggle, are material circumstances. Intuitively, perhaps, Karl Marx felt the burden of determined consciousness in the black, thick hair thrusting from the top of his head like implications and slithering down his chest and back to converge at his crotch, like a conclusion. But, even scrutinizing the hair beneath his fingernails (very like the historical grain in wood), he detected nothing beyond mute, inexorable flux until—striding, smoking—he pushed open his window and noticed Monsieur Grandbouche, his landlord, a figure of bourgeois pieties, who shouted, "When will you pay the rent, my hairball?" Karl Marx strode back and forth and smoked. *La question* Grandbouche burned in his roots, like the residue of a summer rainstorm, quickening the dialectical material of his struggling circumstances. Hair twisted from his ears and whistling nostrils. Angry messages. An idea was occurring. Indeterminable millions would die. Indeterminable millions would eat. Thus, a Parisian landlord, frightened by a smoky blotch in the window, shouted a pathetic joke in the spirit of nervous conviviality, and, as a result, his descendants would be torn to pieces, for he'd epitomized material circumstances by shouting—across generations of Grandbouche—an idea, intensified by repercussions, echoed in concussions of Marxian canons, tearing fascist ligament even in the jungles of the east. *Voilà,* implicit in a landlord's shout is the death rattle of his children's children.

## Business Life

My uncle invested his money in a beauty parlor, began to make a little profit—and the union representative came. My uncle promised to hire union workers soon as the mortgage was paid. Pickets arrived. Back and forth with their signs in front of the beauty parlor. My uncle brought them coffee. They talked about their troubles. A picketer didn't have a soft job. Long apprenticeship; pay wasn't good; and morning to evening, march, march, march, screaming insults at my uncle's customers. The signs didn't look heavy, but try to carry one all day. My uncle agreed: a sign is heavy. Anyhow, business improved. After a while the union bombed the beauty parlor, set fire to my uncle's car, and beat up my aunt. This was reported in the newspaper. Business became much better. My uncle negotiated for a second beauty parlor. One afternoon a picketer leaned against the window of the beauty parlor and lit a cigarette. My uncle started to phone the union, but he hadn't forgotten his life in Russia, his hatred of informers. He put down the phone. The image of that man—slouched against the window, smoking, not carrying the picket sign so that people could read it—seethed in my uncle like moral poison. He soon developed a chronic stomach disturbance. Next came ulcers, doctors, hospitals—all the miseries of a life in business.

## Literary Criticism

Photographs of suspected Jews—men, women, children with hair, teeth, etc.—are available in great sufficiency. If you demand one, either you hate, or do not understand, Borges's critical point, which is that any reader knows stories of this exquisitely general kind. Besides, Borges made his story not from photographable reality—your Polish relatives whose undernourished kosher height never exceeded five feet six inches—but from a stupid story called "The Occurrence at Owl Creek Bridge." My aunt, a schoolgirl, was bleeding on the ground with her mother and father in Brest Litovsk.

## Shrubless Crags

*The Prisoner of Chillon,* by Lord Byron, isn't essentially different from "The Secret Miracle." It too is about a condemned prisoner who becomes ecstatic. Suddenly, after years in a dungeon, Bonnivard transcends his mortality:

> What next befell me then and there
>    I know not well—I never knew—
> First came the loss of light, and air,
>    And then of darkness too:
> I had no thought, no feeling—none—
> Among the stones I stood a stone,
> And was, scarce conscious what I wist,
> As shrubless crags within the mist;
> For all was blank, and bleak, and grey;
> It was not night—it was not day;
> It was not even the dungeon-light,
> So hateful to my heavy sight,
> But vacancy absorbing space,
> And fixedness—without a place.

Like Hladík, in a state of intensified absence, he is a presence.

## Song

Byronic romanticism entered the Russian soul, at the deepest level, as evidenced in the beloved folk song, "Oi yoi, the shrubless crags."

## Blossoms

Metaphysical possibilities—Hladík, Bonnivard—as inherent in the world, are appreciated by Wordsworth when he focuses on shrubless crags and imagines them spiritual entities, theoretical men who neither live nor die. They hover in the mist of universal mind, or the moods of finitude. In a snowstorm outside Smolensk, fighting the Nazis, my uncle was hit in the head by shrapnel, carried to a hospital, and dropped in the dead ward. That night a Jewish woman, who was a surgeon and colonel in the Russian army, discovered him when she left the operating room and, to smoke a cigarette, retreated to the dead ward. A vague moan, "Mama," reached her from shadowy rows of corpses. She ordered a search. Nurses running down the rows, pressing back eyelids, listening at mouth holes, located my uncle. The body wasn't dead; more you couldn't say. The surgeon stepped on her cigarette. "I'll operate." My uncle lived, a hero of the people, guaranteed every right of Russian citizenship. At his first opportunity he fled, walking from Russia to Italy through the confusion of ruined cities; stealing by night across the borders of Poland, Czechoslovakia, Rumania, and Austria; starving, pursued by dogs and police, and always repeating to himself the address of his sister in lower Manhattan. When he got to America he struggled for years, with little English and great anxiety, to make money. Today he owns race tracks and a chain of beauty parlors. He drives a Lincoln Continental. Though he speaks six languages, he isn't much of a conversationalist, but likes a good joke, especially if it comes from life—how, for example, during a Chinese dinner, his brother-in-law's appendix ruptured. Both his sons are doctors and drive Jaguars. He reminds them that his life was saved by a woman less than five feet tall who, during the battle of Smolensk, performed miraculous surgery while standing on ammunition boxes. It could seem, now that he's a big shot, he gives lessons in humility. But how else to defend himself against happiness? He sees terrifying vulnerability in the blossoms of *nachas*.

## The Screams of Children

The New Testament is the best condemned-prisoner story. Jesus, a "suspected" Jew, sublimates at the deadly moment. In two ways, then, he is like Jaromir Hladík. Insofar as the Gestapo gives birth to the ecstatic Hladík, he and Jesus are similar in yet another way. Both are victims of parental ambivalence, which tends to give birth to death. One could savor distinctions here, but the prophetic Kafka hurries me away: humanity, he says, is the growth of death force. For reasons of discretion the trains rolled before dawn, routed through the outskirts of Prague. Nevertheless, you could hear the screams of children.

## Heraclitus, Hegel, Giacometti, Nietzsche, Wordsworth, Stevens

Not considered from the point of view of children, parental ambivalence is a sentimental version of the much admired, familiar principle of destructive generation. According to Heraclitus and Hegel, it is applicable to everything. The Heraclitean dialectic is terse, impetuous, compulsively reiterated, and may be observed in the beautiful statues of Giacometti. Hegel's restatement is logical, passionate, exfoliate, and tremendous.

Despite efforts by Nietzsche, it presently sits on Heraclitus like the buttocks of Clio, squeezing mind and world into one. Wordsworth manages the same—tactfully, however—urging mind and world into lyrical lament:

> A slumber did my spirit seal;
>   I had no human fears:
> She seemed a thing that could not feel
>   The touch of earthly years.
> No motion has she now, no force;
>   She neither hears nor sees;
> Rolled round in earth's diurnal course,
>   With rocks, and stones, and trees.

With rocks and stones, "she"—an intensified absence—is a presence. In the negation of negation, she is. So are Hladík, Bonnivard, and Jesus. My grandfather was a tailor in Brest Litovsk. He vanished. Wallace Stevens says, "Death is the mother of beauty."

### Alienation

In his essay "On the Jewish Question," written in exile, Karl Marx—an alienated Jew assuming the voice of a Hegelienated Jew—says, "Money is the jealous god of Israel." He means, by this oblique smear, the Virgin is a prostitute, her child is capitalism. Hence, it is Jesus—not the exiled Karl Marx—who objectifies alienation. And why not? The life of Jesus, described early and late by the absence of his father, is nothing less than the negation of negation. Marx never gives the least attention to the journey of the Magi, the mystery on the bestial floor, or the ultimate figure of Jesus in the excruciating pictorial epitome. For an execution Roman-style—with three prisoners and ritual paraphernalia—there is Lord Byron's letter.

### Lord Byron's Letter

"The day before I left Rome I saw three robbers guillotined. The ceremony—including the *masqued* priests; the half-naked executioners; the bandaged criminals; the black Christ and his banner; the scaffold; the soldiery; the slow procession, and the quick rattle and heavy fall of the axe; the splash of the blood, and the ghastliness of the exposed heads—is altogether more impressive than the vulgar and ungentlemanly dirty 'new drop' and dog-like agony of infliction upon the sufferers of the English sentence. Two of these men behaved calmly enough, but the first of the three died with great terror and reluctance. What was very horrible, he would not lie down; then his neck was too large for the aperture, and the priest was obliged to drown his exclamations by still louder exhortations. The head was off before the eye could trace the blow; but from an attempt to draw back the head, notwithstanding it was held forward by the hair, the first head was cut off close to the ears: the other two were taken off more cleanly. It is better than the oriental way, and (I should think) than the axe of our ancestors. The pain seems little, and yet the effect to the spectator, and the preparation to the criminal, is very striking and chilling. The first turned me quite hot and thirsty, and made me shake so that I could hardly hold the opera-glass (I was close, but was determined to see, as one should see every thing, once, with attention); the second and third (which shows how dreadfully soon things grow indifferent), I am ashamed to say, had no effect on me as a horror, though I would have saved them if I could."

## Species Being

Casual precision, lucidity, complexity of nuance, smooth coherent speed. I admire the phrase "great terror and reluctance." It makes the prisoner's interior reality and his exterior—or social—reality simultaneous. Surely he felt more than reluctance. But the word stands in contrast to "great terror" and thus acquires the specifically social quality of great terror suffered by an individual at the center of public drama. He could collapse and dissolve into his great terror, but doesn't. Nor does he become ecstatic. Instead, sensitive to the crowd, he tries to join it by conveying an idea of himself—as also watching, like the crowd, a man who is about to get his head chopped off, who is in great terror and who—reluctantly—is himself. He owes the crowd his head. He knows the crowd will have his head. The crowd didn't go to the trouble of gathering itself around him for nothing. He wants to indicate that he is not the sort who is indifferent to what the crowd wants, but, after all, it is his head it wants. Of course he is in no position not to provide it. The crowd sees that he has brought it with him. He would like, just the same, to suggest that he is "reluctant" to do so. At the last instant, he loses poise and pulls back. The result is a messy chop, a bad show. Ethics and aesthetics are inextricable. All this, and much more, is intimated in Byron's letter. Though it is infected, slightly, by ironical preciosity, the letter was written to somebody; therefore, like the prisoner, it participates in a consciousness other than its own; by attitudinizing, it suggests that it sees itself. This is Byron's concession to society; it is justified by his honesty—the childlike, high-spirited allegiance to the facts of the occasion inside and outside *his* head. Compared to the sneering, sarcastic, bludgeoning verbosity of Karl Marx, who walked in Paris, it isn't easy to believe the latter's idea of humanity as social essence is either witty or attractive.

## Dostoevsky

In Dostoevsky's story, a condemned prisoner—at the penultimate instant before a firing squad—is reprieved by the tsar. Dostoevsky says it was his own experience. The reprieve was announced, he says, and the firing squad—not the prisoner Dostoevsky—sublimated. What follows? In life and art at once, the tsar is a champion of imaginative forms. For condemned prisoners—which is all of us—the tsar, a true aristocrat, is godlike in his manifestations. Astonishing, arbitrary, inscrutable. More evil than good—but thus are we saved. From above! Of course, in historical fact the tsar and his family were slaughtered. Trotsky considered this "action" indispensable. Stalin's considerations, regarding Trotsky and his family, were identical. It is impossible to live with or without fictions.

### The Night I Became a Marxist

I heard a voice, turned, saw nobody, walked on, heard the voice again, but didn't turn. Nobody would be there. Or somebody would. In either case—very frightened—I walked faster, stiffened back and neck, expecting a blow, anxious to swivel about, but not doing it until I could no longer, and, walking quickly, stiffly, swiveling to look back, walk on, I noticed street lamps were smashed, blackness took sections of everything, signs were unreadable, windows glossy blotches, doorways like sighs issuing from unimaginable interiors. I felt absolutely outside, savage, and I'd have begun running, but there was the park, the streets beyond. I continued to walk, swivel, walk, saving power, holding self—and then, hearing it, whirled, dropped into a crouch, legs wide, fists raised. I'd have seen nothing, nobody, but—crouched low—realized, suddenly, I was face to face with it, shorter than a midget, speaking mouth, teeth like knives: "Always having fun, aren't you? Night after night, dancing, drinking, fucking. Fun, fun, fun."

### Conclusion

Long before ruling-class, ideological superstructures, there were myths describing ecstasies like those of Jaromir Hladík and Jesus. Nymphs and beautiful boys, fleeing murderous gods, were always sublimating into flowers, trees, rivers, heavenly constellations, etc. The earliest stories, then, already convey an exhilarating apprehension of the world as incessantly created of incessant death. Nothing changes. Stories, myths, ideologies, flowers, rivers, heavenly constellations are the phonemes of a mysterious logos; and the lights of our cultural memory, as upon the surface of black primeval water, flicker and slide into innumerable qualifications. But Jaromir Hladík, among substantial millions, is dead. From a certain point of view, none of this shit matters any more.

# ⁂ ALICE WALKER
## (1944– )

Calling herself a "womanist" rather than a feminist, Alice Walker writes a fiction in the spirit of Zora Neale Hurston, whose work and reputation Walker helped to restore. Walker writes of black women who find the courage, resources, and imagination to claim their lives. It is a fiction that affirms the possibility of healing, change, and hope.

Walker was born in Eatonton, Georgia, the youngest of eight children of sharecroppers, she finished high school in 1961 and enrolled in Spelman College in Atlanta for two years. She transferred to Sarah Lawrence College in New York and graduated in 1965. After a brief visit to East Africa, she began work as a caseworker for the Welfare Department in New York City. She was active in the civil rights movement in the late 1960s and married a white civil rights lawyer with whom she had a daughter. The couple moved to Mississippi, where he prosecuted discrimination cases and she taught at Jackson State College. As an interracial couple in Mississippi, they often faced threats and harassment. They were divorced in 1976.

Walker's first publication was a book of poetry, *Once* (1968). She is best known for her novel *The Color Purple* (1982), which won both the American Book Award and the Pulitzer Prize and was made into a film. Walker has written poetry, short stories, and essays. Her other novels include *The Third Life of Grange Copeland* (1970), *Meridian* (1976), *The Temple of My Familiar* (1989), *Possessing the Secret of Joy* (1992), and *By the Light of My Father's Smile* (1998). Her collections of stories are *In Love & Trouble: Stories of Black Women* (1973), *You Can't Keep a Good Woman Down* (1981), and *The Way Forward Is with a Broken Heart* (2000). Her essays include the influential *In Search of Our Mother's Gardens: Womanist Prose* (1983) and *Living by the Word* (1988). Most recently she has published *The Same River Twice* (1996), a memoir, and *Anything We Love Can Be Saved: A Writer's Activism* (1997).

# To Hell with Dying

"To hell with dying," my father would say. "These children want Mr. Sweet!"

MR. SWEET was a diabetic and an alcoholic and a guitar player and lived down the road from us on a neglected cotton farm. My older brothers and sisters got the most benefit from Mr. Sweet, for when they were growing up he had quite a few years ahead of him and so was capable of being called back from the brink of death any number of times—whenever the voice of my father reached him as he lay expiring. "To hell with dying, man," my father would say, pushing the wife away from the bedside (in tears although she knew the death was not necessarily the last one unless Mr. Sweet really wanted it to be). "These children want Mr. Sweet!" And they did want him, for at a signal from Father they would come crowding around the bed and throw themselves on the covers, and whoever was the smallest at the time would kiss him all over his wrinkled brown face and tickle him so that he would laugh all down in his stomach, and his mustache, which was long and sort of straggly, would shake like Spanish moss and was also that color.

Mr. Sweet had been ambitious as a boy, wanted to be a doctor or lawyer or sailor, only to find that black men fare better if they are not. Since he could become none of these things he turned to fishing as his only earnest career and playing the guitar as his only claim to doing anything extraordinarily well. His son, the only one that he and his wife, Miss Mary, had, was shiftless as the day is long and spent money as if he were trying to see the bottom of the mint, which Mr. Sweet would tell him was the clean brown palm of his hand. Miss Mary loved her "baby," however, and worked hard to get him the "li'l necessaries" of life, which turned out mostly to be women.

Mr. Sweet was a tall, thinnish man with thick kinky hair going dead white. He was dark brown, his eyes were squinty and sort of bluish, and he chewed Brown Mule tobacco. He was constantly on the verge of being blind drunk, for he brewed his own liquor and was not in the least a stingy sort of man, and was always very melancholy and sad, though frequently when he was "feelin' good" he'd dance around the yard with us, usually keeling over just as my mother came to see what the commotion was.

Toward all of us children he was very kind and had the grace to be shy with us, which is unusual in grown-ups. He had great respect for my mother for she never held his drunkenness against him and would let us play with him even when he was about to fall in the fireplace from drink. Although Mr. Sweet would sometimes lose complete or nearly complete control of his head and neck so that he would loll in his chair, his mind remained strangely acute and his speech not too affected. His ability to be drunk and sober at the same time made him an ideal playmate, for he was as weak as we were and we could usually best him in wrestling, all the while keeping a fairly coherent conversation going.

We never felt anything of Mr. Sweet's age when we played with him. We loved his wrinkles and would draw some on our brows to be like him, and his white hair was my special treasure and he knew it and would never come to visit us just after he had had his hair cut off at the barbershop. Once he came to our house for something, probably to see my father about fertilizer for his crops because, although he never paid the slightest attention to his crops, he liked to know what things would be best to use on them if he ever did. Anyhow, he had not come with his hair since he had just had it shaved off at the barbershop. He wore a huge straw hat to keep off the sun and also to keep his head away from me. But as soon as I saw him I ran up and demanded that he take me up and kiss me with his funny beard which smelled so strongly of tobacco. Looking forward to burying my small fingers into his woolly hair, I threw away his hat only to find he had done something to his hair, that it was no longer there! I let out a squall which made my mother think that Mr. Sweet had finally dropped me in the well or something and from that day I've been wary of men in hats. However, not long after, Mr. Sweet showed up with his hair grown out and just as white and kinky and impenetrable as it ever was.

Mr. Sweet used to call me his princess, and I believed it. He made me feel pretty at five and six, and simply outrageously devastating at the blazing age of eight and a half. When he came to our house with his guitar the whole family would stop whatever they were doing to sit around him and listen to him play. He liked to play "Sweet Georgia Brown," that was what he called me sometimes, and also he liked to play "Caldonia" and all sorts of sweet, sad, wonderful songs which he sometimes made up. It was from one of these songs that I heard that he had had to marry Miss Mary when he had in fact loved somebody else (now living in Chi-ca-go, or De-stroy, Michigan). He was not sure that Joe Lee, her "baby," was also his baby. Sometimes he would cry and that was an indication that he was about to die again. And so we would all get prepared, for we were sure to be called upon.

I was seven the first time I remember actually participating in one of Mr. Sweet's "revivals"—my parents told me I had participated before, I had been the one chosen to kiss him and tickle him long before I knew the rite of Mr. Sweet's rehabilitation. He had come to our house, it was a few years after his wife's death, and was very sad, and also, typically, very drunk. He sat on the floor next to me and my older brother, the rest of the children were grown up and lived elsewhere, and began to play his guitar and cry. I held his woolly head in my arms and wished I could have been old enough to have been the woman he loved so much and that I had not been lost years and years ago.

When he was leaving, my mother said to us that we'd better sleep light that night for we'd probably have to go over to Mr. Sweet's before daylight. And we did. For soon after we had gone to bed one of the neighbors knocked on our door and called my father and said that Mr. Sweet was sinking fast and if he wanted to get in a word before the crossover he'd better shake a leg and get over to Mr. Sweet's house. All the neighbors knew to come to our house if something was wrong with Mr. Sweet, but they did not know how we always managed to make him well, or at least stop him from dying, when he was so often near death. As soon as we heard the cry we got up, my brother and I and my mother and father, and put on our clothes. We hurried out of the house and down the road for we were always afraid that we might someday be too late and Mr. Sweet would get tired of dallying.

When we got to the house, a very poor shack really, we found the front room full of neighbors and relatives and someone met us at the door and said it was all very sad that old Mr. Sweet Little (for Little was his family name, although we mostly ignored it) was about to kick the bucket. My parents were advised not to take my brother and me into the "death room," seeing we were so young and all, but we were so much more accustomed to the death room than he that we ignored him and dashed in without giving his warning a second thought. I was almost in tears, for these deaths upset me fearfully, and the thought of how much depended on me and my brother (who was such a ham most of the time) made me very nervous.

The doctor was bending over the bed and turned back to tell us for at least the tenth time in the history of my family that, alas, old Mr. Sweet Little was dying and that the children had best not see the face of implacable death (I didn't know what "implacable" was, but whatever it was, Mr. Sweet was not!). My father pushed him rather abruptly out of the way saying, as he always did and very loudly for he was saying it to Mr. Sweet, "To hell with dying, man, these children want Mr. Sweet"—which was my cue to throw myself upon the bed and kiss Mr. Sweet all around the whiskers and under the eyes and around the collar of his nightshirt where he smelled so strongly of all sorts of things, mostly liniment.

I was very good at bringing him around, for as soon as I saw that he was struggling to open his eyes I knew he was going to be all right, and so could finish my revival sure of success. As soon as his eyes were open he would begin to smile and that way I knew that I had surely won. Once, though, I got a tremendous scare, for he could not open his eyes and later I learned that he had had a stroke and that one side of his face was stiff and hard to get into motion. When he began to smile I could tickle him in earnest because I was sure that nothing would get in the way of his laughter, although once he began to cough so hard that he almost threw me off his stomach, but that was when I was very small, little more than a baby, and my bushy hair had gotten in his nose.

When we were sure he would listen to us we would ask him why he was in bed and when he was coming to see us again and could we play his guitar, which more than likely would be leaning against the bed. His eyes would get all misty and he would sometimes cry out loud, but we never let it embarrass us, for he knew that we loved him and that we sometimes cried too for no reason. My parents would leave the room to just the three of us; Mr. Sweet, by that time, would be propped up in bed with a number of pillows behind his head and with me sitting and lying on his shoulder and along his chest. Even when he had trouble breathing he would not ask me to get down. Looking into my eyes he would shake his white head and run a scratchy old finger all around my hairline, which was rather low down, nearly to my eyebrows, and made some people say I looked like a baby monkey.

My brother was very generous in all this, he let me do all the revivaling—he had done it for years before I was born and so was glad to be able to pass it on to someone new. What he would do while I talked to Mr. Sweet was pretend to play the guitar, in fact pretend that he was a young version of Mr. Sweet, and it always made Mr. Sweet glad to think that someone wanted to be like him—of course, we did not know this then, we played the thing by ear, and whatever he seemed to like, we did. We were desperately afraid that he was just going to take off one day and leave us.

It did not occur to us that we were doing anything special; we had not learned that death was final when it did come. We thought nothing of triumphing over it so many times, and in fact became a trifle contemptuous of people who let themselves be carried away. It did not occur to us that if our father had been dying we could not have stopped it, that Mr. Sweet was the only person over whom we had power.

When Mr. Sweet was in his eighties I was studying in the university many miles from home. I saw him whenever I went home, but he was never on the verge of dying that I could tell and I began to feel that my anxiety for his health and psychological well-being was unnecessary. By this time he not only had a mustache but a long flowing snow-white beard, which I loved and combed and braided for hours. He was very peaceful, fragile, gentle, and the only jarring note about him was his old steel guitar, which he still played in the old sad, sweet, down-home blues way.

On Mr. Sweet's ninetieth birthday I was finishing my doctorate in Massachusetts and had been making arrangements to go home for several weeks' rest. That morning I got a telegram telling me that Mr. Sweet was dying again and could I please drop everything and come home. Of course I could. My dissertation could wait and my teachers would understand when I explained to them when I got back. I ran to the phone, called the airport, and within four hours I was speeding along the dusty road to Mr. Sweet's.

The house was more dilapidated than when I was last there, barely a shack, but it was overgrown with yellow roses which my family had planted many years ago. The air was heavy and sweet and very peaceful. I felt strange walking through the gate and up the old rickety steps. But the strangeness left me as I caught sight of the long white beard I loved so well flowing down the thin body over the familiar quilt coverlet. Mr. Sweet!

His eyes were closed tight and his hands, crossed over his stomach, were thin and delicate, no longer scratchy. I remembered how always before I had run and jumped up on him just anywhere; now I knew he would not be able to support my weight. I looked around at my parents, and was surprised to see that my father and mother also looked old and frail. My father, his own hair very gray, leaned over the quietly sleeping old man, who, incidentally, smelled still of wine and tobacco, and said, as he'd done so many times, "To hell with dying, man! My daughter is home to see Mr. Sweet!" My brother had not been able to come as he was in the war in Asia. I bent down and gently stroked the closed eyes and gradually they began to open. The closed, wine-stained lips twitched a little, then parted in a warm, slightly embarrassed smile. Mr. Sweet could see me and he recognized me and his eyes looked very spry and twinkly for a moment. I put my head down on the pillow next to his and we just looked at each other for a long time.

Then he began to trace my peculiar hairline with a thin, smooth finger. I closed my eyes when his finger halted above my ear (he used to rejoice at the dirt in my ears when I was little), his hand stayed cupped around my cheek. When I opened my eyes, sure that I had reached him in time, his were closed.

Even at twenty-four how could I believe that I had failed? that Mr. Sweet was really gone? He had never gone before. But when I looked at my parents I saw that they were holding back tears. They had loved him dearly. He was like a piece of rare and delicate china which was always being saved from breaking and which finally fell. I looked long at the old face, the wrinkled forehead, the red lips, the hands that still reached out to me. Soon I felt my father pushing something cool into my hands. It was Mr. Sweet's guitar. He had asked them months before to give it to me; he had known that even if I came next time he would not be able to respond in the old way. He did not want me to feel that my trip had been for nothing.

The old guitar! I plucked the strings, hummed "Sweet Georgia Brown." The magic of Mr. Sweet lingered still in the cool steel box. Through the window I could catch the fragrant delicate scent of tender yellow roses. The man on the high old-fashioned bed with the quilt coverlet and the flowing white beard had been my first love.

# JOHN UPDIKE
## (1932– )

Showing remarkable versatility and range, and meeting with both critical and popular success, John Updike's fiction represents a penetrating realist chronicle of the changing morals and manners of American society. Updike's novels and stories continue the long national debate on American civilization and its discontents. Perhaps what is most significant about Updike's work is its depiction of restless and aspiring spirits struggling within the constraints of flesh, of time and gravity, and of changing social conditions, to find something of transcendent value. For Updike, as for many other writers, the conditions and possibilities of love are an index of the conditions and possibilities of faith and belief. As Updike writes in an essay: "Not to be in love, the capital N novel whispers to capital W western man, is to be dying."

Updike was an only child and grew up in the small town of Shillington, Pennsylvania, in rather strained economic conditions. He was a straight-A student, and went to Harvard University in 1950 on a scholarship. He edited the Harvard *Lampoon* and graduated in 1954 with highest honors. After a year on a fellowship to the Ruskin School of Drawing and Fine Arts in Oxford, England, Updike went to work at *The New Yorker*. In 1957 Updike and his family moved to Massachusetts, where he has lived ever since.

Over the years Updike's fiction has won all the major literary prizes in the United States. Some of his many novels include the *Rabbit* series: *Rabbit, Run*

(1960), *Rabbit Redux* (1971), *Rabbit Is Rich* (1981), *Rabbit at Rest* (1990); *The Centaur* (1963); *Couples* (1968); *A Month of Sundays* (1975); *The Coup* (1978); *The Witches of Eastwick* (1984); *Roger's Version* (1986); the *Bech* books: *Bech: A Book* (1970), *Bech Is Back* (1982), *Bech at Bay* (1998); *In the Beauty of the Lilies* (1996); *Toward the End of Time* (1997); and *Gertrude and Claudius* (2000). His many story collections include *The Same Door* (1959), *Pigeon Feathers* (1962), *The Music School* (1966), *Too Far to Go: The Maple Stories* (1979), *Trust Me* (1987), *Afterlife and Other Stories* (1994). A volume of memoirs, *Self-Consciousness,* was published in 1989. His volumes of essays include *Picked-Up Pieces* (1975), *Hugging the Shore: Essays and Criticism* (1983), and *Odd Jobs* (1991).

# Separating

THE DAY was fair. Brilliant. All that June the weather had mocked the Maples' internal misery with solid sunlight—golden shafts and cascades of green in which their conversations had wormed unseeing, their sad murmuring selves the only stain in Nature. Usually by this time of the year they had acquired tans; but when they met their elder daughter's plane on her return from a year in England they were almost as pale as she, though Judith was too dazzled by the sunny opulent jumble of her native land to notice. They did not spoil her homecoming by telling her immediately. Wait a few days, let her recover from jet lag, had been one of their formulations, in that string of gray dialogues—over coffee, over cocktails, over Cointreau—that had shaped the strategy of their dissolution, while the earth performed its annual stunt of renewal unnoticed beyond their closed windows. Richard had thought to leave at Easter; Joan had insisted they wait until the four children were at last assembled, with all exams passed and ceremonies attended, and the bauble of summer to console them. So he had drudged away, in love, in dread, repairing screens, getting the mowers sharpened, rolling and patching their new tennis court.

The court, clay, had come through its first winter pitted and windswept bare of redcoat. Years ago the Maples had observed how often, among their friends, divorce followed a dramatic home improvement, as if the marriage were making one last effort to live; their own worst crisis had come amid the plaster dust and exposed plumbing of a kitchen renovation. Yet, a summer ago, as canary-yellow bulldozers gaily churned a grassy, daisy-dotted knoll into a muddy plateau, and a crew of pigtailed young men raked and tamped clay into a plane, this transformation did not strike them as ominous, but festive in its impudence; their marriage could rend the earth for fun. The next spring, waking each day at dawn to a sliding sensation as if the bed were being tipped, Richard found the barren tennis court—its net and tapes still rolled in the barn—an environment congruous with his mood of purposeful desolation, and the crumbling of handfuls of clay into cracks and holes (dogs had frolicked on the court in a thaw; rivulets had eroded trenches) an activity suitably elemental and interminable. In his sealed heart he hoped the day would never come.

Now it was here. A Friday. Judith was re-acclimated; all four children were assembled, before jobs and camps and visits again scattered them. Joan thought they should be told one by one. Richard was for making an announcement at the table. She said, "I think just making an announcement is a cop-out. They'll start quarrelling and playing to each other instead of focusing. They're each individuals, you know, not just some corporate obstacle to your freedom."

"O.K., O.K. I agree." Joan's plan was exact. That evening, they were giving Judith a belated welcome-home dinner, of lobster and champagne. Then, the party over, they, the two of them, who nineteen years before would push her in a baby carriage along Fifth Avenue to Washington Square, were to walk her out of the house, to the bridge across the salt creek, and tell her, swearing her to secrecy. Then Richard Jr., who was going directly from work to a rock concert in Boston, would be told, either late when he returned on the train or early Saturday morning before he went off to his job; he was seventeen and employed as one of a golf-course maintenance crew. Then the two younger children, John and Margaret, could, as the morning wore on, be informed.

"Mopped up, as it were," Richard said.

"Do you have any better plan? That leaves you the rest of Saturday to answer any questions, pack, and make your wonderful departure."

"No," he said, meaning he had no better plan, and agreed to hers, though to him it showed an edge of false order, a hidden plea for control, like Joan's long chore lists and financial accountings and, in the days when he first knew her, her too-copious lecture notes. Her plan turned one hurdle for him into four—four knife-sharp walls, each with a sheer blind drop on the other side.

All spring he had moved through a world of insides and outsides, of barriers and partitions. He and Joan stood as a thin barrier between the children and the truth. Each moment was a partition, with the past on one side and the future on the other, a future containing this unthinkable *now.* Beyond four knifelike walls a new life for him waited vaguely. His skull cupped a secret, a white face, a face both frightened and soothing, both strange and known, that he wanted to shield from tears, which he felt all about him, solid as the sunlight. So haunted, he had become obsessed with battening down the house against his absence, replacing screens and sash cords, hinges and latches—a Houdini making things snug before his escape.

* * *

The lock. He had still to replace a lock on one of the doors of the screened porch. The task, like most such, proved more difficult than he had imagined. The old lock, aluminum frozen by corrosion, had been deliberately rendered obsolete by manufacturers. Three hardware stores had nothing that even approximately matched the mortised hole its removal (surprisingly easy) left. Another hole had to be gouged, with bits too small and saws too big, and the old hole fitted with a block of wood—the chisels dull, the saw rusty, his fingers thick with lack of sleep. The sun poured down, beyond the porch, on a world of neglect. The bushes already needed pruning, the windward side of the house was shedding flakes of paint, rain would get in when he was gone, insects, rot, death. His family, all those he would lose, filtered through the edges of his awareness as he struggled with screw holes, splinters, opaque instructions, minutiae of metal.

Judith sat on the porch, a princess returned from exile. She regaled them with stories of fuel shortages, of bomb scares in the Underground, of Pakistani workmen loudly lusting after her as she walked past on her way to dance school. Joan came and went, in and out of the house, calmer than she should have been, praising his struggles with the lock as if this were one more and not the last of their long succession of shared chores. The younger of his sons for a few minutes held the rickety screen door while his father clumsily hammered and chiseled, each blow a kind of sob in Richard's ears. His younger daughter, having been at a slumber party, slept on the porch hammock through all the noise—heavy and pink, trusting and forsaken. Time, like the sunlight, continued relentlessly; the sunlight slowly slanted. Today was one of the longest days. The lock clicked, worked. He was through. He had a drink; he drank it on the porch, listening to his daughter. "It was so sweet," she was saying, "during the worst of it, how all the butchers and bakery shops kept open by candlelight. They're all so plucky and cute. From the papers, things sounded so much worse here—people shooting people in gas lines, and everybody freezing."

Richard asked her, "Do you still want to live in England forever?" *Forever:* the concept, now a reality upon him, pressed and scratched at the back of his throat.

"No," Judith confessed, turning her oval face to him, its eyes still childishly far apart, but the lips set as over something succulent and satisfactory. "I was anxious to come home. I'm an American." She was a woman. They had raised her; he and Joan had endured together to raise her, alone of the four. The others had still some raising left in them. Yet it was the thought of telling Judith—the image of her, their first baby, walking between them arm in arm to the bridge—that broke him. The partition between his face and the tears broke. Richard sat down to the celebratory meal with the back of his throat aching; the champagne, the lobster seemed phases of sunshine; he saw them and tasted them through tears. He blinked, swallowed, croakily joked about hay fever. The tears would not stop leaking through; they came not through a hole that could be plugged but through a permeable spot in a membrane, steadily, purely, endlessly, fruitfully. They became, his tears, a shield for himself against these others—their faces, the fact of their assembly, a last time as innocents, at a table where he sat the last time as head. Tears dropped from his nose as he broke the lobster's back; salt flavored his champagne as he sipped it; the raw clench at the back of his throat was delicious. He could not help himself.

His children tried to ignore his tears. Judith, on his right, lit a cigarette, gazed upward in the direction of her too energetic, too sophisticated exhalation; on her other side, John earnestly bent his face to the extraction of the last morsels—legs, tail segments—from the scarlet corpse. Joan, at the opposite end of the table, glanced at him surprised, her reproach displaced by a quick grimace, of forgiveness, or of salute to his superior gift of strategy. Between them, Margaret, no longer called Bean, thirteen and large for her age, gazed from the other side of his pane of tears as if into a shopwindow at something she coveted—at her father, a crystalline heap of splinters and memories. It was not she, however, but John who, in the kitchen, as they cleared the plates and carapaces away, asked Joan the question: *"Why is Daddy crying?"*

Richard heard the question but not the murmured answer. Then he heard Bean cry, "Oh, no-oh!"—the faintly dramatized exclamation of one who had long expected it.

John returned to the table carrying a bowl of salad. He nodded tersely at his father and his lips shaped the conspiratorial words "She told."

"Told what?" Richard asked aloud, insanely.

The boy sat down as if to rebuke his father's distraction with the example of his own good manners. He said quietly, "The separation."

Joan and Margaret returned; the child, in Richard's twisted vision, seemed diminished in size, and relieved, relieved to have had the bogieman at last proved real. He called out to her—the distances at the table had grown immense—"You knew, you always knew," but the clenching at the back of his throat prevented him from making sense of it. From afar he heard Joan talking, levelly, sensibly, reciting what they had prepared: it was a separation for the summer, an experiment. She and Daddy both agreed it would be good for them; they needed space and time to think; they liked each other but did not make each other happy enough, somehow.

Judith, imitating her mother's factual tone, but in her youth off-key, too cool, said, "I think it's silly. You should either live together or get divorced."

Richard's crying, like a wave that has crested and crashed, had become tumultuous; but it was overtopped by another tumult, for John, who had been so reserved, now grew larger and larger at the table. Perhaps his younger sister's being credited with knowing set him off. "Why didn't you *tell* us?" he asked, in a large round voice quite unlike his own. "You should have *told* us you weren't getting along."

Richard was startled into attempting to force words through his tears. "We *do* get along, that's the trouble, so it doesn't show even to us—" *That we do not love each other* was the rest of the sentence; he couldn't finish it.

Joan finished for him, in her style. "And we've always, *especially,* loved our children."

John was not mollified. "What do you care about *us?*" he boomed. "We're just little things you *had.*" His sisters' laughing forced a laugh from him, which he turned hard and parodistic: "Ha ha *ha.*" Richard and Joan realized simultaneously that the child was drunk, on Judith's homecoming champagne. Feeling bound to keep the center of the stage, John took a cigarette from Judith's pack, poked it into his mouth, let it hang from his lower lip, and squinted like a gangster.

"You're not little things we had," Richard called to him. "You're the whole point. But you're grown. Or almost."

The boy was lighting matches. Instead of holding them to his cigarette (for they had never seen him smoke; being "good" had been his way of setting himself apart), he held them to his mother's face, closer and closer, for her to blow out. Then he lit the whole folder—a hiss and then a torch, held against his mother's face. Prismed by tears, the flame filled Richard's vision; he didn't know how it was extinguished. He heard Margaret say, "Oh stop showing off," and saw John, in response, break the cigarette in two and put the halves entirely into his mouth and chew, sticking out his tongue to display the shreds to his sister.

Joan talked to him, reasoning—a fountain of reason, unintelligible. "Talked about it for years . . . our children must help us . . . Daddy and I both want . . ." As the boy listened, he carefully wadded a paper napkin into the leaves of his salad, fashioned a ball of paper and lettuce, and popped it into his mouth, looking around the table for the expected laughter. None came. Judith said, "Be mature," and dismissed a plume of smoke.

Richard got up from this stifling table and led the boy outside. Though the house was in twilight, the outdoors still brimmed with light, the lovely waste light of high summer. Both laughing, he supervised John's spitting out the lettuce and paper and tobacco into the pachysandra. He took him by the hand—a square gritty hand, but for its softness a man's. Yet, it held on. They ran together up into the field, past the tennis court. The raw banking left by the bulldozers was dotted with daisies. Past the court and a flat stretch where they used to play family baseball stood a soft green rise glorious in the sun, each weed and species of grass distinct as illumination on parchment. "I'm sorry, so sorry," Richard cried. "You were the only one who ever tried to help me with all the goddam jobs around this place."

Sobbing, safe within his tears and the champagne, John explained, "It's not just the separation, it's the whole crummy year, I *hate* that school, you can't make any friends, the history teacher's a scud."

They sat on the crest of the rise, shaking and warm from their tears but easier in their voices, and Richard tried to focus on the child's sad year—the weekdays long with homework, the weekends spent in his room with model airplanes, while his parents murmured down below, nursing their separation. How selfish, how blind, Richard thought; his eyes felt scoured. He told his son, "We'll think about getting you transferred. Life's too short to be miserable."

They had said what they could, but did not want the moment to heal, and talked on, about the school, about the tennis court, whether it would ever again be as good as it had been that first summer. They walked to inspect it and pressed a few more tapes more firmly down. A little stiltedly, perhaps trying now to make too much of the moment, Richard led the boy to the spot in the field where the view was best, of the metallic blue river, the emerald marsh, the scattered islands velvety with shadow in the low light, the white bits of beach far away. "See," he said. "It goes on being beautiful. It'll be here tomorrow."

"I know," John answered, impatiently. The moment had closed.

Back in the house, the others had opened some white wine, the champagne being drunk, and still sat at the table, the three females, gossiping. Where Joan sat had become the head. She turned, showing him a tearless face, and asked, "All right?"

"We're fine," he said, resenting it, though relieved, that the party went on without him.

* * *

In bed she explained, "I couldn't cry I guess because I cried so much all spring. It really wasn't fair. It's your idea, and you made it look as though I was kicking you out."

"I'm sorry," he said. "I couldn't stop. I wanted to but couldn't."

"You *didn't* want to. You loved it. You were having your way, making a general announcement."

"I love having it over," he admitted. "God, those kids were great. So brave and funny." John, returned to the house, had settled to a model airplane in his room, and kept shouting down to them, "I'm O.K. No sweat." "And the way," Richard went on, cozy in his relief, "they never questioned the reasons we gave. No thought of a third person. Not even Judith."

"That *was* touching," Joan said.

He gave her a hug. "You were great too. Very reassuring to everybody. Thank you." Guiltily, he realized he did not feel separated.

"You still have Dickie to do," she told him. These words set before him a black mountain in the darkness; its cold breath, its near weight affected his chest. Of the four children, his elder son was most nearly his conscience. Joan did not need to add, "That's one piece of your dirty work I won't do for you."

"I know. I'll do it. You go to sleep."

Within minutes, her breathing slowed, became oblivious and deep. It was quarter to midnight. Dickie's train from the concert would come in at one-fourteen. Richard set the alarm for one. He had slept atrociously for weeks. But whenever he closed his lids some glimpse of the last hours scorched them—Judith exhaling toward the ceiling in a kind of aversion, Bean's mute staring, the sunstruck growth in the field where he and John had rested. The mountain before him moved closer, moved within him; he was huge; momentous. The ache at the back of his throat felt stale. His wife slept as if slain beside him. When, exasperated by his hot lids, his crowded heart, he rose from bed and dressed, she awoke enough to turn over. He told her then, "Joan, if I could undo it all, I would."

"Where would you begin?" she asked. There was no place. Giving him courage, she was always giving him courage. He put on shoes without socks in the dark. The children were breathing in their rooms, the downstairs was hollow. In their confusion they had left lights burning. He turned off all but one, the kitchen overhead. The car started. He had hoped it wouldn't. He met only moonlight on the road; it seemed a diaphanous companion, flickering in the leaves along the roadside, haunting his rearview mirror like a pursuer, melting under his headlights. The center of town, not quite deserted, was eerie at this hour. A young cop in uniform kept company with a gang of T-shirted kids on the steps of the bank. Across from the railroad station, several bars kept open. Customers, mostly young, passed in and out of the warm night, savoring summer's novelty. Voices shouted from cars as they passed; an immense conversation seemed in progress. Richard parked and in his weariness put his head on the passenger seat, out of the commotion and wheeling lights. It was as when, in the movies, an assassin grimly carries his mission through the jostle of a carnival—except the movies cannot show the precipitous, palpable slope you cling to within. You cannot climb back down; you can only fall. The synthetic fabric of the car seat, warmed by his cheek, confided to him an ancient, distant scent of vanilla.

A train whistle caused him to lift his head. It was on time; he had hoped it would be late. The slender drawgates descended. The bell of approach tingled happily. The great metal body, horizontally fluted, rocked to a stop, and sleepy teenagers disembarked, his son among them. Dickie did not show surprise that his father was meeting him at this terrible hour. He sauntered to the car with two friends, both taller than he. He said "Hi" to his father and took the passenger's seat with an exhausted promptness that expressed gratitude. The friends got in the back, and Richard was grateful; a few more minutes' postponement would be won by driving them home.

He asked, "How was the concert?"

"Groovy," one boy said from the back seat.

"It bit," the other said.

"It was O.K.," Dickie said, moderate by nature, so reasonable that in his childhood the unreason of the world had given him headaches, stomach aches, nausea. When the second friend had been dropped off at his dark house, the boy blurted, "Dad, my eyes are killing me with hay fever! I'm out there cutting that mothering grass all day!"

"Do we still have those drops?"

"They didn't do any good last summer."

"They might this." Richard swung a U-turn on the empty street. The drive home took a few minutes. The mountain was here, in his throat. "Richard," he said, and felt the boy, slumped and rubbing his eyes, go tense at his tone, "I didn't come to meet you just to make your life easier. I came because your mother and I have some news for you, and you're a hard man to get ahold of these days. It's sad news."

"That's O.K." The reassurance came out soft, but quick, as if released from the tip of a spring.

Richard had feared that his tears would return and choke him, but the boy's manliness set an example, and his voice issued forth steady and dry: "It's sad news, but it needn't be tragic news, at least for you. It should have no practical effect on your life, though it's bound to have an emotional effect. You'll work at your job, and go back to school in September. Your mother and I are really proud of what you're making of your life; we don't want that to change at all."

"Yeah," the boy said lightly, on the intake of his breath, holding himself up. They turned the corner; the church they went to loomed like a gutted fort. The home of the woman Richard hoped to marry stood across the green. Her bedroom light burned.

"Your mother and I," he said, "have decided to separate. For the summer. Nothing legal, no divorce yet. We want to see how it feels. For some years now, we haven't been doing enough for each other, making each other as happy as we should be. Have you sensed that?"

"No," the boy said. It was an honest, unemotional answer: true or false in a quiz.

Glad for the factual basis, Richard pursued, even garrulously, the details. His apartment across town, his utter accessibility, the split vacation arrangements, the advantages to the children, the added mobility and variety of the summer. Dickie listened, absorbing. "Do the others know?"

"Yes."

"How did they take it?"

"The girls pretty calmly. John flipped out; he shouted and ate a cigarette and made a salad out of his napkin and told us how much he hated school."

His brother chuckled. "He did?"

"Yeah. The school issue was more upsetting for him than Mom and me. He seemed to feel better for having exploded."

"He did?" The repetition was the first sign that he was stunned.

"Yes. Dickie, I want to tell you something. This last hour, waiting for your train to get in, has been about the worst of my life. I hate this. *Hate* it. My father would have died before doing it to me." He felt immensely lighter, saying this. He had dumped the mountain on the boy. They were home. Moving swiftly as a shadow, Dickie was out of the car, through the bright kitchen. Richard called after him, "Want a glass of milk or anything?"

"No thanks."

"Want us to call the course tomorrow and say you're too sick to work?"

"No, that's all right." The answer was faint, delivered at the door to his room; Richard listened for the slam that went with a tantrum. The door closed normally, gently. The sound was sickening.

* * *

Joan had sunk into that first deep trough of deep and was slow to awake. Richard had to repeat, "I told him."

"What did he say?"

"Nothing much. Could you go say goodnight to him? Please."

She left their room, without putting on a bathrobe. He sluggishly changed back into his pajamas and walked down the hall. Dickie was already in bed, Joan was sitting beside him, and the boy's bedside clock radio was murmuring music. When she stood, an inexplicable light—the moon?—outlined her body through the nightie. Richard sat on the warm place she had indented on the child's narrow mattress. He asked him, "Do you want the radio on like that?"

"It always is."

"Doesn't it keep you awake? It would me."

"No."

"Are you sleepy?"

"Yeah."

"Good. Sure you want to get up and go to work? You've had a big night."

"I want to."

Away at school this winter he had learned for the first time that you can go short of sleep and live. As an infant he had slept with an immobile, sweating intensity that had alarmed his babysitters. In adolescence he had often been the first of the four children to go to bed. Even now, he would go slack in the middle of a television show, his sprawled legs hairy and brown. "O.K. Good boy. Dickie, listen. I love you so much; I never knew how much until now. No matter how this works out, I'll always be with you. Really."

Richard bent to kiss an averted face but his son, sinewy, turned and with wet checks embraced him and gave him a kiss, on the lips, passionate as a woman's. In his father's ear he moaned one word, the crucial, intelligent word: *"Why?"*

*Why.* It was a whistle of wind in a crack, a knife thrust, a window thrown open on emptiness. The white face was gone, the darkness was featureless. Richard had forgotten why.

# ⁂ JAMES ALAN McPHERSON
(1943– )

Being born and raised in Savannah, Georgia, a city where several cultures have been uniquely blended, gave James Alan McPherson an ability to transcend racial barriers and to look at particular human experience in universal terms. This is a sensibility he shares with Ralph Ellison, who has praised his fiction and with whom he has collaborated. McPherson writes with deep sympathy for characters so desperate they can do little more than rage impotently against their conditions. Ultimately, however, he is concerned with their plight as human beings and not just as black people.

McPherson received a B.A. from Morris Brown College in 1965 and completed a law degree from the Harvard University School of Law in 1968. He went to the University of Iowa for an M.F.A. in 1969. He taught at a number of colleges, including the University of Iowa, the University of California at Santa Cruz, and the University of Virginia. Since 1981 he has been a faculty member of the Writers' Workshop at the University of Iowa. He also began editing *Double Take* magazine in 1995. In 1997 he went to Stanford University as a behavioral studies fellow. He has had a long association with the *Atlantic Monthly* as a contributing editor. McPherson's Major publications are the story collections *Hue and Cry* (1969) and *Elbow Room* (1977), which was awarded a Pulitzer Prize in 1978. He won a MacArthur Foundation Award in 1981. After a long hiatus he published *Crabcakes* in 1998, a memoir and meditation. He coedited a book with DeWitt Henry called *Fathering Daughters: Reflections by Men* (1998). Most recently he has published *A Region Not Home: Reflections from Exile* (2000).

## Of Cabbages and Kings

CLAUDE SHEATS had been in the Brotherhood all his life and then he had tried to get out. Some of his people and most of his friends were still in the Brotherhood and were still very good members, but Claude was no longer a good member because he had tried to get out after over twenty years. To get away from the Brotherhood and all his friends who were still active in it, he moved to Washington Square and took to reading about being militant. But, living there, he developed a craving for whiteness the way a nicely broke-in virgin craves sex. In spite of this, he maintained a steady black girl, whom he saw at least twice a month to keep up appearances, and once he took both of us with him when he visited his uncle in Harlem who was still in the Brotherhood.

"She's a nice girl, Claude," his uncle's wife had told him that night because the girl, besides being attractive, had some very positive ideas about the Brotherhood. Her name was Marie, she worked as a secretary in my office, and it was on her suggestion that I had moved in with Claude Sheats.

"I'm glad to see you don't waste your time on hippies," the uncle had said. "All our young men are selling out these days."

The uncle was the kind of fellow who had played his cards right. He was much older than his wife, and I had the impression, that night, that he must have given her time to experience enough and to become bored enough before he overwhelmed her with his success. He wore glasses and combed his hair back and had that oily kind of composure that made me think of a waiter waiting to be tipped. He was very proud of his English, I observed, and how he always ended his words with just the right sound. He must have felt superior to people who didn't. He must have felt superior to Claude because he was still with the Brotherhood and Claude had tried to get out.

Claude did not like him and always seemed to feel guilty whenever we visited his uncle's house. "Don't mention any of my girls to him," he told me after our first visit.

"Why would I do that?" I said.

"He'll try to psych you into telling him."

"Why should he suspect you? He never comes over to the apartment."

"He just likes to know what I'm doing. I don't want him to know about my girls."

"I won't say anything," I promised.

He was almost twenty-three and had no steady girls, except for Marie. He was well built, so that he had no trouble in the Village area. It was like going to the market for him. During my first days in the apartment the process had seemed like a game. And once, when he was going out, I said: "Bring back two."

Half an hour later he came back with two girls. He got their drinks and then he called me into his room to meet them.

"This is Doris," he said, pointing to the smaller one, "and I forgot your name," he said to the big blonde.

"Jane," she said.

"This is Howard," he told her.

"Hi," I said. Neither one of them smiled. The big blonde in white pants sat on the big bed and the little one sat on a chair near the window. He had given them his worst bourbon.

"Excuse me a minute," Claude said to the girls. "I want to talk to Howard for a minute." He put on a record before we went outside into the hall between our rooms. He was always extremely polite and gentle, and very soft-spoken in spite of his size.

"Listen," he said to me outside, "you can have the blonde."

"What can I do with that amazon?"

"I don't care. Just get her out of the room."

"She's dirty," I said.

"So you can give her a bath."

"It wouldn't help much."

"Well just take her out and talk to her," he told me. "Remember, you asked for her."

We went back in. "Where you from?" I said to the amazon.

"Brighton."

"What school?"

"No. I just got here."

"From where?"

*"Brighton!"*

"That's not so far," I said.

*"England,"* she said. She looked very bored. Claude Sheats looked at me.

"How did you find Washington Square so fast?"

"I got friends."

She was very superior about it all and seemed to look at us with the same slightly patient irritation of a professional theater critic waiting for a late performance to begin. The little one sat on the chair, her legs crossed, looking up at the ceiling. Her white pants were dirty too. They looked as though they would have been very relieved if we had taken off our clothes and danced for them around the room and across the bed, and made hungry sounds in our throats with our mouths slightly opened.

I said that I had to go out to the drugstore and would be back very soon; but once outside, I walked a whole hour in one direction and then I walked back. I passed them a block away from our apartment. They were walking fast and did not slow down or speak when I passed them.

Claude Sheats was drinking heavily when I came into the apartment.

"What the hell are you trying to pull?" he said.

"I couldn't find a drugstore open."

He got up from the living room table and walked toward me. "You should have asked me," he said. "I got more than enough."

"I wanted some mouthwash too," I said.

He fumed a while longer, and then told me how I had ruined his evening because the amazon would not leave the room to wait for me and the little one would not do anything with the amazon around. He suddenly thought about going down and bringing them back; and he went out for a while. But he came back without them, saying that they had been picked up again.

"When a man looks out for you, you got to look out for him," he warned me.

"I'm sorry."

"A hell of a lot of good *that* does. And that's the last time I look out for *you,* baby," he said. "From now on it's *me* all the way."

"Thanks," I said.

"If she was too much for you I could of taken the amazon."

"It didn't matter that much," I said.

"You could of had Doris if you couldn't handle the amazon."

"They were both too much," I told him.

But Claude Sheats did not answer. He just looked at me.

* * *

After two months of living with him I concluded that Claude hated whites as much as he loved them. And he hated himself with the very same passion. He hated the country and his place in it and he loved the country and his place in it. He loved the Brotherhood and all that being in it had taught him and he still believed in what he had been taught, even after he had left it and did not have to believe in anything.

"This Man is going *down,* Howard," he would announce with conviction.

"Why?" I would ask.

"Because it's the Black Man's time to rule again. They had five thousand years, now we get five thousand years."

"What if I don't *want* to rule?" I asked. "What happens if I don't want to take over?"

He looked at me with pity in his face. "You go down with the rest of the country."

"I guess I wouldn't mind much anyway," I said. "It would be a hell of a place with nobody to hate."

But I could never get him to smile about it the way I tried to smile about it. He was always serious. And, once, when I questioned the mysticism in the teachings of the Brotherhood, Claude almost attacked me. "Another man might kill you for saying that," he had said. "Another man might not let you get away with saying something like that." He was quite deadly and he stood over me with an air of patient superiority. And because he could afford to be generous and forgiving, being one of the saved, he sat down at the table with me under the single light bulb and began to teach me. He told me the stories about how it was in the beginning before the whites took over, and about all the little secret significances of black, and about the subtle infiltration of white superiority into everyday objects.

"You've never seen me eat white bread or white sugar, have you?"

"No," I said. He used brown bread and brown sugar.

"Or use bleached flour or white rice?"

"No."

"You know why, don't you?" He waited expectantly.

"No," I finally said. "I don't know why."

He was visibly shocked, so much so that he dropped that line of instruction and began to draw on a pad before him on the living room table. He moved his big shoulders over the yellow pad to conceal his drawings and looked across the table at me. "Now I'm going to tell you something that white men have paid thousands of dollars to learn," he said. "Men have been killed for telling this but I'm telling you for nothing. I'm warning you not to repeat it because if the whites find out you know, you could be killed too."

"You know me," I said. "I wouldn't repeat any secrets."

He gave me a long thoughtful look.

I gave him back a long, eager, honest look.

Then he leaned across the table and whispered: "Kennedy isn't buried in this country. He was the only President who never had his coffin opened during the funeral. The body was in state all that time and they never opened the coffin once. You know why?"

"No."

"Because he's not *in it!* They buried an empty coffin. Kennedy was a Thirty-third Degree Mason. His body is in Jerusalem right now."

"How do you know?" I asked.

"If I told you it would put your life in danger."

"Did his family know about it?"

"No. His lodge kept it secret."

"No one knew?"

"I'm telling you, *no!*"

"Then how did you find out?"

He sighed, more from tolerance than from boredom with my inability to comprehend the mysticism of pure reality in its most unadulterated form. Of course I could not believe him and we argued about it, back and forth; but to absolutely cap all my uncertainties he drew the thirty-three degree circle, showed me the secret signs that men had died to learn, and spoke about the time when our black ancestors chased an evil genius out of their kingdom and across a desert and onto an island somewhere in the sea; from which, hundreds of years later, this same evil genius sent forth a perfected breed of white-skinned and evil creatures who, through trickery, managed to enslave for five thousand years the one-time Black Masters of the world. He further explained the significance of the East and why all the saved must go there once during their lifetimes, and possibly be buried there, as Kennedy had been.

It was dark and late at night, and the glaring bulb cast his great shadow into the corners so that there was the sense of some outraged spirit, fuming in the halls and dark places of our closets, waiting to extract some terrible and justifiable revenge from him for disclosing to me, an unbeliever, the closest-kept of secrets. But I was aware of them only for an instant, and then I did not believe him again.

The most convincing thing about it all was that he was very intelligent and had an orderly, well regimented lifestyle, and yet *he* had no trouble with believing. He believed in the certainty of statistical surveys, which was his work; the nutritional value of wheat germ sprinkled on eggs; the sensuality of gin; and the dangers inherent in smoking. He was stylish in that he did not believe in God, but he was extremely moral and warm and kind; and I wanted sometimes to embrace him for his kindness and bigness and gentle manners. He lived his life so carefully that no matter what he said, I could not help but believe him sometimes. But I did not want to, because I knew that once I started I could not stop; and then there would be no purpose to my own beliefs and no real conviction or direction in my own efforts to achieve when always in the back of my regular thoughts, there would be a sense of futility and a fear of the unknown all about me. So, for the sake of necessity, I chose not to believe him.

He felt that the country was doomed and that the safe thing to do was to make enough money as soon as possible and escape to the Far East. He forecast summer riots in certain Northern cities and warned me, religiously, to avoid all implicating ties with whites so that I might have a chance to be saved when that time came. And I asked him about *his* ties, and the girls, and how it was never a movie date with coffee afterwards but always his room and the cover-all blanket of Motown sounds late into the night.

"A man has different reasons for doing certain things," he had said.

He never seemed to be comfortable with any of the girls. He never seemed to be in control. And after my third month in the apartment I had concluded that he used his virility as a tool and forged, for however long it lasted, a little area of superiority which could never, it seemed, extend itself beyond the certain confines of his room, no matter how late into the night the records played. I could see him fighting to extend the area, as if an increase in the number of girls he saw could compensate for what he had lost in duration. He saw many girls: curious students, unexpected bus-stop pickups, and assorted other one-nighters. And his rationalizations allowed him to believe that each one was an actual conquest, a physical affirmation of a psychological victory over all he hated and loved and hated in the little world of his room.

But then he seemed to have no happiness, even in this. Even here I sensed some intimations of defeat. After each girl, Claude would almost immediately come out of his room, as if there was no need for aftertalk; as if, after it was over, he felt a brooding, silent emptiness that quickly intensified into nervousness and instantaneous shyness and embarrassment so that the cold which sets in after that kind of emotional drain came in very sharp against his skin, and he could not bear to have her there any longer. And when the girl had gone, he would come into my room to talk. These were the times when he was most like a little boy; and these were the times when he really began to trust me.

"That bitch called me everything but the son of God," he would chuckle. And I would put aside my papers brought home from the office, smile at him, and listen.

He would always eat or drink afterwards and in those early days I was glad for his companionship and the return of his trust, and sometimes we drank and talked until dawn. During these times he would tell me more subleties about the Man and would re-predict the fall of the country. Once, he warned me, in a fatherly way, about reading life from books before experiencing it; and another night he advised me on how to schedule girls so that one could run them without being run in return. These were usually good times of good-natured arguments and predictions; but as we drank more often he tended to grow more excited and quick-tempered, especially after he had just entertained. Sometimes he would seethe hate, and every drink he took gave life to increasingly bitter condemnations of the present system and our place in it. There were actually flying saucers, he told me once, piloted by things from other places in the universe which would eventually destroy the country for what it had done to the black man. He had run into his room, on that occasion, and had brought out a book by a man who maintained that the government was deliberately withholding from the public overwhelming evidence of flying saucers and strange creatures from other galaxies that walked among us every day. Claude emphasized the fact that the writer was a Ph.D. who must know what he was talking about, and insisted that the politicians withheld the information because they knew that their time was almost up and if they made it public the black man would know that he had outside friends who would help him take over the world again. Nothing I said could make him reconsider the slightest bit of his information.

"What are we going to use for weapons when we take over?" I asked him once.

"We've got atomic bombs stockpiled and waiting for the day."

"How can you believe that crap?"

He did not answer, but said instead: "You are the living example of what the Man has done to my people."

"I just try to think things out for myself," I said.

"You can't think. The handkerchief over your head is too big."

I smiled.

"I know," he continued. "I know all there is to know about whites because I've been studying them all my life."

I smiled some more.

"I ought to know," he said slowly. "I have supernatural powers."

"I'm tired," I told him. "I want to go to sleep now."

Claude started to leave the room, then he turned. "Listen," he said at the door. He pointed his finger at me to emphasize the gravity of his pronouncement. "I predict that within the next week something is going to happen to this country that will hurt it even more than Kennedy's assassination."

"Goodnight," I said as he closed the door.

He opened it again. "Remember that I predicted it when it happens," he said. For the first time I noticed that he had been deadly serious all along.

Two days later several astronauts burned to death in Florida. He raced into my room hot with the news.

"Do you believe in me *now?*" he said. "Just two days and look what happened."

I tried to explain, as much to myself as to him, that in any week of the year something unfortunate was bound to occur. But he insisted that this was only part of a divine plan to bring the country to its knees. He said that he intended to send a letter off right away to Jeane Dixon in D.C. to let her know that she was not alone because he also had the same power. Then he thought that he had better not because the FBI knew that he had been active in the Brotherhood before he got out.

At first it was good fun believing that someone important cared enough to watch us. And sometimes when the telephone was dead a long time before the dial tone sounded, I would knock on his door and together we would run through our telephone conversations for that day to see if either of us had said anything implicating or suspect, just in case they were listening. This feeling of persecution brought us closer together and soon the instruction sessions began to go on almost every night. At this point I could not help but believe him a little. And he began to trust me again, like a tolerable little brother, and even confided that the summer riots would break out simultaneously in Harlem and Watts during the second week in August. For some reason, something very difficult to put into words, I spent three hot August nights on the streets of Harlem, waiting for the riot to start.

In the seventh month of our living together, he began to introduce me to his girls again when they came in. Most of them came only once, but all of them received the same mechanical treatment. He only discriminated with liquor, the quality of which improved with the attractiveness or reluctance of the girl: gin for slow starters, bourbon for momentary strangers, and the scotch he reserved for those he hoped would come again. There was first the trek into his room, his own trip out for the ice and glasses while classical music was played within; then after a while the classical piece would be replaced by several Motowns. Finally, there was her trip to the bathroom, his calling a cab in the hall, and the sound of both their feet on the stairs as he walked her down to the cab. Then he would come to my room in his red bathrobe, glass in hand, for the aftertalk.

* * *

Then in the ninth month the trouble started. It would be very easy to pick out one incident, one day, one area of misunderstanding in that month and say: "That was where it began." It would be easy, but not accurate. It might have been one instance or a combination of many. It might have been the girl who came into the living room, when I was going over the proposed blueprints for a new settlement house, and who lingered too long outside his room in conversation because her father was a builder somewhere. Or it might have been nothing at all. But after that time he warned me about being too friendly with his company.

Another night, when I was leaving the bathroom in my shorts, he came out of his room with a girl who smiled.

"Hi," she said to me.

I nodded hello as I ducked back into the bathroom.

When he had walked her down to the door he came to my room and knocked. He did not have a drink.

"Why didn't you speak to my company?" he demanded.

"I was in my shorts."

"She felt bad about it. She asked what the hell was wrong with you. What could I tell her—'He got problems'?"

"I'm sorry," I said. "But I didn't want to stop in my shorts."

"I see through you, Howard," he said. "You're just jealous of me and try to insult my girls to get to me."

"Why should I be jealous of you?"

"Because I'm a man and you're not."

"What makes a man anyway?" I said. "Your fried eggs and wheat germ? Why should I be jealous of you *or* what you bring in?"

"Some people don't need a reason. You're a black devil and you'll get yours. I predict that you'll get yours."

"Look," I told him, "I'm sorry about the girl. Tell her I'm sorry when you see her again."

"You treated her so bad she probably won't come back."

I said nothing more and he stood there silently for a long time before he turned to leave the room. But at the door he turned again and said: "I see through you, Howard. You're a black devil."

It should have ended there and it might have with anyone else. I took great pains to speak to his girls after that, even though he tried to get them into the room as quickly as possible. But a week later he accused me of walking about in his room after he had gone out, some two weeks before.

"I swear I wasn't in your room," I protested.

"I saw your shadow on the blinds from across the street at the bus stop," he insisted.

"I've *never* been in your room when you weren't there," I told him.

"I *saw* you!"

We went into his room and I tried to explain how, even if he could see the window from the bus stop, the big lamp next to the window prevented any shadow from being cast on the blinds. But he was convinced in his mind that at every opportunity I plundered his closets and drawers. He had no respect for simple logic in these matters, no sense of the absurdity of his accusations, and the affair finally ended with my confessing that I might have done it without actually knowing; and if I had, I would not do it again.

But what had been a gesture for peace on my part became a vindication for him, proof that I *was* a black devil, capable of lying and lying until he confronted me with the inescapable truth of the situation. And so he persisted in creating situations from which, if he insisted on a point long enough and with enough self-righteousness, he could draw my inevitable confession.

And I confessed eagerly, goaded on by the necessity of maintaining peace. I confessed to mixing white sugar crystals in with his own brown crystals so that he could use it and violate the teachings of the Brotherhood; I confessed to cleaning the bathroom all the time merely because I wanted to make him feel guilty for not having ever cleaned it. I confessed to telling the faithful Marie, who brought a surprise dinner over for him, that he was working late at his office in order to implicate him with the girls who worked there. I confessed to leaving my papers about the house so that his company could ask about them and develop an interest in me. And I pleaded guilty to a record of other little infamies, which multiplied into countless others, and again subdivided into hundreds of little subtleties until my every movement was a threat to him. If I had a girlfriend to dinner, we should eat in my room instead of at the table because he had to use the bathroom a lot and, besides not wanting to seem as if he were making a pass at my girl by walking through the room so often, he was genuinely embarrassed to be seen going to the bathroom.

If I protested he would fly into a tantrum and shake his big finger at me vigorously. And so I retreated, step by step, into my room, from which I emerged only to go to the bathroom or kitchen or out of the house. I tried to stay out on nights when he had company. But he had company so often that I could not always help being in my room after he had walked her to the door. Then he would knock on my door for his talk. He might offer me a drink, and if I refused, he would go to his room for a while and then come back. He would pace about for a while, like a big little boy who wants to ask for money over his allowance. At these times my mind would move feverishly over all our contacts for as far back as I could make it reach, searching and attempting to pull out that one incident which would surely be the point of his attack. But it was never any use; it might have been anything.

"Howard, I got something on my chest and I might as well get it off."

"What is it?" I asked from my bed.

"You been acting strange lately. Haven't been talking to me. If you got something on your chest, get it off now."

"I have nothing on my chest," I said.

"Then why don't you talk?"

I did not answer.

"You hardly speak to me in the kitchen. If you have something against me, tell me now."

"I have nothing against you."

"Why don't you talk, then?" He looked directly at me. "If a man doesn't talk, you think *something's* wrong!"

"I've been nervous lately, that's all. I got problems and I don't want to talk."

"Everybody's got problems. That's no reason for going around making a man feel guilty."

"For God's sake, I don't want to talk."

"I know what's wrong with you. Your conscience is bothering you. You're so evil that your conscience is giving you trouble. You got everybody fooled but *me*. I know you're a black devil."

"I'm a black devil," I said. "Now will you let me sleep?"

He went to the door. "You dish it out but you can't take it," he said. "That's *your* trouble."

"I'm a black devil," I said.

I lay there, after he left, hating myself but thankful that he hadn't called me into his room for the fatherly talk as he had done another time. That was the worst. He had come to the door and said: "Come out of there, I want to talk to you." He had walked ahead of me into his room and had sat down in his big leather chair next to the lamp with his legs spread wide and his big hands in his lap. He had said: "Don't be afraid. I'm not going to hurt you. Sit down. I'm not going to argue. What are you so nervous about? Have a drink," in his kindest, most fatherly way, and that had been the worst of all. That was the time he had told me to eat in my room. Now I could hear him pacing about in the hall and I knew that it was not over for the night. I began to pray that I could sleep before he came and that he would not be able to wake me, no matter what he did. I did not care what he did as long as I did not have to face him. I resolved to confess to anything he accused me of if it would make him leave sooner. I was about to go out into the hall for my confession when the door was kicked open and he charged into the room.

"You black son-of-a-bitch!" he said. "I ought to *kill* you." He stood over the bed in the dark room and shook his big fist over me. And I lay there hating the overpowering cowardice in me, which kept my body still and my eyes closed, and hoping that he would kill all of it when his heavy fist landed.

"First you insult a man's company, then you ignore him. I been *good* to you. I let you live here, I let you eat my uncle's food, and I taught you things. But you're a ungrateful motherfucker. I ought to *kill* you right now!"

And I still lay there, as he went on, not hearing him, with nothing in me but a loud throbbing which pulsed through the length of my body and made the sheets move with its pounding. I lay there secure and safe in cowardice for as long as I looked up at him with my eyes big and my body twitching and my mind screaming out to him that it was all right, and I thanked him, because now I truly believed in the new five thousand years of Black Rule.

It is night again. I am in bed again, and I can hear the new blonde girl closing the bathroom door. I know that in a minute he will come out in his red robe and call a cab. His muffled voice through my closed door will seem very tired, but just as kind and patient to the dispatcher as it is to everyone, and as it was to me in those old times. I am afraid because when they came up the stairs earlier they caught me working at the living room table with my back to them. I had not expected him back so soon; but then I should have known that he would not go out. I had turned around in the chair and she smiled and said hello and I said "Hi" before he hurried her into the room. I *did* speak and I know that she heard. But I also know that I must have done something wrong; if not to her, then to him earlier today or yesterday or last week, because he glared at me before following her into the room and he almost paused to say something when he came out to get the glasses and ice. I wish that I could remember just what it was. But it does not matter. I *am* guilty and he knows it.

Now that he knows about me I am afraid. I could move away from the apartment and hide my guilt from him, but I know that he would find me. The brainwashed part of my mind tells me to call the police while he is still busy with her, but what could I charge him with when I know that he is only trying to help me. I could move the big, ragged yellow chair in front of the door, but that would not stop him, and it might make him impatient with me. Even if I pretended to be asleep and ignored him, it would not help when he comes. He has not bothered to knock for weeks.

In the black shadows over my bed and in the corners I can sense the outraged spirits who help him when they hover about his arms as he gestures, with his lessons, above my bed. I am determined now to lie here and take it. It is the price I must pay for all the black secrets I have learned, and all the evil I have learned about myself. I *am* jealous of him, of his learning, of his girls. I am not the same handkerchief-head I was nine months ago. I have Marie to thank for that, and Claude, and the spirits. They know about me, and perhaps it is they who make him do it and he cannot help himself. I believe in the spirits now, just as I believe most of the time that I am a black devil.

They are going down to the cab now.

I will not ever blame him for it. He is helping me. But I blame the girls. I blame them for not staying on afterwards, and for letting all the good nice happy love talk cut off automatically after it is over. *I* need to have them there, after it is over. And he needs it; he needs it much more and much longer than they could ever need what he does for them. He should be able to teach them, as he has taught me. And he should have their appreciation, as he has mine. I blame them. I blame them for letting him try and try and never get just a little of the love there is left in the world.

I can hear him coming back from the cab.

# JAMAICA KINCAID
## (1949– )

Jamaica Kincaid was born Elaine Potter Richardson on the Caribbean island of St. John's, Antigua, in the West Indies. This was a British colony during her girlhood, and thus her earliest literary influences were British. Some British writers she loved, others she detested, such as Wordsworth and Milton, though she found the fallen angel of "Paradise Lost" most fascinating. (The protagonist of her novel *Lucy* (1990) delights in the knowledge that she was named after Milton's Lucifer.) At age 17, Kincaid left Antigua for the United States, where she worked briefly as a nanny. After finishing high school by attending night school, she briefly attended the New School for Social Research in New York City. She then spent a year on scholarship at Franconia College in New Hampshire, dropping out in 1974 to educate herself and to work on her writing. She marked that shift by changing her name to Jamaica Kincaid, and began publishing stories in *Rolling Stone, The Paris Review,* and *The New Yorker,* for which she became a staff writer in 1978. In 1979 she married and later moved to Bennington, Vermont, with her family.

Kincaid's first short-story collection, *At the Bottom of the River,* was published in 1983. It was followed by *Annie John,* a book of interrelated stories about a girl's coming of age in the West Indies, in 1985. The novel *The Autobiography of My Mother* appeared in 1996. The memoir about a death from AIDS, *My Brother,* appeared in 1997 and received a nomination for a National Book Award. Her long essay, "A Small Place," an angry attack on colonialism and its effects, appeared in 1988. A recurring theme in Kincaid's work is the conflict between mothers and daughters, which serves as a metaphor for the problems of colonialism.

# Girl

WASH THE white clothes on Monday and put them on the stone heap; wash the color clothes on Tuesday and put them on the clothesline to dry; don't walk barehead in the hot sun; cook pumpkin fritters in very hot sweet oil; soak your little cloths right after you take them off; when buying cotton to make yourself a nice blouse, be sure that it doesn't have gum on it, because that way it won't hold up well after a wash; soak salt fish overnight before you cook it; is it true that you sing benna[1] in Sunday school?; always eat your food in such a way that it won't turn someone else's stomach; on Sundays try to walk like a lady and not like the slut you are so bent on becoming; don't sing benna in Sunday school; you mustn't speak to wharf-rat boys, not even to give directions; don't eat fruits on the street—flies will follow you; *but I don't sing benna on Sundays at all and never in Sunday school;* this is how to sew on a button; this is how to make a button-hole for the button you have just sewed on; this is how to hem a dress when you see the hem coming down and so to prevent yourself from looking like the slut I know you are so bent on becoming; this is how you iron your father's khaki shirt so that it doesn't have a crease; this is how you iron your father's khaki pants so that they don't have a crease; this is how you grow okra—far from the house, because okra tree harbors red ants; when you are growing dasheen, make sure it gets plenty of water or else it makes your throat itch when you are eating it; this is how you sweep a corner; this is how you sweep a whole house; this is how you sweep a yard; this is how you smile to someone you don't like too much; this is how you smile to someone you don't like at all; this is how you smile to someone you like completely; this is how you set a table for tea; this is how you set a table for dinner; this is how you set a table for dinner with an important guest; this is how you set a table for lunch; this is how you set a table for breakfast; this is how to behave in the presence of men who don't know you very well, and this way they won't recognize immediately the slut I have warned you against becoming; be sure to wash every day, even if it is with your own spit; don't squat down to play marbles—you are not a boy, you know; don't pick people's flowers—you might catch something; don't throw stones at blackbirds, because it might not be a blackbird at all; this is how to make a bread pudding; this is how to make doukona[2]; this is how to make pepper pot; this is how to make a good medicine for a cold; this is how to make

1. Calypso music.

2. A spicy plantain pudding.

a good medicine to throw away a child before it even becomes a child; this is how to catch a fish; this is how to throw back a fish you don't like, and that way something bad won't fall on you; this is how to bully a man; this is how a man bullies you; this is how to love a man, and if this doesn't work there are other ways, and if they don't work don't feel too bad about giving up; this is how to spit up in the air if you feel like it, and this is how to move quick so that it doesn't fall on you; this is how to make ends meet; always squeeze bread to make sure it's fresh; *but what if the baker won't let me feel the bread?;* you mean to say that after all you are really going to be the kind of woman who the baker won't let near the bread?

# MAX APPLE
## (1941– )

Born and raised in Grand Rapids, Michigan, of a Jewish baker and his wife, Max Apple grew up in a kosher household in which Yiddish was spoken. He earned a B.A. in English in 1963 from the University of Michigan, and a Ph.D. in 1970. He taught for a year at Reed College in Oregon before moving to Rice University in Houston, Texas, where he has taught since then.

While Apple's fiction provides a comic and satiric look at American obsessions and myths, his tone is marked by amusement and forgiveness rather than by anger and damnation. Juxtaposing and combining historical and pop figures with his made-up ones, Apple writes comedy that is essentially redemptive. His collections of short stories include *The Oranging of America, and Other Stories* (1976) and *Free Agents* (1984). His novels are *Zip: A Novel of the Left and the Right* (1978) and *The Propheteers* (1986). In 1994 he published a loving memoir of his grandfather, *Roommates: My Grandfather's Story,* which was followed in 1998 with *I Love Gootie: My Grandmother's Story.*

# The Oranging of America

I

From the outside it looked like any ordinary 1964 Cadillac limousine. In the expensive space between the driver and passengers, where some installed bars or even bathrooms, Mr. Howard Johnson kept a tidy ice-cream freezer in which there were always at least eighteen flavors on hand, though Mr. Johnson ate only vanilla. The freezer's power came from the battery with an independent auxiliary generator as a back-up system. Although now Howard Johnson means primarily motels, Millie, Mr. HJ, and Otis Brighton, the chauffeur, had not forgotten that ice cream was the cornerstone of their empire. Some of the important tasting was still done in the car. Mr. HJ might have reports in his pocket from sales executives and marketing analysts, from home economists and chemists, but not until Mr. Johnson reached over the lowered Plexiglas to spoon a taste or two into the expert waiting mouth of Otis Brighton did he make any final flavor decision. He might go ahead with butterfly shrimp, with candy kisses, and with packaged chocolate-chip cookies on the opinion of the specialists, but in ice cream he trusted only Otis. From the back seat Howard Johnson would keep his eye on the rearview mirror, where the reflection of pleasure or disgust showed itself in the dark eyes of Otis Brighton no matter what the driving conditions. He could be stalled in a commuter rush with the engine overheating and a dripping oil pan, and still a taste of the right kind never went unappreciated.

When Otis finally said, "Mr. Howard, that shore is sumpin, that one is um-hum. That is it, my man, that is it." Then and not until then did Mr. HJ finally decide to go ahead with something like banana-fudge-ripple royale.

Mildred rarely tasted and Mr. HJ was addicted to one scoop of vanilla every afternoon at three, eaten from his aluminum dish with a disposable plastic spoon. The duties of Otis, Millie, and Mr. Johnson were so divided that they rarely infringed upon one another in the car, which was their office. Neither Mr. HJ nor Millie knew how to drive, Millie and Otis understood little of financing and leasing, and Mr. HJ left the compiling of the "Traveling Reports" and "The Howard Johnson Newsletter" strictly to the literary style of his longtime associate, Miss Mildred Bryce. It was an ideal division of labor, which, in one form or another, had been in continuous operation for well over a quarter of a century.

While Otis listened to the radio behind his soundproof Plexiglas, while Millie in her small, neat hand compiled data for the newsletter, Mr. HJ liked to lean back into the spongy leather seat looking through his specially tinted windshield at the fleeting land. Occasionally, lulled by the hum of the freezer, he might doze off, his large pink head lolling toward the shoulder of his blue suit, but there was not too much that Mr. Johnson missed, even in advanced age.

Along with Millie he planned their continuous itinerary as they traveled. Mildred would tape a large green relief map of the United States to the Plexiglas separating them from Otis. The mountains on the map were light brown and seemed to melt toward the valleys like the crust of a fresh apple pie settling into cinnamon surroundings. The existing HJ houses (Millie called the restaurants and motels houses) were marked by orange dots, while projected future sites bore white dots. The deep green map with its brown mountains and colorful dots seemed much more alive than the miles that twinkled past Mr. Johnson's gaze, and nothing gave the ice-cream king greater pleasure than watching Mildred with her fine touch, and using the original crayon, turn an empty white dot into an orange fulfillment.

"It's like a seed grown into a tree, Millie," Mr. HJ liked to say at such moments when he contemplated the map and saw that it was good.

They had started traveling together in 1925: Mildred, then a secretary to Mr. Johnson, a young man with two restaurants and a dream of hospitality, and Otis, a twenty-year-old busboy and former driver of a Louisiana mule. When Mildred graduated from college, her father, a Michigan doctor who kept his money in a blue steel box under the examining table, encouraged her to try the big city. He sent her a monthly allowance. In those early days she always had more than Mr. Johnson, who paid her $16.50 a week and meals. In the first decade they traveled only on weekends, but every year since 1936 they had spent at least six months on the road, and it might have gone on much longer if Mildred's pain and the trouble in New York with Howard Jr. had not come so close together.

* * *

They were all stoical at the Los Angeles International Airport. Otis waited at the car for what might be his last job while Miss Bryce and Mr. Johnson traveled toward the New York plane along a silent moving floor. Millie stood beside Howard while they passed a mural of a Mexican landscape and some Christmas drawings by fourth graders from Watts. For forty years they had been together in spite of Sonny and the others, but at this most recent appeal from New York Millie urged him to go back. Sonny had cabled, "My God, Dad, you're sixty-nine years old, haven't you been a gypsy long enough? Board meeting December third with or without you. Policy changes imminent."

Normally, they ignored Sonny's cables, but this time Millie wanted him to go, wanted to be alone with the pain that had recently come to her. She had left Howard holding the new canvas suitcase in which she had packed her three notebooks of regional reports along with his aluminum dish, and in a moment of real despair she had even packed the orange crayon. When Howard boarded Flight 965 he looked old to Millie. His feet dragged in the wing-tipped shoes, the hand she shook was moist, the lip felt dry, and as he passed from her sight down the entry ramp Mildred Bryce felt a fresh new ache that sent her hobbling toward the car. Otis had unplugged the freezer, and the silence caused by the missing hum was as intense to Millie as her abdominal pain.

It had come quite suddenly in Albuquerque, New Mexico, at the grand opening of a 210-unit house. She did not make a fuss. Mildred Bryce had never caused trouble to anyone, except perhaps to Mrs. HJ. Millie's quick precise actions, angular face, and thin body made her seem birdlike, especially next to Mr. HJ, six three with splendid white hair accenting his dark blue gabardine suits. Howard was slow and sure. He could sit in the same position for hours while Millie fidgeted on the seat, wrote memos, and filed reports in the small gray cabinet that sat in front of her and parallel to the ice-cream freezer. Her health had always been good, so at first she tried to ignore the pain. It was gas: it was perhaps the New Mexico water or the cooking oil in the fish dinner. But she could not convince away the pain. It stayed like a match burning around her belly, etching itself into her as the round HJ emblem was so symmetrically embroidered into the bedspread, which she had kicked off in the flush that accompanied the pain. She felt as if her sweat would engulf the foam mattress and crisp percale sheet. Finally, Millie brought up her knees and made a ball of herself as if being as small as possible might make her misery disappear. It worked for everything except the pain. The little circle of hot torment was all that remained of her, and when finally at sometime in the early morning it left, it occurred to her that perhaps she had struggled with a demon and been suddenly relieved by the coming of day-light. She stepped lightly into the bathroom and before a full-length mirror (new in HJ motels exclusively) saw herself whole and unmarked, but sign enough to Mildred was her smell, damp and musty, sign enough that something had begun and that something else would therefore necessarily end.

II

Before she had the report from her doctor, Howard Jr.'s message had given her the excuse she needed. There was no reason why Millie could not tell Howard she was sick, but telling him would be admitting too much to herself. Along with Howard Johnson Millie had grown rich beyond dreams. Her inheritance, the $100,000 from her father's steel box in 1939, went directly to Mr. Johnson, who desperately needed it, and the results of that investment brought Millie enough capital to employ two people at the Chase Manhattan with the management of her finances. With money beyond the hope of use, she had vacationed all over the world and spent some time in the company of celebrities, but the reality of her life, like his, was in the back seat of the limousine, waiting for that point at which the needs of the automobile and the human body met the undeviating purpose of the highway and momentarily conquered it.

Her life was measured in rest stops. She, Howard, and Otis had found them out before they existed. They knew the places to stop between Buffalo and Albany, Chicago and Milwaukee, Toledo and Columbus, Des Moines and Minneapolis, they knew through their own bodies, measured in hunger and discomfort in the '30s and '40s when they would stop at remote places to buy land and borrow money, sensing in themselves the hunger that would one day be upon the place. People were wary and Howard had trouble borrowing (her $100,000 had perhaps been the key) but invariably he was right. Howard knew the land, Mildred thought, the way the Indians must have known it. There were even spots along the way where the earth itself seemed to make men stop. Howard had a sixth sense that would sometimes lead them from the main roads to, say, a dark green field in Iowa or Kansas. Howard, who might have seemed asleep, would rap with his knuckles on the Plexiglas, causing the knowing Otis to bring the car to such a quick stop that Millie almost flew into her filing cabinet. And before the emergency brake had settled into its final prong, Howard Johnson was into the field and after the scent. While Millie and Otis waited, he would walk it out slowly. Sometimes he would sit down, disappearing in a field of long and tangled weeds, or he might find a large smooth rock to sit on while he felt some secret vibration from the place. Turning his back to Millie, he would mark the spot with his urine or break some of the clayey earth in his strong pink hands, sifting it like flour for a delicate recipe. She had actually seen him chew the grass, getting down on all fours like an animal and biting the tops without pulling the entire blade from the soil. At times he ran in a slow jog as far as his aging legs would carry him. Whenever he slipped out of sight behind the uneven terrain, Millie felt him in danger, felt that something alien might be there to resist the civilizing instinct of Howard Johnson. Once when Howard had been out of sight for more than an hour and did not respond to their frantic calls, Millie sent Otis into the field and in desperation flagged a passing car.

"Howard Johnson is lost in that field," she told the surprised driver. "He went in to look for a new location and we can't find him now."

"The restaurant Howard Johnson?" the man asked.

"Yes. Help us please."

The man drove off, leaving Millie to taste in his exhaust fumes the barbarism of an ungrateful public. Otis found Howard asleep in a field of light blue wild flowers. He had collapsed from the exertion of his run. Millie brought water to him, and when he felt better, right there in the field, he ate his scoop of vanilla on the very spot where three years later they opened the first fully air-conditioned motel in the world. When she stopped to think about it, Millie knew they were more than businessmen, they were pioneers.

* * *

And once, while on her own, she had the feeling too. In 1951 when she visited the Holy Land there was an inkling of what Howard must have felt all the time. It happened without any warning on a bus crowded with tourists and resident Arabs on their way to the Dead Sea. Past ancient Sodom the bus creaked and bumped, down, down, toward the lowest point on earth, when suddenly in the midst of the crowd and her stomach queasy with the motion of the bus, Mildred Bryce experienced an overwhelming calm. A light brown patch of earth surrounded by a few pale desert rocks overwhelmed her perception, seemed closer to her than the Arab lady in the black flowered dress pushing her basket against Millie at that very moment. She wanted to stop the bus. Had she been near the door she might have actually jumped, so strong was her sensitivity to that barren spot in the endless desert. Her whole body ached for it as if in unison, bone by bone. Her limbs tingled, her breath came in short gasps, the sky rolled out of the bus windows and obliterated her view. The Arab lady spat on the floor and moved a suspicious eye over a squirming Mildred.

When the bus stopped at the Dead Sea, the Arabs and tourists rushed to the soupy brine clutching damaged limbs, while Millie pressed twenty dollars American into the dirty palm of a cab-driver who took her back to the very place where the music of her body began once more as sweetly as the first time. While the incredulous driver waited, Millie walked about the place wishing Howard were there to understand her new understanding of his kind of process. There was nothing there, absolutely nothing but pure bliss. The sun beat her like a wish, the air was hot and stale as a Viennese bathhouse, and yet Mildred felt peace and rest there, and as her cab bill mounted she actually did rest in the miserable barren desert of an altogether unsatisfactory land. When the driver, wiping the sweat from his neck, asked, "Meesez . . . pleeze. Why American woman wants Old Jericho in such kind of heat?" When he said "Jericho," she understood that this was a place where men had always stopped. In dim antiquity Jacob had perhaps watered a flock here, and not far away Lot's wife paused to scan for the last time the city of her youth. Perhaps Mildred now stood where Abraham had been visited by a vision and, making a rock his pillow, had first put the ease into the earth. Whatever it was, Millie knew from her own experience that rest was created here by historical precedent. She tried to buy that piece of land, going as far as King Hussein's secretary of the interior. She imagined a Palestinian HJ with an orange roof angling toward Sodom, a seafood restaurant, and an oasis of fresh fruit. But the land was in dispute between Israel and Jordan, and even King Hussein, who expressed admiration for Howard Johnson, could not sell to Millie the place of her comfort.

That was her single visionary moment, but sharing them with Howard was almost as good. And to end all this, to finally stay in her eighteenth-floor Santa Monica penthouse, where the Pacific dived into California, this seemed to Mildred a paltry conclusion to an adventurous life. Her doctor said it was not so serious, she had a bleeding ulcer and must watch her diet. The prognosis was, in fact, excellent. But Mildred, fifty-six and alone in California, found the doctor less comforting than most of the rest stops she had experienced.

III

California, right after the Second War, was hardly a civilized place for travelers. Millie, HJ, and Otis had a twelve-cylinder '47 Lincoln and snaked along five days between Sacramento and Los Angeles. "Comfort, comfort," said HJ as he surveyed the redwood forest and the bubbly surf while it slipped away from Otis, who had rolled his trousers to chase the ocean away during a stop near San Francisco. Howard Johnson was contemplative in California. They had never been in the West before. Their route, always slightly new, was yet bound by Canada, where a person couldn't get a tax break, and roughly by the Mississippi as a western frontier. Their journeys took them up the eastern seaboard and through New England to the early reaches of the Midwest, stopping at the plains of Wisconsin and the cool crisp edge of Chicago where two HJ lodges twinkled at the lake.

One day in 1947 while on the way from Chicago to Cairo, Illinois, HJ looked long at the green relief maps. While Millie kept busy with her filing, HJ loosened the tape and placed the map across his soft round knees. The map jiggled and sagged, the Mid- and Southwest hanging between his legs. When Mildred finally noticed that look, he had been staring at the map for perhaps fifteen minutes, brooding over it, and Millie knew something was in the air.

HJ looked at that map the way some people looked down from an airplane trying to pick out the familiar from the colorful mass receding beneath them. Howard Johnson's eye flew over the land—over the Tetons, over the Sierra Nevada, over the long thin gouge of the Canyon flew his gaze—charting his course by rest stops the way an antique mariner might have gazed at the stars.

"Millie," he said just north of Carbondale, "Millie . . ." He looked toward her, saw her fingers engaged and her thumbs circling each other in anticipation. He looked at Millie and saw that she saw what he saw. "Millie"—HJ raised his right arm and its shadow spread across the continent like a prophecy—"Millie, what if we turn right at Cairo and go that way?" California, already peeling on the green map, balanced on HJ's left knee like a happy child.

Twenty years later Mildred settled in her eighteenth-floor apartment in the building owned by Lawrence Welk. Howard was in New York, Otis and the car waited in Arizona. The pain did not return as powerfully as it had appeared that night in Albuquerque, but it hurt with dull regularity and an occasional streak of dark blood from her bowels kept her mind on it even on painless days.

Directly beneath her gaze were the organized activities of the golden-age groups, tiny figures playing bridge or shuffleboard or looking out at the water from their benches as she sat on her sofa and looked out at them and the fluffy ocean. Mildred did not regret family life. The HJ houses were her offspring. She had watched them blossom from the rough youngsters of the '40s with steam heat and even occasional kitchenettes into cool mature adults with king-sized beds, color TVs, and room service. Her late years were spent comfortably in the modern houses just as one might enjoy in age the benefits of a child's prosperity. She regretted only that it was probably over.

* * *

But she did not give up completely until she received a personal letter one day telling her that she was eligible for burial insurance until age eighty. A $1000 policy would guarantee a complete and dignified service. Millie crumpled the advertisement, but a few hours later called her Los Angeles lawyer. As she suspected, there were no plans, but as the executor of the estate he would assume full responsibility, subject of course to her approval.

"I'll do it myself," Millie had said, but she could not bring herself to do it. The idea was too alien. In more than forty years Mildred had not gone a day without a shower and change of underclothing. Everything about her suggested order and precision. Her fingernails were shaped so that the soft meat of the tips could stroke a typewriter without damaging the apex of a nail, her arch slid over a 6B shoe like an egg in a shell, and never in her adult life did Mildred recall having vomited. It did not seem right to suddenly let all this sink into the dark earth of Forest Lawn because some organ or other developed a hole as big as a nickel. It was not right and she wouldn't do it. Her first idea was to stay in the apartment, to write it into the lease if necessary. She had the lawyer make an appointment for her with Mr. Welk's management firm, but canceled it the day before. "They will just think I'm crazy," she said aloud to herself, "and they'll bury me anyway."

She thought of cryonics while reading a biography of William Chesebrough, the man who invented petroleum jelly. Howard had known him and often mentioned that his own daily ritual of the scoop of vanilla was like old Chesebrough's two teaspoons of Vaseline every day. Chesebrough lived to be ninety. In the biography it said that after taking the daily dose of Vaseline, he drank three cups of green tea to melt everything down, rested for twelve minutes, and then felt fit as a young man, even in his late eighties. When he died they froze his body and Millie had her idea. The Vaseline people kept him in a secret laboratory somewhere near Cleveland and claimed he was in better condition than Lenin, whom the Russians kept hermetically sealed, but at room temperature.

In the phone book she found the Los Angeles Cryonic Society and asked it to send her information. It all seemed very clean. The cost was $200 a year for maintaining the cold. She sent the pamphlet to her lawyer to be sure that the society was legitimate. It wasn't much money, but, still, if they were charlatans, she didn't want them to take advantage of her even if she would never know about it. They were aboveboard, the lawyer said. "The interest on a ten-thousand-dollar trust fund would pay about five hundred a year," the lawyer said, "and they only charge two hundred dollars. Still, who knows what the cost might be in say two hundred years?" To be extra safe, they put $25,000 in trust for eternal maintenance, to be eternally overseen by Longstreet, Williams, and their eternal heirs. When it was arranged, Mildred felt better than she had in weeks.

## IV

Four months to the day after she had left Howard at the Los Angeles International Airport, he returned for Mildred without the slightest warning. She was in her housecoat and had not even washed the night cream from her cheeks when she saw through the viewing space in her door the familiar long pink jowls, even longer in the distorted glass.

"Howard," she gasped, fumbling with the door, and in an instant he was there picking her up as he might a child or an ice-cream cone while her tears fell like dandruff on his blue suit. While Millie sobbed into his soft padded shoulder, HJ told her the good news. "I'm chairman emeritus of the board now. That means no more New York responsibilities. They still have to listen to me because we hold the majority of the stock, but Howard Junior and Keyes will take care of the business. Our main job is new home-owned franchises. And, Millie, guess where we're going first?"

So overcome was Mildred that she could not hold back her sobs even to guess. Howard Johnson put her down, beaming pleasure through his old bright eyes. "Florida," HJ said, then slowly repeated it, "Flor-idda, and guess what we're going to do?"

"Howard," Millie said, swiping at her tears with the filmy lace cuffs of her dressing gown, "I'm so surprised I don't know what to say. You could tell me we're going to the moon and I'd believe you. Just seeing you again has brought back all my hope." They came out of the hallway and sat on the sofa that looked out over the Pacific. HJ, all pink, kept his hands on his knees like paper-weights.

"Millie, you're almost right. I can't fool you about anything and never could. We're going down near where they launch the rockets from. I've heard . . ." HJ leaned toward the kitchen as if to check for spies. He looked at the stainless-steel-and-glass table, at the built-in avocado appliances, then leaned his large moist lips toward Mildred's ear. "Walt Disney is planning right this minute a new Disneyland down there. They're trying to keep it a secret, but his brother Roy bought options on thousands of acres. We're going down to buy as much as we can as close in as we can." Howard sparkled. "Millie, don't you see, it's a sure thing."

After her emotional outburst at seeing Howard again, a calmer Millie felt a slight twitch in her upper stomach and in the midst of her joy was reminded of another sure thing.

They would be a few weeks in Los Angeles anyway. Howard wanted to thoroughly scout out the existing Disneyland, so Millie had some time to think it out. She could go, as her heart directed her, with HJ to Florida and points beyond. She could take the future as it happened like a Disneyland ride or she could listen to the dismal eloquence of her ulcer and try to make the best arrangements she could. Howard and Otis would take care of her to the end, there were no doubts about that, and the end would be the end. But if she stayed in this apartment, sure of the arrangements for later, she would miss whatever might still be left before the end. Mildred wished there were some clergyman she could consult, but she had never attended a church and believed in no religious doctrine. Her father had been a firm atheist to the very moment of his office suicide, and she remained a passive nonbeliever. Her theology was the order of her own life. Millie had never deceived herself; in spite of her riches all she truly owned was her life, a pocket of habits in the burning universe. But the habits were careful and clean and they were best represented in the body that was she. Freezing her remains was the closest image she could conjure of eternal life. It might not be eternal and it surely would not be life, but that damp, musty feel, that odor she smelled on herself after the pain, that could be avoided, and who knew what else might be saved from the void for a small initial investment and $200 a year. And if you did not believe in a soul, was there not every reason to preserve a body?

* * *

Mrs. Albert of the Cryonic Society welcomed Mildred to a tour of the premises. "See it while you can," she cheerfully told the group (Millie, two men, and a boy with notebook and Polaroid camera). Mrs. Albert, a big woman perhaps in her mid-sixties, carried a face heavy in flesh. Perhaps once the skin had been tight around her long chin and pointed cheekbones, but having lost its spring, the skin merely hung at her neck like a patient animal waiting for the rest of her to join in the decline. From the way she took the concrete stairs down to the vault, it looked as if the wait would be long. "I'm not ready for the freezer yet. I tell every group I take down here, it's gonna be a long time until they get me." Millie believed her. "I may not be the world's smartest cookie"—Mrs. Albert looked directly at Millie—"but a bird in the hand is the only bird I know, huh? That's why when it does come . . . Mrs. A is going to be right here in this facility, and you better believe it. Now, Mr. King on your left"—she pointed to a capsule that looked like a large bullet to Millie—"Mr. King is the gentleman who took me on my first tour, cancer finally but had everything perfectly ready and I would say he was in prime cooling state within seconds and I believe that if they ever cure cancer, and you know they will the way they do most everything nowadays, old Mr. King may be back yet. If anyone got down to low-enough temperature immediately it would be Mr. King." Mildred saw the boy write "Return of the King" in his notebook. "Over here is Mr. and Mizz Winkleman, married sixty years, and went off within a month of each other, a lovely, lovely couple."

While Mrs. Albert continued her necrology and posed for a photo beside the Winklemans, Millie took careful note of the neon-lit room filled with bulletlike capsules. She watched the cool breaths of the group gather like flowers on the steel and vanish without dimming the bright surface. The capsules stood in straight lines with ample walking space between them. To Mrs. Albert they were friends, to Millie it seemed as if she were in a furniture store of the Scandinavian type where elegance is suggested by the absence of material, where straight lines of steel, wood, and glass indicate that relaxation too requires some taste and is not an indifferent sprawl across any soft object that happens to be nearby.

Cemeteries always bothered Millie, but here she felt none of the dread she had expected. She averted her eyes from the cluttered graveyards they always used to pass at the tips of cities in the early days. Fortunately, the superhighways twisted traffic into the city and away from those desolate marking places where used-car lots and the names of famous hotels inscribed on barns often neighbored the dead. Howard had once commented that never in all his experience did he have an intuition of a good location near a cemetery. You could put a lot of things there, you could put up a bowling alley, or maybe even a theater, but never a motel, and Millie knew he was right. He knew where to put his houses but it was Millie who knew how. From that first orange roof angling toward the east, the HJ design and the idea had been Millie's. She had not invented the motel, she had changed it from a place where you had to be to a place where you wanted to be. Perhaps, she thought, the Cryonic Society was trying to do the same for cemeteries.

When she and Howard had started their travels, the old motel courts huddled like so many dark graves around the stone marking of the highway. And what traveler coming into one of those dingy cabins could watch the watery rust dripping from his faucet without thinking of everything he was missing by being a traveler . . . his two-stall garage, his wife small in the half-empty bed, his children with hair the color of that rust. Under the orange Howard Johnson roof all this changed. For about the same price you were redeemed from the road. Headlights did not dazzle you on the foam mattress and percale sheets, your sanitized glasses and toilet appliances sparkled like the mirror behind them. The room was not just there, it awaited you, courted your pleasure, sat like a young bride outside the walls of the city wanting only to please you, you only you on the smoothly pressed sheets, your friend, your one-night destiny.

As if it were yesterday, Millie recalled right there in the cryonic vault the moment when she had first thought the thought that made Howard Johnson Howard Johnson's. And when she told Howard her decision that evening after cooking a cheese soufflé and risking a taste of wine, it was that memory she invoked for both of them, the memory of a cool autumn day in the '30s when a break in their schedule found Millie with a free afternoon in New Hampshire, an afternoon she had spent at the farm of a man who had once been her teacher and remembered her after ten years. Otis drove her out to Robert Frost's farm, where the poet made for her a lunch of scrambled eggs and 7 Up. Millie and Robert Frost talked mostly about the farm, about the cold winter he was expecting and the autumn apples they picked from the trees. He was not so famous then, his hair was only streaked with gray as Howard's was, and she told the poet about what she and Howard were doing, about what she felt about being on the road in America, and Robert Frost said he hadn't been that much but she sounded like she knew and he believed she might be able to accomplish something. He did not remember the poem she wrote in his class but that didn't matter.

"Do you remember, Howard, how I introduced you to him? Mr. Frost, this is Mr. Johnson. I can still see the two of you shaking hands there beside the car. I've always been proud that I introduced you to one another." Howard Johnson nodded his head at the memory, seemed as nostalgic as Millie while he sat in her apartment learning why she would not go to Florida to help bring Howard Johnson's to the new Disneyland.

"And after we left his farm, Howard, remember? Otis took the car in for servicing and left us with some sandwiches on the top of a hill overlooking a town, I don't even remember which one, maybe we never knew the name of it. And we stayed on that hilltop while the sun began to set in New Hampshire. I felt so full of poetry and"—she looked at Howard—"of love, Howard, only about an hour's drive from Robert Frost's farmhouse. Maybe it was just the way we felt then, but I think the sun set differently that night, filtering through the clouds like a big paintbrush making the top of the town all orange. And suddenly I thought what if the tops of our houses were that kind of orange, what a world it would be, Howard, and my God, that orange stayed until the last drop of light was left in it. I didn't feel the cold up there even though it took Otis so long to get back to us. The feeling we had about that orange, Howard, that was ours and that's what I've tried to bring to every house, the way we felt that night. Oh, it makes me sick to think of Colonel Sanders, and Big Boy, and Holiday Inn, and Best Western . . ."

"It's all right, Millie, it's all right." Howard patted her heaving back. Now that he knew about her ulcer and why she wanted to stay behind, the mind that had conjured butterfly shrimp and twenty-eight flavors set himself a new project. He contemplated

Millie sobbing in his lap the way he contemplated prime acreage. There was so little of her, less than one hundred pounds, yet without her Howard Johnson felt himself no match for the wily Disneys gathering near the moonport.

He left her in all her sad resignation that evening, left her thinking she had to give up what remained here to be sure of the proper freezing. But Howard Johnson had other ideas. He did not cancel the advance reservations made for Mildred Bryce along the route to Florida, nor did he remove her filing cabinet from the limousine. The man who hosted a nation and already kept one freezer in his car merely ordered another, this one designed according to cryonic specifications and presented to Mildred housed in a twelve-foot orange U-Haul trailer connected to the rear bumper of the limousine.

"Everything's here," he told the astonished Millie, who thought Howard had left the week before, "everything is here and you'll never have to be more than seconds away from it. It's exactly like a refrigerated truck." Howard Johnson opened the rear door of the U-Haul as proudly as he had ever dedicated a motel. Millie's steel capsule shone within, surrounded by an array of chemicals stored on heavily padded rubber shelves. The California sun was on her back, but her cold breath hovered visibly within the U-Haul. No tears came to Mildred now; she felt relief much as she had felt it that afternoon near ancient Jericho. On Santa Monica Boulevard, in front of Lawrence Welk's apartment building, Mildred Bryce confronted her immortality, a gift from the ice-cream king, another companion for the remainder of her travels. Howard Johnson had turned away, looking toward the ocean. To his blue back and patriarchal white hairs, Mildred said, "Howard, you can do anything," and closing the doors of the U-Haul, she joined the host of the highways, a man with two portable freezers, ready now for the challenge of Disney World.

# BARRY HANNAH
## (1942– )

If one tradition of Southern fiction is humanist and centered on family and relationships, the other explores the underside of violence and nihilism. It is this second tradition that Barry Hannah's fiction follows—an energetic, often surreal, treatment of Southern low life, grim, grotesque, and grisly comic.

Hannah was born in Meridian, Mississippi, where his father was an insurance agent. He completed a B.A. in premed studies in 1964 at Mississippi College, and went on to the University of Arkansas for an M.A. in English in 1966 and an M.F.A. in creative writing in 1967. He has taught at a number of colleges and universities, including Clemson University in South Carolina, Middlebury College in Vermont, the University of Alabama, and the University of Mississippi. He worked as a screenwriter with the filmmaker Robert Altman in 1980.

Hannah's novels include *Geronimo Rex* (1972), *Nightwatchmen* (1973),

*Ray* (1981), *The Tennis Handsome* (1983), *Boomerang* (1989), *Never Die* (1991), and *High Lonesome* (1996). His story collections include *Airships* (1978), *Captain Maximus* (1985), and *Bats Out of Hell* (1993).

# Midnight and I'm Not Famous Yet

I WAS walking around Gon one night, and this C-man—I saw him open the window, and there was a girl in back of him, so I thought it was all right—peeled down on me and shot the back heel off my boot. Nearest I came to getting mailed home when I was there. A jeep came by almost instantly with a thirty cal mounted, couple of allies in it. I pointed over to the window. They shot out about a box and a half on the apartment, just about burned out the dark slot up there. As if the dude was hanging around digging the weather after he shot at me. There were shrieks in the night, etc. But then a man opened the bottom door and started running in the street. This ARVN fellow knocked the shit out of his buddy's head turning the gun to zap the running man. Then I saw something as the dude hit a light: he was fat. I never saw a fat Cong. So I screamed out in Vietnamese. He didn't shoot. I took out my machine pistol and ran after the man, who was up the street by now, and I was hobbling without a heel on my left boot.

Some kind of warm nerve sparklers were getting all over me. I believe in magic, because, million-to-one odds, it was Ike "Tubby" Wooten, from Redwood, a town just north of Vicksburg. He was leaning on a rail, couldn't run anymore. He was wearing the uniform of our Army with a patch on it I didn't even know what was. Old Tubby would remember me. I was the joker at our school. I once pissed in a Dixie cup and eased three drops of it on the library radiator. But Tubby was so serious, reading some photo magazine. He peeped up and saw me do it, then looked down quickly. When the smell came over the place, he asked me, Why? What do you want? What profit is there in that? I guess I just giggled. Sometimes around midnight I'd wake up and think of his questions, and it disturbed me that there was no answer. I giggled my whole youth away. Then I joined the Army. So I thought it was fitting I'd play a Nelda on him now. A Nelda was invented by a corporal when they massacred a patrol up north on a mountain and he was the only one left. The NVA ran all around him and he had this empty rifle hanging on him. They spared him.

"I'm a virgin! Spare me!"

"You, holding the gun? Did you say you were a virgin?" said poor Tubby, trying to get air.

"I am a virgin," I said, which was true, but hoping to get a laugh, anyway.

"And a Southern virgin. A captain. Please to God, don't shoot me," that fat boy said. "I was cheating on my wife for the first time. The penalty shouldn't be death."

"Why'd you run from the house, Tubby?"

"You know me." Up the street they had searchlights moved up all over the apartment house. They shot about fifty rounds into the house. They were shooting tracers now. It must've lit up my face; then a spotlight went by us.

"Bobby Smith," said Tubby. "My God, I thought you were God."

"I'm not. But it seems holy. Here we are looking at each other."

"Aw, Bobby, they were three beautiful girls. I'd never have done the thing with one, but there were *three.*" He was a man with a small pretty face laid around by three layers of jowl and chin. "I heard the machine gun and the guilt struck me. I had to get out. So I just ran."

"Why're you in Nam, anyway?"

"I joined. I wasn't getting anything done but being in love with my wife. That wasn't doing America any good."

"What's that patch on you?"

"Photography." He lifted his hands to hold an imaginary camera. "I'm with the Big Red. I've done a few things out of helicopters."

"You want to see a ground unit? With me. Or does Big Red own you?"

"I have no idea. There hasn't been much to shoot. Some smoking villages. A fire in a bamboo forest. I'd like to see a face."

"You got any pictures of Vicksburg?"

"Oh, well, a few I brought over."

The next day I found out he was doing idlework and Big Red didn't care where he was, so I got him over in my unit. I worried about his weight, etc., and the fact he might be killed. But the boys liked a movie-cameraist being along and I wanted to see the pictures from Vicksburg. It was nice to have Tubby alongside. He was hometown, such as he was. Before we flew out north, he showed me what he had. There was a fine touch in his pictures. There was a cute little Negro on roller skates, and an old woman on a porch, a little boy sleeping in a speedboat with the river in the background. Then there was a blurred picture of his wife naked, just moving through the kitchen, nothing sexy. The last picture was the best. It was John Whitelaw about to crack a golf ball. Tubby had taken it at Augusta, at the Masters. I used to live about five houses away from the Whitelaws. John had his mouth open and his arms, the forearm muscles, were bulked up plain as wires.

John was ten years older than me, but I knew about him. John Whitelaw was our only celebrity since the Civil War. In the picture he wore spectacles. It struck me as something deep, brave, mighty and, well, modern; he had to have the eyeglasses on him to see the mighty thing he was about to do. Maybe I sympathized too much, since I have to wear glasses too, but I thought this picture was worthy of a statue. Tubby had taken it in a striking gray-and-white grain. John seemed to be hitting under a heroic deficiency. You could see the sweat droplets on his neck. His eyes were in an agony. But the thing that got me was that John Whitelaw *cared* so much about what he was doing. It made me love America to know he was in it, and I hadn't loved anything for nigh three years then. Tubby was talking about all this "our country" eagle and stars mooky and had seen all the war movies coming over on the boat. I never saw a higher case of fresh and crazy in my life.

But the picture of John at Augusta, it moved me. It was a man at work and play at the same time, doing his damnedest. And Whitelaw was a beautiful man. They pass that term "beautiful" around like pennies nowadays, but I saw him in the flesh once. It was fall in Baton Rouge, around the campus of LSU. He was getting out of a car with a gypsyish girl on his hand. I was ten, I guess, and he was twenty. We were down for a ball game, Mississippi vs. Louisiana, a classic that makes you goo-goo eyed when you're a full-grown man if your heart's in Dixie, etc. At ten, it's Ozville. So in the middle of it, this feeling, I saw Whitelaw and his woman. My dad stopped the car.

"Wasn't that Johnny Whitelaw?" he asked my grandfather.

"You mean that little peacock who left football for golf? He ought to be quarterbacking Ole Miss right now. It wouldn't be no contest," said my grandfather.

I got my whole idea of what a woman should look like that day . . . and what a man should be. The way John Whitelaw looked, it sort of rebuked yourself ever hoping to call yourself a man. The girl he was with woke up my clammy little dreams about, not even sex, but the perfect thing—it was something like her. As for Whitelaw, his face was curled around by that wild hair the color of beer; his chest was deep, just about to bust out of that collar and bow tie.

"That girl he had, she had a drink in her hand. You could hardly see her for her hair," said my grandfather.

"Johnny got him something Cajun," said my father.

Then my grandfather turned around, looking at me like I was a crab who could say a couple of words. "You look like your mother, but you got gray eyes. What's wrong? You have to take a leak?"

Nothing was wrong with me. I'd just seen John Whitelaw and his girl, that was all.

* * *

Tubby had jumped a half-dozen times at Fort Bragg, but he had that heavy box harnessed on him now and I knew he was going down fast and better know how to hit. I explained to him. I went off the plane four behind him, cupping a joint. I didn't want Tubby seeing me smoking grass, but it's just about the only way to get down. If the Cong saw the plane, you'd fall into a barbecue. They've killed a whole unit before, using shotguns and flame bullets, just like your ducks floating in. You hear a lot of noise going in with a whole unit in the air like this. We start shooting about a hundred feet from ground. If you ever hear one bullet pass you, you get sick thinking there might be a lot of them. All you can do is point your gun down and shoot it all out. You can't reload. You never hit anything. There's a sharpshooter, McIntire, who killed a C shooting from his chute, but that's unlikely. They've got you like a gallery of rabbits if they're down there.

I saw Tubby sinking fast over the wrong part of the field. I had two chutes out, so I cut one off and dropped over toward him, pulling on the left lines so hard I almost didn't have a chute at all for a while. I got level with him and he looked over, pointing down. He was doing his arm up and down. Could have been farmers or just curious rubbernecks down in the field, but there were about ten of them grouped up together, holding things. They weren't shooting, though. I was carrying an experimental gun, me and about ten of my boys. It was a big, light thing; really, it was just a launcher. There were five shells in it, bigger than shotgun shells. If you shot one of them, it was supposed to explode on impact and burn out everything in a twenty-five-yard radius. It was a mean little mother of phosphorus, is what it was. I saw the boys shooting them down into the other side of the field. This stuff would take down a whole tree and you'd chute into a quiet smoking bare area.

I don't know. I don't like a group waiting on me when I jump out of a plane. I almost zapped them, but they weren't throwing anything up. Me and Tubby hit the ground about the same time. They were farmers. I talked to them. They said there were three Cong with them until we were about a hundred feet over. The Cong knew we had the phosphorus shotgun and showed ass, loping out to the woods fifty yards to the north when me and Tubby were coming in.

Tubby took some film of the farmers. All of them had thin chin beards and soft hands because their wives did most of the work. They essentially just lay around and were hung with philosophy, and actually were pretty happy. Nothing had happened around here till we jumped in. These were fresh people. I told them to get everybody out of the huts because we were going to have a thing in the field. It was a crisis point. A huge army of NVA was coming down and they just couldn't avoid us if they wanted to have any run of the valley five miles south. We were there to harass the front point of the army, whatever it was like.

"We're here to check their advance," Tubby told the farmers.

Then we all collected in the woods, five hundred and fifty souls, scared out of mind. What we had going was we knew the NVA general bringing them down was not too bright. He went to the Sorbonne and we had this report from his professor: "Li Dap speaks French very well and had studied Napoleon before he got to me. He knows Robert Lee and the strategy of Jeb Stuart, whose daring circles around an immense army captured his mind. Li Dap wants to be Jeb Stuart. I cannot imagine him in command of more than five hundred troops."

And what we knew stood up. Li Dap had tried to circle left with twenty thousand and got the hell kicked out of him by idle Navy guns sitting outside Gon. He just wasn't very bright. He had half his army climbing around these bluffs, no artillery or air force with them, and it was New Year's Eve for our side.

"So we're here just to kill the edge of their army?" said Tubby.

"That's what I'm here for, why I'm elected. We kill more C's than anybody else in the Army."

"But what if they take a big run at you, all of them?" said Tubby.

"There'll be lots of cooking."

We went out in the edge of the woods and I glassed the field. It was almost night. I saw two tanks come out of the other side and our pickets running back. Pock, pock, pock from the tanks. Then you saw this white glare on one tank where somebody on our team had laid on with one of the phosphorus shotguns. It got white and throbbing, like a little star, and the gun wilted off of it. The other tank ran off a gully into a hell of a cow pond. You wouldn't have known it was that deep. It went underwater over the gun, and they let off the cannon when they went under, raising the water in a spray. It was the silliest-looking thing. Some of them got out and a sergeant yelled for me to come up. It was about a quarter mile out there. Tubby got his camera, and we went out with about fifteen troops.

At the edge of the pond, looking into flashlights, two tankmen sat, one tiny, the other about my size. They were wet, and the big guy was mad. Lot of the troops were chortling, etc. It was awfully damned funny, if you didn't happen to be one of the C-men in the tank.

"Of all the fuck-ups. This is truly saddening." The big guy was saying something like that. I took a flashlight and looked him over. Then I didn't believe it. I told Tubby to get a shot of the big cursing one. Then they brought them on back. I told the boys to tie up the big one and carry him in.

I sat on the ground, talking to Tubby.

"It's so quiet. You'd think they'd be shelling us," he said.

"We're spread out too good. They don't have much ammo now. They really galloped down here. That's the way Li Dap does it. Their side's got big trouble now. And, Tubby, me and you are famous."

"Me, what?"

"You took his picture. You can get some more, more arty angles on him tomorrow."

"Him?"

"It's Li Dap himself. He was in the tank in the pond."

"No. Their general?"

"You want me to go prove it?"

We walked over. They had him tied around a tree. His hands were above his head and he was sitting down. I smelled some hash in the air. The guy who was blowing it was a boy from Detroit I really liked, and I hated to come down on him, but I really beat him up. He never got a lick in. I kicked his rump when he was crawling away and some friends picked him up. You can't have lighting up that shit at night on the ground. Li Dap was watching the fight, still cursing.

"Asshole of the mountains." He was saying something like that. "Fortune's ninny."

"Hi, General. My French isn't too good. You speak English. Honor us."

He wouldn't say anything.

"You have a lot of courage, running out front with the tanks." There were some snickers in the bush, but I cut them out quick. We had a real romantic here and I didn't want him laughed at. He wasn't hearing much, though. About that time two of their rockets flashed into the woods. They went off in the treetops and scattered.

"It was worthy of Patton," I said. "You had some bad luck. But we're glad you made it alive."

"Kiss my ass."

"You want your hands free? Oliver, get his ropes off the tree." The guy I beat up cut him off the tree.

"You scared us very deeply. How many tanks do you have over there?"

"Nonsense," he said.

"What do you have except for a few rockets?"

"I had no credence in the phosphorus gun."

"Your men saw us use them when we landed."

"I had no credence."

"So you just came out to see."

"I say to them never to fear the machine when the cause is just. To throw oneself past the technology tricks of the monsters and into his soft soul."

"And there you will win, huh?"

"Of course. It is our country." He smiled at me. "It's relative to your war in the nineteenth century. The South had slavery. The North must purge it so that it is a healthy region of our country."

"You were out in the tank as an example to your men?"

"Yes!"

All this hero needed was a plumed hat.

"Sleep well," I said, and told Oliver to get him a blanket and feed him, and feed the tiny gunner with him.

* * *

When we got back to my dump, I walked away for a while, not wanting to talk with Tubby. I started crying. It started with these hard sobs coming up like rocks in my throat. I started looking out at forever, across the field. They shot up three more rockets from the woods below the hill. I waited for the things to land on us. They fell on the tops of trees, nothing near me, but there was some howling off to the right. Somebody had got some shrapnel.

I'd killed so many gooks. I'd killed them with machine guns, mortars, howitzers, knives, wire, me and my boys. My boys loved me. They were lying all around me, laying this great cloud of trust on me. The picture of John Whitelaw about to hit that ball at Augusta was jammed in my head. There was such care in his eyes, and it was only a golf ball, a goddamned piece of nothing. But it was wonderful and peaceful. Nobody was being killed. Whitelaw had the right. He had the beloved American right to the pursuit of happiness. The tears were out of my jaws then. Here we shot each other up. All we had going was the pursuit of horror. It seemed to me my life had gone straight from teen-age giggling to horror. I had never had time to be but two things, a giggler and a killer.

Christ, I was crying for myself. I had nothing for the other side, understand that. North Vietnam was a land full of lousy little Commie robots, as far as I knew. A place of the worst propaganda and hypocrisy. You should have read some of their agitprop around Gon, talking about freedom and throwing off the yoke, etc. The gooks went for Communism because they were so ignorant and had nothing to lose. The South Vietnamese, too. I couldn't believe we had them as allies. They were such a pretty and uniformly indecent people. I once saw a little taxi boy, a kid is all, walk into a Medevac with one arm and a hand blown off by a mine he'd picked up. These housewives were walking behind him in the street, right in the middle of Gon. Know what they were doing? They were laughing. They thought it was the most hysterical misadventure they'd ever seen. These people were on our side. These were our friends and lovers. That happened early when I got there. I was a virgin when I got to Nam and stayed a virgin, through a horde of B-girls, the most base and luscious-lipped hustlers. Because I did not want to mingle with this race.

In an ARVN hospital tent you see the hurt officers lined up in front of a private who's holding in his guts with his hands. They'll treat the officer with a bad pimple before they treat the dying private. We're supposed to be shaking hands with these people. Why can't we be fighting for some place like England? When you train yourself to blow gooks away, like I did, something happens, some kind of popping returning dream of murder-with-a-smile.

I needed away. I was sick. In another three months I'd be zapping orphanages.

"Bobby, are you all right?" said Tubby, waddling out to the tree I was hanging on.

"I shouldn't ever've seen that picture of John Whitelaw. I shouldn't've."

"Do you really think we'll be famous?" Tubby got an enchanted look on him, sort of a dumb angel look in that small pretty face amid the fat rolls. It was about midnight.

There was a fine Southern moon lighting up the field. You could see every piece of straw out there. Tubby, by my ass, had the high daze on him. He'd stepped out here in the boonies and put down his foot in Ozville.

"This'll get me Major, anyhow. Sure. Fame. Both of us," I said.

Tubby said: "I tried to get nice touches in with the light coming over his face. These pictures could turn out awfully interesting. I was thinking about the cover of *Time* or *Newsweek.*"

"It'll change your whole life, Tubby," I said.

Tubby was just about to die for love of fate. He was shivering.

* * *

I started enjoying the field again. This time the straws were waving. It was covered with rushing little triangles, these sort of toiling dots. Our side opened up. All the boys came up to join within a minute and it was a sheet of lightning rolling back and forth along the outside of the woods. I could see it all while I was walking back to the radio. I mean humping low. Tubby must've been walking straight up. He took something big right in the square of his back. It rolled him up twenty feet in front of me. He was dead and smoking when I made it to him.

"C'mon, I've got to get the pictures," he said.

I think he was already dead.

I got my phosphorus shotgun. Couldn't think of anything but the radio and getting it over how we were being hit, so we could get dragons—helicopters with fifty cals—in quick. The dragons are nice. They've got searchlights, and you put two of them over a field like we were looking at, they'd clean it out in half an hour. So I made it to the radio and the boys had already called the dragons in, everything was fine. Only we had to hold them for an hour and a half until the dragons got there. I humped up front. Every now and then you'd see somebody use one of the experimental guns. The bad thing was that it lit up the gunner too much at night, too much shine out of the muzzle. I took note of that to tell them when we got back. But the gun really smacked the gook assault. It was good for about seventy-five yards and hit with a huge circle burn about the way they said it would. The gooks' first force was knocked off. You could see men who were still burning running back through the straw, hear them screaming.

I don't remember too well. I was just loitering near the radio, a few fires out in the field, everything mainly quiet. Copters on the way. I decided to go take a look at Li Dap. I thought it was our boys around him, though I didn't know why. They were wearing green and standing up plain as day. There was Oliver, smoking a joint. His rifle was on the ground. The NVA were all around him and he hadn't even noticed. There were so many of them—twenty or so—they were clanking rifles against each other. One of them was going up behind Oliver with a bayonet, just about on him. If I'd had a carbine like usual, I could've taken the bayoneteer off and at least five of the others. Oliver and Li Dap might've ducked and survived.

But I couldn't pick and choose. I hardly even thought. The barrel of the shotgun was up and I pulled on the trigger, aiming at the bayoneteer.

I burned them all up.

Nobody even made a squeak.

There was a flare and they were gone.

Some of my boys rushed over with guns. All they were good for was stomping out the little fires on the edges.

* * *

When we got back, I handed over Tubby's pictures. The old man was beside himself over my killing a general, a captured general. He couldn't understand what kind of laxity I'd allowed to let twenty gooks come up on us like that. They thought I might have a court-martial, and I was under arrest for a week. The story got out to UPI and they were saying things like "atrocity," with my name spelled all over the column.

But it was dropped and I was pulled out and went home a lieutenant.

* * *

That's all right. I've got four hundred and two boys out there—the ones that got back—who love me and know the truth, who love me *because* they know the truth.

It's Tubby's lost fame I dream about.

The Army confiscated the roll and all his pictures. I wrote the Pentagon a letter asking for a print and waited two years here in Vicksburg without even a statement they received the note. I see his wife, who's remarried and is fat herself now, at the discount drugstore every now and then. She has the look of a kind of hopeless cheer. I got a print from the Pentagon when the war was over and it didn't matter. Li Dap looked wonderful—strained, abused and wild, his hair flying over his eyes while he's making a statement full of conviction.

It made me start thinking of faces again.

Since I've been home I've crawled in bed with almost anything that would have me. I've slept with high-school teachers, Negroes and, the other night, my own aunt. It made her smile. All those years of keeping her body in trim came to something, the big naughty surprise that the other women look for in religion, God showing up and killing their neighbors, sparing them. But she knows a lot about things and I think I'll be in love with her.

We were at the John Whitelaw vs. Whitney Maxwell play-off together. It was a piece of wonder. I felt thankful to the wind or God or whoever who brought that fine contest near enough by. When they hit the ball, the sound traveled like a rifle snap out over the bluffs. When it was impossible to hit the ball, that is exactly when they hit it.

My aunt grabbed hold of my fingers when the tension was almost up to a roar. The last two holes. Ah, John lost. I looked over the despondency of the home crowd.

Fools! Fools! I thought. Love it! Love the loss as well as the gain. Go home and dig it. Nobody was killed. We saw victory and defeat, and they were both wonderful.

# ⁂ JAYNE ANNE PHILLIPS
(1952– )

Some of Jayne Anne Phillips' short stories are experiments in what she calls "perception," but Phillips may be at her best in stories and novels that focus on families and relationships that are facing dislocation, disintegration, and loss. *Black Tickets* (1979), the collection that established her reputation, includes stories covering a gamut of sensibilities, from the abnormal to the ordinary. These stories are drawn from her observations and experiences during her own rootless wandering in the mid-1970s, when she traveled from West Virginia to California and back again.

Phillips was born in Buckhannon, West Virginia, where her father was a contractor and her mother a school teacher. She attended West Virginia University and graduated with high honors in 1974. She went to the University of Iowa for an M.F.A., which she completed in 1978. She has taught at a number of institutions in the Boston area, where she resides with her husband and family.

Phillips' major story collections are *Black Tickets* (1979) and *Fast Lanes* (1987). Her novels are *Machine Dreams* (1984), *Shelter* (1994), and *MotherKind* (2000). Her work has won numerous awards, including Pushcart prizes in 1977, 1979, and 1983.

## Souvenir

KATE ALWAYS sent her mother a card on Valentine's Day. She timed the mails from wherever she was so that the cards arrived on February 14th. Her parents had celebrated the day in some small fashion, and since her father's death six years before, Kate made a gesture of compensatory remembrance. At first, she made the cards herself: collage and pressed grass on construction paper sewn in fabric. Now she settled for art reproductions, glossy cards with blank insides. Kate wrote in them with colored inks, "You have always been my Valentine," or simply "Hey, take care of yourself." She might enclose a present as well, something small enough to fit into an envelope; a sachet, a perfumed soap, a funny tintype of a prune-faced man in a bowler hat.

This time, she forgot. Despite the garish displays of paper cupids and heart-shaped boxes in drugstore windows, she let the day nearly approach before remembering. It was too late to send anything in the mail. She called her mother long-distance at night when the rates were low.

"Mom? How are you?"

"It's you! How are *you?*" Her mother's voice grew suddenly brighter; Kate recognized a tone reserved for welcome company. Sometimes it took a while to warm up.

"I'm fine," answered Kate. "What have you been doing?"

"Well, actually I was trying to sleep."

"Sleep? You should be out setting the old hometown on fire."

"The old hometown can burn up without me tonight."

"Really? What's going on?"

"I'm running in-service training sessions for the primary teachers." Kate's mother was a school superintendent. "They're driving me batty. You'd think their brains were rubber."

"They are," Kate said. "Or you wouldn't have to train them. Think of them as a salvation, They create a need for your job."

"Some salvation. Besides, your logic is ridiculous. Just because someone needs training doesn't mean they're stupid."

"I'm just kidding. But *I'm* stupid. I forgot to send you a Valentine's card."

"You did? That's bad. I'm trained to receive one. They bring me luck."

"You're receiving a phone call instead," Kate said. "Won't that do?"

"Of course," said her mother, "but this is costing you money. Tell me quick, how are you?"

"Oh, you know. Doctoral pursuits. Doing my student trip, grooving with the professors."

"The professors? You'd better watch yourself."

"It's a joke, Mom, a joke. But what about you? Any men on the horizon?"

"No, not really. A married salesman or two asking me to dinner when they come through the office. Thank heavens I never let those things get started."

"You should do what you want to," Kate said.

"Sure," said her mother. "And where would I be then?"

"I don't know. Maybe Venezuela."

"They don't even have plumbing in Venezuela."

"Yes, but their sunsets are perfect, and the villages are full of dark passionate men in blousy shirts."

"That's your department, not mine."

"Ha," Kate said, "I wish it were my department. Sounds a lot more exciting than teaching undergraduates."

Her mother laughed. "Be careful," she said. "You'll get what you want. End up sweeping a dirt floor with a squawling baby around your neck."

"A dark baby," Kate said, "to stir up the family blood."

"Nothing would surprise me," her mother said as the line went fuzzy. Her voice was submerged in static, then surfaced. "Listen," she was saying. "Write to me. You seem so far away."

They hung up and Kate sat watching the windows of the neighboring house. The curtains were transparent and flowered and none of them matched. Silhouettes of the window frames spread across them like single dark bars. Her mother's curtains were all the same, white cotton hemmed with a ruffle, tiebacks blousing the cloth into identical shapes. From the street it looked as if the house was always in order.

Kate made a cup of strong Chinese tea, turned the lights off, and sat holding the warm cup in the dark. Her mother kept no real tea in the house, just packets of instant diabetic mixture which tasted of chemical sweetener and had a bitter aftertaste. The packets sat on the shelf next to her mother's miniature scales. The scales were white. Kate saw clearly the face of the metal dial on the front, its markings and trembling needle. Her mother weighed portions of food for meals: frozen broccoli, slices of plastic-wrapped Kraft cheese, careful chunks of roast beef. A dog-eared copy of *The Diabetic Diet* had remained propped against the salt shaker for the last two years.

Kate rubbed her forehead. Often at night she had headaches. Sometimes she wondered if there were an agent in her body, a secret in her blood making ready to work against her.

* * *

The phone blared repeatedly, careening into her sleep. Kate scrambled out of bed, naked and cold, stumbling, before she recognized the striped wallpaper of her bedroom and realized the phone was right there on the bedside table, as always. She picked up the receiver.

"Kate?" said her brother's voice. "It's Robert. Mom is in the hospital. They don't know what's wrong but she's in for tests."

"Tests? What's happened? I just talked to her last night."

"I'm not sure. She called the neighbors and they took her to the emergency room around dawn." Robert's voice still had that slight twang Kate knew was disappearing from her own. He would be calling from his insurance office, nine o'clock their time, in his thick glasses and wide, perfectly knotted tie. He was a member of the million-dollar club and his picture, tiny, the size of a postage stamp, appeared in the Mutual of Omaha magazine. His voice seemed small too over the distance. Kate felt heavy and dull. She would never make much money, and recently she had begun wearing make-up again, waking in smeared mascara as she had in high school.

"Is Mom all right?" she managed now. "How serious is it?"

"They're not sure," Robert said. "Her doctor thinks it could have been any of several things, but they're doing X rays."

"Her doctor *thinks?* Doesn't he know? Get her to someone else. There aren't any doctors in that one-horse town."

"I don't know about that," Robert said defensively. "Anyway, I can't force her. You know how she is about money."

"Money? She could have a stroke and drop dead while her doctor wonders what's wrong."

"Doesn't matter. You know you can't tell her what to do."

"Could I call her somehow?"

"No, not yet. And don't get her all worried. She's been scared enough as it is. I'll tell her what you said about getting another opinion, and I'll call you back in a few hours when I have some news. Meanwhile, she's all right, do you hear?"

The line went dead with a click and Kate walked to the bathroom to wash her face. She splashed her eyes and felt guilty about the Valentine's card. Slogans danced in her head like reprimands. *For A Special One. Dearest Mother. My Best Friend.* Despite Robert, after breakfast she would call the hospital.

* * *

She sat a long time with her coffee, waiting for minutes to pass, considering how many meals she and her mother ate alone. Similar times of day, hundreds of miles apart. Women by themselves. The last person Kate had eaten breakfast with had been someone she'd met in a bar. He was passing through town. He liked his fried eggs gelatinized in the center, only slightly runny, and Kate had studiously looked away as he ate. The night before he'd looked down from above her as he finished and she still moved under him. "You're still wanting," he'd said. "That's nice." Mornings now, Kate saw her own face in the mirror and was glad she'd forgotten his name. When she looked at her reflection from the side, she saw a faint etching of lines beside her mouth. She hadn't slept with anyone for five weeks, and the skin beneath her eyes had taken on a creamy darkness.

She reached for the phone but drew back. It seemed bad luck to ask for news, to push toward whatever was coming as though she had no respect for it.

Standing in the kitchen last summer, her mother had stirred gravy and argued with her.

"I'm thinking of your own good, not mine," she'd said. "Thinking of what you put yourself through. And how can you feel right about it? You were born here, I don't care what you say." Her voice broke and she looked, perplexed, at the broth in the pan.

"But, hypothetically," Kate continued, her own voice unaccountably shaking, "if I'm willing to endure whatever I have to, do you have a right to object? You're my mother. You're supposed to defend my choices."

"You'll have enough trouble without choosing more for yourself. Using birth control that'll ruin your insides, moving from one place to another. I can't defend your choices. I can't even defend myself against you." She wiped her eyes on a napkin.

"Why do you have to make me feel so guilty?" Kate said, fighting tears of frustration. "I'm not attacking you."

"You're not? Then who are you talking to?"

"Oh Mom, give me a break."

"I've tried to give you more than that," her mother said. "I know what your choices are saying to me." She set the steaming gravy off the stove. "You may feel very differently later on. It's just a shame I won't be around to see it."

"Oh? Where will you be?"

"Floating around on a fleecy cloud."

Kate got up to set the table before she realized her mother had already done it.

The days went by. They'd gone shopping before Kate left. Standing at the cash register in an antique shop on Main Street, they bought each other pewter candle holders. "A souvenir," her mother said. "A reminder to always be nice to yourself. If you live alone you should eat by candlelight."

"Listen," Kate said, "I eat in a heart-shaped tub with bubbles to my chin. I sleep on satin sheets and my mattress has a built-in massage engine. My overnight guests are impressed. You don't have to tell me about the solitary pleasures."

They laughed and touched hands.

"Well," her mother said. "If you like yourself, I must have done something right."

* * *

Robert didn't phone until evening. His voice was fatigued and thin. "I've moved her to the university hospital," he said. "They can't deal with it at home."

Kate waited, saying nothing. She concentrated on the toes of her shoes. They needed shining. *You never take care of anything,* her mother would say.

"She has a tumor in her head." He said it firmly, as though Kate might challenge him.

"I'll take a plane tomorrow morning," Kate answered, "I'll be there by noon."

Robert exhaled. "Look," he said, "don't even come back here unless you can keep your mouth shut and do it my way."

"Get to the point."

"The point is they believe she has a malignancy and we're not going to tell her. I almost didn't tell you." His voice faltered. "They're going to operate but if they find what they're expecting, they don't think they can stop it."

For a moment there was no sound except an oceanic vibration of distance on the wire. Even that sound grew still. Robert breathed. Kate could almost see him, in a booth at the hospital, staring straight ahead at the plastic instructions screwed to the narrow rectangular body of the telephone. It seemed to her that she was hurtling toward him.

"I'll do it your way," she said.

* * *

The hospital cafeteria was a large room full of orange Formica tables. Its southern wall was glass. Across the highway, Kate saw a small park modestly dotted with amusement rides and bordered by a narrow band of river. How odd, to build a children's park across from a medical center. The sight was pleasant in a cruel way. The rolling lawn of the little park was perfectly, relentlessly green.

Robert sat down. Their mother was to have surgery in two days.

"After it's over," he said, "they're not certain what will happen. The tumor is in a bad place. There may be some paralysis."

"What kind of paralysis?" Kate said. She watched him twist the green-edged coffee cup around and around on its saucer.

"Facial. And maybe worse."

"You've told her this?"

He didn't answer.

"Robert, what is she going to think if she wakes up and—"

He leaned forward, grasping the cup and speaking through clenched teeth. "Don't you think I thought of that?" He gripped the sides of the table and the cup rolled onto the carpeted floor with a dull thud. He seemed ready to throw the table after it, then grabbed Kate's wrists and squeezed them hard.

"You didn't drive her here," he said. "She was so scared she couldn't talk. How much do you want to hand her at once?"

Kate watched the cup sitting solidly on the nubby carpet.

"We've told her it's benign," Robert said, "that the surgery will cause complications, but she can learn back whatever is lost."

Kate looked at him. "Is that true?"

"They hope so."

"We're lying to her, all of us, more and more." Kate pulled her hands away and Robert touched her shoulder.

"What do *you* want to tell her, Kate? 'You're fifty-five and you're done for'?"

She stiffened. "Why put her through the operation at all?"

He sat back and dropped his arms, lowering his head. "Because without it she'd be in bad pain. Soon." They were silent, then he looked up. "And anyway," he said softly, "we don't *know,* do we? She may have a better chance than they think."

Kate put her hands on her face. Behind her closed eyes she saw a succession of blocks tumbling over.

They took the elevator up to the hospital room. They were alone and they stood close together. Above the door red numerals lit up, flashing. Behind the illuminated shapes droned an impersonal hum of machinery.

Then the doors opened with a sucking sound. Three nurses stood waiting with a lunch cart, identical covered trays stacked in tiers. There was a hot bland smell, like warm cardboard. One of the women caught the thick steel door with her arm and smiled. Kate looked quickly at their rubber-soled shoes. White polish, the kind that rubs off. And their legs seemed only white shapes, boneless and two-dimensional, stepping silently into the metal cage.

* * *

She looked smaller in the white bed. The chrome side rails were pulled up and she seemed powerless behind them, her dark hair pushed back from her face and her forearms delicate in the baggy hospital gown. Her eyes were different in some nearly imperceptible way; she held them wider, they were shiny with a veiled wetness. For a moment the room seemed empty of all else; there were only her eyes and the dark blossoms of the flowers on the table beside her. Red roses with pine. Everyone had sent the same thing.

Robert walked close to the bed with his hands clasped behind his back, as though afraid to touch. "Where did all the flowers come from?" he asked.

"From school, and the neighbors. And Katie." She smiled.

"FTD," Kate said. "Before I left home. I felt so bad for not being here all along."

"That's silly," said their mother. "You can hardly sit at home and wait for some problem to arise."

"Speaking of problems," Robert said, "the doctor tells me you're not eating. Do I have to urge you a little?" He sat down on the edge of the bed and shook the silverware from its paper sleeve.

Kate touched the plastic tray. "Jell-O and canned cream of chicken soup. Looks great. We should have brought you something."

"They don't *want* us to bring her anything," Robert said. "This is a hospital. And I'm sure your comments make her lunch seem even more appetizing."

"I'll eat it!" said their mother in mock dismay. "Admit they sent you in here to stage a battle until I gave in."

"I'm sorry," Kate said. "He's right."

Robert grinned. "Did you hear that? She says I'm right. I don't believe it." He pushed the tray closer to his mother's chest and made a show of tucking a napkin under her chin.

"Of course you're right, dear." She smiled and gave Kate an obvious wink.

"Yeah," Robert said, "I know you two. But seriously, you eat this. I have to go make some business calls from the motel room."

Their mother frowned. "That motel must be costing you a fortune."

"No, it's reasonable," he said. "Kate can stay for a week or two and I'll drive back and forth from home. If you think this food is bad, you should see the meals in that motel restaurant." He got up to go, flashing Kate a glance of collusion. "I'll be back after supper."

His footsteps echoed down the hallway. Kate and her mother looked wordlessly at each other, relieved. Kate looked away guiltily. Then her mother spoke, apologetic. "He's so tired," she said. "He's been with me since yesterday."

She looked at Kate, then into the air of the room. "I'm in a fix," she said. "Except for when the pain comes, it's all a show that goes on without me. I'm like an invalid, or a lunatic."

Kate moved close and touched her mother's arms. "That's all right, we're going to get you through it. Someone's covering for you at work?"

"I had to take a leave of absence. It's going to take a while afterward—"

"I know. But it's the last thing to worry about, it can't be helped."

"Like spilt milk. Isn't that what they say?"

"I don't know what they say. But why didn't you tell me? Didn't you know something was wrong?"

"Yes . . . bad headaches. Migraines, I thought, or the diabetes getting worse. I was afraid they'd start me on insulin." She tightened the corner of her mouth. "Little did I know . . ."

They heard the shuffle of slippers. An old woman stood at the open door of the room, looking in confusedly. She seemed about to speak, then moved on.

"Oh," said Kate's mother in exasperation, "shut that door, please? They let these old women wander around like refugees." She sat up, reaching for a robe. "And let's get me out of this bed."

They sat near the window while she finished eating. Bars of moted yellow banded the floor of the room. The light held a tinge of spring which seemed painful because it might vanish. They heard the rattle of the meal cart outside the closed door, and the clunk-slide of patients with aluminum walkers. Kate's mother sighed and pushed away the half-empty soup bowl.

"They'll be here after me any minute. More tests. I just want to stay with you." Her face was warm and smooth in the slanted light, lines in her skin delicate, unreal; as though a face behind her face was now apparent after many years. She sat looking at Kate and smiled.

"One day when you were about four you were dragging a broom around the kitchen. I asked what you were doing and you told me that when you got old you were going to be an angel and sweep the rotten rain off the clouds."

"What did you say to that?"

"I said that when you were old I was sure God would see to it," Her mother laughed. "I'm glad you weren't such a smart aleck then," she said. "You would have told me my view of God was paternalistic."

"Ah yes," sighed Kate. "God, that famous dude. Here I am, getting old, facing unemployment, alone, and where is He?"

"You're not alone," her mother said, "I'm right here."

Kate didn't answer. She sat motionless and felt her heart begin to open like a box with a hinged lid. The fullness had no edges.

Her mother stood. She rubbed her hands slowly, twisting her wedding rings. "My hands are so dry in the winter," she said softly, "I brought some hand cream with me but I can't find it anywhere, my suitcase is so jumbled. Thank heavens spring is early this year. . . . They told me that little park over there doesn't usually open till the end of March . . ."

She's helping me, thought Kate, I'm not supposed to let her down.

" . . . but they're already running it on weekends. Even past dusk. We'll see the lights tonight. You can't see the shapes this far away, just the motion . . ."

A nurse came in with a wheelchair. Kate's mother pulled a wry face. "This wheelchair is a bit much," she said.

"We don't want to tire you out," said the nurse.

The chair took her weight quietly. At the door she put out her hand to stop, turned, and said anxiously, "Kate, see if you can find that hand cream?"

* * *

It was the blue suitcase from years ago, still almost new. She's brought things she never used for everyday; a cashmere sweater, lace slips, silk underpants wrapped in tissue. Folded beneath was a stack of postmarked envelopes, slightly ragged, tied with twine. Kate opened one and realized that all the cards were there, beginning with the first of the marriage. There were a few photographs of her and Robert, baby pictures almost indistinguishable from each other, and then Kate's homemade Valentines, fastened together with rubber bands. Kate stared. *What will I do with these things?* She wanted air; she needed to breathe. She walked to the window and put the bundled papers on the sill. She'd raised the glass and pushed back the screen when suddenly, her mother's clock radio went off with a flat buzz. Kate moved to switch it off and brushed the cards with her arm. Envelopes shifted and slid, scattering on the floor of the room. A few snapshots wafted silently out the window. They dipped and turned, twirling. Kate didn't try to reach them. They seemed only scraps, buoyant and yellowed, blown away, the faces small as pennies. Somewhere far-off there were sirens, almost musical, drawn out and carefully approaching.

* * *

The nurse came in with evening medication. Kate's mother lay in bed. "I hope this is strong enough," she said. "Last night I couldn't sleep at all. So many sounds in a hospital . . ."

"You'll sleep tonight," the nurse assured her.

Kate winked at her mother. "That's right," she said, "I'll help you out if I have to."

They stayed up for an hour, watching the moving lights outside and the stationary glows of houses across the distant river. The halls grew darker, were lit with night lights, and the hospital dimmed. Kate waited. Her mother's eyes fluttered and finally she slept. Her breathing was low and regular.

Kate didn't move. Robert had said he'd be back; where was he? She felt a sunken anger and shook her head. She'd been on the point of telling her mother everything. The secrets were a travesty. What if there were things her mother wanted done, people she needed to see? Kate wanted to wake her before these hours passed in the dark and confess that she had lied. Between them, through the tension, there had always been a trusted clarity. Now it was twisted. Kate sat leaning forward, nearly touching the hospital bed.

Suddenly her mother sat bolt upright, her eyes open and her face transfixed. She looked blindly toward Kate but seemed to see nothing. "Who are you?" she whispered. Kate stood, at first unable to move. The woman in the bed opened and closed her mouth several times, as though she were gasping. Then she said loudly, "Stop moving the table. Stop it this instant!" Her eyes were wide with fright and her body was vibrating.

Kate reached her. "Mama, wake up, you're dreaming." Her mother jerked, flinging her arms out. Kate held her tightly.

"I can hear the wheels," she moaned.

"No, no," Kate said. "You're here with me."

"It's not so?"

"No," Kate said. "It's not so."

She went limp. Kate felt for her pulse and found it rapid, then regular. She sat rocking her mother. In a few minutes she lay her back on the pillows and smoothed the damp hair at her temples, smoothed the sheets of the bed. Later she slept fitfully in a chair, waking repeatedly to assure herself that her mother was breathing.

Near dawn she got up, exhausted, and left the room to walk in the corridor. In front of the window at the end of the hallway she saw a man slumped on a couch; the man slowly stood and wavered before her like a specter. It was Robert.

"Kate?" he said.

Years ago he had flunked out of a small junior college and their mother sat in her bedroom rocker, crying hard for over an hour while Kate tried in vain to comfort her. Kate went to the university the next fall, so anxious that she studied frantically, outlining whole textbooks in yellow ink. She sat in the front rows of large classrooms to take voluminous notes, writing quickly in her thick notebook. Robert had gone home, held a job in a plant that manufactured business forms and worked his way through the hometown college. By that time their father was dead, and Robert became, always and forever, the man of the house.

"Robert," Kate said, "I'll stay. Go home."

* * *

After breakfast they sat waiting for Robert, who had called and said he'd arrive soon. Kate's fatigue had given way to an intense awareness of every sound, every gesture. How would they get through the day? Her mother had awakened from the drugged sleep still groggy, unable to eat. The meal was sent away untouched and she watched the window as though she feared the walls of the room.

"I'm glad your father isn't here to see this," she said. There was a silence and Kate opened her mouth to speak. "I mean," said her mother quickly, "I'm going to look horrible for a few weeks, with my head all shaved." She pulled an afghan up around her lap and straightened the magazines on the table beside her chair.

"Mom," Kate said, "your hair will grow back."

Her mother pulled the afghan closer. "I've been thinking of your father," she said. "It's not that I'd have wanted him to suffer. But if he had to die, sometimes I wish he'd done it more gently. That heart attack, so finished; never a warning. I wish I'd had some time to nurse him. In a way, it's a chance to settle things."

"Did things need settling?"

"They always do, don't they?" She sat looking out the window, then said softly, "I wonder where I'm headed."

"You're not headed anywhere." Kate said. "I want you right here to see me settle down into normal American womanhood."

Her mother smiled reassuringly. "Where are my grandchildren?" she said. "That's what I'd like to know."

"You stick around," said Kate, "and I promise to start working on it." She moved her chair closer, so that their knees were touching and they could both see out the window. Below them cars moved on the highway and the Ferris wheel in the little park was turning.

"I remember when you were one of the little girls in the parade at the country fair. You weren't even in school yet; you were beautiful in that white organdy dress and pinafore. You wore those shiny black patent shoes and a crown of real apple blossoms. Do you remember?"

"Yes." Kate said. "That long parade. They told me not to move and I sat so still my legs went to sleep. When they lifted me off the float I couldn't stand up. They put me under a tree to wait for you, and you came, in a full white skirt and white sandals, your hair tied back in a red scarf. I can see you yet."

Her mother laughed. "Sounds like a pretty exaggerated picture."

Kate nodded. "I was little. You were big."

"You loved the county fair. You were wild about the carnivals." They looked down at the little park. "Magic, isn't it?" her mother said.

"Maybe we could go see it," said Kate. "I'll ask the doctor."

* * *

They walked across a pedestrian footbridge spanning the highway. Kate had bundled her mother into a winter coat and gloves despite the sunny weather. The day was sharp, nearly still, holding its bright air like illusion. Kate tasted the brittle water of her breath, felt for the cool handrail and thin steel of the webbed fencing. Cars moved steadily under the bridge. Beyond a muted roar of motors the park spread green and wooded, its limits clearly visible.

Kate's mother had combed her hair and put on lipstick. Her mouth was defined and brilliant; she linked arms with Kate like an escort. "I was afraid they'd tell us no," she said. "I was ready to run away!"

"I promised I wouldn't let you. And we only have ten minutes, long enough for the Ferris wheel." Kate grinned.

"I haven't ridden one in years. I wonder if I still know how."

"Of course you do. Ferris wheels are genetic knowledge."

"All right, whatever you say." She smiled. "We'll just hold on."

They drew closer and walked quickly through the sounds of the highway. When they reached the grass it was ankle-high and thick, longer and more ragged than it appeared from a distance. The Ferris wheel sat squarely near a grove of swaying elms, squat and laboring, taller than trees. Its neon lights still burned, pale in the sun, spiraling from inside like an imagined bloom. The naked elms surrounded it, their topmost branches tapping. Steel ribs of the machine were graceful and slightly rusted, squeaking faintly above a tinkling music. Only a few people were riding.

"Looks a little rickety," Kate said.

"Oh, don't worry," said her mother.

Kate tried to buy tickets but the ride was free. The old man running the motor wore an engineer's cap and patched overalls. He stopped the wheel and led them on a short ramp to an open car. It dipped gently, padded with black cushions. An orderly and his children rode in the car above. Kate saw their dangling feet, the girls' dusty sandals and gray socks beside their father's shoes and the hem of his white pants. The youngest one swung her feet absently, so it seemed the breeze blew her legs like fabric hung on a line.

Kate looked at her mother. "Are you ready for the big sky?" They laughed. Beyond them the river moved lazily. Houses on the opposite bank seemed empty, but a few rowboats bobbed at the docks. The surface of the water lapped and reflected clouds, and as Kate watched, searching for a definition of line, the Ferris wheel jerked into motion. The car rocked. They looked into the distance and Kate caught her mother's hand as they ascended.

Far away the hospital rose up white and glistening, its windows catching the glint of the sun. Directly below, the park was nearly deserted. There were a few cars in the parking lot and several dogs chasing each other across the grass. Two or three lone women held children on the teeter-totters and a wind was coming up. The forlorn swings moved on their chains. Kate had a vision of the park at night, totally empty, wind weaving heavily through the trees and children's playthings like a great black fish about to surface. She felt a chill on her arms. The light had gone darker, quietly, like a minor chord.

"Mom," Kate said, "it's going to storm." Her own voice seemed distant, the sound strained through layers of screen or gauze.

"No," said her mother, "it's going to pass over." She moved her hand to Kate's knee and touched the cloth of her daughter's skirt.

Kate gripped the metal bar at their waists and looked straight ahead. They were rising again and she felt she would scream. She tried to breathe rhythmically, steadily. She felt the immense weight of the air as they moved through it.

They came almost to the top and stopped. The little car swayed back and forth.

"You're sick, aren't you," her mother said.

Kate shook her head. Below them the grass seemed to glitter coldly, like a sea. Kate sat wordless, feeling the touch of her mother's hand. The hand moved away and Kate felt the absence of the warmth.

They looked at each other levelly.

"I know all about it," her mother said, "I know what you haven't told me."

The sky circled around them, a sure gray movement. Kate swallowed calmly and let their gaze grow endless. She saw herself in her mother's wide brown eyes and felt she was falling slowly into them.

# ⁂ LESLIE MARMON SILKO
(1948– )

Born in Albuquerque, New Mexico, of ancestry composed of Laguna Pueblo Indian, Mexican, and white, Leslie Marmon Silko grew up on the Laguna Pueblo Reservation. There she heard the many tales, customs, and traditions that came to define her as a human being and writer. She attended Bureau of Indian Affairs schools in Laguna Pueblo and Catholic schools in Albuquerque. She graduated from the University of New Mexico in 1969 with a B.A. in English. She attended law school for three semesters before dropping out to pursue her writing full time. She married an attorney with whom she had two sons, and from whom she was later divorced. After teaching two years at Navajo Community College at Many Farms, Arizona, Silko spent two years in Ketchikan, Alaska, where she began work on her much acclaimed novel *Ceremony* (1977). She has since taught at the University of New Mexico and at the University of Arizona.

Silko has published poetry as well as fiction. Her first publication was *Laguna Woman* (1974), a collection of her poetry. Poems, tales, stories, and photographs are collected in *Storyteller* (1981). Her second novel is the apocalyptic *Almanac of the Dead* (1991). More recently she has published *Sacred Water* (1993), *Yellow Woman and a Beauty of the Spirit: Essays on Native American Life* (1996), and *Gardens in the Dunes* (1999). For Silko, telling stories is essentially a retelling—participating in an ancient and honored Native American activity that defines self and community.

## Storyteller

EVERY DAY the sun came up a little lower on the horizon, moving more slowly until one day she got excited and started calling the jailer. She realized she had been sitting there for many hours, yet the sun had not moved from the center of the sky. The color of the sky had not been good lately; it had been pale blue, almost white, even when there were no clouds. She told herself it wasn't a good sign for the sky to be indistinguishable from the river ice, frozen solid and white against the earth. The tundra rose up behind the river but all the boundaries between the river and hills and sky were lost in the density of the pale ice.

She yelled again, this time some English words which came randomly into her mouth, probably swear words she'd heard from the oil drilling crews last winter. The jailer was an Eskimo, but he would not speak Yupik to her. She had watched people in other cells, when they spoke to him in Yupik he ignored them until they spoke English.

He came and stared at her. She didn't know if he understood what she was telling him until he glanced behind her at the small high window. He looked at the sun, and turned and walked away. She could hear the buckles on his heavy snow-mobile boots jingle as he walked to the front of the building.

It was like the other buildings that white people, the Gussucks, brought with them: BIA and school buildings, portable buildings that arrived sliced in halves, on barges coming up the river. Squares of metal panelling bulged out with the layers of insulation stuffed inside. She had asked once what it was and someone told her it was to keep out the cold. She had not laughed then, but she did now. She walked over to the small double-pane window and she laughed out loud. They thought they could keep out the cold with stringy yellow wadding. Look at the sun. It wasn't moving; it was frozen, caught in the middle of the sky. Look at the sky, solid as the river with ice which had trapped the sun. It had not moved for a long time; in a few more hours it would be weak, and heavy frost would begin to appear on the edges and spread across the face of the sun like a mask. Its light was pale yellow, worn thin by the winter.

She could see people walking down the snow-packed roads, their breath steaming out from their parka hoods, faces hidden and protected by deep ruffs of fur. There were no cars or snowmobiles that day; the cold had silenced their machines. The metal froze; it split and shattered. Oil hardened and moving parts jammed solidly. She had seen it happen to their big yellow machines and the giant drill last winter when they came to drill their test holes. The cold stopped them, and they were helpless against it.

Her village was many miles upriver from this town, but in her mind she could see it clearly. Their house was not near the village houses. It stood alone on the bank upriver from the village. Snow had drifted to the eaves of the roof on the north side, but on the west side, by the door, the path was almost clear. She had nailed scraps of red tin over the logs last summer. She had done it for the bright red color, not for added warmth the way the village people had done. This final winter had been coming even then; there had been signs of its approach for many years.

* * *

She went because she was curious about the big school where the Government sent all the other girls and boys. She had not played much with the village children while she was growing up because they were afraid of the old man, and they ran when her grandmother came. She went because she was tired of being alone with the old woman whose body had been stiffening for as long as the girl could remember. Her knees and knuckles were swollen grotesquely, and the pain had squeezed the brown skin of her face tight against the bones; it left her eyes hard like river stone. The girl asked once what it was that did this to her body, and the old woman had raised up from sewing a sealskin boot, and stared at her.

"The joints," the old woman said in a low voice, whispering like wind across the roof, "the joints are swollen with anger."

Sometimes she did not answer and only stared at the girl. Each year she spoke less and less, but the old man talked more—all night sometimes, not to anyone but himself; in a soft deliberate voice, he told stories, moving his smooth brown hands above the blankets. He had not fished or hunted with the other men for many years, although he was not crippled or sick. He stayed in his bed, smelling like dry fish and urine, telling stories all winter; and when warm weather came, he went to his place on the river bank.

He sat with a long willow stick, poking at the smoldering moss he burned against the insects while he continued with the stories.

The trouble was that she had not recognized the warnings in time. She did not see what the Gussuck school would do to her until she walked into the dormitory and realized that the old man had not been lying about the place. She thought he had been trying to scare her as he used to when she was very small and her grandmother was outside cutting up fish. She hadn't believed what he told her about the school because she knew he wanted to keep her there in the log house with him. She knew what he wanted.

The dormitory matron pulled down her underpants and whipped her with a leather belt because she refused to speak English.

"Those backwards village people," the matron said, because she was an Eskimo who had worked for the BIA a long time, "they kept this one until she was too big to learn." The other girls whispered in English. They knew how to work the showers, and they washed and curled their hair at night. They ate Gussuck food. She lay on her bed and imagined what her grandmother might be sewing, and what the old man was eating in his bed. When summer came, they sent her home.

The way her grandmother had hugged her before she left for school had been a warning too, because the old woman had not hugged or touched her for many years. Not like the old man, whose hands were always hunting, like ravens circling lazily in the sky, ready to touch her. She was not surprised when the priest and the old man met her at the landing strip, to say that the old lady was gone. The priest asked her where she would like to stay. He referred to the old man as her grandfather, but she did not bother to correct him. She had already been thinking about it; if she went with the priest, he would send her away to a school. But the old man was different. She knew he wouldn't send her back to school. She knew he wanted to keep her.

* * *

He told her one time, that she would get too old for him faster than he got too old for her; but again she had not believed him because sometimes he lied. He had lied about what he would do with her if she came into his bed. But as the years passed, she realized what he said was true. She was restless and strong. She had no patience with the old man who had never changed his slow smooth motions under the blankets.

The old man was in his bed for the winter; he did not leave it except to use the slop bucket in the corner. He was dozing with his mouth open slightly; his lips quivered and sometimes they moved like he was telling a story even while he dreamed. She pulled on the sealskin boots, the mukluks with the bright red flannel linings her grandmother had sewn for her, and she tied the braided red yarn tassels around her ankles over the gray wool pants. She zipped the wolfskin parka. Her grandmother had worn it for many years, but the old man said that before she died, she instructed him to bury her in an old black sweater, and to give the parka to the girl. The wolf pelts were creamy colored and silver, almost white in some places, and when the old lady had walked across the tundra in the winter, she was invisible in the snow.

She walked toward the village, breaking her own path through the deep snow. A team of sled dogs tied outside a house at the edge of the village leaped against their chains to bark at her. She kept walking, watching the dusky sky for the first evening stars. It was warm and the dogs were alert. When it got cold again, the dogs would lie curled and still, too drowsy from the cold to bark or pull at the chains. She laughed loudly because it made them howl and snarl. Once the old man had seen her tease the dogs and he shook his head. "So that's the kind of woman you are," he said, "in the wintertime the two of us are no different from those dogs. We wait in the cold for someone to bring us a few dry fish."

She laughed out loud again, and kept walking. She was thinking about the Gussuck oil drillers. They were strange; they watched her when she walked near their machines. She wondered what they looked like underneath their quilted goose-down trousers; she wanted to know how they moved. They would be something different from the old man.

* * *

The old man screamed at her. He shook her shoulders so violently that her head bumped against the log wall. "I smelled it!" he yelled, "as soon as I woke up! I am sure of it now. You can't fool me!" His thin legs were shaking inside the baggy wool trousers; he stumbled over her boots in his bare feet. His toenails were long and yellow like bird claws; she had seen a gray crane last summer fighting another in the shallow water on the edge of the river. She laughed out loud and pulled her shoulder out of his grip. He stood in front of her. He was breathing hard and shaking; he looked weak. He would probably die next winter.

"I'm warning you," he said, "I'm warning you." He crawled back into his bunk then, and reached under the old soiled feather pillow for a piece of dry fish. He lay back on the pillow, staring at the ceiling and chewed dry strips of salmon. "I don't know what the old woman told you," he said, "but there will be trouble." He looked over to see if she was listening. His face suddenly relaxed into a smile, his dark slanty eyes were lost in wrinkles of brown skin. "I could tell you, but you are too good for warnings now. I can smell what you did all night with the Gussucks."

* * *

She did not understand why they came there, because the village was small and so far upriver that even some Eskimos who had been away to school did not want to come back. They stayed downriver in the town. They said the village was too quiet. They were used to the town where the boarding school was located, with electric lights and running water. After all those years away at school, they had forgotten how to set nets in the river and where to hunt seals in the fall. When she asked the old man why the Gussucks bothered to come to the village, his narrow eyes got bright with excitement.

"They only come when there is something to steal. The fur animals are too difficult for them to get now, and the seals and fish are hard to find. Now they come for oil deep in the earth. But this is the last time for them." His breathing was wheezy and fast; his hands gestured at the sky. "It is approaching. As it comes, ice will push across the sky." His eyes were open wide and he stared at the low ceiling rafters for hours without blinking. She remembered all this clearly because he began the story that day, the story he told from that time on. It began with a giant bear which he described muscle by muscle, from the curve of the ivory claws to the whorls of hair at the top of the massive skull. And for eight days he did not sleep, but talked continuously of the giant bear whose color was pale blue glacier ice.

* * *

The snow was dirty and worn down in a path to the door. On either side of the path, the snow was higher than her head. In front of the door there were jagged yellow stains melted into the snow where men had urinated. She stopped in the entry way and kicked the snow off her boots. The room was dim; a kerosene lantern by the cash register was burning low. The long wooden shelves were jammed with cans of beans and potted meats. On the bottom shelf a jar of mayonnaise was broken open, leaking oily white clots on the floor. There was no one in the room except the yellowish dog sleeping in the front of the long glass display case. A reflection made it appear to be lying on the knives and ammunition inside the case. Gussucks kept dogs inside their houses with them; they did not seem to mind the odors which seeped out of the dogs. "They tell us we are dirty for the food we eat—raw fish and fermented meat. But we do not live with dogs," the old man once said. She heard voices in the back room, and the sound of bottles set down hard on tables.

They were always confident. The first year they waited for the ice to break up on the river, and then they brought their big yellow machines up river on barges. They planned to drill their test holes during the summer to avoid the freezing. But the imprints and graves of their machines were still there, on the edge of the tundra above the river, where the summer mud had swallowed them before they ever left sight of the river. The village people had gathered to watch the white men, and to laugh as they drove the giant machines, one by one, off the steel ramp into the bogs; as if sheer numbers of vehicles would somehow make the tundra solid. But the old man said they behaved like desperate people, and they would come back again. When the tundra was frozen solid, they returned.

Village women did not even look through the door to the back room. The priest had warned them. The storeman was watching her because he didn't let Eskimos or Indians sit down at the tables in the back room. But she knew he couldn't throw her out if one of his Gussuck customers invited her to sit with him. She walked across the room. They stared at her, but she had the feeling she was walking for someone else, not herself, so their eyes did not matter. The red-haired man pulled out a chair and motioned for her to sit down. She looked back at the storeman while the red-haired man poured her a glass of red sweet wine. She wanted to laugh at the storeman the way she laughed at the dogs, straining against the chains, howling at her.

The red-haired man kept talking to the other Gussucks sitting around the table, but he slid one hand off the top of the table to her thigh. She looked over at the storeman to see if he was still watching her. She laughed out loud at him and the red-haired man stopped talking and turned to her. He asked if she wanted to go. She nodded and stood up.

Someone in the village had been telling him things about her, he said as they walked down the road to his trailer. She understood that much of what he was saying, but the rest she did not hear. The whine of the big generators at the construction camp sucked away the sound of his words. But English was of no concern to her anymore, and neither was anything the Christians in the village might say about her or the old man. She smiled at the effect of the subzero air on the electric lights around the trailers; they did not shine. They left only flat yellow holes in the darkness.

It took him a long time to get ready, even after she had undressed for him. She waited in the bed with the blankets pulled close, watching him. He adjusted the thermostat and lit candles in the room, turning out the electric lights. He searched through a stack of record albums until he found the right one. She was not sure about the last thing he did: he taped something on the wall behind the bed where he could see it while he lay on top of her. He was shriveled and white from the cold; he pushed against her body for warmth. He guided her hands to his thighs; he was shivering.

She had returned a last time because she wanted to know what it was he stuck on the wall above the bed. After he finished each time, he reached up and pulled it loose, folding it carefully so that she could not see it. But this time she was ready; she waited for his fast breathing and sudden collapse on top of her. She slid out from under him and stood up beside the bed. She looked at the picture while she got dressed. He did not raise his face from the pillow, and she thought she heard teeth rattling together as she left the room.

* * *

She heard the old man move when she came in. After the Gussuck's trailer, the log house felt cool. It smelled like dry fish and cured meat. The room was dark except for the blinking yellow flame in the mica window of the oil stove. She squatted in front of the stove and watched the flames for a long time before she walked to the bed where her grandmother had slept. The bed was covered with a mound of rags and fur scraps the old woman had saved. She reached into the mound until she felt something cold and solid wrapped in a wool blanket. She pushed her fingers around it until she felt smooth stone. Long ago, before the Gussucks came, they had burned whale oil in the big stone lamp which made light and heat as well. The old woman had saved everything they would need when the time came.

In the morning, the old man pulled a piece of dry caribou meat from under the blankets and offered it to her. While she was gone, men from the village had brought a bundle of dry meat. She chewed it slowly, thinking about the way they still came from the village to take care of the old man and his stories. But she had a story now, about the red-haired Gussuck. The old man knew what she was thinking, and his smile made his face seem more round than it was.

"Well," he said, "what was it?"

"A woman with a big dog on top of her."

He laughed softly to himself and walked over to the water barrel. He dipped the tin cup into the water.

"It doesn't surprise me," he said.

* * *

"Grandma," she said, "there was something red in the grass that morning. I remember." She had not asked about her parents before. The old woman stopped splitting the fish bellies open for the willow drying racks. Her jaw muscles pulled so tightly against her skull, the girl thought the old woman would not be able to speak.

"They bought a tin can full of it from the storeman. Late at night. He told them it was alcohol safe to drink. They traded a rifle for it." The old woman's voice sounded like each word stole strength from her. "It made no difference about the rifle. That year the Gussuck boats had come, firing big guns at the walrus and seals. There was nothing left to hunt after that anyway. So," the old lady said, in a low soft voice the girl had not heard for a long time, "I didn't say anything to them when they left that night."

"Right over there," she said, pointing at the fallen poles, half buried in the river sand and tall grass, "in the summer shelter. The sun was high half the night then. Early in the morning when it was still low, the policeman came around. I told the interpreter to tell him that the storeman had poisoned them." She made outlines in the air in front of her, showing how their bodies lay twisted on the sand; telling the story was like laboring to walk through deep snow; sweat shone in the white hair around her forehead. "I told the priest too, after he came. I told him the storeman lied." She turned away from the girl. She held her mouth even tighter, set solidly, not in sorrow or anger, but against the pain, which was all that remained. "I never believed," she said, "not much anyway. I wasn't surprised when the priest did nothing."

The wind came off the river and folded the tall grass into itself like river waves. She could feel the silence the story left, and she wanted to have the old woman go on.

"I heard sounds that night, grandma. Sounds like someone was singing. It was light outside. I could see something red on the ground." The old woman did not answer her; she moved to the tub full of fish on the ground beside the workbench. She stabbed her knife into the belly of a whitefish and lifted it onto the bench. "The Gussuck storeman left the village right after that," the old woman said as she pulled the entrails from the fish, "otherwise, I could tell you more." The old woman's voice flowed with the wind blowing off the river; they never spoke of it again.

When the willows got their leaves and the grass grew tall along the river banks and around the sloughs, she walked early in the morning. While the sun was still low on the horizon, she listened to the wind off the river; its sound was like the voice that day long ago. In the distance, she could hear the engines of the machinery the oil drillers had left the winter before, but she did not go near the village or the store. The sun never left the sky and the summer became the same long day, with only the winds to fan the sun into brightness or allow it to slip into twilight.

She sat beside the old man at his place on the river bank. She poked the smoky fire for him, and felt herself growing wide and thin in the sun as if she had been split from belly to throat and strung on the willow pole in preparation for the winter to come. The old man did not speak anymore. When men from the village brought him fresh fish he hid them deep in the river grass where it was cool. After he went inside, she split the fish open and spread them to dry on the willow frame the way the old woman had done. Inside, he dozed and talked to himself. He had talked all winter, softly and incessantly, about the giant polar bear stalking a lone hunter across Bering Sea ice. After all the months the old man had been telling the story, the bear was within a hundred feet of the man; but the ice fog had closed in on them now and the man could only smell the sharp ammonia odor of the bear, and hear the edge of the snow crust crack under the giant paws.

One night she listened to the old man tell the story all night in his sleep, describing each crystal of ice and the slightly different sounds they made under each paw; first the left and then the right paw, then the hind feet. Her grandmother was there suddenly, a shadow around the stove. She spoke in her low wind voice and the girl was afraid to sit up to hear more clearly. Maybe what she said had been to the old man because he stopped telling the story and began to snore softly the way he had long ago when the old woman had scolded him for telling his stories while others in the house were trying to sleep. But the last words she heard clearly: "It will take a long time, but the story must be told. There must not be any lies." She pulled the blankets up around her chin, slowly, so that her movements would not be seen. She thought her grandmother was talking about the old man's bear story; she did not know about the other story then.

She left the old man wheezing and snoring in his bed. She walked through river grass glistening with frost; the bright green summer color was already fading. She watched the sun move across the sky, already lower on the horizon, already moving away from the village. She stopped by the fallen poles of the summer shelter where her parents had died. Frost glittered on the river sand too; in a few more weeks there would be snow. The predawn light would be the color of an old woman. An old woman sky full of snow. There had been something red lying on the ground the morning they died. She looked for it again, pushing aside the grass with her foot. She knelt in the sand and looked under the fallen structure for some trace of it. When she found it, she would know what the old woman had never told her. She squatted down close to the gray poles and leaned her back against them. The wind made her shiver.

The summer rain had washed the mud from between the logs; the sod blocks stacked as high as her belly next to the log walls had lost their square-cut shape and had grown into soft mounds of tundra moss and stiff-bladed grass bending with clusters of seed bristles. She looked at the northwest, in the direction of the Bering Sea. The cold would come down from there to find narrow slits in the mud, rainwater holes in the outer layer of sod which protected the log house. The dark green tundra stretched away flat and continuous. Somewhere the sea and the land met; she knew by their dark green colors there were no boundaries between them. That was how the cold would come: when the boundaries were gone the polar ice would range across the land into the sky. She watched the horizon for a long time. She would stand in that place on the north side of the house and she would keep watch on the northwest horizon, and eventually she would see it come. She would watch for its approach in the stars, and hear it come with the wind. These preparations were unfamiliar, but gradually she recognized them as she did her own footprints in the snow.

* * *

She emptied the slop jar beside his bed twice a day and kept the barrel full of water melted from river ice. He did not recognize her anymore, and when he spoke to her, he called her by her grandmother's name and talked about people and events from long ago, before he went back to telling the story. The giant bear was creeping across the new snow on its belly, close enough now that the man could hear the rasp of its breathing. On and on in a soft singing voice, the old man caressed the story, repeating the words again and again like gentle strokes.

The sky was gray like a river crane's egg; its density curved into the thin crust of frost already covering the land. She looked at the bright red color of the tin against the ground and the sky and she told the village men to bring the pieces for the old man and her. To drill the test holes in the tundra, the Gussucks had used hundreds of barrels of fuel. The village people split open the empty barrels that were abandoned on the river bank, and pounded the red tin into flat sheets. The village people were using the strips of tin to mend walls and roofs for winter. But she nailed it on the log walls for its color. When she finished, she walked away with the hammer in her hand, not turning around until she was far away, on the ridge above the river banks, and then she looked back. She felt a chill when she saw how the sky and the land were already losing their boundaries, already becoming lost in each other. But the red tin penetrated the thick white color of earth and sky; it defined the boundaries like a wound revealing the ribs and heart of a great caribou about to bolt and be lost to the hunter forever. That night the wind howled and when she scratched a hole through the heavy frost on the inside of the window, she could see nothing but the impenetrable white; whether it was blowing snow or snow that had drifted as high as the house, she did not know.

It had come down suddenly, and she stood with her back to the wind looking at the river, its smoky water clotted with ice. The wind had blown the snow over the frozen river, hiding thin blue streaks where fast water ran under ice translucent and fragile as memory. But she could see shadows of boundaries, outlines of paths which were slender branches of solidity reaching out from the earth. She spent days walking on the river, watching the colors of ice that would safely hold her, kicking the heel of her boot into the snow crust, listening for a solid sound. When she could feel the paths through the soles of her feet, she went to the middle of the river where the fast gray water churned under a thin pane of ice. She looked back. On the river bank in the distance she could see the red tin nailed to the log house, something not swallowed up by the heavy white belly of the sky or caught in the folds of the frozen earth. It was time.

* * *

The wolverine fur around the hood of her parka was white with the frost from her breathing. The warmth inside the store melted it, and she felt tiny drops of water on her face. The storeman came in from the back room. She unzipped the parka and stood by the oil stove. She didn't look at him, but stared instead at the yellowish dog, covered with scabs of matted hair, sleeping in front of the stove. She thought of the Gussuck's picture, taped on the wall above the bed and she laughed out loud. The sound of her laughter was piercing; the yellow dog jumped to its feet and the hair bristled down its back. The storeman was watching her. She wanted to laugh again because he didn't know about the ice. He did not know that it was prowling the earth, or that it had already pushed its way into the sky to seize the sun. She sat down in the chair by the stove and shook her long hair loose. He was like a dog tied up all winter, watching while the others got fed. He remembered how she had gone with the oil drillers, and his blue eyes moved like flies crawling over her body. He held his thin pale lips like he wanted to spit on her. He hated the people because they had something of value, the old man said, something which the Gussucks could never have. They thought they could take it, suck it out of the earth or cut it from the mountains; but they were fools.

There was a matted hunk of dog hair on the floor by her foot. She thought of the yellow insulation coming unstuffed: their defense against the freezing going to pieces as it advanced on them. The ice was crouching on the northwest horizon like the old man's bear. She laughed out loud again. The sun would be down now; it was time.

The first time he spoke to her, she did not hear what he said, so she did not answer or even look up at him. He spoke to her again but his words were only noises coming from his pale mouth, trembling now as his anger began to unravel. He jerked her up and the chair fell over behind her. His arms were shaking and she could feel his hands tense up, pulling the edges of the parka tighter. He raised his fist to hit her, his thin body quivering with rage; but the fist collapsed with the desire he had for the valuable things, which, the old man had rightly said, was the only reason they came. She could hear his heart pounding as he held her close and arched his hips against her, groaning and breathing in spasms. She twisted away from him and ducked under his arms.

She ran with a mitten over her mouth, breathing through the fur to protect her lungs from the freezing air. She could hear him running behind her, his heavy breathing, the occasional sound of metal jingling against metal. But he ran without his parka or mittens, breathing the frozen air; its fire squeezed the lungs against the ribs and it was enough that he could not catch her near his store. On the river bank he realized how far he was from his stove, and the wads of yellow stuffing that held off the cold. But the girl was not able to run very fast through the deep drifts at the edge of the river. The twilight was luminous and he could still see clearly for a long distance; he knew he could catch her so he kept running.

When she neared the middle of the river she looked over her shoulder. He was not following her tracks; he went straight across the ice, running the shortest distance to reach her. He was close then; his face was twisted and scarlet from the exertion and the cold. There was satisfaction in his eyes; he was sure he could outrun her.

She was familiar with the river, down to the instant ice flexed into hairline fractures, and the cracking bone-sliver sounds gathered momentum with the opening ice until the churning gray water was set free. She stopped and turned to the sound of the river and the rattle of swirling ice fragments where he fell through. She pulled off a mitten and zipped the parka to her throat. She was conscious then of her own rapid breathing.

She moved slowly, kicking the ice ahead with the heel of her boot, feeling for sinews of ice to hold her. She looked ahead and all around herself; in the twilight, the dense white sky had merged into the flat snow-covered tundra. In the frantic running she had lost her place on the river. She stood still. The east bank of the river was lost in the sky; the boundaries had been swallowed by the freezing white. But then, in the distance, she saw something red, and suddenly it was as she had remembered it all those years.

* * *

She sat on her bed and while she waited, she listened to the old man. The hunter had found a small jagged knoll on the ice. He pulled his beaver fur cap off his head; the fur inside it steamed with his body heat and sweat. He left it upside down on the ice for the great bear to stalk, and he waited downwind on top of the ice knoll; he was holding the jade knife.

She thought she could see the end of his story in the way he wheezed out the words; but still he reached into his cache of dry fish and dribbled water into his mouth from the tin cup. All night she listened to him describe each breath the man took, each motion of the bear's head as it tried to catch the sound of the man's breathing, and tested the wind for his scent.

* * *

The state trooper asked her questions, and the woman who cleaned house for the priest translated them into Yupik. They wanted to know what happened to the storeman, the Gussuck who had been seen running after her down the road onto the river late last evening. He had not come back, and the Gussuck boss in Anchorage was concerned about him. She did not answer for a long time because the old man suddenly sat up in his bed and began to talk excitedly, looking at all of them—the trooper in his dark glasses and the housekeeper in her corduroy parka. He kept saying, "The story! The story! Eh-ya! The great bear! The hunter!"

They asked her again, what happened to the man from the Northern Commercial store. "He lied to them. He told them it was safe to drink. But I will not lie." She stood up and put on the gray wolfskin parka. "I killed him," she said, "but I don't lie."

* * *

The attorney came back again, and the jailer slid open the steel doors and opened the cell to let him in. He motioned for the jailer to stay to translate for him. She laughed when she saw how the jailer would be forced by this Gussuck to speak Yupik to her. She liked the Gussuck attorney for that, and for the thinning hair on his head. He was very tall, and she liked to think about the exposure of his head to the freezing; she wondered if he would feel the ice descending from the sky before the others did. He wanted to know why she told the state trooper she had killed the storeman. Some village children had seen it happen, he said, and it was an accident. "That's all you have to say to the judge: it was an accident." He kept repeating it over and over again to her, slowly in a loud but gentle voice: "It was an accident. He was running after you and he fell through the ice. That's all you have to say in court. That's all. And they will let you go home. Back to your village." The jailer translated the words sullenly, staring down at the floor. She shook her head. "I will not change the story, not even to escape this place and go home. I intended that he die. The story must be told as it is." The attorney exhaled loudly; his eyes looked tired. "Tell her that she could not have killed him that way. He was a white man. He ran after her without a parka or mittens. She could not have planned that." He paused and turned toward the cell door. "Tell her I will do all I can for her. I will explain to the judge that her mind is confused." She laughed out loud when the jailer translated what the attorney said. The Gussucks did not understand the story; they could not see the way it must be told, year after year as the old man had done, without lapse or silence.

She looked out the window at the frozen white sky. The sun had finally broken loose from the ice but it moved like a wounded caribou running on strength which only dying animals find, leaping and running on bullet-shattered lungs. Its light was weak and pale; it pushed dimly through the clouds. She turned and faced the Gussuck attorney.

"It began a long time ago," she intoned steadily, "in the summertime. Early in the morning, I remember, something red in the tall river grass. . . ."

* * *

The day after the old man died, men from the village came. She was sitting on the edge of her bed, across from the woman the trooper hired to watch her. They came into the room slowly and listened to her. At the foot of her bed they left a king salmon that had been slit open wide and dried last summer. But she did not pause or hesitate; she went on with the story, and she never stopped, not even when the woman got up to close the door behind the village men.

* * *

The old man would not change the story even when he knew the end was approaching. Lies could not stop what was coming. He thrashed around on the bed, pulling the blankets loose, knocking bundles of dried fish and meat on the floor. The hunter had been on the ice for many hours. The freezing winds on the ice knoll had numbed his hands in the mittens, and the cold had exhausted him. He felt a single muscle tremor in his hand that he could not stop, and the jade knife fell; it shattered on the ice, and the blue glacier bear turned slowly to face him.

# ALICE ADAMS
## (1926– )

The fiction of Alice Adams is characterized by finely wrought dialogue and revealing details that chronicle the lives, especially the lives of women, of the middle and upper-middle classes. Adams was born in Fredericksburg, Virginia, but grew up near Chapel Hill, North Carolina, the setting for a lot of her fiction. She attended Radcliffe College from which she graduated in 1945 with a B.A. in English. Married and later divorced, she found herself holding a variety of jobs to support her family. When she achieved literary success, she quit her jobs to devote full time to writing.

Adams' stories have been chosen many times to be in the annual O. Henry Prize anthologies, as well as in *The Best American Short Stories* series. Her novels include *Careless Love* (1966), *Families and Survivors* (1975), *Listening to Billie* (1978), *Rich Rewards* (1980), *Superior Women* (1984), *Second Chances* (1988), *Caroline's Daughters* (1991), *Almost Perfect* (1993), *A Southern Exposure* (1995), and *Medicine Men* (1998). Her story collections include *Beautiful Girls* (1979), *To See You Again* (1982), *Return Trips* (1985), and *After You've Gone* (1989).

# Roses, Rhododendron

ONE DARK and rainy Boston spring of many years ago, I spent all my after-school and evening hours in the living room of our antique-crammed Cedar Street flat, writing down what the Ouija board said to my mother. My father, a spoiled and rowdy Irishman, a sometime engineer, had run off to New Orleans with a girl, and my mother hoped to learn from the board if he would come back. Then, one night in May, during a crashing black thunderstorm (my mother was both afraid and much in awe of such storms), the board told her to move down South, to North Carolina, taking me and all the antiques she had been collecting for years, and to open a store in a small town down there. This is what we did, and shortly thereafter, for the first time in my life, I fell permanently in love: with a house, with a family of three people and with an area of countryside.

Perhaps too little attention is paid to the necessary preconditions of "falling in love"—I mean the state of mind or place that precedes one's first sight of the loved person (or house or land). In my own case, I remember the dark Boston afternoons as a precondition of love. Later on, for another important time, I recognized boredom in a job. And once the fear of growing old.

In the town that she had chosen, my mother, Margot (she picked out her own name, having been christened Margaret), rented a small house on a pleasant back street. It had a big surrounding screened-in porch, where she put most of the antiques, and she put a discreet sign out in the front yard: "Margot—Antiques." The store was open only in the afternoons. In the mornings and on Sundays, she drove around the countryside in our ancient and spacious Buick, searching for trophies among the area's country stores and farms and barns. (She is nothing if not enterprising; no one else down there had thought of doing that before.)

Although frequently embarrassed by her aggression—she thought nothing of making offers for furniture that was in use in a family's rooms—I often drove with her during those first few weeks. I was excited by the novelty of the landscape. The red clay banks that led up to the thick pine groves, the swollen brown creeks half hidden by flowering tangled vines. Bare, shaded yards from which rose gaunt, narrow houses. Chickens that scattered, barefoot children who stared at our approach.

"Hello, there. I'm Mrs. John Kilgore—Margot Kilgore—and I'm interested in buying old furniture. Family portraits. Silver."

Margot a big brassily bleached blonde in a pretty flowered silk dress and high-heeled patent sandals. A hoarse and friendly voice. Me a scrawny, pale, curious girl, about ten, in a blue linen dress with smocking across the bodice. (Margot has always had a passionate belief in good clothes, no matter what.)

On other days, Margot would say, "I'm going to look over my so-called books. Why don't you go for a walk or something, Jane?"

And I would walk along the sleepy, leafed-over streets, on the unpaved sidewalks, past houses that to me were as inviting and as interesting as unread books, and I would try to imagine what went on inside. The families. Their lives.

The main street, where the stores were, interested me least. Two-story brick buildings—dry-goods stores, with dentists' and lawyers' offices above. There was also a drugstore, with round marble tables and wire-backed chairs, at which wilting ladies sipped at their Cokes. (This was to become a favorite haunt of Margot's.) I preferred the civic monuments: a pre-Revolutionary Episcopal chapel of yellowish cracked plaster, and several tall white statues to the Civil War dead—all of them quickly overgrown with ivy or Virginia creeper.

These were the early nineteen-forties, and in the next few years the town was to change enormously. Its small textile factories would be given defense contracts (parachute silk); a Navy preflight school would be established at a neighboring university town. But at that moment it was a sleeping village. Untouched.

My walks were not a lonely occupation, but Margot worried that they were, and some curious reasoning led her to believe that a bicycle would help. (Of course, she turned out to be right.) We went to Sears, and she bought me a big new bike—blue, with balloon tires—on which I began to explore the outskirts of town and the countryside.

The house I fell in love with was about a mile out of town, on top of a hill. A small stone bank that was all overgrown with tangled roses led up to its yard, and pink and white roses climbed up a trellis to the roof of the front porch—the roof on which, later, Harriet and I used to sit and exchange our stores of erroneous sexual information. Harriet Farr was the daughter of the house. On one side of the house, there was what looked like a newer wing, with a bay window and a long side porch, below which the lawn sloped down to some flowering shrubs. There was a yellow rosebush, rhododendron, a plum tree, and beyond were woods—pines, and oak and cedar trees. The effect was rich and careless, generous and somewhat mysterious. I was deeply stirred.

As I was observing all this, from my halted bike on the dusty white hilltop, a small, plump woman, very erect, came out of the front door and went over to a flower bed below the bay window. She sat down very stiffly. (Emily, who was Harriet's mother, had some terrible, never diagnosed trouble with her back; she generally wore a brace.) She was older than Margot, with very beautiful white hair that was badly cut in that butchered nineteen-thirties way.

From the first, I was fascinated by Emily's obvious dissimilarity to Margot. I think I was somehow drawn to her contradictions—the shapeless body held up with so much dignity, even while she was sitting in the dirt. The lovely chopped-off hair. (There were greater contradictions, which I learned of later—she was a Virginia Episcopalian who always voted for Norman Thomas, a feminist who always delayed meals for her tardy husband.)

Emily's hair was one of the first things about the Farr family that I mentioned to Margot after we became friends, Harriet and Emily and I, and I began to spend most of my time in that house.

"I don't think she's ever dyed it," I said, with almost conscious lack of tact.

Of course, Margot was defensive. "I wouldn't dye mine if I thought it would be a decent color on its own."

But by that time Margot's life was also improving. Business was fairly good, and she had finally heard from my father, who began to send sizable checks from New Orleans. He had found work with an oil company. She still asked the Ouija board if she would see him again, but her question was less obsessive.

* * *

The second time I rode past that house, there was a girl sitting on the front porch, reading a book. She was about my age. She looked up. The next time I saw her there, we both smiled. And the time after that (a Saturday morning in late June) she got up and slowly came out to the road, to where I had stopped, ostensibly to look at the view—the sweep of fields, the white highway, which wound down to the thick greenery bordering the creek, the fields and trees that rose in dim and distant hills.

"I've got a bike exactly like that," Harriet said indifferently, as though to deny the gesture of having come out to meet me.

For years, perhaps beginning then, I used to seek my opposite in friends. Inexorably following Margot, I was becoming a big blonde, with some of her same troubles. Harriet was cool and dark, with long gray eyes. A girl about to be beautiful.

"Do you want to come in? We've got some lemon cake that's pretty good."

Inside, the house was cluttered with odd mixtures of furniture. I glimpsed a living room, where there was a shabby sofa next to a pretty, "antique" table. We walked through a dining room that contained a decrepit mahogany table surrounded with delicate fruitwood chairs. (I had a horrifying moment of imagining Margot there, with her accurate eye—making offers in her harsh Yankee voice.) The walls were crowded with portraits and with nineteenth-century oils of bosky landscapes. Books overflowed from rows of shelves along the walls. I would have moved in at once.

We took our lemon cake back to the front porch and ate it there, overlooking that view. I can remember its taste vividly. It was light and tart and sweet, and a beautiful lemon color. With it, we drank cold milk, and then we had seconds and more milk, and we discussed what we liked to read.

We were both at an age to begin reading grown-up books, and there was some minor competition between us to see who had read more of them. Harriet won easily, partly because her mother reviewed books for the local paper, and had brought home Steinbeck, Thomas Wolfe, Virginia Woolf and Elizabeth Bowen. But we also found in common an enthusiasm for certain novels about English children. (Such snobbery!)

"It's the best cake I've ever had!" I told Harriet. I had already adopted something of Margot's emphatic style.

"It's very good," Harriet said judiciously. Then, quite casually, she added, "We could ride our bikes out to Laurel Hill."

We soared dangerously down the winding highway. At the bridge across the creek, we stopped and turned onto a narrow, rutted dirt road that followed the creek through woods as dense and as alien as a jungle would have been—thick pines with low sweeping branches, young leafed-out maples, peeling tall poplars, elms, brambles, green masses of honeysuckle. At times, the road was impassable, and we had to get off our bikes and push them along, over crevices and ruts, through mud or sand. And with all that we kept up our somewhat stilted discussion of literature.

"I love Virginia Woolf!"

"Yes, she's very good. Amazing metaphors."

I thought Harriet was an extraordinary person—more intelligent, more poised and prettier than any girl of my age I had ever known. I felt that she could become anything at all—a writer, an actress, a foreign correspondent (I went to a lot of movies). And I was not entirely wrong; she eventually became a sometimes-published poet.

We came to a small beach, next to a place where the creek widened and ran over some shallow rapids. On the other side, large gray rocks rose steeply. Among the stones grew isolated, twisted trees, and huge bushes with thick green leaves. The laurel of Laurel Hill. Rhododendron. Harriet and I took off our shoes and waded into the warmish water. The bottom squished under our feet, making us laugh, like the children we were, despite all our literary talk.

* * *

Margot was also making friends. Unlike me, she seemed to seek her own likeness, and she found a sort of kinship with a woman named Dolly Murray, a rich widow from Memphis who shared many of Margot's superstitions—fear of thunderstorms, faith in the Ouija board. About ten years older than Margot, Dolly still dyed her hair red; she was a noisy, biased, generous woman. They drank gin and gossiped together, they met for Cokes at the drugstore and sometimes they drove to a neighboring town to have dinner in a restaurant (in those days, still a daring thing for unescorted ladies to do).

I am sure that the Farrs, outwardly a conventional family, saw me as a neglected child. I was so available for meals and overnight visits. But that is not how I experienced my life—I simply felt free. And an important thing to be said about Margot as a mother is that she never made me feel guilty for doing what I wanted to do. And of how many mothers can that be said?

There must have been a moment of "meeting" Emily, but I have forgotten it. I remember only her gentle presence, a soft voice and my own sense of love returned. Beautiful white hair, dark deep eyes and a wide mouth, whose corners turned and moved to express whatever she felt—amusement, interest, boredom, pain. I have never since seen such a vulnerable mouth.

I amused Emily; I almost always made her smile. She must have seen me as something foreign—a violent, enthusiastic Yankee. (I used forbidden words, like "God" and "damn.") Very unlike the decorous young Southern girl that she must have been, that Harriet almost was.

She talked to me a lot; Emily explained to me things about the South that otherwise I would not have picked up. "Virginians feel superior to everyone else, you know," she said, in her gentle (Virginian) voice. "Some people in my family were quite shocked when I married a man from North Carolina and came down here to live. And a Presbyterian at that! Of course, that's nowhere near as bad as a Baptist, but only Episcopalians really count." This was all said lightly, but I knew that some part of Emily agreed with the rest of her family.

* * *

"How about Catholics?" I asked her, mainly to prolong the conversation. Harriet was at the dentist's, and Emily was sitting at her desk answering letters. I was perched on the sofa near her, and we both faced the sweeping green view. But since my father, Johnny Kilgore, was a lapsed Catholic, it was not an entirely frivolous question. Margot was a sort of Christian Scientist (her own sort).

"We hardly know any Catholics." Emily laughed, and then she sighed. "I do sometimes still miss Virginia. You know, when we drive up there I can actually feel the difference as we cross the state line. I've met a few people from South Carolina," she went on, "and I understand that people down there feel the same way Virginians do." (Clearly, she found this unreasonable.)

"West Virginia? Tennessee?"

"They don't seem Southern at all. Neither do Florida and Texas—not to me."

("Dolly says that Mrs. Farr is a terrible snob," Margot told me, inquiringly.

"In a way." I spoke with a new diffidence that I was trying to acquire from Harriet.

"Oh.")

Once, I told Emily what I had been wanting to say since my first sight of her. I said, "Your hair is so beautiful. Why don't you let it grow?"

She laughed, because she usually laughed at what I said, but at the same time she looked surprised, almost startled. I understood that what I had said was not improper but that she was totally unused to attentions of that sort from anyone, including herself. She didn't think about her hair. In a puzzled way, she said, "Perhaps I will."

Nor did Emily dress like a woman with much regard for herself. She wore practical, seersucker dresses and sensible, low shoes. Because her body had so little shape, no indentations (this must have been at least partly due to the back brace), I was surprised to notice that she had pretty, shapely legs. She wore little or no makeup on her sun- and wind-weathered face.

And what of Lawrence Farr, the North Carolina Presbyterian for whom Emily had left her people and her state? He was a small, precisely made man, with fine dark features. (Harriet looked very like him.) A lawyer, but widely read in literature, especially the English nineteenth century. He had a courtly manner, and sometimes a wicked tongue; melancholy eyes, and an odd, sudden, ratchety laugh. He looked ten years younger than Emily; the actual difference was less than two.

* * *

"Well," said Margot, settling into a Queen Anne chair—a new antique—on our porch one stifling hot July morning, "I heard some really interesting gossip about your friends."

Margot had met and admired Harriet, and Harriet liked her, too—Margot made Harriet laugh, and she praised Harriet's fine brown hair. But on some instinct (I am not sure whose) the parents had not met. Very likely, Emily, with her Southern social antennae, had somehow sensed that this meeting would be a mistake.

That morning, Harriet and I were going on a picnic in the woods to the steep rocky side of Laurel Hill, but I forced myself to listen, or half listen, to Margot's story.

"Well, it seems that some years ago Lawrence Farr fell absolutely madly in love with a beautiful young girl—in fact, the orphaned daughter of a friend of his. Terribly romantic. Of course, she loved him, too, but he felt so awful and guilty that they never did anything about it."

I did not like this story much; it made me obscurely uncomfortable, and I think that at some point both Margot and I wondered why she was telling it. Was she pointing out imperfections in my chosen other family? But I asked, in Harriet's indifferent voice, "He never kissed her?"

"Well, maybe. I don't know. But of course everyone in town knew all about it, including Emily Farr. And with her back! Poor woman," Margot added somewhat piously but with real feeling, too.

I forgot the story readily at the time. For one thing, there was something unreal about anyone as old as Lawrence Farr "falling in love." But looking back to Emily's face, Emily looking at Lawrence, I can see that pained watchfulness of a woman who has been hurt, and by a man who could always hurt her again.

In those days, what struck me most about the Farrs was their extreme courtesy to each other—something I had not seen before. Never a harsh word. (Of course, I did not know then about couples who cannot afford a single harsh word.)

* * *

Possibly because of the element of danger (very slight—the slope was gentle), the roof over the front porch was one of the places Harriet and I liked to sit on warm summer nights when I was invited to stay over. There was a country silence, invaded at intervals by summer country sounds—the strangled croak of tree frogs from down in the glen; the crazy baying of a distant hound. There, in the heavy scent of roses, on the scratchy shingles, Harriet and I talked about sex.

"A girl I know told me that if you do it a lot your hips get very wide."

"My cousin Duncan says it makes boys strong if they do it."

"It hurts women a lot—especially at first. But I knew this girl from Santa Barbara, and she said that out there they say Filipinos can do it without hurting."

"Colored people do it a lot more than whites."

"Of course, they have all those babies. But in Boston so do Catholics!"

We are seized with hysteria. We laugh and laugh, so that Emily hears and calls up to us, "Girls, why haven't you-all gone to bed?" But her voice is warm and amused—she likes having us laughing up there.

And Emily liked my enthusiasm for lemon cake. She teased me about the amounts of it I could eat, and she continued to keep me supplied. She was not herself much of a cook—their maid, a young black girl named Evelyn, did most of the cooking.

Once, but only once, I saw the genteel and opaque surface of that family shattered—saw those three people suddenly in violent opposition to each other, like shards of splintered glass. (But what I have forgotten is the cause—what brought about that terrible explosion?)

The four of us, as so often, were seated at lunch. Emily was at what seemed to be the head of the table. At her right hand was the small silver bell that summoned Evelyn to clear, or to bring a new course. Harriet and I across from each other, Lawrence across from Emily. (There was always a tentativeness about Lawrence's posture. He could have been an honored guest, or a spoiled and favorite child.) We were talking in an easy way. I have a vivid recollection only of words that began to career and gather momentum, to go out of control. Of voices raised. Then Harriet rushes from the room. Emily's face reddens dangerously, the corners of her mouth twitch downward and Lawrence, in an exquisitely icy voice, begins to lecture me on the virtues of reading Trollope. I am supposed to help him pretend that nothing has happened, but I can hardly hear what he is saying. I am in shock.

That sudden unleashing of violence, that exposed depth of terrible emotions might have suggested to me that the Farrs were not quite as I had imagined them, not the impeccable family in my mind—but it did not. I was simply and terribly—and selfishly—upset, and hugely relieved when it all seemed to have passed over.

* * *

During that summer, the Ouija board spoke only gibberish to Margot, or it answered direct questions with repeated evasions:

"Will I ever see Johnny Kilgore again, in this life?"

"Yes no perhaps."

"Honey, that means you've got no further need of the board, not right now. You've got to think everything out with your own heart and instincts," Dolly said.

Margot seemed to take her advice. She resolutely put the board away, and she wrote to Johnny that she wanted a divorce.

I had begun to notice that these days, on these sultry August nights, Margot and Dolly were frequently joined on their small excursions by a man named Larry—a jolly, red-faced man who was in real estate and who reminded me considerably of my father.

I said as much to Margot, and was surprised at her furious reaction. "They could not be more different, they are altogether opposite. Larry is a Southern gentleman. You just don't pay any attention to anyone but those Farrs."

A word about Margot's quite understandable jealousy of the Farrs. Much later in my life, when I was unreasonably upset at the attachment of one of my own daughters to another family (unreasonable because her chosen group were all talented musicians, as she was), a wise friend told me that we all could use more than one set of parents—our relations with the original set are too intense, and need dissipating. But no one, certainly not silly Dolly, was around to comfort Margot with this wisdom.

The summer raced on. ("Not without dust and heat," Lawrence several times remarked, in his private ironic voice.) The roses wilted on the roof and on the banks next to the road. The creek dwindled, and beside it honeysuckle leaves lay limply on the vines. For weeks, there was no rain, and then, one afternoon, there came a dark torrential thunderstorm. Harriet and I sat on the side porch and watched its violent start—the black clouds seeming to rise from the horizon, the cracking, jagged streaks of lightning, the heavy, welcome rain. And, later, the clean smell of leaves and grass and damp earth.

Knowing that Margot would be frightened, I thought of calling her, and then remembered that she would not talk on the phone during storms. And that night she told me, "The phone rang and rang, but I didn't think it was you, somehow."

"No."

"I had the craziest idea that it was Johnny. Be just like him to pick the middle of a storm for a phone call."

"There might not have been a storm in New Orleans."

But it turned out that Margot was right.

The next day, when I rode up to the Farrs' on my bike, Emily was sitting out in the grass where I had first seen her. I went and squatted beside her there. I thought she looked old and sad, and partly to cheer her I said, "You grow the most beautiful flowers I've ever seen."

She sighed, instead of smiling as she usually did. She said, "I seem to have turned into a gardener. When I was a girl, I imagined that I would grow up to be a writer, a novelist, and that I would have at least four children. Instead, I grow flowers and write book reviews."

I was not interested in children. "You never wrote a novel?"

She smiled unhappily. "No. I think I was afraid that I wouldn't come up to Trollope. I married rather young, you know."

And at that moment Lawrence came out of the house, immaculate in white flannels.

He greeted me, and said to Emily, "My dear, I find that I have some rather late appointments, in Hillsboro. You won't wait dinner if I'm a trifle late?"

(Of course she would; she always did.)

"No. Have a good time," she said, and she gave him the anxious look that I had come to recognize as the way she looked at Lawrence.

* * *

Soon after that, a lot happened very fast. Margot wrote to Johnny (again) that she wanted a divorce, that she intended to marry Larry. (I wonder if this was ever true.) Johnny telephoned—not once but several times. He told her that she was crazy, that he had a great job with some shipbuilders near San Francisco—a defense contract. He would come to get us, and we would all move out there. Margot agreed. We would make a new life. (Of course, we never knew what happened to the girl.)

I was not as sad about leaving the Farrs and that house, that town, those woods as I was to be later, looking back. I was excited about San Francisco, and I vaguely imagined that someday I would come back and that we would all see each other again. Like parting lovers, Harriet and I promised to write each other every day.

And for quite a while we did write several times a week. I wrote about San Francisco—how beautiful it was: the hills and pastel houses, the sea. How I wished that she could see it. She wrote about school and friends. She described solitary bike rides to places we had been. She told me what she was reading.

In high school, our correspondence became more generalized. Responding perhaps to the adolescent mores of the early nineteen-forties, we wrote about boys and parties; we even competed in making ourselves sound "popular." The truth (my truth) was that I was sometimes popular, often not. I had, in fact, a stormy adolescence. And at that time I developed what was to be a long-lasting habit. As I reviewed a situation in which I had been ill-advised or impulsive, I would re-enact the whole scene in my mind with Harriet in my own role—Harriet, cool and controlled, more intelligent, prettier. Even more than I wanted to see her again, I wanted to *be* Harriet.

Johnny and Margot fought a lot and stayed together, and gradually a sort of comradeship developed between them in our small house on Russian Hill.

I went to Stanford, where I half-heartedly studied history. Harriet was at Radcliffe, studying American literature, writing poetry.

We lost touch with each other.

Margot, however, kept up with her old friend Dolly, by means of Christmas cards and Easter notes, and Margot thus heard a remarkable piece of news about Emily Farr. Emily "up and left Lawrence without so much as a by-your-leave," said Dolly, and went to Washington, D.C., to work in the Folger Library. This news made me smile all day. I was so proud of Emily. And I imagined that Lawrence would amuse himself, that they would both be happier apart.

By accident, I married well—that is to say, a man whom I still like and enjoy. Four daughters came at uncalculated intervals, and each is remarkably unlike her sisters. I named one Harriet, although she seems to have my untidy character.

From time to time, over the years, I would see a poem by Harriet Farr, and I always thought it was marvelous, and I meant to write her. But I distrusted my reaction. I had been (I was) so deeply fond of Harriet (Emily, Lawrence, that house and land) and besides, what would I say—"I think your poem is marvelous"? (I have since learned that this is neither an inadequate nor an unwelcome thing to say to writers.) Of course, the true reason for not writing was that there was too much to say.

Dolly wrote to Margot that Lawrence was drinking "all over the place." He was not happier without Emily. Harriet, Dolly said, was traveling a lot. She married several times and had no children. Lawrence developed emphysema, and was in such bad shape that Emily quit her job and came back to take care of him—whether because of feelings of guilt or duty or possibly affection, I didn't know. He died, lingeringly and miserably, and Emily, too, died, a few years later—at least partly from exhaustion, I would imagine.

* * *

Then, at last, I did write Harriet, in care of the magazine in which I had last seen a poem of hers. I wrote a clumsy, gusty letter, much too long, about shared pasts, landscapes, the creek. All that. And as soon as I had mailed it I began mentally rewriting, seeking more elegant prose.

When for a long time I didn't hear from Harriet, I felt worse and worse, cumbersome, misplaced—as too often in life I had felt before. It did not occur to me that an infrequently staffed magazine could be at fault.

Months later, her letter came—from Rome, where she was then living. Alone, I gathered. She said that she was writing it at the moment of receiving mine. It was a long, emotional and very moving letter, out of character for the Harriet that I remembered (or had invented).

She said, in part: "It was really strange, all that time when Lawrence was dying, and God! so long! and as though 'dying' were all that he was doing—Emily, too, although we didn't know that—all that time the picture that moved me most, in my mind, that moved me to tears, was not of Lawrence and Emily but of you and me. On our bikes at the top of the hill outside our house. Going somewhere. And I first thought that that picture simply symbolized something irretrievable, the lost and irrecoverable past, as Lawrence and Emily would be lost. And I'm sure that was partly it.

"But they were so extremely fond of you—in fact, you were a rare area of agreement. They missed you, and they talked about you for years. It's a wonder that I wasn't jealous, and I think I wasn't only because I felt included in their affection for you. They liked me best with you.

"Another way to say this would be to say that we were all three a little less crazy and isolated with you around, and, God knows, happier."

An amazing letter, I thought. It was enough to make me take a long look at my whole life, and to find some new colors there.

* * *

A postscript: I showed Harriet's letter to my husband. and he said, "How odd. She sounds so much like you."

# 3

# 1980s AND 1990s

## *Centers and Margins*

maybe they were right. That Maltese woman laughed about it, but I noticed she wore only a watch, and that with a leather strap.

The money I give to the church goes in people's stomachs, and on their backs, down in New York City. I have no delusions about the worth of what I do, but I feel it's better to feed somebody than not. There's a priest in Times Square giving shelter to runaway kids, and some Franciscans who run a bread line; actually it's a morning line for coffee and a roll, and Father Paul calls it the continental breakfast for winos and bag ladies. He is curious about how much I am sending, and I know why: he guesses I send a lot, he has said probably more than tithing, and he is right; he wants to know how much because he believes I'm generous and good, and he is wrong about that; he has never had much money and does not know how easy it is to write a check when you have every thing you will ever need, and the figures are mere numbers, and represent no sacrifice at all. Being a real Catholic is too hard; if I were one, I would do with my house and barn what I want the Pope to do with his. So I do not want to impress Father Paul, and when he asks me how much, I say I can't let my left hand know what my right is doing.

He came on Wednesday nights when Gloria and I were married, and the kids were young; Gloria was a very good cook (I assume she still is, but it is difficult to think of her in the present), and I liked sitting at the table with a friend who was also a priest. I was proud of my handsome and healthy children. This was long ago, and they were all very young and cheerful and often funny, and the three boys took care of their baby sister, and did not bully or tease her. Of course they did sometimes, with that excited cruelty children are prone to, but not enough so that it was part of her days. On the Wednesday after Gloria left with the kids and a U-Haul trailer, I was sitting on the front steps, it was summer, and I was watching cars go by on the road, when Father Paul drove around the curve and into the driveway. I was ashamed to see him because he is a priest and my family was gone, but I was relieved too. I went to the car to greet him. He got out smiling, with a bottle of wine, and shook my hand, then pulled me to him, gave me a quick hug, and said: "It's Wednesday, isn't it? Let's open some cans."

With arms about each other we walked to the house, and it was good to know he was doing his work but coming as a friend too, and I thought what good work he had. I have no calling. It is for me to keep horses.

In that other life, anyway. In my real one I go to bed early and sleep well and wake at four forty-five, for an hour of silence. I never want to get out of bed then, and every morning I know I can sleep for another four hours, and still not fail at any of my duties. But I get up, so have come to believe my life can be seen in miniature in that struggle in the dark of morning. While making the bed and boiling water for coffee, I talk to God: I offer Him my day, every act of my body and spirit, my thoughts and moods, as a prayer of thanksgiving, and for Gloria and my children and my friends and two women I made love with after Gloria left. This morning offertory is a habit from my boyhood in a Catholic school; or then it was a habit, but as I kept it and grew older it became a ritual. Then I say the Lord's Prayer, trying not to recite it, and one morning it occurred to me that a prayer, whether recited or said with concentration, is always an act of faith.

I sit in the kitchen at the rear of the house and drink coffee and smoke and watch the sky growing light before sunrise, the trees of the woods near the barn taking shape, becoming single pines and elms and oaks and maples. Sometimes a rabbit comes out of the treeline, or is already sitting there, invisible till the light finds him. The birds are

all trees look alike in the dark

awake in the trees and feeding on the ground, and the little ones, the purple finches and titmice and chickadees, are at the feeder I rigged outside the kitchen window; it is too small for pigeons to get a purchase. I sit and give myself to coffee and tobacco, that get me brisk again, and I watch and listen. In the first year or so after I lost my family, I played the radio in the mornings. But I overcame that, and now I rarely play it at all. Once in the mail I received a questionnaire asking me to write down everything I watched on television during the week they had chosen. At the end of those seven days I wrote in *The Wizard of Oz* and returned it. That was in winter and was actually a busy week for my television, which normally sits out the cold months without once warming up. Had they sent the questionnaire during baseball season, they would have found me at my set. People at the stables talk about shows and performers I have never heard of, but I cannot get interested; when I am in the mood to watch television, I go to a movie or read a detective novel. There are always good detective novels to be found, and I like remembering them next morning with my coffee.

I also think of baseball and hunting and fishing, and of my children. It is not painful to think about them anymore, because even if we had lived together, they would be gone now, grown into their own lives, except Jennifer. I think of death too, not sadly, or with fear, though something like excitement does run through me, something more quickening than the coffee and tobacco. I suppose it is an intense interest, and an outright distrust: I never feel certain that I'll be here watching birds eating at tomorrow's daylight. Sometimes I try to think of other things, like the rabbit that is warm and breathing but not there till twilight. I feel on the brink of something about the life of the senses, but either am not equipped to go further or am not interested enough to concentrate. I have called all of this thinking, but it is not, because it is unintentional; what I'm really doing is feeling the day, in silence, and that is what Father Paul is doing too on his five-to-ten-mile walks.

When the hour ends I take an apple or carrot and I go to the stable and tack up a horse. We take good care of these horses, and no one rides them but students, instructors, and me, and nobody rides the horses we board unless an owner asks me to. The barn is dark and I turn on lights and take some deep breaths, smelling the hay and horses and their manure, both fresh and dried, a combined odor that you either like or you don't. I walk down the wide space of dirt between stalls, greeting the horses, joking with them about their quirks, and choose one for no reason at all other than the way it looks at me that morning. I get my old English saddle that has smoothed and darkened through the years, and go into the stall, talking to this beautiful creature who'll swerve out of a canter if a piece of paper blows in front of him, and if the barn catches fire and you manage to get him out he will, if he can get away from you, run back into the fire, to his stall. Like the smells that surround them, you either like them or you don't. I love them, so am spared having to try to explain why. I feed one the carrot or apple and tack up and lead him outside, where I mount, and we go down the driveway to the road and cross it and turn northwest and walk then trot then canter to St. John's.

A few cars are on the road, their drivers looking serious about going to work. It is always strange for me to see a woman dressed for work so early in the morning. You know how long it takes them, with the makeup and hair and clothes, and I think of them waking in the dark of winter or early light of other seasons, and dressing as they might for an evening's entertainment. Probably this strikes me because I grew up seeing my father put on those suits he never wore on weekends or his two weeks off, and so am accustomed to the men, but when I see these women I think something went wrong, to send all those dressed-up people out on the road when the dew hasn't dried yet. Maybe it's because I so dislike getting up early, but am also doing what I choose to do, while they have no choice. At heart I am lazy, yet I find such peace and delight in it that I believe it is a natural state, and in what looks like my laziest periods I am closest to my center. The ride to St. John's is fifteen minutes. The horses and I do it in all weather; the road is well plowed in winter, and there are only a few days a year when ice makes me drive the pickup. People always look at someone on horseback, and for a moment their faces change and many drivers and I wave to each other. Then at St. John's, Father Paul and five or six regulars and I celebrate the Mass.

Do not think of me as a spiritual man whose every thought during those twenty-five minutes is at one with the words of the Mass. Each morning I try, each morning I fail, and know that always I will be a creature who, looking at Father Paul and the altar, and uttering prayers, will be distracted by scrambled eggs, horses, the weather, and memories and daydreams that have nothing to do with the sacrament I am about to receive. I can receive, though: the Eucharist, and also, at Mass and at other times, moments and even minutes of contemplation. But I cannot achieve contemplation, as some can; and so, having to face and forgive my own failures, I have learned from them both the necessity and wonder of ritual. For ritual allows those who cannot will themselves out of the secular to perform the spiritual, as dancing allows the tongue-tied man a ceremony of love. And, while my mind dwells on breakfast, or Major or Duchess tethered under the church eave, there is, as I take the Host from Father Paul and place it on my tongue and return to the pew, a feeling that I am thankful I have not lost in the forty-eight years since my first Communion. At its center is excitement; spreading out from it is the peace of certainty. Or the certainty of peace. One night Father Paul and I talked about faith. It was long ago, and all I remember is him saying: Belief is believing in God; faith is believing that God believes in you. That is the excitement, and the peace; then the Mass is over, and I go into the sacristy and we have a cigarette and chat, the mystery ends, we are two men talking like any two men on a morning in America, about baseball, plane crashes, presidents, governors, murders, the sun, the clouds. Then I go to the horse and ride back to the life people see, the one in which I move and talk, and most days I enjoy it.

* * *

It is late summer now, the time between fishing and hunting, but a good time for baseball. It has been two weeks since Jennifer left, to drive home to Gloria's after her summer visit. She is the only one who still visits; the boys are married and have children, and sometimes fly up for a holiday, or I fly down or west to visit one of them. Jennifer is twenty, and I worry about her the way fathers worry about daughters but not sons. I want to know what she's up to, and at the same time I don't. She looks athletic, and she is: she swims and runs and of course rides. All my children do. When she comes for six weeks in summer, the house is loud with girls, friends of hers since childhood, and new ones. I am glad she kept the girl friends. They have been young company for me and, being with them, I have been able to gauge her growth between summers. On their riding days, I'd take them back to the house when their lessons were over and they had walked the horses and put them back in the stalls, and we'd have lemonade or Coke, and cookies if I had some, and talk until their parents came to drive them home. One year their breasts grew, so I wasn't startled when I saw Jennifer in July. Then they were driving cars to the stable, and beginning to look like young women, and I was passing out beer and ashtrays and they were talking about college.

When Jennifer was here in summer, they were at the house most days. I would say generally that as they got older they became quieter, and though I enjoyed both, I sometimes missed the giggles and shouts. The quiet voices, just low enough for me not to hear from wherever I was, rising and falling in proportion to my distance from them, frightened me. Not that I believed they were planning or recounting anything really wicked, but there was a female seriousness about them, and it was secretive, and of course I thought: love, sex. But it was more than that: it was womanhood they were entering, the deep forest of it, and no matter how many women and men too are saying these days that there is little difference between us, the truth is that men find their way into that forest only on clearly marked trails, while women move about in it like birds. So hearing Jennifer and her friends talking so quietly, yet intensely, I wanted very much to have a wife.

But not as much as in the old days, when Gloria had left but her presence was still in the house as strongly as if she had only gone to visit her folks for a week. There were no clothes or cosmetics, but potted plants endured my neglectful care as long as they could, and slowly died; I did not kill them on purpose, to exorcise the house of her, but I could not remember to water them. For weeks, because I did not use it much, the house was as neat as she had kept it, though dust layered the order she had made. The kitchen went first: I got the dishes in and out of the dishwasher and wiped the top of the stove, but did not return cooking spoons and pot holders to their hooks on the wall, and soon the burners and oven were caked with spillings, the refrigerator had more space and was spotted with juices. The living room and my bedroom went next; I did not go into the children's rooms except on bad nights when I went from room to room and looked and touched and smelled, so they did not lose their order until a year later when the kids came for six weeks. It was three months before I ate the last of the food Gloria had cooked and frozen: I remember it was a beef stew, and very good. By then I had four cookbooks, and was boasting a bit, and talking about recipes with the women at the stables, and looking forward to cooking for Father Paul. But I never looked forward to cooking at night only for myself, though I made myself do it; on some nights I gave in to my daily temptation, and took a newspaper or detective novel to a restaurant. By the end of the second year, though, I had stopped turning on the radio as soon as I woke in the morning, and was able to be silent and alone in the evening too, and then I enjoyed my dinners.

It is not hard to live through a day, if you can live through a moment. What creates despair is the imagination, which pretends there is a future, and insists on predicting millions of moments, thousands of days, and so drains you that you cannot live the moment at hand. That is what Father Paul told me in those first two years, on some of the bad nights when I believed I could not bear what I had to: the most painful loss was my children, then the loss of Gloria, whom I still loved despite or maybe because of our long periods of sadness that rendered us helpless, so neither of us could break out of it to give a hand to the other. Twelve years later I believe ritual would have healed us more quickly than the repetitious talks we had, perhaps even kept us healed. Marriages have lost that, and I wish I had known then what I know now, and we had performed certain acts together every day, no matter how we felt, and perhaps then we could have subordinated feeling to action, for surely that is the essence of love. I know this from my distractions during Mass, and during everything else I do, so that my actions and feelings are seldom one. It does happen every day, but in proportion to everything else in a day, it is rare, like joy. The third most painful loss, which became second and sometimes first as months passed, was the knowledge that I could never marry again, and so dared not even keep company with a woman.

On some of the bad nights I was bitter about this with Father Paul, and I so pitied myself that I cried, or nearly did, speaking with damp eyes and breaking voice. I believe that celibacy is for him the same trial it is for me, not of the flesh, but the spirit: the heart longing to love. But the difference is he chose it, and did not wake one day to a life with thirty horses. In my anger I said I had done my service to love and chastity, and I told him of the actual physical and spiritual pain of practicing rhythm: nights of striking the mattress with a fist, two young animals lying side by side in heat, leaving the bed to pace, to smoke, to curse, and too passionate to question, for we were so angered and oppressed by our passion that we could see no further than our loins. So now I understand how people can be enslaved for generations before they throw down their tools or use them as weapons, the form of their slavery—the cotton fields, the shacks and puny cupboards and untended illnesses—absorbing their emotions and thoughts until finally they have little or none at all to direct with clarity and energy at the owners and legislators. And I told him of the trick of passion and its slaking: how during what we had to believe were safe periods, though all four children were conceived at those times, we were able with some coherence to question the tradition and reason and justice of the law against birth control, but not with enough conviction to soberly act against it, as though regular satisfaction in bed tempered our revolutionary as well as our erotic desires. Only when abstinence drove us hotly away from each other did we receive an urge so strong it lasted all the way to the drugstore and back; but always, after release, we threw away the remaining condoms; and after going through this a few times, we knew what would happen, and from then on we submitted to the calendar she so precisely marked on the bedroom wall. I told him that living two lives each month, one as celibates, one as lovers, made us tense and short-tempered, so we snapped at each other like dogs.

To have endured that, to have reached a time when we burned slowly and could gain from bed the comfort of lying down at night with one who loves you and whom you love, could for weeks on end go to bed tired and peacefully sleep after a kiss, a touch of the hands, and then to be thrown out of the marriage like a bundle from a moving freight car, was unjust, was intolerable, and I could not or would not muster the strength to endure it. But I did, a moment at a time, a day, a night, except twice, each time with a different woman and more than a year apart, and this was so long ago that I clearly see their faces in my memory, can hear the pitch of their voices, and the way they pronounced words, one with a Massachusetts accent, one midwestern, but I feel as though I only heard about them from someone else. Each rode at the stables and was with me for part of an evening; one was badly married, one divorced, so none of us was free. They did not understand this Catholic view, but they were understanding about my having it, and I remained friends with both of them until the married one left her husband and went to Boston, and the divorced one moved to Maine. After both those evenings, those good women, I went to Mass early while Father Paul was still in the confessional, and received his absolution. I did not tell him who I was, but of course he knew, though I never saw it in his eyes. Now my longing for a wife comes only once in a while, like a cold: on some late afternoons when I am alone in the barn, then I lock up and walk to the house, daydreaming, then suddenly look at it and see it empty, as though for the first time, and all at once I'm weary and feel I do not have the energy to broil meat, and I think of driving to a restaurant, then shake my head and go on to the house, the refrigerator, the oven; and some mornings when I wake in the dark and listen to the silence and run my hand over the cold sheet beside me; and some days in summer when Jennifer is here.

Gloria left first me, then the Church, and that was the end of religion for the children, though on visits they went to Sunday Mass with me, and still do, out of a respect for my life that they manage to keep free of patronage. Jennifer is an agnostic, though I doubt she would call herself that, any more than she would call herself any other name that implied she had made a decision, a choice, about existence, death, and God. In truth she tends to pantheism, a good sign, I think; but not wanting to be a father who tells his children what they ought to believe, I do not say to her that Catholicism includes pantheism, like onions in a stew. Besides, I have no missionary instincts and do not believe everyone should or even could live with the Catholic faith. It is Jennifer's womanhood that renders me awkward. And womanhood now is frank, not like when Gloria was twenty and there were symbols: high heels and cosmetics and dresses, a cigarette, a cocktail. I am glad that women are free now of false modesty and all its attention paid the flesh; but, still, it is difficult to see so much of your daughter, to hear her talk as only men and bawdy women used to, and most of all to see in her face the deep and unabashed sensuality of women, with no tricks of the eyes and mouth to hide the pleasure she feels at having a strong young body. I am certain, with the way things are now, that she has very happily not been a virgin for years. That does not bother me. What bothers me is my certainty about it, just from watching her walk across a room or light a cigarette or pour milk on cereal.

* * *

She told me all of it, waking me that night when I had gone to sleep listening to the wind in the trees and against the house, a wind so strong that I had to shut all but the lee windows, and still the house cooled; told it to me in such detail and so clearly that now, when she has driven the car to Florida, I remember it all as though I had been a passenger in the front seat, or even at the wheel. It started with a movie, then beer and driving to the sea to look at the waves in the night and the wind, Jennifer and Betsy and Liz. They drank a beer on the beach and wanted to go in naked but were afraid they would drown in the high surf. They bought another six-pack at a grocery store in New Hampshire, and drove home. I can see it now, feel it: the three girls and the beer and the ride on country roads where pines curved in the wind and the big deciduous trees swayed and shook as if they might leap from the earth. They would have some windows partly open so they could feel the wind; Jennifer would be playing a cassette, the music stirring them, as it does the young, to memories of another time, other people and places in what is for them the past.

She took Betsy home, then Liz, and sang with her cassette as she left the town west of us and started home, a twenty-minute drive on the road that passes my house. They had each had four beers, but now there were twelve empty bottles in the bag on the floor at the passenger seat, and I keep focusing on their sound against each other when the car shifted speeds or changed directions. For I want to understand that one moment out of all her heart's time on earth, and whether her history had any bearing on it, or whether her heart was then isolated from all it had known, and the sound of those bottles urged it. She was just leaving the town, accelerating past a night club on the right, gaining speed to climb a long, gradual hill, then she went up it, singing, patting the beat on the steering wheel, the wind loud through her few inches of open window, blowing her hair as it did the high branches alongside the road, and she looked up at them and watched the top of the hill for someone drunk or heedless coming over it in part of her lane. She crested to an open black road, and there he was: a bulk, a blur, a thing running across her headlights, and she swerved left and her foot went for the brake and was stomping air above its pedal when she hit him, saw his legs and body in the air, flying out of her light, into the dark. Her brakes were screaming into the wind, bottles clinking in the fallen bag, and with the music and wind inside the car was his sound, already a memory but as real as an echo, that car-shuddering thump as though she had struck a tree. Her foot was back on the accelerator. Then she shifted gears and pushed it. She ejected the cassette and closed the window. She did not start to cry until she knocked on my bedroom door, then called: "Dad?"

Her voice, her tears, broke through my dream and the wind I heard in my sleep, and I stepped into jeans and hurried to the door, thinking harm, rape, death. All were in her face, and I hugged her and pressed her cheek to my chest and smoothed her blown hair, then led her, weeping, to the kitchen and sat her at the table where still she could not speak, nor look at me; when she raised her face it fell forward again, as of its own weight, into her palms. I offered tea and she shook her head, so I offered beer twice, then she shook her head, so I offered whiskey and she nodded. I had some rye that Father Paul and I had not finished last hunting season, and I poured some over ice and set it in front of her and was putting away the ice but stopped and got another glass and poured one for myself too, and brought the ice and bottle to the table where she was trying to get one of her long menthols out of the pack, but her fingers jerked like severed snakes, and I took the pack and lit one for her and took one for myself. I watched her shudder with her first swallow of rye, and push hair back from her face, it is auburn and gleamed in the overhead light, and I remembered how beautiful she looked riding a sorrel; she was smoking fast, then the sobs in her throat stopped, and she looked at me and said it, the words coming out with smoke: "I hit somebody. With the *car.*"

Then she was crying and I was on my feet, moving back and forth, looking down at her, asking *Who? Where? Where?* She was pointing at the wall over the stove, jabbing her fingers and cigarette at it, her other hand at her eyes, and twice in horror I actually looked at the wall. She finished the whiskey in a swallow and I stopped pacing and asking and poured another, and either the drink or the exhaustion of tears quieted her, even the dry sobs, and she told me; not as I tell it now, for that was later as again and again we relived it in the kitchen or living room, and, if in daylight, fled it on horseback out on the trails through the woods and, if at night, walked quietly around in the moonlit pasture, walked around and around it, sweating through our clothes. She told it in bursts, like she was a child again, running to me, injured from play. I put on boots and a shirt and left her with the bottle and her streaked face and a cigarette twitching between her fingers, pushed the door open against the wind, and eased it shut. The wind squinted and watered my eyes as I leaned into it and went to the pickup.

When I passed St. John's I looked at it, and Father Paul's little white rectory in the rear, and wanted to stop, wished I could as I could if he were simply a friend who sold hardware or something. I had forgotten my watch but I always know the time within minutes, even when a sound or dream or my bladder wakes me in the night. It was nearly two; we had been in the kitchen about twenty minutes; she had hit him around one-fifteen. Or her. The road was empty and I drove between blowing trees; caught for an instant in my lights, they seemed to be in panic. I smoked and let hope play its tricks on me: it was neither man nor woman but an animal, a goat or calf or deer on the road; it was a man who had jumped away in time, the collision of metal and body glancing not direct, and he had limped home to nurse bruises and cuts. Then I threw the cigarette and hope both out the window and prayed that he was alive, while beneath that prayer, a reserve deeper in my heart, another one stirred: that if he were dead, they would not get Jennifer.

From our direction, east and a bit south, the road to that hill and the night club beyond it and finally the town is, for its last four or five miles, straight through farming country. When I reached that stretch I slowed the truck and opened my window for the fierce air; on both sides were scattered farmhouses and barns and sometimes a silo, looking not like shelters but like unsheltered things the wind would flatten. Corn bent toward the road from a field on my right, and always something blew in front of me: paper, leaves, dried weeds, branches. I slowed approaching the hill, and went up it in second, staring through my open window at the ditch on the left side of the road, its weeds alive, whipping, a mad dance with the trees above them. I went over the hill and down and, opposite the club, turned right onto a side street of houses, and parked there, in the leaping shadows of trees. I walked back across the road to the club's parking lot, the wind behind me, lifting me as I strode, and I could not hear my boots on pavement. I walked up the hill, on the shoulder, watching the branches above me, hearing their leaves and the creaking trunks and the wind. Then I was at the top, looking down the road and at the farms and fields; the night was clear, and I could see a long way; clouds scudded past the half-moon and stars, blown out to sea.

I started down, watching the tall grass under the trees to my right, glancing into the dark of the ditch, listening for cars behind me; but as soon as I cleared one tree, its sound was gone, its flapping leaves and rattling branches far behind me, as though the greatest distance I had at my back was a matter of feet, while ahead of me I could see a barn two miles off. Then I saw her skid marks: short, and going left and downhill, into the other lane. I stood at the ditch, its weeds blowing; across it were trees and their moving shadows, like the clouds. I stepped onto its slope, and it took me sliding on my feet, then rump, to the bottom, where I sat still, my body gathered to itself, lest a part of me should touch him. But there was only tall grass, and I stood, my shoulders reaching the sides of the ditch, and I walked uphill, wishing for the flashlight in the pickup, walking slowly, and down in the ditch I could hear my feet in the grass and on the earth, and kicking cans and bottles. At the top of the hill I turned and went down, watching the ground above the ditch on my right, praying my prayer from the truck again, the first one, the one I would admit, that he was not dead, was in fact home, and began to hope again, memory telling me of lost pheasants and grouse I had shot, but they were small and the colors of their home, while a man was either there or not; and from that memory I left where I was and while walking in the ditch under the wind was in the deceit of imagination with Jennifer in the kitchen, telling her she had hit no one, or at least had not badly hurt anyone, when I realized he could be in the hospital now and I would have to think of a way to check there, something to say on the phone. I see now that, once hope returned, I should have been certain what it prepared me for: ahead of me, in high grass and the shadows of trees, I saw his shirt. Or that is all my mind would allow itself: a shirt, and I stood looking at it for the moments it took my mind to admit the arm and head and the dark length covered by pants. He lay face down, the arm I could see near his side, his head turned from me, on its cheek.

"Fella?" I said. I had meant to call, but it came out quiet and high lost inches from my face in the wind. Then I said, "Oh God,"and felt Him in the wind and the sky moving past the stars and moon and the fields around me, but only watching me as He might have watched Cain or Job, I did not know which, and I said it again, and wanted to sink to the earth and weep till I slept there in the weeds. I climbed, scrambling up the side of the ditch, pulling at clutched grass, gained the top on hands and knees, and went to him like that, panting, moving through the grass as high and higher than my face, crawling under that sky, making sounds too, like some animal, there being no words to let him know I was here with him now. He was long; that is the word that came to me, not tall. I kneeled beside him, my hands on my legs. His right arm was by his side, his left arm straight out from the shoulder, but turned, so his palm was open to the tree above us. His left cheek was cleanshaven, his eye closed, and there was no blood. I leaned forward to look at his open mouth and saw the blood on it, going down into the grass: I straightened and looked ahead at the wind blowing past me through grass and trees to a distant light, and I stared at the light, imagining someone awake out there, wanting someone to be, a gathering of old friends, or someone alone listening to music or painting a picture, then I figured it was a night light at a farmyard whose house I couldn't see. *Going,* I thought. *Still going.* I leaned over again and looked at dripping blood.

So I had to touch his wrist, a thick one with a watch and expansion band that I pushed up his arm, thinking *he's left-handed,* my three fingers pressing his wrist, and all I felt was my tough finger-tips on that smooth underside flesh and small bones, then relief, then certainty. But against my will, or only because of it, I still don't know, I touched his neck, ran my fingers down it as if petting, then pressed, and my hand sprang back as from fire. I lowered it again, held it there until it felt that faint beating that I could not believe. There was too much wind. Nothing could make a sound in it. A pulse could not be felt in it, nor could mere fingers in that wind feel the absolute silence of a dead man's artery. I was making sounds again; I grabbed his left arm and his waist, and pulled him toward me, and that side of him rose, turned, and I lowered him to his back, his face tilted up toward the tree that was groaning, the tree and I the only sounds in the wind. Turning my face from his, looking down the length of him at his sneakers, I placed my ear on his heart, and heard not that but something else, and I clamped a hand over my exposed ear, heard something liquid and alive, like when you pump a well and after a few strokes you hear air and water moving in the pipe, and I knew I must raise his legs and cover him and run to a phone, while still I listened to his chest, thinking *raise with what? cover with what?* and amid the liquid sound I heard the heart, then lost it, and pressed my ear against bone, but his chest was quiet, and I did not know when the liquid had stopped, and do not know now when I heard air, a faint rush of it, and whether under my ear or at his mouth or whether I heard it at all. I straightened and looked at the light, dim and yellow. Then I touched his throat, looking him full in the face. He was blond and young. He could have been sleeping in the shade of a tree, but for the smear of blood from his mouth to his hair, and the night sky, and the weeds blowing against his head, and the leaves shaking in the dark above us.

I stood. Then I kneeled again and prayed for his soul to join in peace and joy all the dead and living; and, doing so, confronted my first sin against him, not stopping for Father Paul, who could have given him the last rites, and immediately then my second one, or, I saw then, my first, not calling an ambulance to meet me there, and I stood and turned into the wind, slid down the ditch and crawled out of it, and went up the hill and down it, across the road to the street of houses whose people I had left behind forever, so that I moved with stealth in the shadows to my truck.

When I came around the bend near my house, I saw the kitchen light at the rear. She sat as I had left her, the ashtray filled, and I looked at the bottle, felt her eyes on me, felt what she was seeing too: the dirt from my crawling. She had not drunk much of the rye. I poured some in my glass, with the water from melted ice, and sat down and swallowed some and looked at her and swallowed some more, and said: "He's dead."

She rubbed her eyes with the heels of her hands, rubbed the cheeks under them, but she was dry now.

"He was probably dead when he hit the ground. I mean, that's probably what killed—"

"Where was he?"

"Across the ditch, under a tree."

"Was he—did you see his face?"

"No. Not really. I just felt. For life, pulse. I'm going out to the car."

"What for? Oh."

I finished the rye, and pushed back the chair, then she was standing too.

"I'll go with you."

"There's no need."

"I'll go."

I took a flashlight from a drawer and pushed open the door and held it while she went out. We turned our faces from the wind. It was like on the hill, when I was walking, and the wind closed the distance behind me: after three or four steps I felt there was no house back there. She took my hand, as I was reaching for hers. In the garage we let go, and squeezed between the pickup and her little car, to the front of it, where we had more room, and we stepped back from the grill and I shone the light on the fender, the smashed headlight turned into it, the concave chrome staring to the right, at the garage wall.

"We ought to get the bottles," I said.

She moved between the garage and the car, on the passenger side, and had room to open the door and lift the bag. I reached out, and she gave me the bag and backed up and shut the door and came around the car. We sidled to the doorway, and she put her arm around my waist and I hugged her shoulders.

"I thought you'd call the police," she said.

We crossed the yard, faces bowed from the wind, her hair blowing away from her neck, and in the kitchen I put the bag of bottles in the garbage basket. She was working at the table: capping the rye and putting it away, filling the ice tray, washing the glasses, emptying the ashtray, sponging the table.

"Try to sleep now," I said.

She nodded at the sponge circling under her hand, gathering ashes. Then she dropped it in the sink and, looking me full in the face, as I had never seen her look, as perhaps she never had, being for so long a daughter on visits (or so it seemed to me and still does: that until then our eyes had never seriously met), she crossed to me from the sink and kissed my lips, then held me so tightly I lost balance, and would have stumbled forward had she not held me so hard.

* * *

I sat in the living room, the house darkened, and watched the maple and the hemlock. When I believed she was asleep I put on *La Boheme,* and kept it at the same volume as the wind so it would not wake her. Then I listened to *Madame Butterfly,* and in the third act had to rise quickly to lower the sound: the wind was gone. I looked at the still maple near the window, and thought of the wind leaving farms and towns and the coast, going out over the sea to die on the waves. I smoked and gazed out the window. The sky was darker, and at daybreak the rain came. I listened to *Tosca,* and at six-fifteen went to the kitchen where Jennifer's purse lay on the table, a leather shoulder purse crammed with the things of an adult woman, things she had begun accumulating only a few years back, and I nearly wept, thinking of what sandy foundations they were: driver's license, credit card, disposable lighter, cigarettes, checkbook, ballpoint pen, cash, cosmetics, comb, brush, Kleenex, these the rite of passage from childhood, and I took one of them—her keys—and went out, remembering a jacket and hat when the rain struck me, but I kept going to the car, and squeezed and lowered myself into it, pulled the seat belt over my shoulder and fastened it and backed out, turning in the drive, going forward into the road, toward St. John's and Father Paul.

Cars were on the road, the workers, and I did not worry about any of them noticing the fender and light. Only a horse distracted them from what they drove to. In front of St. John's is a parking lot; at its far side, past the church and at the edge of the lawn, is an old pine, taller than the steeple now. I shifted to third, left the road, and, aiming the right headlight at the tree, accelerated past the white blur of church, into the black trunk growing bigger till it was all I could see, then I rocked in that resonant thump she had heard, had felt, and when I turned off the ignition it was still in my ears, my blood, and I saw the boy flying in the wind. I lowered my forehead to the wheel. Father Paul opened the door, his face white in the rain.

"I'm all right."

"What happened?"

"I don't know. I fainted."

I got out and went around to the front of the car, looked at the smashed light, the crumpled and torn fender.

"Come to the house and lie down."

"I'm all right."

"When was your last physical?"

"I'm due for one. Let's get out of this rain."

"You'd better lie down."

"No. I want to receive."

That was the time to say I want to confess, but I have not and will not. Though I could now, for Jennifer is in Florida, and weeks have passed, and perhaps now Father Paul would not feel that he must tell me to go to the police. And, for that very reason, to confess now would be unfair. It is a world of secrets, and now I have one from my best, in truth my only, friend. I have one from Jennifer too, but that is the nature of fatherhood.

Most of that day it rained, so it was only in early evening, when the sky cleared, with a setting sun, that two little boys, leaving their confinement for some play before dinner, found him. Jennifer and I got that on the local news, which we listened to every hour, meeting at the radio, standing with cigarettes, until the one at eight o'clock; when she stopped crying, we went out and walked on the wet grass, around the pasture, the last of sunlight still in the air and trees. His name was Patrick Mitchell, he was nineteen years old, was employed by CETA, lived at home with his parents and brother and sister. The paper next day said he had been at a friend's house and was walking home, and I thought of that light I had seen, then knew it was not for him; he lived on one of the streets behind the club. The paper did not say then, or in the next few days, anything to make Jennifer think he was alive while she was with me in the kitchen. Nor do I know if we—I—could have saved him.

In keeping her secret from her friends, Jennifer had to perform so often, as I did with Father Paul and at the stables, that I believe the acting, which took more of her than our daylight trail rides and our night walks in the pasture, was her healing. Her friends teased me about wrecking her car. When I carried her luggage out to the car on that last morning, we spoke only of the weather for her trip—the day was clear, with a dry cool breeze—and hugged and kissed, and I stood watching as she started the car and turned it around. But then she shifted to neutral and put on the parking brake and unclasped the belt, looking at me all the while, then she was coming to me, as she had that night in the kitchen, and I opened my arms.

I have said I talk with God in the mornings, as I start my day, and sometimes as I sit with coffee, looking at the birds, and the woods. Of course He has never spoken to me, but that is not something I require. Nor does He need to. I know Him, as I know the part of myself that knows Him, that felt Him watching from the wind and the night as I kneeled over the dying boy. Lately I have taken to arguing with Him, as I can't with Father Paul, who, when he hears my monthly confession, has not heard and will not hear anything of failure to do all that one can to save an anonymous life, of injustice to a family in their grief, of deepening their pain at the chance and mystery of death by giving them nothing—no one—to hate. With Father Paul I feel lonely about this, but not with God. When I received the Eucharist while Jennifer's car sat twice-damaged, so redeemed, in the rain, I felt neither loneliness nor shame, but as though He were watching me, even from my tongue, intestines, blood, as I have watched my sons at times in their young lives when I was able to judge but without anger, and so keep silent while they, in the agony of their youth, decided how they must act; or found reasons, after their actions, for what they had done. Their reasons were never as good or as bad as their actions, but they needed to find them, to believe they were living by them, instead of the awful solitude of the heart.

I do not feel the peace I once did: not with God, nor the earth, or anyone on it. I have begun to prefer this state, to remember with fondness the other one as a period of peace I neither earned nor deserved. Now in the mornings while I watch purple finches driving larger titmice from the feeder, I say to Him: I would do it again. For when she knocked on my door, then called me, she woke what had flowed dormant in my blood since her birth, so that what rose from the bed was not a stable owner or a Catholic or any other Luke Ripley I had lived with for a long time, but the father of a girl.

And He says: I am a Father too.

Yes, I say, as You are a Son Whom this morning I will receive; unless You kill me on the way to church, then I trust You will receive me. And as a Son You made Your plea.

Yes, He says, but I would not lift the cup.

True, and I don't want You to lift it from me either. And if one of my sons had come to me that night, I would have phoned the police and told them to meet us with an ambulance at the top of the hill.

Why? Do you love them less?

I tell Him no, it is not that I love them less, but that I could bear the pain of watching and knowing my sons' pain, could bear it with pride as they took the whip and nails. But You never had a daughter and, if You had, You could not have borne her passion.

So, He says, you love her more than you love Me.

I love her more than I love truth.

Then you love in weakness, He says.

As You love me, I say, and I go with an apple or carrot out to the barn.

# SUSAN FROMBERG SCHAEFFER

(1941– )

Susan Fromberg Schaeffer was born in Brooklyn, New York, and was educated in the New York City public schools. After high school she went to the University of Chicago where she completed a B.A. in 1961, an M.A. in 1963, and a Ph.D. in 1966. She taught for several years in Chicago before accepting an appointment to Brooklyn College in 1967. She has taught there ever since. She was married in 1970 and has two children.

Schaeffer is perhaps known more for her novels than for her stories. Her fiction is noteworthy for its strong narrative drive and voice focused on the complexities of family life and its intricate histories. Her novels include *Falling* (1973), *Anya* (1974), *Time in Its Flight* (1978), *Love* (1980), *The Madness of a Seduced Woman* (1983), *Mainland* (1985), *The Injured Party* (1986), *Buffalo Afternoon* (1989), *First Nights* (1993), and *The Golden Rope* (1996). Her stories are collected in *The Queen of Egypt* (1980). Her work has received a number of awards and won her a Guggenheim fellowship.

## The Priest Next Door

In the old neighborhoods, where the houses hide as many as eighteen rooms under their peaked and turreted roofs, silence falls as sweetly on the concrete sidewalks as sunlight; cars are not heard passing under the oak leaves, and it is the sound of wind and rain that people listen to. In neighborhoods like this, it is inevitable that everyone knows the rough lines and perspective of everyone else's lives, for the children belong to the same troops of Girl Scouts, and always have cookies to sell, so that the desperate mothers band together in threes and fours, each mother buying one box of cookies from the other two or three children so that their own child will not have to sell cookies to strangers and cross too many streets. So it is inevitable that not only the rough lines of a life, but the finer details, become common knowledge as well. Yet, on streets where the great tragedies are not deaths, which everyone chronicles in the ledger next to the births of the anonymous infants whose names the neighbors all carefully learn, but the falling of the great oak boughs from the trees in an ice storm, or the sawing off of branches by the telephone company, so they will not pull down the wires, where the truly remarkable event is the late frost aborting the crocuses and forsythias, or the early frost, cracking radiators of automobiles in their garages, themselves the sizes of houses, privacy is always respected.

For the people in the old houses have learned that a yard filled with oak leaves, cinder blocks, and damp cartons may mean the man of the house has had a stroke, and his wife must stay with him, or the woman of the house has been pregnant and confined to her bed and her couch. These events remain hidden, like shoots under leaves, while members of the family stand with their neighbor under an oak tree, admiring the solid ice coating, commenting on the tree's remarkable resemblance to glass. Therefore it is often easier to build a large spiked cedar fence around one's yard than discuss the condition of a neighboring fence with its owner, so that later, it is only possible to see the yard from a few upper windows of one's home, and soon the occupants' eyes learn to avoid the offensive cinder blocks and the thick black-brown sheet of leaves covering the adjoining lawn like a failed and terrible skin.

Still, strange attachments do begin to grow up. One house, which had long been known as the most beautiful on the block, fell into such savage disrepair that its yard was surrounded on two sides by high cedar fences. The neighbors had stopped visiting altogether, claiming the ice on the steps proclaimed the family's distaste for visitors, and no one would go where they were not wanted. In the summer, when everyone else's lawn had turned emerald green, the lawn of this house still blew with dry oak leaves, which would land on the other thick green carpets like dust tongues, each one bleating contempt for the block. So it was a surprise to no one when a *For Sale* sign went up over the door, for by now it was general knowledge that Mrs. Hills had had a heart attack, her oldest son having broken down in the local Catholic school after a month of misbehavior and blurted this out to Sister Grace. From that time on, there were rumors that considerably more of interest was taking place in the house, although no one attempted to find out what it was, since eventually, as is always the rule, the details would publish themselves in the very shingles of the house without anyone troubling to discover them.

The house was eventually sold to a young couple, who fortunately were not superstitious, for on the day they moved in, their baby's crib collapsed, and their own bed, when they sat down on it, fell to the floor in a splatter of splinters. It was a while before they had time to notice anything around them, surrounded as they were by what turned out to be seven truckloads of the Hills family's possessions: medicines abandoned in chests with the spoons beside them sticky, clothes of all sizes, dusty hangers, and, worst of all, in the basement, a trash can with an enormous decapitated doll's head, and, on an abandoned work table, a moose head, one eye torn loose, disgorging chalk powder through its socket, and above the entrance of the loft of the garage, a single leather boxing glove, cracked and peeling, hung from the rafters like a relentless old corpse.

Nevertheless, things settled. The baby who was one year old had stopped peering fuzzily around her new yellow room for the bookshelves of the study she had occupied, because the Zlotnicks' apartment had been much smaller; Mrs. Zlotnick, who was pregnant once again, began to feel the new baby kicking and was vomiting less and less frequently; it had been almost seven months since her last baby had begun growing in her left Fallopian tube, causing the blood explosion that sent her to the hospital for emergency surgery, and she would not be pregnant now if it hadn't been for God's Grace: accidents. Mrs. Zlotnick was beginning to open with the crocuses; less and less often, the emergency room climbed from its frame. Less and less often, she saw herself sitting in the receiving room; less often, she felt herself waiting for the real adults to come out of the cracks in the walls of the new house, although frequently, she did have a dream of a jagged lightning-shaped crack appearing on her stomach, a miniature doctor rising out of it as if on an elevator until he reached the level of her eyes, then menacing her with his stethoscope as if it were a hammer and shouting the names of various things that caused her to lose the baby: bananas! aspirins! antihistamines! turtles! stuffed rabbits! Edith Zlotnick often told her husband, Fred, and her closest friend, Susan, about this dream, carefully enumerating all the small changes in the doctor's list as if it were a grocery list, and always laughing, as if the dream were truly comical. Still, she had it more often than she would have liked.

"Look," Fred said one morning, as they were staring blankly out of their kitchen windows, both of them wondering whether the windows should have curtains or shades, for Fred was a champion of modesty and insisted they must have *something.* Had either of them known they had been thinking about the same thing, they would have been amazed, for, in fact, if they had begun to speak, each would have begun with a different subject. "Look," Fred said, "a fairy priest." "A fairy what?" Edith asked absently, inspecting the sludge of sugar at the bottom of her new china cup, trying to estimate the number of calories she was about to greedily consume. Fred had gone to the window and was staring with greater interest than he had shown in anything since the bathroom sink began its slow menacing leak. Edith got up, holding her stomach, and looked out the window also. In the backyard facing theirs, a priest was putting out paper plate after paper plate and cats were coming toward him through every bush and hedge. "God!" Edith thought, "our cats haven't had their booster shots." "She still hasn't had enough sympathy," Fred thought bitterly, his eyes carefully avoiding Edith, whose hands, he knew, would be supporting her mumpish stomach. "Look at that Persian cat; it's pregnant," Edith pointed, unconsciously adding, "Remember that time I was in the Emergency Room? I never thought a hospital could move so fast. I thought they just filled out forms while you wrote your will on the hospital walls." "The next obstetrician we get is going to give Green Stamps," Fred said absently; "look, he looks just like Mary Martin." "Mary Martin?" Edith echoed, studying the priest moving sideways in little dancing steps, his sharp elbow on his hip jabbing the air. "Mary Martin in *Peter Pan;* he looks like he's on a wire." "Oh." Edith considered politely. One of the cats the priest was feeding looked exactly like a kitten she had given away from her female cat's first and only litter. Zelda Cat had kept her other kitten, and still treated Ophelia as if she were a nursling. The cat Edith was intently watching was white and black patched, although even from a distance she could see he was a terrible mess. Edith assumed the cat was male. "That's a terrible mess," Edith said with more passion than she intended. "The Persian cat's beautiful!" Fred answered in a wounded voice; "it must have cost a fortune." "Anyway, the forsythias are out," Edith sighed. She had been married a long time. "A fairy priest!" Fred wondered out loud again, long after Edith had returned to the table and spooned up the rest of her sugar with her index finger. That night, Edith got into bed slowly and gingerly, not because she was pregnant, but because the shadows from the blinds fell across the floor in unaccustomed patterns, one in particular taking a shape she imagined to be that of a surgeon's knife. Fred was up very late, going over the year's forms, a habit he had developed since their move to the new house.

The next day, which was Sunday, Edith took Cara out into the backyard to rake leaves before the church bells of the neighborhood Catholic school had even begun ringing. The morning chill was beginning to leave the air, and the sky had turned from gray to slate blue and was now shimmering brilliantly at the edges. Her daughter was absorbed in a corner of her outdoor play-pen, which resembled a zoo cage, pulling her doll's red wool hair, when a horrible cat voice sounded at Edith's feet just as she picked up a rake. The black and white cat she had seen from the kitchen was standing in a pile of last year's gray-brown leaves, angrily screaming up at her. It had a shocking pink mouth, a slightly coated pink tongue, and alarmingly shiny pointed teeth. "Good grief!" Edith thought, catching sight of his front paws with their long hooked claws. "I'm not supposed to touch you," she informed the cat defensively; "my husband says you'll give our cats germs." The cat screamed in outrage. "Are you hungry?" Edith asked guiltily. The cat screamed again. "If I feed you this *once,*" Edith asked the cat, "will you go away?" The cat answered loudly. Oppressed, Edith went into the house. She listened carefully, but there was no sound. The cat was screaming his head off on the cement back porch. Edith decided to open his can of tuna with a hand opener, not the electric one, because she was afraid that otherwise Fred would hear, and come down and start a fuss. As she went back out, carrying the paper plate full of cat tuna, blocking her own large cat's exit with her calf, she looked through the window and thought she saw the priest's kitchen curtain pulling back, as if he were watching her.

"You are a terrible mess," she told the black and white cat's shoulders, as he hunched over the plate, gobbling his food. "I wonder how old you are?" she asked the indifferent back of his furry neck. She stopped, thinking what the neighbors might have named him. "Patches?" she whispered. The cat perked up his ears but didn't stop eating. Edith sat down on the step to watch him. The cat slid sideways, toward the edge of the porch, observing her, while chewing, from one large green eye. "Hmmm," Edith observed to the air. The cat raised his head and looked at her. "Nice cat," Edith sighed, getting up and going up to her leaves. Later, when she looked up, the priest's curtains were hanging naturally, and that night, through her kitchen windows, Edith saw him feeding the local army of cats.

The next morning, Edith woke up from a terrible nightmare in which her mother had her committed to an asylum after a violent argument over the decorating of her kitchen windows; she escaped to find her mother driving off with Cara in a purple Pontiac, and found a notice on the front door of the house saying it had been sold to her mother, Mrs. Picarillo, for sixty dollars. While she was trying to pull herself together over the baby bottle and the stove, which along with the rest of the house still belonged to her, an outrageous screaming began at the kitchen door. There was Patches, hanging onto the edge of the back door windows by his front claws. The priest's house had not yet opened for the morning, although two gray cats had taken up their stations on the railings of his porch like two cement lions. Mrs. Zlotnick flew to the back door with a full plate of tuna, then ran up the back steps with Cara's bottle, but as she was feeding her, she was preoccupied with the picture of Patches' desperate face, and her own desire, every moment more desperate, to go down and find him.

Although most of the tuna was gone, Patches was not in the backyard. Mrs. Zlotnick stood still, looking out of the back window, every minute more grimly depressed. When she heard the already-familiar grating scream from the windows of the front porch, and went into the dining room and caught sight of his infuriated face, Edith felt a hot flood of joy, utterly unlike anything she had felt in years. Upstairs, she could hear her daughter crying; she stopped, but only for a second, and went out in her bathrobe and slippers onto the glassed-in front porch. Patches took one look at her and jumped into Cara's red English carriage where, with his chin propped on its edge, he stared defiantly at her. The porch windowpanes rattled in and out in the white gale. "Cold," Edith said out loud, hugging her arms around her breasts; the nipples were cold and were standing up against the terrycloth. Edith sat down on the blue couch the old owner had left marooned against the wall. "I could get pneumonia out here because of this dumb cat," she thought without moving. She was getting colder and colder and more and more miserable, as if everyone in the world she loved had just been destroyed. "I could get pneumonia because of you," she said to Patches accusingly: "look, it's even snowing." Patches looked at her unimpressed, then stood up in the carriage, stretched, arching his back, jumped down and walked over to her. "Well?" Edith asked through chattering teeth as Patches regarded her like a miniature god from the floor. "You're very short," Edith informed him irritably. The cat regarded her without blinking. "You are a Terrible Mess," Edith said with emphasis, a fleeting cloud of guilt streaking across the gray world which held only the two of them; she would never call Cara a terrible mess, although she was, in fact, and most of the time. "A Horrible, Terrible Mess," Edith said loudly. The cat jumped up on to the couch. Joy clawed at Edith's throat. "We'll all get distemper," she warned herself; but without any genuine remorse or fear, her hand went over to him. Immediately, Patches' head twisted back on his neck and his teeth closed on her wrist. "No," she instructed, withdrawing her hand gently: "No. Hand," she said, holding it in front of his face. "Now it's here, and now," she said patiently, raising it over the tips of his ears, "it's here." Patches twisted his head back, but let her hand rest on his back. Edith repeated the lesson twenty times; by then, Patches was lying in her lap, emitting loud squeals, and kneading her swollen stomach. "My mother says cats can carry a virus that can blind a fetus twenty years later," she remembered. "Too bad," she cooed down at Patches, hugging him to her. The cat looked surprised, but did not resist. From a distance, with her head bent gently over the cat, her rapturous look shining through the March morning, Edith and the cat resembled nothing so much as Madonna and Child.

"I don't want that damn animal in the house," Fred told her; "our three cats don't have their boosters." "He doesn't have to come in the house," Edith insisted. "First he's on the porch; next he'll be in the house," Fred predicted unsympathetically. "No he won't," Edith fervently promised, although in fact that was exactly what she had in mind. "When our cats get shots, he can too," Edith sulked, her lower lip out, close to tears. "Do you know a vet who makes house calls," Fred asked sarcastically, "or should we just rent a van from the ASPCA?" "Well," Edith answered, "as a matter of fact, yesterday I was talking to Mrs. Campanella; her daughter dissects the animals? And she said her cousin was a vet who'd come to the house." "I don't want to hear about it," Fred shouted, slamming down his fork; "you'll wind up the crazy cat lady, that's just who Mrs. Campanella is going to tell the vet who makes house calls you are." "Also," Edith went on, more or less unperturbed, "that old lady next door who's always hanging out the laundry and feeding the squirrels? She said Patches used to live in this house. When the man moved, he left five cats." "That's nothing; he left seven truckloads of furniture." "The priest took the Persian," Edith finished. "I don't want to hear about it!" Fred shouted again, this time at the top of his lungs, and stomped up the back stairs to his study on the third floor. Edith tiptoed into the dining room, saw Patches asleep in her daughter's carriage, and with a lovely sense of satisfaction went back to the dishes. "Where's the cat?" Fred bellowed down to her. "Outside!" she shrieked back in an injured voice: "where you wanted him." A peaceable silence fell over the kitchen as Edith smiled to herself at the picture of Patches, stationed in Cara's precious package, and as she washed and rinsed the dishes, listening to the nipples jostle furiously in their sterilizer, she watched the priest dancing with plates of tuna among the chorus of neighborhood cats. It was obvious to her he was looking frantically about the backyard. "Too bad," Edith thought, pressing herself into a corner. The fairy priest was looking directly at her window, and she didn't want to appear either to notice or to gloat.

So the days went by, and if the high point of the day became Edith's early morning visits with Patches, who had taken up permanent residence on the couch under a huge canvasy moving cloth she had provided him with for the rest of the cold weather, she dismissed this oddity in her usual flip way, telling herself she was only meeting the neighbors, and Patches happened to be the only neighbor she liked. Meanwhile, she carried out a relentless war of wills with Fred. "Can't you at least come out and *look* at the poor thing?" she pleaded in horrendous tones. Fred came out and looked. "If your mother could see that, she'd be in the next county," Fred grumbled, watching Patches affectionately place his teeth around Edith's wrist; "God knows what he's picked up." "Do you want him to freeze?" Edith asked rhetorically. "Animal killer," she muttered. "Besides," she went on, "he chases all the other cats out of the yard, doesn't he?" Fred nodded with a bad grace.

"He wouldn't freeze to death," he said; "the priest takes care of him." "He only feeds him," Edith answered, cuddling the cat; "besides, he used to live here; the old woman said so." "She's moving, the old woman," Fred said, as if that canceled out her comment. "And stop calling me an animal killer." "We still need a door for the mail," Edith nagged him. The former owner of the house had put a lock on the porch door, but the bell itself was set into the house door so that daily mail was regularly returned to the post office. "Patches could come in the same door." "Patches can go to France," Fred exploded. "You'll scare him," Edith remonstrated; "will you do it?" "Yes, yes," Fred droned, "but he can't come into the house." Edith nodded. "I don't see what you like so much about that damn cat anyway." Edith kept quiet. "He's a toughy," Fred said with reluctant admiration. "I told you he chased away all the other cats," Edith reminded him, and then proudly began recounting Patches' heroic exploits for the fifteenth time. "And the scars on his nose are healing," she marveled, running her fingers along the long lines of caked blood on his nose, crossing each other in a tick-tack-toe pattern. "Disgusting," Fred said again, shaking his head; "the fairy priest's out in the backyard; he probably wonders where this thing is." "No, he doesn't," Edith answered; "the cat's too filthy to be a house cat. Don't worry; he stays out." "He stays on *our porch,*" Fred corrected pedantically. There was the sound of a baby crying. "Who's going to feed Cara?" he asked. "You do it," Edith answered seraphically. Fred went into the kitchen, and on his third try had a warm bottle for Cara, having boiled the first so hard the plastic sack began leaking, and, having nearly melted the second bottle when he forgot to check to see if it was standing upright in its white enamel pan.

As the days went by, and Patches' visits became more regular, Edith found herself more and more preoccupied with the fairy priest. Did he live alone? Did he live with his mother? She never saw anyone else at the house. "What's he doing up there?" she asked herself from the corner of the kitchen where she often pressed herself and her swelling stomach to secretly observe him. The fairy priest was inching along on his bottom across the shingles of his roof, holding to the shingly surface with one hand and gingerly dipping the other into the metal gutter, putting whatever he fished out into a paper grocery bag. Then he slid onto the sharply inclined roof adjoining and repeated the performance. "Getting leaves out of the gutter," Edith mentally noted, filing this latest picture along with the one of the fake red felt lily she had gotten close enough to observe through the fairy priest's window by pressing her stomach so hard against the heavy diamond-shaped fence she wondered if she was doing damage to their unborn child. Edith now kept a pair of boots on the back porch solely for the purpose of walking around the muddy lawn with Patches, and although she told herself she tried to take Patches for walks when the priest was not home (he now followed her like a dog, jumping up into the air to reach the tips of her fingers) it somehow happened that she was invariably out with the cat when the priest was home, and she either saw his shadow move in the kitchen, or his curtains slowly pulling back until they were at a sharp angle to the sill. Occasionally, when she was balancing on one leg like a distended flamingo, tugging off one boot or gazing down on Patches in her bathrobe, she wondered what the fairy priest thought of her, and invariably she found herself blushing. "His Persian is pregnant," she thought to herself; "it looks like two fat skunks."

The Persian, who was evidently a friend of Patches', since she was the only cat Patches permitted in the yard, now also came to the back porch, but Edith righteously refused to feed her, reasoning she was definitely the priest's responsibility, although lately, the Persian had arrived shepherded by Patches, and Edith was weakening. Once, she arrived alone and Edith fed her in a fury, becoming even more enraged when the pregnant Persian finished the whole can, leaving nothing for Patches. The old woman had told Edith that the Persian, also, used to live in their house, but Edith was sure she was the priest's cat. "There'll be kittens all over," Fred warned her as portentously as he could, but nevertheless, he was making plans to acquire a jigsaw over the weekend and saw out a panel for both the mail and Patches. Domestic relations had become peaceful. "Look at what the fairy priest's doing now," Fred called, peering out the window, while Edith drank her Sanka, pretending not to be interested. She had noticed that lately the priest was always out in the yard wearing only his undershirt and jeans.

Then, one night, Edith, who had gone to bed early after tucking Patches in for the second time on the porch, woke up to hear the loud crying of a cat. "Oh, it's Trembler," she thought, trying to move farther onto her side, falling back asleep as the crying continued. "Edith!" Fred was shouting in the middle of their dark bedroom; "Patches is in the house!" "Patches?" Edith asked groggily. "Patches! He's in the guest room." "Guest room?" Edith echoed; "pushy cat." And she attempted to go back to sleep. "Get up!" Fred thundered; "we have to get him out. Trembler won't let him out of the room." "Oh all right," Edith said, tying Fred's bathrobe around the shifting continents of her stomach. "Trembler," Edith said, addressing her giant calico cat in a firm voice. He blinked his eyes sulkily at her and lay down on the first step of the stairway to the third floor. "See?" Fred said; "you've upset all our cats." "I didn't let him in," Edith said, peering nearsightedly into the guest room. Patches shot by Trembler, down the stairs to the first floor. "Oh fine," Edith sighed, holding the rail, trudging down after him. "He's here," she announced, seeing Trembler's nose pointing under the couch. "Come on, Patches," she said, lying down on the carpet before the couch. Patches looked desperately in her direction. "Do you want me to get a broom?" Fred inquired helpfully. "Who'll carry him out if you scare him with a broom?" Edith asked, inching forward like a worm on her side. "Nice Patches," she cooed, scratching him under the chin. "Just get him out," Fred said in an exhausted voice. "That's what I'm doing," Edith answered, observing Patches, who was beginning to purr. Fred's loud sighs rose like dirigibles, bumping heavily against the ceiling. Edith caught Patches under the front paws, dragged him out from under the couch, and, with an injured stare at Fred, marched off with him toward the three doors leading to the front porch of the house, Fred running in front of her, frantically opening one after another. "What are you doing there?" she called a few minutes later, hearing Fred in the basement. "Sealing up the gas vent to the old dryer; I think that's how he broke in." "Enterprising cat," Edith thought with satisfaction, heavily climbing the steps, taking care to breathe rhythmically, going back to bed.

Two days later Trembler began sneezing and scratching his nose until it bled. "I *told* you," Fred said; "I *told* you." "It's only a cold," Edith insisted, but Ophelia and Linda Cat were sneezing too. When Patches arrived in the afternoon, he was trembling all over; his nose was hot and caked, and his eyes were running. Edith locked him on the porch with a temporary kitty litter box made out of a grocery carton, some food and water, and went in to call Mrs. Campanella, and then the vet who made house calls. Meanwhile, Edith alternated her time between patting the three cats in the house and Patches on the porch, and staring out at the backyard of the fairy priest, which, like hers, was also empty. His shadow was moving about inside regularly and quickly. There were no plates of tuna on his porch. There were no cats in the yard.

"Distemper," Mr. Amadeo said, taking one look at the cats and writing out a prescription for chloromycetin; "the house cats will probably be all right because they've got some immunity, but that black and white cat looks pretty bad." In the days that followed, Trembler, Linda Cat, and Ophelia began to stop sneezing and to eat more and more, but Patches, who had at first been fed through a dropper, now had stopped eating altogether, and lay trembling on the porch couch, his huge head on Edith's hand, looking up at her sadly from his electric green eyes. His breathing was labored. Edith thought about an electric blanket, but then worried that he might put his claws through it and electrocute himself. Edith herself had gone into a frozen panic, and Fred had taken over the care of Cara altogether. "He's toxic," the vet said on his second visit, and from her vigil on the porch, Edith saw him whispering something to Fred. She fell asleep with

Patches' head on her hand, and when she woke up, the cat was rigid, and no longer breathing. "Get up!" she screamed, starting to shake him: "Get up!" And she pressed in and out on his furry chest as she had seen all the television doctors do. The cat lay there, rigid and staring. He was cold to the touch. Finally, Fred had to carry her to their room, where she cried so long she began running a fever. She heard Fred saying "psychiatrist" to her doctor in the hall, and then, "the vet took it away." "It!" Edith began crying, silently and steadily all over again. Her mother was called in; Edith barely noticed her. On the ninth day, she suddenly stopped; her mother began packing to go home and Fred began to look more cheerful. She still had no desire to go near Cara. From the bathroom, she heard Fred telling her mother that the vet had said there was no way of telling, that one of their cats might have picked something up from their clothes or shoes and given it to Patches. "It is my fault," Edith thought to herself, washing her face, rubbing it dry with a vicious terrycloth towel.

Evidently, the doctor had told them to leave her alone, for no one followed her out into the backyard when she wandered out that evening in her robe. As if she had expected it, the priest's door opened, and he walked toward her in his clerical clothes, although by this time of night he usually wore jeans and a blue sweatshirt. "Patches died," she told him. He had a jagged, bony face, red over the cheekbones. He looked at her and snapped a twig from his well-tended hedge, then stubbed it out against the wire fence as if it were a cigarette. "All my cats died," he said, "except the Persian." "Why?" Edith asked. "She had shots from before," he said, "when she lived in your house, and my aunt took her for a booster. She said she was too valuable a cat to take chances with." His bottom lip was chewed and blood-split. "She had five kittens," he added; "do you want one?" "No," Edith answered. "Good," he sighed; "how are your cats?" "They're fine." "That's good," the priest said sadly. They both looked desolately around the empty backyard. Edith thought she heard kittenish mews. "Well," he said. "Mmmmm," Edith murmured, and, supporting her stomach with her hands, she climbed the back porch steps. Just as she was going in, she saw the priest's back door still open, and then his hand carelessly reaching out for it, as if it no longer made any difference to the lives of the creatures on the block whether it was open or shut.

# ANN BEATTIE

## (1947– )

With the beat and lyrics of popular music playing in the background, and filled with the latest upscale accoutrements of the educated middle to upper-middle classes, Ann Beattie's fiction chronicles the lives of the babyboomers, those Americans reaching adulthood in the late 1960s and 1970s and facing their generation's version of disappointment, disillusionment, and loss. Beattie was born in Washington, D.C., where her father worked for the Department of Health, Education, and Welfare, and grew up in nearby Chevy Chase,

Maryland. She went to American University, where she completed a B.A. in 1969. She earned an M.A. in English from the University of Connecticut in 1970. After additional graduate study, she began to submit stories to a variety of magazines and periodicals. Her first publication was in the *Western Humanities Review* in 1972. Since those years, her stories have regularly appeared in *The New Yorker.*

Beattie's first novel, *Chilly Scenes of Winter,* and her first collection of stories, *Distortions,* appeared in 1976. Her story collections include *Secrets and Surprises* (1979), *The Burning House* (1982), *Where You'll Find Me* (1986), *What Was Mine* (1991), *Park City: New and Selected Stories* (1998), and *Perfect Recall: New Stories* (2001). Her novels include *Falling in Place* (1980), *Love Always* (1985), *Picturing Will* (1989), *Another You* (1995), and *My Life, Starring Dara Falcon* (1997).

# Janus

THE BOWL was perfect. Perhaps it was not what you'd select if you faced a shelf of bowls, and not the sort of thing that would inevitably attract a lot of attention at a crafts fair, yet it had real presence. It was as predictably admired as a mutt who has no reason to suspect he might be funny. Just such a dog, in fact, was often brought out (and in) along with the bowl.

Andrea was a real-estate agent, and when she thought that some prospective buyers might be dog-lovers, she would drop off her dog at the same time she placed the bowl in the house that was up for sale. She would put a dish of water in the kitchen for Mondo, take his squeaking plastic frog out of her purse and drop it on the floor. He would pounce delightedly, just as he did every day at home, batting around his favorite toy. The bowl usually sat on a coffee table, though recently she had displayed it on top of a pine blanket chest and on a lacquered table. It was once placed on a cherry table beneath a Bonnard still life, where it held its own.

Everyone who has purchased a house or who has wanted to sell a house must be familiar with some of the tricks used to convince a buyer that the house is quite special: a fire in the fireplace in early evening; jonquils in a pitcher on the kitchen counter, where no one ordinarily has space to put flowers; perhaps the slight aroma of spring, made by a single drop of scent vaporizing from a lamp bulb.

The wonderful thing about the bowl, Andrea thought, was that it was both subtle and noticeable—a paradox of a bowl. Its glaze was the color of cream and seemed to glow no matter what light it was placed in. There were a few bits of color in it—tiny geometric flashes—and some of these were tinged with flecks of silver. They were as mysterious as cells seen under a microscope; it was difficult not to study them, because they shimmered, flashing for a split second, and then resumed their shape. Something about the colors and their random placement suggested motion. People who liked country furniture always commented on the bowl, but then it turned out that people who felt comfortable with Biedermeier loved it just as much. But the bowl was not at all ostentatious, or even so noticeable that anyone would suspect that it had been put in place deliberately. They might notice the height of the ceiling on first entering a room, and only when their eye moved down from that, or away from the refraction of sunlight on a pale wall, would they see the bowl. Then they would go immediately to it and comment. Yet they always faltered when they tried to say something. Perhaps it was because they were in the house for a serious reason, not to notice some object.

Once, Andrea got a call from a woman who had not put in an offer on a house she had shown her. That bowl, she said—would it be possible to find out where the owners had bought that beautiful bowl? Andrea pretended that she did not know what the woman was referring to. A bowl, somewhere in the house? Oh, on a table under the window. Yes, she would ask, of course. She let a couple of days pass, then called back to say that the bowl had been a present and the people did not know where it had been purchased.

When the bowl was not being taken from house to house, it sat on Andrea's coffee table at home. She didn't keep it carefully wrapped (although she transported it that way, in a box); she kept it on the table, because she liked to see it. It was large enough so that it didn't seem fragile, or particularly vulnerable if anyone sideswiped the table or Mondo blundered into it at play. She had asked her husband to please not drop his house key in it. It was meant to be empty.

When her husband first noticed the bowl, he had peered into it and smiled briefly. He always urged her to buy things she liked. In recent years, both of them had acquired many things to make up for all the lean years when they were graduate students, but now that they had been comfortable for quite a while, the pleasure of new possessions dwindled. Her husband had pronounced the bowl "pretty," and he had turned away without picking it up to examine it. He had no more interest in the bowl than she had in his new Leica.

She was sure that the bowl brought her luck. Bids were often put in on houses where she had displayed the bowl. Sometimes the owners, who were always asked to be away or to step outside when the house was being shown, didn't even know that the bowl had been in their house. Once—she could not imagine how—she left it behind, and then she was so afraid that something might have happened to it that she rushed back to the house and sighed with relief when the woman owner opened the door. The bowl, Andrea explained—she had purchased a bowl and set it on the chest for safekeeping while she toured the house with the prospective buyers, and she . . . She felt like rushing past the frowning woman and seizing her bowl. The owner stepped aside, and it was only when Andrea ran to the chest that the lady glanced at her a little strangely. In the few seconds before Andrea picked up the bowl, she realized that the owner must have just seen that it had been perfectly placed, that the sunlight struck the bluer part of it. Her pitcher had been moved to the far side of the chest, and the bowl predominated. All the way home, Andrea wondered how she could have left the bowl behind. It was like leaving a friend at an outing—just walking off. Sometimes there were stories in the paper about families forgetting a child somewhere and driving to the next city. Andrea had only gone a mile down the road before she remembered.

In time, she dreamed of the bowl. Twice, in a waking dream—early in the morning, between sleep and a last nap before rising—she had a clear vision of it. It came into sharp focus and startled her for a moment—the same bowl she looked at every day.

She had a very profitable year selling real estate. Word spread, and she had more clients than she felt comfortable with. She had the foolish thought that if only the bowl were an animate object she could thank it. There were times when she wanted to talk to her husband about the bowl. He was a stockbroker, and sometimes told people that he was fortunate to be married to a woman who had such a fine aesthetic sense and yet could also function in the real world. They were a lot alike, really—they had agreed on that. They were both quiet people—reflective, slow to make value judgments, but almost intractable once they had come to a conclusion. They both liked details, but while ironies attracted her, he was more impatient and dismissive when matters became many-sided or unclear. But they both knew this, it was the kind of thing they could talk about when they were alone in the car together, coming home from a party or after a weekend with friends. But she never talked to him about the bowl. When they were at dinner, exchanging their news of the day, or while they lay in bed at night listening to the stereo and murmuring sleepy disconnections, she was often tempted to come right out and say that she thought that the bowl in the living room, the cream-colored bowl, was responsible for her success. But she didn't say it. She couldn't begin to explain it. Sometimes in the morning, she would look at him and feel guilty that she had such a constant secret.

Could it be that she had some deeper connection with the bowl—a relationship of some kind? She corrected her thinking: how could she imagine such a thing, when she was a human being and it was a bowl? It was ridiculous. Just think of how people lived together and love each other . . . But was that always so clear, always a relationship? She was confused by these thoughts, but they remained in her mind. There was something within her now, something real, that she never talked about.

The bowl was a mystery, even to her. It was frustrating, because her involvement with the bowl contained a steady sense of unrequited good fortune; it would have been easier to respond if some sort of demand were made in return. But that only happened in fairy tales. The bowl was just a bowl. She did not believe that for one second. What she believed was that it was something she loved.

In the past, she had sometimes talked to her husband about a new property she was about to buy or sell—confiding some clever strategy she had devised to persuade owners who seemed ready to sell. Now she stopped doing that, for all her strategies involved the bowl. She became more deliberate with the bowl, and more possessive. She put it in houses only when no one was there, and removed it when she left the house. Instead of just moving a pitcher or a dish, she would remove all the other objects from a table. She had to force herself to handle them carefully, because she didn't really care about them. She just wanted them out of sight.

She wondered how the situation would end. As with a lover, there was no exact scenario of how matters would come to a close. Anxiety became the operative force. It would be irrelevant if the lover rushed into someone else's arms, or wrote her a note and departed to another city. The horror was the possibility of the disappearance. That was what mattered.

She would get up at night and look at the bowl. It never occurred to her that she might break it. She washed and dried it without anxiety, and she moved it often, from coffee table to mahogany corner table or wherever, without fearing an accident. It was clear that she would not be the one who would do anything to the bowl. The bowl was only handled by her, set safely on one surface or another; it was not very likely that anyone would break it. A bowl was a poor conductor of electricity: it would not be hit by lightning. Yet the idea of damage persisted. She did not think beyond that—to what her life would be without the bowl. She only continued to fear that some accident would happen. Why not, in a world where people set plants where they did not belong, so that visitors touring a house would be fooled into thinking that dark corners got sunlight—a world full of tricks?

She had first seen the bowl several years earlier, at a crafts fair she had visited half in secret, with her lover. He had urged her to buy the bowl. She didn't *need* any more things, she told him. But she had been drawn to the bowl, and they had lingered near it. Then she went on to the next booth, and he came up behind her, tapping the rim against her shoulder as she ran her fingers over a wood carving. "You're still insisting that I buy that?" she said. "No," he said. "I bought it for you." He had bought her other things before this—things she liked more, at first—the child's ebony-and-turquoise ring that fitted her little finger; the wooden box, long and thin; beautifully dovetailed, that she used to hold paper clips; the soft gray sweater with a pouch pocket. It was his idea that when he could not be there to hold her hand she could hold her own—clasp her hands inside the lone pocket that stretched across the front. But in time she became more attached to the bowl than to any of his other presents. She tried to talk herself out of it. She owned other things that were more striking or valuable. It wasn't an object whose beauty jumped out at you; a lot of people must have passed it by before the two of them saw it that day.

Her lover had said that she was always too slow to know what she really loved. Why continue with her life the way it was? Why be two-faced, he asked her. He had made the first move toward her. When she would not decide in his favor, would not change her life and come to him, he asked her what made her think she could have it both ways. And then he made the last move and left. It was a decision meant to break her will, to shatter her intransigent ideas about honoring previous commitments.

Time passed. Alone in the living room at night, she often looked at the bowl sitting on the table, still and safe, unilluminated. In its way, it was perfect: the world cut in half, deep and smoothly empty. Near the rim, even in dim light, the eye moved toward one small flash of blue, a vanishing point on the horizon.

# MARY ROBISON

## (1949– )

In a spare, lucid, somewhat detached style, with a keen eye for the small, seemingly insignificant events and details of everyday life, Mary Robison explores the eccentricities and foibles of ordinary middle-class Americans. She creates fictional snapshots or videos of life in the middle. Robison was born and raised in a large family in Washington, D.C. She earned a B.A. in art history at Ohio State University in 1976. She then went to the Johns Hopkins writing program, where she studied with John Barth, and completed an M.A. in 1977. She published her first two stories in *The New Yorker* in 1977.

Like many writers, Robison has had to teach in order to finance her life, and then struggle to find time for her writing. She has had visiting positions at a number of universities and colleges, and a continuing appointment in creative writing at Harvard University. Her story collections include *Days* (1983), *An Amateur's Guide to the Night* (1983), and *Believe Them* (1988). She has also published the novels *Oh!* (1981) and *Subtraction* (1991).

# Coach

I

The August two-a-day practice sessions were sixty-seven days away, Coach calculated. He was drying breakfast dishes. He swabbed a coffee cup and made himself listen to his wife, who was across the kitchen, sponging the stove's burner coils. "I know I'm no Rembrandt," Sherry said, "but I have so damn much fun trying, and this little studio—this room—we can afford. I could get out of your way by going there and get you and Daphne out of my way. No offense."

"I'm thinking," Coach said.

His wife coasted from appliance to appliance. She swiped the face of the oven clock with her sponge. "You're thinking too slow. Your reporter's coming at nine and it's way after eight now. Should I give them a deposit on the studio or not? Yes or no?"

Coach was staring at the sink, at a thread of water that came from one of the taps. He thought of the lake place where they used to go in North Carolina. He saw green water being thickly sliced by a power boat; the boat towing Sherry, who was blonde and laughing on her skis, her rounded back strong, her suit shining red.

"Of course, of course, give them the money," he said.

Their daughter, Daphne, wandered into the kitchen. She was dark-haired, lazy-looking, fifteen. Her eyes were lost behind bangs. She drew open the enormous door of the refrigerator.

"Don't hang, Daphne, you'll unhinge things," her mother said. "What are you after?"

"Food mainly," Daphne said.

Sherry went away, to the little sun patio off the kitchen. Coach pushed the glass door sideways after her and it smacked shut.

"Eat and run," he said to Daphne. "I've got a reporter coming in short order. Get dressed." He spoke firmly but in the smaller voice he always used for his child.

"Yes, sir," Daphne said. She broke into the freezer compartment and ducked to let its gate pass over her head. "Looks bad. Nothing in here but Eggos."

"I ate Eggos. Just hustle up," Coach said.

"Can I be here for this guy?" Daphne asked.

"Who guy? The reporter? Nuh-uh. He's just from the college, Daph. Coming to see if the new freshman coach has three heads or just two."

Daphne was nodding at the food jars racked on the wide refrigerator door. "Hey, lookit," she said. She blew a breath in front of the freezer compartment and made a short jet of mist.

Coach remembered a fall night, a Friday-game night, long ago, when he had put Daphne on the playing field. It was during the ceremonies before his unbeaten squad had taken on Ignatius South High School Parents' Night. He had laced shoulder pads on Daphne and draped the trainer's gag jersey—number 1/2—over her, and balanced Tim-somebody's helmet on her eight-year-old head. She was lost in the getup, a small pile of equipment out on the fifty-yard line. She had applauded when the loudspeaker announced her name, when the p.a. voice, garbled by amplification and echo, had rung out, "Daughter of our coach, Harry Noonan, and his wife—number one-half; Daphne Noonan!" She had stood in the bath of floodlights, shaking as the players and their folks strolled by—the players grim in their war gear, the parents tiny and apologetic-seeming in civilian clothes. The co-captain of the team, awesome in his pads and cleats and steaming from warm-up running, had palmed Daphne's big helmet and twisted it sideways. From behind, from the home stands, Coach had heard, "Haaa!" as Daphne turned circles of happy confusion, trying to right the helmet. Through the ear hole her left eye had twinkled, Coach remembered. He had heard, "God, that's funny," and "Coach's kid."

* * *

On the sun porch now, his wife was doing a set of tennis exercises. She was between Coach and the morning sun, framed by the glass doors. He could see through the careless weave of her caftan, enough to make out the white flesh left by her swimsuit.

"I knew you wouldn't let me," Daphne said. She had poured a glass of chocolate milk. She pulled open a chilled banana. "I bet Mom gets to be here."

"Daph, this isn't a big deal. We've been through it all before," Coach said.

"Not for a college paper," Daphne said. "Wait a minute, I'll be right back." She left the kitchen.

"I'll hold my breath and count the heartbeats," Coach said to the space she had left behind.

They were new to the little town, new to Pennsylvania. Coach was assuming charge of the freshman squad, in a league where freshmen weren't eligible for the varsity. He had taken the job, not sure if it was a step up for him or a serious misstep. The money was so-so. But he wanted the college setting for his family—especially for Daphne. She had been seeming to lose interest in the small celebrity they achieved in high-school towns. She had acted bored at the Noonans' Sunday spaghetti dinners for standout players. She had stopped fetching plates of food for the boys, who were too game-sore to get their own. She had even stopped wearing the charm bracelet her parents had put together for her—a silver bracelet with a tiny megaphone, the numerals 68—a league championship year—and, of course, a miniature football.

Coach took a seat at the kitchen table. He ate grapes from a bowl. He spilled bottled wheat germ into his palm. On the table were four chunky ring binders, their black leatherette covers printed with the college seal—which still looked strange to him. These were his playbooks, and he was having trouble getting the play tactics into his head.

"Will you turn off the radio?" he yelled.

The bleat from Daphne's upstairs bedroom ceased. A minute later she came down and into the kitchen. She had a cardboard folder and some textbooks with her. "Later on, would you look at this stuff and help me? Can you do these?" she asked Coach.

He glanced over one of her papers. It was penciled with algebra equations, smutty with erasures and scribbled-out parts. "I'd have to see the book, but no. Not now, not later. I don't want to and I don't have time."

"That's just great," Daphne said.

"Your mother and I got our algebra homework done already, Daph. We turned ours in," Coach said. "This was in nineteen fifty-six."

"Mom!" Daphne said, pushing aside the glass door.

"Forget it," Sherry said.

II

Toby, the boy sent from *The Rooter* to interview Coach, was unshaven and bleary-eyed. He wore a rumpled cerise polo shirt and faded Levi's. He asked few questions, dragging his words. Now and then he grumbled of a hangover and no sleep. He yawned during Coach's answers. He took no notes.

"You're getting this now?" Coach said.

"Oh, yeah, it's writing itself, I'm such a pro," Toby said, and Coach wasn't certain if the boy was kidding.

"So, you've been here just a little while. Lucky you." Toby said. "Less than a month?"

"Is that like a question? It seems less than a month—less than a week—a day and a half," Coach said. For the interview, he had put on white sports slacks and a maroon pullover with a gold collar—the college's colors. The pullover he had bought at Campus World. The clothes had a snug fit that flattered Coach and showed off his flat stomach and heavy biceps.

He and Toby were on either end of the sofa in the living room of the house, a wooden two-story Coach had found and would be paying off for decades, he was sure.

Toby said, "Well, believe it or not, I've got enough for a couple sticks, which is shoptalk among we press men for two columns. If you're going to be home tomorrow, there's a girl who'll come and take your picture—Marcia. She's a drag, I warn you."

"One thing about this town, there aren't any damn sidewalks, and the cars don't give you much room if you're jogging," Coach said, standing up.

"Hey, tell me about it. When I'm hitching, I wear an orange safety poncho and carry a red flag and paint a big X on my back. Of course, I'm probably just making a better target," the reporter said.

"I jog down at the track now. It's a great facility, comparable to a Big Ten's. I like the layout," Coach said.

"Okay, but the interview's over," Toby said.

"Well, I came from high schools, remember. In Indiana and Ohio—good schools with good budgets, mind you, but high schools, nonetheless."

"Yeah, I got where you're coming from," Toby said.

"Did you need to know what courses I'll be handling? Fall quarter, they've got me lined up for two things: The Atlantic World is the first one, and Colloquium on European Industrial Development, I think it is. Before, I always taught World History. P. O. D.,[1] once or twice."

"That three-eighty-one you're going to teach is a tit course, in case nobody's informed you. It's what we call lunch," Toby said.

"It's, in nature, a refresher class," Coach said.

"Yeah, or out of nature," Toby said.

* * *

Daphne came from the long hall steps into the living room. Her dark hair was brushed and lifting with static. Her eyes seemed to Coach larger than usual, and a little sooty around the lashes.

"You're just leaving, aren't you, buster?" Coach said to her.

"Retrieving a pencil," Daphne said.

"Is your name really Buster?" Toby asked.

"Get your pencil and scoot. This is Toby here. Toby, this is my daughter, Daphne," Coach said.

"Nice to meet you," Daphne said. She slipped into a deep chair at the far corner of the long living room.

"Can she hear us over in that county?" Toby said. "Do you read me?" he shouted.

Daphne smiled. Coach saw bangs and her very white teeth.

"Come on, Daph, hit the trail," he said.

"I've got a joke for her first," Toby said. "What's green and moves very fast"

"Frog in a blender," Daphne said. "Dad? Some friends invited me to go swimming with them at the Natatorium. May I?"

"You've got to see the Nat. It's the best thing," Toby said.

"What about your class, though? She's in makeup school here, Toby, catching up on some algebra that didn't take the first time around."

Toby wrinkled his nose at Daphne, "At first, I thought you meant *makeup* school, like lipstick and rouge."

"I wish," Daphne said.

She slipped her left foot from her leather sandal and casually stroked the toes.

"She's a nut for swimming," Coach said.

"You'll be so bored here. Most nights, your options are either ordering a pizza or slashing your wrists," Toby told Daphne.

"Oh," she said, rolling her chin on her shoulder in a rather seductive way.

"Take it from Toby," he said.

Coach let Toby through the front door, and watched until he was down the street.

"He was nice," Daphne said.

"Aw, Daph. That's what you say about everybody. There's a lot better things you could say—more on-the-beam things."

"I guess you're mad," she said.

Coach went to the kitchen, to sit down with his play-books again. Daphne came after him.

"Aren't you?" she said.

1. Principles of Democracy.

"I guess you thought he was cute," Coach said. He flapped through some mimeographed pages, turning them on the notebook's silver rings. "I don't mean to shock you about it, but you'd be wasting your time there, Daph. You'd be trying to start a fire with a wet match."

Daphne stared at her father. "That's sick!" she said.

"I'm not criticizing him for it. I'm just telling you," Coach said.

III

"This is completely wrong," Coach said sadly. He read further. "Oh, no," he said. He drowned the newspaper in his bath water and slogged the pages over into a corner by the commode.

His wife handed him a dry edition, one of the ten or twelve *Rooters* Daphne had brought home.

Sherry was parallel to Coach on the edge of the tub, sitting with her back braced against the wall. "Oh, cheer up," she said. "Nobody reads a free newspaper."

Coach quartered the dry *Rooter* into a package around Toby's article. "Well, I wasn't head coach at Elmgrove, and I sure wasn't Phi Beta Kappa. And look at this picture," Coach said.

"What's so wrong with it?" Sherry said.

"Where did he get that you were at Mt. Holyoke? And I didn't bitch about the sidewalks this much."

"You didn't?" Sherry said. "That's almost too bad. I thought that was the best part of the article."

Coach slunk farther into the warm water until it crowded his chin. He kept the newspaper aloft, "Oh, come on, give me some credit here! Don't they have any supervision over in journalism? I don't see how he could get away with this shit. It's an unbelievably sloppy job."

"It's just a dinky article in a handout paper, Coach. What do you care? It wouldn't matter if he said we were a bright-green family with scales," Sherry said.

"He didn't think of that or he would have. This breaks my heart," Coach said.

"Daph liked it," Sherry said.

Couch wearily chopped bath water with the side of his hand and threw a splash at the soap recess in the tiled wall. "I tell you, I'm going to be spending my whole first year here explaining how none of it's true."

"What difference does true make?" Sherry said.

IV

Coach was seated awkwardly on an iron stool at a white table on the patio of the Dairy Frost. Daphne was across from him, fighting the early evening heat for her mocha-fudge cone. She tilted her head at the cone, lapping at it.

"You aren't saying anything," Coach said.

"Wait," Daphne said.

She worked on the cone.

"I've been waiting."

"If you two want to separate, it's none of my business," she said.

They were facing the busy parking lot when a new Pontiac turned in off the highway, glided easily onto the gravel, took a parking slot close by. In the driver's seat was a boy with built-up shoulders—a boy who looked very familiar to Coach. In back was a couple in their fifties—the boy's parents, Coach thought—both talking at once.

"Have I been spilling all this breath for nothing! Not a separation," Coach said. "Not anything like it."

"All right, not," Daphne said. She stopped in her attack on the cone long enough to watch the Pontiac boy step out. Dark brown ice cream streamed between her knuckles and down the inside of her wrist.

"You're losing it, honey," Coach said.

Daphne dabbed around the cone and her hand, making repairs.

"Hell, *real* trouble your father wouldn't tell you about at a *Dairy* Frost. This apartment your mom found is like an office or something. A studio for her to go to and get away every now and then. That kid's in my backfield. What the *hell's* his name?"

They watched as the young man took orders from his parents, then went inside the Dairy Frost. He looked both wider and taller than the other patrons, out of their scale. His rump and haunches were thick with muscle. His neck was fat but tight.

"Bobby Stark!" Coach said, and smiled very quickly at the parents in the Pontiac. He turned back to his daughter.

"She wants to get away from us," Daphne said.

"Definitely not. She gave me a list, is how this whole thing started. She's got stuff she wants to do, and you with your school problems and me with the team—we're too much for her, see? She could spend her entire day on us, if you think about it, and never have one second for herself. If you think about it fairly, Daphne, you'll agree."

Daphne seemed to consider. She was focused on the inside of the Dairy Frost building, and for a while she kept still.

"That guy looks dumb. One of the truly dumb," she said.

"My halfback? He's not. He was his class salutatorian," Coach said.

"He doesn't know *you.*"

"Just embarrassed," Coach said. "Can we stick to the point, Daph? And quit rocking the boat. Look what you're doing." Daphne's arm was on the table and she was violently swinging her legs under her chair.

She made a sigh and marched over to a trash can to deposit her slumping cone. Then she washed up at the children's drinking fountain and rejoined Coach, who had finished his Brown Cow but had kept the plastic spoon in his mouth.

"What was on this list of Mom's?" Daphne asked.

"Adult stuff," Coach said.

"Just give me an example."

Coach removed the plastic spoon and cracked it in half.

"Your mother's list is for five years. In that time, she wants to be speaking French regularly. She wants to follow up on her printmaking."

"This is adult stuff?" Daphne said.

Coach raised a hand to Bobby Stark. Stark had three malt cups in a cardboard carrier and he was moving toward the parking lot.

"Hey, those all for you?" Coach called out.

"I got a month to get fat, Coach. You'll have five months to beat it off me," the boy called back.

The people at some of the tables around Coach's lit up with grins. Bobby Stark's parents were grinning.

"Every hit of that junk takes a second off your time in the forty—just remember that!" Coach shouted.

Stark wagged his head ruefully, his cheeks blushing. He pretended to hide the malts behind his arm.

"Duh," Daphne said in a hoarse voice. "Which way to the door, Coach?"

"He can hear you," Coach said.

"Duh, kin I have a candy bar, Coach?" she rasped.

They faced Stark, who smiled a little crookedly at Daphne, and threw her a wink so dazzling, she went silent.

V

Coach was in the basement laundry room, both arms busy hugging a bundle of jogging clothes. He was waiting on the washer, waiting for Sherry to unload her clothes.

"The Cowboys are soaking their players in a sense-deprivation tub of warm saltwater," she said.

"We know," Coach said.

"If Dallas is doing it, I just thought you might want to consider it."

"We have. Hustle up a little with your stuff, will you?" Coach said.

"It's like my apartment," Sherry said. "A place apart."

Coach cut her off "Don't go on about how much you love your apartment."

"I wasn't going to," Sherry said. She slung her wet slacks and blouses into the dryer.

Coach had just two weeks before the start of the heavy practices. His team would have him then, he knew, almost straight through to the Christmas holidays.

"I like that," Coach said. "A place apart."

A half hour later, Coach and his wife were on the side patio. They could hear the tick of the clothes dryer downstairs. Sherry had changed into a halter top. She was taking sun on her back, adding to her tan.

"You know what's odd?" she said. "Daphne's popularity here. I don't mean it's odd."

"She's always done terrific with people, always gone over well," Coach said.

"*Your* people, though. These are hers." Sherry said. "Like that reporter."

"Yeah, they're like sisters," Coach said.

VI

It was a week before the two-a-day practice sessions would begin. The sky was colorless and glazed, like milk glass. When Coach looked at the sun, his eyes ached, his head screamed.

He had run some wind sprints on the stadium field, and now he was doing an easy lap. A stopwatch on a noose of ribbon swung against his chest. He cut through the goalposts and trotted for the sidelines, for the twenty, where he had dumped his clipboard and a towel.

Someone called to him.

Blond Bobby Stark came out from under the stands. His football shoes were laced together and draped around his neck. He wore a midriff-cut T-shirt and shorts. He walked gingerly in white wool socks.

"Did everybody go? Or am I the first one here?" he called to Coach.

" 'Bout a half hour," Coach said, heaving.

Stark sat down to untangle his shoes, and Coach, sweating, stood over him.

Coach spat. He folded his arms in a way that pushed out his muscles. He sniffed, twisting his whole nose and mouth to the left. He said, "You know, Stark, you were salutatorian for your class."

"High school," the boy said. He grinned up at Coach, an eye pinched against the glare.

"That counts, believe me. Maybe we can use you to help some of our slower players along—some of the linemen, maybe I'm thinking."

"What do you mean—tutor?" Stark said.

"Naw. Teach them to eat without biting off their fingers. How to tie a neck-tie. Some of your style." Coach said, and Stark bobbed his head.

Stark settled the fit of his right shoe. He said, "But there aren't any really dumb ones on our squad, because they'd just get flunked out. Recruiters won't touch them in this league. There wouldn't be any percentage in it."

"Then I'm greatly relieved," Coach said.

He planted his feet along a furrow of lime-eaten grass. He faced the open end of the stadium, where the enormous library building stood shimmering and uncertain behind sheets of heat that rose from the parking area.

Stark stood up and studied his shoes as he began jogging in place. He danced twenty yards down the field; loped back.

Other players were arriving for the informal session. Coach meant to time them in the mile, and in some dashes.

Stark looked jittery. He walked in semicircles, crowding Coach.

"What're you worried about?" Coach asked him. "Girl problems you got? You pull a muscle already?"

Stark glanced quickly around them. He said, "I live all my life two doors down from Coach Burton's house. My mom and Burton's wife are best friends, so I always know what's going on."

Burton had been the head coach of the varsity team for over a decade.

"You probably know about it already, anyway," Stark said. "Do you?"

"What the hell are you talking about, Stark?"

"You don't know? Typical. Burton's leaving, see? Like at the end of this year. His wife wants him out real bad, and the alumni want him out because they're tired of losing seasons. So what I heard was you were brought in because of it. And if we do okay this season, like you'll be varsity coach next year."

"That's conjecture," Coach said. But he was excited.

* * *

It was three o'clock, still hot. Coach was moving along a sidewalk with Bobby Stark, who was balanced on a racing bicycle, moving just enough to keep the machine upright.

"Three things," Coach said. "I've seen all the game films from last year, and I came here personally and witnessed the Tech game. No one lost because of the coaching. A coach can work miracles with a good team, but he is *helpless* if his personnel don't want it bad enough. That's the worst part about running a team—you can't climb down into your people's hearts and change them."

Some college girls in a large expensive car went past. They shrieked and whistled at Bobby Stark.

"Lifeguards at the pool," he explained.

"I don't know if Burton's leaving or not," Coach continued. "But if his wife wants him to go, he probably will. If you're ever thinking about a career in coaching someday, Bob, think about that. Your family's either with you or you've had it. And remember, whether you stay someplace or not depends completely on a bunch of *kids.* I swear, I'd give up a leg for a chance to get in a game myself—just one play, with what I know now."

Stark nodded. They went on a block, and he said, "I turn off here. You going to tell your daughter about the job?"

"My daughter?" Coach said, and smiled.

VII

No one was home. A magnet under a plastic ladybug held a note to the face of the refrigerator. The note read:

> Harry, I'm at my place. Daph's with Toby
> K. somewhere, fooling around. Be good now,
> Sherry Baby.

"Dope," Coach said.

He felt very good.

He took a beer upstairs and drank it while he showered. He cinched on a pair of sweat pants and, wearing only these, went back down and fetched another beer.

He watched some of a baseball game on cable. He thought over his conversation with Bobby Stark. "Boy, is that true!" Coach said, and then was not at all sure why he had said it.

He frowned, remembering that in his second year of college, the only year he had been on the varsity team, he had proved an indifferent player.

"Not now," he whispered. "Not anymore."

He squashed the shape out of his beer can and stood it on top of the television.

There was a thump over his head. The ceiling creaked.

"Someone came home while I was in the shower," he said to himself, and ran his hand over his belly, feeling for signs of bloat from the beer.

He took the stairs in three leaps, strode into the master bedroom, calling, "Sherry?"

The dark figure in the room surprised Coach.

He yelled, "Hey!"

Daphne was dancing in front of the full-length mirror. She had improvised a look—sweeping her hair over her right ear, and stretching the neck of her shirt until her right shoulder was bared. A thing by the Commodores shrieked from her transistor.

"Nothing," she said.

"You're not home. Aren't you with whoosis? You're supposed to be out. You are *beet* red," Coach said.

Daphne lowered her head and squared her shirt, which bagged around her small torso. "Okay, Dad," she said.

"No, but how did your audience like the show? I bet they loved it," Coach said. He smiled at himself in the mirror. "I'm just kidding you, Daph. You looked great."

"Come *on,* Dad," she said, and tried to pass.

Coach chimed in with the radio. He shuffled his feet. "Hey, Daph, you know what time it is?" he said.

"Let me out, please," Daphne said.

"It's monkey time!" Coach did a jerky turn, keeping in the way of the exit door. "Do the shing-a-ling. Do the Daphne." He rolled his shoulder vampishly. He kissed his own hand. He sang along.

"Thanks a lot," Daphne said. She gave up on trying to get around him. She leaned over and snapped off her radio. "You've got to use a mirror so you don't look stupid," she said. "Everybody does."

"I was only kidding. Seriously. I know dancing is important," Coach said.

"May I go now? I've got algebra." Daphne brought her hair from behind her ear.

"Before that, you have to hear the news. Here's a news bulletin, flash extra."

"You're drunk. You and Mom are going to live in different cities," Daphne said. "Somebody shot somebody."

"No, this is good news. I'm going to be coach here of the varsity. Me." Coach pointed to his chest.

"Now let me out, please," Daphne said.

Coach let her pass. He followed her down the narrow hallway to her bedroom.

"More money," he said. "I'll even be on TV. I'll have my own show on Sundays. And I'll get written up in the press all the time. By *real* reporters. Hey! Why am I yelling at wood, here?"

VIII

Coach was drunk at the kitchen table. He was enjoying the largeness of the room, and he was making out a roster for his dream team. He had put the best kids from his fifteen years of coaching in the positions they had played for him. He was puzzling over the tight-end spot. "Jim Wyckoff or Jerry Kinney?" he said aloud. He penciled "Kinney" into his diagram.

He heard Daphne on the stairs. It occurred to him to clear the beer cans from the table. Instead, he snapped open a fresh can. "Daphne?" he called.

"Wait a second. What?" she said from the living room.

"Just wondered who else was alive besides me." Coach said. "Your mom's still not home."

Daphne entered the kitchen.

"You're sorry you were rude before? That's perfectly okay, honey, just forget it. All right, Father, but I really am ashamed of myself anyway," Coach said.

"You guzzled all those?" Daphne said.

"Hold still. What've you got on?" Coach asked her. He hauled his chair around so that he could see his daughter.

"Two, four, five," Daphne said, counting the cans.

She was wearing one of the fan shirts that Coach had seen on a few summer coeds. On the front, against a maroon field, in gold, was go. Across the back was griffins.

"Now you're talking," Coach said.

"It was free. This guy I met—well, these two guys, really—who work at Campus World, they gave it to me. It's dumb, but I want you to see I care. I do care. Not just for you, but because I want to stay here. Do you think we can maybe? Do your people look any good this year?"

"Winners," Coach said.

"Yeah," Daphne said.

Coach skidded his chair forward. "Have a beer." he said. "Sit down here and let me show you on paper the material they've given me to work with. Then maybe you'll be a believer. Now these guys are fast and big for once. I'm not overestimating them, either. I've seen what I've seen," Coach said.

A car crept into the drive, and then its engine noise filled the garage. Coach and Daphne were quiet until Sherry bustled down the short hall that connected the garage to the kitchen.

"Really late. Sorry, sorry," she said.

"It's a party in here, I warn you," Coach said.

"So I noticed."Sherry had a grocery sack, but it was almost empty. There were bright streaks of paint on her brown arms.

Daphne plucked a bag of Oreo cookies from the groceries.

"Shoot me one of those." Coach said.

"Is there any beer left for me?" Sherry said. "I want to drown my disappointment. I can't paint!"

"You *can* paint," Coach said.

"Let's face it," Sherry said. "An artist? The wife of a coach?"

# TOBIAS WOLFF

(1945– )

One of the most compelling writers to emerge in the last twenty-five years, Tobias Wolff was born in Birmingham, Alabama, but grew up mostly in Washington state after his parents' divorce. This period of his life was treated in his 1989 memoir *This Boy's Life,* which won awards and was adapted for film in 1993. Dropping out of high school, Wolff was an apprentice seaman and a guesser of ages and weights for a carnival. He served in the U.S. Army paratroopers with duty in Vietnam between 1964 and 1968. He recounts this experience in his book *In Pharaoh's Army: Memories of the Lost War* (1994). After leaving the service he went to Oxford University in England and graduated with First Class Honors in English literature in 1972. He also earned an M.A. there in 1975. He went to Stanford University on a Wallace Stegner fellowship and completed an M.A. there in 1978. He has taught at Goddard College in Vermont, at Arizona State University, and at Syracuse University, where he has had an appointment since 1980.

Wolff's story collections include *In the Garden of North American Martyrs* (1981), *Back in the World* (1985), and *The Night in Question* (1996). His novella *The Barracks Thief* (1984) won the PEN/Faulkner Award for fiction in 1985. His fiction tells the not always admirable truth about fairly ordinary people, but it does so with compassion and understanding.

# Hunters in the Snow

TUB HAD been waiting for an hour in the falling snow. He paced the sidewalk to keep warm and stuck his head out over the curb whenever he saw lights approaching. One driver stopped for him but before Tub could wave the man on he saw the rifle on Tub's back and hit the gas. The tires spun on the ice.

The fall of snow thickened. Tub stood below the overhang of a building. Across the road the clouds whitened just above the rooftops, and the street lights went out. He shifted the rifle strap to his other shoulder. The whiteness seeped up the sky.

A truck slid around the corner, horn blaring, rear end sashaying. Tub moved to the sidewalk and held up his hand. The truck jumped the curb and kept coming, half on the street and half on the sidewalk. It wasn't slowing down at all. Tub stood for a moment, still holding up his hand, then jumped back. His rifle slipped off his shoulder and clattered on the ice, a sandwich fell out of his pocket. He ran for the steps of the building. Another sandwich and a package of cookies tumbled onto the new snow. He made the steps and looked back.

The truck had stopped several feet beyond where Tub had been standing. He picked up his sandwiches and his cookies and slung the rifle and went up to the driver's window. The driver was bent against the steering wheel, slapping his knees and drumming his feet on the floorboards. He looked like a cartoon of a person laughing, except that his eyes watched the man on the seat beside him. "You ought to see yourself," the driver said. "He looks just like a beach ball with a hat on, doesn't he? Doesn't he, Frank?"

The man beside him smiled and looked off.

"You almost ran me down," Tub said. "You could've killed me."

"Come on, Tub," said the man beside the driver. "Be mellow. Kenny was just messing around." He opened the door and slid over to the middle of the seat.

Tub took the bolt out of his rifle and climbed in beside him. "I waited an hour," he said. "If you meant ten o'clock why didn't you say ten o'clock?"

"Tub, you haven't done anything but complain since we got here," said the man in the middle. "If you want to piss and moan all day you might as well go home and bitch at your kids. Take your pick." When Tub didn't say anything he turned to the driver. "Okay, Kenny, let's hit the road."

Some juvenile delinquents had heaved a brick through the windshield on the driver's side, so the cold and snow tunneled right into the cab. The heater didn't work.

They covered themselves with a couple of blankets Kenny had brought along and pulled down the muffs on their caps. Tub tried to keep his hands warm by rubbing them under the blanket but Frank made him stop.

They left Spokane and drove deep into the country, running along black lines of fences. The snow let up, but still there was no edge to the land where it met the sky. Nothing moved in the chalky fields. The cold bleached their faces and made the stubble stand out on their cheeks and along their upper lips. They stopped twice for coffee before they got to the woods where Kenny wanted to hunt.

Tub was for trying someplace different; two years in a row they'd been up and down this land and hadn't seen a thing. Frank didn't care one way or the other, he just wanted to get out of the goddamned truck. "Feel that," Frank said, slamming the door. He spread his feet and closed his eyes and leaned his head way back and breathed deeply. "Tune in on that energy."

"Another thing," Kenny said. "This is open land. Most of the land around here is posted."

"I'm cold," Tub said.

Frank breathed out. "Stop bitching, Tub. Get centered."

"I wasn't bitching."

"Centered," Kenny said. "Next thing you'll be wearing a nightgown, Frank. Selling flowers out at the airport."

"Kenny," Frank said, "you talk too much."

"Okay," Kenny said. "I won't say a word. Like I won't say anything about a certain babysitter."

"What babysitter?" Tub asked.

"That's between us," Frank said, looking at Kenny. "That's confidential. You keep your mouth shut."

Kenny laughed.

"You're asking for it," Frank said.

"Asking for what?"

"You'll see."

"Hey," Tub said, "are we hunting or what?"

They started off across the field. Tub had trouble getting through the fences. Frank and Kenny could have helped him; they could have lifted up on the top wire and stepped on the bottom wire, but they didn't. They stood and watched him. There were a lot of fences and Tub was puffing when they reached the woods.

They hunted for over two hours and saw no deer, no tracks, no sign. Finally they stopped by the creek to eat. Kenny had several slices of pizza and a couple of candy bars: Frank had a sandwich, an apple, two carrots, and a square of chocolate; Tub ate one hard-boiled egg and a stick of celery.

"You ask me how I want to die today," Kenny said, "I'll tell you burn me at the stake." He turned to Tub. "You still on that diet?" He winked at Frank.

"What do you think? You think I like hard-boiled eggs?"

"All I can say is, it's the first diet I ever heard of where you gained weight from it."

"Who said I gained weight?"

"Oh, pardon me. I take it back. You're just wasting away before my very eyes. Isn't he, Frank?"

Frank had his fingers fanned out, tips against the bark of the stump where he'd laid his food. His knuckles were hairy. He wore a heavy wedding band and on his right pinky another gold ring with a flat face and an "F" in what looked like diamonds. He turned the ring this way and that. "Tub," he said, "you haven't seen your own balls in ten years."

Kenny doubled over laughing. He took off his hat and slapped his leg with it.

"What am I supposed to do?" Tub said. "It's my glands."

* * *

They left the woods and hunted along the creek. Frank and Kenny worked one bank and Tub worked the other, moving upstream. The snow was light but the drifts were deep and hard to move through. Wherever Tub looked the surface was smooth, undisturbed, and after a time he lost interest. He stopped looking for tracks and just tried to keep up with Frank and Kenny on the other side. A moment came when he realized he hadn't seen them in a long time. The breeze was moving from him to them; when it stilled he could sometimes hear Kenny laughing but that was all. He quickened his pace, breasting hard into the drifts, fighting away the snow with his knees and elbows. He heard his heart and felt the flush on his face but he never once stopped.

Tub caught up with Frank and Kenny at a bend of the creek. They were standing on a log that stretched from their bank to his. Ice had backed up behind the log. Frozen reeds stuck out, barely nodding when the air moved.

"See anything?" Frank asked.

Tub shook his head.

There wasn't much daylight left and they decided to head back toward the road. Frank and Kenny crossed the log and they started downstream, using the trail Tub had broken. Before they had gone very far Kenny stopped. "Look at that," he said, and pointed to some tracks going from the creek back into the woods. Tub's footprints crossed right over them. There on the bank, plain as day, were several mounds of deer sign. "What do you think that is, Tub?" Kenny kicked at it. "Walnuts on vanilla icing?"

"I guess I didn't notice."

Kenny looked at Frank.

"I was lost."

"You were lost. Big deal."

They followed the tracks into the woods. The deer had gone over a fence half buried in drifting snow. A no hunting sign was nailed to the top of one of the posts. Frank laughed and said the son of a bitch could read. Kenny wanted to go after him but Frank said no way, the people out here didn't mess around. He thought maybe the farmer who owned the land would let them use it if they asked. Kenny wasn't so sure. Anyway, he figured that by the time they walked to the truck and drove up the road and doubled back it would be almost dark.

"Relax," Frank said. "You can't hurry nature. If we're meant to get that deer, we'll get it. If we're not, we won't."

They started back toward the truck. This part of the woods was mainly pine. The snow was shaded and had a glaze on it. It held up Kenny and Frank but Tub kept falling through. As he kicked forward, the edge of the crust bruised his shins. Kenny and Frank pulled ahead of him, to where he couldn't even hear their voices any more. He sat down on a stump and wiped his face. He ate both the sandwiches and half the cookies, taking his own sweet time. It was dead quiet.

* * *

When Tub crossed the last fence into the road the truck started moving. Tub had to run for it and just managed to grab hold of the tailgate and hoist himself into the bed. He lay there, panting. Kenny looked out the rear window and grinned. Tub crawled into the lee of the cab to get out of the freezing wind. He pulled his earflaps low and pushed his chin into the collar of his coat. Someone rapped on the window but Tub would not turn around.

He and Frank waited outside while Kenny went into the farmhouse to ask permission. The house was old and paint was curling off the sides. The smoke streamed westward off the top of the chimney, fanning away into a thin gray plume. Above the ridge of the hills another ridge of blue clouds was rising.

"You've got a short memory," Tub said.

"What?" Frank said. He had been staring off.

"I used to stick up for you."

"Okay, so you used to stick up for me. What's eating you?"

"You shouldn't have just left me back there like that."

"You're a grown-up, Tub. You can take care of yourself. Anyway, if you think you're the only person with problems I can tell you that you're not."

"Is something bothering you, Frank?"

Frank kicked at a branch poking out of the snow. "Never mind," he said.

"What did Kenny mean about the babysitter?"

"Kenny talks too much," Frank said. "You just mind your own business."

Kenny came out of the farmhouse and gave the thumbs-up and they began walking back toward the woods. As they passed the barn a large black hound with a grizzled snout ran out and barked at them. Every time he barked he slid backwards a bit, like a cannon recoiling. Kenny got down on all fours and snarled and barked back at him, and the dog slunk away into the barn, looking over his shoulder and peeing a little as he went.

"That's an old-timer," Frank said. "A real graybeard. Fifteen years if he's a day."

"Too old," Kenny said.

Past the barn they cut off through the fields. The land was unfenced and the crust was freezing up thick and they made good time. They kept to the edge of the field until they picked up the tracks again and followed them into the woods, farther and farther back toward the hills. The trees started to blur with the shadows and the wind rose and needled their faces with the crystals it swept off the glaze. Finally they lost the tracks.

Kenny swore and threw down his hat. "This is the worst day of hunting I ever had, bar none." He picked up his hat and brushed off the snow. "This will be the first season since I was fifteen I haven't got my deer."

"It isn't the deer," Frank said. "It's the hunting. There are all these forces out here and you just have to go with them."

"You go with them," Kenny said. "I came out here to get me a deer, not listen to a bunch of hippie bullshit. And if it hadn't been for dimples here I would have, too."

"That's enough," Frank said.

"And you—you're so busy thinking about that little jailbait of yours you wouldn't know a deer if you saw one."

"Drop dead," Frank said, and turned away.

Kenny and Tub followed him back across the fields. When they were coming up to the barn Kenny stopped and pointed. "I hate that post," he said. He raised his rifle and fired. It sounded like a dry branch cracking. The post splintered along its right side, up towards the top. "There," Kenny said. "It's dead."

"Knock it off," Frank said, walking ahead.

Kenny looked at Tub. He smiled. "I hate that tree," he said, and fired again. Tub hurried to catch up with Frank. He started to speak but just then the dog ran out of the barn and barked at them. "Easy, boy," Frank said.

"I hate that dog." Kenny was behind them.

"That's enough," Frank said. "You put that gun down."

Kenny fired. The bullet went in between the dog's eyes. He sank right down into the snow, his legs splayed out on each side, his yellow eyes open and staring. Except for the blood he looked like a small bearskin rug. The blood ran down the dog's muzzle into the snow.

They all looked at the dog lying there.

"What did he ever do to you?" Tub asked. "He was just barking."

Kenny turned to Tub. "I hate you."

Tub shot from the waist. Kenny jerked backward against the fence and buckled to his knees. He folded his hands across his stomach. "Look," he said. His hands were covered with blood. In the dusk his blood was more blue than red. It seemed to belong to the shadows. It didn't seem out of place. Kenny eased himself onto his back. He sighed several times, deeply. "You shot me," he said.

"I had to," Tub said. He knelt beside Kenny. "Oh God," he said. "Frank. Frank."

Frank hadn't moved since Kenny killed the dog.

"Frank!" Tub shouted.

"I was just kidding around," Kenny said. "It was a joke. Oh!" he said, and arched his back suddenly. "Oh!" he said again, and dug his heels into the snow and pushed himself along on his head for several feet. Then he stopped and lay there, rocking back and forth on his heels and head like a wrestler doing warm-up exercises.

Frank roused himself. "Kenny," he said. He bent down and put his gloved hand on Kenny's brow. "You shot him," he said to Tub.

"He made me," Tub said.

"No no no," Kenny said.

Tub was weeping from the eyes and nostrils. His whole face was wet. Frank closed his eyes, then looked down at Kenny again. "Where does it hurt?"

"Everywhere," Kenny said, "just everywhere."

"Oh God," Tub said.

"I mean where did it go in?" Frank said.

"Here." Kenny pointed at the wound in his stomach. It was welling slowly with blood.

"You're lucky," Frank said. "It's on the left side. It missed your appendix. If it had hit your appendix you'd really be in the soup." He turned and threw up onto the snow, holding his sides as if to keep warm.

"Are you all right?" Tub said.

"There's some aspirin in the truck," Kenny said.

"I'm all right," Frank said.

"We'd better call an ambulance," Tub said.

"Jesus," Frank said. "What are we going to say?"

"Exactly what happened," Tub said. "He was going to shoot me but I shot him first."

"No sir!" Kenny said. "I wasn't either!"

Frank patted Kenny on the arm. "Easy does it, partner." He stood. "Let's go."

Tub picked up Kenny's rifle as they walked down toward the farmhouse. "No sense leaving this around," he said. "Kenny might get ideas."

"I can tell you one thing," Frank said. "You've really done it this time. This definitely takes the cake."

They had to knock on the door twice before it was opened by a thin man with lank hair. The room behind him was filled with smoke. He squinted at them. "You get anything?" he asked.

"No," Frank said.

"I knew you wouldn't. That's what I told the other fellow."

"We've had an accident."

The man looked past Frank and Tub into the gloom. "Shoot your friend, did you?"

Frank nodded.

"I did," Tub said.

"I suppose you want to use the phone."

"If it's okay."

The man in the door looked behind him, then stepped back. Frank and Tub followed him into the house. There was a woman sitting by the stove in the middle of the room. The stove was smoking badly. She looked up and then down again at the child asleep in her lap. Her face was white and damp; strands of hair were pasted across her forehead. Tub warmed his hands over the stove while Frank went into the kitchen to call. The man who had let them in stood at the window, his hands in his pockets.

"My friend shot your dog," Tub said.

The man nodded without turning around. "I should have done it myself. I just couldn't."

"He loved that dog so much," the woman said. The child squirmed and she rocked it.

"You asked him to?" Tub said. "You asked him to shoot your dog?"

"He was old and sick. Couldn't chew his food any more. I would have done it myself but I don't have a gun."

"You couldn't have anyway," the woman said. "Never in a million years."

The man shrugged.

Frank came out of the kitchen. "We'll have to take him ourselves. The nearest hospital is fifty miles from here and all their ambulances are out anyway."

The woman knew a shortcut but the directions were complicated and Tub had to write them down. The man told them where they could find some boards to carry Kenny on. He didn't have a flashlight but he said he would leave the porch light on.

It was dark outside. The clouds were low and heavy-looking and the wind blew in shrill gusts. There was a screen loose on the house and it banged slowly and then quickly as the wind rose again. They could hear it all the way to the barn. Frank went for the boards while Tub looked for Kenny, who was not where they had left him. Tub found him farther up the drive, lying on his stomach. "You okay?" Tub said.

"It hurts."

"Frank says it missed your appendix."

"I already had my appendix out."

"All right," Frank said, coming up to them. "We'll have you in a nice warm bed before you can say Jack Robinson." He put the two boards on Kenny's right side.

"Just as long as I don't have one of those male nurses," Kenny said.

"Ha ha," Frank said. "That's the spirit. Get ready, set, *over you go,*" and he rolled Kenny onto the boards. Kenny screamed and kicked his legs in the air. When he quieted down Frank and Tub lifted the boards and carried him down the drive. Tub had the back end, and with the snow blowing in his face he had trouble with his footing. Also he was tired and the man inside had forgotten to turn the porch light on. Just past the house Tub slipped and threw out his hands to catch himself. The boards fell and Kenny tumbled out and rolled to the bottom of the drive, yelling all the way. He came to rest against the right front wheel of the truck.

"You fat moron," Frank said. "You aren't good for diddly."

Tub grabbed Frank by the collar and backed him hard up against the fence. Frank tried to pull his hands away but Tub shook him and snapped his head back and forth and finally Frank gave up.

"What do you know about fat," Tub said. "What do you know about glands." As he spoke he kept shaking Frank. "What do you know about me."

"All right," Frank said.

"No more," Tub said.

"All right."

"No more talking to me like that. No more watching. No more laughing."

"Okay, Tub. I promise."

Tub let go of Frank and leaned his forehead against the fence. His arms hung straight at his sides.

"I'm sorry, Tub." Frank touched him on the shoulder. "I'll be down at the truck."

Tub stood by the fence for a while and then got the rifles off the porch. Frank had rolled Kenny back onto the boards and they lifted him into the bed of the truck. Frank spread the seat blankets over him. "Warm enough?" he asked.

Kenny nodded.

"Okay. Now how does reverse work on this thing?"

"All the way to the left and up." Kenny sat up as Frank started forward to the cab. "Frank!"

"What?"

"If it sticks don't force it."

The truck started right away. "One thing," Frank said, "you've got to hand it to the Japanese. A very ancient, very spiritual culture and they can still make a hell of a truck." He glanced over at Tub. "Look, I'm sorry. I didn't know you felt that way, honest to God I didn't. You should have said something."

"I did."

"When? Name one time."

"A couple of hours ago."

"I guess I wasn't paying attention."

"That's true, Frank," Tub said. "You don't pay attention very much."

"Tub," Frank said, "what happened back there, I should have been more sympathetic. I realize that. You were going through a lot. I just want you to know it wasn't your fault. He was asking for it."

"You think so?"

"Absolutely. It was him or you. I would have done the same thing in your shoes, no question."

The wind was blowing into their faces. The snow was a moving white wall in front of their lights; it swirled into the cab through the hole in the windshield and settled on them. Tub clapped his hands and shifted around to stay warm, but it didn't work.

"I'm going to have to stop," Frank said. "I can't feel my fingers."

Up ahead they saw some lights off the road. It was a tavern. Outside in the parking lot there were several jeeps and trucks. A couple of them had deer strapped across their hoods. Frank parked and they went back to Kenny. "How you doing, partner," Frank said.

"I'm cold."

"Well, don't feel like the Lone Ranger. It's worse inside, take my word for it. You should get that windshield fixed."

"Look," Tub said, "he threw the blankets off." They were lying in a heap against the tailgate.

"Now look, Kenny," Frank said, "it's no use whining about being cold if you're not going to try and keep warm. You've got to do your share." He spread the blankets over Kenny and tucked them in at the corners.

"They blew off."

"Hold on to them then."

"Why are we stopping, Frank?"

"Because if me and Tub don't get warmed up we're going to freeze solid and then where will you be?" He punched Kenny lightly in the arm. "So just hold your horses."

The bar was full of men in colored jackets, mostly orange. The waitress brought coffee. "Just what the doctor ordered," Frank said, cradling the steaming cup in his hand. His skin was bone white. "Tub, I've been thinking. What you said about me not paying attention, that's true."

"It's okay."

"No. I really had that coming. I guess I've just been a little too interested in old number one. I've had a lot on my mind. Not that that's any excuse."

"Forget it, Frank. I sort of lost my temper back there. I guess we're all a little on edge."

Frank shook his head. "It isn't just that."

"You want to talk about it?"

"Just between us, Tub?"

"Sure, Frank. Just between us."

"Tub, I think I'm going to be leaving Nancy."

"Oh, Frank. Oh, Frank." Tub sat back and shook his head.

Frank reached out and laid his hand on Tub's arm. "Tub, have you ever been really in love?"

"Well—"

"I mean *really* in love." He squeezed Tub's wrist. "With your whole being."

"I don't know. When you put it like that, I don't know."

"You haven't then. Nothing against you, but you'd know it if you had." Frank let go of Tub's arm. "This isn't just some bit of fluff I'm talking about."

"Who is she, Frank?"

Frank paused. He looked into his empty cup. "Roxanne Brewer."

"Cliff Brewer's kid? The babysitter?"

"You can't just put people into categories like that, Tub. That's why the whole system is wrong. And that's why this country is going to hell in a rowboat."

"But she can't be more than—" Tub shook his head.

"Fifteen. She'll be sixteen in May." Frank smiled. "May fourth, three twenty-seven p.m. Hell, Tub, a hundred years ago she'd have been an old maid by that age. Juliet was only thirteen."

"Juliet? Juliet Miller? Jesus, Frank, she doesn't even have breasts. She doesn't even wear a top to her bathing suit. She's still collecting frogs."

"Not Juliet Miller. The real Juliet. Tub, don't you see how you're dividing people up into categories? He's an executive, she's a secretary, he's a truck driver, she's fifteen years old. Tub, this so-called babysitter, this so-called fifteen-year-old has more in her little finger than most of us have in our entire bodies. I can tell you this little lady is something special."

Tub nodded. "I know the kids like her."

"She's opened up whole worlds to me that I never knew were there."

"What does Nancy think about all of this?"

"She doesn't know."

"You haven't told her?"

"Not yet. It's not so easy. She's been damned good to me all these years. Then there's the kids to consider." The brightness in Frank's eyes trembled and he wiped quickly at them with the back of his hand. "I guess you think I'm a complete bastard."

"No, Frank. I don't think that."

"Well, you *ought* to."

"Frank, when you've got a friend it means you've always got someone on your side, no matter what. That's the way I feel about it, anyway."

"You mean that, Tub?"

"Sure I do."

Frank smiled. "You don't know how good it feels to hear you say that."

* * *

Kenny had tried to get out of the truck but he hadn't made it. He was jack-knifed over the tailgate, his head hanging above the bumper. They lifted him back into the bed and covered him again. He was sweating and his teeth chattered. "It hurts, Frank."

"It wouldn't hurt so much if you just stayed put. Now we're going to the hospital. Got that? Say it—I'm going to the hospital."

"I'm going to the hospital."

"Again."

"I'm going to the hospital."

"Now just keep saying that to yourself and before you know it we'll be there."

After they had gone a few miles Tub turned to Frank. "I just pulled a real boner," he said.

"What's that?"

"I left the directions on the table back there."

"That's okay. I remember them pretty well."

The snowfall lightened and the clouds began to roll back off the fields, but it was no warmer and after a time both Frank and Tub were bitten through and shaking. Frank almost didn't make it around a curve, and they decided to stop at the next roadhouse.

There was an automatic hand-dryer in the bathroom and they took turns standing in front of it, opening their jackets and shirts and letting the jet of hot air breathe across their faces and chests.

"You know," Tub said, "what you told me back there, I appreciate it. Trusting me."

Frank opened and closed his fingers in front of the nozzle. "The way I look at it, Tub, no man is an island. You've got to trust someone."

"Frank—"

Frank waited.

"When I said that about my glands, that wasn't true. The truth is I just shovel it in."

"Well, Tub—"

"Day and night, Frank. In the shower. On the freeway." He turned and let the air play over his back. "I've even got stuff in the paper towel machine at work."

"There's nothing wrong with your glands at all?" Frank had taken his boots and socks off. He held first his right, then his left foot up to the nozzle.

"No. There never was."

"Does Alice know?" The machine went off and Frank started lacing up his boots.

"Nobody knows. That's the worst of it, Frank. Not the being fat, I never got any big kick out of being thin, but the lying. Having to lead a double life like a spy or a hit man. This sounds strange but I feel sorry for those guys, I really do. I know what they go through. Always having to think about what you say and do. Always feeling like people are watching you, trying to catch you at something. Never able to just be yourself. Like when I make a big deal about only having an orange for breakfast and then scarf all the way to work. Oreos, Mars Bars, Twinkies. Sugar Babies. Snickers." Tub glanced at Frank and looked quickly away. "Pretty disgusting, isn't it?"

"Tub. Tub." Frank shook his head. "Come on." He took Tub's arm and led him into the restaurant half of the bar. "My friend is hungry," he told the waitress. "Bring four orders of pancakes, plenty of butter and syrup."

"Frank—"

"Sit down."

When the dishes came Frank carved out slabs of butter and just laid them on the pancakes. Then he emptied the bottle of syrup, moving it back and forth over the plates. He leaned forward on his elbows and rested his chin in one hand. "Go on, Tub."

Tub ate several mouthfuls, then started to wipe his lips. Frank took the napkin away from him. "No wiping," he said. Tub kept at it. The syrup covered his chin; it dripped to a point like a goatee. "Weigh in, Tub," Frank said, pushing another fork across the table. "Get down to business." Tub took the fork in his left hand and lowered his head and started really chowing down. "Clean your plate," Frank said when the pancakes were gone, and Tub lifted each of the four plates and licked it clean. He sat back, trying to catch his breath.

"Beautiful," Frank said. "Are you full?"

"I'm full," Tub said. "I've never been so full."

* * *

Kenny's blankets were bunched up against the tailgate again.

"They must have blown off," Tub said.

"They're not doing him any good," Frank said. "We might as well get some use out of them."

Kenny mumbled. Tub bent over him. "What? Speak up."

"I'm going to the hospital," Kenny said.

"Attaboy," Frank said.

The blankets helped. The wind still got their faces and Frank's hands but it was much better. The fresh snow on the road and the trees sparkled under the beam of the headlight. Squares of light from farmhouse windows fell onto the blue snow in the fields.

"Frank," Tub said after a time, "you know that farmer? He told Kenny to kill the dog."

"You're kidding!" Frank leaned forward, considering. "That Kenny. What a card." He laughed and so did Tub. Tub smiled out the back window. Kenny lay with his arms folded over his stomach, moving his lips at the stars. Right overhead was the Big Dipper, and behind, hanging between Kenny's toes in the direction of the hospital, was the North Star, Pole Star, Help to Sailors. As the truck twisted through the gentle hills the star went back and forth between Kenny's boots, staying always in his sight. "I'm going to the hospital," Kenny said. But he was wrong. They had taken a different turn a long way back.

# BOBBIE ANN MASON

## (1940– )

Flannery O'Connor once commented that many of her fellow writers were not "from" any place, by which she meant that general insights about human beings come best through the particularities of time and place. This observation applies to the fiction of Bobbie Ann Mason, which focuses so clearly upon ordinary, barely middle-class people in western Kentucky. Her fiction is the contemporary version of an old tension in American fiction, that between wanderlust and nostalgia. Her people are often caught in the forces of change that have penetrated into the small towns of rural regions, the inescapability of strip-malls and television, harbingers of both threat and promise.

Mason was born and raised on a dairy farm near Mayfield in western Kentucky. She went to the University of Kentucky, majoring in journalism and graduating in 1962. She spent a few years in New York City writing articles about popular entertainers for movie and fan magazines. She earned an M.A. in English from the State University of New York at Binghamton in 1966, and a Ph.D. from the University of Connecticut in 1972. She was a faculty member at Mansfield State College in Pennsylvania from 1972 to 1979, where she wrote and published two books of criticism, one on Nabokov's novel *Ada* (1974) and one on the "girl sleuth" genre of children's fiction (1975). In the late 1970s and early 1980s her fiction began to be published in major magazines such as *The New Yorker, The Atlantic Monthly, Redbook,* and *North American Review.*

Mason's highly acclaimed collection of stories, *Shiloh and Other Stories,* appeared in 1982 and won the National Book Critics Circle Award. Her other story collections include *Love Life* (1989) and *Midnight Magic* (1998). She has also written the novels *In Country* (1985), *Spence + Lila* (1988), and *Feather Crowns* (1993). In 1999 she published *Clear Springs: A Memoir.* Many of her stories have been included in the O. Henry Award annuals and *The Best American Short Stories* series.

# A New-Wave Format

EDWIN CREECH drives a yellow bus, transporting a group of mentally retarded adults to the Cedar Hill Mental Health Center, where they attend training classes. He is away from 7:00 to 9:30 A.M. and from 2:30 to 5:00 P.M. His hours are so particular that Sabrina Jones, the girl he has been living with for several months, could easily cheat on him. Edwin devises schemes to test her. He places a long string of dental floss on her pillow (an idea he got from a mystery novel), but it remains undisturbed. She is away four nights a week, at rehearsals for *Oklahoma!* with the Western Kentucky Little Theatre, and she often goes out to eat afterward with members of the cast. Sabrina won't let him go to rehearsals, saying she wants the play to be complete when he sees it. At home, she sings and dances along with the movie sound track, and she acts out scenes for him. In the play, she's in the chorus, and she has two lines in Act I, Scene 3. Her lines are "And to yer house a dark clubman!" and "Then out of your dreams you'll go." Edwin loves the dramatic way Sabrina waves her arms on her first line. She is supposed to be a fortune teller.

One evening when Sabrina comes home, Edwin is still up, as she puts on the sound track of *Oklahoma!* and sings along with Gordon MacRae while she does splits on the living room floor. Her legs are long and slender, and she still has her summer tan. She is wearing her shorts, even though it is late fall. Edwin suddenly has an overwhelming feeling of love for her. She really seems to believe what she is singing—"Oh, What a Beautiful Mornin'." When the song ends, he tells her that.

"It's the middle of the night," he says, teasing. "And you think it's morning."

"I'm just acting."

"No, you really believe it. You believe it's morning, a beautiful morning."

Sabrina gives him a fishy look, and Edwin feels embarrassed. When the record ends, Sabrina goes into the bedroom and snaps on the radio. Rock music helps her relax before going to sleep. The new rock music she likes is monotonous and bland, but Edwin tells himself that he likes it because Sabrina likes it. As she undresses, he says to her, "I'm sorry. I wasn't accusing you of nothing."

"That's O.K." She shrugs. The T-shirt she sleeps in has a hole revealing a spot of her skin that Edwin would like to kiss, but he doesn't because it seems like a corny thing to do. So many things about Sabrina are amazing: her fennel toothpaste and herbal deodorant; her slim, snaky hips; the way she puts Vaseline on her teeth for a flashier smile, something she learned to do in a beauty contest.

When she sits on the bed, Edwin says, "If I say the wrong things, I want you to tell me. It's just that I'm so crazy about you I can't think sometimes. But if I can do anything better, I will. I promise. Just tell me."

"I don't think of you as the worrying type," she says, lying down beside him. She still has her shoes on.

"I didn't used to be."

"You're the most laid back guy I know."

"Is that some kind of actor talk from your actor friends?"

"No. You're just real laid back. Usually good-looking guys are so stuck up. But you're not." The music sends vibrations through Edwin like a cat's purr. She says, "I brag on you all the time to Jeff and Sue––Curly and Laurey."

"I know who Jeff and Sue are." Sabrina talks constantly about Jeff and Sue, the romantic leads in the play.

Sabrina says, "Here's what I wish. If we had a big pile of money, we could have a house like Sue's. Did I tell you she's got *woven* blinds on her patio that she made herself? Everything she does is so *artistic*." Sabrina shakes Edwin's shoulder. "Wake up and talk to me."

"I can't. I have to get up at six."

Sabrina whispers to him, "Sue has the hots for Jeff. And Jeff's wife is going to have a duck with a rubber tail if she finds out." Sabrina giggles. "He kept dropping hints about how his wife was going to Louisville next week. And he and Sue were eating off the same slice of pizza."

"Is that supposed to mean something?"

"You figure it out."

"Would you do me that way?"

"Don't be silly." Sabrina turns up the radio, then unties her shoes and tosses them over Edwin's head into a corner.

Edwin is forty-three and Sabrina is only twenty, but he does not want to believe age is a barrier between them. Sometimes he cannot believe his good luck, that he has a beautiful girl who finds him still attractive. Edwin has a deep dimple in his chin, which reminded his first wife, Lois Ann, of Kirk Douglas. She had read in a movie magazine that Kirk Douglas has a special attachment for shaving his dimple. But Sabrina thinks Edwin looks like John Travolta, who also has a dimple. Now and then Edwin realizes how much older he is than Sabrina, but time has passed quickly, and he still feels like the same person, unchanged, that he was twenty years ago. His two ex-wives had seemed to drift away from him, and he never tried to hold them back. But with Sabrina, he knows he must make an effort, for it is beginning to dawn on him that sooner or later women get disillusioned with him. Maybe he's too laid back. But Sabrina likes this quality. Sabrina has large round gray eyes and limp, brownish-blond hair, the color of birch paneling, which she highlights with Miss Clairol. They share a love of Fudgsicles, speedboats, and *WKRP in Cincinnati.* At the beginning, he thought that was enough to build a relationship on, because he knew so many couples who never shared such simple pleasures, but gradually he has begun to see that it is more complicated than that. Sabrina's liveliness makes him afraid that she will be fickle. He can't bear the thought of losing her, and he doesn't like the idea that his new possessiveness may be the same uneasy feeling a man would have for a daughter.

Sabrina's parents sent her to college for a year, but her father, a farmer, lost money on his hogs and couldn't afford to continue. When Edwin met her, she was working as a waitress in a steak house. She wants to go back to college, but Edwin does not have the money to send her either. In college, she learned things that make him feel ignorant around her. She said that in an anthropology course, for instance, she learned for a fact that people evolved from animals. But when he tried to argue with her, she said his doubts were too silly to discuss. Edwin doesn't want to sound like a father, so he usually avoids such topics. Sabrina believes in the ERA, although she likes to keep house. She cooks odd things for him, like eggplant, and a weird lasagna with vegetables. She says she knows how to make a Big Mac from scratch, but she never does. Her specialty is pizza. She puts sliced dill pickles on it, which Edwin doesn't dare question. She likes to do things in what she calls an arty way. Now Sabrina is going out for pizza with people in the Theatre. Sabrina talks of "the Theatre."

Until he began driving the bus, Edwin had never worked closely with people. He worked on an offshore oil rig for a time, but kept his distance from the other men. He drove a bulldozer in a logging camp out West. In Kentucky, during his marriages, he worked in an aluminum products company, an automotive machine shop, and numerous gas stations, going from job to job as casually as he did with women. He used to think of himself as an adventurer, but now he believes he has gone through life rather blindly, without much pain or sense of loss.

When he drives the bus, he feels stirred up, perhaps the way Sabrina feels about *Oklahoma!* The bus is a new luxury model with a tape deck, AM-FM, CB, and built-in first-aid kit. He took a first-aid course, so he feels prepared to handle emergencies. Edwin has to stay alert, for anything could happen. The guys who came back from Vietnam said it was like this every moment. Edwin was in the army, but he was never sent to Vietnam, and now he feels that he has bypassed some critical stage in his life: a knowledge of terror. Edwin has never had this kind of responsibility, and he has never been around mentally retarded people before. His passengers are like bizarre, overgrown children, badly behaved and unpredictable. Some of them stare off into space, others are hyperactive. A woman named Freddie Johnson kicks aimlessly at the seat in front of her, spouting her ten-word vocabulary. She can say, "Hot! Shorts," "*Popeye* on?" "*Dukes* on!" "Cook supper," and "Go bed." She talks continuously. A gangly man with a clubfoot has learned to get Hershey bars from a vending machine, and every day he brings home Hershey bars, clutching them in his hand until he squeezes them out of shape. A pretty blond woman shows Edwin the braces on her teeth every day when she gets on the bus. She gets confused if Edwin brings up another topic. The noises on the bus are chaotic and eerie—spurts, gurgles, yelps, squeals. Gradually, Edwin has learned how to keep his distance and keep order at the same time. He plays tape-recorded music to calm and entertain the passengers. In effect, he has become a disc jockey, taking requests and using the microphone, but he avoids fast talk. The supervisors at the center have told him that the developmentally disabled—they always use this term—need a world that is slowed down; they can't keep up with today's fast pace. So he plays mellow old sixties tunes by the Lovin' Spoonful, Joni Mitchell, Donovan. It seems to work. The passengers have learned to clap or hum along with the music. One man, Merle Cope, has been learning to clap his hands in a body-awareness class. Merle is forty-seven years old, and he walks two miles—in an hour—to the bus stop, down a country road. He climbs onto the bus with agonizing slowness. When he gets on, he makes an exaggerated clapping motion, as if to congratulate himself for having made it, but he never lets his hands quite touch. Merle Cope always has an eager grin on his face, and when he tries to clap his hands he looks ecstatic. He looks happier than Sabrina singing "Oh, What a Beautiful Mornin'."

On Thursday, November 14, Edwin stops at the junction of a state road and a gravel road called Ezra Combs Lane to pick up a new passenger. The country roads have shiny new green signs, with the names of the farmers who originally settled there three or four generations ago. The new passenger is Laura Combs, who he has been told is thirty-seven and has never been to school. She will take classes in Home Management and Living Skills. When she gets on the bus, the people who were with her drive off in a blue Pacer. Laura Combs, a large, angular woman with buckteeth, stomps deliberately down the aisle, then plops down beside a young black man named Ray Watson, who has been riding the bus for about three weeks. Ray has hardly spoken, except to say "Have a nice day" to Edwin when he leaves the bus. Ray, who is mildly retarded from a blow on the head in his childhood, is subject to seizures, but so far he has not had one on the bus. Edwin watches him carefully. He learned about convulsions in his first-aid course.

When Laura Combs sits down by Ray Watson, she shoves him and says, "Scoot over. And cheer up."

Her tone is not cheerful. Edwin watches in the rear-view mirror, ready to act. He glides around a curve and slows down for the next passenger. A tape has ended and Edwin hesitates before inserting another. He hears Ray Watson say, "I never seen anybody as ugly as you."

"Shut up or I'll send you to the back of the bus." Laura Combs speaks with a snappy authority that makes Edwin wonder if she is really retarded. Her hair is streaked gray and yellow, and her face is filled with acne pits.

Ray Watson says, "That's fine with me, long as I don't have to set by you."

"Want me to throw you back in the woodpile where you come from?"

"I bet you could throw me plumb out the door, you so big."

It is several minutes before it is clear to Edwin that they are teasing. He is pleased that Ray is talking, but he can't understand why it took a person like Laura Combs to motivate him. She is an imposing woman with a menacing stare. She churns gum, her mouth open.

For a few weeks, Edwin watches them joke with each other, and whenever he decides he should separate them, they break out into big grins and pull at each other's arms. The easy intimacy they develop seems strange to Edwin, but then it suddenly occurs to him what a fool he is being about a twenty-year-old girl, and that seems even stranger. He hears Ray ask Laura," Did you get that hair at the Piggly Wiggly?" Laura's hair is in pigtails, which seem to be freshly plaited on Mondays and untouched the rest of the week. Laura says, "I don't want no birds nesting in *my* hair."

Edwin takes their requests. Laura has to hear "Mister Bojangles" every day, and Ray demands that Edwin play something from Elvis's Christmas album. They argue over tastes. Each says the other's favorite songs are terrible.

Laura tells Ray she never heard of a black person liking Elvis, and Ray says, "There's a lot about black people you don't know."

"What?"

"That's for me to know and you to find out. You belong on the moon. All white peoples belong on the moon."

"You belong in Atlanta," Laura says, doubling over with laughter.

When Edwin reports their antics one day to Sabrina, she says, "That's too depressing for words."

"They're a lot smarter than you'd think."

"I don't see how you can stand it." Sabrina shudders. She says, "Out in the woods, animals that are defective wouldn't survive. Even back in history, deformed babies were abandoned."

"Today's different," says Edwin, feeling alarmed. "Now they have rights."

"Well, I'll say one thing. If I was going to have a retarded baby, I'd get an abortion."

"That's killing."

"It's all in how you look at it," says Sabrina, changing the radio station.

They are having lunch. Sabrina has made a loaf of zucchini bread, because Sue made one for Jeff. Edwin doesn't understand her reasoning, but he takes it as a compliment. She gives him another slice, spreading it with whipped margarine. All of his women were good cooks. Maybe he didn't praise them enough. He suddenly blurts out so much praise for the zucchini bread that Sabrina looks at him oddly. Then he realizes that her attention is on the radio. The Humans are singing a song about paranoia, which begins, "Attention, all you K Mart shoppers, fill your carts, 'cause your time is almost up." It is Sabrina's favorite song.

"Most of my passengers are real poor country people," Edwin says. "Use to, they'd be kept in the attic or out in the barn. Now they're riding a bus, going to school and having a fine time."

"In the attic? I never knew that. *I*'m a poor country girl and I never knew that."

"Everybody knows that," says Edwin, feeling a little pleased. "But don't call yourself a poor country girl."

"It's true. My daddy said he'd give me a calf to raise if I came back home. Big deal. My greatest dread is that I'll end up on a farm, raising a bunch of dirty-faced younguns. Just like some of those characters on your bus."

Edwin does not know what to say. The song ends. The last line is, "They're looking in your picture window."

While Sabrina clears away the dishes, Edwin practices rolling bandages. He has been reviewing his first-aid book. "I want you to help me practice a simple splint," he says to Sabrina.

"If I broke a leg, I couldn't be in *Oklahoma!*"

"You won't break a leg." He holds out the splint. It is a fraternity paddle, a souvenir of her college days. She sits down for him and stretches out her leg.

"I can't stand this," she says.

"I'm just practicing. I have to be prepared. I might have an emergency."

Sabrina, wincing, closes her eyes while Edwin ties the fraternity paddle to her ankle.

"It's perfect," he says, tightening the knot.

Sabrina opens her eyes and wiggles her foot. "Jim says he's sure I can have a part in *Life with Father,*" she says. Jim is the director of *Oklahoma!* She adds, "Jeff is probably going to be the lead."

"I guess you're trying to make me jealous."

"No, I'm not. It's not even a love story."

"I'm glad then. Is that what you want to do?"

"I don't know. Don't you think I ought to go back to school and take a drama class? It'd be a real great experience, and I'm not going to get a job anytime soon, looks like. Nobody's hiring." She shakes her leg impatiently, and Edwin begins untying the bandage. "What do you think I ought to do?"

"I don't know. I never know how to give you advice, Sabrina. What do I know? I haven't been to college like you."

"I wish I were rich, so I could go back to school," Sabrina says sadly. The fraternity paddle falls to the floor, and she says, with her hands rushing to her face, "Oh, God, I can't stand the thought of breaking a leg."

* * *

The play opens in two weeks, during the Christmas season, and Sabrina has been making her costumes—two gingham outfits, virtually identical. She models them for Edwin and practices her dances for him. Edwin applauds, and she gives him a stage bow, as the director has taught her to do. Everything Sabrina does now seems like a performance. When she slices the zucchini bread, sawing at it because it has hardened, it is a performance. When she sat in the kitchen chair with the splint, it was as though she imagined her audience. Edwin has been involved in his own performances, on the bus. He emulates Dr. Johnny Fever, on *WKRP,* because he likes to be low-key, cool. But he hesitates to tell Sabrina about his disc jockey role because she doesn't watch *WKRP in Cincinnati* with him anymore. She goes to rehearsals early.

Maybe it is out of resistance to the sappy *Oklahoma!* sound track, or maybe it is an inevitable progression, but Edwin finds himself playing a few Dylan tunes, some Janis Joplin, nothing too hectic. The passengers shake their heads in pleasure or beat things with their fists. It makes Edwin sad to think how history passes them by, but sometimes he feels the same way about his own life. As he drives along, playing these old songs, he thinks about what his life was like back then. During his first marriage, he worked in a gas station, saving for a down payment on a house. Lois Ann fed him on a TV tray while he watched the war. It was like a drama series. After Lois Ann, and then his travels out West, there was Carolyn and another down payment on another house and more of the war. Carolyn had a regular schedule—pork chops on Mondays, chicken on Tuesdays. Thursday's menu has completely escaped his memory. He feels terrible, remembering his wives by their food, and remembering the war as a TV series. His life has been a delayed reaction. He feels as if he's about Sabrina's age. He plays music he did not understand fifteen years ago, music that now seems full of possibility: the Grateful Dead, the Jefferson Airplane, groups with vision. Edwin feels that he is growing and changing for the first time in years. The passengers on his bus fill him with a compassion he has never felt before. When Freddie Johnson learns a new word—"bus"—Edwin is elated. He feels confident. He could drive his passengers all the way to California if he had to.

One day a stringbean girl with a speech impediment gives Edwin a tape cassette she wants him to play. Her name is Lou Murphy. Edwin has tried to encourage her to talk, but today he hands the tape back to her abruptly.

"I don't like the Plasmatics," he explains, enjoying his authority. "I don't play new-wave. I have a golden-oldie format. I just play sixties stuff."

The girl takes the tape cassette and sits down by Laura Combs. Ray Watson is absent today. She starts pulling at her hair, and the cassette jostles in her lap. Laura is wound up too, jiggling her knees. The pair of them make Edwin think of those vibrating machines that mix paint by shaking the cans.

Edwin takes the microphone and says, "If you want a new wave format, you'll have to ride another bus. Now let's crawl back in the stacks of wax for this oldie but goodie—Janis Joplin and 'A Little Bit Harder.' "

Lou Murphy nods along with the song. Laura's chewing gum pops like BBs. A while later, after picking up another passenger, Edwin glances in the rear-view mirror and sees Laura playing with the Plasmatics tape, pulling it out in a curly heap. Lou seems to be trying to shriek, but nothing comes out. Before Edwin can stop the bus, Laura has thrown the tape out the window.

"You didn't like it, Mr. Creech," Laura says when Edwin, after halting the bus on a shoulder, stalks down the aisle. "You said you didn't like it."

Edwin has never heard anyone sound so matter-of-fact, or look so reasonable. He has heard that since Laura began her classes, she has learned to set a table, make change, and dial a telephone. She even has a job at the training center, sorting seeds and rags. She is as hearty and domineering, yet as delicate and vulnerable, as Janis Joplin must have been. Edwin manages to move Lou to a front seat. She is sobbing silently, her lower jaw jerking, and Edwin realizes he is trembling too. He feels ashamed. After all, he is not driving the bus in order to make a name for himself. Yet it had felt right to insist on the format for his show. There is no appropriate way to apologize, or explain.

Edwin doesn't want to tell Sabrina about the incident. She is preoccupied with the play and often listens to him distractedly. Edwin has decided that he was foolish to suspect that she had a lover. The play is her love. Her nerves are on edge. One chilly afternoon, on the weekend before *Oklahoma!* opens, he suggests driving over to Kentucky Lake.

"You need a break," he tells her. "A little relaxation. I'm worried about you."

"This is nothing," she says. "Two measly lines. I'm not exactly a star."

"What if you were? Would you get an abortion?"

"What are you talking about? I'm not pregnant."

"You said once you would. Remember?"

"Oh. I would if the baby was going to be creepy like those people on your bus."

"But how would you know if it was?"

"They can tell." Sabrina stares at him and then laughs. "Through science."

In the early winter, the lake is deserted. The beaches are washed clean, and the water is clear and gray. Now and then, as they walk by the water, they hear a gunshot from the Land Between the Lakes wilderness area. "The Surrey with the Fringe on Top" is going through Edwin's head, and he wishes he could throw the *Oklahoma!* sound track in the lake, as easily as Laura Combs threw the Plasmatics out the window of the bus. He has an idea that after the play, Sabrina is going to feel a letdown too great for him to deal with.

When Sabrina makes a comment about the "artistic intention" of Rodgers and Hammerstein, Edwin says, "Do you know what Janis Joplin said?"

"No—what?" Sabrina stubs the toe of her jogging shoe in the sand.

"Janis Joplin said, 'I don't write songs. I just make 'em up.' I thought that was clever."

"That's funny, I guess."

"She said she was going to her high school reunion in Port Arthur, Texas. She said, 'I'm going to laugh a lot. They laughed me out of class, out of town, and out of the state.' "

"You sound like you've got that memorized," Sabrina says, looking at the sky.

"I saw it on TV one night when you were gone, an old tape of a Dick Cavett show. It seemed worth remembering." Edwin rests his arm around Sabrina's waist, as thin as a post. He says, "I see a lot of things on TV, when you're not there."

Wild ducks are landing on the water, scooting in like water skiers. Sabrina seems impressed by them. They stand there until the last one lands.

Edwin says, "I bet you can't even remember Janis Joplin. You're just a young girl, Sabrina. *Oklahoma!* will seem silly to you one of these days."

Sabrina hugs his arm. "That don't matter." She breaks into laughter. "You're cute when you're being serious."

Edwin grabs her hand and jerks her toward him. "Look, Sabrina. I was never serious before in my life. I'm just now, at this point in my life—this week—getting to be serious." His words scare him, and he adds with a grin that stretches his dimple, "I'm serious about *you*."

"I know that," she says. She is leading the way along the water, through the trees, pulling him by the hand. "But you never believe how much I care about you," she says, drawing him to her. "I think we get along real good. That's why I wish you'd marry me instead of just stringing me along."

Edwin gasps like a swimmer surfacing. It is very cold on the beach. Another duck skis onto the water.

* * *

*Oklahoma!* has a four-night run, with one matinee. Edwin goes to the play three times, surprised that he enjoys it. Sabrina's lines come off differently each time, and each evening she discusses the impression she made. Edwin tells her that she is the prettiest woman in the cast, and that her lines are cute. He wants to marry Sabrina, although he hasn't yet said he would. He wishes he could buy her a speedboat for a wedding present. She wants him to get a better-paying job, and she has ideas about a honeymoon cottage at the lake. It feels odd that Sabrina has proposed to him. He thinks of her as a liberated woman. The play is old-fashioned and phony. The love scenes between Jeff and Sue are comically stilted, resembling none of the passion and intrigue that Sabrina has reported. She compared them to Bogart and Bacall, but Edwin can't remember if she meant Jeff and Sue's roles or their actual affair. How did Sabrina know about Bogart and Bacall?

At the cast party, at Jeff's house, Jeff and Sue are publicly affectionate, getting away with it by playing their Laurey and Curly roles, but eventually Jeff's wife, who has made ham, potato salad, chiffon cakes, eggnog, and cranberry punch for sixty people, suddenly disappears from the party. Jeff whizzes off in his Camaro to find her. Sabrina whispers to Edwin, "Look how Sue's pretending nothing's happened. She's flirting with the guy who played Jud Fry." Sabrina, so excited that she bounces around on her tiptoes, is impressed by Jeff's house, which has wicker furniture and rose plush carpets.

Edwin drinks too much cranberry punch at the party, and most of the time he sits on a wicker love seat watching Sabrina flit around the room, beaming with the joy of her success. She is out of costume, wearing a sweatshirt with a rainbow on the front and pots of gold on her breasts. He realizes how proud he is of her. Her complexion is as smooth as a white mushroom, and she has crinkled her hair by braiding and unbraiding it. He watches her join some of the cast members around the piano to sing songs from the play, as though they cannot bear it that the play has ended. Sabrina seems to belong with them, these theatre people. Edwin knows they are not really theatre people. They are only local merchants putting on a play in their spare time. But Edwin is just a bus driver. He should get a better job so that he can send Sabrina to college, but he knows that he has to take care of his passengers. Their faces have become as familiar to him as the sound track of *Oklahoma!* He can practically hear Freddie Johnson shouting out her TV shows: "*Popeye* on! *Dukes* on!" He sees Sabrina looking at him lovingly. The singers shout, "Oklahoma, O.K.!"

Sabrina brings him a plastic glass of cranberry punch and sits with him on the love seat, holding his hand. She says, "Jim definitely said I should take a drama course at Murray State next semester. He was real encouraging. He said, 'Why not be in the play *and* take a course or two?' I could drive back and forth, don't you think?"

"Why not? You can have anything you want." Edwin plays with her hand.

"Jeff took two courses at Murray and look how good he was. Didn't you think he was good? I loved that cute way he went into that dance."

Edwin is a little drunk. He finds himself telling Sabrina about how he plays disc jockey on the bus, and he confesses to her his shame about the way he sounded off about his golden-oldie format. His mind is reeling and the topic sounds trivial, compared to Sabrina's future.

"Why *don't* you play a new-wave format?" she asks him. "It's what *every*body listens to." She nods at the stereo, which is playing "You're Living in Your Own Private Idaho," by the B-52s, a song Edwin has often heard on the radio late at night when Sabrina is unwinding, moving into his arms. The music is violent and mindless, with a fast beat like a crazed parent abusing a child, thrashing it senseless.

"I don't know," Edwin says. "I shouldn't have said that to Lou Murphy. It bothers me."

"She don't know the difference," Sabrina says, patting his head. "It's ridiculous to make a big thing out of it. Words are so arbitrary, and people don't say what they mean half the time anyway."

"You should talk, Miss Oklahoma!" Edwin laughs, spurting a little punch on the love seat. "You and your two lines!"

"They're just lines," she says, smiling up at him and poking her finger into his dimple.

* * *

Some of Edwin's passengers bring him Christmas presents, badly wrapped, with tags that say his name in wobbly writing. Edwin puts the presents in a drawer, where Sabrina finds them.

"Aren't you going to open them?" she asks. "I'd be dying to know what was inside."

"I will eventually. Leave them there." Edwin knows what is in them without opening them. There is a bottle of shaving cologne, a tie (he never wears a tie), and three boxes of chocolate-covered cherries (he peeked in one, and the others are exactly the same shape). The presents are so pathetic Edwin could cry. He cannot bring himself to tell Sabrina what happened on the bus.

On the bus, the day before Christmas break, Ray Watson had a seizure. During that week, Edwin had been playing more Dylan and even some Stones. No Christmas music, except the Elvis album as usual for Ray. And then, almost unthinkingly, following Sabrina's advice, Edwin shifted formats. It seemed a logical course, as natural as Sabrina's herbal cosmetics, her mushroom complexion. It started with a revival of The Doors—Jim Morrison singing "Light My Fire," a song that was so long it carried them from the feed mill on one side of town to the rendering plant on the other. The passengers loved the way it stretched out, and some shook their heads and stomped their feet. As Edwin realized later, the whole bus was in a frenzy, and he should have known he was leading the passengers toward disaster, but the music seemed so appropriate. The Doors were a bridge from the past to the present, spanning those empty years—his marriages, the turbulence of the times—and connecting his youth solidly with the present. That day Edwin taped more songs from the radio—Adam and the Ants, Squeeze, the B-52s, the Psychedelic Furs, the Flying Lizards, Frankie and the Knockouts—and he made a point of replacing the Plasmatics tape for Lou Murphy. The new-wave format was a hit. Edwin believed the passengers understood what was happening. The frantic beat was a perfect expression of their aimlessness and frustration. Edwin had the impression that his passengers were growing, expanding, like the corn in *Oklahoma!,* like his own awareness. The new format went on for two days before Ray had his seizure. Edwin did not know exactly what happened, and it was possible Laura Combs had shoved Ray into the aisle. Edwin was in an awkward place on the highway, and he had to shoot across a bridge and over a hill before he could find a good place to stop. Everyone on the bus was making an odd noise, gasping or clapping, some imitating Ray's convulsions. Freddie Johnson was saying, "*Popeye* on! *Dukes* on!" Ray was on the floor, gagging, with his head thrown back, and twitching like someone being electrocuted. Laura Combs stood hunched in her seat, her mouth open in speechless terror, pointing her finger at Edwin. During the commotion, the Flying Lizards were chanting tonelessly, "I'm going to take my problems to the United Nations; there ain't no cure for the summertime blues."

Edwin followed all the emergency steps he had learned. He loosened Ray's clothing, slapped his cheeks, turned him on his side. Ray's skin was the color of the Hershey bars the man with the clubfoot collected. Edwin recalled grimly the first-aid book's ironic assurance that facial coloring was not important in cases of seizure. On the way to the hospital, Edwin clicked in a Donovan cassette. To steady himself, he sang along under his breath. "I'm just wild about saffron," he sang. It was a tune as carefree and lyrical as a field of daffodils. The passengers were screaming. All the way to the hospital, Edwin heard their screams, long and drawn out, orchestrated together into an accusing wail—eerie and supernatural.

Edwin's supervisors commended him for his quick thinking in handling Ray and getting him to the hospital, and everyone he has seen at the center has congratulated him. Ray's mother sent him an uncooked fruitcake made with graham cracker crumbs and marshmallows. She wrote a poignant note, thanking him for saving her son from swallowing his tongue. Edwin keeps thinking: what he did was no big deal; you can't swallow your tongue anyway; and it was Edwin's own fault that Ray had a seizure. He does not feel like a hero. He feels almost embarrassed.

Sabrina seems incapable of embarrassment. She is full of hope, like the Christmas season. *Oklahoma!* was only the beginning for her. She has a new job at McDonald's and a good part in *Life with Father.* She plans to commute to Murray State next semester to take a drama class and a course in Western Civilization that she needs to fulfill a requirement. She seems to assume that Edwin will marry her. He finds it funny that it is up to him to say yes. When she says she will keep her own name, Edwin wonders what the point is.

"My parents would just love it if we got married," Sabrina explains. "For them, it's worse for me to live in sin than to be involved with an older man."

"I didn't think I was really older," says Edwin. "But now I know it. I feel like I've had a developmental disability and it suddenly went away. Something like if Freddie Johnson learned to read. That's how I feel."

"I never thought of you as backward. Laid back is what I said." Sabrina laughs at her joke. "I'm sure you're going to impress Mom and Dad."

Tomorrow, she is going to her parents' farm, thirty miles away, for the Christmas holidays, and she has invited Edwin to go with her. He does not want to disappoint her. He does not want to go through Christmas without her. She has arranged her Christmas cards on a red string between the living room and the kitchen. She is making cookies, and Edwin has a feeling she is adding something strange to them. Her pale, fine hair is falling down in her face. Flour streaks her jeans.

"Let me show you something," Edwin says, bringing out a drugstore envelope of pictures. "One of my passengers, Merle Cope, gave me these."

"Which one is he? The one with the fits?"

"No. The one that claps all the time. He lives with a lot of sisters and brothers down in Langley's Bottom. It's a case of incest. The whole family's backward—your word. He's forty-seven and goes around with this big smile on his face, clapping." Edwin demonstrates.

He pins the pictures on Sabrina's Christmas card line with tiny red and green clothespins. "Look at these and tell me what you think."

Sabrina squints, going down the row of pictures. Her hands are covered with flour and she holds them in front of her, the way she learned from her actor friends to hold an invisible baby.

The pictures are black-and-white snapshots: fried eggs on cracked plates, an oil-clothed kitchen table, a bottle of tomato ketchup, a fence post, a rusted tractor seat sitting on a stump, a corn crib, a sagging door, a toilet bowl, a cow, and finally, a horse's rear end.

"I can't look," says Sabrina. "These are disgusting."

"I think they're arty."

Sabrina laughs. She points to the pictures one by one, getting flour on some of them. Then she gets the giggles and can't stop. "Can you imagine what the developers thought when they saw that horse's ass?" she gasps. Her laughter goes on and on, then subsides with a little whimper. She goes back to the cookies. While she cuts out the cookies, Edwin takes the pictures down and puts them in the envelope. He hides the envelope in the drawer with the Christmas presents. Sabrina sets the cookie sheet in the oven and washes her hands.

Edwin asks, "How long do those cookies take?"

"Twelve minutes. Why?"

"Let me show you something else—in case you ever need to know it. The CPR technique—that's cardio-pulmonary resuscitation, in case you've forgotten."

Sabrina looks annoyed. "I'd rather do the Heimlich maneuver," she says. "Besides, you've practiced CPR on me a hundred times."

"I'm not practicing. I don't have to anymore. I'm beyond that." Edwin notices Sabrina's puzzled face. The thought of her fennel toothpaste, which makes her breath smell like licorice, fills him with something like nostalgia, as though she is already only a memory. He says, "I just want you to feel what it would be like. Come on." He leads her to the couch and sets her down. Her hands are still moist. He says, "Now just pretend. Bend over like this. Just pretend you have the biggest pain, right here, right in your chest, right there."

"Like this?" Sabrina is doubled over, her hair falling to her knees and her fists knotted between her breasts.

"Yes. Right in your heart."

# BLANCHE McCRARY BOYD
## (1945–   )

Blanche McCrary Boyd was born and raised in Charleston, South Carolina. She attended Duke University, but did not graduate. She is divorced. Currently she teaches creative writing at Connecticut College in New London.

Boyd's fiction—written with humor and insight—explores the voyaging female as she makes her way, often painfully but willfully, out of the old world into the new world brought about by the cultural revolutions of the last thirty years, especially those impacting female sexuality and identity. As a Southerner living in New England, Boyd is perhaps in a good position to bear witness to these transitions. Her first two novels, *Nerves* (1973) and *Mourning the Death of Magic* (1977), received little notice or critical attention. But she got both with the publication of *The Redneck Way of Knowledge: Down-Home Tales* in 1981. This collection blends autobiography, essay, and short story into a candid view of an author's return to her "redneck" roots. After a ten-year gap, Boyd returned in 1991 with the acclaimed novel *The Revolution of Little Girls*. Her 1998 novel, *Terminal Velocity*, was also well received.

# The Redneck Way of Knowledge

When I was living in California and still trying to pass as a hip suburban housewife, I got interested in Esalen. I was a graduate student at Stanford, and since Esalen held special weekend workshops right on campus, it was easy to attend some sessions. The first one I went to was an introduction to sensitivity training. In this Esalen buffet, I sampled yoga, screaming, sticking my fingers down my throat without gagging, spinal awareness, and falling down.

The facilitator said that adults, especially American adults, are afraid of falling down. Look how easily kids fall down and recover. Being afraid to fall down makes you stiff. It makes you afraid of risks in general. So we went outside on the grass in front of the Stanford library, the instructor said, *"Fall!"* and we all flopped down in simulated spontaneity. We did this over and over. I was hoping that nobody I knew would see me behaving like this. Of course, in my acting class I'd already had to study a raccoon and spend half an hour crawling around the fountain in front of the bookstore, getting in touch with the raccoon in me; when I found myself rolling around the Stanford lawn with a group of adults who seemed otherwise unremarkable, I was not totally unprepared.

In the second workshop I went to, we did kundalini yoga under self-hypnosis. I already knew something about hypnosis. When I was a teenager I taught myself to hypnotize other people. "Look only at the tip of my cigarette, your eyelids are getting heavy," I said to a young cousin. I kept saying that kind of thing, and then I counted slowly to ten. She went into a trance. I reversed the procedure and she came out of it. Soon I learned to hypnotize willing people with regular success. When I first went to college, I used to do hypnosis as a party trick. At Duke, women were still required to wear skirts, had to be in the dorms by midnight, and were forbidden to smoke cigarettes standing up; they made a new rule about hypnosis by students. Eventually I was asked to leave the Harvard of the South, but before I left I volunteered as a subject at the Parapsychology Laboratory there. At the Parapsychology Lab I was taught self-hypnosis. "Deep body relaxation," Dr. La called it, but I knew better. After a few sessions I could put myself in a trance as easily as I could put others into one.

The kundalini workshop was called "Psychedelic Experiences Through Hypnosis." One reason I took it was that I wanted to have an acid experience without the risk of taking acid. I had left my hypnosis experiments behind because once in a self-induced trance I hallucinated that my arm was ballooning out and I was breathing through my elbow. This experience scared me, but it didn't seem as potentially frightening as LSD. I thought a psychedelic experience through hypnosis would be a good mockup.

The workshop leader taught self-hypnosis and I quickly relocated my ability to go into trances. Then the leader explained the basic theory of kundalini yoga. In kundalini, he said, we conceive of a snake wrapped around the base of the spine. We try to raise this snake up the spine to the top of the head, where it mates with Siva and we reach ecstatic enlightenment. There are seven stages of raising this snake, and seven corresponding places on the spine. Kundalini chants are designed to make each place, or cakra, on the spine vibrate. After chanting all evening Friday and all day Saturday, when I returned on Sunday my mind was enervated. I kept slipping into an eyes-open state that was much like being unconscious. We began to chant again. My legs went to sleep. The instructor told me to lie down on my back. The energy rising through my body, he said, had rendered my legs temporarily useless. As we chanted, I could feel each of the cakras on my spine vibrating. I could feel that snake sliding up. The leader had told us that sometimes the energy gets trapped in the neck and causes headaches. Since I am extremely suggestible, when the snake reached my neck I developed a pulsing flashing pain in the back of my skull. The leader touched my neck for a few minutes and the pain disappeared. We reached the last cakra, and after three days of chanting, there was finally silence. The leader said Om, and I felt as if two hinged flaps on the top of my head opened upward. A white light poured out. The release was unexpected and surprisingly gentle. My mind felt like a countertop that had been wiped clean. For several days I initiated no conversations, and when spoken to, I would sometimes forget to reply.

Noise and falling, scientists say, are the only fears we're born with; all our others are learned, acquired. Maybe my choice of Esalen workshops indicated a personality pattern, because, in the past four months, since I have returned to live in the town where I grew up, I have developed two new interests: skydiving and stock-car racing. Falling and noise. I left South Carolina fifteen years ago, as if it were a burning building. I have returned cautiously, deliberately. What does it mean to love a place? I was grown before I found out Roosevelt didn't cause the Depression; I had lived in the North several years before someone suggested to me that to love the song "Dixie" was racist in itself. In the North I always felt mildly barbaric, a little too earthy, and I worried that I drank too much.

Recently a New York friend came to visit me here in Charleston. We went to a Rites of Spring party on a magnificent plantation on the Ashley River. In the evening there was an oyster roast in a grove of dogwoods, camellias, azaleas. Two young women began to wrestle on the ground and everyone gathered around them chanting, "Rut, rut, rut." My friend said, "I never saw anything quite like it."

Maybe it's the heat, maybe it's the sweat, maybe it's the constant sexual smell of the ocean, but the Puritans didn't have much impact on the South Carolina Lowcountry. The young woman who owns the plantation lived in California for a couple of years, but she got tired of it. "Everybody was always trying to be so laidback. They were always trying to relax, and they tried so *hard.* They don't drink much either. It made me nervous." We were riding around drinking white wine we kept iced down in a cooler. Drinking is a serious pastime here, and so is riding around. When you leave someone's house, it's not uncommon for them to offer you a "traveler," a drink in a paper cup to nurse you to your next destination. I keep a flask in my glove compartment. *Be Here Now* was a radical notion when I was living in California, but the Southerners I have come home to would be bewildered by such advice. Where else would they be? They talk plainer and call the seductions of the moment "having a good time."

Falling and noise. We fall in love, we fall in debt, we fall in with each other, fall out, fall behind, over, ill, short, in battle. We fall from grace. Our faces fall. Our arches fall. It was silly to think I could confront my fear of falling by flopping around on the Stanford lawn. Here in South Carolina, where my past is all around me, I am becoming a connoisseur of the present. I step out of airplanes.

A magazine editor gave me an assignment to learn skydiving. I did it for the money and the dare. I continued it for the thrills. I've jumped more than a dozen times now. Each time the jump master opens the plane door and I climb out onto the wing in an eighty-mile-an-hour wind, each time I experience the purity of freefall, I am so wired I feel luminous. The skydiver falls belly-first, arms and legs stretched back in an ecstatic position. Stepping out of a plane is not like stepping off a roof. The human body does not believe it can fall thousands of feet and survive, but the mind devises a method. In this collision of mind and instinct are moments that are like holes torn in the world. I feel as if I step through them to somewhere else. In freefall, as in orgasm, the conscious mind shrinks in the face of an astounding animal rush. In California a lot of us were talking about altered states. I'm still talking about altered states, but now I want them raw, like oysters.

* * *

I went to the Darlington 500 because I thought it would be better than kundalini yoga under hypnosis. To get ready for Darlington, I went to the Summerville Speedway. The Summerville Speedway is a dirt track, a reddish quarter-mile oval where local boys and local garages compete. Sometimes more important races, like a qualifier for the Sundrop 100, are held here, but mostly this is a neighborhood affair. During the season three classes of races are held every Saturday night. Families come carrying coolers and cushions and kids. It was at Summerville, with my chest rumbling and red dust in my nostrils, that I began to understand racing.

I had smoked a joint in the car. The noise didn't feel so overwhelming at first. During the time trials, only one car was on the track at any given moment. I drank a couple of beers and ate some boiled peanuts. Down in front of the bleachers a gang of kids played peaceably in the loose dirt. Their toys were about fifty crushed beer cans. "REDNECK MONTESSORI!" I screamed at my companion.

I screamed because the race had begun. I had never experienced noise and speed straight up before, like bourbon. My chest cavity was vibrating. So were the bleachers. I began to feel oddly happy. "IT'S LIKE A RAMONES CONCERT WITHOUT THE MUSIC!"

There was a twelve-car wreck. "YAAAAAAYYYYYYY," sang the kids in front of the bleachers. We scrambled down to watch the tow trucks untangle the cars. No one was hurt. "This is nothing!" my friend said. "Wait till you get to Darlington!"

Stock-car racing is a redneck sport. It originated among moonshine runners who souped up their cars so they could escape the feds. (Remember Robert Mitchum in *Thunder Road?*) For fun they tested their driving skills and hand-modified cars against each other. Now dirt tracks are scattered through other parts of the country, and there are a few big speedways in California, Michigan, and Delaware, but stock-car racing has remained primarily a Southern phenomenon. The most important speedways are in Daytona, Darlington, Charlotte, Talladega. These asphalt ovals range in length from a mile and a quarter at Darlington to 2.67 miles at Talladega. The track at Talladega is banked so steeply it would be difficult to walk on the curves. On the big tracks, speeds can go over two hundred miles an hour. Windshields can cave in at speeds like that. Pit crews are so efficient they can change two tires and gas up a car in 13 seconds. They can replace a blown engine in 13 minutes. The metal bodies of these cars are sanded almost paper thin; then the weight that would have been in the hull is redistributed with pieces of lead, to help the car hold the road better.

Going to one of the major races is an event you have to plan for: A remarkable survey at one of the Darlington races revealed that more than three-fourths of the fans had bought their tickets at least a month in advance. This remarkable survey also revealed that 40 percent of the fans drank Anheuser Busch Natural Light beer. Thirty-two percent drank Miller Lite. Coke was favored over Pepsi, and country music was better than any other kind. Twenty-three percent smoked Winstons. One quarter had bought Goodyear tires within the last year. Half used Champion sparkplugs. A quarter used Purolator filters. More than a third cranked up in the morning with Die-Hard batteries. In stock-car racing, as in the Old West, brands matter.

* * *

At Darlington, for a Sunday race, fans begin to arrive on Thursday, when the time trials are held. In the trials, each driver is allowed two laps to qualify. The fastest cars get the best starting positions. On Friday, more fans straggle in. They settle down for the weekend in the parking lot, or they pay $15 extra and park in the infield. Some bring platforms to put on top of their campers. On the platforms they have a good view; they can sunbathe, drink beer, and otherwise feel above it all. Friday night is mildly festive. Cookouts make the air fragrant. There is some drinking, but mostly people are holding out to do their serious partying on Saturday.

On Saturday campers and cars and pickups and vans and even tractor-trailers pour into the infield and the parking lots. The grass disappears. Rednecks pile out of their vehicles. Of course, not everyone at Darlington is working class, and not everyone is white. I did spot four blacks, and, among the 65,000 people attending, I'm sure there were a few others. But mostly these are good ole boys and good ole gals. These folks are real comfortable with that Confederate flag flying over the Speedway. They have decals on their cars and clothes identifying their racing heroes. I saw Darrell Waltrip fans, Buddy Baker fans, Richard Petty fans, Cale Yarborough fans, Dale Earnhardt fans, and fans of both the Allison brothers, Bobby and Donnie. Popular among racing fans are light-weight nylon jackets with patches sewn on them. The patches say the names of races and speedways—"Charlotte International Speedway," "Daytona Firecracker 400," "World 600"—but they also say things like "First National City Traveler's Checks" and "Coburg Dairy."

I went to the Rebel 500 in a camper with two chief petty officers, a Summerville policeman, and their wives. My sister is married to one of the chiefs. Patty had packed barbecued spareribs, boiled peanuts, and deviled eggs. Another of the wives had fried chicken. In our coolers were more than a dozen beers for each person. I popped my first Natural Light at 9 A.M., and by the time we arrived at Darlington at noon, I had a nice buzz going.

It was a gray day. We found our seats on the fourth turn and settled in. I felt a little bored, but the people I was with were already excited. Roger, my brother-in-law, grabbed my arm. "Just wait," he said. "When they say, 'Gentlemen, start your engines,' you won't believe it. The *noise*."

I waited. "Miss Winston" was introduced, "one of the world's most beautiful girls." Then another of the world's most beautiful girls was introduced. Then came the "visiting pacesetter cars," two *Star Wars*-inspired automobiles named Galaxy II and Death Ship II. Galaxy II and Death Ship II are both capable of driving faster than the record speeds at Darlington. They rear up on their tails and scoot along. They look like rockets. Unfortunately, one of them, to quote the announcer, "didn't get it up," and the forces of death prevailed. The pacesetter cars were accompanied by *Star Wars* characters: one guy in white fur, one in black armor, and two young women wearing black bathing suits with silver trim. Apparently women, to be out of this world, don't need as many modifications as men do.

After the *Star Wars* fizzle, the fan club buses paraded by. Then came the parade of tow trucks. Eight of them. I ate a piece of chicken and popped my fifth beer. I was not so much bored now as bewildered. "Why did they bring the tow trucks by?" I asked. No one answered.

It was time for the invocation. The preacher entreated the heavenly father to take the drivers into a new manhood. He talked a long time. Someone in front of me whispered, "He should shut up." Near the end, the preacher said, "May the best *car*—and the best *man—win!*"

A lot of people were wearing earmuffs. I asked Roger about them. "They're radios," he said. "If you listen to the race at the same time you watch it, you know quicker what's happening. If there's an accident on the backstretch or something."

A worn tape of the National Anthem played over the P.A. system. Then the announcer said, *"And now . . . for the most dramatic moment in the world of sports . . . Gentlemen, start your engines!"*

A roar went up from the stands. Behind it was the sharper roar of the cars. The noise was intense, but not what I had prepared for. I was disappointed. Maybe it was because we were high in the stands. Maybe stock-car racing just wasn't as thrilling as skydiving. I'd jumped twice the day before, and maybe I'd taken my edge off. Maybe I just liked dirt-track racing better.

The race started. Soon the noise was relentless, enveloping. It wore away at everything. I watched the fans watch the race. They seemed familiar with every car and driver. They screamed and cheered.

"Pick somebody to root for!" Roger yelled. "You'll have a better time!" Roger's man was Richard Petty, King Richard, No. 43, Mr. STP. I didn't really care who won.

It takes about thirty seconds to run a lap. A 500-mile race at Darlington is 367 laps. With caution flags slowing the action, a race lasts about three hours. I settled in.

After fifty laps my eyes got tired. The cars seemed to come around the track faster and faster while the track got smaller and smaller. The great whine of engines became rhythmical. My eyelids were getting heavy. I tried to concentrate on the gray breeze blowing, on the smell of burned rubber, on smoke drifting from barbecues in the infield. I watched a hefty blonde sunbathing on top of a camper.

One hundred laps. Petty and Waltrip were fighting for the lead. Yarborough was trying to keep up. So was Earnhardt.

My neck ached. I was a whole chorus of inner distractions now, little bladelike pains, grainy eyes, the heaviness of sleep.

"Pit stop!" I yelled at my sister and made my way down the long concrete steps, out of the stands. The bathrooms were under the bleachers. Beer cans and other debris clunked onto the roof like a huge metallic rain. It was funny. I felt better.

When I was back in my seat I ate some chicken. My mind cleared. I began to cheer for Richard Petty. Yarborough had been lapped. "That'll teach that turkey farmer," my sister said. Petty was in the lead. "King Richard," she said, "is definitely the coolest."

A dozen state troopers marched up our aisle. They climbed to the top row and settled in to watch the race. They wore heavy leather boots, gun belts, sunglasses, cowboy hats. The term "state trooper" is much more frightening than "highway patrolman." George Wallace's boys taught me that. One of the troopers was speaking with fatherly benevolence to a fidgety boy who had been throwing beer cans at the people walking below the bleachers.

My head pounded. I wadded up pieces of toilet paper and stuffed them into my ears. My brain felt muffled. I kept rubbing my neck. My sister began to massage it. "Don't want you to go to sleep!" she screamed. Her voice seemed to come from far away.

"I feel like I'm being hypnotized!"

I thought about raising the snake in kundalini. My spine had garbled the message, and the snake was stuck in my neck. It looked like a huge dried worm.

The rookie Earnhardt blew his engine and came into the pits. Cale Yarborough was still trying to regain the lap he'd lost.

In skydiving, there's a term "whuffo." Whuffos are people who hang around skydivers saying, "Whuffo you want to jump out of a perfectly good airplane?" Now I thought, Whuffo these people want to watch this noise? This isn't fun. It's nuts.

When I was a kid I had a gyroscope toy. It was a wheel mounted inside a ring. If you spun the wheel fast, you could set the ring at odd angles and it would stay balanced. I felt out of balance here on the fourth turn. My psyche was leaning. I watched the tiny cars running inside the thunder. I began to see little black dots swimming around.

Maybe I'm sore from jumping yesterday, I thought. On my second jump my muscles had been cramping from so much adrenaline. Not big muscles, but mean tiny ones in my shoulders, in the undersides of my upper arms.

Two hundred laps. My eyes were too far apart; they wouldn't focus right. I was so tired. The noise hammered at me. It seemed to be inside my head now. Cosmic dentistry. The roar was in my chest and ass too, and my legs, but at my neck it was still knotted, blocked.

Cale passed Petty. Both were behind Waltrip. Waltrip's car seemed to be faster. Petty passed Cale again. "He's playing with Cale," Roger said.

Waltrip pitted. The crowd screamed. Petty was leading.

I started to shiver. It wasn't cold. I held my legal pad against my chest.

Two hundred sixty laps. I couldn't stand the headache. I decided to take a walk. Warm up. Look for some coffee. Maybe some aspirin.

I had noticed people standing briefly at the railing below, right above the track. I asked Roger about it. "It's all right to do it," he said, "if you can stand it."

I went down the steps and out the aisle, behind the stands. The ground had begun to disappear under litter. There were lines for Cokes and cigarettes. Beer can't be sold on Sunday in South Carolina. The relative silence was startling. Among the drunk men wandering behind the stands there was a randiness, a bald fuck energy that made me nervous.

I walked past the museum, where earlier I'd paid a quarter for a two-minute simulated ride in Richard Petty's car, and bought a sweatshirt that said "Darlington International Speedway." At the main entrance to the speedway was a tiny diner. I got two BC headache powders and a Coke. I sprinkled the powders on my tongue. They tasted like chewed-up aspirin and reminded me of once when I'd opened a cap of psilocybin and sprinkled the powder on a dish of potato salad.

On my way back to my seat I saw some girls handing out little yellow buttons that said "Happy Easter" to the men lined up to use the bathroom. Then the girls asked each man who took a button for a dollar.

The powders took effect quickly. My head felt cottony, pleasant. I was ready.

I went back into the stands, but I didn't go back to my seat. I walked up to the railing. The noise seemed almost visible. I checked the toilet paper in my ears, and then I grabbed the rail with both hands.

The noise ran up my arms, through my shoulders, past my neck, into my head. It ran down my chest, through my waist and hips, down my legs. It came up through my feet. I felt like a tuning fork. I lasted about ten seconds.

When I got back to my seat, I felt wonderful. "Is Petty winning?" I asked.

David Pearson's pit crew had forgotten to fasten his new tires, and when he drove out of pit row they fell off. He rolled into the wall. Petty and Waltrip were still trading the lead. Donnie Allison was gaining on them.

It began to rain. The noise eased while the cars ran under the caution flag. Petty was leading again. "He's going to win under the caution!" Roger said. "They'll call off the race!"

The rain smelled good. I felt good. I didn't want them to call off the race. "Can't they use windshield wipers?"

Roger laughed. "Wipers don't work at 150 miles an hour."

The caution flag was lifted on lap 321. Petty was in the lead. Waltrip passed Petty. "He's got Waltrip where he wants him," Roger said. "He can slingshot around him."

Thirty laps to go. Petty couldn't seem to get around Waltrip. Cale was one lap back but still crowding them. Donnie Allison had almost caught up.

"Petty's testing him," Roger said. "He'll get him. He's setting him up."

On 349, Petty took the lead. Two photographers in the infield began to jump up and down.

I wasn't cold. My head didn't hurt. I couldn't hear myself shouting. I had begun to scream. Everyone was screaming. Everything shook.

On 360, there was a brief caution. The crowd wailed.

With five laps to go, Waltrip and Petty bumper to bumper, they restarted the race. "I'm gonna have an organism!" Roger shouted.

Petty took it on the first turn. Waltrip took it back. Then Petty took it again. On the last lap, Waltrip shot around him and won.

"My man lost!" Roger said. "I almost had a Pontiac arrest!"

The leaders glided by, in the winning order: Darrell Waltrip, Richard Petty, Donnie Allison. Or, as the cars read, Gatorade, STP, and Hawaiian Tanning Butter.

* * *

After the Rebel 500, I was drunk and tired. We hung out at the camper for a couple of hours, waiting for the traffic to thin out, and then, although we'd already eaten too much, we stopped at Shoney's on the way back to Charleston. Shoney's is a Southern restaurant chain whose trademark is a huge statue of a huge fat boy wearing huge plaid overalls. Over his head he holds a huge hamburger, like a trophy. The chain's slogan is "Shoney's: Home of the Big Boy."

We had gotten away from the Darlington traffic arteries, and the crowd at Shoney's were on their way home from Sunday-evening church. They held their forks furtively over slices of strawberry pie. "Look how guilty they act," my sister whispered. "They're even afraid to eat."

"This is one group I haven't explored yet," I whispered back. "I hope I can skip them."

* * *

I have come home to South Carolina to try to claim my background. I hope I can reclaim what is positive without starting to sing "Rock of Ages" or adopting racist attitudes. The prejudices of white Southerners still startle me.

Recently I went to a wig store in a big shopping mall to buy a wig for a costume party. "I want a blond afro," I told the matronly lady behind the counter. She was wearing a polyester print dress. She had on stockings and white gloves. She might have been part of the Shoney's church crowd, or a kindergarten teacher.

"They can't make blond afros," she said.

I thought she was kidding. "No, like those black ones over there," I said. "Only I want a blond one."

She looked at me compassionately, even kindly. "You don't understand. They can't make blond afros."

"Wait a minute," I said. "Look at those black afros. They're synthetic, right? And those blond wigs, they're synthetic, right? I want a blond one like that."

There was pity in her eyes. "It's scientific," she said. "They can't make blond afros."

I call this anecdote "the limits of reason." Whether I am with aristocrats, rednecks, or the few blacks I've managed to form tentative friendships with, I am aware that we Southerners do not lead with our intellects. Living here in South Carolina, I am afraid that the critical faculties I worked so hard to develop while I was in New York will turn blue and fall off.

* * *

When I stopped trying to pass as a hip suburban housewife, I moved briefly to a commune in Vermont. Then I moved to New York.

In New York I stayed for a month with my friend Penny. Penny was a writer. She had just joined Arica, an organization not entirely dissimilar to Esalen. Penny and I tripped together sometimes. Sometimes we did Arica exercises. Penny rang little brass bells and we sat knees to knees and stared into each other's left eyes. It made us cry.

We both were reading Castaneda. We talked a lot about paths of knowledge, paths of enlightenment. We drank a lot of wine and smoked dope. "Do you think writing can be a path?" we asked each other. "Do you think a guru is necessary?"

Penny moved to California to work in the Arica organization, and I lost track of her for several years. Then I heard she had left Arica and become a follower of the Indian guru Janaka.

In the mid-seventies, I began to see posters for Janaka around New York. He had opened a temporary ashram on the Upper West Side. I saw an old friend on the street who told me Penny was back in town. She'd left a Janaka poster on his door, beckoning him to an audience with her guru.

I called the ashram and asked for Penny. Penny's doing very important work right now, I was told, but audiences with Janaka are held at such and such a time. I'm not interested in Janaka, I said. I'm interested in my old friend Penny. The woman's voice tinkled gaily in my ear. There's nothing left of Penny that's not Janaka, she said. Penny's been reamed out. I'm coming right over, I said. I want to view the carcass for myself.

The ashram was a brownstone. Penny met me in the hall, and we sat on the steps and talked. "I feel as if I'm living the life you left behind," I said. "I'm writing. I have a good shrink. I give dinner parties."

"Do you think that's a path?" She seemed tired. She smelled of decay. She frightened me.

"It's what I need. I've got this heavy Southern past to drag around." I didn't mention the weight of Penny's past, or of anyone else's past, for that matter. "Do you think this is a path?" I asked. "It reminds me of the Baptist church."

"Oh, I know," she said, and laughed absently.

Penny didn't know that I returned to the ashram the next night. Janaka was giving a group audience. Men and women sat shoeless on different sides of the room. Penny had on a sari. She had a red dot painted on her forehead. There was a purple velvet curtain behind the guru, and some white flowers were on a table in front of it.

I sat in the back and watched Penny chant and pray. I listened to Janaka tell a tale about a man whose guru had sent him to graveyards to curse the dead. How did the dead respond? the guru asked. They did not, master. When you respond as the dead did, Janaka said, you will attain enlightenment.

Penny moved to India, and I have come back to South Carolina to seek a funkier transcendence. Call it the redneck way of knowledge. In my refrigerator is a Mason jar of corn liquor, white lightning. It has raisins in it, which make it taste like a fine rum. When I got home from the Rebel 500 it was past midnight. I was still valiantly drinking Natural Light, but I took out the white lightning to go with it.

I went outside and sat on my front steps. I could hear the ocean moving against the sand a block away. I took a sip of the white lightning. My nervous system was jaded, but the 160-proof liquor was still a rush. It burned cleanly, and warmed me.

I wanted to do something to finish the Rebel 500, but I felt too wiped out. I would have sung "Dixie," but it is a racist song, and anyway I can't sing. I hollered once and threw my beer can across the front yard.

I haven't come back to South Carolina to get religion, but I have come back to a total immersion. If I wash in the blood of the past, I tell myself, maybe I'll be free of it. And something has eased in me, being here these past few months. A pain so constant I thought it was a condition of life has begun to wash away. I feel a sense of peace, of aftermath. "Charleston is where the Ashley and the Cooper rivers meet to form the Atlantic Ocean." I heard that when I was a kid.

I still don't know what it means to love a place, but I know I love the salty mouths of these rivers, I love the smells of the long, mournful marshes, I love these romantic palmettos swaying in this postcard moonlight.

One morning soon after I moved home I got up before sunrise and walked over to the beach. Porpoises rolled in the placid water. Everything was bluish—the sand, the water, the sky. Then the sun came up like an opening, a brilliant tear in the horizon, and for a second I thought I could glimpse through it to another place. I was chanting: *rising, rising, rising.*

# LAURIE COLWIN
## (1944–1992)

Laurie Colwin was born and raised in New York City, and this city is the setting of much of her fiction. She attended Bard College and the Columbia University School of General Studies. She married and had one child, a daughter. She worked on the editorial staff of a number of New York City publishing houses and literary agents. She taught writing for a year in the 1980s, and did volunteer work with the Coalition for the Homeless and the Antonio Olivieri Shelter for Homeless Women. In addition to publishing stories in *Mademoiselle, The New Yorker,* and *Redbook,* she wrote a column for *Gourmet* magazine and two books on cooking. She died of a heart attack in 1992.

Is Tolstoy's famous observation that all happy families are alike right? That only unhappy families are interesting and worth writing about? Kafka, too, said that what we need are disturbing stories, that anybody can write stories that make us happy. It would seem, then, that to be taken seriously as a writer one must explore unhappiness. Laurie Colwin, however, took the forms of happiness as her subject and she wrote about them in such a way as to deserve a reader's serious attention. She wrote five novels: *Shine On, Bright & Dangerous Object* (1975), *Happy All the Time* (1978), *Family Happiness* (1982), *Goodbye Without Leaving* (1986), and *A Big Storm Knocked It Over* (1994). Her story collections include *Passion and Affect* (1974), *The Lone Pilgrim* (1981), and *Another Marvelous Thing* (1986).

## Another Marvelous Thing

On a cold, rainy morning in February, Billy Delielle stood by the window of her hospital room looking over Central Park. She was a week and a half from the time her baby was due to be born, and she had been put into the hospital because her blood pressure had suddenly gone up and her doctor wanted her constantly monitored and on bed rest.

A solitary jogger in bright red foul-weather gear ran slowly down the glistening path. The trees were black and the branches were bare. There was not another soul out. Billy had been in the hospital for five days. The first morning she had woken to the sound of squawking. Since her room was next door to the nursery, she assumed this was a sound some newborns made. The next day she got out of bed at dawn and saw that the meadow was full of sea gulls who congregated each morning before the sun came up.

The nursery was an enormous room painted soft yellow. When Billy went to take the one short walk a day allowed her, she found herself averting her eyes from the neat rows of babies in their little plastic bins, but once in a while she found herself hungry for the sight of them. Taped to each crib was a blue (I'M A BOY) or pink (I'M A GIRL) card telling mother's name, the time of birth, and birth weight.

At six in the morning the babies were taken to their mothers to be fed. Billy was impressed by the surprising range of noises they made: mewing, squawking, bleating, piping, and squealing. The fact that she was about to have one of these creatures herself filled her with a combination of bafflement, disbelief, and longing.

For the past two months her chief entertainment had been to lie in bed and observe her unborn child moving under her skin. It had knocked a paperback book off her stomach and caused the saucer of her coffee cup to jiggle and dance.

Billy's husband, Grey, was by temperament and inclination a naturalist. Having a baby was right up his street. Books on neonatology and infant development replaced the astronomy and bird books on his night table. He gave up reading mysteries for texts on childbirth. One of these books had informed him that babies can hear in the womb, so each night he sang "Roll Along Kentucky Moon" directly into Billy's stomach. Another suggested that the educational process could begin before birth. Grey thought he might try to teach the unborn to count.

"Why stop there?" Billy said. "Teach it fractions."

Billy had a horror of the sentimental. In secret, for she would rather have died than showed it, the thought of her own baby brought her to tears. Her dreams were full of infants. Babies appeared everywhere. The buses abounded with pregnant women. The whole process seemed to her one half miraculous and the other half preposterous. She looked around her on a crowded street and said to herself: "Every single one of these people was *born.*"

Her oldest friend, Penny Stern, said to her: "We all hope that this pregnancy will force you to wear maternity clothes, because they will be so much nicer than what you usually wear." Billy went shopping for maternity clothes but came home empty-handed.

She said, "I don't wear puffed sleeves and frilly bibs and ribbons around my neck when I'm not pregnant, so I don't see why I should have to just because I am pregnant." In the end, she wore Grey's sweaters, and she bought two shapeless skirts with elastic waistbands. Penny forced her to buy one nice black dress, which she wore to teach her weekly class in economic history at the business school.

Grey set about renovating a small spare room that had been used for storage. He scraped and polished the floor, built shelves, and painted the walls pale apple green with the ceiling and moldings glossy white. They had once called this room the lumber room. Now they referred to it as the nursery. On the top of one of the shelves Grey put his collection of glass-encased bird's nests. He already had in mind a child who would go on nature hikes with him.

As for Billy, she grimly and without expression submitted herself to the number of advances science had come up with in the field of obstetrics.

It was possible to have amniotic fluid withdrawn and analyzed to find out the genetic health of the unborn and, if you wanted to know, its sex. It was possible to lie on a table and with the aid of an ultrasonic scanner see your unborn child in the womb. It was also possible to have a photograph of this view. As for Grey, he wished Billy could have a sonogram every week, and he watched avidly while Billy's doctor, a handsome, rather melancholy South African named Jordan Bell, identified a series of blobs and clouds as head, shoulders, and back.

Every month in Jordan Bell's office Billy heard the sound of her own child's heart through ultrasound and what she heard sounded like galloping horses in the distance.

Billy went about her business outwardly unflapped. She continued to teach and she worked on her dissertation. In between, when she was not napping, she made lists of baby things: crib sheets, a stroller, baby T-shirts, diapers, blankets. Two months before the baby was due, she and Penny went out and bought what was needed. She was glad she had not saved this until the last minute, because in her ninth month, after an uneventful pregnancy, she was put in the hospital, where she was allowed to walk down the hall once a day. The sense of isolation she had cherished—just herself, Grey, and their unborn child—was gone. She was in the hands of nurses she had never seen before, and she found herself desperate for their companionship because she was exhausted, uncertain, and lonely in her hospital room.

Billy was admitted wearing the nice black dress Penny had made her buy and taken to a private room that overlooked the park. At the bottom of her bed were two towels and a hospital gown that tied up the back. Getting undressed to go to bed in the afternoon made her feel like a child forced to take a nap. She did not put on the hospital gown. Instead, she put on the plaid flannel nightshirt of Grey's that she had packed in her bag weeks ago in case she went into labor in the middle of the night.

"I hate it here already," Billy said.

"It's an awfully nice view," Grey said. "If it were a little further along in the season I could bring my field glasses and see what's nesting."

"I'll never get out of here," Billy said.

"Not only will you get out of here," said Grey, "you will be released a totally transformed woman. You heard Jordan—all babies get born one way or another."

If Grey was frightened, he never showed it. Billy knew that his way of dealing with anxiety was to fix his concentration, and it was now fixed on her and on being cheerful. He had never seen Billy so upset before. He held her hand.

"Don't worry," he said. "Jordan said this isn't serious. It's just a complication. The baby will be fine and you'll be fine. Besides, it won't know how to be a baby and we won't know how to be parents."

Grey had taken off his jacket and he felt a wet place where Billy had laid her cheek. He did not know how to comfort her.

"A mutual learning experience," Billy said into his arm. "I thought nature was supposed to take over and do all this for us."

"It will," Grey said.

Seven o'clock began visiting hours. Even with the door closed Billy could hear shrieks and coos and laughter. With her door open she could hear champagne corks being popped.

Grey closed the door. "You didn't eat much dinner," he said. "Why don't I go downstairs to the delicatessen and get you something?"

"I'm not hungry," Billy said. She did not know what was in front of her, or how long she would be in this room, or how and when the baby would be born.

"I'll call Penny and have her bring something," Grey said.

"I already talked to her," Billy said. "She and David are taking you out to dinner." David was Penny's husband, David Hooks.

"You're trying to get rid of me," Grey said.

"I'm not," Billy said. "You've been here all day, practically. I just want the comfort of knowing that you're being fed and looked after. I think you should go soon."

"It's too early," said Grey. "Fathers don't have to leave when visiting hours are over."

"You're not a father yet," Billy said. "Go."

After he left she waited by the window to watch him cross the street and wait for the bus. It was dark and cold and it had begun to sleet. When she saw him she felt pierced with desolation. He was wearing his old camel's hair coat and the wind blew through his wavy hair. He stood back on his heels as he had as a boy. He turned around and scanned the building for her window. When he saw her, he waved and smiled. Billy waved back. A taxi, thinking it was being hailed, stopped. Grey got in and was driven off.

Every three hours a nurse appeared to take her temperature, blood pressure, and pulse. After Grey had gone, the night nurse appeared. She was a tall, middle-aged black woman named Mrs. Perch. In her hand she carried what looked like a suitcase full of dials and wires.

"Don't be alarmed," Mrs. Perch said. She had a soft West Indian accent. "It is only a portable fetal heart monitor. You get to say good morning and good evening to your baby."

She squirted a blob of cold blue jelly on Billy's stomach and pushed a transducer around in it, listening for the beat. At once Billy heard the sound of galloping hooves. Mrs. Perch timed the beats against her watch.

"Nice and healthy," Mrs. Perch said.

"Which part of this baby is where?" Billy said.

"Well, his head is back here, and his back is there and here is the rump and his feet are near your ribs. Or hers, of course."

"I wondered if that was a foot kicking," Billy said.

"My second boy got his foot under my rib and kicked with all his might," Mrs. Perch said.

Billy sat up in bed. She grabbed Mrs. Perch's hand. "Is this baby going to be all right?" she said.

"Oh my, yes," Mrs. Perch said. "You're not a very interesting case. Many others much more complicated than you have done very well and you will, too."

At four in the morning, another nurse appeared, a florid Englishwoman. Billy had spent a restless night, her heart pounding, her throat dry.

"Your pressure's up, dear," said the nurse, whose tag read "M. Whitely." "Dr. Bell has written orders that if your pressure goes up you're to have a shot of hydralazine. It doesn't hurt baby—did he explain that to you?"

"Yes," said Billy groggily.

"It may give you a little headache."

"What else?"

"That's all," Miss Whitely said.

Billy fell asleep and woke with a pounding headache. When she rang the bell, the nurse who had admitted her appeared. Her name was Bonnie Near and she was Billy's day nurse. She gave Billy a pill and then taped a tongue depressor wrapped in gauze over her bed.

"What's that for?" Billy said.

"Don't ask," said Bonnie Near.

"I want to know."

Bonnie Near sat down at the end of the bed. She was a few years older than Billy, trim and wiry with short hair and tiny diamond earrings.

"It's hospital policy," she said. "The hydralazine gives you a headache, right? You ring to get something to make it go away and because you have high blood pressure everyone assumes that the blood pressure caused it, not the drug. So this thing gets taped above your bed in the one chance in about fifty-five million that you have a convulsion."

Billy turned her face away and stared out the window.

"Hey, hey," said Bonnie Near. "None of this. I noticed yesterday that you're quite a worrier. Are you like this when you're not in the hospital? Listen. I'm a straight shooter and I would tell you if I was worried about you. I'm not. You're just the common garden variety."

* * *

Every morning Grey appeared with two cups of coffee and the morning paper. He sat in a chair and he and Billy read the paper together as they did at home.

"Is the house still standing?" Billy asked after several days. "Are the banks open? Did you bring the mail? I feel I've been here ten months instead of a week."

"The mail was very boring," Grey said. "Except for this booklet from the Wisconsin Loon Society. You'll be happy to know that you can order a record called 'Loon Music.' Would you like a copy?"

"If I moved over," Billy said, "would you take off your jacket and lie down next to me?"

Grey took off his jacket and shoes, and curled up next to Billy. He pressed his nose into her face and looked as if he could drift off to sleep in a second.

"Childworld called about the crib," he said into her neck. "They want to know if we want white paint or natural pine. I said natural."

"That's what I think I ordered," Billy said. "They let the husbands stay over in this place. They call them 'dads.' "

"I'm not a dad yet, as you pointed out," Grey said. "Maybe they'll just let me take naps here."

There was a knock on the door. Grey sprang to his feet and Jordan Bell appeared.

"Don't look so nervous, Billy," he said. "I have good news. I think we want to get this baby born if your pressure isn't going to go down. I think we ought to induce you."

Billy and Grey were silent.

"The way it works is that we put you on a drip of pitocin, which is a synthetic of the chemical your brain produces when you go into labor."

"We know," Billy said. "Katherine went over it in childbirth class." Katherine Walden was Jordan Bell's nurse. "When do you want to do this?"

"Tomorrow," Jordan Bell said. "Katherine will come over and give you your last Lamaze class right here."

"And if it doesn't work?"

"It usually does," said Jordan Bell. "And if it doesn't, we do a second-day induction."

"And if that doesn't work?"

"It generally does. If it doesn't, we do a cesarean, but you'll be awake and Grey can hold your hand."

"Oh what fun," said Billy.

When Jordan Bell left, Billy burst into tears.

"Why isn't anything normal?" she said. "Why do I have to lie here day after day listening to other people's babies crying? Why is my body betraying me like this?"

Grey kissed her and then took her hands. "There is no such thing as normal," he said. "Everyone we've talked to has some story or other—huge babies that won't budge, thirty-hour labors. A cesarean is a perfectly respectable way of being born."

"What about me? What about me getting all stuck up with tubes and cut up into little pieces?" Billy said, and she was instantly ashamed. "I hate being like this. I feel I've lost myself and some whimpering, whining person has taken me over."

"Think about how in two months we'll have a two-month-old baby to take to the park."

"Do you really think everything is going to be all right?" Billy said.

"Yes," said Grey. "I do. In six months we'll be in Maine."

* * *

Billy lay in bed with her door closed reading her brochure from the Loon Society. She thought about the cottage she and Grey rented every August in Jewell Neck, Maine, on a lagoon. There at night with blackness all around them and not a light to be seen, they heard hoot owls and loons calling their night cries to one another. Loon mothers carried their chicks on their back, Billy knew. The last time she had heard those cries she had been just three months pregnant. The next time she heard them she would have a child.

She thought about the baby shower Penny had given her—a lunch party for ten women. At the end of it, Billy and Grey's unborn child had received cotton and wool blankets, little sweaters, tiny garments with feet, and two splendid Teddy bears. The Teddy bears had sat on the coffee table. Billy remembered the strange, light feeling in her chest as she looked at them. She had picked them both up and laughed with astonishment.

At a red light on the way home in a taxi, surrounded by boxes and bags of baby presents, she saw something that made her heart stop: Francis Clemens, who for two years had been Billy's illicit lover.

With the exception of her family. Billy was close only to Grey and Penny Stern. She had never been the subject of anyone's romantic passion. She and Grey, after all, had been fated to marry. She had loved him all her life.

Francis had pursued her: no one had ever pursued her before. The usual signs of romance were as unknown to Billy as the workings of a cyclotron. Crushes, she had felt, were for children. She did not really believe that adults had them.

Without her knowing it, she was incubating a number of curious romantic diseases. One day when Francis came to visit wearing his tweed coat and the ridiculously long paisley scarf he affected, she realized that she had fallen in love.

The fact of Francis was the most exotic thing that had ever happened in Billy's fairly stolid, uneventful life. He was as brilliant as a painted bunting. He was also, in marked contrast to Billy, beautifully dressed. He did not know one tree from another. He felt all birds were either robins or crows. He was avowedly urban and his pleasures were urban. He loved opera, cocktail parties, and lunches. They did not agree about economic theory, either.

Nevertheless, they spent what now seemed to Billy an enormous amount of time together. She had not sought anything like this. If her own case had been presented to her she would have dismissed it as messy, unnecessary, and somewhat sordid, but when she fell in love she fell as if backward into a swimming pool. For a while she felt dazed. Then Francis became a fact in her life. But in the end she felt her life was being ruined.

She had not seen Francis for a long time. In that brief glance at the red light she saw his paisley scarf, its long fringes flapping in the breeze. It was amazing that someone who had been so close to her did not know that she was having a baby. As the cab pulled away, she did not look back at him. She stared rigidly frontward, flanked on either side by presents for her unborn child.

The baby kicked. Mothers-to-be should not be lying in hospital beds thinking about illicit love affairs, Billy thought. Of course, if you were like the other mothers on the maternity floor and probably had never had an illicit love affair, you would not be punished by lying in the hospital in the first place. You would go into labor like everyone else, and come rushing into Maternity Admitting with your husband and your suitcase. By this time tomorrow she would have her baby in her arms, just like everyone else, but she drifted off to sleep thinking of Francis nonetheless.

* * *

At six in the morning, Bonnie Near woke her.

"You can brush your teeth," she said. "But don't drink any water. And your therapist is here to see you, but don't be long."

The door opened and Penny walked in.

"And how are we today?" she said. "Any strange dreams or odd thoughts?"

"How did you get in here?" Billy said.

"I said I was your psychiatrist and that you were being induced today and so forth," Penny said. "I just came to say good luck. Here's all the change we had in the house. Tell Grey to call constantly. I'll see you all tonight."

Billy was taken to the labor floor and hooked up to a fetal heart monitor whose transducers were kept on her stomach by a large elastic cummerbund. A stylish-looking nurse wearing hospital greens, a string of pearls, and perfectly applied pink lipstick poked her head through the door.

"Hi!" she said in a bright voice. "I'm Joanne Kelly. You're my patient today." She had the kind of voice and smile Billy could not imagine anyone's using in private. "Now, how are we? Fine? All right. Here's what we're going to do. First of all, we're going to put this IV into your arm. It will only hurt a little and then we're going to hook you up to something called pitocin. Has Dr. Bell explained any of this to you?" Joanne Kelly said.

"All," said Billy.

"Neat," Joanne Kelly said. "We *like* an informed patient. Put your arm out, please."

Billy stuck out her arm. Joanne Kelly wrapped a rubber thong under her elbow.

"Nice veins," she said. "You would have made a lovely junkie."

"Now we're going to start the pitocin," Joanne Kelly said. "We start off slow to see how you do. Then we escalate." She looked Billy up and down. "Okay," she said. "We're off and running. Now, I've got a lady huffing and puffing in the next room so I have to go and coach her. I'll be back real soon."

Billy lay looking at the clock, or watching the pitocin and glucose drip into her arm. She could not get a comfortable position and the noise of the fetal heart monitor was loud and harsh. The machine itself spat out a continual line of data.

Jordan Bell appeared at the foot of her bed.

"An exciting day—yes, Billy?" he said. "What time is Grey coming?"

"I told him to sleep late," Billy said. "All the nurses told me that this can take a long time. How am I supposed to feel when it starts working?"

"If all goes well, you'll start to have contractions and then they'll get stronger and then you'll have your baby."

"Just like that?" said Billy.

"Pretty much just like that."

But by five o'clock in the afternoon nothing much had happened.

Grey sat in a chair next to the bed. From time to time he checked the data. He had been checking it all day.

"That contraction went right off the paper," he said. "What did it feel like?"

"Intense," Billy said. "It just doesn't hurt."

"You're still in the early stages," said Jordan Bell when he came to check her. "I'm willing to stay on if you want to continue, but the baby might not be born till tomorrow."

"I'm beat," said Billy.

"Here's what we can do," Jordan said. "We can keep going or we start again tomorrow."

"Tomorrow," said Billy.

* * *

She woke up exhausted with her head pounding. The sky was cloudy and the glare hurt her eyes. She was taken to a different labor room.

In the night her blood pressure had gone up. She had begged not to have a shot—she did not see how she could go into labor feeling so terrible, but the shot was given. It had been a long, sleepless night.

She lay alone with a towel covering one eye, trying to sleep, when a nurse appeared by her side. This one looked very young, had curly hair, and thick, slightly rose-tinted glasses. Her tag read "Eva Gottlieb." Underneath she wore a button inscribed EVA: WE DELIVER.

"Hi," said Eva Gottlieb. "I'm sorry I woke you, but I'm your nurse for the day and I have to get you started."

"I'm here for a lobotomy," Billy said. "What are you going to do to me?"

"I'm going to run a line in you," Eva Gottlieb said. "And then I don't know what.

Because your blood pressure is high, I'm supposed to wait until Jordan gets here." She looked at Billy carefully. "I know it's scary," she said. "But the worst that can happen is that you have to be sectioned and that's not bad."

Billy's head throbbed.

"That's easy for you to say," she said. "I'm the section."

Eva Gottlieb smiled. "I'm a terrific nurse," she said. "I'll stay with you."

Tears sprang in Billy's eyes. "Why will you?"

"Well, first of all, it's my job," said Eva. "And second of all, you look like a reasonable person."

Billy looked at Eva carefully. She felt instant, total trust. Perhaps that was part of being in hospitals and having babies. Everyone you came in contact with came very close, very fast.

Billy's eyes hurt. Eva was hooking her up to the fetal heart monitor. Her touch was strong and sure, and she seemed to know Billy did not want to be talked to. She flicked the machine on, and Billy heard the familiar sound of galloping hooves.

"Is there any way to turn it down?" Billy said.

"Sure," said Eva. "But some people find it consoling."

As the morning wore on, Billy's blood pressure continued to rise. Eva was with her constantly.

"What are they going to do to me?" Billy asked.

"I think they're probably going to give you magnesium sulfate to get your blood pressure down and then they're going to section you. Jordan does a gorgeous job, believe me. I won't let them do anything to you without explaining it first, and if you get out of bed first thing tomorrow and start moving around you'll be fine."

Twenty minutes later, a doctor Billy had never seen before administered a dose of magnesium sulfate.

"Can't you do this?" Billy asked Eva.

"It's heavy-duty stuff," Eva said. "It has to be done by a doctor."

"Can they wait until my husband gets here?"

"It's too dangerous," said Eva. "It has to be done. I'll stay with you."

The drug made her hot and flushed, and brought her blood pressure straight down. For the next hour, Billy tried to sleep. She had never been so tired. Eva brought her cracked ice to suck on and a cloth for her head. The baby wiggled and writhed, and the fetal heart monitor gauged its every move. Finally, Grey and Jordan Bell were standing at the foot of her bed.

"Okay, Billy," said Jordan. "Today's the day. We must get the baby out. I explained to Grey about the mag sulfate. We both agree that you must have a cesarean."

"When?" Billy said.

"In the next hour," said Jordan. "I have to check two patients and then we're off to the races."

"What do you think," Billy asked Grey.

"It's right," Grey said.

"And what about you?" Billy said to Eva.

"It has to be done," Eva said.

Jordan Bell was smiling a genuine smile and he looked dashing and happy.

"Why is he so uplifted?" Billy asked Eva after he had dashed down the hall.

"He loves the OR," she said. "He loves deliveries. Think of it this way: you're going to get your baby at last."

* * *

Billy lay on a gurney, waiting to be rolled down the hall. Grey, wearing hospital scrubs, stood beside her holding her hand. She had been prepped and given an epidural anesthetic, and she could no longer feel her legs.

"Look at me," she said to Grey. "I'm a mass of tubes. I'm a miracle of modern science." She put his hand over her eyes.

Grey squatted down to put his head near hers. He looked expectant, exhausted, and worried, but when he saw her scanning his face he smiled.

"It's going to be swell," Grey said. "We'll find out if it's little William or little Ella."

Billy's heart was pounding but she thought she ought to say something to keep her side up. She said, "I knew we never should have had sexual intercourse." Grey gripped her hand tight and smiled. Eva laughed. "Don't you guys leave me," Billy said.

Billy was wheeled down the hall by an orderly. Grey held one hand, Eva held the other. Then they left her to scrub.

She was taken to a large, pale green room. Paint was peeling on the ceiling in the corner. An enormous lamp hung over her head. The anesthetist appeared and tapped her feet.

"Can you feel this?" he said.

"It doesn't feel like feeling," Billy said. She was trying to keep her breathing steady.

"Excellent," he said.

Then Jordan appeared at her feet, and Grey stood by her head.

Eva bent down. "I know you'll hate this, but I have to tape your hands down, and I have to put this oxygen mask over your face. It comes off as soon as the baby's born, and it's good for you and the baby."

Billy took a deep breath. The room was very hot. A screen was placed over her chest.

"It's so you can't see," said Eva. "Here's the mask. I know it'll freak you out, but just breathe nice and easy. Believe me, this is going to be fast."

Billy's arms were taped, her legs were numb, and a clear plastic mask was placed over her nose and mouth. She was so frightened she wanted to cry out, but it was impossible. Instead she breathed as Katherine Walden had taught her to. Every time a wave of panic rose, she breathed it down. Grey held her hand. His face was blank and his glasses were fogged. His hair was covered by a green cap and his brow was wet. There was nothing she could do for him, except squeeze his hand.

"Now, Billy," said Jordan Bell, "you'll feel something cold on your stomach. I'm painting you with Betadine. All right, here we go."

Billy felt something like dull tugging. She heard the sound of foamy water. Then she felt the baby being slipped from her. She turned to Grey. His glasses had unfogged and his eyes were round as quarters. She heard a high, angry scream.

"Here's your baby," said Jordan Bell. "It's a beautiful, healthy boy."

Eva lifted the mask off Billy's face.

"He's perfectly healthy," Eva said. "Listen to those lungs." She took the baby to be weighed and tested. Then she came back to Billy. "He's perfect but he's little—just under five pounds. We have to take him upstairs to the preemie nursery. It's policy when they're not five pounds."

"Give him to me," Billy said. She tried to free her hands but they were securely taped.

"I'll bring him to you," Eva said. "But he can't stay down here. He's too small. It's for the baby's safety, I promise you. Look, here he is."

The baby was held against her forehead. The moment he came near her he stopped shrieking. He was mottled and wet.

"Please let me have him," Billy said.

"He'll be fine," Eva said. They then took him away.

* * *

The next morning Billy rang for the nurse and demanded that her IV be disconnected. Twenty minutes later she was out of bed slowly walking.

"I feel as if someone had crushed my pelvic bones," Billy said.

"Someone did," said the nurse.

Two hours later she was put into a wheelchair and pushed by a nurse into the elevator and taken to the Infant Intensive Care Unit. At the door the nurse said, "I'll wheel you in."

"I can walk," Billy said. "But thank you very much."

Inside, she was instructed to scrub with surgical soap and to put on a sterile gown. Then she walked very slowly and very stiffly down the hall. A Chinese nurse stopped her.

"I'm William Delielle's mother," she said. "Where is he?"

The nurse consulted a clipboard and pointed Billy down a hallway. Another nurse in a side room pointed to an isolette—a large plastic case with porthole windows. There on a white cloth lay her child.

He was fast asleep, his little arm stretched in front of him, an exact replica of Grey's sleeping posture. On his back were two discs the size of nickels hooked up to wires that measured his temperature and his heart and respiration rates on a console above his isolette. He was long and skinny and beautiful.

"He looks like a little chicken," said Billy. "May I hold him?"

"Oh, no," said the nurse. "Not for a while. He mustn't be stressed." She gave Billy a long look and said, "But you can open the windows and touch him."

Billy opened the porthole window and touched his leg. He shivered slightly. She wanted to disconnect his probes, scoop him up, and hold him next to her. She stood quietly, her hand resting lightly on his calf.

The room was bright, hot, and busy. Nurses came and went, washing their hands, checking charts, making notes, diapering, changing bottles of glucose solution. There were three other children in the room. One was very tiny and had a miniature IV attached to a vein in her head. A pink card was taped on her isolette. Billy looked on the side of William's isolette. There was a blue card and in Grey's tiny printing was written "William Delielle."

Later in the morning, when Grey appeared in her room he found Billy sitting next to a glass-encased pump.

"This is the well-known electric breast pump. Made in Switzerland," Billy said.

"It's like the medieval clock at Salisbury Cathedral," Grey said, peering into the glass case. "I just came from seeing William. He's much *longer* than I thought. I called all the grandparents. In fact, I was on the telephone all night after I left you." He gave her a list of messages. "They're feeding him in half an hour."

Billy looked at her watch. She had been instructed to use the pump for three minutes on each breast to begin with. Her milk, however, would not be given to William, who, the doctors said, was too little to nurse. He would be given carefully measured formula, and Billy would eventually have to wean him from the bottle and onto herself. The prospect of this seemed very remote.

As the days went by, Billy's room filled with flowers, but she spent most of her time in the Infant ICU. She could touch William but not hold him. The morning before she was to be discharged, Billy went to William's eight o'clock feeding. She thought how lovely it would be to feed him at home, how they might sit in the rocking chair and watch the birds in the garden below. In William's present home, there was no morning and no night. He had never been in a dark room, or heard bird sounds or traffic noise, or felt a cool draft.

William was asleep on his side wearing a diaper and a little T-shirt. The sight of him seized Billy with emotion.

"You can hold him today," the nurse said.

"Yes?"

"Yes, and you can feed him today, too."

Billy bowed her head. She took a steadying breath. "How can I hold him with all this hardware on him?" she said.

"I'll show you," said the nurse. She disconnected the console, reached into the isolette, and gently untaped William's probes. Then she showed Billy how to change him, put on his T-shirt, and swaddle him in a cotton blanket. In an instant he was in Billy's arms.

He was still asleep, but he made little screeching noises and wrinkled his nose. He moved against her and nudged his head into her arm. The nurse led her to a rocking chair and for the first time she sat down with her baby.

All around her, lights blazed. The radio was on and a sweet male voice sang, "I want you to be mine, I want you to be mine, I want to take you home, I want you to be mine."

William opened his eyes and blinked. Then he yawned and began to cry.

"He's hungry," the nurse said, putting a small bottle into Billy's hand.

She fed him and burped him, and then she held him in her arms and rocked him to sleep. In the process she fell asleep, too, and was woken by the nurse and Grey, who had come from work.

"You must put him back now," said the nurse. "He's been out a long time and we don't want to stress him."

"It's awful to think that being with his mother creates stress," Billy said.

"Oh, no!" the nurse said. "That's not what I mean. I mean, in his isolette it's temperature controlled."

* * *

Once Billy was discharged from the hospital she had to commute to see William. She went to the two morning feedings, came home for a nap, and met Grey for the five o'clock. They raced out for dinner and came back for the eight. Grey would not let Billy stay for the eleven.

Each morning she saw Dr. Edmunds, the head of neonatology. He was a tall, slow-talking, sandy-haired man with horn-rimmed glasses.

"I know you will never want to hear this under any other circumstances," he said to Billy, "but your baby is very boring."

"How boring?"

"Very boring. He's doing just what he ought to do." William had gone to the bottom of his growth curve and was beginning to gain. "As soon as he's a little fatter he's all yours."

Billy stood in front of his isolette watching William sleep.

"This is like having an affair with a married man," Billy said to the nurse who was folding diapers next to her.

The nurse looked at her uncomprehendingly.

"I mean you love the person but can only see him at certain times," said Billy.

The nurse was young and plump. "I guess I see what you mean," she said.

At home William's room was waiting. The crib had been delivered and put together by Grey. While Billy was in the hospital, Grey had finished William's room. The Teddy bears sat on the shelves. A mobile of ducks and geese hung over the crib. Grey had bought a secondhand rocking chair and had painted it red. Billy had thought she would be unable to face William's empty room. Instead she found she could scarcely stay out of it. She folded and refolded his clothes, reorganized his drawers, arranged his crib blankets. She decided what should be his homecoming clothes and set them out on the changing table along with a cotton receiving blanket and a wool shawl.

But even though he did not look at all fragile and he was beginning to gain weight, it often felt to Billy that she would never have him. She and Grey had been told ten days to two weeks from day of birth. One day when she felt she could not stand much more Billy was told that she might try nursing him.

*Touch him on his cheek. He will turn to you. Guide him toward the breast and the magical connection will be made.*

Billy remembered this description from her childbirth books. She had imagined a softly lit room, a sense of peacefulness, some soft, sweet music in the background.

She was put behind a screen in William's room, near an isolette containing an enormous baby who was having breathing difficulties.

She was told to keep on her sterile gown, and was given sterile water to wash her breasts with. At the sight of his mother's naked bosom, William began to howl. The sterile gown dropped onto his face. Billy began to sweat. All around her, the nurses chatted, clattered, and dropped diapers into metal bins and slammed the tops down.

"Come on, William," Billy said. "The books say that this is the blissful union of mother and child."

But William began to scream. The nurse appeared with the formula bottle and William instantly stopped screaming and began to drink happily.

"Don't worry," the nurse said. "He'll catch on."

At night at home she sat by the window. She could not sleep. She had never felt so separated from anything in her life. Grey, to distract himself, was stenciling the wall under the molding in William's room. He had found an early American design of wheat and cornflowers. He stood on a ladder in his blue jeans carefully applying the stencil in pale blue paint.

One night Billy went to the door of the baby's room to watch him, but Grey was not on the ladder. He was sitting in the rocking chair with his head in his hands. His shoulders were shaking slightly. He had the radio on, and he did not hear her.

He had been so brave and cheerful. He had held her hand while William was born. He had told her it was like watching a magician sawing his wife in half. He had taken photos of William in his isolette and sent them to their parents and all their friends. He had read up on growth curves and had bought Billy a book on breast-feeding. He had also purloined his hospital greens to wear each year on William's birthday. Now *he* had broken down.

She made a noise coming into the room and then bent down and stroked his hair. He smelled of soap and paint thinner. She put her arms around him, and she did not let go for a long time.

* * *

Three times a day, Billy tried to nurse William behind a screen and each time she ended up giving him his formula.

Finally she asked a nurse, "Is there some room I could sit in alone with this child?"

"We're not set up for it," the nurse said. "But I could put you in the utility closet."

There amidst used isolettes and cardboard boxes of sterile water, on the second try William nursed for the first time. She touched his cheek. He turned to her, just as it said in the book. Then her eyes crossed.

"Oh, my God!" she said.

A nurse walked in.

"Hurts, right?" she said. "Good for him. That means he's got it. It won't hurt for long."

At his evening feeding he howled again.

"The course of true love never did run smooth," said Grey. He and Billy walked slowly past the park on their way home. It was a cold, wet night.

"I am a childless mother," Billy said.

Two days later William was taken out of his isolette and put into a plastic bin. He had no temperature or heart probes, and Billy could pick him up without having to disconnect anything. At his evening feeding when the unit was quiet, she took him out in the hallway and walked up and down with him.

The next day she was greeted by Dr. Edmunds.

"I've just had a chat with your pediatrician," he said. "How would you like to take your boring baby home with you?"

"When?" said Billy.

"Right now, if you have his clothes," Dr. Edmunds said. "Dr. Jacobson will be up in a few minutes and can officially release him."

She ran down the hall and called Grey.

"Go home and get William's things," she said. "They're springing him. Come and get us."

"You mean we can just walk out of there with him?" Grey said. "I mean, just take him under our arm? He barely knows us."

"Just get here. And don't forget the blankets."

A nurse helped Billy dress William. He was wrapped in a green and white receiving blanket and covered in a white wool shawl. On his head was a blue and green knitted cap. It slipped slightly sideways, giving him a raffish look.

They were accompanied in the elevator by a nurse. It was hospital policy that a nurse hold the baby, and hand it over at the door.

It made Billy feel light-headed to be standing out of doors with her child. She felt she had just robbed a bank and got away with it.

In the taxi, Grey gave the driver their address.

"Not door to door," Billy said. "Can we get out at the avenue and walk down the street just like everyone else?"

When the taxi stopped, they got out carefully. The sky was full of silver clouds and the air was blustery and cold. William squinted at the light and wrinkled his nose.

Then, with William tight in Billy's arms, the three of them walked down the street just like everyone else.

# T. C. BOYLE
## (1948– )

Although sometimes compared with earlier absurdist writers like John Barth, Thomas Pynchon, or Franz Kafka, T. C. Boyle is really his own man with a very distinctive voice. He is known for his wide-ranging interests; an imaginative, even quirky, use of language; and a way of combining the bizarre with the apparently normal for often humorous and satiric effects.

Born Thomas John Boyle in Peekskill, New York, Boyle changed his middle name to Coraghessan when he was 17 years old. He describes himself as having been a "pampered punk" who did not read a book until he was 18. He received his B.A. degree from the State University of New York College at Potsdam in 1968. After a brief stint as a high school teacher, he went on for a Ph.D. from the Writers' Workshop at the University of Iowa, which he completed in 1974. He has been teaching at the University of Southern California since 1977. He is married with three children.

Boyle's stories have appeared in such journals as *Esquire, Paris Review, The Atlantic Monthly,* and *The New Yorker.* His story collections include *The Descent of Man* (1979), *Greasy Lake & Other Stories* (1985), *If the River Was Whiskey* (1990), *Without a Hero* (1994), and *T. C. Boyle Stories* (1998). He has written eight novels: *Water Music* (1981), *Budding Prospects: A Pastoral* (1984), *World's End* (1987), *East Is East* (1991), *The Road to Wellville* (1993), *The Tortilla Curtain* (1995), *Riven Rock* (1998), and *A Friend of the Earth* (2000).

# Greasy Lake

It's about a mile down on the dark side of Route 88.

—BRUCE SPRINGSTEEN

There was a time when courtesy and winning ways went out of style, when it was good to be bad, when you cultivated decadence like a taste. We were all dangerous characters then. We wore torn-up leather jackets, slouched around with toothpicks in our mouths, sniffed glue and ether and what somebody claimed was cocaine. When we wheeled our parents' whining station wagons out into the street we left a patch of rubber half a block long. We drank gin and grape juice, Tango, Thunderbird, and Bali Hai. We were nineteen. We were bad. We read André Gide and struck elaborate poses to show that we didn't give a shit about anything. At night, we went up to Greasy Lake.

Through the center of town, up the strip, past the housing developments and shopping malls, street lights giving way to the thin streaming illumination of the headlights, trees crowding the asphalt in a black unbroken wall: that was the way out to Greasy Lake. The Indians had called it Wakan, a reference to the clarity of its waters. Now it was fetid and murky, the mud banks glittering with broken glass and strewn with beer cans and the charred remains of bonfires. There was a single ravaged island a hundred yards from shore, so stripped of vegetation it looked as if the air force had strafed it. We went up to the lake because everyone went there, because we wanted to snuff the rich scent of possibility on the breeze, watch a girl take off her clothes and plunge into the festering murk, drink beer, smoke pot, howl at the stars, savor the incongruous full-throated roar of rock and roll against the primeval susurrus of frogs and crickets. This was nature.

I was there one night, late, in the company of two dangerous characters. Digby wore a gold star in his right ear and allowed his father to pay his tuition at Cornell; Jeff was thinking of quitting school to become a painter/musician/head-shop proprietor. They were both expert in the social graces, quick with a sneer, able to manage a Ford with lousy shocks over a rutted and gutted blacktop road at eighty-five while rolling a joint as compact as a Tootsie Roll Pop stick. They could lounge against a bank of booming speakers and trade "man"s with the best of them or roll out across the dance floor as if their joints worked on bearings. They were slick and quick and they wore their mirror shades at breakfast and dinner, in the shower, in closets and caves. In short, they were bad.

I drove. Digby pounded the dashboard and shouted along with Toots & the Maytals while Jeff hung his head out the window and streaked the side of my mother's Bel Air with vomit. It was early June, the air soft as a hand on your cheek, the third night of summer vacation. The first two nights we'd been out till dawn, looking for something we never found. On this, the third night, we'd cruised the strip sixty-seven times, been in and out of every bar and club we could think of in a twenty-mile radius, stopped twice for bucket chicken and forty-cent hamburgers, debated going to a party at the house of a girl Jeff's sister knew, and chucked two dozen raw eggs at mailboxes and hitchhikers. It was 2:00 A.M.; the bars were closing. There was nothing to do but take a bottle of lemon-flavored gin up to Greasy Lake.

The taillights of a single car winked at us as we swung into the dirt lot with its tufts of weed and washboard corrugations; '57 Chevy, mint, metallic blue. On the far side of the lot, like the exoskeleton of some gaunt chrome insect, a chopper leaned against its kickstand. And that was it for excitement: some junkie half-wit biker and a car freak pumping his girlfriend. Whatever it was we were looking for, we weren't about to find it at Greasy Lake. Not that night.

But then all of a sudden Digby was fighting for the wheel. "Hey, that's Tony Lovett's car! Hey!" he shouted, while I stabbed at the brake pedal and the Bel Air nosed up to the gleaming bumper of the parked Chevy. Digby leaned on the horn, laughing, and instructed me to put my brights on. I flicked on the brights. This was hilarious. A joke. Tony would experience premature withdrawal and expect to be confronted by grim-looking state troopers with flash-lights. We hit the horn, strobed the lights, and then jumped out of the car to press our witty faces to Tony's windows; for all we knew we might even catch a glimpse of some little fox's tit, and then we could slap backs with red-faced Tony, roughhouse a little, and go on to new heights of adventure and daring.

The first mistake, the one that opened the whole floodgate, was losing my grip on the keys. In the excitement, leaping from the car with the gin in one hand and a roach clip in the other, I spilled them in the grass—in the dark, rank, mysterious nighttime grass of Greasy Lake. This was a tactical error, as damaging and irreversible in its way as Westmoreland's decision to dig in at Khe Sanh. I felt it like a jab of intuition, and I stopped there by the open door, peering vaguely into the night that puddled up round my feet.

The second mistake—and this was inextricably bound up with the first—was identifying the car as Tony Lovett's. Even before the very bad character in greasy jeans and engineer boots ripped out of the driver's door, I began to realize that this chrome blue was much lighter than the robin's-egg of Tony's car, and that Tony's car didn't have rear-mounted speakers. Judging from their expressions, Digby and Jeff were privately groping toward the same inevitable and unsettling conclusion as I was.

In any case, there was no reasoning with this bad greasy character—clearly he was a man of action. The first lusty Rockette kick of his steel-toed boot caught me under the chin, chipped my favorite tooth, and left me sprawled in the dirt. Like a fool, I'd gone down on one knee to comb the stiff hacked grass for the keys, my mind making connections in the most dragged-out, testudineous way, knowing that things had gone wrong, that I was in a lot of trouble, and that the lost ignition key was my grail and my salvation. The three or four succeeding blows were mainly absorbed by my right buttock and the tough piece of bone at the base of my spine.

Meanwhile, Digby vaulted the kissing bumpers and delivered a savage kung-fu blow to the greasy character's collarbone. Digby had just finished a course in martial arts for phys-ed credit and had spent the better part of the past two nights telling us apocryphal tales of Bruce Lee types and of the raw power invested in lightning blows shot from coiled wrists, ankles, and elbows. The greasy character was unimpressed. He merely backed off a step, his face like a Toltecmask, and laid Digby out with a single whistling roundhouse blow . . . but by now Jeff had got into the act, and I was beginning to extricate myself from the dirt, a tinny compound of shock, rage, and impotence wadded in my throat.

Jeff was on the guy's back, biting at his ear. Digby was on the ground, cursing. I went for the tire iron I kept under the driver's seat. I kept it there because bad characters always keep tire irons under the driver's seat, for just such an occasion as this.

Never mind that I hadn't been involved in a fight since sixth grade, when a kid with a sleepy eye and two streams of mucus depending from his nostrils hit me in the knee with a Louisville slugger; never mind that I'd touched the tire iron exactly twice before, to change tires: it was there. And I went for it.

I was terrified. Blood was beating in my ears, my hands were shaking, my heart turning over like a dirtbike in the wrong gear. My antagonist was shirtless, and a single cord of muscle flashed across his chest as he bent forward to peel Jeff from his back like a wet overcoat. "Motherfucker," he spat, over and over, and I was aware in that instant that all four of us—Digby, Jeff, and myself included—were chanting "motherfucker, motherfucker," as if it were a battle cry. (What happened next? the detective asks the murderer from beneath the turned-down brim of his porkpie hat. I don't know, the murderer says, something came over me. Exactly.)

Digby poked the flat of his hand in the bad character's face and I came at him like a kamikaze, mindless, raging, stung with humiliation—the whole thing, from the initial boot in the chin to this murderous primal instant involving no more than sixty hyperventilating, gland-flooding seconds—I came at him and brought the tire iron down across his ear. The effect was instantaneous, astonishing. He was a stunt man and this was Hollywood, he was a big grimacing toothy balloon and I was a man with a straight pin. He collapsed. Wet his pants. Went loose in his boots.

A single second, big as a zeppelin, floated by. We were standing over him in a circle, gritting our teeth, jerking our necks, our limbs and hands and feet twitching with glandular discharges. No one said anything. We just stared down at the guy, the car freak, the lover, the bad greasy character laid low. Digby looked at me; so did Jeff. I was still holding the tire iron, a tuft of hair clinging to the crook like dandelion fluff, like down. Rattled, I dropped it in the dirt, already envisioning the headlines, the pitted faces of the police inquisitors, the gleam of handcuffs, clank of bars, the big black shadows rising from the back of the cell . . . when suddenly a raw torn shriek cut through me like all the juice in all the electric chairs in the country.

It was the fox. She was short, barefoot, dressed in panties and a man's shirt. "Animals!" she screamed, running at us with her fists clenched and wisps of blow-dried hair in her face. There was a silver chain round her ankle, and her toenails flashed in the glare of the headlights. I think it was the toenails that did it. Sure, the gin and the cannabis and even the Kentucky Fried may have had a hand in it, but it was the sight of those flaming toes that set us off—the toad emerging from the loaf in *Virgin Spring,* lipstick smeared on a child: she was already tainted. We were on her like Bergman's deranged brothers—see no evil, hear none, speak none—panting, wheezing, tearing at her clothes, grabbing for flesh. We were bad characters, and we were scared and hot and three steps over the line—anything could have happened.

It didn't.

Before we could pin her to the hood of the car, our eyes masked with lust and greed and the purest primal badness, a pair of headlights swung into the lot. There we were, dirty, bloody, guilty, dissociated from humanity and civilization, the first of the Ur-crimes behind us, the second in progress, shreds of nylon panty and spandex brassiere dangling from our fingers, our flies open, lips licked—there we were, caught in the spotlight. Nailed.

We bolted. First for the car, and then, realizing we had no way of starting it, for the woods. I thought nothing. I thought escape. The headlights came at me like accusing fingers. I was gone.

Ram-bam-bam, across the parking lot, past the chopper and into the feculent undergrowth at the lake's edge, insects flying up in my face, weeds whipping, frogs and snakes and red-eyed turtles splashing off into the night: I was already ankle-deep in muck and tepid water and still going strong. Behind me, the girl's screams rose in intensity, disconsolate, incriminating, the screams of the Sabine women, the Christian martyrs, Anne Frank dragged from the garret. I kept going, pursued by those cries, imagining cops and bloodhounds. The water was up to my knees when I realized what I was doing: I was going to swim for it. Swim the breadth of Greasy Lake and hide myself in the thick clot of woods on the far side. They'd never find me there.

I was breathing in sobs, in gasps. The water lapped at my waist as I looked out over the moon-burnished ripples, the mats of algae that clung to the surface like scabs. Digby and Jeff had vanished. I paused. Listened. The girl was quieter now, screams tapering to sobs, but there were male voices, angry, excited, and the high-pitched ticking of the second car's engine. I waded deeper, stealthy, hunted, the ooze sucking at my sneakers. As I was about to take the plunge—at the very instant I dropped my shoulder for the first slashing stroke—I blundered into something. Something unspeakable, obscene, something soft, wet, moss-grown. A patch of weed? A log? When I reached out to touch it, it gave like a rubber duck, it gave like flesh.

In one of those nasty little epiphanies for which we are prepared by films and TV and childhood visits to the funeral home to ponder the shrunken painted forms of dead grandparents, I understood what it was that bobbed there so inadmissibly in the dark. Understood, and stumbled back in horror and revulsion, my mind yanked in six different directions (I was nineteen, a mere child, an infant, and here in the space of five minutes I'd struck down one greasy character and blundered into the waterlogged carcass of a second), thinking, The keys, the keys, why did I have to go and lose the keys? I stumbled back, but the muck took hold of my feet—a sneaker snagged, balance lost—and suddenly I was pitching face forward into the buoyant black mass, throwing out my hands in desperation while simultaneously conjuring the image of reeking frogs and muskrats revolving in slicks of their own deliquescing juices. AAAAArrrgh! I shot from the water like a torpedo, the dead man rotating to expose a mossy beard and eyes cold as the moon. I must have shouted out, thrashing around in the weeds, because the voices behind me suddenly became animated.

"What was that?"

"It's them, it's them: they tried to, tried to . . . *rape* me!" Sobs.

A man's voice, flat Midwestern accent. "You sons a bitches, we'll kill you!"

Frogs, crickets.

Then another voice, harsh, *r*-less, Lower East Side: "Motherfucker!" I recognized the verbal virtuosity of the bad greasy character in the engineer boots. Tooth chipped, sneakers gone, coated in mud and slime and worse, crouching breathless in the weeds waiting to have my ass thoroughly and definitively kicked and fresh from the hideous stinking embrace of a three-days-dead-corpse. I suddenly felt a rush of joy and vindication: the son of a bitch was alive! Just as quickly, my bowels turned to ice. "Come on out of there, you pansy mother-fuckers!" the bad greasy character was screaming. He shouted curses till he was out of breath.

The crickets started up again, then the frogs. I held my breath. All at once there was a sound in the reeds, a swishing, a splash: thunk-a-thunk. They were throwing rocks. The frogs fell silent. I cradled my head. Swish, swish, thunk-a-thunk. A wedge of feldspar the size of a cue ball glanced off my knee. I bit my finger.

It was then that they turned to the car. I heard a door slam, a curse, and then the sound of the headlights shattering—almost a good-natured sound, celebratory, like corks popping from the necks of bottles. This was succeeded by the dull booming of the fenders, metal on metal, and then the icy crash of the windshield. I inched forward, elbows and knees, my belly pressed to the muck, thinking of guerrillas and commandos and *The Naked and the Dead.* I parted the weeds and squinted the length of the parking lot.

The second car—it was a Trans-Am—was still running, its high beams washing the scene in a lurid stagy light. Tire iron flailing, the greasy bad character was laying into the side of my mother's Bel Air like an avenging demon, his shadow riding up the trunks of the trees. Whomp. Whomp. Whomp-whomp. The other two guys—blond types, in fraternity jackets—were helping out with tree branches and skull-sized boulders. One of them was gathering up bottles, rocks, muck, candy wrappers, used condoms, poptops, and other refuse and pitching it through the window on the driver's side. I could see the fox, a white bulb behind the windshield of the '57 Chevy. "Bobbie," she whined over the thumping, "come *on.*" The greasy character paused a moment, took one good swipe at the left taillight, and then heaved the tire iron halfway across the lake. Then he fired up the '57 and was gone.

Blond head nodded at blond head. One said something to the other, too low for me to catch. They were no doubt thinking that in helping to annihilate my mother's car they'd committed a fairly rash act, and thinking too that there were three bad characters connected with that very car watching them from the woods. Perhaps other possibilities occurred to them as well—police, jail cells, justices of the peace, reparations, lawyers, irate parents, fraternal censure. Whatever they were thinking, they suddenly dropped branches, bottles, and rocks and sprang for their car in unison, as if they'd choreographed it. Five seconds. That's all it took. The engine shrieked, the tires squealed, a cloud of dust rose from the rutted lot and then settled back on darkness.

I don't know how long I lay there, the bad breath of decay all around me, my jacket heavy as a bear, the primordial ooze subtly reconstituting itself to accommodate my upper thighs and testicles. My jaws ached, my knee throbbed, my coccyx was on fire. I contemplated suicide, wondered if I'd need bridgework, scraped the recesses of my brain for some sort of excuse to give my parents—a tree had fallen on the car, I was blindsided by a bread truck, hit and run, vandals had got to it while we were playing chess at Digby's. Then I thought of the dead man. He was probably the only person on the planet worse off than I was. I thought about him, fog on the lake, insects chirring eerily, and felt the tug of fear, felt the darkness opening up inside me like a set of jaws. Who was he, I wondered, this victim of time and circumstance bobbing sorrowfully in the lake at my back. The owner of the chopper, no doubt, a bad older character come to this. Shot during a murky drug deal, drowned while drunkenly frolicking in the lake. Another headline. My car was wrecked; he was dead.

When the eastern half of the sky went from black to cobalt and the trees began to separate themselves from the shadows, I pushed myself up from the mud and stepped out into the open. By now the birds had begun to take over for the crickets, and dew lay slick on the leaves. There was a smell in the air, raw and sweet at the same time, the smell of the sun firing buds and opening blossoms. I contemplated the car. It lay there like a wreck along the highway, like a steel sculpture left over from a vanished civilization. Everything was still. This was nature.

I was circling the car, as dazed and bedraggled as the sole survivor of an air blitz, when Digby and Jeff emerged from the trees behind me. Digby's face was crosshatched with smears of dirt; Jeff's jacket was gone and his shirt was torn across the shoulder. They slouched across the lot, looking sheepish, and silently came up beside me to gape at the ravaged automobile. No one said a word. After a while Jeff swung open the driver's door and began to scoop the broken glass and garbage off the seat. I looked at Digby. He shrugged. "At least they didn't slash the tires," he said.

It was true: the tires were intact. There was no windshield, the headlights were staved in, and the body looked as if it had been sledge-hammered for a quarter a shot at the countyfair, but the tires were inflated to regulation pressure. The car was drivable. In silence, all three of us bent to scrape the mud and shattered glass from the interior. I said nothing about the biker. When we were finished, I reached in my pocket for the keys, experienced a nasty stab of recollection, cursed myself, and turned to search the grass. I spotted them almost immediately, no more than five feet from the open door, glinting like jewels in the first tapering shaft of sunlight. There was no reason to get philosophical about it: I eased into the seat and turned the engine over.

It was at that precise moment that the silver Mustang with the flame decals rumbled into the lot. All three of us froze; then Digby and Jeff slid into the car and slammed the door. We watched as the Mustang rocked and bobbed across the ruts and finally jerked to a halt beside the forlorn chopper at the far end of the lot. "Let's go," Digby said. I hesitated, the Bel Air wheezing beneath me.

Two girls emerged from the Mustang. Tight jeans, stiletto heels, hair like frozen fur. They bent over the motorcycle, paced back and forth aimlessly, glanced once or twice at us, and then ambled over to where the reeds sprang up in a green fence round the perimeter of the lake. One of them cupped her hands to her mouth. "Al," she called. "Hey, Al!"

"Come on," Digby hissed. "Let's get out of here."

But it was too late. The second girl was picking her way across the lot, unsteady on her heels, looking up at us and then away. She was older—twenty-five or -six—and as she came closer we could see there was something wrong with her: she was stoned or drunk, lurching now and waving her arms for balance. I gripped the steering wheel as if it were the ejection lever of a flaming jet, and Digby spat out my name, twice, terse and impatient.

"Hi," the girl said.

We looked at her like zombies, like war veterans, like deaf-and-dumb pencil peddlers.

She smiled, her lips cracked and dry. "Listen," she said, bending from the waist to look in the window, "you guys seen Al?" Her pupils were pinpoints, her eyes glass. She jerked her neck. "That's his bike over there—Al's. You seen him?"

Al. I didn't know what to say. I wanted to get out of the car and retch. I wanted to go home to my parents' house and crawl into bed. Digby poked me in the ribs. "We haven't seen anybody," I said.

The girl seemed to consider this, reaching out a slim veiny arm to brace herself against the car. "No matter," she said, slurring the *t*'s, "he'll turn up." And then, as if she'd just taken stock of the whole scene—the ravaged car and our battered faces, the desolation of the place—she said: "Hey, you guys look like some pretty bad characters—been fightin', huh?" We stared straight ahead, rigid as catatonics. She was fumbling in her pocket and muttering something. Finally she held out a handful of tablets in glassine wrappers: "Hey, you want to party, you want to do some of these with me and Sarah?"

I just looked at her. I thought I was going to cry. Digby broke the silence. "No thanks," he said, leaning over me. "Some other time."

I put the car in gear and it inched forward with a groan, shaking off pellets of glass like an old dog shedding water after a bath, heaving over the ruts on its worn springs, creeping toward the highway. There was a sheen of sun on the lake. I looked back. The girl was still standing there, watching us, her shoulders slumped, hand outstretched.

# CHARLES JOHNSON
## (1948– )

Charles Johnson is one of the most important African-American writers to emerge in the last twenty-five years. He was born in Evanston, Illinois, and was educated at Southern Illinois University, where he finished a B.A. in 1971 and an M.A. in 1973. He did postgraduate work at the State University of New York at Stony Brook from 1973 to 1976. He has been on the faculty of the University of Washington since 1976 and holds an endowed chair in creative writing.

He married in 1970 and has two children. In addition to fiction, Johnson has published criticism, screenplays, and cartoons. He is one of twelve African-American authors to be included on an international stamp series honoring great authors of the twentieth century. In 1998 he was awarded the prestigious MacArthur Fellowship.

Like his teacher John Gardner, under whose guidance he wrote his first novel, *Faith and the Good Thing* (1974), Johnson believes fiction should serve moral ends. Influenced deeply by Eastern philosophy—he has been a practicing Buddhist since 1980—as well as the phenomenology of Edmund Husserl, Johnson seeks to write a fiction that explores classical problems and metaphysical questions in the context of black American life and experience. All his work attests to this ambition, a work equally at home with magic and fantasy and earlier forms of fiction as with contemporary realism. His other novels are *Oxherding Tale* (1982); *Middle Passage* (1990), which won the National Book Award; and *Dreamer* (1998). His stories are collected as *The Sorcerer's Apprentice* (1986).

# Exchange Value

ME AND my brother, Loftis, came in by the old lady's window. There was some kinda boobytrap—boxes of broken glass—that shoulda warned us Miss Bailey wasn't the easy mark we made her to be. She been living alone for twenty years in 4-B down the hall from Loftis and me, long before our folks died—a hincty, halfbald West Indian woman with a craglike face, who kept her door barricaded, shutters closed, and wore the same sorry-looking outfit—black wingtip shoes, cropfingered gloves in winter, and a man's floppy hat—like maybe she dressed half-asleep or in a dark attic. Loftis, he figured Miss Bailey had some grandtheft dough stashed inside, jim, or leastways a shoebox full of money, 'cause she never spent a nickel on herself, not even for food, and only left her place at night.

Anyway, we figured Miss Bailey was gone. Her mailbox be full, and Pookie White, who run the Thirty-ninth Street Creole restaurant, he say she ain't dropped by in days to collect the handouts he give her so she can get by. So here's me and Loftis, tipping around Miss Bailey's blackdark kitchen. The floor be littered with fruitrinds, roaches, old food furred with blue mold. Her dirty dishes be stacked in a sink feathered with cracks, and it looks like the old lady been living, lately, on Ritz crackers and Department of Agriculture (Welfare Office) peanut butter. Her toilet be stopped up, too, and, on the bathroom floor, there's five Maxwell House coffee cans full of shit. Me, I was closing her bathroom door when I whiffed this evil smell so bad, so thick, I could hardly breathe, and what air I breathed was stifling, like solid fluid in my throatpipes, like broth or soup. "Cooter," Loftis whisper, low, across the room, "you smell that?" He went right on sniffing it, like people do for some reason when something be smelling stanky, then took out his headrag and held it over his mouth. "Smells like something crawled up in here and died!" Then, head low, he slipped his long self into the living room. Me, I stayed by the window, gulping for air, and do you know why?

You oughta know, up front, that I ain't too good at this gangster stuff, and I had a real bad feeling about Miss Bailey from the get-go. Mama used to say it was Loftis, not me, who'd go places—I see her standing at the sideboard by the sink now, big as a Frigidaire, white flour to her elbows, a washtowel over her shoulder, while we ate a breakfast of cornbread and syrup. Loftis, he graduated fifth at DuSable High School, had two gigs and, like Papa, he be always wanting the things white people had out in Hyde Park, where Mama did daywork sometimes. Loftis, he be the kind of brother who buys *Esquire,* sews Hart, Schaffner & Marx labels in Robert Hall suits, talks properlike, packs his hair with Murray's; and he took classes in politics and stuff at the Black People's Topographical Library in the late 1960s. At thirty, he make his bed military-style, reads *Black Scholar* on the bus he takes to the plant, and, come hell or high water, plans to make a Big Score. Loftis, he say I'm 'bout as useful on a hustle—or when it comes to getting ahead—as a headcold, and he says he has to count my legs sometimes to make sure I ain't a mule, seeing how, for all my eighteen years, I can't keep no job and sorta stay close to home, watching TV, or reading *World's Finest* comic books, or maybe just laying dead, listening to music, imagining I see faces or foreign places in water stains on the wallpaper, 'cause some days, when I remember Papa, then Mama, killing theyselves for chump change—a pitiful li'l bowl of porridge—I get to thinking that even if I ain't had all I wanted, maybe I've had, you know, all I'm ever gonna get.

"Cooter," Loftis say from the living room. "You best get in here quick."

Loftis, he'd switched on Miss Bailey's bright, overhead living room lights, so for a second I couldn't see and started coughing—the smell be so powerful it hit my nostrils like coke—and when my eyes cleared, shapes come forward in the light, and I thought for an instant like I'd slipped in space. I seen why Loftis called me, and went back two steps. See, 4-B's so small if you ring Miss Bailey's doorbell, the toilet'd flush. But her living room, webbed in dust, be filled to the max with dollars of all denominations, stacks of stock in General Motors, Gulf Oil, and 3M Company in old White Owl cigar boxes, battered purses, or bound in pink rubber bands. It be like the kind of cubbyhole kids play in, but filled with . . . *things:* everything, like a world inside the world, you take it from me, so like picturebook scenes of plentifulness you could seal yourself off in here and settle forever. Loftis and me both drew breath suddenly. There be unopened cases of Jack Daniel's, three safes cemented to the floor, hundreds of matchbooks, unworn clothes, a fuel-burning stove, dozens of wedding rings, rubbish, World War II magazines, a carton of a hundred canned sardines, mink stoles, old rags, a birdcage, a bucket of silver dollars, thousands of books, paintings, quarters in tobacco cans, two pianos, glass jars of pennies, a set of bagpipes, an almost complete Model A Ford dappled with rust, and, I swear, three sections of a dead tree.

"Damn!" My head be light; I sat on an upended peach crate and picked up a bottle of Jack Daniel's.

"Don't you touch *any*thing!" Loftis, he panting a little; he slap both hands on a table. "Not until we inventory this stuff."

"Inventory? Aw, Lord, Loftis," I say, "something ain't *right* about this stash. There could be a curse on it. . . ."

"Boy, sometime you act weak-minded."

"For real, Loftis, I got a feeling. . . ."

Loftis, he shucked off his shoes, and sat down heavily on the lumpy arm of a stuffed chair. "Don't say *any*thing." He chewed his knuckles, and for the first time Loftis looked like he didn't know his next move. "Let me think, okay?" He squeezed his nose in a way he has when thinking hard, sighed, then stood up and say, "There's something you better see in that bedroom yonder. Cover up your mouth."

"Loftis, I ain't going in there."

He look at me right funny then. "She's a miser, that's all. She saves things."

"But a tree?" I say. "Loftis, a *tree* ain't normal!"

"Cooter, I ain't gonna tell you twice."

Like always, I followed Loftis, who swung his flashlight from the plant—he a night watchman—into Miss Bailey's bedroom, but me, I'm thinking how trippy this thing is getting, remembering how, last year, when I had a paper route, the old lady, with her queer, crablike walk, pulled my coat for some change in the hallway, and when I give her a handful of dimes, she say, like one of them spooks on old-time radio. "Thank you, Co-o-oter," then gulped the coins down like aspirin, no lie, and scurried off like a hunchback. Me, I wanted no parts of this squirrely old broad, but Loftis, he holding my wrist now, beaming his light onto a low bed. The room had a funny, museumlike smell. Real sour. It was full of dirty laundry. And I be sure the old lady's stuff had a terrible string attached when Loftis, looking away, lifted her bedsheets and a knot of black flies rose. I stepped back and held my breath. Miss Bailey be in her long-sleeved flannel nightgown, bloated, like she'd been blown up by a bicycle pump, her old face caved in with rot, flyblown, her fingers big and colored like spoiled bananas. Her wristwatch be ticking softly beside a half-eaten hamburger. Above the bed, her wall had roaches squashed in little swirls of bloodstain. Maggots clustered in her eyes, her ears, and one fist-sized rat hissed inside her flesh. My eyes snapped shut. My knees failed; then I did a Hollywood faint. When I surfaced, Loftis, he be sitting beside me in the living room, where he'd drug me, reading a wrinkled, yellow article from the *Chicago Daily Defender.*

"Listen to this," Loftis say. "'Elnora Bailey, forty-five, a Negro housemaid in the Highland Park home of Henry Conners, is the beneficiary of her employer's will. An old American family, the Conners arrived in this country on the *Providence* shortly after the voyage of the *Mayflower.* The family flourished in the early days of the 1900s.' . . ." He went on, getting breath: " 'A distinguished and wealthy industrialist, without heirs or a wife, Conners willed his entire estate to Miss Bailey of 3347 North Clark Street for her twenty years of service to his family.' . . ." Loftis, he give that Geoffrey Holder laugh of his, low and deep; then it eased up his throat until it hit a high note and tipped his head back onto his shoulders. "Cooter, that was before we was born! Miss Bailey kept this in the Bible next to her bed."

Standing, I braced myself with one hand against the wall. "She didn't earn it?"

"Naw." Loftis, he folded the paper—"Not one penny"—and stuffed it in his shirt pocket. His jaw looked tight as a horseshoe. "Way *I* see it," he say, "this was her one shot in a lifetime to be rich, but being country, she had backward ways and blew it." Rubbing his hands, he stood up to survey the living room. "Somebody's gonna find Miss Bailey soon, but if we stay on the case—Cooter, don't square up on me now—we can tote everything to our place before daybreak. Best we start with the big stuff."

"But why didn't she *use* it, huh? Tell me that?"

Loftis, he don't pay me no mind. When he gets an idea in his head, you can't dig it out with a chisel. How long it took me and Loftis to inventory, then haul Miss Bailey's queer old stuff to our crib, I can't say, but that cranky old ninnyhammer's hoard come to $879,543 in cash money, thirty-two bank books (some deposits be only $5), and me, I wasn't sure I was dreaming or what, but I suddenly flashed on this feeling, once we left her flat, that all the fears Loftis and me had about the future be gone, 'cause Miss Bailey's property was the past—the power of that fellah Henry Conners trapped like a bottle spirit—which we could live off, so it was the future, too, pure potential: can *do.* Loftis got to talking on about how that piano we pushed home be equal to a thousand bills, jim, which equals, say, a bad TEAC A-3340 tape deck, or a down payment on a deuce-and-a-quarter. Its value be (Loftis say) that of a universal standard of measure, relational, unreal as number, so that tape deck could turn, magically, into two gold lamé suits, a trip to Tijuana, or twenty-five blow jobs from a ho—we had $879,543 worth of wishes, if you can deal with that. Be like Miss Bailey's stuff is raw energy, and Loftis and me, like wizards, could transform her stuff into anything else at will. All we had to do, it seemed to me, was decide exactly what to exchange it for.

While Loftis studied this over (he looked funny, like a potato trying to say something, after the inventory, and sat, real quiet, in the kitchen), I filled my pockets with fifties, grabbed me a cab downtown to grease, yum, at one of them high-hat restaurants in the Loop. . . . But then I thought better of it, you know, like I'd be out of place—just another jig putting on airs—and scarfed instead at a ribjoint till both my eyes bubbled. This fat lady making fishburgers in the back favored an old hardleg baby-sitter I once had, a Mrs. Paine who made me eat ocher, and I wanted so bad to say, "Loftis and me Got Ovuh," but I couldn't put that in the wind, could I, so I hatted up. Then I copped a boss silk necktie, cashmere socks, and a whistle-slick maxi leather jacket on State Street, took cabs *every*where, but when I got home that evening, a funny, Pandora-like feeling hit me. I took off the jacket, boxed it—it looked trifling in the hallway's weak light—and, tired, turned my key in the door. I couldn't get in. Loftis, he'd changed the lock and, when he finally let me in, looking vaguer, crabby, like something out of the Book of Revelations, I seen this elaborate, booby-trapped tunnel of cardboard and razor blades behind him, with a two-foot space just big enough for him or me to crawl through. That wasn't all. Two bags of trash from the furnace room downstairs be sitting inside the door. Loftis, he give my leather jacket this evil look, hauled me inside, and hit me upside my head.

"How much this thing set us back?"

"Two fifty." My jaws got tight; I toss him my receipt. "You want me to take it back? Maybe I can get something else. . . ."

Loftis, he say, not to me, but to the receipt, "Remember the time Mama give me that ring we had in the family for fifty years? And I took it to Merchandise Mart and sold it for a few pieces of candy?" He hitched his chair forward and sat with his elbows on his knees. "That's what you did, Cooter. You crawled into a Clark bar." He commence to rip up my receipt, then picked up his flashlight and keys. "As soon as you buy something you *lose* the power to buy something." He button up his coat with holes in the elbows, showing his blue shirt, then turned 'round at the tunnel to say, "Don't touch Miss Bailey's money, or drink her splo, or do *any*thing until I get back."

"Where you going?"

"To work. It's Wednesday, ain't it?"

"You going to work?"

"Yeah."

"You got to go *really?* Loftis," I say, "what you brang them bags of trash in here for?"

"It ain't trash!" He cut his eyes at me. "There's good clothes in there. Mr. Peterson tossed them out, he don't care, but I saw some use in them, that's all."

"Loftis . . ."

"Yeah?"

"What we gonna do with all this money?"

Loftis pressed his fingers to his eyelids, and for a second he looked caged, or like somebody'd kicked him in his stomach. Then he cut me some slack: "Let me think on it tonight—it don't pay to rush—then we can TCB, okay?"

Five hours after Loftis leave for work, that old blister Mr. Peterson, our landlord, he come collecting rent, find Mrs. Bailey's body in apartment 4-B, and phoned the fire department. Me, I be folding my new jacket in tissue paper to keep it fresh, adding the box to Miss Bailey's unsunned treasures when two paramedics squeezed her on a long stretcher through a crowd in the hallway. See, I had to pin her from the stairhead, looking down one last time at this dizzy old lady, and I seen something in her face, like maybe she'd been poor as Job's turkey for thirty years, suffering that special Negro fear of using up what little we get in this life—Loftis, he call that entropy—believing in her belly, and for all her faith, jim, that there just ain't no more coming tomorrow from grace, or the Lord, or from her own labor, like she can't kill nothing, and won't nothing die . . . so when Conners will her his wealth, it put her through changes, she be spellbound, possessed by the promise of life, panicky about depletion, and locked now in the past 'cause *every* purchase, you know, has to be a poor buy: a loss of life. Me, I wasn't worried none. Loftis, he got a brain trained by years of talking trash with people in Frog Hudson's barbershop on Thirty-fifth Street. By morning, I knew, he'd have some kinda wheeze worked out.

But Loftis, he don't come home. Me, I got kinda worried. I listen to the hi-fi all day Thursday, only pawing outside to peep down the stairs, like that'd make Loftis come sooner. So Thursday go by; and come Friday the head's out of kilter—first there's an ogrelike belch from the toilet bowl, then water bursts from the bathroom into the kitchen—and me, I can't call the super (How do I explain the tunnel?), so I gave up and quit bailing. But on Saturday, I could smell greens cooking next door. Twice I almost opened Miss Bailey's sardines, even though starving be less an evil than eating up our stash, but I waited till it was dark and, with my stomach talking to me, stepped outside to Pookie White's, lay a hard-luck story on him, and Pookie, he give me some jambalaya and gumbo. Back home in the living room, finger-feeding myself, barricaded in by all that hope-made material, the Kid felt like a king in his counting room, and I copped some Zs in an armchair till I heard the door move on its hinges, then bumping in the tunnel, and a heavy-footed walk thumped into the bedroom.

"Loftis?" I rubbed my eyes. "You back?" It be Sunday morning. Six-thirty sharp. Darkness dissolved slowly into the strangeness of twilight, with the rays of sunlight surging at exactly the same angle they fall each evening, as if the hour be an island, a moment outside time. Me, I'm afraid Loftis gonna fuss 'bout my not straightening up, letting things go. I went into the bathroom, poured water in the one-spigot washstand—brown rust come bursting out in flakes—and rinsed my face. "Loftis, you supposed to be home four days ago. Hey," I say, toweling my face, "you okay?" How come he don't answer me? Wiping my hands on the seat on my trousers, I tipped into Loftis's room. He sleeping with his mouth open. His legs be drawn up, both fists clenched between his knees. He'd kicked his blanket on the floor. In his sleep, Loftis laughed, or moaned, it be hard to tell. His eyelids, not quite shut, show slits of white. I decided to wait till Loftis wake up for his decision, but turning, I seen his watch, keys, and what looked in the first stain of sunlight to be a carefully wrapped piece of newspaper on his nightstand. The sunlight swelled to a bright shimmer, focusing the bedroom slowly like solution do a photographic image in the developer. And then something so freakish went down I ain't sure it took place. Fumble-fingered, I unfolded the paper, and inside be a blemished penny. It be like suddenly somebody slapped my head from behind. Taped on the penny be a slip of paper, and on the paper be the note "Found while walking down Devon Avenue." I hear Loftis mumble like he trapped in a nightmare. "Hold tight," I whisper. "It's all right." Me, I wanted to tell Loftis how Miss Bailey looked four days ago, that maybe it didn't have to be like that for us—did it?—because we could change. Couldn't we? Me, I pull his packed sheets over him, wrap up the penny, and, when I locate Miss Bailey's glass jar in the living room, put it away carefully, for now, with the rest of our things.

# ⁂ SUSAN SONTAG
## (1933–    )

Born Susan Rosenblatt in New York City, Susan Sontag was raised by a nanny in the city while her parents lived most of the year in China where her father was a fur trader. When Susan was 12, her father died of tuberculosis, and her mother remarried, to Captain Nathan Sontag, an Army Air Corps pilot. Susan took his name. Extremely bright and curious as a child, she read voraciously. She entered the University of California at Berkeley at age 15, and went on to the University of Chicago and completed a B.A. at age 18. When she was 17, she married the sociologist Philip Rieff and had one child. When Rieff took an appointment at Brandeis University, Sontag continued her studies at Harvard University. She earned two M.A.s, one in English and one in philosophy. She divorced her husband in 1958 and moved to New York City, where she involved herself in the new currents of art of the late 1950s and early 1960s. She spent summers in Paris and steeped herself in the new French thought.

Sontag is perhaps best known for her essays on art and culture. Her two collections of essays, *Against Interpretation* (1966) and *Styles of Radical Will* (1969), established her reputation as an influential if controversial thinker. A leftist politically in the 1960s, she traveled to Hanoi and wrote sympathetically of the North Vietnamese. In the late 1970s she faced a bout with cancer, which led to her book *Illness as Metaphor* (1978), an issue she explored again in her 1989 book *AIDS and Its Metaphors.* Her criticism argued for an aesthetics of form to break out of the prison of interpretation, an idea she sought to express and illustrate in her first two novels, *The Benefactor* (1963) and *Death Kit* (1967).

More recently her work shows a renewed interest in realism and history as seen in *The Volcano Lover: A Romance* (1992) and *In America* (2000). A first collection of her stories is *I, Etcetera* (1978). Sontag has also written screenplays and a play. She has been awarded distinguished fellowships including the Rockefeller, the Guggenheim, and a five-year MacArthur Foundation Award, 1990–1995. Her 1977 book *On Photography* won a National Book Critics Circle prize. Her story "The Way We Live Now" was published in *The New Yorker* in 1987.

# The Way We Live Now

AT FIRST he was just losing weight, he felt only a little ill, Max said to Ellen, and he didn't call for an appointment with his doctor, according to Greg, because he was managing to keep on working at more or less the same rhythm, but he did stop smoking, Tanya pointed out, which suggests he was frightened, but also that he wanted, even more than he knew, to be healthy, or healthier, or maybe just to gain back a few pounds, said Orson, for he told her, Tanya went on, that he expected to be climbing the walls (isn't that what people say?) and found, to his surprise, that he didn't miss cigarettes at all and reveled in the sensation of his lungs' being ache-free for the first time in years. But did he have a good doctor, Stephen wanted to know, since it would have been crazy not to go for a checkup after the pressure was off and he was back from the conference in Helsinki, even if by then he was feeling better. And he said, to Frank, that he would go, even though he was indeed frightened, as he admitted to Jan, but who wouldn't be frightened now, though, odd as that might seem, he hadn't been worrying until recently, he avowed to Quentin, it was only in the last six months that he had the metallic taste of panic in his mouth, because becoming seriously ill was something that happened to other people, a normal delusion, he observed to Paolo, if one was thirty-eight and had never had a serious illness; he wasn't, as Jan confirmed, a hypochondriac. Of course, it was hard not to worry, everyone was worried, but it wouldn't do to panic, because, as Max pointed out to Quentin, there wasn't anything one could do except wait and hope, wait and start being careful, be careful, and hope. And even if one did prove to be ill, one shouldn't give up, they had new treatments that promised an arrest of the disease's inexorable course, research was progressing. It seemed that everyone was in touch with everyone else several times a week, checking in, I've never spent so many hours at a time on the phone, Stephen said to Kate, and when I'm exhausted after the two or three calls made to me, giving me the latest, instead of switching off the phone to give myself a respite I tap out the number of another friend or acquaintance, to pass on the news. I'm not sure I can afford to think so much about it, Ellen said, and I suspect my own motives, there's something morbid I'm getting used to, getting excited by, this must be like what people felt in London during the Blitz. As far as I know, I'm not at risk, but you never know, said Aileen. This thing is totally unprecedented, said Frank. But don't you think he ought to see a doctor, Stephen insisted. Listen, said Orson, you can't force people to take care of themselves, and what makes you think the worst, he could be just run down, people still do get ordinary illnesses, awful ones, why are you assuming it has to be that. But all I want to be sure, said Stephen, is that he understands the options, because most people don't, that's why they won't see a doctor or have the test, they think there's nothing one can do. But is there anything one can do, he said to Tanya (according to Greg), I mean what do I gain if I go to the doctor; if I'm really ill, he's reported to have said, I'll find out soon enough.

* * *

And when he was in the hospital, his spirits seemed to lighten, according to Donny. He seemed more cheerful than he had been in the last months, Ursula said, and the bad news seemed to come almost as a relief, according to Ira, as a truly unexpected blow, according to Quentin, but you'd hardly expect him to have said the same thing to all his friends, because his relation to Ira was so different from his relation to Quentin (this according to Quentin, who was proud of their friendship), and perhaps he thought Quentin wouldn't be undone by seeing him weep, but Ira insisted that couldn't be the reason he behaved so differently with each, and that maybe he was feeling less shocked, mobilizing his strength to fight for his life, at the moment he saw Ira but overcome by feelings of hopelessness when Quentin arrived with flowers, because anyway the flowers threw him into a bad mood, as Quentin told Kate, since the hospital room was choked with flowers, you couldn't have crammed another flower into that room, but surely you're exaggerating, Kate said, smiling, everybody likes flowers. Well, who wouldn't exaggerate at a time like this, Quentin said sharply. Don't you think this is an exaggeration. Of course I do, said Kate gently, I was only teasing, I mean I didn't mean to tease. I know that, Quentin said, with tears in his eyes, and Kate hugged him and said well, when I go this evening I guess I won't bring flowers, what does he want, and Quentin said, according to Max, what he likes best is chocolate. Is there anything else, asked Kate, I mean like chocolate but not chocolate. Licorice, said Quentin, blowing his nose. And besides that. Aren't you exaggerating now, Quentin said, smiling. Right, said Kate, so if I want to bring him a whole raft of stuff, besides chocolate and licorice, what else. Jelly beans, Quentin said.

* * *

He didn't want to be alone, according to Paolo, and lots of people came in the first week, and the Jamaican nurse said there were other patients on the floor who would be glad to have the surplus flowers, and people weren't afraid to visit, it wasn't like the old days, as Kate pointed out to Aileen, they're not even segregated in the hospital anymore, as Hilda observed, there's nothing on the door of his room warning visitors of the possibility of contagion, as there was a few years ago; in fact, he's in a double room and, as he told Orson, the old guy on the far side of the curtain (who's clearly on the way out, said Stephen) doesn't even have the disease, so, as Kate went on, you really should go and see him, he'd be happy to see you, he likes having people visit, you aren't not going because you're afraid, are you. Of course not, Aileen said, but I don't know what to say, I think I'll feel awkward, which he's bound to notice, and that will make him feel worse, so I won't be doing him any good, will I. But he won't notice anything, Kate said, patting Aileen's hand, it's not like that, it's not the way you imagine, he's not judging people or wondering about their motives, he's just happy to see his friends. But I never was really a friend of his, Aileen said, you're a friend, he's always liked you, you told me he talks about Nora with you, I know he likes me, he's even attracted to me, but he respects you. But, according to Wesley, the reason Aileen was so stingy with her visits was that she could never have him to herself, there were always others there already and by the time they left still others had arrived, she'd been in love with him for years, and I can understand, said Donny, that Aileen should feel bitter that if there could have been a woman friend he did more than occasionally bed, a woman he really loved, and my God, Victor said, who had known him in those years, he was crazy about Nora, what a heart-rending couple they were, two surly angels, then it couldn't have been she.

* * *

And when some of the friends, the ones who came every day, waylaid the doctor in the corridor, Stephen was the one who asked the most informed questions, who'd been keeping up not just with the stories that appeared several times a week in the *Times* (which Greg confessed to have stopped reading, unable to stand it anymore) but with articles in the medical journals published here and in England and France, and who knew socially one of the principal doctors in Paris who was doing some much-publicized research on the disease, but his doctor said little more than that the pneumonia was not life-threatening, the fever was subsiding, of course he was still weak but he was responding well to the antibiotics, that he'd have to complete his stay in the hospital, which entailed a minimum of twenty-one days on the IV, before she could start him on the new drug, for she was optimistic about the possibility of getting him into the protocol; and when Victor said that if he had so much trouble eating (he'd say to everyone when they coaxed him to eat some of the hospital meals, that food didn't taste right, that he had a funny metallic taste in his mouth) it couldn't be good that friends were bringing him all that chocolate, the doctor just smiled and said that in these cases the patient's morale was also an important factor, and if chocolate made him feel better she saw no harm in it, which worried Stephen, as Stephen said later to Donny, because they wanted to believe in the promises and taboos of today's high-tech medicine but here this reassuringly curt and silver-haired specialist in the disease, someone quoted frequently in the papers, was talking like some old-fangled country GP who tells the family that tea with honey or chicken soup may do as much for the patient as penicillin, which might mean, as Max said, that they were just going through the motions of treating him, that they were not sure about what to do, or rather, as Xavier interjected, that they didn't know what the hell they were doing, that the truth, the real truth, as Hilda said, upping the ante, was that they didn't, the doctors, really have any hope.

* * *

Oh, no, said Lewis, I can't stand it, wait a minute, I can't believe it, are you sure, I mean are they sure, have they done all the tests, it's getting so when the phone rings I'm scared to answer because I think it will be someone telling me someone else is ill; but did Lewis really not know until yesterday, Robert said testily, I find that hard to believe, everybody is talking about it, it seems impossible that someone wouldn't have called Lewis; and perhaps Lewis did know, was for some reason pretending not to know already, because, Jan recalled, didn't Lewis say something months ago to Greg, and not only to Greg, about his not looking well, losing weight, and being worried about him and wishing he'd see a doctor, so it couldn't come as a total surprise. Well, everybody is worried about everybody now, said Betsy, that seems to be the way we live, the way we live now. And, after all, they were once very close, doesn't Lewis still have the keys to his apartment, you know the way you let someone keep the keys after you've broken up, only a little because you hope the person might just saunter in, drunk or high, late some evening, but mainly because it's wise to have a few sets of keys strewn around town, if you live alone, at the top of a former commercial building that, pretentious as it is, will never acquire a doorman or even a resident superintendent, someone whom you can call on for the keys late one night if you find you've lost yours or have locked yourself out. Who else has keys, Tanya inquired, I was thinking somebody might drop by tomorrow before coming to the hospital and bring some treasures, because the other day, Ira said, he was complaining about how dreary the hospital room was, and how it was like being locked up in a motel room, which got everybody started telling funny stories about motel rooms they'd known, and at Ursula's story, about the Luxury Budget Inn in Schenectady, there was an uproar of laughter around his bed, while he watched them in silence, eyes bright with fever, all the while, as Victor recalled, gobbling that damned chocolate. But, according to Jan, whom Lewis's keys enabled to tour the swank of his bachelor lair with an eye to bringing over some art consolation to brighten up the hospital room, the Byzantine icon wasn't on the wall over his bed, and that was a puzzle until Orson remembered that he'd recounted without seeming upset (this disputed by Greg) that the boy he'd recently gotten rid of had stolen it, along with four of the *maki-e* lacquer boxes, as if these were objects as easy to sell on the street as a TV or a stereo. But he's always been very generous, Kate said quietly, and though he loves beautiful things isn't really attached to them, to things, as Orson said, which is unusual in a collector, as Frank commented, and when Kate shuddered and tears sprang to her eyes and Orson inquired anxiously if he, Orson, had said something wrong, she pointed out that they'd begun talking about him in a retrospective mode, summing up what he was like, what made them fond of him, as if he were finished, completed, already a part of the past.

* * *

Perhaps he was getting tired of having so many visitors, said Robert, who was, as Ellen couldn't help mentioning, someone who had come only twice and was probably looking for a reason not to be in regular attendance, but there could be no doubt, according to Ursula, that his spirits had dipped, not that there was any discouraging news from the doctors, and he seemed now to prefer being alone a few hours of the day; and he told Donny that he'd begun keeping a diary for the first time in his life, because he wanted to record the course of his mental reactions to this astonishing turn of events, to do something parallel to what the doctors were doing, who came every morning and conferred at his bedside about his body, and that perhaps it wasn't so important what he wrote in it, which amounted, as he said wryly to Quentin, to little more than the usual banalities about terror and amazement that this was happening to him, to him also, plus the usual remorseful assessments of his past life, his pardonable superficialities, capped by resolves to live better, more deeply, more in touch with his work and his friends, and not to care so passionately about what people thought of him, interspersed with admonitions to himself that in this situation his will to live counted more than anything else and that if he really wanted to live, and trusted life, and liked himself well enough (down, ol' debbil Thanatos!), he *would* live, he would be an exception; but perhaps all this, as Quentin ruminated, talking on the phone to Kate, wasn't the point, the point was that by the very keeping of the diary he was accumulating something to reread one day, slyly staking out his claim to a future time, in which the diary would be an object, a relic, in which he might not actually reread it, because he would want to have put this ordeal behind him, but the diary would be there in the drawer of his stupendous Majorelle desk, and he could already, he did actually say to Quentin one late sunny afternoon, propped up in the hospital bed, with the stain of chocolate framing one corner of a heartbreaking smile, see himself in the penthouse, the October sun streaming through those clear windows instead of this streaked one, and the diary, the pathetic diary, safe inside the drawer.

* * *

It doesn't matter about the treatment's side effects, Stephen said (when talking to Max), I don't know why you're so worried about that, every strong treatment has some dangerous side effects, it's inevitable, you mean otherwise the treatment wouldn't be effective, Hilda interjected, and anyway, Stephen went on doggedly, just because there *are* side effects it doesn't mean he has to get them, or all of them, each one, or even some of them. That's just a list of all the possible things that could go wrong, because the doctors have to cover themselves, so they make up a worst-case scenario, but isn't what's happening to him, and to so many other people, Tanya interrupted, a worst-case scenario, a catastrophe no one could have imagined, it's too cruel, and isn't everything a side effect, quipped Ira, even *we* are all side effects, but we're not bad side effects, Frank said, he likes having his friends around, and we're helping each other, too; because his illness sticks us all in the same glue, mused Xavier, and, whatever the jealousies and grievances from the past that have made us wary and cranky with each other, when something like this happens (the sky is falling, the sky is falling!) you understand what's really important. I agree, Chicken Little, he is reported to have said. But don't you think, Quentin observed to Max, that being as close to him as we are, making time to drop by the hospital every day, is a way of our trying to define ourselves more firmly and irrevocably as the well, those who aren't ill, who aren't going to fall ill, as if what's happened to him couldn't happen to us, when in fact the chances are that before long one of us will end up where he is, which is probably what he felt when he was one of the cohort visiting Zack in the spring (you never knew Zack, did you?), and, according to Clarice, Zack's widow, he didn't come very often, he said he hated hospitals, and didn't feel he was doing Zack any good, that Zack would see on his face how uncomfortable he was. Oh, he was one of those, Aileen said. A coward. Like me.

* * *

And after he was sent home from the hospital, and Quentin had volunteered to move in and was cooking meals and taking telephone messages and keeping the mother in Mississippi informed, well, mainly keeping her from flying to New York and heaping her grief on her son and confusing the household routine with her oppressive ministrations, he was able to work an hour or two in his study, on days he didn't insist on going out, for a meal or a movie, which tired him. He seemed optimistic, Kate thought, his appetite was good, and what he said, Orson reported, was that he agreed when Stephen advised him that the main thing was to keep in shape, he was a fighter, right, he wouldn't be who he was if he weren't, and was he ready for the big fight, Stephen asked rhetorically (as Max told it to Donny), and he said you bet, and Stephen added it could be a lot worse, you could have gotten the disease two years ago, but now so many scientists are working on it, the American team and the French team, everyone bucking for that Nobel Prize a few years down the road, that all you have to do is stay healthy for another year or two and then there will be good treatment. Yes, he said, Stephen said, my timing is good. And Betsy, who had been climbing on and rolling off macrobiotic diets for a decade, came up with a Japanese specialist she wanted him to see but thank God, Donny reported, he'd had the sense to refuse, but he did agree to see Victor's visualization therapist, although what could one possibly visualize, said Hilda, when the point of visualizing disease was to see it as an entity with contours, borders, here rather than there, something limited, something you were the host of, in the sense that you could disinvite the disease, while this was so total; or would be, Max said. But the main thing, said Greg, was to see that he didn't go the macrobiotic route, which might be harmless for plump Betsy but could only be devastating for him, lean as he'd always been, with all the cigarettes and other appetite-suppressing chemicals he'd been welcoming into his body for years; and now was hardly the time, as Stephen pointed out, to be worried about cleaning up his act, and eliminating the chemical additives and other pollutants that we're all blithely or not so blithely feasting on, blithely since we're healthy, healthy as we can be; so far, Ira said. Meat and potatoes is what I'd be happy to see him eating, Ursula said wistfully. And spaghetti and clam sauce, Greg added. And thick cholesterol-rich omelets with smoked mozzarella, suggested Yvonne, who had flown from London for the weekend to see him. Chocolate cake, said Frank. Maybe not chocolate cake, Ursula said, he's already eating so much chocolate.

* * *

And when, not right away but still only three weeks later, he was accepted into the protocol for the new drug, which took considerable behind-the-scenes lobbying with the doctors, he talked less about being ill, according to Donny, which seemed like a good sign, Kate felt, a sign that he was not feeling like a victim, feeling not that he *had* a disease but, rather, was living *with* a disease (that was the right cliché, wasn't it?), a more hospitable arrangement, said Jan, a kind of cohabitation which implied that it was something temporary, that it could be terminated, but terminated how, said Hilda, and when you say hospitable, Jan, I hear hospital. And it was encouraging, Stephen insisted, that from the start, at least from the time he was finally persuaded to make the telephone call to his doctor, he was willing to say the name of the disease, pronounce it often and easily, as if it were just another word, like boy or gallery or cigarette or money or deal, as in no big deal, Paolo interjected, because, as Stephen continued, to utter the name is a sign of health, a sign that one has accepted being who one is, mortal, vulnerable, not exempt, not an exception after all, it's a sign that one is willing, truly willing, to fight for one's life. And we must say the name, too, and often, Tanya added, we mustn't lag behind him in honesty, or let him feel that, the effort of honesty having been made, it's something done with and he can go on to other things. One is so much better prepared to help him, Wesley replied. In a way he's fortunate, said Yvonne, who had taken care of a problem at the New York store and was flying back to London this evening, sure, fortunate, said Wesley, no one is shunning him, Yvonne went on, no one's afraid to hug him or kiss him lightly on the mouth, in London we are, as usual, a few years behind you, people I know, people who would seem to be not even remotely at risk, are just terrified, but I'm impressed by how cool and rational you all are; you find us cool, asked Quentin. But I have to say, he's reported to have said, I'm terrified, I find it very hard to read (and you know how he loves to read, said Greg; yes, reading is his television, said Paolo) or to think, but I don't feel hysterical. I feel quite hysterical, Lewis said to Yvonne. But you're able to *do* something for him, that's wonderful, how I wish I could stay longer, Yvonne answered, it's rather beautiful, I can't help thinking, this utopia of friendship you've assembled around him (this pathetic utopia, said Kate), so that the disease, Yvonne concluded, is not, anymore, out there. Yes, don't you think we're more at home here, with him, with the disease, said Tanya, because the imagined disease is so much worse than the reality of him, whom we all love, each in our fashion, having it. I know for me his getting it has quite demystified the disease, said Jan, I don't feel afraid, spooked, as I did before he became ill, when it was only news about remote acquaintances, whom I never saw again after they became ill. But you know you're not going to come down with the disease, Quentin said, to which Ellen replied, on her behalf, that's not the point, and possibly untrue, my gynecologist says that everyone is at risk, everyone who has a sexual life, because sexuality is a chain that links each of us to many others, unknown others, and now the great chain of being has become a chain of death as well. It's not the same for you, Quentin insisted, it's not the same for you as it is for me or Lewis or Frank or Paolo or Max, I'm more and more frightened, and I have every reason to be. I don't think about whether I'm at risk or not, said Hilda, I know that I was afraid to know someone with the disease, afraid of what I'd see, what I'd feel, and after the first day I came to the hospital I felt so relieved. I'll never feel that way, that fear, again; he doesn't seem different from me. He's not, Quentin said.

* * *

According to Lewis, he talked more often about those who visited more often, which is natural, said Betsy, I think he's even keeping a tally. And among those who came or checked in by phone every day, the inner circle as it were, those who were getting more points, there was still a further competition, which was what was getting on Betsy's nerves, she confessed to Jan; there's always that vulgar jockeying for position around the bedside of the gravely ill, and though we all feel suffused with virtue at our loyalty to him (speak for yourself, said Jan), to the extent that we're carving time out of every day, or almost every day, though some of us are dropping out, as Xavier pointed out, aren't we getting at least as much out of this as he is. Are we, said Jan. We're rivals for a sign from him of special pleasure over a visit, each stretching for the brass ring of his favor, wanting to feel the most wanted, the true nearest and dearest, which is inevitable with someone who doesn't have a spouse and children or an official in-house lover, hierarchies that no one would dare contest, Betsy went on, so we are the family he's founded, without meaning to, without official titles and ranks (we, we, snarled Quentin); and is it so clear, though some of us, Lewis and Quentin and Tanya and Paolo, among others, are ex-lovers and all of us more or less than friends, which one of us he prefers, Victor said (now it's us, raged Quentin), because sometimes I think he looks forward more to seeing Aileen, who has visited only three times, twice at the hospital and once since he's been home, than he does you or me; but, according to Tanya, after being very disappointed that Aileen hadn't come, now he was angry, while, according to Xavier, he was not really hurt but touchingly passive, accepting Aileen's absence as something he somehow deserved. But he's happy to have people around, said Lewis; he says when he doesn't have company he gets very sleepy, he sleeps (according to Quentin), and then perks up when someone arrives, it's important that he not feel ever alone. But, said Victor, there's one person he hasn't heard from, whom he'd probably like to hear from more than most of us; but she didn't just vanish, even right after she broke away from him, and he knows exactly where she lives now, said Kate, he told me he put in a call to her last Christmas Eve, and she said it's nice to hear from you and Merry Christmas, and he was shattered, according to Orson, and furious and disdainful, according to Ellen (what do you expect of her, said Wesley, she was burned out), but Kate wondered if maybe he hadn't phoned Nora in the middle of a sleepless night, what's the time difference, and Quentin said no, I don't think so, I think he wouldn't want her to know.

* * *

And when he was feeling even better and had regained the pounds he'd shed right away in the hospital, though the refrigerator started to fill up with organic wheat germ and grapefruit and skimmed milk (he's worried about his cholesterol count, Stephen lamented), and told Quentin he could manage by himself now, and did, he started asking everyone who visited how he looked, and everyone said he looked great, so much better than a few weeks ago, which didn't jibe with what anyone had told him at that time; but then it was getting harder and harder to know how he looked, to answer such a question honestly when among themselves they wanted to be honest, both for honesty's sake and (as Donny thought) to prepare for the worst, because he'd been looking like *this* for so long, at least it seemed so long, that it was as if he'd always been like this, how did he look before, but it was only a few months, and those words, pale and wan looking and fragile, hadn't they always applied? And one Thursday Ellen, meeting Lewis at the door of the building, said, as they rode up together in the elevator, how is he *really?* But you see how he is, Lewis said tartly, he's fine, he's perfectly healthy, and Ellen understood that of course Lewis didn't think he was perfectly healthy but that he wasn't worse, and that was true, but wasn't it, well, almost heartless to talk like that. Seems inoffensive to me, Quentin said, but I know what you mean, I remember once talking to Frank, somebody, after all, who has volunteered to do five hours a week of office work at the Crisis Center (I know, said Ellen), and Frank was going on about this guy, diagnosed almost a year ago, and so much further along, who'd been complaining to Frank on the phone about the indifference of some doctor, and had gotten quite abusive about the doctor, and Frank was saying there was no reason to be so upset, the implication being that *he,* Frank, wouldn't behave so irrationally, and I said, barely able to control my scorn, but Frank, Frank, he has every reason to be upset, he's dying, and Frank said, said according to Quentin, oh, I don't like to think about it that way.

* * *

And it was while he was still home, recuperating, getting his weekly treatment, still not able to do much work, he complained, but, according to Quentin, up and about most of the time and turning up at the office several days a week, that bad news came about two remote acquaintances, one in Houston and one in Paris, news that was intercepted by Quentin on the ground that it could only depress him, but Stephen contended that it was wrong to lie to him, it was so important for him to live in the truth; that had been one of his first victories, that he was candid, that he was even willing to crack jokes about the disease, but Ellen said it wasn't good to give him this end-of-the-world feeling, too many people were getting ill, it was becoming such a common destiny that maybe some of the will to fight for his life would be drained out of him if it seemed to be as natural as, well, death. Oh, Hilda said, who didn't know personally either the one in Houston or the one in Paris, but knew *of* the one in Paris, a pianist who specialized in twentieth-century Czech and Polish music, I have his records, he's such a valuable person, and, when Kate glared at her, continued defensively, I know every life is equally sacred, but that *is* a thought, another thought, I mean, all these valuable people who aren't going to have their normal four score as it is now, these people aren't going to be replaced, and it's such a loss to the culture. But this isn't going to go on forever, Wesley said, it can't, they're bound to come up with something (they, they, muttered Stephen), but did you ever think, Greg said, that if some people don't die, I mean even if they can keep them alive (they, they, muttered Kate), they continue to be carriers, and that means, if you have a conscience, that you can never make love, make love fully, as you'd been wont—wantonly, Ira said—to do. But it's better than dying, said Frank. And in all his talk about the future, when he allowed himself to be hopeful, according to Quentin, he never mentioned the prospect that even if he didn't die, if he were so fortunate as to be among the first generation of the disease's survivors, never mentioned, Kate confirmed, that whatever happened it was over, the way he had lived until now, but, according to Ira, he did think about it, the end of bravado, the end of folly, the end of trusting life, the end of taking life for granted, and of treating life as something that, samurai-like, he thought himself ready to throw away lightly, impudently; and Kate recalled, sighing, a brief exchange she'd insisted on having as long as two years ago, huddling on a banquette covered with steel-gray industrial carpet on an upper level of The Prophet and toking up for their next foray onto the dance floor: she'd said hesitantly, for it felt foolish asking a prince of debauchery to, well, take it easy, and she wasn't keen on playing big sister, a role, as Hilda confirmed, he inspired in many women, are you being careful, honey, you know what I mean. And he replied, Kate went on, no, I'm not, listen, I can't, I just can't, sex is too important to me, always has been (he started talking like that, according to Victor, after Nora left him), and if I get it, well, I get it. But he wouldn't talk like that now, would he, said Greg; he must feel awfully foolish now, said Betsy, like someone who went on smoking, saying I can't give up cigarettes, but when the bad X-ray is taken even the most besotted nicotine addict can stop on a dime. But sex isn't like cigarettes, is it, said Frank, and, besides, what good does it do to remember that he was reckless, said Lewis angrily, the appalling thing is that you just have to be unlucky once, and wouldn't he feel even worse if he'd stopped three years ago and had come down with it anyway, since one of the most terrifying features of the disease is that you don't know when you contracted it, it could have been ten years ago, because surely this disease has existed for years and years, long before it was recognized; that is, named. Who knows how long (I think a lot about that, said Max) and who knows (I know what you're going to say, Stephen interrupted) how many are going to get it.

* * *

I'm feeling fine, he's reported to have said whenever someone asked him how he was, which was almost always the first question anyone asked. Or: I'm feeling better, how are you? But he said other things, too, I'm playing leapfrog with myself, he is reported to have said, according to Victor. And: There must be a way to get something positive out of this situation, he's reported to have said to Kate. How American of him, said Paolo. Well, said Betsy, you know the old American adage: When you've got a lemon, make lemonade. The one thing I'm sure I couldn't take, Jan said he said to her, is becoming disfigured, but Stephen hastened to point out the disease doesn't take that form very often anymore, its profile is mutating, and, in conversation with Ellen, wheeled up words like blood-brain barrier; I never thought there was a barrier *there,* said Jan. But he mustn't know about Max, Ellen said, that would really depress him, please don't tell him, he'll have to know, Quentin said grimly, and he'll be furious not to have been told. But there's time for that, when they take Max off the respirator, said Ellen; but isn't it incredible, Frank said, Max was fine, not feeling ill at all, and then to wake up with a fever of a hundred and five, unable to breathe, but that's the way it often starts, with absolutely no warning, Stephen said, the disease has so many forms. And when, after another week had gone by, he asked Quentin where Max was, he didn't question Quentin's account of a spree in the Bahamas, but then the number of people who visited regularly was thinning out, partly because the old feuds that had been put aside through the first hospitalization and the return home had resurfaced, and the flickering enmity between Lewis and Frank exploded, even though Kate did her best to mediate between them; and also because he himself had done something to loosen the bonds of love that united the friends around him, by seeming to take them all for granted, as if it were perfectly normal for so many people to carve out so much time and attention for him, visit him every few days, talk about him incessantly on the phone with each other; but, according to Paolo, it wasn't that he was less grateful, it was just something he was getting used to, the visits. It had become, with time, a more ordinary kind of situation, a kind of ongoing party, first at the hospital and now since he was home, barely on his feet again, it being clear, said Robert, that I'm on the B list; but Kate said, that's absurd, there's no list; and Victor said, but there is, only it's not he, it's Quentin who's drawing it up. He wants to see us, we're helping him, we have to do it the way he wants, he fell down yesterday on the way to the bathroom, he mustn't be told about Max (but he already knew, according to Donny), it's getting worse.

* * *

When I was home, he is reported to have said, I was afraid to sleep, as I was dropping off each night it felt like just that, as if I were falling down a black hole, to sleep felt like giving in to death, I slept every night with the light on; but here, in the hospital, I'm less afraid. And to Quentin he said, one morning, the fear rips through me, it tears me open; and, to Ira, it presses me together, squeezes me toward myself. Fear gives everything its hue, its high. I feel so, I don't know how to say it, exalted, he said to Quentin. Calamity is an amazing high, too. Sometimes I feel *so* well, so powerful, it's as if I could jump out of my skin. Am I going crazy, or what? Is it all this attention and coddling I'm getting from everybody, like a child's dream of being loved? Is it the drugs? I know it sounds crazy but sometimes I think this is a *fantastic* experience, he said shyly; but there was also the bad taste in the mouth, the pressure in the head and at the back of the neck, the red, bleeding gums, the painful, if pink-lobed, breathing, and his ivory pallor, color of white chocolate. Among those who wept when told over the phone that he was back in the hospital were Kate and Stephen (who'd been called by Quentin), and Ellen, Victor, Aileen, and Lewis (who were called by Kate), and Xavier and Ursula (who were called by Stephen). Among those who didn't weep were Hilda, who said that she'd just learned that her seventy-five-year-old aunt was dying of the disease, which she'd contracted from a transfusion given during her successful double bypass of five years ago, and Frank and Donny and Betsy, but this didn't mean, according to Tanya, that they weren't moved and appalled, and Quentin thought they might not be coming soon to the hospital but would send presents; the room, he was in a private room this time, was filling up with flowers, and plants, and books, and tapes. The high tide of barely suppressed acrimony of the last weeks at home subsided into the routines of hospital visiting, though more than a few resented Quentin's having charge of the visiting book (but it was Quentin who had the idea, Lewis pointed out); now, to insure a steady stream of visitors, preferably no more than two at a time (this, the rule in all hospitals, wasn't enforced here, at least on this floor; whether out of kindness or inefficiency, no one could decide), Quentin had to be called first, to get one's time slot, there was no more casual dropping by. And his mother could no longer be prevented from taking a plane and installing herself in a hotel near the hospital; but he seemed to mind her daily presence less than expected, Quentin said; said Ellen it's we who mind, do you suppose she'll stay long. It was easier to be generous with each other visiting him here in the hospital, as Donny pointed out, than at home, where one minded never being alone with him; coming here, in our twos and twos, there's no doubt about what our role is, how we should be, collective, funny, distracting, undemanding, light, it's important to be light, for in all this dread there is gaiety, too, as the poet said, said Kate. (His eyes, his glittering eyes, said Lewis.) His eyes looked dull, extinguished, Wesley said to Xavier, but Betsy said his face, not just his eyes, looked soulful, warm; whatever is there, said Kate, I've never been so aware of his eyes; and Stephen said, I'm afraid of what my eyes show, the way I watch him, with too much intensity, or a phony kind of casualness, said Victor. And, unlike at home, he was clean-shaven each morning, at whatever hour they visited him; his curly hair was always combed; but he complained that the nurses had changed since he was here the last time, and that he didn't like the change, he wanted everyone to be the same. The room was furnished now with some of his personal effects (odd word for one's things, said Ellen), and Tanya brought drawings and a letter from her nine-year-old dyslexic son, who was writing now, since she'd purchased a computer; and Donny brought champagne and some helium balloons, which were anchored to the foot of his bed; tell me about something that's going on, he said, waking up from a nap to find Donny and Kate at the side of his bed, beaming at him; tell me a story, he said wistfully, said Donny, who couldn't think of anything to say; *you're* the story, Kate said. And Xavier brought an eighteenth-century Guatemalan wooden statue of Saint Sebastian with upcast eyes and open mouth, and when Tanya said what's that, a tribute to eros past, Xavier said where I come from Sebastian is venerated as a protector against pestilence. Pestilence symbolized by arrows? Symbolized by arrows. All people remember is the body of a beautiful youth bound to a tree, pierced by arrows (of which he always seems oblivious, Tanya interjected), people forget that the story continues, Xavier continued, that when the Christian women came to bury the martyr they found him still alive and nursed him back to health. And he said, according to Stephen, I didn't know Saint Sebastian didn't die. It's undeniable, isn't it, said Kate on the phone to Stephen, the fascination of the dying. It makes me ashamed. We're learning how to die, said Hilda, I'm not ready to learn, said Aileen; and Lewis, who was coming straight from the other hospital, the hospital where Max was still being kept in ICU, met Tanya getting out of the elevator on the tenth floor, and as they walked together down the shiny corridor past the open doors, averting their eyes from the other patients sunk in their beds, with tubes in their noses, irradiated by the bluish light from the television sets, the thing I can't bear to think about, Tanya said to Lewis, is someone dying with the TV on.

* * *

He has that strange, unnerving detachment now, said Ellen, that's what upsets me, even though it makes it easier to be with him. Sometimes he was querulous. I can't stand them coming in here taking my blood every morning, what are they doing with all that blood, he is reported to have said; but where was his anger, Jan wondered. Mostly he was lovely to be with, always saying how are *you,* how are you feeling. He's so sweet now, said Aileen. He's so nice, said Tanya. (Nice, nice, groaned Paolo.) At first he was very ill, but he was rallying, according to Stephen's best information, there was no fear of his not recovering this time, and the doctor spoke of his being discharged from the hospital in another ten days if all went well, and the mother was persuaded to fly back to Mississippi, and Quentin was readying the penthouse for his return. And he was still writing his diary, not showing it to anyone, though Tanya, first to arrive one late-winter morning, and finding him dozing, peeked, and was horrified, according to Greg, not by anything she read but by a progressive change in his handwriting: in the recent pages, it was becoming spidery, less legible, and some lines of script wandered and tilted about the page. I was thinking, Ursula said to Quentin, that the difference between a story and a painting or photograph is that in a story you can write, He's still alive. But in a painting or a photo you can't show "still." You can just show him being alive. He's still alive, Stephen said.

# GARRISON KEILLOR
(1942– )

From 1974 to 1987, Garrison Keillor was the host and principal writer for the weekly radio program *A Prairie Home Companion* broadcast live by Minnesota Public Radio. At the height of its popularity it was broadcast by two hundred stations with an audience of some four million listeners. The highlight of each show was Keillor's winsome monologue, "News from Lake Wobegon," essentially straight-faced humor and gentle satire of the absurdities and pathos of life in a small town. These monologues, as well as stories and sketches, were gathered and published in several collections: *Happy to Be Here* (1982), *Leaving Home* (1987), and *We Are Still Married: Stories & Letters* (1989). His 1985 novel *Lake Wobegon Days* was a best-seller, as were *WLT: A Radio Romance* (1991); *Wobegon Boy* (1997); *The Book of Guys* (1993), a series of sketches on men; and *Me: By Jimmy (Big Boy) Valente, Governor of Minnesota, as Told to Garrison Keillor* (1999), a satire on the just-elected Jesse (The Body) Ventura, governor of Minnesota.

Gary Edward Keillor was born in Anoka, Minnesota, to parents who were members of a strict fundamentalist sect, the Plymouth Brethren. He studied at the University of Minnesota, where he worked at the campus radio station. He received a B.A. in 1966 and pursued graduate work for another two years. He married in 1965, had one child, and divorced in 1976. He remarried in 1985. In 1987 he left Minnesota and his radio show to live in New York City and to devote more time to his writing. He returned to Minnesota in 1989 to resume production of his radio program.

## The Tip-Top Club

THE IDEA of pouring warm soapy water into overshoes and wearing them around the house to give yourself a relaxing footbath while you work is one that all fans of WLT's

"The Tip-Top Club" seem to have remembered over the years, along with the idea that if you're depressed you should sit down and write a letter to yourself praising all of your good qualities, and the idea of puffing cigarette smoke at violets to prevent aphids.

Every evening, Sunday through Thursday, at 10:00 P.M. ("and now . . . direct from the Tip-Top studio in downtown Minneapolis . . ."), WLT played the Tip-Top theme song—

Whenever you feel blue, think of something nice to do;
That's the motto of the Tip-Top crew.
Don't let it get you down, wear a smile and not a frown,
And you'll be feeling tip-top too.

—and Bud Swenson came on the air with his friendly greeting: "Good evening, Tip-Toppers, and welcome to *your* show. This is your faithful recording secretary, chief cook and bottle-washer, Bud Swenson, calling the Club to order and waiting to hear from you." And of the hundreds of calls that came in on the Tip-Top line (847-8677, or T-I-P-T-O-P-S), and of the fifty or sixty that actually got on the air, many were from listeners who simply wanted Bud to know they were doing fine, feeling good, and enjoying the show. "And—oh yes," they might add, "we got our boots on," referring to overshoes.

Every night, Bud got at least one request for a copy of the poem a woman had written about writing a letter to yourself. It was called "Dear Me," it was a hundred and eight lines long, WLT mailed out 18,000 copies of it in the six months after it was written (May 18, 1956), and it began:

When I look around these days
And hear blame instead of praise
(For to bless is so much harder than to damn),
It makes me feel much better
To write myself a letter
And tell myself how good I really am.

Dear Me, Sorry it's been
So long since I took pen
In hand and scribbled off a word or two.
I'm busy with my work and such,
But I need to keep in touch
Cause the very closest friend I have is you.

Through times of strife and toil,
You've always remained loyal.
And stuck with me when other friends were far,
And because we are so close,
I think of you the most
And of just how near and dear to me you are.

As for puffing smoke at violets, it touched off a debate that lasted for years. For months after it was suggested by an elderly woman, Bud got call after call from listeners who said that smoke-puffing would *not* discourage aphids; that even if it would, there are *better* ways to discourage aphids; and, worse, that it might encourage young people to take up smoking.

The pro-puffers replied hotly that: (1) you don't have to *inhale* in order to *puff* on a plant; (2) the treatment should be given only once a week or so; and (3) anyone who wants to smoke probably will go ahead and do it *anyway,* violets or *no* violets.

As time passed, the issue became confused in the minds of some Tip-Toppers, who came to think that Bud himself was a smoker (he was not). To the very end (November 26, 1969), he got calls from listeners wanting to know if he didn't agree with them that smoking is a filthy habit. (He did.)

At Bud's retirement party, Roy Elmore, Jr., president of WLT, presented him with twenty-five potted violet plants, one for each year of service.

Controversy was the very thing that distinguished "The Tip-Top Club." It had none. Edgar Elmore, the founder of WLT, abhorred controversy, and the terms of his will bound his heir, Roy Jr., to abhor it also. Though Edgar never heard Bud's show, having died in 1940, eleven years before the Club was formed, he certainly would have enjoyed it very much, as Roy Jr. told Bud frequently. No conversation about religion or politics was permitted, nor were callers allowed to be pessimistic or moody on the air. If a person started in to be moody, he or she was told firmly and politely to hang up and *listen* to the show and it would cheer him or her up. Few had to be told.

Vacations and pets were favorite Tip-Top topics, along with household hints, children, gardening, memories of long ago, favorite foods, great persons, good health and how to keep it, and of course the weather. Even when the weather was bad, even in times of national crisis, the Tip-Toppers always came up with cheerful things to talk about.

One reason for the show's cheery quality and the almost complete absence of crank calls was Bud's phone policy. After the first year he never divulged the Tip-Top phone number over the air (nor, for that matter, over the phone). In fact, it was an unlisted number, and one could obtain it only from another Tip-Topper. This tended to limit participation to those who understood the rules and accepted them.

The main reason for the show's cheery quality was Bud himself and his radio personality. His voice wasn't deep but his style of speaking was warm and reassuring, and he always tried to look on the bright side, even as host of "The Ten O'Clock News" (starting July 1, 1944). On the newscast, Bud played up features and human-interest stories and he skimmed over what he called "The grim stuff." He might devote fifteen seconds to a major earthquake and three minutes to a story about a chimpanzee whose finger paintings had been exhibited at a New York gallery and fooled all the critics. His approach offended a few listeners ("the *New York Times* crowd," he called them), but most people liked it. Bud pulled in fifty or sixty fan letters a week, more than all other WLT newscasters combined.

After reading a few headlines, he'd say, "Oh, here's something you might be interested in," and he'd tell about a dog that had actually learned to sing and sing on key, or read a story about the world's largest known tomato, or about a three-year-old kid who was a whiz at chess; and then he'd talk about a dog that *he* knew, or a kid *he* knew, or a tomato *he* had seen, and then he'd say, "Well, I don't know. Let me know what *you* think."

At first, some letters said, "What happened to the news?" but they quickly dwindled. ("Anger doesn't last," Roy Jr. said. "Only love is lasting. Angry people spout off once and then get over it. The people who love you are loyal to the end.") Most of the letters were about a story Bud had read: the letter writer described a similar experience that *he* had had, or quoted a poem or a saying that the story had reminded *her* of—and Bud made sure to read every one of those letters on the air. One day in the winter of 1950, Roy Jr. said, "It's time to close down the News. You need a new shingle."

* * *

According to Bud, the Tip-Top Club was the idea of a woman in St. Paul. "We love your show," she wrote in January 1951, "and feel that truly it is our show too. When I listen, as I do every night, I feel as if I am among friends and we are all members of a club that gathers around our radios. We share ideas and experiences, we inspire each other with beautiful thoughts, and I only wish I could meet personally every one of the wonderful people who also write to you, for when they write to you, they are truly writing to me also."

Bud read her letter on the air, and listeners responded favorably to the idea of a club. (Since he had often referred to his stories as "News-Toppers," Bud suggested the name Tip-Top Club and it stuck.)

Nobody at WLT quite remembers who came up with the phone idea. WLT had been doing remote broadcasts over telephone lines for years, starting with the "WLT Barn Dance and Bean Feed" in 1938; all that needed to be done to put a telephone signal on the air was wrap the bare end of one wire around the bare end of another. One night, Bud's engineer, Harlan, did just that, and a woman's voice came on describing dark thunderstorm clouds moving east toward Minneapolis.

"Is it raining there yet?" asked Bud.

"No," she said, "but it will be, any minute now. But I've got my boots on!"

Roy Jr. was leery of the phone idea from the start. "Every foulmouth in town will be slobbering into his telephone for the chance to get on the air," he told Bud. "Every creep who writes on toilet walls, every dummy, every drunken son-of-a-bitch from hell to breakfast. We'll be running a nuthouse. We'll lose our license in a week."

Then Harlan came forward with his tape loop. Harlan was one who seldom cracked a smile, but when WLT bought its first tape recorders, two big Ampexes, in 1949, he was like a boy with a new toy. He recorded everything on tape, and he played around with it, and his favorite game was to play around with Bud's voice. At first, he got a kick out of playing Bud's voice at a faster speed so he sounded like a hysterical woman; then backward, which sounded like Russian; then slower, so Bud sounded drunk; and then Harlan became fascinated with editing Bud. With a razor blade in hand, Harlan went through thousands of feet of Bud tape, finding a word here and a word there, and a vowel sound here and a consonant there, making new words, and snipping and splicing hundreds of little bits of tape to form a few sentences spoken in Bud's own voice, in which Bud spoke, in his own warm and reassuring tones, about having carnal relations with dogs, cats, tomatoes, small boys, chimpanzees, overshoes, fruit jars, lawn mowers. It was disgusting, and also an amazing feat of patience. In two years, Harlan assembled just three minutes of Bud.

Harlan solved the problem of loonies by the simple trick of threading a continuous loop of tape through two machines sitting side by side. Bud and his telephone caller could be recorded on the first machine, which fed the tape to the second machine, which played it back on the air three seconds later. If the caller said something not befitting the show, Harlan, listening to the first machine, would have three seconds in which to turn off the second. "Can't beat it," said Harlan. "I hit the button and they die like rats."

Nevertheless, Roy Jr. was on hand for the first taped show and supervised the Stop button personally. "I trust you," he told Harlan, "but the way you talk, you might not notice profanity until it is too late." Bud explained the tape loop on the air and invited calls as Roy Jr. hunched over the machine, his finger in position, like a ship's gunner waiting for incoming aircraft. The first caller was a man who wanted to know more about the loop and if it might have useful applications in the home. He got flustered in mid-call and stopped. On his radio at home, he heard his own voice, delayed by tape, saying what he had said three seconds before. "Please turn your radio down," Bud said. It was a line that he was to repeat thousands of times in the next eighteen years.

"This has been an historic event," Roy Jr. said proudly when the show was over. He had cut off just two calls, the first one after the words "What in hell—" and the second at the mention of the Pope ("Probably nothing, but I wasn't about to take chances," he explained to Harlan).

Most of the calls were about the tape loop, with all callers favoring its use, howbeit with some trepidation that a mechanical failure or employee carelessness might lead to tragedy. Several were worried that certain persons might try to fool Bud, opening their calls with a few innocuous remarks and then slipping in a fast one. ("Thanks for the tip," said Bud. "I'm confident we can handle them.")

Communists, people agreed, might be particularly adept at subverting the tape loop. Communists, one man reported, learned these techniques at special schools, including how to insinuate their beliefs into a conversation without anyone being the wiser. ("Appreciate your concern, sir, and, believe me, we'll be on guard.")

* * *

It was three weeks before Roy Jr. turned over the guard duty to Harlan and Alice the switchboard girl. Alice was to screen all callers: no kids, no foreign accents, and nobody who seemed unusually intense or determined to get on the air. Harlan was the second line of defense. Roy Jr. instructed him to listen carefully to each call and try to anticipate what the caller was driving at; and if the conversation should drift toward deep waters—hit the button. No politics. No religion except for general belief in the Almighty, thankfulness for His gifts, wonder at His creation, etc. No criticism of others, not even the caller's kith and kin. Roy Jr. didn't want them to get dragged into family squabbles and maybe have to give equal time to a miffed husband or mother-in-law giving *their* side of it. No promotion of products, services, clubs, fund drives, or events.

"What's left to talk about?" Harlan wondered. "Not a goddamn helluva lot."

And, at first, the Tip-Toppers seemed unsure of what to talk about too. "Just thought I'd call and say hi," one would say. "Great. What are you doing tonight?" Bud would ask. "Oh, not much," the caller would reply. "Just sitting here listening to the show."

Gradually, though, they loosened up, and when Bud said to a caller, "Tell me about yourself," the caller generally did. Most Tip-Toppers seemed to be older persons leading quiet lives and keeping busy with hobbies and children and grandchildren, and, judging from the interest in household hints, their homes were neat as a pin and in good repair. They were unfailingly courteous ("The distinguished gentleman who spoke earlier on cats was very well-informed on most points, but I feel he may have overlooked the fact that cats will not shed if brushed regularly"), and soon Harlan was taking his finger off the button and relaxing in the control room and even leaving for a smoke now and then. The few nuts who called in Alice soon recognized by voice—she enjoyed talking with them, and after a few conversations they always asked for her and not for Bud. They sent her gifts, usually pamphlets or books but occasionally a box of cookies or a cake, which, on Harlan's advice, she did not eat. Three months went by, and not a single nut got past the loop; Roy Jr. raised Bud's salary and even gave him a contract—six months with an option of renewing for three more.

"It is so pleasant in this day and age when we are subjected to so much dissension and mud-slinging to take a rest and listen to a show that follows the old adage 'If you can't say something nice, don't say anything at all,' " a woman wrote to Bud. "I am a faithful listener-in and now have a telephone in my bedroom so that I can participate after turning in. I go to sleep listening to the show, and I believe I sleep better knowing it is there."

Sleep was a major item on the Tip-Top agenda: how much is needed? how to get it? what position is best? Many scorned the eight-hour quota as wasteful and self-indulgent and said four or five is enough for any adult. "The secret of longevity is to stay out of bed," said one oldster.

Most members disagreed; they felt they needed more sleep, and one call asking for a cure for insomnia would set off an avalanche of sleep tips—warm milk, a hot bath, a brisk walk, a brief prayer, a mild barbiturate—each of which had gotten the caller through some difficult nights. A doctor (he called in often, usually to settle somebody's hash on the value of vitamins, chiropractic medicine, and vegetarian diets) offered the opinion that worry causes 95 percent of all sleeplessness. He suggested that Tip-Toppers who go to bed with restless thoughts should fill their minds instead with pleasant memories and plans for vacations.

As for vacations, there were strong voices in the Club who argued that a Minnesotan's vacation money should be kept at home, not spent abroad. The rest of the world, it was said, could be seen perfectly well in the pages of the *National Geographic*. There was general agreement, however, that the purpose of a vacation is to rest and enjoy yourself and not necessarily to visit family members or to catch up on work around the house.

Housework was important, though, a sure antidote for grief and worry and feeling sorry for yourself. To scrub a floor or paint a wall or make a pie was better than going to a psychiatrist. At the same time, there was no use taking more time than necessary to get the job done, and every job had its shortcuts. "What's a quick way to get bubble gum out of hair?" a woman would ask, and minutes later, a legion of women who had faced that very problem would rally to her side. Give the Club a problem, and in short order the Club solved it, whether it be a wobbly table, a grape-juice stain, or a treacherous stair tread, and then it suggested two or three things you could do in the time you had saved, such as making lovely and useful gifts from egg cartons, Popsicle sticks, and bottle caps.

And then there were hobbies. Bud often asked callers, particularly the shyer ones, to talk about their hobbies. He *never* asked about their occupations, not after the first few times: the answers were always apologetic-sounding—"Oh, I'm just a truck driver," or "Oh, I just work for the Post Office. But ask someone what he did in his spare time and the answer might be good for five or ten minutes.

Club members tended to be collectors. It seemed as if every object of which there was more than one sort, type, shape, brand, color, or configuration was the object of some collector's affection. "I have matchbook covers from more than thirty-five countries." "Some of my fruit jars have been appraised at ten dollars and more." "I hope someday to open a license-plate museum." "I plan to donate my nails to the historical society."

Bird-watching, a sort of collecting, was also popular, and Bud had to put a damper on the bird people, they were so fanatical. One might call in and say, "I wonder if anyone out there can help me identify a bird I heard this morning. Its call sounded something like this—" and then whistle, *"twee-twee, twee-twee,"* and suddenly Alice was swamped with calls, some identifying the bird, some saying they had heard it too and didn't know what it was either, and others wondering if the bird's call perhaps wasn't more of a *"twee-it, twee-it."*

* * *

Five nights a week, from 10:00 P.M. to sign-off, Bud sat in Studio B behind a table, the earphones clamped on, and scribbled notes on a pad as one Tip-Topper after another poured it out. After the first few months of the tape loop, he quit reading news stories, and after the Club had hit full stride, telephonically speaking, he himself said very little, aside from an occasional question. He became a listener. For eighteen years, from 1951 to 1969, he sat in the same chair, in the same position (slightly hunched, head down and supported with one hand, the other hand writing, feet on the floor), and heard the same stuff, until he seemed to lose whatever personality he had in the beginning. He became neutral. "A goddamn ghost," Harlan said. "When he comes in, I don't even see him anymore. He don't really exist, except on the air."

At the age of sixty-five he quietly retired. He didn't mention his retirement on "The Tip-Top Club." Tip-Toppers didn't know he was gone until they tuned in one night and heard Wayne Bargy. Wayne was the only WLT announcer willing to take the show. Others had subbed for Bud before when he took vacations and they noted a certain snideness, a meanness, among the Tip-Toppers, who implied in their conversations that the new man, while adequate, was certainly no Bud. "Bud would *know* that," a caller might say. "Bud wouldn't have said that." "Maybe I'll talk to Bud about it. When is Bud coming back?"

So one night out of the clear blue it was "The Tip-Top Club with Wayne Bargy," and one can only imagine the shock that Bud's fans felt to hear a new theme song (Simon and Garfunkel's "Sounds of Silence") instead of the old Tip-Top song, and then Wayne Bargy delivering a tribute to Bud as if Bud were dead. He called him "an innovator" and "a genius" and "a man who was totally concerned about others." "I loved him," said Wayne. "He was a totally understanding, giving type of man. He was someone I could always talk to about my problems.

"Friends, I know you're as disappointed as I am that Bud won't be here with us anymore, and let me tell you, I'd give anything if he were, and I want to be honest with you and admit that I've never done this type of show before and I don't know how good I am at talking with people, and maybe some of you will even wonder what I'm doing in the radio business and I have to admit that you may have a point there, but I would rather be honest about this than sit here and pretend that I'm somebody that I'm not, because I think that honesty has a place in radio, I don't think a radio personality has to be some sort of star or an idol or anything, I think he can be a real person, and even if I should fail and would quit this show tomorrow, I'd still be satisfied knowing I had done it my way and not tried to be like somebody else."

The Tip-Toppers heard him out; there was a minute or so of lull at the switchboard (perhaps they were too dazed to dial, or else they were composing carefully what they would say); and then the first wave struck. Even Harlan was surprised by the abuse Wayne got.

First call: "Why wait until tomorrow? Why not quit tonight?" (Wayne: "Thanks for calling.") A man said, "Oh, don't worry that we'll consider you a star, Wayne. Don't worry about that for one minute!" (Wayne: "Okay, I won't.") A woman said it was the worst night of her life. (Wayne: "It's hard for all of us.") "You make me absolutely sick. You're the biggest mistake they've made down there!" ("I appreciate your honesty, sir. I don't necessarily agree with that statement, but I think it's important that you feel you can be honest with me.")

By midnight, Wayne had logged almost a hundred calls, most of them quite brief and most cut off by Harlan. The longest exchange was with a woman who wanted to know where Bud was. Wayne said that Bud had retired.

SHE: Then I'd like his number.

HE: I'm sorry?

SHE: I want Bud's phone number.

HE: I—ma'am. I wish I could give you that but I can't, it's against company policy. We don't give out announcers' home numbers to the general public.

SHE: Well, *I'm* not the general public. I'm Grace Ritter and he knows me even if you don't.

HE: I'm sorry, but—

SHE: And this is his show, and I think he has a right to know what you're doing to it! (click)

During the midnight newscast, Roy Jr. called and told Wayne he was doing great. "I knew it'd be tough sledding the first night," he said, "but you stick in there. They're sore about Bud, but in three weeks they'll get tired and give up and all you'll get is flowers."

It didn't work that way. For one thing, Wayne had little interest in the old Tip-Top topics. He was divorced and lived in an efficiency apartment (no lawn to keep up, no maintenance responsibilities) and had no pets or children. His major interest was psychology. "People fascinate me," he said. ("You don't fascinate *me,*" someone said.) He read psychology books and talked about them on the air. He said that he was undergoing therapy, and it had helped him to understand himself better. ("What's to understand?")

His other interests were eating out in foreign restaurants, attending films, and planning a trip to the Far East. ("How about leaving tomorrow?") Occasionally, he got a friendly caller who also liked Szechuan cuisine or Carl Rogers or Woody Allen movies, and he reached out and hung onto that call for dear life. Those calls would last for fifteen, twenty minutes, as if the caller were an old college chum he hadn't heard from in ages, but when he hung up, the Tip-Toppers were waiting, more determined than ever.

THEM: This show is so boring. You talk about stuff that nobody but you is interested in.

HIM: I really think you're mistaken about that, at least I hope you are, but more importantly, I think that I would have no business being here if I *didn't* talk about things that interest me, because, when all is said and done, I do have to be myself.

THEM: That's the problem, Wayne. Yourself. You're dull.

HIM: Well, I grant you I'm not slick or polished, and I'm not a comedian, but that's not my job. Basically, I'm a communicator, and whatever my faults or failures in relating to people, I do try to be positive.

THEM: You're positively boring.

HIM: Well, let's talk about that. Define your terms. What do you mean by "boring"?

What they meant was Wayne Bargy. For all he said about keeping an open mind ("You got a hole in your head, Wayne!") and not condemning others but trying to understand people who may be different from ourselves ("You're different from everybody, Wayne! You're a different species!"), the Club kept a united front against him.

One night, Wayne casually mentioned that it was his first anniversary hosting the show. The switchboard sizzled. One man said it was time for Club members to take action, and before Harlan could cut him off he announced a time and a place for the meeting.

Word came back that the Tip-Toppers had elected officers and were putting together a mailing list for a monthly newsletter. It was said the Club was assigning members to "listening squads" with each squad assigned two hours of "Wayne duty" a week. The squad members were responsible for listening to the show and calling in frequently. The newsletter printed a list of things to say.

It was harder on Harlan than on Wayne. Harlan had started to assemble a special Wayne Bargy tape, but he had no time to work on it. What with Wayne giving out the phone number every fifteen minutes, the show was attracting oddballs, in addition to the legions of Tip-Toppers, and Harlan was cutting calls off the air by the dozens. One night, after Wayne had talked about his divorce (he said that he and his wife didn't "relate to each other sexually"), there passed a long half hour during which no call was fit to broadcast. "I was slapping them down like barnyard flies. We were up to our ears in crazies," said Harlan. "Finally, my fingers got sore, and Alice pulled the plug on the switchboard and her and me sat down and had a cup of coffee and left that poor dumb SOB sit and die by himself."

Wayne talked a long time that night. He said he'd had a typical middle-class upbringing until he went to college, which opened his mind up to new possibilities. He said he had gone into radio because it had tremendous possibilities for creative communication. This show was a tremendous opportunity to get people to open up their minds. He viewed himself as an educator of sorts.

"I'll be honest," he said. "The past year has been rough. There's a lot of anger and violence out there—and I don't say people shouldn't feel that way, but I do feel people should be willing to change. Life is change. We all change. I've changed. Frankly, when I started doing this show, I didn't come off very well. I didn't communicate well. I had a hard time relating to working-class people. I think I've improved. I'm learning. I've put my feelings on the line, and I've benefited from it. I'm going to keep on trying."

He did keep on trying, and the Tip-Toppers kept calling—"We won't go away, Wayne!" they said, and he said, "I don't want you to go away. I want you to stay and let's get to know each other." That summer WLT did a survey that showed that most of the Tip-Top Club audience was over forty (72 percent), the least desirable age group to advertisers, and in July the station switched the Tip-Top slot to what it called "a modified middle-of-the-road pop-rock format" with a disc jockey who never talked except to give time, temperature, and commercials. His name was Michael Keske, but he never said it on the air.

# TIM O'BRIEN
(1946– )

The long U.S. military involvement in Vietnam was one of the most culture-wrenching experiences of American history. It haunts the fiction of Tim O'Brien, and few writers have explored its impact and effects more imaginatively and thoughtfully than he. O'Brien's work has been an ongoing attempt to find a language and narrative form for an often maddening, absurd, and tragic experience that has affected us all.

William Timothy O'Brien was born in Austin, Minnesota, son of an insurance salesman and a teacher. He attended Macalester College and graduated summa cum laude in 1968. He was immediately drafted into the army and served in combat in Vietnam. He rose to the rank of sergeant and won a Purple Heart after a shrapnel wound near My Lai. After his discharge in 1970, he began graduate work at Harvard.

O'Brien's first book was a mixture of memoir and fiction, *If I Die in a Combat Zone, Box Me Up and Ship Me Home* (1973). His first novel, *Northern Lights* (1975), met mostly critical reviews, but his second, *Going After Cacciato* (1978), won the National Book Award. His other publications include *The Nuclear Age* (1985), a novel; *The Things They Carried* (1990), a series of interlocking stories; *In the Lake of the Woods* (1994), a novel; and *Tomcat in Love* (1998), his most recent novel. O'Brien lives and works in Boston.

## The Things They Carried

First Lieutenant Jimmy Cross carried letters from a girl named Martha, a junior at Mount Sebastian College in New Jersey. They were not love letters, but Lieutenant Cross was hoping, so he kept them folded in plastic at the bottom of his rucksack. In the late afternoon, after a day's march, he would dig his foxhole, wash his hands under a canteen, unwrap the letters, hold them with the tips of his fingers, and spend the last hour of light pretending. He would imagine romantic camping trips into the White Mountains in New Hampshire. He would sometimes taste the envelope flaps, knowing her tongue had been there. More than anything, he wanted Martha to love him as he loved her, but the letters were mostly chatty, elusive on the matter of love. She was a virgin, he was almost sure. She was an English major at Mount Sebastian, and she wrote beautifully about her professors and roommates and midterm exams, about her respect for Chaucer and her great affection for Virginia Woolf. She often quoted lines of poetry; she never mentioned the war, except to say, Jimmy, take care of yourself. The letters weighed ten ounces. They were signed "Love, Martha," but Lieutenant Cross understood that "Love" was only a way of signing and did not mean what he sometimes pretended it meant. At dusk, he would carefully return the letters to his rucksack. Slowly, a bit distracted, he would get up and move among his men, checking the perimeter, then at full dark he would return to his hole and watch the night and wonder if Martha was a virgin.

The things they carried were largely determined by necessity. Among the necessities or near necessities were P-38 can openers, pocket knives, heat tabs, wrist watches, dog tags, mosquito repellant, chewing gum, candy, cigarettes, salt tablets, packets of Kool-Aid, lighters, matches, sewing kits, Military Payment Certificates, C rations, and two or three canteens of water. Together, these items weighed between fifteen and twenty pounds, depending upon a man's habits or rate of metabolism. Henry Dobbins, who was a big man, carried extra rations; he was especially fond of canned peaches in heavy syrup over pound cake. Dave Jensen, who practiced field hygiene, carried a tooth-brush, dental floss, and several hotel-size bars of soap he'd stolen on R&R in Sydney, Australia. Ted Lavender, who was scared, carried tranquilizers until he was shot in the head outside the village of Than Khe in mid-April. By necessity, and because it was SOP, they all carried steel helmets that weighed five pounds including the liner and camouflage cover. They carried the standard fatigue jackets and trousers. Very few carried underwear. On their feet they carried jungle boots—2.1 pounds—and Dave Jensen carried three pairs of socks and a can of Dr. Scholl's foot powder as a precaution against trench foot. Until he was shot, Ted Lavender carried six or seven ounces of premium dope, which for him was a necessity. Mitchell Sanders, the RTO, carried condoms. Norman Bowker carried a diary. Rat Kiley carried comic books. Kiowa, a devout Baptist, carried an illustrated New Testament that had been presented to him by his father, who taught Sunday school in Oklahoma City, Oklahoma. As a hedge against bad times, however, Kiowa also carried his grandmother's distrust of the white man, his grandfather's old hunting hatchet. Necessity dictated. Because the land was mined and booby-trapped, it was SOP for each man to carry a steel-centered, nylon-covered flak jacket, which weighed 6.7 pounds, but which on hot days seemed much heavier. Because you could die so quickly, each man carried at least one large compress bandage, usually in the helmet band for easy access. Because the nights were cold, and because the monsoons were wet, each carried a green plastic poncho that could be used as a raincoat or ground sheet or makeshift tent. With its quilted liner, the poncho weighed almost two pounds, but it was worth every ounce. In April, for instance, when Ted Lavender was shot, they used his poncho to wrap him up, then to carry him across the paddy, then to lift him into the chopper that took him away.

* * *

They were called legs or grunts.

To carry something was to "hump" it, as when Lieutenant Jimmy Cross humped his love for Martha up the hills and through the swamps. In its intransitive form, "to hump" meant "to walk," or "to march," but it implied burdens far beyond the intransitive.

Almost everyone humped photographs. In his wallet, Lieutenant Cross carried two photographs of Martha. The first was a Kodachrome snapshot signed "Love," though he knew better. She stood against a brick wall. Her eyes were gray and neutral, her lips slightly open as she stared straight-on at the camera. At night, sometimes, Lieutenant Cross wondered who had taken the picture, because he knew she had boyfriends, because he loved her so much, and because he could see the shadow of the picture taker spreading out against the brick wall. The second photograph had been clipped from the 1968 Mount Sebastian yearbook. It was an action shot—women's volleyball—and Martha was bent horizontal to the floor, reaching, the palms of her hands in sharp focus, the tongue taut, the expression frank and competitive. There was no visible sweat. She wore white gym shorts. Her legs, he thought, were almost certainly the legs of a virgin, dry and without hair, the left knee cocked and carrying her entire weight, which was just over one hundred pounds. Lieutenant Cross remembered touching that left knee. A dark theater, he remembered, and the movie was *Bonnie and Clyde,* and Martha wore a tweed skirt, and during the final scene, when he touched her knee, she turned and looked at him in a sad, sober way that made him pull his hand back, but he would always remember the feel of the tweed skirt and the knee beneath it and the sound of the gunfire that killed Bonnie and Clyde, how embarrassing it was, how slow and oppressive. He remembered kissing her good night at the dorm door. Right then, he thought, he should've done something brave. He should've carried her up the stairs to her room and tied her to the bed and touched that left knee all night long. He should've risked it. Whenever he looked at the photographs, he thought of new things he should've done.

* * *

What they carried was partly a function of rank, partly of field specialty.

As a first lieutenant and platoon leader, Jimmy Cross carried a compass, maps, code books, binoculars, and a .45-caliber pistol that weighed 2.9 pounds fully loaded. He carried a strobe light and the responsibility for the lives of his men.

As an RTO, Mitchell Sanders carried the PRC-25 radio, a killer, twenty-six pounds with its battery.

As a medic, Rat Kiley carried a canvas satchel filled with morphine and plasma and malaria tablets and surgical tape and comic books and all the things a medic must carry, including M&M's for especially bad wounds, for a total weight of nearly twenty pounds.

As a big man, therefore a machine gunner, Henry Dobbins carried the M-60, which weighed twenty-three pounds unloaded, but which was almost always loaded. In addition, Dobbins carried between ten and fifteen pounds of ammunition draped in belts across his chest and shoulders.

As PFCs or Spec 4s, most of them were common grunts and carried the standard M-16 gas-operated assault rifle. The weapon weighed 7.5 pounds unloaded, 8.2 pounds with its full twenty-round magazine. Depending on numerous factors, such as topography and psychology, the riflemen carried anywhere from twelve to twenty magazines, usually in cloth bandoliers, adding on another 8.4 pounds at minimum, fourteen pounds at maximum. When it was available, they also carried M-16 maintenance gear—rods and steel brushes and swabs and tubes of LSA oil—all of which weighed about a pound. Among the grunts, some carried the M-79 grenade launcher, 5.9 pounds unloaded, a reasonably light weapon except for the ammunition, which was heavy. A single round weighed ten ounces. The typical load was twenty-five rounds. But Ted Lavender, who was scared, carried thirty-four rounds when he was shot and killed outside Than Khe, and he went down under an exceptional burden, more than twenty pounds of ammunition, plus the flak jacket and helmet and rations and water and toilet paper and tranquilizers and all the rest, plus the unweighed fear. He was dead weight. There was no twitching or flopping. Kiowa, who saw it happen, said it was like watching a rock fall, or a big sandbag or something—just boom, then down—not like the movies where the dead guy rolls around and does fancy spins and goes ass over teakettle—not like that, Kiowa said, the poor bastard just flat-fuck fell. Boom. Down. Nothing else. It was a bright morning in mid-April. Lieutenant Cross felt the pain. He blamed himself. They stripped off Lavender's canteens and ammo, all the heavy things, and Rat Kiley said the obvious, the guy's dead, and Mitchell Sanders used his radio to report one U.S. KIA and to request a chopper. Then they wrapped Lavender in his poncho. They carried him out to a dry paddy, established security, and sat smoking the dead man's dope until the chopper came. Lieutenant Cross kept to himself. He pictured Martha's smooth young face, thinking he loved her more than anything, more than his men, and now Ted Lavender was dead because he loved her so much and could not stop thinking about her. When the dust-off arrived, they carried Lavender aboard. Afterward they burned Than Khe. They marched until dusk, then dug their holes, and that night Kiowa kept explaining how you had to be there, how fast it was, how the poor guy just dropped like so much concrete. Boom-down, he said. Like cement.

* * *

In addition to the three standard weapons—the M-60, M-16, and M-79—they carried whatever presented itself, or whatever seemed appropriate as a means of killing or staying alive. They carried catch-as-catch-can. At various times, in various situations, they carried M-14s and CAR-15s and Swedish Ks and grease guns and captured AK-47s and Chi-Coms and RPGs and Simonov carbines and black-market Uzis and .38-caliber Smith & Wesson handguns and 66 mm LAWs and shotguns and silencers and blackjacks and bayonets and C-4 plastic explosives. Lee Strunk carried a slingshot; a weapon of last resort, he called it. Mitchell Sanders carried brass knuckles. Kiowa carried his grandfather's feathered hatchet. Every third or fourth man carried a Claymore antipersonnel mine—3.5 pounds with its firing device. They all carried fragmentation grenades—fourteen ounces each. They all carried at least one M-18 colored smoke grenade—twenty-four ounces. Some carried CS or teargas grenades. Some carried white-phosphorus grenades. They carried all they could bear, and then some, including a silent awe for the terrible power of the things they carried.

In the first week of April, before Lavender died, Lieutenant Jimmy Cross received a good-luck charm from Martha. It was a simple pebble, an ounce at most. Smooth to the touch, it was a milky-white color with flecks of orange and violet, oval-shaped, like a miniature egg. In the accompanying letter, Martha wrote that she had found the pebble on the Jersey shoreline, precisely where the land touched water at high tide, where things came together but also separated. It was this separate-but-together quality, she wrote, that had inspired her to pick up the pebble and to carry it in her breast pocket for several days, where it seemed weightless, and then to send it through the mail, by air, as a token of her truest feelings for him. Lieutenant Cross found this romantic. But he wondered what her truest feelings were, exactly, and what she meant by separate-but-together. He wondered how the tides and waves had come into play on that afternoon along the Jersey shoreline when Martha saw the pebble and bent down to rescue it from geology. He imagined bare feet. Martha was a poet, with the poet's sensibilities, and her feet would be brown and bare, the toenails unpainted, the eyes chilly and somber like the ocean in March, and though it was painful, he wondered who had been with her that afternoon. He imagined a pair of shadows moving along the strip of sand where things came together but also separated. It was phantom jealousy, he knew, but he couldn't help himself. He loved her so much. On the march, through the hot days of early April, he carried the pebble in his mouth, turning it with his tongue, tasting sea salts and moisture. His mind wandered. He had difficulty keeping his attention on the war. On occasion he would yell at his men to spread out the column, to keep their eyes open, but then he would slip away into daydreams, just pretending, walking barefoot along the Jersey shore, with Martha, carrying nothing. He would feel himself rising. Sun and waves and gentle winds, all love and lightness.

* * *

What they carried varied by mission.

When a mission took them to the mountains, they carried mosquito netting, machetes, canvas tarps, and extra bug juice.

If a mission seemed especially hazardous, or if it involved a place they knew to be bad, they carried everything they could. In certain heavily mined AOs, where the land was dense with Toe Poppers and Bouncing Betties, they took turns humping a twenty-eight-pound mine detector. With its headphones and big sensing plate, the equipment was a stress on the lower back and shoulders, awkward to handle, often useless because of the shrapnel in the earth, but they carried it anyway, partly for safety, partly for the illusion of safety.

On ambush, or other night missions, they carried peculiar little odds and ends. Kiowa always took along his New Testament and a pair of moccasins for silence. Dave Jensen carried night-sight vitamins high in carotin. Lee Strunk carried his slingshot; ammo, he claimed, would never be a problem. Rat Kiley carried brandy and M&M's. Until he was shot, Ted Lavender carried the starlight scope, which weighed 6.3 pounds with its aluminum carrying case. Henry Dobbins carried his girlfriend's pantyhose wrapped around his neck as a comforter. They all carried ghosts. When dark came, they would move out single file across the meadows and paddies to their ambush coordinates, where they would quietly set up the Claymores and lie down and spend the night waiting.

Other missions were more complicated and required special equipment. In mid-April, it was their mission to search out and destroy the elaborate tunnel complexes in the Than Khe area south of Chu Lai. To blow the tunnels, they carried one-pound blocks of pentrite high explosives, four blocks to a man, sixty-eight pounds in all. They carried wiring, detonators, and battery-powered clackers. Dave Jensen carried earplugs. Most often, before blowing the tunnels, they were ordered by higher command to search them, which was considered bad news, but by and large they just shrugged and carried out orders. Because he was a big man, Henry Dobbins was excused from tunnel duty. The others would draw numbers. Before Lavender died there were seventeen men in the platoon, and whoever drew the number seventeen would strip off his gear and crawl in head first with a flashlight and Lieutenant Cross's .45-caliber pistol. The rest of them would fan out as security. They would sit down or kneel, not facing the hole, listening to the ground beneath them, imagining cobwebs and ghosts, whatever was down there—the tunnel walls squeezing in—how the flashlight seemed impossibly heavy in the hand and how it was tunnel vision in the very strictest sense, compression in all ways, even time, and how you had to wiggle in—ass and elbows—a swallowed-up feeling—and how you found yourself worrying about odd things—will your flashlight go dead? Do rats carry rabies? If you screamed, how far would the sound carry? Would your buddies hear it? Would they have the courage to drag you out? In some respects, though not many, the waiting was worse than the tunnel itself. Imagination was a killer.

On April 16, when Lee Strunk drew the number seventeen, he laughed and muttered something and went down quickly. The morning was hot and very still. Not good, Kiowa said. He looked at the tunnel opening, then out across a dry paddy toward the village of Than Khe. Nothing moved. No clouds or birds or people. As they waited, the men smoked and drank Kool-Aid, not talking much, feeling sympathy for Lee Strunk but also feeling the luck of the draw. You win some, you lose some, said Mitchell Sanders, and sometimes you settle for a rain check. It was a tired line and no one laughed.

Henry Dobbins ate a tropical chocolate bar. Ted Lavender popped a tranquilizer and went off to pee.

After five minutes, Lieutenant Jimmy Cross moved to the tunnel, leaned down, and examined the darkness. Trouble, he thought—a cave-in maybe. And then suddenly, without willing it, he was thinking about Martha. The stresses and fractures, the quick collapse, the two of them buried alive under all that weight. Dense, crushing love. Kneeling, watching the hole, he tried to concentrate on Lee Strunk and the war, all the dangers, but his love was too much for him, he felt paralyzed, he wanted to sleep inside her lungs and breathe her blood and be smothered. He wanted her to be a virgin and not a virgin, all at once. He wanted to know her. Intimate secrets—why poetry? Why so sad? Why the grayness in her eyes? Why so alone? Not lonely, just alone—riding her bike across campus or sitting off by herself in the cafeteria. Even dancing, she danced alone—and it was the aloneness that filled him with love. He remembered telling her that one evening. How she nodded and looked away. And how, later, when he kissed her, she received the kiss without returning it, her eyes wide open, not afraid, not a virgin's eyes, just flat and uninvolved.

Lieutenant Cross gazed at the tunnel. But he was not there. He was buried with Martha under the white sand at the Jersey shore. They were pressed together, and the pebble in his mouth was her tongue. He was smiling. Vaguely, he was aware of how quiet the day was, the sullen paddies, yet he could not bring himself to worry about matters of security. He was beyond that. He was just a kid at war, in love. He was twenty-two years old. He couldn't help it.

A few moments later Lee Strunk crawled out of the tunnel. He came up grinning, filthy but alive. Lieutenant Cross nodded and closed his eyes while the others clapped Strunk on the back and made jokes about rising from the dead.

Worms, Rat Kiley said. Right out of the grave. Fuckin' zombie.

The men laughed. They all felt great relief.

Spook City, said Mitchell Sanders.

Lee Strunk made a funny ghost sound, a kind of moaning, yet very happy, and right then, when Strunk made that high happy moaning sound, when he went *Ahhooooo,* right then Ted Lavender was shot in the head on his way back from peeing. He lay with his mouth open. The teeth were broken. There was a swollen black bruise under his left eye. The cheekbone was gone. Oh shit, Rat Kiley said, the guy's dead. The guy's dead, he kept saying, which seemed profound—the guy's dead. I mean really.

* * *

The things they carried were determined to some extent by superstition. Lieutenant Cross carried his good-luck pebble. Dave Jensen carried a rabbit's foot. Norman Bowker, otherwise a very gentle person, carried a thumb that had been presented to him as a gift by Mitchell Sanders. The thumb was dark brown, rubbery to the touch, and weighed four ounces at most. It had been cut from a VC corpse, a boy of fifteen or sixteen. They'd found him at the bottom of an irrigation ditch, badly burned, flies in his mouth and eyes. The boy wore black shorts and sandals. At the time of his death he had been carrying a pouch of rice, a rifle, and three magazines of ammunition.

You want my opinion, Mitchell Sanders said, there's a definite moral here.

He put his hand on the dead boy's wrist. He was quiet for a time, as if counting a pulse, then he patted the stomach, almost affectionately, and used Kiowa's hunting hatchet to remove the thumb.

Henry Dobbins asked what the moral was.

Moral?

You know. *Moral.*

Sanders wrapped the thumb in toilet paper and handed it across to Norman Bowker. There was no blood. Smiling, he kicked the boy's head, watched the flies scatter, and said, It's like with that old TV show—Paladin. Have gun, will travel.

Henry Dobbins thought about it.

Yeah, well, he finally said. I don't see no moral.

There it *is,* man.

Fuck off.

* * *

They carried USO stationery and pencils and pens. They carried Sterno, safety pins, trip flares, signal flares, spools of wire, razor blades, chewing tobacco, liberated joss sticks and statuettes of the smiling Buddha, candles, grease pencils, *The Stars and Stripes,* fingernail clippers, Psy Ops leaflets, bush hats, bolos, and much more. Twice a week, when the resupply choppers came in, they carried hot chow in green Mermite cans and large canvas bags filled with iced beer and soda pop. They carried plastic water containers, each with a two-gallon capacity. Mitchell Sanders carried a set of starched tiger fatigues for special occasions. Henry Dobbins carried Black Flag insecticide. Dave Jensen carried empty sandbags that could be filled at night for added protection. Lee Strunk carried tanning lotion. Some things they carried in common. Taking turns, they carried the big PRC-77 scrambler radio, which weighed thirty pounds with its battery. They shared the weight of memory. They took up what others could no longer bear. Often, they carried each other, the wounded or weak. They carried infections. They carried chess sets, basketballs, Vietnamese-English dictionaries, insignia of rank, Bronze Stars and Purple Hearts, plastic cards imprinted with the Code of Conduct. They carried diseases, among them malaria and dysentery. They carried lice and ringworm and leeches and paddy algae and various rots and molds. They carried the land itself—Vietnam, the place, the soil—a powdery orange-red dust that covered their boots and fatigues and faces. They carried the sky. The whole atmosphere, they carried it, the humidity, the monsoons, the stink of fungus and decay, all of it, they carried gravity. They moved like mules. By daylight they took sniper fire, at night they were mortared, but it was not battle, it was just the endless march, village to village, without purpose, nothing won or lost. They marched for the sake of the march. They plodded along slowly, dumbly, leaning forward against the heat, unthinking, all blood and bone, simple grunts, soldiering with their legs, toiling up the hills and down into the paddies and across the rivers and up again and down, just humping, one step and then the next and then another, but no volition, no will, because it was automatic, it was anatomy, and the war was entirely a matter of posture and carriage, the hump was everything, a kind of inertia, a kind of emptiness, a dullness of desire and intellect and conscience and hope and human sensibility. Their principles were in their feet. Their calculations were biological. They had no sense of strategy or mission. They searched the villages without knowing what to look for, not caring, kicking over jars of rice, frisking children and old men, blowing tunnels, sometimes setting fires and sometimes not, then forming up and moving on to the next village, then other villages, where it would always be the same. They carried their own lives. The pressures were enormous. In the heat of early afternoon, they would remove their helmets and flak jackets, walking bare, which was dangerous but which helped ease the strain. They would often discard things along the route of march. Purely for comfort, they would throw away rations, blow their Claymores and grenades, no matter, because by nightfall the resupply choppers would arrive with more of the same, then a day or two later still more, fresh watermelons and crates of ammunition and sunglasses and woolen sweaters—the resources were stunning—sparklers for the Fourth of July, colored eggs for Easter. It was the great American war chest—the fruits of science, the smoke-stacks, the canneries, the arsenals at Hartford, the Minnesota forests, the machine shops, the vast fields of corn and wheat—they carried like freight trains; they carried it on their backs and shoulders—and for all the ambiguities of Vietnam, all the mysteries and unknowns, there was at least the single abiding certainty that they would never be at a loss for things to carry.

* * *

After the chopper took Lavender away, Lieutenant Jimmy Cross led his men into the village of Than Khe. They burned everything. They shot chickens and dogs, they trashed the village well, they called in artillery and watched the wreckage, then they marched for several hours through the hot afternoon, and then at dusk, while Kiowa explained how Lavender died, Lieutenant Cross found himself trembling.

He tried not to cry. With his entrenching tool, which weighed five pounds, he began digging a hole in the earth.

He felt shame. He hated himself. He had loved Martha more than his men, and as a consequence Lavender was now dead, and this was something he would have to carry like a stone in his stomach for the rest of the war.

All he could do was dig. He used his entrenching tool like an ax, slashing, feeling both love and hate, and then later, when it was full dark, he sat at the bottom of his foxhole and wept. It went on for a long while. In part, he was grieving for Ted Lavender, but mostly it was for Martha, and for himself, because she belonged to another world, which was not quite real, and because she was a junior at Mount Sebastian College in

New Jersey, a poet and a virgin and uninvolved, and because he realized she did not love him and never would.

* * *

Like cement, Kiowa whispered in the dark. I swear to God—boom-down. Not a word.

I've heard this, said Norman Bowker.

A pisser, you know? Still zipping himself up. Zapped while zipping.

All right, fine. That's enough.

Yeah, but you had to see it, the guy just—

I *heard,* man. Cement. So why not shut the fuck *up?*

Kiowa shook his head sadly and glanced over at the hole where Lieutenant Jimmy Cross sat watching the night. The air was thick and wet. A warm, dense fog had settled over the paddies and there was the stillness that precedes rain.

After a time Kiowa sighed.

One thing for sure, he said. The Lieutenant's in some deep hurt. I mean that crying jag—the way he was carrying on—it wasn't fake or anything, it was real heavy-duty hurt. The man cares.

Sure, Norman Bowker said.

Say what you want, the man does care.

We all got problems.

Not Lavender.

No, I guess not, Bowker said. Do me a favor, though.

Shut up?

That's a smart Indian. Shut up.

Shrugging, Kiowa pulled off his boots. He wanted to say more, just to lighten up his sleep, but instead he opened his New Testament and arranged it beneath his head as a pillow. The fog made things seem hollow and unattached. He tried not to think about Ted Lavender, but then he was thinking how fast it was, no drama, down and dead, and how it was hard to feel anything except surprise. It seemed un-Christian. He wished he could find some great sadness, or even anger, but the emotion wasn't there and he couldn't make it happen. Mostly he felt pleased to be alive. He liked the smell of the New Testament under his cheek, the leather and ink and paper and glue, whatever the chemicals were. He liked hearing the sounds of night. Even his fatigue, it felt fine, the stiff muscles and the prickly awareness of his own body, a floating feeling. He enjoyed not being dead. Lying there, Kiowa admired Lieutenant Jimmy Cross's capacity for grief. He wanted to share the man's pain, he wanted to care as Jimmy Cross cared. And yet when he closed his eyes, all he could think was Boom-down, and all he could feel was the pleasure of having his boots off and the fog curling in around him and the damp soil and the Bible smells and the plush comfort of night.

After a moment Norman Bowker sat up in the dark.

What the hell, he said. You want to talk, *talk.* Tell it to me.

Forget it.

No, man, go on. One thing I hate, it's a silent Indian.

* * *

For the most part they carried themselves with poise, a kind of dignity. Now and then, however, there were times of panic, when they squealed or wanted to squeal but couldn't, when they twitched and made moaning sounds and covered their heads and said Dear Jesus and flopped around on the earth and fired their weapons blindly and cringed and sobbed and begged for the noise to stop and went wild and made stupid promises to themselves and to God and to their mothers and fathers, hoping not to die. In different ways, it happened to all of them. Afterward, when the firing ended, they would blink and peek up. They would touch their bodies, feeling shame, then quickly hiding it. They would force themselves to stand. As if in slow motion, frame by frame, the world would take on the old logic—absolute silence, then the wind, then sunlight, then voices. It was the burden of being alive. Awkwardly, the men would reassemble themselves, first in private, then in groups, becoming soldiers again. They would repair the leaks in their eyes. They would check for casualties, call in dust-offs, light cigarettes, try to smile, clear their throats and spit and begin cleaning their weapons. After a time someone would shake his head and say, No lie, I almost shit my pants, and someone else would laugh, which meant it was bad, yes, but the guy had obviously not shit his pants, it wasn't that bad, and in any case nobody would ever do such a thing and then go ahead and talk about it. They would squint into the dense, oppressive sunlight. For a few moments, perhaps, they would fall silent, lighting a joint and tracking its passage from man to man, inhaling, holding in the humiliation. Scary stuff, one of them might say. But then someone else would grin or flick his eyebrows and say, Roger-dodger, almost cut me a new asshole, *almost.*

There were numerous such poses. Some carried themselves with a sort of wistful resignation, others with pride or stiff soldierly discipline or good humor or macho zeal. They were afraid of dying but they were even more afraid to show it.

They found jokes to tell.

They used a hard vocabulary to contain the terrible softness. *Greased,* they'd say. *Offed, lit up, zapped while zipping.* It wasn't cruelty, just stage presence. They were actors and the war came at them in 3-D. When someone died, it wasn't quite dying, because in a curious way it seemed scripted, and because they had their lines mostly memorized, irony mixed with tragedy, and because they called it by other names, as if to encyst and destroy the reality of death itself. They kicked corpses. They cut off thumbs. They talked grunt lingo. They told stories about Ted Lavender's supply of tranquilizers, how the poor guy didn't feel a thing, how incredibly tranquil he was.

There's a moral here, said Mitchell Sanders.

They were waiting for Lavender's chopper, smoking the dead man's dope.

The moral's pretty obvious, Sanders said, and winked. Stay away from drugs. No joke, they'll ruin your day every time.

Cute, said Henry Dobbins.

Mind-blower, get it? Talk about wiggy—nothing left, just blood and brains.

They made themselves laugh.

There it is, they'd say, over and over, as if the repetition itself were an act of poise, a balance between crazy and almost crazy, knowing without going. There it is, which meant be cool, let it ride, because oh yeah, man, you can't change what can't be changed, there it is, there it absolutely and positively and fucking well *is.*

They were tough.

They carried all the emotional baggage of men who might die. Grief, terror, love, longing—these were intangibles, but the intangibles had their own mass and specific gravity, they had tangible weight. They carried shameful memories. They carried the common secret of cowardice barely restrained, the instinct to run or freeze or hide, and in many respects this was the heaviest burden of all, for it could never be put down, it required perfect balance and perfect posture. They carried their reputations. They carried the soldier's greatest fear, which was the fear of blushing. Men killed, and died, because they were embarrassed not to. It was what had brought them to the war in the first place, nothing positive, no dreams of glory or honor, just to avoid the blush of dishonor. They died so as not to die of embarrassment. They crawled into tunnels and walked point and advanced under fire. Each morning, despite the unknowns, they made their legs move. They endured. They kept humping. They did not submit to the obvious alternative, which was simply to close the eyes and fall. So easy, really. Go limp and tumble to the ground and let the muscles unwind and not speak and not budge until your buddies picked you up and lifted you into the chopper that would roar and dip its nose and carry you off to the world. A mere matter of falling, yet no one ever fell. It was not courage, exactly; the object was not valor. Rather, they were too frightened to be cowards.

By and large they carried these things inside, maintaining the masks of composure. They sneered at sick call. They spoke bitterly about guys who had found release by shooting off their own toes or fingers. Pussies, they'd say. Candyasses. It was fierce, mocking talk, with only a trace of envy or awe, but even so, the image played itself out behind their eyes.

They imagined the muzzle against flesh. They imagined the quick, sweet pain, then the evacuation to Japan, then a hospital with warm beds and cute geisha nurses.

They dreamed of freedom birds.

At night, on guard, staring into the dark, they were carried away by jumbo jets. They felt the rush of takeoff. *Gone!* they yelled. And then velocity, wings and engines, a smiling stewardess—but it was more than a plane, it was a real bird, a big sleek silver bird with feathers and talons and high screeching. They were flying. The weights fell off, there was nothing to bear. They laughed and held on tight, feeling the cold slap of wind and altitude, soaring, thinking *It's over, I'm gone!*—they were naked, they were light and free—it was all lightness, bright and fast and buoyant, light as light, a helium buzz in the brain, a giddy bubbling in the lungs as they were taken up over the clouds and the war, beyond duty, beyond gravity and mortification and global entanglements—*Sin loi!* they yelled, *I'm sorry, motherfuckers, but I'm out of it, I'm goofed, I'm on a space cruise, I'm gone!*—and it was a restful, disencumbered sensation, just riding the light waves, sailing that big silver freedom bird over the mountains and oceans, over America, over the farms and great sleeping cities and cemeteries and highways and the golden arches of McDonald's. It was flight, a kind of fleeing, a kind of falling, falling higher and higher, spinning off the edge of the earth and beyond the sun and through the vast, silent vacuum where there were no burdens and where everything weighed exactly nothing. *Gone!* they screamed, *I'm sorry but I'm gone!* And so at night, not quite dreaming, they gave themselves over to lightness, they were carried, they were purely borne.

* * *

On the morning after Ted Lavender died, First Lieutenant Jimmy Cross crouched at the bottom of his foxhole and burned Martha's letters. Then he burned the two photographs. There was a steady rain falling, which made it difficult, but he used heat tabs and Sterno to build a small fire, screening it with his body, holding the photographs over the tight blue flame with the tips of his fingers.

He realized it was only a gesture. Stupid, he thought. Sentimental, too, but mostly just stupid.

Lavender was dead. You couldn't burn the blame.

Besides, the letters were in his head. And even now, without photographs, Lieutenant Cross could see Martha playing volleyball in her white gym shorts and yellow T-shirt. He could see her moving in the rain.

When the fire died out, Lieutenant Cross pulled his poncho over his shoulders and ate breakfast from a can.

There was no great mystery, he decided.

In those burned letters Martha had never mentioned the war, except to say, Jimmy, take care of yourself. She wasn't involved. She signed the letters "Love," but it wasn't love, and all the fine lines and technicalities did not matter.

The morning came up wet and blurry. Everything seemed part of everything else, the fog and Martha and the deepening rain.

It was a war, after all.

Half smiling, Lieutenant Jimmy Cross took out his maps. He shook his head hard, as if to clear it, then bent forward and began planning the day's march. In ten minutes, or maybe twenty, he would rouse the men and they would pack up and head west, where the maps showed the country to be green and inviting. They would do what they had always done. The rain might add some weight, but otherwise it would be one more day layered upon all the other days.

He was realistic about it. There was that new hardness in his stomach.

No more fantasies, he told himself.

Henceforth, when he thought about Martha, it would be only to think that she belonged elsewhere. He would shut down the daydreams. This was not Mount Sebastian, it was another world, where there were no pretty poems or midterm exams, a place where men died because of carelessness and gross stupidity. Kiowa was right. Boom-down, and you were dead, never partly dead.

Briefly, in the rain, Lieutenant Cross saw Martha's gray eyes gazing back at him.

He understood.

It was very sad, he thought. The things men carried inside. The things men did or felt they had to do.

He almost nodded at her, but didn't.

Instead he went back to his maps. He was now determined to perform his duties firmly and without negligence. It wouldn't help Lavender, he knew that, but from this point on he would comport himself as a soldier. He would dispose of his good-luck pebble. Swallow it, maybe, or use Lee Strunk's slingshot, or just drop it along the trail. On the march he would impose strict field discipline. He would be careful to send out flank security, to prevent straggling or bunching up, to keep his troops moving at the proper pace and at the proper interval. He would insist on clean weapons. He would confiscate the remainder of Lavender's dope. Later in the day, perhaps, he would call the men together and speak to them plainly. He would accept the blame for what had happened to Ted Lavender. He would be a man about it. He would look them in the eyes, keeping his chin level, and he would issue the new SOPs in a calm, impersonal tone of voice, an officer's voice, leaving no room for argument or discussion. Commencing immediately, he'd tell them, they would no longer abandon equipment along the route of march. They would police up their acts. They would get their shit together, and keep it together, and maintain it neatly and in good working order.

He would not tolerate laxity. He would show strength, distancing himself.

Among the men there would be grumbling, of course, and maybe worse, because their days would seem longer and their loads heavier, but Lieutenant Cross reminded himself that his obligation was not to be loved but to lead. He would dispense with love; it was not now a factor. And if anyone quarreled or complained, he would simply tighten his lips and arrange his shoulders in the correct command posture. He might give a curt little nod. Or he might not. He might just shrug and say Carry on, then they would saddle up and form into a column and move out toward the villages of Than Khe.

# JOY WILLIAMS
(1944– )

Born in Chelmsford, Massachusetts, where her father was a minister, Joy Williams went to Marietta College in Ohio and graduated with high honors in 1963. She then earned an M.F.A. from the Writers' Workshop of the University of Iowa in 1965. For two years, 1967 to 1969, she was a data analyst at the U.S. Navy marine laboratory at Siesta Key, Florida. Since then she has concentrated on writing, publishing stories in many major periodicals, such as *The New Yorker, Esquire, The Paris Review, Ms.*, and others. She was awarded a fellowship from the National Endowment of the Arts in 1974 and a Guggenheim Fellowship in 1975. She is married to writer and editor Rust Hills and has one child. They have homes in Florida and Massachusetts.

Williams' publications include the story collections *Taking Care* (1982) and *Escapes* (1990). Her first novel, *State of Grace* (1973), was a National Book Award nominee. Her second novel, *The Changeling* (1978), received mixed reviews. Her most recent work is the novel *The Quick and the Dead* (2000). Her fiction often explores the ways ordinary lives are exposed to vulnerability and terror. She writes in a style that is intense and surreal.

## Health

PAMMY IS in an unpleasant Texas city, the city where she was born, in the month of her twelfth birthday. It is cold and cloudy. Soon it will rain. The rain will wash the film of ash off the car she is traveling in, volcanic ash that has drifted across the Gulf of Mexico, all the way from the Yucatán. Pammy is a stocky gray-eyed blonde, a daughter, traveling in her father's car, being taken to her tanning lesson.

This is her father's joke. She is being taken to a tanning session, twenty-five minutes long. She had requested this for her birthday, ten tanning sessions in a health spa. She had also asked for and received new wheels for her skates. They are purple Rannalli's. She had dyed her stoppers to match although the match was not perfect. The stoppers were a duller, cruder purple. Pammy wants to be a speed skater but she worries that she doesn't have the personality for it. "You've gotta have gravel in your gut to be in speed," her coach said. Pammy has mastered the duck walk but still doesn't have a good, smooth crossover, and sometimes she fears that she never will.

Pammy and her father, Morris, are following a truck which is carrying a jumble of television sets. There is a twenty-four-inch console facing them on the open tailgate, restrained by rope, with a bullet hole in the exact center of the screen.

Morris drinks coffee from a plastic-lidded cup that fits into a bracket mounted just beneath the car's radio. Pammy has a friend, Wanda, whose stepfather has the same kind of plastic cup in his car, but he drinks bourbon and water from his. Wanda had been adopted when she was two months old. Pammy is relieved that neither her father nor Marge, her mother, drinks. Sometimes they have wine. On her birthday, even Pammy had wine with dinner. Marge and Morris seldom quarrel and she is grateful for this. This morning, however, she had seen them quarrel. Once again, her mother had borrowed her father's hairbrush and left long, brown hairs in it. Her father had taken the brush and cleaned it with a comb over the clean kitchen sink. Her father had left a nest of brown hair in the white sink.

In the car, the radio is playing a song called "Tainted Love," a song Morris likes to refer to as "Rancid Love." The radio plays constantly when Pammy and her father drive anywhere. Morris is a good driver. He is fast and doesn't bear grudges. He enjoys driving still, after years and years of it. Pammy looks forward to learning how to drive now, but after a few years, who knows? She can't imagine it being that enjoyable after a while. Her father is skillful here, on the freeways and streets, and on the terrifying, wide two-lane highways and narrow mountain roads in Mexico, and even on the rutted, soiled beaches of the Gulf Coast. One weekend, earlier that spring, Morris had rented a Jeep in Corpus Christi and he and Pammy and Marge had driven the length of Padre Island. They sped across the sand, the only people for miles and miles. There was plastic everywhere.

"You will see a lot of plastic," the man who rented them the Jeep said, "but it is plastic from all over the world."

Morris had given Pammy a lesson in driving the Jeep. He taught her how to shift smoothly, how to synchronize acceleration with the depression and release of the clutch. "There's a way to do things right," Morris told her and when he said this she was filled with a sort of fear. They were just words, she knew, words that anybody could use, but behind words were always things, sometimes things you could never tell anyone, certainly no one you loved, frightening things that weren't even true.

"I'm sick of being behind this truck," Morris says. The screen of the injured television looks like dirty water. Morris pulls to the curb beside an Oriental market. Pammy stares into the market where shoppers wait in line at a cash register. Many of the women wear scarves on their heads. Pammy is deeply disturbed by Orientals who kill penguins to make gloves and murder whales to make nail polish. In school, in social studies class, she is reading eyewitness accounts of the aftermath of the atomic bombing of Hiroshima. She reads about young girls running from their melting city, their hair burnt off, their burnt skin in loose folds, crying, "Stupid Americans." Morris sips his coffee, then turns the car back onto the street, a street now free from fatally wounded television sets.

Pammy gazes at the backs of her hands which are tan, but, she feels, not tan enough. They are a dusky peach color. This will be her fifth tanning lesson. In the health spa, there are ten colored photographs on the wall showing a woman in a bikini, a pale woman being transformed into a tanned woman. In the last photograph she has plucked the bikini slightly away from her hipbone to expose a sliver of white skin and she is smiling down at the sliver.

Pammy tans well. Without a tan, her face seems grainy and uneven for she has freckles and rather large pores. Tanning draws her together, completes her. She has had all kinds of tans—golden tans, pool tans, even a Florida tan which seemed yellow back in Texas. She had brought all her friends the same present from Florida—small plywood crates filled with tiny oranges which were actually chewing gum. The finest tan Pammy has ever had, however, was in Mexico six months ago. She had gone there with her parents for two weeks, and she had gotten a truly remarkable tan and she had gotten tuberculosis. This has caused some tension between Morris and Marge as it had been Morris's idea to swim at the spas in the mountains rather than in the pools at the more established hotels. It was believed that Pammy had become infected at one particular public spa just outside the small dusty town where they had gone to buy tiles, tiles of a dusky orange with blue rays flowing from the center, tiles which are now in the kitchen of their home where each morning Pammy drinks her juice and takes three hundred milligrams of isoniazid.

"Here we are," Morris says. The health spa is in a small, concrete block building with white columns, salvaged from the wrecking of a mansion, adorning the front. There are gift shops, palmists and all-night restaurants along the street, as well as an exterminating company that has a huge fiberglass bug with Xs for eyes on the roof. This was not the company that had tented Wanda's house for termites. That had been another company. When Pammy was in Mexico getting tuberculosis, Wanda and her parents had gone to San Antonio for a week while their house was being tented. When they returned, they'd found a dead robber in the living room, the things he was stealing piled neatly nearby. He had died from inhaling the deadly gas used by the exterminators.

"Mommy will pick you up," Morris says. "She has a class this afternoon so she might be a little late. Just stay inside until she comes."

Morris kisses her on the cheek. He treats her like a child. He treats Marge like a mother, her mother.

Marge is thirty-five but she is still a student. She takes courses in art history and film at one of the city's universities, the same university where Morris teaches petroleum science. Years ago when Marge had first been a student, before she had met Morris and Pammy had been born, she had been in Spain, in a museum studying a Goya and a piece of the painting had fallen at her feet. She had quickly placed it in her pocket and now has it on her bureau in a small glass box. It is a wedge of greenish-violet paint, as large as a thumbnail. It is from one of Goya's nudes.

Pammy gets out of the car and goes into the health spa. There is no equipment here except for the tanning beds, twelve tanning beds in eight small rooms. Pammy has never had to share a room with anyone. If asked to, she would probably say no, hoping that she would not hurt the other person's feelings. The receptionist is an old, vigorous woman behind a scratched metal desk, wearing a black jumpsuit and feather earrings. Behind her are shelves of powders and pills in squat brown bottles with names like DYNAMIC STAMINA BUILDER and DYNAMIC SUPER STRESS–END and LIVER CONCENTRATE ENERGIZER.

The receptionist's name is Aurora. Pammy thinks that the name is magnificent and is surprised that it belongs to such an old woman. Aurora leads her to one of the rooms at the rear of the building. The room has a mirror, a sink, a small stool, a white rotating fan and the bed, a long bronze coffinlike apparatus with a lid. Pammy is always startled when she sees the bed with its frosted ultraviolet tubes, its black vinyl headrest. In the next room, someone coughs. Pammy imagines people lying in all the rooms, wrapped in white light, lying quietly as though they were being rested for a long, long journey. Aurora takes a spray bottle of disinfectant and a scrap of toweling from the counter above the sink and cleans the surface of the bed. She twists the timer and the light leaps out, like an animal in a dream, like a murderer in a movie.

"There you are, honey," Aurora says. She pats Pammy on the shoulder and leaves.

Pammy pushes off her sandals and undresses quickly. She leaves her clothes in a heap, her sweatshirt on top of the pile. Her sweatshirt is white with a transfer of a skater on the back. The skater is a man wearing a helmet and kneepads, side-surfing goofy-footed. She lies down and with her left hand pulls the lid to within a foot of the bed's cool surface. She can see the closed door and the heap of clothing and her feet. Pammy considers her feet to be her ugliest feature. They are skinny and the toes are too far apart. She and Wanda had painted their toes the same color, but Wanda's feet were pretty and hers were not. Pammy thought her feet looked like they belonged to a dead person and there wasn't anything she could do about them. She closes her eyes.

Wanda, who read a lot, told Pammy that tuberculosis was a very romantic disease, the disease of artists and poets and "highly sensitive individuals."

"Oh yeah," her stepfather had said. "Tuberculosis has mucho cachet."

Wanda's stepfather speaks loudly and his eyes glitter. He is always joking, Pammy thinks. Pammy feels that Wanda's parents are pleasant but she's always a little uncomfortable around them. Wanda wasn't the first child they had adopted. There had been another baby, but it was learned that the baby's background had been misrepresented. Or perhaps it had been a boring baby. In any case the baby had been returned and they got Wanda. Pammy doesn't think Wanda's parents are very steadfast. She is surprised that they don't make Wanda nervous.

The tanning bed is warm but not uncomfortably so. Pammy lies with her arms straight by her sides, palms down. She hears voices in the hall and footsteps. When she first began coming to the health spa, she was afraid that someone would open the door to the room she was in by mistake. She imagined exactly what it would be like. She would see the door open abruptly out of the corner of her eye, then someone would say, "Sorry," and the door would close again. But this had not happened. The voices pass by.

Pammy thinks of Snow White lying in her glass coffin. The queen had deceived her how many times? Three? She had been in disguise, but still. And then Snow White had choked on an apple. In the restaurants she sometimes goes to with her parents there are posters on the walls which show a person choking and another person trying to save him. The posters take away Pammy's appetite.

Snow White lay in a glass coffin, not naked of course but in a gown, watched over by dwarfs. But surely they had not been real dwarfs. That had just been a word that had been given to them.

When Pammy had told Morris that tuberculosis was a romantic disease, he had said, "There's nothing romantic about it. Besides, you don't have it."

It seems to be a fact that she both has and doesn't have tuberculosis. Pammy had been given the tuberculin skin test along with her classmates when she began school in the fall and within forty-eight hours had a large swelling on her arm.

"Now that you've come in contact with it, you don't have to worry about getting it," the pediatrician had said in his office, smiling.

"You mean the infection constitutes immunity," Marge said.

"Not exactly," the pediatrician said, shaking his head, still smiling.

Her lungs are clear. She is not ill but has an illness. The germs are in her body, but in a resting state, still alive but rendered powerless, successfully overcome by her healthy body's strong defenses. Outwardly, she is the same, but within, a great drama had taken place and Pammy feels herself in possession of a bright, secret, and unspeakable knowledge.

She knows other things too, things that would break her parents' hearts, common, ugly, easy things. She knows a girl in school who stole her mother's Green Stamps and bought a personal massager with the books. She knows another girl whose brother likes to wear her clothes. She knows a boy who threw a can of motor oil at his father and knocked him unconscious.

Pammy stretches. Her head tingles. Her body is about a foot and a half off the floor and appears almost gray in the glare from the tubes. She has heard of pills one could take to acquire a tan. One just took two pills a day and after twenty days one had a wonderful tan which could be maintained by continuing to take the pills. You ordered them from Canada. It was some kind of food-coloring substance. How gross, Pammy thinks. When she had been little she had bought a quarter of an acre of land in Canada by mail for fifty cents. That had been two years ago.

Pammy hears voices from the room next to hers, coming through the thin wall. A woman talking rapidly says, "Pete went up to Detroit two days ago to visit his brother who's dying up there in the hospital. Cancer. The brother's always been a nasty type, I mean very unpleasant. Younger than Pete and always mean. Tried to commit suicide twice. Then he learns he has cancer and decides he doesn't want to die. Carries on and on. Is miserable to everyone. Puts the whole family through hell, but nothing can be done about it, he's dying of cancer. So Pete goes up to see him his last days in the hospital and you know what happens? Pete's wallet gets stolen. Right out of a dying man's room. Five hundred dollars in cash and all our credit cards. That was yesterday. What a day."

Another woman says, "If it's not one thing, it's something else."

Pammy coughs. She doesn't want to hear other people's voices. It is as though they are throwing away junk, the way some people use words, as though one word were as good as another.

"Things happen so abruptly anymore," the woman says. "You know what I mean?"

Pammy does not listen and she does not open her eyes for if she did she would see this odd bright room with her clothes in a heap and herself lying motionless and naked. She does not open her eyes because she prefers imagining that she is a magician's accomplice, levitating on a stage in a coil of pure energy. If one thought purely enough, one could create one's own truth. That's how people accomplished astral travel, walked over burning coals, cured warts. There was a girl in Pammy's class at school, Bonnie Black, a small owlish looking girl who was a Christian Scientist. She raised rabbits and showed them at fairs, and was always wearing the ribbons they had won to school, pinned to her blouse. She had warts all over her hands, but one day Pammy noticed that the warts were gone and Bonnie Black had told her that the warts disappeared after she had clearly realized that in her true being as God's reflection, she couldn't have warts.

It seemed that people were better off when they could concentrate on something, hold something in their mind for a long time and really believe it. Pammy had once seen a radical skater putting on a show at the opening of a shopping mall. He leapt over cars and pumped up the sides of buildings. He did flips and spins. A disc jockey who was set up for the day in the parking lot interviewed him. "I'm really impressed with your performance," the disc jockey said, "and I'm impressed that you never fall. Why don't you fall?" The skater was a thin boy in baggy cutoff jeans. "I don't fall," the boy said, looking hard at the microphone, "because I've got a deep respect for the concrete surface and because when I make a miscalculation, instead of falling, I turn it into a new trick."

Pammy thinks it is wonderful that the boy was able to say something which would keep him from thinking he might fall.

The door to the room opened. Pammy had heard the turning of the knob. At first she lies without opening her eyes, willing the sound of the door shutting, but she hears nothing, only the ticking of the bed's timer. She swings her head quickly to the side and looks at the door. There is a man standing there, staring at her. She presses her right hand into a fist and lays it between her legs. She puts her left arm across her breasts.

"What?" she says to the figure, frightened. In an instant she is almost panting with fear. She feels the repetition of something painful and known, but she has not known this, not ever. The figure says nothing and pulls the door shut. With a flurry of rapid ticking, the timer stops. The harsh lights of the bed go out.

Pammy pushes the lid back and hurriedly gets up. She dresses hastily and smooths her hair with her fingers. She looks at herself in the mirror, her lips parted. Her teeth are white behind her pale lips. She stares at herself. She can be looked at and not discovered. She can speak and not be known. She opens the door and enters the hall. There is no one there. The hall is so narrow that by spreading her arms she can touch the walls with her fingertips. In the reception area by Aurora's desk, there are three people, a stoop-shouldered young woman and two men. The woman was signing up for a month of unlimited tanning which meant that after the basic monthly fee she only had to pay a dollar a visit. She takes her checkbook out of a soiled handbag, which is made out of some silvery material, and writes a check. The men look comfortable lounging in the chairs, their legs stretched out. They know one another, Pammy guesses, but they do not know the woman. One of them has dark spikey hair like a wet animal's. The other wears a red tight T-shirt. Neither is the man she had seen in the doorway.

"What time do you want to come back tomorrow, honey?" Aurora asks Pammy. "You certainly are coming along nicely. Isn't she coming along nicely?"

"I'd like to come back the same time tomorrow," Pammy says. She raises her hand to her mouth and coughs slightly.

"Not the same time, honey. Can't give you the same time. How about an hour later?"

"All right," Pammy says. The stoop-shouldered woman sits down in a chair. There are no more chairs in the room. Pammy opens the door and steps outside. It has rained and the street is dark and shining. She walks slowly down the street and smells the rain lingering in the trees. By a store called Imagine, there's a clump of bamboo with some beer cans glittering in its ragged, grassy center. Imagine sells neon palm trees and silk clouds and stars. It sells greeting cards and chocolate in shapes children aren't allowed to see and it sells children stickers and shoelaces. Pammy looks in the window at a satin pillow in the shape of a heart with a heavy zipper running down the center of it. Pammy turns and walks back to the building that houses the tanning beds. Her mother pulls up in their car. "Pammy!" she calls. She is leaning toward the window on the passenger side which she has rolled down. She unlocks the car's door. Pammy gets in and the door locks again.

The car speeds down the street and Pammy sits in it, a little stunned. Her father will teach her how to drive, and she will drive around. Her mother will continue to take classes at the university. Whenever she meets someone new, she will mention the Goya. "I have a small Goya," she will say, and laugh. Pammy will grow older, she is older now. But the world will remain as young as she was once, infinite in its possibilities, and uncaring. She never wants to see that figure looking at her again, so coldly staring, but she knows she will, for already its features are becoming more indistinct, more general. It could be anything. And it will be somewhere else now, something else. She coughs, but it is not the cough of a sick person because Pammy is a healthy girl. It is the kind of cough a person might make if they were at a party and there was no one there but strangers.

# MAXINE HONG KINGSTON
## (1940– )

One of the noteworthy developments in American literature in the last decades of the twentieth century was the emergence of Chinese-American authors. One of the most acclaimed is Maxine Hong Kingston, whose work engages powerfully and imaginatively the problems of gender and ethnicity. Her first two books, *The Woman Warrior* (1976) and *China Men* (1980), are called nonfiction, but really are an amalgam of autobiography, fiction, and mythology, which demonstrate the discovery of voice and the assertion of self in the engagement with a two-culture history.

Kingston was born in Stockton, California, the eldest of six children. Her father, trained as a scholar in China, was a laundry man and manager of a gambling house. Her mother had medical and midwife training in China, but worked as a field hand and in a laundry in the United States. Kingston earned a B.A. from the University of California at Berkeley in 1962 and a teaching certificate in 1965. In 1962 she married Earl Kingston, an actor; they have one child. Kingston taught in high schools in California and Hawaii. She is currently Chancellor's Distinguished Professor at Berkeley. Her novel *Tripmaster Monkey: His Fake Book* came out in 1988.

## On Mortality

As YOU know, any plain person you chance to meet can prove to be a powerful immortal in disguise come to test you.

Li Fu-yen told a story about Tu Tzu-chun, who lived from A.D. 558 to 618, during the Northern Chou and Sui dynasties. Tu's examiner was a Taoist monk, who made him rich twice, and twice Tu squandered his fortune though it took him two lifetimes to do so. The third time the Taoist gave him money, he bought a thousand li of good land, plowed it himself, seeded it, built houses, roads, and bridges, then welcomed widows and orphans to live on it. With the left-over money, he found a husband for each spinster and a wife for every bachelor in his family, and also paid for the weddings. When he met the Taoist again, he said, "I've used up all your money on the unfortunates I've come across."

"You'll have to repay me by working for me," said the Taoist monk. "I need your help on an important difficult task." He gave Tu three white pills. "Swallow these," he said, pouring him a cup of wine. "All that you'll see and feel will be illusions. No matter what happens, don't speak; don't scream. Remember the saying 'Hide your broken arms in your sleeves.' "

"How easy," said Tu as he swallowed the pills in three gulps of wine. "Why should I scream if I know they're illusions?"

Level by level he descended into the nine hells. At first he saw oxheads, horsefaces, and the heads of generals decapitated in war. Illusions. Only illusions, harmless. He laughed at the heads. He had seen heads before. Soon fewer heads whizzed through the dark until he saw no more of them.

Suddenly his wife was being tortured. Demons were cutting her up into pieces, starting with her toes. He heard her scream; he heard her bones crack. He reminded himself that she was an illusion. *Illusion,* he thought. She was ground into bloodmeal.

Then the tortures on his own body began. Demons poured bronze down his throat and beat him with iron clubs and chains. They mortar-and-pestled and packed him into a pill.

He had to walk over mountains of knives and through fields of knives and forests of swords. He was killed, his head chopped off, rolling into other people's nightmares.

He heard gods and goddesses talking about him, "This man is too wicked to be reborn a man. Let him be born a woman." He saw the entrance of a black tunnel and felt tired. He would have to squeeze his head and shoulders down into that enclosure and travel a long distance. He pushed head first through the entrance, only the beginning. A god kicked him in the butt to give him a move on. (This kick is the reason many Chinese babies have a blue-gray spot on their butts or lower backs, the "Mongolian spot.") Sometimes stuck in the tunnel, sometimes shooting helplessly through it, he emerged again into light with many urgent things to do, many messages to deliver, but his hands were useless baby's hands, his legs wobbly baby's legs, his voice a wordless baby's cries. Years had to pass before he could regain adult powers; he howled as he began to forget the cosmos, his attention taken up with mastering how to crawl, how to stand, how to walk, how to control his bowel movements.

He discovered that he had been reborn a deaf-mute female named Tu. When she became a woman, her parents married her to a man named Lu, who at first did not mind. "Why does she need to talk," said Lu, "to be a good wife? Let her set an example for women." They had a child. But years later, Lu tired of Tu's dumbness. "You're just being stubborn," he said, and lifted their child by the feet. "Talk, or I'll dash its head against the rocks." The poor mother held her hand to her mouth. Lu swung the child, broke its head against the wall.

Tu shouted out, "Oh! Oh!"—and he was back with the Taoist, who sadly told him that at the moment when she had said, "Oh! Oh!" the Taoist was about to complete the last step in making the elixir for immortality. Now that Tu had broken his silence, the formula was spoiled, no immortality for the human race. "You overcame joy and sorrow, anger, fear, and evil desire, but not love," said the Taoist, and went on his way.

# BHARATI MUKHERJEE

## (1940– )

Immigration is perhaps the major defining and shaping force in American history. So much of American literature concerns the migrations of peoples from Old Worlds to a New World and the discovery, abandonment, and remarking of all sorts of boundaries. Such migrations involve the encounter of diverse cultures and the attendant struggles over identity and tradition. Bharati Mukherjee's fiction thoughtfully and imaginatively explores the complexities of the experience of the more recent waves of immigrations of Third World peoples to North America.

Mukherjee was born a Bengali Brahmin in Calcutta, India. Her father was a wealthy businessman and chemist. Later the family lived for over two years in London before returning to India in 1951. Mukherjee attended an English convent school and the University of Calcutta, where she majored in English and ancient Indian culture. She completed a B.A. in 1959. She earned an M.A. from the University of Baroda in 1961. She continued her studies at the University of Iowa's Writers' Workshop, where she earned an M.F.A. in 1963 and a Ph.D. in 1969. While at Iowa she met and married the writer and teacher Clark Blaise, with whom she has two children. The family lived in Montreal and later in Toronto until 1980. Mukherjee taught at McGill University and wrote her first two novels, *The Tiger's Daughter* (1972) and *Wife* (1975).

The admission into Canada of some five thousand Asians from Uganda led to the emergence of strong anti-Asian attacks, which made Mukherjee's and her family's life there increasingly difficult. The family finally moved to the United States, where Mukherjee taught at Skidmore College, Columbia University, and Queens College of the City University of New York. She became an American citizen in 1988, and since 1990 has been a professor at the University of California at Berkeley.

Mukherjee and her husband spent a year in India in the late 1970s, after which they collaborated on a journal-book, *Days and Nights in Calcutta* (1977), which describes their different impressions of the country. They also collaborated on a book about a terrorist attack, *The Sorrow and the Terror: The Haunting Legacy of the Air India Tragedy* (1987). Mukherjee's novels, besides those already mentioned, include *Jasmine* (1989), *The Holder of the World* (1993), and *Leave It to Me* (1997). Her two collections of short stories are

*Darkness* (1985) and *The Middleman and Other Stories* (1988), which won the National Book Critics Circle Award in 1989.

# The Management of Grief

A WOMAN I don't know is boiling tea the Indian way in my kitchen. There are a lot of women I don't know in my kitchen, whispering and moving tactfully. They open doors, rummage through the pantry, and try not to ask me where things are kept. They remind me of when my sons were small, on Mother's Day or when Vikram and I were tired, and they would make big, sloppy omelets. I would lie in bed pretending I didn't hear them.

Dr. Sharma, the treasurer of the Indo-Canada Society, pulls me into the hallway. He wants to know if I am worried about money. His wife, who has just come up from the basement with a tray of empty cups and glasses, scolds him. "Don't bother Mrs. Bhave with mundane details." She looks so monstrously pregnant her baby must be days overdue. I tell her she shouldn't be carrying heavy things. "Shaila," she says, smiling, "this is the fifth." Then she grabs a teenager by his shirttails. He slips his Walkman off his head. He has to be one of her four children; they have the same domed and dented foreheads. "What's the official word now?" she demands. The boy slips the headphones back on. "They're acting evasive, Ma. They're saying it could be an accident or a terrorist bomb."

All morning, the boys have been muttering, Sikh bomb, Sikh bomb. The men, not using the word, bow their heads in agreement. Mrs. Sharma touches her forehead at such a word. At least they've stopped talking about space debris and Russian lasers.

Two radios are going in the dining room. They are tuned to different stations. Someone must have brought the radios down from my boys' bedrooms. I haven't gone into their rooms since Kusum came running across the front lawn in her bathrobe. She looked so funny, I was laughing when I opened the door.

The big TV in the den is being whizzed through American networks and cable channels.

"Damn!" some man swears bitterly. "How can these preachers carry on like nothing's happened?" I want to tell him we're not that important. You look at the audience, and at the preacher in his blue robe with his beautiful white hair, the potted palm trees under a blue sky, and you know they care about nothing.

The phone rings and rings. Dr. Sharma's taken charge. "We're with her," he keeps saying. "Yes, yes, the doctor has given calming pills. Yes, yes, pills are having necessary effect." I wonder if pills alone explain this calm. Not peace, just a deadening quiet. I was always controlled, but never repressed. Sound can reach me, but my body is tensed, ready to scream. I hear their voices all around me. I hear my boys and Vikram cry, "Mommy, Shaila!" and their screams insulate me, like headphones.

The woman boiling water tells her story again and again. "I got the news first. My cousin called from Halifax before six A.M., can you imagine? He'd gotten up for prayers and his son was studying for medical exams and heard on a rock channel that something had happened to a plane. They said first it had disappeared from the radar, like a giant eraser just reached out. His father called me, so I said to him, what do you mean, 'something bad'? You mean a hijacking? And he said, *Behn,* there is no confirmation of anything yet, but check with your neighbors because a lot of them must be on that plane. So I called poor Kusum straight-away. I knew Kusum's husband and daughter were booked to go yesterday."

Kusum lives across the street from me. She and Satish had moved in less than a month ago. They said they needed a bigger place. All these people, the Sharmas and friends from the Indo-Canada Society, had been there for the housewarming. Satish and Kusum made tandoori on their big gas grill and even the white neighbors piled their plates high with that luridly red, charred, juicy chicken. Their younger daughter had danced, and even our boys had broken away from the Stanley Cup telecast to put in a reluctant appearance. Everyone took pictures for their albums and for the community newspapers—another of our families had made it big in Toronto—and now I wonder how many of those happy faces are gone. "Why does God give us so much if all along He intends to take it away?" Kusum asks me.

I nod. We sit on carpeted stairs, holding hands like children. "I never once told him that I loved him," I say. I was too much the well-brought-up woman. I was so well brought up I never felt comfortable calling my husband by his first name.

"It's all right," Kusum says. "He knew. My husband knew. They felt it. Modern young girls have to say it because what they feel is fake."

Kusum's daughter Pam runs in with an overnight case. Pam's in her McDonald's uniform. "Mummy! You have to get dressed!" Panic makes her cranky. "A reporter's on his way here."

"Why?"

"You want to talk to him in your bathrobe?" She starts to brush her mother's long hair. She's the daughter who's always in trouble. She dates Canadian boys and hangs out in the mall, shopping for tight sweaters. The younger one, the goody-goody one according to Pam, the one with a voice so sweet that when she sang *bhajans* for Ethiopian relief even a frugal man like my husband wrote out a hundred-dollar check, *she* was on that plane. *She* was going to spend July and August with grandparents because Pam wouldn't go. Pam said she'd rather waitress at McDonald's. "If it's a choice between Bombay and Wonderland, I'm picking Wonderland," she'd said.

"Leave me alone," Kusum yells. "You know what I want to do? If I didn't have to look after you now, I'd hang myself."

Pam's young face goes blotchy with pain. "Thanks," she says, "don't let me stop you."

"Hush," pregnant Mrs. Sharma scolds Pam. "Leave your mother alone. Mr. Sharma will tackle the reporters and fill out the forms. He'll say what has to be said."

Pam stands her ground. "You think I don't know what Mummy's thinking? *Why her?* That's what. That's sick! Mummy wishes my little sister were alive and I were dead."

Kusum's hand in mine is trembly hot. We continue to sit on the stairs.

* * *

She calls before she arrives, wondering if there's anything I need. Her name is Judith Templeton and she's an appointee of the provincial government. "Multiculturalism?" I ask, and she says "partially," but that her mandate is bigger. "I've been told you knew many of the people on the flight," she says. "Perhaps if you'd agree to help us reach the others . . . ?"

She gives me time at least to put on tea water and pick up the mess in the front room. I have a few *samosas* from Kusum's housewarming that I could fry up, but then I think, why prolong this visit?

Judith Templeton is much younger than she sounded. She wears a blue suit with a white blouse and a polka-dot tie. Her blond hair is cut short, her only jewelry is pearl-drop earrings. Her briefcase is new and expensive looking, a gleaming cordovan leather. She sits with it across her lap. When she looks out the front windows onto the street, her contact lenses seem to float in front of her light blue eyes.

"What sort of help do you want from me?" I ask. She has refused the tea, out of politeness, but I insist, along with some slightly stale biscuits.

"I have no experience," she admits. "That is, I have an M.S.W. and I've worked in liaison with accident victims, but I mean I have no experience with a tragedy of this scale—"

"Who could?" I ask.

"—and with the complications of culture, language, and customs. Someone mentioned that Mrs. Bhave is a pillar—because you've taken it more calmly."

At this, perhaps, I frown, for she reaches forward, almost to take my hand. "I hope you understand my meaning, Mrs. Bhave. There are hundreds of people in Metro directly affected, like you, and some of them speak no English. There are some widows who've never handled money or gone on a bus, and there are old parents who still haven't eaten or gone outside their bedrooms. Some houses and apartments have been looted. Some wives are still hysterical. Some husbands are in shock and profound depression. We want to help, but our hands are tied in so many ways. We have to distribute money to some people, and there are legal documents—these things can be done. We have interpreters, but we don't always have the human touch, or maybe the right human touch. We don't want to make mistakes, Mrs. Bhave, and that's why we'd like to ask you to help us."

"More mistakes, you mean," I say.

"Police matters are not in my hands," she answers.

"Nothing I can do will make any difference," I say. "We must all grieve in our own way."

"But you are coping very well. All the people said, Mrs. Bhave is the strongest person of all. Perhaps if the others could see you, talk with you, it would help them."

"By the standards of the people you call hysterical, I am behaving very oddly and very badly, Miss Templeton." I want to say to her, *I wish I could scream, starve, walk into Lake Ontario, jump from a bridge.* "They would not see me as a model. I do not see myself as a model."

I am a freak. No one who has ever known me would think of me reacting this way. This terrible calm will not go away.

She asks me if she may call again, after I get back from a long trip that we all must make. "Of course," I say. "Feel free to call, anytime."

* * *

Four days later, I find Kusum squatting on a rock overlooking a bay in Ireland. It isn't a big rock, but it juts sharply out over water. This is as close as we'll ever get to them.

June breezes balloon out her sari and unpin her knee-length hair. She has the bewildered look of a sea creature whom the tides have stranded.

It's been one hundred hours since Kusum came stumbling and screaming across my lawn. Waiting around the hospital, we've heard many stories. The police, the diplomats, they tell us things thinking that we're strong, that knowledge is helpful to the grieving, and maybe it is. Some, I know, prefer ignorance, or their own versions. The plane broke into two, they say. Unconsciousness was instantaneous. No one suffered. My boys must have just finished their breakfasts. They loved eating on planes, they loved the smallness of plates, knives, and forks. Last year they saved the airline salt and pepper shakers. Half an hour more and they would have made it to Heathrow.

Kusum says that we can't escape our fate. She says that all those people—our husbands, my boys, her girl with the nightingale voice, all those Hindus, Christians, Sikhs, Muslims, Parsis, and atheists on that plane—were fated to die together off this beautiful bay. She learned this from a swami in Toronto.

I have my Valium.

Six of us "relatives"—two widows and four widowers—choose to spend the day today by the waters instead of sitting in a hospital room and scanning photographs of the dead. That's what they call us now: relatives. I've looked through twenty-seven photos in two days. They're very kind to us, the Irish are very understanding. Sometimes understanding means freeing a tourist bus for this trip to the bay, so we can pretend to spy our loved ones through the glassiness of waves or in sun-speckled cloud shapes.

I could die here, too, and be content.

"What is that, out there?" She's standing and flapping her hands, and for a moment I see a head shape bobbing in the waves. She's standing in the water, I, on the boulder. The tide is low, and a round, black, head-sized rock has just risen from the waves. She returns, her sari end dripping and ruined and her face is a twisted remnant of hope, the way mine was a hundred hours ago, still laughing but inwardly knowing that nothing but the ultimate tragedy could bring two women together at six o'clock on a Sunday morning. I watch her face sag into blankness.

"That water felt warm, Shaila," she says at length.

"You can't," I say. "We have to wait for our turn to come."

I haven't eaten in four days, haven't brushed my teeth.

"I know," she says. "I tell myself I have no right to grieve. They are in a better place than we are. My swami says I should be thrilled for them. My swami says depression is a sign of our selfishness."

Maybe I'm selfish. Selfishly I break away from Kusum and run, sandals slapping against stones, to the water's edge. What if my boys aren't lying pinned under the debris? What if they aren't stuck a mile below that innocent blue chop? What if, given the strong currents. . . .

Now I've ruined my sari, one of my best. Kusum has joined me, knee-deep in water that feels to me like a swimming pool. I could settle in the water, and my husband would take my hand and the boys would slap water in my face just to see me scream.

"Do you remember what good swimmers my boys were, Kusum?"

"I saw the medals," she says.

One of the widowers, Dr. Ranganathan from Montreal, walks out to us, carrying his shoes in one hand. He's an electrical engineer. Someone at the hotel mentioned his work is famous around the world, something about the place where physics and electricity come together. He has lost a huge family, something indescribable. "With some good luck," Dr. Ranganathan suggests to me, "a good swimmer could make it safely to some island. It is quite possible that there may be many, many microscopic islets scattered around."

"You're not just saying that?" I tell Dr. Ranganathan about Vinod, my elder son. Last year he took diving as well.

"It's a parent's duty to hope," he says. "It is foolish to rule out possibilities that have not been tested. I myself have not surrendered hope."

Kusum is sobbing once again. "Dear lady," he says, laying his free hand on her arm, and she calms down.

"Vinod is how old?" he asks me. He's very careful, as we all are. *Is,* not was.

"Fourteen. Yesterday he was fourteen. His father and uncle were going to take him down to the Taj and give him a big birthday party. I couldn't go with them because I couldn't get two weeks off from my stupid job in June." I process bills for a travel agent. June is a big travel month.

Dr. Ranganathan whips the pockets of his suit jacket inside out. Squashed roses, in darkening shades of pink, float on the water. He tore the roses off creepers in somebody's garden. He didn't ask anyone if he could pluck the roses, but now there's been an article about it in the local papers. When you see an Indian person, it says, please give him or her flowers.

"A strong youth of fourteen," he says, "can very likely pull to safety a younger one."

My sons, though four years apart, were very close. Vinod wouldn't let Mithun drown. *Electrical engineering,* I think, foolishly perhaps: this man knows important secrets of the universe, things closed to me. Relief spins me lightheaded. No wonder my boys' photographs haven't turned up in the gallery of photos of the recovered dead. "Such pretty roses," I say.

"My wife loved pink roses. Every Friday I had to bring a bunch home. I used to say, Why? After twenty-odd years of marriage you're still needing proof positive of my love?" He has identified his wife and three of his children. Then others from Montreal, the lucky ones, intact families with no survivors. He chuckles as he wades back to shore. Then he swings around to ask me a question. "Mrs. Bhave, you are wanting to throw in some roses for your loved ones? I have two big ones left."

But I have other things to float: Vinod's pocket calculator; a half-painted model B-52 for my Mithun. They'd want them on their island. And for my husband? For him I let fall into the calm, glassy waters a poem I wrote in the hospital yesterday. Finally he'll know my feelings for him.

"Don't tumble, the rocks are slippery," Dr. Ranganathan cautions. He holds out a hand for me to grab.

Then it's time to get back on the bus, time to rush back to our waiting posts on hospital benches.

* * *

Kusum is one of the lucky ones. The lucky ones flew here, identified in multiplicate their loved ones, then will fly to India with the bodies for proper ceremonies. Satish is one of the few males who surfaced. The photos of faces we saw on the walls in an office at Heathrow and here in the hospital are mostly of women. Women have more body fat, a nun said to me matter-of-factly. They float better.

Today I was stopped by a young sailor on the street. He had loaded bodies, he'd gone into the water when—he checks my face for signs of strength—when the sharks were first spotted. I don't blush, and he breaks down. "It's all right," I say. "Thank you." I heard about the sharks from Dr. Ranganathan. In his orderly mind, science brings understanding, it holds no terror. It is the shark's duty. For every deer there is a hunter, for every fish a fisherman.

The Irish are not shy; they rush to me and give me hugs and some are crying. I cannot imagine reactions like that on the streets of Toronto. Just strangers, and I am touched. Some carry flowers with them and give them to any Indian they see.

After lunch, a policeman I have gotten to know quite well catches hold of me. He says he thinks he has a match for Vinod. I explain what a good swimmer Vinod is.

"You want me with you when you look at photos?" Dr. Ranganathan walks ahead of me into the picture gallery. In these matters, he is a scientist, and I am grateful. It is a new perspective. "They have performed miracles," he says. "We are indebted to them."

The first day or two the policemen showed us relatives only one picture at a time; now they're in a hurry, they're eager to lay out the possibles, and even the probables.

The face on the photo is of a boy much like Vinod; the same intelligent eyes, the same thick brows dipping into a V. But this boy's features, even his cheeks, are puffier, wider, mushier.

"No." My gaze is pulled by other pictures. There are five other boys who look like Vinod.

The nun assigned to console me rubs the first picture with a fingertip. "When they've been in the water for a while, love, they look a little heavier." The bones under the skin are broken, they said on the first day—try to adjust your memories. It's important.

"It's not him. I'm his mother. I'd know."

"I know this one!" Dr. Ranganathan cries out, and suddenly from the back of the gallery. "And this one!" I think he senses that I don't want to find my boys. "They are the Kutty brothers. They were also from Montreal." I don't mean to be crying. On the contrary, I am ecstatic. My suitcase in the hotel is packed heavy with dry clothes for my boys.

The policeman starts to cry. "I am so sorry, I am so sorry, ma'am. I really thought we had a match."

With the nun ahead of us and the policeman behind, we, the unlucky ones without our children's bodies, file out of the makeshift gallery.

* * *

From Ireland most of us go on to India. Kusum and I take the same direct flight to Bombay, so I can help her clear customs quickly. But we have to argue with a man in uniform. He has large boils on his face. The boils swell and glow with sweat as we argue with him. He wants Kusum to wait in line and he refuses to take authority because his boss is on a tea break. But Kusum won't let her coffins out of sight, and I shan't desert her though I know that my parents, elderly and diabetic, must be waiting in a stuffy car in a scorching lot.

"You bastard!" I scream at the man with the popping boils. Other passengers press closer. "You think we're smuggling contraband in those coffins!"

Once upon a time we were well-brought-up women; we were dutiful wives who kept our heads veiled, our voices shy and sweet.

* * *

In India, I become, once again, an only child of rich, ailing parents. Old friends of the family come to pay their respects. Some are Sikh, and inwardly, involuntarily, I cringe. My parents are progressive people; they do not blame communities for a few individuals.

In Canada it is a different story now.

"Stay longer," my mother pleads. "Canada is a cold place. Why would you want to be all by yourself?" I stay.

Three months pass. Then another.

"Vikram wouldn't have wanted you to give up things!" they protest. They call my husband by the name he was born with. In Toronto he'd changed to Vik so the men he worked with at his office would find his name as easy as Rod or Chris. "You know, the dead aren't cut off from us!"

My grandmother, the spoiled daughter of a rich zamindar, shaved her head with rusty razor blades when she was widowed at sixteen. My grandfather died of childhood diabetes when he was nineteen, and she saw herself as the harbinger of bad luck. My mother grew up without parents, raised indifferently by an uncle, while her true mother slept in a hut behind the main estate house and took her food with the servants. She grew up a rationalist. My parents abhor mindless mortification.

The zamindar's daughter kept stubborn faith in Vedic rituals; my parents rebelled. I am trapped between two modes of knowledge. At thirty-six, I am too old to start over and too young to give up. Like my husband's spirit, I flutter between worlds.

* * *

Courting aphasia, we travel. We travel with our phalanx of servants and poor relatives. To hill stations and to beach resorts. We play contract bridge in dusty gymkhana clubs. We ride stubby ponies up crumbly mountain trails. At tea dances, we let ourselves be twirled twice round the ballroom. We hit the holy spots we hadn't made time for before. In Varanasi, Kalighat, Rishikesh, Hardwar, astrologers and palmists seek me out and for a fee offer me cosmic consolations.

Already the widowers among us are being shown new bride candidates. They cannot resist the call of custom, the authority of their parents and older brothers. They must marry; it is the duty of a man to look after a wife. The new wives will be young widows with children, destitute but of good family. They will make loving wives, but the men will shun them. I've had calls from the men over crackling Indian telephone lines. "Save me," they say, these substantial, educated, successful men of forty. "My parents are arranging a marriage for me." In a month they will have buried one family and returned to Canada with a new bride and partial family.

I am comparatively lucky. No one here thinks of arranging a husband for an unlucky widow.

Then, on the third day of the sixth month into this odyssey, in an abandoned temple in a tiny Himalayan village, as I make my offering of flowers and sweetmeats to the god of a tribe of animists, my husband descends to me. He is squatting next to a scrawny sadhu in moth-eaten robes. Vikram wears the vanilla suit he wore the last time I hugged him. The sadhu tosses petals on a butter-fed flame, reciting Sanskrit mantras, and sweeps his face of flies. My husband takes my hands in his.

*You're beautiful,* he starts. Then, *What are you doing here?*

*Shall I stay?* I ask. He only smiles, but already the image is fading. *You must finish alone what we started together.* No seaweed wreathes his mouth. He speaks too fast, just as he used to when we were an envied family in our pink split-level. He is gone.

In the windowless altar room, smoky with joss sticks and clarified butter lamps, a sweaty hand gropes for my blouse. I do not shriek. The sadhu arranges his robe. The lamps hiss and sputter out.

When we come out of the temple, my mother says, "Did you feel something weird in there?"

My mother has no patience with ghosts, prophetic dreams, holy men, and cults.

"No," I lie. "Nothing."

But she knows that she's lost me. She knows that in days I shall be leaving.

* * *

Kusum's put up her house for sale. She wants to live in an ashram in Hardwar. Moving to Hardwar was her swami's idea. Her swami runs two ashrams, the one in Hardwar and another here in Toronto.

"Don't run away," I tell her.

"I'm not running away," she says. "I'm pursuing inner peace. You think you or that Ranganathan fellow are better off?"

Pam's left for California. She wants to do some modeling, she says. She says when she comes into her share of the insurance money she'll open a yoga-cum-aerobics studio in Hollywood. She sends me postcards so naughty I daren't leave them on the coffee table. Her mother has withdrawn from her and the world.

The rest of us don't lose touch, that's the point. Talk is all we have, says Dr. Ranganathan, who has also resisted his relatives and returned to Montreal and to his job, alone. He says, Whom better to talk with than other relatives? We've been melted down and recast as a new tribe.

He calls me twice a week from Montreal. Every Wednesday night and every Saturday afternoon. He is changing jobs, going to Ottawa. But Ottawa is over a hundred miles away, and he is forced to drive two hundred and twenty miles a day from his home in Montreal. He can't bring himself to sell his house. The house is a temple, he says; the king-sized bed in the master bedroom is a shrine. He sleeps on a folding cot. A devotee.

* * *

There are still some hysterical relatives. Judith Templeton's list of those needing help and those who've "accepted" is in nearly perfect balance. Acceptance means you speak of your family in the past tense and you make active plans for moving ahead with your life. There are courses at Seneca and Ryerson we could be taking. Her gleaming leather briefcase is full of college catalogues and lists of cultural societies that need our help. She has done impressive work, I tell her.

"In the textbooks on grief management," she replies—I am her confidante, I realize, one of the few whose grief has not sprung bizarre obsessions—"there are stages to pass through: rejection, depression, acceptance, reconstruction." She has compiled a chart and finds that six months after the tragedy, none of us still rejects reality, but only a handful are reconstructing. "Depressed acceptance" is the plateau we've reached. Remarriage is a major step in reconstruction (though she's a little surprised, even shocked, over *how* quickly some of the men have taken on new families). Selling one's house and changing jobs and cities is healthy.

How to tell Judith Templeton that my family surrounds me, and that like creatures in epics, they've changed shapes? She sees me as calm and accepting but worries that I have no job, no career. My closest friends are worse off than I. I cannot tell her my days, even my nights, are thrilling.

She asks me to help with families she can't reach at all. An elderly couple in Agincourt whose sons were killed just weeks after they had brought their parents over from a village in Punjab. From their names, I know they are Sikh. Judith Templeton and a translator have visited them twice with offers of money for airfare to Ireland, with bank forms, power-of-attorney forms, but they have refused to sign, or to leave their tiny apartment. Their sons' money is frozen in the bank. Their sons' investment apartments have been trashed by tenants, the furnishings sold off. The parents fear that anything they sign or any money they receive will end the company's or the country's obligations to them. They fear they are selling their sons for two airline tickets to a place they've never seen.

The high-rise apartment is a tower of Indians and West Indians, with a sprinkling of Orientals. The nearest bus-stop kiosk is lined with women in saris. Boys practice cricket in the parking lot. Inside the building, even I wince a bit from the ferocity of onion fumes, the distinctive and immediate Indianness of frying ghee, but Judith Templeton maintains a steady flow of information. These poor old people are in imminent danger of losing their place and all their services.

I say to her, "They are Sikh. They will not open up to a Hindu woman." And what I want to add is, as much as I try not to, I stiffen now at the sight of beards and turbans. I remember a time when we all trusted each other in this new country, it was only the new country we worried about.

* * *

The two rooms are dark and stuffy. The lights are off, and an oil lamp sputters on the coffee table. The bent old lady has let us in, and her husband is wrapping a white turban over his oiled, hip-length hair. She immediately goes to the kitchen, and I hear the most familiar sound of an Indian home, tap water hitting and filling a teapot.

They have not paid their utility bills, out of fear and inability to write a check. The telephone is gone, electricity and gas and water are soon to follow. They have told Judith their sons will provide. They are good boys, and they have always earned and looked after their parents.

We converse a bit in Hindi. They do not ask about the crash and I wonder if I should bring it up. If they think I am here merely as a translator, then they may feel insulted. There are thousands of Punjabi speakers, Sikhs, in Toronto to do a better job. And so I say to the old lady, "I too have lost my sons, and my husband, in the crash."

Her eyes immediately fill with tears. The man mutters a few words which sound like a blessing. "God provides and God takes away," he says.

I want to say, But only men destroy and give back nothing. "My boys and my husband are not coming back," I say. "We have to understand that."

Now the old woman responds. "But who is to say? Man alone does not decide these things." To this her husband adds his agreement.

Judith asks about the bank papers, the release forms. With a stroke of the pen, they will have a provincial trustee to pay their bills, invest their money, send them a monthly pension.

"Do you know this woman?" I ask them.

The man raises his hand from the table, turns it over, and seems to regard each finger separately before he answers. "This young lady is always coming here, we make tea for her, and she leaves papers for us to sign." His eyes scan a pile of papers in the corner of the room. "Soon we will be out of tea, then will she go away?"

The old lady adds, "I have asked my neighbors and no one else gets *angrezi* visitors. What have we done?"

"It's her job," I try to explain. "The government is worried. Soon you will have no place to stay, no lights, no gas, no water."

"Government will get its money. Tell her not to worry, we are honorable people."

I try to explain the government wishes to give money, not take. He raises his hand. "Let them take," he says. "We are accustomed to that. That is no problem."

"We are strong people," says the wife. "Tell her that."

"Who needs all this machinery?" demands the husband. "It is unhealthy, the bright lights, the cold air on a hot day, the cold food, the four gas rings. God will provide, not government."

"When our boys return," the mother says.

Her husband sucks his teeth. "Enough talk," he says.

Judith breaks in. "Have you convinced them?" The snaps on her cordovan briefcase go off like firecrackers in that quiet apartment. She lays the sheaf of legal papers on the coffee table. "If they can't write their names, an X will do—I've told them that."

Now the old lady has shuffled to the kitchen and soon emerges with a pot of tea and two cups. "I think my bladder will go first on a job like this," Judith says to me, smiling. "If only there was some way of reaching them. Please thank her for the tea. Tell her she's very kind."

I nod in Judith's direction and tell them in Hindi, "She thanks you for the tea. She thinks you are being very hospitable but she doesn't have the slightest idea what it means."

I want to say, Humor her. I want to say, My boys and my husband are with me too, more than ever. I look in the old man's eyes and I can read his stubborn, peasant's message: *I have protected this woman as best I can. She is the only person I have left. Give to me or take from me what you will, but I will not sign for it. I will not pretend that I accept.*

In the car, Judith says, "You see what I'm up against? I'm sure they're lovely people, but their stubbornness and ignorance are driving me crazy. They think signing a paper is signing their sons' death warrants, don't they?"

I am looking out the window. I want to say, *In our culture, it is a parent's duty to hope.*

"Now Shaila, this next woman is a real mess. She cries day and night, and she refuses all medical help. We may have to—"

"Let me out at the subway," I say.

"I beg your pardon?" I can feel those blue eyes staring at me.

It would not be like her to disobey. She merely disapproves, and slows at a corner to let me out. Her voice is plaintive. "Is there anything I said? Anything I did?"

I could answer her suddenly in a dozen ways, but I choose not to. "Shaila? Let's talk about it," I hear, then slam the door.

* * *

A wife and mother begins her life in a new country, and that life is cut short. Yet her husband tells her: Complete what we have started. We, who stayed out of politics and came half way around the world to avoid religious and political feuding, have been the first in the New World to die from it. I no longer know what we started, nor how to complete it. I write letters to the editors of local papers and to members of Parliament. Now at least they admit it was a bomb. One MP answers back, with sympathy, but with a challenge. You want to make a difference? Work on a campaign. Work on mine. Politicize the Indian voter.

My husband's old lawyer helps me set up a trust. Vikram was a saver and a careful investor. He had saved the boys' boarding school and college fees. I sell the pink house at four times what we paid for it and take a small apartment downtown. I am looking for a charity to support.

* * *

We are deep in the Toronto winter, gray skies, icy pavements. I stay indoors, watching television. I have tried to assess my situation, how best to live my life, to complete what we began so many years ago. Kusum has written me from Hardwar that her life is now serene. She has seen Satish and has heard her daughter sing again. Kusum was on a pilgrimage, passing through a village, when she heard a young girl's voice, singing one of her daughter's favorite *bhajans*. She followed the music through the squalor of a Himalayan village, to a hut where a young girl, an exact replica of her daughter, was fanning coals under the kitchen fire. When she appeared, the girl cried out, "Ma!" and ran away. What did I think of that?

I think I can only envy her.

Pam didn't make it to California, but writes me from Vancouver. She works in a department store, giving makeup hints to Indian and Oriental girls. Dr. Ranganathan has given up his commute, given up his house and job, and accepted an academic position in Texas, where no one knows his story and he has vowed not to tell it. He calls me now once a week.

I wait, I listen and I pray, but Vikram has not returned to me. The voices and the shapes and the nights filled with visions ended abruptly several weeks ago.

I take it as a sign.

One rare, beautiful, sunny day last week, returning from a small errand on Yonge Street, I was walking through the park from the subway to my apartment. I live equidistant from the Ontario Houses of Parliament and the University of Toronto. The day was not cold, but something in the bare trees caught my attention. I looked up from the gravel, into the branches and the clear blue sky beyond. I thought I heard the rustling of larger forms, and I waited a moment for voices. Nothing.

"What?" I asked.

Then as I stood in the path looking north to Queen's Park and west to the university, I heard the voices of my family one last time. *Your time has come,* they said. *Go, be brave.*

I do not know where this voyage I have begun will end. I do not know which direction I will take. I dropped the package on a park bench and started walking.

# CHARLES BAXTER
(1947– )

Charles Baxter was born in Minneapolis, Minnesota. He graduated from Macalester College in St. Paul in 1969, and earned a Ph.D. from the State University of New York at Buffalo in 1974. He taught for five years at Wayne State University in Detroit before moving to Ann Arbor, where he is currently directing the writing program at the University of Michigan. He is married with one child.

Baxter's first publications were collections of poetry, *Chameleon* (1970) and *The South Dakota Guidebook* (1974). He published another volume of poems in 1989, *Imaginary Paintings.* He has written the novels *First Light* (1987) and *Shadow Play* (1993) and has published four short-story collections: *Harmony of the World* (1984), *Through the Safety Net* (1985), *A Relative Stranger* (1990), and *Believers* (1997). Many of his stories have been honored by inclusion in prize-winning annual anthologies. A collection of essays on fiction, *Burning Down the House,* appeared in 1997. Most of Baxter's fiction explores ordinary if troubled Middle Westerners, about whom he writes with generosity and compassion. In compelling language, his stories, as the writer Lorrie Moore has observed in a review, "capture the stranded inner lives of the Middle West's repressed eccentrics," people facing difficulty negotiating their way through a complex and often confusing world.

· teacher exposes students to new ideas
· kids → exposed to good & evil

## Gryphon

ON WEDNESDAY afternoon, between the geography lesson in ancient Egypt's hand-operated irrigation system and an art project that involved drawing a model city next to a mountain, our fourth-grade teacher, Mr. Hibler, developed a cough. This cough began with a series of muffled throat-clearings and progressed to propulsive noises contained within Mr. Hibler's closed mouth. "Listen to him," Carol Peterson whispered to me.

"He's gonna blow up." Mr. Hibler's laughter—dazed and infrequent—sounded a bit like his cough, but as we worked on our model cities we would look up, thinking he was enjoying a joke, and see Mr. Hibler's face turning red, his cheeks puffed out. This was not laughter. Twice he bent over, and his loose tie, like a plumb line, hung down straight from his neck as he exploded himself into a Kleenex. He would excuse himself, then go on coughing. "I'll bet you a dime," Carol Peterson whispered, "we get a substitute tomorrow."

Carol sat at the desk in front of mine and was a bad person—when she thought no one was looking she would blow her nose on notebook paper, then crumple it up and throw it into the wastebasket—but at times of crisis she spoke the truth. I knew I'd lose the dime.

"No deal," I said.

When Mr. Hibler stood us in formation at the door just prior to the final bell, he was almost incapable of speech. "I'm sorry, boys and girls," he said. "I seem to be coming down with something."

"I hope you feel better tomorrow, Mr. Hibler," Bobby Kryzanowicz, the faultless brown-noser, said, and I heard Carol Peterson's evil giggle. Then Mr. Hibler opened the door and we walked out to the buses, a clique of us starting noisily to hawk and *cough* as soon as we thought we were a few feet beyond Mr. Hibler's earshot.

* * *

Since Five Oaks was a rural community, and in Michigan, the supply of substitute teachers was limited to the town's unemployed community college graduates, a pool of about four mothers. These ladies fluttered, provided easeful class days, and nervously covered material we had mastered weeks earlier. Therefore it was a surprise when a woman we had never seen came into the class the next day, carrying a purple purse, a checkerboard lunchbox, and a few books. She put the books on one side of Mr. Hibler's desk and the lunchbox on the other, next to the Voice of Music phonograph. Three of us in the back of the room were playing with Heever, the chameleon that lived in a terrarium and on one of the plastic drapes, when she walked in.

She clapped her hands at us. "Little boys," she said, "why are you bent over together like that?" She didn't wait for us to answer. "Are you tormenting an animal? Put it back. Please sit down at your desks. I want no cabals this time of the day." We just stared at her. "Boys," she repeated, "I asked you to sit down."

I put the chameleon in his terrarium and felt my way to my desk, never taking my eyes off the woman. With white and green chalk, she had started to draw a tree on the left side of the blackboard. She didn't look usual. Furthermore, her tree was outsized, disproportionate, for some reason.

"This room needs a tree," she said, with one line drawing the suggestion of a leaf. "A large, leafy, shady, deciduous . . . oak."

Her fine, light hair had been done up in what I would learn years later was called a chignon, and she wore gold-rimmed glasses whose lenses seemed to have the faintest blue tint. Harold Knardahl, who sat across from me, whispered, "Mars," and I nodded slowly, savoring the imminent weirdness of the day. The substitute drew another branch with an extravagant arm gesture, then turned around and said, "Good morning. I don't believe I said good morning to all of you yet."

Facing us, she was no special age—an adult is an adult—but her face had two prominent lines, descending vertically from the sides of her mouth to her chin. I knew where I had seen those lines before: *Pinocchio.* They were marionette lines. "You may stare at me," she said to us, as a few more kids from the last bus came into the room, their eyes fixed on her, "for a few more seconds, until the bell rings. Then I will permit no more staring. Looking I will permit. Staring, no. It is impolite to stare, and a sign of bad breeding. You cannot make a social effort while staring."

Harold Knardahl did not glance at me, or nudge, but I heard him whisper "Mars" again, trying to get more mileage out of his single joke with the kids who had just come in.

When everyone was seated, the substitute teacher finished her tree, put down her chalk fastidiously on the phonograph, brushed her hands, and faced us. "Good morning," she said. "I am Miss Ferenczi, your teacher for the day. I am fairly new to your community, and I don't believe any of you know me. I will therefore start by telling you a story about myself."

While we settled back, she launched into her tale. She said her grandfather had been a Hungarian prince; her mother had been born in some place called Flanders, had been a pianist, and had played concerts for people Miss Ferenczi referred to as "crowned heads." She gave us a knowing look. "Grieg," she said, "the Norwegian master, wrote a concerto for piano that was . . ."—she paused—"my mother's triumph at her debut concert in London." Her eyes searched the ceiling. Our eyes followed. Nothing up there but ceiling tile. "For reasons that I shall not go into, my family's fortunes took us to Detroit, then north to dreadful Saginaw, and now here I am in Five Oaks, as your substitute teacher, for today, Thursday, October the eleventh. I believe it will be a good day: all the forecasts coincide. We shall start with your reading lesson. Take out your reading book. I believe it is called *Broad Horizons,* or something along those lines."

Jeannie Vermeesch raised her hand. Miss Ferenczi nodded at her. "Mr. Hibler always starts the day with the Pledge of Allegiance," Jeannie whined.

"Oh, does he? In that case," Miss Ferenczi said, "you must know it *very* well by now, and we certainly need not spend our time on it. No, no allegiance pledging on the premises today, by my reckoning. Not with so much sunlight coming into the room. A pledge does not suit my mood." She glanced at her watch. "Time *is* flying. Take out *Broad Horizons.*"

* * *

She disappointed us by giving us an ordinary lesson, complete with vocabulary and drills, comprehension questions, and recitation. She didn't seem to care for the material, however. She sighed every few minutes and rubbed her glasses with a frilly handkerchief that she withdrew, magician-style, from her left sleeve.

After reading we moved on to arithmetic. It was my favorite time of the morning, when the lazy autumn sunlight dazzled its way through ribbons of clouds past the windows on the east side of the classroom and crept across the linoleum floor. On the playground the first group of children, the kindergartners, were running on the quack grass just beyond the monkey bars. We were doing multiplication tables. Miss Ferenczi had made John Wazny stand up at his desk in the front row. He was supposed to go through the tables of six. From where I was sitting, I could smell the Vitalis soaked into John's plastered hair. He was doing fine until he came to six times eleven and six times twelve. "Six times eleven," he said, "is sixty-eight. Six times twelve is . . ." He put his fingers to his head, quickly and secretly sniffed his fingertips, and said, ". . . seventy-two." Then he sat down.

"Fine," Miss Ferenczi said. "Well now. That was very good."

"Miss Ferenczi!" One of the Eddy twins was waving her hand desperately in the air. "Miss Ferenczi! Miss Ferenczi!"

"Yes?"

"John said that six times eleven is sixty-eight and you said he was right!"

"*Did* I?" She gazed at the class with a jolly look breaking across her marionette's face. "Did I say that? Well, what *is* six times eleven?"

"It's sixty-six!"

She nodded. "Yes. So it is. But, and I know some people will not entirely agree with me, at some times it is sixty-eight."

"When? When is it sixty-eight?"

We were all waiting.

"In higher mathematics, which you children do not yet understand, six times eleven can be considered to be sixty-eight." She laughed through her nose. "In higher mathematics numbers are . . . more fluid. The only thing a number does is contain a certain amount of something. Think of water. A cup is not the only way to measure a certain amount of water, is it?" We were staring, shaking our heads. "You could use saucepans or thimbles. In either case, the water *would be the same.* Perhaps," she started again, "it would be better for you to think that six times eleven is sixty-eight only when I am in the room."

"Why is it sixty-eight," Mark Poole asked, "when you're in the room?"

"Because it's more interesting that way," she said, smiling very rapidly behind her blue-tinted glasses. "Besides, I'm your substitute teacher, am I not?" We all nodded. "Well, then, think of six times eleven equals sixty-eight as a substitute fact."

"A substitute fact?"

"Yes." Then she looked at us carefully. "Do you think," she asked, "that anyone is going to be hurt by a substitute fact?"

We looked back at her.

"Will the plants on the windowsill be hurt?" We glanced at them. There were sensitive plants thriving in a green plastic tray, and several wilted ferns in small clay pots. "Your dogs and cats, or your moms and dads?" She waited. "So," she concluded, "what's the problem?"

"But it's wrong," Janice Weber said, "isn't it?"

"What's your name, young lady?"

"Janice Weber."

"And you think it's wrong, Janice?"

"I was just asking."

"Well, all right. You were just asking. I think we've spent enough time on this matter by now, don't you, class? You are free to think what you like. When your teacher, Mr. Hibler, returns, six times eleven will be sixty-six again, you can rest assured. And it will be that for the rest of your lives in Five Oaks. Too bad, eh?" She raised her eyebrows and glinted herself at us. "But for now, it wasn't. So much for that. Let us go on to your assigned problems for today, as painstakingly outlined, I see, in Mr. Hibler's lesson plan. Take out a sheet of paper and write your names on the upper left-hand corner."

For the next half hour we did the rest of our arithmetic problems. We handed them in and then went on to spelling, my worst subject. Spelling always came before lunch. We were taking spelling dictation and looking at the clock. "Thorough," Miss Ferenczi said. "Boundary." She walked in the aisles between the desks, holding the spelling book open and looking down at our papers. "Balcony." I clutched my pencil. Somehow, the way she said those words, they seemed foreign, mis-voweled and mis-consonanted. I stared down at what I had spelled. *Balconie.* I turned the pencil upside down and erased my mistake. *Balconey.* That looked better, but still incorrect. I cursed the world of spelling and tried erasing it again and saw the paper beginning to wear away. *Balkony.* Suddenly I felt a hand on my shoulder.

"I don't like that word either," Miss Ferenczi whispered, bent over, her mouth near my ear. "It's ugly. My feeling is, if you don't like a word, you don't have to use it." She straightened up, leaving behind a slight odor of Clorets.

At lunchtime we went out to get our trays of sloppy joes, peaches in heavy syrup, coconut cookies, and milk, and brought them back to the classroom, where Miss Ferenczi was sitting at the desk, eating a brown sticky thing she had unwrapped from tightly rubber-banded waxed paper, "Miss Ferenczi," I said, raising my hand. "You don't have to eat with us. You can eat with the other teachers. There's a teacher's lounge," I ended up, "next to the principal's office."

"No, thank you," she said. "I prefer it here."

"We've got a room monitor," I said. "Mrs. Eddy." I pointed to where Mrs. Eddy, Joyce and Judy's mother, sat silently at the back of the room, doing her knitting.

"That's fine," Miss Ferenczi said. "But I shall continue to eat here, with you children. I prefer it," she repeated.

"How come?" Wayne Razmer asked without raising his hand.

"I talked to the other teachers before class this morning," Miss Ferenczi said, biting into her brown food. "There was a great rattling of the words for the fewness of the ideas. I didn't care for their brand of hilarity. I don't like ditto-machine jokes."

"Oh," Wayne said.

"What's that you're eating?" Maxine Sylvester asked, twitching her nose. "Is it food?"

"It most certainly *is* food. It's a stuffed fig. I had to drive almost down to Detroit to get it. I also brought some smoked sturgeon. And this," she said, lifting some green leaves out of her lunchbox, "is raw spinach, cleaned this morning."

"Why're you eating raw spinach?" Maxine asked.

"It's good for you," Miss Ferenczi said. "More stimulating than soda pop or smelling salts." I bit into my sloppy joe and stared blankly out the window. An almost invisible moon was faintly silvered in the daytime autumn sky. "As far as food is concerned," Miss Ferenczi was saying, "you have to shuffle the pack. Mix it up. Too many people eat . . . well, never mind."

"Miss Ferenczi," Carol Peterson said, "what are we going to do this afternoon?"

"Well," she said, looking down at Mr. Hibler's lesson plan. "I see that your teacher, Mr. Hibler, has you scheduled for a unit on the Egyptians." Carol groaned. "Yessss,"

Miss Ferenczi continued, "that is what we will do: the Egyptians. A remarkable people. Almost as remarkable as the Americans. But not quite." She lowered her head, did her quick smile, and went back to eating her spinach.

* * *

After noon recess we came back into the classroom and saw that Miss Ferenczi had drawn a pyramid on the blackboard close to her oak tree. Some of us who had been playing baseball were messing around in the back of the room, dropping the bats and gloves into the playground box, and Ray Schontzeler had just slugged me when I heard Miss Ferenczi's high-pitched voice, quavering with emotions. "Boys," she said, "come to order right this minute and take your seats. I do not wish to waste a minute of class time. Take out your geography books." We trudged to our desks and, still sweating, pulled out *Distant Lands and Their People.* "Turn to page forty-two." She waited for thirty seconds, then looked over at Kelly Munger. "Young man," she said, "why are you still fossicking in your desk?"

Kelly looked as if his foot had been stepped on. "Why am I what?"

"Why are you . . . burrowing in your desk like that?"

"I'm lookin' for the book, Miss Ferenczi."

Bobby Kryzanowicz, the faultless brown-noser who sat in the first row by choice, softly said, "His name is Kelly Munger. He can't ever find his stuff. He always does that."

"I don't care what his name is, especially after lunch," Miss Ferenczi said. *"Where is your book?"*

"I just found it." Kelly was peering into his desk and with both hands pulled at the book, shoveling along in front of it several pencils and crayons, which fell into his lap and then to the floor.

"I hate a mess," Miss Ferenczi said. "I hate a mess in a desk or a mind. It's . . . unsanitary. You wouldn't want your house at home to look like your desk at school, now, would you?" She didn't wait for an answer. "I should think not. A house at home should be as neat as human hands can make it. What were we talking about? Egypt. Page forty-two. I note from Mr. Hibler's lesson plan that you have been discussing the modes of Egyptian irrigation. Interesting, in my view, but not so interesting as what we are about to cover. The pyramids, and Egyptian slave labor. A plus on one side, a minus on the other." We had our books open to page forty-two, where there was a picture of a pyramid, but Miss Ferenczi wasn't looking at the book. Instead, she was staring at some object just outside the window.

"Pyramids," Miss Ferenczi said, still looking past the window. "I want you to think about pyramids. And what was inside. The bodies of the pharaohs, of course, and their attendant treasures. Scrolls. Perhaps," Miss Ferenczi said, her face gleeful but unsmiling, "these scrolls were novels for the pharaohs, helping them to pass the time in their long voyage through the centuries. But then, I am joking." I was looking at the lines on Miss Ferenczi's skin. "Pyramids," Miss Ferenczi went on, "were the repositories of special cosmic powers. The nature of a pyramid is to guide cosmic energy forces into a concentrated point. The Egyptians knew that; we have generally forgotten it. Did you know," she asked, walking to the side of the room so that she was standing by the coat closet, "that George Washington had Egyptian blood, from his grandmother? Certain features of the Constitution of the United States are notable for their Egyptian ideas."

Without glancing down at the book, she began to talk about the movement of souls in Egyptian religion. She said that when people die, their souls return to Earth in the form of carpenter ants or walnut trees, depending on how they behaved—"well or ill"—in life. She said that the Egyptians believed that people act the way they do because of magnetism produced by tidal forces in the solar system, forces produced by the sun and by its "planetary ally," Jupiter. Jupiter, she said, was a planet, as we had been told, but had "certain properties of stars." She was speaking very fast. She said that the Egyptians were great explorers and conquerors. She said that the greatest of all the conquerors, Genghis Khan, had had forty horses and forty young women killed on the site of his grave. We listened. No one tried to stop her. "I myself have been in Egypt," she said, "and have witnessed much dust and many brutalities." She said that an old man in Egypt who worked for a circus had personally shown her an animal in a cage, a monster, half bird and half lion. She said that this monster was called a gryphon and that she had heard about them but never seen them until she traveled to the outskirts of Cairo. She wrote the word out on the blackboard in large capital letters: GRYPHON. She said that Egyptian astronomers had discovered the planet Saturn but had not seen its rings. She said that the Egyptians were the first to discover that dogs, when they are ill, will not drink from rivers, but wait for rain, and hold their jaws open to catch it.

* * *

"She lies."

We were on the school bus home. I was sitting next to Carl Whiteside, who had bad breath and a huge collection of marbles. We were arguing. Carl thought she was lying. I said she wasn't, probably.

"I didn't believe that stuff about the bird," Carl said, "and what she told us about the pyramids? I didn't believe that, either. She didn't know what she was talking about."

"Oh yeah?" I had liked her. She was strange. I thought I could nail him. "If she was lying," I said, "what'd she say that was a lie?"

"Six times eleven isn't sixty-eight. It isn't ever. It's sixty-six, I know for a fact."

"She said so. She admitted it. What else did she lie about?"

"I don't know," he said. "Stuff."

"What stuff?"

"Well." He swung his legs back and forth. "You ever see an animal that was half lion and half bird?" He crossed his arms. "It sounded real fakey to me."

"It could happen," I said. I had to improvise, to outrage him. "I read in this newspaper my mom bought in the IGA about this scientist, this mad scientist in the Swiss Alps, and he's been putting genes and chromosomes and stuff together in test tubes, and he combined a human being and a hamster." I waited, for effect. "It's called a humster."

"You never." Carl was staring at me, his mouth open, his terrible bad breath making its way toward me. "What newspaper was it?"

*"The National Enquirer,"* I said, "that they sell next to the cash registers." When I saw his look of recognition, I knew I had him. "And this mad scientist," I said, "his name was, um, Dr. Frankenbush." I realized belatedly that this name was a mistake and

waited for Carl to notice its resemblance to the name of the other famous mad master of permutations, but he only sat there.

"A man and a hamster?" He was staring at me, squinting, his mouth opening in distaste. "Jeez. What'd it look like?"

* * *

When the bus reached my stop, I took off down our dirt road and ran up through the backyard, kicking the tire swing for good luck. I dropped my books on the back steps so I could hug and kiss our dog, Mr. Selby. Then I hurried inside. I could smell brussels sprouts cooking, my unfavorite vegetable. My mother was washing other vegetables in the kitchen sink, and my baby brother was hollering in his yellow playpen on the kitchen floor.

"Hi, Mom," I said, hopping around the playpen to kiss her. "Guess what?"

"I have no idea."

"We had this substitute today, Miss Ferenczi, and I'd never seen her before, and she had all these stories and ideas and stuff."

"Well. That's good." My mother looked out the window in front of the sink, her eyes on the pine woods west of our house. That time of the afternoon her skin always looked so white to me. Strangers always said my mother looked like Betty Crocker, framed by the giant spoon on the side of the Bisquick box. "Listen, Tommy," she said. "Would you please go upstairs and pick your clothes off the floor in the bathroom, and then go outside to the shed and put the shovel and ax away that your father left outside this morning?"

"She said that six times eleven was sometimes sixty-eight!" I said. "And she said she once saw a monster that was half lion and half bird." I waited. "In Egypt."

"Did you hear me?" my mother asked, raising her arm to wipe her forehead with the back of her hand. "You have chores to do."

"I know," I said. "I was just telling you about the substitute."

"It's very interesting," my mother said, quickly glancing down at me, "and we can talk about it later when your father gets home. But right now you have some work to do."

"Okay, Mom." I took a cookie out of the jar on the counter and was about to go outside when I had a thought. I ran into the living room, pulled out a dictionary next to the TV stand, and opened it to the Gs. After five minutes I found it. *Gryphon:* variant of griffin. *Griffin:* "a fabulous beast with the head and wings of an eagle and the body of a lion." Fabulous was right. I shouted with triumph and ran outside to put my father's tools in their proper places.

* * *

Miss Ferenczi was back the next day, slightly altered. She had pulled her hair down and twisted it into pigtails, with red rubber bands holding them tight one inch from the ends. She was wearing a green blouse and pink scarf, making her difficult to look at for a full class day. This time there was no pretense of doing a reading lesson or moving on to arithmetic. As soon as the bell rang, she simply began to talk.

She talked for forty minutes straight. There seemed to be less connection between her ideas, but the ideas themselves were, as the dictionary would say, fabulous. She said she had heard of a huge jewel, in what she called the antipodes, that was so brilliant that when light shone into it at a certain angle it would blind whoever was looking at its center. She said the biggest diamond in the world was cursed and had killed everyone who owned it, and that by a trick of fate it was called the Hope Diamond. Diamonds are magic, she said, and this is why women wear them on their fingers, as a sign of the magic of womanhood. Men have strength, Miss Ferenczi said, but no true magic. That is why men fall in love with women but women do not fall in love with men: they just love being loved. George Washington had died because of a mistake he made about a diamond. Washington was not the first *true* President, but she didn't say who was. In some places in the world, she said, men and women still live in the trees and eat monkeys for breakfast. Their doctors are magicians. At the bottom of the sea are creatures thin as pancakes who have never been studied by scientists because when you take them up to air, the fish explode.

There was not a sound in the classroom, except for Miss Ferenczi's voice, and Donna DeShano's coughing. No one even went to the bathroom.

Beethoven, she said, had not been deaf; it was a trick to make himself famous, and it worked. As she talked, Miss Ferenczi's pigtails swung back and forth. There are trees in the world, she said, that eat meat: their leaves are sticky and close up on bugs like hands. She lifted her hands and brought them together, palm to palm. Venus, which most people think is the next closest planet to the sun, is not always closer, and, besides, it is the planet of greatest mystery because of its thick cloud cover. "I know what lies underneath those clouds," Miss Ferenczi said, and waited. After the silence, she said, "Angels. Angels live under those clouds." She said that angels were not invisible to everyone and were in fact smarter than most people. They did not dress in robes as was often claimed but instead wore formal evening clothes, as if they were about to attend a concert. Often angels *do* attend concerts and sit in the aisles, where, she said, most people pay no attention to them. She said the most terrible angel had the shape of the Sphinx. "There is no running away from that one," she said. She said that unquenchable fires burn just under the surface of the earth in Ohio, and that the baby Mozart fainted dead away in his cradle when he first heard the sound of a trumpet. She said that someone named Narzim al Harrardim was the greatest writer who ever lived. She said that planets control behavior, and anyone conceived during a solar eclipse would be born with webbed feet.

"I know you children like to hear these things," she said; "these secrets, and that is why I am telling you all this." We nodded. It was better than doing comprehension questions for the readings in *Broad Horizons.*

"I will tell you one more story," she said, "and then we will have to do arithmetic." She leaned over, and her voice grew soft. "There is no death," she said. "You must never be afraid. Never. That which is, cannot die. It will change into different earthly and unearthly elements, but I know this as sure as I stand here in front of you, and I swear it: you must not be afraid. I have seen this truth with these eyes. I know it because in a dream God kissed me. Here." And she pointed with her right index finger to the side of her head, below the mouth where the vertical lines were carved into her skin.

* * *

Absentmindedly we all did our arithmetic problems. At recess the class was out on the playground, but no one was playing. We were all standing in small groups, talking about

Miss Ferenczi. We didn't know if she was crazy, or what. I looked out beyond the playground, at the rusted cars piled in a small heap behind a clump of sumac, and I wanted to see shapes there, approaching me.

* * *

On the way home, Carl sat next to me again. He didn't say much, and I didn't either. At last he turned to me. "You know what she said about the leaves that close up on bugs?"

"Huh?"

"The leaves," Carl insisted. "The meat-eating plants. I know it's true. I saw it on television. The leaves have this icky glue that the plants have got smeared all over them and the insects can't get off 'cause they're stuck. I saw it." He seemed demoralized. "She's tellin' the truth."

"Yeah."

"You think she's seen all those angels?"

I shrugged.

"I don't think she has," Carl informed me. "I think she made that part up."

"There's a tree," I suddenly said. I was looking out the window at the farms along County Road H. I knew every barn, every broken windmill, every fence, every anhydrous ammonia tank, by heart. "There's a tree that's . . . that I've seen . . ."

"Don't you try to do it," Carl said. "You'll just sound like a jerk."

* * *

I kissed my mother. She was standing in front of the stove. "How was your day?" she asked.

"Fine."

"Did you have Miss Ferenczi again?"

"Yeah."

"Well?"

"She was fine. Mom," I asked, "can I go to my room?"

"No," she said, "not until you've gone out to the vegetable garden and picked me a few tomatoes." She glanced at the sky. "I think it's going to rain. Skedaddle and do it now. Then you come back inside and watch your brother for a few minutes while I go upstairs. I need to clean up before dinner." She looked down at me. "You're looking a little pale, Tommy." She touched the back of her hand to my forehead and I felt her diamond ring against my skin. "Do you feel all right?"

"I'm fine," I said, and went out to pick the tomatoes.

* * *

Coughing mutedly, Mr. Hibler was back the next day, slipping lozenges into his mouth when his back was turned at forty-five-minute intervals and asking us how much of his prepared lesson plan Miss Ferenczi had followed. Edith Atwater took the responsibility for the class of explaining to Mr. Hibler that the substitute hadn't always done exactly what he, Mr. Hibler, would have done, but we had worked hard even though she talked a lot. About what? he asked. All kinds of things, Edith said. I sort of forgot. To our relief, Mr. Hibler seemed not at all interested in what Miss Ferenczi had said to fill the day. He probably thought it was woman's talk: unserious and not suited for school. It was enough that he had a pile of arithmetic problems from us to correct.

For the next month, the sumac turned a distracting red in the field, and the sun traveled toward the southern sky, so that its rays reached Mr. Hibler's Halloween display on the bulletin board in the back of the room, fading the pumpkin head scarecrow from orange to tan. Every three days I measured how much farther the sun had moved toward the southern horizon by making small marks with my black Crayola on the north wall, ant-sized marks only I knew were there.

And then in early December, four days after the first permanent snowfall, she appeared again in our classroom. The minute she came in the door, I felt my heart begin to pound. Once again, she was different: this time, her hair hung straight down and seemed hardly to have been combed. She hadn't brought her lunchbox with her, but she was carrying what seemed to be a small box. She greeted all of us and talked about the weather. Donna DeShano had to remind her to take her overcoat off.

When the bell to start the day finally rang, Miss Ferenczi looked out at all of us and said, "Children, I have enjoyed your company in the past, and today I am going to reward you." She held up the small box. "Do you know what this is?" She waited. "Of course you don't. It is a Tarot pack."

Edith Atwater raised her hand. "What's a Tarot pack, Miss Ferenczi?"

"It is used to tell fortunes," she said. "And that is what I shall do this morning. I shall tell your fortunes, as I have been taught to do."

"What's fortune?" Bobby Kryzanowicz asked.

"The future, young man. I shall tell you what your future will be. I can't do your whole future, of course. I shall have to limit myself to the five-card system, the wands, cups, swords, pentacles, and the higher arcanes. Now who wants to be first?"

There was a long silence. Then Carol Peterson raised her hand.

"All right," Miss Ferenczi said. She divided the pack into five smaller packs and walked back to Carol's desk, in front of mine. "Pick one card from each one of these packs," she said. I saw that Carol had a four of cups and a six of swords, but I couldn't see the other cards. Miss Ferenczi studied the cards on Carol's desk for a minute. "Not bad," she said. "I do not see much higher education. Probably an early marriage. Many children. There's something bleak and dreary here, but I can't tell what. Perhaps just the tasks of a housewife life. I think you'll do very well, for the most part." She smiled at Carol, a smile with a certain lack of interest. "Who wants to be next?"

Carl Whiteside raised his hand slowly.

"Yes," Miss Ferenczi said, "let's do a boy." She walked over to where Carl sat. After he picked his five cards, she gazed at them for a long time. "Travel," she said. "Much distant travel. You might go into the army. Not too much romantic interest here. A late marriage, if at all. But the Sun in your major arcana, that's a very good card." She giggled. "You'll have a happy life."

Next I raised my hand. She told me my future. She did the same with Bobby Kryzanowicz, Kelly Munger, Edith Atwater, and Kim Foor. Then she came to Wayne Razmer. He picked his five cards, and I could see that the Death card was one of them.

"What's your name?" Miss Ferenczi asked.

"Wayne."

"Well, Wayne," she said, "you will undergo a great metamorphosis, a change, before you become an adult. Your earthly element will no doubt leap higher, because you seem to be a sweet boy. This card, this nine of swords, tells me of suffering and desolation. And this ten of wands, well, that's a heavy load."

"What about this one?" Wayne pointed at the Death card.

"It means, my sweet, that you will die soon." She gathered up the cards. We were all looking at Wayne. "But do not fear," she said. "It is not really death. Just change. Out of your earthly shape." She put the cards on Mr. Hibler's desk. "And now, let's do some arithmetic."

* * *

At lunchtime Wayne went to Mr. Faegre, the principal, and informed him of what Miss Ferenczi had done. During the noon recess, we saw Miss Ferenczi drive out of the parking lot in her rusting green Rambler American. I stood under the slide, listening to the other kids coasting down and landing in the little depressive bowls at the bottom. I was kicking stones and tugging at my hair right up to the moment when I saw Wayne come out to the playground. He smiled, the dead fool, and with the fingers of his right hand he was showing everyone how he had told on Miss Ferenczi.

I made my way toward Wayne, pushing myself past two girls from another class. He was watching me with his little pinhead eyes.

"You told," I shouted at him. "She was just kidding."

"She shouldn't have," he shouted back. "We were supposed to be doing arithmetic."

"She just scared you," I said. "You're a chicken. You're a chicken, Wayne. You are. Scared of a little card," I sing-songed.

Wayne fell at me, his two fists hammering down on my nose. I gave him a good one in the stomach and then I tried for his head. Aiming my fist, I saw that he was crying. I slugged him.

"She was right," I yelled. "She was always right! She told the truth!" Other kids were whooping. "You were just scared, that's all!"

And then large hands pulled at us, and it was my turn to speak to Mr. Faegre.

* * *

In the afternoon Miss Ferenczi was gone, and my nose was stuffed with cotton clotted with blood, and my lip had swelled, and our class had been combined with Mrs. Mantei's sixth-grade class for a crowded afternoon science unit on insect life in ditches and swamps. I knew where Mrs. Mantei lived: she had a new house trailer just down the road from us, at the Clearwater Park. She was no mystery. Somehow she and Mr. Bodine, the other fourth-grade teacher, had managed to fit forty-five desks into the room. Kelly Munger asked if Miss Ferenczi had been arrested, and Mrs. Mantei said no, of course not. All that afternoon, until the buses came to pick us up, we learned about field crickets and two-striped grasshoppers, water bugs, cicadas, mosquitoes, flies, and moths. We learned about insects' hard outer shell, the exoskeleton, and the usual parts of the mouth, including the labrum, mandible, maxilla, and glossa. We learned about compound eyes, and the four-stage metamorphosis from egg to larva to pupa to adult. We learned something, but not much, about mating. Mrs. Mantei drew, very skillfully, the internal anatomy of the grasshopper on the blackboard. We learned about the dance of the honeybee, directing other bees in the hive to pollen. We found out about which insects were pests to man, and which were not. On lined white pieces of paper we made lists of insects we might actually see, then a list of insects too small to be clearly visible, such as fleas; Mrs. Mantei said that our assignment would be to memorize these lists for the next day, when Mr. Hibler would certainly return and test us on our knowledge.

# AMY TAN

## (1952– )

Amy Tan's work, like that of Maxine Hong Kingston, has been much acclaimed. Her novel, *The Joy Luck Club* (1989), like Louise Erdrich's *Love Medicine,* consists of a sequence of interrelated stories. Focusing on mother-daughter relationships, Tan vividly explores the ethnic, gender, and intergenerational issues associated with an American-born child growing up with immigrant parents—an old American story made new again by a new generation of Asian writers.

Amy Tan was born in Oakland, California, the daughter of Chinese immigrants. Her father, trained as an electrical engineer as well as a Baptist minister, came to the United States in 1947. Her mother fled China just before the Communist takeover in 1949, leaving behind three daughters of a previous marriage. The family lived in a number of cities around the San Francisco bay area. Tan's father and older brother died of brain tumors before she was 15. He mother took her and her younger brother to live in Europe, and Tan graduated from high school in Montreux, Switzerland, in 1969. Upon returning to the United States, She attended Linfield College in Oregon, where she met her husband. She transferred to San José State University, where she earned degrees in English and linguistics in 1973 and 1974. After some graduate study at the University of California at Berkeley, Tan worked as a language development consultant to programs for disabled children, and then as a free-lance technical writer for various companies during most of the 1980s. Dissatisfied with the high-tech world, she turned to more creative endeavors, like studying jazz piano and writing fiction.

Tan's best-selling *The Joy Luck Club* was followed by *The Kitchen God's Wife* in 1991, *The Hundred Secret Senses* in 1995, and *The Bonesetter's Daughter* in 2001. Tan has also published two children's books. She and her husband have residences in San Francisco and New York.

## Rules of the Game

I WAS six when my mother taught me the art of invisible strength. It was a strategy for winning arguments, respect from others, and eventually, though neither of us knew it at the time, chess games.

"Bite back your tongue," scolded my mother when I cried loudly, yanking her hand toward the store that sold bags of salted plums. At home, she said, "Wise guy, he not go against wind. In Chinese we say, Come from South, blow with wind—poom!—North will follow. Strongest wind cannot be seen."

The next week I bit back my tongue as we entered the store with the forbidden candies. When my mother finished her shopping, she quietly plucked a small bag of plums from the rack and put it on the counter with the rest of the items.

* * *

My mother imparted her daily truths so she could help my older brothers and me rise above our circumstances. We lived in San Francisco's Chinatown. Like most of the other Chinese children who played in the back alleys of restaurants and curio shops, I didn't think we were poor. My bowl was always full, three five-course meals every day, beginning with a soup full of mysterious things I didn't want to know the names of.

We lived on Waverly Place, in a warm, clean, two-bedroom flat that sat above a small Chinese bakery specializing in steamed pastries and dim sum. In the early morning, when the alley was still quiet, I could smell fragrant red beans as they were cooked down to a pasty sweetness. By daybreak, our flat was heavy with the odor of fried sesame balls and sweet curried chicken crescents. From my bed, I would listen as my father got ready for work, then locked the door behind him, one-two-three clicks.

At the end of our two-block alley was a small sandlot playground with swings and slides well-shined down the middle with use. The play area was bordered by wood-slat benches where old-country people sat cracking roasted watermelon seeds with their golden teeth and scattering the husks to an impatient gathering of gurgling pigeons. The best playground, however, was the dark alley itself. It was crammed with daily mysteries and adventures. My brothers and I would peer into the medicinal herb shop, watching old Li dole out onto a stiff sheet of white paper the right amount of insect shells, saffron-colored seeds, and pungent leaves for his ailing customers. It was said that he once cured a woman dying of an ancestral curse that had eluded the best of American doctors. Next to the pharmacy was a printer who specialized in gold-embossed wedding invitations and festive red banners.

Farther down the street was Ping Yuen Fish Market. The front window displayed a tank crowded with doomed fish and turtles struggling to gain footing on the slimy green-tiled sides. A hand-written sign informed tourists, "Within this store, is all for food, not for pet." Inside, the butchers with their bloodstained white smocks deftly gutted the fish while customers cried out their orders and shouted, "Give me your freshest," to which the butchers always protested, "All are freshest." On less crowded market days, we would inspect the crates of live frogs and crabs which we were warned not to poke, boxes of dried cuttlefish, and row upon row of iced prawns, squid, and slippery fish. The sanddabs made me shiver each time; their eyes lay on one flattened side and reminded me of my mother's story of a careless girl who ran into a crowded street and was crushed by a cab. "Was smash flat," reported my mother.

At the corner of the alley was Hong Sing's, a four-table café with a recessed stairwell in front that led to a door marked "Tradesmen." My brothers and I believed the bad people emerged from this door at night. Tourists never went to Hong Sing's, since the menu was printed only in Chinese. A Caucasian man with a big camera once posed me and my playmates in front of the restaurant. He had us move to the side of the picture window so the photo would capture the roasted duck with its head dangling from a juice-covered rope. After he took the picture, I told him he should go into Hong Sing's and eat dinner. When he smiled and asked me what they served, I shouted, "Guts and duck's feet and octopus gizzards!" Then I ran off with my friends, shrieking with laughter as we scampered across the alley and hid in the entryway grotto of the China Gem Company, my heart pounding with hope that he would chase us.

My mother named me after the street that we lived on: Waverly Place Jong, my official name for important American documents. But my family called me Meimei, "Little Sister." I was the youngest, the only daughter. Each morning before school, my mother would twist and yank on my thick black hair until she had formed two tightly wound pigtails. One day, as she struggled to weave a hard-toothed comb through my disobedient hair, I had a sly thought.

I asked her, "Ma, what is Chinese torture?" My mother shook her head. A bobby pin was wedged between her lips. She wetted her palm and smoothed the hair above my ear, then pushed the pin in so that it nicked sharply against my scalp.

"Who say this word?" she asked without a trace of knowing how wicked I was being. I shrugged my shoulders and said, "Some boy in my class said Chinese people do Chinese torture."

"Chinese people do many things," she said simply. "Chinese people do business, do medicine, do painting. Not lazy like American people. We do torture. Best torture."

* * *

My older brother Vincent was the one who actually got the chess set. We had gone to the annual Christmas party held at the First Chinese Baptist Church at the end of the alley. The missionary ladies had put together a Santa bag of gifts donated by members of another church. None of the gifts had names on them. There were separate sacks for boys and girls of different ages.

One of the Chinese parishioners had donned a Santa Claus costume and a stiff paper beard with cotton balls glued to it. I think the only children who thought he was the real thing were too young to know that Santa Claus was not Chinese. When my turn came up, the Santa man asked me how old I was. I thought it was a trick question; I was seven according to the American formula and eight by the Chinese calendar. I said I was born on March 17, 1951. That seemed to satisfy him. He then solemnly asked if I had been a very, very good girl this year and did I believe in Jesus Christ and obey my parents. I knew the only answer to that. I nodded back with equal solemnity.

Having watched the other children opening their gifts, I already knew that the big gifts were not necessarily the nicest ones. One girl my age got a large coloring book of biblical characters, while a less greedy girl who selected a smaller box received a glass vial of lavender toilet water. The sound of the box was also important. A ten-year-old boy had chosen a box that jangled when he shook it. It was a tin globe of the world with a slit for inserting money. He must have thought it was full of dimes and nickels, because when he saw that it had just ten pennies, his face fell with such undisguised disappointment that his mother slapped the side of his head and led him out of the church hall, apologizing to the crowd for her son who had such bad manners he couldn't appreciate such a fine gift.

As I peered into the sack, I quickly fingered the remaining presents, testing their weight, imagining what they contained. I chose a heavy, compact one that was wrapped in shiny silver foil and a red satin ribbon. It was a twelve-pack of Life Savers and I spent the rest of the party arranging and rearranging the candy tubes in the order of my favorites. My brother Winston chose wisely as well. His present turned out to be a box of intricate plastic parts; the instructions on the box proclaimed that when they were properly assembled he would have an authentic miniature replica of a World War II submarine.

Vincent got the chess set, which would have been a very decent present to get at a church Christmas party, except it was obviously used and, as we discovered later, it was missing a black pawn and a white knight. My mother graciously thanked the unknown benefactor, saying, "Too good. Cost too much." At which point, an old lady with fine white, wispy hair nodded toward our family and said with a whistling whisper, "Merry, merry Christmas."

When we got home, my mother told Vincent to throw the chess set away. "She not want it. We not want it," she said, tossing her head stiffly to the side with a tight, proud smile. My brothers had deaf ears. They were already lining up the chess pieces and reading from the dog-eared instruction book.

* * *

I watched Vincent and Winston play during Christmas week. The chessboard seemed to hold elaborate secrets waiting to be untangled. The chessmen were more powerful than old Li's magic herbs that cured ancestral curses. And my brothers wore such serious faces that I was sure something was at stake that was greater than avoiding the tradesmen's door to Hong Sing's.

"Let me! Let me!" I begged between games when one brother or the other would sit back with a deep sigh of relief and victory, the other annoyed, unable to let go of the outcome. Vincent at first refused to let me play, but when I offered my Life Savers as replacements for the buttons that filled in for the missing pieces, he relented. He chose the flavors: wild cherry for the black pawn and peppermint for the white knight. Winner could eat both.

As our mother sprinkled flour and rolled out small doughy circles for the steamed dumplings that would be our dinner that night, Vincent explained the rules, pointing to each piece. "You have sixteen pieces and so do I. One king and queen, two bishops, two knights, two castles, and eight pawns. The pawns can only move forward one step, except on the first move. Then they can move two. But they can only take men by moving crossways like this, except in the beginning, when you can move ahead and take another pawn."

"Why?" I asked as I moved my pawn. "Why can't they move more steps?"

"Because they're pawns," he said.

"But why do they go crossways to take other men? Why aren't there any women and children?"

"Why is the sky blue? Why must you always ask stupid questions?" asked Vincent. "This is a game. These are the rules. I didn't make them up. See. Here. In the book." He jabbed a page with a pawn in his hand. "Pawn. P-A-W-N. Pawn. Read it yourself."

My mother patted the flour off her hands. "Let me see book," she said quietly. She scanned the pages quickly, not reading the foreign English symbols, seeming to search deliberately for nothing in particular.

"This American rules," she concluded at last. "Every time people come out from foreign country, must know rules. You not know, judge say, Too bad, go back. They not telling you why so you can use their way go forward. They say, Don't know why, you find out yourself. But they knowing all the time. Better you take it, find out why yourself." She tossed her head back with a satisfied smile.

I found out about all the whys later. I read the rules and looked up all the big words in a dictionary. I borrowed books from the Chinatown library. I studied each chess piece, trying to absorb the power each contained.

I learned about opening moves and why it's important to control the center early on; the shortest distance between two points is straight down the middle. I learned about the middle game and why tactics between two adversaries are like clashing ideas; the one who plays better has the clearest plans for both attacking and getting out of traps. I learned why it is essential in the endgame to have foresight, a mathematical understanding of all possible moves, and patience; all weaknesses and advantages become evident to a strong adversary and are obscured to a tiring opponent. I discovered that for the whole game one must gather invisible strengths and see the endgame before the game begins.

I also found out why I should never reveal "why" to others. A little knowledge withheld is a great advantage one should store for future use. That is the power of chess. It is a game of secrets in which one must show and never tell.

I loved the secrets I found within the sixty-four black and white squares. I carefully drew a handmade chessboard and pinned it to the wall next to my bed, where at night I would stare for hours at imaginary battles. Soon I no longer lost any games or Life Savers, but I lost my adversaries. Winston and Vincent decided they were more interested in roaming the streets after school in their Hopalong Cassidy cowboy hats.

* * *

On a cold spring afternoon, while walking home from school, I detoured through the playground at the end of our alley. I saw a group of old men, two seated across a folding table playing a game of chess, others smoking pipes, eating peanuts, and watching. I ran home and grabbed Vincent's chess set, which was bound in a cardboard box with rubber bands. I also carefully selected two prized rolls of Life Savers. I came back to the park and approached a man who was observing the game.

"Want to play?" I asked him. His face widened with surprise and he grinned as he looked at the box under my arm.

"Little sister, been a long time since I play with dolls," he said, smiling benevolently. I quickly put the box down next to him on the bench and displayed my retort.

Lau Po, as he allowed me to call him, turned out to be a much better player than my brothers. I lost many games and many Life Savers. But over the weeks, with each diminishing roll of candies, I added new secrets. Lau Po gave me the names. The Double Attack from the East and West Shores. Throwing Stones on the Drowning Man. The Sudden Meeting of the Clan. The Surprise from the Sleeping Guard. The Humble Servant Who Kills the King. Sand in the Eyes of Advancing Forces. A Double Killing Without Blood.

There were also the fine points of chess etiquette. Keep captured men in neat rows, as well-tended prisoners. Never announce "Check" with vanity, lest someone with an unseen sword slit your throat. Never hurl pieces into the sandbox after you have lost a game, because then you must find them again, by yourself, after apologizing to all around you. By the end of the summer, Lau Po had taught me all he knew, and I had become a better chess player.

A small weekend crowd of Chinese people and tourists would gather as I played and defeated my opponents one by one. My mother would join the crowds during these outdoor exhibition games. She sat proudly on the bench, telling my admirers with proper Chinese humility, "Is luck."

A man who watched me play in the park suggested that my mother allow me to play in local chess tournaments. My mother smiled graciously, an answer that meant nothing. I desperately wanted to go, but I bit back my tongue. I knew she would not let me play among strangers. So as we walked home I said in a small voice that I didn't want to play in the local tournament. They would have American rules. If I lost, I would bring shame on my family.

"Is shame you fall down nobody push you," said my mother.

During my first tournament, my mother sat with me in the front row as I waited for my turn. I frequently bounced my legs to unstick them from the cold metal seat of the folding chair. When my name was called, I leapt up. My mother unwrapped something in her lap. It was her *chang,* a small tablet of red jade which held the sun's fire. "Is luck," she whispered, and tucked it into my dress pocket. I turned to my opponent, a fifteen-year-old boy from Oakland. He looked at me, wrinkling his nose.

As I began to play, the boy disappeared, the color ran out of the room, and I saw only my white pieces and his black ones waiting on the other side. A light wind began blowing past my ears. It whispered secrets only I could hear.

"Blow from the South," it murmured. "The wind leaves no trail." I saw a clear path, the traps to avoid. The crowd rustled. "Shhh! Shhh!" said the corners of the room. The wind blew stronger. "Throw sand from the East to distract him." The knight came forward ready for the sacrifice. The wind hissed, louder and louder. "Blow, blow, blow. He cannot see. He is blind now. Make him lean away from the wind so he is easier to knock down."

"Check," I said, as the wind roared with laughter. The wind died down to little puffs, my own breath.

* * *

My mother placed my first trophy next to a new plastic chess set that the neighborhood Tao society had given to me. As she wiped each piece with a soft cloth, she said, "Next time win more, lose less."

"Ma, it's not how many pieces you lose," I said. "Sometimes you need to lose pieces to get ahead."

"Better to lose less, see if you really need."

At the next tournament, I won again, but it was my mother who wore the triumphant grin.

"Lost eight piece this time. Last time was eleven. What I tell you? Better off lose less!" I was annoyed, but I couldn't say anything.

I attended more tournaments, each one farther away from home. I won all games, in all divisions. The Chinese bakery downstairs from our flat displayed my growing collection of trophies in its window, amidst the dust-covered cakes that were never picked up. The day after I won an important regional tournament, the window encased a fresh sheet cake with whipped-cream frosting and red script saying "Congratulations, Waverly Jong, Chinatown Chess Champion." Soon after that, a flower shop, headstone engraver, and funeral parlor offered to sponsor me in national tournaments. That's when my mother decided I no longer had to do the dishes. Winston and Vincent had to do my chores.

"Why does she get to play and we do all the work," complained Vincent.

"Is new American rules," said my mother. "Meimei play, squeeze all her brains out for win chess. You play, worth squeeze towel."

By my ninth birthday, I was a national chess champion. I was still some 429 points away from grand-master status, but I was touted as the Great American Hope, a child prodigy and a girl to boot. They ran a photo of me in *Life* magazine next to a quote in which Bobby Fischer said, "There will never be a woman grand master." "Your move, Bobby," said the caption.

The day they took the magazine picture I wore neatly plaited braids clipped with plastic barrettes trimmed with rhinestones. I was playing in a large high school auditorium that echoed with phlegmy coughs and the squeaky rubber knobs of chair legs sliding across freshly waxed wooden floors. Seated across from me was an American man, about the same age as Lau Po, maybe fifty. I remember that his sweaty brow seemed to weep at my every move. He wore a dark, malodorous suit. One of his pockets was stuffed with a great white kerchief on which he wiped his palm before sweeping his hand over the chosen chess piece with great flourish.

In my crisp pink-and-white dress with scratchy lace at the neck, one of two my mother had sewn for these special occasions, I would clasp my hands under my chin, the delicate points of my elbows poised lightly on the table in the manner my mother had shown me for posing for the press. I would swing my patent leather shoes back and forth like an impatient child riding on a school bus. Then I would pause, suck in my lips, twirl my chosen piece in midair as if undecided, and then firmly plant it in its new threatening place, with a triumphant smile thrown back at my opponent for good measure.

* * *

I no longer played in the alley of Waverly Place. I never visited the playground where the pigeons and old men gathered. I went to school, then directly home to learn new chess secrets, cleverly concealed advantages, more escape routes.

But I found it difficult to concentrate at home. My mother had a habit of standing over me while I plotted out my games. I think she thought of herself as my protective ally. Her lips would be sealed tight, and after each move I made, a soft "Hmmmmph" would escape from her nose.

"Ma, I can't practice when you stand there like that," I said one day. She retreated to the kitchen and made loud noises with the pots and pans. When the crashing stopped, I could see out of the corner of my eye that she was standing in the doorway. "Hmmmph!" Only this one came out of her tight throat.

My parents made many concessions to allow me to practice. One time I complained that the bedroom I shared was so noisy that I couldn't think. Thereafter, my brothers slept in a bed in the living room facing the street. I said I couldn't finish my rice; my head didn't work right when my stomach was too full. I left the table with half-finished bowls and nobody complained. But there was one duty I couldn't avoid. I had to accompany my mother on Saturday market days when I had no tournament to play. My mother would proudly walk with me, visiting many shops, buying very little. "This my daughter Wave-ly Jong," she said to whoever looked her way.

One day after we left a shop I said under my breath, "I wish you wouldn't do that, telling everybody I'm your daughter." My mother stopped walking. Crowds of people with heavy bags pushed past us on the sidewalk, bumping into first one shoulder, then another.

"Aiii-ya. So shame be with mother?" She grasped my hand even tighter as she glared at me.

I looked down. "It's not that, it's just so obvious. It's just so embarrassing."

"Embarrass you be my daughter?" Her voice was cracking with anger.

"That's not what I meant. That's not what I said."

"What you say?"

I knew it was a mistake to say anything more, but I heard my voice speaking, "Why do you have to use me to show off? If you want to show off, then why don't you learn to play chess?"

My mother's eyes turned into dangerous black slits. She had no words for me, just sharp silence.

I felt the wind rushing around my hot ears. I jerked my hand out of my mother's tight grasp and spun around, knocking into an old woman. Her bag of groceries spilled to the ground.

"Aii-ya! Stupid girl!" my mother and the woman cried. Oranges and tin cans careened down the sidewalk. As my mother stooped to help the old woman pick up the escaping food, I took off.

I raced down the street, dashing between people, not looking back as my mother screamed shrilly, "Meimei! Meimei!" I fled down an alley, past dark, curtained shops and merchants washing the grime off their windows. I sped into the sunlight, into a large street crowded with tourists examining trinkets and souvenirs. I ducked into another dark alley, down another street, up another alley. I ran until it hurt and I realized I had nowhere to go, that I was not running from anything. The alleys contained no escape routes.

My breath came out like angry smoke. It was cold. I sat down on an upturned plastic pail next to a stack of empty boxes, cupping my chin with my hands, thinking hard. I imagined my mother, first walking briskly down one street or another looking for me, then giving up and returning home to await my arrival. After two hours, I stood up on creaking legs and slowly walked home.

The alley was quiet and I could see the yellow lights shining from our flat like two tiger's eyes in the night. I climbed the sixteen steps to the door, advancing quietly up each so as not to make any warning sounds. I turned the knob; the door was locked. I heard a chair moving, quick steps, the locks turning—click! click! click!—and then the door opened.

"About time you got home," said Vincent. "Boy, are you in trouble."

He slid back to the dinner table. On a platter were the remains of a large fish, its fleshy head still connected to bones swimming upstream in vain escape. Standing there waiting for my punishment, I heard my mother speak in a dry voice.

"We not concerning this girl. This girl not have concerning for us."

Nobody looked at me. Bone chopsticks clinked against the inside of bowls being emptied into hungry mouths.

I walked into my room, closed the door, and lay down on my bed. The room was dark, the ceiling filled with shadows from the dinnertime lights of neighboring flats.

In my head, I saw a chessboard with sixty-four black and white squares. Opposite me was my opponent, two angry black slits. She wore a triumphant smile. "Strongest wind cannot be seen," she said.

Her black men advanced across the plane, slowly marching to each successive level as a single unit. My white pieces screamed as they scurried and fell off the board one by one. As her men drew closer to my edge, I felt myself growing light. I rose up into the air and flew out the window. Higher and higher, above the alley, over the tops of tiled roofs, where I was gathered up by the wind and pushed up toward the night sky until everything below me disappeared and I was alone.

I closed my eyes and pondered my next move.

# RICHARD FORD
## (1944– )

Born in Jackson, Mississippi, and raised in Arkansas, Richard Ford studied at Michigan State University where he received a B.A. in English in 1966. He attended law school for a year before enrolling in the creative writing program at the University of California at Irvine, where he completed an M.F.A. in 1970. He was married in 1968. Ford has taught briefly at a number of schools, including the University of Michigan, Williams College in Massachusetts, Princeton University, and Harvard University, and has published stories in such periodicals as *The New Yorker, Granta, Esquire, Antaeus, Tri-Quarterly, Michigan Quarterly Review,* and *The Paris Review.* He makes his home in Montana.

Ford's first novel, *A Piece of My Heart,* was published in 1976 to mixed reviews. Set in Mississippi, the novel was accused of being "neo-Faulknerian." Ford, however, has resisted regional labels or categories for his work. His second novel, *The Ultimate Good Luck* (1981), was set in Mexico. It was his third novel, *The Sportswriter* (1986), set in New Jersey, that elevated his reputation to the first rank of contemporary writers. *Time* chose it as one of the best five books of 1986, and it won the PEN/Faulkner Award for fiction in 1987. Ford's much acclaimed collection of stories, *Rock Springs,* was published in 1987. The novel *Wildlife* appeared in 1990. A sequel to *The Sportswriter, Indepen-*

*dence Day,* was published to great acclaim in 1995 and won the Pulitzer Prize. In 1997 Ford published *Women with Men: Three Stories.* Ford's best work concerns wounded men attempting to comprehend and cope with loss, disappointment, and ruptured relationships while still maintaining a belief in a sense of duty, responsibility, and what was once called honor.

# Rock Springs

EDNA AND I had started down from Kalispell, heading for Tampa–St. Pete where I still had some friends from the old glory days who wouldn't turn me in to the police. I had managed to scrape with the law in Kalispell over several bad checks—which is a prison crime in Montana. And I knew Edna was already looking at her cards and thinking about a move, since it wasn't the first time I'd been in law scrapes in my life. She herself had already had her own troubles, losing her kids and keeping her ex-husband, Danny, from breaking in her house and stealing her things while she was at work, which was really why I had moved in in the first place, that and needing to give my little daughter, Cheryl, a better shake in things.

I don't know what was between Edna and me, just beached by the same tides when you got down to it. Though love has been built on frailer ground than that, as I well know. And when I came in the house that afternoon, I just asked her if she wanted to go to Florida with me, leave things where they sat, and she said, "Why not? My datebook's not that full."

Edna and I had been a pair eight months, more or less man and wife, some of which time I had been out of work, and some when I'd worked at the dog track as a lead-out and could help with the rent and talk sense to Danny when he came around. Danny was afraid of me because Edna had told him I'd been in prison in Florida for killing a man, though that wasn't true. I had once been in jail in Tallahassee for stealing tires and had gotten into a fight on the country farm where a man had lost his eye. But I hadn't done the hurting, and Edna just wanted the story worse than it was so Danny wouldn't act crazy and make her have to take her kids back, since she had made a good adjustment to not having them, and I already had Cheryl with me. I'm not a violent person and would never put a man's eye out, much less kill someone. My former wife, Helen, would come all the way from Waikiki Beach to testify to that. We never had violence, and I believe in crossing the street to stay out of trouble's way. Though Danny didn't know that.

But we were half down through Wyoming, going toward I-80 and feeling good about things, when the oil light flashed on in the car I'd stolen, a sign I knew to be a bad one.

I'd gotten us a good car, a cranberry Mercedes I'd stolen out of an ophthalmologist's lot in Whitefish, Montana. I stole it because I thought it would be comfortable over a long haul, because I thought it got good mileage, which it didn't, and because I'd never had a good car in my life, just old Chevy junkers and used trucks back from when I was a kid swamping citrus with Cubans.

The car made us all high that day. I ran the windows up and down, and Edna told us some jokes and made faces. She could be lively. Her features would light up like a beacon and you could see her beauty, which wasn't ordinary. It all made me giddy, and I drove clear down to Bozeman, then straight on through the park to Jackson Hole. I rented us the bridal suite in the Quality Court in Jackson and left Cheryl and her little dog, Duke sleeping while Edna and I drove to a rib barn and drank beer and laughed till after midnight.

It felt like a whole new beginning for us, bad memories left behind and a new horizon to build on. I got so worked up, I had a tattoo done on my arm that said famous times, and Edna bought a Bailey hat with an Indian feather band and a little turquoise-and-silver bracelet for Cheryl, and we made love on the seat of the car in the Quality Court parking lot just as the sun was burning up on the Snake River, and everything seemed then like the end of the rainbow.

It was that very enthusiasm, in fact, that made me keep the car one day longer instead of driving it into the river and stealing another one, like I should've done and *had* done before.

Where the car went bad there wasn't a town in sight or even a house, just some low mountains maybe fifty miles away or maybe a hundred, a barbed-wire fence in both directions, hardpan prairie, and some hawks riding the evening air seizing insects.

I got out to look at the motor, and Edna got out with Cheryl and the dog to let them have a pee by the car. I checked the water and checked the oil stick, and both of them said perfect.

"What's that light mean, Earl?" Edna said. She had come and stood by the car with her hat on. She was just sizing things up for herself.

"We shouldn't run it," I said. "Something's not right in the oil."

She looked around at Cheryl and Little Duke, who were peeing on the hardtop side by side like two little dolls, then out at the mountains, which were becoming black and lost in the distance. "What're we doing?" she said. She wasn't worried yet, but she wanted to know what I was thinking about.

"Let me try it again."

"That's a good idea," she said, and we all got back in the car.

When I turned the motor over, it started right away and the red light stayed off and there weren't any noises to make you think something was wrong. I let it idle a minute, then pushed the accelerator down and watched the red bulb. But there wasn't any light on, and I started wondering if maybe I hadn't dreamed I saw it, or that it had been the sun catching an angle off the window chrome, or maybe I was scared of something and didn't know it.

"What's the matter with it, Daddy?" Cheryl said from the backseat. I looked back at her and she had on her turquoise bracelet and Edna's hat set back on the back of her head and that little black-and-white Heinz dog on her lap. She looked like a little cowgirl in the movies.

"Nothing, honey, everything's fine now," I said.

"Little Duke tinkled where I tinkled," Cheryl said, and laughed.

"You're two of a kind," Edna said, not looking back. Edna was usually good with Cheryl, but I knew she was tired now. We hadn't had much sleep, and she had a tendency to get cranky when she didn't sleep. "We oughta ditch this damn car first chance we get" she said.

"What's the first chance we got?" I asked, because I knew she'd been at the map.

"Rock Springs, Wyoming," Edna said with conviction. "Thirty miles down this road." She pointed out ahead.

I had wanted all along to drive the car into Florida like a big success story. But I knew Edna was right about it, that we shouldn't take crazy chances. I had kept thinking of it as my car and not the ophthalmologist's, and that was how you got caught in these things.

"Then my belief is we ought to go to Rock Springs and negotiate ourselves a new car," I said. I wanted to stay upbeat, like everything was panning out right.

"That's a great idea," Edna said, and she leaned over and kissed me hard on the mouth.

"That's a great idea," Cheryl said. "Let's pull on out of here right now."

* * *

The sunset that day I remember as being the prettiest I'd ever seen. Just as it touched the rim of the horizon, it all at once fired the air into jewels and red sequins the precise likes of which I had never seen before and haven't seen since. The West has it all over everywhere for sunsets, even Florida, where it's supposedly flat but where half the time trees block your view.

"It's cocktail hour," Edna said after we'd driven a while. "We ought to have a drink and celebrate something." She felt better thinking we were going to get rid of the car. It certainly had dark troubles and was something you'd want to put behind you.

Edna had out a whiskey bottle and some plastic cups and was measuring levels on the glove box lid. She liked drinking, and she liked drinking in the car, which was something you got used to in Montana, where it wasn't against the law, but where, strangely enough, a bad check would land you in Deer Lodge Prison for a year.

"Did I ever tell you I once had a monkey?" Edna said, setting my drink on the dashboard where I would reach it when I was ready. Her spirits were already picked up. She was like that, up one minute and down the next.

"I don't think you ever did tell me that," I said. "Where were you then?"

"Missoula," she said. She put her bare feet on the dash and rested the cup on her breasts. "I was waitressing at the AmVets. This was before I met you. Some guy came in one day with a monkey. A spider monkey. And I said, just to be joking, 'I'll roll you for that monkey.' And the guy said, 'Just one roll?' And I said, 'Sure.' He put the monkey down on the bar, picked up the cup, and rolled out boxcars. I picked it up and rolled out three fives. And I just stood there looking at the guy. He was just some guy passing through, I guess a vet. He got a strange look on his face—I'm sure not as strange as the one I had—but he looked kind of sad and surprised and satisfied all at once. I said, 'We can roll again,' But he said, 'No, I never roll twice for anything.' And he sat and drank a beer and talked about one thing and another for a while, about nuclear war and building a stronghold somewhere up in the Bitterroot, whatever it was, while I just watched the monkey, wondering what I was going to do with it when the guy left. And pretty soon he got up and said, 'Well, good-bye, Chipper'—that was his monkey's name, of course. And then he left before I could say anything. And the monkey just sat on the bar all that night. I don't know what made me think of that, Earl. Just something weird. I'm letting my mind wander."

"That's perfectly fine," I said. I took a drink of my drink. "I'd never own a monkey," I said after a minute. "They're too nasty. I'm sure Cheryl would like a monkey, though, wouldn't you, honey?" Cheryl was down on the seat playing with Little Duke. She used to talk about monkeys all the time then. "What'd you ever do with that monkey?" I said, watching the speedometer. We were having to go slower now because the red light kept fluttering on. And all I could do to keep it off was go slower. We were going maybe thirty-five and it was an hour before dark, and I was hoping Rock Springs wasn't far away.

"You really want to know?" Edna said. She gave me a quick glance, then looked back at the empty desert as if she was brooding over it.

"Sure," I said. I was still upbeat. I figured I could worry about breaking down and let other people be happy for a change.

"I kept it a week." And she seemed gloomy all of a sudden, as if she saw some aspect of the story she had never seen before. "I took it home and back and forth to the Am Vets on my shifts. And it didn't cause any trouble. I fixed a chair up for it to sit on, back of the bar, and people liked it. It made a nice little clicking noise. We changed its name to Mary because the bartender figured out it was a girl. Though I was never really comfortable with it at home. I felt like it watched me too much. Then one day a guy came in, some guy who'd been in Vietnam, still wore a fatigue coat. And he said to me, 'Don't you know that a monkey'll kill you? It's got more strength in its fingers than you got in your whole body.' He said people had been killed in Vietnam by monkeys, bunches of them marauding while you were asleep, killing you and covering you with leaves. I didn't believe a word of it, except that when I got home and got undressed I started looking over across the room at Mary on her chair in the dark watching me. And I got the creeps. And after a while I got up and went out to the car, got a length of clothesline wire, and came back in and wired her to the doorknob through her little silver collar, then went back and tried to sleep. And I guess I must've slept the sleep of the dead—though I don't remember it—because when I got up I found Mary had tipped off her chair-back and hanged herself on the wire line. I'd made it too short."

Edna seemed badly affected by that story and slid low in the seat so she couldn't see out over the dash. "Isn't that a shameful story, Earl, what happened to that poor little monkey?"

"I see a town! I see a town!" Cheryl started yelling from the back seat, and right up Little Duke started yapping and the whole car fell into a racket. And sure enough she had seen something I hadn't, which was Rock Springs, Wyoming, at the bottom of a long hill, a little glowing jewel in the desert with I-80 running on the north side and the black desert spread out behind.

"That's it, honey," I said. "That's where we're going. You saw it first."

"We're hungry," Cheryl said. "Little Duke wants some fish, and I want spaghetti." She put her arms around my neck and hugged me.

"Then you'll just get it," I said. "You can have anything you want. And so can Edna and so can Little Duke." I looked over at Edna, smiling, but she was staring at me with eyes that were fierce with anger. "What's wrong?" I said.

"Don't you care anything about that awful thing that happened to me?" Her mouth was drawn tight, and her eyes kept cutting back at Cheryl and Little Duke, as if they had been tormenting her.

"Of course I do," I said. "I thought that was an awful thing." I didn't want her to be unhappy. We were almost there, and pretty soon we could sit down and have a real meal without thinking somebody might be hurting us.

"You want to know what I did with that monkey?" Edna said.

"Sure I do," I said.

"I put her in a green garbage bag, put it in the trunk of my car, drove to the dump, and threw her in the trash." She was staring at me darkly, as if the story meant something to her that was real important but that only she could see and that the rest of the world was a fool for.

"Well, that's horrible," I said. "But I don't see what else you could do. You didn't mean to kill it. You'd have done it differently if you had. And then you had to get rid of it, and I don't know what else you could have done. Throwing it away might seem unsympathetic to somebody, probably, but not to me. Sometimes that's all you can do, and you can't worry about what somebody else thinks." I tried to smile at her, but the red light was staying on if I pushed the accelerator at all, and I was trying to gauge if we could coast to Rock Springs before the car gave out completely. I looked at Edna again. "What else can I say?" I said.

"Nothing," she said, and stared back at the dark highway. "I should've known that's what you'd think. You've got a character that leaves something out, Earl. I've known that a long time."

"And yet here you are," I said. "And you're not doing so bad. Things could be a lot worse. At least we're all together here."

"Things could always be worse," Edna said. "You could go to the electric chair tomorrow."

"That's right," I said. "And somewhere somebody probably will. Only it won't be you."

"I'm hungry," said Cheryl. "When're we gonna eat? Let's find a motel. I'm tired of this. Little Duke's tired of it too."

Where the car stopped rolling was some distance from the town, though you could see the clear outline of the interstate in the dark with Rock Springs lighting up the sky behind. You could hear the big tractors hitting the spacers in the overpass, revving up for the climb to the mountains.

I shut off the lights.

"What're we going to do now?" Edna said irritably, giving me a bitter look.

"I'm figuring it," I said. "It won't be hard, whatever it is. You won't have to do anything."

"I'd hope not," she said and looked the other way.

Across the road and across a dry wash a hundred yards was what looked like a huge mobile-home town, with a factory or a refinery of some kind lit up behind it and in full swing. There were lights on in a lot of the mobile homes, and there were cars moving along an access road that ended near the freeway overpass a mile the other way. The lights in the mobile homes seemed friendly to me, and I knew right then what I should do.

"Get out," I said, opening my door.

"Are we walking?" Edna said.

"We're pushing."

"I'm not pushing." Edna reached up and locked her door.

"All right," I said. "Then you just steer."

"You're pushing us to Rock Springs, are you, Earl? It doesn't look like it's more than about three miles."

"I'll push," Cheryl said from the back.

"No, hon. Daddy'll push. You just get out with Little Duke and move out of the way."

Edna gave me a threatening look, just as if I'd tried to hit her. But when I got out she slid into my seat and took the wheel, staring angrily ahead straight into the cottonwood scrub.

"Edna can't drive that car," Cheryl said from out in the dark. "She'll run it in the ditch."

"Yes, she can, hon. Edna can drive it as good as I can. Probably better."

"No she can't," Cheryl said. "No she can't either." And I thought she was about to cry, but she didn't.

I told Edna to keep the ignition on so it wouldn't lock up and to steer into the cottonwoods with the parking lights on so she could see. And when I started, she steered it straight off into the trees, and I kept pushing until we were twenty yards into the cover and the tires sank in the soft sand and nothing at all could be seen from the road.

"Now where are we?" she said, sitting at the wheel. Her voice was tired and hard, and I knew she could have put a good meal to use. She had a sweet nature, and I recognized that this wasn't her fault but mine. Only I wished she could be more hopeful.

"You stay right here, and I'll go over to that trailer park and call us a cab," I said.

"What cab?" Edna said, her mouth wrinkled as if she'd never heard anything like that in her life.

"There'll be cabs," I said, and tried to smile at her. "There's cabs everywhere."

"What're you going to tell him when he gets here? Our stolen car broke down and we need a ride to where we can steal another one? That'll be a big hit, Earl."

"I'll talk," I said. "You just listen to the radio for ten minutes and then walk on out to the shoulder like nothing was suspicious. And you and Cheryl act nice. She doesn't need to know about this car."

"Like we're not suspicious enough already, right?" Edna looked up at me out of the lighted car. "You don't think right, did you know that, Earl? You think the world's stupid and you're smart. But that's not how it is. I feel sorry for you. You might've *been* something, but things just went crazy someplace."

I had a thought about poor Danny. He was a vet and crazy as a shit-house mouse, and I was glad he wasn't in for all this. "Just get the baby in the car," I said, trying to be patient. "I'm hungry like you are."

"I'm tired of this," Edna said. "I wish I'd stayed in Montana."

"Then you can go back in the morning," I said. "I'll buy the ticket and put you on the bus. But not till then."

"Just get on with it, Earl." She slumped down in the seat, turning off the parking lights with one foot and the radio on with the other.

* * *

The mobile home community was as big as any I'd ever seen. It was attached in some way to the plant that was lighted up behind it, because I could see a car once in a while leave one of the trailer streets, turn in the direction of the plant, then go slowly into it. Everything in the plant was white, and you could see that all the trailers were painted white and looked exactly alike. A deep hum came out of the plant, and I thought as I got closer that it wouldn't be a location I'd ever want to work in.

I went right to the first trailer where there was a light, and knocked on the metal door. Kids' toys were lying in the gravel around the little wood steps, and I could hear talking on TV that suddenly went off. I heard a woman's voice talking, and then the door opened wide.

A large Negro woman with a wide, friendly face stood in the doorway. She smiled at me and moved forward as if she was going to come out, but she stopped at the top step. There was a little Negro boy behind her peeping out from behind her legs, watching me with his eyes half closed. The trailer had that feeling that no one else was inside, which was a feeling I knew something about.

"I'm sorry to intrude," I said. "But I've run up on a little bad luck tonight. My name's Earl Middleton."

The woman looked at me, then out into the night toward the freeway as if what I had said was something she was going to be able to see. "What kind of bad luck?" she said, looking down at me again.

"My car broke down out on the highway," I said. "I can't fix it myself, and I wondered if I could use your phone to call for help."

The woman smiled at me knowingly. "We can't live without cars, can we?"

"That's the honest truth," I said.

"They're like our hearts," she said, her face shining in the little bulb light that burned beside the door. "Where's your car situated?"

I turned and looked over into the dark, but I couldn't see anything because of where we'd put it. "It's over there," I said. "You can't see it in the dark."

"Who all's with you now?" the woman said. "Have you got your wife with you?"

"She's with my little girl and our dog in the car," I said. "My daughter's asleep or I would have brought them."

"They shouldn't be left in the dark by themselves," the woman said and frowned. "There's too much unsavoriness out there."

"The best I can do is hurry back." I tried to look sincere, since everything except Cheryl being asleep and Edna being my wife was the truth. The truth is meant to serve you if you'll let it, and I wanted it to serve me. "I'll pay for the phone call," I said. "If you'll bring the phone to the door I'll call from right here."

The woman looked at me again as if she was searching for a truth of her own, then back out into the night. She was maybe in her sixties, but I couldn't say for sure. "You're not going to rob me, are you, Mr. Middleton?" She smiled like it was a joke between us.

"Not tonight," I said, and smiled a genuine smile. "I'm not up to it tonight. Maybe another time."

"Then I guess Terrel and I can let you use our phone with Daddy not here, can't we, Terrel? This is my grandson, Terrel Junior, Mr. Middleton." She put her hand on the boy's head and looked down at him. "Terrel won't talk. Though if he did he'd tell you to use our phone. He's a sweet boy." She opened the screen for me to come in.

The trailer was a big one with a new rug and a new couch and a living room that expanded to give the space of a real house. Something good and sweet was cooking in the kitchen, and the trailer felt like it was somebody's comfortable new home instead of just temporary. I've lived in trailers, but they were just snailbacks with one room and no toilet, and they always felt cramped and unhappy—though I've thought maybe it might've been me that was unhappy in them.

There was a big Sony TV and a lot of kids' toys scattered on the floor. I recognized a Greyhound bus I'd gotten for Cheryl. The phone was beside a new leather recliner, and the Negro woman pointed for me to sit down and call and gave me the phone book. Terrel began fingering his toys and the woman sat on the couch while I called, watching me and smiling.

There were three listings for cab companies, all with one number different. I called the numbers in order and didn't get an answer until the last one, which answered with the name of the second company. I said I was on the highway beyond the interstate and that my wife and family needed to be taken to town and I would arrange for a tow later. While I was giving the location, I looked up the name of a tow service to tell the driver in case he asked.

When I hung up, the Negro woman was sitting looking at me with the same look she had been staring with into the dark, a look that seemed to want truth. She was smiling, though. Something pleased her and I reminded her of it.

"This is a very nice home," I said, resting in the recliner, which felt like the driver's seat of the Mercedes, and where I'd have been happy to stay.

"This isn't *our* house, Mr. Middleton," the Negro woman said. "The company owns these. They give them to us for nothing. We have our own home in Rockford, Illinois."

"That's wonderful," I said.

"It's never wonderful when you have to be away from home, Mr. Middleton, though we're only here three months, and it'll be easier when Terrel Junior begins his special school. You see, our son was killed in the war, and his wife ran off without Terrel Junior. Though you shouldn't worry. He can't understand us. His little feelings can't be hurt." The woman folded her hands in her lap and smiled in a satisfied way. She was an attractive woman, and had on a blue-and-pink floral dress that made her seem bigger than she could've been, just the right woman to sit on the couch she was sitting on. She was good nature's picture, and I was glad she could be, with her little brain-damaged boy, living in a place where no one in his right mind would want to live a minute. "Where do *you* live, Mr. Middleton?" she said politely, smiling in the same sympathetic way.

"My family and I are in transit," I said. "I'm an ophthalmologist, and we're moving back to Florida, where I'm from. I'm setting up practice in some little town where it's warm year-round. I haven't decided where."

"Florida's a wonderful place," the woman said. "I think Terrel would like it there."

"Could I ask you something?" I said.

"You certainly may," the woman said. Terrel had begun pushing his Greyhound across the front of the TV screen, making a scratch that no one watching the set could miss. "Stop that, Terrel Junior," the woman said quietly. But Terrel kept pushing his bus on the glass, and she smiled at me again as if we both understood something sad. Except I knew Cheryl would never damage a television set. She had respect for nice things, and I was sorry for the lady that Terrel didn't. "What did you want to ask?" the woman said.

"What goes on in that plant or whatever it is back there beyond these trailers, where all the lights are on?"

"Gold," the woman said and smiled.

"It's what?" I said.

"Gold," the Negro woman said, smiling as she had for almost all the time I'd been there. "It's a gold mine."

"They're mining gold back there?" I said, pointing.

"Every night and every day." She smiled in a pleased way.

"Does your husband work there?" I said.

"He's the assayer," she said. "He controls the quality. He works three months a year, and we live the rest of the time at home in Rockford. We've waited a long time for this. We've been happy to have our grandson, but I won't say I'll be sorry to have him go. We're ready to start our lives over." She smiled broadly at me and then at Terrel, who was giving her a spiteful look from the floor. "You said you had a daughter," the Negro woman said. "And what's her name?"

"Irma Cheryl," I said. "She's named for my mother."

"That's nice. And she's healthy, too. I can see it in your face." She looked at Terrel Junior with pity.

"I guess I'm lucky," I said.

"So far you are. But children bring you grief, the same way they bring you joy. We were unhappy for a long time before my husband got his job in the gold mine. Now, when Terrel starts to school, we'll be kids again." She stood up. "You might miss your cab, Mr. Middleton," she said, walking toward the door, though not to be forcing me out. She was too polite. "If *we* can't see your car, the cab surely won't be able to."

"That's true." I got up off the recliner, where I'd been so comfortable. "None of us have eaten yet, and your food makes me know how hungry we probably all are."

"There are fine restaurants in town, and you'll find them," the Negro woman said. "I'm sorry you didn't meet my husband. He's a wonderful man. He's everything to me."

"Tell him I appreciate the phone," I said. "You saved me."

"You weren't hard to save," the woman said. "Saving people is what we were all put on earth to do. I just passed you on to whatever's coming to you."

"Let's hope it's good," I said, stepping back into the dark.

"I'll be hoping, Mr. Middleton. Terrel and I will both be hoping."

I waved to her as I walked out into the darkness toward the car where it was hidden in the night.

* * *

The cab had already arrived when I got there. I could see its little red-and-green roof lights all the way across the dry wash, and it made me worry that Edna was already saying something to get us in trouble, something about the car or where we'd come from, something that would cast suspicion on us. I thought, then, how I never planned things well enough. There was always a gap between my plan and what happened, and I only responded to things as they came along and hoped I wouldn't get in trouble. I was an offender in the law's eyes. But I always *thought* differently, as if I weren't an offender and had no intention of being one, which was the truth. But as I read on a napkin once, between the idea and the act a whole kingdom lies. And I had a hard time with my acts, which were oftentimes offender's acts, and my ideas, which were as good as the gold they mined there where the bright lights were blazing.

"We're waiting for you, Daddy," Cheryl said when I crossed the road. "The taxicab's already here."

"I see, hon," I said, and gave Cheryl a big hug. The cabdriver was sitting in the driver's seat having a smoke with the lights on inside. Edna was leaning against the back of the cab between the taillights, wearing her Bailey hat. "What'd you tell him?" I said when I got close.

"Nothing," she said. "What's there to tell?"

"Did he see the car?"

She glanced over in the direction of the trees where we had hid the Mercedes. Nothing was visible in the darkness, though I could hear Little Duke combing around in the underbrush tracking something, his little collar tinkling. "Where're we going?" she said. "I'm so hungry I could pass out."

"Edna's in a terrible mood," Cheryl said. "She already snapped at me."

"We're tired, honey," I said. "So try to be nicer."

"She's never nice," Cheryl said.

"Run go get Little Duke," I said. "And hurry back."

"I guess *my* questions come last here, right?" Edna said.

I put my arm around her. "That's not true."

"Did you find somebody over there in the trailers you'd rather stay with? You were gone long enough."

"That's not a thing to say," I said. "I was just trying to make things look right, so we don't get put in jail."

"So *you* don't, you mean." Edna laughed a little laugh I didn't like hearing.

"That's right. So I don't," I said. "I'd be the one in Dutch." I stared out at the big, lighted assemblage of white buildings and white lights beyond the trailer community, plumes of white smoke escaping up into the heartless Wyoming sky, the whole company of buildings looking like some unbelievable castle, humming away in a distorted dream. "You know what all those buildings are there?" I said to Edna, who hadn't moved and who didn't really seem to care if she ever moved anymore ever.

"No. But I can't say it matters, because it isn't a motel and it isn't a restaurant."

"It's a gold mine," I said, staring at the gold mine, which, I knew now, was a greater distance from us than it seemed, though it seemed huge and near, up against the cold sky. I thought there should've been a wall around it with guards instead of just the lights and no fence. It seemed as if anyone could go in and take what they wanted, just the way I had gone up to that woman's trailer and used the telephone, though that obviously wasn't true.

Edna began to laugh then. Not the mean laugh I didn't like, but a laugh that had something caring behind it, a full laugh that enjoyed a joke, a laugh she was laughing the first time I laid eyes on her, in Missoula in the East Gate Bar in 1979, a laugh we used to laugh together when Cheryl was still with her mother and I was working steady at the track and not stealing cars or passing bogus checks to merchants. A better time all around. And for some reason it made me laugh just hearing her, and we both stood there behind the cab in the dark, laughing at the gold mine in the desert, me with my arm around her and Cheryl out rustling up Little Duke and the cabdriver smoking in the cab and our stolen Mercedes-Benz, which I'd had such hopes for in Florida, stuck up to its axle in sand, where I'd never get to see it again.

"I always wondered what a gold mine would look like when I saw it," Edna said, still laughing, wiping a tear from her eye.

"Me too," I said. "I was always curious about it."

"We're a couple of fools, aren't we, Earl?" she said, unable to quit laughing completely. "We're two of a kind."

"It might be a good sign, though," I said.

"How could it be? It's not our gold mine. There aren't any drive-up windows." She was still laughing.

"We've seen it," I said, pointing. "That's it right there. It may mean we're getting closer. Some people never see it at all."

"In a pig's eye, Earl," she said. "You and me see it in a pig's eye."

And she turned and got in the cab to go.

* * *

The cabdriver didn't ask anything about our car or where it was, to mean he'd noticed something queer. All of which made me feel like we had made a clean break from the car and couldn't be connected with it until it was too late, if ever. The driver told us a lot about Rock Springs while he drove, that because of the gold mine a lot of people had moved there in just six months, people from all over, including New York, and that most of them lived out in the trailers. Prostitutes from New York City, who he called "B-girls," had come into town, he said, on the prosperity tide, and Cadillacs with New York plates cruised the little streets every night, full of Negroes with big hats who ran the women. He told us that everybody who got in his cab now wanted to know where the women were, and when he got our call he almost didn't come because some of the trailers were brothels operated by the mine for engineers and computer people away from home. He said he got tired of running back and forth out there just for vile business. He said that *60 Minutes* had even done a program about Rock Springs and that a blow-up had resulted in Cheyenne, though nothing could be done unless the boom left town. "It's prosperity's fruit," the driver said. "I'd rather be poor, which is lucky for me."

He said all the motels were sky-high, but since we were a family he could show us a nice one that was affordable. But I told him we wanted a first-rate place where they took animals, and the money didn't matter because we had had a hard day and wanted to finish on a high note. I also knew that it was in the little nowhere places that the police look for you and find you. People I'd known were always being arrested in cheap hotels and tourist courts with names you'd never heard of before. Never in Holiday Inns or TraveLodges.

I asked him to drive us to the middle of town and back out again so Cheryl could see the train station, and while we were there I saw a pink Cadillac with New York plates and a TV aerial being driven slowly by a Negro in a big hat down a narrow street where there were just bars and a Chinese restaurant. It was an odd sight, nothing you could ever expect.

"There's your pure criminal element," the cabdriver said and seemed sad. "I'm sorry for people like you to see a thing like that. We've got a nice town here, but there're some that want to ruin it for everybody. There used to be a way to deal with trash and criminals, but those days are gone forever."

"You said it," Edna said.

"You shouldn't let it get *you* down," I said to him. "There's more of you than them.

And there always will be. You're the best advertisement this town has. I know Cheryl will remember you and not *that* man, won't you, honey?" But Cheryl was asleep by then, holding Little Duke in her arms on the taxi seat.

The driver took us to the Ramada Inn on the interstate, not far from where we'd broken down. I had a small pain of regret as we drove under the Ramada awning that we hadn't driven up in a cranberry-colored Mercedes but instead in a beat-up old Chrysler taxi driven by an old man full of complaints. Though I knew it was for the best. We were better off without that car; better, really, in any other car but that one, where the signs had turned bad.

I registered under another name and paid for the room in cash so there wouldn't be any questions. On the line where it said "Representing" I wrote "Ophthalmologist" and put "M.D." after the name. It had a nice look to it, even though it wasn't my name.

When we got to the room, which was in the back where I'd asked for it, I put Cheryl on one of the beds and Little Duke beside her so they'd sleep. She'd missed dinner, but it only meant she'd be hungry in the morning, when she could have anything she wanted. A few missed meals don't make a kid bad. I'd missed a lot of them myself and haven't turned out completely bad.

"Let's have some fried chicken," I said to Edna when she came out of the bathroom. "They have good fried chicken at Ramadas, and I noticed the buffet was still up. Cheryl can stay right here, where it's safe, till we're back."

"I guess I'm not hungry anymore," Edna said. She stood at the window staring out into the dark. I could see out the window past her some yellowish foggy glow in the sky. For a moment I thought it was the gold mine out in the distance lighting the night, though it was only the interstate.

"We could order up," I said. "Whatever you want. There's a menu on the phone book. You could just have a salad."

"You go ahead," she said. "I've lost my hungry spirit." She sat on the bed beside Cheryl and Little Duke and looked at them in a sweet way and put her hand on Cheryl's cheek just as if she'd had a fever. "Sweet little girl," she said. "Everybody loves you."

"What do you want to do?" I said. "I'd like to eat. Maybe *I'll* order up some chicken."

"Why don't you do that?" she said. "It's your favorite." And she smiled at me from the bed.

I sat on the other bed and dialed room service. I asked for chicken, garden salad, potato and a roll, plus a piece of hot apple pie and iced tea. I realized I hadn't eaten all day. When I put down the phone I saw that Edna was watching me, not in a hateful way or a loving way, just in a way that seemed to say she didn't understand something and was going to ask me about it.

"When did watching me get so entertaining?" I said and smiled at her. I was trying to be friendly. I knew how tired she must be. It was after nine o'clock.

"I was just thinking how much I hated being in a motel without a car that was mine to drive. Isn't that funny? I started feeling like that last night when that purple car wasn't mine. That purple car just gave me the willies, I guess, Earl."

"One of those cars *outside* is yours," I said. "Just stand right there and pick it out."

"I know," she said. "But that's different, isn't it?" She reached and got her blue Bailey hat, put it on her head, and set it way back like Dale Evans. She looked sweet. "I used to like to go to motels, you know," she said. "There's something secret about them and free—I was never paying, of course. But you felt safe from everything and free to do what you wanted because you'd made the decision to be there and paid that price, and all the rest was the good part. Fucking and everything, you know." She smiled at me in a good-natured way.

"Isn't that the way this is?" I was sitting on the bed, watching her, not knowing what to expect her to say next.

"I don't guess it is, Earl," she said and stared out the window. "I'm thirty-two and I'm going to have to give up on motels. I can't keep that fantasy going anymore."

"Don't you like this place?" I said and looked around at the room. I appreciated the modern paintings and the lowboy bureau and the big TV. It seemed like a plenty nice enough place to me, considering where we'd been.

"No, I don't," Edna said with real conviction. "There's no use in my getting mad at you about it. It isn't your fault. You do the best you can for everybody. But every trip teaches you something. And I've learned I need to give up on motels before some bad thing happens to me. I'm sorry."

"What does that mean?" I said, because I really didn't know what she had in mind to do, though I should've guessed.

"I guess I'll take that ticket you mentioned," she said, and got up and faced the window. "Tomorrow's soon enough. We haven't got a car to take me anyhow."

"Well, that's a fine thing," I said, sitting on the bed, feeling like I was in shock. I wanted to say something to her, to argue with her, but I couldn't think what to say that seemed right. I didn't want to be mad at her, but it made me mad.

"You've got a right to be mad at me, Earl," she said, "but I don't think you can really blame me." She turned around and faced me and sat on the windowsill, her hands on her knees. Someone knocked on the door, and I just yelled for them to set the tray down and put it on the bill.

"I guess I *do* blame you," I said, and I was angry. I thought about how I could've disappeared into that trailer community and hadn't, had come back to keep things going, had tried to take control of things for everybody when they looked bad.

"Don't. I wish you wouldn't," Edna said and smiled at me like she wanted me to hug her. "Anybody ought to have their choice in things if they can. Don't you believe that, Earl? Here I am out here in the desert where I don't know anything, in a stolen car, in a motel room under an assumed name, with no money of my own, a kid that's not mine, and the law after me. And I have a choice to get out of all of it by getting on a bus. What would you do? I know exactly what you'd do."

"You think you do," I said. But I didn't want to get into an argument about it and tell her all I could've done and didn't do. Because it wouldn't have done any good. When you get to the point of arguing, you're past the point of changing anybody's mind, even though it's supposed to be the other way, and maybe for some classes of people it is, just never mine.

Edna smiled at me and came across the room and put her arms around me where I was sitting on the bed. Cheryl rolled over and looked at us and smiled, then closed her eyes, and the room was quiet. I was beginning to think of Rock Springs in a way I knew I would always think of it, a lowdown city full of crimes and whores and disappointments, a place where a woman left me, instead of a place where I got things on the straight track once and for all, a place I saw a gold mine.

"Eat your chicken, Earl," Edna said. "Then we can go to bed. I'm tired, but I'd like to make love to you anyway. None of this is a matter of not loving you, you know that."

* * *

Sometime late in the night, after Edna was asleep, I got up and walked outside into the parking lot. It could've been anytime because there was still the light from the interstate frosting the low sky and the big red Ramada sign humming motionlessly in the night and no light at all in the east to indicate it might be morning. The lot was full of cars all nosed in, a couple of them with suitcases strapped to their roofs and their trunks weighed down with belongings the people were taking someplace, to a new home or a vacation resort in the mountains. I had laid in bed a long time after Edna was asleep, watching the Atlanta Braves on television, trying to get my mind off how I'd feel when I saw that bus pull away the next day, and how I'd feel when I turned around and there stood Cheryl and Little Duke and no one to see about them but me alone, and that the first thing I had to do was get hold of some automobile and get the plates switched, then get them some breakfast and get us all on the road to Florida, all in the space of probably two hours, since that Mercedes would certainly look less hid in the daytime than the night, and word travels fast. I've always taken care of Cheryl myself as long as I've had her with me. None of the women ever did. Most of them didn't even seem to like her, though they took care of me in a way so that I could take care of her. And I knew that once Edna left, all that was going to get harder. Though what I wanted most to do was not think about it just for a little while, try to let my mind go limp so it could be strong for the rest of what there was. I thought that the difference between a successful life and an unsuccessful one, between me at that moment and all the people who owned the cars that were nosed into their proper places in the lot, maybe between me and that woman out in the trailers by the gold mine, was how well you were able to put things like this out of your mind and not be bothered by them, and maybe, too, by how many troubles like this one you had to face in a lifetime. Through luck or design they had all faced fewer troubles, and by their own characters, they forgot them faster. And that's what I wanted for me. Fewer troubles, fewer memories of trouble.

I walked over to a car, a Pontiac with Ohio tags, one of the ones with bundles and suitcases strapped to the top and a lot more in the trunk, by the way it was riding. I looked inside the driver's window. There were maps and paperback books and sunglasses and the little plastic holders for cans that hang on the window wells. And in the back there were kids' toys and some pillows and a cat box with a cat sitting in it staring up at me like I was the face of the moon. It all looked familiar to me, the very same things I would have in my car if I had a car. Nothing seemed surprising, nothing different. Though I had a funny sensation at that moment and turned and looked up at the windows along the back of the motel. All were dark except two. Mine and another one. And I wondered, because it seemed funny, what would you think a man was doing if you saw him in the middle of the night looking in the windows of cars in the parking lot of the Ramada Inn? Would you think he was trying to get his head cleared? Would you think he was trying to get ready for a day when trouble would come down on him? Would you think his girlfriend was leaving him? Would you think he had a daughter? Would you think he was anybody like you?

# ⁂ LORRIE MOORE
(1957– )

In these peculiar postmodern times, it may be that comedy and irony provide a refuge of sorts for those who are removed or cut off from the consolations of faith or religion. In the fiction of Lorrie Moore, such a refuge offers little or no help for her intelligent, or at least well-educated, but rather feckless characters. Being smart is no guarantee of success; indeed, it may be a handicap in coping with life's disappointments and mistakes. Is ironic humor sufficient for the remedylessness of life? Such are the concerns of an author whose three collections of stories, *Self-Help* (1985), *Like Life* (1990), and *Birds of America* (1998), have propelled her into the front ranks of fiction writers today.

Moore was born in Glen Falls, New York, the daughter of an insurance executive and a housewife. She went to St. Lawrence University and graduated with highest honors in 1978. She completed an M.F.A. at Cornell University in 1982. She has been teaching at the University of Wisconsin since 1984. Her stories have appeared regularly in such magazines as *The New Yorker, Cosmopolitan,* and *Ms.* Her first novel, *Anagrams,* was published in 1987, and her second, *Who Will Run the Frog Hospital?,* appeared in 1994.

## People Like That Are the Only People Here
### *Canonical Babbling in Peed Onk*

A BEGINNING, an end: there seems to be neither. The whole thing is like a cloud that just lands and everywhere inside it is full of rain. A start: the Mother finds a blood clot in the Baby's diaper. What is the story? Who put this here? It is big and bright, with a broken khaki-colored vein in it. Over the weekend, the Baby had looked listless and spacey, clayey and grim. But today he looks fine—so what is this thing, startling against the white diaper, like a tiny mouse heart packed in snow? Perhaps it belongs to someone else. Perhaps it is something menstrual, something belonging to the Mother or to the Baby-sitter, something the Baby has found in a wastebasket and for his own demented baby reasons stowed away here. (Babies: they're crazy! What can you do?) In her mind, the Mother takes this away from his body and attaches it to someone else's. There. Doesn't that make more sense?

* * *

Still, she phones the clinic at the children's hospital. "Blood in the diaper," she says, and, sounding alarmed and perplexed, the woman on the other end says, "Come in now."

Such pleasingly instant service! Just say "blood." Just say "diaper." Look what you get!

In the examination room, pediatrician, nurse, head resident—all seem less alarmed and perplexed than simply perplexed. At first, stupidly, the Mother is calmed by this. But soon, besides peering and saying "Hmmmm," the pediatrician, nurse, and head resident are all drawing their mouths in, bluish and tight—morning glories sensing noon. They fold their arms across their white-coated chests, unfold them again and jot things down. They order an ultrasound. Bladder and kidneys. "Here's the card. Go downstairs; turn left."

* * *

In Radiology, the Baby stands anxiously on the table, naked against the Mother as she holds him still against her legs and waist, the Radiologist's cold scanning disc moving about the Baby's back. The Baby whimpers, looks up at the Mother. *Let's get out of here,* his eyes beg. *Pick me up!* The Radiologist stops, freezes one of the many swirls of oceanic gray, and clicks repeatedly, a single moment within the long, cavernous weather map that is the Baby's insides.

"Are you finding something?" asks the Mother. Last year, her uncle Larry had had a kidney removed for something that turned out to be benign. These imaging machines! They are like dogs, or metal detectors: they find everything, but don't know what they've found. That's where the surgeons come in. They're like the owners of the dogs. "Give me that," they say to the dog. "What the heck is that?"

"The surgeon will speak to you," says the Radiologist.

"Are you finding something?"

"The surgeon will speak to you," the Radiologist says again. "There seems to be something there, but the surgeon will talk to you about it."

"My uncle once had something on his kidney," says the Mother. "So they removed the kidney and it turned out the something was benign."

The Radiologist smiles a broad, ominous smile. "That's always the way it is," he says. "You don't know exactly what it is until it's in the bucket."

" 'In the bucket,' " the Mother repeats.

The Radiologist's grin grows scarily wider—is that even possible? "That's doctor talk," he says.

"It's very appealing," says the Mother. "It's a very appealing way to talk." Swirls of bile and blood, mustard and maroon in a pail, the colors of an African flag or some exuberant salad bar: *in the bucket*—she imagines it all.

"The Surgeon will see you soon," he says again. He tousles the Baby's ringletty hair. "Cute kid," he says.

* * *

"Let's see now," says the Surgeon in one of his examining rooms. He has stepped in, then stepped out, then come back in again. He has crisp, frowning features, sharp bones, and a tennis-in-Bermuda tan. He crosses his blue-cottoned legs. He is wearing clogs.

The Mother knows her own face is a big white dumpling of worry. She is still wearing her long, dark parka, holding the Baby, who has pulled the hood up over her head because he always thinks it's funny to do that. Though on certain windy mornings she would like to think she could look vaguely romantic like this, like some French Lieutenant's Woman of the Prairie, in all of her saner moments she knows she doesn't. Ever. She knows she looks ridiculous—like one of those animals made out of twisted party balloons. She lowers the hood and slips one arm out of the sleeve. The Baby wants to get up and play with the light switch. He fidgets, fusses, and points.

"He's big on lights these days," explains the Mother.

"That's okay," says the Surgeon, nodding toward the light switch. "Let him play with it." The Mother goes and stands by it, and the Baby begins turning the lights off and on, off and on.

"What we have here is a Wilms' tumor," says the Surgeon, suddenly plunged into darkness. He says "tumor" as if it were the most normal thing in the world.

"Wilms'?" repeats the Mother. The room is quickly on fire again with light, then wiped dark again. Among the three of them here, there is a long silence, as if it were suddenly the middle of the night. "Is that apostrophe *s* or *s* apostrophe?" the Mother says finally. She is a writer and a teacher. Spelling can be important—perhaps even at a time like this, though she has never before been at a time like this, so there are barbarisms she could easily commit and not know.

The lights come on: the world is doused and exposed.

"*S* apostrophe," says the Surgeon. "I think." The lights go back out, but the Surgeon continues speaking in the dark. "A malignant tumor on the left kidney."

Wait a minute. Hold on here. The Baby is only a baby, fed on organic applesauce and soy milk—a little prince!—and he was standing so close to her during the ultrasound. How could he have this terrible thing? It must have been *her* kidney. A fifties kidney. A DDT kidney. The Mother clears her throat. "Is it possible it was my kidney on the scan? I mean, I've never heard of a baby with a tumor, and, frankly, I was standing very close." She would make the blood hers, the tumor hers; it would all be some treacherous, farcical mistake.

"No, that's not possible," says the Surgeon. The light goes back on.

"It's not?" says the Mother. Wait until it's *in the bucket,* she thinks. Don't be so sure. *Do we have to wait until it's in the bucket to find out a mistake has been made?*

"We will start with a radical nephrectomy," says the Surgeon, instantly thrown into darkness again. His voice comes from nowhere and everywhere at once. "And then we'll begin with chemotherapy after that. These tumors usually respond very well to chemo."

"I've never heard of a baby having chemo," the Mother says. *Baby* and *Chemo,* she thinks: they should never even appear in the same sentence together, let alone the same life. In her other life, her life before this day, she had been a believer in alternative medicine. Chemotherapy? Unthinkable. Now, suddenly, alternative medicine seems the wacko maiden aunt to the Nice Big Daddy of Conventional Treatment. How quickly the old girl faints and gives way, leaves one just standing there. Chemo? Of course: chemo! Why by all means: chemo. Absolutely! Chemo!

The Baby flicks the switch back on, and the walls reappear, big wedges of light checkered with small framed watercolors of the local lake. The Mother has begun to cry: all of life has led her here, to this moment. After this, there is no more life. There is something else, something stumbling and unlivable, something mechanical, something for robots, but not life. Life has been taken and broken, quickly, like a stick. The room goes dark again, so that the Mother can cry more freely. How can a baby's body be stolen so fast? How much can one heaven-sent and unsuspecting child endure? Why has he not been spared this inconceivable fate?

Perhaps, she thinks, she is being punished: too many baby-sitters too early on. ("Come to Mommy! Come to Mommy-Baby-sitter!" she used to say. But it was a joke!) Her life, perhaps, bore too openly the marks and wigs of deepest drag. Her unmotherly thoughts had all been noted: the panicky hope that his nap would last longer than it did; her occasional desire to kiss him passionately on the mouth (to make out with her baby!); her ongoing complaints about the very vocabulary of motherhood, how it degraded the speaker ("Is this a poopie onesie! Yes, it's a very poopie onesie!"). She had, moreover, on three occasions used the formula bottles as flower vases. She twice let the Baby's ears get fudgy with wax. A few afternoons last month, at snacktime, she placed a bowl of Cheerios on the floor for him to eat, like a dog. She let him play with the Dustbuster. Just once, before he was born, she said, "Healthy? I just want the kid to be rich." A joke, for God's sake! After he was born she announced that her life had become a daily sequence of mind-wrecking chores, the same ones over and over again, like a novel by Mrs. Camus. Another joke! These jokes will kill you! She had told too often, and with too much enjoyment, the story of how the Baby had said "Hi" to his high chair, waved at the lake waves, shouted "Goody-goody-goody" in what seemed to be a Russian accent, pointed at his eyes and said "Ice." And all that nonsensical baby talk: wasn't it a stitch? "Canonical babbling," the language experts called it. He recounted whole stories in it—totally made up, she could tell. He embroidered; he fished; he exaggerated. What a card! To friends, she spoke of his eating habits (carrots yes, tuna no). She mentioned, too much, his sidesplitting giggle. Did she have to be so boring? Did she have no consideration for others, for the intellectual demands and courtesies of human society? Would she not even attempt to be more interesting? It was a crime against the human mind not even to try.

Now her baby, for all these reasons—lack of motherly gratitude, motherly judgment, motherly proportion—will be taken away.

The room is fluorescently ablaze again. The Mother digs around in her parka pocket and comes up with a Kleenex. It is old and thin, like a mashed flower saved from a dance; she dabs it at her eyes and nose.

"The Baby won't suffer as much as you," says the Surgeon.

And who can contradict? Not the Baby, who in his Slavic Betty Boop voice can say only *mama, dada, cheese, ice, bye-bye, outside, boogie-boogie, goody-goody, eddy-eddy,* and *car.* (Who is Eddy? They have no idea.) This will not suffice to express his mortal suffering. Who can say what babies do with their agony and shock? Not they themselves. (Baby talk: isn't it a stitch?) They put it all no place anyone can really see. They are like a different race, a different species: they seem not to experience pain the way *we* do. Yeah, that's it: their nervous systems are not as fully formed, and *they just don't experience pain the way we do.* A tune to keep one humming through the war. "You'll get through it," the Surgeon says.

"How?" asks the Mother. "How does one get through it?"

"You just put your head down and go," says the Surgeon. He picks up his file folder. He is a skilled manual laborer. The tricky emotional stuff is not to his liking. The babies. The babies! What can be said to console the parents about the babies? "I'll go phone the oncologist on duty to let him know," he says, and leaves the room.

"Come here, sweetie," the Mother says to the Baby, who has toddled off toward a gum wrapper on the floor. "We've got to put your jacket on." She picks him up and he reaches for the light switch again. Light, dark. Peekaboo: where's baby? Where did baby go?

* * *

At home, she leaves a message—"Urgent! Call me!"—for the Husband on his voice mail. Then she takes the Baby upstairs for his nap, rocks him in the rocker. The Baby waves good-bye to his little bears, then looks toward the window and says, "Bye-bye, outside." He has, lately, the habit of waving good-bye to everything, and now it seems as if he senses an imminent departure, and it breaks her heart to hear him. *Bye-bye!* She sings low and monotonously, like a small appliance, which is how he likes it. He is drowsy, dozy, drifting off. He has grown so much in the last year, he hardly fits in her lap anymore; his limbs dangle off like a pietà. His head rolls slightly inside the crook of her arm. She can feel him falling backward into sleep, his mouth round and open like the sweetest of poppies. All the lullabies in the world, all the melodies threaded through with maternal melancholy now become for her—abandoned as a mother can be by working men and napping babies—the songs of hard, hard grief. Sitting there, bowed and bobbing, the Mother feels the entirety of her love as worry and heartbreak. A quick and irrevocable alchemy: there is no longer one unworried scrap left for happiness. "If you go," she keens low into his soapy neck, into the ranunculus coil of his ear, "we are going with you. We are nothing without you. Without you, we are a heap of rocks. We are gravel and mold. Without you, we are two stumps, with nothing any longer in our hearts. Wherever this takes you, we are following. We will be there. Don't be scared. We are going, too. That is that."

* * *

"Take Notes," says the Husband, after coming straight home from work, midafternoon, hearing the news, and saying all the words out loud—*surgery, metastasis, dialysis, transplant*—then collapsing in a chair in tears. "Take notes. We are going to need the money."

"Good God," cries the Mother. Everything inside her suddenly begins to cower and shrink, a thinning of bones. Perhaps this is a soldier's readiness, but it has the whiff of death and defeat. It feels like a heart attack, a failure of will and courage, a power failure: a failure of everything. Her face, when she glimpses it in a mirror, is cold and bloated with shock, her eyes scarlet and shrunk. She has already started to wear sunglasses indoors, like a celebrity widow. From where will her own strength come? From some philosophy? From some frigid little philosophy? She is neither stalwart nor realistic and has trouble with basic concepts, such as the one that says events move in one direction only and do not jump up, turn around, and take themselves back.

The Husband begins too many of his sentences with "What if." He is trying to piece everything together like a train wreck. He is trying to get the train to town.

"We'll just take all the steps, move through all the stages. We'll go where we have to go. We'll hunt; we'll find; we'll pay what we have to pay. What if we can't pay?"

"Sounds like shopping."

"I cannot believe this is happening to our little boy," he says, and starts to sob again. "Why didn't it happen to one of us? It's so unfair. Just last week, my doctor declared me in perfect health: the prostate of a twenty-year-old, the heart of a ten-year-old, the brain of an insect—or whatever it was he said. What a nightmare this is."

What words can be uttered? You turn just slightly and there it is: the death of your child. It is part symbol, part devil, and in your blind spot all along, until, if you are unlucky, it is completely upon you. Then it is a fierce little country abducting you; it holds you squarely inside itself like a cellar room—the best boundaries of you are the boundaries of it. Are there windows? Sometimes aren't there windows?

* * *

The Mother is not a shopper. She hates to shop, is generally bad at it, though she does like a good sale. She cannot stroll meaningfully through anger, denial, grief, and acceptance. She goes straight to bargaining and stays there. How much? she calls out to the ceiling, to some makeshift construction of holiness she has desperately, though not uncreatively, assembled in her mind and prayed to; a doubter, never before given to prayer, she must now reap what she has not sown; she must assemble from scratch an entire altar of worship and begging. She tries for noble abstractions, nothing too anthropomorphic, just some Higher Morality, though if this particular Highness looks something like the manager at Marshall Field's, sucking a Frango mint, so be it. Amen. Just tell me what you want, requests the Mother. And how do you want it? More charitable acts? A billion starting now. Charitable thoughts? Harder, but of course! Of course! I'll do the cooking, honey; I'll pay the rent. Just tell me. *Excuse me?* Well, if not to you, to whom do I speak? Hello? To whom do I have to speak around here? A higher-up? A superior? Wait? I can wait. I've got all day. I've got the whole damn day.

The Husband now lies next to her in bed, sighing. "Poor little guy could survive all this, only to be killed in a car crash at the age of sixteen," he says.

The wife, bargaining, considers this. "We'll take the car crash," she says.

"What?"

"Let's Make a Deal! Sixteen Is a Full Life! We'll take the car crash. We'll take the car crash, in front of which Carol Merrill is now standing."

Now the Manager of Marshall Field's reappears. "To take the surprises out is to take the life out of life," he says.

The phone rings. The Husband gets up and leaves the room.

"But I don't want these surprises," says the Mother. "Here! You take these surprises!"

"To know the narrative in advance is to turn yourself into a machine," the Manager continues. "What makes humans human is precisely that they do not know the future. That is why they do the fateful and amusing things they do: who can say how anything will turn out? Therein lies the only hope for redemption, discovery, and—let's be frank—fun, fun, fun! There might be things people will get away with. And not just motel towels. There might be great illicit loves, enduring joy, faith-shaking accidents with farm machinery. But you have to not know in order to see what stories your life's efforts bring you. The mystery is all."

The Mother, though shy, has grown confrontational. "Is this the kind of bogus, random crap they teach at merchandising school? We would like fewer surprises, fewer efforts and mysteries, thank you. K through eight; can we just get K through eight?" It now seems like the luckiest, most beautiful, most musical phrase she's ever heard: K through eight. The very lilt. The very thought.

The Manager continues, trying things out. "I mean, the whole conception of 'the story,' of cause and effect, the whole idea that people have a clue as to how the world works is just a piece of laughable metaphysical colonialism perpetrated upon the wild country of time."

Did they own a gun? The Mother begins looking through drawers.

The Husband comes back into the room and observes her. "Ha! The Great Havoc that is the Puzzle of all Life!" he says of the Marshall Field's management policy. He has just gotten off a conference call with the insurance company and the hospital. The surgery will be Friday. "It's all just some dirty capitalist's idea of a philosophy."

"Maybe it's just a fact of narrative and you really can't politicize it," says the Mother. It is now only the two of them.

"Whose side are you on?"

"I'm on the Baby's side."

"Are you taking notes for this?"

"No."

"You're not?"

"No. I can't. Not this! I write fiction. This isn't fiction."

"Then write nonfiction. Do a piece of journalism. Get two dollars a word."

"Then it has to be true and full of information. I'm not trained. I'm not that skilled. Plus, I have a convenient personal principle about artists not abandoning art. One should never turn one's back on a vivid imagination. Even the whole memoir thing annoys me."

"Well, make things up, but pretend they're real."

"I'm not that insured."

"You're making me nervous."

"Sweetie, darling, I'm not that good. I can't *do this.* I can do—what can I do? I can do quasi-amusing phone dialogue. I can do succinct descriptions of weather. I can do screwball outings with the family pet. Sometimes I can do those. Honey, I only do what I can. I do *the careful ironies of daydream.* I do *the marshy ideas upon which intimate life is built.* But this? Our baby with cancer? I'm sorry. My stop was two stations back. This is irony at its most gaudy and careless. This is a Hieronymus Bosch of facts and figures and blood and graphs. This is a nightmare of narrative slop. This cannot be designed. This cannot even be noted in preparation for a design—"

"We're going to need the money."

"To say nothing of the moral boundaries of pecuniary recompense in a situation such as this—"

"What if the other kidney goes? What if he needs a transplant? Where are the moral boundaries there? What are we going to do, have bake sales?"

"We can sell the house. I hate this house. It makes me crazy."

"And we'll live—where again?"

"The Ronald McDonald place. I hear it's nice. It's the least McDonald's can do."

"You have a keen sense of justice."

"I try. What can I say?" She pauses. "Is all this really happening? I keep thinking that soon it will be over—the life expectancy of a cloud is supposed to be only twelve hours—and then I realize something has occurred that can never ever be over."

The Husband buries his face in his hands: "Our poor baby. How did this happen to him?" He looks over and stares at the bookcase that serves as the nightstand. "And do you think even one of these baby books is any help?" He picks up the Leach, the Spock, the *What to Expect.* "Where in the pages or index of any of these does it say 'chemotherapy' or 'Hickman catheter' or 'renal sarcoma'? Where does it say 'carcinogenesis'? You know what these books are obsessed with? *Holding a fucking spoon.*" He begins hurling the books off the night table and against the far wall.

"Hey," says the Mother, trying to soothe. "Hey, hey, hey." But compared to his stormy roar, her words are those of a backup singer—a Shondell, a Pip—a doo-wop ditty. Books, and now more books, continue to fly.

* * *

Take Notes.

Is *fainthearted* one word or two? Student prose has wrecked her spelling.

It's one word. Two words—*Faint Hearted*—what would that be? The name of a drag queen.

* * *

Take Notes. In the end, you suffer alone. But at the beginning you suffer with a whole lot of others. When your child has cancer, you are instantly whisked away to another planet: one of bald-headed little boys. Pediatric Oncology. Peed Onk. You wash your hands for thirty seconds in antibacterial soap before you are allowed to enter through the swinging doors. You put paper slippers on your shoes. You keep your voice down. A whole place has been designed and decorated for your nightmare. Here is where nightmare will occur. We've got a room all ready for you. We have cots. We have refrigerators. "The children are almost entirely boys," says one of the nurses. "No one knows why. It's been documented, but a lot of people out there still don't realize it." The little boys are all from sweet-sounding places—Janesville and Appleton—little heartland towns with giant landfills, agricultural runoff, paper factories, Joe McCarthy's grave (Alone, a site of great toxicity, thinks the Mother. The soil should be tested).

All the bald little boys look like brothers. They wheel their IVs up and down the single corridor of Peed Onk. Some of the lively ones, feeling good for a day, ride the lower bars of the IV while their large, cheerful mothers whiz them along the halls. *Wheee!*

* * *

The Mother does not feel large and cheerful. In her mind, she is scathing, acid-tongued, wraith-thin, and chain-smoking out on a fire escape somewhere. Beneath her lie the gentle undulations of the Midwest, with all its aspirations to be—to be what? To be Long Island. How it has succeeded! Strip mall upon strip mall. Lurid water, poisoned potatoes. The Mother drags deeply, blowing clouds of smoke out over the disfigured cornfields. When a baby gets cancer, it seems stupid ever to have given up smoking. When a baby gets cancer, you think, Whom are we kidding? Let's all light up. When a baby gets cancer, you think, Who came up with *this* idea? What celestial abandon gave rise to *this?* Pour me a drink, so I can refuse to toast.

The Mother does not know how to be one of these other mothers, with their blond hair and sweatpants and sneakers and determined pleasantness. She does not think that she can be anything similar. She does not feel remotely like them. She knows, for instance, too many people in Greenwich Village. She mail-orders oysters and tiramisu from a shop in SoHo. She is close friends with four actual homosexuals. Her husband is asking her to Take Notes.

Where do these women get their sweatpants? She will find out.

She will start, perhaps, with the costume and work from there.

She will live according to the bromides. Take one day at a time. Take a positive attitude. *Take a hike!* She wishes that there were more interesting things that were useful and true, but it seems now that it's only the boring things that are useful and true. *One day at a time.* And *at least we have our health.* How ordinary. How obvious. One day at a time. You need a brain for that?

* * *

While the Surgeon is fine-boned, regal, and laconic—they have correctly guessed his game to be doubles—there is a bit of the mad, overcaffeinated scientist to the Oncologist. He speaks quickly. He knows a lot of studies and numbers. He can do the math. Good! Someone should be able to do the math! "It's a fast but wimpy tumor," he explains. "It typically metastasizes to the lung." He rattles off some numbers, time frames, risk statistics. Fast but wimpy: the Mother tries to imagine this combination of traits, tries to think and think, and can only come up with Claudia Osk from the fourth grade, who blushed and almost wept when called on in class, but in gym could outrun everyone in the quarter-mile fire-door-to-fence dash. The Mother thinks now of this tumor as Claudia Osk. They are going to get Claudia Osk, make her sorry. All right! Claudia Osk must die. Though it has never been mentioned before, it now seems clear that Claudia Osk should have died long ago. Who was she anyway? So conceited: not letting anyone beat her in a race. Well, hey, hey, hey: don't look now, Claudia!

The Husband nudges her. "Are you listening?"

"The chances of this happening even just to one kidney are one in fifteen thousand. Now given all these other factors, the chances on the second kidney are about one in eight."

"One in eight," says the Husband. "Not bad. As long as it's not one in fifteen thousand."

The Mother studies the trees and fish along the ceiling's edge in the Save the Planet wallpaper border. Save the Planet. Yes! But the windows in this very building don't open and diesel fumes are leaking into the ventilating system, near which, outside, a delivery truck is parked. The air is nauseous and stale.

"Really," the Oncologist is saying, "of all the cancers he could get, this is probably the best."

"We win," says the Mother.

"*Best,* I know, hardly seems the right word. Look, you two probably need to get some rest. We'll see how the surgery and histology go. Then we'll start with chemo the week following. A little light chemo: vincristine and—"

"Vincristine?" interrupts the Mother. "Wine of Christ?"

"The names are strange, I know. The other one we use is actinomycin-D. Sometimes called 'dactinomycin.' People move the *D* around to the front."

"They move the *D* around to the front," repeats the Mother.

"Yup!" the Oncologist says. "I don't know why—they just do!"

"Christ didn't survive his wine," says the Husband.

"But of course he did," says the Oncologist, and nods toward the Baby, who has now found a cupboard full of hospital linens and bandages and is yanking them all out onto the floor. "I'll see you guys tomorrow, after the surgery." And with that, the Oncologist leaves.

"Or, rather, Christ *was* his wine," mumbles the Husband. Everything he knows about the New Testament, he has gleaned from the sound track of *Godspell.* "His blood was the wine. What a great beverage idea."

"A little light chemo. Don't you like that one?" says the Mother. "*Eine kleine* dactinomycin. I'd like to see Mozart write that one up for a big wad o' cash."

"Come here, honey," the Husband says to the Baby, who has now pulled off both his shoes.

"It's bad enough when they refer to medical science as 'an inexact science,' " says the Mother. "But when they start referring to it as 'an art,' I get extremely nervous."

"Yeah. If we wanted art, Doc, we'd go to an art museum." The Husband picks up the Baby. "You're an artist," he says to the Mother, with the taint of accusation in his voice. "They probably think you find creativity reassuring."

The Mother sighs. "I just find it inevitable. Let's go get something to eat." And so they take the elevator to the cafeteria, where there is a high chair, and where, not noticing, they all eat a lot of apples with the price tags still on them.

* * *

Because his surgery is not until tomorrow, the Baby likes the hospital. He likes the long corridors, down which he can run. He likes everything on wheels. The flower carts in the lobby! ("Please keep your boy away from the flowers," says the vendor. "We'll buy the whole display," snaps the Mother, adding, "Actual children in a children's hospital—unbelievable, isn't it?") The Baby likes the other little boys. Places to go! People to see! Rooms to wander into! There is Intensive Care. There is the Trauma Unit. The Baby smiles and waves. What a little Cancer Personality! Bandaged citizens smile and wave back. In Peed Onk, there are the bald little boys to play with. Joey, Eric, Tim, Mort, and Tod (Mort! Tod!). There is the four-year-old, Ned, holding his little deflated rubber ball, the one with the intriguing curling hose. The Baby wants to play with it. "It's mine. Leave it alone," says Ned. "Tell the Baby to leave it alone."

"Baby, you've got to share," says the Mother from a chair some feet away.

Suddenly, from down near the Tiny Tim Lounge, comes Ned's mother, large and blond and sweatpanted. "Stop that! Stop it!" she cries out, dashing toward the Baby and Ned and pushing the Baby away. "Don't touch that!" she barks at the Baby, who is only a Baby and bursts into tears because he has never been yelled at like this before.

Ned's mom glares at everyone. "This is drawing fluid from Neddy's liver!" She pats at the rubber thing and starts to cry a little.

"Oh my God," says the Mother. She comforts the Baby, who is also crying. She and Ned, the only dry-eyed people, look at each other. "I'm so sorry," she says to Ned and then to his mother. "I'm so stupid. I thought they were squabbling over a toy."

"It does look like a toy," agrees Ned. He smiles. He is an angel. All the little boys are angels. Total, sweet, bald little angels, and now God is trying to get them back for himself. Who are they, mere mortal women, in the face of this, this powerful and overwhelming and inscrutable thing, God's will? They are the mothers, that's who. You can't have him! they shout every day. You dirty old man! *Get out of here! Hands off!*

"I'm so sorry," says the Mother again. "I didn't know."

Ned's mother smiles vaguely. "Of course you didn't know," she says, and walks back to the Tiny Tim Lounge.

* * *

The Tiny Tim Lounge is a little sitting area at the end of the Peed Onk corridor. There are two small sofas, a table, a rocking chair, a television and a VCR. There are various videos: *Speed, Dune,* and *Star Wars.* On one of the lounge walls there is a gold plaque with the singer Tiny Tim's name on it: his son was treated once at this hospital and so, five years ago, he donated money for this lounge. It is a cramped little lounge, which, one suspects, would be larger if Tiny Tim's son had actually lived. Instead, he died here, at this hospital and now there is this tiny room which is part gratitude, part generosity, part *fuck-you.*

Sifting through the videocassettes, the Mother wonders what science fiction could begin to compete with the science fiction of cancer itself—a tumor with its differentiated muscle and bone cells, a clump of wild nothing and its mad, ambitious desire to be something: something inside you, instead of you, another organism, but with a monster's architecture, a demon's sabotage and chaos. Think of leukemia, a tumor diabolically taking liquid form, better to swim about incognito in the blood. George Lucas, direct that!

Sitting with the other parents in the Tiny Tim Lounge, the night before the surgery, having put the Baby to bed in his high steel crib two rooms down, the Mother begins to hear the stories: leukemia in kindergarten, sarcomas in Little League, neuroblastomas discovered at summer camp. "Eric slid into third base, but then the scrape didn't heal." The parents pat one another's forearms and speak of other children's hospitals as if they were resorts. "You were at St. Jude's last winter? So were we. What did you think of it? We loved the staff." Jobs have been quit, marriages hacked up, bank accounts ravaged; the parents have seemingly endured the unendurable. They speak not of the *possibility* of comas brought on by the chemo, but of the *number* of them. "He was in his first coma last July," says Ned's mother. "It was a scary time, but we pulled through."

Pulling through is what people do around here. There is a kind of bravery in their lives that isn't bravery at all. It is automatic, unflinching, a mix of man and machine, consuming and unquestionable obligation meeting illness move for move in a giant even-steven game of chess—an unending round of something that looks like shadowboxing, though between love and death, which is the shadow? "Everyone admires us for our courage," says one man. "They have no idea what they're talking about."

I could get out of here, thinks the Mother. I could just get on a bus and go, never come back. Change my name. A kind of witness relocation thing.

"Courage requires options," the man adds.

The Baby might be better off.

"There are options," says a woman with a thick suede head-band. "You could give up. You could fall apart."

"No, you can't. Nobody does. I've never seen it," says the man. "Well, not *really* fall apart." Then the lounge falls quiet. Over the VCR someone has taped the fortune from a fortune cookie. "Optimism," it says, "is what allows a teakettle to sing though up to its neck in hot water." Underneath, someone else has taped a clipping from a summer horoscope. "Cancer rules!" it says. Who would tape this up? Somebody's twelve-year-old brother. One of the fathers—Joey's father—gets up and tears them both off, makes a small wad in his fist.

There is some rustling of magazine pages.

The Mother clears her throat. "Tiny Tim forgot the wet bar," she says.

Ned, who is still up, comes out of his room and down the corridor, whose lights dim at nine. Standing next to her chair, he says to the Mother, "Where are you from? What is wrong with your baby?"

* * *

In the tiny room that is theirs, she sleeps fitfully in her sweatpants, occasionally leaping up to check on the Baby. This is what the sweatpants are for: leaping. In case of fire. In case of anything. In case the difference between day and night starts to dissolve, and there is no difference at all, so why pretend? In the cot beside her, the Husband, who has taken a sleeping pill, is snoring loudly, his arms folded about his head in a kind of origami. How could either of them have stayed back at the house, with its empty high chair and empty crib? Occasionally the Baby wakes and cries out, and she bolts up, goes to him, rubs his back, rearranges the linens. The clock on the metal dresser shows that it is five after three. Then twenty to five. And then it is really morning, the beginning of this day, nephrectomy day. Will she be glad when it's over, or barely alive, or both? Each day this week has arrived huge, empty, and unknown, like a spaceship, and this one especially is lit a bright gray.

"He'll need to put this on," says John, one of the nurses, bright and early, handing the Mother a thin greenish garment with roses and teddy bears printed on it. A wave of nausea hits her; this smock, she thinks, will soon be splattered with—with what?

The Baby is awake but drowsy. She lifts off his pajamas. "Don't forget, *bubeleh,*" she whispers, undressing and dressing him. "We will be with you every moment, every step. When you think you are asleep and floating off far away from everybody, Mommy will still be there." If she hasn't fled on a bus. "Mommy will take care of you. And Daddy, too." She hopes the Baby does not detect her own fear and uncertainty, which she must hide from him, like a limp. He is hungry, not having been allowed to eat, and he is no longer amused by this new place, but worried about its hardships. Oh, my baby, she thinks. And the room starts to swim a little. The Husband comes in to take over. "Take a break," he says to her. "I'll walk him around for five minutes."

She leaves but doesn't know where to go. In the hallway, she is approached by a kind of social worker, a customer-relations person, who had given them a video to watch about the anesthesia: how the parent accompanies the child into the operating room, and how gently, nicely the drugs are administered.

"Did you watch the video?"

"Yes," says the Mother.

"Wasn't it helpful?"

"I don't know," says the Mother.

"Do you have any questions?" asks the video woman. "Do you have any questions?" asked of someone who has recently landed in this fearful, alien place seems to the Mother an absurd and amazing little courtesy. The very specificity of a question would give a lie to the overwhelming strangeness of everything around her.

"Not right now," says the Mother. "Right now, I think I'm just going to go to the bathroom."

When she returns to the Baby's room, everyone is there: the surgeon, the anesthesiologist, all the nurses, the social worker. In their blue caps and scrubs, they look like a clutch of forget-me-nots, and forget them, who could? The Baby, in his little teddy-bear smock, seems cold and scared. He reaches out and the Mother lifts him from the Husband's arms, rubs his back to warm him.

"Well, it's time!" says the Surgeon, forcing a smile.

"Shall we go?" says the Anesthesiologist.

What follows is a blur of obedience and bright lights. They take an elevator down to a big concrete room, the anteroom, the greenroom, the backstage of the operating room. Lining the walls are long shelves full of blue surgical outfits. "Children often become afraid of the color blue," says one of the nurses. But of course. Of course! "Now, which one of you would like to come into the operating room for the anesthesia?"

"I will," says the Mother.

"Are you sure?" asks the Husband.

"Yup." She kisses the Baby's hair. "Mr. Curlyhead," people keep calling him here, and it seems both rude and nice. Women look admiringly at his long lashes and exclaim, "Always the boys! Always the boys!"

Two surgical nurses put a blue smock and a blue cotton cap on the Mother. The Baby finds this funny and keeps pulling at the cap. "This way," says another nurse, and the Mother follows. "Just put the Baby down on the table."

In the video, the mother holds the baby and fumes are gently waved under the baby's nose until he falls asleep. Now, out of view of camera or social worker, the Anesthesiologist is anxious to get this under way and not let too much gas leak out into the room generally. The occupational hazard of this, his chosen profession, is gas exposure and nerve damage, and it has started to worry him. No doubt he frets about it to his wife every night. Now he turns the gas on and quickly clamps the plastic mouthpiece over the baby's cheeks and lips.

The Baby is startled. The Mother is startled. The Baby starts to scream and redden behind the plastic, but he cannot be heard. He thrashes. "Tell him it's okay," says the nurse to the Mother.

Okay? "It's okay," repeats the Mother, holding his hand, but she knows he can tell it's not okay, because he can see not only that she is still wearing that stupid paper cap but that her words are mechanical and swallowed, and she is biting her lips to keep them from trembling. Panicked, he attempts to sit. He cannot breathe; his arms reach up. *Bye-bye, outside.* And then, quite quickly, his eyes shut; he untenses and has fallen not *into* sleep but aside to sleep, an odd, kidnapping kind of sleep, his terror now hidden someplace deep inside him.

"How did it go?" asks the social worker, waiting in the concrete outer room. The Mother is hysterical. A nurse has ushered her out.

"It wasn't at all like the filmstrip!" she cries. "It wasn't like the filmstrip at all!"

"The filmstrip? You mean the video?" asks the social worker.

"It wasn't like that at all! It was brutal and unforgivable."

"Why that's terrible," she says, her role now no longer misinformational but janitorial, and she touches the Mother's arm, though the Mother shakes it off and goes to find the Husband.

* * *

She finds him in the large mulberry Surgery Lounge, where he has been taken and where there is free hot chocolate in small Styrofoam cups. Red cellophane garlands festoon the doorways. She has totally forgotten it is as close to Christmas as this. A pianist in the corner is playing "Carol of the Bells," and it sounds not only unfestive but scary, like the theme from *The Exorcist.*

There is a giant clock on the far wall. It is a kind of porthole into the operating room, a way of assessing the Baby's ordeal: forty-five minutes for the Hickman implant; two and a half hours for the nephrectomy. And then, after that, three months of chemotherapy. The magazine on her lap stays open at a ruby-hued perfume ad.

"Still not taking notes," says the Husband.

"Nope."

"You know, in a way, this is the kind of thing you've *always* written about."

"You are really something, you know that? This is life. This isn't a 'kind of thing.' "

"But this is the kind of thing that fiction is: it's the unlivable life, the strange room tacked onto the house, the extra moon that is circling the earth unbeknownst to science."

"I told you that."

"I'm quoting you."

She looks at her watch, thinking of the Baby. "How long has it been?"

"Not long. Too long. In the end, maybe those're the same things."

"What do you suppose is happening to him right this second?"

Infection? Slipping knives? "I don't know. But you know what? I've gotta go. I've gotta just walk a bit." The Husband gets up, walks around the lounge, then comes back and sits down.

The synapses between the minutes are unswimmable. An hour is thick as fudge. The Mother feels depleted; she is a string of empty tin cans attached by wire, something a goat would sniff and chew, something now and then enlivened by a jolt of electricity.

She hears their names being called over the intercom. "Yes? Yes?" She stands up quickly. Her words have flown out before her, an exhalation of birds. The piano music has stopped. The pianist is gone. She and the Husband approach the main desk, where a man looks up at them and smiles. Before him is a xeroxed list of patients' names. "That's our little boy right there," says the Mother, seeing the Baby's name on the list and pointing at it. "Is there some word? Is everything okay?"

"Yes," says the man. "Your boy is doing fine. They've just finished with the catheter, and they are moving on to the kidney."

"But it's been two hours already! Oh my God, did something go wrong? What happened? What went wrong?"

"Did something go wrong?" The Husband tugs at his collar.

"Not really. It just took longer than they expected. I'm told everything is fine. They wanted you to know."

"Thank you," says the Husband. They turn and walk back toward where they were sitting.

"I'm not going to make it." The Mother sighs, sinking into a fake leather chair shaped somewhat like a baseball mitt. "But before I go, I'm taking half this hospital out with me."

"Do you want some coffee?" asks the Husband.

"I don't know," says the Mother. "No, I guess not. No. Do you?"

"Nah, I don't, either, I guess," he says.

"Would you like part of an orange?"

"Oh, maybe, I guess, if you're having one." She takes an orange from her purse and just sits there peeling its difficult skin, the flesh rupturing beneath her fingers, the juice trickling down her hands, stinging the hangnails. She and the Husband chew and swallow, discreetly spit the seeds into Kleenex, and read from photocopies of the latest medical research, which they begged from the intern. They read, and underline, and sigh and close their eyes, and after some time, the surgery is over. A nurse from Peed Onk comes down to tell them.

"Your little boy's in recovery right now. He's doing well. You can see him in about fifteen minutes."

* * *

How can it be described? How can any of it be described? The trip and the story of the trip are always two different things. The narrator is the one who has stayed home, but then, afterward, presses her mouth upon the traveler's mouth, in order to make the mouth work, to make the mouth say, say, say. One cannot go to a place and speak of it; one cannot both see and say, not really. One can go, and upon returning make a lot of hand motions and indications with the arms. The mouth itself, working at the speed of light, at the eye's instructions, is necessarily struck still; so fast, so much to report, it hangs open and dumb as a gutted bell. All that unsayable life! That's where the narrator comes in. The narrator comes with her kisses and mimicry and tidying up. The narrator comes and makes a slow, fake song of the mouth's eager devastation.

It is a horror and a miracle to see him. He is lying in his crib in his room, tubed up, splayed like a boy on a cross, his arms stiffened into cardboard "no-no's" so that he cannot yank out the tubes. There is the bladder catheter, the nasal-gastric tube, and the Hickman, which, beneath the skin, is plugged into his jugular, then popped out his chest wall and capped with a long plastic cap. There is a large bandage taped over his abdomen. Groggy, on a morphine drip, still he is able to look at her when, maneuvering through all the vinyl wiring, she leans to hold him, and when she does, he begins to cry, but cry silently, without motion or noise. She has never seen a baby cry without motion or noise. It is the crying of an old person: silent, beyond opinion, shattered. In someone so tiny, it is frightening and unnatural. She wants to pick up the Baby and run—out of there, out of there. She wants to whip out a gun: *No-no's, eh? This whole thing is what I call a no-no.* Don't you touch him! she wants to shout at the surgeons and the needle nurses. Not anymore! No more! No more! She would crawl up and lie beside him in the crib if she could. But instead, because of all his intricate wiring, she must lean and cuddle, sing to him, songs of peril and flight: "We gotta get out of this place, if it's the last thing we ever do. We gotta get out of this place . . . there's a better life for me and you."

Very 1967. She was eleven then and impressionable.

The Baby looks at her, pleadingly, his arms splayed out in surrender. To where? Where is there to go? Take me! Take me!

* * *

That night, postop night, the Mother and Husband lie afloat in the cot together. A fluorescent lamp near the crib is kept on in the dark. The Baby breathes evenly but thinly in his drugged sleep. The morphine in its first flooding doses apparently makes him feel as if he were falling backward—or so the Mother has been told—and it causes the Baby to jerk, to catch himself over and over, as if he were being dropped from a tree. "Is this right? Isn't there something that should be done?" The nurses come in hourly, different ones—the night shifts seem strangely short and frequent. If the Baby stirs or frets, the nurses give him more morphine through the Hickman catheter, then leave to tend to other patients. The Mother rises to check on him in the low light. There is gurgling from the clear plastic suction tube coming out of his mouth. Brownish clumps have collected in the tube. What is going on? The Mother rings for the nurse. Is it Renée or Sarah or Darcy? She's forgotten.

"What, what is it?" murmurs the Husband, waking up.

"Something is wrong," says the Mother. "It looks like blood in his N-G tube."

"What?" The Husband gets out of bed. He, too, is wearing sweatpants.

The nurse—Valerie—pushes open the heavy door to the room and enters quietly. "Everything okay?"

"There's something wrong here. The tube is sucking blood out of his stomach. It looks like it may have perforated his stomach and that now he's bleeding internally. Look!"

Valerie is a saint, but her voice is the standard hospital saint voice: an infuriating, pharmaceutical calm. It says, Everything is normal here. Death is normal. Pain is normal. Nothing is abnormal. So there is nothing to get excited about. "Well now, let's see." She holds up the plastic tube and tries to see inside it. "Hmmm," she says. "I'll call the attending physician."

Because this is a research and teaching hospital, all the regular doctors are at home sleeping in their Mission-style beds. Tonight, as is apparently the case every weekend night, the attending physician is a medical student. He looks fifteen. The authority he attempts to convey, he cannot remotely inhabit. He is not even in the same building with it. He shakes everyone's hands, then strokes his chin, a gesture no doubt gleaned from some piece of dinner theater his parents took him to once. As if there were an actual beard on that chin! As if beard growth on that chin were even possible! *Our Town! Kiss Me Kate! Barefoot in the Park!* He is attempting to convince, if not to impress.

"We're in trouble," the Mother whispers to the Husband. She is tired, tired of young people grubbing for grades. "We've got Dr. 'Kiss Me Kate,' here."

The Husband looks at her blankly, a mix of disorientation and divorce.

The medical student holds the tubing in his hands. "I don't really see anything," he says.

He flunks! "You don't?" The Mother shoves her way in, holds the clear tubing in both hands. "That," she says. "Right here and here." Just this past semester, she said to one of her own students, "If you don't see how this essay is better than that one, then I want you just to go out into the hallway and stand there until you do." Is it important to keep one's voice down? The Baby stays asleep. He is drugged and dreaming, far away.

"Hmmm," says the medical student. "Perhaps there's a little irritation in the stomach."

"A little irritation?" The Mother grows furious. "This is blood. These are clumps and clots. This stupid thing is sucking the life right out of him!" Life! She is starting to cry.

They turn off the suction and bring in antacids, which they feed into the Baby through the tube. Then they turn the suction on again. This time on low.

"What was it on before?" asks the Husband.

"High," says Valerie. "Doctor's orders, though I don't know why. I don't know why these doctors do a lot of the things they do."

"Maybe they're . . . not all that bright?" suggests the Mother. She is feeling relief and rage simultaneously: there is a feeling of prayer and litigation in the air. Yet essentially, she is grateful. Isn't she? She thinks she is. And still, and still: look at all the things you have to do to protect a child, a hospital merely an intensification of life's cruel obstacle course.

* * *

The Surgeon comes to visit on Saturday morning. He steps in and nods at the Baby, who is awake but glazed from the morphine, his eyes two dark unseeing grapes. "The boy looks fine," the Surgeon announces. He peeks under the Baby's bandage. "The stitches look good," he says. The Baby's abdomen is stitched all the way across like a baseball. "And the other kidney, when we looked at it yesterday face-to-face, looked fine. We'll try to wean him off the morphine a little, and see how he's doing on Monday." He clears his throat. "And now," he says, looking about the room at the nurses and medical students, "I would like to speak with the Mother, alone."

The Mother's heart gives a jolt. "Me?"

"Yes," he says, motioning, then turning.

She gets up and steps out into the empty hallway with him, closing the door behind her. What can this be about? She hears the Baby fretting a little in his crib. Her brain fills with pain and alarm. Her voice comes out as a hoarse whisper. "Is there something—"

"There is a particular thing I need from you," says the Surgeon, turning and standing there very seriously.

"Yes?" Her heart is pounding. She does not feel resilient enough for any more bad news.

"I need to ask a favor."

"Certainly," she says, attempting very hard to summon the strength and courage for this occasion, whatever it is; her throat has tightened to a fist.

From inside his white coat, the surgeon removes a thin paperback book and thrusts it toward her. "Will you sign my copy of your novel?"

The Mother looks down and sees that it is indeed a copy of a novel she has written, one about teenaged girls.

She looks up. A big, spirited grin is cutting across his face. "I read this last summer," he says, "and I still remember parts of it! Those girls got into such trouble!"

Of all the surreal moments of the last few days, this, she thinks, might be the most so.

"Okay," she says, and the Surgeon merrily hands her a pen.

"You can just write 'To Dr.'—Oh, I don't need to tell you what to write."

The Mother sits down on a bench and shakes ink into the pen. A sigh of relief washes over and out of her. Oh, the pleasure of a sigh of relief, like the finest moments of love; has anyone properly sung the praises of sighs of relief? She opens the book to the title page. She breathes deeply. What is he doing reading novels about teenaged girls, anyway? And why didn't he buy the hardcover? She inscribes something grateful and true, then hands the book back to him.

"Is he going to be okay?"

"The boy? The boy is going to be fine," he says, then taps her stiffly on the shoulder. "Now you take care. It's Saturday. Drink a little wine."

* * *

Over the weekend, while the Baby sleeps, the Mother and Husband sit together in the Tiny Tim Lounge. The Husband is restless and makes cafeteria and sundry runs, running errands for everyone. In his absence, the other parents regale her further with their sagas. Pediatric cancer and chemo stories: the children's amputations, blood poisoning, teeth flaking like shale, the learning delays and disabilities caused by chemo frying the young, budding brain. But strangely optimistic codas are tacked on—endings as stiff and loopy as carpenter's lace, crisp and empty as lettuce, reticulate as a net—ah, words. "After all that business with the tutor, he's better now, and fitted with new incisors by my wife's cousin's husband, who did dental school in two and a half years, if you can believe that. We hope for the best. We take things as they come. Life is hard."

"Life's a big problem," agrees the Mother. Part of her welcomes and invites all their tales. In the few long days since this nightmare began, part of her has become addicted to disaster and war stories. She wants only to hear about the sadness and emergencies of others. They are the only situations that can join hands with her own; everything else bounces off her shiny shield of resentment and unsympathy. Nothing else can even stay in her brain. From this, no doubt, the philistine world is made, or should one say recruited? Together, the parents huddle all day in the Tiny Tim Lounge—no need to watch *Oprah.* They leave Oprah in the dust. Oprah has nothing on them. They chat matter-of-factly, then fall silent and watch *Dune* or *Star Wars,* in which there are bright and shiny robots, whom the Mother now sees not as robots at all but as human beings who have had terrible things happen to them.

* * *

Some of their friends visit with stuffed animals and soft greetings of "Looking good" for the dozing baby, though the room is way past the stuffed-animal limit. The Mother arranges, once more, a plateful of Mint Milano cookies and cups of take-out coffee for guests. All her nutso pals stop by—the two on Prozac, the one obsessed with the word *penis* in the word *happiness,* the one who recently had her hair foiled green. "Your friends put the *de* in *fin de siècle,*" says the husband. Overheard, or recorded, all marital conversation sounds as if someone must be joking, though usually no one is.

She loves her friends, especially loves them for coming, since there are times they all fight and don't speak for weeks. Is this friendship? For now and here, it must do and is, and is, she swears it is. For one, they never offer impromptu spiritual lectures about death, how it is part of life, its natural ebb and flow, how we all must accept that, or other such utterances that make her want to scratch out some eyes. Like true friends, they take no hardy or elegant stance loosely choreographed from some broad perspective. They get right in there and mutter "Jesus Christ!" and shake their heads. Plus, they are the only people who not only will laugh at her stupid jokes but offer up stupid ones of their own. *What do you get when you cross Tiny Tim with a pit bull?* A child's illness is a strain on the mind. They know how to laugh in a fluty, desperate way—unlike the people who are more her husband's friends and who seem just to deepen their sorrowful gazes, nodding their heads with Sympathy. How exiling and estranging are everybody's Sympathetic Expressions! When anyone laughs, she thinks, Okay! Hooray: a buddy. In disaster as in show business.

Nurses come and go; their chirpy voices both startle and soothe. Some of the other Peed Onk parents stick their heads in to see how the Baby is and offer encouragement.

Green Hair scratches her head. "Everyone's so friendly here. Is there someone in this place who isn't doing all this airy, scripted optimism—or are people like that the only people here?"

"It's Modern Middle Medicine meets the Modern Middle Family," says the Husband. "In the Modern Middle West."

Someone has brought in take-out lo mein, and they all eat it out in the hall by the elevators.

* * *

Parents are allowed use of the Courtesy Line.

"You've got to have a second child," says a different friend on the phone, a friend from out of town. "An heir and a spare. That's what we did. We had another child to ensure we wouldn't off ourselves if we lost our first."

"Really?"

"I'm serious."

"A formal suicide? Wouldn't you just drink yourself into a lifelong stupor and let it go at that?"

"Nope. I knew how I would do it even. For a while, until our second came along, I had it all planned."

"What did you plan?"

"I can't go into too much detail, because—Hi, honey!—the kids are here now in the room. But I'll spell out the general idea: R-O-P-E."

* * *

Sunday evening, she goes and sinks down on the sofa in the Tiny Tim Lounge next to Frank, Joey's father. He is a short, stocky man with the currentless, flatlined look behind the eyes that all the parents eventually get here. He has shaved his head bald in solidarity with his son. His little boy has been battling cancer for five years. It is now in the liver, and the rumor around the corridor is that Joey has three weeks to live. She knows that Joey's mother, Heather, left Frank years ago, two years into the cancer, and has remarried and had another child, a girl named Brittany. The Mother sees Heather here sometimes with her new life—the cute little girl and the new, young, full-haired husband who will never be so maniacally and debilitatingly obsessed with Joey's illness the way Frank, her first husband, was. Heather comes to visit Joey, to say hello and now good-bye, but she is not Joey's main man. Frank is.

Frank is full of stories—about the doctors, about the food, about the nurses, about

Joey. Joey, affectless from his meds, sometimes leaves his room and comes out to watch TV in his bathrobe. He is jaundiced and bald, and though he is nine, he looks no older than six. Frank has devoted the last four and a half years to saving Joey's life. When the cancer was first diagnosed, the doctors gave Joey a 20 percent chance of living six more months. Now here it is, almost five years later, and Joey's still here. It is all due to Frank, who, early on, quit his job as vice president of a consulting firm in order to commit himself totally to his son. He is proud of everything he's given up and done, but he is tired. Part of him now really believes things are coming to a close, that this is the end. He says this without tears. There are no more tears.

"You have probably been through more than anyone else on this corridor," says the Mother.

"I could tell you stories," he says. There is a sour odor between them, and she realizes that neither of them has bathed for days.

"Tell me one. Tell me the worst one." She knows he hates his ex-wife and hates her new husband even more.

"The worst? They're all the worst. Here's one: one morning, I went out for breakfast with my buddy—it was the only time I'd left Joey alone ever; left him for two hours is all—and when I came back, his N-G tube was full of blood. They had the suction on too high, and it was sucking the guts right out of him."

"Oh my God. That just happened to us," said the Mother.

"It did?"

"Friday night."

"You're kidding. They let that happen again? I gave them such a chewing-out about that!"

"I guess our luck is not so good. We get your very worst story on the second night we're here."

"It's not a bad place, though."

"It's not?"

"Naw. I've seen worse. I've taken Joey everywhere."

"He seems very strong." Truth is, at this point, Joey seems like a zombie and frightens her.

"Joey's a fucking genius. A biological genius. They'd given him six months, remember."

The Mother nods.

"Six months is not very long," says Frank. "Six months is nothing. He was four and a half years old."

All the words are like blows. She feels flooded with affection and mourning for this man. She looks away, out the window, out past the hospital parking lot, up toward the black marbled sky and the electric eyelash of the moon. "And now he's nine," she says. "You're his hero."

"And he's mine," says Frank, though the fatigue in his voice seems to overwhelm him. "He'll be that forever. Excuse me," he says, "I've got to go check. His breathing hasn't been good. Excuse me."

* * *

"Good news and bad," says the Oncologist on Monday. He has knocked, entered the room, and now stands there. Their cots are unmade. One wastebasket is overflowing with coffee cups. "We've got the pathologist's report. The bad news is that the kidney they removed had certain lesions, called 'rests,' which are associated with a higher risk for disease in the other kidney. The good news is that the tumor is stage one, regular cell structure, and under five hundred grams, which qualifies you for a national experiment in which chemotherapy isn't done but your boy is monitored with ultrasound instead. It's not all that risky, given that the patient's watched closely, but here is the literature on it. There are forms to sign, if you decide to do that. Read all this and we can discuss it further. You have to decide within four days."

Lesions? Rests? They dry up and scatter like M&M's on the floor. All she hears is the part about no chemo. Another sigh of relief rises up in her and spills out. In a life where there is only the bearable and the unbearable, a sigh of relief is an ecstasy.

"No chemo?" says the Husband. "Do you recommend that?"

The Oncologist shrugs. What casual gestures these doctors are permitted! "I know chemo. I like chemo," says the Oncologist. "But this is for you to decide. It depends how you feel."

The Husband leans forward. "But don't you think that now that we have the upper hand with this thing, we should keep going? Shouldn't we stomp on it, beat it, smash it to death with the chemo?"

The Mother swats him angrily and hard. "Honey, you're delirious!" She whispers, but it comes out as a hiss. "This is our lucky break!" Then she adds gently, "We don't want the Baby to have chemo."

The Husband turns back to the Oncologist. "What do *you* think?"

"It could be," he says, shrugging. "It could be that this is your lucky break. But you won't know for sure for five years."

The Husband turns back to the Mother. "Okay," he says. "Okay."

* * *

The Baby grows happier and strong. He begins to move and sit and eat. Wednesday morning, they are allowed to leave, and leave without chemo. The Oncologist looks a little nervous. "Are you nervous about this?" asks the Mother.

"Of course I'm nervous." But he shrugs and doesn't look that nervous. "See you in six weeks for the ultrasound," he says, waves and then leaves, looking at his big black shoes as he does.

The Baby smiles, even toddles around a little, the sun bursting through the clouds, an angel chorus crescendoing. Nurses arrive. The Hickman is taken out of the Baby's neck and chest; antibiotic lotion is dispensed. The Mother packs up their bags. The Baby sucks on a bottle of juice and does not cry.

"No chemo?" says one of the nurses. "Not even a *little* chemo?"

"We're doing watch and wait," says the Mother.

The other parents look envious but concerned. They have never seen any child get out of there with his hair and white blood cells intact.

"Will you be okay?" asks Ned's mother.

"The worry's going to kill us," says the Husband.

"But if all we have to do is worry," chides the Mother, "every day for a hundred years, it'll be easy. It'll be nothing. I'll take all the worry in the world, if it wards off the thing itself."

"That's right," says Ned's mother. "Compared to everything else, compared to all the actual events, the worry is nothing."

The Husband shakes his head. "I'm such an amateur," he moans.

"You're both doing admirably," says the other mother. "Your baby's lucky, and I wish you all the best."

The Husband shakes her hand warmly. "Thank you," he says. "You've been wonderful."

Another mother, the mother of Eric, comes up to them. "It's all very hard," she says, her head cocked to one side. "But there's a lot of collateral beauty along the way."

*Collateral beauty?* Who is entitled to such a thing? A child is ill. No one is entitled to any collateral beauty!

"Thank you," says the Husband.

Joey's father, Frank, comes up and embraces them both. "It's a journey," he says. He chucks the Baby on the chin. "Good luck, little man."

"Yes, thank you so much," says the Mother. "We hope things go well with Joey." She knows that Joey had a hard, terrible night.

Frank shrugs and steps back. "Gotta go," he says. "Goodbye!"

"Bye," she says, and then he is gone. She bites the inside of her lip, a bit tearily, then bends down to pick up the diaper bag, which is now stuffed with little animals; helium balloons are tied to its zipper. Shouldering the thing, the Mother feels she has just won a prize. All the parents have now vanished down the hall in the opposite direction. The Husband moves close. With one arm, he takes the Baby from her; with the other, he rubs her back. He can see she is starting to get weepy.

"Aren't these people nice? Don't you feel better hearing about their lives?" he asks.

Why does he do this, form clubs all the time; why does even this society of suffering soothe him? When it comes to death and dying, perhaps someone in this family ought to be more of a snob.

"All these nice people with their brave stories," he continues as they make their way toward the elevator bank, waving good-bye to the nursing staff as they go, even the Baby waving shyly. *Bye-bye! Bye-bye!* "Don't you feel consoled, knowing we're all in the same boat, that we're all in this together?"

But who on earth would want to be in this boat? the Mother thinks. This boat is a nightmare boat. Look where it goes: to a silver-and-white room, where, just before your eye-sight and hearing and your ability to touch or be touched disappear entirely, you must watch your child die.

Rope! Bring on the rope.

"Let's make our own way," says the Mother, "and not in this boat."

Woman Overboard! She takes the Baby back from the Husband, cups the Baby's cheek in her hand, kisses his brow and then, quickly, his flowery mouth. The Baby's heart—she can hear it—drums with life. "For as long as I live," says the Mother, pressing the elevator button—up or down, everyone in the end has to leave this way—"I never want to see any of these people again."

* * *

There are the notes.

Now where is the money?

# ⁜ LOUISE ERDRICH
(1954– )

Exploring, in often poetic prose, the intricate and complex fatedness of family and tribal history, Louise Erdrich's fiction, like that of Faulkner, employs multiple narration and a shifting, nonchronological structure. Erdrich grew up listening to the many tribal tales told by her grandfather and others of the Chippewa tribe of the Turtle Mountain Reservation in North Dakota. Her novels are made up of many interrelated and overlapping stories focusing on three Chippewa families from about 1912 to the 1980s.

Erdrich was born in Little Falls, Minnesota, and was raised in Wahpeton, North Dakota. Her mother was a Chippewa Indian and her father was of German descent. They both worked for the Bureau of Indian Affairs. Erdrich received a B.A. from Dartmouth College in 1976 and an M.A. from Johns Hopkins University in 1979. In 1981 she married Michael Dorris, an anthropologist and the head of Dartmouth's Native American Studies Program. They collaborated closely on a number of projects, and cowrote the novel *The Crown of Columbus* (1991). Dorris committed suicide in 1997, and Erdrich now lives in Minnesota.

In 1984, Erdrich published a volume of poetry, *Jacklight,* and her first novel, *Love Medicine,* which won the National Book Critics Circle Award for fiction. Her other novels include *The Beet Queen* (1986), *Tracks* (1988), *The Bingo Palace* (1994), and *Tales of Burning Love* (1996). In 1995, she published a memoir on her experiences in mothering, *The Blue Jay's Dance.*

## Saint Marie
## *(1934)*

### MARIE LAZARRE

So when I went there, I knew the dark fish must rise. Plumes of radiance had soldered on me. No reservation girl had ever prayed so hard. There was no use in trying to ignore me any longer. I was going up there on the hill with the black robe women. They were not any lighter than me. I was going up there to pray as good as they could. Because I don't have that much Indian blood. And they never thought they'd have a girl from this reservation as a saint they'd have to kneel to. But they'd have me. And I'd be carved in pure gold. With ruby lips. And my toenails would be little pink ocean shells, which they would have to stoop down off their high horse to kiss.

I was ignorant. I was near age fourteen. The length of sky is just about the size of my ignorance. Pure and wide. And it was just that—the pure and wideness of my ignorance—that got me up the hill to Sacred Heart Convent and brought me back down alive. For maybe Jesus did not take my bait, but them Sisters tried to cram me right down whole.

You ever see a walleye strike so bad the lure is practically out its back end before you reel it in? That is what they done with me. I don't like to make that low comparison, but I have seen a walleye do that once. And it's the same attempt as Sister Leopolda made to get me in her clutch.

I had the mail-order Catholic soul you get in a girl raised out in the bush, whose only thought is getting into town. For Sunday Mass is the only time my aunt brought us children in except for school, when we were harnessed. Our soul went cheap. We were so anxious to get there we would have walked in on our hands and knees. We just craved going to the store, slinging bottle caps in the dust, making fool eyes at each other. And of course we went to church.

Where they have the convent is on top of the highest hill, so that from its windows the Sisters can be looking into the marrow of the town. Recently a windbreak was planted before the bar "for the purposes of tornado insurance." Don't tell me that. That poplar stand was put up to hide the drinkers as they get the transformation. As they are served into the beast of their burden. While they're drinking, that body comes upon them, and then they stagger or crawl out the bar door, pulling a weight they can't move past the poplars. They don't want no holy witness to their fall.

Anyway, I climbed. That was a long-ago day. There was a road then for wagons that wound in ruts to the top of the hill where they had their buildings of painted brick. Gleaming white. So white the sun glanced off in dazzling display to set forms whirling behind your eyelids. The face of God you could hardly look at. But that day it drizzled, so I could look all I wanted. I saw the homelier side. The cracked whitewash and swallows nesting in the busted ends of caves. I saw the boards sawed the size of broken windowpanes and the fruit trees, stripped. Only the tough wild rhubarb flourished. Goldenrod rubbed up their walls. It was a poor convent. I didn't see that then but I know that now. Compared to others it was humble, ragtag, out in the middle of no place. It was the end of the world to some. Where the maps stopped. Where God had only half a hand in the creation. Where the Dark One had put in thick bush, liquor, wild dogs, and Indians.

I heard later that the Sacred Heart Convent was a catchall place for nuns that don't get along elsewhere. Nuns that complain too much or lose their mind. I'll always wonder now, after hearing that, where they picked up Sister Leopolda. Perhaps she had scarred someone else, the way she left a mark on me. Perhaps she was just sent around to test her Sister's faith, here and there, like the spot-checker in a factory. For she was the definite most-hard trial to anyone's endurance, even when they started out with veils of wretched love upon their eyes.

I was that girl who thought the black hem of her garment would help me rise. Veils of love which was only hate petrified by longing—that was me. I was like those bush Indians who stole the holy black hat of a Jesuit and swallowed little scraps of it to cure their fevers. But the hat itself carried smallpox and was killing them with belief. Veils of faith! I had this confidence in Leopolda. She was different. The other Sisters had long ago gone blank and given up on Satan. He slept for them. They never noticed his comings and goings. But Leopolda kept track of him and knew his habits, minds he burrowed in, deep spaces where he did. She knew as much about him as my grandma, who called him by other names and was not afraid.

In her class, Sister Leopolda carried a long oak pole for opening high windows. It had a hook made of iron on one end that could jerk a patch of your hair out or throttle you by the collar—all from a distance. She used this deadly hook-pole for catching Satan by surprise. He could have entered without your knowing it—through your lips or your nose or any one of your seven openings—and gained your mind. But she would see him. That pole would brain you from behind. And he would gasp, dazzled, and take the first thing she offered, which was pain.

She had a stringer of children who could only breathe if she said the word. I was the worst of them. She always said the Dark One wanted me most of all, and I believed this. I stood out. Evil was a common thing I trusted. Before sleep sometimes he came and whispered conversation in the old language of the bush. I listened. He told me things he never told anyone but Indians. I was privy to both worlds of his knowledge. I listened to him, but I had confidence in Leopolda. She was the only one of the bunch he even noticed.

There came a day, though, when Leopolda turned the tide with her hook-pole.

It was a quiet day with everyone working at their desks, when I heard him. He had sneaked into the closets in the back of the room. He was scratching around, tasting crumbs in our pockets, stealing buttons, squirting his dark juice in the linings and the boots. I was the only one who heard him, and I got bold. I smiled. I glanced back and smiled and looked up at her sly to see if she had noticed. My heart jumped. For she was looking straight at me. And she sniffed. She had a big stark bony nose stuck to the front of her face for smelling out brimstone and evil thoughts. She had smelled him on me. She stood up. Tall, pale, a blackness leading into the deeper blackness of the slate wall behind her. Her oak pole had flown into her grip. She had seen me glance at the closet. Oh, she knew. She knew just where he was. I watched her watch him in her mind's eye. The whole class was watching now. She was staring, sizing, following his scuffle. And all of a sudden she tensed down, posed on her bent kneesprings, cocked her arm back. She threw the oak pole singing over my head, through my braincloud. It cracked through the thin wood door of the back closet, and the heavy pointed hook drove through his heart. I turned. She'd speared her own black rubber overboot where he'd taken refuge in the tip of her darkest toe.

Something howled in my mind. Loss and darkness. I understood. I was to suffer for my smile.

He rose up hard in my heart. I didn't blink when the pole cracked. My skull was tough. I didn't flinch when she shrieked in my ear. I only shrugged at the flowers of hell. He wanted me. More than anything he craved me. But then she did the worst. She did what broke my mind to her. She grabbed me by the collar and dragged me, feet flying, through the room and threw me in the closet with her dead black overboot. And I was there. The only light was a crack beneath the door. I asked the Dark One to enter into me and boost my mind. I asked him to restrain my tears, for they was pushing behind my eyes. But he was afraid to come back there. He was afraid of her sharp pole. And I was afraid of Leopolda's pole for the first time, too. I felt the cold hook in my heart.

How it could crack through the door at any minute and drag me out, like a dead fish on a gaff, drop me on the floor like a gunshot squirrel.

I was nothing. I edged back to the wall as far as I could. I breathed the chalk dust. The hem of her full black cloak cut against my cheek. He had left me. Her spear could find me any time. Her keen ears would aim the hook into the beat of my heart.

What was that sound?

It filled the closet, filled it up until it spilled over, but I did not recognize the crying wailing voice as mine until the door cracked open, brightness, and she hoisted me to her camphor-smelling lips.

"He *wants* you," she said. "That's the difference. I give you love."

Love. The black hook. The spear singing through the mind. I saw that she had tracked the Dark One to my heart and flushed him out into the open. So now my heart was an empty nest where she could lurk.

Well, I was weak. I was weak when I let her in, but she got a foothold there. Hard to dislodge as the year passed. Sometimes I felt him—the brush of dim wings—but only rarely did his voice compel. It was between Marie and Leopolda now, and the struggle changed. I began to realize I had been on the wrong track with the fruits of hell. The real way to overcome Leopolda was this: I'd get to heaven first. And then, when I saw her coming, I'd shut the gate. She'd be out! That is why, besides the bowing and the scraping I'd be dealt, I wanted to sit on the altar as a saint.

To this end, I went up on the hill. Sister Leopolda was the consecrated nun who had sponsored me to come there.

"You're not vain," she said. "You're too honest, looking into the mirror, for that. You're not smart. You don't have the ambition to get clear. You have two choices. One, you can marry a no-good Indian, bear his brats, die like a dog. Or two, you can give yourself to God."

"I'll come up there," I said, "but not because of what you think."

I could have had any damn man on the reservation at the time. And I could have made him treat me like his own life. I looked good. And I looked white. But I wanted Sister Leopolda's heart. And here was the thing: sometimes I wanted her heart in love and admiration. Sometimes. And sometimes I wanted her heart to roast on a black stick.

* * *

She answered the back door where they had instructed me to call. I stood there with my bundle. She looked me up and down.

"All right," she said finally. "Come in."

She took my hand. Her fingers were like a bundle of broom straws, so thin and dry, but the strength of them was unnatural. I couldn't have tugged loose if she was leading me into rooms of white-hot coal. Her strength was a kind of perverse miracle, for she got it from fasting herself thin. Because of this hunger practice her lips were a wounded brown and her skin deadly pale. Her eye sockets were two deep lashless hollows in a taut skull. I told you about the nose already. It stuck out far and made the place her eyes moved even deeper, as if she stared out the wrong end of a gun barrel. She took the bundle from my hands and threw it in the corner.

"You'll be sleeping behind the stove, child."

It was immense, like a great furnace. There was a small cot close behind it.

"Looks like it could get warm there," I said.

"Hot. It does."

"Do I get a habit?"

I wanted something like the thing she wore. Flowing black cotton. Her face was strapped in white bandages, and a sharp crest of starched white cardboard hung over her forehead like a glaring beak. If possible, I wanted a bigger, longer, whiter beak than hers.

"No," she said, grinning her great skull grin. "You don't get one yet. Who knows, you might not like us. Or we might not like you."

But she had loved me, or offered me love. And she had tried to hunt the Dark One down. So I had this confidence.

"I'll inherit your keys from you," I said.

She looked at me sharply, and her grin turned strange. She hissed, taking in her breath. Then she turned to the door and took a key from her belt. It was a giant key, and it unlocked the larder where the food was stored.

Inside there was all kinds of good stuff. Things I'd tasted only once or twice in my life. I saw sticks of dried fruit, jars of orange peel, spice like cinnamon. I saw tins of crackers with ships painted on the side. I saw pickles. Jars of herring and the rind of pigs. There was cheese, a big brown block of it from the thick milk of goats. And besides that there was the everyday stuff, in great quantities, the flour and the coffee.

It was the cheese that got to me. When I saw it my stomach hollowed. My tongue dripped. I loved that goat-milk cheese better than anything I'd ever ate. I stared at it. The rich curve in the buttery cloth.

"When you inherit my keys," she said sourly, slamming the door in my face, "you can eat all you want of the priest's cheese."

Then she seemed to consider what she'd done. She looked at me. She took the key from her belt and went back, sliced a hunk off, and put it in my hand.

"If you're good you'll taste this cheese again. When I'm dead and gone," she said.

Then she dragged out the big sack of flour. When I finished that heaven stuff she told me to roll my sleeves up and begin doing God's labor. For a while we worked in silence, mixing up the dough and pounding it out on stone slabs.

"God's work," I said after a while. "If this is God's work, then I've done it all my life."

"Well, you've done it with the Devil in your heart then," she said. "Not God."

"How do you know?" I asked. But I knew she did. And I wished I had not brought up the subject.

"I see right into you like a clear glass," she said. "I always did."

"You don't know it," she continued after a while, "but he's come around here sulking. He's come around here brooding. You brought him in. He knows the smell of me, and he's going to make a last ditch try to get you back. Don't let him." She glared over at me. Her eyes were cold and lighted. "Don't let him touch you. We'll be a long time getting rid of him."

So I was careful. I was careful not to give him an inch. I said a rosary, two rosaries, three, underneath my breath. I said the Creed. I said every scrap of Latin I knew while we punched the dough with our fists. And still, I dropped the cup. It rolled under that monstrous iron stove, which was getting fired up for baking.

And she was on me. She saw he'd entered my distraction.

"Our good cup," she said. "Get it out of there, Marie."

I reached for the poker to snag it out from beneath the stove. But I had a sinking feel in my stomach as I did this. Sure enough, her long arm darted past me like a whip. The poker lighted in her hand.

"Reach," she said. "Reach with your arm for that cup. And when your flesh is hot, remember that the flames you feel are only one fraction of the heat you will feel in his hellish embrace."

She always did things this way, to teach you lessons. So I wasn't surprised. It was playacting, anyway, because a stove isn't very hot underneath right along the floor. They aren't made that way. Otherwise a wood floor would burn. So I said yes and got down on my stomach and reached under. I meant to grab it quick and jump up again, before she could think up another lesson, but here it happened. Although I groped for the cup, my hand closed on nothing. That cup was nowhere to be found. I heard her step toward me, a slow step. I heard the creak of thick shoe leather, the little *plat* as the folds of her heavy skirts met, a trickle of fine sand sifting, somewhere, perhaps in the bowels of her, and I was afraid. I tried to scramble up, but her foot came down lightly behind my ear, and I was lowered. The foot came down more firmly at the base of my neck, and I was held.

"You're like I was," she said. "He wants you very much."

"He doesn't want me no more," I said. "He had his fill. I got the cup!"

I heard the valve opening, the hissed intake of breath, and knew that I should not have spoke.

"You lie," she said. "You're cold. There is a wicked ice forming in your blood. You don't have a shred of devotion for God. Only wild cold dark lust. I know it. I know how you feel. I see the beast . . . the beast watches me out of your eyes sometimes. Cold."

The urgent scrape of metal. It took a moment to know from where. Top of the stove. Kettle. Lessons. She was steadying herself with the iron poker. I could feel it like pure certainty, driving into the wood floor. I would not remind her of pokers. I heard the water as it came, tipped from the spout, cooling as it fell but still scalding as it struck. I must have twitched beneath her foot, because she steadied me, and then the poker nudged up beside my arm as if to guide. "To warm your cold ash heart," she said. I felt how patient she would be. The water came. My mind went dead blank. Again. I could only think the kettle would be cooling slowly in her hand. I could not stand it. I bit my lip so as not to satisfy her with a sound. She gave me more reason to keep still.

"I will boil him from your mind if you make a peep," she said, "by filling up your ear."

* * *

Any sensible fool would have run back down the hill the minute Leopolda let them up from under her heel. But I was snared in her black intelligence by then. I could not think straight. I had prayed so hard I think I broke a cog in my mind. I prayed while her foot squeezed my throat. While my skin burst. I prayed even when I heard the wind come through, shrieking in the busted bird nests. I didn't stop when pure light fell, turning slowly behind my eyelids. God's face. Even that did not disrupt my continued praise. Words came. Words came from nowhere and flooded my mind.

Now I could pray much better than any one of them. Than all of them full force. This was proved. I turned to her in a daze when she let me up. My thoughts were gone, and yet I remember how surprised I was. Tears glittered in her eyes, deep down, like the sinking reflection in a well.

"It was so hard, Marie," she gasped. Her hands were shaking. The kettle clattered against the stove. "But I have used all the water up now. I think he is gone."

"I prayed," I said foolishly. "I prayed very hard."

"Yes," she said. "My dear one, I know."

* * *

We sat together quietly because we had no more words. We let the dough rise and punched it down once. She gave me a bowl of mush, unlocked the sausage from a special cupboard, and took that in to the Sisters. They sat down the hall, chewing their sausage, and I could hear them. I could hear their teeth bite through their bread and meat. I couldn't move. My shirt was dry but the cloth stuck to my back, and I couldn't think straight. I was losing the sense to understand how her mind worked. She'd gotten past me with her poker and I would never be a saint. I despaired. I felt I had no inside voice, nothing to direct me, no darkness, no Marie. I was about to throw that cornmeal mush out to the birds and make a run for it, when the vision rose up blazing in my mind.

I was rippling gold. My breasts were bare and my nipples flashed and winked. Diamonds tipped them. I could walk through panes of glass. I could walk through windows. She was at my feet, swallowing the glass after each step I took. I broke through another and another. The glass she swallowed ground and cut until her starved insides were only a subtle dust. She coughed. She coughed a cloud of dust. And then she was only a black rag that flapped off, snagged in bobwire, hung there for an age, and finally rotted into the breeze.

I saw this, mouth hanging open, gazing off into the flagged boughs of trees.

"Get up!" she cried. "Stop dreaming. It is time to bake."

Two other Sisters had come in with her, wide women with hands like paddles. They were evening and smoothing out the firebox beneath the great jaws of the oven.

"Who is this one?" they asked Leopolda. "Is she yours?"

"She is mine," said Leopolda. "A very good girl."

"What is your name?" one asked me.

"Marie."

"Marie. Star of the Sea."

"She will shine," said Leopolda, "when we have burned off the dark corrosion."

The others laughed, but uncertainly. They were mild and sturdy French, who did not understand Leopolda's twisted jokes, although they muttered respectfully at things she said. I knew they wouldn't believe what she had done with the kettle. There was no question. So I kept quiet.

*"Elle est docile,"* they said approvingly as they left to starch the linens.

"Does it pain?" Leopolda asked me as soon as they were out the door.

I did not answer. I felt sick with the hurt.

"Come along," she said.

The building was wholly quiet now. I followed her up the narrow staircase into a hall of little rooms, many doors. Her cell was the quietest, at the very end. Inside, the air smelled stale, as if the door had not been opened for years. There was a crude straw mattress, a tiny bookcase with a picture of Saint Francis hanging over it, a ragged palm, a stool for sitting on, a crucifix. She told me to remove my blouse and sit on the stool. I did so. She took a pot of salve from the bookcase and began to smooth it upon my burns. Her hands made slow, wide circles, stopping the pain. I closed my eyes. I expected to see blackness. Peace. But instead the vision reared up again. My chest was still tipped with diamonds. I was walking through windows. She was chewing up the broken litter I left behind.

"I am going," I said. "Let me go."

But she held me down.

"Don't go," she said quickly. "Don't. We have just begun."

I was weakening. My thoughts were whirling pitifully. The pain had kept me strong, and as it left me I began to forget it; I couldn't hold on. I began to wonder if she'd really scalded me with the kettle. I could not remember. To remember this seemed the most important thing in the world. But I was losing the memory. The scalding. The pouring. It began to vanish. I felt like my mind was coming off its hinge, flapping in the breeze, hanging by the hair of my own pain. I wrenched out of her grip.

"He was always in you," I said. "Even more than in me. He wanted you even more. And now he's got you. Get thee behind me!"

I shouted that, grabbed my shirt, and ran through the door throwing the cloth on my body. I got down the stairs and into the kitchen, even, but no matter what I told myself, I couldn't get out the door. It wasn't finished. And she knew I would not leave. Her quiet step was immediately behind me.

"We must take the bread from the oven now," she said.

She was pretending nothing happened. But for the first time I had gotten through some chink she'd left in her darkness. Touched some doubt. Her voice was so low and brittle it cracked off at the end of her sentence.

"Help me, Marie," she said slowly.

But I was not going to help her, even though she had calmly buttoned the back of my shirt up and put the big cloth mittens in my hands for taking out the loaves. I could have bolted for it then. But I didn't. I knew that something was nearing completion. Something was about to happen. My back was a wall of singing flame. I was turning. I watched her take the long fork in one hand, to tap the loaves. In the other hand she gripped the black poker to hook the pans.

"Help me," she said again, and I thought, Yes, this is part of it. I put the mittens on my hands and swung the door open on its hinges. The oven gaped. She stood back a moment, letting the first blast of heat rush by. I moved behind her. I could feel the heat at my front and at my back. Before, behind. My skin was turning to beaten gold. It was coming quicker than I thought. The oven was like the gate of a personal hell. Just big enough and hot enough for one person, and that was her. One kick and Leopolda would fly in headfirst. And that would be one-millionth of the heat she would feel when she finally collapsed in his hellish embrace.

Saints know these numbers.

She bent forward with her fork held out. I kicked her with all my might. She flew in. But the outstretched poker hit the back wall first, so she rebounded. The oven was not so deep as I had thought.

There was a moment when I felt a sort of thin, hot disappointment, as when a fish slips off the line. Only I was the one going to be lost. She was fearfully silent. She whirled. Her veil had cutting edges. She had the poker in one hand. In the other she held that long sharp fork she used to tap the delicate crusts of loaves. Her face turned upside down on her shoulders. Her face turned blue. But saints are used to miracles. I felt no trace of fear.

If I was going to be lost, let the diamonds cut! Let her eat ground glass!

"Bitch of Jesus Christ!" I shouted. "Kneel and beg! Lick the floor!"

That was when she stabbed me through the hand with the fork, then took the poker up alongside my head, and knocked me out.

* * *

It must have been a half an hour later when I came around. Things were so strange. So strange I can hardly tell it for delight at the remembrance. For when I came around this was actually taking place. I was being worshiped. I had somehow gained the altar of a saint.

I was lying back on the stiff couch in the Mother Superior's office. I looked around me. It was as though my deepest dream had come to life. The Sisters of the convent were kneeling to me. Sister Bonaventure. Sister Dympna. Sister Cecilia Saint-Claire. The two French with hands like paddles. They were down on their knees. Black capes were slung over some of their heads. My name was buzzing up and down the room, like a fat autumn fly lighting on the tips of their tongues between Latin, humming up the heavy blood-dark curtains, circling their little cosseted heads. Marie! Marie! A girl thrown in a closet. Who was afraid of a rubber overboot. Who was half overcome. A girl who came in the back door where they threw their garbage. Marie! Who never found the cup. Who had to eat their cold mush. Marie! Leopolda had her face buried in her knuckles. Saint Marie of the Holy Slops! Saint Marie of the Bread Fork! Saint Marie of the Burnt Back and Scalded Butt!

I broke out and laughed.

They looked up. All holy hell burst loose when they saw I'd woke. I still did not understand what was happening. They were watching, talking, but not to me.

"The marks . . ."

"She has her hand closed."

*"Je ne peux pas voir."*

I was not stupid enough to ask what they were talking about. I couldn't tell why I was lying in white sheets. I couldn't tell why they were praying to me. But I'll tell you this: it seemed entirely natural. It was me. I lifted up my hand as in my dream. It was completely limp with sacredness.

"Peace be with you."

My arm was dried blood from the wrist down to the elbow. And it hurt. Their faces turned like flat flowers of adoration to follow that hand's movements. I let it swing through the air, imparting a saint's blessing. I had practiced. I knew exactly how to act.

They murmured. I heaved a sigh, and a golden beam of light suddenly broke through the clouded window and flooded down directly on my face. A stroke of perfect luck! They had to be convinced.

Leopolda still knelt in the back of the room. Her knuckles were crammed halfway down her throat. Let me tell you, a saint has senses honed keen as a wolf. I knew that she was over my barrel now. How it happened did not matter. The last thing I remembered was how she flew from the oven and stabbed me. That one thing was most certainly true.

"Come forward, Sister Leopolda." I gestured with my heavenly wound. Oh, it hurt. It bled when I reopened the slight heal. "Kneel beside me," I said.

She kneeled, but her voice box evidently did not work, for her mouth opened, shut, opened, but no sound came out. My throat clenched in noble delight I had read of as befitting a saint. She could not speak. But she was beaten. It was in her eyes. She stared at me now with all the deep hate of the wheel of devilish dust that rolled wild within her emptiness.

"What is it you want to tell me?" I asked. And at last she spoke.

"I have told my Sisters of your passion," she managed to choke out. "How the stigmata . . . the marks of the nails . . . appeared in your palm and you swooned at the holy vision. . . ."

"Yes," I said curiously.

And then, after a moment, I understood.

Leopolda had saved herself with her quick brain. She had witnessed a miracle. She had hid the fork and told this to the others. And of course they believed her, because they never knew how Satan came and went or where he took refuge.

"I saw it from the first," said the large one who put the bread in the oven. "Humility of the spirit. So rare in these girls."

"I saw it, too," said the other one with great satisfaction. She sighed quietly. "If only it was me."

Leopolda was kneeling bolt upright, face blazing and twitching, a barely held fountain of blasting poison.

"Christ has marked me," I agreed.

I smiled the saint's smirk into her face. And then I looked at her. That was my mistake.

For I saw her kneeling there. Leopolda with her soul like a rubber overboot. With her face of a starved rat. With the desperate eyes drowning in the deep wells of her wrongness. There would be no one else after me. And I would leave. I saw Leopolda kneeling within the shambles of her love.

My heart had been about to surge from my chest with the blackness of my joyous heat. Now it dropped. I pitied her. I pitied her. Pity twisted in my stomach like that hook-pole was driven through me. I was caught. It was a feeling more terrible than any amount of boiling water and worse than being forked. Still, still, I could not help what I did. I had already smiled in a saint's mealy forgiveness. I heard myself speaking gently.

"Receive the dispensation of my sacred blood," I whispered.

But there was no heart in it. No joy when she bent to touch the floor. No dark leaping. I fell back into the white pillows. Blank dust was whirling through the light shafts. My skin was dust. Dust my lips. Dust the dirty spoons on the ends of my feet.

Rise up! I thought. Rise up and walk! There is no limit to this dust!

# ⁜ FRANK CHIN
## (1940– )

To young Asian-American writers of the late 1960s and 1970s, Frank Chin was known as the "godfather" and as the conscience of Asian-American writing. While sometimes criticized for being angry and bitter, Chin's work is hip, iconoclastic, satiric, and demythologizing in its project to explore new possibilities of Asian-American identities in the fast-changing American cultural landscape.

Chin was born in Berkeley, California, and attended the University of California there from 1958 to 1961. He went to the Writers' Workshop at the University of Iowa from 1961 to 1963. He returned to California and finished his degree work at the University of California at Santa Barbara in 1965. He worked on the Southern Pacific Railroad as a clerk and, later, as the first Chinese-American brakeman. In Seattle between 1966 and 1969, Chin worked as a writer for KING-TV. Returning to California, he taught Asian-American studies at San Francisco State University and at the University of California at Davis, among other institutions. He founded and led the Asian-American Theater Workshop from 1973 to 1977.

Chin's unpublished novel *A Chinese Lady Dies* won the Jackson Award from the San Francisco Foundation in 1965. His play *The Chickencoop Chinaman* (1972) was the first Asian-American play produced on the New York legitimate stage. His second play, *The Year of the Dragon* (1974), was staged at the American Place Theater and filmed for television by PBS in 1975. His fiction includes the story collection *The Chinamen Pacific & Frisco R.R. Co.* (1988) and the novels *Donald Duk* (1991) and *Gunga Din Highway* (1994). He has coedited anthologies of Asian-American literature and published a collection of essays, *Bulletproof Buddhists and Other Essays,* in 1998.

# The Only Real Day

THE MEN played mah-jong or passed the waterpipe, their voices low under the sound of the fish pumps thudding into the room from the tropical fish store. Voices became louder over other voices in the thickening heat. Yuen was with his friends now, where he was always happy and loud every Tuesday night. All the faces shone of skin oily from the heat and laughter, the same as last week, the same men and room and waterpipe. Yuen knew them. Here it was comfortable after another week of that crippled would-be Hollywood Oriental-for-a-friend in Oakland. He hated the sight of cripples on his night and day off, and one had spoken to him as he stepped off the A-train into the tinny breath of the Key System Bay Bridge Terminal. Off the train in San Francisco into the voice of a cripple. "Count your blessings!" The old white people left to die at the Eclipse Hotel, and the old waitresses who worked there often said "Count your blessings" over sneezes and little ouches and bad news. Christian resignation. Yuen was older than many of the white guests of the Eclipse. He washed dishes there without ever once counting his blessings.

"That's impossible," Huie said to Yuen.

Yuen grinned at his friend and said, "Whaddaya mean? It's true! You don't know because you were born here."

"Whaddaya mean 'born here'? Who was born here?"

"Every morning, I woke up with my father and my son, and we walked out of our house to the field, and stood in a circle around a young peach tree and lowered our trousers and pissed on the tree, made bubbles in the dirt, got the bark wet, splattered on the roots and watched our piss sink in. That's how we fertilized the big one the day I said I was going to Hong Kong tomorrow with my wife and son, and told them I was leaving my father and mother, and I did. I left. Then I left Hong Kong and left my family there, and came to America to make money," Yuen said. "Then after so much money, bring them over."

"Nobody gets over these days, so don't bang your head about not getting people over. What I want to know is did you make money?"

"Make money?"

"Yes, did you make money?"

"I'm still here, my wife is dead . . . but my son is still in Hong Kong, and I send him what I can."

"You're too good a father! He's a big boy now. Has to be a full-grown man. You don't want to spoil him."

Yuen looked up at the lightbulb and blinked. "It's good to get away from those *lo fan* women always around the restaurant. Waitresses, hotel guests crying for Rose. Ha ha." He didn't want to talk about his son or China. Talk of white women he'd seen changing in the corridor outside his room over the kitchen, and sex acts of the past, would cloud out what he didn't want to talk about. Already the men in the room full of fish tanks were speaking loudly, shouting when they laughed, throwing the sound of their voices loud against the spongy atmosphere of fish pumps and warm-water aquariums. Yuen enjoyed the room when it was loud and blunt. The fishtanks and gulping and chortling pumps sopped up the sound of the clickety clickety of the games and kept the voices, no matter how loud, inside. The louder the closer, thicker, fleshier, as the night wore on. This was the life after a week of privacy with the only real Chinese speaker being paralyzed speechless in a wheelchair. No wonder the boy doesn't speak Chinese, he thought, not making sense. The boy should come here sometime. He might like the fish.

"Perhaps you could," Huie said, laughing, "Perhaps you could make love to them, Ah-Yuen gaw." The men laughed, showing gold and aged yellow teeth. "Love!" Yuen snorted against the friendly laugh.

"That's what they call it if you do it for free," Huie said.

"Not me," Yuen said taking the bucket and water pipe from Huie. "Free or money. No love. No fuck. Not me." He lifted the punk from the tobacco, then shot off the ash with a blast of air into the pipe that sent a squirt of water up the stem. "I don't even like talking to them. Why should I speak their language? They don't think I'm anything anyway. They change their clothes and smoke in their slips right outside my door in the hallway, and don't care I live there. So what?" His head lifted to face his friends, and his nostrils opened, one larger than the other as he spoke faster. "And anyway, they don't care if I come out of my room and see them standing half-naked in the hall. They must know they're ugly. They all have wrinkles and you can see all the dirt on their skins and they shave their armpits badly, and their powder turns brown in the folds of their skin. They're not like Chinese women at all." Yuen made it a joke for his friends.

"I have always wanted to see a real naked American woman for free. There's something about not paying money to see what you see," Huie said. "Ahhh and what I want to see is bigger breasts. Do these free peeks have bigger breasts than Chinese women? Do they have nipples as pink as calendar girls' sweet suckies?" Huie grunted and put his hands inside his jacket and hefted invisible breasts, "Do they have . . . ?"

"I don't know. I don't look. All the ones at my place are old, and who wants to look inside the clothes of the old for their parts? And you can't tell about calendar pictures . . ." Yuen pulled at the deep smoke of the waterpipe. The water inside gurgled loudly, and singed tobacco ash jumped when Yuen blew back into the tube. He lifted his head and licked the edges of his teeth. He always licked the edges of his teeth before speaking. He did not think it a sign of old age. Before he broke the first word over his licked teeth, Huie raised his hand. "Jimmy Chan goes out with *lo fan* women . . . blonde ones with blue eyelids too. And he smokes cigars," Huie said.

"He smokes cigars. So what? What's that?"

"They light his cigars for him."

"That's because he has money. If Chinese have money here, everybody likes them," Yuen said. "Blue nipples, pink eyelids, everybody likes them."

"Not the Jews."

"Not the Jews." Yuen said. "I saw a cripple. Screamed 'Count your blessings!' Could have been a Jew, huh? I should have looked . . . Who cares? So what?"

"The Jews don't like anybody," Huie said. "They call us, you and me, the Tang people 'Jews of the Orient.' Ever hear that?"

"Because the Jews don't like anybody?"

"Because nobody likes the Jews!" Huie said. He pulled the tip of his nose down with his fingers. "Do I look like a Jew of the Orient, for fuckin out loud? What a life!" The men at the mah-jong table laughed and shook the table with the pounding of their hands. Over their laughter, Yuen spoke loudly, licking the edges of his teeth and smiling, "What do you want to be Jew for? You're Chinese! That's bad enough!" And the room full of close men was loud with the sound of tables slapped with night-pale hands and belly laughter shrinking into wheezes and silent empty mouths breathless and drooling. "We have a Jew at the Eclipse Hotel. They look white like the other *lo fan gwai* to me," Yuen said, and touched the glowing punk to the tobacco and inhaled through his mouth, gurgling the water. He let the smoke drop from his nostrils and laughed smoke out between his teeth, and leaned back into the small spaces of smoke between the men and enjoyed the whole room.

Yuen was a man of neat habits, but always seemed disheveled with his dry mouth, open with the lower lip shining, dry and dangling below yellow teeth. Even today, dressed in his day-off suit that he kept hung in his closet with butcher paper over it and a hat he kept in a box, he had seen people watching him and laughing behind their hands at his pulling at the shoulders of the jacket and lifting the brim of his hat from his eyes. He had gathered himself into his own arms and leaned back into his seat to think about the room in San Francisco; then he slept and was ignorant of the people, the conductor, and all the people he had seen before, watching him and snickering, and who might have been, he thought, jealous of him for being tall for a Chinese, or his long fingers, exactly what he did not know or worry about in his half-stupor between wakefulness and sleep with his body against the side of the train, the sounds of the steel wheels, and the train pitching side to side, all amazingly loud and echoing in his ears, through his body before sleep.

Tuesday evening Yuen took the A-train from Oakland to San Francisco. He walked to the train stop right after work at the restaurant and stood, always watching to the end of the street for the train's coming, dim out of the darkness from San Francisco. The train came, its cars swaying side to side and looked like a short snake with a lit stripe of lights squirming past him, or like the long dragon that stretched and jumped over the feet of the boys carrying it. He hated the dragon here, but saw it when it ran, for the boy's sake. The train looked like that, the glittering dragon that moved quickly like the sound of drum rolls and dangled its staring eyes out of its head with a flurry of beard; the screaming bird's voice of the train excited in him his idea of a child's impulse to run, to grab, to destroy.

Then he stood and listened to the sound of the train's steel wheels, the sound of an invisible cheering crowd being sucked after the lights of the train toward the end of the line, leaving the quiet street more quiet and Yuen almost superstitiously anxious. Almost. The distance from superstitious feeling a loss or an achievement, he wasn't sure.

He was always grateful for the Tuesdays Dirigible walked him to the train stop. They left early on these nights and walked past drugstores, bought comic books, looked into the windows of closed shops and dimly lit used bookstores, and looked at shoes or suits on dummies. "How much is that?" Yuen would ask.

"I don't know what you're talking," Dirigible, the boy of the unpronounceable name, would say. "I don't know what you're talking" seemed the only complete phrase he commanded in Cantonese.

"What a stupid boy you are; can't even talk Chinese," Yuen would say, and "Too moochie shi-yet," adding his only American phrase. "Come on, I have a train to catch." They would laugh at each other and walk slowly, the old man lifting his shoulders and leaning his head far back on his neck, walking straighter, when he remembered. The boy. "Fay Gay" in Cantonese, Flying Ship, made him remember.

A glance back to Dirigible as he boarded the train, a smile, a wave, the boy through the window a silent thing in the noise of the engines. Yuen would shrug and settle himself against the back, against the seat, and still watch Dirigible, who would be walking now, back toward the restaurant. Tonight he realized again how young the Flying Ship was to be walking home alone at night through the city back to the kitchen entrance of the hotel. He saw Dirigible not walking the usual way home, but running next to the moving train, then turning the corner to walk up a street with more lights and people. Yuen turned, thinking he might shout out the door for the boy to go home the way they had come, but the train was moving, the moment gone. Almost. Yuen had forgotten something. The train was moving. And he had no right. Dirigible had heard his mother say that Yuen had no right so many times that Dirigible was saying it too. In Chinese. Badly spoken and bungled, but Chinese. That he was not Yuen's son. That this was not China. Knowing the boy was allowed to say such things by his only speaking parent made Yuen's need to scold and shout more urgent, his silence in front of the spoiled punk more humiliating. Yuen was still and worked himself out of his confusion. The beginning of his day off was bad; nothing about it right or usual; all of it bad, no good, wrong. Yuen chewed it out of his mind until the memory was fond and funny, then relaxed.

"Jimmy Chan has a small Mexican dog too, that he keeps in his pocket," Huie said. "It's lined with rubber."

"The little dog?" Yuen asked. And the men laughed.

"The dog . . ." Huie said and chuckled out of his chinless face, "No, his pocket, so if the dog urinates . . ." He shrugged, "You know."

"Then how can he make love to his blonde *fangwai* woman with blue breasts if his pocket is full of dogpiss?"

"He takes off his coat!" The men laughed with their faces up into the falling smoke. The men seemed very close to Yuen, as if with the heat and smoke they swelled to crowding against the walls, and Yuen swelled and was hot with them, feeling tropically close and friendly, friendlier, until he was dizzy with friendship and forgot names. No, don't forget names. "A Chinese can do anything with *fangwai* if he has money," Yuen said.

"Like too moochie shi-yet, he can," Huie shouted, almost falling off his seat. "He can't make himself white!" Huie jabbed his finger at Yuen and glared. The men at the table stopped. The noise of the mah-jong and voices stopped to the sound of rumps shifting over chairs and creaks of table legs. Heavy arms were leaned onto the tabletops. Yuen was not sure whether he was arguing with his friend or not. He did not want to argue on his day off, yet he was constrained to say something. He knew that whatever he said would sound more important than he meant it. He licked his teeth and said, "Who want to be white when they can have money?" He grinned. The man nodded and sat quiet a moment, listening to the sound of boys shouting at cars to come and park in their lots. "Older brother, you always know the right thing to say in a little pinch, don't you."

"You mother's twat! Play!" And the men laughed and in a burst of noise returned to their game.

The back room was separated from the tropical fish store by a long window shade drawn over the doorway. Calendars with pictures of Chinese women holding peaches the size of basketballs, calendars with pictures of nude white women with large breasts of all shapes, and a picture someone thought was funny, showing a man with the breasts of a woman, were tacked to the walls above the stacked glass tanks of warm-water fish. The men sat on boxes, in chairs, at counters with a wall of drawers full of stuff for tropical fish, and leaned inside the doorway and bits of wall not occupied by a gurgling tank of colorful little swimming things. They sat and passed the waterpipe and tea and played mah-jong or talked. Every night the waterpipe, the tea, the mah-jong, the talk.

"Wuhay! Hey, Yuen, older brother," a familiar nameless voice shouted through the smoke and thumping pumps. "Why're you so quiet tonight?"

"I thought I was being loud and obnoxious," Yuen said. "Perhaps it's my boss's son looking sick again."

"The boy?" Huie said.

Yuen stood and removed his jacket, brushed it and hung it on a nail. "He has this trouble with his stomach . . . makes him bend up and he cries and won't move. It comes and goes," Yuen said.

"Bring him over to me, and I'll give him some herbs, make him well in a hurry."

"His mother, my boss, is one of these new-fashioned people giving up the old ways. She speaks nothing but American if she can help it, and has *lo fan* women working for her at her restaurant. She laughs at me when I tell her about herbs making her son well, but she knows . . ."

"Herbs make me well when I'm sick."

"They can call you 'mass hysteria' crazy in the head. People like her mean well, but don't know what's real and what's phony."

"Herbs made my brother well, but he died anyway," Huie said. He took off his glasses and licked the lenses.

"Because he wanted to," Yuen said.

"He shot himself."

"Yes, I remember," Yuen said. He scratched his Adam's apple noisily a moment. "He used to come into the restaurant in the mornings. I'd fix him scrambled eggs. He always use to talk with bits of egg on his lips and shake his fork and tell me that I could learn English good enough to be cook at some good restaurant. I could too, but the cook where I wash dishes is Chinese already, and buys good meat, so I have a good life."

Huie sighed and said, "Good meat is important I suppose." Then put his mouth to the mouth of the waterpipe.

"What?" Yuen asked absently at Huie's sigh. He allowed his eyes to unfocus on the room now, tried to remember Huie's brother's face with bits of egg on the lips and was angry. Suddenly an angry old man wanting to be alone screamed. He wiped his own lips with his knuckles and looked back to Huie the herbalist. Yuen did not want to talk about Huie's brother. He wanted to listen to music, or jokes, or breaking bones, something happy or terrible.

"His fine American talk," Huie said. "He used to go to the Oakland High School at night to learn."

My boss wants me to go there too," Yuen said. "You should only talk English if you have money to talk to them with . . . I mean, only fools talk buddy buddy with the *lo fan* when they don't have money. If you talk to them without money, all you'll hear is what they say behind your back, and you don't want to listen to that."

"I don't."

"No."

"He received a letter one day, did he tell you that? He got a letter from the American Immigration, and he took the letter to Jimmy Chan, who reads government stuff well . . . and Jimmy said that the Immigration wanted to know how he came into the country and wanted to know if he was sending money to Communists or not." Huie smiled wanly and stared between his legs. Yuen watched Huie sitting on the box; he had passed the pipe and now sat with his short legs spread slightly apart. He was down now, his eyes just visible to Yuen. Huie's slumped body looked relaxed, only the muscles of his hands and wrists were tight and working. To Yuen, Huie right now looked as calm as if he were sitting on a padded crapper. Yuen smiled and tried to save the pleasure of his day-off visit that was being lost in morbid talk. "Did he have his dog with him?" he asked.

"His dog? My brother never had a dog."

"I mean Jimmy Chan with his rubber pocket."

"How can you talk about Jimmy Chan's stupid dog when I'm talking about my brother's death."

"Perhaps I'm worried about the boy," Yuen said. "I shouldn't have let him wait for the train tonight."

"Was he sick?"

"That too maybe. Who can tell?" Yuen said without a hint, not a word more of the cripple shouting "Count your blessings!" at the end of the A-train's line in Frisco. It wouldn't be funny, and Yuen wanted a laugh.

"Bring the boy to me next week, and I'll fix him up," Huie said quickly, and put on his glasses again. Yuen, out of his day-off, loud, cheerful mood, angry and ashamed of his anger, listened to Huie. "My brother was very old, you remember? He was here during the fire and earthquake, and he told this to Jimmy Chan." Huie stopped speaking and patted Yuen's knee. "Yes, he did have his little dog in his pocket . . ." The men looked across to each other, and Yuen nodded. They were friends, had always been friends. They were friends now. "And my brother told Jimmy that all his papers had been burned in the fire and told about how he came across the bay in a sailboat that was so full that his elbows, just over the side of the boat, were in the water, and about the women crying and then shouting, and that no one thought about papers, and some not even of their gold."

"Yes. I know."

"And Jimmy Chan laughed at my brother and told him that there was nothing he could do, and that my brother would have to wait and see if he would be sent back to China or not. So . . ." Huie put his hands on his knees and rocked himself forward, lifting and setting his thin rump onto the wooden box, sighed and swallowed, "my brother shot himself." Huie looked up to Yuen; they licked their lips at the same moment, watching each other's tongues. "He died very messy," Huie said, and Yuen heard it through again for his friend, as he had a hundred times before. But tonight it made him sick.

The talk about death and the insides of a head spread wet all over the floor, the head of someone he knew, the talk was not relaxing; it was incongruous to the room of undershirted men playing mah-jong and pai-gow. And the men, quieter since the shout, were out of place in their undershirts. Yuen wanted to relax, but everything was frantic that should not be; perhaps he was too sensitive, Yuen thought, and wanted to be numb. "You don't have to talk about it if it bothers," Yuen said.

"He looked messy, for me that was enough . . . and enough of Jimmy Chan for me too. He could've written and said my brother was a good citizen or something . . ." Huie stopped and flicked at his ear with his fingertips. "You don't want to talk anymore about it?"

"No," Yuen said.

"How did we come to talk about my brother's death anyhow?"

"Jimmy Chan and his Mexican dog."

"I don't want to talk about that anymore, either."

"How soon is Chinese New Year's?"

"I don't think I want to talk about anything anymore," Huie said, "New Year's is a long ways off. Next year."

"Yes, I know that."

"I don't want to talk about it," Huie said. Each man sat now, staring toward and past each other without moving their eyes, as if moving their eyes would break their friendship. He knew that whatever had happened had been his fault; perhaps tonight would have been more congenial if he had not taken Dirigible to the used bookstore where he found a pile of sunshine and nudist magazines, or if the cripple had fallen on his face, or not been there. Yuen could still feel the presence of the cripple, how he wanted still to push him over, crashing to the cement. The joy it would have given him was embarrassing, new, unaccountable, like being in love.

"Would you like a cigar, ah-dai low?" Huie asked, with a friendly Cantonese "Older Brother."

"No, I like the waterpipe." Yuen watched Huie spit the end of the cigar out onto the floor.

"You remind me of my brother, Yuen."

"How so?"

"Shaking your head, biting your lips, always shaking your head . . . you do too much thinking about nothing. You have to shake the thinking out to stop, eh?"

"And I rattle my eyes, too." Yuen laughed, knowing he had no way with a joke, but the friendliness botched in expression was genuine, and winning. "So what can I do without getting arrested?"

"I don't know," Huie said and looked around, "Mah-jong?"

"No."

"Are you unhappy?"

"What kind of question is that? I have my friends, right? But sometimes I feel . . . Aww, everybody does . . ."

"Just like my brother . . . too much thinking, and thinking becomes worry. You should smoke cigars and get drunk and go help one of your *lo fan* waitresses shave her armpits properly and put your head inside and tickle her with your tongue until she's silly. I'd like to put my face into the armpit of some big *fangwai* American woman . . . with a big armpit!"

"But I'm not like your brother." Yuen said. "I don't shoot myself in the mouth and blow the back of my head out with a gun."

"You only have to try once."

Yuen waited a moment, then stood. "I should be leaving now," he said. Tonight had been very slow, but over quickly. He did not like being compared to an old man who had shot himself.

Huie stood and shook Yuen's hand, held Yuen's elbow and squeezed Yuen's hand hard. "I didn't mean to shout at you, dailow."

Yuen smiled his wet smile. Huie held onto Yuen's hand and stood as if he was about to sit again. He had an embarrassingly sad smile. Yuen did not mean to twist his friend's face into this muscular contortion; he had marred Huie's happy evening of gambling, hoarse laughter, and alcoholic wheezings. "I shouted too," Yuen said finally.

"You always know the right things to say, older brother." Huie squeezed Yuen's hand and said, "Goodnight, dailow." And Yuen was walking, was out of the back room and into the tropical fish store. He opened the door to the alley and removed his glasses, blew on them in the sudden cold air to fog them, then wiped them clean.

For a long time he walked the always-damp alleys, between glittering streets of Chinatown. Women with black coats walked with young children. This Chinatown was taller than Oakland's, had more fire escapes and lights, more music coming from the street vents. He usually enjoyed walking at this hour every Wednesday of every week. But this was Tuesday evening, and already he had left his friends, yet it looked like Wednesday with the same paper vendors coming up the hills, carrying bundles of freshly printed Chinese papers. He walked down the hill to Portsmouth Square on Kearney Street to sit in the park and read the paper. He sat on a wooden bench and looked up the trunk of a palm tree, looking toward the sounds of pigeons. He could hear the fat birds cooing over the sound of the streets, and the grass snap when their droppings dropped fresh. Some splattered on the bronze plaque marking the location of the birth of the first white child in San Francisco, a few feet away. He looked up and down the park once, then moved to the other side of the tree out of the wind and sat to read the paper by the streetlight before walking. Tonight he was glad to be tired; to Yuen tiredness was the only explanation for his nervousness. Almost anger. Almost. He would go home early; there was nothing else to do here, and he would sleep through his day off, or at least, late into the morning.

* * *

He entered the kitchen and snorted a breath through his nose. He was home to the smell of cooking and the greasy sweat of waitresses. His boss wiped her forehead with the back of her arm and asked him why he had come back so early; she did not expect him back until dinnertime tomorrow and was he sick? He answered, "Yes," lying to avoid conversation. All warfare is based on deception, he thought, quoting the strategist Sun Tzu, the grandson. He asked the young woman where her son the Flying Ship was, and she said he was upstairs in his room sleeping, where he belonged. Yuen nodded, "Of course, it's late isn't it," he said, avoiding the stare of her greasy eyes, and went upstairs to his room across the hall from the waitresses' wardrobe. He looked once around the kitchen before turning the first landing. He saw the large refrigerators and the steam table, and realized he was truly tired, and sighed the atmosphere of his day off out of his body. "You're trying to walk too straight, anyway, Ah-bok," his boss, Rose, said, calling him uncle from the bottom of stairs. He did not understand her joke or criticism or what she meant and went on up the stairs.

At the top of the stairs he turned and walked down the hall, past the room of his boss and her paralyzed husband, and past Dirigible's room, toward his own room across the hall from the wardrobe and next to the bathroom. Facing the door was the standup wardrobe, a fancy store-bought box with two doors, a mirror on the inside, and a rack for clothes, where the waitresses kept their white-and-black uniforms and changed. A redheaded waitress was sitting inside the wardrobe smoking a cigarette. She sat between hanging clothes with her back against the back of the wardrobe, her legs crossed and stretched out of the box. One naked heel turned on the floor, back and forth, making her legs wobble and jump to the rhythm of her nervous breathing.

Yuen walked slowly down the hall, his head down, like a car full of gunmen down a dark street, his fingers feeling the edges of his long hair that tickled the tops of his ears. He looked down to the floor but could no longer see the bare legs jutting from out of the box, the long muscles under the thighs hanging limp and shaking slowly to the turning heel. He knew she was ugly. He snorted and walked close to the far wall; he would walk past her and not at her. She did not move her legs. He stopped and leaned against the wall and lifted one foot after the other and gingerly swung them over the waitress's legs.

As his second foot went over her ankles, he glanced into the box and saw her pull a strap over her shoulder and giggle. Dry rock and unnatural white teeth in there. He hopped to keep his balance. She kicked. "Hiya, Yuen," she said to him stumbling down. He felt his shoe scrape the waitress's leg, skin it a little, heard her yelp, and fell on her. "Oh, my God!" she growled and went crazy, tangling her legs and arms with his, jumping into the box to stamp out the cigarette she had let fall from her mouth laughing. The smell was sweet, dusty, and flowery inside the box, like a stale funeral. Huie wanted to stuff his head into a *fangwai* woman's armpit, did he? Yuen looked, as he stumbled to his feet out of the sweet choking smell, and could not make out any distinct armpits in the flurry of flesh and shiny nylon slip and uniforms, and flying shoes, shouting and pounding after her cigarette. He couldn't find his hat. He looked under the waitress.

The waitress stood from out of the wardrobe up to her skinny and flabby self and pulled her slip straight around her belly. She looked down to Yuen, his head nodding and dangling on his neck. He looked like a large bird feeding on something dead, and the waitress laughed. "Come on there, Yuen," the waitress said. "I was just playing." She bent to help the man up. She took his shoulders with her hands and began pulling gently. The door to the bathroom was open and the light through the doorway shone white on the front of her powdered face. Yuen saw her face looking very white with flecks of powder falling from light hairs over her grin, a very white face on a grey wrinkled neck and a chest warped with skin veined like blue cheese. He did not like her smiling and chuckling her breathing into his face or her being so comfortably undressed in front of him.

"Are you all right now, Yuen?" she asked. He did not understand. He felt her holding him and saw her smiling and saw her old breasts quiver and dangle against her slip and the skin stretch across her ribs, not at all like the women in the calendars and magazines, Yuen thought. He took his shoulders closer to his body and she still held him, squeezing the muscle of his arm with strong hands, and pulled him toward her and muttered something in her rotten-throated voice. He leaned away from her and patted his head to show her he was looking for his hat. He chanced a grin.

She looked at his head and moved her fingers through his hair. "I don't see a bump, honey. Where does it hurt?"

Her body was too close to his face for him to see. The smell of her strong soap, stale perfume, layers of powder hung into his breathing. He was angry. "My hat! My hat!" he shouted in Chinese. He took an invisible hat and put it on his head and tapped the brim with his hands.

The waitress, also on her knees now, moved after him and felt his head. "Where does it hurt?" she said. "I don't feel anything but your head."

He stood quickly and leaned against the wall and glared stupidly at her.

"I was just trying to see if you're hurt, Yuen," the waitress said. "Did I touch your sore or something?" She held her arms out and stood. A strap fell from her shoulder; she ignored it and stretched her neck and reached toward him with her fingers. "I was just joking when I kicked you, honey. I thought it was funny, the way you were stepping over me, see?" All Yuen heard were whines and giggles in her voice. He shook his head. He held his coat closed with his hands and shoved at her with his head. "*Chiyeah!* Go way! *Hooey la!*"

A door opened and Dirigible stepped into the hall in his underwear. "What'sa wrong?" he asked. The waitress turned then, fixed her slip, and brushed her dry hair out of her face. "Make him understand, will you?" she said pointing at Yuen. She jabbed her arm at Yuen again. "Him. He's . . ." She crossed her eyes and pointed at her head.

"She's drunk!" Yuen said. "Tell her to go away."

"I was joking! Tell him I didn't mean to hurt his old head."

"Don't let her touch you, she's crazy tonight. Ask her why she here so late. What's she been doing here all night?"

"Do something! I can't."

"What? What?" Dirigible said. "What? I don't know what you're talking," sounding as if he were being accused of something.

The waitress was in front of the boy now and trying to explain. Yuen stepped quickly down the hall and pushed the boy into his room and closed the door. "Go to sleep . . . you'll get a stomach ache," he said.

"What'd you push me for?" the boy asked in English. He kicked the door and tried to open it, but Yuen held the knob. The boy shouted. His anger burst into tears.

"Coffee," Yuen said to the waitress and pointed at her, meaning that she should go have coffee. The waitress nodded quickly, took a robe from the wardrobe, and went downstairs.

Yuen went to his room without looking for his hat. The boy opened his door and followed the old man. He stood in the doorway and watched Yuen hang his overcoat in his closet. Yuen did not notice the boy and locked the door in his face.

The old man put a hand under his shirt and rubbed the sweat under his armpit. He loosened his belt and flapped the waist of his underwear before lying on top of his bed. He felt under the pillow for his revolver; it was big in his hand. Then he swallowed to slow his breath and sat up to take off his shoes and socks.

He saw the dark stain of blood on the heel of his right shoe, and dropped it onto the floor. "I guess, I can't tell," he thought. "She'll say I kicked her." He rapped the wall to speak to Dirigible. "*Wuhay! Ah-Fay Shurn ahh,* don't tell nutting, okay?"

"I don't know what you're talking. You . . ." Yuen heard nothing through the wall. He wished that Dirigible spoke Chinese better than he did. What the hell was he learning at that Chinese school if not Chinese?

"You hit me in the face," Dirigible said.

"I did not."

"You did, and it hurt," the boy said. Dirigible. The flying ship that doesn't fly anymore. The boy had the name of an extinct species. He was playing himself more hurt and younger than he was. "Don't be a baby," Yuen said.

"You hit me in the face."

"Uhhh," Yuen groaned, and rolled away from the wall. He would buy the little Dirigible a funnybook in the morning. He would buy Dirigible a dozen funnybooks and a candy bar in the morning. He leaned back into bed and began unbuttoning his shirt.

He stopped and blinked. Someone knocked at his door again. He'd almost heard it the first time. He almost felt for his revolver. He heard, "Ah Yuen bok, ahhh! I got some coffee, uncle. Are you all right? Anna says you hurt your head?" Rose, his boss, Dirigible's mother.

"Go away, I'm sleeping."

"But Anna says you asked for coffee. Have you been drinking?"

"I don't want any coffee."

"Since you're here, I told the colored boy not to come in tomorrow morning . . . What's your hat doing in the bathroom?"

"Leave it," Yuen said. "Just leave it. I'll get it in the morning." He coughed and rolled over on the bed and coughed once into the pillow.

"By the way, you got a letter today. Your American name on it. Nelson Yuen Fong . . . Your name looks nice," the voice outside said.

"What?"

"Nothing. I'll keep it until tomorrow for you."

He coughed phlegm up from his chest, held it in his mouth, then swallowed it. His face was warm in his own breath against the pillow. He relaxed the grip of his lids on his eyes for sleep. The hat was probably all dirty if it was in the bathroom, he thought and did not get up to urinate, get his hat, or shut off the light.

The hallway outside was quiet now. He felt his eyes smarting and felt stale and sour. He was not sure whether or not he was asleep. It was late; the night was wider, higher without lights on the horizon or lengths of sound stretching down the streets. The air was not silent but excited, jittery without noise. Yuen heard sounds on the edge of hearing, and listened for them, the small sounds of almost voices and cars somewhere. He occasionally heard nothing. Perhaps he was sleeping when he heard nothing. If he opened his eyes now, he would know . . . but he could not open his eyes now. He decided he was asleep, and was sleeping, finally.

What had the waitress been doing up here all this time? Entertaining the man who would never play a Japanese general or Chinese sissy sidekick who dies in the movies ever again, if he ever did, by inflicting her flesh on his mute, immobile, trapped, paralyzed self? Or perhaps a show, a long striptease for the boy to watch from his room through his keyhole. Or had she been inside his room? He had no right. How had they met? Come up the stairs one day from a smoke of the waterpipe in the cool dry room where the potatoes and onions were kept and peeled, looking forward to an hour on his bed with one or two picture magazines full of strippers showing their breasts. The sight of the boy, nine or ten years old, holding his revolver stopped the man from stepping into his own room. The unexpected boy caught Yuen dirty-minded, his mental pecker hanging out. He had a loaded gun in his hand, between Yuen and his girlie magazines. His son. The knees. The boy's knees. That was funny. That was laughable now.

*Tomorrow he would buy Dirigible a dozen funnybooks and a big candy bar, even if he was not angry or scared anymore.*

And now truly asleep, he was sitting at a table with this boy, but the boy was his son, then Huie's dead brother with bits of scrambled eggs drying on his lips. The flesh all over the skull looked as if it had been boiled in soup to fall off the bone. Yuen wiped the boy's lip but more egg came up where he had wiped the egg off. Then the lips were gone. The lipless boy laughed, took Yuen's hand, and pulled him up. They walked from the table and were in a field with not a bird in the sky above them, smooth as skin, blue as veins. The boy pointed, and there, on the edge of the world was the peach tree. They dropped their trousers, aimed their peckers to the horizon, and pissed the long distance to the tree and watched the streams of their yellow liquid gleam and flash under the bright sky before it arched into the shadow of the mountains. They pissed a very long time without beginning to run out. Yuen was surprised he was still pissing. He squinted to see if he was reaching the tree. The boy was laughing and pissing on Yuen's feet. Yuen was standing in a mud of piss. "What are you doing?"

"Coffee," the boy answered in the waitress's voice and laughed. Birds. They were in the sky out of nowhere and dove on him, silent except for their wings breaking the dive. I'm going to die. Too moochie shi-yet. I'm going to die. And continued fertilizing the peach tree on the horizon. He had not shouted. "It's true!" He woke up to the sound of his voice, he was sure, and heard only the curtains shuffling in front of his open window. He felt under the sheets around his ankles to see if there was any wet. There was not. He hadn't wet the bed. He got up and spat into the wash basin in the corner. He didn't curse the spring handles on the taps. He turned out the light, sat on the edge of his bed, and listened for a hint of waitresses lurking in the silence outside his door, then returned to sleep.

He bathed with his underwear on this morning and plugged the keyhole with toilet paper. He combed his hair and returned to his room. He had found his hat on the lid of the toilet. He did not like the hat any longer; it was too big and the band was dirty. The dream had left him by the time he went downstairs for breakfast, but he knew he had dreamed.

He sat down at a table at the end of the long steam table. He could hear a waitress laughing shrilly outside in the dining room, not the same waitress as last night, he knew, for the breakfast waitresses were different from the ones at dinner. He took a toothpick from a tin can nailed to the end of the steam table and put it in his mouth and sucked the taste of wood and read his Chinese paper. He did not goodmorning his boss. She was younger and should be the first to give greetings, out of respect. But she was his boss. So what. He was reading about Chiang Kai-shek making a speech to his army again. He liked Chiang Kai-shek. He decided he liked Chiang Kai-shek. Chiang Kai-shek was familiar and pleasant in his life, and he enjoyed it. "He made another speech to his army," Yuen said.

Dirigible said, "He made one last week to the army."

He's forgotten last night, Yuen thought, and answered, "That was to the farmers. This time it's to the army. Next week to everybody." This was part of every morning also.

Rose wiped her hands on her apron and sat down next to Yuen. She took an envelope from her pocket and unfolded it. Before removing the letter, she turned to Dirigible and said, "Go upstairs, change your pants. And comb your hair for a change."

"I'll be late for school. I gotta eat breakfast."

"Go upstairs, huh? I don't have time to argue!" Rose said.

"Can I use your comb, ah-bok?"

"You have your own comb. Don't bother people. I wanta talk to ah-bok."

Yuen gave Dirigible his comb, which he kept in a case. Rose watched the boy go past the first landing and out of sight and then took the letter out of the envelope. "I read this letter of yours," she said. She looked straight at Yuen as she spoke, and Yuen resented her look and the way she held his letter. "Who said you could?" he asked, "It might have been from my son. What do you want to read my mail for, when you don't care what else I do?"

"Now, you know that's not so!" Rose said. "Anyway, it's addressed to your American name, and it's from the U.S. Immigration."

"Well . . . What did Anna tell you about last night? You know what she was really trying to do, don't you? I'll tell you I don't believe a word that woman says. She eats scraps too. Right off the dirty dishes.

"Oh, Yuen bok, you're so old, your brain's busting loose. She was just trying to see if you had a cut or a hurt on your head was all."

"Aww, I don't like her no matter what," Yuen said. He went to the steam table and ladled cream of wheat into a bowl and sat down to eat it. "What are you looking at? You never seen me eat before?"

"Don't you use milk?" Rose asked.

"No, you should know that."

"But your letter, Yuen bok. You're in trouble."

"What for?"

"It's from the immigrators, I told you. They want to know if you came into this country legally."

Yuen looked up from his cereal to the powder and rouge of her face. The oil from her Chinese skin had soaked through and messed it all up. She smiled with her lips shut and cheeks pulled in as if sucking something in her mouth. He did not like Rose because she treated him with disdain and made bad jokes, and thought she was beautiful, a real femme fatale behind the steam table with an apron and earrings. And now she did not seem natural to Yuen, being so kind and trying so to soften the harshness in her voice. "That's a bad joke," Yuen said.

"I'm not joking. Do I look like I'm joking, ah-bok? Here, you can read it for yourself if you don't believe me." She shoved the letter to him. He pushed his cereal bowl aside and flattened the letter on the table. He put his glasses on, then without touching the letter, bent over it and stared. He saw a printed seal with an eagle. The paper was very white, and had a watermark that made another eagle. He removed his glasses and licked his teeth. "You know I don't read English."

"I know," Rose said. "So why don't you eat your breakfast and I'll tell you what the letter says. Then you can get the dishes done."

Yuen nodded and did as she said. She wiped her hands on her apron and told him that the letter said the immigrators wanted to know if he had any criminal record with the police in the City of Oakland and that he was to go to the Oakland Police and have his fingerprints taken and get a letter from them about his criminal record yes or no. "I will talk to Mrs. Walker who was a legal secretary and she can help me write a watcha-call, a character reference for you."

"Why tell people?"

"They ask for letters making good references about you, don't they? You want to stay in this country, don't you?" She folded the letter and ran her thumb along the creases, leaving grey marks where her fingers had touched. Yuen took the letter and unfolded it again and put on his glasses again and stared down at the piece of paper. He took a pencil and copied something he saw in the letter on a napkin. "What's this?" he asked, pointing at the napkin.

"That's a T," Rose said.

"What's it mean?"

"It doesn't mean anything. It's just a T."

"Did I make it right?"

"You are not going to learn to read and write English before this afternoon, ah-bok."

Yuen lost interest in his T and wiped his face with his napkin. "T Zone wahh. Camel cigarette!" he mumbled. He remembered cigarette ads with the pictures of actors' heads with a T over their mouths and down their throats. Rose didn't know everything. She was not his friend. He sighed and straightened in his seat. He was sure Rose heard all the little gurgles and slopping sounds inside him. It ached to sit straight. He had to sit straight to feel any strength in his muscles now. The ache gave a certain bite to the fright. He thought about aching and wanting to ache, like nobody else. Every white muscle in his body felt raw and tender, from the base of his spine, and the muscles from his neck down to his shoulder, and the hard muscles behind his armpit. He was conscious of every corner and bend in his body, and all this was inside him, private, the only form of reliable relaxation he had. He wanted to sit back and enjoy himself, ignore the letter and travel the countries of his aches. He looked to Rose. She looked away. He saw she knew he was frightened. He did not want her pity, her face to smile some simpering kindly smile for his sake, for he had always pitied her, with her reasonable good looks, her youth, and a husband she keeps in a room like a bug in a jar, who won't be going to Hollywood after all. He didn't want to need her English, her letter full of nice things about him, her help.

Rose patted Yuen's shoulder and stood up and went to the foot of the stairs and called for Dirigible to come down. "You'll be late for school!" Then to the old man, "I'm going to have to tell him, you know."

"Dritchable?" Yuen said, botching the name.

"Everyone will know sooner or later. They come and ask people questions. The immigrators do that," Rose said. They could hear Dirigible stamping on the floor above them.

Yuen put the letter in his shirt pocket and removed his glasses and put them and the case in the tin can with the toothpicks. His place. He went around the steam table to the dishwashing area, lit the fires under the three sinks full of water, and started the electric dishwashing machine slung like an outboard motor in the well of the washing sink.

He put a teaspoonful of disinfectant into the washwater, then a cup of soap powder. He watched the yellow soap turn the water green and raise a cloud of green to the top of the water. He turned and saw Dirigible sitting at the table again. "*Wuhay!* Good morning, kid," he shouted over the noise of the dishwashing machine. Dirigible looked up and waved back, then looked back at the breakfast his mother had set in front of him. "Come here, Dritch'ble, I got money for funnybooks!" Yuen switched off the machine and repeated what he'd said in a lower voice.

"Dirigible's late for school. He has to eat and run," Rose said. She turned to Dirigible and said, "Be sure you come right home from school. Don't go to Chinese school today, hear?"

"It's not my day to read to Pa."

"Just come home from school, like I told you, hear me? She leaned through a space between a shelf and the steam table to see the boy, and steam bloomed up her face and looked like a beard.

"Oh, boy!" Dirigible said, and Yuen saw that the boy was happy.

"What did you tell him?" he asked Rose.

"That he didn't have to go to Chinese school today."

"Why? Don't you want him to be able to talk Chinese?"

"I want him to take you to the city hall this afternoon and do what the letter says," Rose said. She lifted her head back on her neck to face Yuen, and Yuen looking at her without his glasses on saw her face sitting atop the rising steam.

"I don't want a little boy to help me," he said. "You think I'm a fool? I'll call Jimmy Chan and ask him to help me. Dritch'ble too young to do anything for me."

Rose flickered a smile then twisted herself out from between the shelf and the steam table. "You've been watching too much television, ah-bok. Chinatown's not like that anymore. You can't hide there like you used to. Everything's orderly and businesslike now."

"How do you know Chinatown? You watch television, not me. I know Chinatown. Not everybody talks about the Chinese like the *lo fan* and you. You should know what you're talking about before talking sometimes. Chie!"

"Ham and!" a waitress shouted through the door.

"Ham and!" Rose repeated. "I'm just as much Chinese as you, ah-bok, but this is America!"

"The truth is still the truth, in China, America, on Mars . . . Two and two don't make four in America, just because you're Chinese."

"What?" the waitress said, jutting her head through the kitchen door, in the rhythm of its swing.

"Eggs how?" Margie asked.

"Oh, basted."

"Basted," Margie said, and reached for the eggs. "Listen, ah-bok. I don't want to get in trouble because of you. I worked hard to get this restaurant, and I gave you a job. Who else do you think would give you a job, and a room? You're too old to work anywhere else, and you'd have to join the union and learn English. You don't want to learn English. That's your business, but if you get in trouble here, I'm in trouble too. Now just do what the letter says. And just don't argue with me about it. No one is trying to hurt you." She brought three cooking strips of bacon from the back of grill toward the center where she kept the iron hot.

"Me make trouble for you? You said I am in trouble already."

"I am trying to help you the best way I can. Now let me alone to cook, and you get back to the dishes. Can't you see I'm nervous? Listen, take the day off. I'll call the colored boy. I shouldn't have told him not to come in. I don't know what I was thinking . . . Now, please, ah-bok, leave me finish breakfast, will you?"

"I'm sorry, I'll get the dishes . . ." Yuen said.

"I said take the day off." Rose said. "Please." She quickly slid the spatula under another egg order on the griddle and flopped them onto a plate. She forgot the bacon.

"The bacon," Yuen said.

She ignored him and said, "Dirigible, you don't have time to finish your breakfast. Take that little pie in the icebox for your teacher and go to school now."

Dirigible looked to Yuen. "I'll walk you to school," Yuen said. Rose snapped, "Be back in time for the dinner dishes . . . Oh, what . . . Forget I said that, but both of you be back after school."

Looking down the street, they could see the morning sun shattered in the greasy shimmer of Lake Merritt. The grass on the shore was covered with black coots and staggering seagulls. Yuen had his glasses on and could see the trees on the other side of the lake and sailors walking with girls, and he could smell the stagnant water as he walked the other way with Dirigible.

The boy watched the ground and stayed inside Yuen's shadow as they walked. Yuen glanced at the boy and saw him playing his game with his shadow and knew the boy had forgotten last night, the waitress. They were beyond the smell of the lake now and inside the smell of water drying off the sides of washed brick buildings, and Yuen's morning was complete and almost gone. "What're you carrying there?" Yuen asked.

"A pie for teacher," Dirigible said.

Yuen smiled his wet smile. They stopped at the street that had the train tracks in the center. "Mommy said your hat was in the toilet."

"Do you want to go to San Francisco with me?"

"I can't. I have to go home right after school. You too."

"I mean right now. Would you like to go to San Francisco on the train, right now?"

"I have to go to school."

"I'll take you to my friend's and he'll give you some herbs that will make your stomach stop hurting again." Yuen put a hand on the boy's shoulder and stood in front of him. What happens to boys born here? Are they all little bureaucrats by ten years old? They no longer dreamed of the Marvelous Traveler from the outlaws of Leongsahn Marsh come to deliver an invitation to adventure? "I'll buy you five funnybooks and a candy bar."

"But it doesn't hurt."

"For when your stomach does hurt. These herbs and it won't hurt again." Then inspiration in his instinct had the words out of his mouth before they'd come to mind. "How about I buy you special Chinese funnybooks? Chinese fighters with swords and bows and arrows, spears, big wars, heads cut off. And the head cut off spits blood in the face of its killer. You'll like them."

There were more people on the train now than at night. The train was dirtier in the day. They caught the A-train at the end of the line near Dirigible's school. As the train started to pull, it rang its electric bell, screeching like a thousand trapped birds. They hummed and rattled across Oakland, onto the lower level of the Bay Bridge toward San Francisco. Dirigible ate the little pie and Yuen put his arm over the boy's shoulders when people boarded, and let go on the bridge. He was glad to have the boy with him. Good company. He was young and didn't have to know what Yuen was doing to have a little adventure. Yuen enjoyed being with the boy. That was something he could still enjoy.

The train moved quickly, swaying its cars side to side over the tracks. Yuen looked only once out of the window to the street full of people. He had been in Oakland for twenty years now, and he still felt uncomfortable, without allies in the streets. On the train he could sit and did not have to walk among people with hands out of their pockets all around him. The train moved him quickly out of the moldy shadows between tall buildings, and was moving down a street lined with low wooden houses now. He could see Negro women with scarves around their large heads. Elephant-hipped women with fat legs walking old and slow down the street. The feelings he had for them were vague and nothing personal, but haunted him. The train passed them, and now there were no more houses. They whirred into the train yards, and the A screamed its crazed electric birds toward the bridge.

They passed broken streetcars and empty trains in the yards, and saw bits of grass growing up between the crossties. Beyond the yards they saw the flat bay and the thick brown carpet of dung floating next to the shore. And they could smell the bay, the cooking sewage, the oily steel. Last night he slept past this part of the trip. "Shi-yet," he said sniffing. The boy smiled. Yuen realized now what he was doing. He was trying to be brave, and knew he would fail. He felt the letter in his coat pocket without touching the letter and thought of how he would take the letter from his pocket to show Jimmy Chan.

The sounds of the wheels on the rails changed in pitch and they were on the bridge now, with shadows of steelwork skipping over their faces. They were above the bay and could see the backs of seagulls gliding and soaring parallel to them, their beaks split in answer to the electric bell. Yuen could see the birds stop and hang on the air with their wings stiff, then fall and keep falling until the bridge blocked his vision, and in his mind he counted the splashes on the bay the seagulls made. He looked down to Dirigible again and saw pie on the boy's lips. Dirigible took his hand out of the paper bag and grinned. "That's bad for your stomach," Yuen said. Too nervous to smile. No, not nervous, he thought, angry. Calm, numbly angry. It wasn't unpleasant or aggravating or lonely, but moving very fast, train or no train, he without a move felt himself hurtling home. The electric birds screamed and they were moving in a slow curve toward the terminal at the San Francisco end of the line.

Chinatown was very warm and the streets smelled of vegetables and snails set out in front of the shops. Among the shopping Chinese women, Yuen saw small groups of *lo fan* white tourists with bright neckties and cameras pointing into windows and playing with bamboo flutes or toy dragons inside the curio shops. Yuen stopped in front of a bookstore with several different poster portraits of a redfaced potbellied, longbearded soldier in green robes. "Know him?" Yuen asked. The boy glanced, "Sure, I've seen him around."

"Who is he?"

"He's you," the boy said, looking caught again. Yuen took him inside and bought an expensive set of paperbound Chinese funnybooks that looked like little books and came in a box. Yuen opened up one of the books to the pictures and chuckled, delighted. "See, here?" He snatched at the tale of the 108 outlaw heroes of legendary Leongsahn Marsh in curt, chugging Cantonese babytalk the boy might understand. "Heh heh, look like a Buddhist monk fella, huh? Very bad temper this guy . . . Now this guy, look. He catch cold, get drunk on knock out 'Mickey Finn' kind of booze, not knock out, and gotta cross the mountain. *Don't cross that mountain alone!* they say. *Fuck you!* he says. *Oooh, big tiger eat you up there. Better not go!* they say him. *Don't try to fool me!* he says and he goes and they can't stop him go. Up the mountain at night. The tiger jump him! Whoo! He gotta sniffle and sneeze. Runny eyes and cough. And he drunk too much wine suppose to knock people out. And he thinks maybe he should not have come up to the mountaintop after all, but gotta fight anyway, and *kawk kawk kawk kawk!* punch and kick and push the tiger's face in the dirt and punch and kick 'em and kill that tiger. They call that one Tiger Jung. He's my favorite of the 108 heroes," Yuen said and sighed, smiling. "One by one, you know, all the heroes are accused of crimes by the government. They say he commit a crime he didn't and they make him run, see? And one by one, all the good guys made outlaw by the bad government come to Leongsahn Marsh and join the good guy, Soong Gong. Yeah, sure. *Sam Gawk Yun Yee, Sir Woo Jun,* I memorize 'em all. All the boys like to see who know more. Then you see them in the opera, and . . ." Yuen signed again and wouldn't finish that thought. "Soong Gong. They call him the Timely Rain, Gup Sir Yur. Every boy like you in the world for awhile is like these guys. Before you lie, before you betray, before you steal. You know if you stay honest, don't sell out, don't betray, don't give up even if it means you run all alone, someday, someone will tap you on the shoulder and, *You!* the Marvelous Traveler will say. *Our leader, the Timely Rain, has long admired your gallantry. Soong Gong says he is a man of no talent, but asks you to join us and our rebel band and do great things.* But you grow up. You sell out, you betray, you kill . . . just a little bit. But too much to expect the Marvelous Traveler to come with any message from the Timely Rain."

The dining room of Jimmy Chan's restaurant was dark with the shadows of chairs stacked and tangled on the tabletops. A white-jacketed busboy led Yuen and the boy between the tables sprouting trees of chairs to the office. Yuen left Dirigible outside to read his funnybooks, then went inside after removing his hat. Rose's lessons in American servility got to him at the oddest times.

Jimmy Chan's bow tie was very small against his fat bellying throat. The tie wriggled like the wings of a tropical moth when he spoke. Jimmy Chan's dog walked all over his desk and Jimmy laughed at it when Yuen came in. Instead of greeting Yuen, he said, "It's a chee-wah-wah. How about that? Please, have a seat."

"How are you?" Yuen asked. "I've been trying to catch you to ask you out for coffee and see how you are. But a busy man about town, like Jimmy Chan . . ." Yuen said, opening with a courtesy, he hoped. The knack for saying the right thing. Huie said Yuen had it. Or had Huie just been saying the right thing himself?

"I'm busy all right. Busy going bankrupt to hell and damn."

Yuen nodded, then too quickly put his hand into his coat pocket, as if he'd been bitten there. Then, "I got a letter from the United States of America," Yuen said.

"I can't help with letters from the government. I can't tamper with the government. I'm going to be naturalized next year, but I know people who think I'm a communist. Why? Because I have a big restaurant. What kind of communist owns a restaurant with a floor show and a fan dancer? I'm going bust, I tell you the truth. People say Jimmy Chan is a smuggler. I'm not a goddamn-all-to-hell smuggler any more than you are. But what the hellfuck are my problems compared to yours? Where's a crooked cop when you need one, huh? You need money for a lawyer? What you need is a lawyer to tamper with the government, you know that?"

"Maybe you could read the letter?" Yuen held the letter out. Jimmy Chan put a cigar into his mouth and took the letter. The dog walked over to sniff Jimmy's hands and sniffed at the letter. "Don't let the dog dirty the letter," Yuen said.

"You should let him piss on it. Ha ha. It's a chee-wah-wah. You think I'd let my chee-wah-wah walk on my desk if it was going to dirty things up? You think these papers I have on my desk mean nothing? . . . I'm sorry if I seemed short-tempered just then, uncle, you asked with such force. You see, men with letters like this have come in before, and never, ever, have they ordered me or asked me anything straight out. I was surprised. You should be in business. You should be a general!" Jimmy turned and held the letter up to the light and stared at the watermark. "Fine paper they use," he said, and patted the dog.

"I thought you could give me some advice,"

"You don't want advice," Jimmy Chan said. "You want me to help you. Perform a miracle. But you said advice. I'll take you on your word and give you advice. If you have no criminal record, you have nothing to worry about. There is no advice to give you. Just do what the letter says. Want me to translate it? It says go to the police. Get your fingerprints made and sent to Washington. Get your record of arrests and have the police send a copy to the government. It says it's only routine. Right here, just like this. I am routine."

"They might send me back to China."

"Not if you're all legal."

"Well, still . . ."

"Uncle, my sympathy is free. My advice too. I sympathize with you. You can't hide from them. They even have Chinese working for them, so you can't hide. I sympathize with you, but the only Chinese that get ahead are those who are professional Christian Chinese, or, you know, cater to that palate, right? You didn't know that when you came here, and now you're just another Chinaman that's all Chinese and in trouble. I can't help you."

"You could write a letter for me telling them I'm all right," Yuen said. He leaned back as Jimmy Chan pushed papers to both sides with his hands and elbows.

"Uncle, I don't know you're all right. And I don't want to know. I can help when I can help because I don't ask for secrets, I don't ask questions, and I don't trust anybody. I'd like to help you. I'm grateful to your generation, but your day is over. You could have avoided all your trouble if you had realized that the *lo fan* like the Chinese as novelties. Toys. Look at me. I eat, dress, act, and talk like a fool. I smell like rotten flower shop. And the *lo fan* can't get into my restaurant fast enough. They all call me Jimmy. I'm becoming an American citizen, not because I want to be like them, but because it's good business. It makes me wealthy enough to go bankrupt in style, to make the *lo fan* think I belong to them. Look! They like the Chinese better than Negroes because we're not many and we're not black. They don't like us as much as Germans or Norwegians because we're not white. They like us better than Jews because we can't be white like the Jews and disappear among the *lo fan.* But! They don't like a Chinaman being Chinese about life because they remind them of the Indians who, thirty-five thousand years ago, were Chinese themselves, see? So . . . !" Jimmy Chan clapped his hands together and spread them with the effect of climaxing a magic trick and looked about his office. He adjusted his bow tie and grinned. "This is being a professional Christian Chinese!"

"Indians?" was all Yuen could say that made sense.

"But helping you would be bad for me. So I write a letter for you. I get investigated, and then I get a letter. I don't want to be investigated. I want to become a citizen next year. Nobody likes me. Your people don't like me anymore because I'm really nobody, and you'll say I stepped on you to become a citizen and a professional Chinese. I have no friends, you see? I'm in more trouble than you."

"I'm going then. Thanks," Yuen said, and stood.

"Listen, uncle," Jimmy said from his seat, "don't do anything goddamn silly. If I can help with anything else, I'll be happy to do it. Want a loan? A job?"

"No," Yuen said and started to leave.

"Uncle, I trust you. You know what I mean. I know you have a job and keep your word and all that." Jimmy stood and took a long time to walk around his desk to Yuen's side. He put an arm around his shoulders. "You are a wise man. . . . If you die, die of old age. I feel bad when I can't help, and I feel real bad when men die." He grinned and opened the door for the old man. "But you are a wise man."

"Didn't even offer a drink," Yuen said outside with the boy.

Pigeons dropped from the sky to walk between the feet of people and peck at feed dropped from the cages of squabs and chickens in front of the poultry shops. "Stupid birds," Yuen said. "Someone will catch one and eat it." He laughed and the boy laughed.

"I'm hungry," Dirigible said.

As they left the restaurant, Yuen walked quickly. He held Dirigible's hand and pulled him down the streets and pointed at fire escapes and told him what Tongs were there and what he had seen when he had been at parties there, and he walked over iron gratings in the sidewalk and pointed down inside and told Dirigible that at night music could be heard down there. They passed men sitting next to magazine stands and shook hands. Then Yuen went to the bank and withdrew all his money in a money order and borrowed a sheet of paper and an envelope, and in Chinese wrote his song: "This is all the money I have. You will not get anymore. I'm dead. Your father," and signed it. He put the letter and the money order in the envelope, addressed it, then went to the post office branch and mailed it. San Francisco was nothing to him now. He had said goodbye to his friends and seen the places he used to visit. They were all dirty in this daylight. The value of his death, to himself, was that nothing in his life was important; he had finished with his son that he hadn't seen in twenty years or more, and his friends, and San Francisco. Now he was going home. The tops of the buildings sparkled with their white tile and flags, Yuen saw. Jimmy Chan was wrong, he thought. But he helped me start the finish. The Grandson, Sun Tzu, the strategist says, "In death ground, fight." I am. I'm a very lucky man to know when all I am to do in life is done and my day is over. Jimmy Chan is too professional to know that. He doesn't see the difference between me and Huie's dead brother. Too bad. No cringing. No excuses. He walked quickly down the hill, believing himself to the bus stop. Dirigible had to run to keep up with him.

"What did you take him to San Francisco for? And why go to San Francisco, anyway? Do you know I had to wash all the dishes and cook, too? That colored boy wasn't home, you know," Rose said. "Criminey sakes, you think I'm a machine or something?"

"I'm sorry," Yuen said. Rose wouldn't understand anything he said right now. Better she not know what good shape he was in. No explanations.

"Well, you have to hurry, if you're going to get back in time to help me with the dinner dishes. I'm sorry, I didn't mean that, ah-bok, I'm just worried. All right?" She put a hand on his shoulder.

"All right."

Rose took the letter from Yuen's pocket and sat down at the kitchen table and read it over. Yuen sat down next to her and put a toothpick in his mouth. Rose stared down at the letter and began scratching a slow noisy circle around her breast. She talked to Dirigible without looking at the boy. "Uncle's in trouble, dear, I mean ah-bok has to go to the police and get his pictures taken. And you have to take him there and help him answer the questions the police will ask in this letter."

"I've been walking all day, Mommy. I don't wanta walk no more," Dirigible said. "Why don't you go?"

"You got a car," Dirigible said, stepping backward.

"Listen," Rose said. "You take this letter." She lifted the letter and pinned it with a safety pin inside Dirigible's coat. "And you go to where the fingerprint place is and you tell them to read the letter, that the United States Immigrators want them to read it, and that everybody, everybody, likes Yuen-bok, okay? And you take him." She gave the boy some crackers to eat on the way and helped Yuen to his feet.

"Do you know how to get there?" Yuen asked at every corner. They walked streets full of rush-hour traffic, walked past parking meters and a bodybuilding gymnasium. Yuen put an arm about Dirigible and held him. "Where are we in all this?" Yuen asked and pushed Dirigible toward the edge of the sidewalk with each word.

"We have to go fast now, ah-bok, or the police will close," the boy said.

The streets were not crowded, but everywhere on the sidewalks along the sides of the buildings Yuen saw people walking, all of their eyes staring somewhere beyond him, the pads of fat next to their stiff mouths trembling with their steps. They all moved past him easily, without actually avoiding him. Yuen held the boy's hand and walked, numbing himself to the people.

The long corridor of the city hall was full of the sound of feet and shaking keys against leather-belted hips, and waxed reflections of the outside light through the door at the corridor's end, shrunk and twisted on the floor, as they walked further down, past men with hats on and briefcases, policemen picking their noses, newspaper vendors with aprons. "Where do we go?" Yuen asked.

"I don't know," Dirigible said. "I can't read all the doors."

In a low voice, almost as smooth as an old woman's, Yuen said, "Do you see any Chinese around? Ask one, he'll help us." His hand rested on the back of the boy's neck, and was very still there as they walked.

"Excuse me . . ." a large man said, walking into them. They all tried to walk through each other a moment, then fell with the large man holding Dirigible's head and shouting a grunted "excuse me." Their legs all tangled, and they fell together in a soft crash. The man stood and brushed himself off. "I'm terribly sorry. Just barged out of my office, not thinking. Or thinking when I should have been watching my step. Are you all right? Your father looks a little sick."

"I have a letter," Dirigible said, and opened his jacket to show the letter pinned to the inside of his lapel.

"What's this?" the man asked, bending again. "A safety pin. All you people are safety pinning each other, my god!" he muttered. He took the letter and took a long grunt to stand up. Dirigible turned and helped Yuen, who was still on the floor, waiting, and staring with drool over his lip up at the strange *lo fan.* Yuen lifted himself to a crouch, rested, then stood and held himself steady, leaning on the boy.

"Immigration people want him fingerprinted," the man said. "You poor kid." He brushed his hair under his hat as he spoke. "I'll take you there. It's upstairs. Don't worry, if things go badly, you can call me, Councilman Papagannis." He adjusted his hat with his fat fingertips and walked quickly upstairs, swinging his arms with each step. They walked into a narrow hall with benches. At a desk, sitting on a high stool, in front of a typewriter, his sleeves rolled sloppily over his elbows, was a police sergeant, typing. "You can wash that ink stuff off your fingers in there, through that office, you see?" he was saying as they walked up to his desk. "What do you want? You'll have to wait in line. All these men here are in a hurry to get fingerprinted too."

"But I got a letter and supposed to tell you how people like Yuen-bok. Him." Dirigible pulled Yuen to the desk.

"What?" the police sergeant asked.

"Immigration people want him fingerprinted, photographed, and a copy of his record," Councilman Papagannis said. "Here's the letter. I'm Councilman Papagannis. I'd like to see them out of here in a hurry, you know, for the boy's sake." The councilman shook the sergeant's hand, then removed his tight-fitting hat.

"It says here, they want a copy of his record, too," the sergeant said.

"Well, do it!" the councilman said, stuffing himself between Yuen and the boy. The police sergeant took out a form and put it in the typewriter; then he picked up the telephone and asked for the city's record on Nelson Yuen Fong. He put the telephone down and looked up to the councilman. "Never heard of him," he said.

"Surely you have a form for that contingency, sergeant."

"Surely."

"Who said, 'The mills of the gods grind slow, but they grind exceedingly fine'? or something like that. The mills of the system are a-grinding, young man," the councilman said, marveling at the sergeant's checking boxes on a form. The police sergeant removed Yuen's hat with a short motion of his arm, "Hair color, grey," he said and began typing. He dropped the hat onto Yuen's head.

Yuen took the hat from his head and looked inside the brim. "What for?" he asked.

"Nothing," Dirigible said and took the hat and held it. Yuen watched now, his eyes wide with the lids almost folding over backwards. This was a fine joke for Yuen now. They were all so somber for his sake, and he had finished already. He could say anything and they would not understand, but Dirigible might understand a little, and Dirigible was too young to see the humor of the situation. Dirigible shouldn't be here, Yuen thought. I'll buy him a funnybook on the way home. He'll like that and won't feel so bad.

Dirigible yanked Yuen up to the edge of the police sergeant's desk and held his sleeve tightly. "How much do you weigh?" the police sergeant asked.

"He don't talk American," Dirigible said.

"What is he?"

"He's alien," Dirigible said.

"I mean, is he Filipino, Japanese, Hawaiian?"

"He's Chinese."

"Fine people, the Chinese," the councilman said.

"Fine," the police sergeant said and typed. "Now ask him how much he weighs."

Dirigible pulled at Yuen's coat until the man half-knelt. Dirigible's first word was in English and jittery. Yuen frowned, then smiled to relax the boy. The boy stamped his foot and snapped his glare burning from the police sergeant to Yuen. Yuen should have known the boy would hate him for not being able to speak English Longtime Californ'.

"You how heavy?" Dirigible said, blushing, sounding stupid to everybody, and cracked the accent on the *choong* word for "heavy" in a flat accent, but meaning "onion" when high-toned. Both the boy and Yuen heard "heavy" waver into "onion" and blushed. "What do you mean?" Yuen asked instead of laughing. "Take it easy, kid."

"You are how many pounds?"

"What's your old man say, boy?"

"We don't talk good together yet," Dirigible said, crunching his tongue into English, while still lugging his tongue in gutless Chinese, "You are HOW MANY POUNDS?" The boy stood straight and shouted, "How heavy the pounds?" as if shouting made it more Chinese.

"Oh, how many pounds do I weigh?" Yuen grinned and nodded to the police sergeant and the councilman. The police sergeant nodded and pointed at Yuen's stomach then patted his own belly. "Hundred and thirty pounds heavy," Yuen said.

"One hundred and thirty pounds," Dirigible said. The police sergeant typed.

After the questions, the police sergeant stepped down from his high stool and held Yuen's arms. "Tell him we're going to take his picture now, boy." Dirigible told Yuen what he'd heard old Chinese say to children all the time, and Yuen asked Dirigible to ask the police sergeant if he could comb his hair before being photographed. The men laughed when Dirigible asked.

Dirigible stepped away from Yuen and snuck a pinch of the blue stripe of the police sergeant's trousers, to see if what looked like shiny wire was metallic to the fingertips and wasn't sure. Yuen turned his head and combed his hair with his pocketcomb.

The police sergeant kicked a lever that turned Yuen's seat around. He snapped a picture. Yuen yelled once as the chair spun ninety degrees with the snap and stunned humm of a huge spring in the floor. "Atta boy, Nelson!" the police sergeant cheered. "Now for the fingerprints." He took the frames from the camera and tapped Dirigible next to the ear. "Tell your father to get down now."

"Ah-bok ahhh, get down now."

They walked home with the first blue of the dark night coming. Yuen patted the boy's shoulder and kept asking him to stop and buy some funnybooks, but the boy pulled Yuen's sleeve and walked on quickly, saying he was hungry and wanted to get back to the hotel kitchen. "Come on, ah-bok. I'm hungry," Dirigible said whenever the old man stopped to sit on a garbage can and nod his head at every streetcorner with a city trashcan. He sat as if he would sit forever, without moving his body or fixing the odd hairs the wind had loosened, his head nodding slowly like a sleeping pigeon's. "Are you mad at me?"

"No," the boy said in a hurry.

"Your mother's waiting for us, isn't she?" Yuen said. He stood and walked a little and said, "You're a funny son. . . ." He muttered to himself louder as they neared the Eclipse Hotel. All his old age shook and fattened up the veins in his hands as he tried to touch Dirigible's nose or his ears or poke the soft of the boy's cheeks. "You're almost as tall as me . . . Did you see the policeman's face when he saw me?" In his slouching walk Yuen and the boy were very close to the same height. Yuen took a breath and tried to straighten up a thousand years, then sighed. He was too tired. Not important. "And that chair . . ."

He walked slower as they came to the back door of the restaurant. He looked up to the light over the door with pigeon droppings painting the hood. That light had gone out only once while he lived here, and he had changed the bulb himself. He had polished the hood and wiped the bulb. It was his favorite light in the whole restaurant, perhaps because it was the light that helped him open the door when he returned tipsy from San Francisco, or perhaps because it was the only light outside, back of the building. Thinking about a light bulb is stupid, he thought. He could enjoy stupidity now, after all this time of trying to be smart, trying to be tall, stupidity was inevitably on the way to rounding out the circle and resting it in silence.

Yuen could hear Margie shouting the names of foods back to the waitresses as if cussing them out and didn't seem to hear a thing. He could hear the little screech of ice-cold meat slapped flat onto a hot steel griddle before the grease cackles, running water, the insulated door of the walk-in refrigerator stomping shut, and didn't hear a thing. He held Dirigible's wrists together with one hand. Then to his horror, both his hands and all his strength, which felt considerable, twisted Dirigible's wrists. He could see from the ease with which the boy moved his arms that his considerable strength was nothing. "Help me upstairs," he said. "I don't feel well."

He leaned heavily on the boy, pushed himself upright against the wall as they climbed. Dirigible was very strong, Yuen felt, very strong. And very angry. The boy pushed at Yuen, upping the old man onto the next step up, up the stairs to his room.

In his room, Yuen did nothing but sigh and sigh and fall backward onto his bed. He stared a moment at the ceiling. The boy did not leave the room. Yuen closed his eyes and pulled at his nose and wiped it with his fingers and stared at the boy. He saw the boy clearly now, and the smile on his face closed shut, then the mouth opened to breathe. It no longer felt like his face he was feeling, no part of him. The old man's fingers, nothing felt like anything of his now. It all felt like old books in old stores. "I have an idea," he said slowly, and took the gun from under his pillow. "We used to try to swallow our tongues to choke ourselves when we were scared, but we always spit them out, or couldn't get them down. I want you to watch so you can tell them I wanted to."

"I don't know what you're talking." Dirigible eyed the gun.

"I'm going to die by myself," Yuen attempted in Chinese for dummies.

The boy stared, eyes big as black olives, "Who? You . . . What are you doing?"

"Your mother can find another dishwasher. She's a good businesswoman."

"Who'll buy me books?"

Yuen pointed the gun at one ear, then switched hands, and pointed the gun at the other ear. He looked at the gun and held it with both hands and pointed it at his mouth, aiming it into his mouth, toward the bulge at the back of his head. He could be angry at the boy, even knowing the boy knew nothing else to say, he could be angry, but wasn't. Dirigible hit himself with a first and shouted, "Ah-bok!" Dirigible leaned and fell backward, stepped once toward the old man before stopping against the towel rack. The boy was weeping and groaning, holding an imaginary pain in his shoulder.

Yuen looked over the gun and watched the boy's rhythmless stumblings in the close room. He eased the hammer to safe and sighed a longer sigh than he had breath. He went to the boy and pulled him to the bed and sat him and wiped his face with his hand. "It's all right, Dritch'ble." Yuen worked for enough breath to speak. "Get up. Go downstairs, now." He bent to untie his shoelaces, dropping the gun to the floor when his fingers could not work them. "Wait. Will you help me bathe? I feel very weak." He'd failed. But he had known he would. He'd expected it.

"Yes."

"I have soap. All kinds. You can have some . . ."

"I have soap too."

He patted the boy's shoulders with his hands and clutched into them with his fingers as he pulled himself to standing. You're an odd son," Yuen said, before turning to undress. "Help me with this."

Dirigible held a towel about Yuen's pale waist as he took him out of his room to the bathroom and helped him into the tub. Dirigible plugged the tub and turned on the water, with Yuen curled up on the bottom, waiting. He didn't complain about the temperature. He leaned forward and asked the boy to scrub his back. His body was loose over his bones, and the same color as his colorless wrists with fat spongy veins piping through the skin. He took the boy's hand and looked into his face with eyes covered with raw eggwhite. "You didn't write me," he said clearly and, his body quivering, rippling water away from his waist, Yuen died. He closed his eyes with his mouth opening to breathe or sigh, and at the end, his chest was low, his ribs showed, and he was dead. There was no more for him. He had finished it.

Dirigible lifted his hands from the water and put his cheek on the edge of the tub. Yuen's death had seemed nothing special, nothing personal. He had given up the boy also. The boy tried to work a tear loose. He felt he should. Tears not all for Yuen, but for himself, because Yuen had been *his.*

Rose came up the stairs and walked down the hall noisily, saying, "Well, how did it go, you two?" before she leaned her head into the bathroom.

# FRANCINE PROSE

## (1947– )

Francine Prose was born in Brooklyn, New York, to parents who were both physicians. She received a B.A. from Radcliffe College in 1968 and an M.A. from Harvard University in 1969. She married Howard Michels, a sculptor, in 1976. She taught briefly at Harvard and at the University of Arizona before taking a full-time position at Warren Wilson College in Swannanon, North Carolina, in 1984.

Prose's stories have appeared in a number of periodicals, including *Mademoiselle, Redbook, Harper's Bazaar, Glamour, The Atlantic Monthly,* and *Commentary.* Her early fiction reflects her interest in the Jewish folktale tradition and ranges widely in place and time. Her novels include *Judah the Pious* (1973), *The Glorious Ones* (1974), *Animal Magnetism* (1978), *Household Saints* (1981), *Hungry Hearts* (1983), *Bigfoot Dreams* (1986), *Primitive People* (1992), *Hunters and Gatherers* (1995), *Guided Tours of Hell: Novellas* (1997), and *Blue Angel* (2000). Her more recent fiction takes a satirical look at contemporary forms of hypocrisy and the many ways individuals and institutions break down.

## Everyday Disorders

WHEN GILDA tries to imagine what Phoebe Morrow looks like, she pictures Amelia Earhart in her rumpled jumpsuit, those fetching goggles and helmet rising straight from the cockpit, long scarf floating straight back, until Gilda realizes that what she's seeing isn't Phoebe or Amelia Earhart at all, but, rather, Snoopy as the Red Baron. Lately Gilda's been troubled by this confusion of images. This winter she reread *Madame Bovary,* and Emma's swoony romantic airs kept bringing to mind Miss Piggy. Gilda blames this on how much of the last dozen years she's spent among children. Childless women have other problems, she knows, but she's pretty sure that the inability to distinguish the mythic from the cartoon isn't one of them. When Phoebe Morrow aims her camera at the horizon, she's not seeing an untrustworthy line which may at any moment turn into a tightrope for Koko the Clown to bounce on; when Phoebe took those famous photographs of the dead Marines in Beirut, she knew she wasn't shooting GI Joe.

Making a square with her fingers, Gilda frames her living room to see what in that mass of discarded clothes and sports equipment and chewed-up baseball cards might catch Phoebe's eye. Nothing, she realizes, and anyway, Nathan's already taken that shot. Nathan's made his name as a chronicler of everyday disorder, so sometimes it seems unfair that he should chide Gilda for being, alternately, too fussy and not neat enough. The worst argument they ever had was years ago, when Gilda asked Nathan if he'd clean up the downstairs—in fact he *had* been cleaning, but the children were too much for them both—and he'd said, "After the revolution you'll be the commissar of cleanliness, the minister who makes sure that everyone keeps their houses neat and tidy." By now they know there won't be any revolution, not here in northern Pennsylvania, anyway, and if there is, they won't be the ones to lead it. Since then they've had more serious fights, meaner and closer to the bone. But the reason she still considers that one the worst is that whenever she straightens up—as she is doing now, as she does fairly often, to be sure—she remembers what Nathan said, and it spoils her pleasure in the work and in the look of things when she's done.

Gilda's looking for reasons to be angry at Nathan because the real reason seems so meanspirited and small: she's upset that he's gotten Phoebe Morrow a one-year job at the college, that he's picking her up at the airport and they're headed back here for lunch. At times like this she feels like one of those wives who work to send their husbands through medical or law school and then the husbands take their fancy practices and split. It's not that Nathan's about to leave her—things feel solid enough, he's not looking for someone else—or that she's ever supported him, but rather that his whole career has been built on his photos of her and their family and their house. What cinched his reputation was that series he took when Gilda's grandfather came to live with them, that terrible year at the end of her grandfather's life; it seems incredible now that the first time she really knew Pop was dying was when she read it in a review of Nathan's show. Nathan's never understood why it bothered her so when critics wrote of Gilda's face as balancing on the border between the beautiful and the impossibly ugly. But all that, Gilda understands now, was nothing compared to how she's felt lately when Nathan, criticizing his own work, says it's all trivial, meaningless, small, come to nothing; Gilda can't help thinking he means her. She knows it's why he pressured his colleagues to hire Phoebe Morrow, who's been to Beirut, Nicaragua, Iraq, whose specialties are guerrilla encampments, free-fire zones, and risking her neck. Not only does Nathan admire Phoebe's work; he wishes he'd led her life.

That's what Gilda's thinking when the doorbell rings and why she has a rictus grin on her face and someone else's tight voice in her mouth as she says, "Nathan, sweetheart, why didn't you use your key?" What strikes Gilda right away is that Phoebe *does* look a bit like Amelia Earhart, that same clear wide forehead, those friendly wide-open eyes, and also a little—Gilda's veering towards the cartoon again—like Betty Boop. What Gilda has been hoping for, of course, was someone more serious-looking, and homelier. Phoebe's wearing a pink silk shirt, tight jeans, little heels. When Nathan introduces them, Phoebe grasps Gilda's hand in both of hers, and Gilda wonders how those delicate arms can possibly heft all that heavy camera equipment.

"Gilda?" Phoebe has enormous blue eyes and is shining them straight at Gilda. "Don't tell me. Your mother saw Rita Hayworth in *Gilda* right before you were born."

"You got it," says Gilda graciously, because she thinks she's scored one off Phoebe: lots of people—movie buffs and nearly everyone over thirty-five—say the same thing. Gilda glances at Nathan to see if he's noticed, but he's too busy looking for somewhere to put Phoebe's expensive-looking luggage. Then Phoebe says, "You know what I can't stop thinking about? Rita Hayworth having Alzheimer's. Forgetting all those beautiful nightgowns and how red her hair was and riding around in Ali Khan's fast cars and getting her picture taken kneeling on those messed-up satin sheets . . ."

Gilda, who's been half-poised for a retreat to the kitchen, turns and stops, and it's at this point that it occurs to her that she might actually *like* Phoebe Morrow. Not only has she been thinking, on and off for months and in much the same terms, about Rita Hayworth's Alzheimer's, but there's something about that kind of thinking—a frank taste for celebrity gossip combined with a certain way of paying attention to the world and in particular to those ironies so appalling they seem both predictable and ultimately bizarre—which appeals to her in people.

"As a matter of fact," Phoebe says, "I wanted to go out to wherever she is and take pictures—"

"That'd be a real change of pace for you," says Nathan with a kind of desperate hopefulness which suddenly makes Gilda think of how their youngest son Danny—for years, afraid of the water—would brighten when he heard the other kids deciding it was too cold for them to swim, too.

"But I didn't think I could handle it," says Phoebe, and then, noticing the surprise on both Gilda's and Nathan's faces, says, "It's easier taking pictures of dead people."

There's a silence during which Gilda thinks—and wonders if Nathan's thinking—of the bitter disagreement they had when Nathan wanted to take pictures of Gilda's grandfather in his coffin. Later, when Gilda was finally able to look at them, she understood that the photos were very moving and beautiful and really not ghoulish at all. Nevertheless, when she leafs through the book of Nathan's photos, as she still occasionally does, she finds herself skipping that page.

"You must be starving," she says to Phoebe. "Come on, let's eat."

It's only within the last year or so that Gilda's been able to set the table before guests arrive. She used to wait till they got there, then set out stacks of plates, silverware in a pile; it was a way of pretending she didn't care. All that casualness was planned; that's how nervous she is when strangers come to her house. Today she brings out an enormous tureen of hot mushroom soup she spent all yesterday making with heavy cream and mushrooms and fresh-grated nutmeg. She told herself she was giving the flavors an extra day to meld but the truth is, when she cooks the same day guests are coming she can't eat, can't even pretend; and though she explains all that, she often wonders if strangers suspect her of covering up some life-threatening appetite disorder.

"Hey," Nathan says, "this is unbelievably great," and Gilda thinks how like him that is. He's generous with everything—with praise, with blame, with enthusiasm, attention for the children. She wants to reach out and touch his hand, but finds it no easier now than it was twenty years ago when they first fell in love. Then it was shyness restraining her; now it's the tactlessness of indulging in that cozy married-couple stuff in front of the unattached.

"These are real mushrooms, aren't they?" says Phoebe. "I mean, fresh mushrooms, you must have made this from scratch." When Gilda nods, Phoebe says, "I've never had this before. Not real mushroom soup from scratch. Oh, Gilda, this is perfect, I can't tell you what it means to me, it's just what I needed, real hot homemade soup, it's been years, I don't think anyone but my mother's ever made me homemade soup, and even she never made mushroom. When you're living alone and traveling a lot you don't get homemade anything."

The forlornness of this last bit makes Gilda glad she didn't touch Nathan's hand. At the same time she's listening for a hint of the patronizing in all this talk of Mom's hot homemade soup, and, when she doesn't hear any, decides Phoebe's pleasure is genuine. Suddenly Phoebe gets up and, standing on tiptoe, peers down into the soup tureen. It's a peculiar gesture. Small as she is, Phoebe could see into the tureen if she just stayed flat on her feet. It's meant to be childlike, meant to charm, but what interests Gilda is that a woman who's gone on commando raids with Sandinista guerrillas would act like an eight-year-old to charm them. "All this soup for us?" Phoebe says.

"I thought I'd make extra in case the students are hungry when they get here," says Gilda and immediately regrets it, hating this image of herself: the homey, solid, faculty wife cooking nourishing soup for the students.

"What students?" Phoebe asks.

"We talked about this in the car," Nathan says. "Some students begged me to let them come by a little later and meet you. I warned them you'd probably be exhausted. But you said it was okay. *Is* it okay? If it isn't, if you're tired or anything, it's fine, I can call and ask them to come some other time—"

"Sure it's okay. I just forgot." Phoebe's voice has taken on such an odd drifty tone that Gilda begins to wonder if she might be suffering slightly from jet lag.

"How long was your trip?" Gilda says.

"Thirty-six hours," says Phoebe. "We got hung up in the Athens airport. Hijack check. The worst part was sitting next to this big fat Palestinian businessman who kept trying to get me to go back and blow him in the airplane bathroom."

There's a silence. Neither Gilda nor Nathan knows quite how to respond. Finally Gilda says, "Yuck," realizing it's a word she's learned from the children. Suddenly she feels the need to bring the children—in spirit—into the room. She knows they've become a kind of talisman for her; when things turn unpleasant or even just socially strained, she runs through their names the way Catholics click off their rosaries.

"You know," Gilda says, "it's a pleasure to cook soup like this for a change. Mostly I don't get a chance. The children wouldn't touch it with a stick."

"How many kids do you have?" Phoebe says, and Gilda's—surprisingly—a little stung that Nathan didn't tell her this in the car. Gilda can't imagine riding for an hour with a stranger and not getting around to that. Though maybe he did, and maybe Phoebe forgot it the way she forgot the students.

"Four," Gilda says. "Sophie's thirteen and Brian's eleven and Ruthie's nine and Danny's seven." Naming them like this makes Gilda acutely aware of how many there are; she feels like Phoebe's a late arrival she's just introduced to a roomful of guests whose names she'll never remember.

"Four?" says Phoebe, and Gilda waits for her to say more. What she's found is that people's responses are so predictable—and so repetitive. In that way having four children is rather like being named Gilda: you get to have the same conversation again and again.

But all Phoebe says is, "That takes courage." This isn't dazzlingly original, either. Lots of people tell Gilda that, but so far none of them have been women who've spent the last ten years careening from war zone to war zone. Gilda almost wants to make Phoebe repeat it for Nathan's benefit since he doesn't seem to be listening, but then Nathan says, "Courage? Stupidity's more like it."

Though Nathan clearly means it as a joke, Gilda's stunned by his betrayal. She knows he doesn't feel that way about her or himself or the kids. She's so shocked she hears herself babbling things she can't believe she's saying.

"It really wasn't courage," she says. "What happened was, I became a kind of junkie. I got hooked on being pregnant and having babies and nursing, and once I got started I couldn't quit. I'd miss the way newborns smell—their breath and the tops of their heads have this sweet smell, like candy—and the next thing I knew I was pregnant again."

Gilda looks over at Nathan, who's smiling slightly and nodding. He knows what she means, and she feels that this shared knowledge shames him a little for what he's just said. When Gilda was pregnant, he couldn't get enough of her—of touching her, of taking her picture. The sad thing is that now, when she looks at his book, she skips over those photos too. Nathan also knows that what Gilda's said is only three-quarters true. Danny was really an accident. By then they'd decided to stop having kids, not because they wanted to, but because they'd gotten superstitious. They'd been so lucky with the first three; they were frightened of pushing their luck. In fact, Danny turned out okay, but Gilda's afraid he inherited all the terrors of that pregnancy; although he's begun to outgrow it, he's been, at one time or another, scared of nearly everything. Once, late at night in bed, Nathan referred to Danny as the runt of the litter and Gilda was horrified at first, then laughed, because his speaking her own worst fear out loud made her feel very close to him; it's something only the other parent can get away with.

Nathan says, "Gilda was the most beautiful pregnant woman you could imagine," and it occurs to Gilda that Phoebe—that anyone who knows Nathan's work—knows *exactly* how she looked pregnant. Though Gilda's aware that they're very consciously not talking shop here, she's hoping that Phoebe will mention those pictures. But what Phoebe says is, "If you can't cook the children mushroom soup, what *can* you cook them?"

"Pizza," says Nathan. "Endless pizza."

"What's *your* favorite meal?" Phoebe asks Gilda, who's so surprised that Phoebe would be interested that the only answer she can come up with is, "Linguine and steamed mussels with hot pepper flakes and garlic and parsley." It's true, she realizes, but if she'd thought a moment longer, she wouldn't have been able to decide.

"That sounds wonderful," says Phoebe. "Maybe you can make it for me sometime."

"And yours?" Gilda says. "Your favorite?"

Phoebe thinks for a while. "Airplane food," she says at last, and her voice goes so vague and drifty again, it's as if she's flying away from them even as they sit there. Gilda's afraid they've bored her with all this talk of children, and knows the time has come to ask about *Phoebe*'s courage—her career, her work. But what's stopping her is this: if people repeat themselves so on the subject of Gilda's name and four children, how much more repetitious must be the questions Phoebe hears all the time. Gilda longs to frame *her* question in a way no one's happened on yet, but so much dead air's flowing by that eventually she panics and says, "Have you ever been hit?"

Phoebe looks at her strangely. "Only by my lovers," she says. Gilda wonders if this is all Phoebe intends to say on the subject, and has the odd sensation that Phoebe's saving her war stories for a larger and more satisfying audience. But then Phoebe says, "I'll tell you a funny thing. Sometimes out in the field I get this feeling I'm invisible. That no one sees me, that I don't exist. A bullet, a rocket—a bomb couldn't find me. And in a way, I guess, I've learned to make myself invisible. It's like I'm not there—it's how I get all my best shots."

"What a great trick to know," says Gilda. "How do you do it?"

"It's hard to explain," Phoebe says. "But I know when I started feeling that way: as a kid growing up in New York. I used to have to walk home from school along the Bowery, and the bums would all say these dirty things to me. I was *terrified.* So I'd practice making myself disappear so the bums wouldn't see me—and that's how I learned how to do it."

Gilda loves this story, this tale of childhood terror mined for power in later life. She hopes—and is embarrassed for reducing everything to this level again, but there it is—that something similar may work for Danny. She glances over at Nathan, who's got the strangest look on his face. It's hardly enchantment—that much seems clear. But that's all Gilda knows. All those years of practice reading Nathan's mind, and she hasn't a clue to what's on it.

Just then the doorbell rings. "That'll be the students," says Nathan.

"We'll have dessert later," Gilda says, and jumps up from the table.

With each passing year Gilda finds herself avoiding Nathan's students more determinedly. Mostly she's disturbed that they stay the same age while she keeps getting older, but there's also their dogged insistence on calling her Mrs. Wilson no matter how often she asks them to call her Gilda. It makes her feel like Dennis the Menace's neighbor, or like the headmaster's wife in some British public-school novel. One thing she knows is that she doesn't want them calling her Mrs. Wilson in front of Phoebe, so she busies herself cleaning dishes while Nathan introduces Phoebe to the students—six of them, Gilda counts, three boys, three girls, though their nearly identical short punky haircuts and designer paratrooper clothes make this difficult to say for sure. It strikes Gilda as ironic that they are the ones dressed like Green Berets while Phoebe, who's probably actually jumped out of airplanes, is wearing silk and those tiny high heels. Making extra trips so as to have something involving to do, Gilda imagines that she's the downstairs maid, and might as well be for all the attention anyone pays her until she shoos them into the living room, urging them to talk and relax while she makes coffee and whips the cream for dessert.

The noise of the electric beater is wonderfully soothing. It blots out everything else as Gilda concentrates on the small miracle of white liquid turning into white solid. She watches the coffee brew, drip by drip, and when she turns away from the counter, she's touched to find Nathan leaning against the doorway between the kitchen and living room, as if he's reluctant to leave her alone in there, working. Hearing Phoebe's clear voice ringing from the other room, Gilda goes and stands beside Nathan to look at what he's watching: Phoebe on the sofa with all the students seated in a circle on the floor, literally at her feet.

Phoebe's in the middle of a story, and it takes Gilda a while to get the gist of it, to realize that Phoebe's volunteering all this, or else the students have been less circumspect than Gilda and Nathan in grilling her for the details of her paramilitary career.

"I had a lover," Phoebe's saying, "a Palestinian commando, trained as a fighter pilot. He'd take me on missions with him so I could take aerial shots of all the bases. Most of them I sold to *Newsweek.* When things calmed down we'd make love everywhere, even standing up in the airplane bathroom."

"Bathrooms on fighter planes?" Gilda whispers to Nathan, but Nathan puts a finger to her lips and says, "Shhh."

"Then one day," says Phoebe, "we took some Israeli fire. We got hit, we went down. My lover was killed. The next thing I knew, I was in an Israeli medivac unit with sixty-two pieces of shrapnel in my back, one in this really strategic place near the base of my spine."

The students make various appreciative, prayerful noises. Wow. Jesus. God. Holy Christ.

"They told me," Phoebe continues, "that I'd been in a coma for thirty-six hours. But here's what I remember: when I opened my eyes, there was this beautiful Israeli nurse. A redhead. She looked just like Rita Hayworth. She had on this great perfume—it smelled like a newborn baby, like candy. And she was bringing me food—homemade mushroom soup, made with real mushrooms from scratch. I'd never had it before, and oh, it was just what I needed. I got to be a kind of junkie for it; once I got started I couldn't stop. And when I began to feel better, she brought me—without my even asking for it—my favorite food: linguine with steamed mussels, hot pepper flakes, garlic, and parsley."

Gilda and Nathan linger a moment to see if Phoebe realizes they're watching her from the doorway. But she's focused on the middle distance, completely intent on her story; she doesn't know they're there.

Gilda grabs Nathan's hand and pulls him into the kitchen and lets the door swing shut behind them. Gilda's got chills running down her spine, but before she says anything, she wants to be accurate, to know precisely what kind of chills they are. At first she thinks this is how she might feel if she'd come home to find Phoebe trying on all her clothes. But what's happened, she realizes, is less frightening, eerier and more distant—more like the startled, upset way she felt last summer when she found a bird's nest into which had been woven, unmistakably, swatches of that red plaid shirt of Danny's that had mysteriously disappeared from the line. Mostly what concerns Gilda now is that Phoebe be gone before the children get back. How different from her earlier fantasy: that they'd come home early enough for her to show them off. Now Gilda's afraid that if Phoebe meets them, she'll steal something from them too.

Nathan says, "Do me a favor. Don't offer those kids out there any of that mushroom soup. Then they'll really know something's weird."

Gilda nods, then says, "Did you know about this?"

"She said a couple of strange things on the drive back from the airport," Nathan answers. "But I wasn't sure till she started in on that stuff about making herself invisible so the bums wouldn't see her. That's a famous Dorothea Lange story. The other thing is, Phoebe didn't grow up in New York, she grew up in some Nebraska hick town where if a bum ever walked down Main Street, the sheriff would have escorted him onto the first boxcar out of there."

"Is this just starting?" Gilda says. "Has she always been this way? Could she have done all those things she's done—taken all those great pictures—and have always been this way?"

"I don't know." Nathan shrugs. "What difference does it make?"

Gilda wants to tell him that it does make a difference, that, disturbing as the whole thing is, there's reason for relief and possibly even rejoicing here. For the fact is, Phoebe Morrow isn't anyone to be envied; by no means is her life a model life. In no way is her approach to the world any better than Nathan's. The fact is, there's something wrong with her. Some essential component of self is so desperately missing she keeps trying to patch it with borrowed scraps from other people's lives.

Nathan sighs and says, "It's going to be quite a year." And all at once Gilda realizes how childish she's being. Nathan's right; what difference does any of it make? They're too old for easy and false consolations, for the small, mean pleasures of learning that someone whose achievements you've always admired and envied is homely or cursed with an unhappy private life. If Nathan's afraid he's wasted his life, who cares what Phoebe Morrow's done with hers?

Nathan goes to the window and, turning his back to her, looks out. Gilda can't see what he's seeing, but knows, without having to look, there's a rusted swing set and a tangle of bicycles on the lawn. When Danny gets home, he'll cry for Nathan to pull his bicycle out from the bottom, where it always is, its pedal caught in someone else's spoke, and Nathan will study it awhile, then find a way to unhook it.

And now Gilda wants to tell Nathan something else. Quick, before she forgets. She opens her mouth to speak and her hands move as if she's already speaking. She wants to tell him: there is a kind of heroism in everyday life, in facing the daily messes which Gilda would often gladly have turned away from.

She's thinking of how, near the end, her grandfather kept falling. How the trim little body he'd always tended so carefully turned first to fat, then useless weight, and fell and fell, so that for a while she feared her house would always seem like a museum of places Pop went down: the guest room, the bathroom, the tight spot between sink and stove she thought they'd never get him out of. She remembers how gently Nathan would lift Pop and walk with him till he stopped feeling embarrassed and shaken, and of how, watching, seeking some way to comfort herself, she'd think of how children learn to walk, how they fell, too—especially Danny, who was so scared. She'd think of herself and Nathan facing each other and calling, Come to Mama, Come to Papa, to the baby tottering back and forth as its parents move farther and farther and farther apart until one or another of them suddenly steps aside and the child, tricked into it, just keeps going.

# RAYMOND CARVER
## (1938–1988)

Influenced by the fiction of Ernest Hemingway and Sherwood Anderson, Raymond Carver became a master of the short story. He did so out of desperate necessity, not of preference. He literally had no time to write anything longer than a short story while trying to provide for his wife and two children by holding down a series of low-paying jobs. It was not until his success brought him financial security that his work became more expansive and he could begin work on a novel. Carver told stories of desperate, essentially inarticulate, lower-middle-class people who were often only a click away from bankruptcy and who had little capacity to comprehend their fates. He told these stories in a style that was flat and unemotional, in a language that was spare and unadorned, giving little more than the mundane details of life, a style that implied disorder and desperation and rarely showed glimpses of hope. The style became known as "minimalism" or K-Mart realism, and it suggested a world where human possibility was minimal at best. Not appreciated by some critics and writers, Carver's minimalism has nevertheless had a great influence on the renewal of short fiction in the 1970s and 1980s.

Carver was born in the logging town of Clatskanie, Oregon, where his father worked in a sawmill and his mother held odd jobs. By age 19 Carver had married and fathered two children. In 1958 he and his family moved to California and enrolled at Chico State College (now University), where he took an influential writing class taught by the young writer John Gardner. He completed a B.A. at Humboldt State College in 1963. With a stipend he was able to attend the Writers' Workshop at the University of Iowa, but had to leave after six months to support his family.

Carver's first success came in 1967 when his story, "Will You Please Be Quiet, Please?," was included in *The Best American Short Stories of 1967*. Grants and fellowships gave him more time to write and led to teaching jobs at the University of California at Santa Cruz in 1971–1972 and at Berkeley in 1972–1973. In 1975, however, Carver declared bankruptcy, and over the next two years he was frequently hospitalized for alcohol abuse.

Carver's first story collection, *Will You Please Be Quiet, Please?,* was nominated for the National Book Award in 1976. As his first marriage failed, he began to live with the poet Tess Gallagher, and together they taught writing at Syracuse University. He and Gallagher were living in Port Angeles, Washington, at the time of his death in 1988 from lung cancer. Carver's other story collections include *Furious Seasons* (1977), *What We Talk About When We Talk About Love* (1981), *Cathedral* (1983), and *Where I'm Calling From:*

(1988). In 1992, *No Heroics, Please: Uncollected Writings* was published. Carver also published a number of volumes of poetry, including *Near Klamath* (1968), *Winter Insomnia* (1970), *Where Water Comes Together with Other Water* (1985), *Ultramarine* (1986), and *A New Path to the Waterfall* (1989).

# What We Talk About When We Talk About Love

MY FRIEND Mel McGinnis was talking. Mel McGinnis is a cardiologist, and sometimes that gives him the right.

The four of us were sitting around his kitchen table drinking gin. Sunlight filled the kitchen from the big window behind the sink. There were Mel and me and his second wife, Teresa—Terri, we called her—and my wife, Laura. We lived in Albuquerque then. But we were all from somewhere else.

There was an ice bucket on the table. The gin and the tonic water kept going around, and we somehow got on the subject of love. Mel thought real love was nothing less than spiritual love. He said he'd spent five years in a seminary before quitting to go to medical school. He said he still looked back on those years in the seminary as the most important years in his life.

Terri said the man she lived with before she lived with Mel loved her so much he tried to kill her. Then Terri said, "He beat me up one night. He dragged me around the living room by my ankles. He kept saying, 'I love you, I love you, you bitch.' He went on dragging me around the living room. My head kept knocking on things." Terri looked around the table. "What do you do with love like that?"

She was a bone-thin woman with a pretty face, dark eyes, and brown hair that hung down her back. She liked necklaces made of turquoise, and long pendant earrings.

"My God, don't be silly. That's not love, and you know it," Mel said. "I don't know what you'd call it, but I sure know you wouldn't call it love."

"Say what you want to, but I know it was," Terri said. Terri said, "It may sound crazy to you, but it's true just the same. People are different, Mel. Sure, sometimes he may have acted crazy. Okay. But he loved me. In his own way maybe; but he loved me. There was love there, Mel. Don't say there wasn't."

Mel let out his breath. He held his glass and turned to Laura and me. "The man threatened to kill me," Mel said. He finished his drink and reached for the gin bottle. "Terri's a romantic. Terri's of the kick-me-so-I'll-know-you-love-me school. Terri, hon, don't look that way." Mel reached across the table and touched Terri's cheek with his fingers. He grinned at her.

"Now he wants to make up," Terri said.

"Make up what?" Mel said. "What is there to make up? I know what I know. That's all."

"How'd we get started on this subject, anyway?" Terri said. She raised her glass and drank from it. "Mel always has love on his mind," she said. "Don't you, honey?" She smiled, and I thought that was the last of it.

"I just wouldn't call Ed's behavior love. That's all I'm saying, honey," Mel said. "What about you guys?" Mel said to Laura and me. "Does that sound like love to you?"

"I'm the wrong person to ask," I said. "I didn't even know the man. I've only heard his name mentioned in passing. I wouldn't know. You'd have to know the particulars. But I think what you're saying is that love is an absolute."

Mel said, "The kind of love I'm talking about is. The kind of love I'm talking about, you don't try to kill people."

Laura said, "I don't know anything about Ed, or anything about the situation. But who can judge anyone else's situation?"

I touched the back of Laura's hand. She gave me a quick smile. I picked up Laura's hand. It was warm, the nails polished, perfectly manicured. I encircled the broad wrist with my fingers, and I held her.

* * *

"When I left, he drank rat poison," Terri said. She clasped her arms with her hands. "They took him to the hospital in Santa Fe. That's where we lived then, about ten miles out. They saved his life. But his gums went crazy from it. I mean they pulled away from his teeth. After that, his teeth stood out like fangs. My God," Terri said. She waited a minute, then let go of her arms and picked up her glass.

"What people won't do!" Laura said.

"He's out of the action now," Mel said. "He's dead."

Mel handed me the saucer of limes. I took a section, squeezed it over my drink, and stirred the ice cubes with my finger.

"It gets worse," Terri said. "He shot himself in the mouth. But he bungled that too. Poor Ed," she said. Terri shook her head.

"Poor Ed nothing," Mel said. "He was dangerous."

Mel was forty-five years old. He was tall and rangy with curly soft hair. His face and arms were brown from the tennis he played. When he was sober, his gestures, all his movements, were precise, very careful.

"He did love me though, Mel. Grant me that," Terri said. "That's all I'm asking. He didn't love me the way you love me. I'm not saying that. But he loved me. You can grant me that, can't you?"

"What do you mean, he bungled it?" I said.

Laura leaned forward with her glass. She put her elbows on the table and held her glass in both hands. She glanced from Mel to Terri and waited with a look of bewilderment on her open face as if amazed that such things happened to people you were friendly with.

"How'd he bungle it when he killed himself?" I said.

"I'll tell you what happened," Mel said. "He took this twenty-two pistol he'd bought to threaten Terri and me with. Oh, I'm serious, the man was always threatening. You should have seen the way we lived in those days. Like fugitives. I even bought a gun myself. Can you believe it? A guy like me? But I did. I bought one for self-defense and carried it in the glove compartment. Sometimes I'd have to leave the apartment in the middle of the night. To go to the hospital, you know? Terri and I weren't married then, and my first wife had the house and kids, the dog, everything, and Terri and I were living in this apartment here. Sometimes, as I say, I'd get a call in the middle of the night and have to go in to the hospital at two or three in the morning. It'd be dark out there in the parking lot, and I'd break into a sweat before I could even get to my car. I never knew if he was going to come up out of the shrubbery or from behind a car and start shooting. I mean, the man was crazy. He was capable of wiring a bomb, anything. He used to call my service at all hours and say he needed to talk to the doctor, and when I'd return the call, he'd say, 'Son of a bitch, your days are numbered.' Little things like that. It was scary, I'm telling you."

"I still feel sorry for him," Terri said.

"It sounds like a nightmare," Laura said. "But what exactly happened after he shot himself?"

Laura is a legal secretary. We'd met in a professional capacity. Before we knew it, it was a courtship. She's thirty-five, three years younger than I am. In addition to being in love, we like each other and enjoy one another's company. She's easy to be with.

* * *

"What happened?" Laura said.

Mel said, "He shot himself in the mouth in his room. Someone heard the shot and told the manager. They came in with a passkey, saw what had happened, and called an ambulance. I happened to be there when they brought him in, alive but past recall. The man lived for three days. His head swelled up to twice the size of a normal head. I'd never seen anything like it, and I hope I never do again. Terri wanted to go in and sit with him when she found out about it. We had a fight over it. I didn't think she should see him like that. I didn't think she should see him, and I still don't."

"Who won the fight?" Laura said.

"I was in the room with him when he died," Terri said. "He never came up out of it. But I sat with him. He didn't have anyone else."

"He was dangerous," Mel said. "If you call that love, you can have it."

"It was love," Terri said. "Sure, it's abnormal in most people's eyes. But he was willing to die for it. He did die for it."

"I sure as hell wouldn't call it love," Mel said. "I mean, no one knows what he did it for. I've seen a lot of suicides, and I couldn't say anyone ever knew what they did it for."

Mel put his hands behind his neck and tilted his chair back. "I'm not interested in that kind of love," he said. "If that's love, you can have it."

Terri said, "We were afraid. Mel even made a will out and wrote to his brother in California who used to be a Green Beret. Mel told him who to look for if something happened to him."

Terri drank from her glass. She said, "But Mel's right—we lived like fugitives. We were afraid. Mel was, weren't you, honey? I even called the police at one point, but they were no help. They said they couldn't do anything until Ed actually did something. Isn't that a laugh?" Terri said.

She poured the last of the gin into her glass and waggled the bottle. Mel got up from the table and went to the cupboard. He took down another bottle.

* * *

"Well, Nick and I know what love is," Laura said. "For us, I mean," Laura said. She bumped my knee with her knee. "You're supposed to say something now," Laura said, and turned her smile on me.

For an answer, I took Laura's hand and raised it to my lips. I made a big production out of kissing her hand. Everyone was amused.

"We're lucky," I said.

"You guys," Terri said. "Stop that now. You're making me sick. You're still on the honeymoon, for God's sake. You're still gaga, for crying out loud. Just wait. How long have you been together now? How long has it been? A year? Longer than a year?"

"Going on a year and a half," Laura said, flushed and smiling.

"Oh, now," Terri said. "Wait awhile."

She held her drink and gazed at Laura.

"I'm only kidding," Terri said.

Mel opened the gin and went around the table with the bottle.

"Here, you guys," he said. "Let's have a toast. I want to propose a toast. A toast to love. To true love," Mel said.

We touched glasses.

"To love," we said.

* * *

Outside in the backyard, one of the dogs began to bark. The leaves of the aspen that leaned past the window ticked against the glass. The afternoon sun was like a presence in this room, the spacious light of ease and generosity. We could have been anywhere, somewhere enchanted. We raised our glasses again and grinned at each other like children who had agreed on something forbidden.

"I'll tell you what real love is," Mel said. "I mean, I'll give you a good example. And then you can draw your own conclusions." He poured more gin into his glass. He added an ice cube and a sliver of lime. We waited and sipped our drinks. Laura and I touched knees again. I put a hand on her warm thigh and left it there.

"What do any of us really know about love?" Mel said. "It seems to me we're just beginners at love. We say we love each other and we do, I don't doubt it. I love Terri and Terri loves me, and you guys love each other too. You know the kind of love I'm talking about now. Physical love, that impulse that drives you to someone special, as well as love of the other person's being, his or her essence, as it were. Carnal love and, well, call it sentimental love; the day-to-day caring about the other person. But sometimes I have a hard time accounting for the fact that I must have loved my first wife too. But I did, I know I did. So I suppose I am like Terri in that regard. Terri and Ed." He thought about it and then he went on. "There was a time when I thought I loved my first wife more than life itself. But now I hate her guts. I do. How do you explain that? What happened to that love? What happened to it, is what I'd like to know. I wish someone could tell me. Then there's Ed. Okay, we're back to Ed. He loves Terri so much he tries to kill her and he winds up killing himself." Mel stopped talking and swallowed from his glass. "You guys have been together eighteen months and you love each other. It shows all over you. You glow with it. But you both loved other people before you met each other. You've both been married before, just like us. And you probably loved other people before that too, even. Terri and I have been together five years, been married for four. And the terrible thing, the terrible thing, is, but the good thing too, the saving grace, you might say, is that if something happened to one of us—excuse me for saying this—but if something happened to one of us tomorrow, I think the other one, the other person, would grieve for a while, you know, but then the surviving party would go out and love again, have someone else soon enough. All this, all of this love we're talking about, it would just be a memory. Maybe not even a memory. Am I wrong? Am I way off base? Because I want you to set me straight if you think I'm wrong. I want to know. I mean, I don't know anything, and I'm the first one to admit it."

"Mel, for God's sake," Terri said. She reached out and took hold of his wrist. "Are you getting drunk? Honey? Are you drunk?"

"Honey, I'm just talking," Mel said. "All right? I don't have to be drunk to say what I think. I mean, we're all just talking, right?" Mel said. He fixed his eyes on her.

"Sweetie, I'm not criticizing," Terri said.

She picked up her glass.

"I'm not on call today," Mel said. "Let me remind you of that. I am not on call," he said.

"Mel, we love you," Laura said.

Mel looked at Laura. He looked at her as if he could not place her, as if she was not the woman she was.

"Love you too, Laura," Mel said. "And you, Nick, love you too. You know something?" Mel said. "You guys are our pals," Mel said.

He picked up his glass.

* * *

Mel said, "I was going to tell you about something. I mean, I was going to prove a point. You see, this happened a few months ago, but it's still going on right now, and it ought to make us feel ashamed when we talk like we know what we're talking about when we talk about love."

"Come on now," Terri said. "Don't talk like you're drunk if you're not drunk."

"Just shut up for once in your life," Mel said very quietly. "Will you do me a favor and do that for a minute? So as I was saying, there's this old couple who had this car wreck out on the interstate. A kid hit them and they were all torn to shit and nobody was giving them much chance to pull through."

Terri looked at us and then back at Mel. She seemed anxious, or maybe that's too strong a word.

Mel was handling the bottle around the table.

"I was on call that night," Mel said. "It was May or maybe it was June. Terri and I had just sat down to dinner when the hospital called. There'd been this thing out on the interstate. Drunk kid, teenager, plowed his dad's pickup into this camper with this old couple in it. They were up in their mid-seventies, that couple. The kid—eighteen, nineteen, something—he was DOA. Taken the steering wheel through his sternum. The old couple, they were alive, you understand. I mean, just barely. But they had everything. Multiple fractures, internal injuries, hemorrhaging, contusions, lacerations, the works, and they each of them had themselves concussions. They were in a bad way, believe me. And, of course, their age was two strikes against them. I'd say she was worse off than he was. Ruptured spleen along with everything else. Both kneecaps broken. But they'd been wearing their seatbelts and, God knows, that's what saved them for the time being."

"Folks, this is an advertisement for the National Safety Council," Terri said. "This is your spokesman, Dr. Melvin R. McGinnis, talking." Terri laughed. "Mel," she said, "sometimes you're just too much. But I love you, hon," she said.

"Honey, I love you," Mel said.

He leaned across the table. Terri met him halfway. They kissed.

"Terri's right," Mel said as he settled himself again. "Get those seatbelts on. But seriously, they were in some shape, those oldsters. By the time I got down there, the kid was dead, as I said. He was off in a corner, laid out on a gurney. I took one look at the old couple and told the ER nurse to get me a neurologist and an orthopedic man and a couple of surgeons down there right away."

He drank from his glass. "I'll try to keep this short," he said. "So we took the two of them up to the OR and worked like fuck on them most of the night. They had these incredible reserves, those two. You see that once in a while. So we did everything that could be done, and toward morning we're giving them a fifty-fifty chance, maybe less than that for her. So here they are, still alive the next morning. So, okay, we move them into the ICU, which is where they both kept plugging away at it for two weeks, hitting it better and better on all the scopes. So we transfer them out to their own room."

Mel stopped talking. "Here," he said, "let's drink this cheapo gin the hell up. Then we're going to dinner, right? Terri and I know a new place. That's where we'll go, to this new place we know about. But we're not going until we finish up this cut-rate, lousy gin."

Terri said, "We haven't actually eaten there yet. But it looks good. From the outside, you know."

"I like food," Mel said. "If I had it to do all over again, I'd be a chef, you know? Right, Terri?" Mel said.

He laughed. He fingered the ice in his glass.

"Terri knows," he said. "Terri can tell you. But let me say this. If I could come back again in a different life, a different time and all, you know what? I'd like to come back as a knight. You were pretty safe wearing all that armor. It was all right being a knight until gunpowder and muskets and pistols came along."

"Mel would like to ride a horse and carry a lance," Terri said.

"Carry a woman's scarf with you everywhere," Laura said.

"Or just a woman," Mel said.

"Shame on you," Laura said.

Terri said, "Suppose you came back as a serf. The serfs didn't have it so good in those days," Terri said.

"The serfs never had it good," Mel said. "But I guess even the knights were vessels to someone. Isn't that the way it worked? But then everyone is always a vessel to someone. Isn't that right? Terri? But what I liked about knights, besides their ladies, was that they had that suit of armor, you know, and they couldn't get hurt very easy. No cars in those days, you know? No drunk teenagers to tear into your ass."

* * *

"Vassals," Terri said.

"What?" Mel said.

"Vassals," Terri said. "They were called vassals, not vessels."

"Vassals, vessels," Mel said, "what the fuck's the difference? You knew what I meant anyway. All right," Mel said. "So I'm not educated. I learned my stuff. I'm a heart surgeon, sure, but I'm just a mechanic. I go in and I fuck around and I fix things. Shit," Mel said.

"Modesty doesn't become you," Terri said.

"He's just a humble sawbones," I said. "But sometimes they suffocated in all that armor, Mel. They'd even have heart attacks if it got too hot and they were too tired and worn out. I read somewhere that they'd fall off their horses and not be able to get up because they were too tired to stand with all that armor on them. They got trampled by their own horses sometimes."

"That's terrible," Mel said. "That's a terrible thing, Nicky. I guess they'd just lay there and wait until somebody came along and made a shish kebab out of them."

"Some other vessel," Terri said.

"That's right," Mel said. "Some vassal would come along and spear the bastard in the name of love. Or whatever the fuck it was they fought over in those days."

"Same things we fight over these days," Terri said.

Laura said, "Nothing's changed."

The color was still high in Laura's cheeks. Her eyes were bright. She brought her glass to her lips.

Mel poured himself another drink. He looked at the label closely as if studying a long row of numbers. Then he slowly put the bottle down on the table and slowly reached for the tonic water.

* * *

"What about the old couple?" Laura said. "You didn't finish that story you started."

Laura was having a hard time lighting her cigarette. Her matches kept going out.

The sunshine inside the room was different now, changing, getting thinner. But the leaves outside the window were still shimmering, and I stared at the pattern they made on the panes and on the Formica counter. They weren't the same patterns, of course.

"What about the old couple?" I said.

"Older but wiser," Terri said.

Mel stared at her.

Terri said, "Go on with your story, hon. I was only kidding. Then what happened?"

"Terri, sometimes," Mel said.

"Please, Mel," Terri said. "Don't always be so serious, sweetie. Can't you take a joke?"

"Where's the joke?" Mel said.

He held his glass and gazed steadily at his wife.

"What happened?" Laura said.

Mel fastened his eyes on Laura. He said, "Laura, if I didn't have Terri and if I didn't love her so much, and if Nick wasn't my best friend, I'd fall in love with you. I'd carry you off, honey," he said.

"Tell your story," Terri said. "Then we'll go to that new place, okay?"

"Okay," Mel said. "Where was I?" he said. He stared at the table and then he began again.

"I dropped in to see each of them every day, sometimes twice a day if I was up doing other calls anyway. Casts and bandages, head to foot, the both of them. You know, you've seen it in the movies. That's just the way they looked, just like in the movies. Little eye-holes and nose-holes and mouth-holes. And she had to have her legs slung up on top of it. Well, the husband was very depressed for the longest while. Even after he found out that his wife was going to pull through, he was still very depressed.

Not about the accident, though. I mean, the accident was one thing, but it wasn't everything. I'd get up to his mouth-hole, you know, and he'd say no, it wasn't the accident exactly but it was because he couldn't see her through his eye-holes. He said that was what was making him feel so bad. Can you imagine? I'm telling you, the man's heart was breaking because he couldn't turn his goddamn head and *see* his goddamn wife."

Mel looked around the table and shook his head at what he was going to say.

"I mean, it was killing the old fart just because he couldn't *look* at the fucking woman."

We all looked at Mel.

"Do you see what I'm saying?" he said.

Maybe we were a little drunk by then. I know it was hard keeping things in focus. The light was draining out of the room, going back through the window where it had come from. Yet nobody made a move to get up from the table to turn on the overhead light.

"Listen," Mel said. "Let's finish this fucking gin. There's about enough left here for one shooter all around. Then let's go eat. Let's go to the new place."

"He's depressed," Terri said. "Mel, why don't you take a pill?"

Mel shook his head. "I've taken everything there is."

"We all need a pill now and then," I said.

"Some people are born needing them," Terri said.

She was using her finger to rub at something on the table. Then she stopped rubbing.

"I think I want to call my kids," Mel said. "Is that all right with everybody? I'll call my kids," he said.

Terri said, "What if Marjorie answers the phone? You guys, you've heard us on the subject of Marjorie? Honey, you know you don't want to talk to Marjorie. It'll make you feel even worse."

"I don't want to talk to Marjorie," Mel said. "But I want to talk to my kids."

"There isn't a day goes by that Mel doesn't say he wishes she'd get married again. Or else die," Terri said. "For one thing," Terri said, "she's bankrupting us. Mel says it's just to spite him that she won't get married again. She has a boyfriend who lives with her and the kids, so Mel is supporting the boyfriend too."

"She's allergic to bees," Mel said. "If I'm not praying she'll get married again, I'm praying she'll get herself stung to death by a swarm of fucking bees."

"Shame on you," Laura said.

"Bzzzzzzz," Mel said, turning his fingers into bees and buzzing them at Terri's throat. Then he let his hands drop all the way to his sides.

"She's vicious," Mel said. "Sometimes I think I'll go up there dressed like a beekeeper. You know, that hat that's like a helmet with the plate that comes down over your face, the big gloves, and the padded coat? I'll knock on the door and let loose a hive of bees in the house. But first I'd make sure the kids were out, of course."

He crossed one leg over the other. It seemed to take him a lot of time to do it. Then he put both feet on the floor and leaned forward, elbows on the table, his chin cupped in his hands.

"Maybe I won't call the kids, after all. Maybe it isn't such a hot idea. Maybe we'll just go eat. How does that sound?"

"Sounds fine to me," I said. "Eat or not eat. Or keep drinking. I could head right on out into the sunset."

"What does that mean, honey?" Laura said.

"It just means what I said," I said. "It means I could just keep going. That's all it means."

"I could eat something myself," Laura said. "I don't think I've ever been so hungry in my life. Is there something to nibble on?"

"I'll put out some cheese and crackers," Terri said.

But Terri just sat there. She did not get up to get anything.

Mel turned his glass over. He spilled it out on the table.

"Gin's gone," Mel said.

Terri said, "Now what?"

I could hear my heart beating. I could hear everyone's heart. I could hear the human noise we sat there making, not one of us moving, not even when the room went dark.

# Cathedral

THIS BLIND man, an old friend of my wife's, he was on his way to spend the night. His wife had died. So he was visiting the dead wife's relatives in Connecticut. He called my wife from his in-laws'. Arrangements were made. He would come by train, a five-hour trip, and my wife would meet him at the station. She hadn't seen him since she worked for him one summer in Seattle ten years ago. But she and the blind man had kept in touch. They made tapes and mailed them back and forth. I wasn't enthusiastic about his visit. He was no one I knew. And his being blind bothered me. My idea of blindness came from the movies. In the movies, the blind moved slowly and never laughed. Sometimes they were led by seeing-eye dogs. A blind man in my house was not something I looked forward to.

That summer in Seattle she had needed a job. She didn't have any money. The man she was going to marry at the end of the summer was in officers' training school. He didn't have any money, either. But she was in love with the guy, and he was in love with her, etc. She'd seen something in the paper: HELP WANTED—*Reading to Blind Man,* and a telephone number. She phoned and went over, was hired on the spot. She'd worked with this blind man all summer. She read stuff to him, case studies, reports, that sort of thing. She helped him organize his little office in the country social-service department. They'd become good friends, my wife and the blind man. How do I know these things? She told me. And she told me something else. On her last day in the office, the blind man asked if he could touch her face. She agreed to this. She told me he touched his fingers to every part of her face, her nose—even her neck! She never forgot it. She even tried to write a poem about it. She was always trying to write a poem. She wrote a poem or two every year, usually after something really important had happened to her.

When we first started going out together, she showed me the poem. In the poem, she recalled his fingers and the way they had moved around over her face. In the poem, she talked about what she had felt at the time, about what went through her mind when the blind man touched her nose and lips. I can remember I didn't think much of the poem. Of course, I didn't tell her that. Maybe I just don't understand poetry. I admit it's not the first thing I reach for when I pick up something to read.

Anyway, this man who'd first enjoyed her favors, the officer-to-be, he'd been her childhood sweetheart. So okay. I'm saying that at the end of the summer she let the blind man run his hands over her face, said goodbye to him, married her childhood etc., who was now a commissioned officer, and she moved away from Seattle. But they'd kept in touch, she and the blind man. She made the first contact after a year or so. She called him up one night from an Air Force base in Alabama. She wanted to talk. They talked. He asked her to send him a tape and tell him about her life. She did this. She sent the tape. On the tape, she told the blind man about her husband and about their life together in the military. She told the blind man she loved her husband but she didn't like it where they lived and she didn't like it that he was a part of the military-industrial thing. She told the blind man she'd written a poem and he was in it. She told him that she was writing a poem about what it was like to be an Air Force officer's wife. The poem wasn't finished yet. She was still writing it. The blind man made a tape. He sent her the tape. She made a tape. This went on for years. My wife's officer was posted to one base and then another. She sent tapes from Moody AFB, McGuire, McConnell, and finally Travis, near Sacramento, where one night she got to feeling lonely and cut off from people she kept losing in that moving-around life. She got to feeling she couldn't go it another step. She went in and swallowed all the pills and capsules in the medicine chest and washed them down with a bottle of gin. Then she got into a hot-bath and passed out.

But instead of dying, she got sick. She threw up. Her officer—why should he have a name? he was the childhood sweetheart, and what more does he want?—came home from somewhere, found her, and called the ambulance. In time, she put it all on a tape and sent the tape to the blind man. Over the years, she put all kinds of stuff on tapes and sent the tapes off lickety-split. Next to writing a poem every year, I think it was her chief means of recreation. On one tape, she told the blind man she'd decided to live away from her officer for a time. On another tape, she told him about her divorce. She and I began going out, and of course she told her blind man about it. She told him everything, or so it seemed to me. Once she asked me if I'd like to hear the latest tape from the blind man. This was a year ago. I was on the tape, she said. So I said okay, I'd listen to it. I got us drinks and we settled down in the living room. We made ready to listen. First she inserted the tape into the player and adjusted a couple of dials. Then she pushed a lever. The tape squeaked and someone began to talk in this loud voice. She lowered the volume. After a few minutes of harmless chitchat, I heard my own name in the mouth of this stranger, this blind man I didn't even know! And then this: "From all you've said about him, I can only conclude—" "But we were interrupted, a knock at the door, something, and we didn't ever get back to the tape. Maybe it was just as well. I'd heard all I wanted to.

Now this same blind man was coming to sleep in my house.

"Maybe I could take him bowling," I said to my wife. She was at the draining board doing scalloped potatoes. She put down the knife she was using and turned around.

"If you love me," she said, "You can do this for me. If you don't love me, okay. But if you had a friend, any friend, and the friend came to visit, I'd make him feel comfortable." She wiped her hands with the dish towel.

"I don't have any blind friends," I said.

"You don't have *any* friends," she said, "Period. Besides," she said, "Goddamn it, his wife's just died! Don't you understand that? That man's lost his wife!"

I didn't answer. She'd told me a little about the blind man's wife. Her name was Beulah. Beulah! That's a name for a colored woman.

"Was his wife a Negro?" I asked.

"Are you crazy?" my wife said. "Have you just flipped or something?" She picked up a potato. I saw it hit the floor, then roll under the stove. "What's wrong with you?" she said. "Are you drunk?"

"I'm just asking," I said.

Right then my wife filled me in with more details than I cared to know. I made a drink and sat at the kitchen table to listen. Pieces of the story began to fall into place.

Beulah had gone to work for the blind man the summer after my wife had stopped working for him. Pretty soon Beulah and the blind man had themselves a church wedding. It was a little wedding—who'd want to go to such a wedding in the first place?—just the two of them, plus the minister and the minister's wife. But it was a church wedding just the same. It was what Beulah had wanted, he'd said. But even then Beulah must have been carrying the cancer in her glands. After they had been inseparable for eight years—my wife's word, *inseparable*—Beulah's health went into a rapid decline. She died in a Seattle hospital room, the blind man sitting beside the bed and holding on to her hand. They'd married, lived and worked together, slept together—had sex, sure—and then the blind man had to bury her. All this without his having ever seen what the goddamned woman looked like. It was beyond my understanding. Hearing this, I felt sorry for the blind man for a little bit. And then I found myself thinking what a pitiful life this woman must have led. Imagine a woman who could never see herself as she was seen in the eyes of her loved one. A woman who could go on day after day and never receive the smallest compliment from her beloved. A woman whose husband could never read the expression on her face, be it misery or something better. Someone who could wear makeup or not—what difference to him? She could, if she wanted, wear green eye-shadow around one eye, a straight pin in her nostril, yellow slacks and purple shoes, no matter. And then to slip off into death, the blind man's hand on her hand, his blind eyes streaming tears—I'm imagining now—her last thought maybe this: that he never even knew what she looked like, and she on an express to the grave. Robert was left with a small insurance policy and half of a twenty-peso Mexican coin. The other half of the coin went into the box with her. Pathetic.

So when the time rolled around, my wife went to the depot to pick him up. With nothing to do but wait—sure, I blamed him for that—I was having a drink and watching the TV when I heard the car pull into the drive. I got up from the sofa with my drink and went to the window to have a look.

I saw my wife laughing as she parked the car. I saw her get out of the car and shut the door. She was still wearing a smile. Just amazing. She went around to the other side of the car to where the blind man was already starting to get out. This blind man, feature this, he was wearing a full beard! A beard on a blind man! Too much, I say. The blind man reached into the back seat and dragged out a suitcase. My wife took his arm, shut the car door, and, talking all the way, moved him down the drive and then up the steps to the front porch. I turned off the TV. I finished my drink, rinsed the glass, dried my hands. Then I went to the door.

My wife said, "I want you to meet Robert. Robert, this is my husband. I've told you all about him." She was beaming. She had this blind man by his coat sleeve.

The blind man let go of his suitcase and up came his hand.

I took it. He squeezed hard, held my hand, and then he let it go.

"I feel like we've already met," he boomed.

"Likewise," I said. I didn't know what else to say. Then I said "Welcome. I've heard a lot about you." We began to move then, a little group, from the porch into the living room, my wife guiding him by the arm. The blind man was carrying his suitcase in his other hand. My wife said things like, "To your left here, Robert. That's right. Now watch it, there's a chair. That's it. Sit down right here. This is the sofa. We just bought this sofa two weeks ago."

I started to say something about the old sofa. I'd liked that old sofa. But I didn't say anything. Then I wanted to say something else, small talk, about the scenic ride along the Hudson. How going to New York, you should sit on the right-hand side of the train, and coming *from* New York, the left-hand side.

"Did you have a good train ride?" I said. "Which side of the train did you sit on, by the way?"

"What a question, which side!" my wife said. "What's it matter which side?" she said.

"I just asked," I said,

"Right side," the blind man said. "I hadn't been on a train in nearly forty years. Not since I was a kid. With my folks. That's been a long time. I'd nearly forgotten the sensation. I have winter in my beard now," he said. "So I've been told, anyway. Do I look distinguished, my dear?" the blind man said to my wife.

"You look distinguished, Robert," she said. "Robert," she said. "Robert, it's just so good to see you."

My wife finally took her eyes off the blind man and looked at me. I had the feeling she didn't like what she saw. I shrugged.

I've never met, or personally known, anyone who was blind. This blind man was late forties, a heavy-set, balding man with stooped shoulders, as if he carried a great weight there. He wore brown slacks, brown shoes, a light-brown shirt, a tie, a sports coat. Spiffy. He also had this full beard. But he didn't use a cane and he didn't wear dark glasses. I'd always thought dark glasses were a must for the blind. Fact was, I wished he had a pair. At first glance, his eyes looked like anyone else's eyes. But if you looked close, there was something different about them. Too much white in the iris, for one thing, and the pupils seemed to move around in the sockets without his knowing it or being able to stop it. Creepy. As I stared at his face, I saw the left pupil turn in toward his nose while the other made an effort to keep in one place. But it was only an effort, for that eye was on the roam without his knowing it or wanting it to be.

I said, "Let me get you a drink. What's your pleasure? We have a little of everything. It's one of our pastimes."

"Bub, I'm a Scotch man myself," he said fast enough in this big voice.

"Right," I said. Bub! "Sure you are. I knew it."

He let his fingers touch his suitcase, which was sitting alongside the sofa. He was taking his bearings. I didn't blame him for that.

"I'll move that up to your room," my wife said.

"No, that's fine," the blind man said loudly. "It can go up when I go up."

"A little water with the Scotch?" I said.

"Very little," he said.

"I knew it," I said.

He said, "Just a tad. The Irish actor Barry Fitzgerald? I'm like that fellow. When I drink water, Fitzgerald said, I drink water. When I drink whiskey, I drink whiskey." My wife laughed. The blind man brought his hand up under his beard. He lifted his beard slowly and let it drop.

I did the drinks, three big glasses of Scotch with a splash of water in each. Then we made ourselves comfortable and talked about Robert's travels. First the long flight from the West Coast to Connecticut, we covered that. Then from Connecticut up here by train. We had another drink concerning that leg of the trip.

I remembered having read somewhere that the blind didn't smoke because, as speculation had it, they couldn't see the smoke they exhaled. I thought I knew that much and that much only about blind people. But this blind man smoked his cigarette down to the nubbin and then lit another one. This blind man filled his ashtray and my wife emptied it.

When we sat down at the table for dinner, we had another drink. My wife heaped Robert's plate with cube steak, scalloped potatoes, green beans. I buttered him up two slices of bread. I said, "Here's bread and butter for you." I swallowed some of my drink. "Now let us pray," I said, and the blind man lowered his head. My wife looked at me, her mouth agape. "Pray the phone won't ring and food doesn't get cold," I said.

We dug in. We ate everything there was to eat on the table. We ate like there was no tomorrow. We didn't talk. We ate. We scarfed. We grazed that table. We were into serious eating. The blind man had right away located his foods, he knew just where everything was on his plate. I watched with admiration as he used his knife and fork on the meat. He'd cut two pieces of meat, fork the meat into his mouth, and then go all out for the scalloped potatoes, the beans next, and then he'd tear off a hunk of buttered bread and eat that. He'd follow this up with a big drink of milk. It didn't seem to bother him to use his fingers once in a while, either.

We finished everything including half a strawberry pie. For a few moments, we sat as if stunned. Sweat beaded on our faces. Finally, we got up from the table and left the dirty plates. We didn't look back. We took ourselves into the living room and sank into our places again. Robert and my wife sat on the sofa. I took the big chair. We had us two or three more drinks while they talked about the major things that had come to pass for them in the past ten years. For the most part, I just listened. Now and then I joined in. I didn't want him to think I'd left the room, and I didn't want her to think I was feeling left out. They talked of things that had happened to them—to them!—these past ten years. I waited in vain to hear my name on my wife's sweet lips. "And then my dear husband came into my life"—something like that. But I heard nothing of the sort. More talk of Robert. Robert had done a little of everything, it seemed, a regular blind jack-of-all-trades. But most recently he and his wife had had an Amway distributorship, from which, I gathered, they'd earned their living, such as it was. The blind man was also a ham radio operator. He talked in his loud voice about conversations he'd had with fellow operators in Guam, in the Philippines, in Alaska, and even in Tahiti. He said he'd have a lot of friends there if he ever wanted to go visit those places. From time to time, he'd turn his blind face toward me, put his hand under his beard, ask me something. How long had I been in my present position? (Three years.) Did I like my work? (I didn't.) Was I going to stay with it? (What were the options?) Finally, when I thought he was beginning to run down, I got up and turned on the TV.

My wife looked at me with irritation. She was heading toward a boil. Then she looked at the blind man and said, "Robert, do you have a TV?"

The blind man said, "My dear, I have two TVs. I have a color set and a black-and-white thing, an old relic. It's funny, but if I turn the TV on, and I'm always turning it on, I turn on the color set. It's funny, don't you think?"

I didn't know what to say to that. I had absolutely nothing to say to that. No opinion. So I watched the news program and tried to listen to what the announcer was saying.

"This is a color TV," the blind man said. "Don't ask me how but I can tell."

"We traded up a while ago," I said.

The blind man had another taste of his drink. He lifted his beard, sniffed it, and let it fall. He leaned forward on the sofa. He positioned his ashtray on the coffee table, then put the lighter to his cigarette. He leaned back on the sofa and crossed his legs at the ankles.

My wife covered her mouth, and then she yawned. She stretched. She said, "I think I'll go upstairs and put on my robe. I think I'll change into something else. Robert, you make yourself comfortable," she said.

"I'm comfortable," the blind man said.

"I want you to feel comfortable in this house," she said.

"I am comfortable," the blind man said.

After she'd left the room, he and I listened to the weather report and then to the sports roundup. By that time, she'd been gone so long I didn't know if she was going to come back. I thought she might have gone to bed. I wished she'd come back downstairs. I didn't want to be left alone with a blind man. I asked him if he wanted another drink, and he said sure. Then I asked if he wanted to smoke some dope with me. I said I'd just rolled a number. I hadn't, but I planned to do so in about two shakes.

"I'll try some with you," he said.

"Damn right," I said. "That's the stuff."

I got our drinks and sat down on the sofa with him. Then I rolled us two fat numbers. I lit one and passed it. I brought it to his fingers. He took it and inhaled.

"Hold it as long as you can," I said. I could tell he didn't know the first thing.

My wife came back downstairs wearing her pink robe and her pink slippers.

"What do I smell?" she said.

"We thought we'd have us some cannabis," I said.

My wife gave me a savage look. Then she looked at the blind man and said, "Robert, I didn't know you smoked."

He said, "I do now, my dear. There's a first time for everything. But I don't feel anything yet."

"This stuff is pretty mellow," I said. "This stuff is mild. It's dope you can reason with," I said. "It doesn't mess you up."

"Not much it doesn't, bub," he said, and laughed.

My wife sat on the sofa between the blind man and me. I passed her the number. She took it and toked and then passed it back to me. "Which way is this going?" she said. Then she said, "I shouldn't be smoking this. I can hardly keep my eyes open as it is. That dinner did me in. I shouldn't have eaten so much."

"It was the strawberry pie," the blind man said. "That's what did it," he said, and he laughed his big laugh. Then he shook his head.

"There's more strawberry pie," I said.

"Do you want some more, Robert?" my wife said.

"Maybe in a little while," he said.

We gave our attention to the TV. My wife yawned again. She said, "Your bed is made up when you feel like going to bed, Robert. I know you must have had a long day. When you're ready to go to bed, say so." She pulled his arm. "Robert?"

He came to and said "I've had a real nice time. This beats tapes, doesn't it?"

I said, "Coming at you," and I put the number between his fingers. He inhaled, held the smoke, and then let it go. It was like he'd been doing it since he was nine years old.

"Thanks, bub," he said. "But I think this is all for me. I think I'm beginning to feel it," he said. He held the burning roach out for my wife.

"Same here," she said. "Ditto. Me, too." She took the roach and passed it to me. "I may just sit here for a while between you two guys with my eyes closed. But don't let me bother you, okay? Either one of you. If it bothers you, say so. Otherwise, I may just sit here with my eyes closed until you're ready to go to bed," she said. "Your bed's made up, Robert, when you're ready. It's right next to our room at the top of the stairs. We'll show you up when you're ready. You wake me up now, you guys, if I fall asleep." She said that and then she closed her eyes and went to sleep.

The news program ended. I got up and changed the channel. I sat back down on the sofa. I wished my wife hadn't pooped out. Her head lay across the back of the sofa, her mouth open. She'd turned so that her robe had slipped away from her legs, exposing a juicy thigh. I reached to draw her robe back over her, and it was then that I glanced at the blind man. What the hell! I flipped the robe open again.

"You say when you want some strawberry pie," I said.

"I will," he said.

I said, "Are you tired? Do you want me to take you up to your bed? Are you ready to hit the hay?"

"Not yet," he said. "No, I'll stay up with you, bub. If that's all right. I'll stay up until you're ready to turn in. We haven't had a chance to talk. Know what I mean? I feel like me and her monopolized the evening." He lifted his beard and he let it fall. He picked up his cigarettes and his lighter.

"That's all right," I said. Then I said, "I'm glad for the company."

And I guess I was. Every night I smoked dope and stayed up as long as I could before I fell asleep. My wife and I hardly ever went to bed at the same time. When I did go to sleep, I had these dreams. Sometimes I'd wake up from one of them, my heart going crazy.

Something about the church and the Middle Ages was on the TV. Not your run-of-the-mill TV fare. I wanted to watch something else. I turned to the other channels. But there was nothing on them, either. So I turned back to the first channel and apologized.

"Bub, it's all right," the blind man said. "It's fine with me. Whatever you want to watch is okay. I'm always learning something. Learning never ends. It won't hurt me to learn something tonight. I got ears," he said.

We didn't say anything for a time. He was leaning forward with his head turned at me, his right ear aimed in the direction of the set. Very disconcerting. Now and then his eyelids drooped and then they snapped open again. Now and then he put his fingers into his beard and tugged, like he was thinking about something he was hearing on the television.

On the screen, a group of men wearing cowls was being set upon and tormented by men dressed in skeleton costumes and men dressed as devils. The men dressed as devils wore devil masks, horns, and long tails. This pageant was part of a procession. The Englishman who was narrating the thing said it took place in Spain once a year. I tried to explain to the blind man what was happening.

"Skeletons," he said. "I know about skeletons," he said, and he nodded.

The TV showed this one cathedral. Then there was a long, slow look at another one. Finally, the picture switched to the famous one in Paris, with its flying buttresses and its spires reaching up to the clouds. The camera pulled away to show the whole of the cathedral rising above the skyline.

There were times when the Englishman who was telling the thing would shut up, would simply let the camera move around over the cathedrals. Or else the camera would tour the countryside, men in the fields walking behind oxen. I waited as long as I could. Then I felt I had to say something. I said, "They're showing the outside of this cathedral now. Gargoyles. Little statues carved to look like monsters. Now I guess they're in Italy. Yeah, they're in Italy. There's paintings on the walls of this one church."

"Are those fresco paintings, bub?" he asked, and he sipped from his drink.

I reached for my glass. But it was empty. I tried to remember what I could remember. "You're asking me are those frescoes?" I said. "That's a good question. I don't know."

The camera moved to a cathedral outside Lisbon. The differences in the Portuguese cathedral compared with the French and Italian were not that great. But they were there. Mostly the interior stuff. Then something occurred to me, and I said, "Something has occurred to me. Do you have any idea what a cathedral is? What they look like, that is? Do you follow me? If somebody says cathedral to you, do you have any notion what they're talking about? Do you know the difference between that and a Baptist church, say?"

He let the smoke dribble from his mouth. "I know they took hundreds of workers fifty or a hundred years to build," he said. "I just heard the man say that, of course. I know generations of the same families worked on a cathedral. I heard him say that, too. Then men who began their life's work on them, they never lived to see the completion of their work. In that wise, bub, they're no different from the rest of us, right?" He laughed. Then his eyelids drooped again. His head nodded. He seemed to be snoozing. Maybe he was imagining himself in Portugal. The TV was showing another cathedral now. This one was in Germany. The Englishman's voice droned on. "Cathedrals," the blind man said. He sat up and rolled his head back and forth. "If you want the truth, bub; that's about all I know. What I just said. What I heard him say. But maybe you could describe one to me? I wish you'd do it. I'd like that. If you want to know, I really don't have a good idea."

I stared hard at the shot of the cathedral on the TV. How could I even begin to describe it? But say my life depended on it. Say my life was being threatened by an insane guy who said I had to do it or else.

I stared some more at the cathedral before the picture flipped off into the countryside. There was no use. I turned to the blind man and said, "To begin with, they're very tall." I was looking around the room for clues. "They reach way up. Up and up. Toward the sky. They're so big, some of them, they have to have these supports. To help hold them up, so to speak. These supports are called buttresses. They remind me of viaducts, for some reason. But maybe you don't know viaducts, either? Sometimes the cathedrals have devils and such carved into the front. Sometimes lords and ladies. Don't ask me why this is," I said.

He was nodding. The whole upper part of his body seemed to be moving back and forth.

"I'm not doing so good, am I?" I said.

He stopped nodding and leaned forward on the edge of the sofa. As he listened to me, he was running his fingers through his beard. I wasn't getting through to him, I could see that. But he waited for me to go on just the same. He nodded; like he was trying to encourage me. I tried to think what else to say. "They're really big," I said. "They're massive. They're built of stone. Marble, too, sometimes. In those olden days, when they built cathedrals, men wanted to be close to God. In those olden days, God was an important part of everyone's life. You could tell this from their cathedral building. I'm sorry," I said, "but it looks like that's the best I can do for you. I'm just no good at it."

"That's all right, bub," the blind man said. "Hey, listen. I hope you don't mind my asking you. Can I ask you something? Let me ask you a simple question, yes or no. I'm just curious and there's no offense. You're my host. But let me ask if you are in any way religious? You don't mind my asking?"

I shook my head. He couldn't see that, though. A wink is the same as a nod to a blind man. "I guess I don't believe in it. In anything. Sometimes it's hard. You know what I'm saying?"

"Sure, I do," he said.

"Right," I said.

The Englishman was still holding forth. My wife sighed in her sleep. She drew a long breath and went on with her sleeping.

"You'll have to forgive me," I said. "But I can't tell you what a cathedral looks like. It just isn't in me to do it. I can't do any more than I've done."

The blind man sat very still, his head down, as he listened to me.

I said, "The truth is, cathedrals don't mean anything special to me. Nothing. Cathedrals. They're something to look at on late-night TV. That's all they are."

It was then that the blind man cleared his throat. He brought something up. He took a handkerchief from his back pocket. Then he said, "I get it, bub. It's okay. It happens. Don't worry about it," he said. "Hey, listen to me. Will you do me a favor? I got an idea. Why don't you find us some heavy paper? And a pen. We'll do something. We'll draw one together. Get us a pen and some heavy paper. Go on, bub, get the stuff," he said.

So I went upstairs. My legs felt like they didn't have any strength in them. They felt like they did after I'd done some running. In my wife's room, I looked around. I found some ballpoints in a little basket on her table. And then I tried to think where to look for the kind of paper he was talking about.

Downstairs, in the kitchen, I found a shopping bag with onion skins in the bottom of the bag. I emptied the bag and shook it. I brought it into the living room and sat down with it near his legs. I moved some things, smoothed the wrinkles from the bag, spread it out on the coffee table.

The blind man got down from the sofa and sat next to me on the carpet.

He ran his fingers over the paper. He went up and down the sides of the paper. The edges, even the edges. He fingered the corners.

"All right," he said. "All right, let's do her."

He found my hand, the hand with the pen. He closed his hand over my hand. "Go ahead, bub, draw," he said. "Draw. You'll see. I'll follow along with you. It'll be okay. Just begin now like I'm telling you. You'll see. Draw," the blind man said.

So I began. First I drew a box that looked like a house. It could have been the house I lived in. Then I put a roof on it. At either end of the roof, I drew spires. Crazy.

"Swell," he said. "Terrific. You're doing fine," he said. "Never thought anything like this could happen in your lifetime, did you, bub? Well, it's a strange life, we all know that. Go on now. Keep it up."

I put in windows with arches. I drew flying buttresses. I hung great doors. I couldn't stop. The TV station went off the air. I put down the pen and closed and opened my fingers. The blind man felt around over the paper. He moved the tips of his fingers over the paper, all over what I had drawn, and he nodded.

"Doing fine," the blind man said.

I took up the pen again, and he found my hand. I kept at it. I'm no artist. But I kept drawing just the same.

My wife opened up her eyes and gazed at us. She sat up on the sofa, her robe hanging open. She said, "What are you doing? Tell me, I want to know."

I didn't answer her.

The blind man said, "We're drawing a cathedral. Me and him are working on it. Press hard," he said to me. "That's right. That's good," he said. "Sure. You got it, bub. I can tell. You didn't think you could. But you can, can't you? You're cooking with gas now. You know what I'm saying? We're going to really have us something here in a minute. How's the old arm?" he said "Put some people in there now. What's a cathedral without people?"

My wife said, "What's going on? Robert, what are you doing? What's going on?"

"It's all right," he said to her. "Close your eyes now," the blind man said to me.

I did it. I closed them just like he said.

"Are they closed?" he said. "Don't fudge."

"They're closed," I said.

"Keep them that way," he said. He said, "Don't stop now. Draw."

So we kept on with it. His fingers rode my fingers as my hand went over the paper. It was like nothing else in my life up to now.

Then he said, "I think that's it. I think you got it," he said. "Take a look. What do you think?"

But I had my eyes closed. I thought I'd keep them that way for a little longer. I thought it was something I ought to do.

"Well?" he said. "Are you looking?"

My eyes were still closed. I was in my house. I knew that. But I didn't feel like I was inside anything.

"It's really something," I said.

⁂ AMY HEMPEL
(1951– )

Dr. William Carlos Williams' famous poem "The Red Wheelbarrow" begins: "so much depends/upon," and is then followed by a twelve-word verbal snapshot of a yard scene. Something analogous can be applied to the fiction of Amy Hempel, which truly makes brevity the soul of her wit. Influenced by such writers as Raymond Carver, Hempel writes fiction that is an art of compression. She attempts to see what is there clearly, even if what is there is so frequently sad and painful. Even so, the exactitude of her perceptions of our risk-filled world is tempered by humor and small acts of love and courage.

Hempel was born in Chicago but grew up in California, where she attended four colleges before moving to New York City to attend one more. A fiction workshop at Columbia University in 1982 with the editor Gordon Lish led to her publishing her first collection of stories, *Reasons to Live,* in 1985. Her work has appeared in such periodicals as *Esquire, Harper's, Vanity Fair,* and *Vogue.* Her second collection, *At the Gates of the Animal Kingdom,* was published in 1990, and *Tumble Home: A Novella and Short Stories* appeared in 1997. She lives with her husband in New York City.

·hospital. Death, fear of death,

## In the Cemetery Where Al Jolson Is Buried

"TELL ME things I won't mind forgetting," she said. "Make it useless stuff or skip it."

I began. I told her insects fly through rain missing every drop, never getting wet. I told her no one in America owned a tape recorder before Bing Crosby did. I told her the shape of the moon is like a banana—you see it looking full, you're seeing it end-on.

The camera made me self-conscious and I stopped. It was trained on us from a ceiling mount—the kind of camera banks use to photograph robbers. It played us to the nurses down the hall in Intensive Care.

"Go on, girl," she said. "You get used to it."

I had my audience. I went on. Did she know that Tammy Wynette had changed her tune? Really. That now she sings "Stand By Your Friends"? That Paul Anka did it too, I said. Does "You're Having *Our* Baby." That he got sick of all that feminist bitching.

"What else?" she said. "Have you got something else?"

Oh, yes.

For her I would always have something else.

"Did you know that when they taught the first chimp to talk, it lied? That when they asked her who did it on the desk, she signed back Max, the janitor. And that when they pressed her, she said she was sorry, that it was really the project director. But she was a mother, so I guess she had her reasons."

"Oh, that's good," she said. "A parable."

"There's more about the chimp," I said. "But it will break your heart."

"No, thanks," she says, and scratches at her mask.

* * *

We look like good-guy outlaws. Good or bad, I am not used to the mask yet. I keep touching the warm spot where my breath, thank God, comes out. She is used to hers. She only ties the strings on top. The other ones—a pro by now—she lets hang loose.

We call this place the Marcus Welby Hospital. It's the white one with the palm trees under the opening credits of all those shows. A Hollywood hospital, though in fact it is several miles west. Off camera, there is a beach across the street.

* * *

She introduces me to a nurse as the Best Friend. The impersonal article is more intimate. It tells me that *they* are intimate, the nurse and my friend.

"I was telling her we used to drink Canada Dry ginger ale and pretend we were in Canada."

"That's how dumb *we* were," I say.

"You could be sisters," the nurse says.

So how come, I'll bet they are wondering, it took me so long to get to such a glamorous place? But do they ask?

They do not ask.

Two months, and how long is the drive?

The best I can explain it is this—I have a friend who worked one summer in a mortuary. He used to tell me stories. The one that really got to me was not the grisliest, but it's the one that did. A man wrecked his car on 101 going south. He did not lose consciousness. But his arm was taken down to the wet bone—and when he looked at it—it scared him to death.

I mean, he died.

So I hadn't dared to look any closer. But now I'm doing it—and hoping that I will live through it.

* * *

She shakes out a summer-weight blanket, showing a leg you did not want to see. Except for that, you look at her and understand the law that requires two people to be with the body at all times.

"I thought of something," she says. "I thought of it last night. I think there is a real and present need here. You know," she says, "like for someone to do it for you when you can't do it yourself. You call them up whenever you want—like when push comes to shove."

She grabs the bedside phone and loops the cord around her neck.

"Hey," she says, "the end o' the line."

She keeps on, giddy with something. But I don't know with what.

"I can't remember," she says. "What does Kübler-Ross say comes after Denial?"

It seems to me Anger must be next. Then Bargaining, Depression, and so on and so forth. But I keep my guesses to myself.

"The only thing is," she says, "is where's Resurrection? God knows, I want to do it by the book. But she left out Resurrection."

* * *

She laughs, and I cling to the sound the way someone dangling above a ravine holds fast to the thrown rope.

"Tell me," she says, "about that chimp with the talking hands. What do they do when the thing ends and the chimp says, 'I don't want to go back to the zoo'?"

When I don't say anything, she says, "Okay—then tell me another animal story. I like animal stories. But not a sick one—I don't want to know about all the seeing-eye dogs going blind."

No, I would not tell her a sick one.

"How about the hearing-ear dogs?" I say. "They're not going deaf, but they are getting very judgmental. For instance, there's this golden retriever in New Jersey, he wakes up the deaf mother and drags her into the daughter's room because the kid has got a flashlight and is reading under the covers."

"Oh, you're killing me," she says. "Yes, you're definitely killing me."

"They say the smart dog obeys, but the smarter dog knows when to disobey."

"Yes," she says, "the smarter anything knows when to disobey. Now, for example."

* * *

She is flirting with the Good Doctor, who has just appeared. Unlike the Bad Doctor, who checks the I.V. drip before saying good morning, the Good Doctor says things like "God didn't give epileptics a fair shake." The Good Doctor awards himself points for the cripples he could have hit in the parking lot. Because the Good Doctor is a little in love with her, he says maybe a year. He pulls a chair up to her bed and suggests I might like to spend an hour on the beach.

"Bring me something back," she says. "Anything from the beach. Or the gift shop. Taste is no object."

He draws the curtain around her bed.

"Wait!" she cries.

I look in at her.

"Anything," she says, "except a magazine subscription."

The doctor turns away.

I watch her mouth laugh.

* * *

What seems dangerous often is not—black snakes, for example, or clear-air turbulence. While things that just lie there, like this beach, are loaded with jeopardy. A yellow dust rising from the ground, the heat that ripens melons overnight—this is earthquake weather. You can sit here braiding the fringe on your towel and the sand will all of a sudden suck down like an hourglass. The air roars. In the cheap apartments on-shore, bathtubs fill themselves and gardens roll up and over like green waves. If nothing happens, the dust will drift and the heat deepen till fear turns to desire. Nerves like that are only bought off by catastrophe.

* * *

"It never happens when you're thinking about it," she once observed. "Earthquake, earthquake, earthquake," she said.

"Earthquake, earthquake, earthquake," I said.

Like the aviaphobe who keeps the plane aloft with prayer, we kept it up until an aftershock cracked the ceiling.

That was after the big one in '72. We were in college; our dormitory was five miles from the epicenter. When the ride was over and my jabbering pulse began to slow, she served five parts champagne to one part orange juice, and joked about living in Ocean View, Kansas. I offered to drive her to Hawaii on the new world psychics predicted would surface the next time, or the next.

I could not say that now—next.

Who's next? she could ask.

* * *

Was I the only one who noticed that the experts had stopped saying *if* and now spoke of *when?* Of course not; the fearful ran to thousands. We watched the traffic of Japanese beetles for deviation. Deviation might mean more natural violence.

I wanted her to be afraid with me. But she said, "I don't know. I'm just not."

She was afraid of nothing, not even of flying.

I have this dream before a flight where we buckle in and the plane moves down the runway. It takes off at thirty-five miles an hour, and then we're airborne, skimming the tree tops. Still, we arrive in New York on time.

It is so pleasant.

One night I flew to Moscow this way.

* * *

She flew with me once. That time she flew with me she ate macadamia nuts while the wings bounced. She knows the wing tips can bend thirty feet up and thirty feet down without coming off. She believes it. She trusts the laws of aerodynamics. My mind stampedes. I can almost accept that a battleship floats when everybody knows steel sinks.

I see fear in her now, and am not going to try to talk her out of it. She is right to be afraid.

After a quake, the six o'clock news airs a film clip of first-graders yelling at the broken playground per their teacher's instructions.

"*Bad* earth!" they shout, because anger is stronger than fear.

* * *

But the beach is standing still today. Everyone on it is tranquilized, numb, or asleep. Teenaged girls rub coconut oil on each other's hard-to-reach places. They smell like macaroons. They pry open compacts like clamshells; mirrors catch the sun and throw a spray of white rays across glazed shoulders. The girls arrange their wet hair with silk flowers the way they learned in *Seventeen.* They pose.

A formation of low-riders pulls over to watch with a six-pack. They get vocal when the girls check their tan lines. When the beer is gone, so are they—flexing their cars on up the boulevard.

Above this aggressive health are the twin wrought-iron terraces, painted flamingo pink, of the Palm Royale. Someone dies there every time the sheets are changed. There's an ambulance in the driveway, so the remaining residents line the balconies, rocking and not talking, one-upped.

The ocean they stare at is dangerous, and not just the undertow. You can almost see the slapping tails of sand sharks keeping cruising bodies alive.

If she looked, she could see this, some of it, from her window. She would be the first to say how little it takes to make a thing all wrong.

* * *

There was a second bed in the room when I got back to it!

For two beats I didn't get it. Then it hit me like an open coffin.

She wants every minute, I thought. She wants my life.

"You missed Gussie," she said.

Gussie is her parents' three-hundred-pound, narcoleptic maid. Her attacks often come at the ironing board. The pillowcases in that family are all bordered with scorch.

"It's a hard trip for her," I said. "How is she?"

"Well, she didn't fall asleep, if that's what you mean. Gussie's great—you know what she said? She said, 'Darlin, stop this worriation. Just keep prayin, down on your knees'—me, who can't even get out of bed."

She shrugged. "What am I missing?"

"It's earthquake weather," I told her.

"The best thing to do about earthquakes," she said, "is not to live in California."

"That's useful," I said. "You sound like Reverend Ike—'The best thing to do for the poor is not be one of them.' "

We're crazy about Reverend Ike.

I noticed her face was bloated.

"You know," she said, "I feel like hell. I'm about to stop having fun."

* * *

"The ancients have a saying," I said. "'There are times when the wolves are silent; there are times when the moon howls.'"

"What's that, Navajo?"

"Palm Royale lobby graffiti," I said. "I bought a paper there. I'll read you something."

"Even though I care about nothing?"

I turned to the page with the trivia column. I said, "Did you know the more shrimp flamingo birds eat, the pinker their feathers get?" I said, "Did you know that Eskimos need refrigerators? Do you know *why* Eskimos need refrigerators? Did you know that Eskimos need refrigerators because how else would they keep their food from freezing?"

I turned to page three, to a UPI filler datelined Mexico City. I read her "Man Robs Bank with Chicken," about a man who bought a barbecued chicken at a stand down the block from a bank. Passing the bank, he got the idea. He walked in and approached a teller. He pointed the brown paper bag at her and she handed over the day's receipts. It was the smell of barbecue sauce that eventually led to his capture.

* * *

The story had made her hungry, she said—so I took the elevator down six floors to the cafeteria, and brought back all the ice cream she wanted. We lay side by side, adjustable beds cranked up for optimal TV-viewing, littering the sheets with Good Humor wrappers, picking toasted almonds out of the gauze. We were Lucy and Ethel, Mary and Rhoda in extremis. The blinds were closed to keep light off the screen.

We watched a movie starring men we used to think we wanted to sleep with. Hers was a tough cop out to stop mine, a vicious rapist who went after cocktail waitresses.

"This is a good movie," she said when snipers felled them both.

I missed her already.

* * *

A Filipino nurse tiptoed in and gave her an injection. The nurse removed the pile of popsicle sticks from the nightstand—enough to splint a small animal.

The injection made us both sleepy. We slept.

I dreamed she was a decorator, come to furnish my house. She worked in secret, singing to herself. When she finished, she guided me proudly to the door. "How do you like it?" she asked, easing me inside.

Every beam and sill and shelf and knob was draped in gay bunting, with streamers of pastel crepe looped around bright mirrors.

* * *

"I have to go home," I said when she woke up.

She thought I meant home to her house in the Canyon, and I had to say No, *home* home. I twisted my hands in the time-honored fashion of people in pain. I was supposed to offer something. The Best Friend. I could not even offer to come back.

I felt weak and small and failed.

Also exhilarated.

I had a convertible in the parking lot. Once out of that room, I would drive it too fast down the Coast highway through the crab-smelling air. A stop in Malibu for sangria. The music in the place would be sexy and loud. They'd serve papaya and shrimp and watermelon ice. After dinner I would shimmer with lust, buzz with heat, vibrate with life, and stay up all night.

* * *

Without a word, she yanked off her mask and threw it on the floor. She kicked at the blankets and moved to the door. She must have hated having to pause for breath and balance before slamming out of Isolation, and out of the second room, the one where you scrub and tie on the white masks.

A voice shouted her name in alarm, and people ran down the corridor. The Good Doctor was paged over the intercom. I opened the door and the nurses at the station stared hard, as if this flight had been my idea.

"Where is she?" I asked, and they nodded to the supply closet.

I looked in. Two nurses were kneeling beside her on the floor, talking to her in low voices. One held a mask over her nose and mouth, the other rubbed her back in slow circles. The nurses glanced up to see if I was the doctor—and when I wasn't, they went back to what they were doing.

"There, there, honey," they cooed.

* * *

On the morning she was moved to the cemetery, the one where Al Jolson is buried, I enrolled in a Fear of Flying class. "What is your worst fear?" the instructor asked, and I answered, "That I will finish this course and still be afraid."

* * *

I sleep with a glass of water on the nightstand so I can see by its level if the coastal earth is trembling or if the shaking is still me.

* * *

What do I remember?

I remember only the useless things I hear—that Bob Dylan's mother invented Wite-Out, that twenty-three people must be in a room before there is a fifty-fifty chance two will have the same birthdate. Who cares whether or not it's true? In my head there are bath towels swaddling this stuff. Nothing else seeps through.

I review those things that will figure in the re-telling: a kiss through surgical gauze, the pale hand correcting the position of the wig. I noted these gestures as they happened, not in any retrospect—though I do not know why looking back should show us more than looking at.

It is just possible I will say I stayed the night.

And who is there that can say that I did not?

* * *

I think of the chimp, the one with the talking hands.

In the course of the experiment, that chimp had a baby. Imagine how her trainers must have thrilled when the mother, without prompting, began to sign to her newborn.

Baby, drink milk.

Baby, play ball.

And when the baby died, the mother stood over the body, her wrinkled hands moving with animal grace, forming again and again the words, Baby, come hug, Baby, come hug, fluent now in the language of grief.

# ⁂ RON HANSEN
(1947– )

Ron Hansen was born in Omaha, Nebraska, where his father was an electrical engineer and his mother a stenographer. He earned a B.A. in English at Creighton University in 1970, and then served as a lieutenant in the U.S. Army. He completed an M.F.A. at the Writers' Workshop of the University of Iowa in 1974, where his teachers were John Irving and John Cheever. He did further graduate study at Standford University on a Wallace Stegner Creative Writing Fellowship in 1977–1978. He taught at several universities before going to the University of California at Santa Cruz in 1989, where he is now the Gerard Manley Hopkins Professor of Writing.

Hansen's first novel, *Desperadoes,* was published in 1979, and was followed by *The Assassination of Jesse James by the Coward Robert Ford* in 1983, *Mariette in Ecstasy* in 1991, *Mexican Mystery* in 1993, *Atticus* in 1996, and *Hitler's Niece* in 1999. Crossing borders and blending genres, Hansen's fiction ranges widely in theme and setting and reflects his deep interest in the essentially religious issues of human sinfulness and redemption, as well as the mysteries of love and forgiveness.

## Wickedness

AT THE end of the nineteenth century a girl from Delaware got on a milk train in Omaha and took a green wool seat in the second-class car. August was outside the window, and sunlight was a yellow glare on the trees. Up front, a railway conductor in a navy-blue uniform was gingerly backing down the aisle with a heavy package in a gunnysack that a boy was helping him with. They were talking about an agreeable seat away from the hot Nebraska day that was persistent outside, and then they were setting their cargo across the runnered aisle from the girl and tilting it against the shellacked wooden wall of the railway car before walking back up the aisle and elsewhere into August.

She was sixteen years old and an Easterner just recently hired as a county schoolteacher, but she knew enough about prairie farming to think the heavy package was a crank-and-piston washing machine or a boxed plowshare and coulter, something no higher than the bloody stump where the poultry were chopped with a hatchet and then wildly high-stepped around the yard. Soon, however, there was a juggling movement and the gunnysack slipped aside, and she saw an old man sitting there, his limbs hacked away, and dark holes where his ears ought to have been, the skin pursed at his jaw hinge like pink lips in a kiss. The milk train jerked into a roll through the railway yard, and the old man was jounced so that his gray cheek pressed against the hot window glass. Although he didn't complain, it seemed an uneasy position, and the girl wished she had the courage to get up from her seat and tug the jolting body upright. She instead got to her page in *Quo Vadis* and pretended to be so rapt by the book that she didn't look up again until Columbus, where a doctor with liquorice on his breath sat heavily beside her and openly stared over his newspaper before whispering that the poor man was a carpenter in Genoa who'd been caught out in the great blizzard of 1888. Had she heard of that one?

The girl shook her head.

She ought to look out for their winters, the doctor said. Weather in Nebraska could be the wickedest thing she ever saw.

She didn't know what to say, so she said nothing. And at Genoa a young teamster got on in order to carry out the old man, whose half body was heavy enough that the boy had to yank the gunnysack up the aisle like sixty pounds of mail.

* * *

In the year 1888, on the twelfth day of January, a pink sun was up just after seven and southeastern zephyrs of such soft temperature were sailing over the Great Plains that squatters walked their properties in high rubber boots and April jackets and some farmhands took off their Civil War greatcoats to rake silage into the cattle troughs. However, sheep that ate whatever they could the night before raised their heads away from food and sniffed the salt tang in the air. And all that morning streetcar mules were reported to be acting up, nipping each other, jingling the hitch rings, foolishly waggling their dark manes and necks as though beset by gnats and horseflies.

A Danish cattleman named Axel Hansen later said he was near the Snake River and tipping a teaspoon of saleratus into a yearling's mouth when he heard a faint groaning in the north that was like the noise of a high waterfall at a fair distance. Axel looked toward Dakota, and there half the sky was suddenly gray and black and indigo blue with great storm clouds that were seething up as high as the sun and wrangling toward him at horse speed. Weeds were being uprooted, sapling trees were bullwhipping, and the top inches of snow and prairie soil were being sucked up and stirred like the dirty flour that was called red dog. And then the onslaught hit him hard as furniture, flying him onto his back so that when Axel looked up, he seemed to be deep undersea and in icehouse cold. Eddying snow made it hard to breathe any way but sideways, and getting up to just his knees and hands seemed a great attainment. Although his sod house was but a quarter-mile away, it took Axel four hours to get there. Half his face was frozen gray and hard as weatherboarding so the cattleman was speechless until nightfall, and then Axel Hansen simply told his wife, That was not pleasant.

Cow tails stuck out sideways when the wind caught them. Sparrows and crows whumped hard against the windowpanes, their jerking eyes seeking out an escape, their wings fanned out and flattened as though pinned up in an ornithologist's display. Cats died, dogs died, pigeons died. Entire farms of cattle and pigs and geese and chickens were wiped out in a single night. Horizontal snow that was hard and dry as salt dashed and seethed over everything, sloped up like rooftops, tricked its way across creek beds and ditches, milkily purled down city streets, stole shanties and coops and pens from a bleak landscape that was even then called the Great American Desert. Everything about the blizzard seemed to have personality and hateful intention. Especially the cold. At six A.M., the temperature at Valentine, Nebraska, was thirty degrees above zero. Half a day later the temperature was fourteen below, a drop of forty-four degrees and the difference between having toes and not, between staying alive overnight and not, between ordinary concerns and one overriding idea.

Ainslie Classen was hopelessly lost in the whiteness and tilting low under the jamming gale when his right elbow jarred against a joist of his pigsty. He walked around the sty by skating his sore red hands along the upright shiplap and then squeezed inside through the slops trough. The pigs scampered over to him, seeking his protection, and Ainslie put himself among them, getting down in their stink and their body heat, socking them away only when they ganged up or when two or three presumed he was food. Hurt was nailing into his finger joints until he thought to work his hands into the pigs' hot wastes, then smeared some onto his skin. The pigs grunted around him and intelligently snuffled at his body with their pink and tender noses, and Ainslie thought, *You are not me but I am you,* and Ainslie Classen got through the night without shame or injury.

Whereas a Hartington woman took two steps out her door and disappeared until the snow sank away in April and raised her body up from her garden patch.

An Omaha cigar maker got off the Leavenworth Street trolley that night, fifty yards from his own home and five yards from another's. The completeness of the blizzard so puzzled him that the cigar maker tramped up and down the block more than twenty times and then slept against a lamppost and died.

A cattle inspector froze to death getting up on his quarter horse. The next morning he was still tilting the saddle with his upright weight, one cowboy boot just inside the iced stirrup, one bear-paw mitten over the horn and reins. His quarter horse apparently kept waiting for him to complete his mount, and then the quarter horse died too.

A Chicago boy visiting his brother for the holidays was going to a neighbor's farm to borrow a scoop shovel when the night train of blizzard raged in and overwhelmed him. His tracks showed the boy mistakenly slanted past the sod house he'd just come from, and then tilted forward with perhaps the vain hope of running into some shop or shed or railway depot. His body was found four days later and twenty-seven miles from home.

A forty-year-old wife sought out her husband in the open range land near O'Neill and days later was found standing up in her muskrat coat and black bandanna, her scarf-wrapped hands tightly clenching the top strand of rabbit wire that was keeping her upright, her blue eyes still open but cloudily bottled by a half inch of ice, her jaw unhinged as though she'd died yelling out a name.

The one A.M. report from the Chief Signal Officer in Washington, D.C., had said Kansas and Nebraska could expect "fair weather, followed by snow, brisk to high southerly winds gradually diminishing in force, becoming westerly and warmer, followed by colder."

* * *

Sin Thomas undertook the job of taking Emily Flint home from their Holt County schoolhouse just before noon. Sin's age was sixteen, and Emily was not only six years younger but also practically kin to him, since her stepfather was Sin's older brother. Sin took the girl's hand and they haltingly tilted against the uprighting gale on their walk to a dark horse, gray-maned and gray-tailed with ice. Sin cracked the reins loose of the crowbar tie-up and helped Emily up onto his horse, jumping up onto the croup from a soapbox and clinging the girl to him as though she were groceries he couldn't let spill.

Everything she knew was no longer there. She was in a book without descriptions. She could put her hand out and her hand would disappear. Although Sin knew the general direction to Emily's house, the geography was so duned and drunk with snow that Sin gave up trying to nudge his horse one way or another and permitted its slight adjustments away from the wind. Hours passed and the horse strayed southeast into Wheeler County, and then in misery and pneumonia it stopped, planting its overworked legs like four parts of an argument and slinging its head away from Sin's yanks and then hanging its nose in anguish. Emily hopped down into the snow and held on to the boy's coat pocket as Sin uncinched the saddle and jerked off a green horse blanket and slapped it against his iron leggings in order to crack the ice from it. And then Sin scooped out a deep nook in a snow slope that was as high and steep as the roof of a New Hampshire house. Emily tightly wrapped herself in the green horse blanket and slumped inside the nook in the snow, and the boy crept on top of her and stayed like that, trying not to press into her.

Emily would never say what was said or was cautiously not said that night. She may have been hysterical. In spite of the fact that Emily was out of the wind, she later said that the January night's temperature was like wire-cutting pliers that snipped at her ears and toes and fingertips until the horrible pain became only a nettling and then a kind of sleep and her feet seemed as dead as her shoes. Emily wept, but her tears froze cold as penny nails and her upper lip seemed candlewaxed by her nose and she couldn't stop herself from feeling the difference in the body on top of her. She thought Sin Thomas was responsible, that the night suited his secret purpose, and she so complained of the bitter cold that Sin finally took off his Newmarket overcoat and tailored it around the girl; but sixty years later, when Emily wrote her own account of the ordeal, she forgot to say anything about him giving her his overcoat and only said in an ordinary way that they spent the night inside a snowdrift and that "by morning the storm had subsided."

With daybreak Sin told Emily to stay there and, with or without his Newmarket overcoat, the boy walked away with the forlorn hope of chancing upon his horse. Winds were still high, the temperature was thirty-five degrees below zero, and the snow was deep enough that Sin pulled lopsidedly with every step and then toppled over just a few yards away. And then it was impossible for him to get to his knees, and Sin only sank deeper when he attempted to swim up into the high wave of snow hanging over him. Sin told himself that he would try again to get out, but first he'd build up his strength by napping for just a little while. He arranged his body in the snow gully so that the sunlight angled onto it, and then Sin Thomas gave in to sleep and within twenty minutes died.

His body was discovered at noon by a Wheeler County search party, and shortly after that they came upon Emily. She was carried to a nearby house where she slumped in a kitchen chair while girls her own age dipped Emily's hands and feet into pans of ice water. She could look up over a windowsill and see Sin Thomas's body standing upright on the porch, his hands woodenly crossed at his chest, so Emily kept her brown eyes on the pinewood floor and slept that night with jars of hot water against her skin. She could not walk for two months. Even scissoring tired her hands. She took a cashier's job with the Nebraska Farm Implements Company and kept it for forty-five years, staying all her life in Holt County. She died in a wheelchair on a hospital porch in the month of April. She was wearing a glamorous sable coat. She never married.

* * *

The T. E. D. Schusters' only child was a seven-year-old boy named Cleo who rode his Shetland pony to the Westpoint school that day and had not shown up on the doorstep by two P.M., when Mr. Schuster went down into the root cellar, dumped purple sugar beets onto the earthen floor, and upended the bushel basket over his head as he slung himself against the onslaught in his second try for Westpoint. Hours later Mrs. Schuster was tapping powdered salt onto the night candles in order to preserve the wax when the door abruptly blew open and Mr. Schuster stood there without Cleo and utterly white and petrified with cold. She warmed him up with okra soup and tenderly wrapped his frozen feet and hands in strips of gauze that she'd dipped in kerosene, and they were sitting on milking stools by a red-hot stove, their ankles just touching, only the usual sentiments being expressed, when they heard a clopping on the wooden stoop and looked out to see the dark Shetland pony turned gray and shaggy-bearded with ice, his legs as wobbly as if he'd just been born. Jammed under the saddle skirt was a damp, rolled-up note from the Scottish schoolteacher that said, Cleo is safe. The Schusters invited the pony into the house and bewildered him with praises as Cleo's mother scraped ice from the pony's shag with her own ivory comb, and Cleo's father gave him sugar from the Dresden bowl as steam rose up from the pony's back.

* * *

Even at six o'clock that evening, there was no heat in Mathias Aachen's house, and the seven Aachen children were in whatever stockings and clothing they owned as they put their hands on a Hay-burner stove that was no warmer than soap. When a jar of apricots burst open that night and the iced orange syrup did not ooze out, Aachen's wife told the children, You ought now to get under your covers. While the seven were crying and crowding onto their dirty floor mattresses, she rang the green tent cloth along the iron wire dividing the house and slid underneath horse blankets in Mathias Aachen's gray wool trousers and her own gray dress and a ghastly muskrat coat that in hot weather gave birth to insects.

Aachen said, Every one of us will be dying of cold before morning. Freezing here. In Nebraska.

His wife just lay there, saying nothing.

Aachen later said he sat up bodingly until shortly after one P.M., when the house temperature was so exceedingly cold that a gray suede of ice was on the teapot and his pretty girls were whimpering in their sleep. You are not meant to stay here, Aachen thought, and tilted hot candle wax into his right ear and then his left, until he could only hear his body drumming blood. And then Aachen got his Navy Colt and kissed his wife and killed her. And then walked under the green tent cloth and killed his seven children, stopping twice to capture a scuttling boy and stopping once more to reload.

* * *

Hattie Benedict was in her Antelope County schoolyard overseeing the noon recess in a black cardigan sweater and gray wool dress when the January blizzard caught her unaware. She had been impatiently watching four girls in flying coats playing Ante I Over by tossing a spindle of chartreuse yarn over the one-room schoolhouse, and then a sharp cold petted her neck and Hattie turned toward the open fields of hoarfrosted scraggle and yellow grass. Just a half mile away was a gray blur of snow underneath a dark sky that was all hurry and calamity, like a nighttime city of sin-black buildings and havoc in the streets. Wind tortured a creekside cottonwood until it cracked apart. A tin water pail rang in a skipping roll to the horse path. One quarter of the tar-paper roof was torn from the schoolhouse and sailed southeast forty feet. And only then did Hattie yell for the older boys with their cigarettes and clay pipes to hurry in from the prairie twenty rods away, and she was hustling a dallying girl inside just as the snowstorm socked into her Antelope County schoolhouse, shipping the building awry off its timber skids so that the southwest side heavily dropped six inches and the oak-plank floor became a slope that Hattie ascended unsteadily while ordering the children to open their *Webster Franklin Fourth Reader* to the Lord's Prayer in verse and to say it aloud. And then Hattie stood by her desk with her pink hands held theatrically to her cheeks as she looked up at the walking noise of bricks being jarred from the chimney and down the roof. Every window view was as white as if butchers' paper had been tacked up. Winds pounded into the windowpanes and dry window putty trickled onto the unpainted sills. Even the slough grass fire in the Hay-burner stove was sucked high into the tin stack pipe so that the soot on it reddened and snapped. Hattie could only stare. Four of the boys were just about Hattie's age, so she didn't say anything when they ignored the reading assignment and earnestly got up from the wooden benches in order to argue *oughts* and *ought nots* in the cloakroom. She heard the girls saying Amen and then she saw Janusz Vasko, who was fifteen years old and had grown up in Nebraska weather, gravely exiting the cloakroom with a cigarette behind one ear and his right hand raised high overhead. Hattie called on him, and Janusz said the older boys agreed that they could get the littler ones home, but only if they went out right away. And before she could even give it thought, Janusz tied his red handkerchief over his nose and mouth and jabbed his orange corduroy trousers inside his antelope boots with a pencil.

Yes, Hattie said, please go, and Janusz got the boys and girls to link themselves together with jump ropes and twine and piano wire, and twelve of Hattie Benedict's pupils walked out into a nothingness that the boys knew from their shoes up and dully worked their way across as though each crooked stump and tilted fence post was a word they could spell in a plain-spoken sentence in a book of practical knowledge. Hours later the children showed up at their homes, aching and crying in raw pain. Each was given cocoa or the green tea of the elder flower and hot bricks were put next to their feet while they napped and newspapers printed their names incorrectly. And then, one by one, the children disappeared from history.

Except for Johan and Alma Lindquist, aged nine and six, who stayed behind in the schoolhouse, owing to the greater distance to their ranch. Hattie opened a week-old Omaha newspaper on her desktop and with caution peeled a spotted yellow apple on it, eating tan slices from her scissor blade as she peered out at children who seemed irritatingly sad and pathetic. She said, You wish you were home.

The Lindquists stared.

Me too, she said. She dropped the apple core onto the newspaper page and watched it ripple with the juice stain. Have you any idea where Pennsylvania is?

East, the boy said. Johan was eating pepper cheese and day-old rye bread from a tin lunch box that sparked with electricity whenever he touched it. And his sister nudged him to show how her yellow hair was beguiled toward her green rubber comb whenever she brought it near.

Hattie was talking in such quick English that she could tell the Lindquists couldn't quite understand it. She kept hearing the snow pinging and pattering against the windowpanes, and the storm howling like clarinets down the stack pipe, but she perceived the increasing cold in the room only when she looked to the Lindquists and saw their Danish sentences grayly blossoming as they spoke. Hattie went into the cloakroom and skidded out the poorhouse box, rummaging from it a Scotch plaid scarf that she wrapped twice around her skull and ears just as a squaw would, and snipping off the fingertips of some red knitted gloves that were only slightly too small. She put them on and then she got into her secondhand coat and Alma whispered to her brother but Hattie said she'd have no whispering, she hated that, she couldn't wait for their kin to show up for them, she had too many responsibilities, and nothing interesting ever happened in the country. Everything was stupid. Everything was work. She didn't even have a girlfriend. She said she'd once been sick for four days, and two by two practically every woman in Neligh mistrustfully visited her rooming house to squint at Hattie and palm her forehead and talk about her symptoms. And then they'd snail out into the hallway and prattle and whisper in the hawk and spit of the German language.

Alma looked at Johan with misunderstanding and terror, and Hattie told them to get out paper and pencils; she was going to say some necessary things and the children were going to write them down. She slowly paced as she constructed a paragraph, one knuckle darkly striping the blackboard, but she couldn't properly express herself. She had forgotten herself so absolutely that she thought forgetting was a yeast in the air; or that the onslaught's only point was to say over and over again that she was next to nothing. Easily bewildered. Easily dismayed. The Lindquists were shying from the crazy woman and concentrating their shame on a nickel pad of Wisconsin paper. And Hattie thought, *You'll give me an ugly name and there will be cartoons and snickering and the older girls will idly slay me with jokes and imitations.*

She explained she was taking them to her rooming house, and she strode purposefully out into the great blizzard as if she were going out to a garden to fetch some strawberries, and Johan dutifully followed, but Alma stayed inside the schoolhouse with her purple scarf up over her mouth and nose and her own dark sandwich of pepper cheese and rye bread clutched to her breast like a prayer book. And then Johan stepped out of the utter whiteness to say Alma had to hurry up, that Miss Benedict was angrily asking him if his sister had forgotten how to use her legs. So Alma stepped out of the one-room schoolhouse, sinking deep in the snow and sloshing ahead in it as she would in a pond until she caught up with Hattie Benedict, who took the Lindquists' hands in her own and walked them into the utter whiteness and night of the afternoon. Seeking to blindly go north to her rooming house, Hattie put her high button shoes in the deep tracks that Janusz and the schoolchildren had made, but she misstepped twice, and that was enough to get her on a screw-tape path over snow humps and hillocks that took her south and west and very nearly into a great wilderness that was like a sea in high gale.

Hattie imagined herself reaching the Elkhorn River and discovering her rooming house standing high and honorable under the sky's insanity. And then she and the

Lindquist children would duck over their teaspoons of tomato soup and soda crackers as the town's brooms and scarecrows teetered over them, hooking their green hands on the boy and girl and saying, Tell us about it. She therefore created a heroine's part for herself and tried to keep to it as she floundered through drifts as high as a four-poster bed in a white room of piety and weeping. Hattie pretended gaiety by saying once, See how it swirls! but she saw that the Lindquists were tucking deep inside themselves as they trudged forward and fell and got up again, the wind drawing tears from their squinting eyes, the hard, dry snow hitting their skin like wildly flying pencils. Hours passed as Hattie tipped away from the press of the wind into country that was a puzzle to her, but she kept saying, Just a little farther, until she saw Alma playing Gretel by secretly trailing her right hand along a high wave of snow in order to secretly let go yet another crumb of her rye bread. And then, just ahead of her, she saw some pepper cheese that the girl dropped some time ago. Hissing spindrifts tore away from the snow swells and spiked her face like sharp pins, but then a door seemed to inch ajar and Hattie saw the slight, dark change of a haystack and she cut toward it, announcing that they'd stay there for the night.

She slashed away an access into the haystack and ordered Alma to crawl inside, but the girl hesitated as if she were still thinking of the gingerbread house and the witch's oven, and Hattie acidly whispered, You'll be a dainty mouthful. She meant it as a joke but her green eyes must have seemed crazy, because the little girl was crying when Hattie got inside the haystack next to her, and then Johan was crying, too, and Hattie hugged the Lindquists to her body and tried to shush them with a hymn by Dr. Watts, gently singing, Hush, my dears, lie still and slumber. She couldn't get her feet inside the haystack, but she couldn't feel them anyway just then, and the haystack was making everything else seem right and possible. She talked to the children about hot pastries and taffy and Christmas presents, and that night she made up a story about the horrible storm being a wicked old man whose only thought was to eat them up, but he couldn't find them in the haystack even though he looked and looked. The old man was howling, she said, because he was so hungry.

At daybreak a party of farmers from Neligh rode out on their high plowhorses to the Antelope County schoolhouse in order to get Hattie and the Lindquist children, but the room was empty and the bluetick hound that was with them kept scratching up rye bread until the party walked along behind it on footpaths that wreathed around the schoolyard and into a haystack twenty rods away where the older boys smoked and spit tobacco juice at recess. The Lindquist girl and the boy were killed by the cold, but Hattie Benedict had stayed alive inside the hay, and she wouldn't come out again until the party of men yanked her by the ankles. Even then she kept the girl's body hugged against one side and the boy's body hugged to the other, and when she was put up on one horse, she stared down at them with green eyes that were empty of thought or understanding and inquired if they'd be okay. Yes, one man said. You took good care of them.

Bent Lindquist ripped down his kitchen cupboards and carpentered his own triangular caskets, blacking them with shoe polish, and then swaddled Alma and Johan in black alpaca that was kindly provided by an elder in the Church of Jesus Christ of Latter-Day Saints. And all that night Danish women sat up with the bodies, sopping the Lindquists' skin with vinegar so as to impede putrefaction.

Hattie Benedict woke up in a Lincoln hospital with sweet oil of spermaceti on her hands and lips, and weeks later a Kansas City surgeon amputated her feet with a polished silver hacksaw in the presence of his anatomy class. She was walking again by June, but she was attached to cork-and-iron shoes and she sighed and grunted with every step. Within a year she grew so overweight that she gave up her crutches for a wicker-backed wheelchair and stayed in Antelope County on a pension of forty dollars per month, letting her dark hair grow dirty and leafy, reading one popular romance per day. And yet she complained so much about her helplessness, especially in winter, that the Protestant churches took up a collection and Hattie Benedict was shipped by train to Oakland, California, whence she sent postcards saying she'd married a trolley repairman and she hated Nebraska, hated their horrible weather, hated their petty lives.

* * *

On Friday the thirteenth some pioneers went to the upper stories of their houses to jack up the windows and crawl out onto snow that was like a jeweled ceiling over their properties. Everything was sloped and planed and caped and whitely furbelowed. One man couldn't get over his boyish delight in tramping about on deer-hide snowshoes at the height of his roof gutters, or that his dogwood tree was forgotten but for twigs sticking out of the snow like a skeleton's fingers. His name was Eldad Alderman, and he jabbed a bamboo fishing pole in four likely spots a couple of feet below his snowshoes before the bamboo finally thumped against the plank roof of his chicken coop. He spent two hours spading down to the coop and then squeezed in through the one window in order to walk among the fowl and count up. Half his sixty hens were alive; the other half were still nesting, their orange beaks lying against their white hackles, sitting there like a dress shop's hats, their pure white eggs not yet cold underneath them. In gratitude to those thirty chickens that withstood the ordeal, Eldad gave them Dutch whey and curds and eventually wrote a letter praising their constitutions in the *American Poultry Yard.*

Anna Shevschenko managed to get oxen inside a shelter sturdily constructed of oak scantling and a high stack of barley straw, but the snow powder was so fine and fiercely penetrating that it sifted through and slowly accumulated on the floor. The oxen tamped it down and inchingly rose toward the oak scantling rafters, where they were stopped as the snow flooded up, and by daybreak were overcome and finally asphyxiated. Widow Shevschenko decided then that an old woman could not keep a Nebraska farm alone, and she left for the East in February.

One man lost three hundred Rhode Island Red chickens; another lost two hundred sixty Hereford cattle and sold their hides for two dollars apiece. Hours after the Hubenka boy permitted twenty-one hogs to get out of the snowstorm and join their forty Holsteins in the upper barn, the planked floor in the cattle linter collapsed under the extra weight and the livestock perished. Since even coal picks could no more than chip the earth, the iron-hard bodies were hauled aside until they could be put underground in April, and just about then some Pawnee Indians showed up outside David City. Knowing their manner of living, Mr. Hubenka told them where the carcasses were rotting in the sea wrack of weed tangles and thaw-water jetsam, and the Pawnee rode their ponies onto the property one night and hauled the carrion away.

And there were stories about a Union Pacific train being arrested by snow on a railway siding near Lincoln, and the merchandisers in the smoking car playing euchre, high five, and flinch until sunup; about cowboys staying inside a Hazard bunk-house for three days and getting bellyaches from eating so many tins of anchovies and saltine crackers; about the Omaha YMCA where shop clerks paged through inspirational pamphlets or played checkers and cribbage or napped in green leather Chesterfield chairs until the great blizzard petered out.

Half a century later, in Atkinson, there was a cranky talker named Bates, who maintained he was the fellow who first thought of attaching the word *blizzard* to the onslaught of high winds and slashing dry snow and ought to be given credit for it. And later, too, a Lincoln woman remembered herself as a little girl peering out through yellowed window paper at a yard and countryside that were as white as the first day of God's creation. And then a great white Brahma bull with street-wide horns trotted up to the house, the night's snow puffing up from his heavy footsteps like soap flakes, gray funnels of air flaring from his nostrils and wisping away in the horrible cold. With a tilt of his head the great bull sought out the hiding girl under a Chesterfield table and, having seen her, sighed and trotted back toward Oklahoma.

Wild turkey were sighted over the next few weeks, their wattled heads and necks just above the snow like dark sticks, some of them petrified that way but others simply waiting for happier times to come. The onslaught also killed prairie dogs, jackrabbits, and crows, and the coyotes that relied upon them for food got so hungry that skulks of them would loiter like juveniles in the yards at night and yearn for scraps and castaways in old songs of agony that were always misunderstood.

* * *

Addie Dillingham was seventeen and irresistible that January day of the great blizzard, a beautiful English girl in an hourglass dress and an ankle-length otter-skin coat that was sculpted brazenly to display a womanly bosom and bustle. She had gently agreed to join an upperclassman at the Nebraska School of Medicine on a journey across the green ice of the Missouri River to Iowa, where there was a party at the Masonic Temple in order to celebrate the final linking of Omaha and Council Bluffs. The medical student was Repler Hitchcock of Council Bluffs—a good companion, a Republican, and an Episcopalian—who yearned to practice electro-therapeutics in Cuernavaca, Mexico. He paid for their three-course luncheon at the Paxton Hotel and then the couple strolled down Douglas Street with four hundred other partygoers, who got into cutters and one-horse open sleighs just underneath the iron legs and girders of what would eventually be called the Ak-Sar-Ben Bridge. At a cap-pistol shot the party jerked away from Nebraska and there were champagne toasts and cheers and yahooing, but gradually the party scattered and Addie could only hear the iron shoes of the plowhorse and the racing sleigh hushing across the shaded window glass of river, like those tropical flowers shaped like saucers and cups that slide across the green silk of a pond of their own accord.

At the Masonic Temple there were coconut macaroons and hot syllabub made with cider and brandy, and quadrille dancing on a puncheon floor to songs like the "Butterfly Whirl" and "Cheater Swing" and "The Girl I Left Behind Me." Although the day was getting dark and there was talk about a great snowstorm roistering outside, Addie insisted on staying out on the dance floor until only twenty people remained and the quadrille caller had put away his violin and his sister's cello. Addie smiled and said, Oh what fun! as Repler tidily helped her into her mother's otter-skin coat and then escorted her out into a grand empire of snow that Addie thought was thrilling. And then, although the world by then was wrathfully meaning everything it said, she walked alone to the railroad depot at Ninth and Broadway so she could take the one-stop train called The Dummy across to Omaha.

Addie sipped hot cocoa as she passed sixty minutes up close to the railroad depot's coal stoker oven and some other party-goers sang of Good King Wenceslaus over a parlor organ. And then an old yardman who was sheeped in snow trudged through the high drifts by the door and announced that no more trains would be going out until morning.

Half the couples stranded there had family in Council Bluffs and decided to stay overnight, but the idea of traipsing back to Repler's house and sleeping in his sister's trundle bed seemed squalid to Addie, and she decided to walk the iron railway trestle across to Omaha.

Addie was a half hour away from the Iowa railway yard and up on the tracks over the great Missouri before she had second thoughts. White hatchings and tracings of snow flew at her horizontally. Wind had rippled snow up against the southern girders so that the high white skin was pleated and patterned like oyster shell. Every creosote tie was tented with snow that angled down into dark troughs that Addie could fit a leg through. Everything else was night sky and mystery, and the world she knew had disappeared. And yet she walked out onto the trestle, teetering over to a catwalk and sidestepping along it in high-button shoes, forty feet above the ice, her left hand taking the yield from one guy wire as her right hand sought out another. Yelling winds were yanking at her, and the iron trestle was swaying enough to tilt her over into nothingness, as though Addie Dillingham were a playground game it was just inventing. Halfway across, her gray tam-o'-shanter was snagged out just far enough into space that she could follow its spider-drop into the night, but she only stared at the great river that was lying there moon-white with snow and intractable. Wishing for her jump.

Years later Addie thought that she got to Nebraska and did not give up and was not overfrightened because she was seventeen and could do no wrong, and accidents and dying seemed a government you could vote against, a mother you could ignore. She said she panicked at one jolt of wind and sank down to her knees up there and briefly touched her forehead to iron that hurt her skin like teeth, but when she got up again, she could see the ink-black stitching of the woods just east of Omaha and the shanties on timber piers just above the Missouri River's jagged stacks of ice. And she grinned as she thought how she would look to a vagrant down there plying his way along a rope in order to assay his trotlines for gar and catfish and then, perhaps, appraising the night as if he'd heard a crazy woman screaming in a faraway hospital room. And she'd be jauntily up there on the iron trestle like a new star you could wish on, and as joyous as the last high notes of "The Girl I Left Behind Me."

# ⁑ STEPHANIE VAUGHN
(1943– )

Stephanie Vaughn was born in Millersburg, Ohio. Because her father was an army officer, she grew up on a number of military bases in Ohio, New York, Oklahoma, Texas, the Philippines, and Italy. She completed a B.A. at Ohio State University and an M.F.A. at the University of Iowa's Writers' Workshop. She did additional study at Stanford University on a Wallace Stegner Creative Writing Fellowship. She now teaches fiction writing and literature at Cornell University.

Vaughn's stories have appeared in *Antaeus, The New Yorker,* and *Redbook* and in the O. Henry and Pushcart Prize collections. Her collection of stories, *Sweet Talk,* was published in 1990. In prose that is clean, crisp, and unsentimental, Vaughn's stories treat women confronting life's contingencies with a mixture of humor and sadness.

## Able, Baker, Charlie, Dog

WHEN I was twelve years old, my father was tall and awesome. I can see him walking across the parade ground behind our quarters. The wind blew snow into the folds of his coat and made the hem swoop around his legs. He did not lower his head, he did not jam his hands into the pockets. He was coming home along a diagonal that would cut the parade ground into perfect triangles, and he was not going to be stopped by any snowstorm. I stood at the kitchen door and watched him through a hole I had rubbed in the steamy glass.

My grandmother and mother fidgeted with pans of food that had been kept warm too long. It was one o'clock on Saturday and he had been expected home at noon.

"You want to know what this chicken looks like?" said my grandmother. "It looks like it died last year."

My mother looked into the pan but didn't say anything.

My grandmother believed my mother should have married a minister, not an Army officer. Once my mother had gone out with a minister, and now he was on the radio every Sunday in Ohio. My grandmother thought my father had misrepresented himself as a religious man. There was a story my mother told about their first date. They went to a restaurant and my father told her that he was going to have twelve sons and name them Peter, James, John, et cetera. "And I thought, Twelve sons!" said my mother. "Boy, do I pity your poor wife." My mother had two miscarriages and then she had me. My father named me Gemma, which my grandmother believed was not even a Christian name.

"You want to know what this squash looks like?" said my grandmother.

"It'll be fine," said my mother.

Just then the wind gusted on the parade ground, and my father veered to the left. He stopped and looked up. How is it possible you have caught me off guard, he seemed to ask. Exactly where have I miscalculated the velocities, how have I misjudged the vectors?

"It looks like somebody peed in it," my grandmother said.

* * *

"Keep your voice low," my father told me that day as we ate the ruined squash and chicken. "Keep your voice low and you can win any point."

We were living in Fort Niagara, a little Army post at the juncture of the Niagara River and Lake Ontario. We had been there through the fall and into the winter, as my father, who was second in command, waited for his next promotion. It began to snow in October. The arctic winds swept across the lake from Canada and shook the windows of our house. Snow drifted across the parade ground, and floes of ice piled up against each other in the river, so that if a person were courageous enough, or foolhardy enough, and also lucky, he could walk the mile across the river to Canada.

"And always speak in sentences," he told me. "You have developed a junior-high habit of speaking in fragments. Learn to come to a full stop when you complete an idea. Use semicolons and periods in your speech."

My mother put down her fork and knife. Her hands were so thin and light they seemed to pass through the table as she dropped them in her lap. "Zachary, perhaps we could save some of the lecture for dessert?" she said.

My grandmother leaned back into her own heaviness. "The poor kid never gets to eat a hot meal," she said. She was referring to the rule that said I could not cut my food or eat while I was speaking or being spoken to. My father used mealtimes to lecture on the mechanics of life, the how-tos of a civilized world. Normally I was receptive to his advice, but that day I was angry with him.

"You know, Dad," I said, "I don't think my friends are going to notice a missing semicolon."

I thought he would give me a fierce look, but instead he winked. "And don't say 'you know,' " he said.

He never said "you know," never spoke in fragments, never slurred his speech, even years later when he had just put away a fifth of scotch and was trying to describe the Eskimo custom of chewing up the meat before it was given to the elders, who had no teeth. He spoke with such calculation and precision that his sentences hung over us like high vaulted ceilings, or rolled across the table like ornaments sculptured from stone. It was a huge cathedral of a voice, full of volume and complexity.

* * *

He taught me the alphabet. Able, Baker, Charlie, Dog. It was the alphabet the military used to keep b's separate from v's and i's separate from y's. He liked the music of it, the way it sounded on his fine voice. I was four years old and my grandmother had not come to live with us yet. We were stationed in Manila, and living in a house the Army had built on squat stilts to protect us from the insects. There was a typhoon sweeping inland, and we could hear the hoarse sound of metal scraping across the Army's paved street. It was the corrugated roof of the house next door.

"Don't you think it's time we went under the house?" my mother said. She was sitting on a duffel bag that contained our tarps and food rations. The house had a loose plank in the living-room floor, so that if the roof blew away, or the walls caved in, we could escape through the opening and sit in the low space between the reinforced floor and the ground until the military rescue bus came.

My father looked at me and said, "Able, Baker, Charlie, Dog. Can you say it, Gemma?"

I looked up at the dark slope of our own metal roof.

"Can you say it?"

"Able, Baker, Charlie, Dog," I said.

The metal rumbled on the road outside. My mother lifted the plank.

"We will be all right," he said. "Easy, Fox, George, How."

"Anybody want to join me?" said my mother.

"Easy."

"Rachel, please put that plank back."

"Easy, Fox, George, How," I said.

My mother replaced the plank and sat on the floor beside me. The storm grew louder, the rain fell against the roof like handfuls of gravel.

"Item, Jig, King." My father's voice grew lower, fuller. We sat under the sound of it and felt safe. "Love, Mike, Nan."

But then we heard another sound—something that went *whap-whap,* softly, between the gusts of rain. We tilted our heads toward the shuttered windows.

"Well," said my father, standing up to stretch. "I think we are losing a board or two off the side of the house."

"Where are you going?" said my mother. "Just where do you think you're going?"

He put on his rain slicker and went into the next room. When he returned, he was carrying a bucket of nails and a hammer. "Obviously," he said, "I am going fishing."

* * *

We moved back to the States when I was six, and he taught me how to play Parcheesi, checkers, chess, cribbage, dominoes, and twenty questions. "When you lose," he told me, "don't cry. When you win, don't gloat."

He taught me how to plant tomatoes and load a shotgun shell. He showed me how to gut a dove, turning it inside out as the Europeans do, using the flexible breastbone for a pivot. He read a great many books and never forgot a fact or a technical description. He explained the principles of crop rotation and the flying buttress. He discussed the Defenestration of Prague.

When I was in elementary school, he was sent abroad twice on year-long tours—once to Turkey and once to Greenland, both strategic outposts for America's Early Warning System. I wanted to, but I could not write him letters. His came to me every week, but without the rhythms of his voice the words seemed pale and flat, like the transparent shapes of cells under a microscope. He did not write about his work, because his work was secret. He did not send advice, because that he left to my mother and grandmother in his absence. He wrote about small things—the smooth white rocks he found on a mountainside in Turkey, the first fresh egg he ate in Greenland. When I reread the letters after he died, I was struck by their grace and invention. But when I read them as a child, I looked through the words—"eggs . . . shipment . . . frozen"—and there was nothing on the other side but the great vacuum of his missing voice.

"I can't think of anything to say," I told my mother the first time she urged me to write to him. He had already been in Turkey for three months. She stood behind me at the heavy library table and smoothed my hair, touched my shoulders. "Tell him about your tap lessons," she said. "Tell him about ballet."

"Dear Dad," I wrote. "I am taking tap lessons. I am also taking ballet." I tried to imagine what he looked like. I tried to put a face before my face, but it was gray and featureless, like the face of a statue worn flat by wind and rain. "And I hope you have a Happy Birthday next month," I concluded, hoping to evade the necessity of writing him again in three weeks.

* * *

The autumn I turned twelve, we moved to Fort Niagara, which was the administrative base for the missile sites strung along the Canadian border between Lake Erie and Lake Ontario. It was a handsome post, full of oak trees, brick buildings, and history. The French had taken the land from the Indians and built the original fort. The British took the fort from the French, and the Americans took it from the British. My father recounted the battles for us as we drove there along the wide sweep of the Niagara River, past apple orchards and thick pastures. My grandmother sat in the back seat and made a note of each red convertible that passed. I was supposed to be counting the white ones. When we drove through the gate and saw the post for the first time—the expanses of clipped grass, the tall trees, the row of Colonial houses overlooking the river—my grandmother put down her tablet and said, "This is some post." She looked at my father admiringly, the first indication she had ever given that he might be a good match for my mother after all. She asked to be taken to the far end of the post, where the Old Fort was. It sat on a point of land at the juncture of the lake and river, and looked appropriately warlike, with its moat and tiny gun windows, but it was surprisingly small—a simple square of yellow stone, a modest French château. "Is this all there is?" I said as my grandmother and I posed for pictures on the drawbridge near two soldiers dressed in Revolutionary War costumes. It was hard to imagine that chunks of a vast continent had been won and lost within the confines of a fortress hardly bigger than Sleeping Beauty's castle at Disneyland. Later, as we drove back along the river, my father said in his aphoristic way, "Sometimes the biggest battles are the smallest ones."

The week after we settled in our quarters, we made the obligatory trip to the Falls. It was a sultry day—Indian summer—and our eyes began to water as we neared the chemical factories that surrounded the city of Niagara Falls. We stopped for iced tea and my father explained how the glaciers had formed the escarpment through which the Falls had cut a deep gorge. *Escarpment*—that was the term he used, instead of *cliff.* It skidded along the roof of his mouth and entered the conversation with a soft explosion.

We went to the Niagara Falls Museum and examined the containers people had used successfully to go over the Falls early in the century, when there was a thousand-dollar prize given to survivors. Two were wooden barrels strapped with metal bands. One was a giant rubber ball reinforced with a steel cage. A fourth was a long steel capsule. On the walls were photographs of each survivor and plaques explaining who had been injured and how. The steel capsule was used by a man who had broken every bone in his body. The plaque said that he was in the hospital for twenty-three weeks and then took his capsule around the world on a speaking tour. One day when he was in New Zealand, he slipped on an orange peel, broke his leg, and died of complications.

We went next to Goat Island and stood on the open bank to watch the leap and dive of the white water. My mother held her handbag close to her breasts. She had a habit of always holding things this way—a stack of dinner plates, the dish towel, some mail she had brought in from the porch; she hunched over slightly, so that her body seemed at once to be protective and protected. "I don't like the river," she said. "I think it wants to hypnotize you." My father put his hands in his pockets to show how at ease he was, and my grandmother went off to buy an ice-cream cone.

At the observation point, we stood at a metal fence and looked into the frothing water at the bottom of the gorge. We watched bits and pieces of rainbows appear and vanish in the sunlight that was refracted off the water through the mist. My father pointed to a black shape in the rapids above the Horseshoe Falls. "That's a river barge," he said. He lowered his voice so that he could be heard under the roar of the water. "A long time ago, there were two men standing on that barge waiting to see whether in the next moment of their lives they would go over."

He told us the story of the barge then—how it had broken loose from a tug near Buffalo and floated down-river, gathering speed. The two men tore at the air, waved and shouted to people on shore, but the barge entered the rapids. They bumped around over the rocks, and the white water rose in the air. One man—"He was the thinking man," said my father—thought they might be able to wedge the barge among the rocks if they allowed the hull to fill with water. They came closer to the Falls—four hundred yards, three hundred—before the barge jerked broadside and stopped. They were there all afternoon and night, listening to the sound of the water pounding into the boulders at the bottom of the gorge. The next morning they were rescued, and one of the men, the thinking man, told the newspapers that he had spent the night playing poker in his head. He played all the hands, and he bluffed himself. He drew to inside straights. If the barge had torn loose from the rocks in the night, he was going to go over the Falls saying, "Five-card draw, jacks or better to open." The other man sat on the barge, his arms clasped around his knees, and watched the mist blow back from the edge of the Falls in the moonlight. He could not speak.

"The scream of the water entered his body," said my father. He paused to let us think about that.

"Well, what does that mean?" my grandmother said at last.

My father rested his arms on the fence and gazed pleasantly at the Falls. "He went insane."

The river fascinated me. I often stood between the yellow curtains of my bedroom and looked down upon it and thought about how deep and swift it was, how black under the glittering surface. The newspaper carried stories about people who jumped over the Falls, fourteen miles upriver from our house. I thought of their bodies pushed along the soft silt of the bottom, tumbling silently, huddled in upon themselves like fetuses—jilted brides, unemployed factory workers, old people who did not want to go to rest homes, teenagers who got bad grades, young women who fell in love with married men. They floated invisibly past my bedroom window, out into the lake.

* * *

That winter, I thought I was going to die. I thought I had cancer of the breasts. My mother had explained to me about menstruation, she had given me a book about the reproductive systems of men and women, but she had not told me about breasts and how they begin as invisible lumps that become tender and sore.

I thought the soreness had begun in a phys. ed. class one day in December when I was hit in the chest with a basketball. I didn't worry about it, and it went away by New Year's. In January, I found a pamphlet at the bus stop. I was stamping my feet in the cold, looking down at my boots, when I saw the headline—CANCER: SEVEN WARNING SIGNALS. When I got home, I went into the bathroom and undressed. I examined myself for enlarged moles and small wounds that wouldn't heal. I was systematic. I sat on the edge of the tub with the pamphlet by my side and began with my toenails, looking under the tips of them. I felt my soles, arches, ankles. I worked my way up my body and then I felt the soreness again, around both nipples. At dinner that night I didn't say anything all through the meal. In bed I slept on my back, with my arms stiff against my sides.

The next Saturday was the day my father came home late for lunch. The squash sat on the back of the stove and turned to ocher soup. The chicken fell away from the bones. After lunch he went into the living room and drank scotch and read a book. When I came down for supper, he was still sitting there, and he told my mother he would eat later. My grandmother, my mother, and I ate silently at the kitchen table. I took a long bath. I scrubbed my chest hard.

I went straight to my bedroom, and after a while my mother came upstairs and said, "What's wrong?"

I didn't say anything.

She stood in front of me with her hands clasped in front of her. She seemed to lean toward her own hands. "But you've been acting, you know"—and here she laughed self-consciously, as she used the forbidden phrase—"you know, you've been acting different. You were so quiet today."

I went to my chest of drawers and took the pamphlet out from under a stack of folded underpants and gave it to her.

"What's this?" she said.

"I think I have Number Four," I said.

She must have known immediately what the problem was, but she didn't smile. She asked me to raise my nightgown and she examined my chest, pressing firmly, as if she were a doctor. I told her about the soreness. "Here?" she said. "And here? What about here, too?" She told me I was beginning to "develop." I knew what she meant, but I wanted her to be precise.

"You're getting breasts," she said.

"But I don't *see* anything."

"You will."

"You never told me it would hurt."

"Oh, dear. I just forgot. When you're grown up you just forget what it was like."

I asked her whether, just to be safe, I could see a doctor. She said that of course I could, and I felt better, as if I had had a disease and already been cured. As she was leaving the room, I said, "Do you think I need a bra?" She smiled. I went to sleep watching the snow fall past the window. I had my hands cupped over my new breasts.

* * *

When I awoke, I did not recognize the window. The snow had stopped and moonlight slanted through the glass. I could not make out the words, but I heard my father's voice filling up the house. I tiptoed down the back staircase that led to the kitchen and stood in the slice of shadow near the doorjamb. My grandmother was telling my mother to pack her bags. He was a degenerate, she said—she had always seen that in him. My mother said, "Why, Zachary, why are you doing this?"

"Just go pack your bags," my grandmother said. "I'll get the child."

My father said conversationally, tensely, "Do I have to break your arms?"

I leaned into the light. He was holding on to a bottle of scotch with one hand, and my mother was trying to pull it away with both of hers. He jerked his arm back and forth, so that she was drawn into a little dance, back and forth across the linoleum in front of him.

"The Lord knows the way of righteousness," said my grandmother.

"Please," said my mother. "Please, please."

"And the way of the ungodly shall perish," said my grandmother.

"Whose house is this?" said my father. His voice exploded. He snapped his arm back, trying to take the bottle from my mother in one powerful gesture. It smashed against the wall, and I stepped into the kitchen. The white light from the ceiling fixture burned across the smooth surfaces of the refrigerator, the stove, the white Formica countertops. It was as if an atom had been smashed somewhere and a wave of radiation was rolling through the kitchen. I looked him in the eye and waited for him to speak. I sensed my mother and grandmother on either side of me, in petrified postures. At last, he said, "Well." His voice cracked. The word split in two. "Wel-el." He said it again. His face took on a flatness.

"I am going back to bed," I said. I went up the narrow steps, and he followed me. My mother and grandmother came along behind, whispering. He tucked in the covers, and sat on the edge of the bed, watching me. My mother and grandmother stood stiff against the door. "I am sorry I woke you up," he said finally, and his voice was deep and soothing. The two women watched him go down the hall, and when I heard his steps on the front staircase I rolled over and put my face in the pillow. I heard them turn off the lights and say good-night to me. I heard them go to their bedrooms. I lay there for a long time, listening for a sound downstairs, and then it came—the sound of the front door closing.

I went downstairs and put on my hat, coat, boots. I followed his footsteps in the snow, down the front walk, and across the road to the riverbank. He did not seem surprised to see me next to him. We stood side by side, hands in our pockets, breathing frost into the air. The river was filled from shore to shore with white heaps of ice, which cast blue shadows in the moonlight.

"This is the edge of America," he said, in a tone that seemed to answer a question I had just asked. There was a creak and crunch of ice as two floes below us scraped each other and jammed against the bank.

"You knew all week, didn't you? Your mother and your grandmother didn't know, but I knew that you could be counted on to know."

I hadn't known until just then, but I guessed the unspeakable thing—that his career was falling apart—and I knew. I nodded. Years later, my mother told me what she had learned about the incident, not from him but from another Army wife. He had called a general a son of a bitch. That was all. I never knew what the issue was or whether he had been right or wrong. Whether the defense of the United States of America had been at stake, or merely the pot in a card game. I didn't even know whether he had called the general a son of a bitch to his face or simply been overheard in an unguarded moment. I only knew that he had been given a 7 instead of a 9 on his Efficiency Report and then passed over for promotion. But that night I nodded, not knowing the cause but knowing the consequences, as we stood on the riverbank above the moonlit ice. "I am looking at that thin beautiful line of Canada," he said. "I think I will go for a walk."

"No," I said. I said it again. "No." I wanted to remember later that I had told him not to go.

"How long do you think it would take to go over and back?" he said.

"Two hours."

He rocked back and forth in his boots, looked up at the moon, then down at the river. I did not say anything.

He started down the bank, sideways, taking long, graceful sliding steps, which threw little puffs of snow in the air. He took his hands from his pockets and hopped from the bank to the ice. He tested his weight against the weight of the ice, flexing his knees. I watched him walk a few yards from the shore and then I saw him rise in the air, his long legs scissoring the moonlight, as he crossed from the edge of one floe to the next. He turned and waved to me, one hand making a slow arc.

I could have said anything. I could have said "Come back" or "I love you." Instead, I called after him, "Be sure and write!" The last thing I heard, long after I had lost sight of him far out on the river, was the sound of his laugh splitting the cold air.

* * *

In the spring he resigned his commission and we went back to Ohio. He used his savings to invest in a chain of hardware stores with my uncle. My uncle arranged the contracts with builders and plumbers, and supervised the employees. My father controlled the inventory and handled the books. He had been a logistics officer, and all the skills he might have used in supervising the movement of land, air, and sea cargoes, or in calculating the disposition of several billion dollars' worth of military supplies, were instead brought to bear on the deployment of nuts and bolts, plumbers' joints and nipples, No. 2 pine, Con-Tact paper, acrylic paint, caulking guns, and rubber dishpans. He learned a new vocabulary—traffic builders, margins, end-cap displays, perfboard merchandisers, seasonal impulse items—and spoke it with the ostentation and faint amusement of a man who has just mastered a foreign language.

"But what I really want to know, Mr. Jenkins," I heard him tell a man on the telephone one day, "is why you think the Triple Gripper Vegetable Ripper would make a good loss-leader item in mid-winter." He had been in the hardlines industry, as it was called, for six months, and I was making my first visit to his office, and then only because my mother had sent me there on the pretext of taking him a midmorning snack during a busy Saturday. I was reluctant to confront him in his civilian role, afraid I would find him somehow diminished. In fact, although he looked incongruous among the reds, yellows, and blues that the previous owner had used to decorate the office, he sounded much like the man who had taught me to speak in complete sentences.

"Mr. Jenkins, I am not asking for a discourse on coleslaw."

When he hung up, he winked at me and said, "Your father is about to become the emperor of the building-and-housewares trade in Killbuck, Ohio."

I nodded and took a seat in a red-and-blue chair.

Then he looked at his hands spread upon the spotless ink blotter and said, "Of course, you know that I do not give a damn about the Triple Gripper Vegetable Ripper."

I had skipped a grade and entered high school. I saw less and less of him, because I ate dinner early so that I could go to play rehearsals, basketball games, dances. In the evenings he sat in a green chair and smoked cigarettes, drank scotch, read books—the same kinds of books, year after year. They were all about Eskimos and Arctic explorations—an interest he had developed during his tour in Greenland. Sometimes, when I came in late and was in the kitchen making a snack, I watched him through the doorway. Often he looked away from the book and gazed toward the window. He would strike a match and let it burn to his thumb and fingertip, then wave it out. He would raise the glass but not drink from it. I think he must have imagined himself to be in the Arctic during those moments, a warrior tracking across the ice for bear or seal. Sometimes he was waiting for me to join him. He wanted to tell me about the techniques the Eskimos had developed for survival, the way they stitched up skins to make them watertight vessels. He became obsessive on the subject of meat. The Eskimo diet was nearly all protein. "Eat meat," he said. Two professors at Columbia had tested the value of the Eskimo diet by eating nothing but caribou for a year and claimed they were healthier at the end of the experiment than they had been before.

Later, when I went to college, he developed the habit of calling me long distance when my mother and grandmother had gone to bed and he was alone downstairs with a drink. "Are you getting enough protein?" he asked me once at three in the morning. It was against dorm rules to put through calls after midnight except in cases of emergency, but his deep, commanding voice was so authoritative ("This is Gemma Jackson's father, and I must speak with her immediately") that it was for some time believed on my corridor that the people in my family were either accident-prone or suffering from long terminal illnesses.

* * *

He died the summer I received my master's degree. I had accepted a teaching position at a high school in Chicago, and I went home for a month before school began. He was overweight and short of breath. He drank too much, smoked too many cigarettes. The doctor told him to stop, my mother told him, my grandmother told him.

My grandmother was upstairs watching television and my mother and I were sitting on the front porch. He was asleep in the green chair, with a book in his lap. I left the porch to go to the kitchen to make a sandwich, and as I passed by the chair I heard him say, "Ahhhh. Ahhhhh." I saw his fist rise to his chest. I saw his eyes open and dilate in the lamplight. I knelt beside him.

"Are you okay?" I said. "Are you dreaming?"

We buried him in a small cemetery near the farm where he was born. In the eulogy he was remembered for having survived the first wave of the invasion of Normandy. He was admired for having been the proprietor of a chain of excellent hardware stores.

"He didn't have to do this," my mother said after the funeral. "He did this to himself."

"He was a good man," said my grandmother. "He put a nice roof over our heads. He sent us to Europe twice."

Afterward I went alone to the cemetery. I knelt beside the heaps of wilting flowers—mostly roses and gladiolus, and one wreath of red, white, and blue carnations.

Above me, the maple pods spun through the sunlight like wings, and in the distance the corn trumpeted green across the hillsides. I touched the loose black soil at the edge of the flowers. Able, Baker, Charlie, Dog. I could remember the beginning of the alphabet, up through Mike and Nan. I could remember the end. X-ray, Yoke, Zebra. I was his eldest child, and he taught me what he knew. I wept then, but not because he had gone back to Ohio to read about the Eskimos and sell the artifacts of civilized life to homeowners and builders. I wept because when I was twelve years old I had stood on a snowy riverbank as he became a shadow on the ice, and waited to see whether he would slip between the cracking floes into the water.

# HELENA MARÍA VIRAMONTES

(1954– )

Part of the resurgence of Hispanic writers in the 1970s and 1980s, Helena María Viramontes writes fiction that powerfully addresses social issues, especially the forms of oppression—economic, racial, and sexual—that affect the lives of mostly Chicana women in the Los Angeles area. For Viramontes, fiction is a means of spurring social change.

Viramontes was born and raised in East Los Angeles, daughter of a construction worker and a homemaker. After graduating from Garfield High School, she attended Immaculate Heart College while working twenty hours a week. She completed a B.A. in 1975, one of five Chicanas in her class. She enrolled in the creative writing program at the University of California at Irvine, but did not complete an M.F.A. until after the publication of her collection, *The Moths and Other Stories,* in 1985. She coedited a volume on Chicana writers, *Chicana Creativity and Criticism* (1988). A second collection of stories, *Paris Rats in E.L.A.*, appeared in 1993. Her first novel, *Under the Feet of Jesus,* was published in 1995, followed in 2000 with the novel *Their Dogs Came with Them.* She currently teaches at Cornell University.

## The Cariboo Cafe

I.

They arrived in the secrecy of night, as displaced people often do, stopping over for a week, a month, eventually staying a lifetime. The plan was simple. Mother would work too until they saved enough to move into a finer future where the toilet was one's own and the children needn't be frightened. In the meantime, they played in the back alleys, among the broken glass, wise to the ways of the streets. Rule one: never talk to strangers, not even the neighbor who paced up and down the hallways talking to himself. Rule two: the police, or "polie" as Sonya's popi pronounced the word, was La Migra in disguise and thus should always be avoided. Rule three: keep your key with you at all times—the four walls of the apartment were the only protection against the streets until Popi returned home.

Sonya considered her key a guardian saint and she wore it around her neck as such until this afternoon. Gone was the string with the big knot. Gone was the key. She hadn't noticed its disappearance until she picked up Macky from Mrs. Avila's house and walked home. She remembered playing with it as Amá walked her to school. But lunch break came, and Lalo wrestled her down so that he could see her underwear, and it probably fell somewhere between the iron rings and sandbox. Sitting on the front steps of the apartment building, she considered how to explain the missing key without having to reveal what Lalo had seen, for she wasn't quite sure which offense carried the worse penalty.

She watched people piling in and spilling out of the buses, watched an old man asleep on the bus bench across the street. He resembled a crumbled ball of paper, huddled up in the security of a tattered coat. She became aware of their mutual loneliness and she rested her head against her knees blackened by the soot of the playground asphalt.

The old man eventually awoke, yawned like a lion's roar, unfolded his limbs and staggered to the alley where he urinated between two trash bins. (She wanted to peek, but it was Macky who turned to look.) He zipped up, drank from a paper bag and she watched him until he disappeared around the corner. As time passed, buses came less frequently, and every other person seemed to resemble Popi. Macky became bored. He picked through the trash barrel; later, and to Sonya's fright, he ran into the street after a pigeon. She understood his restlessness for waiting was as relentless as long lines to the bathroom. When a small boy walked by, licking away at a scoop of vanilla ice cream, Macky ran after him. In his haste to outrun Sonya's grasp, he fell and tore the knee of his denim jeans. He began to cry, wiping snot against his sweater sleeve.

"See?" She asked, dragging him back to the porch steps by his wrist. "See? God punished you!" It was a thing she always said because it seemed to work. Terrified by the scrawny tortured man on the cross, Macky wanted to avoid his wrath as much as possible. She sat him on the steps in one gruff jerk. Seeing his torn jeans, and her own scraped knees, she wanted to join in his sorrow, and cry. Instead she snuggled so close to him, she could hear his stomach growling.

"Coke," he asked. Mrs. Avila gave him an afternoon snack which usually held him over until dinner. But sometimes Macky got lost in the midst of her own six children and . . .

Mrs. Avila! It took Sonya a few moments to realize the depth of her idea. They could wait there, at Mrs. Avila's. And she'd probably have a stack of flour tortillas, fresh off the comal, ready to eat with butter and salt. She grabbed his hand. "Mrs. Avila has Coke."

"Coke!" He jumped up to follow his sister. "Coke," he cooed.

At the major intersection, Sonya quietly calculated their next move while the scores of adults hurried to their own destinations. She scratched one knee as she tried retracing her journey home in the labyrinth of her memory. Things never looked the same when backwards and she searched for familiar scenes. She looked for the newspaperman who sat in a little house with a little T.V. on and selling magazines with naked girls holding beach balls. But he was gone. What remained was a little closet-like shed with chains and locks, and she wondered what happened to him, for she thought he lived there with the naked ladies.

They finally crossed the street at a cautious pace, the colors of the street lights brighter as darkness descended, a stereo store blaring music from two huge, blasting speakers. She thought it was the disco store she passed, but she didn't remember if the sign was green or red. And she didn't remember it flashing like it was now. Studying the neon light, she bumped into a tall, lanky dark man. Maybe it was Raoul's Popi. Raoul was a dark boy in her class that she felt sorry for because everyone called him sponge head. Maybe she could ask Raoul's Popi where Mrs. Avila lived, but before she could think it all out, red sirens flashed in their faces and she shielded her eyes to see the polie.

The polie is men in black who get kids and send them to Tijuana, says Popi. Whenever you see them, run, because they hate you, says Popi. She grabs Macky by his sleeve and they crawl under a table of bargain cassettes. Macky's nose is running, and when he sniffles, she puts her finger to her lips. She peeks from behind the poster of Vincente Fernandez to see Raoul's father putting keys and stuff from his pockets onto the hood of the polie car. And it's true, they're putting him in the car and taking him to Tijuana. Popi, she murmured to herself. Mamá.

"Coke." Macky whispered, as if she had failed to remember.

"Ssssh. Mi'jo, when I say run, you run, okay?" She waited for the tires to turn out, and as the black and white drove off, she whispered "Now," and they scurried out from under the table and ran across the street, oblivious to the horns.

They entered a maze of alleys and dead ends, the long, abandoned warehouses shadowing any light. Macky stumbled and she continued to drag him until his crying, his untied sneakers, and his raspy breathing finally forced her to stop. She scanned the boarded up boxcars, the rows of rusted rails to make sure the polie wasn't following them. Tired, her heart bursting, she leaned him against a tall, chainlink fence. Except for the rambling of some railcars, silence prevailed, and she could hear Macky sniffling in the darkness. Her mouth was parched and she swallowed to rid herself of the metallic taste of fear. The shadows stalked them, hovering like nightmares. Across the tracks, in the distance, was a room with a yellow glow, like a beacon light at the end of a dark sea. She pinched Macky's nose with the corner of her dress, took hold of his sleeve. At least the shadows will be gone, she concluded, at the zero zero place.

II.

Don't look at me. I didn't give it the name. It was passed on. Didn't even know what it meant until I looked it up in some library dictionary. But I kinda liked the name. It's, well, romantic, almost like the name of a song, you know, so I kept it. That was before JoJo turned fourteen even. But now if you take a look at the sign, the paint's peeled off 'cept for the two O's. The double zero cafe. Story of my life. But who cares, right? As long as everyone 'round the factories know I run an honest business.

The place is clean. That's more than I can say for some people who walk through that door. And I offer the best prices on double burger deluxes this side of Main Street. Okay, so its not pure beef. Big deal, most meat markets do the same. But I make no bones 'bout it. I tell them up front, "yeah, it ain't dogmeat, but it ain't sirloin either." Cause that's the sort of guy I am. Honest.

That's the trouble. It never pays to be honest. I tried scrubbing the stains off the floor, so that my customers won't be reminded of what happened. But they keep walking as if my cafe ain't fit for lepers. And that's the thanks I get for being a fair guy.

Not once did I hang up all those stupid signs. You know, like "We reserve the right to refuse service to anyone," or "No shirt, no shoes, no service." To tell you the truth—which is what I always do though it don't pay—I wouldn't have nobody walking through that door. The streets are full of scum, but scum gotta eat too is the way I see it. Now, listen. I ain't talkin 'bout out-of-luckers, weirdos, whores, you know. I'm talking 'bout five-to-lifers out of some tech. I'm talking Paulie.

I swear Paulie is thirty-five, or six. JoJo's age if he were still alive, but he don't look a day over ninety. Maybe why I let him hang out 'cause he's JoJo's age. Shit, he's okay as long as he don't bring his wigged out friends whose voices sound like a record at low speed. Paulie's got too many stories and they all get jammed up in his mouth so I can't make out what he's saying. He scares the other customers too, acting like he is shadow boxing, or like a monkey hopping on a frying pan. You know, nervous, jumpy, his jaw all falling and his eyes bulgy and dirt yellow. I give him the last booth, coffee and yesterday's donut holes to keep him quiet. After a few minutes, out he goes, before lunch. I'm too old, you know, too busy making ends meet to be nursing the kid. And so is Delia.

That Delia's got these unique titties. One is bigger than another. Like an orange and grapefruit. I kid you not. They're like that on account of when she was real young she had some babies, and they all sucked only one favorite tittie. So one is bigger than the other, and when she used to walk in with Paulie, huggy huggy and wearing those tight leotard blouses that show the nipple dots, you could see the difference. You could tell right off that Paulie was proud of them, the way he'd hang his arm over her shoulder and squeeze the grapefruit. They kill me, her knockers. She'd come in real queen-like, smacking gum and chewing the fat with the illegals who work in that garment warehouse. They come in real queen-like too, sitting in the best booth near the window, and order cokes. That's all. Cokes. Hey, but I'm a nice guy, so what if they mess up my table, bring their own lunches and only order small cokes, leaving a dime as tip? So sometimes the place ain't crawling with people, you comprende buddy? A dime's a dime as long as it's in my pocket.

Like I gotta pay my bills too, I gotta eat. So like I serve anybody whose got the greens, including that crazy lady and the two kids that started all the trouble. If only I had closed early. But I had to wash the dinner dishes on account of I can't afford a dishwasher. I was scraping off some birdshit glue stuck to this plate, see, when I hear the bells jingle against the door. I hate those fucking bells. That was Nell's idea. Nell's my wife; my ex-wife. So people won't sneak up on you, says my ex. Anyway, I'm standing behind the counter staring at this short woman. Already I know that she's bad news because she looks street to me. Round face, burnt toast color, black hair that hangs like straight ropes. Weirdo, I've had enough to last me a lifetime. She's wearing a shawl and a dirty slip is hanging out. Shit if I have to dish out a free meal. Funny thing, but I didn't see the two kids 'til I got to the booth. All of a sudden I see these big eyes looking over the table's edge at me. It shook me up, the way they kinda appeared. Aw, maybe they were there all the time.

The boy's a sweetheart. Short Order don't look nothing like his mom. He's got dried snot all over his dirty cheeks and his hair ain't seen a comb for years. She can't take care of herself, much less him or the doggie of a sister. But he's a tough one, and I pinch his nose 'cause he's a real sweetheart like JoJo. You know, my boy.

It's his sister I don't like. She's got these poking eyes that follow you 'round 'cause she don't trust no one. Like when I reach for Short Order, she flinches like I'm 'bout to tear his nose off, gives me a nasty, squinty look. She's maybe five, maybe six, I don't know, and she acts like she owns him. Even when I bring the burgers, she doesn't let go of his hand. Finally, the fellow bites it and I wink at him. A real sweetheart.

In the next booth, I'm twisting the black crud off the top of the ketchup bottle when I hear the lady saying something in Spanish. Right off I know she's illegal, which explains why she looks like a weirdo. Anyway, she says something nice to them 'cause it's in the same tone that Nell used when I'd rest my head on her lap. I'm surprised the illegal's got a fiver to pay, but she and her tail leave no tip. I see Short Order's small bites on the bun.

You know, a cafe's the kinda business that moves. You get some regulars but most of them are on the move, so I don't pay much attention to them. But this lady's face sticks like egg yolk on a plate. It ain't 'til I open a beer and sit in front of the B & W to check out the wrestling matches that I see this news bulletin 'bout two missing kids. I recognize the mugs right away. Short Order and his doggie sister. And all of a sudden her face is out of my mind. Aw fuck, I say, and put my beer down so hard that the foam spills onto last month's Hustler. Aw fuck.

See, if Nell was here, she'd know what to do: call the cops. But I don't know. Cops ain't exactly my friends, and all I need is for bacon to be crawling all over my place. And seeing how her face is vague now, I decide to wait 'til the late news. Short Order don't look right neither. I'll have another beer and wait for the late news.

The alarm rings at four and I have this headache, see, from the sixpak, and I gotta get up. I was supposed to do something, but I got all suck-faced and forgot. Turn off the T.V., take a shower, but that don't help my memory any.

Hear sirens near the railroad tracks. Cops. I'm supposed to call the cops. I'll do it after I make the coffee, put away the eggs, get the donuts out. But Paulie strolls in looking partied out. We actually talk 'bout last night's wrestling match between BoBo Brazil and the Crusher. I slept through it, you see. Paulie orders an O.J. on account of he's catching a cold. I open up my big mouth and ask about De. Drinks the rest of his O.J., says real calm like, that he caught her eaglespread with the Vegetable fatso down the block. Then, very polite like, Paulie excuses himself. That's one thing I gotta say about Paulie. He may be one big Fuck-up, but he's got manners. Juice gave him shit cramps, he says.

Well, leave it to Paulie. Good ole Mr. Fuck-Up himself to help me with the cops. The prick O.D.'s in my crapper; vomits and shits are all over—I mean all over the fuckin' walls. That's the thanks I get for being Mr. Nice Guy. I had the cops looking up my ass for the stash; says one, the one wearing a mortician's suit, We'll be back, we'll be back when you ain't looking. If I was pushing, would I be burning my goddamn balls off with spitting grease? So fuck 'em, I think. I ain't gonna tell you nothing 'bout the lady. Fuck you, I say to them as they drive away. Fuck your mother.

That's why Nell was good to have 'round. She could be a pain in the ass, you know, like making me hang those stupid bells, but mostly she knew what to do. See, I go bananas. Like my mind fries with the potatoes and by the end of the day, I'm deader than dogshit. Let me tell you what I mean. A few hours later, after I swore I wouldn't give the fuckin' pigs the time of day, the green vans roll up across the street. While I'm stirring the chili con carne I see all these illegals running out of the factory to hide, like roaches when the lightswitch goes on. I taste the chile, but I really can't taste nothing on account of I've lost my appetite after cleaning out the crapper, when three of them run into the Cariboo. They look at me as if I'm gonna stop them, but when I go on stirring the chile, they run to the bathroom. Now look, I'm a nice guy, but I don't like to be used, you know? Just 'cause they're regulars don't mean jackshit. I run an honest business. And that's what I told them Agents. See, by that time, my stomach being all dizzy, and the cops all over the place, and the three illegals running in here, I was all confused, you know. That's how it was, and well, I haven't seen Nell for years, and I guess that's why I pointed to the bathroom.

I don't know. I didn't expect handcuffs and them agents putting their hands up and down their thighs. When they walked passed me, they didn't look at me. That is the two young ones. The older one, the one that looked silly in the handcuffs on account of she's old enough to be my grandma's grandma, looks straight at my face with the same eyes Short Order's sister gave me yesterday. What a day. Then, to top off the potatoes with the gravy, the bells jingle against the door and in enters the lady again with the two kids.

III.

He's got lice. Probably from living in the detainers. Those are the rooms where they round up the children and make them work for their food. I saw them from the window. Their eyes are cut glass, and no one looks for sympathy. They take turns, sorting out the arms from the legs, heads from the torsos. Is that one your mother? one guard asks, holding a mummified head with eyes shut tighter than coffins. But the children no longer cry. They just continue sorting as if they were salvaging cans from a heap of trash. They do this until time is up and they drift into a tunnel, back to the womb of sleep, while a new group comes in. It is all very organized. I bite my fist to keep from retching. Please God, please don't let Geraldo be there.

For you see, they took Geraldo. By mistake, of course. It was my fault. I shouldn't have sent him out to fetch me a mango. But it was just to the corner. I didn't even bother to put his sweater on. I hear his sandals flapping against the gravel. I follow him with my eyes, see him scratching his buttocks when the wind picks up swiftly, as it often does at such unstable times, and I have to close the door.

The darkness becomes a serpent's tongue, swallowing us whole. It is the night of La Llorona. The women come up from the depths of sorrow to search for their children. I join them, frantic, desperate, and our eyes become scrutinizers, our bodies opiated with the scent of their smiles. Descending from door to door, the wind whips our faces. I hear the wailing of the women and know it to be my own. Geraldo is nowhere to be found.

Dawn is not welcomed. It is a drunkard wavering between consciousness and sleep. My life is fleeing, moving south towards the sea. My tears are now hushed and faint.

The boy, barely a few years older than Geraldo, lights a cigarette, rests it on the edge of his desk, next to all the other cigarette burns. The blinds are down to keep the room cool. Above him hangs a single bulb that shades and shadows his face in such a way as to mask his expressions. He is not to be trusted. He fills in the information, for I cannot write. Statements delivered, we discuss motives.

"Spies," says he, flicking a long burning ash from the cigarette onto the floor, then wolfing the smoke in as if his lungs had an unquenchable thirst for nicotine. "We arrest spies. Criminals." He says this with cigarette smoke spurting out from his nostrils like a nose bleed.

"Spies? Criminal?" My shawl falls to the ground. "He is only five and a half years old." I plead for logic with my hands. "What kind of crimes could a five year old commit?"

"Anyone who so willfully supports the contras in any form must be arrested and punished without delay." He knows the line by heart.

I think about moths and their stupidity. Always attracted by light, they fly into fires, or singe their wings with the heat of the single bulb and fall on his desk, writhing in pain. I don't understand why nature has been so cruel as to prevent them from feeling warmth. He dismisses them with a sweep of a hand. "This," he continues, "is what we plan to do with the contras, and those who aid them." He inhales again.

"But, Señor, he's just a baby."

"Contras are tricksters. They exploit the ignorance of people like you. Perhaps they convinced your son to circulate pamphlets. You should be talking to them, not us." The cigarette is down to his yellow finger tips, to where he can no longer continue to hold it without burning himself. He throws the stub on the floor, crushes it under his boot. "This," he says, screwing his boot into the ground, "is what the contras do to people like you."

"Señor. I am a washer woman. You yourself see I cannot read or write. There is my X. Do you think my son can read?" How can I explain to this man that we are poor, that we live as best we can? "If such a thing has happened, perhaps he wanted to make a few centavos for his mamá. He's just a baby."

"So you are admitting his guilt?"

"So you are admitting he is here?" I promise, once I see him, hold him in my arms again, I will never, never scold him for wanting more than I can give. "You see, he needs his sweater . . ." The sweater lies limp on my lap.

"Your assumption is incorrect."

"May I check the detainers for myself?"

"In time."

"And what about my Geraldo?"

"In time." He dismisses me, placing the forms in a big envelope crinkled by the day's humidity.

"When?" I am wringing the sweater with my hands.

"Don't be foolish, woman. Now off with your nonsense. We will try to locate your Pedro."

"Geraldo."

* * *

Maria came by today with a bowl of hot soup. She reports in her usual excited way, that the soldiers are now eating the brains of their victims. It is unlike her to be so scandalous. So insane. Geraldo must be cold without his sweater.

"Why?" I ask as the soup gets cold. I will write Tavo tonight.

At the plaza a group of people are whispering. They are quiet when I pass, turn to one another and put their finger to their lips to cage their voices. They continue as I reach the church steps. To be associated with me is condemnation.

Today I felt like killing myself, Lord. But I am too much of a coward. I am a washer woman, Lord. My mother was one, and hers too. We have lived as best we can, washing other people's laundry, rinsing off other people's dirt until our hands crust and chap. When my son wanted to hold my hand, I held soap instead. When he wanted to play, my feet were in pools of water. It takes such little courage, being a washer woman. Give me strength, Lord.

What have I done to deserve this, Lord? Raising a child is like building a kite. You must bend the twigs enough, but not too much, for you might break them. You must find paper that is delicate and light enough to wave on the breath of the wind, yet must withstand the ravages of a storm. You must tie the strings gently but firmly so that it may not fall apart. You must let the string go, eventually, so that the kite will stretch its ambition. It is such delicate work, Lord, being a mother. This I understand, Lord, because I am, but you have snapped the cord, Lord. It was only a matter of minutes and my life is lost somewhere in the clouds. I don't know, I don't know what games you play, Lord.

These four walls are no longer my house, the earth beneath it, no longer my home. Weeds have replaced all good crops. The irrigation ditches are clodded with bodies. No matter where we turn, there are rumors facing us and we try to live as best we can, under the rule of men who rape women, then rip their fetuses from their bellies. Is this our home? Is this our country? I ask Maria. Don't these men have mothers, lovers, babies, sisters? Don't they see what they are doing? Later, Maria says, these men are babes farted out from the Devil's ass. We check to make sure no one has heard her say this.

Without Geraldo, this is not my home, the earth beneath it, not my country. This is why I have to leave. Maria begins to cry. Not because I am going, but because she is staying.

Tavo. Sweet Tavo. He has sold his car to send me the money. He has just married and he sold his car for me. Thank you, Tavo. Not just for the money. But also for making me believe in the goodness of people again . . . The money is enough to buy off the border soldiers. The rest will come from the can. I have saved for Geraldo's schooling and it is enough for a bus ticket to Juarez. I am to wait for Tavo there.

I spit. I do not turn back.

Perhaps I am wrong in coming. I worry that Geraldo will not have a home to return to, no mother to cradle his nightmares away, soothe the scars, stop the hemorrhaging of his heart. Tavo is happy I am here, but it is crowded, the three of us, and I hear them arguing behind their closed door. There is only so much a nephew can provide. I must find work. I have two hands willing to work. But the heart. The heart wills only to watch the children playing in the street.

The machines, their speed and dust, make me ill. But I can clean. I clean toilets, dump trash cans, sweep. Disinfect the sinks. I will gladly do whatever is necessary to repay Tavo. The baby is due any time and money is tight. I volunteer for odd hours, weekends, since I really have very little to do. When the baby comes I know Tavo's wife will not let me hold it, for she thinks I am a bad omen. I know it.

Why would God play such a cruel joke, if he isn't my son? I jumped the curb, dashed out into the street, but the street is becoming wider and wider. I've lost him once and can't lose him again and to hell with the screeching tires and the horns and the headlights barely touching my hips. I can't take my eyes off him because, you see, they are swift and cunning and can take your life with a snap of a finger. But God is a just man and His mistakes can be undone.

My heart pounds in my head like a sledge hammer against the asphalt. What if it isn't Geraldo? What if he is still in the detainer waiting for me? A million questions, one answer: Yes. Geraldo, yes. I want to touch his hand first, have it disappear in my own because it is so small. His eyes look at me in total bewilderment. I grab him because the earth is crumbling beneath us and I must save him. We both fall to the ground.

A hot meal is in store. A festival. The cook, a man with shrunken cheeks and the hands of a car mechanic, takes a liking to Geraldo. Its like birthing you again, mi'jo. My baby.

I bathe him. He flutters in excitement, the water grey around him. I scrub his head with lye to kill off the lice, comb his hair out with a fine tooth comb. I wash his rubbery penis, wrap him in a towel and he stands in front of the window, shriveling and sucking milk from a carton, his hair shiny from the dampness.

He finally sleeps. So easily, she thinks. On her bed next to the open window he coos in the night. Below the sounds of the city become as monotonous as the ocean waves. She rubs his back with warm oil, each stroke making up for the days of his absence. She hums to him softly so that her breath brushes against his face, tunes that are rusted and crack in her throat. The hotel neon shines on his back and she covers him.

All the while the young girl watches her brother sleeping. She removes her sneakers, climbs into the bed, snuggles up to her brother, and soon her breathing is raspy, her arms under her stomach.

The couch is her bed tonight. Before switching the light off, she checks once more to make sure this is not a joke. Tomorrow she will make arrangements to go home. Maria will be the same, the mango stand on the corner next to the church plaza will be the same. It will all be the way it was before. But enough excitement. For the first time in years, her mind is quiet of all noise and she has the desire to sleep.

The bells jingle when the screen door slaps shut behind them. The cook wrings his hands in his apron, looking at them. Geraldo is in the middle, and they sit in the booth farthest away from the window, near the hall where the toilets are, and right away the small boy, his hair now neatly combed and split to the side like an adult, wrinkles his nose at the peculiar smell. The cook wipes perspiration off his forehead with the corner of his apron, finally comes over to the table.

She looks so different, so young. Her hair is combed slick back into one thick braid and her earrings hang like baskets of golden pears on her finely sculptured ears. He can't believe how different she looks. Almost beautiful. She points to what she wants on the menu with a white, clean fingernail. Although confused, the cook is sure of one thing—it's Short Order all right, pointing to him with a commanding finger, saying his only English word: coke.

His hands tremble as he slaps the meat on the grill; the patties hiss instantly. He feels like vomiting. The chile overboils and singes the fires, deep red trail of chile crawling to the floor and puddling there. He grabs the handles, burns himself, drops the pot on the wooden racks of the floor. He sucks his fingers, the patties blackening and sputtering grease. He flips them, and the burgers hiss anew. In some strange way he hopes they have disappeared, and he takes a quick look only to see Short Order's sister, still in the same dress, still holding her brother's hand. She is craning her neck to peek at what is going on in the kitchen.

Aw, fuck, he says, in a fog of smoke his eyes burning tears. He can't believe it, but he's crying. For the first time since JoJo's death, he's crying. He becomes angry at the lady for returning. At JoJo. At Nell for leaving him. He wishes Nell here, but doesn't know where she's at or what part of Vietnam JoJo is all crumbled up in. Children gotta be with their parents, family gotta be together, he thinks. It's only right. The emergency line is ringing.

Two black and whites roll up and skid the front tires against the curb. The flashing lights carousel inside the cafe. She sees them opening the screen door, their guns taut and cold like steel erections. Something is wrong, and she looks to the cowering cook. She has been betrayed, and her heart is pounding like footsteps running, faster, louder, faster and she can't hear what they are saying to her. She jumps up from the table, grabs Geraldo by the wrist, his sister dragged along because, like her, she refuses to release his hand. Their lips are mouthing words she can't hear, can't comprehend. Run, Run is all she can think of to do, Run through the hallway, out to the alley, Run because they will never take him away again.

But her legs are heavy and she crushes Geraldo against her, so tight, as if she wants to conceal him in her body again, return him to her belly so that they will not castrate him and hang his small, blue penis on her door, not crush his face so that he is unrecognizable, not bury him among the heaps of bones, and ears, and teeth, and jaws, because no one, but she, cared to know that he cried. For years he cried and she could hear him day and night. Screaming, howling, sobbing, shriveling and crying because he is only five years old, and all she wanted was a mango.

But the crying begins all over again. In the distance, she hears crying.

She refuses to let go. For they will have to cut her arms off to take him, rip her mouth off to keep her from screaming for help. Without thinking, she reaches over to where two pots of coffee are brewing and throws the streaming coffee into their faces. Outside, people begin to gather, pressing their faces against the window glass to get a good view. The cook huddles behind the counter, frightened, trembling. Their faces become distorted and she doesn't see the huge hand that takes hold of Geraldo and she begins screaming all over again, screaming so that the walls shake, screaming enough for all the women of murdered children, screaming, pleading for help from the people outside, and she pushes an open hand against an officer's nose, because no one will stop them and he pushes the gun barrel to her face.

And I laugh at his ignorance. How stupid of him to think that I will let them take my Geraldo away, just because he waves that gun like a flag. Well, to hell with you, you pieces of shit, do you hear me? Stupid, cruel pigs. To hell with you all, because you can no longer frighten me. I will fight you for my son until I have no hands left to hold a knife. I will fight you all because you're all farted out of the Devil's ass, and you'll not take us with you. I am laughing, howling at their stupidity. Because they should know by now that I will never let my son go and then I hear something crunching like broken glass against my forehead and I am blinded by the liquid darkness. But I hold onto his hand. That I can feel, you see, I'll never let go. Because we are going home. My son and I.

# ⁂ SANDRA CISNEROS
(1954– )

The only daughter in a family of seven children, Sandra Cisneros was born in Chicago to a Mexican father and Chicana mother. The family moved often between Chicago and Mexico City. Cisneros completed a B.A. at Loyola University in Chicago in 1976 and an M.F.A. at the University of Iowa's Writers' Workshop in 1978. After working as a teacher of high school dropouts, counselor and college recruiter, artist/poet in residence, and art administrator, she taught writing at the University of Michigan, the University of California at Irvine, and the University of New Mexico.

Cisneros has published several volumes of poetry: *Bad Boys* (1980), *The Rodrigo Poems* (1983), *My Wicked Wicked Ways* (1987), and *Loose Women* (1994). Her story collections include *The House on Mango Street* (1984) and *Woman Hollering Creek* (1991). Her prose is lyrical and poetic, a compact expression of feeling in its exploration of growing up female in a male-dominated Chicano culture and its connections with the dominant Anglo society. In 1995 Cisneros was awarded a MacArthur Fellowship. She lives in San Antonio.

## One Holy Night

> About the truth, if you give it to a person, then he has power over you. And if someone gives it to you, then they have made themselves your slave. It is a strong magic. You can never take it back.
>
> —CHAQ UXMAL PALOQUÍN

HE SAID his name was Chaq. Chaq Uxmal Paloquín. That's what he told me. He was of an ancient line of Mayan kings. Here, he said, making a map with the heel of his boot, this is where I come from, the Yucatán, the ancient cities. This is what Boy Baby said.

It's been eighteen weeks since Abuelita chased him away with the broom, and what I'm telling you I never told nobody, except Rachel and Lourdes, who know everything. He said he would love me like a revolution, like a religion. Abuelita burned the push-cart and sent me here, miles from home, in this town of dust, with one wrinkled witch woman who rubs my belly with jade, and sixteen nosy cousins.

I don't know how many girls have gone bad from selling cucumbers. I know I'm not the first. My mother took the crooked walk too, I'm told, and I'm sure my Abuelita has her own story, but it's not my place to ask.

Abuelita says it's Uncle Lalo's fault because he's the man of the family and if he had come home on time like he was supposed to and worked the pushcart on the days he was told to and watched over his goddaughter, who is too foolish to look after herself, nothing would've happened, and I wouldn't have to be sent to Mexico. But Uncle Lalo says if they had never left Mexico in the first place, shame enough would have kept a girl from doing devil things.

I'm not saying I'm not bad. I'm not saying I'm special. But I'm not like the Allport Street girls, who stand in doorways and go with men into alleys.

All I know is I didn't want it like that. Not against the bricks or hunkering in somebody's car. I wanted it come undone like gold thread, like a tent full of birds. The way it's supposed to be, the way I knew it would be when I met Boy Baby.

But you must know, I was no girl back then. And Boy Baby was no boy. Chaq Uxmal Paloquín. Boy Baby was a man. When I asked him how old he was he said he didn't know. The past and the future are the same thing. So he seemed boy and baby and man all at once, and the way he looked at me, how do I explain?

I'd park the pushcart in front of the Jewel food store Saturdays. He bought a mango on a stick the first time. Paid for it with a new twenty. Next Saturday he was back. Two mangoes, lime juice, and chili powder, keep the change. The third Saturday he asked for a cucumber spear and ate it slow. I didn't see him after that till the day he brought me Kool-Aid in a plastic cup. Then I knew what I felt for him.

Maybe you wouldn't like him. To you he might be a bum. Maybe he looked it. Maybe. He had broken thumbs and burnt fingers. He had thick greasy fingernails he never cut and dusty hair. And all his bones were strong ones like a man's. I waited every Saturday in my same blue dress. I sold all the mango and cucumber, and then Boy Baby would come finally.

What I knew of Chaq was only what he told me, because nobody seemed to know where he came from. Only that he could speak a strange language that no one could understand, said his name translated into boy, or boy-child, and so it was the street people nicknamed him Boy Baby.

I never asked about his past. He said it was all the same and didn't matter, past and the future all the same to his people. But the truth has a strange way of following you, of coming up to you and making you listen to what it has to say.

Night time. Boy Baby brushes my hair and talks to me in his strange language because I like to hear it. What I like to hear him tell is how he is Chaq, Chaq of the people of the sun, Chaq of the temples, and what he says sounds sometimes like broken clay, and at other times like hollow sticks, or like the swish of old feathers crumbling into dust.

He lived behind Esparza & Sons Auto Repair in a little room that used to be a closet—pink plastic curtains on a narrow window, a dirty cot covered with newspapers, and a cardboard box filled with socks and rusty tools. It was there, under one bald bulb, in the back room of the Esparza garage, in the single room with pink curtains, that he showed me the guns—twenty-four in all. Rifles and pistols, one rusty musket, a machine gun, and several tiny weapons with mother-of-pearl handles that looked like toys. So you'll see who I am, he said, laying them all out on the bed of newspapers. So you'll understand. But I didn't want to know.

The stars foretell everything, he said. My birth. My son's. The boy-child who will bring back the grandeur of my people from those who have broken the arrows, from those who have pushed the ancient stones off their pedestals.

Then he told how he had prayed in the Temple of the Magician years ago as a child when his father had made him promise to bring back the ancient ways. Boy Baby had cried in the temple dark that only the bats made holy. Boy Baby who was man and child among the great and dusty guns lay down on the newspaper bed and wept for a thousand years. When I touched him, he looked at me with the sadness of stone.

You must not tell anyone what I am going to do, he said. And what I remember next is how the moon, the pale moon with its one yellow eye, the moon of Tikal, and Tulum, and Chichén, stared through the pink plastic curtains. Then something inside bit me, and I gave out a cry as if the other, the one I wouldn't be anymore, leapt out.

So I was initiated beneath an ancient sky by a great and mighty heir—Chaq Uxmal Paloquín. I, Ixchel, his queen.

* * *

The truth is, it wasn't a big deal. It wasn't any deal at all. I put my bloody panties inside my T-shirt and ran home hugging myself. I thought about a lot of things on the way home. I thought about all the world and how suddenly I became a part of history and wondered if everyone on the street, the sewing machine lady and the *panadería* saleswomen and the woman with two kids sitting on the bus bench didn't all know. *Did I look any different? Could they tell?* We were all the same somehow, laughing behind our hands, waiting the way all women wait, and when we find out, we wonder why the world and a million years made such a big deal over nothing.

I know I was supposed to feel ashamed, but I wasn't ashamed. I wanted to stand on top of the highest building, the top-top floor, and yell, *I know.*

Then I understood why Abuelita didn't let me sleep over at Lourdes's house full of too many brothers, and why the Roman girl in the movies always runs away from the soldier, and what happens when the scenes in love stories begin to fade, and why brides blush, and how it is that sex isn't simply a box you check *M* or *F* on in the test we get at school.

I was wise. The corner girls were still jumping into their stupid little hopscotch squares. I laughed inside and climbed the wooden stairs two by two to the second floor rear where me and Abuelita and Uncle Lalo live. I was still laughing when I opened the door and Abuelita asked, Where's the pushcart?

And then I didn't know what to do.

* * *

It's a good thing we live in a bad neighborhood. There are always plenty of bums to blame for your sins. If it didn't happen the way I told it, it really could've. We looked and looked all over for the kids who stole my pushcart. The story wasn't the best, but since I had to make it up right then and there with Abuelita staring a hole through my heart, it wasn't too bad.

For two weeks I had to stay home. Abuelita was afraid the street kids who had stolen the cart would be after me again. Then I thought I might go over to the Esparza garage and take the pushcart out and leave it in some alley for the police to find, but I was never allowed to leave the house alone. Bit by bit the truth started to seep out like a dangerous gasoline.

First the nosy woman who lives upstairs from the laundromat told my Abuelita she thought something was fishy, the pushcart wheeled into Esparza & Sons every Saturday after dark, how a man, the same dark Indian one, the one who never talks to anybody, walked with me when the sun went down and pushed the cart into the garage, that one there, and yes we went inside, there where the fat lady named Concha, whose hair is dyed a hard black, pointed a fat finger.

I prayed that we would not meet Boy Baby, and since the gods listen and are mostly good, Esparza said yes, a man like that had lived there but was gone, had packed a few things and left the pushcart in a corner to pay for his last week's rent.

We had to pay $20 before he would give us our pushcart back. Then Abuelita made me tell the real story of how the cart had disappeared, all of which I told this time, except for that one night, which I would have to tell anyway, weeks later, when I prayed for the moon of my cycle to come back, but it would not.

* * *

When Abuelita found out I was going to *dar a luz,* she cried until her eyes were little, and blamed Uncle Lalo, and Uncle Lalo blamed this country, and Abuelita blamed the infamy of men. That is when she burned the cucumber pushcart and called me a *sinvergüenza* because I *am* without shame.

Then I cried too—Boy Baby was lost from me—until my head was hot with headaches and I fell asleep. When I woke up, the cucumber pushcart was dust and Abuelita was sprinkling holy water on my head.

Abuelita woke up early every day and went to the Esparza garage to see if news about that *demonio* had been found, had Chaq Uxmal Paloquín sent any letters, any, and when the other mechanics heard that name they laughed, and asked if we had made it up, that we could have some letters that had come for Boy Baby, no forwarding address, since he had gone in such a hurry.

There were three. The first, addressed "Occupant," demanded immediate payment for a four-month-old electric bill. The second was one I recognized right away—a brown envelope fat with cake-mix coupons and fabric-softener samples—because we'd gotten one just like it. The third was addressed in a spidery Spanish to a Señor C. Cruz, on paper so thin you could read it unopened by the light of the sky. The return address a convent in Tampico.

This was to whom my Abuelita wrote in hopes of finding the man who could correct my ruined life, to ask if the good nuns might know the whereabouts of a certain Boy Baby—and if they were hiding him it would be of no use because God's eyes see through all souls.

We heard nothing for a long time. Abuelita took me out of school when my uniform got tight around the belly and said it was a shame I wouldn't be able to graduate with the other eighth graders.

Except for Lourdes and Rachel, my grandma and Uncle Lalo, nobody knew about my past. I would sleep in the big bed I share with Abuelita same as always. I could hear Abuelita and Uncle Lalo talking in low voices in the kitchen as if they were praying the rosary, how they were going to send me to Mexico, to San Dionisio de Tlaltepango, where I have cousins and where I was conceived and would've been born had my grandma not thought it wise to send my mother here to the United States so that neighbors in San Dionisio de Tlaltepango wouldn't ask why her belly was suddenly big.

I was happy. I liked staying home. Abuelita was teaching me to crochet the way she had learned in Mexico. And just when I had mastered the tricky rosette stitch, the letter came from the convent which gave the truth about Boy Baby—however much we didn't want to hear.

He was born on a street with no name in a town called Miseria. His father, Eusebio, is a knife sharpener. His mother, Refugia, stacks apricots into pyramids and sells them on a cloth in the market. There are brothers. Sisters too of which I know little. The youngest, a Carmelite, writes me all this and prays for my soul, which is why I know it's all true.

Boy Baby is thirty-seven years old. His name is Chato which means fat-face. There is no Mayan blood.

* * *

I don't think they understand how it is to be a girl. I don't think they know how it is to have to wait your whole life. I count the months for the baby to be born, and it's like a ring of water inside me reaching out and out until one day it will tear from me with its own teeth.

Already I can feel the animal inside me stirring in his own uneven sleep. The witch woman says it's the dreams of weasels that make my child sleep the way he sleeps. She makes me eat white bread blessed by the priest, but I know it's the ghost of him inside me that circles and circles, and will not let me rest.

* * *

Abuelita said they sent me here just in time, because a little later Boy Baby came back to our house looking for me, and she had to chase him away with the broom. The next thing we hear, he's in the newspaper clippings his sister sends. A picture of him looking very much like stone, police hooked on either arm . . . *on the road to Las Grutas de Xtacumbilxuna, the Caves of the Hidden Girl . . . eleven female bodies . . . the last seven years . . .*

Then I couldn't read but only stare at the little black-and-white dots that make up the face I am in love with.

* * *

All my girl cousins here either don't talk to me, or those who do, ask questions they're too young to know *not* to ask. What they want to know really is how it is to have a man, because they're too ashamed to ask their married sisters.

They don't know what it is to lay so still until his sleep breathing is heavy, for the eyes in the dim dark to look and look without worry at the man-bones and the neck, the man-wrist and man-jaw thick and strong, all the salty dips and hollows, the stiff hair of the brow and sour swirl of sideburns, to lick the fat earlobes that taste of smoke, and stare at how perfect is a man.

I tell them, "It's a bad joke. When you find out you'll be sorry."

* * *

I'm going to have five children. Five. Two girls. Two boys. And one baby.

The girls will be called Lisette and Maritza. The boys I'll name Pablo and Sandro.

And my baby. My baby will be named Alegre, because life will always be hard.

* * *

Rachel says that love is like a big black piano being pushed off the top of a three-story building and you're waiting on the bottom to catch it. But Lourdes says it's not that way at all. It's like a top, like all the colors in the world are spinning so fast they're not colors anymore and all that's left is a white hum.

There was a man, a crazy who lived upstairs from us when we lived on South Loomis. He couldn't talk, just walked around all day with this harmonica in his mouth. Didn't play it. Just sort of breathed through it, all day long, wheezing, in and out, in and out.

This is how it is with me. Love I mean.

# ROBERT OLEN BUTLER (1944– )

Robert Butler was born in Granite City, Illinois, near St. Louis, where his father was a college professor and his mother an executive secretary. He went to Northwestern University and graduated with a B.A. in 1967, and then completed an M.A. in playwriting at the Writers' Workshop of the University of Iowa in 1969. He enlisted in the U.S. Army and studied the Vietnamese language as part of his training which began his long interest in Vietnamese culture. He served three years, 1969–1972, in army intelligence in Vietnam and as assistant to the American advisor to the mayor of Saigon. After leaving the service in 1973 he moved to New York City, worked variously as a high school teacher and an editor of a business newspaper, and wrote fiction whenever he could. In 1985, Butler accepted an appointment to the faculty at McNeece State University at Lake Charles, Louisiana, where he made contact with a Vietnamese refugee community that had settled in the area. This gave him material for his first collection of stories.

Butler produced six novels that achieved some critical success but low sales: *The Alleys of Eden* (1981), *Sun Dogs* (1982), *Countrymen of Bones* (1983), *On Distant Ground* (1985), *Wabash* (1987), and *The Deuce* (1989).

While he was known mostly as a novelist, it was his Pulitzer Prize–winning collection of stories, *A Good Scent from a Strange Mountain,* in 1993, that elevated his reputation to national prominence. Since then he has published the novels *They Whisper* (1994) and *The Deep Green Sea* (1998), as well as the collection of stories *Tabloid Dreams* (1996), each story of which takes off from a tabloid-like headline for a title and explores bizarre and unusual occurrences and ideas, a merging of the popular with the serious. Most of Butler's fiction deals with his Vietnam experiences, but his subject is not combat but rather the intersection of two cultures, the ways we both understand and fail to understand the other, as well as the loneliness and longing that often come from that meeting and the search for a meaningful identity.

# Relic

YOU MAY be surprised to learn that a man from Vietnam owns one of John Lennon's shoes. Not only one of John Lennon's shoes. One shoe that he was wearing when he was shot to death in front of the Dakota apartment building. That man is me, and I have money, of course, to buy this thing. I was a very wealthy man in my former country, before the spineless poor threw down their guns and let the communists take over. Something comes into your head as I speak: This is a hard man, a man of no caring; how can he speak of the "spineless poor"? I do not mean to say that these people are poor because they are cowards. I am saying that being poor can take away a man's courage. For those who are poor, being beaten down, robbed of rights, repressed under the worst possible form of tyranny is not enough worse than just being poor. Why should they risk the pain and the maiming and the death for so little benefit? If I was a poor man, I, too, would be spineless.

But I had wealth in Vietnam and that gave me courage enough even to sail away on the South China Sea, sail away from all those things I owned and come to a foreign country and start again with nothing. That is what I did. I came at last to New Orleans, Louisiana, and because I was once from North Vietnam and was Catholic, I ended up among my own people far east in Orleans Parish, in a community called Versailles, named after an apartment complex they put us in as refugees. I lived in such a place for a time. The ceilings were hardly eight feet high and there was no veranda, nowhere even to hang a wind chime. The emptiness of the rooms threatened to cast me down, take my courage. In Saigon, I owned many wonderful things: furniture of teak, inlaid with scenes made of tiles of ivory and pearl, showing how the Tru'ng sisters threw out the Chinese from our country in the year 40 A.D.; a part of an oracle bone from the earliest times of my country, the bone of some animal killed by ritual and carved with the future in Chinese characters; a dagger with a stag's antler handle in bronze. You might think that things like this should have protected me from what happened. There is much power in objects. My church teaches that clearly. A fragment of bone from a saint's body, a bit of skin, a lock of hair—all of these things have great power to do miracles, to cure, to heal.

But you see, though the Tru'ng sisters threw the Chinese out, just one year later the Chinese returned and the Tru'ng sisters had to retreat, and finally, in the year 43, they threw themselves into a river and drowned. And the oracle bone, though I did not know exactly what it said, probably dealt with events long past or maybe even foresaw this very world where I have ended up. And the dagger looked ceremonial and I'm sure was never drawn in anger. It would have been better if I had owned the tiniest fragment of some saint's body, but the church does not sell such things.

And here I sit, at the desk in the study in my house. I am growing rich once more and in the center of my desk sits this shoe. It is more like a little boot, coming up to the ankle and having no laces but a loop of leather at the back where John Lennon's forefinger went through to pull the shoe onto his foot, even that morning which was his last morning on this earth. Something comes into your head when I tell you this. It is my talent in making wealth to know what others are thinking. You wonder how I should come to have this shoe, how I know it is really what I say it is. I cannot give away the names of those who I dealt with, but I can tell you this much. I am a special collector of things. A man in New York who sells to me asked if I was interested in something unusual. When he told me about this shoe, I had the same response—how can I know for sure? Well, I met the man who provided the shoe, and I have photographs and even a newspaper article that identifies him as a very close associate of John Lennon. He says that certain items were very painful for the family, so they were disposed of and he was in possession of them and he knew that some people would appreciate them very much. He, too, is a Catholic. The other shoe was already gone, which is unfortunate, but this shoe was still available, and I paid much money for it.

Of course, I have made much money in my new country. It is a gift I have, and America is the land of opportunity. I started in paper lanterns and firecrackers and cay nêu, the New Year poles. I sold these at the time of Têt, our Vietnam New Year celebration, when the refugees wanted to think about home. I also sold them sandwiches and drinks and later I opened a restaurant and then a parlor with many video games. Versailles already has a pool hall, run by another good businessman, but I have video games in my place and the young men love these games, fighting alien spaceships and wizards and kung-fu villains with much greater skill than their fathers fought the communists. And I am now doing other things, bigger things, mostly in the shrimp industry. In ten years people from Vietnam will be the only shrimp fishermen in the Gulf of Mexico. I do not need an oracle bone to tell you this for sure. And when this is so, I will be making even more money.

I may even be able to break free of Versailles. I sit at my desk and I look beyond John Lennon's shoe, through the window, and what do I see? My house, unlike the others on this street, has two stories. I am on the second story at the back and outside is my carefully trimmed yard, the lush St. Augustine grass faintly tinted with blue, and there is my brick barbecue pit and my setting of cypress lawn furniture. But beyond is the bayou that runs through Versailles and my house is built at an angle on an acre and a half and I can see all the other backyards set side by side for the quarter mile to the place where the lagoon opens up and the Versailles apartments stand. All the backyards of these houses—all of them—are plowed and planted as if this was some provincial village in Vietnam. Such things are not done in America. In America a vegetable garden is a hobby. Here in Versailles the people of Vietnam are cultivating their backyards as a way of life. And behind the yards is a path and beyond the path is the border of city land along the bayou and on this land the people of Vietnam have planted a community garden stretching down to the lagoon and even now I can see a scattering of conical straw hats there, the women crouched flat-footed and working the garden, and I expect any moment to see a boy riding a water buffalo down the path or perhaps a sampan gliding along the bayou, heading for the South China Sea. Do you understand me? I am living in the past.

I have enough money to leave Versailles and become the American that I must be. But I have found that it isn't so simple. Something is missing. I know I am wrong when I say that still more money, from shrimp or from whatever else, will finally free me from the past. Perhaps the problem is that my businesses are all connected to the Vietnam community here. There was no way around that when I started. And perhaps it's true that I should find some American business to invest in. But there is nothing to keep me in this place even if my money is made here. I do not work the cash registers in my businesses.

Perhaps it is the absence of my family. But this is something they chose for themselves. My wife was a simple woman and she would not leave her parents and she feared America greatly. The children came from her body. They belong with her, and she felt she belonged in Vietnam. My only regret is that I have nothing of hers to touch, not a lock of hair or a ring or even a scarf—she had so many beautiful scarves, some of which she wore around her waist. But if my family had come with me, would they not in fact be a further difficulty in my becoming American? As it is, I have only myself to consider in this problem and that should make things simpler.

But there are certain matters in life that a man is not able to control on his own. My religion teaches this clearly. For a rich man, for a man with the gift to become rich even a second time, this is a truth that is sometimes difficult to see. But he should realize that he is human and dependent on forces beyond himself and he should look to the opportunity that his wealth can give him.

I do not even know John Lennon's music very well. I have heard it and it is very nice, but in Vietnam I always preferred the popular singers in my own language, and in America I like the music they call "easy listening," though sometimes a favorite tune I will hear from the Living Strings or Percy Faith turns out to be a song of John Lennon. It is of no matter to a man like John Lennon that I did not know his music well before I possessed his shoe. The significance of this object is the same. He is a very important figure. This is common knowledge. He wrote many songs that affected the lives of people in America and he sang about love and peace and then he died on the streets of New York as a martyr.

I touch his shoe. The leather is smooth and is the color of teakwood and my forefinger glides along the instep to the toe, where there is a jagged scrape. I lift my finger and put it on the spot where the scrape begins, at the point of the toe, and I trace the gash, follow the fuzzy track of the exposed underside of the leather. All along it I feel a faint grinding inside me, as if this is a wound in flesh that I touch. John Lennon's wound. I understand this scrape on the shoe. John Lennon fell and his leg pushed out on the pavement as he died. This is the stigmata of the shoe, the sign of his martyrdom.

With one hand I cup the shoe at its back and slide my other hand under the toe and I lift and the shoe always surprises me at its lightness, just as one who has moments before died a martyr's death might be surprised at the lightness of his own soul. I angle the shoe toward the light from my window and I look inside. I see the words SAVILE ROW on the lining, but that is all. There is no size recorded here and I imagine that this shoe was made special for John Lennon, that they carefully measured his foot and this is its purest image in the softest leather. I am very quiet inside but there is this great pressure in my chest, coming from something I cannot identify as myself. This is because of what I will now do.

I wait until I can draw an adequate breath. Then I turn in my chair and gently lower the shoe to the floor and I place it before my bare right foot. I make the sign of the cross and slip my foot into John Lennon's shoe, sliding my forefinger into the loop at the back and pulling gently, just as John Lennon did on the day he joined the angels. The lining is made of something as soft as silk and there is a chill from it. I stand up before my desk and the shoe is large for me, but that's as it should be. I take one step and then another and I am in the center of my room and I stand there and my heart is very full and I wait for what I pray will one day be mine, a feeling about what has happened to me that I cannot even imagine until I actually feel it. I have asked the man in New York to look for another of John Lennon's shoes, a left shoe. Even if it is from some other pair, I want to own just one more shoe. Then I will put both of John Lennon's shoes on my feet and I will go out into the street and I will walk as far as I need to go to find the place where I belong.

# ROBERT STONE
## (1937– )

Likened to such authors as Graham Greene, Joseph Conrad, and Herman Melville, Robert Stone is in the front ranks of contemporary American fiction writers. He was born in New York City. He never knew his father and, because his mother was frequently institutionalized for schizophrenia, he spent time in Catholic-run orphanages and was educated in Catholic schools. At age 17 he joined the navy and served for three years. Leaving the service in 1958, Stone worked for the *New York Daily News* and attended New York University. He married in 1959, and he and his wife lived in New Orleans for awhile, then got involved in the emerging bohemian scene back in New York. He was friends with Jack Kerouac, and went on the road with Ken Kesey and the Merry Pranksters. A Wallace Stegner fellowship brought him to Stanford University to study writing from 1962 to 1964. He now lives and works in Connecticut.

Stone's first novel, *A Hall of Mirrors* (1967), won a William Faulkner Foundation Award; his second novel, *Dog Soldiers* (1974), won a National Book Award; and his third, *A Flag for Sunrise* (1981), won the PEN/Faulkner Award. In 1986 he published *Children of Light,* and in 1989 *Outerbridge Reach.* A collection of stories, *Bear and His Daughter,* appeared in 1997. His most recent novel, *Damascus Gate,* was published in 1998 to high critical praise.

Even though Stone's fiction explores political themes, its deepest concerns are religious and theological. Stone's vision of the human condition is often harsh and pessimistic as he seeks to show ideas and morality in action in darkly extreme circumstances, to probe the spiritual depths of the American experience. He does so through characters who feel lost and confused but yet quest for some sort of confirmation, some coherence, some explanation of the price they pay to survive. Desperate, even despairing, they remain seekers.

# Helping

ONE GRAY November day, Elliot went to Boston for the afternoon. The wet streets seemed cold and lonely. He sensed a broken promise in the city's elegance and verve. Old hopes tormented him like phantom limbs, but he did not drink. He had joined Alcoholics Anonymous fifteen months before.

Christmas came, childless, a festival of regret. His wife went to Mass and cooked a turkey. Sober, Elliot walked in the woods.

In January, blizzards swept down from the Arctic until the weather became too cold for snow. The Shawmut Valley grew quiet and crystalline. In the white silences, Elliot could hear the boards of his house contract and feel a shrinking in his bones. Each dusk, starveling deer came out of the wooded swamp behind the house to graze his orchard for whatever raccoons had uncovered and left behind. At night he lay beside his sleeping wife listening to the baying of dog packs running them down in the deep moonshadowed snow.

Day in, day out, he was sober. At times it was almost stimulating. But he could not shake off the sensations he had felt in Boston. In his mind's eye he could see dead leaves rattling along brick gutters and savor that day's desperation. The brief outing had undermined him.

Sober, however, he remained, until the day a man named Blankenship came into his office at the state hospital for counseling. Blankenship had red hair, a brutal face and a sneaking manner. He was a sponger and petty thief whom Elliot had seen a number of times before.

"I been having this dream," Blankenship announced loudly. His voice was not pleasant. His skin was unwholesome. Every time he got arrested the court sent him to the psychiatrists and the psychiatrists, who spoke little English, sent him to Elliot.

Blankenship had joined the army after his first burglary but had never served east of the Rhine. After a few months in Wiesbaden, he had been discharged for reasons of unsuitability, but he told everyone he was a veteran of the Vietnam War. He went about in a tiger suit. Elliot had had enough of him.

"Dreams are boring," Elliot told him.

Blankenship was outraged. "Whaddaya mean?" he demanded.

During counseling sessions Elliot usually moved his chair into the middle of the room in order to seem accessible to his clients. Now he stayed securely behind his desk. He did not care to seem accessible to Blankenship. "What I said, Mr. Blankenship. Other people's dreams are boring. Didn't you ever hear that?"

"Boring?" Blankenship frowned. He seemed unable to imagine a meaning for the word.

Elliot picked up a pencil and set its point quivering on his desktop blotter. He gazed into his client's slack-jawed face. The Blankenship family made their way through life as strolling litigants, and young Blankenship's specialty was slipping on ice cubes. Hauled off the pavement, he would hassle the doctors in Emergency for pain pills and hurry to a law clinic. The Blankenships had threatened suit against half the property owners in the southern part of the state. What they could not extort at law they stole. But even the Blankenship family had abandoned Blankenship. His last visit to the hospital had been subsequent to an arrest for lifting a case of hot-dog rolls from Woolworth's. He lived in a Goodwill depository bin in Wyndham.

"Now I suppose you want to tell me your dream. Is that right, Mr. Blankenship?"

Blankenship looked left and right like a dog surrendering eye contact. "Don't you want to hear it?" he asked humbly.

Elliot was unmoved. "Tell me something, Blankenship. Was your dream about Vietnam?"

At the mention of the word "Vietnam," Blankenship customarily broke into a broad smile. Now he looked guilty and guarded. He shrugged. "Ya."

"How come you have dreams about that place, Blankenship? You were never there."

"Whaddaya mean?" Blankenship began to say, but Elliot cut him off.

"You were never there, my man. You never saw the goddamn place. You have no business dreaming about it! You better cut it out!"

He had raised his voice to the extent that the secretary outside his open door paused at her computer.

"Lemme alone," Blankenship said fearfully. "Some doctor you are."

"It's all right," Elliot assured him. "I'm not a doctor."

"Everybody's on my case," Blankenship said. His moods were volatile. He began to weep.

Elliot watched the tears roll down Blankenship's chapped, pitted cheeks. He cleared his throat. "Look, fella . . ." he began. He felt at a loss. He felt like telling Blankenship that things were tough all over.

Blankenship sniffed and telescoped his neck and after a moment looked at Elliot. His look was disconcertingly trustful; he was used to being counseled.

"Really, you know, it's ridiculous for you to tell me your problems have to do with Nam. You were never over there. It was me over there, Blankenship. Not you."

Blankenship leaned forward and put his forehead on his knees.

"Your troubles have to do with here and now," Elliot told his client. "Fantasies aren't helpful."

His voice sounded overripe and hypocritical in his own ears. What a dreadful business, he thought. What an awful job this is. Anger was driving him crazy.

Blankenship straightened up and spoke through his tears. "This dream . . ." he said. "I'm scared."

Elliot felt ready to endure a great deal in order not to hear Blankenship's dream.

"I'm not the one you see about that," he said. In the end he knew his duty. He sighed. "OK. All right. Tell me about it."

"Yeah?" Blankenship asked with leaden sarcasm. "Yeah? You think dreams are friggin' boring!"

"No, no," Elliot said. He offered Blankenship a tissue and Blankenship took one. "That was sort of off the top of my head. I didn't really mean it."

Blankenship fixed his eyes on dreaming distance. "There's a feeling that goes with it. With the dream." Then he shook his head in revulsion and looked at Elliot as though he had only just awakened. "So what do you think? You think it's boring?"

"Of course not," Elliot said. "A physical feeling?"

"Ya. It's like I'm floating in rubber."

He watched Elliot stealthily, aware of quickened attention. Elliot had caught dengue in Vietnam and during his weeks of delirium had felt vaguely as though he were floating in rubber.

"What are you seeing in this dream?"

Blankenship only shook his head. Elliot suffered a brief but intense attack of rage.

"Hey, Blankenship," he said equably, "here I am, man. You can see I'm listening."

"What I saw was black," Blankenship said. He spoke in an odd tremolo. His behavior was quite different from anything Elliot had come to expect from him.

"Black? What was it?"

"Smoke. The sky maybe."

"The sky?" Elliot asked.

"It was all black. I was scared."

In a waking dream of his own, Elliot felt the muscles on his neck distend. He was looking up at a sky that was black, filled with smoke-swollen clouds, lit with fires, damped with blood and rain.

"What were you scared of?" he asked Blankenship.

"I don't know," Blankenship said.

Elliot could not drive the black sky from his inward eye. It was as though Blankenship's dream had infected his own mind.

"You don't know? You don't know what you were scared of?"

Blankenship's posture was rigid. Elliot, who knew the aspect of true fear, recognized it there in front of him.

"The Nam," Blankenship said.

"You're not even old enough," Elliot told him.

Blankenship sat trembling with joined palms between his thighs. His face was flushed and not in the least ennobled by pain. He had trouble with alcohol and drugs. He had trouble with everything.

"So wherever your black sky is, it isn't Vietnam."

Things were so unfair, Elliot thought. It was unfair of Blankenship to appropriate the condition of a Vietnam veteran. The trauma inducing his post-traumatic stress had been nothing more serious than his own birth, a routine procedure. Now, in addition to the poverty, anxiety and confusion that would always be his life's lot, he had been visited with irony. It was all arbitrary and some people simply got elected. Everyone knew that who had been where Blankenship had not.

"Because, I assure you, Mr. Blankenship, you were never there."

"Whaddaya mean?" Blankenship asked.

* * *

When Blankenship was gone, Elliot leafed through his file and saw that the psychiatrists had passed him upstairs without recording a diagnosis. Disproportionately angry, he went out to the secretary's desk.

"Nobody wrote up that last patient," he said. "I'm not supposed to see people without a diagnosis. The shrinks are just passing the buck."

The secretary was a tall, solemn redhead with prominent front teeth and a slight speech disorder. "Dr. Sayyid will have kittens if he hears you call him a shrink, Chas. He's already complained. He hates being called a shrink."

"Then he came to the wrong country," Elliot said. "He can go back to his own."

The woman giggled. "He *is* the doctor, Chas."

"Hates being called a shrink!" He threw the file on the secretary's table and stormed back toward his office. "That fucking little zip couldn't give you a decent haircut. He's a prescription clerk."

The secretary looked about her guiltily and shook her head. She was used to him.

Elliot succeeded in calming himself down after a while, but the image of black sky remained with him. At first he thought he would be able to shrug the whole thing off. After a few minutes, he picked up his phone and dialed Blankenship's probation officer.

"The Vietnam thing is all he has," the probation officer explained. "I guess he picked it up around."

"His descriptions are vivid," Elliot said.

"You mean they sound authentic?"

"I mean he had me going today. He was ringing my bells."

"Good for Blanky. Think he believes it himself?"

"Yes," Elliot said. "He believes it himself now."

Elliot told the probation officer about Blankenship's current arrest, which was for showering illegally at midnight in the Wyndham Regional High School. He asked what Probation knew about Blankenship's present relationship with his family.

"You kiddin'?" the P.O. asked. "They're all locked down. The whole family's inside. The old man's in Bridgewater. Little Donny's in San Quentin or somewhere. Their dog's in the pound."

Elliot had lunch alone in the hospital staff cafeteria. On the far side of the double-glazed windows, the day was darkening as an expected snowstorm gathered. Along Route 7, ancient elms stood frozen against the gray sky. When he had finished his sandwich and coffee, he sat staring out at the winter afternoon. His anger had given way to an insistent anxiety.

On the way back to his office, he stopped at the hospital gift shop for a copy of *Sports Illustrated* and a candy bar. When he was inside again, he closed the door and put his feet up. It was Friday and he had no appointments for the remainder of the day, nothing to do but write a few letters and read the office mail.

Elliot's cubicle in the social services department was windowless and lined with bookshelves. When he found himself unable to concentrate on the magazine and without any heart for his paperwork, he ran his eye over the row of books beside his chair. There were volumes by Heinrich Muller and Carlos Castaneda, Jones's life of Freud and *The Golden Bough.* The books aroused a revulsion in Elliot. Their present uselessness repelled him.

Over and over again, detail by detail, he tried to recall his conversation with Blankenship.

"You were never there," he heard himself explaining. He was trying to get the whole incident straightened out after the fact. Something was wrong. Dread crept over him like a paralysis. He ate his candy bar without tasting it. He knew that the craving for sweets was itself a bad sign.

Blankenship had misappropriated someone else's dream and made it his own. It made no difference whether you had been there, after all. The dreams had crossed the ocean. They were in the air.

He took his glasses off and put them on his desk and sat with his arms folded, looking into the well of light from his desk lamp. There seemed to be nothing but whirl inside him. Unwelcome things came and went in his mind's eye. His heart beat faster. He could not control the headlong promiscuity of his thoughts.

It was possible to imagine larval dreams traveling in suspended animation undetectable in a host brain. They could be divided and regenerate like flatworms, hide in seams and bedding, in war stories, laughter, snapshots. They could rot your socks and turn your memory into a black and green blister. Green for the hills, black for the sky above. At daybreak they hung themselves up in rows like bats. At dusk they went out to look for dreamers.

Elliot put his jacket on and went into the outer office, where the secretary sat frowning into the measured sound and light of her machine. She must enjoy its sleekness and order, he thought. She was divorced. Four red-headed kids between ten and seventeen lived with her in an unpainted house across from Stop & Shop. Elliot liked her and had come to find her attractive. He managed a smile for her.

"Ethel, I think I'm going to pack it in," he declared. It seemed awkward to be leaving early without a reason.

"Jack wants to talk to you before you go, Chas."

Elliot looked at her blankly.

Then his colleague, Jack Sprague, having heard his voice, called from the adjoining cubicle. "Chas, what about Sunday's games? Shall I call you with the spread?"

"I don't know," Elliot said. "I'll phone you tomorrow."

"This is a big decision for him," Jack Sprague told the secretary. "He might lose twenty-five bucks."

At present, Elliot drew a slightly higher salary than Jack Sprague, although Jack had a Ph.D. and Elliot was only an M.S.W. Different branches of the state government employed them.

"Twenty-five bucks," said the woman. "If you guys have no better use for twenty-five bucks, give it to me."

"Where are you off to, by the way?" Sprague asked.

Elliot began to answer, but for a moment no reply occurred to him. He shrugged. "I have to get back," he finally stammered. "I promised Grace."

"Was that Blankenship I saw leaving?"

Elliot nodded.

"It's February," Jack said. "How come he's not in Florida?"

"I don't know," Elliot said. He put on his coat and walked to the door. "I'll see you."

"Have a nice weekend," the secretary said. She and Sprague looked after him indulgently as he walked toward the main corridor.

"Are Chas and Grace going out on the town?" she said to Sprague. "What do you think?"

"That would be the day," Sprague said. "Tomorrow he'll come back over here and read all day. He spends every weekend holed up in this goddamn office while she does something or other at the church." He shook his head. "Every night he's at A.A. and she's home alone."

Ethel savored her overbite. "Jack," she said teasingly, "are you thinking what I think you're thinking? Shame on you."

"I'm thinking I'm glad I'm not him, that's what I'm thinking. That's as much as I'll say."

"Yeah, well, I don't care," Ethel said. "Two salaries and no kids, that's the way to go, boy."

* * *

Elliot went out through the automatic doors of the emergency bay and the cold closed over him. He walked across the hospital parking lot with his eyes on the pavement, his hands thrust deep in his overcoat pockets, skirting patches of shattered ice. There was no wind, but the motionless air stung; the metal frames of his glasses burned his skin. Curlicues of mud-brown ice coated the soiled snowbanks along the street. Although it was still afternoon, the street lights had come on.

The lock on his car door had frozen and he had to breathe on the keyhole to fit the key. When the engine turned over, Jussi Björling's recording of the Handel Largo filled the car interior. He snapped it off at once.

Halted at the first stoplight, he began to feel the want of a destination. The fear and impulse to flight that had got him out of the office faded, and he had no desire to go home. He was troubled by a peculiar impatience that might have been with time itself. It was as though he were waiting for something. The sensation made him feel anxious; it was unfamiliar but not altogether unpleasant. When the light changed he drove on, past the Gulf station and the firehouse and between the greens of Ilford Common. At the far end of the common he swung into the parking lot of the Packard Conway Library and stopped with the engine running. What he was experiencing, he thought, was the principle of possibility.

He turned off the engine and went out again into the cold. Behind the leaded library windows he could see the librarian pouring coffee in her tiny private office. The librarian was a Quaker of socialist convictions named Candace Music, who was Elliot's cousin.

The Conway Library was all dark wood and etched mirrors, a Gothic saloon. Years before, out of work and booze-whipped, Elliot had gone to hide there. Because Candace was a classicist's widow and knew some Greek, she was one of the few people in the valley with whom Elliot had cared to speak in those days. Eventually, it had seemed to him that all their conversations tended toward Vietnam, so he had gone less and less often. Elliot was the only Vietnam veteran Candace knew well enough to chat with, and he had come to suspect that he was being probed for the edification of the East Ilford Friends Meeting. At that time he had still pretended to talk easily about his war and had prepared little discourses and picaresque anecdotes to recite on demand. Earnest seekers like Candace had caused him great secret distress.

Candace came out of her office to find him at the checkout desk. He watched her brow furrow with concern as she composed a smile. "Chas, what a surprise. You haven't been in for an age."

"Sure I have, Candace. I went to all the Wednesday films last fall. I work just across the road."

"I know, dear," Candace said. "I always seem to miss you."

A cozy fire burned in the hearth, an antique brass clock ticked along on the marble mantel above it. On a couch near the fireplace an old man sat upright, his mouth open, asleep among half a dozen soiled plastic bags. Two teenage girls whispered over their homework at a table under the largest window.

"Now that I'm here," he said, laughing, "I can't remember what I came to get."

"Stay and get warm," Candace told him. "Got a minute? Have a cup of coffee."

Elliot had nothing but time, but he quickly realized that he did not want to stay and pass it with Candace. He had no clear idea of why he had come to the library. Standing at the checkout desk, he accepted coffee. She attended him with an air of benign supervision, as though he were a Chinese peasant and she a medical missionary, like her father. Candace was tall and plain, more handsome in her middle sixties than she had ever been.

"Why don't we sit down?"

He allowed her to gentle him into a chair by the fire. They made a threesome with the sleeping old man.

"Have you given up translating, Chas? I hope not."

"Not at all," he said. Together they had once rendered a few fragments of Sophocles into verse. She was good at clever rhymes.

"You come in so rarely, Chas. Ted's books go to waste."

After her husband's death, Candace had donated his books to the Conway, where they reposed in a reading room inscribed to his memory, untouched among foreign-language volumes, local genealogies and books in large type for the elderly.

"I have a study in the barn," he told Candace. "I work there. When I have time." The lie was absurd, but he felt the need of it.

"And you're working with Vietnam veterans," Candace declared.

"Supposedly," Elliot said. He was growing impatient with her nodding solicitude.

"Actually," he said, "I came in for the new Oxford *Classical World.* I thought you'd get it for the library and I could have a look before I spent my hard-earned cash."

Candace beamed. "You've come to the right place, Chas, I'm happy to say." He thought she looked disproportionately happy. "I have it."

"Good," Elliot said, standing. "I'll just take it, then. I can't really stay."

Candace took his cup and saucer and stood as he did. When the library telephone rang, she ignored it, reluctant to let him go. "How's Grace?" she asked.

"Fine," Elliot said. "Grace is well."

At the third ring she went to the desk. When her back was turned, he hesitated for a moment and then went outside.

The gray afternoon had softened into night, and it was snowing. The falling snow whirled like a furious mist in the headlight beams on Route 7 and settled implacably on Elliot's cheeks and eyelids. His heart, for no good reason, leaped up in childlike expectation. He had run away from a dream and encountered possibility. He felt in possession of a promise. He began to walk toward the roadside lights.

Only gradually did he begin to understand what had brought him there and what the happy anticipation was that fluttered in his breast. Drinking, he had started his evenings from the Conway Library. He would arrive hung over in the early afternoon to browse and read. When the old pain rolled in with dusk, he would walk down to the Midway Tavern for a remedy. Standing in the snow outside the library, he realized that he had contrived to promise himself a drink.

Ahead, through the storm, he could see the beer signs in the Midway's window warm and welcoming. Snowflakes spun around his head like an excitement.

Outside the Midway's package store, he paused with his hand on the doorknob. There was an old man behind the counter whom Elliot remembered from his drinking days. When he was inside, he realized that the old man neither knew nor cared who he was. The package store was thick with dust; it was on the counter, the shelves, the bottles themselves. The old counterman looked dusty. Elliot bought a bottle of King William Scotch and put it in the inside pocket of his overcoat.

Passing the windows of the Midway Tavern, Elliot could see the ranks of bottles aglow behind the bar. The place was crowded with men leaving the afternoon shifts at the shoe and felt factories. No one turned to note him when he passed inside. There was a single stool vacant at the bar and he took it. His heart beat faster. Bruce Springsteen was on the jukebox.

The bartender was a club fighter from Pittsfield called Jackie G., with whom Elliot had often gossiped. Jackie G. greeted him as though he had been in the previous evening. "Say, babe?"

"How do," Elliot said.

A couple of the men at the bar eyed his shirt and tie. Confronted with the bartender, he felt impelled to explain his presence. "Just thought I'd stop by," he told Jackie G. "Just thought I'd have one. Saw the light. The snow . . ." He chuckled expansively.

"Good move," the bartender said. "Scotch?"

"Double," Elliot said.

When he shoved two dollars forward along the bar, Jackie G. pushed one of the bills back to him. "Happy hour, babe."

"Ah," Elliot said. He watched Jackie pour the double. "Not a moment too soon."

* * *

For five minutes or so, Elliot sat in his car in the barn with the engine running and his Handel tape on full volume. He had driven over from East Ilford in a Baroque ecstasy, swinging and swaying and singing along. When the tape ended, he turned off the engine and poured some Scotch into an apple juice container to store providentially beneath the car seat. Then he took the tape and the Scotch into the house with him. He was lying on the sofa in the dark living room, listening to the Largo, when he heard his wife's car in the driveway. By the time Grace had made her way up the icy back-porch steps, he was able to hide the Scotch and rinse his glass clean in the kitchen sink. The drinking life, he thought, was lived moment by moment.

Soon she was in the tiny cloakroom struggling off with her overcoat. In the process she knocked over a cross-country ski, which stood propped against the cloakroom wall. It had been more than a year since Elliot had used the skis.

She came into the kitchen and sat down at the table to take off her boots. Her lean, freckled face was flushed with the cold, but her eyes looked weary. "I wish you'd put those skis down in the barn," she told him. "You never use them."

"I always like to think," Elliot said, "that I'll start the morning off skiing."

"Well, you never do," she said. "How long have you been home?"

"Practically just walked in," he said. Her pointing out that he no longer skied in the morning enraged him. "I stopped at the Conway Library to get the new Oxford *Classical World.* Candace ordered it."

Her look grew troubled. She had caught something in his voice. With dread and bitter satisfaction, Elliot watched his wife detect the smell of whiskey.

"Oh God," she said. "I don't believe it."

Let's get it over with, he thought. Let's have the song and dance.

She sat up straight in her chair and looked at him in fear.

"Oh, Chas," she said, "how could you?"

For a moment he was tempted to try to explain it all.

"The fact is," Elliot told his wife, "I hate people who start the day cross-country skiing."

She shook her head in denial and leaned her forehead on her palm and cried.

He looked into the kitchen window and saw his own distorted image. "The fact is I think I'll start tomorrow morning by stringing head-high razor wire across Anderson's trail."

The Andersons were the Elliots' nearest neighbors. Loyall Anderson was a full professor of government at the state university, thirty miles away. Anderson and his wife were blond and both of them were over six feet tall. They had two blond children, who qualified for the gifted class in the local school but attended regular classes in token of the Andersons' opposition to elitism.

"Sure," Elliot said. "Stringing wire's good exercise. It's life-affirming in its own way."

The Andersons started each and every day with a brisk morning glide along a trail that they partly maintained. They skied well and presented a pleasing, wholesome sight. If, in the course of their adventure, they encountered a snowmobile, Darlene Anderson would affect to choke and cough, indicating her displeasure. If the snowmobile approached them from behind and the trail was narrow, the Andersons would decline to let it pass, asserting their statutory right-of-way.

"I don't want to hear your violent fantasies," Grace said.

Elliot was picturing razor wire, the army kind. He was picturing the decapitated Andersons, their blood and jaunty ski caps bright on the white trail. He was picturing their severed heads, their earnest blue eyes and large white teeth reflecting the virginal morning snow. Although Elliot hated snowmobiles, he hated the Andersons far more.

He looked at his wife and saw that she had stopped crying. Her long, elegant face was rigid and lipless.

"Know what I mean? One string at mommy-and-daddy level for Loyall and Darlene. And a bitty wee string at kiddie level for Skippy and Samantha, those cunning little whizzes."

"Stop it," she said to him.

"Sorry," Elliot told her.

Stiff with shame, he went and took his bottle out of the cabinet into which he had thrust it and poured a drink. He was aware of her eyes on him. As he drank, a fragment from old Music's translation of *Medea* came into his mind. "Old friend, I have to weep. The gods and I went mad together and made things as they are." It was such a waste; eighteen months of struggle thrown away. But there was no way to get the stuff back in the bottle.

"I'm very sorry," he said. "You know I'm very sorry, don't you, Grace?"

The delectable Handel arias spun on in the next room.

"You must stop," she said. "You must make yourself stop before it takes over."

"It's out of my hands," Elliot said. He showed her his empty hands. "It's beyond me."

"You'll lose your job, Chas." She stood up at the table and leaned on it, staring wide-eyed at him. Drunk as he was, the panic in her voice frightened him. "You'll end up in jail again."

"One engages," Elliot said, "and then one sees."

"How can you have done it?" she demanded. "You promised me."

"First the promises," Elliot said, "and then the rest."

"Last time was supposed to be the last time," she said.

"Yes," he said, "I remember."

"I can't stand it," she said. "You reduce me to hysterics." She wrung her hands for him to see. "See? Here I am, I'm in hysterics."

"What can I say?" Elliot asked. He went to the bottle and refilled his glass. "Maybe you shouldn't watch."

"You want me to be forbearing, Chas? I'm not going to be."

"The last thing I want," Elliot said, "is an argument."

"I'll give you a fucking argument. You didn't have to drink. All you had to do was come home."

"That must have been the problem," he said.

Then he ducked, alert at the last possible second to the missile that came for him at hairline level. Covering up, he heard the shattering of glass, and a fine rain of crystals enveloped him. She had sailed the sugar bowl at him; it had smashed against the wall above his head and there was sugar and glass in his hair.

"You bastard!" she screamed. "You are undermining me!"

"You ought not to throw things at me," Elliot said. "I don't throw things at you."

He left her frozen into her follow-through and went into the living room to turn the music off. When he returned she was leaning back against the wall, rubbing her right elbow with her left hand. Her eyes were bright. She had picked up one of her boots from the middle of the kitchen floor and stood holding it.

"What the hell do you mean, that must have been the problem?"

He set his glass on the edge of the sink with an unsteady hand and turned to her. "What do I mean? I mean that most of the time I'm putting one foot in front of the other like a good soldier and I'm out of it from the neck up. But there are times when I don't think I will ever be dead enough—or dead long enough—to get the taste of this life off my teeth. That's what I mean!"

She looked at him dry-eyed. "Poor fella," she said.

"What you have to understand, Grace, is that this drink I'm having"—he raised the glass toward her in a gesture of salute—"is the only worthwhile thing I've done in the last year and a half. It's the only thing in my life that means jack shit, the closest thing to satisfaction I've had. Now how can you begrudge me that? It's the best I'm capable of."

"You'll go too far," she said to him. "You'll see."

"What's that, Grace? A threat to walk?" He was grinding his teeth. "Don't make me laugh. You, walk? You, the friend of the unfortunate?"

"Don't you hit me," she said when she looked at his face. "Don't you dare."

"You, the Christian Queen of Calvary, walk? Why, I don't believe that for a minute."

She ran a hand through her hair and bit her lip. "No, we stay,"she said. Anger and distraction made her look young. Her cheeks blazed rosy against the general pallor of her skin. "In my family we stay until the fella dies. That's the tradition. We stay and pour it for them and they die."

He put his drink down and shook his head.

"I thought we'd come through," Grace said. "I was sure."

"No," Elliot said. "Not altogether."

They stood in silence for a minute. Elliot sat down at the oilcloth-covered table. Grace walked around it and poured herself a whiskey.

"You are undermining me, Chas. You are making things impossible for me and I just don't know." She drank and winced. "I'm not going to stay through another drunk. I'm telling you right now. I haven't got it in me. I'll die."

He did not want to look at her. He watched the flakes settle against the glass of the kitchen door. "Do what you feel the need of," he said.

"I just can't take it," she said. Her voice was not scolding but measured and reasonable. "It's February. And I went to court this morning and lost Vopotik."

Once again, he thought, my troubles are going to be obviated by those of the deserving poor. He said, "Which one was that?"

"Don't you remember them? The three-year-old with the broken fingers?"

He shrugged. Grace sipped her whiskey.

"I told you. I said I had a three-year-old with broken fingers, and you said, 'Maybe he owed somebody money.' "

"Yes," he said, "I remember now."

"You ought to see the Vopotiks, Chas. The woman is young and obese. She's so young that for a while I thought I could get to her as a juvenile. The guy is a biker. They believe the kid came from another planet to control their lives. They believe this literally, both of them."

"You shouldn't get involved that way," Elliot said. "You should leave it to the caseworkers."

"They scared their first caseworker all the way to California. They were following me to work."

"You didn't tell me."

"Are you kidding?" she asked. "Of course I didn't." To Elliot's surprise, his wife poured herself a second whiskey. "You know how they address the child? As 'dude.' She says to it, 'Hey, dude.' " Grace shuddered with loathing. "You can't imagine! The woman munching Twinkies. The kid smelling of shit. They're high morning, noon and night, but you can't get anybody for that these days."

"People must really hate it," Elliot said, "when somebody tells them they're not treating their kids right."

"They definitely don't want to hear it," Grace said. "You're right." She sat stirring her drink, frowning into the glass. "The Vopotik child will die, I think."

"Surely not," Elliot said.

"This one I think will die," Grace said. She took a deep breath and puffed out her cheeks and looked at him forlornly. "The situation's extreme. Of course, sometimes you wonder whether it makes any difference. That's the big question, isn't it?"

"I would think," Elliot said, "that would be the one question you didn't ask."

"But you do," she said. "You wonder: Ought they to live at all? To continue the cycle?" She put a hand to her hair and shook her head as if in confusion. "Some of these folks, my God, the poor things cannot put Wednesday on top of Tuesday to save their lives."

"It's a trick," Elliot agreed, "a lot of them can't manage."

"And kids are small, they're handy and underfoot. They make noise. They can't hurt you back."

"I suppose child abuse is something people can do together," Elliot said.

"Some kids are obnoxious. No question about it."

"I wouldn't know," Elliot said.

"Maybe you should stop complaining. Maybe you're better off. Maybe your kids are better off unborn."

"Better off or not," Elliot said, "it looks like they'll stay that way."

"I mean our kids, of course," Grace said. "I'm not blaming you, understand? It's just that here we are with you drunk again and me losing Vopotik, so I thought why not get into the big unaskable questions." She got up and folded her arms and began to pace up and down the kitchen. "Oh," she said when her eye fell upon the bottle, "that's good stuff, Chas. You won't mind if I have another? I'll leave you enough to get loaded on."

Elliot watched her pour. So much pain, he thought; such anger and confusion. He was tired of pain, anger and confusion; they were what had got him in trouble that very morning.

The liquor seemed to be giving him a perverse lucidity when all he now required was oblivion. His rage, especially, was intact in its salting of alcohol. Its contours were palpable and bleeding at the borders. Booze was good for rage. Booze could keep it burning through the darkest night.

"What happened in court?" he asked his wife.

She was leaning on one arm against the wall, her long, strong body flexed at the hip. Holding her glass, she stared angrily toward the invisible fields outside. "I lost the child," she said.

Elliot thought that a peculiar way of putting it. He said nothing.

"The court convened in an atmosphere of high hilarity. It may be Hate Month around here but it was buddy-buddy over at Ilford Courthouse. The room was full of bikers and bikers' lawyers. A colorful crowd. There was a lot of bonding." She drank and shivered. "They didn't think too well of me. They don't think too well of broads as lawyers. Neither does the judge. The judge has the common touch. He's one of the boys."

"Which judge?" Elliot asked.

"Buckley. A man of about sixty. Know him? Lots of veins on his nose?"

Elliot shrugged.

"I thought I had done my homework," Grace told him. "But suddenly I had nothing but paper. No witnesses. It was Margolis at Valley Hospital who spotted the radiator burns. He called us in the first place. Suddenly he's got to keep his reservation for a campsite in St. John. So Buckley threw his deposition out." She began to chew on a fingernail. "The caseworkers have vanished—one's in L.A., the other's in Nepal. I went in there and got run over. I lost the child."

"It happens all the time," Elliot said. "Doesn't it?"

"This one shouldn't have been lost, Chas. These people aren't simply confused. They're weird. They stink."

"You go messing into anybody's life," Elliot said, "that's what you'll find."

"If the child stays in that house," she said, "he's going to die."

"You did your best," he told his wife. "Forget it."

She pushed the bottle away. She was holding a water glass that was almost a third full of whiskey.

"That's what the commissioner said."

Elliot was thinking of how she must have looked in court to the cherry-faced judge and the bikers and their lawyers. Like the schoolteachers who had tormented their childhoods, earnest and tight-assed, humorless and self-righteous. It was not surprising that things had gone against her.

He walked over to the window and faced his reflection again. "Your optimism always surprises me."

"My optimism? Where I grew up our principal cultural expression was the funeral. Whatever keeps me going, it isn't optimism."

"No?" he asked. "What is it?"

"I forget," she said.

"Maybe it's your religious perspective. Your sense of the divine plan."

She sighed in exasperation. "Look, I don't think I want to fight anymore. I'm sorry I threw the sugar at you. I'm not your keeper. Pick on someone your own size."

"Sometimes," Elliot said, "I try to imagine what it's like to believe that the sky is full of care and concern."

"You want to take everything from me, do you?" She stood leaning against the back of her chair. "That you can't take. It's the only part of my life you can't mess up."

He was thinking that if it had not been for her he might not have survived. There could be no forgiveness for that. "Your life? You've got all this piety strung out between Monadnock and Central America. And look at yourself. Look at your life."

"Yes," she said, "look at it."

"You should have been a nun. You don't know how to live."

"I know that," she said. "That's why I stopped doing counseling. Because I'd rather talk the law than life." She turned to him. "You got everything I had, Chas. What's left I absolutely require."

"I swear I would rather be a drunk," Elliot said, "than force myself to believe such trivial horseshit."

"Well, you're going to have to do it without a straight man," she said, "because this time I'm not going to be here for you. Believe it or not."

"I don't believe it," Elliot said. "Not my Grace."

"You're really good at this," she told him. "You make me feel ashamed of my own name."

"I love your name," he said.

The telephone rang. They let it ring three times, and then Elliot went over and answered it.

"Hey, who's that?" a good-humored voice on the phone demanded.

Elliot recited their phone number.

"Hey, I want to talk to your woman, man. Put her on."

"I'll give her a message," Elliot said.

"You put your woman on, man. Run and get her."

Elliot looked at the receiver. He shook his head. "Mr. Vopotik?"

"Never you fuckin' mind, man. I don't want to talk to you. I want to talk to the skinny bitch."

Elliot hung up.

"Is it him?" she asked.

"I guess so."

They waited for the phone to ring again and it shortly did.

"I'll talk to him," Grace said. But Elliot already had the phone.

"Who are you, asshole?" the voice inquired. "What's your fuckin' name, man?"

"Elliot," Elliot said.

"Hey, don't hang up on me, Elliot. I won't put up with that. I told you go get that skinny bitch, man. You go do it."

There were sounds of festivity in the background on the other end of the line—a stereo and drunken voices.

"Hey," the voice declared. "Hey, don't keep me waiting, man."

"What do you want to say to her?" Elliot asked.

"That's none of your fucking business, fool. Do what I told you."

"My wife is resting," Elliot said. "I'm taking her calls."

He was answered by a shout of rage. He put the phone aside for a moment and finished his glass of whiskey. When he picked it up again the man on the line was screaming at him. "That bitch tried to break up my family, man! She almost got away with it. You know what kind of pain my wife went through?"

"What kind?" Elliot asked.

For a few seconds he heard only the noise of the party. "Hey, you're not drunk, are you, fella?"

"Certainly not," Elliot insisted.

"You tell that skinny bitch she's gonna pay for what she did to my family, man. You tell her she can run but she can't hide. I don't care where you go—California, anywhere—I'll get to you."

"Now that I have you on the phone," Elliot said, "I'd like to ask you a couple of questions. Promise you won't get mad?"

"Stop it!" Grace said to him. She tried to wrench the phone from his grasp, but he clutched it to his chest.

"Do you keep a journal?" Elliot asked the man on the phone. "What's your hat size?"

"Maybe you think I can't get to you," the man said. "But I can get to you, man. I don't care who you are, I'll get to you. The brothers will get to you."

"Well, there's no need to go to California. You know where we live."

"For God's sake," Grace said.

"Fuckin' right," the man on the telephone said. "Fuckin' right I know."

"Come on over," Elliot said.

"How's that?" the man on the phone asked.

"I said come on over. We'll talk about space travel. Comets and stuff. We'll talk astral projection. The moons of Jupiter."

"You're making a mistake, fucker."

"Come on over," Elliot insisted. "Bring your fat wife and your beat-up kid. Don't be embarrassed if your head's a little small."

The telephone was full of music and shouting. Elliot held it away from his ear.

"Good work," Grace said to him when he had replaced the receiver.

"I hope he comes," Elliot said. "I'll pop him."

He went carefully down the cellar stairs, switched on the overhead light and began searching among the spiderwebbed shadows and fouled fishing line for his shotgun. It took him fifteen minutes to find it and his cleaning case. While he was still downstairs, he heard the telephone ring again and his wife answer it. He came upstairs and spread his shooting gear across the kitchen table. "Was that him?"

She nodded wearily. "He called back to play us the chain saw."

"I've heard that melody before," Elliot said.

He assembled his cleaning rod and swabbed out the shotgun barrel. Grace watched him, a hand to her forehead. "God," she said. "What have I done? I'm so drunk."

"Most of the time," Elliot said, sighting down the barrel, "I'm helpless in the face of human misery. Tonight I'm ready to reach out."

"I'm finished," Grace said. "I'm through, Chas. I mean it."

Elliot rammed three red shells into the shotgun and pumped one forward into the breech with a satisfying report. "Me, I'm ready for some radical problem-solving. I'm going to spray that no-neck Slovak all over the yard."

"He isn't a Slovak," Grace said. She stood in the middle of the kitchen with her eyes closed. Her face was chalk white.

"What do you mean?" Elliot demanded. "Certainly he's a Slovak."

"No he's not," Grace said.

"Fuck him anyway. I don't care what he is. I'll grease his ass."

He took a handful of deer shells from the box and stuffed them in his jacket pockets.

"I'm not going to stay with you, Chas. Do you understand me?"

Elliot walked to the window and peered out at his driveway. "He won't be alone. They travel in packs."

"For God's sake!" Grace cried, and in the next instant bolted for the downstairs bathroom. Elliot went out, turned off the porch light and switched on a spotlight over the barn door. Back inside, he could hear Grace in the toilet being sick. He turned off the light in the kitchen.

He was still standing by the window when she came up behind him. It seemed strange and fateful to be standing in the dark near her, holding the shotgun. He felt ready for anything.

"I can't leave you alone down here drunk with a loaded shotgun," she said. "How can I?"

"Go upstairs," he said.

"If I went upstairs it would mean I didn't care what happened. Do you understand? If I go it means I don't care anymore. Understand?"

"Stop asking me if I understand," Elliot said. "I understand fine."

"I can't think," she said in a sick voice. "Maybe I don't care. I don't know. I'm going upstairs."

"Good," Elliot said.

* * *

When she was upstairs, Elliot took his shotgun and the whiskey into the dark living room and sat down in an armchair beside one of the lace-curtained windows. The powerful barn light illuminated the length of his driveway and the whole of the back yard. From the window at which he sat, he commanded a view of several miles in the direction of East Ilford. The two-lane blacktop road that ran there was the only one along which an enemy could pass.

He drank and watched the snow, toying with the safety of his 12-gauge Remington. He felt neither anxious nor angry now but only impatient to be done with whatever the night would bring. Drunkenness and the silent rhythm of the falling snow combined to make him feel outside of time and syntax.

Sitting in the dark room, he found himself confronting Blankenship's dream. He saw the bunkers and wire of some long-lost perimeter. The rank smell of night came back to him, the dread evening and quick dusk, the mysteries of outer darkness: fear, combat and death. Enervated by liquor, he began to cry. Elliot was sympathetic with other people's tears but ashamed of his own. He thought of his own tears as childish and excremental. He stifled whatever it was that had started them.

Now his whiskey tasted thin as water. Beyond the lightly frosted glass, illuminated snowflakes spun and settled sleepily on weighted pine boughs. He had found a life beyond the war after all, but in it he was still sitting in darkness, armed, enraged, waiting.

His eyes grew heavy as the snow came down. He felt as though he could be drawn up into the storm and he began to imagine that. He imagined his life with all its artifacts and appetites easing up the spout into white oblivion, everything obviated and foreclosed. He thought maybe he could go for that.

When he awakened, his left hand had gone numb against the trigger guard of his shotgun. The living room was full of pale, delicate light. He looked outside and saw that the storm was done with and the sky radiant and cloudless. The sun was still below the horizon.

Slowly Elliot got to his feet. The throbbing poison in his limbs served to remind him of the state of things. He finished the glass of whiskey on the windowsill beside his easy chair. Then he went to the hall closet to get a ski jacket, shouldered his shotgun and went outside.

There were two cleared acres behind his house; beyond them a trail descended into a hollow of pine forest and frozen swamp. Across the hollow, white pastures stretched to the ridge line, lambent under the lightening sky. A line of skeletal elms weighted with snow marked the course of frozen Shawmut Brook.

He found a pair of ski goggles in a jacket pocket and put them on and set out toward the tree line, gripping the shotgun, step by careful step in the knee-deep snow. Two raucous crows wheeled high overhead, their cries exploding the morning's silence. When the sun came over the ridge, he stood where he was and took in a deep breath. The risen sun warmed his face and he closed his eyes. It was windless and very cold.

Only after he had stood there for a while did he realize how tired he had become. The weight of the gun taxed him. It seemed infinitely wearying to contemplate another single step in the snow. He opened his eyes and closed them again. With sunup the world had gone blazing blue and white, and even with his tinted goggles its whiteness dazzled him and made his head ache. Behind his eyes, the hypnagogic patterns formed a monsoon-heavy tropical sky. He yawned. More than anything, he wanted to lie down in the soft, pure snow. If he could do that, he was certain he could go to sleep at once.

He stood in the middle of the field and listened to the crows. Fear, anger and sleep were the three primary conditions of life. He had learned that over there. Once he had thought fear the worst, but he had learned that the worst was anger. Nothing could fix it, neither alcohol nor medicine. It was a worm. It left him no peace. Sleep was the best.

He opened his eyes and pushed on until he came to the brow that overlooked the swamp. Just below, gliding along among the frozen cattails and bare scrub maple, was a man on skis. Elliot stopped to watch the man approach.

The skier's face was concealed by a red and blue ski mask. He wore snow goggles, a blue jumpsuit and a red woollen Norwegian hat. As he came, he leaned into the turns of the trail, moving silently and gracefully along. At the foot of the slope on which Elliot stood, the man looked up, saw him and slid to a halt. The man stood staring at him for a moment and then began to herringbone up the slope. In no time at all the skier stood no more than ten feet away, removing his goggles, and inside the woollen mask Elliot recognized the clear blue eyes of his neighbor, Professor Loyall Anderson. The shotgun Elliot was carrying seemed to grow heavier. He yawned and shook his head, trying unsuccessfully to clear it. The sight of Anderson's eyes gave him a little thrill of revulsion.

"What are you after?" the young professor asked him, nodding toward the shotgun Elliot was cradling.

"Whatever there is," Elliot said.

Anderson took a quick look at the distant pasture behind him and then turned back to Elliot. The mouth hole of the professor's mask filled with teeth. Elliot thought that Anderson's teeth were quite as he had imagined them earlier. "Well, Polonski's cows are locked up," the professor said. "So they at least are safe."

Elliot realized that the professor had made a joke and was smiling. "Yes," he agreed.

Professor Anderson and his wife had been the moving force behind an initiative to outlaw the discharge of firearms within the boundaries of East Ilford Township. The initiative had been defeated, because East Ilford was not that kind of town.

"I think I'll go over by the river," Elliot said. He said it only to have something to say, to fill the silence before Anderson spoke again. He was afraid of what Anderson might say to him and of what might happen.

"You know," Anderson said, "that's all bird sanctuary over there now."

"Sure," Elliot agreed.

Outfitted as he was, the professor attracted Elliot's anger in an elemental manner. The mask made him appear a kind of doll, a kachina figure or a marionette. His eyes and mouth, all on their own, were disagreeable.

Elliot began to wonder if Anderson could smell the whiskey on his breath. He pushed the little red bull's-eye safety button on his gun to Off.

"Seriously," Anderson said, "I'm always having to run hunters out of there. Some people don't understand the word 'posted.' "

"I would never do that," Elliot said. "I would be afraid."

Anderson nodded his head. He seemed to be laughing. "Would you?" he asked Elliot merrily.

In imagination, Elliot rested the tip of his shotgun barrel against Anderson's smiling teeth. If he fired a load of deer shot into them, he thought, they might make a noise like broken china. "Yes," Elliot said. "I wouldn't know who they were or where they'd been. They might resent my being alive. Telling them where they could shoot and where not."

Anderson's teeth remained in place. "That's pretty strange," he said. "I mean, to talk about resenting someone for being alive."

"It's all relative," Elliot said. "They might think, 'Why should he be alive when some brother of mine isn't?' Or they might think, 'Why should he be alive when I'm not?' "

"Oh," Anderson said.

"You see?" Elliot said. Facing Anderson, he took a long step backward. "All relative."

"Yes," Anderson said.

"That's so often true, isn't it?" Elliot asked. "Values are often relative."

"Yes," Anderson said. Elliot was relieved to see that he had stopped smiling.

"I've hardly slept, you know," Elliot told Professor Anderson. "Hardly at all. All night. I've been drinking."

"Oh," Anderson said. He licked his lips in the mouth of the mask. "You should get some rest."

"You're right," Elliot said.

"Well," Anderson said, "got to go now."

Elliot thought he sounded a little thick in the tongue. A little slow in the jaw.

"It's a nice day," Elliot said, wanting now to be agreeable.

"It's great," Anderson said, shuffling on his skis.

"Have a nice day," Elliot said.

"Yes," Anderson said, and pushed off.

Elliot rested the shotgun across his shoulders and watched Anderson withdraw through the frozen swamp. It was in fact a nice day, but Elliot took no comfort in the weather. He missed night and the falling snow.

As he walked back toward his house, he realized that now there would be whole days to get through, running before the antic energy of whiskey. The whiskey would drive him until he dropped. He shook his head in regret. "It's a revolution," he said aloud. He imagined himself talking to his wife.

Getting drunk was an insurrection, a revolution—a bad one. There would be outsize bogus emotions. There would be petty moral blackmail and cheap remorse. He had said dreadful things to his wife. He had bullied Anderson with his violence and unhappiness, and Anderson would not forgive him. There would be damn little justice and no mercy.

Nearly to the house, he was startled by the desperate feathered drumming of a pheasant's rush. He froze, and out of instinct brought the gun up in the direction of the sound. When he saw the bird break from its cover and take wing, he tracked it, took a breath and fired once. The bird was a little flash of opulent color against the bright blue sky. Elliot felt himself flying for a moment. The shot missed.

Lowering the gun, he remembered the deer shells he had loaded. A hit with the concentrated shot would have pulverized the bird, and he was glad he had missed. He wished no harm to any creature. Then he thought of himself wishing no harm to any creature and began to feel fond and sorry for himself. As soon as he grew aware of the emotion he was indulging, he suppressed it. Pissing and moaning, mourning and weeping, that was the nature of the drug.

The shot echoed from the distant hills. Smoke hung in the air. He turned and looked behind him and saw, far away across the pasture, the tiny blue and red figure of Professor Anderson motionless against the snow. Then Elliot turned again toward his house and took a few labored steps and looked up to see his wife at the bedroom window. She stood perfectly still, and the morning sun lit her nakedness. He stopped where he was. She had heard the shot and run to the window. What had she thought to see? Burnt rags and blood on the snow. How relieved was she now? How disappointed?

Elliot thought he could feel his wife trembling at the window. She was hugging herself. Her hands clasped her shoulders. Elliot took his snow goggles off and shaded his eyes with his hand. He stood in the field staring.

The length of the gun was between them, he thought. Somehow she had got out in front of it, to the wrong side of the wire. If he looked long enough he would find everything out there. He would find himself down the sight.

How beautiful she is, he thought. The effect was striking. The window was so clear because he had washed it himself, with vinegar. At the best of times he was a difficult, fussy man.

Elliot began to hope for forgiveness. He leaned the shotgun on his forearm and raised his left hand and waved to her. Show a hand, he thought. Please just show a hand.

He was cold, but it had got light. He wanted no more than the gesture. It seemed to him that he could build another day on it. Another day was all you needed. He raised his hand higher and waited.

# ⁂ PAM HOUSTON
(1962– )

Pam Houston was born in New Jersey. Her father was a businessman and her mother an actress. She graduated with a B.A. from Denison University in Ohio and received a Ph.D. from the University of Utah. She has lived a vigorous and challenging life as a hunting and rafting guide in the American West and Alaska. She learned the ropes of outdoor living for herself and to be with the kind of men who infatuated her. She married a man from South Africa who was a former safari guide.

Houston describes a cowboy as someone who is a ruggedly handsome but emotionally inarticulate outdoorsman, the kind of man, she says, who couldn't use the word "love" in a sentence. The stories in her well-received collection, *Cowboys Are My Weakness* (1992), portray a more rugged form of female endurance than shown in traditional domestic contexts. Houston brings humor and wit and a new perspective to an old American story—characters seeking something in the wilds of nature. Her other books include a novel, *Waltzing the Cat* (1998), and a book of essays, *A Little More About Me* (1999).

## How to Talk to a Hunter

WHEN HE says "Skins or blankets?" it will take you a moment to realize that he's asking which you want to sleep under. And in your hesitation he'll decide that he wants to see your skin wrapped in the big black moose hide. He carried it, he'll say, soaking wet and heavier than a dead man, across the tundra for two—was it hours or days or weeks? But the payoff, now, will be to see it fall across one of your white breasts. It's December, and your skin is never really warm, so you will pull the bulk of it around you and pose for him, pose for his camera, without having to narrate this moose's death.

You will spend every night in this man's bed without asking yourself why he listens to top-forty country. Why he donated money to the Republican Party. Why he won't play back his messages while you are in the room. You are there so often the messages pile up. Once you noticed the bright green counter reading as high as fifteen.

He will have lured you here out of a careful independence that you spent months cultivating; though it will finally be winter, the dwindling daylight and the threat of Christmas, that makes you give in. Spending nights with this man means suffering the long face of your sheepdog, who likes to sleep on your bed, who worries when you don't come home. But the hunter's house is so much warmer than yours, and he'll give you a key, and just like a woman, you'll think that means something. It will snow hard for thirteen straight days. Then it will really get cold. When it is sixty below there will be no wind and no clouds, just still air and cold sunshine. The sun on the windows will lure you out of bed, but he'll pull you back under. The next two hours he'll devote to your body. With his hands, with his tongue, he'll express what will seem to you like the most eternal of loves. Like the house key, this is just another kind of lie. Even in bed; especially in bed, you and he cannot speak the same language. The machine will answer the incoming calls. From under an ocean of passion and hide and hair you'll hear a woman's muffled voice between the beeps.

* * *

Your best female friend will say, "So what did you think? That a man who sleeps under a dead moose is capable of commitment?"

* * *

This is what you learned in college: A man desires the satisfaction of his desire; a woman desires the condition of desiring.

The hunter will talk about spring in Hawaii, summer in Alaska. The man who says he was always better at math will form the sentences so carefully it will be impossible to tell if you are included in these plans. When he asks you if you would like to open a small guest ranch way out in the country, understand that this is a rhetorical question. Label these conversations future perfect, but don't expect the present to catch up with them. Spring is an inconceivable distance from the December days that just keep getting shorter and gray.

He'll ask you if you've ever shot anything, if you'd like to, if you ever thought about teaching your dog to retrieve. Your dog will like him too much, will drop the stick at his feet every time, will roll over and let the hunter scratch his belly.

* * *

One day he'll leave you sleeping to go split wood or get the mail and his phone will ring again. You'll sit very still while a woman who calls herself something like Janie Coyote leaves a message on his machine: She's leaving work, she'll say, and the last thing she wanted to hear was the sound of his beautiful voice. Maybe she'll talk only in rhyme. Maybe the counter will change to sixteen. You'll look a question at the mule deer on the wall, and the dark spots on either side of his mouth will tell you he shares more with this hunter than you ever will. One night, drunk, the hunter told you he was sorry for taking that deer, that every now and then there's an animal that isn't meant to be taken, and he should have known that deer was one.

* * *

Your best male friend will say, "No one who needs to call herself Janie Coyote can hold a candle to you, but why not let him sleep alone a few nights, just to make sure?"

* * *

The hunter will fill your freezer with elk burger, venison sausage, organic potatoes, fresh pecans. He'll tell you to wear your seat belt, to dress warmly, to drive safely. He'll say you are always on his mind, that you're the best thing that's ever happened to him, that you make him glad that he's a man.

Tell him it don't come easy, tell him freedom's just another word for nothing left to lose.

* * *

These are the things you'll know without asking: The coyote woman wears her hair in braids. She uses words like "howdy." She's man enough to shoot a deer.

* * *

A week before Christmas you'll rent *It's a Wonderful Life* and watch it together, curled on your couch, faces touching. Then you'll bring up the word "monogamy." He'll tell you how badly he was hurt by your predecessor. He'll tell you he couldn't be happier spending every night with you. He'll say there's just a few questions he doesn't have the answers for. He'll say he's just scared and confused. Of course this isn't exactly what he means. Tell him you understand. Tell him you are scared too. Tell him to take all the time he needs. Know that you could never shoot an animal; and be glad of it.

* * *

Your best female friend will say, "You didn't tell him you loved him, did you?" Don't even tell her the truth. If you do you'll have to tell her that he said this: "I feel exactly the same way."

* * *

Your best male friend will say, "Didn't you know what would happen when you said the word 'commitment'?"

But that isn't the word that you said.

He'll say, "Commitment, monogamy, it all means just one thing."

The coyote woman will come from Montana with the heavier snows. The hunter will call you on the day of the solstice to say he has a friend in town and can't see you. He'll leave you hanging your Christmas lights; he'll give new meaning to the phrase "longest night of the year." The man who has said he's not so good with words will manage to say eight things about his friend without using a gender-determining pronoun. Get out of the house quickly. Call the most understanding person you know who will let you sleep in his bed.

* * *

Your best female friend will say, "So what did you think? That he was capable of living outside his gender?"

* * *

When you get home in the morning there's a candy tin on your pillow. Santa, obese and grotesque, fondles two small children on the lid. The card will say something like "From your not-so-secret admirer." Open it. Examine each carefully made truffle. Feed them, one at a time, to the dog. Call the hunter's machine. Tell him you don't speak chocolate.

* * *

Your best female friend will say, "At this point, what is it about him that you could possibly find appealing?"

* * *

Your best male friend will say, "Can't you understand that this is a good sign? Can't you understand that this proves how deep he's in with you?" Hug your best male friend. Give him the truffles the dog wouldn't eat.

* * *

Of course the weather will cooperate with the coyote woman. The highways will close, she will stay another night. He'll tell her he's going to work so he can come and see you. He'll even leave her your number and write "Me at Work" on the yellow pad of paper by his phone. Although you shouldn't, you'll have to be there. It will be you and your nauseous dog and your half-trimmed tree all waiting for him like a series of questions.

* * *

This is what you learned in graduate school: In every assumption is contained the possibility of its opposite.

* * *

In your kitchen he'll hug you like you might both die there. Sniff him for coyote. Don't hug him back.

* * *

He will say whatever he needs to to win. He'll say it's just an old friend. He'll say the visit was all the friend's idea. He'll say the night away from you has given him time to think about how much you mean to him. Realize that nothing short of sleeping alone will ever make him realize how much you mean to him. He'll say that if you can just be a little patient, some good will come out of this for the two of you after all. He still won't use a gender-specific pronoun.

Put your head in your hands. Think about what it means to be patient. Think about the beautiful, smart, strong, clever woman you thought he saw when he looked at you. Pull on your hair. Rock your body back and forth. Don't cry.

He'll say that after holding you it doesn't feel right holding anyone else. For "holding," substitute "fucking." Then take it as a compliment.

He will get frustrated and rise to leave. He may or may not be bluffing. Stall for time. Ask a question he can't immediately answer. Tell him you want to make love on the floor. When he tells you your body is beautiful say, "I feel exactly the same way." Don't, under any circumstances, stand in front of the door.

Your best female friend will say, "They lie to us, they cheat on us, and we love them more for it." She'll say, "It's our fault; we raise them to be like that."

* * *

Tell her it can't be your fault. You've never raised anything but dogs.

* * *

The hunter will say it's late and he has to go home to sleep. He'll emphasize the last word in the sentence. Give him one kiss that he'll remember while he's fucking the coyote woman. Give him one kiss that ought to make him cry if he's capable of it, but don't notice when he does. Tell him to have a good night.

* * *

Your best male friend will say, "We all do it. We can't help it. We're self-destructive. It's the old bad-boy routine. You have a male dog, don't you?"

* * *

The next day the sun will be out and the coyote woman will leave. Think about how easy it must be for a coyote woman and a man who listens to top-forty country. The coyote woman would never use a word like "monogamy"; the coyote woman will stay gentle on his mind.

* * *

If you can, let him sleep alone for at least one night. If you can't, invite him over to finish trimming your Christmas tree. When he asks how you are, tell him you think it's a good idea to keep your sense of humor during the holidays.

Plan to be breezy and aloof and full of interesting anecdotes about all the other men you've ever known. Plan to be hotter than ever before in bed, and a little cold out of it. Remember that necessity is the mother of invention. Be flexible.

* * *

First, he will find the faulty bulb that's been keeping all the others from lighting. He will explain, in great detail, the most elementary electrical principles. You will take turns placing the ornaments you and other men, he and other women, have spent years carefully choosing. Under the circumstances, try to let this be a comforting thought.

He will thin the clusters of tinsel you put on the tree. He'll say something ambiguous like "Next year you should string popcorn and cranberries." Finally, his arm will stretch just high enough to place the angel on the top of the tree.

* * *

Your best female friend will say, "Why can't you ever fall in love with a man who will be your friend?"

Your best male friend will say, "You ought to know this by now: Men always cheat on the best women."

* * *

This is what you learned in the pop psychology book: Love means letting go of fear.

Play Willie Nelson's "Pretty Paper." He'll ask you to dance, and before you can answer he'll be spinning you around your wood stove, he'll be humming in your ear. Before the song ends he'll be taking off your clothes, setting you lightly under the tree, hovering above you with tinsel in his hair. Through the spread of the branches the all-white lights you insisted on will shudder and blur, outlining the ornaments he brought: a pheasant, a snow goose, a deer.

The record will end. Above the crackle of the wood stove and the rasp of the hunter's breathing you'll hear one long low howl break the quiet of the frozen night: your dog, chained and lonely and cold. You'll wonder if he knows enough to stay in his doghouse. You'll wonder if he knows that the nights are getting shorter now.

# DON DELILLO
(1936– )

Don DeLillo was born in New York City and grew up in the Bronx Italian-American neighborhood he describes in his recent novel *Underworld* (1997). He attended Fordham University, graduating in 1958. He worked for an advertising agency until 1964, when he quit to devote more time to his writing. Struggling to get by, he finally published his first novel, *Americana,* in 1971. A year later he published a second novel, *End Zone*. He also began publishing stories in such magazines as *Esquire* and *Harper's*. His next five novels—*Great Jones Street* (1973), *Ratner's Star* (1976), *Players* (1977), *Running Dog* (1978), *The Names* (1982)—received high critical praise but little popular or financial success. However, his novel *White Noise* (1985) established DeLillo's reputation and was awarded the National Book Award. His novel *Libra* (1988) explored the life of the assassin Lee Harvey Oswald. In 1991, the novel *Mao II* appeared and was awarded the PEN/Faulkner Award. Early in his career, DeLillo came to feel that language was a subject as well as an instrument in his work. As a result, his fiction explores our entrapment in various systems of signification, plots and conspiracies that may not have real-world connections. For DeLillo, fiction is all about reliving things, an act that enables a deep exploration of the often ominous currents of our time, but also one that may be an agent of redemption.

## Videotape

IT SHOWS a man driving a car. It is the simplest sort of family video. You see a man at the wheel of a medium Dodge.

It is just a kid aiming her camera through the rear window of the family car at the windshield of the car behind her.

You know about families and their video cameras. You know how kids get involved, how the camera shows them that every subject is potentially charged, a million things they never see with the unaided eye. They investigate the meaning of inert objects and dumb pets and they poke at family privacy. They learn to see things twice.

It is the kid's own privacy that is being protected here. She is twelve years old and her name is being withheld even though she is neither the victim nor the perpetrator of the crime but only the means of recording it.

It shows a man in a sport shirt at the wheel of his car. There is nothing else to see. The car approaches briefly, then falls back.

You know how children with cameras learn to work the exposed moments that define the family cluster. They break every trust, spy out the undefended space, catching Mom coming out of the bathroom in her cumbrous robe and turbaned towel, looking bloodless and plucked. It is not a joke. They will shoot you sitting on the pot if they can manage a suitable vantage.

The tape has the jostled sort of noneventness that marks the family product. Of course the man in this case is not a member of the family but a stranger in a car, a random figure, someone who has happened along in the slow lane.

It shows a man in his forties wearing a pale shirt open at the throat, the image washed by reflections and sunglint, with many jostled moments.

It is not just another video homicide. It is a homicide recorded by a child who thought she was doing something simple and maybe halfway clever, shooting some tape of a man in a car.

He sees the girl and waves briefly, wagging a hand without taking it off the wheel—an underplayed reaction that makes you like him.

It is unrelenting footage that rolls on and on. It has an aimless determination, a persistence that lives outside the subject matter. You are looking into the mind of home video. It is innocent, it is aimless, it is determined, it is real.

He is bald up the middle of his head, a nice guy in his forties whose whole life seems open to the hand-held camera.

But there is also an element of suspense. You keep on looking not because you know something is going to happen—of course you do know something is going to happen and you do look for that reason but you might also keep on looking if you came across this footage for the first time without knowing the outcome. There is a crude power operating here. You keep on looking because things combine to hold you fast—a sense of the random, the amateurish, the accidental, the impending. You don't think of the tape as boring or interesting. It is crude, it is blunt, it is relentless. It is the jostled part of your mind, the film that runs through your hotel brain under all the thoughts you know you're thinking.

The world is lurking in the camera, already framed, waiting for the boy or girl who will come along and take up the device, learn the instrument, shooting old Granddad at breakfast, all stroked out so his nostrils gape, the cereal spoon baby-gripped in his pale fist.

It shows a man alone in a medium Dodge. It seems to go on forever.

There's something about the nature of the tape, the grain of the image, the sputtering black-and-white tones, the starkness—you think this is more real, truer-to-life than anything around you. The things around you have a rehearsed and layered and cosmetic look. The tape is superreal, or maybe underreal is the way you want to put it. It is what lies at the scraped bottom of all the layers you have added. And this is another reason why you keep on looking. The tape has a searing realness.

It shows him giving an abbreviated wave, stiff-palmed, like a signal flag at a siding.

You know how families make up games. This is just another game in which the child invents the rules as she goes along. She likes the idea of videotaping a man in his car. She has probably never done it before and she sees no reason to vary the format or terminate early or pan to another car. This is her game and she is learning it and playing it at the same time. She feels halfway clever and inventive and maybe slightly intrusive as well, a little bit of brazenness that spices any game.

And you keep on looking. You look because this is the nature of the footage, to make a channeled path through time, to give things a shape and a destiny.

Of course if she had panned to another car, the right car at the precise time, she would have caught the gunman as he fired.

The chance quality of the encounter. The victim, the killer, and the child with a camera. Random energies that approach a common point. There's something here that speaks to you directly, saying terrible things about forces beyond your control, lines of intersection that cut through history and logic and every reasonable layer of human expectation.

She wandered into it. The girl got lost and wandered clear-eyed into horror. This is a children's story about straying too far from home. But it isn't the family car that serves as the instrument of the child's curiosity, her inclination to explore. It is the camera that puts her in the tale.

You know about holidays and family celebrations and how somebody shows up with a camcorder and the relatives stand around and barely react because they're numbingly accustomed to the process of being taped and decked and shown on the VCR with the coffee and cake.

He is hit soon after. If you've seen the tape many times you know from the handwave exactly when he will be hit. It is something, naturally, that you wait for. You say to your wife, if you're at home and she is there, Now here is where he gets it. You say, Janet, hurry up, this is where it happens.

Now here is where he gets it. You see him jolted, sort of wire-shocked—then he seizes up and falls toward the door or maybe leans or slides into the door is the proper way to put it. It is awful and unremarkable at the same time. The car stays in the slow lane. It approaches briefly, then falls back.

You don't usually call your wife over to the TV set. She has her programs, you have yours. But there's a certain urgency here. You want her to see how it looks. The tape has been running forever and now the thing is finally going to happen and you want her to be here when he's shot.

Here it comes, all right. He is shot, head-shot, and the camera reacts, the child reacts—there is a jolting movement but she keeps on taping, there is a sympathetic response, a nerve response, her heart is beating faster but she keeps the camera trained on the subject as he slides into the door and even as you see him die you're thinking of the girl. At some level the girl has to be present here, watching what you're watching, unprepared—the girl is seeing this cold and you have to marvel at the fact that she keeps the tape rolling.

It shows something awful and unaccompanied. You want your wife to see it because it is real this time, not fancy movie violence—the realness beneath the layers of cosmetic perception. Hurry up, Janet, here it comes. He dies so fast. There is no accompaniment of any kind. It is very stripped. You want to tell her it is realer than real but then she will ask what that means.

The way the camera reacts to the gunshot—a startle reaction that brings pity and terror into the frame, the girl's own shock, the girl's identification with the victim.

You don't see the blood, which is probably trickling behind his ear and down the back of his neck. The way his head is twisted away from the door, the twist of the head gives you only a partial profile and it's the wrong side, it's not the side where he was hit.

And maybe you're being a little aggressive here, practically forcing your wife to watch. Why? What are you telling her? Are you making a little statement? Like I'm going to ruin your day out of ordinary spite. Or a big statement? Like this is the risk of existing. Either way you're rubbing her face in this tape and you don't know why.

It shows the car drifting toward the guardrail and then there's a jostling sense of two other lanes and part of another car, a split-second blur, and the tape ends here, either because the girl stopped shooting or because some central authority, the police or the district attorney or the TV station, decided there was nothing else you had to see.

This is either the tenth or eleventh homicide committed by the Texas Highway Killer. The number is uncertain because the police believe that one of the shootings may have been a copycat crime.

And there is something about videotape, isn't there, and this particular kind of serial crime? This is a crime designed for random taping and immediate playing. You sit there and wonder if this kind of crime became more possible when the means of taping and playing an event—playing it immediately after the taping—became part of the culture. The principal doesn't necessarily commit the sequence of crimes in order to see them taped and played. He commits the crimes as if they were a form of taped-and-played event. The crimes are inseparable from the idea of taping and playing. You sit there thinking that this is a crime that has found its medium, or vice versa—cheap mass production, the sequence of repeated images and victims, stark and glary and more or less unremarkable.

It shows very little in the end. It is a famous murder because it is on tape and because the murderer has done it many times and because the crime was recorded by a child. So the child is involved, the Video Kid as she is sometimes called because they have to call her something. The tape is famous and so is she. She is famous in the modern manner of people whose names are strategically withheld. They are famous without names or faces, spirits living apart from their bodies, the victims and witnesses, the underage criminals, out there somewhere at the edges of perception.

Seeing someone at the moment he dies, dying unexpectedly. This is reason alone to stay fixed to the screen. It is instructional, watching a man shot dead as he drives along on a sunny day. It demonstrates an elemental truth, that every breath you take has two possible endings. And that's another thing. There's a joke locked away here, a note of cruel slapstick that you are completely willing to appreciate. Maybe the victim's a chump, a dope, classically unlucky. He had it coming, in a way, like an innocent fool in a silent movie.

You don't want Janet to give you any crap about it's on all the time, they show it a thousand times a day. They show it because it exists, because they have to show it, because this is why they're out there. The horror freezes your soul but this doesn't mean that you want them to stop.

# ⁂ THOM JONES
(1945–   )

Thom Jones was born in Aurora, Illinois. He served in the U.S. Marine Corps and was a boxer. He married in 1968 and has one child. He earned a B.A. from the University of Washington in 1970 and an M.F.A. from the Writers' Workshop at the University of Iowa in 1973. He currently teaches at the University of Iowa.

Jones' stories have appeared in a number of periodicals, including *The New Yorker, Playboy,* and *Esquire,* and have been included in the Best American Stories Award annuals as well as receiving an O. Henry Award. They vividly capture raw and basic emotions, mostly of men trying to cope with their sense of despair, desperation, and rage in a world that often makes no sense. His story collections are *The Pugilist at Rest* (1993), *Cold Snap: Stories* (1995), and *Sonny Liston Was a Friend of Mine* (1999).

## Cold Snap

Son of a bitch, there's a cold snap and I do this number where I leave all the faucets running because my house, and most houses out here on the West Coast, aren't "real"—they don't have windows that go up and down, or basements (which protect the pipes in a way that a crawl space can't), or sidewalks out in the front with a nice pair of towering oak trees or a couple of elms, which a real house will have, one of those good old Midwest houses. Out here the windows go side to side. You get no basement. No sidewalk and no real trees, just evergreens, and when it gets cold and snows, nobody knows what to do. An inch of snow and they cancel school and the community is paralyzed. "Help me, I'm helpless!" Well, it's cold for a change and I guess that's not so bad, because all the fleas and mosquitoes will freeze, and also because any change is *something,* and maybe it will help snap me out of this bleak post-Africa depression—oh, baby, I'm so depressed—but I wake up at three in the morning and think, Oh, no, a pipe is gonna bust, so I run the water and let the faucets drip and I go outside and turn on the outdoor faucets, which are the most vulnerable. Sure enough, they were caking up, and I got to them just in the nick of time, which was good, since in my condition there was no way I could possibly cope with a broken water pipe. I just got back from Africa, where I was playing doctor to the natives, got hammered with a nasty case of malaria, and lost thirty pounds, but it was a manic episode I had that caused Global Aid to send me home. It was my worst attack to date, and on lithium I get such a bad case of psoriasis that I look like alligator man. You can take Tegretol for mania but it once wiped out my white count and almost killed me, so what I like to do when I get all revved up is skin-pop some morphine, which I had with me by the gallon over there and which will keep you calm—and, unlike booze, it's something I can keep under control. Although I must confess I lost my medical license in the States for substance abuse and ended up with Global Aid when the dust settled over that one. God's will, really. Fate. Karma. Whatever. Anyhow, hypomania is a good thing in Africa, a real motivator, and you can do anything you want over there as long as you keep your feet on the ground and don't parade naked on the president's lawn in Nairobi and get expelled (which I did and which will get you expelled; okay, I lied, you can't do *anything*—so sue me). On lithium, while you don't crash so bad, you never get high, either, and all you can do is sit around sucking on Primus beer bottles, bitching about how hot it is when there's so much work to do.

While I'm outside checking my faucets, I look my Oldsmobile over and wonder was it last year I changed the antifreeze? Back in bed, it strikes me that it's been three years, so I go out and run the engine and sit in the car with my teeth chattering—it's thirteen below, geez! And pretty soon the warm air is defrosting the car and I drive over to the hardware section at Safeway and get one of those antifreeze testers with the little balls in it. At four in the morning I'm sitting in my kitchen trying to get it out of the plastic jacket, and it comes out in two parts, with the bulb upside down. No doubt some know-nothing Central American put it in upside down for twenty cents an hour in some slave factory. I know he's got problems—fact is, I've been there and could elucidate his problems—but how about me and my damn antifreeze? I mean, too bad about you, buddy, how about me? And I'm trying to jury-rig it when I realize there is a high potential for breaking the glass and cutting my thumb, and just as that voice that is me, that is always talking to me, my ego, I guess, tells me, "Be careful, Richard, so you don't cut your thumb"—at that instant, I slice my thumb down to the bone. So the next thing you know I'm driving to the hospital with a towel on my thumb thinking, A minute ago everything was just fine, and now I'm driving myself to the emergency room!

Some other guy comes in with this awful burn because a pressure cooker exploded in his face, and he's got this receding hairline, and you can see the way the skin is peeled back—poached-looking. The guy's going to need a hairpiece for sure. A doctor comes out eating a sandwich, and I hear him tell the nurse to set up an I.V. line and start running some Dilaudid for the guy, which he deserves, considering. I would like some for my thumb, but all I get is Novocain, and my doctor says, "You aren't going to get woozy on me, are you?" I tell him no, I'm not like that, but I have another problem, and he says, "What's that?" and I tell him I can't jack off left-handed. Everybody laughs, because it's the graveyard shift, when that kind of joke is appropriate—even in mixed company. Plus, it's true.

After he stitches me up, I'm in no pain, although I say, "I'll bet this is going to hurt tomorrow," and he says no, he'll give me some pain medication, and I'm thinking, What a great doctor. He's giving me *pain medication.* And while he's in a giving mood I hit him up for some prostate antibiotics because my left testicle feels very heavy.

"Your left testicle feels *heavy?*" he says skeptically.

Yeah, every guy gets it, shit; I tell him my left nut feels like an anvil. I mean, I want to cradle it in my hand when I'm out and about, or rest it on a little silk pillow when I'm stationary. It doesn't really hurt, but I'm very much conscious of having a left testicle, whereas I have teeth and a belly button and a right testicle and I don't even know. I tell him I don't want a finger wave, because I've been through this a thousand times. My prostate is backing up into the seminal vesicles, and if you don't jerk off it builds up and gets worse, and the doctor agrees—that does happen, and he doesn't really want to give me a finger wave, especially when I tell him that a urologist checked it out a couple of months back. He puts on a plastic glove and feels my testicle, pronounces it swollen, and writes a script for antibiotics, after which he tells me to quit drinking coffee. I was going to tell him that I don't jerk off because I'm a sex fiend; I have low sex drive, and it's actually not that much fun. I just do it to keep the prostate empty. Or should I tell him I'm a doctor myself, albeit defrocked, that I just got back from Africa and my nut could be infected with elephantiasis? Highly unlikely, but you never know. But he won't know diddle about tropical medicine—that's my department, and I decide I will just shut my mouth, which is a first for me.

The duty nurse is pretty good-looking, and she contradicts the doctor's orders—gives me a cup of coffee anyhow, plus a roll, and we're sitting there quietly, listening to the other doctor and a nurse fixing the guy with the burned forehead. A little human interaction is taking place and my depression is gone as I begin to feel sorry for the guy with the burn, who is explaining that he was up late with insomnia cooking sweet potatoes when the pressure cooker blew. He was going to candy them with brown sugar and eat them at six in the morning and he's laughing, too, because of the Dilaudid drip. After Linda Ronstadt sings "Just One Look" on the radio, the announcer comes on and says that we've set a record for cold—it's thirteen and a half below at the airport—and I notice that the announcer is happy, too; there's a kind of solidarity that occurs when suffering is inflicted on the community by nature.

My own thing is the Vincent van Gogh effect. I read where he "felt like a million" after he cut off his ear. It only lasted for a couple of days. They always show you the series of four self-portraits that he painted at different times in his life as his mental condition went progressively downhill. Van Gogh One is a realistic-looking pic, but as life goes on and his madness gets worse he paints Van Gogh Four and it looks as though he's been doing some kind of bad LSD, which is how the world had been looking to me until I cut my thumb. It gave me a three-day respite from the blues, and clarity came into my life, and I have to remind myself by writing this down that all the bad stuff does pass if you can wait it out. You forget when you're in the middle of it, so during that three-day break I slapped this note on the refrigerator door: "Richard, you are a good and loving person, and all the bad stuff does pass, so remember that the next time you get down and think that you've always been down and always will be down, since that's paranoia and it gets you nowhere. You're just in one of your Fyodor Dostoyevski moods—do yourself a favor and forget it!"

* * *

I felt so good I actually had the nerve to go out and buy a new set of clothes and see a movie, and then, on the last day before the depression came back, I drove out to Western State and checked my baby sister, Susan, out for a day trip. Susan was always a lot worse than me; she heard voices and pulled I don't know how many suicide attempts until she took my squirrel pistol and put a .22 long-rifle slug through the temple—not really the temple, because at the last minute you always flinch, but forward of the temple, and it was the most perfect lobotomy. I remember hearing the gun pop and how she came into my room (I was home from college for the summer) and said, "Richard, I just shot myself, how come I'm not dead?" Her voice was calm instead of the usual fingernails-on-the-chalkboard voice, the when-she-was-crazy (which was almost always) voice, and I realized later that she was instantly cured, the very moment the bullet zipped through her brain. Everyone said it was such a shame because she was so beautiful, but what good are looks if you are in hell? And she let her looks go at the hospital because she really didn't have a care in the world, but she was still probably the most beautiful patient at Western State. I had a fresh occasion to worry about her on this trip when I saw an attendant rough-handling an old man to stop him from whining, which it did. She'd go along with anything, and she had no advocate except me. And then I almost regretted going out there, in spite of my do-good mood, because Susan wanted to go to the Point Defiance Zoo to see Cindy, the elephant that was on the news after they transferred the attendant who took care of her, for defying orders and actually going into the elephant pen on the sly to be her friend.

There are seven hundred elephants in North American zoos, and although Cindy is an Asian elephant and a female and small, she is still considered the most dangerous elephant in America. Last year alone, three people were killed by elephants in the United States, and this is what Susan had seen and heard on the color television in the ward dayroom, and she's like a child—she wants to go out and see an elephant when it's ten below zero. They originally had Cindy clamped up in a pen tighter than the one they've got John Gotti in down in Marion, Illinois, and I don't remember that the catalogue of Cindy's crimes included human murder. She was just a general troublemaker, and they were beating her with a two-by-four when some animal activist reported it and there was a big scandal that ended with Cindy getting shipped down to the San Diego Zoo; I think there was some kind of escape (don't quote me on that) where Cindy was running around on a golf course in between moves, and then a capture involving tranquilizer darts, and when they couldn't control Cindy in San Diego they shipped her back up here to Tacoma and put her in maximum-security confinement. It was pretty awful. I told Susan that over in India Cindy would have a job hauling logs or something, and there would be an elephant boy to scrub her down at night with a big brush while she lay in the river, and the elephant boy would be with her at all times, her constant companion. Actually, the elephant would be more important than the boy, I told her, and that's how you should handle an elephant in America—import an experienced elephant boy for each one, give the kids a green card, pay them a lot of overtime, and have them stay with the elephants around the clock. You know, quality time. How could you blame Cindy for all the shit she pulled? And in the middle of this, Susan has a tear floating off her cheek and I don't know if it's a tear caused by the cold or if she was touched by Cindy's plight. The reason they sent my sister to the nuthouse was that you could light a fire on the floor in front of her and she would just sit there and watch it burn. When our parents died, I took her to my place in Washington state and hired helpers to look after her, but they would always quit—quit while I was over in the Third World, where it's impossible to do anything. It was like, *Meanwhile, back in the jungle/Meanwhile, back in the States. . . .* Apart from her lack of affect, Susan was always logical and made perfect sense. She was kind of like a Mr. Spock who just didn't give a shit anymore except when it came to childish fun and games. All bundled up, with a scarf over her ears, in her innocence she looked like Eva Marie Saint in *On the Waterfront.*

We drove over to Nordstrom's in the University District and I bought Suz some new threads and then took her to a hair salon where she got this chic haircut, and she was looking so good that I almost regretted it, 'cause if those wacked-out freaks at the hospital weren't hitting on her before they would be now. It was starting to get dark and time to head back when Susan spots the Space Needle from I-5—she's never been there, so I took her to the top and she wandered outside to the observation deck, where the wind was a walking razor blade at five hundred and eighteen feet, but Susan is grooving on the lights of Seattle and with her homemade lobotomy doesn't experience pain in quite the way a normal person does, and I want her to have a little fun, but I'm freezing out there, especially my thumb, which ached. I didn't want to pop back inside in the sheltered part and leave her out there, though, because she might want to pitch herself over the side. I mean, they've got safety nets, but what if she's still got some vestige of a death wish? We had dinner in the revolving dining room, and people were looking at us funny because of Susan's eating habits, which deteriorate when you live in a nuthouse, but we got through that and went back to my place to watch TV, and after that I was glad to go to sleep—but I couldn't sleep because of my thumb. I was thinking I still hadn't cashed in the script for the pain pills when Susan comes into my bedroom naked and sits down on the edge of the bed.

"Ever since I've been shot, I feel like those animals in the zoo. I want to set them free," she says, in a remarkable display of insight, since that scar in her frontal lobes has got more steel bars than all the prisons of the world, and, as a rule, folks with frontal-lobe damage don't have much insight. I get her to put on her pajamas, and I remember what it used to be like when she stayed at home—you always had to have someone watching her—and I wished I had gotten her back to the hospital that very night, because she was up prowling, and suddenly all my good feelings of the past few days were gone. I felt crappy, but I had to stay vigilant while my baby sister was tripping around the house with this bullet-induced, jocular euphoria.

At one point she went outside barefoot. Later I found her eating a cube of butter. Then she took out all the canned foods in my larder and stacked them up—Progresso black beans (*beaucoup*), beef-barley soup, and canned carrot juice—playing supermarket. I tell her, "Mrs. Ma'am, I'll take one of those, and one of those, and have you got any peachy pie?"

She says, "I'm sorry, Richard, we haven't got any peachy pie."

"But, baby, I would sure like a nice big piece of peachy pie, heated up, and some vanilla ice cream with some rum sauce and maybe something along the lines of a maraschino cherry to put on the top for a little garnish. Nutmeg would do. Or are you telling me this is just a soup, beans, and carrot-juice joint? Is that all you got here?"

"Yes, Richard. Just soup and beans. They're very filling, though."

"Ahhm gonna have to call Betty Crocker, 'cause I'm in the mood for some pie, darlin'."

Suzie looks at me sort of worried and says that she thinks Betty Crocker is dead. Fuck. I realized I just had to sit on the couch and watch her, and this goes on and on, and of course I think I hear someone crashing around in the yard, so I get my .357 out from under my pillow and walk around the perimeter of the house, my feet crunching on the frozen snow. There was nobody out there. Back inside I checked on Susan, who was asleep in my bed. When I finally saw the rising of the sun and heard birds chirping to greet the new day, I went to the refrigerator, where I saw my recent affirmation: "Richard, you are a good and loving person," etc. I ripped it off the refrigerator and tore it into a thousand tiny pieces. Only an idiot would write something like that. It was like, I can't hack it in Africa, can't hack it at home—all I can hack is dead. So I took all the bullets out of the .357 except one, spun the chamber, placed the barrel against my right temple, and squeezed the trigger. When I heard the click of the hammer—voilà! I instantly felt better. My thumb quit throbbing. My stomach did not burn. The dread of morning and of sunlight had vanished, and I saw the dawn as something good, the bird-song wonderful. Even the obscure, take-it-for-granted objects in my house—the little knickknacks covered in an inch of dust, a simple wooden chair, my morning coffee cup drying upside down on the drainboard—seemed so relevant, so alive and necessary. I was glad for life and glad to be alive, especially when I looked down at the gun and saw that my bullet had rotated to the firing chamber. The Van Gogh effect again. I was back from Van Gogh Four to Van Gogh One.

* * *

They're calling from the hospital, because I kept Susan overnight: "Where is Susan?" "She's watching *Days of Our Lives,*" I say as I shove the .357 into a top drawer next to the phone book. "Is she taking her Stelazine?" "Yes," I say. "Absolutely. Thanks for your concern. Now, goodbye!"

Just then the doorbell rings, and what I've got is a pair of Jehovah's Witnesses. I've seen enough of them on the Dark Continent to overcome an instinctive dread, since they seem to be genuinely content, proportionately—like, if you measured a bunch of them against the general population they are very happy people, and so pretty soon we're drinking Sanka and Susan comes out and they are talking about Christ's Kingdom on Earth where the lion lies down with the lamb, and Susan buys every word of it, 'cause it's like that line "Unless they come to me as little children. . . ." Susan is totally guileless and the two Witnesses are without much guile, and I, the king of agnostics, listen and think, How's a lion going to eat straw? It's got a G.I. system designed to consume flesh, bones, and viscera—it's got sharp teeth, claws, and predatory instincts, not twenty-seven stomachs, like some bovine Bossie the Cow or whatever. And while I'm paging through a copy of *Awake!,* I see a little article from the correspondent in Nigeria entitled "The Guinea Worm—Its Final Days." As a doctor of tropical medicine, I probably know more about *Dracunculus medinensis,* the "fiery serpent," or Guinea worm, than anyone in the country. Infection follows ingestion of water containing crustacea (*Cyclops*). The worms penetrate the gut wall and mature in the retroperitoneal space, where they can grow three feet in length, and then generally migrate to the lower legs, where they form a painful blister. What the Africans do is burst the ulcer and extract the adult worm by hooking a stick under it and ever so gently tugging it out, since if you break it off the dead body can become septic and the leg might have to be removed. The pain of the Guinea worm is on a par with the pain of gout, and it can take ten days to nudge one out. The bad part is they usually come not in singles but in multiples. I've seen seven come out of an old man's leg.

If and when Global Aid sends me back to Africa, I will help continue the worm-eradication program, and as the Witnesses delight Susan with tales of a Heaven on Earth I'm thinking of the heat and the bugs in the equatorial zone, and the muddy water that the villagers take from rivers—they pour it in jugs and let the sediment settle for an hour and then dip from the top, where it looks sort of clean; it's hard to get through to them that *Cyclops* crustacea may be floating about invisibly and one swallow could get you seven worms, a swallow you took three years ago. You can talk to the villagers until you're blue in the face and they'll drink it anyhow. So you have to poison the *Cyclops* without over-poisoning the water. I mean, it can be done, but, given the way things work over there, you have to do everything yourself if you want it done right, which is why I hate the idea of going back: you have to come on like a one-man band.

On the other hand, Brother Bogue and the other brothers in the home office of Global Aid don't trust me; they don't like it when I come into the office irrepressibly happy, like Maurice Chevalier in his tuxedo and straw hat—"*Jambo jambo, bwana, jambo bonjour!*"—and give everyone one of those African soft handshakes, and then maybe do a little turn at seventy-eight revolutions per minute: "Oh, *oui oui,* it's delightful for me, walking my baby back home!" or "Hey, ain't it great, after staying out late? Zangk heffen for leetle gorls." Etc. They hate it when I'm high and they hate it when I'm low, and they hate it most if I'm feeling crazy/paranoid and come in and say, "You won't believe what happened to me now!" To face those humorless brothers every day and stay forever in a job as a medical administrator, to wear a suit and tie and drive I-5 morning and night, to climb under the house and tape those pipes with insulation—you get in the crawl space and the dryer-hose vent is busted and there's lint up the ass, a time bomb for spontaneous combustion, funny the house hasn't blown already (and furthermore, no wonder the house is dusty), and, hey, what, carpenter ants, too? When I think of all that: Fair America, I bid you adieu!

But things are basically looking up when I get Suz back to the hospital. As luck has it, I meet an Indian psychiatrist who spent fifteen years in Kampala, Uganda—he was one of the three shrinks in the whole country—and I ask him how Big Daddy Idi Amin is doing. Apparently, he's doing fine, living in Saudi Arabia with paresis or something, and the next thing you know the doc is telling me he's going to review Susan's case file, which means he's going to put her in a better ward and look out for her, and that's a load off my mind. Before I go, Suz and I take a little stroll around the spacious hospital grounds—it's a tranquil place. I can't help thinking that if Brother Bogue fires me—though I'm determined to behave myself after my latest mishap—I could come here and take Haldol and lithium, watch color TV, and drool. Whatever happened to that deal where you just went off to the hospital for a "little rest," with no stigma attached? Maybe all I need is some rest.

Susan still has those Jehovah's Witnesses on her mind. As we sit on a bench, she pulls one of their booklets out of her coat and shows me scenes of cornucopias filled with fruit and bounty, rainbows, and vividly colored vistas of a heaven on earth. Vistas that I've seen in a way, however paradoxically, in these awful Third World places, and I'm thinking, Let them that have eyes see; and let them that have ears hear—that's how it is, and I start telling Suz about Africa, maybe someday I can take her there, and she gets excited and asks me what it's like. Can you see lions?

And I tell her, "Yeah, baby, you'll see lions, giraffes, zebras, monkeys, and parrots, and the Pygmies." And she really wants to see Pygmies. So I tell her about a Pygmy chief who likes to trade monkey meat for tobacco, T-shirts, candy, and trinkets, and about how one time when I went manic and took to the bush I stayed with this tribe, and went on a hunt with them, and we found a honeycomb in the forest; one of the hunters climbed up the tree to knock it down, oblivious of all the bees that were biting him. There were about five of us in the party and maybe ten pounds of honey and we ate all of it on the spot, didn't save an ounce, because we had the munchies from smoking dope. I don't tell Suz how it feels to take an airplane to New York, wait four hours for a flight to London, spend six hours in a transient lounge, and then hop on a nine-hour flight to Nairobi, clear customs, and ride on the back of a feed truck driven by a kamikaze African over potholes, through thick red dust, mosquitoes, black flies, tsetse flies, or about river blindness, bone-break fever, bilharziasis, dumdum fever, tropical ulcers, AIDS, leprosy, etc. To go through all that to save somebody's life and maybe have them spit in your eye for the favor—I don't tell her about it, the way you don't tell a little kid that Santa Claus is a fabrication. And anyhow if I had eyes and could see, and ears and could hear—it very well might *be* the Garden of Eden. I mean, I can fuck up a wet dream with my attitude. I don't tell her that lions don't eat straw, never have, and so she's happy. And it's a nice moment for me, too, in a funny-ass way. I'm beginning to feel that with her I might find another little island of stability.

* * *

Another hospital visit: winter has given way to spring and the cherry blossoms are out. In two weeks it's gone from ten below to sixty-five, my Elavil and lithium are kicking in, and I'm feeling fine, calm, feeling pretty good. (I'm ready to go back and rumble in the jungle, yeah! *Sha-lah la-la-la-lah.*) Susan tells me she had a prophetic dream. She's unusually focused and articulate. She tells me she dreamed the two of us were driving around Heaven in a blue '67 Dodge.

"A '67 Dodge. Baby, what were we, the losers of Heaven?"

"Maybe, but it didn't really matter because we were there and we were happy."

"What were the other people like? Who was there? Was Arthur Schopenhauer there?"

"You silly! We didn't see other people. Just the houses. We drove up this hill and everything was like in a Walt Disney cartoon and we looked at one another and smiled because we were in Heaven, because we made it, because there wasn't any more shit."

"Now, let me get this straight. We were driving around in a beat-up car—"

"Yes, Richard, but it didn't matter."

"Let me finish. You say people lived in houses. That means people have to build houses. Paint them, clean them, and maintain them. Are you telling me that people in Heaven have jobs?"

"Yes, but they like their jobs."

"Oh, God, does it never end? A *job!* What am I going to do? I'm a doctor. If people don't get sick there, they'll probably make me a coal miner or something."

"Yes, but you'll love it." She grabs my arm with both hands, pitches her forehead against my chest, and laughs. It's the first time I've heard Susan laugh, ever—since we were kids, I mean.

"Richard, it's just like Earth but with none of the bad stuff. You were happy, too. So please don't worry. Is Africa like the Garden of Eden, Richard?"

"It's lush all right, but there's lots and lots of dead time," I say. "It's a good place to read *Anna Karenina.* Do you get to read novels in Heaven, hon? Have they got a library? After I pull my shift in the coal mine, do I get to take a nice little shower, hop in the Dodge, and drive over to the library?"

Susan laughs for the second time. "We will travel from glory to glory, Richard, and you won't be asking existential questions all the time. You won't have to anymore. And Mom and Dad will be there. You and me, all of us in perfect health. No coal mining. No wars, no fighting, no discontent. Satan will be in the Big Pit. He's on the earth now tormenting us, but these are his last days. Why do you think we are here?"

"I often ask myself that question."

"Just hold on for a little while longer, Richard. Can you do that? Will you do it for me, Richard? What good would Heaven be if you're not there? Please, Richard, tell me you'll come."

I said, "Okay, baby, anything for you. I repent."

"No more Fyodor Dostoyevski?"

"I'll be non-Dostoyevski. It's just that, in the meantime, we're just sitting around here—waiting for Godot?"

"No, Richard, don't be a smart-ass. In the meantime we eat lunch. What did you bring?"

I opened up a deli bag and laid out chicken-salad-sandwich halves on homemade bread wrapped in white butcher paper. The sandwiches were stuffed with alfalfa sprouts and grated cheese, impaled with toothpicks with red, blue, and green cellophane ribbons on them, and there were two large, perfect, crunchy garlic pickles on the side. And a couple of cartons of strawberry Yoplait, two tubs of fruit salad with fresh whipped cream and little wooden spoons, and two large cardboard cups of aromatic, steaming, fresh black coffee.

It begins to rain, and we have to haul ass into the front seat of my Olds, where Suz and I finish the best little lunch of a lifetime and suddenly the Shirelles are singing, "This is dedicated to the one I love," and I'm thinking that I'm gonna be all right, and in the meantime what can be better than a cool, breezy, fragrant day, rain-splatter diamonds on the wraparound windshield of a Ninety-eight Olds with a view of cherry trees blooming in the light spring rain?

# SHERMAN ALEXIE

## (1966– )

Part of a younger generation of Native American writers, Sherman Alexie writes fiction and poetry that graphically portray contemporary Indian life both on and off the reservation. His work blends realism and surrealism, subverts conventional expectations and forms, and mixes a wry humor with an earned anger for the lingering consequences of historical injustice. The anger is tempered by a belief in the healing and restorative power of love.

Alexie was born in Spokane, Washington, and grew up on the Spokane reservation in Wellpinit, Washington. His parents were alcoholics, though his mother has recovered and works as a substance abuse counselor. Alexie spent most of his childhood reading all the books in the Wellpinit school library. He attended Spokane's Jesuit Gonzaga University from 1985 to 1987, most of which time he wasted in alcohol abuse. After transferring to Washington State University in 1987, he quit drinking and began to develop his writing talents under the influence of his teacher Alex Kuo, a poet. Alexie received his B.A. in 1991.

Alexie's first two books, *The Business of Fancydancing: Stories and Poems* and *I Would Steal Horses* were published in 1992, followed by *First Indian on the Moon* (1993), *Old Shirts & New Skins* (1993), *Water Flowing Home* (1994), and *The Summer of Black Widows* (1996). His first story collection, *The Lone Ranger and Tonto Fistfight in Heaven* (1993), won a PEN/Hemingway Award for best first book of fiction. His novel *Reservation Blues* (1994) won the American Book Award. His next novel was *Indian Killer* (1996). More recently he published the collection of stories *The Toughest Indian in the World* (2000). He also produced the film *Smoke Signals* based on part of his first story collection, and plans to produce and direct a film of his novel *Indian Killer.*

father / son story - father dies

# This Is What It Means to Say Phoenix, Arizona

tradition / history → society

JUST AFTER Victor lost his job at the BIA, he also found out that his father had died of a heart attack in Phoenix, Arizona. Victor hadn't seen his father in a few years, only talked to him on the telephone once or twice, but there still was a genetic pain, which was soon to be pain as real and immediate as a broken bone.

Victor didn't have any money. Who does have money on a reservation, except the cigarette and fireworks salespeople? His father had a savings account waiting to be claimed, but Victor needed to find a way to get to Phoenix. Victor's mother was just as poor as he was, and the rest of his family didn't have any use at all for him. So Victor called the Tribal Council.

"Listen," Victor said. "My father just died. I need some money to get to Phoenix to make arrangements."

"Now, Victor," the council said. "You know we're having a difficult time financially."

"But I thought the council had special funds set aside for stuff like this."

"Now, Victor, we do have some money available for the proper return of tribal members' bodies. But I don't think we have enough to bring your father all the way back from Phoenix."

"Well," Victor said. "It ain't going to cost all that much. He had to be cremated. Things were kind of ugly. He died of a heart attack in his trailer and nobody found him for a week. It was really hot, too. You get the picture."

"Now, Victor, we're sorry for your loss and the circumstances. But we can really only afford to give you one hundred dollars."

"That's not even enough for a plane ticket."

"Well, you might consider driving down to Phoenix."

"I don't have a car. Besides, I was going to drive my father's pickup back up here."

"Now, Victor," the council said. "We're sure there is somebody who could drive you to Phoenix. Or is there somebody who could lend you the rest of the money?"

"You know there ain't nobody around with that kind of money."

"Well, we're sorry, Victor, but that's the best we can do."

Victor accepted the Tribal Council's offer. What else could he do? So he signed the proper papers, picked up his check, and walked over to the Trading Post to cash it.

While Victor stood in line, he watched Thomas Builds-the-Fire standing near the magazine rack, talking to himself. Like he always did. Thomas was a storyteller that nobody wanted to listen to. That's like being a dentist in a town where everybody has false teeth.

Victor and Thomas Builds-the-Fire were the same age, had grown up and played in the dirt together. Ever since Victor could remember, it was Thomas who always had something to say.

Once, when they were seven years old, when Victor's father still lived with the family, Thomas closed his eyes and told Victor this story: "Your father's heart is weak. He is afraid of his own family. He is afraid of you. Late at night he sits in the dark. Watches the television until there's nothing but that white noise. Sometimes he feels like he wants to buy a motorcycle and ride away. He wants to run and hide. He doesn't want to be found."

Thomas Builds-the-Fire had known that Victor's father was going to leave, knew it before anyone. Now Victor stood in the Trading Post with a one-hundred-dollar check in his hand, wondering if Thomas knew that Victor's father was dead, if he knew what was going to happen next.

Just then Thomas looked at Victor, smiled, and walked over to him.

"Victor, I'm sorry about your father," Thomas said.

"How did you know about it?" Victor asked.

"I heard it on the wind. I heard it from the birds. I felt it in the sunlight. Also, your mother was just in here crying."

"Oh," Victor said and looked around the Trading Post. All the other Indians stared, surprised that Victor was even talking to Thomas. Nobody talked to Thomas anymore because he told the same damn stories over and over again. Victor was embarrassed, but he thought that Thomas might be able to help him. Victor felt a sudden need for tradition.

"I can lend you the money you need," Thomas said suddenly. "But you have to take me with you."

"I can't take your money," Victor said. "I mean, I haven't hardly talked to you in years. We're not really friends anymore."

"I didn't say we were friends. I said you had to take me with you."

"Let me think about it."

Victor went home with his one hundred dollars and sat at the kitchen table. He held his head in his hands and thought about Thomas Builds-the-Fire, remembered little details, tears and scars, the bicycle they shared for a summer, so many stories.

* * *

Thomas Builds-the-Fire sat on the bicycle, waited in Victor's yard. He was ten years old and skinny. His hair was dirty because it was the Fourth of July.

"Victor," Thomas yelled. "Hurry up. We're going to miss the fireworks."

After a few minutes, Victor ran out of his house, jumped the porch railing, and landed gracefully on the sidewalk.

"And the judges award him a 9.95, the highest score of the summer," Thomas said, clapped, laughed.

"That was perfect, cousin," Victor said. "And it's my turn to ride the bike."

Thomas gave up the bike and they headed for the fair-grounds. It was nearly dark and the fireworks were about to start.

"You know," Thomas said. "It's strange how us Indians celebrate the Fourth of July. It ain't like it was *our* independence everybody was fighting for."

"You think about things too much," Victor said. "It's just supposed to be fun. Maybe Junior will be there."

"Which Junior? Everybody on this reservation is named Junior."

And they both laughed.

The fireworks were small, hardly more than a few bottle rockets and a fountain. But it was enough for two Indian boys. Years later, they would need much more.

Afterwards, sitting in the dark, fighting off mosquitoes, Victor turned to Thomas Builds-the-Fire.

"Hey," Victor said. "Tell me a story."

Thomas closed his eyes and told this story: "There were these two Indian boys who wanted to be warriors. But it was too late to be warriors in the old way. All the horses were gone. So the two Indian boys stole a car and drove to the city. They parked the stolen car in front of the police station and then hitchhiked back home to the reservation. When they got back, all their friends cheered and their parents' eyes shone with pride. *You were very brave,* everybody said to the two Indian boys. *Very brave.*"

"Ya-hey," Victor said. "That's a good one. I wish I could be a warrior."

"Me, too," Thomas said.

They went home together in the dark, Thomas on the bike now, Victor on foot. They walked through shadows and light from streetlamps.

"We've come a long ways," Thomas said. "We have outdoor lighting."

"All I need is the stars," Victor said. "And besides, you still think about things too much."

They separated then, each headed for home, both laughing all the way.

* * *

Victor sat at his kitchen table. He counted his one hundred dollars again and again. He knew he needed more to make it to Phoenix and back. He knew he needed Thomas Builds-the-Fire. So he put his money in his wallet and opened the front door to find Thomas on the porch.

"Ya-hey, Victor," Thomas said. "I knew you'd call me."

Thomas walked into the living room and sat down on Victor's favorite chair.

"I've got some money saved up," Thomas said. "It's enough to get us down there, but you have to get us back."

"I've got this hundred dollars," Victor said. "And my dad had a savings account I'm going to claim."

"How much in your dad's account?"

"Enough. A few hundred."

"Sounds good. When we leaving?"

* * *

When they were fifteen and had long since stopped being friends, Victor and Thomas got into a fistfight. That is, Victor was really drunk and beat Thomas up for no reason at all. All the other Indian boys stood around and watched it happen. Junior was there and so were Lester, Seymour, and a lot of others. The beating might have gone on until Thomas was dead if Norma Many Horses hadn't come along and stopped it.

"Hey, you boys," Norma yelled and jumped out of her car. "Leave him alone."

If it had been someone else, even another man, the Indian boys would've just ignored the warnings. But Norma was a warrior. She was powerful. She could have picked up any two of the boys and smashed their skulls together. But worse than that, she would have dragged them all over to some tipi and made them listen to some elder tell a dusty old story.

The Indian boys scattered, and Norma walked over to Thomas and picked him up.

"Hey, little man, are you okay?" she asked.

Thomas gave her a thumbs up.

"Why they always picking on you?"

Thomas shook his head, closed his eyes, but no stories came to him, no words or music. He just wanted to go home, to lie in his bed and let his dreams tell his stories for him.

* * *

Thomas Builds-the-Fire and Victor sat next to each other in the airplane, coach section. A tiny white woman had the window seat. She was busy twisting her body into pretzels. She was flexible.

"I have to ask," Thomas said, and Victor closed his eyes in embarrassment.

"Don't," Victor said.

"Excuse me, miss," Thomas asked. "Are you a gymnast or something?"

"There's no something about it," she said. "I was first alternate on the 1980 Olympic team."

"Really?" Thomas asked.

"Really."

"I mean, you used to be a world-class athlete?" Thomas asked.

"My husband still thinks I am."

Thomas Builds-the-Fire smiled. She was a mental gymnast, too. She pulled her leg straight up against her body so that she could've kissed her kneecap.

"I wish I could do that," Thomas said.

Victor was ready to jump out of the plane. Thomas, that crazy Indian storyteller with ratty old braids and broken teeth, was flirting with a beautiful Olympic gymnast. Nobody back home on the reservation would ever believe it.

"Well," the gymnast said. "It's easy. Try it."

Thomas grabbed at his leg and tried to pull it up into the same position as the gymnast. He couldn't even come close, which made Victor and the gymnast laugh.

"Hey," she asked. "You two are Indian, right?"

"Full-blood," Victor said.

"Not me," Thomas said. "I'm half magician on my mother's side and half clown on my father's."

They all laughed.

"What are your names?" she asked.

"Victor and Thomas."

"Mine is Cathy. Pleased to meet you all."

The three of them talked for the duration of the flight. Cathy the gymnast complained about the government, how they screwed the 1980 Olympic team by boycotting.

"Sounds like you all got a lot in common with Indians," Thomas said.

Nobody laughed.

After the plane landed in Phoenix and they had all found their way to the terminal, Cathy the gymnast smiled and waved good-bye.

"She was really nice," Thomas said.

"Yeah, but everybody talks to everybody on airplanes," Victor said. "It's too bad we can't always be that way."

"You always used to tell me I think too much," Thomas said. "Now it sounds like you do."

"Maybe I caught it from you."

"Yeah."

Thomas and Victor rode in a taxi to the trailer where Victor's father died.

"Listen," Victor said as they stopped in front of the trailer. "I never told you I was sorry for beating you up that time."

"Oh, it was nothing. We were just kids and you were drunk."

"Yeah, but I'm still sorry."

"That's all right."

Victor paid for the taxi and the two of them stood in the hot Phoenix summer. They could smell the trailer.

"This ain't going to be nice," Victor said. "You don't have to go in."

"You're going to need help."

Victor walked to the front door and opened it. The stink rolled out and made them both gag. Victor's father had lain in that trailer for a week in hundred-degree temperatures before anyone found him. And the only reason anyone found him was because of the smell. They needed dental records to identify him. That's exactly what the coroner said. They needed dental records.

"Oh, man," Victor said. "I don't know if I can do this."

"Well, then don't."

"But there might be something valuable in there."

"I thought his money was in the bank."

"It is. I was talking about pictures and letters and stuff like that."

"Oh," Thomas said as he held his breath and followed Victor into the trailer.

* * *

When Victor was twelve, he stepped into an underground wasp nest. His foot was caught in the hole, and no matter how hard he struggled, Victor couldn't pull free.

He might have died there, stung a thousand times, if Thomas Builds-the-Fire had not come by.

"Run," Thomas yelled and pulled Victor's foot from the hole. They ran then, hard as they ever had, faster than Billy Mills, faster than Jim Thorpe, faster than the wasps could fly.

Victor and Thomas ran until they couldn't breathe, ran until it was cold and dark outside, ran until they were lost and it took hours to find their way home. All the way back, Victor counted his stings.

"Seven," Victor said. "My lucky number."

* * *

Victor didn't find much to keep in the trailer. Only a photo album and a stereo. Everything else had that smell stuck in it or was useless anyway.

"I guess this is all," Victor said. "It ain't much."

"Better than nothing," Thomas said.

"Yeah, and I do have the pickup."

"Yeah," Thomas said. "It's in good shape."

"Dad was good about that stuff."

"Yeah, I remember your dad."

"Really?" Victor asked. "What do you remember?"

Thomas Builds-the-Fire closed his eyes and told this story: "I remember when I had this dream that told me to go to Spokane, to stand by the Falls in the middle of the city and wait for a sign. I knew I had to go there but I didn't have a car. Didn't have a license. I was only thirteen. So I walked all the way, took me all day, and I finally made it to the Falls. I stood there for an hour waiting. Then your dad came walking up. *What the hell are you doing here?* he asked me. I said, *Waiting for a vision.* Then your father said, *All you're going to get here is mugged.* So he drove me over to Denny's, bought me dinner, and then drove me home to the reservation. For a long time I was mad because I thought my dreams had lied to me. But they didn't. Your dad was my vision. *Take care of each other* is what my dreams were saying. *Take care of each other.*"

Victor was quiet for a long time. He searched his mind for memories of his father, found the good ones, found a few bad ones, added it all up, and smiled.

"My father never told me about finding you in Spokane," Victor said.

"He said he wouldn't tell anybody. Didn't want me to get in trouble. But he said I had to watch out for you as part of the deal."

"Really?"

"Really. Your father said you would need the help. He was right."

"That's why you came down here with me, isn't it?" Victor asked.

"I came because of your father."

Victor and Thomas climbed into the pickup, drove over to the bank, and claimed the three hundred dollars in the savings account.

* * *

Thomas Builds-the-Fire could fly.

Once, he jumped off the roof of the tribal school and flapped his arms like a crazy eagle. And he flew. For a second, he hovered, suspended above all the other Indian boys who were too smart or too scared to jump.

"He's flying," Junior yelled, and Seymour was busy looking for the trick wires or mirrors. But it was real. As real as the dirt when Thomas lost altitude and crashed to the ground.

He broke his arm in two places.

"He broke his wing," Victor chanted, and the other Indian boys joined in, made it a tribal song.

"He broke his wing, he broke his wing, he broke his wing," all the Indian boys chanted as they ran off, flapping their wings, wishing they could fly, too. They hated Thomas for his courage, his brief moment as a bird. Everybody has dreams about flying. Thomas flew.

One of his dreams came true for just a second, just enough to make it real.

* * *

Victor's father, his ashes, fit in one wooden box with enough left over to fill a cardboard box.

"He always was a big man," Thomas said.

Victor carried part of his father and Thomas carried the rest out to the pickup. They set him down carefully behind the seats, put a cowboy hat on the wooden box and a Dodgers cap on the cardboard box. That's the way it was supposed to be.

"Ready to head back home," Victor asked.

"It's going to be a long drive."

"Yeah, take a couple days, maybe."

"We can take turns," Thomas said.

"Okay," Victor said, but they didn't take turns. Victor drove for sixteen hours straight north, made it halfway up Nevada toward home before he finally pulled over.

"Hey, Thomas," Victor said. "You got to drive for a while."

"Okay."

Thomas Builds-the-Fire slid behind the wheel and started off down the road. All through Nevada, Thomas and Victor had been amazed at the lack of animal life, at the absence of water, of movement.

"Where is everything?" Victor had asked more than once.

Now when Thomas was finally driving they saw the first animal, maybe the only animal in Nevada. It was a long-eared jackrabbit.

"Look," Victor yelled. "It's alive."

Thomas and Victor were busy congratulating themselves on their discovery when the jackrabbit darted out into the road and under the wheels of the pickup.

"Stop the goddamn car," Victor yelled, and Thomas did stop, backed the pickup to the dead jackrabbit.

"Oh, man, he's dead," Victor said as he looked at the squashed animal.

"Really dead."

"The only thing alive in this whole state and we just killed it."

"I don't know," Thomas said. "I think it was suicide."

Victor looked around the desert, sniffed the air, felt the emptiness and loneliness, and nodded his head.

"Yeah," Victor said. "It had to be suicide."

"I can't believe this," Thomas said. "You drive for a thousand miles and there ain't even any bugs smashed on the windshield. I drive for ten seconds and kill the only living thing in Nevada."

"Yeah," Victor said. "Maybe I should drive."

"Maybe you should."

* * *

Thomas Builds-the-Fire walked through the corridors of the tribal school by himself. Nobody wanted to be anywhere near him because of all those stories. Story after story.

Thomas closed his eyes and this story came to him: "We are all given one thing by which our lives are measured, one determination. Mine are the stories which can change or not change the world. It doesn't matter which as long as I continue to tell the stories. My father, he died on Okinawa in World War II, died fighting for this country, which had tried to kill him for years. My mother, she died giving birth to me, died while I was still inside her. She pushed me out into the world with her last breath. I have no brothers or sisters. I have only my stories which came to me before I even had the words to speak. I learned a thousand stories before I took my first thousand steps. They are all I have. It's all I can do."

Thomas Builds-the-Fire told his stories to all those who would stop and listen. He kept telling them long after people had stopped listening.

* * *

Victor and Thomas made it back to the reservation just as the sun was rising. It was the beginning of a new day on earth, but the same old shit on the reservation.

"Good morning," Thomas said.

"Good morning."

The tribe was waking up, ready for work, eating breakfast, reading the newspaper, just like everybody else does. Willene LeBret was out in her garden wearing a bathrobe. She waved when Thomas and Victor drove by.

"Crazy Indians made it," she said to herself and went back to her roses.

Victor stopped the pickup in front of Thomas Builds-the-Fire's HUD house. They both yawned, stretched a little, shook dust from their bodies.

"I'm tired," Victor said.

"Of everything," Thomas added.

They both searched for words to end the journey. Victor needed to thank Thomas for his help, for the money, and make the promise to pay it all back.

"Don't worry about the money," Thomas said. "It don't make any difference anyhow."

"Probably not, enit?"

"Nope."

Victor knew that Thomas would remain the crazy storyteller who talked to dogs and cars, who listened to the wind and pine trees. Victor knew that he couldn't really be friends with Thomas, even after all that had happened. It was cruel but it was real. As real as the ashes, as Victor's father, sitting behind the seats.

"I know how it is," Thomas said. "I know you ain't going to treat me any better than you did before. I know your friends would give you too much shit about it."

Victor was ashamed of himself. Whatever happened to the tribal ties, the sense of community? The only real thing he shared with anybody was a bottle and broken dreams. He owed Thomas something, anything.

"Listen," Victor said and handed Thomas the cardboard box which contained half of his father. "I want you to have this."

Thomas took the ashes and smiled, closed his eyes, and told this story: "I'm going to travel to Spokane Falls one last time and toss these ashes into the water. And your father will rise like a salmon, leap over the bridge, over me, and find his way home. It will be beautiful. His teeth will shine like silver, like a rainbow. He will rise, Victor, he will rise."

Victor smiled.

"I was planning on doing the same thing with my half," Victor said. "But I didn't imagine my father looking anything like a salmon. I thought it'd be like cleaning the attic or something. Like letting things go after they've stopped having any use."

"Nothing stops, cousin," Thomas said. "Nothing stops."

Thomas Builds-the-Fire got out of the pickup and walked up his driveway. Victor started the pickup and began the drive home.

"Wait," Thomas yelled suddenly from his porch. "I just got to ask one favor."

Victor stopped the pickup, leaned out the window, and shouted back. "What do you want?"

"Just one time when I'm telling a story somewhere, why don't you stop and listen?" Thomas asked.

"Just once?"

"Just once."

Victor waved his arms to let Thomas know that the deal was good. It was a fair trade, and that was all Victor had ever wanted from his whole life. So Victor drove his father's pickup toward home while Thomas went into his house, closed the door behind him, and heard a new story come to him in the silence afterwards.

# RON CARLSON

## (1947– )

Ron Carlson was born in Logan, Utah. He attended the University of Utah, completing a B.A. in 1970 and an M.A. in 1972. He married in 1969 and has two sons. He taught at the Hotchkins School in Lakeville, Connecticut, from 1971 to 1981. He devoted full time to his writing for five years before taking a permanent teaching position at Arizona State University in 1986, where he continues to live and teach.

Carlson's fiction is a careful blend of the comic and the serious. It is witty and observant, keeping a careful tension between sentiment and cynicism, the tender and the cruel, often examining the universal human longing that is never fully understood. Carlson published his first novel, *Betrayed by F. Scott Fitzgerald,* in 1977, and his second, *Truants,* in 1981. Two one-act plays were produced off-off Broadway in 1987. A collection of stories, *The News of the World,* appeared in 1987, followed by *Plan B for the Middle Class* in 1992 and *The Hotel Eden* in 1997.

# Oxygen

IN 1967, the year before the year that finally cracked the twentieth century once and for all, I had as my summer job delivering medical oxygen in Phoenix, Arizona. I was a sophomore at the University of Montana in Missoula, but my parents lived in Phoenix, and my father, as a welding engineer, used his contacts to get me a job at Ayr Oxygen Company. I started there doing what I called dumbbell maintenance, the kind of make-work assigned to college kids. I cleared debris from the back lot, mainly crushed packing crates that had been discarded. That took a week, and on the last day, as I was raking, I put a nail through the bottom of my foot and had to go for a tetanus shot. Next, I whitewashed the front of the supply store and did such a good job that I began a month of painting my way around the ten-acre plant.

These were good days for me. I was nineteen years old and this was the hardest work I had ever done. The days were stunning, starting hot and growing insistently hotter. My first week two of the days had been 116. The heat was a pure physical thing, magnified by the steel and pavement of the plant, and in that first week, I learned what not to touch, where not to stand, and I found the powerhouse heat simply bracing. I lost some of the winter dormitory fat and could feel myself browning and getting into shape. It felt good to pull on my Levi's and workshoes every morning (I'd tossed my tennies after the nail incident), and not to have any papers due for any class.

Of course, during this time I was living at home, that is arriving home from work sometime after six and then leaving for work sometime before seven the next morning. My parents and I had little use for each other. They were in their mid-forties then, an age I've since found out that can be oddly taxing, and besides they were in the middle of a huge career decision which would make their fortune and allow them to live the way they live now. I was nineteen, as I said, which in this country is not a real age at all, and effectively disqualifies a person for one year from meaningful relationship with any other human being.

I was having a hard ride through the one relationship I had begun during the school year. Her name was Linda Enright, a classmate, and we had made the mistake of sleeping together that spring, just once, but it wrecked absolutely everything. We were dreamy beforehand, the kind of couple who walked real close, bumping foreheads. We read each other's papers. I'm not making this up: we read poetry on the library lawn under a tree. I had met her in a huge section of Western Civilization taught by a young firebrand named Whisner, whose credo was "Western civilization is what you personally are doing." He'd defined it that way the first day of class and some wit had called out, "Then Western Civ is watching television." But Linda and I had taken it seriously, the way we took all things I guess, and we joined the Democratic Student Alliance and worked on a grape boycott, though it didn't seem that there were that many grapes to begin with in Montana that chilly spring.

And then one night in her dorm room we went ahead with it, squirming out of our clothes on her hard bed, and we did something for about a minute that changed everything. After that we weren't even the same people. She wasn't she and I wasn't I; we were two young citizens in the wrong country. I see now that a great deal of it was double- and triple-think, that is I thought she thought it was my fault and I thought that she might be right with that thought and I should be sorry and that I was sure she didn't know how sorry I was already, regret like a big burning house on the hill of my conscience, or something like that, and besides all I could think through all my sorrow and compunction was that I wanted it to happen again, soon. It was confusing. All I could remember from the incident itself was Linda stopping once and undoing my belt and saying, "Here, I'll get it."

The coolness of that practical phrase repeated in my mind after I'd said goodbye to Linda and she'd gone off to Boulder, where her summer job was working in her parents' cookie shop. I called her every Sunday from a pay phone at an Exxon Station on Indian School Road, and we'd fight and if you asked me what we fought about I couldn't tell you. We both felt misunderstood. I knew I was misunderstood, because I didn't understand myself. It was a glass booth, the standard phone booth, and at five in the afternoon on a late-June Sunday the sun torched the little space into a furnace. The steel tray was too hot to fry eggs on, you'd have ruined them. It gave me little-burns along my forearms. I'd slump outside the door as far as the steel cord allowed, my skin running to chills in the heat, and we'd argue until the operator came on and then I'd dump eight dollars of quarters into the blistering mechanism and go home.

The radio that summer played a strange mix, "Little Red Riding Hood," by Sam the Sham and the Pharaohs, over and over, along with songs by the Animals, even "Sky Pilot." This was not great music and I knew it at the time, but it all set me on edge. After work I'd shower and throw myself on the couch in my parents' dark and cool living room and read and sleep and watch the late movies, making a list of the titles eventually in the one notebook I was keeping.

About the third week of June, I burned myself. I'd graduated to the paint sprayer and was coating the caustic towers in the oxygen plant. These were two narrow, four-story tanks that stood beside the metal building where the oxygen was bottled. The towers were full of a viscous caustic material that air was forced through to remove nitrogen and other elements until the gas that emerged was 99 percent oxygen. I was forty feet up an extension ladder reaching right and left to spray the tops of the tanks. Beneath me was the pump station that ran the operation, a nasty tangle of motors, belts, and valving. The mistake I made was to spray where the ladder arms met the curved surface of the tank, and as I reached out then to hit the last and farthest spot, I felt the ladder slide in the new paint. Involuntarily I threw my arms straight out in a terrific hug against the superheated steel. Oddly I didn't feel the burn at first nor did I drop the spray gun. I looked down at what seemed now to be the wicked machinery of my death. It certainly would have killed me to fall. After a moment, and that's the right span here, a moment, seconds or a minute, long enough to stablilize my heartbeat and sear my cheekbone and the inside of both elbows, I slid one foot down one rung and began to descend.

All the burns were the shapes of little footballs, the one on my face a three-inch oval below my left eye, but after an hour with the doctor that afternoon, I didn't miss a day of work. They've all healed extraordinarily well, though they darken first if I'm not careful with the sun. That summer I was proud of them, the way I was proud not to have dropped the spray gun, and proud of my growing strength, of the way I'd broken in my workshoes, and proud in a strange way of my loneliness.

Where does loneliness live in the body? How many kinds of loneliness are there? Mine was the loneliness of the college student in a summer job at once very far from and very close to the thing he will become. I thought my parents were hopelessly bourgeois, my girlfriend a separate race, my body a thing of wonder and terror, and as I went through the days, my loneliness built. Where? In my heart? It didn't feel like my heart. The loneliness in me was a dryness in the back of my mouth that could not be slaked.

And what about lust, that thing that seemed to have defeated me that spring, undermined my sense of the good boy I'd been, and rinsed the sweetness from my relationship with Linda? Lust felt related to the loneliness, part of the dry, bittersweet taste in the lava-hot air. It went with me like an aura as I strode with my three burns across the paved yard of Ayr Oxygen Company, and I felt it as a certain tension in the tendons in my legs, behind the knees, a tight, wired feeling that I knew to be sexual.

* * *

The loading dock at Ayr Oxygen was a huge rotting concrete slab under an old corrugated-metal roof. Mr. Mac Bonner ran the dock with two Hispanic guys that I got to know pretty well, Victor and Jesse, and they kept the place clean and well organized in a kind of military way. Industrial and medical trucks were always delivering full or empty cylinders or taking them away, and the tanks had to be lodged in neat squadrons which would not be in the way. Victor, who was the older man, taught me how to roll two cylinders at once while I walked, turning my hands on the caps and kick-turning the bottom of the rear one. As soon as I could do that, briskly moving two at a time, I was accepted there and fell into a week of work with them, loading and unloading trucks. They were quiet men who knew the code and didn't have to speak or call instructions when a truck backed in. I followed their lead.

The fascinating thing about Victor and Jesse was their lunches. I had been eating my lunch at a little patio behind the main building, alone, not talking to the five or six other employees who sat in groups at the other metal tables. I was the college kid and they were afraid of me because they knew my dad knew one of the bosses. It seemed there had been some trouble in previous summers, and so I just ate my tuna sandwiches and drank my iced tea while the sweat dried on my forehead and I pulled my wet T-shirt away from my shoulders. After I burned my face, people were friendlier, but then I was transferred up to the dock.

There were dozens of little alcoves amid the gas cylinders standing on the platform, and that is where I ate my lunches now. Victor and Jesse had milk crates and they found one for me and we'd sit out of sight up there from eleven-thirty to noon and eat. There was a certain uneasiness at first, as if they weren't sure if I should be joining them, but then Victor saw it was essentially a necessity. I wasn't going to get my lunch out of the old fridge on the dock and walk across the yard to eat with the supply people. On the dock was where I learned the meaning of *whitebread,* the way it's used now. I'd open my little bag, two tuna sandwiches and a baggie of chips, and then I'd watch the two men open their huge sacks of burritos and tacos and other items I didn't know the names of and which I've never seen since. I mean these were huge lunches that their wives had prepared, everything wrapped in white paper. No baggies. Jesse and I traded a little bit; he liked my mother's tuna. And I loved the big burritos. I was hungry and thirsty all the time and the hefty food seemed to make me well for a while. The burritos were packed with roast beef and onions and a fiery salsa rich with cilantro. During these lunches Victor would talk a little, telling me where to keep my gloves so that the drivers didn't pick them up, and where not to sit even on break.

"There was a kid here last year," he said. "Used to take his breaks right over there." He shook his head. "Right in front of the boss's window." It was cool and private sitting behind the walls of cylinders.

"He didn't stay," Jesse said. "The boss don't know you're on break."

"Come back in here," Victor said. "Or don't sit down." He smiled at me. I looked at Jesse and he shrugged and smiled too. They hadn't told the other kid where not to sit. Jesse handed me a burrito rolled in white paper. I was on the inside now; they'd taken me in.

That afternoon there was a big Linde Oxygen semi backed against the dock and we were rolling the hot cylinders off when I heard a crash. Jesse yelled from back in the dock and I saw his arms flash and Victor, who was in front of me, laid the two tanks he was rolling on the deck of the truck and jumped off the side and ran into the open yard. I saw the first rows of tanks start to tumble wildly, a chain reaction, a murderous thundering domino chase. As the cylinders fell off the dock, they cart-wheeled into the air crazily, heavily tearing clods from the cement dock ledge and thudding into the tarry asphalt. A dozen plummeted onto somebody's Dodge rental car parked too close to the action. It was crushed. The noise was ponderous, painful, and the session continued through a minute until there was only one lone bank of brown nitrogen cylinders standing like a little jury on the back corner of the loading dock. The space looked strange that empty.

The yard was full of people standing back in a crescent. Then I saw Victor step forward and walk toward where I stood on the back of the semi. I still had my hands on the tanks.

He looked what? Scared, disgusted, and a little amused. "Mi amigo," he said, climbing back on the truck. "When they go like that, run away." He pointed back to where all of the employees of Ayr Oxygen Company were watching us. "Away, get it?"

"Yes, sir," I told him. "I do."

"Now you can park those," he said, tapping the cylinders in my hand. "And we'll go pick up all these others."

It took the rest of the day and still stands as the afternoon during which I lifted more weight than any other in this life. It felt a little funny setting the hundreds of cylinders back on the old pitted concrete. "They should repour this," I said to Victor as we were finishing.

"They should," he said. "But if accidents are going to follow you, a new floor won't help." I wondered if he meant that I'd been responsible for the catastrophe. I had rolled and parked a dozen tanks when things blew, but I never considered that it might have been my fault, one cockeyed tank left wobbling.

"I'm through with accidents," I told him. "Don't worry. This is my third. I'm finished."

The next day I was drafted to drive one of the two medical oxygen trucks. One of the drivers had quit and our foreman, Mac Bonner, came out onto the dock in the morning and told me to see Nadine, who ran Medical, in her little office building out front. She was a large woman who had one speed: gruff. I was instructed in a three-minute speech to go get my commercial driver's license that afternoon and then stop by the uniform shop on Bethany Home Road and get two sets of the brown trousers and short-sleeved yellow shirts worn by the delivery people. On my way out I went by and got my lunch and saw Victor. "They want me to drive the truck. Dennis quit, I guess." This was new to me and I was still working it over in my mind; I mean, it seemed like good news.

"Dennis wouldn't last," Victor said. "We'll have the Ford loaded for you by nine."

The yellow shirt had a name oval over the heart pocket: David. And the brown pants had a crease that will outlast us all. It felt funny going to work in those clothes and when I came up to the loading dock after picking up the truck keys and my delivery list, Jesse and Victor came out of the forest of cylinders grinning. Jesse saluted. I was embarrassed and uneasy. "One of you guys take the truck," I said.

"No way, David." Victor stepped up and pulled my collar straight. "You look too good. Besides, this job needs a white guy." I looked helplessly at Jesse.

"Better you than me," he said. They had the truck loaded: two groups of ten medical blue cylinders chain-hitched into the front of the bed. They'd used the special cardboard sleeves we had for medical gas on all the tanks; these kept them from getting too beat up. These tanks were going to be in people's bedrooms. Inside each was the same oxygen as in the dinged-up green cylinders that the welding shops used.

I climbed in the truck and started it up. Victor had already told me about allowing a little more stopping time because of the load. "Here he comes, ladies," Jesse called. I could see his hand raised in the rearview mirror as I pulled onto McDowell and headed for Sun City.

At that time, Sun City was set alone in the desert, a weird theme park for retired white people, and from the beginning it gave me an eerie feeling. The streets were like toy streets, narrow and clean, running in huge circles. No cars, no garage doors open, and, of course, in the heat, no pedestrians. As I made my rounds, wheeling the hot blue tanks up the driveways and through the carpeted houses to the bedroom, uncoupling the old tank, connecting the new one, I felt peculiar. In the houses I was met by the wife or the husband and was escorted along the way. Whoever was sick was in the other room. It was all very proper. These people had come here from the midwest and the east. They had been doctors and professors and lawyers and wanted to live among their own kind. No one under twenty could reside in Sun City. When I'd made my six calls, I fled that town, heading east on old Bell Road, which in those days was miles and miles of desert and orchards, not two traffic lights all the way to Scottsdale Road.

Mr. Rensdale was the first of my customers I ever saw in bed. He lived in one of the many blocks of townhouses they were building in Scottsdale. These were compact units with two stories and a pool in the small private yard. All of Scottsdale shuddered under bulldozers that year; it was dust and construction delays, as the little town began to see the future. I rang the bell and was met by a young woman in a long silk shirt who saw me and said, "Oh, yeah. Come on in. Where's Dennis?"

I had the hot blue cylinder on the single dolly and pulled it up the step and into the dark, cool space. I had my pocket rag and wiped the wheels as soon as she shut the door. I could see her knees and they seemed to glow in the near dark. "I'm taking his route for a while," I said, standing up. I couldn't see her face, but she had a hand on one hip.

"Right," she said. "He got fired."

"I don't know about that," I said. I pointed down the hall. "Is it this way?"

"No, upstairs, first door on your right. He's awake, David." She said my name just the way you read names off shirts. Then she put her hand on my sleeve and said, "Who hit you?" My burn was still raw across my cheekbone.

"I got burned."

"Cute," she said. "They're going to love that back at . . . where?"

"University of Montana," I said.

"University of what?" she said. "There's a university there?" She cocked her head at me. I couldn't tell what she was wearing under that shirt. She smiled. "I'm kidding. I'm a snob, but I'm kidding. What year are you?"

"I'll be a junior," I said.

"I'm a senior at Penn," she said. I nodded, my mind whipping around for something clever. I didn't even know where Penn was.

"Great," I said. I started up the stairs.

"Yeah," she said, turning. "Great."

I drew the dolly up the carpeted stair carefully, my first second story, and entered the bedroom. It was dim in there, but I could see the other cylinder beside the bed and a man in the bed, awake. He was wearing pajamas, and immediately upon seeing me, he said, "Good. Open the blinds, will you?"

"Sure thing," I said, and I went around the bed and turned the miniblind wand. The Arizona day fell into the room. The young woman I'd spoken to walked out to the pool beneath me. She took her shirt off and hung it on one of the chairs. Her breasts were white in the sunlight. She set out her magazine and drink by one of the lounges and lay facedown in a shiny green bikini bottom. I only looked down for a second or less, but I could feel the image in my body.

While I was disconnecting the regulator from the old tank and setting up the new one, Mr. Rensdale introduced himself. He was a thin, handsome man with dark hair and mustache and he looked like about three or four of the actors I was seeing those nights in late movies after my parents went to bed. He wore an aspirator with the two small nostril tubes, which he removed while I changed tanks. I liked him immediately. "Yeah," he went on, "it's good you're going back to college. Though there's a future, believe me, in this stuff." He knocked the oxygen tank with his knuckle.

"What field are you in?" I asked him. He seemed so absolutely worldly there, his wry eyes and his East Coast accent, and he seemed old the way people did then, but I realize now he wasn't fifty.

"I, lad, am the owner of Rensdale Foundations, which my father founded," his whisper was rich with humor, "and which supplies me with more money than my fine daughters will ever be able to spend." He turned his head toward me. "We make ladies' undergarments, lots of them."

The dolly was loaded and I was ready to go. "Do you enjoy it? Has it been a good thing to do?"

"Oh, for chrissakes," he wheezed a kind of laugh, "give me a week on that, will you? I didn't know this was going to be an interview. Come after four and it's worth a martini to you, kid, and we'll do some career counseling."

"You all set?" I said as I moved to the door.

"Set," he whispered now, rearranging his aspirator. "Oh absolutely. Go get them, champ." He gave me a thin smile and I left. Letting myself out of the dark downstairs, I did an odd thing. I stood still in the house. I had talked to her right here. I saw her breasts again in the bright light. No one knew where I was.

Of course, Elizabeth Rensdale, seeing her at the pool that way, so casually naked, made me think of Linda and the fact that I had no idea of what was going on. I couldn't remember her body, though, that summer, I gave it some thought. It was worse not being a virgin, because I should have then had some information to fuel my struggles with loneliness. I had none, except Linda's face and her voice, *"Here, let me get it."*

From the truck I called Nadine, telling her I was finished with Scottsdale and was heading—on schedule—to Mesa. "Did you pick up Mr. Rensdale's walker? Over."

"No, ma'am. Over." We had to say "Over."

"Why not? You were supposed to. Over."

The heat in the early afternoon as I dropped through the river bottom and headed out to Mesa was gigantic, an enormous, unrelenting thing, and I took a kind of perverse pleasure from it. I could feel a heartbeat in my healing burns. My truck was not air-conditioned, a thing that wouldn't fly now, but then I drove with my arm out the window through the traffic of these desert towns. "I'm sorry. I didn't know. Should I go back? Over." I could see going back, surprising the girl. I wanted to see that girl again.

"It was on your sheet. Let it go this week. But let's read the sheet from now on. Over and out."

"Over and out," I said into the air, hanging up the handset.

Half the streets in Mesa were dirt, freshly bladed into the huge grid which now is paved wall to wall. I made several deliveries and ended up at the torn edge of the known world, the road just a track, a year maybe two at most from the first ripples of the growth which would swallow hundreds of miles of the desert. The house was an old block home gone to seed, the lawn dirt, the shrubs dead, the windows brown with dust and cobwebs. From the front yard I had a clear view of the Santan Mountains to the south. I was fairly sure I had a wrong address and that the property was abandoned. I knocked on the greasy door and after five minutes a stooped, red-haired old man answered. This was Gil, and I have no idea how old he was that summer, but it was as old as you get. Plus he was sick with the emphysema and liver disease. His skin, stretched tight and translucent on his gaunt body, was splattered with brown spots. On his hands several had been picked raw.

I didn't want to go into the house. This was the oddest call of my first day driving oxygen. There had been something regular about the rest of it, even the sanitized houses in Sun City, the upscale apartments in Scottsdale so new the paint hadn't dried, and the other houses I'd been to, magazines on a coffee table, a wife paying bills in the kitchen.

I pulled my dolly into the house, dark inside against the crushing daylight, and was hit by the roiling smell of dog hair and urine. I didn't kneel to wipe the wheels. "Right in here," the old man said, leading me back into the house toward a yellow light in the small kitchen, where I could hear a radio chattering. He had his oxygen set up in the corner of the kitchen; it looked like he lived in the one room. There was a fur of fine red dust on everything, the range, the sink, except half the kitchen table where he had his things arranged, some brown vials of prescription medicine, two decks of cards, a pencil or two on a small pad, a warped issue of *Field & Stream,* a little red Bible, and a box of cough drops. In the middle of the table was a fancy painted plate, maybe a seascape, with a line of Oreos on it. I got busy changing out the tanks. You take the cardboard sleeve off, un-hook the regulator, open the valve on the new tank for one second, blasting dust from the mouth, screw the regulator on it, open the pressure so it reads the same as you came, sleeve the old tank, load it up, and go. The new tank was always hot, too hot to touch from being in the sun, and it seemed wrong to leave such a hot thing in someone's bedroom. Nadine handled all the paperwork.

The cookies had scared me and I was trying to get out. Meanwhile the old man sat down at the kitchen table and started talking. "I'm Gil Benson," his speech began, "and I'm glad to see you, David. My lungs got burned in France in 1919 and it took them all these years to buckle." He spoke like so many of my customers in a hoarse whisper. "I've lived all over the world, including the three A's: Africa, Cairo, Australia, Burberry, and Alaska, Point Barrow. My favorite place was Montreal, Canada, because I was in love there and married the woman, had children. She's dead. My least favorite place is right here because of this. One of my closest friends was young Jack Kramer, the tennis player. That was many years ago. I've flown almost every plane made between the years 1938 and 1958. I don't fly anymore with all this." He indicated the oxygen equipment. "Sit down. Have a cookie."

I had my dolly ready. "I shouldn't, sir," I said. "I've got a schedule and better keep it."

"Grab that pitcher out of the fridge before you sit down. I made us some Kool-Aid. It's good."

I opened his refrigerator. Except for the Tupperware pitcher, it was empty. Nothing. I put the pitcher on the table. "I really have to go," I said. "I'll be late."

Gil lifted the container of Kool-Aid and raised it into a jittery hover above the two plastic glasses. There was going to be an accident. His hands were covered with purple scabs. I took the pitcher from him and filled the glasses.

"Sit down," he said. "I'm glad you're here, young fella." When I didn't move he said, "Really. Nadine said you were a good-looking kid." He smiled, and leaning on both hands, he sat hard into the kitchen chair. "This is your last stop today. Have a snack."

So began my visits with old Gil Benson. He was my last delivery every fourth day that summer, and as far as I could tell, I was the only one to visit his wretched house. On one occasion I placed one of the Oreos he gave me on the corner of my chair as I left and it was right there next time when I returned. Our visits became little three-part dramas: my arrival and the bustle of intrusion; the snack and his monologue; his hysteria and weeping.

The first time he reached for my wrist across the table as I was standing to get up, it scared me. Things had been going fine. He'd told me stories in an urgent voice, one story spilling into the other without a seam, because he didn't want me to interrupt. I had *I've got to go* all over my face, but he wouldn't read it. He spoke as if placing each word in the record, as if I were going to write it all down when I got home. It always started with a story of long ago, an airplane, a homemade repair, an emergency landing, a special cargo, an odd coincidence, each part told with pride, but his voice would gradually change, slide into a kind of whine as he began an escalating series of complaints about his doctors, the insurance, his children—naming each of the four and relating their indifference, petty greed, or cruelty. I nodded through all of this: I've got to go. He leaned forward and picked at the back of his hands. When he tired after forty minutes, I'd slide my chair back and he'd grab my wrist. By then I could understand his children pushing him away and moving out of state. I wanted out. But I'd stand—while he still held me—and say, "That's interesting. Save some of these cookies for next time." And then I'd move to the door, hurrying the dolly, but never fast enough to escape. Crying softly and carrying his little walker bottle of oxygen, he'd see me to the door and then out into the numbing heat to the big white pickup. He'd continue his monologue while I chained the old tank in the back and while I climbed in the cab and started the engine and then while I'd start to pull away. I cannot describe how despicable I felt doing that, gradually moving away from old Gil on that dirt lane, and when I hit the corner and turned west for the shop, I tromped it: forty-five, fifty, fifty-five, raising a thick red dust train along what would someday be Chandler Boulevard.

Backing up to the loading dock late on those days with a truck of empties, I was full of animal happiness. The sun was at its worst, blasting the sides of everything, and I moved with the measured deliberation the full day had given me. My shirt was crusted with salt, but I wasn't sweating anymore. When I bent to the metal fountain beside the dock, gulping the water, I could feel it bloom on my back and chest and come out along my hairline. Jesse or Victor would help me sort the cylinders and reload for tomorrow, or many days, everyone would be gone already except Gene, the swing man, who'd talk to me while I finished up. His comments were always about overtime, which I'd be getting if I saw him, and what was I going to do with all my money.

What I was doing was banking it all, except for pocket money and the eight dollars I spent every Sunday calling Linda Enright. I became tight and fit, my burns finally scabbed up so that by mid-July I looked like a young boxer, and I tried not to think about anything.

A terrible thing happened in my phone correspondence with Linda. We stopped fighting. We'd talk about her family; the cookie business was taking off, but her father wouldn't let her take the car. He was stingy. I told her about my deliveries, the heat. She was looking forward to getting the fall bulletin. Was I going to major in geology as I'd planned? As I listened to us talk, I stood and wondered: Who are these people? The other me wanted to interrupt, to ask: Hey, didn't we have sex? I mean, was that sexual intercourse? Isn't the world a little different for you now? But I chatted with her. Neither one of us mentioned other people, that is boys she might have met, and I didn't mention Elizabeth Rensdale. I shifted my feet in the baking phone booth and chatted. When the operator came on, I was crazy with Linda's indifference, but unable to say anything but "Take care, I'll call."

Meanwhile the summer assumed a regularity that was nothing but comfort. I drove my routes: hospitals Mondays, rest homes Tuesdays, residences the rest of the week. Sun City, Scottsdale, Mesa. Nights I'd stay up and watch the old movies, keeping a list of titles and great lines. It was as much of a life of the mind as I wanted. Then it would be six a.m. and I'd have Sun City, Scottsdale, Mesa. I was hard and brown and lost in the routine.

I was used to sitting with Gil Benson and hearing his stories, pocketing the Oreos secretly to throw them from the truck later; I was used to the new-carpet smell of all the little homes in Sun City, everything clean, quiet, and polite; I was used to Elizabeth Rensdale showing me her white breasts, posturing by the pool whenever she knew I was upstairs with her father. By the end of July I had three or four of her little moves memorized, the way she rolled on her back, the way she kneaded them with oil sitting with her long legs on each side of the lounge chair. Driving the valley those long summer days, each window of the truck a furnace, listening to "Paperback Writer" and "Last Train to Clarksville," I delivered oxygen to the paralyzed and dying, and I felt so alive and on edge at every moment that I could have burst. I liked the truck, hopping up unloading the hot cylinders at each address and then driving to the next stop. I knew what I was doing and wanted no more.

Rain broke the summer. The second week in August I woke to the first clouds in ninety days. They massed and thickened and by the time I left Sun City, it had begun, a crashing down-pour. It never rains lightly in the desert. The wipers on the truck were shot with sun rot and I had to stop and charge a set at a Chevron station on the Black Canyon Freeway and then continue east toward Scottsdale, crawling along in the stunned traffic, water everywhere over the highway.

I didn't want to be late at the Rensdales'. I liked the way Elizabeth looked at me when she let me in, and I liked looking at her naked by the pool. It didn't occur to me that today would be any different until I pulled my dolly toward their door through the warm rain. I was wiping down the tank in the covered entry when she opened the door and disappeared back into the dark house. I was wet and coming into the air-conditioned house ran a chill along my sides. The blue light of the television pulsed against the darkness. When my eyes adjusted and I started backing up the stairway with the new cylinder, I saw Elizabeth sitting on the couch in the den, her knees together up under her chin, watching me. She was looking right at me. I'd never seen her like this, and she'd never looked at me before.

"This is the worst summer of my entire life," she said.

"Sorry," I said, coming down a step. "What'd you say?"

"David! Is that you?" Mr. Rensdale called from his room. His voice was a ghost. I liked him very much and it had become clear over the summer that he was not going back to Pennsylvania. He'd lost weight. His face had become even more angular and his eyes had sunken. "David."

Elizabeth Rensdale whispered across the room to me, "I don't want to be here." She closed her eyes and rocked her head. I stood the cylinder on the dolly and went over to her. I didn't like leaving it there on the carpet. It wasn't what I wanted to do. She was sitting in her underpants on the couch. "He's dying," she said to me.

"Oh," I said, trying to make it simply a place holder, let her know that I'd heard her. It was the wrong thing, but anything, even silence, would have been wrong. She put her face in her hands and lay over on the couch. I dropped to a knee and, putting my hand on her shoulder, I said, "What can I do?"

This was the secret side that I suspected from this summer. Elizabeth Rensdale put her hand on mine and turned her face to mine so slowly that I felt my heart drop a gear, grinding now heavily uphill in my chest. The rain was like a pressure on the roof.

Mr. Rensdale called my name again. Elizabeth's face on mine so close and open made it possible for me to move my hand around her back and pull her to me. It was like

I knew what I was doing. I didn't take my eyes from hers when she rolled onto her back and guided me onto her. It was different in every way from what I had imagined. The dark room closed around us. Her mouth came to mine and stayed there. This wasn't education; this was need. And later, when I felt her hand on my bare ass, her heels rolling in the back of my knees, I knew it was the mirror of my cradling her in both my arms as we rocked along the edge of the couch, moving it finally halfway across the den as I pushed into her. I wish I could get this right here, but there is no chance. We stayed together for a moment afterward and my eyes opened and focused. She was still looking at me, holding me, and her look was simply serious. Her father called, "David?" from upstairs again, and I realized he must have been calling steadily. Still, we were slow to move. I stood without embarrassment and dressed, tucking my shirt in. That we were intent, that we were still rapt, made me confident in a way I'd never been. I grabbed the dolly and ascended the stairs.

Mr. Rensdale lay white and twisted in the bed. He looked the way the dying look, his face parched and sunken, the mouth a dry orifice, his eyes little spots of water. I saw him acknowledge me with a withering look, more power than you'd think could rise from such a body. I felt it a cruel scolding, and I moved in the room deliberate with shame, avoiding his eyes. The rain drummed against the window in waves. After I had changed out the tanks, I turned to him and said, "There you go."

He rolled his hand in a little flip toward the bedtable and his glass of water. His chalky mouth was in the shape of an O, and I could hear him breathing, a thin rasp. Who knows what happened in me then, because I stood in the little bedroom with Mr. Rensdale and then I just rolled the dolly and the expired tank out and down the stairs. I didn't go to him; I didn't hand him the glass of water. I burned; who would ever know what I had done?

When I opened the door downstairs on the world of rain, Elizabeth came out of the dark again, naked, to stand a foot or two away. I took her not speaking as just part of the intensity I felt and the way she stood with her arms easy at her sides was the way I felt when I'd been naked before her. We looked at each other for a moment; the rain was already at my head and the dolly and tank was between us in the narrow entry, and then something happened that sealed the way I feel about myself even today. She came up and we met beside the tank and there was no question about the way we went for each other what was going on. I pushed by the oxygen equipment and followed her onto the entry tile, then a moment later turning in adjustment so that she could climb me, get her bare back off the floor.

So the last month of that summer I began seeing Elizabeth Rensdale every day. My weekly visits to the Rensdale townhouse continued, but then I started driving out to Scottsdale nights. I told my parents I was at the library, because I wanted it to sound like a lie and have them know it was a lie. I came in after midnight; the library closed at nine. After work I'd shower and put on a clean shirt, something without my name on it, and I'd call back from the door, "Going to the library." And I knew they knew I was up to something. It was like I wanted them to challenge me, to have it out.

Elizabeth and I were hardy and focused lovers. I relished the way every night she'd meet my knock at the door and pull me into the room and then, having touched, we didn't stop. Knowing we had two hours, we used every minute of it and we became experts at each other. For me these nights were the first nights in my new life, I mean,

I could tell then that there was no going back, that I had changed my life forever and I could not stop it. We never went out for a Coke, we never took a break for a glass of water, we rarely spoke. There was admiration and curiosity in my touch and affection and gratitude in hers or so I assumed, and I was pleased, even proud, at the time that there was so little need to speak. There was one time when I arrived a little early when Mr. Rensdale's nurse was still there and Elizabeth and I sat in the den watching television two feet apart on the couch, and even then we didn't speak. I forget what program was on, but Elizabeth asked me if it was okay, and I said fine and that was all we said while we waited for the nurse to leave.

On the way home with my arm out in the hot night, I drove like the young king of the desert. Looking into my car at a traffic light, other drivers could read it all on my face and the way I held my head cocked back. I was young those nights, but I was getting over it.

Meanwhile Gil Benson had begun clinging to me worse than ever and those prolonged visits were full of agony and desperation. As the Arizona monsoon season continued toward Labor Day, the rains played hell with his old red road, and many times I pulled up in the same tracks I'd left the week before. He stopped putting cookies out, which at first I took as a good sign, but then I realized that he now considered me so familiar that cookies weren't necessary. A kind of terror had inhabited him, and it was fed by the weather. Now most days I had to go west to cross the flooded Salt River at the old Mill Avenue Bridge to get to Mesa late and by the time I arrived, Gil would be on the porch, frantic. Not because of oxygen deprivation; he only needed to use the stuff nights. But I was his oxygen now, his only visitor, his only companion. I'd never had such a thing happen before and until it did I'd thought of myself as a compassionate person. I watched myself arrive at his terrible house and wheel the tank toward the door and I searched myself for compassion, the smallest shred of fellow feeling, kindness, affection, pity, but all I found was repulsion, impatience. I thought, surely I would be kind, but that was a joke, and I saw that compassion was a joke too along with fidelity and chastity and all the other notions I'd run over this summer. Words, I thought, big words. Give me the truck keys and a job to do, and the words can look out for themselves. I had no compassion for Gil Benson and that diminished over the summer. His scabby hands, the dried spittle in the ruined corners of his mouth, his crummy weeping in his stinking house. He always grabbed my wrist with both hands, and I shuffled back toward the truck. His voice, already a whisper, broke and he cried, his face a twisted ugliness which he wiped at with one hand while holding me with the other. I tried to nod and say, "You bet," and "That's too bad. I'll see you next week." But he wouldn't hear me any more than I was listening to him. His voice was so nakedly plaintive it embarrassed me. I wanted to push him down in the mud and weeds of his yard and drive away, but I never did that. What I finally did was worse.

The summer already felt nothing but old as Labor Day approached, the shadows in the afternoon gathering reach although the temperature was always 105. I could see it when I backed into the dock late every day, the banks of cylinders stark in the slanted sunlight, Victor and Jesse emerging from a world which was only black and white, sun and long shadow. The change gave me a feeling that I can only describe as anxiety. Birds flew overhead, three and four at a time, headed somewhere. There were huge banks of clouds in the sky every afternoon and after such a long season of blanched white heat, the shadows beside things seemed ominous. The cars and buildings and the massive tin roof of the loading dock were just things, but their shadows seemed like meanings. Summer, whatever it had meant, was ending. The fact that I would be going back to Montana and college in three weeks became tangible. It all felt complicated.

I sensed this all through a growing curtain of fatigue. The long hot days and the sharp extended nights with Elizabeth began to shave my energy. At first it took all the extra that I had being nineteen, and then I started to cut into the principal. I couldn't feel it mornings, which passed in a flurry, but afternoons, my back solid sweat against the seat of my truck, I felt it as a weight, my body going leaden as I drove the streets of Phoenix. Unloading became an absolute drag. I stopped jumping off the truck and started climbing down, stopped skipping up onto the dock, started walking, and every few minutes would put my hands on my waist and lean against something, the tailgate, the dock, a pillar.

"Oy, amigo," Jesse said one day late in August as I rested against the shipping desk in back of the dock. "Qué pasa?"

"Nothing but good things," I said. "How're you doing?"

He came closer and looked at my face, concerned. "You sick?"

"No, I'm great. Long day."

Victor appeared with the cargo sheet and handed me the clipboard to sign. He and Jesse exchanged glances. I looked up at them. Victor put his hand on my chin and let it drop. "Too much tail." He was speaking to Jesse. "He got the truck and forgot what I told him. Remember?" He turned to me. "Remember? Watch what you're doing." Victor took the clipboard back and tapped it against his leg. "When the tanks start to fall, run the *other* way."

A moment later as I was getting ready to move the truck, Jesse came out with his white lunch bag and gave me his leftover burrito. It was heavy as a book and I ate it like a lesson.

But it was a hot heedless summer and I showered every night like some animal born of it, heedless and hot, and I pulled a cotton T-shirt over my ribs, combed my wet hair back, and without a word to my parents, who were wary of me now it seemed, drove to Scottsdale and buried myself in Elizabeth Rensdale.

* * *

The Sunday before Labor Day, I didn't call Linda Enright. This had been my custom all these many weeks and now I was breaking it. I rousted around the house, finally raking the yard, sweeping the garage, and washing all three of the cars, before rolling onto the couch in the den and watching some of the sad, throwaway television of a summer Sunday. In each minute of the day, Linda Enright, sitting in her father's home office, which she'd described to me on the telephone many times (we always talked about where we were; I told her about my phone booth, the heat, graffiti, and passing traffic), was in my mind. I saw her there in her green sweater by her father's rolltop. We always talked about what we were wearing and she always said the green sweater, saying it innocently as if wearing the sweater that I'd helped pull over her head that night in her dorm room was of little note, a coincidence, and not the most important thing that she'd say in the whole eight-dollar call, and I'd say just Levi's and a T-shirt, hoping she'd imagine the belt, the buckle, the trouble it could all be in the dark. I saw her sitting still in the afternoon shadow, maybe writing some notes in her calendar or reading, and right over there, the telephone. I lay there in my stocking feet knowing I could get up and hit the phone booth in less than ten minutes and make that phone ring, have her reach for it, but I didn't. I stared at the television screen as if this was some kind of work and I had to do it. It was the most vivid that Linda had appeared before me the entire summer. Green sweater in the study through the endless day. I let her sit there until the last sunlight rocked through the den, broke, and disappeared. I hated the television, the couch, my body which would not move. I finally got up sometime after nine and went to bed.

Elizabeth Rensdale and I kept at it. Over the Labor Day weekend, I stayed with her overnight and we worked and reworked ourselves long past satiation. She was ravenous and my appetite for her was relentless. That was how I felt it all: relentless. Moments after coming hard into her, I would begin to palm her bare hip as if dreaming and then still dreaming begin to mouth her ear and her hand would play over my genitals lightly and then move in dreamily sorting me around in the dark and we would shift to begin again. I woke from a brief nap sometime after four in the morning with Elizabeth across me, a leg between mine, her face in my neck, and I felt a heaviness in my arm as I slid it down her tight back that reminded me of what Victor had said. I was tired in a way I'd never known. My blood stilled and I could feel a pressure running in my head like sand, and still my hand descended in the dark. There was no stopping. Soon I felt her hand, as I had every night for a month, and we labored toward dawn.

In the morning, Sunday, I didn't go home, but drove way down by Ayr Oxygen Company to the Roadrunner, the truck stop there on McDowell adjacent to the freeway. It was the first day I'd ever been sore and I walked carefully to the coffee shop. I sat alone at the counter, eating eggs and bacon and toast and coffee, feeling the night tick away in every sinew the way a car cools after a long drive. It was an effort to breathe and at times I had to stop and gulp some air, adjusting myself on the counter stool. Around me it was only truck drivers who had driven all night from Los Angeles, Sacramento, Albuquerque, Salt Lake City. There was only one woman in the place, a large woman in a white waitress dress who moved up and down the counter pouring coffee. When she poured mine, I looked up at her and our eyes locked, I mean her head tipped and her face registered something I'd never seen before. If I used such words I'd call it *horror,* but I don't. My old heart bucked. I thought of my Professor Whisner and Western Civ; if it was what I was personally doing, then it was in tough shape. The gravity of the moment between the waitress and myself was such that I was certain to my toenails I'd been seen: she knew all about me.

* * *

That week I gave Nadine my notice, reminding her that I would be leaving in ten days, mid-September, to go back to school. "Well, sonnyboy, I hope we didn't work your wheels off." She leaned back, letting me know there was more to say.

"No, ma'am. It's been a good summer."

"We think so too," she said. "Come by and I'll have your last check cut early, so we don't have to mail it."

"Thanks, Nadine." I moved to the door; I had a full day of deliveries.

"Old Gil Benson is going to miss you, I think."

"I've met a lot of nice people," I said. I wanted to deflect this and get going.

"No," she said, "you've been good to him; it's important. Some of these old guys don't have much to look forward to. He's called several times. I might as well tell you. Mr. Ayr heard about it and is writing you a little bonus."

I stepped back toward her. "What?"

"Congratulations." She smiled. "Drive carefully."

I walked slowly out to the truck. I cinched the chain hitches in the back of my Ford, securing the cylinders, climbed wearily down to the asphalt, which was already baking at half past eight, and pulled myself into the driver's seat. In the rearview mirror I could see Victor and Jesse standing in the shadows. I was tired.

Some of my customers knew I was leaving and made kind remarks or shook my hand or had their wife hand me an envelope with a twenty in it. I smiled and nodded gratefully and then turned businesslike to the dolly and left. These were strange good-byes, because there was no question that we would ever see each other again. It had been a summer and I had been their oxygen guy. But there was more: I was young and they were ill. I stood in the bedroom doors in Sun City and said, "Take care," and I moved to the truck and felt something, but I couldn't even today tell you what it was. The people who didn't know, who said, "See you next week, David," I didn't correct them. I said, "See you," and I left their homes too. It all had me on edge.

The last day of my job in the summer of 1967, I drove to work under a cloud cover as thick as twilight in winter and still massing. It began to rain early and I made the quick decision to beat the Salt River flooding by hitting Mesa first and Scottsdale in the afternoon. I had known for a week that I did not want Gil Benson to be my last call for the summer, and this rain, steady but light, gave me the excuse I wanted. Of course, it was nuts to think I could get out to Mesa before the crossings were flooded. And by now, mid-September, all the drivers were wise to the monsoon and headed for the Tempe Bridge as soon as they saw overcast. The traffic was colossal, and I crept in a huge column of cars east across the river, noting it was twice as bad coming back, everyone trying to get to Phoenix for the day. My heart was only heavy, not fearful or nervous, as I edged forward. What I am saying is that I had time to think about it all, this summer, myself, and it was a powerful stew. The radio wouldn't finish a song, "Young Girl," by Gary Puckett and the Union Gap or "Cherish," by the Association without interrupting with a traffic bulletin about crossing the river.

I imagined it raining in the hills of Boulder, Colorado, Linda Enright selling cookies in her apron in a shop with curtains, a Victorian tearoom, ten years ahead of itself as it turned out, her sturdy face with no expression telling she wasn't a virgin anymore, and that now she had been for thirty days betrayed. I thought, and this is the truth, I thought for the first time of what I was going to say *last* to Elizabeth Rensdale. I tried to imagine it, and my imagination failed. I tried again, I mean, I really tried to picture us there in the entry of the Scottsdale townhouse speaking to each other, which we had never, ever done. When I climbed from her bed the nights I'd gone to her, it was just that, climbing out, dressing, and crossing to the door. She didn't get up. This wasn't *Casablanca* or *High Noon,* or *Captain Blood,* which I had seen this summer, this was getting laid in a hot summer desert town by your father's oxygen deliveryman. There was no way to make it anything else, and it was too late as I moved through Tempe toward Mesa and Gil Benson's outpost to make it anything else. We were not going to hold each other's faces in our hands and whisper; we were not going to stand speechless in the shadows. I was going to try to get her pants off one more time and let her see me. That was it. I shifted in my truck seat and drove.

Even driving slowly, I fishtailed through the red clay along Gil's road. The rain had moved in for the day, persistent and even, and the temperature stalled and hovered at about a hundred. I thought Gil would be pleased to see me so soon in the day, because he was always glad to see me, welcomed me, but I surprised him this last Friday knocking at the door for five full minutes before he unlocked the door, looking scared. Though I had told him I would eventually be going back to college, I hadn't told him this was my last day. I didn't want any this or that, just the little visit and the drive away. I wanted to get to Scottsdale.

Shaken up like he was, things went differently. There was no chatter right off the bat, no sitting down at the table. He just moved things out of the way as I wheeled the oxygen in and changed tanks. He stood to one side, leaning against the counter. When I finished, he made no move to keep me there, so I just kept going. I wondered for a moment if he knew who I was or if he was just waking up. At the front door, I said, "There you go, good luck, Gil." His name quickened him and he came after me with short steps in his slippers.

"Well, yes," he started as always, "I wouldn't need this stuff at all if I'd stayed out of the war." And he was off and cranking. But when I went outside, he followed me into the rain. "Of course, I was strong as a horse and came back and got right with it. I mean, there wasn't any sue-the-government then. We were happy to be home. I was happy." He went on, the rain pelting us both. His slippers were all muddy.

"You gotta go," I told him. "It's wet out here." His wet skin in the flat light looked raw, the spots on his forehead brown and liquid; under his eyes the skin was purple. I'd let him get too close to the truck and he'd grabbed the door handle.

"I wasn't sick a day in my life," he said. "Not as a kid, not in the army. Ask my wife. When this came on," he patted his chest, "it came on bang! Just like that and here I am. Somewhere." His eyes, which had been looking everywhere past me, found mine and took hold. "This place!" He pointed at his ruined house. "This place!" I put my hand on his on the door handle and I knew that I wasn't going to be able to pry it off without breaking it.

Then there was a hitch in the rain, a gust of wet wind, and hail began to rattle through the yard, bouncing up from the mud, bouncing off the truck and our heads. "Let me take you back inside," I said. "Quick, Gil, let's get out of this weather." The hail stepped up a notch, a million mothballs ringing every surface. Gil Benson pulled the truck door open, and with surprising dexterity, he stepped up into the vehicle, sitting on all my paperwork. He wasn't going to budge and I hated pleading with him. I wouldn't do it. Now the hail had tripled, quadrupled, in a crashfest off the hood. I looked at Gil, shrunken and purple in the darkness of the cab; he looked like the victim of a fire.

"Well, at least we're dry in here, right?" I said. "We'll give it a minute." And that's what it took, about sixty seconds for the hail to abate, and after a couple of heavy curtains of the rain ripped across the hood as if they'd been thrown from somewhere, the world went silent and we could hear only the patter of the last faint drops. "Gil," I said. "I'm late. Let's go in." I looked at him but he did not look at me. "I've got to go." He sat still, his eyes timid, frightened, smug. It was an expression you use when you want someone to hit you.

I started the truck, hoping that would scare him, but he did not move. His eyes were still floating and it looked like he was grinning, but it wasn't a grin. I crammed the truck into gear and began to fishtail along the road. I didn't care for that second if we went off the road; the wheels roared mud. At the corner, we slid in the wet clay across the street and stopped.

I kicked my door open and jumped down into the red mud and went around the front of the truck. When I opened his door, he did not turn or look at me, which was fine with me. I lifted Gil like a bride and he clutched me, his wet face against my face. I carried him to the weedy corner lot. He was light and bony like an old bird and I was strong and I felt strong, but I could tell this was an insult the old man didn't need. When I stood him there he would not let go, his hands clasped around my neck, and I peeled his hands apart carefully, easily, and I folded them back toward him so he wouldn't snag me again. "Goodbye, Gil," I said. He was an old wet man alone in the desert. He did not acknowledge me.

I ran to the truck and eased ahead for traction and when I had traction, I floored it, throwing mud behind me like a rocket.

By the time I lined up for the Tempe Bridge, the sky was torn with blue vents. The Salt River was nothing but muscle, a brown torrent four feet over the river-bottom roadway. The traffic was thick. I merged and merged again and finally funneled onto the bridge and across toward Scottsdale. A ten-mile rainbow had emerged over the McDowell Mountains.

I radioed Nadine that the rain had slowed me up and I wouldn't make it back before five.

"No problem, sonnyboy," she said. "I'll leave your checks on my desk. Have you been to Scottsdale yet? Over."

"Just now," I said. "I'll hit the Rensdales' and on in. Over."

"Sonnyboy," she said. "Just pick up there. Mr. Rensdale died yesterday. Remember the portable unit, okay? And good luck at school. Stop in if you're down for Christmas break. Over."

I waited a minute to over and out to Nadine while the news subsided in me. I was on Scottsdale Road at Camelback, where I turned right. That corner will always be that radio call. "Copy. Over," I said.

I just drove. Now the sky was ripped apart the way I've learned only a western sky can be, the glacial cloud cover broken and the shreds gathering against the Superstition Mountains, the blue air a color you don't see twice a summer in the desert, icy and clear, no dust or smoke. All the construction crews in Scottsdale had given it up and the bright lumber on the sites sat dripping in the afternoon sun. They had taken the day off from changing this place.

In front of the Rensdales' townhouse I felt odd going to the door with the empty dolly. I rang the bell, and after a moment Elizabeth appeared. She was barefoot in jeans and a T-shirt, and she just looked at me. "I'm sorry about your father," I said. "This is tough." She stared at me and I held the gaze. "I mean it. I'm sorry."

She drifted back into the house. It felt for the first time strange and cumbersome to be in the dark little townhouse. She had the air conditioning cranked way up so that I could feel the edge of a chill on my arms and neck as I pulled the dolly up the stairs to Mr. Rensdale's room. It had been taken apart a little bit, the bed stripped, our gear all standing in the corner. With Mr. Rensdale gone you could see what the room was, just a little box in the desert. Looking out the window over the pool and the two dozen tiled roofs before the edge of the Indian reservation and the sage and creosote bushes, it seemed clearly someplace to come and die. The mountains, now all rinsed by rain, were red and purple, a pretty lie.

"I'm going back Friday." Elizabeth had come into the room. "I guess I'll go back to school."

"Good," I said. "Good idea." I didn't know what I was saying. The space in my heart about returning to school was nothing but dread.

"They're going to bury him tomorrow." She sat on the bed. "Out here somewhere."

I started to say something about that, but she pointed at me. "Don't come. Just do what you do, but don't come to the funeral. You don't have to."

"I want to," I said. Her tone had hurt, made me mad.

"My mother and sister will be here tonight," she said.

"I want to," I said. I walked to the bed and put my hands on her shoulders.

"Don't."

I bent and looked into her face.

"Don't."

I went to pull her toward me to kiss her and she leaned away sharply. "Don't, David." But I followed her over onto the bed, and though she squirmed, tight as a knot, I held her beside me, adjusting her, drawing her back against me. We'd struggled in every manner, but not this. Her arms were tight cords and it took more strength than I'd ever used to pin them both against her chest while I opened my mouth on her neck and ran my other hand flat inside the front of her pants. I reached deep and she drew a sharp breath and stretched her legs out along mine, bumping at my ankles with her heels. Then she gave way and I knew I could let go of her arms. We lay still that way, nothing moving but my finger. She rocked her head back.

About a minute later she said, "What are you doing?"

"It's okay," I said.

Then she put her hand on my wrist, stopping it. "Don't," she said. "What are you doing?"

"Elizabeth," I said, kissing at her nape. "This is what we do. Don't you like it?"

She rose to an elbow and looked at me, her face rock-hard, unfamiliar. "This is what we do?" Our eyes were locked. "Is this what you came for?" She lay back and thumbed off her pants until she was naked from the waist down. "Is it?"

"Yes," I said. It was the truth and there was pleasure in saying it.

"Then go ahead. Here." She moved to the edge of the bed, a clear display. The moment had fused and I held her look and I felt seen. I felt known. I stood and undid my belt and went at her, the whole time neither of us changing expression, eyes open, though I studied her as I moved looking for a signal of the old ways, the pleasure, a lowered eyelid, the opening mouth, but none came. Her mouth was open but as a challenge to me, and her fists gripped the mattress but simply so she didn't give ground. She didn't move when I pulled away, just lay there looking at me. I remember it as the moment in this life when I was farthest from any of my feelings. I gathered the empty cylinder and the portable gear with the strangest thought: *It's going to take me twenty years to figure out who I am now.*

I could feel Elizabeth Rensdale's hatred, as I would feel it dozens of times a season for many years. It's a kind of dread for me that has become a rudder and kept me out of other troubles. That next year at school, I used it to treat Linda Enright correctly, as a gentleman, and keep my distance, though I came to know I was in love with her and had been all along. I had the chance to win her back and I did not take it. We worked together several times with the Democratic Student Alliance, and it is public record that our organization brought Robert Kennedy to the Houck Center on campus that March. Professor Whisner introduced him that night, and at the reception I shook Robert Kennedy's hand. It felt, for one beat, like Western Civilization.

* * *

That bad day at the Rensdales' I descended the stair, carefully, not looking back, and I let myself out of the townhouse for the last time. The mud on the truck had dried in brown fans along the sides and rear. The late afternoon in Scottsdale had been scrubbed and hung out to dry, the air glassy and quick, the color of everything distinct, and the brown folds of the McDowell Mountains magnified and looming. It was fresh, the temperature had dropped twenty degrees, and the elongated shadows of the short new imported palms along the street printed themselves eerily in the wet lawns. Today those trees are as tall as those weird shadows. I just wanted to close this whole show down.

But as I drove through Scottsdale, block by block, west toward Camelback Mountain, I was torn by a nagging thought of Gil Benson. I shouldn't have left him out there. At a dead end by the Indian School canal I stopped and turned off the truck. The grapefruit grove there was being bladed under. Summer was over; I was supposed to be happy.

Back at Ayr Oxygen, I told Gene, the swing man, to forget it and I unloaded the truck myself. It was the one good hour of that day, one hour of straight work, lifting and rolling my empties into the ranks at the far end of the old structure. Victor and Jesse would find them tomorrow. They would be the last gas cylinders I would ever handle. I locked the truck and walked to the office in my worn-out workshoes. I found two envelopes on Nadine's desk: my check and the bonus check. It was two hundred and fifty dollars. I put them in my pocket and left my keys, pulling the door locked behind me.

I left for my junior year of college at Missoula three days later. The evening before my flight, my parents took me to dinner at a steakhouse on a mesa, a western place where they cut your tie off if you wear one. The barn-plank walls were covered with the clipped ends of ties. It was a good dinner, hearty, the baked potatoes big as melons and the charred edges of the steaks dropping off the plates. My parents were giddy, ebullient, because their business plans which had so consumed them were looking good. Every loan they'd positioned was ready; the world was right. They were proud of me, they said, working hard like this all summer away from my friends. I was changing, they said, and they could tell it was for the better.

After dinner we went back to the house and had a drink on the back terrace, which was a new thing in our lives. I didn't drink very much and I had never had a drink with my parents. My father made a toast to my success at school and then my mother made a toast to my success at school and to my success with Linda Enright, and she smiled at me, a little friendly joke, and she clinked her scotch and water against my bottle of Bud and tossed it back. "I'm serious," she said. Then she stood and threw her glass out back and we heard it shatter against the stucco wall. A moment later she hugged me and she and my father went in to bed.

I cupped my car keys and went outside. I drove the dark streets. The radio played a steady rotation of exactly the same songs heard today on every fifty-thousand-watt station in this country; every fifth song was the Supremes. I knew where I was going. Beyond the bright rough edge of the lights of Mesa I drove until the pavement ended, and then I dropped onto the red clay roads and found Gil Benson's house. It was as dark as some final place, and there was no disturbance in the dust on the front walk or in the network of spiderwebs inside the broken storm door. I knocked and called for minutes. Out back, I kicked through the debris and weeds until I found one of the back bedroom windows unlocked and I slid it open and climbed inside. In the stale heat, I knew immediately that the house was abandoned. I called Gil's name and picked my way carefully to the hall. The lights did not work, and in the kitchen when I opened the fridge, the light was out and the humid stench hit me and I closed the door. I wasn't scared, but I was something else. Standing in that dark room where I had palmed old Oreos all summer long, I now had proof, hard proof, that I had lost Gil Benson. He hadn't made it back and I couldn't wish him back.

Outside, the cooked air filled my lungs and the bright dish of Phoenix glittered to the west. I drove toward it carefully. Nothing had cooled down. In every direction the desert was being torn up, and I let the raw night rip through the open car window. At home my suitcases were packed. Some big thing was closing down in me; I'd spent the summer as someone else, someone I knew I didn't care for and I would be glad when he left town. We would see each other from time to time, but I also knew he was no friend of mine. I eased along the empty roadways trying simply to gather what was left, to think, but it was like trying to fold a big blanket alone. I kept having to start over.

# ANDREA BARRETT
(1965– )

Andrea Barrett was born in Boston, Massachusetts, and grew up largely on Cape Cod. She left high school in her junior year and enrolled at Union College in Schenectady, New York, from which she graduated, at 19, with a degree in biology. She did graduate work in zoology at the University of Massachusetts in Amherst, but did not complete a degree. Later she returned to Amherst to do graduate work in medieval and Reformation theological history. Barrett lives in Rochester, New York, with her husband, the biologist Barry Goldstein. She teaches part-time in a low-residency MFA program at Warren Wilson College in Rochester.

Barrett was National Endowment for the Arts Fellow in 1992 and won a Guggenheim Award. Before publishing her National Book Award–winning collection of stories, *Ship Fever* (1995), Barrett published four novels: *Lucid Stars*

(1988), *Secret Harmonies* (1989), *The Middle Kingdom* (1991), and *The Forms of Water* (1993). All of her work reflects thorough research and often blends historical and fictional characters. The stories in *Ship Fever* explore the confluence of history, science, family, and memory, and Barrett likens the stories to a sort of laboratory notebook. She is one of the few contemporary writers whose work makes a knowledgeable and provocative use of science and of characters who are scientists, in the sense that they are seekers and explorers. Her latest novel, *The Voyage of the Narwhal* (1998), shows these interests very well.

# The Littoral Zone

WHEN THEY met, fifteen years ago, Jonathan had a job teaching botany at a small college near Albany, and Ruby was teaching invertebrate zoology at a college in the Berkshires. Both of them, along with an ornithologist, an ichthyologist, and an oceanographer, had agreed to spend three weeks of their summer break at a marine biology research station on an island off the New Hampshire coast. They had spouses, children, mortgages, bills; they went, they later told each other, because the pay was too good to refuse. Two-thirds of the way through the course, they agreed that the pay was not enough.

How they reached that first agreement is a story they've repeated to each other again and again and told, separately, to their closest friends. Ruby thinks they had this conversation on the second Friday of the course, after Frank Kenary's slide show on the abyssal fish and before Carol Dagliesh's lecture on the courting behavior of herring gulls. Jonathan maintains that they had it earlier—that Wednesday, maybe, when they were still recovering from Gunnar Erickson's trawling expedition. The days before they became so aware of each other have blurred in their minds, but they agree that their first real conversation took place on the afternoon devoted to the littoral zone.

The tide was all the way out. The students were clumped on the rocky, pitted apron between the water and the ledges, peering into the tidal pools and listing the species they found. Gunnar was in the equipment room, repairing one of the sampling claws. Frank was setting up dissections in the tiny lab; Carol had gone back to the mainland on the supply boat, hoping to replace the camera one of the students had dropped. And so the two of them, Jonathan and Ruby, were left alone for a little while.

They both remember the granite ledge where they sat, and the raucous quarrels of the nesting gulls. They agree that Ruby was scratching furiously at her calves and that Jonathan said, "Take it easy, okay? You'll draw blood."

Her calves were slim and tan, Jonathan remembers. Covered with blotches and scrapes.

I folded my fingers, Ruby remembers. Then I blushed. My throat felt sunburned.

Ruby said, "I know, it's so embarrassing. But all this salt on my poison ivy—God, what I wouldn't give for a bath! They never told me there wouldn't be any *water* here. . . ."

Jonathan gestured at the ocean surrounding them and then they started laughing. *Hysteria,* they have told each other since. They were so tired by then, twelve days into the course, and so dirty and overworked and strained by pretending to the students that these things didn't matter, that neither of them could understand that they were also lonely. Their shared laughter felt like pure relief.

"No water?" Jonathan said. "I haven't been dry since we got here. My clothes are damp, my sneakers are damp, my hair never dries. . . ."

His hair was beautiful, Ruby remembers. Thick, a little too long. Part blond and part brown.

"I know," she said. "But you know what I mean. I didn't realize they'd have to bring our drinking water over on a boat."

"Or that they'd expect us to wash in the ocean," Jonathan said. Her forearms were dusted with salt, he remembers. The down along them sparkled in the sun.

"And those cots," Ruby said. "Does yours have a sag in it like a hammock?"

"Like a slingshot," Jonathan said.

For half an hour they sat on their ledge and compared their bubbling patches of poison ivy and the barnacle wounds that scored their hands and feet. Nothing healed out here, they told each other. Everything got infected. When one of the students called, "Look what I found!" Jonathan rose and held his hand out to Ruby. She took it easily and hauled herself up and they walked down to the water together. Jonathan's hand was thick and blunt-fingered, with nails bitten down so far that the skin around them was raw. Odd, Ruby remembers thinking. Those bitten stumps attached to such a good-looking man.

* * *

They have always agreed that the worst moment, for each of them, was when they stepped from the boat to the dock on the final day of the course and saw their families waiting in the parking lot. Jonathan's wife had their four-year-old daughter balanced on her shoulders. Their two older children were leaning perilously over the guardrails and shrieking at the sight of him. Jessie had turned nine in Jonathan's absence, and Jonathan can't think of her eager face without remembering the starfish he brought as his sole, guilty gift.

Ruby's husband had parked their car just a few yards from Jonathan's family. Her sons were wearing baseball caps, and what Ruby remembers is the way the yellow linings lit their faces. For a minute she saw the children squealing near her sons as faceless, inconsequential; Jonathan later told her that her children had been similarly blurred for him. Then Jonathan said, "That's my family, there," and Ruby said, "That's mine, right next to yours," and all the faces leapt into focus for both of them.

Nothing that was to come—not the days in court, nor the days they moved, nor the losses of jobs and homes—would ever seem so awful to them as that moment when they first saw their families standing there, unaware and hopeful. Deceitfully, treacherously, Ruby and Jonathan separated and walked to the people awaiting them. They didn't introduce each other to their spouses. They didn't look at each other—although, they later admitted, they cast covert looks at each other's families. They thought they were invisible, that no one could see what had happened between them. They thought their families would not remember how they had stepped off the boat and stood, for an instant, together.

On that boat, sitting dumb and miserable in the litter of nets and equipment, they had each pretended to be resigned to going home. Each foresaw (or so they later told each other) the hysterical phone calls and the frenzied, secret meetings. Neither foresaw how much the sight of each other's family would hurt. "Sweetie," Jonathan remembers Ruby's husband saying. "You've lost so much weight." Ruby remembers staring over her husband's shoulder and watching Jessie butt her head like a dog under Jonathan's hand.

* * *

For the first twelve days on the island, Jonathan and Ruby were so busy that they hardly noticed each other. For the next few days, after their conversation on the ledge, they sat near each other during faculty lectures and student presentations. These were held in the library, a ramshackle building separated from the bunkhouse and the dining hall by a stretch of wild roses and poison ivy.

Jonathan had talked about algae in there, holding up samples of *Fucus* and *Hildenbrandtia.* Ruby had talked about the littoral zone, that space between high and low watermarks where organisms struggled to adapt to the daily rhythm of immersion and exposure. They had drawn on the blackboard in colored chalk while the students, itchy and hot and tired, scratched their arms and legs and feigned attention.

Neither of them, they admitted much later, had focused fully on the other's lecture. "It was *before,*" Ruby has said ruefully. "I didn't know that I was going to want to have listened." And Jonathan has laughed and confessed that he was studying the shells and skulls on the walls while Ruby was drawing on the board.

The library was exceedingly hot, they agreed, and the chairs remarkably uncomfortable; the only good spot was the sofa in front of the fireplace. That was the spot they commandeered on the evening after their first conversation, when dinner led to a walk and then the walk led them into the library a few minutes before the scheduled lecture.

Erika Moorhead, Ruby remembers. Talking about the tensile strength of byssus threads.

Walter Schank, Jonathan remembers. Something to do with hydrozoans.

They both remember feeling comfortable for the first time since their arrival. And for the next few days—three by Ruby's accounting; four by Jonathan's—one of them came early for every lecture and saved a seat on the sofa for the other.

They giggled at Frank Kenary's slides, which he'd arranged like a creepy fashion show: abyssal fish sporting varied blobs of luminescent flesh. When Gunnar talked for two hours about subduction zones and the calcium carbonate cycle, they amused themselves exchanging doodles. They can't remember, now, whether Gunnar's endless lecture came before Carol Dagliesh's filmstrip on the herring gulls, or which of the students tipped over the dissecting scope and sent the dish of copepods to their deaths. But both of them remember those days and nights as being almost purely happy. They swam in that odd, indefinite zone where they were more than friends, not yet lovers, still able to deny to themselves that they were headed where they were headed.

* * *

Ruby made the first phone call, a week after they left the island. At eleven o'clock on a Sunday night, she told her husband she'd left something in her office that she needed to prepare the next day's class. She drove to campus, unlocked her door, picked up the phone and called Jonathan at his house. One of his children—Jessie, she thinks—

answered the phone. Ruby remembers how, even through the turmoil of her emotions, she'd been shocked at the idea of a child staying up so late.

There was a horrible moment while Jessie went to find her father; another when Jonathan, hearing Ruby's voice, said, "Wait, hang on, I'll just be a minute," and then negotiated Jessie into bed. Ruby waited, dreading his anger, knowing she'd been wrong to call him at home. But Jonathan, when he finally returned, said, "Ruby. You got my letter."

"What letter?" she asked. He wrote to tell me good-bye, she remembers thinking.

"My *letter,*" he said. "I wrote you, I have to see you. I can't stand this."

Ruby released the breath she hadn't known she was holding.

"You didn't get it?" he said. "You just called?" It wasn't only me, he remembers thinking. She feels it too.

"I had to hear your voice," she said.

Ruby called, but Jonathan wrote. And so when Jonathan's youngest daughter, Cora, later fell in love and confided in Ruby, and then asked her, "Was it like this with you two? Who started it—you or Dad?" all Ruby could say was, "It happened to both of us."

* * *

Sometimes, when Ruby and Jonathan sit on the patio looking out at the hills above Palmyra, they will turn and see their children watching them through the kitchen window. Before the children went off to college, the house bulged with them on weekends and holidays and seemed empty in between; Jonathan's wife had custody of Jessie and Gordon and Cora, and Ruby's husband took her sons, Mickey and Ryan, when he remarried. Now that the children are old enough to come and go as they please, the house is silent almost all the time.

Jessie is twenty-four, and Gordon is twenty-two; Mickey is twenty-one, and Cora and Ryan are both nineteen. When they visit Jonathan and Ruby they spend an unhealthy amount of time talking about their past. In their conversations they seem to split their lives into three epochs: the years when what they think of as their real families were whole; the years right after Jonathan and Ruby met, when their parents were coming and going, fighting and making up, separating and divorcing; and the years since Jonathan and Ruby's marriage, when they were forced into a reconstituted family. Which epoch they decide to explore depends on who's visiting and who's getting along with whom.

"But we were happy," Mickey may say to Ruby, if he and Ryan are visiting and Jonathan's children are absent. "We were, we were fine."

"It wasn't like you and Mom ever fought," Cora may say to Jonathan, if Ruby's sons aren't around. "You could have worked it out if you'd tried."

When they are all together, they tend to avoid the first two epochs and to talk about their first strained weekends and holidays together. They've learned to tolerate each other, despite their forced introductions; Cora and Ryan, whose birthdays are less than three months apart, seem especially close. Ruby and Jonathan know that much of what draws their youngest children together is shared speculation about what happened on that island.

They look old to their children, they know. Both of them are nearing fifty. Jonathan has grown quite heavy and has lost much of his hair; Ruby's fine-boned figure has gone gaunt and stringy. They know their children can't imagine them young and strong and wrung by passion. The children can't think—can't stand to think—about what happened on the island, but they can't stop themselves from asking questions.

"Did you have other girlfriends?" Cora asks Jonathan. "Were you so unhappy with Mom?"

"Did you know him before?" Ryan asks Ruby. "Did you go there to be with him?"

"We met there," Jonathan and Ruby say. "We had never seen each other before. We fell in love." That is all they will say, they never give details, they say "yes" or "no" to the easy questions and evade the hard ones. They worry that even the little they offer may be too much.

* * *

Jonathan and Ruby tell each other the stories of their talk by the tidal pool, their walks and meals, the sagging sofa, the moment in the parking lot, and the evening Ruby made her call. They tell these to console themselves when their children chide them or when, alone in the house, they sit quietly near each other and struggle to conceal their disappointments.

Of course they have expected some of these. Mickey and Gordon have both had trouble in school, and Jessie has grown much too close to her mother; neither Jonathan nor Ruby has found jobs as good as the ones they lost, and their new home in Palmyra still doesn't feel quite like home. But all they have lost in order to be together would seem bearable had they continued to feel the way they felt on the island.

They're sensible people, and very well-mannered; they remind themselves that they were young then and are middle-aged now, and that their fierce attraction would naturally ebb with time. Neither likes to think about how much of the thrill of their early days together came from the obstacles they had to overcome. Some days, when Ruby pulls into the driveway still thinking about her last class and catches sight of Jonathan out in the garden, she can't believe the heavyset figure pruning shrubs so meticulously is the man for whom she fought such battles. Jonathan, who often wakes very early, sometimes stares at Ruby's sleeping face and thinks how much more gracefully his ex-wife is aging.

They never reproach each other. When the tension builds in the house and the silence becomes overwhelming, one or the other will say, "Do you remember . . . ?" and then launch into one of the myths on which they have founded their lives. But there is one story they never tell each other, because they can't bear to talk about what they have lost. This is the one about the evening that has shaped their life together.

Jonathan's hand on Ruby's back, Ruby's hand on Jonathan's thigh, a shirt unbuttoned, a belt undone. They never mention this moment, or the moments that followed it, because that would mean discussing who seduced whom, and any resolution of that would mean assigning blame. Guilt they can handle; they've been living with guilt for fifteen years. But blame? It would be more than either of them could bear, to know the exact moment when one of them precipitated all that has happened to them. The most either of them has ever said is, "How could we have known?"

But the night in the library is what they both think about, when they lie silently next to each other and listen to the wind. It must be summer for them to think about it; the children must be with their other parents and the rain must be falling on the cedar shingles overhead. A candle must be burning on the mantel above the bed and the maple branches outside their window must be tossing against each other. Then they think of the story they know so well and never say out loud.

There was a huge storm three nights before they left the island, the tail end of a hurricane passing farther out to sea. The cedar trees creaked and swayed in the wind beyond the library windows. The students had staggered off to bed, after the visitor from Woods Hole had finished his lecture on the explorations of the *Alvin* in the Cayman Trough, and Frank and Gunnar and Carol had shrouded themselves in their rain gear and left as well, sheltering the visitor between them. Ruby sat at one end of the long table, preparing bottles of fixative for their expedition the following morning, and Jonathan lay on the sofa writing notes. The boat was leaving just after dawn and they knew they ought to go to bed.

The wind picked up outside, sweeping the branches against the walls. The windows rattled. Jonathan shivered and said, "Do you suppose we could get a fire going in that old fireplace?"

"I bet we could," said Ruby, which gave both of them the pretext they needed to crouch side by side on the cracked tiles, brushing elbows as they opened the flue and crumpled paper and laid kindling in the form of a grid. The logs Jonathan found near the lobster traps were dry and the fire caught quickly.

Who found the green candle in the drawer below the microscope? Who lit the candle and turned off the lights? And who found the remains of the jug of wine that Frank had brought in honor of the visitor? They sat there side by side, poking at the burning logs and pretending they weren't doing what they were doing. The wind pushed through the window they'd opened a crack, and the tan window shade lifted and then fell back against the frame. The noise was soothing at first; later it seemed irritating.

Jonathan, whose fingernails were bitten to the quick, admired the long nail on Ruby's right little finger and then said, half-seriously, how much he'd love to bite a nail like that. When Ruby held her hand to his mouth he took the nail between his teeth and nibbled through the white tip, which days in the water had softened. Ruby slipped her other hand inside his shirt and ran it up his back. Jonathan ran his mouth up her arm and down her neck.

They started in front of the fire and worked their way across the floor, breaking a glass, knocking the table askew. Ruby rubbed her back raw against the rug and Jonathan scraped his knees, and twice they paused and laughed at their wild excesses. They moved across the floor from east to west and later from west to east, and between those two journeys, during the time when they heaped their clothes and the sofa cushions into a nest in front of the fire, they talked.

This was not the kind of conversation they'd had during walks and meals since that first time on the rocks: who they were, where they'd come from, how they'd made it here. This was the talk where they instinctively edited out the daily pleasures of their lives on the mainland and spliced together the hard times, the dark times, until they'd constructed versions of themselves that could make sense of what they'd just done.

For months after this, as they lay in stolen, secret rooms between houses and divorces and jobs and lives, Jonathan would tell Ruby that he swallowed her nail. The nail dissolved in his stomach, he'd say. It passed into his villi and out to his blood and then flowed to bone and muscle and nerve, where the molecules that had once been part of her became part of him. Ruby, who always seemed to know more acutely than Jonathan that they'd have to leave whatever room this was in an hour or a day, would argue with him.

"Nails are keratin," she'd tell him. "Like hooves and hair. Like wool. We can't digest wool."

"Moths can," Jonathan would tell her. "Moths eat sweaters."

"Moths have a special enzyme in their saliva," Ruby would say. This was true, she knew it for a fact. She'd been so taken by Jonathan's tale that she'd gone to the library to check out the details and discovered he was wrong.

But Jonathan didn't care what the biochemists said. He held her against his chest and said, "I have an enzyme for you."

That night, after the fire burned out, they slept for a couple of hours. Ruby woke first and watched Jonathan sleep for a while. He slept like a child, with his knees bent toward his chest and his hands clasped between his thighs. Ruby picked up the tipped-over chair and swept the fragments of broken glass onto a sheet of paper. Then she woke Jonathan and they tiptoed back to the rooms where they were supposed to be.

# MARY GAITSKILL

## (1954– )

The world Mary Gaitskill's fiction portrays is one of violation, of bad behavior, where true human intimacy is elusive though often sought. Her characters are both victims and perpetrators of violations and, out of some inner confusion or depravity, are unable to discern the signals of modern life, especially in interpersonal relationships. It is a world absent of authority and explanation—America at the end of the twentieth century.

Gaitskill was born in Lexington, Kentucky, the daughter of a teacher and a social worker. She describes her adolescence as troubled. She ran away from home at age 16, became a stripper, and spent time in mental hospitals. This experience, she says, has limited relevance to her work: "My experience of life as essentially unhappy and uncontrollable taught me to examine the way people, including myself, create survival systems and psychologically safe places for themselves in unorthodox and sometimes apparently self-defeating ways. These inner worlds, although often unworkable and unattractive in social terms, can have a unique beauty and courage." In 1981 Gaitskill completed a B.A. at the University of Michigan, where she won an award for an unpublished collection of stories called *The Woman Who Knew Judo, and Other Stories.* Her first collection of stories, *Bad Behavior,* was published in 1988, followed in 1991 by her novel *Two Girls, Fat and Thin.* Her second collection of stories, *Because They Wanted To,* appeared in 1997.

# The Girl on the Plane

John Morton came down the aisle of the plane, banging his luggage into people's knees and sweating angrily under his suit. He had just run through the corridors of the airport, cursing and struggling with his luggage, slipping and flailing in front of the vapid brat at the seat assignment desk. Too winded to speak, he thrust his ticket at the boy and readjusted his luggage in his sticky hands. "You're a little late for a seat assignment," said the kid snottily. "I hope you can get on board before it pulls away."

He took his boarding pass and said, "Thanks, you little prick." The boy's discomfiture was made more obvious by his pretense of hauteur; it both soothed and fed John's anger.

At least he was able to stuff his bags into the compartment above the first seat he found. He sat down, grunting territorially, and his body slowly eased into a normal dull pulse and ebb. He looked at his watch; desk attendant to the contrary, the plane was sitting stupidly still, twenty minutes after takeoff time. He had the pleasing fantasy of punching the little bastard's face.

He was always just barely making his flight. His wife had read in one of her magazines that habitual lateness meant lack of interest in life or depression or something. Well, who could blame him for lack of interest in the crap he was dealing with?

He glanced at the guy a seat away from him on the left, an alcoholic-looking old shark in an expensive suit, who sat staring fixedly at a magazine photograph of a grinning blonde in a white jumpsuit. The plane continued to sit there, while stewardesses fiddled with compartments and women rolled up and down the aisles on trips to the bathroom. They were even boarding a passenger; a woman had just entered, flushed and vigorously banging along the aisle with her luggage. She was very pretty, and he watched her, his body still feebly sending off alarm signals in response to its forced run.

"Hi," she said. "I'm in the middle there."

"By all means." The force of his anger entered his magnanimity and swelled it hugely; he pinched his ankles together to let her by. She put her bag under the seat in front of her, sat down, and rested her booted feet on its pale leather. The old shark by the window glanced appraisingly at her breasts through her open coat. He looked up at her face and made smile movements. The stewardess did her parody of a suffocating person reaching for an air mask, the pilot mumbled, the plane prepared to assert its unnatural presence in nature.

"They said I'd missed my flight by fifteen minutes," she said. "But I knew I'd make it. They're never on time." Her voice was unexpectedly small, with a rough, gravelly undertone that was seedy and schoolgirlish at once.

"It's bullshit," he said. "Well, what can you do?" She had large hazel eyes.

She smiled a tight, rueful smile that he associated with women who'd been fucked too many times and which he found sexy. She cuddled more deeply into her seat, produced a *People* magazine, and intently read it. He liked her profile—which was an interesting combination of soft (forehead, chin) and sharp (nose, cheekbones)—her shoulder-length, pale-brown hair, and her soft Mediterranean skin. He liked the coarse quality in the subtle downturn of her lips, and the heavy way her lids sat on her eyes. She was older than he'd originally thought, probably in her early thirties.

Who did she remind him of? A girl from a long time ago, an older version of some date or crush or screw. Or love, he thought gamely.

The pilot said they would be leaving the ground shortly. She was now reading a feature that appeared to be about the wedding of two people who had AIDS. He thought of his wife, at home in Minneapolis, at the stove poking at something, in the living room reading, the fuzzy pink of her favorite sweater. The plane charged and tore a hole in the air.

He reviewed his mental file of girls he'd known before his wife and paused at the memory of Andrea, the girl who'd made an asshole of him. It had been twelve years, and only now could he say that phrase to himself, the only phrase that accurately described the situation. With stale resentment, he regarded her: a pale, long-legged thing with huge gray eyes, a small mouth, long red hair, and the helpless manner of a pampered pet let loose in the wilderness.

The woman next to him was hurriedly flipping the pages of *People,* presumably looking for something as engrossing as the AIDS wedding. When she didn't find it, she closed the magazine and turned to him in a way that invited conversation.

She said she'd lived in L.A. for eight years and that she liked it, even though it was "gross."

"I've never been to L.A.," he said. "I picture it being like *L.A. Law.* Is it like that?"

"I don't know. I've never seen *L.A. Law.* I don't watch TV. I don't own one."

He had never known a person who didn't own a TV, not even an old high school friend who lived in a slum and got food stamps. "You must read the newspapers a lot."

"No. I don't read them much at all."

He was incredulous. "How do you connect with the rest of the world? How do you know anything?"

"I'm part of the world. I know a lot of things."

He expelled a snort of laughter. "That's an awfully small perspective you've got there."

She shrugged and turned her head, and he was sorry he'd been rude. He glanced at her profile to read her expression and—of course; she reminded him of Patty LaForge, poor Patty.

* * *

He had met Patty at Meadow Community College in Coate, Minnesota. He was in his last semester; she had just entered. They worked in the student union cafeteria, preparing, serving, and snacking on denatured food. She was a slim, curvy person with dark-blond hair, hazel eyes, and remarkable legs and hips. Her beauty was spoiled by the aggressive resignation that held her features in a fixed position and made all her expressions stiff. Her full mouth had a bitter downturn, and her voice was quick, low, self-deprecating, and sarcastic. She presented her beautiful body statically, as if it were a shield, and the effort of this presentation seemed to be the source of her animation.

Most of the people he knew at Meadow were kids he'd gone to high school and even junior high with. They still lived at home and still drove their cars around together at night, drank in the small bars of Coate, adventured in Minneapolis, and made love to each other. This late-adolescent camaraderie gave their time at Meadow a fraught emotional quality that was like the shimmering fullness of a bead of water before it falls. They were all about to scatter and become different from one another, and this made them exult in their closeness and alikeness.

* * *

The woman on the plane was flying to Kentucky to visit her parents and stopping over in Cincinnati.

"Did you grow up in Kentucky?" he asked. He imagined her as a big-eyed child in a cotton shift, playing in some dusty, sunny alley, some rural Kentucky-like place. Funny she had grown up to be this wan little bun with too much makeup in black creases under her eyes.

"No. I was born there, but I grew up mostly in Minnesota, near Minneapolis."

He turned away, registered the little shock of coincidence, and turned back. The situation compounded: she had gone to Redford Community College in Thorold, a suburb much like Coate. She had grown up in Thorold, like Patty. The only reason Patty had gone to Meadow was that Redford didn't exist yet.

He felt a surge of commonality. He imagined that she had experienced his adolescence, and this made him experience it for a moment. He had loved walking the small, neat walkways of the campus through the stiffly banked hedges of snow and harsh morning austerity, entering the close, food-smelling student union with the hard winter air popping off his skin. He would see his friends standing in a conspiratorial huddle, warming their hands on cheap cups of coffee; he always remembered the face of a particular girl, Layla, turning to greet him, looking over her frail sloped shoulder, her hair a bunched dark tangle, her round eyes ringed with green pencil, her perfectly ordinary face compelling in its configurations of girlish curiosity, maternal license, sexual knowledge, forgiveness, and femininity. A familiar mystery he had meant to explore sometime and never did, except when he grabbed her butt at a Halloween party and she smiled like a mother of four who worked as a porn model on the side. He loved driving with his friends to the Red Owl to buy alcohol and bagged salty snacks, which they consumed as they drove around Coate playing the tape deck and yelling at each other, the beautiful ordinary landscape unpeeling before them, revealing the essential strangeness of its shadows and night movements. He loved driving with girls to the deserted housing development they called "the Spot," loved the blurred memories of the girls in the back seat with their naked legs curled up to their chests, their shirts bunched about their necks, their eyes wide with ardor and alcohol, beer and potato chips spilled on the floor of the car, the tape deck singing of love and triumph. He getting out of the car for a triumphant piss, while the girl daintily replaced her pants. In the morning his mother would make him "cowboy eggs," eggs fried on top of bacon, and he would go through the cold to Meadow, to sit in a fluorescent classroom and dream.

* * *

"Did you like growing up in that area?" she asked.

"Like it? It was the greatest time of my life." Some extremity in his voice made her look away, and as she did, he looked more fully at her profile. She didn't look that much like Patty; she wasn't even blond. But the small physical resemblance was augmented by a less tangible affinity, a telling similarity of speech and movement.

* * *

Patty belonged to a different crowd at Meadow. They were rougher than the Coate people, but the two groups were friendly. Patty was a strange, still presence within her group, with her hip thrust out and a cigarette always bleeding smoke from her hand. She was loose even by seventies standards; she had a dirty sense of humor, and she wore pants so tight you could see the swollen outline of her genitals. She was also shy. When she talked she pawed the ground with her foot and pulled her hair over her mouth; she looked away from you and then snuck a look back to see what you thought of her. She was accepted by the Thorold people the way you accept what you've always known. The stiffness of her face and body contradicting her loose reputation, her coarse language expressed in her timid voice and shy manners, her beauty and her ordinariness, all gave her a disconnected sexiness that was aggravating.

But he liked her. They were often a team at work, and he enjoyed having her next to him, her golden-haired arms plunged in greasy black dishwater or flecked with garbage as she plucked silverware from vile plates on their way to the dishwasher. She spooned out quivering red Jell-O or drew long bland snakes of soft ice cream from the stainless-steel machine, she smoked, wiped her nose, and muttered about a fight with her mother or a bad date. Her movements were resigned and bitter, yet her eyes and her nasty humor peeked impishly from under this weight. There was something pleasing in this combination, something congruent with her spoiled beauty.

It was a long time before he realized she had a crush on him. All her conversation was braided together with a fly strip of different boys she had been with or was involved with, and she talked of all of them with the same tone of fondness and resentment. He thought nothing of it when she followed him outside to the field behind the union, where they would walk along the narrow wet ditch, smoking pot and talking. It was early spring; dark, naked trees pressed intensely against the horizon, wet weeds clung to their jeans, and her small voice bobbed assertively on the vibrant air. The cold wind gave her lips a swollen raw look and made her young skin grainy and bleached. "So why do you let him treat you like that?" "Ah, I get back at him. It's not really him, you know, I'm just fixated on him. I'm working out something through him. Besides, he's a great lay." He never noticed how often she came up behind him to walk him to class or sat on the edge of his chair as he lounged in the union. Then one day she missed work, and a buddy of his said, "Hey, where's your little puppy dog today?" and he knew.

* * *

"Did you like Thorold?" he asked the girl next to him.

"No, I didn't." She turned toward him, her face a staccato burst of candor. "I didn't know what I was doing, and I was a practicing alcoholic. I kept trying to fit in and I couldn't."

"That doesn't sound good." He smiled. How like Patty to answer a polite question from a stranger with this emotional nakedness, this urgent excess of information. She was always doing that, especially after the job at the cafeteria ended. He'd see her in a hallway or the union lounge, where normal life was happening all around them, and she'd swoop into a compressed communication, intently twining her hair around her finger as she quickly muttered that she'd had the strangest dream about this guy David, in which a nuclear war was going on, and he, John, was in it too, and—

* * *

"What did you do after Redford?" he asked the girl next to him.

"Screwed around, basically. I went to New York pretty soon after that and did the same things I was doing in Thorold. Except I was trying to be a singer."

"Yeah?" He felt buoyed by her ambition. He pictured her in a tight black dress, lips parted, eyes closed, bathed in cheap, sexy stage light. "Didja ever do anything with it?"

"Not much." She abruptly changed expression, as though she'd just remembered not to put herself down. "Well, some stuff. I had a good band once, we played the club circuit in L.A. for a while six years ago." She paused. "But I'm mostly a paralegal now."

"Well, that's not bad, either. Do you ever sing now?"

"I haven't for a long time. But I was thinking of trying again." Just like Patty, she looked away and quickly looked back as if to check his reaction. "I've been auditioning. Even though . . . I don't know."

"It sounds great to me," he said. "At least you're trying. It sounds better than what I do." His self-deprecation annoyed him, and he bulled his way through an explanation of what he did, making it sound more interesting than selling software.

A stewardess with a small pink face asked if they'd like anything to drink, and he ordered two little bottles of Jack Daniel's. Patty's shadow had a compressed can of orange juice and an unsavory packet of nuts; their silent companion by the window had vodka straight. He thought of asking her if she was married, but he bet the answer was no, and he didn't want to make her admit her loneliness. Of course, not every single person was lonely, but he guessed that she was. She seemed in need of comfort and care, like a stray animal that gets fed by various kindly people but never held.

"Will you get some mothering while you're at home?" he asked.

"Oh, yes. My mother will make things I like to eat and . . . stuff like that."

He thought of telling her that she reminded him of someone he'd known in Coate, but he didn't. He sat silently, knocking back his whiskey and watching her roll a greasy peanut between two fingers.

* * *

Out in the field, they were sitting on a fallen branch, sharing a wet stub of pot. "I don't usually say stuff like this," said Patty. "I know you think I do, because of the way I talk, but I don't. But I'm really attracted to you, John." The wind blew a piece of hair across her cheek, and its texture contrasted acutely with her cold-bleached skin.

"Yeah, I was beginning to notice."

"I guess it was kind of obvious, huh?" She looked down and drew her curtain of hair. "And I've been getting these mixed signals from you. I can't tell if you're attracted to me or not." She paused. "But I guess you're not, huh?"

Her humility embarrassed and touched him. "Well, I am attracted to you. Sort of. I mean, you're beautiful and everything. I'm just not attracted enough to do anything. Besides, there's Susan."

"Oh. I thought you didn't like her that much." She sniffed and dropped the roach on the raw grass; her lipstick had congealed into little chapped bumps on her lower lip. "Well, I'm really disappointed. I thought you liked me."

"I do like you, Patty."

"You know what I meant." Pause. "I'm more attracted to you than I've been to anybody for two years. Since Paul."

A flattered giggle escaped him.

"Well, I hope we can be friends," she said. "We can still talk and stuff, can't we?"

* * *

"Patty LaForge? I wouldn't touch her, man. The smell alone."

He was driving around with a carload of drunk boys who were filled with a tangle of goodwill and aggression.

"Ah, LaForge is okay."

He was indignant for Patty, but he laughed anyway.

* * *

"Were you really an alcoholic when you lived in Thorold?" he asked.

"I still am, I just don't drink now. But then I did. Yeah."

He had stepped into a conversation that had looked nice and solid, and his foot had gone through the floor and into the basement. But he couldn't stop. "I guess I drank too much then too. But it wasn't a problem. We just had a lot of fun."

She smiled with tight, terse mystery.

"How come you told me that about yourself? It seems kind of personal." He attached his gaze to hers as he said this; sometimes women said personal things to you as a way of coming on.

But instead of becoming soft and encouraging, her expression turned proper and institutional, like a kid about to recite. "If I'm going to admit it to other alcoholics in the program, I can admit it in regular life too. It humbles you, sort of."

What a bunch of shit, he thought.

* * *

He was drinking with some guys at the Winners Circle, a rough pickup bar, when suddenly Patty walked up to him, really drunk.

"John," she gasped."John, John, John." She lurched at him and attached her nail-bitten little claws to his jacket. "John, this guy over there really wants to fuck me, and I was going to go with him, but I don't want him, I want you, I want you." Her voice wrinkled into a squeak, her face looked like you could smear it with your hand.

"Patty," he mumbled, "you're drunk."

"That's not why. I always feel like this." Her nose and eyelashes and lips touched his cheek in an alcoholic caress. "Just let me kiss you. Just hold me."

He put his hands on her shoulders. "C'mon, stop it."

"It doesn't have to mean anything. You don't have to love me. I love you enough for both of us."

He felt the presence of his smirking friends. "Patty, these guys are laughing at you. I'll see you later." He tried to push her away.

"I don't care. I love you, John. I mean it." She pressed her taut body against his, one sweaty hand under his shirt, and arched her neck until he could see the small veins and bones. "Please. Just be with me. Please." Her hand stroked him, groped between his legs. He took her shoulders and shoved her harder than he had meant to. She staggered back, fell against a table, knocked down a chair, and almost fell again. She straightened and looked at him as if she'd known him and hated him all her life.

* * *

He leaned back in his seat and closed his eyes, an overweight, prematurely balding salesman getting drunk on an airplane.

"Look at the clouds," said the girl next to him. "Aren't they beautiful?"

He opened his eyes and silently looked.

Shrewdness glimmered under her gaze.

"What's your name?" he asked.

"Lorraine."

"I'm John." He extended his hand and she took it, her eyes unreadable, her hand exuding sweet feminine sweat.

"Why do you want to talk about your alcoholism publicly? I mean, if nobody asks or anything?"

Her eyes were steadfast, but her body was hesitant. "Well, I didn't have to just now. It's just the first thing I thought of when you asked me about Thorold. In general, it's to remind me. It's easy to bullshit yourself that you don't have a problem."

He thought of the rows and rows of people in swivel chairs on talk-show stages, admitting their problems. Wife beaters, child abusers, dominatrixes, porn stars. In the past it probably was a humbling experience to stand up and tell people you were an alcoholic. Now it was just something else to talk about. He remembered Patty tottering through a crowded party on smudged red high heels, bragging about what great blow jobs she gave. Some girl rolled her eyes and said, "Oh, no, not again." Patty disappeared into a bedroom with a bottle of vodka and Jack Spannos.

He remembered a conversation with his wife before he married her, a conversation about his bachelor party. "It was no women allowed," he'd told her. "Unless they wanted to give blow jobs."

"Couldn't they just jump naked out of a cake?" she asked.

"Nope. Blow jobs for everybody."

They were at a festive restaurant, drinking margaritas. Nervously, she touched her tiny straws. "Wouldn't that be embarrassing? In front of each other? I can't imagine Henry doing that in front of you all."

He smiled at the mention of his shy friend in this context. "Yeah," he said. "It probably would be embarrassing. Group sex is for teenagers."

Her face rose away from her glass in a kind of excited alarm, her lips parted. "You had group sex when you were a teenager?"

"Oh. Not really. Just a gang bang once."

She looked like an antelope testing the wind with its nose in the air, ready to fly. "It wasn't rape," she said.

"Oh, no, no." Her body relaxed and released a warm, sensual curiosity, like a cat against his leg. "The girl liked it."

"Are you sure?"

"Yeah. She liked having sex with a lot of guys. We all knew her, she knew us."

He felt her shiver inwardly, shocked and fascinated by this dangerous pack-animal aspect of his masculinity.

"What was it like?" she asked.

He shrugged. "It was a good time with the guys. It was a bunch of guys standing around in their socks and underwear."

* * *

Some kid he didn't know walked up and put his arm around him while he was talking to a girl named Chrissie. The kid's eyes were boyish and drunkenly enthusiastic, his face heavy and porous. He whispered something about Patty in John's ear and said, "C'mon."

The girl's expression subtly withdrew.

"What?" said John.

"Come on," said the kid.

"Bye-bye," said Chrissie, with a gingerly wag of her fingers.

He followed the guy through the room, seizing glimpses of hips and tits sheathed in bright, cheap cloth, girls doing wiggly dances with guys who jogged helplessly from foot to foot, holding their chests proudly aloof from their lower bodies. On the TV, a pretty girl gyrated in her black bra, sending a clean bolt of sex into the room. The music made his organs want to leap in and out of his body in time. His friends were all around him.

A door opened and closed behind him, muffling the music. The kid who'd brought him in sat in an armchair, smiling. Patty lay on a bed with her skirt pulled up to her waist and a guy with his pants down straddling her face. Without knowing why, he laughed. Patty twisted her legs about and bucked slightly. For a moment he felt frightened that this was against her will—but no, she would have screamed. He recognized the boy on her as Pete Kopiekin, who was thrusting his flat, hairy butt in the same dogged, earnest, woeful manner with which he played football. His heart was pounding.

Kopiekin got off her and the other guy got on; between them he saw her chin sticking up from her sprawled body, pivoting to and fro on her neck while she muttered and groped blindly up and down her body. Kopiekin opened the door to leave, and a fist of music punched the room. John's body jumped in shocked response, and the door shut. The guy on top of Patty was talking to her; to John's amazement, he seemed to be using love words. "You're so beautiful, baby." He saw Patty's hips moving. She wasn't being raped, he thought. When the guy finished, he stood and poured the rest of his beer in her face.

"Hey," said John lamely, "hey."

"Oh, man, don't tell me that. I've known her a long time."

When the guy left, he thought of wiping her face, but he didn't. She sighed fitfully and rolled on her side, as if there was something under the mattress, disturbing her sleep, but she was too tired to remove it. His thoughts spiraled inward, and he let them be chopped up by muffled guitar chords. He sat awhile, watching guys swarm over Patty and talking to the ones waiting. Music sliced in and out of the room. Then some guy wanted to pour maple syrup on her, and John said, "No, I didn't go yet." He sat on the bed and, for the first time, looked at her, expecting to see the sheepish bitter look he knew. He didn't recognize her. Her rigid face was weirdly slack; her eyes fluttered open, rolled, and closed; a mix of half-formed expressions flew across her face like swarming ghosts. "Patty," he said, "hey." He shook her shoulder. Her eyes opened, her gaze raked his face. He saw tenderness, he thought. He lay on her and tried to embrace her. Her body was leaden and floppy. She muttered and moved, but in ways he didn't understand. He massaged her breasts; they felt like they could come off and she wouldn't notice.

He lay there, supporting himself on his elbows, and felt the deep breath in her lower body meeting his own breath. Subtly, he felt her come to life. She lifted her head and said something; he heard his name. He kissed her on the lips. Her tongue touched his, gently, her sleeping hands woke. He held her and stroked her pale, beautiful face.

He got up in such a good mood that he slapped the guy coming in with the maple syrup a high five, something he thought was stupid and usually never did.

The next time he saw Patty was at a Foreigner concert in Minneapolis; he saw her holding hands with Pete Kopiekin.

Well, now she could probably be on a talk show about date rape. It was a confusing thing. She may have wanted to kiss him or to give Jack Spannos a blow job, but she probably didn't want maple syrup poured on her. Really, though, if you were going to get blind drunk and let everybody fuck you, you had to expect some nasty stuff. On the talk shows they always said it was low self-esteem that made them do it. If he had low self-esteem, he sure wouldn't try to cure it like that. His eyes rested on Lorraine's hands; she was wadding the empty nut package and stuffing it in her empty plastic cup.

"Hey," he said, "what did you mean when you said you kept trying to fit in and you couldn't? When you were in Thorold?"

"Oh, you know." She seemed impatient. "Acting the part of the pretty, sexy girl."

"When in fact you were not a pretty, sexy girl?"

She started to smile, then caught his expression and gestured dismissively. "It was complicated."

It was seductive, the way she drew him in and then shut him out. She picked up her magazine again. Her slight arm movement released a tiny cloud of sweat and deodorant, which evaporated as soon as he inhaled it. He breathed in deeply, hoping to smell her again. Sunlight pressed in with viral intensity and exaggerated the lovely contours of her face, the fine lines, the stray cosmetic flecks, the marvelous profusion of her pores. He thought of the stories he'd read in sex magazines about strangers on airplanes having sex in the bathroom or masturbating each other under blankets.

The stewardess made a sweep with a gaping white garbage bag and cleared their trays of bottles and cups.

She put down the magazine. "You've probably had the same experience yourself," she said. Her face was curiously determined, as if it were very important that she make herself understood. "I mean doing stuff for other people's expectations or just to feel you have a social identity because you're so convinced who you are isn't right."

"You mean low self-esteem?"

"Well, yeah, but more than that." He sensed her inner tension and felt an empathic twitch.

"It's just that you get so many projections onto yourself of who and what you're supposed to be that if you don't have a strong support system it's hard to process it."

"Yeah," he said. "I know what you mean. I've had that experience. I don't know how you can't have it when you're young. There's so much crap in the world." He felt embarrassed, but he kept talking, wanting to tell her something about himself, to return her candor. "I've done lots of things I wish I hadn't done, I've made mistakes. But you can't let it rule your life."

She smiled again, with her mouth only. "Once, a few years ago, my father asked me what I believed to be the worst mistakes in my life. This is how he thinks, this is his favorite kind of question. Anyway, it was really hard to say, because I don't know from this vantage point what would've happened if I'd done otherwise in most situations. Finally, I came up with two things: my relationship with this guy named Jerry and the time I turned down an offer to work with this really awful band that became famous. He was totally bewildered. He was expecting me to say 'dropping out of college.'"

"You didn't make a mistake dropping out of college." The vehemence in his voice almost made him blush; then nameless urgency swelled forth and quelled embarrassment. "That wasn't a mistake," he repeated.

"Well, yeah, I know."

"Excuse me." The silent business shark to their left rose in majestic self-containment and moved awkwardly past their knees, looking at John with pointed irony as he did so. Fuck you, thought John.

"And about that relationship," he went on. "That wasn't your loss. It was his." He had meant these words to sound light and playfully gallant, but they had the awful intensity of a maudlin personal confession. He reached out to gently pat her hand, to reassure her that he wasn't a nut, but instead he grabbed it and held it. "If you want to talk about mistakes—shit, I raped somebody. Somebody I liked."

Their gaze met in a conflagration of reaction. She was so close he could smell her sweating, but at the speed of light she was falling away, deep into herself where he couldn't follow. She was struggling to free her hand.

"No," he said, "it wasn't a real rape. It was what you were talking about—it was complicated."

She wrenched her hand free and held it protectively close to her chest. "Don't touch me again." She turned tautly forward. He imagined her heart beating in alarm. His body felt so stiff he could barely feel his own heart. Furiously, he wondered if the people around them had heard any of this. Staring ahead of him, he hissed, "Do you think I was dying to hear about your alcoholism? You were the one who started this crazy conversation."

He felt her consider this. "It's not the same thing," she hissed back.

"But it wasn't really a rape." He struggled to say what it was. He recalled Patty that night at the Winners Circle, her neck arched and exposed, her feelings extended and flailing the air where she expected his feelings to be.

"You don't understand," he finished lamely.

She was silent. He thought he dimly felt her body relax, emitting some possibility of forgiveness. But he couldn't tell. He closed his eyes. He thought of Patty's splayed body, her half-conscious kiss. He thought of his wife, her compact scrappy body, her tough-looking flat nose and chipped nail polish, her smile, her smell, her embrace, which was both soft and fierce. He imagined the hotel room he would sleep in tonight, its stifling grid of rectangles, oblongs, and windows that wouldn't open. He leaned back and closed his eyes.

The pilot roused him with a command to fasten his seat belt. He sat up and blinked.

Nothing had changed. The woman at his side was sitting slightly hunched, with her hands resolutely clasped.

"God, I'll be glad when we're on the ground," he said.

She sniffed in reply.

They descended, ears popping. They landed with a flurry of baggage-grabbing. He stood, bumped his head, and tried to get into the aisle to escape, but it was too crowded. He sat back down. Not being able to leave made him feel that he had to say something else. "Look, don't be upset. What I said came out wrong."

"I don't want to talk."

Neither do I, he thought. But he felt disoriented and depressed amid these shifting, lunging, grabbing people from all over the country, who had been in his life for hours and were now about to disappear, taking their personal items and habits with them.

"Excuse me." She butted her way past him and into the aisle. He watched a round, vulnerable piece of her head move between the obstructions of shoulders and arms. She glanced backward, possibly to see if he was going to try to follow her. The sideways movement of her hazel iris prickled him. They burst from the plane and scattered, people picking up speed as they bore down on their destination. He caught up with her as they entered the terminal. "I'm sorry," he said to the back of her head. She moved farther away, into memory and beyond.

# DAVID LEAVITT
## (1961– )

The 1980s saw the movement of gay writers from the margins to the mainstream of American cultural attention. David Leavitt has been a leading figure in that movement. His fiction has skillfully explored the experiences of gay men and women in families and society. Resisting the label "gay writer," Leavitt believes his work has met with success because the situations of his characters have been more important than their sexuality. Mostly conventional in form, Leavitt's stories address what he calls "an age of ironic hopelessness," with the possibilities of love and hope and the legitimate claims of human communities caught between the tensions of loyalty and betrayal.

Leavitt was born in Pittsburgh, Pennsylvania, but was raised in Palo Alto, California, where his father was a professor at Stanford University. He graduated from Yale University in 1983, and spent time working for a publisher in New York City. He began publishing his stories in *The New Yorker, Esquire,* and *Harper's*. His first collection of stories, *Family Dancing,* appeared in 1984. His novels include *The Lost Language of Cranes* (1986), *Equal Affections* (1989), *While England Sleeps* (1993). *Arkansas: Three Novellas* (1997), and *The Page Turner* (1998). His second collection of stories, *A Place I've Never Been,* was published in 1990. He lives in East Hampton, Long Island, and spends a lot of time in Florence, Italy.

# A Place I've Never Been

I HAD known Nathan for years—too many years, since we were in college—so when he went to Europe I wasn't sure how I'd survive it; he was my best friend, after all, my constant companion at Sunday afternoon double bills at the Thalia, my ever-present source of consolation and conversation. Still, such a turn can prove to be a blessing in disguise. It threw me off at first, his not being there—I had no one to watch *Jeopardy!* with, or talk to on the phone late at night—but then, gradually, I got over it, and I realized that maybe it was a good thing after all, that maybe now, with Nathan gone, I would be forced to go out into the world more, make new friends, maybe even find a boyfriend. And I had started: I lost weight, I went shopping. I was at Bloomingdale's one day on my lunch hour when a very skinny black woman with a French accent asked me if I'd like to have a makeover. I had always run away from such things, but this time, before I had a chance, this woman put her long hands on my cheeks and looked into my face—not my eyes, my face—and said, "You're really beautiful. You know that?" And I absolutely couldn't answer. After she was through with me I didn't even know what I looked like, but everyone at my office was amazed. "Celia," they said, "you look great. What happened?" I smiled, wondering if I'd be allowed to go back every day for a makeover, if I offered to pay.

There was even some interest from a man—a guy named Roy who works downstairs, in contracts—and I was feeling pretty good about myself again, when the phone rang, and it was Nathan. At first I thought he must have been calling me from some European capital, but he said no, he was back in New York. "Celia," he said, "I have to see you. Something awful has happened."

Hearing those words, I pitched over—I assumed the worst. (And why not? He had been assuming the worst for over a year.) But he said, "No, no, I'm fine. I'm perfectly healthy. It's my apartment. Oh, Celia, it's awful. Could you come over?"

"Were you broken into?" I asked.

"I might as well have been!"

"Okay," I said. "I'll come over after work."

"I just got back last night. This is too much."

"I'll be there by six, Nathan."

"Thank you," he said, a little breathlessly, and hung up.

I drummed my nails—newly painted by another skinny woman at Bloomingdale's—against the black Formica of my desk, mostly to try out the sound. In truth I was a little happy he was back—I had missed him—and not at all surprised that he'd cut his trip short. Rich people are like that, I've observed; because they don't have to buy bargain-basement tickets on weird charter airlines, they feel free to change their minds. Probably he just got bored tooting around Europe, missed his old life, missed *Jeopardy!*, his friends. Oh, Nathan! How could I tell him the Thalia had closed?

I had to take several buses to get from my office to his neighborhood—a route I had once traversed almost daily, but which, since Nathan's departure, I hadn't had much occasion to take. Sitting on the Madison Avenue bus, I looked out the window at the rows of unaffordable shops, some still exactly what they'd been before, others boarded up, or reopened under new auspices—such a familiar panorama, unfolding, block by block, like a Chinese scroll I'd once been shown on a museum trip in junior high school. It was raining a little, and in the warm bus the long, unvarying progress of my love for Nathan seemed to unscroll as well—all the dinners and lunches and arguments, and all the trips back alone to my apartment, feeling ugly and fat, because Nathan had once again confirmed he could never love me the way he assured me he would someday love a man. How many hundreds of times I received that confirmation! And yet, somehow, it never occurred to me to give up that love I had nurtured for him since our earliest time together, that love which belonged to those days just past the brink of childhood, before I understood about Nathan, or rather, before Nathan understood about himself. So I persisted, and Nathan, in spite of his embarrassment at my occasional outbursts, continued to depend on me. I think he hoped that my feeling for him would one day transform itself into a more maternal kind of affection, that I would one day become the sort of woman who could tend to him without expecting anything in return. And that was, perhaps, a reasonable hope on his part, given my behavior. But: "If only," he said to me once, "you didn't have to act so crazy, Celia—" And that was how I realized I had to get out.

I got off the bus and walked the block and a half to his building—its façade, I noted, like almost every façade in the neighborhood, blemished by a bit of scaffolding—and, standing in that vestibule where I'd stood so often, waited for him to buzz me up. I read for diversion the now familiar list of tenants' names. The only difference today was that there were ragged ends of Scotch tape stuck around Nathan's name; probably his subletter had put his own name over Nathan's, and Nathan, returning, had torn the piece of paper off and left the ends of the tape. This didn't seem like him, and it made me suspicious. He was a scrupulous person about such things.

In due time—though slowly, for him—he let me in, and I walked the three flights of stairs to find him standing in the doorway, unshaven, looking as if he'd just gotten out of bed. He wasn't wearing any shoes, and he'd gained some weight. Almost immediately he fell into me—that is the only way to describe it, his big body limp in my arms. "Oh, God," he murmured into my hair, "am I glad to see you."

"Nathan," I said. "Nathan." And held him there. Usually he wriggled out of physical affection; kisses from him were little nips; hugs were tight, jerky chokeholds. Now he lay absolutely still, his arms slung under mine, and I tried to keep from gasping from the weight of him. But finally—reluctantly—he let go, and putting his hand on his forehead, gestured toward the open door. "Prepare yourself," he said. "It's worse than you can imagine."

He led me into the apartment. I have to admit, I was shocked by what I saw. Nathan, unlike me, is a chronically neat person, everything in its place, all his perfect furniture glowing, polished, every state-of-the-art fountain pen and pencil tip-up in the blue glass jar on his desk. Today, however, the place was in havoc—newspapers and old Entenmann's cookie boxes spread over the floor, records piled on top of each other, inner sleeves crumpled behind the radiator, the blue glass jar overturned. The carpet was covered with dark mottlings, and a stench of old cigarette smoke and sweat and urine inhabited the place. "It gets worse," he said. "Look at the kitchen." A thick, yellowing layer of grease encrusted the stove-top. The bathroom was beyond the pale of my descriptive capacity for filth.

"Those bastards," Nathan was saying, shaking his head.

"Hold on to the security deposit," I suggested. "Make them pay for it."

He sat down on the sofa, the arms of which appeared to have been ground with cigarette butts, and shook his head. "There is no security deposit," he moaned. "I didn't take one because supposedly Denny was my friend, and this other guy—Hoop, or whatever his name was—he was Denny's friend. And look at this!" From the coffee table he handed me a thick stack of utility and phone bills, all unopened. "The phone's disconnected," he said. "Two of the rent checks have bounced. The landlord's about to evict me. I'm sure my credit rating has gone to hell. Jesus, why'd I do it?" He stood, marched into the corner, then turned again to face me. "You know what? I'm going to call my father. I'm going to have him sick every one of his bastard lawyers on those assholes until they pay."

"Nathan," I reminded, "they're unemployed actors. They're poor."

"Then let them rot in jail!" Nathan screamed. His voice was loud and sharp in my ears. It had been a long time since I'd had to witness another person's misery, a long time since anyone had asked of me what Nathan was now asking of me: to take care, to resolve, to smooth. Nonetheless I rallied my energies. I stood. "Look," I said. "I'm going to go out and buy sponges, Comet, Spic and Span, Fantastik, Windex. Everything. We're going to clean this place up. We're going to wash the sheets and shampoo the rug, we're going to scrub the toilet until it shines. I promise you, by the time you go to sleep tonight, it'll be what it was."

He stood silent in the corner.

"Okay?" I said.

"Okay."

"So you wait here," I said. "I'll be right back."

"Thank you."

I picked up my purse and closed the door, thus, once again, saving him from disaster.

* * *

But there were certain things I could not save Nathan from. A year ago, his ex-lover Martin had called him up and told him he had tested positive. This was the secret fact he had to live with every day of his life, the secret fact that had brought him to Xanax and Halcion, Darvon and Valium—all crude efforts to cut the fear firing through his blood, exploding like the tiny viral time bombs he believed were lying in wait, expertly planted. It was the day after he found out that he started talking about clearing out. He had no obligations—he had quit his job a few months before and was just doing freelance work anyway—and so, he reasoned, what was keeping him in New York? "I need to get away from all this," he said, gesturing frantically at the air. I believe he really thought back then that by running away to somewhere where it was less well known, he might be able to escape the disease. This is something I've noticed: The men act as if they think the power of infection exists in direct proportion to its publicity, that in places far from New York City it can, in effect, be outrun. And who's to say they are wrong, with all this talk about stress and the immune system? In Italy, in the countryside, Nathan seemed to feel he'd feel safer. And probably he was right; he would feel safer. Over there, away from the American cityscape with its streets full of gaunt sufferers, you're able to forget the last ten years, you can remember how old the world is and how there was a time when sex wasn't something likely to kill you.

It should be pointed out that Nathan had no symptoms; he hadn't even had the test for the virus itself. He refused to have it, saying he could think of no reason to give up at least the hope of freedom. Not that this made any difference, of course. The fear itself is a brutal enough enemy.

But he gave up sex. No sex, he said, was safe enough for him. He bought a VCR and began to hoard pornographic videotapes. And I think he was having phone sex too, because once I picked up the phone in his apartment and before I could say hello, a husky-voiced man said, "You stud," and then, when I said "Excuse me?" got flustered-sounding and hung up. Some people would probably count that as sex, but I'm not sure I would.

All the time, meanwhile, he was frenzied. I could never guess what time he'd call—six in the morning, sometimes, he'd drag me from sleep. "I figured you'd still be up," he'd say, which gave me a clue to how he was living. It got so bad that by the time he actually left I felt as if a great burden had been lifted from my shoulders. Not that I didn't miss him, but from that day on my time was, miraculously, my own. Nathan is a terrible correspondent—I don't think he's sent me one postcard or letter in all the time we've known each other—and so for months my only news of him came through the phone. Strangers would call me, Germans, Italians, nervous-sounding young men who spoke bad English, who were staying at the YMCA, who were in New York for the first time and to whom he had given my number. I don't think any of them actually wanted to see me; I think they just wanted me to tell them which bars were good and which subway lines were safe—information I happily dispensed. Of course, there was a time when I would have taken them on the subways, shown them around the bars, but I have thankfully passed out of that phase.

And of course, as sex became more and more a possibility, then a likelihood once again in my life, I began to worry myself about the very things that were torturing Nathan. What should I say, say, to Roy in contracts, when he asked me to sleep with him, which I was fairly sure he was going to do within a lunch or two? Certainly I wanted to sleep with him. But did I dare ask him to use a condom? Did I dare even broach the subject? I was frightened that he might get furious, that he might overreact, and I considered saying nothing, taking my chances. Then again, for me in particular, it was a very big chance to take; I have a pattern of falling in love with men who at some point or other have fallen in love with other men. All trivial, selfish, this line of worry, I recognize now, but at that point Nathan was gone, and I had no one around to remind me of how high the stakes were for other people. I slipped back into a kind of women's-magazine attitude toward the whole thing: for the moment, at least, *I* was safe, and I cherished that safety without even knowing it, I gloried in it. All my speculations were merely matters of prevention; that place where Nathan had been exiled was a place I'd never been. I am ashamed to admit it, but there was even a moment when I took a kind of vengeful pleasure in the whole matter—the years I had hardly slept with anyone, for which I had been taught to feel ashamed and freakish, I now wanted to rub in someone's face: I was right and you were wrong! I wanted to say. I'm not proud of having had such thoughts, and I can only say, in my defense, that they passed quickly—but a strict accounting of all feelings, at this point, seems to me necessary. We have to be rigorous with ourselves these days.

In any case, Nathan was back, and I didn't dare think about myself. I went to the grocery store, I bought every cleaner I could find. And when I got back to the apartment he was still standing where he'd been standing, in the corner. "Nate," I said, "here's everything. Let's get to work."

"Okay," he said glumly, even though he is an ace cleaner, and we began.

As we cleaned, the truth came out. This Denny to whom he'd sublet the apartment, Nathan had had a crush on. "To the extent that a crush is a relevant thing in my life anymore," he said, "since God knows, there's nothing to be done about it. But there you are. The libido doesn't stop, the heart doesn't stop, no matter how hard you try to make them."

None of this—especially that last part—was news to me, though Nathan had managed to overlook that aspect of our relationship for years. I had understood from the beginning about the skipping-over of the security payment, the laxness of the setup, because these were the sorts of things I would have willingly done for Nathan at a different time. I think he was privately so excited at the prospect of this virile young man, Denny, sleeping, and perhaps having sex, between his sheets, that he would have taken any number of risks to assure it. Crush: what an oddly appropriate word, considering what it makes you do to yourself. His apartment was, in a sense, the most Nathan could offer, and probably the most Denny would accept. I understood: You want to get as close as you can, even if it's only at arm's length. And when you come back, maybe, you want to breathe in the smell of the person you love loving someone else.

Europe, he said, had been a failure. He had wandered, having dinner with old friends of his parents, visiting college acquaintances who were busy with exotic lives. He'd gone to bars, which was merely frustrating; there was nothing to be done. "What about safe sex?" I asked, and he said, "Celia, please. There is no such thing, as far as I'm concerned." Once again this started a panicked thumping in my chest as I thought about Roy, and Nathan said, "It's really true. Suppose something lands on you—you know what I'm saying—and there's a microscopic cut in your skin. Bingo."

"Nathan, come on," I said. "That sounds crazy to me."

"Yeah?" he said. "Just wait till some ex-lover of yours calls you up with a little piece of news. Then see how you feel."

He returned to his furious scrubbing of the bathroom sink. I returned to my furious scrubbing of the tub. Somehow, even now, I'm always stuck with the worst of it.

Finally we were done. The place looked okay—it didn't smell anymore—though it was hardly what it had been. Some long-preserved pristineness was gone from the apartment, and both of us knew without saying a word that it would never be restored. We breathed in exhausted—no, not exhausted triumph. It was more like relief. We had beaten something back, yet again.

My hands were red from detergents, my stomach and forehead sweaty. I went into the now-bearable bathroom and washed up, and then Nathan said he would take me out to dinner—my choice. And so we ended up, as we had a thousand other nights, sitting by the window at the Empire Szechuan down the block from his apartment, eating cold noodles with sesame sauce, which, when we had finished them, Nathan ordered more of. "God, how I've missed these," he said, as he scooped the brown slimy noodles into his mouth. "You don't know."

In between slurps he looked at me and said, "You look good, Celia. Have you lost weight?"

"Yes, as a matter of fact," I said.

"I thought so."

I looked back at him, trying to recreate the expression on the French woman's face, and didn't say anything, but as it turned out I didn't need to. "I know what you're thinking," he said, "and you're right. Twelve pounds since you last saw me. But I don't care. I mean, you lose weight when you're sick. At least this way, gaining weight, I know I don't have it."

He continued eating. I looked outside. Past the plate-glass window that separated us from the sidewalk, crowds of people walked, young and old, good-looking and bad-looking, healthy and sick, some of them staring in at our food and our eating. Suddenly—urgently—I wanted to be out among them, I wanted to be walking in that crowd, pushed along in it, and not sitting here, locked into this tiny two-person table with Nathan. And yet I knew that escape was probably impossible. I looked once again at Nathan, eating happily, resigned, perhaps, to the fate of his apartment, and the knowledge that everything would work out, that this had, in fact, been merely a run-of-the-mill crisis. For the moment he was appeased, his hungry anxiety sated; for the moment. But who could guess what would set him off next? I steadied my chin on my palm, drank some water, watched Nathan eat like a happy child.

* * *

The next few weeks were thorny with events. Nathan bought a new sofa, had his place recarpeted, threw several small dinners. Then it was time for Lizzie Fischman's birthday party—one of the few annual events in our lives. We had known Lizzie since college—she was a tragic, trying sort of person, the sort who carries with her a constant aura of fatedness, of doom. So many bad things happen to Lizzie you can't help but wonder, after a while, if she doesn't hold out a beacon for disaster. This year alone, she was in a taxi that got hit by a bus; then she was mugged in the subway by a man who called her an "ugly dyke bitch"; then she started feeling sick all the time, and no one could figure out what was wrong, until it was revealed that her building's heating system was leaking small quantities of carbon monoxide into her awful little apartment. The tenants sued, and in the course of the suit, Lizzie, exposed as an illegal subletter, was evicted. She now lived with her father in one half of a two-family house in Plainfield, New Jersey, because she couldn't find another apartment she could afford. (Her job, incidentally, in addition to being wretchedly low-paying, is one of the dreariest I know of: proofreading accounting textbooks in an office on Forty-second Street.)

Anyway, each year Lizzie threw a big birthday party for herself in her father's house in Plainfield, and we all went, her friends, because of course we couldn't bear to disappoint her and add ourselves to her roster of worldwide enemies. It was invariably a miserable party—everyone drunk on bourbon, and Lizzie, eager to recreate the slumber parties of her childhood, dancing around in pink pajamas with feet. We were making s'mores over the gas stove—shoving the chocolate bars and the graham crackers onto fondue forks rather than old sticks—and *Beach Blanket Bingo* was playing on the VCR and no one was having a good time, particularly Nathan, who was overdressed in a beige Giorgio Armani linen suit he'd bought in Italy, and was standing in the corner idly pressing his neck, feeling for swollen lymph nodes. Lizzie's circle dwindled each year, as her friends moved on, or found ways to get out of it. This year eight of us had made it to the party, plus a newcomer from Lizzie's office, a very fat girl with very red nails named Dorrie Friedman, who, in spite of her heaviness, was what my mother would have called dainty. She ate a lot, but unless you were observant, you'd never have noticed it. The image of the fat person stuffing food into her face is mythic: I know from experience, when fat you eat slowly, chew methodically, in order not to draw attention to your mouth. Over the course of an hour I watched Dorrie Friedman put away six of those s'mores with a tidiness worthy of Emily Post, I watched her dab her cheek with her napkin after each bite, and I understood: This was shame, but also, in some peculiar way, this was innocence. A state to envy.

There is a point in Lizzie's parties when she invariably suggests we play Deprivation, a game that had been terribly popular among our crowd in college. The way you play it is you sit in a big circle, and everyone is given ten pennies. (In this case the pennies were unceremoniously taken from a huge bowl that sat on top of Lizzie's mother's refrigerator, and that she had upended on the linoleum floor—no doubt a long-contemplated act of desecration.) You go around the circle, and each person announces something he or she has never done, or a place they've never been—"I've never been to Borneo" is a good example—and then everyone who has been to Borneo is obliged to throw you a penny. Needless to say, especially in college, the game degenerates rather quickly to matters of sex and drugs.

I remembered the first time I ever played Deprivation, my sophomore year, I had been reading Blake's *Songs of Innocence* and *Songs of Experience.* Everything in our lives seemed a question of innocence and experience back then, so this seemed appropriate. There was a tacit assumption among my friends that "experience"—by that term we meant, I think, almost exclusively sex and drugs—was something you strove to get as much of as you could, that innocence, for all the praise it received in literature, was a state so essentially tedious that those of us still stuck in it deserved the childish recompense of shiny new pennies. (None of us, of course, imagining that five years from now the "experiences" we urged on one another might spread a murderous germ, that five years from now some of our friends, still in their youth, would be lost. Youth! You were supposed to sow your wild oats, weren't you? Those of us who didn't—we were the ones who failed, weren't we?)

One problem with Deprivation is that the older you get, the less interesting it becomes; every year, it seemed, my friends had fewer gaps in their lives to confess, and as our embarrassments began to stack up on the positive side, it was what we *had* done that was titillating. Indeed, Nick Walsh, who was to Lizzie what Nathan was to me, complained as the game began, "I can't play this. There's nothing I haven't done." But Lizzie, who has a naive faith in ritual, merely smiled and said, "Oh come on, Nick. No one's done *everything.* For instance, you could say, 'I've never been to Togo,' or 'I've never been made love to simultaneously by twelve Arab boys in a back alley on Mott Street.' "

"Well, Lizzie," Nick said, "it is true that I've never been to Togo." His leering smile surveyed the circle, and of course, there *was* someone there—Gracie Wong, I think—who had, in fact, been to Togo.

The next person in the circle was Nathan. He's never liked this game, but he also plays it more cleverly than anyone. "Hmm," he said, stroking his chin as if there were a beard there, "let's see . . . Ah, I've got it. I've never had sex with anyone in this group." He smiled boldly, and everyone laughed—everyone, that is,except for me and Bill Darlington, and Lizzie herself—all three of us now, for the wretched experiments of our early youth, obliged to throw Nathan a penny.

Next was Dorrie Friedman's turn, which I had been dreading. She sat on the floor, her legs crossed under her, her very fat fingers intertwined, and said, "Hmm . . . Something I've never done. Well—I've never ridden a bicycle."

An awful silence greeted this confession, and then a tinkling sound, like wind chimes, as the pennies flew. "Gee," Dorrie Friedman said, "I won big that time." I couldn't tell if she was genuinely pleased.

And as the game went on, we settled, all of us, into more or less parallel states of innocence and experience, except for Lizzie and Nick, whose piles had rapidly dwindled, and Dorrie Friedman, who, it seemed, by virtue of lifelong fatness, had done nearly nothing. She had never been to Europe; she had never swum; she had never played tennis; she had never skied; she had never been on a boat. Even someone else's turn could be an awful moment for Dorrie, as when Nick said, "I've never had a vaginal orgasm." But fortunately, there, she did throw in her penny. I was relieved; I don't think I could have stood it if she hadn't.

After a while, in an effort not to look at Dorrie and her immense pile of pennies, we all started trying to trip up Lizzie and Nick, whose respective caches of sexual experience seemed limitless. "I've never had sex in my parents' bed," I offered. The pennies flew. "I've never had sex under a dry-docked boat." "I've never had sex with more than one other person." "Two other people." "Three other people." By then Lizzie was out of pennies, and declared the game over.

"I guess I won," Dorrie said rather softly. She had her pennies neatly piled in identically sized stacks.

I wondered if Lizzie was worried. I wondered if she was thinking about the disease, if she was frightened, the way Nathan was, or if she just assumed death was coming anyway, the final blow in her life of unendurable misfortunes. She started to gather the pennies back into their bowl, and I glanced across the room at Nathan, to see if he was ready to go. All through the game, of course, he had been looking pretty miserable—he always looks miserable at parties. Worse, he has a way of turning his misery around, making me responsible for it. Across the circle of our nearest and dearest friends he glared at me angrily, and I knew that by the time we were back in his car and on our way home to Manhattan he would have contrived a way for the evening to be my fault. And yet tonight, his occasional knowing sneers, inviting my complicity in looking down on the party, only enraged me. I was angry at him, in advance, for what I was sure he was going to do in the car, and I was also angry at him for being such a snob, for having no sympathy toward this evening, which, in spite of all its displeasures, was nevertheless an event of some interest, perhaps the very last hurrah of our youth, our own little big chill. And that was something: Up until now I had always assumed Nathan's version of things to be the correct one, and cast my own into the background. Now his perception seemed meager, insufficient: Here was an historic night, after all, and all he seemed to want to think about was his own boredom, his own unhappiness.

Finally, reluctantly, Lizzie let us go, and relinquished from her grip, we got into Nathan's car and headed onto the Garden State Parkway. "Never again," Nathan was saying, "will I allow you to convince me to attend one of Lizzie Fischman's awful parties. This is the last." I didn't even bother answering, it all seemed so predictable. Instead I just settled back into the comfortable velour of the car seat and switched on the radio. Dionne Warwick and Elton John were singing "That's What Friends Are For," and Nathan said, "You know, of course, that that's the song they wrote to raise money for AIDS."

"I'd heard," I said.

"Have you seen the video? It makes me furious. All these famous singers up there, grinning these huge grins, rocking back and forth. Why the hell are they smiling, I'd like to ask?"

For a second, I considered answering that question, then decided I'd better not. We were slipping into the Holland Tunnel, and by the time we got through to Manhattan I was ready to call it a night. I wanted to get back to my apartment and see if Roy had left a message on my answering machine. But Nathan said, "It's Saturday night, Celia, it's still early. Won't you have a drink with me or something?"

"I don't want to go to any more gay bars, Nathan, I told you that."

"So we'll go to a straight bar. I don't care. I just can't bear to go back to my apartment at eleven o'clock." We stopped for a red light, and he leaned closer to me. "The truth is, I don't think I can bear to be alone. Please."

"All right," I said. What else could I say?

"Goody," Nathan said.

We parked the car in a garage and walked to a darkish café on Greenwich Avenue, just a few doors down from the huge gay bar Nathan used to frequent, and which he jokingly referred to as "the airport." No mention was made of that bar in the café, however, where he ordered latte machiato for both of us. "Aren't you going to have some dessert?" he said. "I know I am. Babu au rhum, perhaps. Or tiramisu. You know '*tirami su*' means 'pick me up,' but if you want to offend an Italian waiter, you say 'I'll have the *tiramilo su,*' which means 'pick up my dick.' "

"I'm trying to lose weight, Nathan," I said. "Please don't encourage me to eat desserts."

"Sorry." He coughed. Our latte machiatos came, and Nathan raised his cup and said, "Here's to us. Here's to Lizzie Fischman. Here's to never playing that dumb game again as long as we live." These days, I noticed, Nathan used the phrase "as long as we live" a bit too frequently for comfort.

Reluctantly I touched my glass to his. "You know," he said, "I think I've always hated that game. Even in college, when I won, it made me jealous. Everyone else had done so much more than me. Back then I figured I'd have time to explore the sexual world. Guess the joke's on me, huh?"

I shrugged. I wasn't sure.

"What's with you tonight, anyway?" he said. "You're so distant."

"I just have things on my mind, Nathan, that's all."

"You've been acting weird ever since I got back from Europe, Celia. Sometimes I think you don't even want to see me."

Clearly he was expecting reassurances to the contrary. I didn't say anything.

"Well," he said, "is that it? You don't want to see me?"

I twisted my shoulders in confusion. "Nathan—"

"Great," he said, and laughed so that I couldn't tell if he was kidding. "Your best friend for nearly ten years. Jesus."

"Look, Nathan, don't melodramatize," I said. "It's not that simple. It's just that I have to think a little about myself. My own life, my own needs. I mean, I'm going to be thirty soon. You know how long it's been since I've had a boyfriend?"

"I'm not against your having a boyfriend," Nathan said. "Have I ever tried to stop you from having a boyfriend?"

"But, Nathan," I said, "I never get to meet anyone when I'm with you all the time. I love you and I want to be your friend, but you can't expect me to just keep giving and giving and giving my time to you without anything in return. It's not fair."

I was looking away from him as I said this. From the corner of my vision I could see him glancing to the side, his mouth a small, tight line.

"You're all I have," he said quietly.

"That's not true, Nathan," I said.

"Yes it is true, Celia."

"Nathan, you have lots of other friends."

"But none of them count. No one but you counts."

The waitress arrived with his goblet of tiramisu, put it down in front of him. "Go on with your life, you say," he was muttering. "Find a boyfriend. Don't you think I'd do the same thing if I could? But all those options are closed to me, Celia. There's nowhere for me to go, no route that isn't dangerous. I mean, getting on with my life—I just can't talk about that simply anymore, the way you can." He leaned closer, over the table. "Do you want to know something?" he said. "Every time I see someone I'm attracted to I go into a cold sweat. And I imagine that they're dead, that if I touch them, the part of them I touch will die. Don't you see? It's bad enough to be afraid you might get it. But to be afraid you might give it—and to someone you loved—" He shook his head, put his hand to his forehead.

What could I say to that? What possibly was there to say? I took his hand, suddenly, I squeezed his hand until the edges of his fingers were white. I was remembering how Nathan looked the first time I saw him, in line at a college dining hall, his hands on his hips, his head erect, staring worriedly at the old lady dishing out food, as if he feared she might run out, or not give him enough. I have always loved the boyish hungers—for food, for sex—because they are so perpetual, so faithful in their daily revival, and even though I hadn't met Nathan yet, I think, in my mind, I already understood: I wanted to feed him, to fill him up; I wanted to give him everything.

Across from us, now, two girls were smoking cigarettes and talking about what art was. A man and a woman, in love, intertwined their fingers. Nathan's hand was getting warm and damp in mine, so I let it go, and eventually he blew his nose and lit a cigarette.

"You know," he said after a while, "it's not the sex, really. That's not what I regret missing. It's just that—Do you realize, Celia, I've never been in love? Never once in my life have I actually been in love?" And he looked at me very earnestly, not knowing, not having the slightest idea, that once again he was counting me for nothing.

"Nathan," I said. "Oh, my Nathan." Still, he didn't seem satisfied, and I knew he had been hoping for something better than my limp consolation. He looked away from me, across the café, listening, I suppose, for that wind-chime peal as all the world's pennies flew his way.

# CREDITS

"The Lottery," from *The Lottery* by Shirley Jackson. Copyright © 1976, 1977 by Laurence Hyman, Barry Hyman, Mrs. Sarah Webster, and Mrs. Janne Schnurer. Reprinted by permission of Farrar, Straus and Giroux, LLC, and Linda Allen Literary Agency.

"Why I Live at the P.O.," from *A Curtain of Green, and Other Stories,* copyright © 1941 and renewed © 1969 by Eudora Welty, reprinted by permission of Harcourt Inc.

"The Spinoza of Market Street," from *The Spinoza of Market Street* by Isaac Baschevis Siner. Copyright © 1961 and copyright renewed © 1989 by Isaac Bashevis Singer. Reprinted by permission of Farrar, Straus and Giroux, LLC, and The Random House Group Ltd.

"I Stand Here Ironing," copyright © 1956, 1957, 1960, 1961 by Tillie Olsen. From *Tell Me a Riddle* by Tillie Olsen. Introduction by John Leonard. Used by permission of Delacorte Press/Seymour Lawrence, a division of Random House, Inc., and The Elaine Markson Literary Agency, Inc.

"Battle Royal," from *Invisible Man* by Ralph Ellison. Copyright © 1948 by Ralph Ellison. Reprinted by permission of Random House, Inc.

"An Interest in Life," from *The Little Disturbances of Man* by Grace Paley. Copyright © 1956, 1957, 1958, 1959 by Grace Paley. Used by permission of Viking Penguin, a division of Penguin Putnam Inc., and by The Elaine Markson Literary Agency, Inc.

"The Prince of Darkness," from *The Prince of Darkness, and Other Stories* by J. F. Powers. Reprint permission granted by The Estate of J. F. Powers.

"Don't Call Me by My Right Name" by James Purdy, from *The Color of Darkness*. Copyright © 1956 by The Andreas Foundation. Reprinted permission of New Directions Publishing Corp. and James Purdy.

"The Jew Bird," from *The Complete Stories* by Bernard Malamud. Copyright © 1997 by Ann Malamud.

"The Old Forest," from *The Old Forest, and Other Stories* by Peter Taylor. Copyright © 1941, 1945, 1947, 1951, 1958, 1959, 1979, 1981 by Peter Taylor. Used by permission of Doubleday, a division of Random House, Inc.

"A Good Man Is Hard to Find," from *A Good Man Is Hard to Find,* copyright © 1953 by Flannery O'Connor and renewed © 1981 by Regina O'Connor, reprinted by permission of Harcourt Inc.

"Revelation," from *Everything That Rises Must Converge* by Flannery O'Connor. Copyright © 1964, 1965 by Estate of Mary Flannery O'Connor. Copyright renewed © 1993 by Regina O'Connor. Reprinted by permission of Farrar, Straus and Giroux, LLC, and Harold Matson Co., Inc.

"A Ram in the Thicket," from *Collected Stories, 1948–1986.* Reprinted by the permission of Russel & Volkening as agents for the author. Copyright © 1948 by Wright Morris, renewed © 1986 by Wright Morris. Story originally appeared in *Harper's Bazaar,* May 1948.

"The Country Husband," from *The Stories of John Cheever* by John Cheever. Copyright © 1954 by John Cheever. Reprinted by permission of Alfred A. Knopf, a division of Random House, Inc.

"The Housebreaker of Shady Hill," from *The Stories of John Cheever* by John Cheever. Copyright © 1956 by John Cheever. Reprinted by permission of Alfred A. Knopf, a division of Random House, Inc.

"Defender of the Faith," from *Goodbye, Columbus* by Philip Roth. Copyright © 1959 by Philip Roth. Reprinted by permission of Houghton Mifflin Co. All rights reserved.

"Sonny's Blues" was originally pubished in *Partisan Review.* Collected in *Going to Meet the Man,* copyright © 1965 by James Baldwin. Copyright renewed. Published by Vintage Books. Reprinted by arrangement with the James Baldwin Estate.

Hisaye Yamamoto, *Seventeen Syllables, and Other Stories,* copyright © 1988 by Hisaye Yamamoto. Reprinted by permission of Rutgers University Press.

"Looking for Mr. Green," copyright, renewed © 1979 by Saul Bellow, from *Mosby's Memoirs, and Other Stories* by Saul Bellow. Used by permission of Viking Penguin, a division of Penguin Putnam Inc.

"In the Heart of the Heart of the Country," from *In the Heart of the Heart of the Country* by William H. Gass. Reprinted by permission of David R. Godine, Publisher, Inc. Copyright © 1984 by William H. Gass.

"The Sky Is Gray," copyright © 1963 by Ernest J. Gaines. From *Bloodline* by Ernest J. Gaines. Used by permission of Doubleday, a division of Random House, Inc.

"The Babysitter," from *Pricksongs and Descants* by Robert Coover (New York: E.P. Dutton & Co., Inc.). Copyright © 1969 by Robert Coover. Reprinted by permission of Georges Borchardt, Inc.

"Night-Sea Journey," copyright © 1966 by John Barth (first published in *Esquire Magazine*). From *Lost in the Funhouse* by John Barth. Used by permission of Doubleday, a division of Random House, Inc.

"The Ones Who Walk Away from Omelas," by Ursula K. Le Guin. Copyright © 1973 by Ursula K. Le Guin; first appeared in *New Dimensions 3*; from *The Wind's Twelve Quarters*; reprinted by permission of the author and the author's agents, the Virginia Kidd Agency, Inc.

"The Shawl," from *The Shawl* by Cynthia Ozick. Copyright © 1980, 1983 by Cynthia Ozick. Reprinted by permission of Alfred A. Knopf, a division of Random House, Inc.

"Come on Back," from *The Art of Living* by John Gardner (New York: Alfred A. Knopf, 1981). Copyright © 1974, 1976, 1977, 1979, 1981 by John Gardner.

"Where Are You Going, Where Have You Been?," by Joyce Carol Oates. Published in *The Wheel of Love, and Other Stories* by Vanguard (1970). Reprinted by permission of John Hawkins & Associates, Inc.

"The Lesson", from *Gorilla, My Love* by Toni Cade Bambara. Copyright © 1972 by Toni Cade Bambara. Reprinted by permission of Random House, Inc.

"I Would Have Saved Them If I Could," from *I Would Have Saved Them If I Could* by Leonard Michaels. Copyright © 1975 by Leonard Michaels. Reprinted by permission of Farrar, Straus and Giroux, LLC.

"To Hell with Dying," from *In Love & Trouble: Stories of Black Women*, copyright © 1967 and renewed © 1995 by Alice Walker, reprinted by permission of Harcourt Inc.

"Separating," from *Problems, and Other Stories* by John Updike. Copyright © 1972, 1973, 1974, 1975, 1976, 1978, 1979 by John Updike. Reprinted by permission of Alfred A. Knopf, a division of Random House, Inc.

"Of Cabbages and Kings," from *Hue and Cry* by James Alan McPherson (1969). Reprinted by permission of James Alan McPherson.

"Girl," from *At the Bottom of the River* by Jamaica Kincaid. Copyright © 1983 by Jamaica Kincaid. Reprinted by permission of Farrar, Straus and Giroux, LLC.

"The Oranging of America," from *The Oranging of America* by Max Apple. Copyright © 1974, 1975, 1976 by Max Apple. Used by permission of Viking Penguin, a division of Penguin Putnam Inc.

"Midnight and I'm Not Famous Yet," from *Airships* by Barry Hannah. Copyright © 1978 by Barry Hannah. Reprinted by permission of Grove/Atlantic, Inc.

"Souvenir," from *Black Tickets* by Jayne Anne Phillips. Reprinted by permission of Dell Books, a division of Random House, Inc.

"Storyteller," from *Storyteller* by Leslie Marmon Silko. Copyright © 1981 by Leslie Marmon Silko. Reprint permission granted by The Wylie Agency.

"Roses, Rhododendron," from *Beautiful Girls* by Alice Adams. Copyright © 1977 by Alice Adams. Reprinted by permission of Alfred A. Knopf, a division of Random House, Inc.

"A Father's Story," by Andre Dubus. Reprinted by permission of David R. Godine, Publisher, Inc. Copyright © 1993 by Andre Dubus.

"The Priest Next Door," by Susan Fromberg Schaeffer. From *The Queen of Egypt.*

"Janus," from *Where You'll Find Me, and Other Stories*, by Ann Beattie. Copyright © 1986 by Irony & Pity, Inc. Reprinted with the permission of Simon & Schuster and International Creative Management, Inc.

"Coach," from *An Amateur's Guide to the Night* by Mary Robinson. Copyright © 1981, 1982, 1983 by Mary Robinson. Reprinted by permission of Alfred A. Knopf, a division of Random House, Inc.

"Hunters in the Snow," from *In the Garden of the North Martyrs* by Tobias Wolff. Copyright © 1976, 1978, 1980, 1981 by Tobias Wolff. Reprinted by permission of The Ecco Press and International Creative Management, Inc.

"A New-Wave Format," from *Shiloh, and Other Stories* by Bobbie Ann Mason. Reprinted by permission of International Creative Management, Inc.

"The Redneck Way of Knowledge" by Blanche McCrary. From *The Redneck Way of Knowledge.*

"Another Marvelous Thing," from *Another Marvelous Thing* by Laurie Colwin. Copyright © 1986 by Laurie Colwin. Reprinted by permission of Alfred A. Knopf, a division of Random House, Inc.

"Greasy Lake," from *Greasy Lake, and Other Stories* by T. Coraghessan Boyle. Copyright © 1979, 1981, 1982, 1983, 1984, 1985 by T. Coraghessan Boyle. Used by permission of Viking Penguin, a division of Penguin Putnam Inc., and Sheil Land Associates Ltd.

"Exchange Value," from *The Sorcerer's Apprentice* by Charles Johnson. Reprinted with the permission of Scribner, a division of Simon & Schuster, from *The Sorcerer's Apprentice* by Charles Johnson. Copyright © 1981, 1986 by Charles Johnson.

"The Way We Live Now" from *The Way We Live Now* by Susan Sontag. Copyright © 1986 by Susan Sontag. First published in *The New Yorker.* Reprinted by permission of Farrar, Straus and Giroux, LLC, and The Wylie Agency.

"The Tip-Top Club," copyright © 1981 by Garrison Keillor, from *Happy to Be Here* by Garrison Keillor. Used by permission of Viking Penguin, a division of Penguin Putnam Inc.

"The Things They Carried," from *The Things They Carried* by Tim O'Brien. Copyright © 1990 by Tim O'Brien. Reprinted by permission of Houghton Mifflin Company. All rights reserved.

"Health," from *Escape* by Joy Williams.

"On Morality," from *China Men* by Maxine Hong Kingston. Copyright © 1980 by Maxine Hong Kingston. Reprinted by permission of Alfred A. Knopf, a division of Random House, Inc.

"The Management of Grief," from *The Middleman, and Other Stories* by Bharati Mukherjee. Copyright © 1988 by Bharati Mukherjee. Reprinted by permission of Grove/Atlantic, Inc.

"Gryphon," from *Through the Safety Net* by Charles Baxter. Permission granted by The Darhansoff & Verrill Literary Agency.

"Rules of the Game," from *The Joy Luck Club* by Amy Tan. Reprinted by permission of Abner Stein.

"Rock Springs," from *Rock Springs* by Richard Ford. Copyright © 1987 by Richard Ford. Reprinted by permission of Grove/Atlantic, Inc., and International Creative Management, Inc.

"People Like That Are the Only People Here: Canonical Babbling in Peed Onk," from *Birds of America* by Lorrie Moore. Copyright © 1988 by Lorrie Moore. Reprinted by permission of Alfred A. Knopf, a division of Random House, Inc., and Faber and Faber.

"Saint Marie," from *Love Medicine*, New and Expanded Edition by Louise Erdrich. Copyright © 1984, 1993 by Louise Erdrich. Reprinted by permission of Henry Holt and Company, LLC.

"The Only Real Day," from *The Chinaman Pacific & Frisco R.R.* by Frank Chin. Reprinted by permission of Coffee House Press.

"Everyday Disorders," from *Women and Children First* by Francine Prose. Reprinted by permission of International Creative Management.

"What We Talk About When We Talk About Love," from *What We Talk About When We Talk About Love* by Raymond Carver. Copyright © 1981 by Raymond Carver. Reprinted by permission of Alfred A. Knopf, a division of Random House, Inc., and International Creative Management, Inc.

"Cathedral," from *Cathedral* by Raymond Carver. Copyright © 1983 by Raymond Carver. Reprinted by permission of Alfred A. Knopf, a division of Random House, Inc., and International Creative Management, Inc.

"In the Cemetery Where Al Jolson Is Buried" by Amy Hempel. Reprinted by permission of The Darhansoff & Verrill Literary Agency.

"Wickedness," from *Nebraska* by Ron Hansen. Copyright by Ron Hansen. Reprinted by permission of Sterling Lord Literistic, Inc.

"Able, Baker, Charlie, Dog," from *Sweet Talk* by Stephanie Vaughn (New York: Random House, 1990). Copyright © 1978, 1979, 1981, 1990 by Stephanie Vaughn. Reprinted by permission of Georges Brochardt, Inc., for the author.

"The Cariboo Cafe" by Helena María Viramontes is reprinted with permission from the publisher of *The Moths, and Other Stories* (Houston: Arte Publico Press—University of Houston, 1985).

"One Holy Night," from *Woman Hollering Creek* by Sandra Cisneros. Copyright © 1991 by Sandra Cisneros. Published by Vintage Books, a division of Random House, Inc., and originally in hardcover by Random House, Inc. Reprinted by permission of Susan Bergholz Literary Services, New York. All rights reserved.

"Relic," from *A Good Scent from a Strange Mountain* by Robert Olen Butler. Copyright © 1992 by Robert Olen Butler. Reprinted by permission of Henry Holt and Company, LLC.

"Helping," from *Bear and His Daughters: Stories* by Robert Stone. Copyright © 1997 by Robert Stone. Reprinted by permission of Houghton Mifflin Company. All rights reserved.

"How to Talk to a Hunter," from *Cowboys Are My Weakness* by Pam Houston. Copyright © 1992 by Pam Houston. Reprinted by permission of W.W. Norton & Company, Inc., and The Darhansoff & Verrill Literary Agency.

"Videotape," reprinted with the permission of Scribner, a division of Simon & Schuster, from *Underworld* by Don DeLillo. Copyright © 1997 by Don DeLillo.

"Cold Snap," from *Cold Snap* by Thom Jones. Copyright © 1995 by Thom Jones; first appeared in *The New Yorker*. Reprinted by permission of Little, Brown and Company Inc.

"This Is What It Means to Say Phoenix, Arizona," from *The Lone Ranger and Tonto Fistfight in Heaven* by Sherman Alexie. Copyright © 1993 by Sherman Alexie. Reprinted by permission of Grove/Atlantic, Inc.

"Oxygen," from *The Hotel Eden: Stories* by Ron Carlson. Copyright © 1997 by Ron Carlson. Reprinted by permission of W.W. Norton & Company, Inc., and Brandt & Brandt Literary Agents, Inc.

"The Littoral Zone," from *Ship Fever, and Other Stories* by Andrea Barrett. Copyright © 1996 by Andrea Barrett. Reprinted by permission of W.W. Norton & Company, Inc., and David Higham Associates.

"The Girl on the Plane," reprinted with the permission of Simon & Schuster from *Because They Wanted To* by Mary Gaitskill. Copyright © 1997 by Mary Gaitskill.

"A Place I've Never Been," from *A Place I've Never Been* by David Leavitt. Copyright © 1990 by David Leavitt. Used by permission of Viking Penguin, a division of Penguin Putnam Inc.